I0822289

THE MOONSHINE TASK FORCE COMPLETE SERIES

BOOKS 1-6 OF THE MOONSHINE TASK FORCE SERIES

LARAMIE BRISCOE

Edited by: Elfwerks Editing

Cover Art by: Kari Ayasha, Cover to Cover Designs

Proofread by: Dawn Bourgeois

Beta Read by: Keyla Handley & Danielle Wentworth

Cover Photography: RLS Photography

Cover Model: Max Rai Fitness

Created with Vellum

For everyone who never gives up on what they want, no matter what it is. And for those little jokes each of us have in relationships – may you always 'pew pew' with the love of your life!

AUTHOR'S NOTE

While the series is called The Moonshine Task Force Series, please be aware the task force is what bought most of these men together. It's the catalyst (if you will) that has made the friendship of the five men you'll meet in the series.

Like most of my recent books, these are character-driven. The action, as it is, advances the storyline or sets up the storyline for subsequent books. There won't be manufactured drama or manufactured storyline. These are very much what you see, is what you get. Each book follows one member, and you'll get to see how they change and grow through-out the course of the series.

I hope you'll love all these stories featuring these alpha men and the women they love!

Enjoy!

Laramie

RENEGADE - BOOK I

BLURB

When you fall in love with the most unexpected person, at the most unexpected time...

Ryan "Renegade" Kepler

I'm the type of man who knows what I want. I make up my mind and stay in my lane, never veering off the course I set for myself.

Going into the military? Did it. Youngest member of the Moonshine Task Force? That's me. Get my best friend's older sister in bed? It was my pleasure.

Age means nothing to me. I've seen and done things men twice my age never will. What I want more than anything is someone to share my life with, and that person is my best friend's older sister, Whitney.

Whitney Trumbolt

Ryan may be ten years my junior, but damn, my first time being a cougar will never be forgotten. Now I'm struggling with wanting things to either go back to the way they were or spend every night in his arms.

Make my wedding planning company the best in the south? Did it. Ignore the way my body trembles when I see Ryan? Epic fail. Freak out when I see a positive pregnancy test staring back at me? Complete with mascara running down my face and clutching my pearls.

Looks like things will never be the same. There's a man in my life who doesn't take no for an answer. He's the one who makes my blood run hot, cheeks turn red, and heart beat wildly within my chest. His name is Renegade.

CHAPTER ONE

WHITNEY

LATE MARCH

"Ryan, I'm tellin' you, I need my hair pulled, a red handprint across my ass, someone licking my nipples, a dick in my treasure cove. I need it all."

Drunk. I am drunk. Like way past the legal limit – otherwise I wouldn't be sitting here spilling all my secrets to my baby brother's best friend. The baby brother who had been totally unplanned by my parents. Ten years my junior, baby brother. He and Ryan are the same age; twenty-five to my thirty-five. Makes me feel so much older just thinking about it. Not only by age, but by life experience, too, although they've probably got me beat. They're cops and have served overseas in the military. Dear Lord, I think I sound like Julia Sugarbaker from Designing Women. I'm three sheets to the wind, and nobody stopped me.

I see him try to suppress a grin as he brings his beer up to his lips, taking a nice long pull off the wide mouth. I am mesmerized by the way his throat muscles move when he swallows, pushing the liquid down his throat. No denying he's all man. None of the boyhood shyness he always had with me is anywhere near us tonight. The palm of his hand completely covers the label, the one drink he takes drains half the bottle. For a second he focuses on my face, squinting as he watches me. "How many of those have you had to drink?" He points the neck of his beer to the wine glass in my hand.

His voice is as smooth as the red liquid I swirl in my glass. I tilt my head to the side, realizing the whole room goes right along with it. Counting back, I try to think how many I had before he took the seat next to mine, and I can't remember. "Five or six?" I ask him, like he should know. "What's it to you, Ren-e-gade," I sound out his name by syllables. My words sound slightly slurred to my own ears. "Renegade," I grin. "Anybody ever tell you, you little boys and your nicknames are cute? Just like playing cops and robbers...you with your Renegade, Trevor with his Tank," I'm giggling for real now. "Pew, pew!" I fake shoot him with my finger gun, thinking how pissed off my brother would be if he were here right now. Not Ryan, though, he's patient. God bless him.

"You think maybe it's time you quit for the night?" He gently moves to take what I have left away from me.

His fingers are soft as they try to pry mine from around the stem, but I resist his attempts and pull it closer to my chest. The liquid sloshes and I inhale deeply, hoping not to lose any of it. I'm like a two-year-old with my blankie. This glass of wine is my security and at this moment I'll protect it with everything I have. Once the security is gone, I'm left with nothing. I can't be transparent tonight, I need something shielding me from my reality. I'm a woman on the prowl, and a woman on the prowl is confident in her abilities.

"Quit?" I ask, running my tongue over my dry lips, trying to moisten them so I can form words more easily. "Quitting is not something I do. That's what my ex-husband did. My mama did. That's what my former boss did," I shake my head and try to stand on four-inch stilettos. He reaches out and grabs my elbow, steadying me, being a rock when I haven't had one in a very long time. "Whitney Trumbolt is not a fuckin' quitter." I make my voice as strong and as clear as possible, I fear though that it comes out a slurred mess.

I can see Ryan try again to keep the smile from his face. The corners of his lips twitch, and it pisses me off. Not because I'm mad, but because he thinks it's funny. He thinks this is a joke, and it's not. It's my life. The life I've been trying so desperately to get out from under or save. I'm not sure which yet. All I know is I haven't been living and I'm damn sick of the in-between.

"You think this is funny?" I take another drink from my wine glass. It's a big one this time, I drain it. There's not one drop left when I set it back down on the bar, slapping my lips together with a satisfied pop.

"No, Whit, I think you're having a bad night." His tone is one someone would use with a kindergartner, talking them down from a temper tantrum. It pisses me off too.

A bad night? Try a bad decade. If I could do anything, it would go back to the night I turned twenty-five and be the age that Ryan is again. I would do so many things differently, I would change so much about the choices I made back then. "You know nothing about me, other than the fact that I'm Tank's older sister."

He grabs me by the wrist, locking his hand around the flesh. I feel his fingers lightly touch the skin and bone. It's more of a caress than a warning. I never realized until this moment how much bigger he is than me. Never really paid any kind of attention to it – oh I've paid attention to him off and on through-out the years, but never like this.

Ryan "Renegade" Kepler rises to his full height, towering over me as I do my best to keep my footing and ignore the way my skin tingles where he grips my wrist. He leans in close – so close I can feel his breath on my skin.

"I know a lot of things about you that you don't think I know."

His voice is hard and soft at the same time. I close my eyes to savor it, to try and figure out how he's able to do both. Maybe it's my drunken mind, but he's magic to me in this instant. The deep timbre rushes over me as I try to understand his words, but I'm having a hard time. This is the closest I've been to a man in a very long time. My body is at attention, as is my libido. I press my thighs together as I dig my heels in deeper, not because I don't want him to move me, because I ache. It's an ache that's never been fulfilled, if I'm honest.

"I know that you love your mama's fried chicken, your grandmother's homemade mac and cheese, Alabama football, and Dale Earnhardt Jr. I know that you have a soft heart. Hallmark movies make you cry, you pick up strays on the side of the road, and you always buy that homeless man near the Starbucks a morning coffee," he lulls me into a sense of security. Making me want to believe there is someone out there who listens when I talk, someone who looks at me and sees a brain behind my blonde hair.

I'm wrapped up in his voice, in the things he does know about me. Things I never knew he paid attention to. I'm swaying, but it's because his voice is doing weird things to my equilibrium. His other hand cups my hip and I can feel the heat of his body through the material of my skirt. My thighs burn as they're pressed against his where we stand.

"I know that your ex-husband was a piece of shit. I know that your ex-boss didn't know what the hell to do with the creative genius that is your mind, and I know that your mama will never forgive you for giving up pageants, but she'll never forgive herself for pushing you that damn hard," he stops and pulls back, giving me his eyes and face to stare at.

Our eyes meet – his brown to my blue – and I realize with clarity that I'm breathing hard, hard enough that it feels as if I've run a marathon. The loss of his strong body against mine makes me want to cry. I want to grasp at his clothing, pull him back in, and let him heat up parts of me that have been cold for so long.

"You wanna know what else I know?" The question is asked in a way that says he's not sure if he wants an answer. The way his face closes off and he withdraws slightly into himself make me think this is a secret he's not shared with anyone. Tonight, I want him to share it with me; I want to be the person he confides in. He knows so much about me, I want to know everything about him too. There's a string of awareness stretched between us, and it's pulling me closer.

I'm captivated by the way the dim lights of the bar make his brown eyes darker, I'm enthralled by the fact that it looks like it's been a few days since he shaved, and I'm even more fascinated by the cut he has on his cheek. He and Tank went out on a call last night, and I can't help but wonder if that cut is the result of a dangerous night doing a dangerous job.

I shake my head and then nod, because I'm conflicted in my drunkenness, but I do want to find out what else he knows. I step forward, put my arms around his neck, and lean up so that now I'm the one in his ear. The truth of the matter is I need to feel close to him, I want the heat back he's taken away from me. I'm cold without it, and I'm sick to death of being cold. "Tell me what else you know."

I see him look around the bar, checking to make sure that we're not being paid any attention to. He bends with his knees and grips my ass cheeks in the palms of his hands, bringing us flush together so our bodies touch. His voice is dark as he all but growls. "I know I'm the one who can put my dick in that treasure cove. I know I'm the one that can pull that hair, I can pull on those nipples, and I can smack this ass," he squeezes my flesh like he owns it, where his hands rest. "The question is – will you let me?"

It's not a question I can say *no* to. The way the air crackles between us, the alcohol I've consumed, and the sudden fascination I have with his heat. There's not any way that I can say no nor is there any desire on my part to deny it. I've denied myself a lot of things in this life and this right here is not something that I want to brush off. This is God giving me what I want on a silver platter, a sacrificial offering for the shit I've gone through the past few years. This is my Cinderella moment and my SEC Championship all tied together into one great big bow. Over six feet and two hundred pounds of bow. If I say no, Lord, never offer me anything else because I'm gonna be a nun for the rest of my life.

"You're what?" He asks, a glimmer of surprise and playfulness in his eyes.

I said that out loud? Never mind, I can fix this.

"Yes," I breath out, adding on a "please."

"Oh baby, you don't have to beg. I'll do whatever you need me to," Ryan says as I find my hand in his and stumble to keep up as he pulls us out of the bar. We pass people we've known our whole lives, clients I've helped to the altar, and I'm pretty sure we just passed the Deacon of the church. No one stops us as we hit the front door. I gulp in the fresh air, sure as the world my senses are going to come to me.

Guess what? They don't. I'm in for whatever this full moon-lit night is going to bring us. Safe Whitney is not putting the brakes on a ride crazier than a lap at Talladega. No, Wild Whitney has taken her place. Funny how both are four letter words, yet they couldn't be further apart.

In mere minutes I'm in his truck, and we're headed towards my house. I will myself not to pass out, because for the first time in years, I want to be here and present for this experience that's about to happen. I want to remember every damn detail. If it's only going to be for this one night, I don't want to miss a thing.

CHAPTER TWO
RENEGADE

FUN FACT: All of the material from my teenage spank bank is sitting in my truck next to me right now. Whitney Trumbolt (thank God she took back her maiden name) was the star of every fantasy I'd ever had when I'd been a young, horny guy. Back then I'd been skinnier and much less confident in myself, and if I'd ever been able to get inside her, I probably would have lasted all of three seconds.

Now, I go by the nickname Renegade and I'm a member of a specialized task force, along with my regular job as a cop here in Laurel Springs, Alabama. My job is sometimes dangerous and allows me to put my military training to good use. I get to use my hands, brain, and best of all, I get to arrest dumbasses that love to break the law. All in all – it's a win-win. We're not a large enough town to have to worry about crime, but Jesus do we have a booming illegal moonshine business. Even though it's not illegal to make anymore, it's sure as fuck illegal not to pay taxes on it and not keep it below the maximum alcoholic volume.

"You still live over here on Magnolia?" I ask. I want her to think I haven't been keeping track of her, but the truth of the matter is – I have. The fact that Tank is my best friend lets me keep tabs without seeming like a fucking stalker. I simply like to know how she's doing.

"Yup," she giggles. "That's the one thing the motherfucker didn't get in the divorce."

My eyebrows raise to my hairline as I hear the words coming out of her mouth. Wow, her tongue has loosened. Normally Whitney is the epitome of a true southern debutante. She wears her pearls, her blonde hair is curled just so, and you won't catch her skirt over her knee or those words ever being spoken. Maybe I should get her drunk more often. So far it's been a revelation. "We'll be there in a few minutes." I look over at her, realizing she's leaning against the glass of the window. "Don't pass out on me now."

She doesn't say anything and I wonder if maybe she's rethought what she offered. Since we got into the truck, she hasn't turned towards me, she hasn't tried to touch me, and if I didn't know better, I'd say she's almost gone for the night. Part of me expects to hear soft snores coming from her side of the truck. Turning on my blinker, I pull into her drive and let it idle there for a few moments before turning it off. "If you've had second thoughts about this..." I start. I'm nothing if not a gentleman and truthfully, I don't want there to be any weirdness between us. I spend holidays with the Trumbolts. Maybe time and a little bit of sobering up has changed her mind.

God I hope not. When I walked into the bar tonight, I couldn't believe my eyes. Tank had a date, and I hadn't wanted my own company, so I'd decided to go have a beer. Imagine my surprise when I walked in and saw Whitney holding court over almost every man there. I'd shot them all looks of death and then taken the seat next to her. When I realized exactly how drunk she was, I made it my mission to find out what the hell was going on.

I steel myself against the realization that this is probably going to backfire in a big way. Allowing myself to glance over at her, I'm surprised as hell when she meets my eyes, offers me a saucy smile and lifts her hips off the leather of the seat. My dick, which has been a good guy throughout all the talk of treasure coves and nipple play, makes itself known at that moment as it punches against the denim encasing it. I reach down and palm the hardness laying beneath the hard ridge of my jeans, hoping to find a more comfortable position for it to lay. When you're faced with your teenage dreams coming true, you man up and do whatever it takes to make them happen.

"Change my mind?" I watch as she pulls her shirt down, flashing me a little skin. "Not a chance, Renegade. Tonight I'm gonna do things I've never done before." She lifts her hands up like she did at the bar, making finger guns as she *pew pew*'s me again, laughing so hard she lets out an unladylike snort.

With that, she's shrieking and jumping down from my truck, running into her house.

It takes me all of five seconds to follow her. When she playfully slams the door in my face, I wonder if she's going to lock it, but I test the knob and find out that I can easily turn it. As soon as I enter the darkened house, I'm on high alert. This is what I do for a living, chase people. My hearing is exceptional, my night vision is incredible, and I can sense where someone is, usually within a few inches. This woman has nothing on me. Tilting my head to the side, I hear her, she's breathing – not as hard as she will be later, if she lets me follow through, but it's loud enough that I can hear it.

I turn my body to face hers, let my eyes adjust, and see her standing just inside the hallway with her back pressed tightly against the wall. It's almost like she's trying to blend in, but Whitney's never been able to blend in. She's always had a spark about her, always stood tall and beautiful in the face of any storm. Why she thinks she'll be hiding in the dark right now is beyond me. Stalking over to her, I box her in by placing my hands on either side of her shoulders and lean forward so close that our lips are almost touching. I tilt my head sideways, almost capturing the kiss I want. We're sharing breath we're so close, but I don't take it. I want the decision to be hers and hers alone.

"Last chance to back out. Otherwise, prepare to have everything you told me about in the bar come true," I give her five seconds, because that's all I can wait. It's all I have the patience for. Teenage me is seeing every one of his wet dreams come true, while adult me is ready to show this woman what I have in my repertoire. "What's it gonna be, Whit?"

Whitney

His words taunt me, his body tempts me. There are so many voices telling me I shouldn't want this, that this won't end well, but fuck those voices. Those same voices told me that my marriage would last forever and that I'd be a mother by now. They told me that it was my responsibility to be a good wife. I was and the asshole ruined me – he completely broke my heart – and I'm doing everything I can to get a little piece of the old Whitney back. Is this my best idea ever? Probably not, but damnit, I want this, I need this.

Sober Whitney would be telling Ryan to take himself somewhere else, that he's too young and I'm too damaged, but Doormat Whitney isn't in charge right now. This Whitney wants everything she's never had. She wants to experience all the things she's heard about. Giving myself up for the night is exactly what I want. It's only one night...right? After this, I can go back to being the woman who makes dreams come true for everyone else. For one night, I can feel like a real woman. I can feel like someone who's wanted instead of someone that was thrown away and forgotten about.

My voice is breathless. "I don't want to back out. I wanna know what you taste like, what you feel like, how your fingers grip me when you're fucking me. Tonight, I want it all."

Truthfully, I don't even recognize my own voice, I don't recognize the decisions I'm making. These are the desperate decisions of a woman who's been pushed too far – a woman who's been told too many times that she's not worth it. I want to be worth it. I want to feel worthy, even if it's only once.

"Relax," he whispers as his hands come off the wall and bury themselves in my hair, making me glad I wore it down and loose tonight.

His fingertips massage my scalp in a motion that lulls me into a sense of security before he tugs slightly, tilting my head back so that I expose my neck to his lips. His mouth is hungry, his tongue wet as it laps at the skin there. I can feel the rasp of his five o'clock shadow, the sharpness of his teeth as he scores the flesh, and then the warmth of his tongue as he soothes the burn.

My arms go around him, holding onto his neck and pushing my fingers up into the short hair on his head, threading them through so I can hold him closer to me. I want him to inhale me, I want him to eat me up and not make any apologies about it. If there's anything he could give me, it would be the wild rush into passion. I've never felt that before. I've never had one of those movie love scenes where the two people just can't keep their hands off one another. I want that tonight, more than I've ever wanted anything in my life.

His hands move from my hair down my shoulders, grasping the edges of my collar. The plaid button-down I have on is only held together by snaps which easily release when he pulls roughly on the seams. Pushing the useless fabric from my body, he devours me. I can feel his gaze on me, but I'm not happy with that. I want to see it, the hunger, the way he looks upon me. Prying my eyes open, I take in the look on his face and hold it tightly. His face says it all; this is a man who enjoys what he's looking at. His gaze is hot and hungry. It makes me self-conscious and it takes everything I have not to cover myself up. I've never felt this exposed before. While it's frightening, it's also a huge turn on, especially when I look down and see the hard-on tenting his jeans.

"I'm not young like you're used to," I make the excuse, diverting my gaze. So far he hasn't given me any indication he's not turned on by me, but some men can get it up no matter who they're with. "But I work out four times a week," because I have to, otherwise my anxiety ramps up too much and I can't even live with myself.

His hands cup my hips, curling in at my waist, squeezing the firm skin before moving them up, towards the material that holds the heavy weight of my chest up. His hands don't stop as he uses his fingers to push my flesh up over the lacy tops before he leans in and swipes the hard tips with the edge of his tongue. I slap my palms back against the wall, grasping for something to hold onto in order to anchor myself. If this were a movie, it would be Top Gun, you know that scene where all you see is tongue in the moonlight as a shadow? I always loved that damn movie, and I always envisioned having that very sex scene.

"You're gorgeous."

I want to believe it, because the way he says it, makes me want to. His voice is raw, the words raspy and gravelly as he breathes them out. They make me want to revel in them. If I were brave, I'd thrust my tits out, spread my legs a little, and welcome him into the cradle of them. Unfortunately, inviting him in here has taken up all my bravado tonight.

"I bet you say that to all the women," I give him a shy smile, not fishing for a compliment. I'm not used to them, and I have no idea how to react to them. Something tells me that Ryan Kepler is a very generous lover with a totally silver tongue.

"No," he shakes his head, face serious. "Normally, I just tell them to flip over, stick their ass up, and prepare to be fucked. You," he stops, running his tongue along his bottom lip as he steps closer into my personal space. "For you I'll make an exception."

All of a sudden I'm scared to death, but this fear is something I'll never run from.

CHAPTER THREE
RENEGADE

I CAN'T BELIEVE this woman doesn't know how beautiful, how gorgeous, or how sexy she is. I can see it in her eyes; she questions it. I know from being around the family what an asshole her ex-husband was, but I didn't know it was *this* bad. In my mind I try to think back to the times I saw them together, but nothing ever stood out at me. Whitney just got quieter and quieter over the years, but I figured that was her personality changing. Now I'm wondering if it was all due to her marriage. I'm not sure even they know it was this bad. My mission tonight is clear. Show this woman how gorgeous she is and how bad I want to get deep inside her body.

"Which way's the bedroom?" Most of the time I've been around her has been at her family's home, not this one she's made for herself. As a couple, she and Stephen never invited anyone over. I always thought it was because they liked to keep their private life private – as in they were just private people. Now I'm beginning to wonder if there wasn't something else going on behind the scenes. The way she's reacting to me is throwing up all kinds of red flags. I purposely keep my touch on her light.

Bashfully, she buries her face in my neck, inhaling deeply before she points down the hallway. "On the right," she tells me, her voice muffled against my skin.

I turn to my right and walk us through the doorway. Once I'm there, I take a look around and my jaw almost drops. It's the most feminine thing I have ever seen in my life. It's completely and totally Whitney in every way possible. I'm surprised the fucking sheets don't have monograms on them. From where I stand, I can see that they are Tiffany blue. Once upon a time, I didn't know what that color was – I called it blue green – and you would have thought it was the end of the world. As a teenager, I didn't know how important the distinction would be. She made sure I knew the difference; she takes this shit seriously.

I let her body slide down mine until she's on her high heels, steadying her. "Take those off, Whit, you're not gonna need them the rest of the night."

She listens, turning to kick them in the general direction of her closet and it's then that I realize how much smaller she is than me. With those shoes gone, she barely reaches my collarbone. It's not that I haven't known but being this close, knowing that I'm going to cover her with my body in a few minutes and take what we both want, makes me worry about hurting her. I fight the urge to pull her in, cradle her head against my chest, and tell her everything is going to be okay. That's not what she needs tonight, that's not what she wants, and it sure as fuck isn't what she's asked me for. Her body wants to use mine, and I'm down for doing whatever is needed to make that happen.

"What do you want me to do to you? What's your fantasy?" I ask, my voice low as I move in behind her and wrap my arms around her waist. Not giving her time to overthink, I move my hands to her tits, palming them, teasing the nipples as I wait for her answer. When she doesn't speak, I make a vow again, pulling her head back against my shoulder and tilting her chin up so I can see her in the dim light the moon is casting through the curtains. "I'm going to give you whatever you want."

Her voice is breathless when she answers me. It's rough, raw, but it's firm, so I know there's no second-guessing here. "I want everything you would do with a one-night stand; everything I talked about at the bar. Use me the way I want to use you." I turn her around to face me so I can make sure she's being truthful. She's never had much of a poker face.

The rosy blush that's covering her cheeks tells me those words were hard for her to say and I'll be fucking damned if I'm going to use her, but I'll give her the best night of her life...or pull my groin trying. Lowering my face to hers, I brush a soft kiss against her mouth. "Birth control?" I ask.

Her chin wobbles, lower lip sticks a teeny bit farther out than her upper one. The words she speaks are low, and thick with sadness. "You're covered. I can't have kids."

The words hit my gut like I've been shot, but I recover quickly. This is something I'm not even sure Tank knows and I'll take it to the grave with me if I have to. "Doesn't matter to me," I answer shooting her a hot smile, hoping to bring the mood back up.

I look into her eyes, memorizing the way they appear in this moment. In the muted light of the room, I can't see the color, but I can see her pupils are dilated and cloudy with desire. I want to keep that look there and possibly add aroused and hungry to it as well. "You ready, Whit?" I ask.

"For what?" Her voice is hushed in the quiet room.

Leaning in, I put my lips at her ear, nibbling softly on the lobe. "Everything."

Whitney

My body shivers as his breath washes over the skin of my ear. I can feel the heat everywhere, I want him like I've never wanted anyone before. There is a part of me that wants him to take me, but there's also a part of me that wants to be a participant, and give him everything I've never been able to give another man. Reaching my arms up, I wrap them around his neck and pull him down so we're face-to-face. I lean in so our lips are millimeters apart; we're breathing the same air, and I want so badly to touch his skin to mine but I pull back at the last second.

Ryan's lips chase me, causing my heart to pound, my pulse to skyrocket, and a wetness between my thighs. When they catch mine, I let him swallow me up, I let him take the lead. His tongue is smooth velvet as it glides against mine, devouring me in a way I've never been devoured before. When he pulls away, I chase him. I'm dying to be closer to him. So when he palms my ass with his hands, I let my weight rest there as I lift my legs and wrap them around his waist, pushing against him as he pulls me closer.

There's an urgency in our movements, in the way we're kissing, and the way our hands are suddenly fighting with one another. One arm loosens its hold from his neck and moves down to the waistband of his jeans, shoving his shirt up over what I feel are tight abs. As I pull it up to his collarbone, he wrenches his mouth from mine, allowing me to finish bringing it up and over his head.

"Wow," I'm looking at his chest and abs like I've never seen a man's body before. In reality I've not seen one that looks like his. He's cut in ways I've only dreamed about, all lined muscle and tone flesh with a tattoo on his left pec and another that wraps around his right bicep all the way down to his elbow. I can't make out what either is, and right now I don't much care. Tattoos have never been a thing for me, but right now I'd like to color both of these in with the tip of my tongue. I realize I've blurted those words out loud when he chuckles against me, small puffs of hot air gusting against my face.

"Whatever you want, Whit," he tells me again as he sets me down softly on my feet. My toes curl into the plush carpet, almost like they know what I'm about to do. They're getting prepared to curl for a different reason.

I want everything and more. A lot that we don't have time for, and a lot that I'm not emotionally prepared to handle. We have one night, and I want it to count. The way my life has gone means I might never get this chance again. I make quick work of his belt and unbutton his shorts, slipping them off the lower part of his body and letting it drop in a puddle at our feet. Our eyes meet and I'm breathless as I make out the passion glowing from his. Whatever this is between us, he's taking it seriously. "I want you to show me what I've been missing."

He growls – a rough noise that lifts the hairs on my forearms – as he sinks down to his knees in front of me, slightly pushing me back so I land on the bed. The force is enough that I let my elbows take my weight. Gazing at him over the edge of my body, I wonder what he's going to do with me once he gets my legs spread. A vague thought that he's going to not only worship but ravage me races through my mind. I'm completely on board with whatever he wants to do. Strong hands pull me forward on the bed, almost far enough that I can touch the floor with my feet, but instead, he stops before my feet can make the connection again. He leaves me hanging, suspended, and even that excites me. Getting up from his knees, he moves so that he's kneeling between my thighs and places a kiss on my stomach before he lifts his eyes to mine.

"Lift up your arms, sweetheart," his voice is low, seductive, and fucking sexy as he brings my tank top over my head. My bra is meant for sin; a hot pink number that is cut low. If I make one move too fast, you can see a nipple. I know, because I checked. My underwear? They match. I had a plan tonight. It's up in the air if I would have gone through with it had I not run into Ryan.

"Shit, why do you keep these covered up?" he asks, bringing his palms up to the sides of my breasts, using his thumbs to agitate my nipples into hard buds. They're pulling taut, begging for his mouth.

"Please, Ryan," I use my elbows to push myself towards him. He doesn't need to know my shyness, doesn't need to know that it took me a shot of vodka and a shot of Jim Beam to even put these clothes on and walk out of my house tonight. All he needs to know is that I want his lips on my nipples, I want his length inside my body, and I want to be screaming with release as soon as possible.

I don't have to ask twice as he leans forward and captures my flesh in between his teeth, scoring the nub lightly, before he soothes it with his tongue. I dig my fingers into his shoulders as he leans closer to me, spreading my legs further apart. I dent those strong shoulders with my nails, yanking against his skin, wanting his weight on top of me, wanting to feel it more than I've ever wanted to feel anything.

He makes one nipple stand at attention before he does the same to the other, causing me to grasp him under his arms and pull him up and over me. I'm holding him as tightly and as closely as I can. My subconscious is scared he'll leave before he's done, before I'm done. "Now, Ryan, I can't wait. Now, please," I beg him.

He spreads out over top of me. Grasping my hands, he puts our palms together and stretches them up over my head, entwining our fingers. "Hold on," he rasps as he slides deep inside me.

It takes my breath, the feeling of him stretching my core, of his hardness inside me. It's something I wanted, but until this moment, I never knew I did. I feel tears prick the back of my eyes, because Ryan is a thousand times more tender than my ex-husband ever was, even being as rough as he is. It's something I want, something I need. I hook my legs around his hips, urging him on, digging my heels into his ass. Even the words I'm thinking are dirtier tonight than they've ever been. Finally, I've given myself permission to be a woman who knows what she wants. Damn the consequences.

"Faster," I breathe out against the heat of his neck as I bury my mouth there. "I haven't come from anything other than my hand in such a long time, even when I was married. Ryan, get me there," I'm straining against him, wanting to let the feeling wash over me, dying for this orgasm.

"C'mon Whit, you're feelin' it, baby. I can feel you tightening against me."

He's right, I am. He's thrusting and withdrawing at such a pace, I feel like I'm in a souped up foreign car running the quarter mile. I'm heading on a one-way course to coming, and I want it so bad I can taste it.

"Just let it go, babe, let it go," he tells me as he shoves deep inside me, and let's go of my hands to tilt my ass. He bottoms out and grinds against my clit. It's a move no one's ever used on me before, and good gracious, if they had, I'd know what a spectacular orgasm was before now.

That's all I need. All the tension breaks loose and I arch into his caress, closing my eyes tightly, letting the feeling wash over me.

"Ryan!" I moan, feeling him spill inside me, as I pulse against him.

Like that, my world brightens, changes, and spins so far off its axis that I'm not sure it'll ever be straight again. As I try to come to grips with what I've done, all I can do is smile a sappy grin. For once, I did something for myself – damn the consequences. For once, I'm happy. With a giggle, I make a soft little *pew pew* because if it hadn't been for Renegade, I wouldn't be here.

CHAPTER FOUR

WHITNEY

HOT, I'm so hot, burning up in fact. I don't remember ever being this hot in my life, and there's something pressing against me. A gentle pressure that I'm feeling at the core of my body. Using my hand, I move down to where I feel the pressure, and feel hair. Prying my eyes open, I look down, only to see Ryan's head between my legs.

"Oh my God," I breathe out as I feel his tongue lick up against my clit. His fingers grip the flesh of my thighs, holding them open with his shoulders to give himself room. "Don't stop," I beg him, grasping the tips of his hair, yanking his mouth closer to me.

I'm grinding against his tongue, wondering how long he's been doing this because I'm there already. Normally it takes me a while to loosen up, to let myself go and feel. My ex-husband, he never went down, so this is a treat I wasn't expecting. I've also never been woken up for sex, so I'm going to enjoy this while I can. Three ticks off the "never done before" list in less than twenty-four hours. I'm feeling mighty proud of myself.

Pressing my body down against his face, I'm trying to widen my thighs even more when he inserts two fingers inside of me and then uses his tongue to flick my clit. That's all it takes. I can't stop moving, rotating my thighs to try to get closer. I'm screaming, grasping hold of his hair. He's with me the entire way, never letting up no matter which way I move. Ryan sticks with me, his lips never detach from mine.

Pushing against his head, I move him. "Please, so sensitive." My words are still slurred, but I think this time I'm sex drunk instead of wine drunk.

He lets go, then uses his hands on my thighs to flip me over onto my stomach.

In the darkness, I hear his words, rough with sleep and hard with arousal. "Grab the headboard, Whitney."

Ohhh, this is also something I've only ever done a few times. I like this side of Ryan. I try to tell him, but as he thrusts inside me, the breath and words are taken from my throat. "Shit," I let my head fall against the headboard, resting my hot cheek against the cool wood. It's the one thing that's keeping me grounded. The way he's pounding into me makes me feel like I can fly.

"What did you say to me earlier tonight, Whit?" he pants into my ear as he layers himself over my body. His sweaty chest slips against my back. "You needed a red handprint on your ass?"

I'm trying to think as I tilt my head back, sucking in air, trying to focus my eyes. "I think, oh God," he grips my hip as he pushes even deeper. "I think that's what I said," I pant, grabbing for anything I can use to anchor myself.

He lifts himself up and that's when I feel his palm connect with my ass cheek. It shocks me, making me scream, but in a really good way.

"That what you wanted?"

It's everything I wanted and more. "Yes!"

And then I can't form anymore words as he smacks my flesh again before he grips my hips, resting his forehead on my back. The only thing I can hear are his grunts and the deep intake of both our lungs trying to get oxygen, before I feel him erupt inside of me.

Turning me onto my side, he spoons me from behind, using his index finger to flick my clit. I feel myself fly again as I explode.

One thing is for sure. I won't ever forget this night. Those are the last thoughts I have before sleep overtakes me again.

THE SUN IS bright as it tries to invade the darkness of my closed eyes. I moan, those rays feel like safety pins poking small holes in the blanket of my eye lids. I've never felt like this before, even when I was a college co-ed and indulged in a few frat parties. My tongue is stuck to the roof of my mouth, and I am hot, so hot. Which is weird, because I'm usually freezing. I reach down to pull the cover off me, only to figure out that I can't pull it off, it's heavy – as if something has pinned it down or snagged the edge. Even as I grunt and yank with all my might, I can't make it budge.

I pry an eye open and glance to the other side of the bed. Laying there, with the blanket down to his waist and half of it wrapped around him is Ryan Kepler. What in the world is he doing in my bed? I gasp, because there's nothing else for me to do, as I move away from him. It's then that I feel the soreness between my thighs and memories of the night before flash through my head like a movie. It's almost as if I'm outside my body watching us as they flood back to me. I slept with my little brother's best friend. Holy shit! My movements must disturb him because he rolls so he's facing me and gives me the hottest smile I've ever seen in my life. It makes every part of my body tingle and tremble. Every part he touched last night relives it right there in that moment.

"Morning."

His voice is everything, it makes me close my eyes as I let it run through me. It's rough and deep with sleep, tinted with the southern accent of our hometown, and I can hear all the words he said to me last night as he thrust his body into mine. It causes my face to burn, and I know right now that I have to get him out of my bed, out of my house, out of my life. I can't believe what I've done. I'm an addict that's taken her first hit of heroin.

"Morning," I tell him back as I get up, hugging the comforter to my naked body. I push the sheet towards him, hoping he remains covered. My eyes don't meet his. I can't bring myself to do it, I can't make myself look at him and lay myself bare, it's not how I'm hardwired – not after five years of marriage to a man who ended up either scaring or humiliating me on an almost daily basis.

There's a sigh, and I realize that it's not mine. It's his.

"So that's how it's going to be?" His tone doesn't mask the hurt.

"What do you mean?" I can plainly hear the disappointment. I'm still not meeting his eyes, can't stand to see what the look in them must be.

"You know exactly what I mean, Whitney," this time it's clipped and pissed.

I hear him fling the sheet off and brace myself for the raised voice, the accusation, the humiliation, but it doesn't come. Nothing happens and that makes me even more nervous. Finally curiosity wins out and I have to know what's going on. I lift my eyes and see him looking at me as he quietly puts his clothes on with jerky movements.

"I'm sorry," I whisper, because I am. I wish this could be different; wish like hell that *I* could be different. But I'm not. I haven't been able to move on that far yet, and I don't know when I'll ever be able to.

His face is dark, the beard growth covering his cheeks and chin, his hair is an absolute mess, and he looks dangerous with his chest exposed, tattoo showing. "You got what you wanted didn't you? You proved to yourself that the fuckface you married didn't break you completely. That's what you needed – right?"

He has this all wrong. It is what I needed, but not this way. Yes it was about using each other, but I never wanted it to feel cheap, and this morning, that's exactly how it feels. "You don't understand," I shake my head. "You're too young to get it."

His head snaps up, and *now* he's pissed. Before he had been irritated, now there's a rage. I can feel it coming off him in waves, see it in the way his eyes narrow. The words he flings with his irritation exposed, hits me harder than any fists ever could. "Don't tell me how young I am, Whitney. I've seen and done things you can't even imagine."

While I'm sure that's true, I have ten years of life experience on him and I can't say that I'm proud of what I did last night. If someone had slept with my brother and they were my age, there would definitely be some judgement – mine included – pointed toward them. I can't change that I feel a little dirty about what I've done.

I try again, using the tone I use with customers who are upset about the service they've received. It doesn't happen often, but I do know how to soothe ruffled feathers. "I don't want to offend you."

"Too late, sweetheart," he says as he yanks the shirt over his head, blocking my view of that tattoo.

"This isn't how I meant for this to go," I try again, holding the blanket against my middle. I can recognize that I'm bent over trying to disappear into myself, making my body smaller as not to attract his attention. I always have to explain myself, I always have to make sure that I'm understood, it gives me anxiety not to be understood.

He finishes putting his clothes on and then sits down on the bed, covering his feet with boots. When he gets up and buttons his jeans, he walks over to me. Ryan raises his hands and I immediately pull into myself, flinching away from him, without meaning to.

Awareness flashes in his eyes, and then his jaw sets even harder than it was. "Jesus, Whit," he whispers.

I try to keep the tears out of my eyes, but it doesn't work. "Yeah," I pull my bottom lip between my teeth, looking anywhere but at him. There's nothing else to say. He now knows every humiliation I've suffered.

His touch is tender as he cups my face in his palms. They're warm and I want to bury myself there, let him make all of my hurts better. I'm not sure I can ever give anyone that power over me again, though. "I think I do understand, and you shouldn't have kept that from anyone," he swallows hard, sighing again. "And if this is what you needed, then I'm glad I could be the man to give it to you."

"Thank you," I tell him. I'm so grateful for him. I'm so thankful that he gave me back this part of myself, even if only for a few hours.

"Doesn't mean that it doesn't kill me, because there's so much I want to say to you right now, but I know you aren't ready for it."

He's right, I'm not ready for anything more than this, at all, and I'm lucky that he recognizes it and is man enough to realize this isn't about him. It's about me. This is all completely about me.

"I'll never forget what you did for me," I tell him, clearing my throat. "Last night means the world to me."

He opens his mouth but doesn't say anything. He rocks on the balls of his feet, then shakes his head.

Leaning forward he kisses me, softly but thoroughly, leaving an imprint on me that I'm not sure will ever go away.

He lets me go and walks towards the doorway of the bedroom, but he turns at the last minute. "I'm gonna be honest, because this could be my only chance," he stops and takes a breath, seems to collect himself. "You'll never know how much this," he waves his arms towards the bed, "means to me."

With that he's gone, and I'm left to try and process just what in the world I've done. Those consequences I was damning last night hurt in the harsh daylight of the morning.

CHAPTER FIVE

WHITNEY

"WHAT BRINGS YOU HERE TODAY?" the female Doc Miller asks me. I purposely requested her when I called for an emergency appointment. The receptionist went to high school with me and knew by the shock in my voice I needed to see someone today, although I didn't tell her about my positive pregnancy tests. I'm just lucky the clinic is open until seven at night.

I try to fight back the tears that are threatening. "I thought I was depressed," I whisper as I think back to the thoughts that were so clear hours ago. Back when I'd tried to convince myself it was seasonal.

"Okay, what's going on?" she asks, opening up the chart in front of her.

"I'm tired all the time, some days I don't want to get out of bed. You and I both know that's not like me. Running my own business is all I ever wanted to do. Now that Whitney's Weddings has taken off, I'm busier than ever but some days it's a struggle. I'm crying very easily, like at the drop of a hat, I feel nauseated some mornings, and sometimes it's a struggle to eat. I just feel off," I tell her, listing my symptoms. "And this afternoon I took five positive pregnancy tests," I swallow against the lump in my throat. "But they can't be right because I can't have kids."

Her eyes are wide as I tell her about the five positive pregnancy tests. She lets out a breath and gives me a small smile. "Okay, then let's get the basic info first. When was your last period?" she asks.

Pulling my phone out of my pocket, I glance at the app, giving her the date. "It's never been regular, and I've never been able to get pregnant before. Maybe I'm going through early menopause?" I'm grasping at straws because thinking I'm pregnant and then finding out that I'm not will obliterate me.

"We can test for that. It's simple and just a blood test. We'll do the lab in-office that way we'll know quicker. At least we'll have a starting point. How's that sound?" she asks.

"Great," I tell her. I honestly just want answers. I'm sick of being so tired, and I need to know an official answer before I get my hopes up too far.

I sit there through getting pricked with the needle, having the blood withdrawn, and wait while the results come back. The whole time a million things are playing over and over again in my brain. I'm exhausted and drifting off when the door opens and Doc Miller comes in, papers in her hand.

"Whitney, let me ask you a question."

I'm trying very hard to give her my full attention, to not drift off in the middle of this doctor's appointment. That's all I need. "Sure."

"Who told you that you couldn't have children?" She asks carefully, almost as if she's trying to gauge my reaction.

I run my hand through my blonde hair thinking back to all the things that had gone on. All the months that we'd tried. Every month a negative pregnancy test. "Stephen and I tried for four out of the five years that we were married. I could never get pregnant."

"Did you ever get tested?" She asks carefully.

Shame burns my face as I try valiantly to push back the tears threatening to spill over. My voice is strangled, my breath gusting faster as I explain. "We were going to, but he told me there wasn't a reason to because it was all my fault. And if I was any kind of woman, I'd be giving her man an heir to carry on the family name. I was so upset that we never went to the appointment. You have to understand about him..." I go back to my old MO of trying to make excuses for the man that I was once married to.

"Don't excuse him, Whitney. I see men like him every day."

She stops for a minute and levels me with a stare. It's equal parts disbelieving and what looks like happiness. It scares me.

"So were the tests true then? Was it him who had the problem and not me?" I put on a brave face, but inside, I'm coming apart.

She comes over and grabs my hand, and that's when I know it. Something is majorly wrong, I'm probably dying. Or maybe she's going to tell me exactly what I want to hear.

"Congratulations, Whitney! You're pregnant."

The world tilts as I pass out against the examination table.

Renegade

Betty is pushing papers at myself and Trevor. "I need you to sign this so we can send it to the worker's comp company since this was a work injury," she's telling Trevor who looks at her like she's grown another head.

"With what hand? Fucker got my dominant one," he gestures at the thick padding and ace bandage that now covers the ten stitches in his skin.

"Here," I laugh. "Let me sign your name, sweetheart."

"Thanks, baby," he winks, puckering his lips to give me an air kiss and causing her to laugh at us.

"You two are too much. Here," she hands us a packet. "You'll need to give this to Holden, because it is worker's comp, and here's your next appointment to get the stitches out," she hands Trevor an appointment card.

"Thanks," he tells her. "If I have trouble, should I call here or go to the ER?" Doc Miller told us that there was a high risk of infection considering where the he'd been sliced, as well as the condition of the blade.

She looks down. "Notes say go straight to the ER."

"Great," he says, quirking a brow. "Let's hope that doesn't happen."

I start to say something, but the door beside us opens and someone else comes out of the examination rooms. We're holding up progress, so I quickly sign Trevor's name and grab the paperwork we need. I'm trying not to listen in on what's going on behind us, but we're so close that I can't help it.

"Here's your first round of prenatals. Let's see how you handle these, and then we'll get more. Stop by Betty and make your first follow-up. At your age, we'll have to monitor you closely."

Curiosity gets the better of me, and both Trevor and I turn around at the same time, our eyes meeting Whitney's.

"You're pregnant?" we both ask at the same time.

Her face is a mask of panic, and once more, she looks like she wants to escape.

I'll be damned.

Whitney

"Seems like it," I do my best to smile at both my brother and the father of my unborn child. God I never thought I'd say those words. For so many years I had hoped that I would, but with Stephen nothing ever happened and it had always been my fault. For five seconds, I have the urge to call him, tell him that some other man got the job done, and then hang up.

But the sensible side to my brain tells me that he'll find some way to make it a mistake. He'll find a way for me to doubt myself, my words, and my life, and I've worked too hard to put all that behind me, to put *him* behind me. Glancing into Ryan's clear, brown eyes, I can see that he has questions, but I can't go into it right here, right now. Not with Trevor looking at me like he can see into my soul.

"I didn't even know that you were seeing anyone," Trevor pins me with his gaze.

I might be ten years older than him, but he has always seen himself as my protector, and damn whoever gets in the way. From the time he was old enough to put up his fists and fight, he's been my fiercest ally. "It's new and completely unexpected." That's not a lie at all.

"How are you feeling?" he asks. "You look a little pale."

I laugh almost in a crazy way. It's the only thing keeping me from crying, and right now I'm not sure if they're tears of happiness or tears of oh-my-God-what-am-I-doing? "I passed out when she told me. I couldn't believe it."

Trevor gestures to his hand. "We gotta get back, but I'm calling you later on and we're having a talk."

For the first time, I notice that it's wrapped in thick gauze and he's holding it gingerly. "Oh my gosh, what happened to you?"

"We were serving a summons and a seventy-year-old man took offense to us dismantling his still," Trevor shook his head. "Still can't believe he had a knife."

He reaches in and hugs me. "I'm glad you're okay."

I realize now more than ever how dangerous what they do is, and one of them is now the father of my unborn child. It's enough to cause tears to spring to my eyes. Damn these hormones to hell.

"Don't cry," he pulls me in for another hug, wrapping his good hand around my neck. "I'm good, Whit."

I valiantly try to still the trembling of my chin. "I know, just emotional," I clear my throat and try to get myself together.

"I gotta go," he tells me. "Love you."

"Love you, too. Be very careful. You have a niece or nephew to worry about now," I shakily smile at him.

He and Ryan go to leave the office, but Ryan grabs my hand.

"Congratulations, Whit," he says loud enough for everyone to hear, but then he lowers his voice. "I'll be by your house after I square up things with Trevor. We need to talk."

I nod, because I know he's right. I know he has questions but I don't have any answers.

Renegade

"You're quiet," Trevor speaks twenty minutes after we get into the truck. I've said all of two words to him. I want to press the gas, go one hundred miles an hour, drop him off, and then get to Whitney's. I have a million thoughts running through my head, but I am in no way ready to tell Trevor that I'm the father of his soon-to-be niece or nephew. I haven't discussed it with Whitney, I don't know how we're going to play this, and above all, I'm in fucking shock.

"Got a lot on my mind, man."

"Anything you want to talk about?" Trevor is the best friend I've ever had, and it doesn't feel good not being completely honest with him. It really fucking sucks.

"Nothing I can talk about right now, but when I can, you'll be the first to know."

God, I'm a dick. No matter what I do though, it's going to piss off one of the Trumbolts, and I'd rather not do that now. I sigh in relief as I see headquarters over the hill. I can drop Trevor off, go to Whitney's, and finally get some answers.

It feels like an eternity as I answer the questions for Holden about what the doctor said so he's in the loop about Trevor's injury. Holden, thank God, is going to drive him home, leaving me free to do what I need to do. Since I've been on this team, I've never ran out so fast, ready to get to another facet of my life. This crew, this team, has been my life.

A few traffic laws are broken as I make my way to Whitney's house. I try to play the potential conversation in my brain, before I even get there, because I want to be prepared for what she might say to me. I want to make sure I sound like an adult, not her little brother's best friend. I have a feeling, a very strong feeling, that this is going to take a lot of sweet-talking on my part. She's not been shy about the fact that I'm younger than her.

What should have taken me thirty minutes has taken me fifteen. I park my truck in her driveway and stop for a few moments, collecting myself, my thoughts, fuck my manhood, as I step down from the running board and go up her walkway. I feel like a man with a plan, nothing is going to derail or deter me.

Until I knock, and knock, and knock on her front door and she doesn't answer.

"Whitney, your SUV is parked out front, I know you're in there," I tell her through the heavy thickness of wood that separates us.

I knock a few more minutes, still she doesn't answer. "Don't think I can't get in there, Whit," I laugh. "You do realize that I did special ops, right?"

When she doesn't answer, I realize that she doesn't know who she's dealing with. "Fuck it," I mumble as I make my way to the back of the house. If I'm going to be breaking and entering, I don't want to do it in full view of her neighbors.

I'm amused as I open her unlocked gate and jog up her back porch. What she doesn't realize is breaking the law and getting paid to do it is kinda my thing. "Game on, baby doll," I whisper as I grab my tool kit out of my back pocket. Never leave home without it.

CHAPTER SIX

WHITNEY

I'M SITTING at my kitchen table with my latest client file in front of me, earbuds in, and Spotify on. When I'm stressed this is what I do best, bury myself in work and let the stress go. Now that the pregnancy has been confirmed, I have a surge of energy I haven't had in weeks. It makes me want to get back to work. Whitney's Weddings has become one of the most sought after wedding and event planning businesses in the Birmingham area. I serve all the small surrounding counties and have handled events all the way to Gulf Shores and Orange Beach, as well. My business is growing, it's become enough that I'm making more money and living better than I was when I was married.

Which makes me smile, because it was a big issue that Stephen held over my head for the longest time. I couldn't take care of myself. There wouldn't be money for vacations, or the manicures and pedicures I enjoy. How wrong he was – I've thrived without his negativity.

I reach down to cup my non-existent bump and I make a promise to myself and this child. I will not fail us, I will do whatever it takes to make our lives work. For years I've lived my life for other people, but now I'm doing whatever it takes to make me happy. For so long I've made the fairy tale for other people, it's time I make the fairy tale for myself – even if there isn't a Prince Charming in the picture. A vision of Ryan flashes before me, but I shake my head. There's no way in this world we could work out. Instead, I'm going to do what makes me happy.

Which is planning weddings.

I pick up the white piece of fabric the bride has chosen for her tablecloths and hold it against a rose gold place setting. The bride requested elegant and I love the way this looks together. Hoping that she does too, I lean down and make notes in the notebook I have specified for this wedding. Noticing that I've made another note to check a local vendor for customized necklaces, I pick up my phone and begin typing out a message to a friend who works there. One thing this business has given me is an extended network of women who are changing the world with a smartphone, Wi-Fi, and a little bit of imagination. It's a great time to be a woman in business, and I'm proud to be one of them.

It's then I feel someone watching me. This is a feeling I know all too well. It's one I grew accustomed to in my marriage. Swallowing against the lump that's formed in my throat, I turn around, facing where I feel the gaze coming from. When I see Ryan, I scream and jump a mile in my chair.

"Ryan, what the hell are you doing in here?" I ask, putting my hand to my heart, realizing it's beating fast enough to give me a heart attack. "I thought we were meeting later on."

"Yeah," he gives me a smile that I can only describe as smart ass. "I did too, but when you didn't answer the door, I decided to let myself in," he holds up a tool that I've seen Trevor use on occasion.

Glancing down at my phone, I realize I got so involved in my work that I completely lost track of time, but it doesn't excuse what he's done. Letting a man run all over me isn't something I'm going to allow to happen again. Too many years I've wasted, and I refuse to do it any longer. "You broke into my house? You broke the law you're bound to uphold."

"Let myself in," he corrects me. "I was worried you were avoiding me."

I can see where he's coming from and at least he's not feeding me a line about worrying for my safety. I'm sure Trevor's told him that I've learned to take care of myself. One of the first things I did after getting divorced was take self-defense classes and got my concealed carry license. "I simply lost track of time," I'm apologetic and I hope he realizes that it had nothing to do with him.

"Mind if I have a seat?" he indicates the seat across from me at the table.

I shake my head no. I'd rather our conversation be in my own space, where I have control over the situation. Control is something I've lacked so often in my life. Now I hang onto it with both hands and refuse to let it go. Quickly grabbing the materials off the table, I put them into the labeled box that I have for every client. "I'm sorry, when I work sometimes it's to the detriment of everything else."

"Trevor told me your business is doing well," he smiles softly at me as he has a seat.

"It is," I try not to notice how big he is sitting at my dining room table, how much room he takes up. If I let myself notice that, then I get too deep inside my head and I scare myself. Ryan is not here to hurt me. He had the perfect chance, and he didn't take it. With my back to him, earbuds in, and completely engrossed in what I was doing, he could have done anything he wanted.

Instead, he let me work and simply watched. While it creeps me out a little, I know above all I can trust him. He's never given me a reason not to, and if I'm honest with myself – breaking in like that is something Trevor would have done. "I can, without a doubt, take care of myself and this baby."

There, I've thrown down the gauntlet, and my hands are shaking as I grip the edges of the table. Taking a stand isn't easy when you've been verbally beaten down every other time you tried to do it. I'm proud as I hide the shaking of my hands and keep my bottom lip stiff.

Renegade

She's skittish as a newborn colt, and I'm doing my best not to frighten her. The way she's been reacting to me tells me her marriage must have been hell for her. It must have been a situation she hadn't been able to escape, and I'm immediately pissed at Trevor. He should have gotten her out before it did this much damage. I've seen this all too often with domestic cases we've worked.

"I have no doubt that you can take care of yourself and the baby," I tell her, my voice soft and coaxing, doing my best not to spook her. This is out of character for me, I'm used to taking whatever I want, but there's one thing I've learned in the professions I've had. You have to make people trust you; you can't go in guns blazing and expect them to not see you as an overbearing asshole. "But I'm prepared to help."

"Ryan," her voice is raspy and I watch as she adjusts herself in her seat, pushing her back up straighter and folding her hands in front of her. This is an ice queen pose if I've ever seen one. "You're in the prime of your life, I don't expect you to take on this responsibility."

"That's too damn bad, because I happen to think this is the biggest responsibility in life that I have," my voice is harder than I mean for it to be. I try to talk myself down, Whitney doesn't know my past like Trevor does. She has absolutely no idea what this whole situation means to me, and I'm not about to lay my soul bare to her right now. The words she's just spoken tells me that she sees me as nothing more than a boy, playing the role of a man. That's fine. I can prove it to her, how serious I am. I've had to prove my worth to almost everyone in my life. I'm not scared to prove it to her.

"I don't want to force you into a situation that you don't want to be in," she tries again, this time giving me that bullshit tone that people use to placate you when they've pissed you off.

I put my hand on top of hers, trying to ignore the electricity that sparks between us. It's palpable and I have a feeling it could burn both of us if we aren't careful. "Don't tell me what you're forcing me to do, what you think I'm prepared for, or what you think I can handle," I soften my own voice. "I haven't told you how to feel about this situation. Don't tell me how to feel about it."

"I don't want anything from you," she tries again, face getting red with either embarrassment or frustration. Right now I'm unsure which it is.

"Whitney," I stop her. I can't sit here and let her push me out of this child's life. My child's life. I can't, not when it means the world to me to be a part of it. "I want everything from you."

I see tears come to her eyes, and I want to kick my own ass.

"Ryan," she brushes the edges of her eyes, cleaning up the mascara that's slightly smudged. "That's exactly what I'm afraid of."

"I don't want to take it from you," I try to explain. "I want to live it with you."

The look on her face tells me that may scare her even more, and damned if I know how to ease her discomfort, how to make this better, or even how to bridge the gap. Both of us are hanging on to a cliff, and neither one of us want to let go and make the jump.

The set of our jaws match, and at this moment I think we both realize how strong the other is.

CHAPTER SEVEN
RENEGADE

THE NEXT MORNING I'm raw after talking with Whitney. All night, I tossed and turned because nothing has been resolved, and I fucking hate it. I'm the type of guy that likes not to have anything up in the air. I have a plan for everything and I even account for most contingencies. It's how I've lived my life since I turned eighteen and got out from under my parents' roof, it's why I excelled in the military, and it's how I plan on living my life, including this pregnancy.

Whitney thinks she just handed me a rude awakening.

I have never in my life let someone push me out of anything the way I let her potentially push me out of my child's life yesterday. It had a purpose, though. After talking with her for a few minutes, I realized I need to re-group – I need a new game plan. Obviously Whitney isn't the type of woman who wants a man to take care of her any longer. She is strong, independent, and ready to take on the world without someone at her side. My thoughts are interrupted when my cell phone rings beside me, adrenaline immediately flowing as I see Holden's name on the caller ID.

"Renegade," I answer, because above anything else, that's who I am. It's who I became when Ryan couldn't deal with the hand life dealt him. In times of fear, chaos, deep sadness, and emotional turmoil, it became my shield against the world. It became my alter ego; the part of my personality that's not scared of anything.

"Everyone needs to report to base," his voice is urgent over the line. "Judge Hawthorne wants us to raid that property over on Old Mill Road."

Shit. These people have been working with the Strathers, and right now, they aren't my favorite family. We've raided that property twice before, and each time we find that their operation has grown more sophisticated. But that operation, they don't pay taxes, and the state of Alabama just can't abide by that. For every cent of profit it makes, the government wants their cut, too. When the government doesn't get their piece, they call us in.

"I'll be there, ASAP," I tell him, flipping on the KC lights embedded into the front grill of my truck.

This is exactly what I need, I realize as I push my foot down on the accelerator. Feeling and hearing the engine respond, the way my tires eat up the miles between myself and our home base, soothes me. The lights give me the ability to weave in and out of traffic, and I do it with abandon, driving faster than I probably should, but it's what I'm craving right now. An out of control ride I'm really in control of. The adrenaline courses through my veins, giving me the high I only get from being the junkie I am.

Within minutes I'm at our base, and I can't help the grin that covers my face as I see the rest of the team roaring into the parking lot, tires squealing and lights blaring.

"Let's do this shit," Ace, another member of our team, yells as he steps out of his Dodge Charger.

I hold out my hand for him to slap and he does as he walks towards me. "Agreed, I need something to take the edge off," I move my head from side to side, loosening my neck as I try to stretch out my shoulders.

"You okay?" he asks, looking at me closely.

I nod. "It'll all work out." And it will, I know it will. It's the getting there that's going to be the difficult part.

"SURVEILLANCE PHOTOS from yesterday show they've moved deeper into the woods. From up above, it looks like they've fortified the property next to the natural spring. Not sure if they've trapped it, but we'll know as soon as we get there," Holden tells us as he passes out information packets of what we need.

"How are they armed?" I ask. Normally that's not the question I ask, but now it means something. I need to make sure I make it out of this and home at the end of the day. That's never been something I've worried about before, but my life changed yesterday, in a way I never imagined.

Holden flips over his own packet, skimming whatever's on it. Looking up at me, his gaze meets me head on. "Eyes on the ground have told us that there is a lot of fire power, but they aren't formally trained. Chances are they're going to react, and that's it. If we can go in quiet, we'll have the element of surprise on our side and hopefully be able to subdue them without using our own fire power. The goal is take them peacefully."

Ace pipes up from where he sits. "Isn't that always the goal? Sometimes dudes with big guns though, they have that little man syndrome and get all fucked up with it."

"You do what you have to do to get your ass back here," Holden levels us all with a glare. "That's number one, above anything else. Whatever happens, we get back here. Let's suit up and head out."

PUTTING on my vest has never meant so much to me. It has always protected me and been a major part of my life, but today it means more. *Renegade, get your shit together*, I tell myself. I can't let my head get in the middle of this game; if I let my head get into the middle of it, I'm dead. When I'm out there, I can't let myself think about anything other than the job at hand. Letting personal thoughts creep in gets people hurt or killed. I have way too much to fucking live for right now.

Checking my gun, I put extra ammunition in my cargo pants pocket and grab my KA-BAR knife, sticking it in my waistband. At points there have been times when I've had to do hand-to-hand combat, and I want to make sure I'm prepared. I want to leave nothing to chance. I plan for all contingencies; in one of my pockets I even carry a Taser. If it gets bad, you want whatever it takes to get out of a situation alive.

"You ready?" Holden asks as he holds out a piece of gum towards me.

I chew it because it helps with my nerves, it allows me to focus on the rhythm of that rather than the beating of my heart or the adrenaline making my hands shake. I open the paper and pop it into my mouth. "I'm ready," I tell him, putting my earpiece in my ear.

"Then let's ride, brother," he says as he tags me on the chest. The hit of his knuckles is almost like a timer going off in my head. It puts me on high alert and sets my heart pounding. With those words, everything kicks into high gear and all of us make our way out to the garage, loading up into our armored vehicle.

The ride to Old Mill Road is quiet as we're all focused on our own thoughts. Mine centered on how I'm going to subdue and enforce, how I'm going to make it out without taking a bullet, and how I'm going to go home at the end of the day. I close my eyes; we've been to this property enough that I know the layout. I envision how I'm going to move once we get out of this vehicle. In my mind, I see the places danger could be hiding, where they could have made improvements, where they could have put traps. My focus and goal is not to leave anything to chance.

Pulling my cell phone out of my pocket, my finger lingers over Whitney's name. I've not had a woman in my life since I started this job. It's always been a couple of nights here, a couple of nights there. One girl was a week, but by the end of that week, I felt so fucking suffocated I couldn't wait to let her go. Whitney though, she holds a piece of me – literally – and for the first time it hits me – what if I don't make it out of this alive. She won't even know where I was going, what I was doing.

Decision made, I fire off a quick message letting her know I'm out on a job, not to worry, but telling her that I want her to know what I'm doing. If something happens what she needs to do. Maybe it's morbid to be thinking about these things right now, but my life has done a complete one-eighty in the last twenty-four hours. With great clarity, I realize I need to change my beneficiaries as soon as possible with not only this place, but with my military pension.

I want to be a thousand percent honest with her, because I feel like Stephen wasn't that way. The good things, the bad things, the things that we aren't sure about. I want to share those with her – even if she doesn't want to share that with me yet.

"Two minutes out," I hear and now I know I need to let everything go. I'm not religious but in these moments before we reach a target, I always say a little prayer and give it to God. It's the only thing that lets me get through what are sometimes hairy parts.

I shut down the phone and put it in my tactical vest. Leaning my forehead down against the butt of my AK 47, I let my mind clear. I let it become blank and it's then that my hearing becomes superhuman; I'm completely aware of everything that's going on around me.

This heightened sense of awareness has saved my life many times and helped me through more missions that I care to count.

It's what makes me Renegade.

CHAPTER EIGHT
WHITNEY

WHAT I WOULDN'T GIVE for a glass of wine, but let's face it, that's what got me into this situation in the first place. I'm emotionally and mentally raw after talking to Ryan yesterday. So many times in my life I've had to deal with things on my own. Nobody knew how horrible my marriage was, because I kept it all to myself. I've never wanted to be the type of woman who needs someone to clean up her messes, and that ended up with me in the biggest mess of my life.

Beside me, my phone buzzes, and I see Addison's smiling face. Somehow she always knows when I need to talk.

"Thank God," I answer the phone, sniffing as I say the words. "How do you always get it right?"

"Because, we were twins separated at birth," she jokes, a laugh in her voice. "Tell Addison all about it. Did you go to the doctor? Have you found out what the hell's going on with you?"

I haven't told anyone about my night with Ryan, not even the doctor who just confirmed my pregnancy, and I desperately need to. I've kept this inside for six long weeks, and this woman, I know I can trust her with my life. That's how close we are. When I left Stephen, she was the person who went with me to the attorney and held my hand while I filed for divorce. She was the person I sent pictures to the two times he hit me, keeping the situation in her best friend vault while I formulated a plan to leave him. If there's anyone I know I can trust, it's her.

"I'm having a baby with Ryan Kepler." Best to get it out in the open. This is one thing I don't want to brush under the rug. No matter how it ended up, I'm kind of proud of myself for stepping out on a limb and having the guts to tell a man what I wanted. To tell him, because if anyone is definitely a man, it's him.

There's silence on the phone and I'm wondering if I've shocked her into speechlessness. It wasn't what I meant to do and I've truly never known her to not have any kind of reaction. "Addison?"

She clears her throat. "I'm here," she answers. "Did I hear you correctly? You and Renegade did the nasty?"

I breathe through my nose heavily. "It wasn't like that, I swear."

"Wait," she interrupts me. "I'm coming over. I want to see your face when you tell me this tale. I need to know what you're feeling, not wonder about while I'm on the other end of a phone line."

This is exactly what I don't want to happen, because Addison knows me so well, but damned if I can stop it. "I'll see you in a few," I tell her quietly. While I wait for her to get here, I'm going to come to grips with the fact she's going to see everything. I won't be able to hide anything from her.

IT'S LESS than ten minutes later when Addison pulls into my driveway. I hear the car door slam and I can even hear her all but run to my front door. She knows me well enough to know that my front door isn't unlocked. She's laying on the doorbell in seconds.

"I'm coming!" I yell.

Opening the door, I wait for the explosion that I know is coming.

"Whitney Trumbolt, what in the hell has gotten into you?" Addison stops, her mouth moving like she's a fish gasping for air until she finally presses the words out. "Tell me what happened and I'm talkin' now – don't leave anything out."

My palms are sweaty as I have a seat on my couch and face her. It's hard to admit to others what I've done. I don't like disappointing people, and this feels like a huge one. Even bigger than when I quit my job and started my own business, when I finally left my husband and asked for a divorce, and when I was a teenager and told my mom that I wouldn't be doing pageants again. This feels insurmountable.

"One night I was at a bar," I start, gathering my thoughts. "Stephen had left a message on my cell phone and it bothered me, like it always does."

"How many times have I told you, Whit?" She interrupts me. "He's nothing to you anymore. He has no power over you."

Running my fingers through my hair, I squeeze my eyes shut. "I know, I know, but it's not that easy, Addison. Not when you lived what I did for so many years. It's hard to admit, but with the therapy I've had, I can honestly say, I'm owning the fact that I have issues. I'm trying to work through them, but that's neither here nor there. You asked me what lead me to Ryan. It was Stephen."

A smile forms on Addison's face. "How fuckin' ironic."

Ignoring her, I move forward. "There was way too much drinking going on. I told Ryan things I've never told anyone before, including you."

"You trust him a little bit then," she interjects.

"He's Trevor's best friend. Why would I not trust him? I've known him since he was a kid – which brings me to another problem. He's ten years younger than me."

"One thing at a time," she gets me back on track. "I gotta know about conception night."

I'm not sure how comfortable I am telling her how bare we laid ourselves that night. How bare I laid myself. I've thought about it since then, and I realized I gave a piece of myself to Ryan that I've never given to another person and I'm trying to process that still.

"I asked him to end my long drought, he brought me back here, and did everything I asked him to."

Her eyebrows are in her hairline. "That's it? You're not going to give me details?" Her voice squeaks with disbelief.

"I think you know what happened, it's been happening since the beginning of time." I brush it off. If anyone asks me, I'll say it was a coming together of two bodies in the age-old dance of time, but God it was so much more than that. It was me getting a piece of myself back and the best sex I've ever had in my life. And while I'm being honest, I've woken up at least once a week since our encounter having dreams of Ryan. He did things to me I won't even admit in the light of day.

She leans in with this look on her face that I recognize. I think I'm about to get a lecture.

"Whitney, how could you not use protection? He's a young guy who's been all over the world. I'm sure he's sticking his dick in anything that walks."

"Gee, Addison, thanks!" The thought had crossed my mind, but I don't think we're giving him enough credit. There was something about the way he'd treated me, the way he'd touched me. It made me think that it had been a while for him too, like I wasn't a one-night stand.

"Sorry," she shrugs but I can tell she isn't.

"Stephen and I tried to get pregnant for years and we couldn't. I was always lead to believe that I couldn't have children," I explain, tears popping into my eyes again. Hormones are going to kill me.

"Oh, Whitney," she shakes her head, letting it fall back on her shoulders. "Let me guess, by Stephen?"

I can't meet her eyes as I nod, my chin trembling with the magnitude of feelings my marriage caused me. It's an embarrassment to know that he's still so deep in my head, even a year after the divorce. I should be stronger than this. "Needless to say," I shrug, a small smile on my face. "I'm pregnant, and it's his."

Addison scoots forward and grabs my hand in hers. "Are you happy, Whit? This is what you've wanted for so long. So what's got you upset?"

I swallow roughly and realize that what I'm about to say sounds stupid, even to my own ears. "He wants to be a part of the baby's life."

Throwing her head back, Addison cracks up. "Oh girl, you try to keep this man away from you or his child, you're in for the fight of your life. You might as well give in. Renegade Kepler gets what he wants. He's wanted you for years and damned if he didn't get you – at least for a night."

The realization that she's right has me more scared than before.

CHAPTER NINE
RENEGADE

FILLING out paperwork is my least favorite thing about this job, but it's a necessity. I usually try to get it done immediately after we finish a raid, but tonight, my mind is somewhere else. It's on a southern debutante who looked like a porn star on her knees.

Shaking my head, I lean back over that paperwork and continue writing up my report.

I'm quiet as I move deeper into the woods. My breathing is slow and steady, I'm not winded and I'm on high alert. All my senses are attuned to what's going on around me. Adrenaline is pumping through my veins, making sweat trickle along my back and run down under the bullet proof vest I wear. This is exactly why I wear leather gloves, so that the gun doesn't slip between them when my heart pounds the fastest and my head runs through every scenario.

I stop for a moment and focus on chewing my gum, let it regain my equilibrium. I spot Ace up ahead and he motions to me to stop. My reaction is immediate. I hear what he hears. People are talking, but we can't make out the words. Looking around at the trees around us, I see that they've turned black – it's a reaction that happens when people are running a still. We're close.

In the silence, we hear a shot. Ace and I immediately hit the ground, and I hear the bullet hit a tree somewhere behind me.

"Motherfucker," I mumble under my breath. They've got a lookout this time.

Bringing myself back to the present, I continue filling out my incident reports, shaking my head at how brazen some of the people we go up against are. In the end, we breached the compound and took our suspects into custody. Long day, long night, and now all I want is a shower and my bed.

"You outta here?" Holden asks as I digitally sign my paperwork, upload it to the server, and close my work laptop.

"Sure am, unless you need me to do anything else?"

I grab my jacket, but don't put it on because I'm dirty and I don't like to do laundry.

"No, just wanted to let you know you did good today," he tells me, giving my hand a shake. That means a lot coming from him. I'm the newest on the team and the youngest. Trevor is six months older than me and holds it over my head whenever possible.

"Thank you," I feel a rush of pride. I never had pride in anything I did while I was growing up. Not in the shitty trailer we lived in, not in the piece of shit rusted truck my Dad sometimes drove me to school in, and not in the fucking free lunch I got every day in the cafeteria. Since I took off on my own, pride is something I never take for granted. I want to feel that rush in my chest whenever possible. "I appreciate that and I'm working hard to show you that I belong here."

"Trust me," Holden tells me. "It's not going unnoticed. We appreciate the work you're putting in."

That means more to me than I can say. I take satisfaction in my work and how I hold myself, because it's the only thing in my life I've ever had control of. "I won't let you down," I tell him as we walk to the parking lot.

"Never crossed my mind, my man."

I get into my truck and let myself shut off. It's then that I realize how fucking tired I am and how much I've been through in the last few days. It's a lot to take in, and I need to decompress in a bad way. My bed is definitely calling my name.

MY APARTMENT ISN'T MUCH, but it's mine. I don't have to worry about a drunk or high dad appearing around a corner when I least expect it. I don't have to listen for the tears of a mom who's not strong enough to leave or to escape her own demons. The quiet is my friend. I'm not one of those people who constantly has to have something playing in the background. I appreciate the silence.

I've had so little of it in my life.

Putting my keys on the breakfast bar, I reach into the pocket of my jeans and pull my cell phone out, seeing that I've missed a text from Whitney.

"Damnit."

W: *Maybe we can have dinner tomorrow night in a neutral spot and come to an agreement about what we both want. I have no intention of making this difficult for you and I believe we should be able to meet each other halfway.*

She's issued an olive branch, and I'd be a dumbfuck not to take it. I need to grab on and hold it with both hands. This is what I want, I want to be a part of my child's life. There is nothing negotiable about that; at this point I'll do what she asks just to get my foot in the door.

R: *I'll pick you up at six tomorrow night. We can go to Birmingham, that way we won't run into anyone we know. We've got to work this out before we announce it. I want us to tell Trevor together.*

I hope she's agreeable to what I've laid out. It means a lot that we tell Trevor; I don't like hiding things from him, I never have. He's always been there for me, no matter what's gone on in my life. He was one of the only people in my teenage years who knew exactly what was going on in my home. He never betrayed my trust, and I don't want to betray his.

My phone beeps as she comes back to me.

W: *Sounds good, but I'll drive myself. If things don't go well, I don't want us to have to drive back in stony silence. We'll talk about it all tomorrow night.*

Feeling better about things than I have all day, I finish emptying out my pockets and take off my boots, setting them next to the door in the hallway. The military and my upbringing makes me want to be an organized man. I don't like clutter, I don't like things not in their places, and I hate having loose ends dangling. That's part of the reason why I need to get this situated with Whitney – I need to know where my place is in her life. After not knowing my place for so long, I vowed to myself I would always know where I stand.

Grabbing a towel, I take off my clothes and put them in the hamper. Reaching into the shower, I turn on the hot water and wait for it to regulate to the temperature I want it to be. More than anything today, I need this shower to wash the dirt off of me and reveal the man I've become instead of the boy that I was.

CHAPTER TEN
WHITNEY

I DON'T THINK I've ever been this nervous in my life. Running my hands down the jeans I'm wearing, I hope to dry some of the sweat off of them. As I pull my SUV into the parking lot and find a parking spot, I see Ryan's truck already there. That boy is nothing, if not punctual. I look down at the clock on my dashboard to see that I'm fifteen minutes early myself. Makes me wonder how long he's been here; he was probably wondering if I'd show up or not.

He sees me and gets out of his truck, walking over towards my vehicle. I can't help but watch him as he strolls across the blacktop. There's something about the way he walks that shows his authority. He doesn't look down, his gaze is always straight ahead, even though his hands are tucked into his pockets. The jeans he wears are just the right amount of loose, the black t-shirt he wears hugs his body tight. The aviators covering his eyes give him an air of mystery. With the boots on, he looks like he owns the place. My hands shake as I take my key out of the ignition and reach over for my purse. That walk tells me that he's here to play hardball with me, that he's not going to give up as easily as I hoped he would.

My door opens, and he offers his hand to me. "Hey," he grins, pushing his sunglasses up further on his head and I see again why I gave into him so easily that night. Those soulful brown eyes and that damn grin. When he grins, it brings up memories of his head between my thighs and twisted sheets. So what I don't need to be remembering right now.

"Hi yourself," I take his hand and let him help me down. There's a part of me that wants to give him nothing of myself, to let him see the ice queen portrayal I can give when I need to keep my feelings out of situations, but there's another part of me that wants to live in this moment. Ryan enjoys life and I wish so much I could be like him. Maybe I can let him teach me things outside of the bedroom. The only thing I have to do is give him a chance – the chance though is the hardest damn part.

"Are you hungry?" he asks, trying to fill the awkward silence stretching between us.

I haven't eaten much today because I've been so nervous and I answer him truthfully. "Starving, but I'm nervous about our conversation."

"Hell, Whit, I don't want you to be nervous about it. Nothing has to be decided tonight, but I think we do have to respect each other's wishes or at least try to come to an understanding of our own positions."

It's a mature stance to take, and I have to admit that I'm proud of him for taking it, but it doesn't make it much easier for me. I wish he was being unreasonable, that he was giving me cause to tell him to get out of my life for good, but he's not. He doesn't want me to do this alone, and he's being more than understanding about it.

"I hope we can do that, too."

Renegade

I feel like I'm failing at some sort of test that I didn't even know I was taking. We've been sitting at this table for over an hour and have yet to approach any subject that surrounds this unborn child we're having. Conversation has been stilted and polite. Whitney is the consummate southern debutante not wanting to rock the boat, but that fucker needs to be capsized.

"We've eaten, we've had polite conversation, now can we talk about what we really came here to talk about?" I ask, situating myself in my seat so that I'm a little closer to her. I see her stiffen as she closes off a part of herself.

"I guess we should," she admits, but I can tell that this is the last thing she wants to do.

I wait for her to open up the lines of communication, but she doesn't take the first step, and I realize that this is where I'm supposed to man up and make sure this is talked through. Her floundering is her request for help, and I can't mistake the way her eyes flutter at mine, nervous energy shining brightly in them. "I'm going to tell you what I want, and you tell me if it's possible, okay?"

She nods, taking a healthy drink of her water.

"I want to be a part of this baby's life. Doctor's appointments and Lamaze classes, I want to be there. In a perfect world, we would live together, because I don't want you to have to go through everything by yourself, but I know that's not in the cards for us right now."

Her eyes grow round, her face goes ghostly white. "Live together? Like a real couple?"

"Yeah," I admit. "I didn't have the best childhood growing up, I don't know if Trevor's ever told you anything about it. For the most part, I don't share that with many people."

She shakes her head. "Trevor's never mentioned a word to me about it."

"He's a good friend. Right now, I don't want to get into it, but let's just say I always wanted to do kids the right way."

Whitney shifts closer to me. "I did too, but it looks like fate had other plans for us. I promise to keep you updated on what's going on with the baby, but I can't guarantee you we'll ever have a relationship, Ryan. I just can't do that."

A piece of my teenage heart breaks off in my chest and floats around in there, banging against the bone. I literally put my hand to my sternum and rub. Hearing those words was a thousand times more painful than I ever assumed they would be. "I understand," I tell her.

"And I want you to understand, it's not because I don't find you attractive. I do. I think you're a great guy, but desperate situations sometimes throw people into things they would never be a part of otherwise."

I want this woman to know I'm not some dumb kid. I've got a good head on my shoulders, I've been to war for fuck's sake. "Like an eighteen-year-old joining the Army so he can get away from the pieces of shit that raised him? Trust me, Whit, I know all about desperate situations. This isn't my first."

Shock is written on her face and that kind of makes a part of me happy. No one should ever assume they know another person's life. They should never assume that by all outward appearances someone is okay. A smile – it hides a shit ton of pain.

"I'll text you my appointment times," she tells me, resolve now on her face.

Good, she knows I'm not going anywhere now, and that's exactly how I want it to be.

CHAPTER ELEVEN
WHITNEY

SO FAR I'VE been pretty lucky. Other than a few times, morning sickness hasn't been a blip on my radar. Today that changed in a major way. I take a look at myself in the mirror and squeeze my cheeks, hoping to put some color into them. I still have the nasty taste in my mouth since I have no toothpaste or mouthwash. I hope it doesn't cause me to get sick again. I have to figure this out, I have to pull myself together and make this work.

"Are you sure you don't want to go home?" Addison, asks as I come out of the ladies room for the third time in the last hour. I hope that no one has noticed and that no one thinks I was on a bender the night before. That's the last thing that I need right now.

I shake my head. Being able to do my job, being able to support myself is the only thing that's kept me going for years. It was the one thing that pulled me through my divorce. It forced me to get up every morning, put my feet on the floor, and face the day. It didn't matter how crappy that day was, I faced it because I knew I had to. If I give up that piece of myself now, where will I be? Besides in a few months, I'll be a single mother. No matter what Ryan says, I'll still be getting up at night by myself and doing things on my own. No matter what he thinks, what he wants to give, or what he feels I deserve, I don't expect anything from him. I won't because I'm used to doing for myself. I pop a peppermint into my mouth, the only thing I've found that's halfway soothing my stomach today and square my shoulders.

"I'm fine," I tell her. "This is something I'm going to have to live with, something I'm going to have to learn to maneuver around. This kid isn't going anywhere." It's the same thing I've been telling myself all morning.

"Are we ready, Whitney?"

I turn around, facing the mother of the bride and hope that I don't look as awful as I did a few minutes ago in the restroom or as awful I still feel. This is one of the most important clients I've ever had, and I can't screw this up.

"We are," I tell her, going through my mental checklist. At least I'm pretty positive I'm not lying. I can do this job to the best of my ability without anyone knowing that the child in my womb is wrecking my stomach. "Tell Peyton that it's okay for her to come out, and I'll get everything situated. This is going to go off without a hitch."

I watch as the mother of the bride goes back into the bridal suite and give myself a talking to. Nothing that I'm going through can ruin my client's experience. I have to put my own issues aside and make this the perfect day for the people who are paying me. My reputation counts on it, and my business needs it. With a looming maternity leave, I'm going to need to bank everything I can.

Addison is beside me, holding my arm. I'm not sure whether it's to get my attention or if she just wants to make sure that I stay upright. "I'll make sure everything is set up, but if everyone has done their job we should be fine."

I employ only the best, and I know without a doubt that we should be. I'm through with the peppermint, so I grab a cracker out of my emergency stash and will it to stay down. I will never again be relying on someone else to make my way through this world. Even if that person is named Renegade, has arms of steel, and eyes I could lose myself in. I have to prove that I can do this for me.

Renegade

I'm in my element at the shooting range. It's a place where I can control all the variables, and it's also a place that I can let my anger and anxiety go as I focus on the piece of paper in front of me. It's important that all of us keep our skills sharp, but it's also something that's carried over since my military days.

"Did you ever think about being a sniper?" Holden asks as he stands next to me, examining my shots.

I've put a few rounds into the heart and head of this piece of paper and it feels good to know I haven't lost my touch. No matter what the situation, I'm still good under pressure and I can protect whoever needs it. "I thought about it, even applied to school, but I couldn't bring myself to go," I tell him.

It's hard to explain to people who aren't familiar with the military way of life that – at least for me – kill or be killed was different than being a contract killer. To me being a sniper was no more than someone putting a bounty on someone else's head, and my conscience couldn't take it.

Looking back, it probably had to do with the fact that my parents would purposely put me in situations where I was forced to make a decision, taking away options for me. I had a really hard time taking away options for someone else, which was why I never wanted to put a bullet in someone else's head.

I think that's why I'm having an issue with letting Whitney call the shots on everything having to do with this baby. I'm trying though, trying to tamp down the need inside that says if she won't offer it to me, I'll be forced to take it.

"You alright?" Holden asks. I realize then that I'm standing there like an idiot, holding my gun, looking at nothing in particular.

Holden is our leader. If something is bothering me, realistically he's the first person I should go to when I've needed to talk to someone. Obviously Trevor is out of the question, which explains why I blurt it out.

"Tank's sister and I are having a baby, and he doesn't know yet."

Holden is quiet for a minute, before he whistles through his teeth. "Son of a bitch, Renegade, he's gonna kill you."

Don't I know it. At least being here at the gun range says that I'm preparing for the inevitable.

Whitney

It's close to ten at night when I turn onto my street. I'm yawning and I'm exhausted, but happy. The wedding went off flawlessly. The bride was happy, the groom was happy, and the flower girl made it all the way down the aisle before she had a meltdown. All in all, it was an amazing night. My team and I did our job to the best of our abilities, but it took a lot out of me. When the wedding party looks back at the pictures, they hopefully won't see how tired and pale I look. They won't pay attention to how dead my team is on their feet, if we're somehow in the background. Hopefully all they'll see that we made their dreams come true and gave them the best time of their lives.

"Shit," I whisper as I pull into my driveway and turn off my SUV. Parked in the back far enough away that you can't see it from the street near the storage building is Ryan's truck, and given that there's a light on in the house, I see he's let himself in again.

Grabbing my purse and shoes, which I took off hours ago and replaced with flip flops because my feet hurt too much, I get out of my SUV. I'm slow as I walk up to the back door and let myself in. I'm not prepared for what's waiting for me.

Ryan is standing at my stove, cooking something that smells delicious. My mouth waters and I realize then how long it's been since I've eaten.

"I see you've made yourself at home," I joke, putting my purse on the counter along with my expensive heels.

"You should just give me a key, sweetheart. Then I won't have to keep breaking into your back door," he picks up his keyring and jingles it at me.

I'm not quite sure how I feel about him possibly having a key to my house.

It doesn't instill fear or anxiety in me, so there's that, but at the same time I'm not sure I want to give up any of the freedom I've become accustomed to. Instead of answering him, I give him a small smile and a non-committal "We'll see." I pull out the chair I have at the breakfast bar, gratefully sinking into it, sighing as I do so.

"Long day?"

I nod as I take a good look at him. He's as mouthwatering as whatever it is he's cooking. The jeans he wears hugs his ass in an almost loving caress, and the shirt covering his torso clings to his back just enough to make me want to go tear it off of him. Since the night with him, my dreams have been plagued. While I've never been a sexually needy type person in the past, now all my dreams are filled with a play-by-play of what we did to create this child.

"Are you hungry?" He turns around, and I'm breathless. Renegade is a good-looking man.

"Famished." It's then that I realize I don't have to lie. Whatever was making it difficult for me to eat earlier in the day is now gone, and I think I could attack him and gnaw off his arm.

"Good," he gives me a panty-melting smile. "Dinner is served."

I slowly get up from the bar and follow him over to the table where he has two place settings already prepared. Experience with my ex has me questioning what this is all about, but for once, I'm going to put the part of me that's wary about all things nice in a box and enjoy this for what I hope it is. A nice guy cooking dinner for the woman who accidentally got pregnant with his baby.

CHAPTER TWELVE
RENEGADE

SHE LOOKS EXHAUSTED, even in the candlelight surrounding us. Unfortunately, I don't know much about her job, but given the way she brought her shoes into the house with flip flops on her feet, I assume that she stands for a good portion of any event she's planned.

"How was your day?" I take a bite of the asparagus, almost moaning. There are three things I do well. Cook, fuck, and take down bad guys.

I watch her take a bite of her cream of mushroom covered pork chop and daintily swallow. The movement of her throat muscles mesmerize me, and I have to adjust my seat, which is almost embarrassing.

"It was long, but good."

She doesn't offer more than that, and honestly that's not enough for me. If we're going to do this, I want to know as much as I can about her daily life. Right now I know what she tells her brother, and what he in turn bitches to me about. "Did you have an event?"

"A wedding," she smiles. "It was gorgeous, too. They were a young couple, extremely in love, and not yet ruined by the reality of life. It was nice to see."

I get the feeling she has been ruined, and I think about whether I want to call her on it. In the end, I'm the kind of guy that has to know everything. I don't shy away from the bad parts and expect to be told only about the rainbows and flowers. Bad things, good things – they all make up what we call life, and I've been alive long enough to know you can't have the good without the bad or vice versa.

"Have you been ruined by the reality of life?"

The question seems to startle her. Her water glass stops halfway to her mouth and she puts it down on the table, along with her fork and knife. Pushing her hair back from her face, her blue eyes search mine. "You want honesty?"

"I always want honesty. I didn't make it home from two tours in Iraq by lying to myself," I take a drink of my beer to calm the pounding of my heart.

"I don't really know that I was ever in love with Stephen the way the couple that I helped get married today are in love with each other," she says softly.

This is a break-through, and I'm unsure of the reason, but I'm thankful for it. She's still talking, and I have to tell myself to pay attention.

"When a man asks you to marry him, you get so caught up in the pomp and circumstance of it. Mom and dad were so excited and happy for me."

"What about you?" I think I'm the first person who's ever thought to ask her that question.

She shrugs, those eyes of hers shiny. "I felt like an adult. It was the logical next step in my life, and I felt as if it was one I should take," she breathes deeply. "Trevor asked me about it the day before the wedding. He asked if I was sure I wanted to do it, and I told him he was crazy to ask me that question. When I look back now, I think he's the only one who knew that Stephen wasn't the man everyone thought he was."

We're quiet for a long moment, and then by mutual agreement, we continue eating.

I wait a long time before I say anything else, because I don't know how the declaration will be perceived, but I know I have to say it. "Whit, I want you to know that I'm everything you think I am, and everything you think I'm not."

Her brows draw together in question. "I don't know if I get what you mean, Ryan."

"That's okay. You will."

That's a promise I make to both of us. I won't be erased from her life the way Stephen was. I won't have to be.

Whitney

I am beyond tired, but at the same time I don't want Ryan to go. It's been nice spending the evening with him. Someone having dinner ready when I get home is a new concept for me. Stephen sure as hell never did that. He expected it on the table when he got home, no matter what kind of a day I was having. I defied him once and that's all it took for me to learn never to do it again. Hiding my yawn behind my hand, I glance over at Ryan.

"Are you tired?" he asks softly.

He does it in such a way that makes me think he knows the answer, but he wants me to admit that I'm not Superwoman. Sometimes I want to admit that too, and I think out of anyone I've ever been with, it's okay for me to answer that question honestly with him.

I nod before answering. He wanted honesty earlier, and there's no reason for me to believe he won't want honesty again. "Exhausted," I smile. "But this is the kind of exhausted I love. I've done a good job, my team has done a good job, and the bride was happy. I can go to bed tonight with a smile on my face."

We're sitting on the couch and Ryan has my feet in his hands, working the tired ball of pain. His fingers are doing amazing things, loosening the tight bunch of muscles and it's putting me to sleep. I'm more relaxed than I've been in weeks, he could be a masseuse if this whole task force thing doesn't work out for him. Just as I'm sinking down into the feeling of euphoria he's giving me, he looks over at me, his eyebrow raised.

"Do you go to bed very often with a smile on your face?"

Damn him and his questions, he wants to go deeper than I want. I know it's his way of getting to know me, his way of proving to me I can't do everything on my own, but I'm having such a good time with him tonight that it pisses me off. I'm tempted to tell him to fuck off, but that's not me and I'm trying to be better than I was before. I'm stronger than I've ever been, and I don't want to shy away from anything.

"Sometimes," I answer honestly. "More now than I did. When I was with Stephen, it was hard to be happy about anything because I walked around on eggshells so much. I didn't ever want to do anything to upset him, so I kind of forgot what happy really was. I'm learning to be happy again, though. Every day I find something that makes me giggle or puts a smile on my face, and I hold it tightly. The therapist I saw back when he and I first got divorced told me I'd remember how to be happy again, and she's right. It comes easier every day." I flex my foot against his hand. "If you keep rubbing my feet the way you are, I'll definitely go to bed with a smile on my face."

He flashes me his own smile, his teeth white against the dark stubble covering his face. I never noticed, but he's got smile lines, which means he knows how to be happy. Maybe he can teach me, and maybe we can be happy together. With this life we've created, with the way our worlds will be entwined in the future, possibly the two of us can build something I never could with my ex-husband. I bring myself out of my thoughts as I realize he's speaking. "My plan is to make myself invaluable to you. I wanna show you how good I am to have around."

In a moment of clarity that I'm sure I'll want to take back in the morning, I lean in and kiss him softly on the lips. I feel closer to him than I have anyone else in years. I don't want to question too much why I feel this way. I know a part of it is the child I carry, part of it is the way he's taken care of me tonight, but there's another part I don't want to look at too closely. When I'm ready, I will. "You're already there, whether you know it or not."

His hands stop, and he chases my lips when I pull away. His breath is hot as he forces my lips open, and I stop fighting. I give in, because I'm tired of so many things tonight. I let myself melt against the cushions when he pushes me back to them, holding himself over my body. He's careful not to put his weight on me, but the heat rolling off him is enough to make me wind my arms around his neck and pull him deeper into the kiss. For a fraction of a moment I feel his tongue flirt with mine and I feel the sharp jolt of electricity when he runs it against the roof of my mouth, leaving no space untouched. He owns my mouth the way he owned my body. If I'm not careful, this man will own me in a different way Stephen ever hoped to. It lasts both forever and not long enough. I feel his hand cup my cheek as he disengages our embrace. I moan when our lips finally part.

His forehead drops to mine, and he breathes heavily against me. When he lifts his head and looks into my eyes, they're dark with desire, but soft at the same time. "You're tired Whit, let's get you to bed."

I grin up at him, feeling a little brazen. I'm not sure what I want tonight, I just know I don't necessarily want to be alone. "Am I going down the hall by myself tonight?"

It seems as if I've taken him by surprise with my words. He doesn't say anything for the next few moments. "It's your decision, just know we won't be getting naked. You need your sleep."

I can't help the way my stomach drops at his words. I'd wanted to get naked with him, I'd wanted to feel his heat again, but he's right. I'm more tired than I thought I was and if I let myself relax, I know I'll be fading fast. An idea pops into my head before I can push the words back into my throat.

"You saying you'll hold me?"

I want him to answer this question badly, I want him to say the right thing, because so far he's said all the perfect things. For once I want someone to not disappoint me. Stephen never held me when I needed to be held. God, there had been so many nights when I'd needed it. The few times I'd asked him, he'd laughed at me and told me I was weak for asking. I want desperately for Ryan to be the man I hope he is. I want us to be able to be around one another. With Stephen, I'd started to hate him, and towards the end, I couldn't even stand to be around him. That's when I'd known we had to divorce. I couldn't take living that life any longer.

The getting through the divorce had been the hard part. He'd fought me every step of the way for any of the things I'd wanted to keep. Then he'd decided not to sign the papers. Every night for a year and a half, I'd asked God what I'd done wrong. How had I accepted a man like this into my life, my heart, and my bed. Was I really that bad at reading personalities and telling bad from good? It'd made me question every damn thing I'd ever done. But here, tonight, with Ryan, I want him to be the man I think he is. I don't want to question him,

I want to believe he's exactly everything he says he is. Tonight, I'll believe it for me and this child I'm carrying.

His voice is deep when he answers. I can see honesty and truth in his eyes. If I'm looking deep enough, I can also see he's surprised I've made this request. I am too, but if I don't start correcting the pattern now, I don't know what my child is going to be born into. I need to be strong for him or her. I need to learn to not only stand on my own two feet, but also know when to ask for help. Tonight, I want his arms around me, I want to lean on him and let him help me. "For as long as you let me, or at least until you force me to let go."

Here, in the muted light of my living room, with him staring at me like he is, I'm not sure I ever want him to let go.

CHAPTER THIRTEEN
RENEGADE

ALL NIGHT I've slept maybe three hours. I haven't wanted to miss anything, because Whitney letting me in her bed to do this isn't going to be a regular occurrence. With everything I have in me, I know that to be a fact. Last night, she'd been weak. She'd needed someone to take care of her, and she'd been strong enough to let me do it.

I have no doubt as soon as she wakes up and realizes I'm still in her bed, she's gonna kick me out. Am I okay with that? Not really, but I'm not in any position to make demands. I want the two of us to have an amicable relationship. She holds all the power to let me see my child too, so I want to be the type of guy she can get along with and be proud to have in her corner.

Her ex-husband wasn't like that, from everything I can gather. I want to be different, be a much better man than he ever thought he could be.

There's one thing I can't deny though. How right it feels to have her in my arms. Sometime in the middle of the night, she snuggled up to me. Taking advantage of it, I pulled her into my chest and I haven't let her go since. So many of my teenage dreams involve this – hell, I'm not ashamed to say it got me through some hard nights in Iraq, too. Over there, it's whatever gets you through the night, and Whitney got me there.

She's stirring and it's making me nervous, I don't want to go yet. There are things I want to know about her. How does she take her coffee? What's the first thing she does in the morning? What does she have for breakfast? Does she wear a robe? Is she a morning shower person? These are all questions most people in relationships learn about each other, but I'm not sure if I'll be afforded the same opportunity most people have.

"Ryan, you gotta let me go," she says, an urgency in her voice.

I'm not sure why, but I don't even question it. In a flash, she's out of the bed and she's running for the bathroom. Seconds later, I hear her emptying her stomach. The sound is awful and it makes me want to puke, but I man up. This is something I've been fighting to be a part of – I need to be in there with her.

Getting up, I stumble in behind her, cringing when I hear another round. Ryan Kepler can handle this shit – I figure if I say it enough, it'll stick. She's leaning over the porcelain and I do what any man worth his salt would do. I lean behind her and grab her hair out of the way, rubbing her back as she heaves.

"You don't have to stay," she tells me as she tries to catch her breath.

"Get the fuck outta here. I'm not going anywhere."

I hope she realizes how true the words I speak are.

"I KNOW you can't have caffeinated coffee, but do you have decaf?" I ask as I navigate Whitney's kitchen. It's starting to become as familiar to me as my own. If this is the only way she'll let me take care of her, then so be it. I'll take what I can get.

She's leaning on the bar, her head in her hands. "It's to your left."

I open the cabinet door and spot the bag of coffee. "You need anything else? Would toast make you feel better?"

I'm trying not to pay attention to the fact I'm wearing no shirt and she's in her pajamas. Granted, I've seen her naked, and she's seen me naked, but this is so much more intimate than anything else we've ever done.

"Toast would be great," she gives me a small smile.

She's so pale and she's shaky. It occurs to me, she does this by herself every morning. Nobody's here to take care of her; she does what she has to do and then she goes to work, comes home, and takes care of herself again. It's wrong. It's not how I want this to be, and I hope she'll feel the same way. The only way I can prove how invaluable I am is to be here when she needs me. "Coming right up. Dry?"

"Yeah," she laughs softly. "I tried butter one day. Our child didn't like that at all."

It makes my breath catch as she mentions our child. I don't know how to respond to what she's said, but I do my best. "Already a picky eater, huh? Totally didn't take after me," I joke, a smile on my own face.

"How true is that statement?" she lifts her head off her hands and gives me a fond look. "I remember you and Trevor eating pizza rolls with honey. I mean who in the world does that? It looks so nasty."

"It's the sweet and salty thing," I defend my food choices. "Besides, that's a cheat meal now. I can't eat like that these days and still have this body," I run my hand down my abs. "I have to do extra sit ups and lots of weights to keep these now."

Her eyes have followed my hand, and I can't help but to feel a little cocky and conceited. She likes my body? I can work with that. The toast pops and I grab the two pieces, putting them on a Styrofoam plate. Grabbing the coffee pot that's finished brewing, I bring that over as well.

"Look at you being all domesticated and making me breakfast," she pours her coffee and begins doctoring it.

"I made you dinner last night, too. There's a lot I can do for you, if you let me," I wink, hoping those words didn't sound as provocative to her as they did to me.

She takes a drink of her coffee, seeming to think about what I'm saying. "We're gonna have to take it one day at a time, Ryan. I understand how badly you want to be a part of my life, of this child's life, and I've told you I don't want to keep you away. I won't keep you away. Please understand though, I need to protect myself, too. Just because you'll be there for our child doesn't necessarily mean you'll be there for me, and I understand that."

I don't know what to say to her. Anything I can think of sounds like I'm a fucking stalker, and I don't want to scare her off.

"As long as you'll allow me, I'll be there for the both of you. Whit, I think you know, whether you want to admit it or not, how I feel about you. I don't see that changing, since it hasn't really changed since I was old enough to know what that tickle in my stomach was when I saw you," she looks like she wants to protest. Putting my hand up, I stop her. "I understand you're not there yet, and you may never be there. I'm starting to understand what an ass your ex was. I'm willing to put the time in, just let me do it. Let me be here when you need help, and I'll prove you can count on me."

She takes a drink of her coffee, pondering my words. I can almost see the inner workings of her head. I'm surprised smoke and steam isn't rising from her forehead. At some point I realize I have a shot. Her eyes have softened and she's giving me a real smile. The one that shows the laugh lines on her face. My hope meter is off the charts.

"Okay," she stops my words with a hand in my face. "I'm willing to give you a shot. If you want to prove to me you're in this for the long haul, then I'll let you be here. Starting out we can have dinner together every Tuesday and Thursday night," she finishes. "If you already have plans, I only ask that you let me know."

I can do anything she asks of me. This will be a piece of cake.

"I'm not asking you to cook for me all the time either," she's saying. "We work as a team, because Ryan, we've got to figure out how to be a team."

I grab her hand and kiss the back of it. "I think we've proven what a good team we can be."

She throws me a look. "We've got to prove we can get along outside the bedroom, too. We've got at least eighteen years to put up with each other."

If it's up to me, it'll be the rest of our lives, but I know she's not ready to hear that right now. She may never be ready to hear those words, and it's a bridge I'll cross if we ever come to it. For now, I'll take this gift she's given me and I will impress the fuck outta this woman.

She won't know what hit her. In a really good way.

CHAPTER FOURTEEN
RENEGADE

"IT'S BEEN A SLOW FUCKING DAY," Tank yawns as the two of us sit in our patrol car, clocking speed on a side street off of a main thoroughfare. The town's had complaints about speeding being a problem in this residential area, but so far we've seen nothing.

There's no lie in his statement. It's been one of the slowest days in recent memory for me. After the past week though I'm enjoying it. Every time I'm with him, I have a rush of guilt and I'm scared I'll blow the cover on the baby. This is one thing Whitney and I haven't really talked about, and I plan on bringing it up at our first dinner tonight.

I smile slightly, thinking about the dinner we'll be having tonight. She said she'd like to cook on Tuesdays, leaving me with Thursdays. Off and on we've texted a little, trying to figure out if there's anything either of us absolutely hate, anything we both love. It's been mundane conversation, but to know I'm on her mind, even that way, is worth it.

"It has, I'm ready to put this nine hours behind us," I grab my cell phone, and check the time. Two more hours to go.

"Wanna come over and grill out tonight? I got some steaks at the butcher the other day."

Damn, I love steaks from the butcher Tank goes to, but Whitney's way more important. "Sorry man, I have plans."

"What's her name?" He asks as he takes a look at me.

"Why do you think it's a woman?"

"Only a woman can put a stupid smile like that on your face."

I squirm, knowing if he keeps this up, I'll probably break. I'm weak when it comes to my best friend, he knows me better than anyone else in the world. "Get outta here with that bullshit. I'll open my vault, but only if you're gonna open your vault about Blaze," I mention the name of the paramedic who helped us when he got stabbed in the palm.

Immediately I know there won't be any kind of vaults being opened today. "I'd rather not," he grabs a piece of gum, sticking it in his mouth, chewing so hard I'm sure his jaw is going to dislocate.

My phone vibrates in my hand, and I quickly check it, excited to see a text from Whitney.

W: *I hope you like roast. I saw it at the grocery and my mouth watered.*

She's had some cravings lately, telling me there are some things she has to have when she realizes she wants it. I get the feeling this is one of those cravings. Looking to my left, I make sure Tank's focused on clocking the drivers on the road in front of us, as I type a reply.

R: *That sounds amazing, I haven't had anything home cooked in a very long time. At least nothing I haven't cooked myself.*

W: *Great! See you then!*

I put the phone back in my pocket, trying to wipe the grin off my face before I'm met with the judgement on Tank's.

"Who was that?"

I know I can't tell him, but I want to. I've never been great at keeping things from the people I care about. Not having him in the loop, not having him to go to is hard. He's my best friend, and I want him to be a part of this. "I'll let you know soon."

He makes a sound – something that's a cross between a mumble and a grunt. "She must be hot stuff, you never keep your women a secret."

"It's because I know they won't be sticking around."

"You think this one will be?"

For at least eighteen years...is on the tip of my tongue, but if I put it out there in the open he's going to want to know the whole story. Instead, I give him a smile, turning my gaze back to the street in front of us. "How's your hand?" I change the subject.

"Sore, but I can drive now, obviously," he gestures to the driver's seat he's sitting in.

"I'm surprised they're letting you drive to be honest," as far as I know he hasn't been back to the doctor, but lately we aren't up in each other's business as we normally are.

He offers me a grin. I'm about to say something when a pickup flies by us in nothing but a streak of black. "Holy shit, how fast was he going?"

Tank checks his radar. "Clocked it runnin' at eighty-five."

"In a motherfuckin' thirty-five. Kids play out here," I'm pissed.

Tank puts the car in gear, flips the lights, and I hang on for dear life. The truck's already almost out of our line of vision. He steps on the gas, and I can feel the police package in our Dodge Charger respond, eating up the miles as we chase down the asshole with the lead foot.

I'm busy calling in our position and the description of the vehicle, while Tank is navigating the intersections, watching for bystanders. School just let out and we're about to cross into a school zone.

Thumbing the radio, I speak calmly and clearly. "Dispatch, be advised we're traveling at a high rate of speed toward Laurel Springs Elementary, can you notify them to clear that crosswalk?"

My hearts beating out of my chest as we advance on the truck. We're close enough now I can see the license plate. Calling in the number, I wait for dispatch to get back to me.

"I'm coming back with a 2009 Ford F150 registered to Merle Strather."

Tank and I glance at each other. There's no way in hell Merle's drivin' this truck. "10-4."

I put the radio down. "Gotta be his grandson."

Tank groans and so do I. We've had run-ins with this kid before. For an eighteen-year-old punk, he's got the smartest mouth I've ever heard in my life. Totally could have been me had I not found the military.

Finally we're on the bumper of the truck. He can see our lights, I know he can, because I can see him glance at us in his rearview. I push my arm to the side of the road. "Pull the fuck over!"

Approaching the elementary school, I see they've cleared the crosswalk and key my radio. "Passing Laurel Springs Elementary – still traveling south high rate of speed. Continue or disengage?"

We're coming into a very crowded and congested part of the city. Kids are getting out of school, parents are coming to get them, teenagers just left the high school – which is where this shithead just left from. "We can deliver the ticket to the residence. We can see the registrant's grandson, Brooks Strather, driving the vehicle."

Holden's voice comes over the radio. He also doubles his time up when we aren't busting up moonshine stills. "Let it go guys, we'll have the closest uniforms deliver the ticket. What did you clock him at?"

"Eighty-five in a thirty-five."

"Disengage, no reason for someone to get killed because he's got a lead foot. C'mon back with your reports."

Tank bangs on the steering wheel with his good hand. He absolutely hates to give something up when he knows the other person is in the wrong.

"Fuckin' pisses me off. He could have killed somebody, and we just gotta let him go. That whole family is off the rails."

"They always have been. Now the law's just cracking down and catching up, they'll keep doing stupid shit. We give them enough rope, they'll hang themselves."

He glances over at me. "At what cost? Before someone gets hurt?"

These are both questions I don't know the answers to and instead of feeding him a line of bullshit, I just sit with my mind in my own thoughts. Dinner with Whitney is all I'm looking forward to, and it's the one thing I can focus on without feeling like a failure.

I DEBATED for fifteen minutes while I was at the grocery picking up some fresh bread, if I should get her flowers. I mean debated like I've never debated anything before in my life. I wondered if it would make me seem desperate. But then again, I've already been there and done that. I wondered if she would read too much into it, then realize there is no reading too much into it – we're having a damn baby. I decide she deserves the flowers, regardless of where we are in our own relationship right now. Grabbing the wildflower bouquet, because it seems much less serious than the roses, I hoof it to the checkout lane and throw them both down on the conveyor belt before I change my mind.

Letting out a deep breath, I realize I'm fucking nervous. What do we talk about? What kind of a conversation do we have? Any other time we've been together we've had either family or the awkward situation of our night of passion as a buffer. How do we become two people forming a relationship? All of a sudden I get it; this is what she's been worried about, what's been weighing so heavily on her mind. Why she can't seem to get on board with me truly wanting to be a part of the baby's life.

It's clear now, crystal fucking clear and I get it. It's why she sees me as too young to be able to deal with this, why she doesn't think we can be a couple. It's okay though, because now that I'm aware of the problem, I can fix it.

The whole way to her house I think of the man I need to be. Try to put myself in her shoes and figure out what's expected of me. It's hard because her family was my example growing up, and they were the quintessential loving family straight out of a fucking sitcom. I realize quickly that's what I want, but I have to make sure she's there and ready for it too. If I rush this, I hurt everybody involved.

Pulling into Whitney's driveway, I give myself a pep talk, tell my pounding heart it's going to be fine, and wipe my sweaty palms on my jeans. I've done shit scarier, tougher, and more life-threatening than this before, but as I knock on her door, I wonder just how much these dinners are going to change my life.

CHAPTER FIFTEEN
WHITNEY

I'VE BEEN anxious since I heard his truck pull in the driveway. It's not overly loud, but loud enough. I'm pretty sure he doesn't have one of those annoying mufflers like Trevor put on his. Like all of the things they share in life, they both have a love for big trucks. Both blacked out with chrome, but Ryan's is lifted a little higher to accommodate his height. Trevor makes jokes about how Ryan has little man syndrome, but I know better. A flash of heat runs through my body as I think about his size. God, I miss the feeling he gave me as he thrust into me that night, the welcome weight of him laying on top of me, the way our eyes locked when he made me come. Damn, it's hot in here now.

Fanning my hand in front of my face, I try to cool my wayward thoughts. This past week has been awful. If I didn't know better, I'd think I'm a teenage boy. After looking it up on the internet though, I know I'm good. This is completely normal, no matter how unnatural it feels.

Putting my palms to my cheeks, I pace in front of the door as I wait for him to knock. Opening it before he gets there would be a total rookie move on my part. I'm the older one here, the supposedly more experienced one, and I should be able to keep my crap together. The knock I've been waiting for finally comes, so I take a deep breath and wait at least thirty seconds before I say "coming". That's right, Whitney, act like you haven't been waiting on him to get here.

The image I'm greeted with is absolutely mouthwatering. Starting from the bottom, I let my gaze eat him up, for lack of a better term. His feet are encased in leather boots, maybe motorcycle (definitely not cowboy), leading into dark jeans that don't fit snuggly but they aren't loose either (he can move in them), up past a gray and black open flannel shirt that's rolled up to his elbows, and a white undershirt shows off the dark tan he has. He must not have had time to shave because he's sporting the tiniest little bit of stubble. I shiver, remembering how it felt against my neck the morning we woke up together. I would love to feel it again. I want to make it a reality, but I don't know how to go about propositioning him. His hair is adorably mussed, like he spent the entire ride over here running his hands through it.

"These are for you," he thrusts the bouquet of wildflowers in his hand at me. "And this is for us," his other hand holds a loaf of fresh bread.

I'd completely missed he was holding them, the only thing I could focus on was the corded strength of his forearm. "Thank you," when I grab them our fingertips touch and the spark is back, the one that burned so bright the night we were together. The flame so strong it sucks out the oxygen in the room, and both of us gasp.

I'm the first one to pull away. "C'mon in," I motion him inside. "I'll put these in some water and then we can eat, dinner's ready."

"It smells delicious," he comes in, shutting the door behind him. "You look gorgeous by the way, Princess."

That nickname he's given me takes up a space in my heart that I never thought would be big enough for anyone again. It'd closed and a lock had been placed around it, tightly squeezing the joy out of most things when I'd been with my ex-husband. Ryan though, just the sound of his voice chips away some of the stone. I can't tell if it's the southern lilt so much like mine, or if it's the slightly teasing tone he uses with me. No one ever teases me. As soon as they see me, they see debutante and assume I can't have a little fun.

"Thanks, I wore it because it's so hot today," I look down at my pale pink sundress, noticing for the first time that I may, in fact, look a little like a princess.

"Damn, I know. Tank and I were bitching about the heat. We had to check the calendar and make sure it's May, not August. Wearing our vests and all our gear is miserable."

A feeling of dread comes over me, and I stop a moment to put my hand over my heart. "Promise me both of you will wear those vests from now on without complaining. You both have something to live for, and two people who want you to come home at the end of a shift."

His eyes soften and a smile spreads across his face. "Believe me, I'll do everything I can to get home unscathed and so will Tank. I just have to make sure he doesn't kill me when he finds out the truth."

"I'm going to tell him," I assure Ryan. "It just hasn't come up yet."

"I don't want you to tell him without me there. If he gets upset, he needs to get upset with both of us, and you shouldn't have to deal with it on your own."

This man says all the right words at all the right times. It makes me nervous – maybe he's better than I deserve. I've been willing to write him off at every turn because of his age – almost refused him a chance to let him get to know his child. I'm seeing I was wrong in presuming I know him. In the end, maybe he's more mature and better equipped to handle our situation than me.

Renegade

My stomach growls loudly, causing me to put my hand over it and a blush to cover my cheeks. "Sorry."

She giggles, grabbing our two drinks as she makes her way over to the dining room table. "I'm glad I'm feeding the beast."

In my jeans, my cock twitches. She has no idea which beast wants to come out and play. Whitney Trumbolt has always been a beautiful woman, but she has no clue how hot she looks in the dress she's wearing tonight. Pale pink lace shimmers over her body, the length skims just above her knee, and her fuck me shoes? Shit, I don't know how she keeps wearing them, but my cock appreciates the effort. I never understood what people meant about a glow when women were pregnant, but tonight I get it. She's absolutely radiant, and if I didn't know better, I would think she was glowing. My eyes rake over her body one more time, hoping she doesn't see me as I get my plate full of potatoes, carrots, pot roast, and the bread I brought. With my hand on the ladle, halfway between pulling it out of the crockpot and putting it on my plate, I stall. She's taken my drink over to the table and bent over, facing me, giving me a view down the front of her dress, only obscured by a pink lace bra. Her tits are bigger than they had been, not by much, but by enough they are trying to free themselves from their prison. My fingers itch to let them loose.

"Did you need something else?" she asks as she sees me looking over at her.

You sprawled out on the kitchen table with your dress around your waist, panties pushed to the side, and me with my pants down far enough to get my cock out. That's exactly what I need. I have to remind myself she's talking about food. "Nope, got everything right here."

With a few fortifying breaths, I gather myself together and walk over to the table, pulling her seat out for her. "You go ahead and sit down. If there's anything else you need, let me know and I'll grab it."

"Thanks," she smiles up at me, and it's enough to make my stomach flutter. "I have it all," she gestures to the plate in front of her.

As we sit down, I realize how fucking awkward I feel right now. I've seen this woman naked, I made a meal out of what's between her legs, but I've never had so much as a real conversation with her. Not really – not when there's an age difference like there is between her and Tank.

"I hope you like it."

The soft words are spoken in a way that makes me think she's nervous, like it matters what I think. Maybe she wants to please me. Again, the word *please* does things to me. I've gotta get this shit under control. Maybe next time before I come over, I need to jack it in the shower at least twice. Taking a bite of the food in front of me, I moan as the flavors hit my tongue. It's an explosion of amazingly seasoned and cooked meat, much better than the microwave shit I do most of the time. It's hard to cook for just one person and not have enough to feed an army – so I normally buy single serve that cooks up fast. "Damn, you can cook a meal."

"You like it? I seasoned it a different way than I normally do. Something I found on Pinterest."

"Fucking amazing," are the only words I can get out before I go back in for another bite. It's been hours since I last ate, and the amount of working out I do, I usually like to eat every few hours.

We're quiet for the next few minutes. I'm shoving food down my throat, and she seems lost in her own thoughts. When my stomach is no longer clawing at itself in hunger, I set my fork down and chew slower, grabbing a piece of the bread.

"How was your day?"

Whitney glances up at me, like she's surprised I asked. Maybe she's surprised I care.

"Good," she takes a drink of her ice water. "I had a meeting with a new client. She's interested me in doing both a wedding and a business event for her."

"You don't do business events usually, do you?"

She shakes her head. "Not so much anymore. When I first started, it was more of an event planning business, but it slowly evolved to weddings. Which is what I like to do more than anything. It's hands on, and I get to work directly with the bride and groom. Sometimes it can be plain and simple, sometimes it's black tie and Cinderella fancy. I never know what my day is going to bring – that's what I like about it."

"Kinda why I like police work and the task force," I can relate. "No day is routine, there's always something different about every shift."

"What do you do when you're bored?"

The question catches me off guard and I want to clarify what she's asking. "When I'm at work or when I'm at home?"

"Either. We don't know a whole lot about each other except what we have in common with Trevor and what we look like with our clothes off."

I laugh because she's right. "If I'm at work, I'm normally with Trevor. We read news articles to each other, or we talk about sports. Sometimes we'll park the patrol car and take a walk, just to get out and do something different for a while. If I'm at home, I either Netflix something, go workout, or go work in the wood shop I put in behind my apartment."

"You do woodwork?" her eyes light up.

This is a part of myself I keep quiet, not because I'm embarrassed, but because it's important to me. Not many people know I do it. My grandfather taught me as a kid before he passed on, and what he didn't teach me, I taught myself. "Yeah," I grin at her enthusiasm. "I'm not super good at it, but I enjoy it. Once or twice a year I'll set up at one of the festivals, usually the winter one since people want Christmas gifts."

"Do you do well?" she asks, very interested in what I'm telling her.

"Usually sell out," my voice is quiet. I don't want her to think I'm bragging. I don't do it for the money, I do it because it's fun and it makes me feel closer to the one man who gave a damn about me.

"Ryan that's amazing."

"Everybody has that one thing they're good at, right?" I shrug.

"From where I sit you're good at a number of things."

I try not to let those words mean as much as they do, but I can't wait to show her what else I'm good at. When I put my mind to something, I conquer it, and I can't wait to be great at being a father to our child, along with a reliable partner for her.

CHAPTER SIXTEEN
WHITNEY

TUESDAY NIGHT HAS NOW BECOME my favorite night of the week, followed by Thursday. For a month Ryan and I have been doing dinner. The first week was awkward, but now we've settled into a pattern. I cook on Tuesday and he cooks on Thursday. I try not look too deeply into why Tuesday is my favorite night, but I know it's because I get to take care of him.

We've still managed to keep our secret, but it's not going to be much longer. The morning sickness has finally gone away and now I'm starting to gain weight. My clothes are fitting more tightly now that we're almost into the fourth month. We're going to need to start decorating a nursery and making plans soon. I'm a planner, obviously, and we both want to know the gender of the baby, can't even begin to tell you how excited I'm becoming about this new season of life.

I check the clock on my SUV as I pull into the driveway. I have about forty-five minutes before Ryan gets here, which is nice, because that means I'll be able to figure out something to wear that fits. As I'm letting myself into the house, my phone rings. Flipping it over, I see my brother's smiling face.

"Hey Trevor," I answer, closing the door, setting my stuff on the counter, and making my way upstairs.

"I haven't heard from you in a while, Sis. I was gettin' a little worried."

I love him, I do, but my brother has this uncanny ability to call me when I'm about to let my guard down. He knows exactly the questions to ask me in order for me to fess up and I can't let that happen right now. Pregnancy brain is a real thing for me, and I have no doubt somehow he'll know, and then I'm screwed.

"I'm good," I answer, hoping I don't sound as winded as I feel after walking the length of the hallway and reaching down to take my shoes off. I'm not sure why I thought it would be a good idea to wear the high heels with the buckle straps today.

"Mom said you haven't been over for Sunday dinner in a few weeks."

Trevor is as subtle as a spaceship landing outside on my front yard.

"I've been busy. You know this is my busy season, and it's not easy running my own business," I make the excuse. Truth is I'm so tired that all I wanna do on the weekends is sleep, and I'm scared my mom will be able to look at me and see what's going on. Usually I'm the one laying this guilt trip on Trevor so I have no idea what's happening here.

"Are you sure that's all it is? Most of the time when you're busy you at least have time to send me a text to let me know you're okay. I know you haven't told mom about the baby yet," he drops his bomb. "And even though I've asked, you still haven't told me who the dad is."

"Because it's none of your business. Right now he and I are trying to figure things out, and I don't need you in the middle of it, trying to fix this for me. I love you, Trevor, but you've got to let me deal with my own life."

He's quiet for a few minutes and I can almost hear him gripping the phone, can hear his teeth grinding against one another. "I didn't know what Stephen was doing to you, and I'll never forgive myself for it. If anyone could have helped you, it was me."

My heart almost breaks as I hear the tortured timbre of his voice. I forget he has in some ways been affected even more than I was by not only the breakup of my marriage, but what he suspects has happened. I hope Ryan didn't tell him anything I told him in confidence.

"Trev, I'm a big girl. I can take care of myself. Regardless of what you think, I always have been. I don't blame anyone but myself for the situation I was in. Truthfully, it made me a stronger person. Now I know what I want, and I won't settle for less again."

And I won't because I took less the first time around, and even if it means being a single mother for the rest of my life, I will be. It doesn't scare me, not like it probably would other women. What scares me is giving up my independence and handing it over to a man who'll snuff it out.

"Just know I'm always here to talk. It doesn't matter what time of the day or night it is, Whit. I couldn't be there for you the first time around, but I can be there for you now."

Damn emotions – what he said brings tears to my eyes. "I know," I strangle out against a tight throat. "And I appreciate it, but please respect my decision when I say I'll tell you everything when I'm ready."

"I'm gonna hold you to those words, Whit. I just need to know you're taken care of."

"I appreciate the sentiment, but I gotta go," I've got to get off the phone with him before he makes me cry.

"Love you, Whit."

Damn him.

"Love you too, Trev."

I hang up before I put my face in my hands and sob. I don't know why I'm crying, I'm not even sure why the emotions are coming at me so hard tonight. Maybe I'm tired. I haven't been sleeping well and I've been missing out on my afternoon nap. Another thought creeps into my subconscious and I do my best to block it out, but it's there, making its presence known.

Maybe I miss Ryan.

That can't be it, I tell myself, but there's no mistaking the way my heart beats faster on Tuesdays and Thursdays. I purposely don't work late on those days, either. In fact, I've started taking off earlier on those days so I can get home and get changed before he arrives. It's not necessarily that I want to look cute for him, but – shit – let's face it, I do. I plop down across the bed, letting my head fall off the other side.

What the hell am I going to do? I'm the one who said there wouldn't be any kind of relationship and look what I'm doing.

"Okay, Whit, here's what you do. You keep track of how you feel when he's around tonight."

Saying the words out loud seems stupid, but there's no one else here for me to talk to, and I decide this is my plan of attack. I'm going to gauge my feelings and see exactly what they are while he's around. That way – if I lie to anyone – it's only to myself.

"DO YOU LIKE IT?"

I tried a new recipe tonight, roast beef and gravy sandwiches. They simmered in the crockpot all day while I was at work. When I came home, I didn't have to do much to throw dinner on the table.

"It's not healthy, but damn that's good," he speaks carefully around the food in his mouth, moaning as he takes another bite.

"Sometimes I need to eat whatever I feel like. Tonight felt like comfort food," I take a bite of my own sandwich, moaning along with him.

The taste of food has gotten sharper, and I swear sometimes I can tell individual ingredients. I've never been like this before, but from reading information on the internet, I know it's from the pregnancy.

"Is anything wrong?"

How do I bring this up to him? How do I explain at thirty-five years old, I'm scared to tell my parents what I've done? I'm worried about the judgment, and another part of me is worried that he won't stick around. "Trevor called me tonight, giving me a hard time about not going to Sunday dinners at my mom's."

His green gaze pierces mine. I want to hide from the depth of his stare, because I feel as if he looks directly into my soul. "Is it because of me?"

Honesty time apparently. "No, not directly. It's because of the baby," I reach down, cupping my hand over my small bump. "I don't know how they'll react."

"Whit, you're thirty-five years old. What's it going to matter?"

It's frustrating. He doesn't come from the type of family I do. "You don't have to hear their judgment, about how they're so disappointed in me. I waited until I was divorced and then got knocked up."

"I don't have to hear it because you won't let me," his voice is quiet in the space of the kitchen.

I'm not entirely sure how we got here, angrily whispering words back and forth with one another. I put my fork down, appetite gone. He's not lying, I've deliberately kept him away, because maybe this is my dirty little secret. Then again maybe this is something I wanted for me, and not to share with everyone else. Whatever it is, I realize I'm not being fair, but I'm still not sure I want to open us up to whatever our friends and family might dish out.

"It's a simple decision, Princess. You either want me to be your secret, or you want me to be the father of your child. I can't and won't be both," he slams his own fork down. "I thought that by spending time with you, you'd realize how serious I am about us co-parenting, or maybe even having a relationship. Obviously we can make it work between the sheets."

"Don't be crude, Ryan."

"What was it you told me that night? You needed a dick in your treasure cove? Who was crude then? How come you get a different set of rules than I do?"

"That's not fair," I'm getting hot in my anger and stand up to fan my fingers in front of my face.

I look around as he gets up, too. Instinctively I move further back into the kitchen, until my waist hits the countertop on the far side.

"Don't act like I'm about to hit you, Whit. I'm not that asshole you were married to. I think I've proven to you in the last few months that I'm different. I'd prove it to everyone if you'd let me. We're two consenting adults having a conversation," he runs his fingers through his hair.

My mouth is poised open to speak, but he continues.

"You wanna talk about what's not fair? That's mine," he points to my stomach as he inches closer. "The child you carry is mine and yours, but you're the one who gets to experience everything. I'm relegated to what you allow me to experience and you call all the shots. There's nothing I can take for granted, because you won't let me."

My mind tells me to find a way out, my heart thumps against my chest, and my breath becomes pants as he's finally close enough to touch me.

"Wanna know what else was mine?" His eyes are dark, voice soft, hands gentle as one reaches out to cup the back of my neck while the other slides against my cheek.

"No," I whisper as I nod my head yes. Everything about Ryan and me is highlighted in this exchange. My voice is saying no, while my body says yes.

"You do," he moves his mouth to my ear. "You wanna know. Stop fighting it, Princess. For those few hours that night, you were mine, and they were the best hours of my life. I had everything I'd ever wanted at my fingertips. I gorged on you, I lived in you, and I left a piece of myself behind," he breathes deeply, a sigh that moves the hair at my temple. "Damnit, Princess, I'd be everything you need if you'd just give me the fucking chance."

It all sounds so good to hear him talk. I move my hands up to his biceps, curling my fingers in the skin, denting them with my fingernails. "I want to," I mouth, but I know he doesn't hear me, because I don't let the words escape.

CHAPTER SEVENTEEN
RENEGADE

I'VE BEEN GOOD. Since this started I've let her call the shots, let her decide what part I get to play, what she'll allow me to do. I've never been the type of person to just sit back and let others direct me in my personal life. Doing what I do for a job, I have to be able to take, execute, and adjust my orders. I don't like it so much when I'm cut off at the knees in my personal life. It hits me like a freight train, the need to show this woman what I want from her.

Her finger nails are cutting into my flesh she's holding me so tightly. The weight of her body is leaning into me, and I'm taking it. I want to show her how much I support her, how invaluable I am when she needs someone to lean on. I'm not the kind of guy to run when things get tough. Never in my life have I backed away from a fight, whether it be between me and my dad, me and gunfire in the middle of the night, or me and a perp. Ryan Kepler hangs around and gets the job done, no matter how difficult it is.

"Whit," my voice is tight. I've been holding my feelings, my instincts back for a long time. It's been hard, it's taken its toll. The tension between us isn't even thick anymore; it's a solid force, a concrete wall that we need to either plow through or scale the fuck over.

"Ryan," I can barely hear the words. Her breath fans against my neck, where she's buried her face. If it hadn't been for the soft stir, I might not have even heard my name whispered against my skin. She's holding herself so still and close, she's starting to mold around my muscles.

My arms go around her, holding her tighter, our bodies touching from toes to head. Every part of her is tucked against me, and I feel more protective of her than I've ever felt for anyone else. I also want her more than I've ever wanted another person in my life.

"Fuck it all," I mumble as I move my hands to her hair, dig my fingers against her scalp, and tilt it back.

She's surprised because she opens her mouth on a gasp, and when she does, I capture her lips with mine. What I meant to be a slow kiss is a fast drop into passion. My tongue invades her space, sweeping against the roof of her mouth, tasting the juice she prefers to drink right now. I breathe deeply, inhaling the apple-scented lotion she likes to wear. Pushing against her body, we stop when she collides with the counter of the breakfast bar. Her hands are gripping my waist, her fingers tightening in the cloth of my t-shirt. Disentangling my hands from her hair, I move them down to her waist holding them there for a few seconds before I realize I don't want to be a gentleman anymore. I want her to know me, the real me, who took what he wanted the night we spent together. Trailing my hands down to the curve of her ass, I cup the flesh and pull her into the cradle of my thighs, letting her feel how much she affects me.

Tearing her lips from mine, she moans. "Jesus, Ryan, you're..." she trails off, biting her bottom lip as she lets her head fall back, thrusts her pussy into me.

"Hard as a rock," I supply for her, grasping the lobe of her ear in between my lips, using my teeth to tug slightly. "Happens every damn time I'm around you."

I bend with my knees, grasping her ass tighter, and lift her so that she's perched on the countertop. Here, she's eye-level with me. I take a moment to look into her eyes, make sure she's okay with all of this and it's not just her hormones. What I see when I look is passion, need, desire, and maybe a little bit of disbelief. Deciding she's into it, I move my hands to her thighs, pushing the same pink sundress she wore the first night we met for dinner at her house up around her waist.

"From the bottom of my heart, thank you for wearing this dress. The first night I saw you in it, I wanted to do this with you," I admit, latching onto her neck as I push her thighs apart already feeling the heat from her core.

"I wanted you to," her voice is low, strained, and full of need. "I wanted this to happen. I've wanted this to happen every time we've been together since the first time. I don't know what you did to me, Ryan, but I wake up at night wishing you were there. I'm hot, horny, and so fucking frustrated," she bites her lip as I move the panel of her panties aside and let my finger tip dip into her heat.

"I can take care of all those problems for you, Princess, you've only got to be honest with me. Tell me what you need, tell me what I can do to make it better."

Her fingers grip my shoulders as she presses against my invasion before moving down. "Keep doing that, don't stop. Please," with one hand she grabs hold of my shirt at my stomach. "Just let me get this one first," she's thrusting against my fingers, letting the stretch of my shirt give her leverage as she pushes and pulls away.

"Take what you need, Whit."

And with those words out of my mouth, she does exactly what I've told her to do. She's never looked more gorgeous as she reaches up with her hand to expose one of her breasts, continuing to thrust against me. The invitation there, I lean forward, nosing aside the lace of her bra and the flesh of her finger, capturing the taut nipple in between my lips.

"Yes," she breathes, sighing deeply.

Using my teeth, I nip slightly before soothing the burn with my tongue, moaning when she takes my fingers deeper into her core. Turning my fingers, I allow my thumb to stroke her clit, knowing that will get her off faster. When I flick my wrist, she pulls so roughly on my shirt I'm afraid she's going to either rip it or strangle me with the neck of it.

"Don't stop, Ryan," she chants. "Please don't stop, please don't stop."

I can feel her opening, can feel her getting wetter, lubing my fingers to go deeper, allowing me to reach into her body. I want to take my fingers out, unbutton my jeans, shove them down around my thighs and plunge home. I want her pussy hugging my cock the way it's hugging my fingers, but I know without a doubt this is about her and I have to let it be about her.

Moaning against her nipple, I lick the turgid nub with my tongue, growing harder behind the zipper of my jeans as I feel her nipple grow harder. She's wild on the countertop and I'm wondering if I should get us down, but to do that, I'm going to have to stop everything I'm doing to her body. Right now, it's out of the question – I want her to feel this.

Her body is strung tight as a bow, her thighs are open wide, her mouth is hanging open panting at the things I'm doing to her.

"Never felt like this before, Ryan, can't get close enough," she's thrusting towards my fingers, opening her thighs wider to get as close to me as she can.

"C'mon, Princess," I grasp her around the neck, pulling her head down to rest on my shoulder as I continue to tongue her nipple and finger fuck her pussy. "Let it go."

My words are muffled by my mouth against her skin, but she gets it as she pumps against my fingers, and that's when I feel the crest. Her body slumps, she screams against the fabric of my shirt, and bites the flesh of my shoulder as she comes so hard she stops everything once it's done.

I'm worried she's passed out, until I feel her body shuddering against mine. When I pull back, she's got a bright smile on her face and she's laughing.

"You okay?" I push her sweat-drenched hair out of her face.

"Perfect," she grins at me, decidedly evil as she reaches down and grasps my crotch with her hand. "Why don't you unleash that weapon and show me how good you use it, Officer Kepler."

With fucking pleasure.

DOWN THE HALL, in her bedroom, I try to slow things down, try to be gentle with her. It's hard because I feel so much for her. I've held things back for so long, and I feel them coming to the forefront of this relationship. If this is the only way I can show her how I feel, I'll take it.

Her body is stretched out underneath mine, naked as the day she was born, the soft light from across the room bathing her in a glow. "You're so fucking gorgeous," I whisper in her ear as I move my mouth over the smooth skin of her neck, nipping at the point that's pulsing out of control.

"God," her voice is strangled. "You are too, if you could've seen what you looked like walking into my house tonight," she throws her head back as I continue to make love to the elegant expanse of neck she's exposed to me. "Those jeans, that shirt, the cocky look you have all the time when you look at my stomach...shit," she flexes her hands in my hair. "I was wet as soon as I saw you."

If nothing else, Whitney makes me feel like I could scale a wall and take on an entire army by myself. Pulling my lips away from her flesh, I reach down, positioning my length at her pussy. "That might've been what you saw babe, but what I saw was an extremely sexy woman looking at me like she wanted to eat me up. Immediate hard-on," I push inside, groaning as she squeezes me.

I don't want to hurt her, but tonight I'm in touch with my feelings more than I normally am. There's not a reason I can pinpoint, but maybe it's the fact I feel more comfortable with her. She exploded against me in the kitchen, giving me every piece of her in a way she never has before. It was nothing she said, nothing about the way she acted – it was a physical shift in the air between us. Now, I want her to feel it. I want to give her every part of me, pour myself into her.

Picking up speed, I continue to plunge into her body, and then withdraw. Keeping a steady pace, I push up on my knees, grabbing her around the shoulders and pull her up so we face one another.

"Oh my God," she sighs.

My sigh answers hers. I'm deeper in this position; it allows me to feel every part of her body, every grip of her pussy against me. "Don't close those eyes," I command, holding her face in my hands. "Let me see what I do to you, Whit. Let me see it."

Our eyes drill into one another, and it's the most intense thing I've ever experienced in my life. I can see her pupils get darker, bigger as she continues thrusting against me. Letting go of her face, I move one hand behind her back, letting her recline partially as my other hand goes to her breast. My fingers pluck at the taut nipple, and that's all it takes for her to grind against me, moving her hips in a circle. As I thrust and thrust harder, each time letting her pull me deeper, she's smashing her clit against my body. As hard as she came before, I think we're both about to come even harder.

"Feel good?" I twist her nipple harder, grinning as she groans, trying to close her eyes against the sensation. "Keep those blue eyes open, baby."

"You know it does," her voice is strangled again.

"Feels good for me, too. You wanna come, Princess?"

"Fuck yes," the words are ripped from her body. There's always something so hot about hearing her say fuck. The image she presents is so buttoned up. When I can pop one of those buttons, it makes me feel like the manliest man in the world.

Grabbing her hips, I piston into her without slowing, even as hers start to match mine. Sweat rolls down my body, sliding against hers as I push her back to the bed, and climb on top of her again. I stop thinking about everything and let my mind completely blank out to concentrate on how good the act between us feels. I don't expect it when my rhythm falters and the orgasm takes me by surprise. Not wanting her to be left behind, I stick my hand between us, flattening my thumb against Whitney's clit as I continue to pound into her. That's when I feel the rush of wetness against me, the loss of tension in her body, and the small moan she makes. As we stop pushing against one another, she fights for breath.

"I feel like I owe you for that one," she giggles against my neck.

Suddenly an idea pops into my head, panting against her as well, I pull back. "Let me take you out on a date."

It's one of the most important questions I've ever asked her. Going out on a date means she isn't ashamed to be seen with me. If we're honest, that's what I fear – that I'm okay to fuck while nobody knows, but never okay to be seen with in public.

Her face gives away the surprise at my request. "If you want to take me out, and aren't scared to be seen with an older woman, then I'd love to go out with you."

Hearing her words and knowing my own fear, it makes me realize possibly we were both scared of the same thing, just on opposite sides of the spectrum. "Tomorrow," I kiss her cheek. "Tomorrow I take you on a date."

CHAPTER EIGHTEEN

RENEGADE

"THESE ARE FOR YOU," I hand Whitney the flowers I brought over. I figured if we're going to do the dating thing, I might as well pull out all the stops. Even if I did get her flowers last night. Every woman deserves to be wooed, and I will totally woo the fuck outta her.

She smiles as she dips her head down to inhale the scent permeating the plastic they're in. "You always get me the best smelling flowers."

"I wanted to be sure you remember this occasion. It's our first date," I remind her, following her into her house.

After being relegated to indoor dinners, I can't believe I finally got her to agree to appear in public with me. I'm happier about it than I probably should be, because it still doesn't mean anything in the grand scheme of things. She's still unsure of me, and I know that, but I'll prove to her I'm the real deal.

"I'm excited about our date," she says as she adds the flowers to the same vase with the ones from last night, before grabbing her purse and walking out of the house.

"I am too, but I do have to say, I never took you for a bingo player."

When she told me she wanted to play bingo, I thought maybe she was pulling my leg, but after talking with Tank, I found out Whitney's kind of a bingo aficionado. It was hard, talking to him about her without giving anything away, but I asked in passing acting like I was taking another girl out on a date, wondering if Whitney liked it. Imagine my surprise, when Tank told me everything I wanted to know.

"Oh no, I love bingo; especially since they outlawed cigarettes. Now my hair doesn't smell like smoke when I go home."

We get into the truck and I notice for the first time, she's carrying a small bag along with her purse. "Whatcha got there?"

Her face turns a pretty pink, and I wonder what I've hit on.

She smirks, a twinkle coming to her eyes that I've never seen before. There's an air of mystery there, and a little bit of sin if I'm being honest.

Her blue eyes cut over to me, I can see them in the dim light of the evening sky when I risk a glance at her. She unbuckles her seat belt, scooting over to sit next to me on the bench seat, before she clasps the lap belt. Whitney leans in closer, and my pulse quickens when I feel her breath, hot at my ear.

"Lingerie. I'm gonna proposition you in the ladies room between the second and fifth game, you won't see it coming. Nobody goes to the restroom during the game because they don't want to miss out on any money. We'll be completely by ourselves, and given the noise of that bingo hall, we can probably scream as loud as we want," she drops a soft kiss on my neck as she pulls back.

I'm clutching the wheel so tightly my knuckles are white, and as we come to a stop at a red light, I shift it in park before I lift up in my seat, adjusting my jeans. "Goddamn woman," I'm speechless, I don't even know what to say.

At a loss, I clear my throat. "What in the hell do you really have in that bag?"

She giggles, before she pulls it across the seat, putting it in her lap. Winking as she puts her hand into the opening, she pulls out a zip up hoodie.

"In case I get cold, and these," she shows me five dabbers, all different colors. "They're lucky and they help me keep my games straight," she explains.

"You're killin' me, smalls," I joke. I roll the window down, wishing it was winter weather, but enjoying the cool breeze as much as I can, hoping like hell it cools my libido before we get there.

We're quiet as we drive along the streets of a town that could be confused with Mayberry, but on Friday, Saturday, and Sunday nights it looks like NASCAR'S come to town with the amount of cars and trucks parked along the sides of the roads. Judging by how far back I'm going to have to leave my truck, we probably should have left for this particular bingo hall around noon.

"Will they still have a place for us to sit?" I tease her as I sling my arm over her shoulders, checking the road before we cross and making sure I walk next to the traffic.

"Yes," she laughs. "It's just popular. You'll see, once we get inside, it's huge. I mean we could probably fit a football field in there if we truly wanted to."

"I had no idea this many people loved bingo," I whistle through my teeth, gazing at the couples, ages ranging from teenagers to about ninety, make their way towards the front doors.

"Me neither until I started going," she admits.

Tugging on the ends of her hair, I make her look up at me as I look down at her. She rests her head on my shoulder as we continue walking slowly. "Why did you start going?"

"Loneliness mostly," smiling in the sad way she does sometimes. "After the divorce, I needed to be around people, and bless his heart, I couldn't take hanging out with Tank anymore. So I lied and told him I joined a singles group."

I chuckle loudly. "Instead you started playing bingo?"

She laughs so hard she has to stop for a second. "Yeah, but what can I say? I got good at it and ended up making enough money to help finance part of my business."

"And you go to church on Sunday with that sinning heart," I tease her again.

Whitney moves in front of me, turning to face me. Leaning in, she goes up on the tips of her toes to kiss me softly. "Sinning here is nothing like what I've done with you. The world needs more sinners like us."

I shove my fingers into her hair, cupping the nape of her neck with my fingers. "Sinning with you is my favorite thing to do."

Her eyes close and she leans her forehead against my nose, because that's as far as she gets, even on tiptoe. "Mine, too."

My dumbass heart swells, and I bite back all the romantic words I want to tell her, because I know she still isn't ready. I disentangle my hands from her hair, running them down her back, until I let them rest on her ass. "C'mon," I give her a tap. "Show me what all the fuss is about."

"Get ready, Ryan," she says over her shoulder as she drags me towards the door. "You ain't never seen anything like this before in your life."

Whitney

I wonder if I looked the same way Ryan does right now when I walked through the doors of this place for the first time. It's overwhelming to say the least, all the noise and people. And did I mention the noise? Tables are as far as the eye can see in the main room, and then in other rooms there are different games of bingo going on.

He leans down so I can hear him. "Holy fucking shit, Whitney. This is bananas."

"I know," I laugh. "I love it! Let's go get our game cards."

As we stand in line, Ryan lightly touches me, his arm over my shoulder holding my back to his front. It feels good, knowing he's here with me, letting him touch me this way. This is what I've missed more than anything. Having someone who stands behind me and supports me. With this guy, I know I never have to worry if he's going to support me. He's made me believe it with everything he's done. It's hard for me to put those words out into the open, but I know one day I will. One day I'm going to tell him how I feel, but until then I'll show him.

My hand grasps his where it rests against my chest. When he mindlessly begins rubbing my fingers, I nuzzle my chin towards our clasped hands. If I'm not careful, this man could be big trouble for me.

"How many do you want Whitney?"

The cashier recognizes me and I'm trying not to show my embarrassment. He already knows I come here a lot. "Let's get four," I tell him. "Two for me, and two for my friend."

I'm reaching into my purse to grab my wallet, when Ryan's hands stop me. "Don't even think about it, Princess." It's weird, even in my marriage, I paid for things. Not that we didn't have a joint checking account, but it was always up to me to take my card out and pay for things.

I like Ryan taking care of me, love the fact he treats me like someone special. I'm not just a good time to him, and I think above everything I'm truly learning that, if nothing else.

We grab our game boards and thread through the crowd, waving at people we know along the way, trying to find a place to sit. One thing about this man of mine – and I do admit he's mine, at least for right now – he doesn't let go of my hand in a crowd. He brings me along as he looks for some empty seats.

"Over there," I point to him, gesturing towards the back of the bingo hall.

It takes us another ten minutes to get over there, but once we do, the loudness of the place has been cut in half. Over here, out of the way, it isn't nearly as bad as in the thick of everything. "We'll have to wait for the new game," I explain as we get our stuff set up. Glancing over at him, I notice he doesn't have his own dabber. "Do you want to use my blue one?" I hold it out to him, almost as if I'm offering him a sacred piece of a puzzle.

"You sure?" he quirks an eyebrow at me. "These are lucky and all, what if some of the luck rubs off on me?"

Turning my head to him, I smile. "Maybe you need some luck, Ren-e-gade," I tease him the way I did when we met at the bar.

"Please *pew pew* for me," he ruins it and makes me stick my tongue out at him.

"I'm never going to live that down."

"No," he agrees. "Not in a million fucking years. That's okay though, it was the cutest thing I've ever seen someone do."

We're quiet for a few minutes as we watch the comings and goings, ebbing and flow, of the crowd. "You want something to munch on while we play?" he asks, motioning towards the concession stand.

"Nachos and whatever drink they have that's lemon lime would be amazing."

As I watch him walk away, I realize other women watch him too, and I want to scream out he's mine. I have a claim on him, and for one of the first times since this all started, I truly realize I want the claim. I want him to tell people about me, I want to tell others about him. And with great clarity, I realize I'm also the one that's been holding us back.

It's hard, but as I sit there in the crowd of people, I vow I'm not going to hold us back anymore. Whatever happens is going to happen, and if it's good, I have to be open to it. If it's bad, I'll live through it the same way I've lived through all the other shit in my life. But it's very clear that if I do nothing, I'm going to lose out on something amazing.

And I refuse to lose out on a chance at happiness. I've gone through enough loneliness and sadness in my life. Happy is where I want to be, and if this man walking back towards me now with a goofy smile on my face is my happy – I'm going to hold on with both hands and never let go.

CHAPTER NINETEEN
RENEGADE

"FUCK I FEEL like I'm about to serve a warrant," I tell Whitney as I listen to the caller giving us our letters and numbers. "My heart is going to beat out of my chest, I'm so close to a damn bingo."

She laughs at my side. "It's addicting, isn't it?"

"Like fucking heroin," I agree as I hear the next spot we can mark. Damnit, it's not the one I need.

"This is seriously what got me into it," she admits. "I won once and then I wanted to win again and again. So I just kept coming back. At one point, I could play like ten cards at once."

"No way," I take my eyes off my own cards for a split second. "How?"

"Obsession?" she shrugs. "You just learn to do it, and then you don't want to stop. I'm not saying this is the best thing for someone with an addictive personality, but it's fun for a while."

The caller calls out B-32 and *holy shit*. "Bingo! Bingo!" I yell to be heard above the loud room. Holding my hand up.

"Yes!" Whitney squeals next to me. "You did it!"

We wait as they come over and inspect my card. Like I'm going to lie about a damn bingo? Apparently it's a thing, though.

"You're good," the worker tells me. "Go ahead and go to the desk to get your money."

"Wait, I win money? I was excited about winning period."

Whitney laughs. "Yes! C'mon let's go get it."

She drags me to the payout desk and when they tell me I've won a thousand bucks, my mouth hangs open. "Are you fucking kidding me?"

"I told you I was able to finance some of my business with my bingo winnings," she reminds me.

I'm putting the cash in my wallet as I glance at her. "How much did you win exactly?"

She runs her tongue over her lips. "Five figures."

"Damn, babe," I turn back to the bingo floor. "Do you want to go back and try our hand some more?"

"Nah, I think we did what we came here to do. We had a great time, you won some money, and I got to indulge my addiction."

We exit the building, and I hold the door open for the couple behind us. They're older and the man is using a walker, his wife holding onto his elbow as she slowly walks beside him.

"Thank you," she smiles up at me.

"No problem ma'am. Do y'all need help to your car?"

"No," he answers, shaking his head. "But thank you for asking young man. Our son's coming to pick us up and should be here in a few minutes."

"There he is," the lady points to a car. "Thank you for holding the door and the offer."

As we watch them get into the car, Whitney slips her hand in mine. "What would it be like to be with someone that long? To still love someone at that age so much you want to hang onto them?"

"You've never thought of it?" I question as we slowly walk back to my truck.

She's quiet and I wonder if I've overstepped my boundaries. We don't much talk about Stephen and that's fine with me, but it's not like I avoid it on purpose. I avoid it because I don't think she wants to talk about him.

"I did at one time. I mean you don't go into a marriage thinking it's not going to last forever, ya know? Especially with my parents and the family I come from. But the longer it went on, the more unhappy I got, I just couldn't keep pretending."

"What about now," I ask before I can stop myself. "Is it something you want now?"

"With the right person," she answers carefully. "If I had it for the right reasons and it was good timing, I would definitely get married again. I would gladly spend my life with someone else. Would I have said that a few months ago? No, but things change."

I wonder if she's talking about me, I wonder if I'm one of the reasons her feelings on the subject have changed. Part of me wants to ask her, but the other part doesn't want to hear it in case I'm not.

We fall into an easy silence as we make our way back to the truck.

"Can I be forward?" she turns to me after we've almost made it back to her house.

"You can always tell me whatever it is you want to tell me. You don't have to ever censor yourself for me. Just say what you want."

She struggles, I can tell by the way she opens her mouth, and then shuts it, three times before words come from her throat. "I don't want this night to end. I've had a really good time with you. I feel like we've turned a corner here. Will you spend the night with me?"

My heart almost stops as she asks me with uncertainty in her voice. I know with everything I am, she doesn't understand what this means to me. There's no fucking way she can feel the way my heart thuds in my chest as I look over at her, seeing glimpses of her as the street lights brighten the interior of my truck. This feels like an invitation to take things with us a little more serious, a step further. I won't push her, but I do want to tell her parents and Tank about this baby before it's born. I've wondered a few times if she'd just like to show up one day holding a bundle of baby and then let people ask her where it came from.

"You don't have to ask me like that, Whit. I'll stay whenever you want me to. Hell, if it were up to me, I'd move in."

"I don't know if I'm ready for that," she says hesitantly, biting her nail.

"I know, but I'm just telling you I'm willing to stay. You want me there? I'll be there, any and every time you need me."

Whitney

My hands shake as I brush my teeth and hair, getting ready for bed. I'm not sure what it is about tonight that's different from all the other times Ryan and I have hung out. Maybe it's the way he wasn't afraid to touch me in public, he wasn't scared to be with an older woman. Not once did he make me feel like I was second best. He treated me like I was number one to him and as if I were his main concern tonight. I haven't had that kind of attention in a long time, and I have to admit it was nice.

Him opening the door, being polite to the older couple, buying my stuff, touching me every time he could – if it were from anyone else, I'd think they were playing a game. But I know every time I look into Ryan's eyes, there's nothing there but honesty. I've tried to ignore it, tried to explain it away and told myself I'm ten kinds of an idiot for seeking him out. Truth of the matter is, I can't help it. The more we're together, the longer he stays in this with me, the more I'm going to count on him. Summer is beating down on us and before we know it, it'll be Christmas. When our baby is due.

I don't want to go through this alone, never did, and for the first time I'm feeling like Ryan is right where he wants to be. I put aside all my own preconceived notions tonight and truly paid attention to how he acted around me, how he treated me, and what he was saying. I stopped thinking ahead and stopped doing my own interpretation of everything. Instead I let my instincts do the talking, and they said this guy is the real deal. I'd be stupid not to take this and see where it may go.

For fifteen minutes I debated on if I wanted to dress sexy or wear my normal t-shirt to bed. In the end, I had to go with the t-shirt. I'm tired, and tonight won't be a night where we're burning up the sheets – I just don't have it in me.

Opening the door, I shut off the bathroom light and walk out into the bedroom. Ryan's already lying down, checking his phone in the light cast by the lamp on my nightstand.

"You look ridiculous in my Tiffany-Blue Damask comforter," I smile as I walk over to my side and pull back the sheets.

"Never let it be said I haven't done emasculating things for you, Whit. This is probably at the top of them so far. I feel like I need to hand Tank my nuts next time I see him."

"No need for that," I curl up next to him without even thinking about it. "I kinda like them and want you to keep them for a little while longer," I snuggle into the indention of his arm and throw my leg over his. "I hope you don't mind, but I'm a cuddler."

"Please, cuddle me if it makes you feel good," his breath is warm against my forehead.

I only wish I could tell him how good it really does make me feel. Cherished actually, but I keep that to myself.

CHAPTER TWENTY
RENEGADE

"WHAT'S WRONG?" I ask when I feel her turn over for maybe the hundredth time tonight. I'd thought being invited into her bed and sleeping here tonight would be a smooth ride, but she's probably traveled three miles in her quest for sleep.

"Can't sleep," she huffs, disentangling herself from me and pushing her pillow further up into the headboard. "No matter which way I lay, I can't get comfortable. Those chairs tonight were hard."

"Isn't that supposed to happen later on in the pregnancy?" I drawl, trying to wake myself up to deal with her plight.

"I guess it can happen whenever because my hip is freakin' killing me, and now I can't go back to sleep."

I know by the way she huffs again that this is going to be a long night. Forcing my eyes open, I focus on the clock at the bedside table. Two in the morning. If I can get her back to sleep within an hour, I can at least get four more before I have to be up and down at the station. "Would talking help you go to sleep?" I ask, rolling over so that I'm facing her. She's irritated and it could be the cutest thing I've ever seen in my life. I can tell by the circles under her eyes, she wouldn't appreciate me saying this is cute.

"Maybe?" her voice is doubtful.

An idea pops into my head. A game I haven't played since I was in Iraq. "Do you want to play a little game?"

"Ryan, I'm not interested in getting naked with you right now. I'm not in the mood." Her voice is annoyed and I can't help the laugh that escapes my throat.

"Not that kind of game," I explain as I sit up, leaning back against the head board. "In Iraq when we couldn't sleep, we'd play a game called truth or lie, because ya know, there wasn't much you could do for a dare in the middle of a war zone. The person would say truth or lie, if it was truth, they got to tell you from what point in your life the truth had to be from, and if it was a lie, anything was fair game. So you tell me. Truth or lie."

She's interested, I can tell because she's quit squirming and she's giving me her full attention. "Truth," she finally says.

"From what period in my life."

Frankly I'm a little scared at what she's going to ask me. Most of my life is an open book where she's concerned but there are definitely times and situations that I've wanted to keep to myself. Maybe that isn't fair, because I've asked her to open her whole life up to me.

"Why did you sometimes sleep in Trevor's room on the floor when you were younger?" she asks quietly.

Goddamn. She went in for the kill. I can tell by the way she's reluctantly asked she doesn't know whether I'll answer or not, and she's unsure if she should have questioned it. Maybe I'm quiet for too long because she rubs her hand up and down my shoulder.

"You don't have to answer if you don't want. It's just something I've always wondered."

"Nah," I clear my throat, removing the boulder that's lodged itself there. "I'll tell you, it just might take me a while to get it out."

"I've got all night," she fluffs her pillow, showing me that she won't be going anywhere any time soon.

"When I was eight, my dad started suffering from PTSD," I start, my voice so rough it sounds like I swallowed a quarry full of fucking rocks.

"Was he in the military?" she asks. "For some reason I didn't think you joined because it was a family tradition."

"No, he wasn't in the military. He was a night clerk at a convenience store off of I-65. One night he was robbed at gunpoint, beaten, and left for dead."

She gasps and for a split-second I want her sympathy. I want her to think he'd been a good guy who'd been at the wrong place at the wrong time. But I've never been the type of person to shy away from my past. "You don't have to keep going."

"I do, because he doesn't deserve your sympathy," she grabs hold of my hand as she hears me speak, starting to gently rub the palm. "The men who robbed and beat him did it because he owed them money. My dad had a bad drug habit. He begged, borrowed, and stole to get his next fix."

"I had no idea," she whispers.

"Not many people did." Although I wish they had. I dreamed so many nights someone would come and take me away from him. He'd clean up just enough every time child services was called. "Eventually my mom couldn't handle it anymore."

"What did she do?" The tone of Whitney's voice tells me she doesn't truly want to know, she probably dreads this little game, but it's better to get this out in the open than to let it fester. We all have our demons, and I think it's better for her to see mine haunt me just as much as hers haunt her.

"She left, but she wasn't perfect either. Mom had her own problems, alcohol usually, but she also made bad decisions. I heard through the grapevine a few years back that she died, but her body remains unclaimed as a Jane Doe down by the gulf," I squeeze Whitney's hand hard. "I can't bring myself to ever go and see if it's truly her. It's easier to think she's still out there, maybe happy with the choices she made, even if she left me."

I hope that by telling Whitney this story she realizes how important it is for me to be there for my own child. She understands it's not something I want to hold over her, but something I want to be a part of.

"Did my parents know?" she finally asks, her tone strained. She grabs my hand, and I'm not sure if it's to comfort me or her.

I tilt my head back, looking up at the ceiling because it's easier not to look into her eyes when I talk. "Eventually. For the longest time they thought my dad worked late – which he did – but then he never came home. By the time your mom understood, and I think she told your dad, I was a teenager," I swallow hard, fighting back emotion I hardly ever allow myself to feel. "God, Whit, your parents saved my life. There were days I would have gone hungry had they not let me eat at their table. Your mom got to the point where she didn't just buy me clothes and pass them off as extras Trevor didn't need. She'd wait until I was at the house and take both of us shopping. I found out later that she talked to the school resource center about me and asked what it would take to be my guardian, but because they could never get anything to stick on my dad, it would never happen. She made sure Trevor and I were in the same classes, so if he had a field trip, she could send money in with my name on it. Your parents...." I stop, shaking my head at a loss for words for everything they've done for me. I don't talk about it much because it's so emotional for me. "Saved a teenage kid who had nowhere to go."

"Mom's always been fond of you," her voice trembles as she speaks. "And dad's always spoken highly of you, I guess I just never thought to ask why."

"I've never told Tank this, so it stays between us," I turn to my side, so I can look at her, because I want her to see the truth in my eyes. "When I turned eighteen, your dad took me aside and told me he'd pay for school for me, just like he had you and Tank. It broke me, Whit," I shake my head, swallowing hard to dislodge the bad taste it gives me in my mouth. My parents should have been the people to do that, not my best friend's dad. "I asked him how and like the man he is, he was honest. Told me they'd take a second mortgage out on their home to send me, a child that wasn't their own, to college. I wanted to go, but I couldn't put that burden on them. Not when they'd already done so much for me. I had good test scores for the Army, so I decided to join and Tank followed, because we do everything together," I laugh, but no one will know how much it meant to me when he went to boot camp with me. I'd expected to go alone in that venture of my life, but Tank's closer to me than even a brother could be. "When I got home from Iraq, your dad had bought me a whole workshop for the woodwork I do. He said it cost less than a college education, and since I hadn't taken him up on his offer, he could at least pay for something I'd enjoy doing."

"That's when he bought Trevor his boat," she grins, wiping tears from her eyes.

"It's the money he'd put aside for Tank for college, and he spent some of it on me. Do you know what that means to me?" I'm not even sure I can voice what it means, and to know I've kept a secret from all of them is killing me. Knowing I so badly want to be a part of their family, that I'm lying by omission isn't going well for me.

"I can tell by the way you're getting emotional and the way you've always treated my parents with respect," she runs a hand down my chest.

"Which is why it's been hard for me to keep this secret from them. If there's anyone's advice I want – it's Stanley's because your dad has been more of a dad to me than anyone else in this world. He doesn't say it much, but he does tell me he loves me every once in a while," I wipe at my chin, fighting the emotions that have welled up all night.

She laughs, a watery sound as she reaches out and cups my face. "He's a man of few words, but when he wants you to know how he feels, he definitely does."

"We have to tell them soon, Princess," I draw a line in the sand, so to speak. "It don't feel good, not having them involved in our lives. Not when they've done so much."

She nods, sniffling slightly. "Next week at the Fourth of July cookout they always have. We'll tell them then."

I drag her over to me, holding her in my arms, tucking her head under my chin. "Next week."

And finally, I breathe a sigh of relief.

CHAPTER TWENTY-ONE

WHITNEY

"DO YOU LIKE THIS COLOR?" I hold up a piece of pale yellow fabric next to an off-white. "Does it wash this out?"

"I like them together, especially for a spring or early summer wedding. When is this one?" Addison asks, grabbing the appointment book from my table.

We're in my kitchen today, working on some of the things we've unintentionally let pile up. I have a whole list I want to get through today, and Addison, bless her heart, brought me an iced decaf coffee from our local shop. We're checking stuff off our list like nobody's business. "I think it's in April of next year, but I'm meeting her next week to talk about color. I want to give her some options."

"You're right, it is April. Ohhhh," she reaches over grabbing another piece of fabric. "What about the yellow and either a mint or a light blue? It's unusual, but it could be striking with the right back drop."

I grab my notebook, jotting down notes. "I love that!"

"So what are your colors gonna be when you marry Ryan?" She smirks at me over her coffee cup.

I'm speechless for a full minute because I'm shocked and I'm not sure what to say. "We're not getting married. We're having a baby. Those are two very different things."

"If it were the fifties you'd be getting married," she reminds me, giving me a wink.

"Good thing we're not in the fifties," I retort.

She's quiet for a beat, then she asks another question that takes me off my game. "Do you think you'd wanna marry him someday?"

"What the hell, Addison?"

"We're wedding planners, I can't help but think about it. I mean obviously you thought enough of him to sleep with him. You haven't been with anyone since you got divorced. Am I wrong?"

I don't know how to explain to her how I feel about Ryan. He's becoming important to me in ways that don't have anything to do with him being the father of my child. He's showed me he's caring and an overall good person. If I ever decided to marry someone else, he wouldn't be a bad choice, I'm just unsure if he'd be willing to be with an older woman for the rest of his life. "I'm older than him," I shrug.

"Lame," Addison throws a dish towel at me. "That is such a lame-ass cop out. Tell me how you really feel, you need to get it off your chest, Whitney. What do you truly think of Ryan?"

No one's ever asked me that question, and I'm not exactly sure how to answer it. "Ryan is one of the best people I've ever met."

"That's all I'm gonna get? C'mon Whit, I know he's been staying here. His truck is always here."

I wonder if people drive by and see that, I wonder if Trevor's seen it. "I count on him more than I should," I let the words fall from my lips. "He's wormed his way into a part of my heart I didn't know still existed. I thought I'd locked it away when I got divorced, but he's gotten under my skin. I'm not saying I'm in love with him or anything like that, but I enjoy the time I spend with him. He's going to be a great father to our child, and hopefully a good partner for me. If anything comes of it, then so be it."

Addison gives me a sappy look before she points at me. "Girl, you've got it bad. Keep tellin' yourself all that bullshit you just told me. Sooner or later though, you're gonna admit it. You want him, and not for the remainder of your pregnancy. You want him forever."

I can't dispute what she's saying, but at the same time I'm not going to tell her that. "Look, we're figuring it out. Whatever it's going to be, it will be. Stop trying to put what Ryan and I have in a box."

"I know you, and I know you won't mess around forever, Whitney."

She's right, but I also don't want to discuss that with her. If I discuss it with anyone, it should be Ryan.

Renegade

"You coming over for mom and dad's cookout?" Tank asks as we patrol the streets of Laurel Springs.

"Yeah, I'm gonna stop by at least." It's not like I can tell him I'm going to actually be there with his sister. He'll ask why I'm riding with her, and then I'll have to admit what's been going on. I know how he works.

"I think Whit said she's bringing a friend. She didn't say whether it was female or male."

I hit him in the knee. "It's not your business who she's bringing."

"Yes, it is. What if it's a hot chick? I could potentially get a date."

The snort I let out is so loud we both laugh. "Yeah right, what will Blaze say about that?"

"Doesn't matter," he shrugs. "She doesn't want to date me, she's made that painfully obvious."

The tone he uses says not to ask him what he means, but I want to. He's my friend and I can tell he's keeping something in his vault, and not knowing what it is makes me feel like a piece of shit. Especially when I know exactly what I'm keeping in mine.

We turn off onto a side street that connects the county with the highway, parking in an abandoned lot. This is just for show, you can see our cruiser for miles along either side east or west of us. Anyone who plans on speeding will have to make a concentrated decision to do so. Really the reason we sit here is to deter it, to try and keep the roads safer.

"What's been going on with you lately? I feel like you have this secret life you're keeping from me," Tank sets up the radar detector, calibrating it so that it can be used properly.

"Busy more than anything, been doing my woodworking stuff. There's a show in August. You know how much I sell when I go to the shows."

It hurts and sucks lying to my friend, but at least I know the lying will end in a few days. Then I'll be lucky if he speaks to me again. The thought has crossed my mind. I don't like it, but I've committed to my choices and I will stick with them, regardless if they hurt or not.

"You do fuckin' great at those. You should probably quit this bullshit and do that full time."

I'm about to make a smartass comment when a black truck screams by us so fast the only thing we see is the color.

"Again?" Tank growls as he flips our lights on and jams his foot on the accelerator.

Quickly I key the radio and call in our position, letting them know which vehicle we're behind. This time I know who it is, I remember the license plate from last time, and I'm not surprised when they give us the name Merle Strather.

"The question is, will he stop this time?" Tank takes a turn on what feels like two wheels as he asks the question.

"Fuckin' A man, I want to make it out of this shift alive," I shoot him a look before I radio in again. "Dispatch, be advised we're in excess of eighty miles an hour, out on Highway 5. Going east.

He's obviously headed for his grandfather's still.

"If he hits that still, y'all back off," Holden's voice comes over the line. "We need probable cause to go in there. If he yanks that fucking truck into the drive, we have our probable cause. I'm pretty sure they've already started a new batch."

Tank and I do our best to keep up with the truck. There's something about this kid and the way he drives with such abandon. He has no regard for life, no thought to anyone else who's on the road with him. It makes him dangerous, and I wonder for a split second what will stop him. Will it be the road itself? A wreck? A ticket? Growing up and becoming a man?

"He's bailing down the dirt road leading to the operation," Tank points to the truck turning off the road.

"Holden, he took the access road," I radio in, waiting to hear from our commander.

"Excellent. We'll have orders in the next few weeks. Y'all give it up and go back to patrolling."

I know this is a means to an end, but it bothers me that we weren't able to give him a ticket. Any of the times we've pursued him and given chase, we've been told to suspend it or use it for other things. I feel like we're failing the kid, letting him think it's okay to keep going when in all honesty, he should be facing the music for what he's doing.

Worry gnaws at my gut. What if one day he does something he can't take back and we could have stopped him by giving him a piece of paper? By giving him a fucking slap on the wrist and a cash fine. Sometimes it's all people need to straighten up. With him, it feels like we'll never know.

"One day we're gonna get that little piece of shit," Tank takes a drink of his water sitting next to us in the console. "It pisses me off that he keeps getting away."

"Same, but we have to do what they want us to."

"Doesn't mean it doesn't suck."

I chuckle as I put notes on a piece of paper for our report. "I'm gonna put that in the report. It sucks that you keep making us suspend our chase. We want blood, goddamnit."

Tank laughs along with me. "Feel like we're in the fucking Army again, so much regulation bullshit."

I quietly agree as we go back to our regular patrol. Glancing over at him, I hope like hell that we can still be friends when all this with Whitney is said and done.

CHAPTER TWENTY-TWO

WHITNEY

"ARE YOU NERVOUS?"

Ryan's quiet as he sits in the driver seat, navigating us along the back roads to my parents' house. They've lived in the split-level ranch home since I was ten years old and mom was pregnant with Trevor. Back when I was younger, mom had her own roadside vegetable stand, but she's given it up in the last few years. Now she caters for my company on occasion when I need her to. Nearing sixty, I hope dad's looking to retire, and I know mom's ready to buy a beach house along the gulf.

"You think I should be?" His tone is one of nonchalance, a man completely at ease with the choices he's made.

I scoot closer, grabbing his free hand with my own, and hold it in my lap. There's just something I love when a truck has a bench seat. "Maybe. I mean, you did get me pregnant. Even if I am thirty-five, I'll always be his little girl. Isn't that what dads always say?"

He looks my way, taking his gaze off the road for a split second, but I can't see his eyes behind the aviators he's wearing. "If we have a daughter, I'll let you know," he drawls out, moving his hand down to my leg, lazily stroking my thigh left bare by the shorts I'm wearing.

"You truly aren't nervous?"

Now I feel like maybe I'm a freak of nature, because I am nervous. What if telling my family ruins Ryan's relationship with Trevor? If I'm honest, that's my biggest fear. I've never wanted to come in between the two of them, and every time I think about the child I'm carrying, that's the first thought that comes to mind.

"Princess," he smiles slowly as he faces back towards the road. "Regardless of what they say, it's not going to change anything about the relationship we have. At least on my end. They may be upset you've kept it a secret for almost four months, but if they're the people I know they are, they're going to be excited for you. If anything, they know how badly you've wanted a baby. There's no way in hell they're going to begrudge you something you've wanted this much."

I know he's right, but I can't help but feel he's making it simpler than it really is.

"If you're okay then I am, too," I nod, moving my head up and down in an affirmative action.

He laughs, and the sound causes goose bumps to break out on my arms. God, sometimes he's the sexiest man in the world, and I can't believe he sleeps with me almost every night. "You keep telling yourself that, baby. It's okay though, I believe enough for the both of us."

Changing the subject, I ask him another question I've been wondering since we left the house. "Do you think it's okay that I wore a bikini? I mean I know you can definitely tell I'm having a baby now, but it still fit. Should I have grabbed a one piece?"

His hand grasps mine again. "Fuck no, you looked hot when you tried it on the other day. I have a feeling you're gonna need to show that belly off so people believe we're actually having a baby. Otherwise they're gonna think I've tricked you into lying."

This time I laugh, because I know if anyone knew what kind of a guy Ryan is, they would be wondering why he's with me. He doesn't give himself enough credit. "Maybe I tricked you," I lift our hands up and place a kiss on his knuckles.

Since our date, I've felt closer to him, feel like maybe this can be a real relationship. Like we have enough in common to have a life together. Before I was worried all this was merely a physical reaction to one another. Those never last and lie to myself as I might, I want this to last with Ryan. I just can't voice the words to him yet, but I will, when the time is right.

"Nah," he shakes his head. "I went completely of my own free will as soon as you offered yourself to me on a silver platter. Nothing about that night is a regret, as is nothing since."

I still don't know what I've done to deserve this man, but I hope every day that I don't let my inability to express my feelings ruin it. I worry I'll push him away by protecting myself, and I truly hope it doesn't come down to that. "Same here," my voice is soft as I let go of some of the tight control I keep over myself.

We stop at the turn off to my parents and he glances over at me, a slow smile spreading across his face. "I can't believe you actually admitted it, Princess. I'll win you over before this is all said and done."

He has truly no idea how close he is to already doing it.

MY STOMACH IS in knots as my mom, dad, brother, Ryan, myself and two cousins sit around the table, talking after we've had our lunch. My two cousins will leave in a few minutes and then, as per tradition, the rest of us will swim, eat ice cream, and nap until the sun starts going down. Then we'll make our way down to the local ball field where we'll sit in the back of the pickups and watch the fireworks show our town puts on. We've done this every year since I can remember, and I've always enjoyed it. Right now, though, I wish my two cousins would stay for the rest of the afternoon and into the night.

Stop being a wuss, Whitney, I berate myself. You can't just show up one day with a belly poking out five inches and then the next time with a baby in your arms, and expect nobody to wonder what in the world happened to you.

"You okay?" Ryan asks as he has a seat next to me. He's taken off his shirt and sweat runs down his body, making little rivers until they pool into the lines of his stomach. My dad convinced him and Trevor to help him get some work done while he had both the boys around. I lick my lips and then move my gaze back up to his.

"Yeah, I'm good."

He offers me a smile. I'm pretty sure he knew exactly what I was looking at, exactly what my thoughts were. "Just checking."

It's then that I realize my cousins are gone, and it's only the immediate family left. But before I can open my mouth, my mom sets down some ice cream in front of us and my stomach clenches sharply. I want that ice cream like I've never wanted anything in my life.

"It's so good to have everyone around again," she says as she doles out spoons. "It seems like forever since we've all been together."

"We've been busy with the task force and workin'," Trevor glances at Ryan.

"He's right, Mona. They have us on OT right now."

I'm surprised they both got the day off, especially with it being a holiday, but I won't question it. I'm enjoying my chocolate sauce when my mom turns her gaze on me. "Where in the world have you been child? We ain't seen you around here in almost two months."

One more bite of my ice cream and I've fortified myself enough to tell everybody what's been going on with me. It's not a secret I can continue to keep, not even one I want to keep any longer. I push away the bowl and put my hands in my lap.

"I have something I need to tell all of you."

Nervously I glance at Ryan, but the ball is in my court. I'm the one who needs to tell my family what's going on here. He gives me a nod of encouragement and then reaches over to grab my hand, entwining our fingers together.

"What the fuck?" Trevor mumbles, his eyes going wide as his gaze locks on our entwined fingers. I can almost feel the energy coming from him, even though a table separates us.

I shoot him a glare and then glance back at my mom and dad. "The reason I haven't been coming around is because I haven't been feeling all that great. A week ago, that stopped, and I've got more energy than I've had in a while."

"What's wrong with you?" My dad asks, his eyes not moving from mine and Ryan's entwined fingers.

Ryan sits forward in his chair, moving closer so that our knees touch. I take comfort from the warmth of his skin. It gives me the courage to take a deep breath and move forward.

"I'm pregnant," I smile shakily. "Ryan and I are having a baby."

There's silence and shock, but my mom's hands go to her mouth and she gasps in what I think is a happy sound all before I hear the words of my brother.

"You fucking son of a bitch," he stands, advancing on Ryan who also stands with arms at his sides.

Seeing the two of them standing nose-to-nose causes my stomach to turn. They're almost matched in height; Ryan's taller, but that's where it ends. Where Ryan is dark Trevor is light – longer blonde hair, lighter skin, a little bit of a smaller build. I have no doubt Ryan can take my brother and shove him into the ground. He's had a harder life, lived through more than my brother's ever had to face. But Trevor's got a temper and I've only seriously ever seen him let go of once – and that was on Stephen. Nobody knows about that night, and I'll take it with me to my grave.

"Trevor," I warn him, but he doesn't hear me. He presses up against Ryan, their noses hitting, but Ryan doesn't take a step back.

"Whatever you feel like you gotta do, do it," he gives Trevor a hard gaze, one I never thought I'd see between the two of them. "But know, I don't regret a single second of it."

I scream when my brother lays the father of my child flat on his back with one punch to the chin. It kills me that Ryan didn't block it and hasn't fought back. He won't fight his friend.

"Damnit, Trevor," I'm up out of my chair, grabbing him by the arm, where he's standing over Ryan. "What's wrong with you?"

"Me?" He turns to face me. His normally laughing face and smiling mouth are dark and in a deep frown. "What the fuck's wrong with him? What the fuck's wrong with *you*? It's in the best friend code – you don't fuck your best friend's sister!"

Now I'm pissed. Even though it was a one-night stand, it's turned into so much more. How dare he cheapen it by calling it fucking? I'm ready to lay into him, but Ryan's on his feet now, not even wiping the blood off his face.

"I'm willing to let you beat me down and call me names and not put up a fight because we've been through some shit together, Tank," his voice steely as he pushes me behind him, protecting me from the wrath of a pissed-off brother. "But you'll not talk about her like that ever again. You don't know what happened between us, or what's been happening between us. So not knowing means keep your mouth shut. Just because you go around fucking women and throwing them away when they don't do what you want them to doesn't mean I do the same thing. Treat your sister with some damn respect."

I look over Ryan's shoulder, not believing what I'm seeing from my brother. "I'm really disappointed in you, Trevor," I'm close to tears because I'm hormonal and I don't want them to be at odds with one another. "Out of everyone I know I have to tell, I was most excited to tell you because you know how much I've always wanted a baby. You were there numerous times when I would take a negative pregnancy test before." I take a fortifying breath and make myself more vulnerable than I have in a long time. "Hell, I called you while you were overseas and cried to you – in so many ways you were my support system. How can you not be excited for me?"

Trevor's eyes meet mine and I can see the war he's fighting within himself. He wants to be happy, I can tell. He wants to enjoy this with me, be excited for me, but he's holding himself back. "With Ryan?"

I nod, giving him a small smile. "He's your best friend," I remind him. "If he's the best for you, why wouldn't he be the best for me?"

"This is just going to take some getting used to," he admits, running a hand through his hair. "Shit, I can't believe the two of you..." He trails off, shaking his head.

"Trust us," Ryan pulls me forward so that I stand next to him, his arm around my waist. "We've had months. You've had a few minutes."

There's silence, and then I hear my dad speak. "Even if your brother's not excited baby girl, we are." He stands with his arm around my mom. "When you walked in today you were lit from the inside out. I haven't seen you look this way in years, and if Ryan's the one making you happy, then so be it. He's been in this family a long time, and it's good to know he's going to have a permanent spot. He's one of the best men I know, and if he's given you two of the things you've always wanted, a baby and commitment, then who am I to judge? Now would I have preferred the two of you been married and then announced this? Yeah, but life never goes quite the way we plan. It's too short. Your brother will learn that sooner or later."

I walk over to my parents, giving them both hugs as I let a few more tears fall. The breath comes to my lungs easier and I can finally relax, let myself be excited without this dark cloud hanging over me. Now that it's all out in the open, I'm ready to start truly enjoying life.

CHAPTER TWENTY-THREE

RENEGADE

"**A**RE you okay with not sitting with your family?" I take Whitney's hand in mine as we wait for the fireworks to start. We're sitting on the tailgate of my truck, in the back of the football field away from everyone, but still where we can be a part of the celebration.

Around us families are eating leftover bar-b-que, kids are running around with sparklers, dogs are giving them chase, and parents are taking a few minutes to breathe, knowing this is a safe spot for those kids. Someone's set up a kiddie pool and slide to the left of us, and I laugh as I see Holden take his shirt off, taking a ride down the slip-n-slide. Something about the summer air and the Fourth of July makes everyone festive.

"Yeah, I think we both need to have our own separate conversations with Trevor, but tonight I'm not up for it."

I can tell, she looks like she's wilting in the heat. "You look like you're about to fall over," I offer her the bottle of water I'm drinking.

"It's just been a long day, but I definitely wanna see the fireworks."

"Do you want to sit in the truck and turn on the air for a minute?" It's the easiest thing I can think to do.

"No, I'll just be even hotter when I get out," she turns around and glances at the concession stand. "I would *love* a snow cone, though."

The cute little smirk on her face is my undoing. I'm already off the truck and on my feet. "You want grape, right?"

"It amazes me how well you know me, when I didn't think you ever paid attention."

Leaning in, I pull her down for a quick kiss. "I told you babe, I been paying attention for a long time."

I let my thoughts drift as I walk over to the concession stand. Normally, it sells snacks and drinks for the football games, but tonight it's doing a hopping business for the fireworks show. The line is long, but it swings around to where the ambulances are parked. I see Blaze talking to Tank. I also know they will probably have an ice pack, which will feel good to Whitney. Regardless of how Tank and I feel about each other, I want her to be comfortable.

"I don't want to interrupt," I approach them. "But do you have an ice pack I could give to Whit? She's really hot."

Blaze looks up at Tank and then back at me. "Congratulations are in order, I hear," she grins before she gets up and walks back into the ambulance. When she comes out, she carries an ice pack. "Just crack it and shake it up. Put it down the back of her shirt. That's a good point for her to start cooling off."

"She probably shouldn't be out in this damn heat," Tank mumbles, looking at me with open animosity.

"I don't want to fight with you, and I'm willing to take your anger, but place it where it needs to be. Not at her."

"Oh, I'm plenty fucking pissed at the both of you. Someone should have told me. I was there when she found out she was pregnant. What? You couldn't pull me aside and be like 'dude, it was me'?"

I shake my head. "It wasn't your business, Tank," I'm getting irritated, and I can tell he is, too.

"She's my business."

I stand face-to-face with him. "She's mine too, and the baby she carries, also mine. You, of all fucking people..." I cut off, not sure I can finish my sentence, because Tank knows so much about my home life when I was a kid. "Know what having a child means to me. You know I want to be in this kid's life, and you know I'm not going to do anything to threaten any of it." I let my voice drop as I get closer. "You also know I've had it bad for her for years. Why can't you be happy for me?"

Some of the anger has drained out of his face, and I know I've hit on the one soft spot he might have where this is concerned.

"This is gonna be your niece or nephew man. Be pissed at me for a few days, be irritated at her for a few days, but find a way to get over it. Finally, we're going to be family, like we always talked about when we were little. I understand you're shocked – I was, too. She told me she couldn't have kids, but you know where in the fuck that came from."

"Yeah," he runs a hand through his longish blonde hair. "I do know where that came from, and I'm glad as fuck she didn't have this kid with him."

"There, I have something going for me already."

Silence stretches between us for what feels like three long beats and I know I need to get back to Whitney.

"I'll let y'all get back to whatever it was you were talking about," I hold the ice pack in my hands, using it to gesture with. "But know you're always gonna be my best friend, Trevor, and I'm going to need you now more than ever. And so will she."

When I turn around, I can feel his gaze on me, can tell he's still fighting with himself. But I was honest, and I have to let him get over the shock on his own. It's the only way we'll be able to salvage a friendship out of this.

Whitney

"Thank you for the snow cone and the ice pack. It's made a huge difference," I snuggle next to Ryan as we lay in the back of his pickup. He found a blanket and a couple of jackets. Now we're snuggled up, him leaning against the back and me laying against his chest, waiting on the fireworks.

The night sky has finally turned an inky black. I wasn't sure whether that sun would ever go completely down. It lingered on the horizon forever, almost as if it didn't want to say goodbye.

Fireworks have always been my favorite part of the Fourth of July.

"Do you think Trevor will forgive us?" I whisper as I play with the material of his shirt.

"Oh yeah," he answers immediately. "Trevor's in shock, just like we were when we found out. It's going to take him a little while, but he'll be the most excited uncle there ever was when he gets over it."

"Do you think he'll get over it soon? I hate when he's mad at me, and he hasn't been this mad at me in a while."

He laughs, soft puffs of air against my forehead. "He's mad at you? I have to patrol with him in the morning. That's going to be an interesting ride."

"I'm sorry," I tuck my bottom lip between my teeth, hoping to keep in the emotion I'm feeling. I hate being emotional all the time, but it's the curse of this pregnancy for me. "I never wanted to come between the two of you."

"You haven't," he tilts my chin up, forcing me to meet his gaze. "Tank knows how I feel about you, has always known how I felt about you. I've never tried to hide it."

Which is crazy to me. "How did I not know? The one person who should have?"

"You didn't want to know?" He tightens his arms around me. "You were a married woman and before that I was a teenage kid. It's not something you would have been looking for, and it definitely wasn't something I wanted to tell you."

The only thing I can think about is how much time I wasted with Stephen when he tells me these things. I do understand where he's coming from, the age difference would have kept me away more than anything else. It still makes me uneasy, I can't imagine how I would have reacted as a thirty-year-old and him being a twenty-year-old. Maybe we both had to grow up in order to accept the tenuous relationship we have now. I want to say something else, but the lights at the field shut off.

"Ooh, it's time!"

I jump as the first firework explodes in the air, bright colors of pink and green, holding onto Ryan tightly as another batch explode to our left. This group is red, white, and blue. I've always felt patriotic because of Trevor, but being held in this man's arms who served his country, it means a lot more to me now.

Tearing my eyes away from the beautiful sky, I look up at him, only to see he's looking at me. Our gazes meet, and then I don't care about the damn fireworks anymore. The look in his eyes is so soft, so passionate, that I can't take it anymore. I grip his shirt, hauling myself to him, fusing our lips together in one of the hottest kisses we've ever shared.

"Nobody's watching," he breathes into my ear as I jerk my mouth away from his, straddling him and start canting my hips.

I've never done anything like this before, but Ryan does this to me, makes me this wild person who wants nothing but him. I know the fireworks are at least a fifteen-minute show and when his hands grip my ass, pushing me against the hardening length in his shorts, I can't help it. Fuck it, I grind against it, fusing my mouth with his again. The noise of the booms encourages me, sending me further on my journey as I thrust against him.

Fully clothed, we're like two teenage kids dry humping in the back of their dad's truck at the Fourth of July. Thank God we parked so far away from everyone else. I groan loudly as he slips one hand off my ass and trails it up my tank top and underneath to where he grasps my bikini covered breast with the palm of his hand. My nipples are more sensitive than they've ever been, and as I feel the warmth of his skin, it pulls tight, stabbing into him.

"Oh God," I shake as I pull out of the kiss, throwing my head back as I continue to ride his shorts.

His fingertips grasp the nub, pulling almost painfully, but damnit if that's not what I need right now. I can feel my body speeding up to the fireworks in the sky. I know the crescendo is coming for both me and the show that we should be watching. Increasing my speed, I sit up, using my knees for leverage and move his hand out of the way, grasping my own tits, worrying the nipples between my own fingers.

"C'mon Whit, the shows almost over," he moves his hand down to the leg of my shorts, sneaking two fingers up, not even going under the barrier of my swimsuit bottoms. When the tips of his fingers graze my clit I explode, falling down on top of him, burying my face in his throat, and latching on tightly as I suck the flesh to keep myself from screaming. I don't want people to know what we've been doing over here.

"Fuck," he flexes his other hand against my ass, as I continue to rock slowly against him.

"Jesus," I breathe out, rubbing against him like I'm a cat, my body is still sparking. If we were at my house by ourselves, I'd want it again. I can feel him hard against me.

"Let's get in the truck," he says before the lights come back on.

We scramble, me on shaky legs, feeling the wetness between my thighs. My gaze is a little unfocused and I wonder just what in the hell this man drives me to do, even in public. Getting into the truck, he unbuttons his jeans and slips them down, lower on his hips.

"Fuckin' hell that feels so much better," He breathes out as he throws the truck into drive. We realize we're one of the first trucks out of the gate, we don't even have to wait in line. When we're on the open highway, I reach over, grasping his cock in my hand.

"Whitney, holy shit. You don't have to do this."

"I want to. I want you to have what I had, I want to feel you come against me."

"I'd rather come *in* you," he lets his head fall back against the seat of the truck for a second.

Challenge accepted. I move to unbuckle my seatbelt and then kneel, pushing his boxers down and take him in my mouth.

"Jesus fuck," he grasps my hair in one of his hands.

"Watch the road," I laugh as I pull my mouth off his length.

I've never been one to enjoy this particular act, but with Ryan I love it. His taste is like bourbon, hot and spicy on my tongue. I hollow out my cheeks as I suck him down, and he groans loudly.

"Ain't gonna be long, Princess. You got me pretty worked up back there."

If the way he's thrusting his hips into my mouth is any indication, this will be over even quicker than he thinks it will be. One more shove into my mouth and I feel him spilling against my throat. With no other choice but to swallow, I do so happily.

"Son of a bitch, Whitney," he pants, keeping both hands on the wheel as I let him go with a pop of my mouth.

"Happy Fourth of July," I grin over at him, wiping at my chin.

He gathers me next to him, and we ride home. Me with a silly grin on my lips and a happy flutter in my heart.

CHAPTER TWENTY-FOUR
RENEGADE

I'M SORT OF surprised when I show up at the station to get into our car the next morning and see Tank already there. I figured he'd call in or get someone to switch with him instead of being stuck with me for the day.

"Morning," I hand him the cup of coffee I always bring both of us.

He grunts something to me that may be morning back, but I'm not sure. If this is any indication on how this ride is going to go, maybe I ought to turn around and go back home. For the first three hours, we ride in complete silence. When my cell phone chimes with a new text message, I'm excited that it gives me someone to talk to.

W: *Hey handsome! How's it going with my brother?*

R: *We haven't said but two words to one another. He took my coffee though, so maybe it's a good sign? How are you today? You were sleeping hard when I left this morning.*

W: *It's because someone wore me out last night.*

R: *No, I'm pretty sure that was you humping my dick in the back of my truck, and then you giving me road head as we went home. Kinda think you wore me out.*

"Can you at least wipe the stupid ass smirk off your face when you're texting her?"

Tank's cool voice dims the excitement I had at her texting me a small amount. "I can, but it's not going to change how I feel about her, how she makes me feel in return. Why don't you tell me what your deal is?"

He's quiet for a long time, longer than I would like for him to be, and I wonder if he's going to be honest. Finally, after giving up on it, he starts to speak. "I know how your parents were when we were growing up, and I know you desperately want to right the wrongs they did to you with your own kid. But I worry, what if those demons come for you? We don't know what happened with your mom – not really – and your dad is a piece of shit on a good day. I don't want my sister and niece or nephew to be touched by that," he ends with a hand beat heavily against the steering wheel. "And I feel like a fucking piece of shit for even saying it, because I know what a good man you are, Renegade. I know I'd lay my life down for you, and I know you'd lay yours down for me. But those thoughts are keeping me awake."

"Don't you think they're keeping me awake, too? But if there's one thing I've learned over the past few years, it's that I can't let where I come from dictate who I end up being. Not in that way. I can't let it make me live my life in fear, but I can use the shit I went through to make me a better person. There's no way I'll make it through the world if I let fear override every bit of happiness I've ever had," I stop for a second. "Whitney makes me happy, Trev, and I think I make her happy, too."

"I know you do. Dad was right; she was lit from the inside out when I saw her yesterday. She hasn't looked that light, that carefree in years. And you – you're not carrying around the tension you always seem to be tight with either. You've stopped taking everything so seriously. Except on the raids. I've noticed when we do summons or raids, or whatever, you make sure your vest is on, you make sure you're careful. Anything else, you're laughing more, frowning less. Happiness looks great on the both of you, and I don't want to spoil it or ruin it," he finishes. "But I also don't want either of you to get hurt."

"There are no guarantees in life, both of us know that," I wonder if what I say next will piss him off or be the olive branch he's been wanting extended in his direction. "But if push comes to shove and I do have to protect her, you're the only other person I would want at my side. Don't let this come between us."

It takes a minute, but he turns to me, a sly smile on his face. "The part of me that's not her brother is the one saying this. Holy shit, Renegade, you tapped the one girl you've always wanted to tap. How did that feel?"

"Probably the same way it felt when you tapped Blaze," I laugh, because this is my friend, this is the guy I've gone to war and come back home with. He's the dude that let me sleep on his floor and didn't tell me I was a pussy when I would cry about my parents as a kid. This is my brother.

"Pretty damn good then," he grins back over at me. "Now the part of me that is her brother is going to tell you this once, and that's it. You treat her like Stephen did, you break her heart, you make her cry? I'll break your face. You'll be wearing a lot more than the bruise you're sporting today. I don't even care how pretty that face is."

He holds his hand out for a shake. I return the gesture. "You have my word. I'm not going to screw up something I've wanted my whole damn life."

"Good to hear it. Now we know where we both stand."

Whitney

Ryan's not coming over tonight, he has some stuff he has to take care of at his apartment and a few orders he has to fill for his woodworking business. I know he takes orders now and then, but what I really want to do is see what he does in person. He's very shy about it though, and I'm not sure he ever shows it to anyone.

I hadn't realized before tonight how much I enjoy having Ryan around. The house is too quiet, and I'm not used to being by myself after six o'clock at night. Normally he's gone and grabbed clothes, dinner, or whatever, and he's already here. We're usually trying to figure out what we're going to do for the night, or we're stealing kisses in the guise of watching TV.

I'm lying on my couch, flipping through the TV channels, and bored out of my mind when my doorbell rings. Knowing it's not Ryan, I don't necessarily rush to answer it, but when I fling back the door and see Trevor, my palms go sweaty.

"Mind if I come in?" He's still wearing his uniform, and for some reason that makes him seem vulnerable to me.

"Sure," I open the door the rest of the way.

"I had a talk with Ryan today," he rushes right into whatever it is he wants to talk about. "And I won't say I'm a hundred percent there with the two of you right now, but I'm close. I just need to hear what you have to say."

There's been moments where I've been laid bare before my brother. He's seen me in some dark instances where I know he'll never speak of them again. I know once he has answers to his questions, he'll be okay. I clear my throat. "What do you want to know?"

"Did he take advantage of you?" He has a seat on my couch, pulling the man-bun he keeps his hair in out. "It's something that's been nagging at me since yesterday. Did he take advantage of you feeling low?"

I have a seat next to him, envious of the hair he has. I always have been. He could be a model, he's dead ringer for that Jax Teller guy on Sons of Anarchy. "No," I think back to that night, feeling a little thrill at the way things had gone down. "If anything, I took advantage of him. I'm just going to be honest with you, Trev. I was drunk, horny, and feeling sorry for myself. You know my marriage with Stephen, especially towards the end, wasn't anything to write home about. I asked Ryan to give me all the things I'd always wanted and never had," I shrug. "He did."

"He didn't mistreat you? Wasn't rough with you? Didn't do anything you didn't want to do?" I can see the worry in his eyes, and I know this isn't about his friend, it's about his sister.

"He only got as rough with me as I asked him to," I answer truthfully. "I told you it's not something you want to hear about, but it's true. Ryan did nothing out of the way and if it's anybody's fault I'm pregnant, it's mine. I told him I couldn't have kids."

"Because that's what the fucker you were married to made you believe," he growls, cracking his knuckles loudly.

I realize now that yes, he did make me believe that. He made me believe a lot of things, and I can't help but send up a little prayer, thanking God for getting me out of that nasty situation. "It's true, he made me believe a lot and I was naïve enough to take at his word. Luckily for all of us, Ryan's showing me not all men are like him."

"Ryan's a good one," Trevor agrees, reaching over to grab my hand. "If I trust you with anyone, it's him. I just had to know...ya know?"

"I get it, I really do."

I take his hand and put it to my stomach. "I can kinda feel the baby move around in there sometimes, and I feel it now. Can you?"

His brows pull together in concentration and then I see a wide smile break out across his face. "Oh my god, that's such a strong kick. You've got a punter for Alabama in there," he laughs.

"We find out in three weeks when I go to the doctor. They couldn't get me in before the first week of August."

"That's why Ryan asked off? He never asks off."

I reach over, giving my brother a hug. "He's a good guy who's one thousand percent here for this pregnancy. Please don't make this any harder on us than it has to be."

His hand grips my stomach again. "I won't. Please keep me in the loop and let me know what gender I need to be buying stuff for. I'm excited for you, Sis, don't ever think I wasn't."

"I didn't, but I'm glad to know I have your blessing. It does mean the world to me."

He hugs me again before he gets up, walking towards my door.

"Maybe one day you'll have this with that girl you've told me about."

A wistful look comes into his eyes as he opens the door. "You never know, crazier shits happened. I mean, look at you."

I throw my pillow at him as he shuts the door quickly, waving goodbye.

Left alone with my thoughts, I go down the hallway to the empty room in my house I've always wanted to use for a nursery. I can't wait to find out what we're having so I can start decorating, but I feel restless right now.

Grabbing all the stuff I use to plan weddings, I sit down in the middle of the empty room, spending the next few hours on designing the perfect boy's room and the perfect girl's room.

Hopefully Ryan will go along with what I've picked, but knowing what I do about him now, I know it won't be too hard to work my feminine wiles and convince him of almost anything.

CHAPTER TWENTY-FIVE

WHITNEY

AUGUST

"Thanks for picking me up," I lean in, buckling my lap band, kissing Ryan on the cheek.

I'd had a meeting with a client at The Café in town, and instead of driving two cars, I'd had Trevor drop me off on his way to work and gotten Ryan to pick me up. Today, we get to find out what our baby is going to be.

"Like you had to ask me twice to pick you up? You're vibrating with excitement," he laughs as he eases his truck into traffic, putting his arm around my shoulders.

"I'm so excited, I could barely sleep last night. It was bad enough you weren't there," I put my hand on his thigh as we drive through downtown. Even though it's almost noon, it's not yet bustling with activity.

"Well, trust me, working the night shift last night sucked. I don't like riding with Ace as much as I like riding with Tank, but luckily it was a slow night either way. I had trouble sleeping last night, too," he indicates the back seat of the crew cab. "Totally packed a bag for tonight. I don't like sleeping away from you."

I curl against him in the truck, inhaling deeply. I love his scent, it's all over my sheets and I slept with his pillow tucked into my arms last night. There's something about the scent that makes me feel safe, loved, and sexy all at the same time. "I don't either, I'm glad you packed it. Maybe you could pack all your stuff up and move it over sometime."

He inhales loudly. "Are you shitting me, Whit?"

"No," I shake my head, offering him a smile. "Whenever you're ready, I'd love for you to move in. I don't like being without you."

And right now that's as close as I can get to telling him I love him without saying the words. Looking at his sunglass covered eyes, I think he knows it too.

"We can for sure make this happen. I won't crowd you."

I lean up, flicking his ear with my tongue. "I kinda like when you crowd me."

He pulls me closer. "Then be prepared for all kinds of crowding, because you've just made my entire year."

We make good time to the medical building where my OB/GYN is housed. As he parks along the square, he taps my leg. "Come out over here, people don't watch on that side of the road."

He helps me scoot out of the driver's side and I almost swoon at the way he makes sure I'm good, regardless of where we are. I straighten my skirt and grab my purse before he shuts the door and entwines our fingers together as we walk up the street. I love that he doesn't care who sees us strolling along. He stops as we see the local baby boutique.

"After we finish with our appointment, we should come here and pick out the furniture. You know, so we can figure out what in the world that room you've planned is going to be male or female."

I bashfully hide my face in his shoulder. "I can't believe I did that without asking you, I really am sorry."

"Don't be babe, you're the planner between us. At least we got to agree on the names together."

I think back to the night I showed him the rooms I'd planned while I'd been bored and wishing he was with me. He'd laughed and told me he was surprised it'd taken me that long to figure out what I wanted the rooms to look like. I'd been embarrassed but we'd had a seat in the room and got the feel of it together, discussing names. We were bound and determined not to tell anyone what the name would be until we found out the gender.

"Well I didn't want to keep you out of the loop on everything."

He pulls me closer, kissing me on the forehead. "You keep me in the loop on everything that matters, Princess. We're doing pretty good together, don't you think?"

"Yeah," I smile up at him. "We are. Better than I ever thought we would."

We stop at the front of the office, both taking a deep breath. "You ready?" he asks.

"If you are."

"I don't know if you know this or not, but I'd face a firing squad for you and our kid. I'm beyond ready."

Leaning up on my tiptoes I give him a kiss. "Then I'm ready, too."

WE'RE WAITING in the back for the ultrasound tech to show up and we're both totally nervous. "Do you feel like your heart could beat out of your chest?" I ask him, running a hand through my hair.

"Yes! I've done missions with the MTF and the Army and not ever felt this nervous. I feel like every part of my life depends on this picture we're about to see."

I reach over for his hand. "I feel the same way, and maybe it does mean that much. Maybe we're placing too much importance on it, but it's us, Ryan. It's what we think it should be. We know how much we already love this child, whether it's a boy or a girl makes no difference to me."

"But it does to me," his face gets red. "If it's a boy I only have to worry about him sticking his dick in other girls. If it's a girl I gotta worry about all the other dicks of the world. I mean that's a lot of pressure, babe."

I throw my head back, laughing hysterically, making my shoulders jerk with the force of it. "How long have you worried about this?"

"Like every night for the past two months," he runs a hand through his hair. "On my mind all the damn time."

"Why didn't you tell me?" I giggle, feeling sorry for him. "Don't make me laugh, I have to pee so bad."

"I didn't want to worry you with my crazy, too. I mean I figured you had a lot of shit going through your own mind."

I'm wiping tears I've laughed so hard, and oh my God, was it a good laugh. I needed it to get rid of all that nervous energy. "I would have helped you get through your fears. We're in this together, remember?"

"I do remember that, but I felt like I was being a pussy."

I chuckle some more as the tech makes her way into the room. "I can hear you two laughing outside. These are the types of parents I like," she claps her hands as she sits down.

"We're pretty excited," I tell her jumping when she reaches down to lift up my shirt and puts the cold gel on it.

"Sorry, probably should have warned you about that, I'm a little frazzled. The people in front of you found out they're having four instead of two."

"Oh holy fuck," Ryan mumbles from beside me. "What if we're having more than one?" He questions, his eyebrows in his hair line.

"We're good," I tell him, even though I just got even more scared myself. "We're good." I'm not sure if I'm trying to calm his fears or my own.

"Well," the tech gives us a wink. "We'll definitely find out."

Both of us are as quiet as I've ever heard us as we wait for her to turn the machine on. Then we hear the loud thumping of the heartbeat and we both look at each other. "It's fast," I comment as I wait for a picture to come up on the screen.

"It's perfect," she says as she presses some buttons, and that's when we see it. The picture of our baby.

"So let me show you what we've got here," she situates herself so we can both see everything she's doing.

I grip Ryan's hand tightly in mine, waiting for what feels like forever until she speaks again.

"We have the head, legs, arms, all that stuff looks perfect. You're right on target with size and all. Now, for the most important part of today. You two want to know the sex of the baby?"

"Yes," we answer together.

"Congratulations you two, you're having a girl."

Beside me Ryan let's out a sigh with a groan. "Guess I'm gonna have to worry about all the dicks."

I laugh, wiping tears from my eyes. "But Stella will know exactly which one she wants."

He leans forward, kissing me on the forehead. "I'm not sure if that makes me feel better or not."

The tech laughs at the two of us. "Do you want some pictures?"

We both nod, and as she hands one to Ryan, he takes a picture of it on his phone. "Do you mind if I send this to Tank?"

"Not at all," I want Ryan to feel like he's a part of this, and letting him tell my brother is probably more important to him than it is to me.

He waits while I get dressed and cleaned up, then we head down to the children's boutique where we pick out everything but a crib.

Neither one of us can agree on the crib, but we're both excited to get home, and put together what we've bought for Stella. As we get into the truck, I text Trevor, asking if he wants to come help.

Finally, I feel like we're all one big happy family.

CHAPTER TWENTY-SIX
RENEGADE

"TRUTH OR LIE?" I ask her, running my hand along her shoulder. It's hot tonight, and we're both still sweating from the workout we just put in with one another. But I know we're both energized and neither one of us will be sleeping for a while. Back to playing our game.

"Umm," she rolls closer to me, tugging the sheet up to her chest before she scrunches her nose in the most adorable way. "Sometimes I love the elaborate lies you make up, but I want a truth tonight."

"Ahhh," I throw my head back against the pillow, wondering what kind of truth I should tell her. "How old does the truth have to be?"

She sucks that full bottom lip in between her teeth and sits up crisscrossing her legs while she makes sure the sheet still covers her bare breasts. "Teenage truth," she throws down the gauntlet.

"Shhiiitttt," I breathe out, sitting up myself, but I lean against her headboard. I go back through my teenager years, trying to figure out what the hell I want to tell her. So much of my adolescence is wrapped up in her and she doesn't even know it.

"C'mon, Ryan, or are you scared?" she teases.

"I'm not scared," I throw her a look. "I'm trying to figure out what I want to tell you."

"If you're scared, I'll let you lie," she offers.

"I don't need your charity." And that's when the perfect truth hits me.

"Trevor's sixteenth birthday. I was still fifteen, jealous as all fuck because he could drive now. You remember?" I ask, hoping to put her back almost ten years ago.

Tilting her head to the side, she purses her lips. "Vaguely."

"Damn woman, that was like your coming out party for me," I whistle. "One minute I'm pissed at Tank, mad as hell that Stanley and Mona got him a truck and now he can go to the movies with his flavor of the week. The next, I glance up and you've walked down from the house to the pool, wearing that turquoise blue bikini."

Her eyes widen. "Oh my God, you remember that?"

"There's not much I forget about you, Princess."

My voice gets deeper as I continue on with my story. "I was doing good, fighting off the most embarrassing hard-on of my adolescent life until you came over and wished Trevor a Happy Birthday. You hugged him, then you hugged me, and I was done for. The feel of your tits against my chest? I wanted to reach down and cup your ass, even though I wasn't sure what that meant."

"Ryan!" She laughs as she bashfully pulls the sheet up over her head, fanning her cheeks. "I can't believe this."

"Believe it," I laugh, even though it's strangled because I still remember the frustrated teenage boy I was. "I went and jacked off in your mom's beach-themed bathroom."

"OH MY GOD! That was my bathroom when I lived at home," she's laughing, her face a red that I can make out even in the semi-darkness.

"You wanted the truth, babe," I grin over at her, stealing the sheet from her fingers. "The truth is I've wanted you for as long as I can remember, and now that I've got you, I'm going to do my best to keep you."

She reaches over to grab the sheet back, but instead, I grasp her hand in mine and pull her so that she's straddling my hips. Burying my hands in her hair, I pull her down so our lips can meet. "You undo me sometimes, Ryan," she whispers against my lips as they chase one another.

"It's only fair," I answer, as I bury my face in her neck. "You undo me all the time."

I'M CHOMPING on my gum, hoping it regulates the sweat rolling down the back of my vest and the way my mind is racing at what we're about to do. We finally got the order from the judge signed to raid the still off of Highway 5.

Nervousness courses through me, and I'm unsure as to why. This isn't a sneak attack, we're rolling up and bailing out. There's no hiding anything we have going on. Maybe it's the way Whitney and I talked last night, where I admitted something I thought I would take to my grave. I feel vulnerable today, like my insides are fileted open for anyone to see.

"You good?" Tank asks me as we sit next to each other.

I adjust the hat on my head, hoping it stops some of the sweat from pouring down my face. It's all adrenaline, I know this more than anything. "I'm good, just nervous. I've never had people to get home to before, ya know?"

"Hopefully it'll make you smarter in the field," Holden says from where he sits.

We've told everybody about the baby. It wasn't like this big huge announcement, but a week ago she brought me dinner when we were having a meeting about a raid, and of course everyone saw her stomach. They witnessed me giving her a kiss goodbye, and none of them have stopped their teasing since. "I was already pretty damn smart."

"You were," Ace says from across the way. "But you're going to be even more so now, because you have the baby and the girl to get home to. I gotta tell ya, it was so sickening sweet it almost gave me a toothache, watching the two of you. Crumbled this black heart I have."

Everyone laughs, some of the tension gone. "Stop it," I can't help the grin that spreads across my face.

"So when are you gonna marry her?" Holden teases.

I look over at Tank because this is something we haven't discussed, it's not an issue I've wanted to bring up. I'm not sure how she'll take it. Marriage wasn't happy for her before. "I don't know, we haven't talked about it."

"He'll be lucky if my sister doesn't run screaming – you know she's divorced."

Tank tries to divert talk away from me. I'm thankful, because if there's one thing, I hate it's to be the center of damn attention like this.

"Two minutes out," the driver yells over our talking.

Just like that everybody zips up, gets focused, and thinks about the job at hand we have to do. "Be careful out there," Holden tells us all as we pull up on the dirt road.

I can feel it bumping beneath us and when we come to stop, we all exit the vehicle, guns at the ready. Prepared for anything that might happen to us this day, but guns start to drop as we see who's in front of us. Instead of facing a firing squad, we're all surprised.

What we're faced with is the scared face of Leighton Strather, all by herself.

"Where's your daddy and Merle?" Holden asks, going over to her, turning her around to put cuffs on her wrists. Regardless if she's a young girl who probably knows nothing about what's going on here, we still have to treat her like a suspect.

"I don't know," her voice is soft as she bends her head down. "They were supposed to be here an hour ago."

"Leighton," Holden starts carefully. "You know we're gonna bust this still up and take you in. You're the only one here."

She cries softly as the reality of the situation comes down on her. I went to school with her some, even though she's younger than me. She's always been smart, and I wonder what the hell a twenty-two-year-old like her is doing caught up in a business like this.

I watch as Holden puts her in the back of the patrol car that's come with us. Tears roll down her cheeks, and he's being nicer to her than I've ever seen him be to anyone before. I think he knows just like we do – she's a pawn in the game. Her family has fucked her over big time.

Later on, Tank and I are pouring out the containers of moonshine and waiting for the rest of the still to drain.

"Ya know, if I hadn't gotten the chance I did from your family, I have no doubt I'd be in the same situation as Leighton. Taking the fall for something I didn't do and not even realizing it until it was too late," I let the last of my bottle empty and then look up at him. "I feel bad for her."

"I do, too," he answers. "But what can we do?"

The truth of the matter is I don't know. Never before have I felt as lucky as I do now, and I can't wait to get home so I can put my arms around the family I've formed. I hope one day Leighton can find her own.

CHAPTER TWENTY-SEVEN

WHITNEY

"**E**VERYTHING'S ready for her to be here, Ryan."

I spin in a circle, eyeing what will be Stella's nursery when she decides to come in December. Who cares if I'm a few months early. Before I know it, September will be over and I'll be looking down the barrel of my thirty-sixth birthday, wondering where all the time went. If I can get as much done now as possible, that's less I have to do later.

It looks exactly like I planned for it to. Pink, white, and grey chevron on one wall, the other three walls alternating those colors. The hardwood floor has the huge pink shag rug I wanted, a chandelier hangs from the ceiling. The dresser and changing table are set up, the closet has clothes ready for her to wear. Trevor, myself, and Ryan have done a lot of work, almost completely on our own. It's been fun, watching their friendship evolve.

"The only thing we're missing is a crib." I put my hands on my hips, with a frown on my face. It's all we need to make this room perfect.

"It's because we could never agree on one," he reminds me.

His arms circle me from behind, his chin resting on my shoulder. I turn so I can give him a smooch. "That's because you didn't like any of my ideas."

"No babe, you didn't like any of my ideas," he accuses.

It's then I notice right there where the crib should be, there's a large structure with a white sheet over it. How I missed it before, I'm not sure, but I'm not as observant as I once was. "Ryan, what's that?" I point to it, using our interlocked fingers.

His voice is shaky and unsure as he answers. "Why don't you go look at it?"

Suddenly I'm nervous and I don't even know why. Something about the way he said the words has my heart ready to beat out of my chest, not sure if it's adrenaline or anxiousness. My feet feel heavy as I make my way over to whatever this is, but I feel Ryan's arm behind me, offering me silent strength.

I look back at him, not sure what to do.

"Take the sheet off, Whit, it's not gonna bite."

With shaking hands I grip the sheet, pulling it off, letting it fall to the floor. Once it registers what it is, I turn to him, my mouth hanging wide open. "Did you make this?"

He turns me back around so that I'm facing the most beautiful crib I've ever seen. It's got very distinctive woodwork, which makes me think Ryan has done this himself.

"Yeah," he offers me a shy smile. I've never been able to see one of the pieces he's made before. Knowing he's made this for our daughter? It's one of the most amazing things I've ever felt in my life. "It's re-claimed barn wood. Before you worry that it doesn't meet safety expectations, I have a friend in the industry that I talk to sometimes when I'm making custom pieces – he helped me get it up to code. It's completely safe."

The wood grain fits in amazingly well against the color and style of the nursery, giving it a country chic vibe. I can almost tell by looking at it how much love he put into every piece. It's flowing from where it sits.

"I don't even know what to say," I fight back tears. This is one of the most thoughtful things anyone has ever done for me. "It's beautiful."

"You're beautiful, she's beautiful, and the two of you are my world. I knew I had to give you the best, and if I make it with my own two hands, I know it's the best."

I turn around, grasping him in the strongest hug I can with my big belly between us. "This is the most amazing gift anyone has ever given me."

He pulls back, dropping his hand to my stomach. "Good, because this is the best gift you could have ever given me."

Renegade

To be honest, I've never given a fuck either way what people think of me. I've always kind of stayed in my own lane and done things on my own time, at my own pace. It's never been that big of a deal, but to see Whitney cry over something I've made fills a hole in my heart I didn't even realize I had. This woman with her soft smiles, her stoic ways, and the passion with which she comes to me is enough to break me down. It's enough to make me want to tear down every single wall she has erected around her heart and beg her to let me in. There have been times when I've seen her look at me, and I think it's love in her eyes. It's something other than acceptance. I know at night when we sleep, she reaches for me whether she knows it or not. She can start out on the other side of the bed, and by the time morning rolls around, she's all the way next to me. Her arms wrapped around my waist, her legs tangled in mine. I do give a fuck what Whitney thinks about me. And the way she stared at me, like I'd made her the happiest woman in the world, fills me with the most pride I've ever had in my life.

"You okay?" She asks when I stood there for too long without speaking.

For the first time in my life, I'm truly feeling like I could conquer the world and not do it on my own. "Just excited for her to be here, excited for us to be parents."

"I am too, Ryan, more than you know." She smiles at me with true happiness, and a pride I've never seen her have before. I put those emotions there, and it's almost too much for me to bear.

"It just kinda hit me tonight, ya know? I've never really given a fuck what people think of me, but I care what you think about me. I want to make Stella proud of me, want to be the type of father she's proud to bring her friend's home to meet. I never wanted to bring my friends home to meet my dad or mom. Hell, Tank's only met them a handful of times, and how long have we been friends? Most of our lives," I stop a second and turn to face the door because I can't stand the look on her face anymore.

I'm trying to keep my shit together. Obviously I didn't realize how much it meant to me to explain myself to her. When I feel her arms come around my waist, I clasp my hands over hers.

"You never have to wonder about our daughter being embarrassed by her dad. Never. You're one of the most amazing men I've ever met in my life. To come from the things you've dealt with to become the man you are today? You're amazing, Ryan, and I'm lucky to have you in my life."

I inhale deeply, facing her again, tilting her chin up. "I think we're both pretty damn lucky."

She doesn't pull away when I fuse our lips together. I'm exactly right where I want to be and who I want to be. I hope like hell the same is true for her.

CHAPTER TWENTY-EIGHT
RENEGADE

"PLEASE DON'T HURT YOURSELVES," Whitney looks at Tank and me over the top of her sunglasses.

"We're cleaning out your gutters and taking care of your fall yardwork," Tank shoots her a look. "How in the world do you think we're going to hurt ourselves? We're in great shape."

"That cocky attitude is it right there," she puts her hands on her hips, giving him a stare down. Showing her own attitude.

"Don't worry about us. Go hang out with your friends, take their gifts, and when you get home, we'll put them in the nursery and then we'll relax," I send her off with a kiss on the cheek as she strolls over to her SUV.

"How in the hell did you get out of a baby shower?" Tank asks as he watches her leave.

I turn, a sly grin on my face. "No fuckin' clue dude. All I know is the second week of September, somebody called, and said that they thought it'd be too difficult to do a baby shower with her birthday next month, Thanksgiving, and then Christmas. Since all of us think she'll go before Christmas, she agreed. Two hours later, they'd planned a lunch, a very informal baby shower. It ain't like we need anything anyway. Your mom kinda spearheaded it, I guess. Either way, I don't have to go. In fact, they told me no men allowed. I'll take it," I laugh as I walk back towards the storage garage.

"Dad's here," he says, when we hear a car turn into the driveway.

We watch as he gets out of the car, holding his coffee mug. He's wearing flip flops and a pair of shorts, even though tomorrow is October first.

"What kinda work you plan on doing in those flip flops?" Tank gives him shit.

"Boy, you aren't too old for me to bust in the mouth. I'm supervisin'."

Tank and I glance at one another. Supervising means he's going to tell us what to do all afternoon. It'll be a replay of our youth, but to be honest, I'm looking forward to it.

"Shit," Tank walks back towards the house. "I'm gonna need another cup of coffee for this."

I laugh, shaking my head at the two of them, unlocking the storage shed and grabbing the leaf blower and a couple of bags. As I bring them out and set them on the driveway, Stanley comes over to me.

"While he's inside, I thought I might have a little talk with you," he sticks one hand in his pocket, still holding his coffee cup in the other.

This makes me nervous. Stanley hardly ever wants to have a talk with me, and to be honest, he hasn't since I turned him down for that college money.

"Look," he starts. "I know you probably wonder what we think about Whitney having your baby, but you're trying too much not to dwell on it. I've treated you like my own for a long time, Ryan, and God's truth, you know if Mona and I could have adopted you, we would have. There's no one else I'd want my daughter to have a child with. We're extremely excited for the two of you, and if there's anything you need, please let us know."

I don't know what to say. Truth be told, I'm scared I might cry.

"You don't have to say anything, just know that Mona and I support both of you and there's absolutely no animosity. Whitney's a grown woman, she can make her own decisions, and if you're her decision, we're more than happy to back her up."

"Thank you," I'm finally able to clear my throat enough to get the words out. I reach over, hugging him tightly. I haven't hugged him since he offered me the money for school, but his hug is still solid and steady, the pillar of the family that everyone needs sometimes. "You don't know how much that means to me."

"I have some idea, son. I watched you boldly turn down money for an education to go fight a war because you didn't want to make life hard for me. You're one of the best men I know, and that's not a damn lie."

"C'mon you two, let's get this show on the road," Tank yells as he holds his coffee, coming down off the porch. "I got plans tonight. We need to get done in time for me to go take a shower."

"Does Blaze know you have plans?" I shoot him a smirk.

"Shut the fuck up and start that leaf blower."

I do as he asks, shooting all the leaves at him while he makes a run for it. "You're an ass, Renegade."

Stanley's laughing at the two of us as he leans against his truck. "This takes me back to your teenage years. You two ain't grown up at all."

Whitney

"Truth or lie?" I ask, yawning slightly. I'm tired tonight, but wired at the same time. Fall is fast approaching and with that is the due date of our baby girl. I'm tired more often than not, but find I don't fall asleep as easily as I used to.

"Truth," he winks, even though I can tell he's tired, too. When I came home to find my entire yard done, my gutters cleared, and my porches cleaned too, I realize how much work the guys did for me. It was enough to almost make me cry. Damn hormones.

We haven't played this game since he had to admit to jacking off in my mom's bathroom. I know he's probably expecting something like that from me, but I have another truth I want to share with him. "When I was married, there was only one thing I ever asked for, for my birthday," I start.

He's sitting up, completely at attention because I don't talk about my marriage often. Lately it hasn't come up at all, and I'm happy for that. I'm no longer living in the past and neither is Ryan. We're making a life for ourselves separate from the jerk I was married to for so long.

"What is it that you've always wanted, Princess?"

His words are a caress, letting me know maybe one day I'll have what I've wanted. If there's anything Ryan does well, it's make me happy, less stressed, and enjoy life more. "My whole life I've wanted to go to an Alabama football game. The UT game always falls on my birthday weekend and I've dreamed of heading to Tuscaloosa wearing my pearls and red lipstick to cheer on the home team."

"Like any good sorority girl would," he laughs as he nods. "That's a pretty legit dream to have."

"Every year I want it, and every year nobody listens," I smile ruefully. "They always plan an elaborate birthday party for me, and while I appreciate it, it's not what I want," I sigh. "Maybe someday, I'll take our daughter," I rub my stomach.

"Nobody has ever given you that, Whit?" he asks softly, as he strokes my arm. It's the patch of skin he can find easiest with the tips of his fingers. "It's such an easy wish to grant."

"Right?" I become halfway emotional. That's what I've never understood. All it would take would be a little planning on the person's part who gives me the gift. Instead I get the same thing every year. "But it seems to be the hardest thing for me to get people to listen."

He's quiet for a long time as he lets my words sink in. I want to know what he's thinking, but I fall asleep before I can ask.

CHAPTER TWENTY-NINE

RENEGADE

I'M NERVOUS THIS MORNING, even though Whitney has been banging around the house since she woke up. I think it's because she assumes this day will be like all her other birthdays. What she doesn't know is this is a game changer. I've gone to a lot of trouble to surprise her and make this day special. I hope like hell I've done enough.

Two weeks before

"I hope you don't mind," I tell the Trumbolt family. I've asked them to meet me for lunch when I know Whitney's made a trip to Birmingham. The last thing I need for her is come upon this meeting of the minds, so to speak, and figure out what the hell I'm doing for her.

"I know you all like to do a party for her, and it's kind of a tradition, but she told me she wants to go to the Alabama game her birthday weekend. I got lucky and got tickets," I show them the tickets to prove I really do have them. "But I don't want to step on anyone's toes."

"She'll love it," Tank answers first. "She's always wanted to go to a game, but she never got around to it."

I want to tell him she's asked for her it for a long time, but nobody's ever listened. Instead I nod my head enthusiastically. "Exactly. Who knows when the next time we can do this will be? With the baby coming soon, we don't know how life is going to go. This may be the last time she can do anything carefree for a while."

I'm playing on their want to make her happy and reminding them they have a new member of the family coming very soon.

"I just want y'all to not be mad and let her have something she may never get to have again."

Mona smiles and I know I've got them in my hand now. "That sounds amazing, and we all know she'd love it. Have fun Ryan. Take pictures for us."

"I will," I promise them as I leave The Café.

Pulling my phone out, I text my contact, hoping like hell they still have that parking pass they said I could use.

"Princess, would you stop slamming doors and c'mere," I yell from where I still lie in bed. I'm deliberately being lazy, I don't want her to think I have anything planned. When in reality I have jeans and socks on, and all I need is a shirt and shoes.

"What?" she asks, attitude thick today.

"The attitude is strong with this one," I tease as I watch her face turn an angry red. "Your face is turning Alabama red," I tease again, sitting up in the bed and grabbing a card from the bedside table.

"Ryan, I'm not in the mood today." Her gaze looks confused as she sees my jeans. I grab the shirt I have laying over to the side, and slip my feet into my running shoes.

"Too bad," I hand her the card. "Would be a perfect shade of red for the game today."

She eyes me, opening up the card, before a smile spreads across her face when she realizes what she holds. It's the most genuine smile I've ever seen, aside from when it's for our daughter.

"Is this real? You're taking me to an Alabama football game today?" Her smile is brighter than the sun shining in through the bedroom window and I feel like I've just given her the whole world.

I nod, standing up to take her in my arms. "It's one of the things you've always wanted, right?"

Tears pool in her eyes and I'm scared I've done something wrong. She sniffs, holding the tickets in her hands. "It is," she whispers. "But nobody has ever listened to what I want, Ryan. They hear me talk all the time, but they never really listen."

Grasping the back of her head with my fingers, digging through the platinum locks, I tilt it back so her eyes have to meet mine. "Every sound you make, every word that comes out of your mouth, is deeply ingrained into my memory. When you speak, you have my full attention."

She closes her eyes, letting the tears fall.

"C'mon Princess, don't cry about it, let's go watch some football."

Tugging on my hand, she stops my momentum, pulling me back to her. Her arms wrap around my neck and she plasters herself against me. "Thank you for being everything I've always wanted, but never had."

The emotion is too much for me, and I can't respond. Instead I kiss her softly on the cheek. Hopefully one day she'll realize the reason I do all these things.

One day she'll realize I'm so head over heels in love with her I can barely see straight. And maybe on that day she'll realize she's in love with me, too.

"I have two more things for you."

Her smile is impatient. "What else could you have for me that I'll love more than these tickets?" she waves them in my face like she's won the lottery.

"Do you remember that truth or lie?" I ask her, hoping to dig some into her memory. "You told me you wanted to be that girl wearing her pearls and red lipstick, going to the Alabama game," I hand her a bag. "I hope I did okay."

Her hands shake as she opens the bag. "Ryan," she breathes as she pulls out a tube of her favorite red lipstick. "I had to do some sneaking to get that information out of Addison. You may want to explain to her what I was doing. She may possibly have the wrong idea about me," I rub my neck, a grimace on my face. "Keep going, Princess."

The next box she pulls out is the blue/teal color that all women love. She eyes me as she takes the lid off of it, squealing as she sees the pearl earrings I picked out just for her.

"Oh my God, Ryan. This," she waves a hand in front of her face. "Is the best birthday ever. I don't know how you're ever going to top this in the years to come."

My heart expands in my chest because she's talking about a future, and I don't allow myself to think about it that much. There's a part of me that doesn't want to get my hopes up, a part of me that doesn't want the colossal disappointment of her realizing how much better she is than me. The other part of me, the cocky guy who arrests people for a living, kicks that other dude to the street and gives her a smile. "I have all kinds of ideas up my sleeve, Princess. You'll need eighty or so years to see what they all are."

"When do we leave?" she asks, putting the earrings on.

"Right now. We have to leave right now in order to make it. Is there anything you need?"

"Do you think I look okay?"

She's wearing an Alabama football shirt and a pair of ripped leggings that have become her favorite. I know they're leggings because I once called them pajama jeans (like the ones I saw on an infomercial one night) and that was a huge mistake. This is as dressed down as Whitney gets.

"You have your pearls and your red lipstick, babe you're ready to go," I hold my hand out to her, pulling her towards the truck.

THE RIDE to Tuscaloosa is quiet because Whitney decides to take a nap to rest up for the game. I'm great with that; I want her to have the time of her life and not be tired. I sneak looks at her as we eat up the miles on the interstate, still unable to believe I'm making one of her dreams come true. I haven't been able to do that for anyone else but her.

As we get closer to the stadium, traffic picks up, but I have the parking tag a friend on the force got me. Actually, he helped me get the tickets too, promising me they were on the lower level, near the field so Whit wouldn't have to climb the stairs.

Miracle of all miracles, they see my tag and let me through, directing me to some section of parking I never even imagined would be this close. I can see the damn field from where we park.

"Whit babe, we're here," I gently shake her awake.

It takes her a minute, but as she acclimates back to where she is, I can feel her excitement. "Let's go," she grabs her bag and meets me at the front of the truck.

"This is crazy," I'm in awe as I see the amount of people around us. I hold her hand tighter, not wanting us to get lost.

"I knew it would be this way," she says as we walk towards the entrance, with the mass of people making their way into the stadium. "I feel like I'm with my people."

"Wait," she stops as we make our way through the vendors selling things the closer we get to the front. "I need a shaker, Ryan. I can't go into a football game here without a shaker."

She points to a booth where a guy is selling what she needs. "How many do you need?" he asks her, when he sees her walk up.

"Two," she grins up at me. "He needs one, too."

The man grabs the two shakers, or whatever they are, and then takes a good look at her.

"You havin' a boy or a girl?" He nods to her stomach.

"Little girl," I answer, and realize it's one of the first times I've ever answered that question. Pride swells in my chest and I puff it out a little further.

"First baby?" he asks us. He's an older gentleman, lines of age cross across his dark colored face contrast with the white of his fuzzy hair.

"Yeah," she answers, putting her hand on her stomach in the way she does that endears me to her every time. "Unplanned, but supremely loved."

"It'll be five dollars for the shakers, and this for free," He says as he pushes a small Alabama shirt our way. It's made to look like one of the cheerleader uniforms, so small it makes my heart stop. I hadn't ever thought about our baby being that small.

I fish a five out of my wallet and give it to him, with a very heartfelt thank you. Poor Whitney looks like she's about to either cry or throw her arms around this man and profess her love to him. "C'mon babe, let's get inside. Thank you again, Sir."

I don't think I've ever seen Whitney so alive in my life, at least besides the times she's been in my arms. As the game starts, she claps with the crowd, boos when a call pisses her off, and gets so irritated she slams her drink down at one point. "Should I worry about you going into early labor on me?" I joke, catching the stormy look on her face.

"No, but I normally watch the games on my own. You're usually working so you never see me get all riled up like this. Stella moves like crazy when I watch though," she grabs hold of my hand and puts it on her tight abdomen.

"Holy shit," I laugh as I feel the movement. "Is she doing flips in there?"

"Sometimes I wonder," she grins.

Pulling her in close with my arm around her neck, I grab my phone, turning us around so the field is our backdrop, and take a selfie of us. We don't have many pictures together and this is one moment I want to remember. If we don't make it, I want her smile at an Alabama football game to be one of those things I never forget.

The game goes by quicker than I imagine, and I'm pretty sure it's because while she's watching it, I'm watching her.

"It's the fourth quarter," she grins over at me, pretty late in the fourth. The game has pretty much been a blowout and Alabama has no chance to not win this.

"Do you want to leave early?" I ask, not sure why she's looking at me like she is.

"No, my favorite part of the home games is coming up."

I'm about to ask her what she means when I distinctly hear something that sounds like "Dixieland Delight" coming from somewhere. "Are they gonna sing this?" I question as I watch her clapping along.

"Kinda," she grins again, but this time it's a little evil.

That's when everyone starts singing and I realize they've altered the lyrics. My eyes bugging out as I hear what people are singing.

Loud and proud, I hear Whitney scream, "On beer!" as she joins in.

I sit back and watch her, the smile on her face, the rosy color of her cheeks, and the happiness in her eyes. I realize I put all those things there. I made her happy, and if I can make her happy today, then I know can make her happy forever.

She's just got to give me the chance. And judging by the way she clings to me as we leave the stadium. I'm closer to that chance than I've ever been.

CHAPTER THIRTY
RENEGADE

"I'M STILL NOT sure about this," I pull the truck into the brick building, shutting it off as I look over at Whitney.

She laughs and like always it grabs me by the heart. I love to hear her laugh. I love a lot of things about her, but her laugh is in the top three. "Why are you so scared? We'll get to see what she looks like."

I shrug, running my hands over the steering wheel. "It freaks me out slightly. What if she looks like an alien? I don't know if I'm prepared for it."

"Chances are she'll be born in the next month, Ryan. I have a feeling she's going to look now exactly like she will then. Don't you want to make sure she looks like a Stella before she becomes a Stella?"

Whitney has a point. We don't want to stick her with a name that doesn't scream it's her name, but we can figure that out after she's born – right? "I guess."

She gets out of the truck and comes over to the driver's side, opening the door. Pulling at me, she gets me out of the driver's seat and then turns me to face her. Her bottom lip is poking out slightly as she bats her eyes up at me. "Please? For me?"

And that's where she's got me, because I will do absolutely anything for this woman standing in front of me. "Okay," I sigh. "But if I have nightmares about this, know I blame you."

"I will fully take the blame," she crosses her finger over her heart. "But I really think you'll like it."

I HAVEN'T PAID much attention since we came into the room, because it still freaks me out. I can't even say why it bothers me, but I've seen other 4D Ultrasound pictures and they look so weird to me. Everyone says it'll be different with my own child. I doubt it, but I'll keep those thoughts to myself.

"You ready?" Whitney asks as I get comfortable in the chair, and grab hold of her out-stretched hand.

"As I'll ever be."

She laughs, looking over at the technician. "He's scared she'll look like an alien and then he'll be scarred for life."

"I won't lie," the other woman says. "Sometimes it's a bit weird to see things like this, but then you get to pick out features. That's the fun part, you'll see."

I give her a raised brow, but don't say anything else. I won't be convinced until I see for myself, but I'll still go through with it, because it's what Whitney wants. The machine comes on, and I watch as they manipulate her stomach. A loud thumping is heard throughout the room.

"Her heartbeat is good. Let's see if we can get a face," the tech moves the wand around and I find my eyes glued to the screen on the wall.

"Here we go," she zooms in on a face.

It's like a kick to the heart. She has my lips. "Oh my God, Whitney," I squeeze her hand. "She has my lips."

"She does," Whitney agrees. "And look, she's grabbing her toes! No wonder I feel like she's doing gymnastics in there sometimes."

"It's because she is," I grin at her. All those alien comments and fears I had previously are now gone. I can totally see why anyone who can would do this.

I was already in love with her, was already in love with her mom, but after seeing this I know I've absolutely fallen as hard as I can. There's no going back.

Whitney

He falls in love with her in that moment. I can see it, by the way his eyes soften, by the way he grips my hand. Ryan falls head over heels in love with his daughter. There's a part of me that wishes he'd do the same with me, but I know everything has to happen with us organically. We can't force an issue. When we tried to force things in the beginning, it took us too long to get comfortable with each other.

When we stopped forcing feelings, we settled into the easy comradery we have now. I can say with complete certainty. He is my best friend. I've never had one like him. He's seen me at my best, will see me at worst, and everywhere in between. I've never had this with anyone else. Not with my ex-husband, not with my parents, not with my brother. No one.

"I have to go back to work," I tell him, pushing my bottom lip out a little.

Addison's been keeping us on track by herself, but today she's decorating for a wedding we have coming up over the weekend.

"Sucks that I'm off today and you have to work," he frowns as he holds my hands in front of him.

"You're welcome to come hang out with me. It's not like you'll be in the way, I'll definitely put you to work."

He thinks it over for a minute and then nods. "Why the hell not, all I'm gonna do is go home and watch Netflix. When you ask me if I've caught up on Blue Bloods I'll say no and you'll know I'm lying."

It warms my heart in a million ways to know he thinks of my house as his home. For someone like him who's never really had a spot to call his own besides his apartment, it means something. To know I've given him stability that no one else ever has can almost bring me to my knees. "Let's get going," I grab hold of his shirt sleeve. "And don't you be watching Blue Bloods without me. We talked about that already."

"I get bored without you there," he complains good-naturedly.

"Pretty soon we won't be bored at all," I remind him. "All the hours of our days will be filled with taking care of Stella, preparing to take care of Stella, or trying to catch up on our sleep. We probably need to enjoy it while we can."

He shakes his head as we make our way back to his truck. "I'd much rather spend time with you."

WHEN WE GET to the wedding hall, I direct him on where to park and then grab my change of clothes. Walking in, I see our crew already at work and wave Addison over.

"I'm gonna go change, but he's come to help us today since he doesn't have to work. Tell him what to do while I go get more comfortable."

As I walk back to the bathroom, I think about how this could be my life from now on, Ryan and I helping each other through situations and being a support when we both need it. I never had that with Stephen, never would have even thought to ask him to come work with me. He wouldn't have, even if I had begged. He was that selfish.

Ryan is that selfless. Always has been, and I pray to God our daughter gets his empathy and willingness to work hard. They're both such great characteristics to have, and I hope he's rubbed off on me, too. I can be a southern lady, but I can also be a lady who helps people. After changing, I go in search of Addison, stopping when I see her watching our crew from the door.

"How's it going?"

"With your superhero baby daddy out there, it's going a lot faster. God, but he is strong," she gives me a look with her lips pursed. "Tight ass, makes you just want to grab it."

"Stop!" I laugh, smacking her in the arm. "You said it right, he is my baby daddy. Hands off, sister."

I watch as he works alongside our team, never backing away from anything they ask him to do. Even when I'm doing my own thing, I don't let him go too far out of my vision.

If he's willing to work this hard on something that isn't his, I can't help but imagine how hard he'll work something that is. Like maybe the love he and I can share.

The thought is enough to startle me. It's been there, in the back of my mind for a while, but I've not been able to bring myself to tell him, and I know I won't be able to now either. Love got me hurt in a bad way before, and I know that with him, it would hurt even worse.

Making myself vulnerable in that way just isn't possible yet. No matter how badly I want it.

CHAPTER THIRTY-ONE

WHITNEY

I HEAR Ryan come home through the back door, hear his keys hit the bar, and his shoes hit the spot next to the door where we keep them.

I've been thinking about him the past few hours. I have no idea what it is, but he sent me a selfie at lunch with the sexiest smirk I've ever seen him wear. Since then I've been on edge, my nipples rubbing the inside of my bra almost made me come twice.

People told me that once I hit the third trimester, I would want sex, but they didn't tell me how much. Today I feel like a horndog, and I'm almost mad that it took him an extra thirty minutes to get home tonight. Something about a call they had. I know it's crazy I would be upset about it, but I literally ache with the need to have him inside me.

"Whitney, you in the bedroom?" he yells as he makes his way down the hall way.

"Yeah," I answer as he enters the room, whistling as he sees me.

I'm naked as the day I was born because I didn't want to waste any time getting clothes off my body.

"What's going on?" he starts unbuttoning his shirt, and I'm amazed when he takes it off, revealing his Adam's apple, the tattoo I love, and the wide expanse of skin that are his abs.

Sauntering over to him, I notice he's already removed his gun belt and I'm thankful for it. Moving my hands to the button of his pants, I start the task of taking them off. "That picture you sent me earlier was the hottest smile I've ever seen. All day long I've thought about you," I lift up on my toes to kiss him, driving my tongue into his mouth.

"Ohh Princess," he pulls back, and judging by the way his eyes darken, he's with the program now. "You need me, don't you?"

"Yes," the word is a hiss as I feel his button let loose.

Within seconds, he's got his pants down around his ankles and I'm pushing his boxers that way. "Need you is too weak a phrase," I admit, moaning as the palms of his hands lift the hot, heaviness of my breasts.

"How do you want it tonight?" he buries his face in my neck, pulling on the skin, then soothing it with his tongue.

"You behind me, I'll hang onto the headboard. Don't worry about being romantic, I can't stand it tonight."

Doing what I've asked, he threads his fingers through my hair, pushing me back towards the bed. I'm too big for him to pick up now, and I kind of miss it. Tonight I'd love for him to manhandle me and throw me on the bed. Instead, when the backs of my knees hit the mattress, he turns me around, hand still in my hair. He keeps hold as I knee-walk over to the headboard. When I'm there, I wrap my hands around it, before looking back at him over my shoulder.

"Fuck me, Renegade."

The breath he inhales through his nose is sharp, and enough to make my nipples peak harder.

"Hold on, Princess, it's gonna be a wild ride."

I can distinctly remember him saying something like that the first time we ever had sex, and my body responds. It responds in a big way. Moisture flushes against my core, and it eases him in as he seeks passage. He thrusts deeply against me and we both moan as he crowds me against the wood of the headboard.

"You're so fuckin' wet, Whit. What the hell has gotten into you?"

I throw my head back against his shoulder. "That bad boy smile you gave me. It's all I needed. My mind thought up a million fantasies about it," I pant as he wraps an arm around my thighs, moving his fingers to my clit, fingering the protruding nub, making all my pleasure spots light up.

"Like this one?"

"Just like this one," I answer, thrusting back against his cock and then forward against his fingers. I have no shame at all, none where he's concerned. All I want to feel is the release I know he can give my body. "Except you were pulling my hair."

"I can make that happen," he grabs hold of my hair again, pulling tightly.

Between the sensation of the hair pulling at my scalp, his fingers at my clit, and his cock in my pussy, I'm done. I don't think I can take anymore. My ears are ringing as he pounds into me, and out of nowhere my orgasm hits me.

"Fuck, Whit, me too," he groans as he pitches forward, grasping the headboard to keep from squishing me under his weight.

As our bodies press into one another, coming down from our high, his heart hammers against my back, and it's the best sense of completion I've ever had.

Renegade

I'm draggin' ass this morning because it's normally my day off. This week though, I've switched a shift with Ace's partner, and we're riding together today.

"Do you hate Trevor for being off today while you have to work six on?" Whitney questions as she strolls into the bathroom, standing next to me at the double vanity.

I shake my head. "No, nothing could have kept me from being at your ultrasound on Thursday. Seeing our little girl? Highlight of my life."

I can tell by the way her cheeks turn a pink hue she enjoys the answer I've given. I don't think I'll ever forget seeing our daughter's face so clearly on screen yesterday. When Whitney had approached me with the 4D appointment and shown me some of the pictures, it'd freaked me out and I had almost declined her offer. Now? I have a picture of Stella in my wallet that I'll never let go of. She fuckin' looks like me. Has my lips and everything. Nothing could have prepared me nor taken away from anything that happened yesterday.

"It was pretty amazing, wasn't it?" Whitney puts her hand on her stomach before she bends over and grabs the toothpaste, doing her morning rituals.

"Amazing isn't the word for it, but either way, I'm glad to work my sixth day in a row if it let me be there for you and her."

Our eyes meet in the mirror as she finishes brushing her teeth. The pull I've felt with her since the night we conceived the child in her belly is still there and it's only getting stronger. She turns around, leaning her back against the counter. Taking advantage, I move in, putting my arms around her waist. Immediately, her arms go around my neck and she rests her head against my shoulder.

"I'm so tired," she yawns, burrowing deep against the indention where shoulder and neck meet.

"Me too," I answer, brushing my lips against the skin of her forehead. "I won't keep you up late tonight." There's a smile in my voice as I think about the hours we spent wrapped up in each other. I'd had Whitney on her knees while she'd gripped the edge of the headboard, begging me to ease the ache she's feeling more now that she's further along in the pregnancy. Some of the guys at the station told me third trimester sex was going to be the best sex of my life – they were not joking. "Where are you meeting your client again? If things run slow, I might pop in and say hi, see how my girls are doing."

She burrows a little deeper and I can feel the smile spread across her face as her cheeks pull against my skin. "The Café. Mom's meeting them with me since she's going to be handling the catering. They're calling for rain most of the day, so she wants to drive me," she pulls back and rolls her eyes. "Mom said she doesn't want me out in my condition."

"I'd have to agree with her. If someone can drive you, then all the better."

Whitney purses her lips, putting her hand on her hip before sticking it out. "We still have a couple of weeks to go, Ryan. You can't be around me 24/7."

"You're right, but when there's the option of someone being around, I'll take it. Besides Thanksgiving is this week. People are out and about and being stupid while they run their errands. Just let your mom dote on you. Soon you won't be her little girl anymore. You ever think of that?"

"I'm thirty-six years old," she argues.

"But now, you're responsible for another human being. It's a change, and I'm sure it's taking her some getting used to."

Whitney reaches up, kissing my jawline as she nuzzles the rough skin there. "Don't shave, I kinda like it."

Works for me, less time to get ready. "You know I live to please you."

She pulls me in by grabbing the fabric of the boxers I'm still wearing, before she circles her arms around my waist. "That you do, and you pleasure me so well."

I can feel myself responding to her, responding to the chemistry that flows between our bodies, no matter what we're doing. "The pleasure is going to have to wait," I groan because I want nothing more than to spend the day with her.

"I know," she sighs. "We both have to get ready for our day."

CHAPTER THIRTY-TWO
RENEGADE

I'VE HAD a cup of coffee and I could be on my second Monster of the day, but I'll neither confirm or deny that to anyone. I am tired as fuck.

"You okay over there?" Ace asks as we continue making our rounds through town. We drive back and forth, up and down a grid pattern, before we make our way out of the more populated edges of town. Once we're on what's considered a back road, Ace presses the accelerator, letting us speed up and down the hills, making me grab hold of my oh shit handle as we take a curve faster than we need to.

"Perfect."

"Am I scaring you?" Ace asked, a grin in his voice as he straightens the car out when we hit another straight stretch.

"I'd like to live to see my child born, if that's what you're asking," I take a healthy drink of the Monster before setting it down again.

"Figured I'd wake up you. Why are you so tired anyway?" He looks over the console at me, genuine question and concern in his eyes.

No way I'm going to tell him what I was doing, instead I answer. "Getting the last of the nursery done and it's my sixth day on." He doesn't have to know the nursery has been done for months.

"Oh yeah, how did the ultrasound go?"

I struggle with not pulling the picture out of my wallet and showing him with a dumb smile on my face. "It went great. She looks like the perfect mix of both me and her."

"You seem happy, Renegade. I'm thrilled for you." Judging by the sincerity in his voice, I believe him. It's nice to have friends who like it when you do good, and Stella is the best thing I've ever done in my life.

"Thanks man," I smile because it's all true. "I'm very happy. If someone had told me a year ago I'd be where I am now, I'd say they were fucking crazy," I laugh, because sometimes I truly can't believe it. "But I'm happier now than I've ever been."

Whitney

I hear a sharp catcall as I get out of my mom's car. Used to dealing with that type of thing, I turn around, ready to give the person a piece of my mind, when I see Trevor. The harsh lines of my face relax and I grin at my younger brother.

"Hey," I hold my arms open to him, hugging him as well as I can with the belly I sport.

"Hey, Sis," he lets me go and gives mom a hug too. "Didn't expect to see the two of you here."

"Meeting a client," I explain, hooking a thumb at The Café. "What are you doing here?"

He lifts up a brown paper bag. "Grabbing some sandwiches. I think I'm gonna see if the fish bite today."

I can see he's dressed for fishing – an old band t-shirt covers his torso, holes in it here and there. Old camo pants have been turned into shorts and a hat rests on his head.

"How's it going to be without your fishing buddy?" I know Ryan usually fishes with him.

Trevor gives me a tight smile. "Guess I'm going to have to figure it out. In a few weeks he won't have much time to fish, now will he?"

I'm shocked by the tone Trevor uses. "He'll have plenty of time to do whatever you want him to do with you. Just because we'll have a baby doesn't mean either one of us won't have time for you. You're one of the most important people in our lives, and not only are you Stella's uncle, but you'll be her Godfather, too. Don't even think that."

He gives me a disbelieving look. "I know, just gonna take some getting used to."

"You're tellin' me? I'm gonna be a mom." Some days it still hasn't sunk in, other days I can't wait to hold her in my arms.

"You've wanted it for years, you were born to be a mom. There's absolutely no reason you won't blow motherhood out the park."

I giggle because I'm not sure I've ever knocked anything out of the park, but leave it to him to use a sports analogy. "I love you, Trev."

"Love you too. I gotta get goin'. See ya, Mama," he leans down and gives our mom a kiss on the cheek.

Mom heads for The Café, but I stand there a few minutes, watching him as he goes to his truck and gets in. For a split-second I have a feeling of suffocation, like I want to grab him and hold him close to me, never let him go. I've never felt anything like it before, but I also know my emotions are crazy because of the pregnancy, and I don't need to push my craziness off on him. Shaking my head, I go in, smiling as I see mom greeting our mutual client.

"Hey Ashley," I wave to the bride as I have a seat. It's time to get to work and push anything besides doing my job out of my brain.

Renegade

"You ever wonder why we have slow days?" Ace asks as he yawns. "I mean why are some days so busy we can't even take a break to piss, but then you have days like today when we've not had one call."

"I think we should be thankful for it. In the grand scheme of things it means no one's in trouble or needs help. Maybe everybody is following the law to the letter, we shouldn't question it."

"I think I want to know more for the psychological side of things. You know? Why do people commit crimes? What makes one day worse than the next? Why does a full moon bring out all the crazies? I don't know." he shrugs. "This is the shit I think about."

"Dude, you need to go on Dr. Phil or some shit like that," I laugh. "You've got too many questions in your head."

"I've been told that before," he doesn't deny. "Just the type of person I am."

I open my mouth to say something to him, but just as I do, a black pickup drives by in a blur of speed. Literally the only thing I can see is the color as it flies by.

"Holy fuck," Ace yells as he flips on his lights and takes off after it.

I can see the license plate and know immediately who it is, but I call Brooks Strather in anyway. "He ain't gonna stop," I tell Ace. "He never fuckin' stops."

"How many tickets have you and Tank had a uniform deliver?"

"Probably around five at this point, but you know other people have tried to stop him, too."

We're both quiet as we give chase. This is a dangerous part of the county. S-curves lead to a low-lying creek with a small two-lane bridge that links the two pieces of land together.

"I might be able to get him in the curves. He's gonna have to slow down. No way in hell he'll be able to handle them."

"Dispatch, we're in pursuit of Brooks Strather, near the bottoms on the S-curves going south. He's in excess of ninety miles an hour," I shake my head as I glance at the speedometer. Looking over at Ace, I'm disgusted. "He's going to kill himself or someone else."

Again silence takes over the cab of the car. All those Monsters I've drank and the coffee I've had is rolling through my system as I white-knuckle the console and the handle at my side, sending up a prayer they tell us to stop this pursuit. Nothing about this feels good.

"He's outta control," Ace mumbles as he attempts to both keep up and maintain a safe distance back from the truck.

I watch in horror as Brooks gets too far to the right, his passenger side rear tire off the road. "Don't yank that fuckin' wheel!" I scream out at him, knowing he can't hear me. I'm pressing an imaginary break in the floorboard, wanting to stop him as I see him overcorrect.

"He's lost it," Ace grimaces as he slows and both of us watch whatever's about to happen in what feels like slow motion.

"Dispatch suspect has wrecked – oh fuck!"

Out of the blind spot on the curve another truck appears northbound right as Brooks crosses the yellow line. They hit head on, pieces of wreckage flying everywhere. It feels like it takes two hours for the two vehicles to come to a stop as we watch one of them barrel roll. "Be advised dispatch we have two. I repeat two cars involved in this accident. Suspect hit another truck going estimated eighty to ninety miles an hour head on. We need assistance."

Ace pulls our car at an angle, blocking the road until another unit can get there. "You go to Brooks, I'll check on the other one," I unbuckle my seat belt and take off at a run, adrenaline pumping through my veins. I hate accidents, but it's a part of the job we have to deal with.

The truck has turned in the opposite direction and the back is now facing me, the mass of metal sitting on the driver's side. For a moment I take in what's left of the back windshield and of the tailgate. Something looks damn familiar to me, and that's when I see it.

It's Tank's truck. He's the only person I know with a 'lake life' sticker on the back, right next to one that says 'I brake for Auburn fans – so I can talk to them about their life choices'.

My throat drops into my stomach and my stomach drops somewhere around my knees. I gag as I try not to throw up, but everything I've had today is threatening to show itself.

"Dispatch," I key the radio again, this time not able to recognize my own voice. "Be advised the other person involved is one of ours off-duty. Get help here a-fuckin'-sap."

Immediately I know I want to get to him, assess the damage. I've done it in a war zone, I know without a doubt I can do it for my best friend. The wind has picked up on this overcast day and there's a storm coming, it's rocking the truck, and suddenly it rolls completely over. The driver's side is no longer resting in the ground.

I'm running as fast as I can, and when I get to the driver's side door, I feel bile rise up in my throat again. Tank's out cold, and he's at a weird angle.

"Don't fuckin' do this to me," I whisper, hands shaking as I dig through the mud, grabbing the handle, but the door doesn't budge when I try to open it.

Tears spring to my eyes and I tell myself not to show the emotion, to keep my shit together because that's what Tank needs right now. Getting up, I run to the back. The tailgate is a tangled mess, but it's twisted enough that I can see to squeeze up through there and go in through the back window.

Lying on the ground, I realize I haven't done this type of shit since BASIC. Shimmying halfway up, I curse because with my vest on, I'm not going to fit. For the first time since I found out about Stella, I'm taking it off on-duty. But I have to check on my friend, make sure my daughter's uncle is okay.

Ripping my shirt off and unhooking the vest, leaving my undershirt on to protect me from the elements. I lay back on the ground and start my shimmy again. This time I fit, and thank God I'm not claustrophobic. If I were this would be hell. Getting to the back window, I test the glass and see it's partway broken. Unhooking my nightstick from my side, I extend it and push against the glass, hooking it in a hole, and pulling it back towards me. It falls, but not on the side Tank is on. If anyone's going to get cut up, it's me.

Turning my body in ways I've never known it would go, I wiggle myself in, and finally reach Tank. My world stops in this moment because I'm not sure if he's breathing. I can't hear it, and that scares me more than anything.

"Trevor, wake up, wake up," I plead, using two fingers to search for a pulse. It takes forever to find one, and once I do, it's erratic, but I'll take what I can get.

"Dispatch advise EMS the officer has a very weak pulse and is trapped inside the wreckage. I'm kind of in here, but we're gonna need the jaws of life to get him out."

Putting the radio to my side, I take stock of what's going on. His breathing is just as erratic as his heartbeat, but I say a little thank you that he's breathing. Now I can hear it, but it's a wheeze that makes me more worried, if that's even possible. "Don't you give up on me, Trev. Please don't give up on me. You have a niece to meet. When I finally convince Whitney to marry me, I'm gonna need a best man. Don't you dare fuckin' give up on me."

It's then I feel the wetness of the tears streaming down my face. We've been to war and back, we've been on many dangerous calls as police officers and members of the Moonshine Task Force. I'll be damned if I let my best friend die on the side of the road because some little piece of shit couldn't obey a speed limit.

"Ryan, they're here. EMS needs you to come out so the fire department can use the jaws. It's time to turn him over to someone else.'

I grip Trevor's hand, promising him things I'm not sure will come true. "I'm gonna be right here, and then I'm gonna go get your sister and momma. You're gonna be fine, brother. Hang in there for me."

I extricate myself as quickly as possible, and as I come out, my eyes meet Blaze's.

"It's Trevor?" she asks, a look of devastation on her face.

"It's Trevor," I confirm. "Get our boy safely to the hospital and give him a fighting chance. I have to go notify his family."

"What do we do about Brooks?" Ace asks.

For the first time I look over and see Brooks standing on the side of the road, blood running down his face from a gash at his hairline, but he's fine. He's not going to be fighting for his life like Trevor will be. It takes everything I have not to run over and lay that boy out, to hold my gun to his head and ask him to plead for his life. I remind myself he's someone else's kid, and he's made a stupid decision, but fuck if I'm going to let him be comfortable while Trevor is stuck in the fuckin' mud.

"I don't give two shits. Let him rot out here until transport comes. I'm taking our car."

CHAPTER THIRTY-THREE

WHITNEY

THE MEETING IS GOING WELL and we've just signed contracts with the happy couple and I've scanned them with my phone, sending them to Addison. "Please don't think the fact I'll have a newborn then will be a problem."

"You've always been an amazing and fair business woman, Whitney, I have no doubt you will make it work as a mother."

I can't help but smile, feeling excited and happy people still trust me. "I'm anxious to get started. I know we have a few months, but I'll probably have something for you to look at next week. I'm not one to wait until the last second and I'll keep you up to date."

We stand, ready to end our meeting when a group of older men come in. "Ernie, turn the scanner on,"

Oh good grief, something must be happening and they want to be nosey. One of the disadvantages of living in a small town. I turn to grab my bag, when another group of men come in, this one a little younger than the previous.

"Ernie is the scanner on? We just tried to come through the bottoms and there's been a bad wreck."

"I'm turning it on," Ernie yells from behind the counter.

"Did y'all hear one of the cars involved was an officer and they died?" One of the group of older men asked the other group.

"Mom," my heart drops and I reach out, grabbing her mom by the arm. "Did he say what I think he said?"

"Yes," my mom nods slowly. "And none of them should be talking about it unless they know for sure," she says loud enough that the group could hear them.

"Oh honey, is your boy workin' today? He's normally off, I didn't think nothin' of it." One of the men at the counter says, looking over at me, with sympathy in his eyes.

"He switched because we had an ultrasound," I put my hand on my stomach, feeling Stella kick.

"Have a seat," Mom scoots a chair underneath me, while I'm fumbling in my purse. "I know," I grab my phone. "I'll just call and see if they can patch me through. He'll answer, and things will be fine."

But they don't feel fine, and my fingers shake as I dial the number. Dread pools in my stomach and I think immediately of all the things I should have said. The things I wanted to say but never did. I've never even told Ryan I love him, even though I do. I didn't want to open myself up to the potential hurt putting my feelings out there may cause. The regret eats at me as I listen to the phone ring.

"Laurel County Dispatch."

I go into my spiel, telling them who I am and telling her I just want to know if Ryan's okay or if they can patch me through to him.

"I'm sorry, if you aren't immediate family we can't give that info out while someone's on shift."

"We may not be blood related, but I carry his baby," I tell the woman on the other end of the line.

"Unless you wear his ring, have his last name, or a marriage license, I simply can't give you the information you're asking for."

I hang up because it's not in me to be rude to this woman. I still remember how my mom raised me and the fact she's sitting right next to me. "I'll call Trevor," I decide. "He'll know."

As I listen to the phone go to voicemail, the tears come, they glide down my face and neck, until they're stopped by the pearls I always wear. Reaching up, I grab hold of the pearl stud Ryan gave me for my birthday before the Alabama game.

"I never told him I love him, mom. I never told him. What if he died wondering? I didn't tell him," I bury my head in my hands, sobbing, letting my entire body take on the regret I feel.

"Honey, he knows," Mom rubs my back, speaking to me in soothing tones.

I can't breathe, I feel the suffocation of the room, of all the eyes on me. "Not if he's dead, mom."

"Why don't we go home?" She offers. "That way you're there if they come for you."

"No," I stiffen my chin, hoping it stops trembling as I grip the edge of the table, daring her to drag me out of there if she has to. "Ryan knew I was going to be here today. If they're looking for me, Ryan would tell them where I am."

I'm aware that I make no sense. I've just told my mom he's dead, but I can't make myself leave in case he's not. Why would God do this to me? Why would he give me something worth holding onto if he was just going to take him away from me? I can't understand.

I grab my purse and phone, running outside as much as I can run. When I get into the fresh air, rain falls like tears from the sky, I inhale deep breathes, trying to regulate my heartbeat. I put my hands over my head, clasping my fingers, expanding my ribcage, and hope I don't have this baby weeks early because if Ryan's dead, a part of me just died, too.

In the distance, I see blue lights and know they're coming to tell me my baby has no father. They're coming to make a notification.

Wiping the tears off my neck and face, I pull my bottom lip in between my teeth. I absolutely will not be complete and total mess when they tell me. I will make Ryan proud of how I handle this.

The car comes to a screeching halt in front of the cafe, and I do a double-take as Ryan gets out of the driver's seat. He's dirty, covered in mud, blood, and I have no idea what else, but he's alive.

I run to him, crushing my white dress to the front of his once-white shirt. "You're alive," I run my hands through his hair.

He grabs hold of me tightly, holding me against him. "It wasn't me, Princess. It wasn't me, I'm here."

I can't say anything, I bury my face in his chest, sobbing. Relief flowing through me, but despair for the other person's family.

"I have bad news though, Whit."

Suddenly I look up at him. Now I notice the tension on his face, the utter devastation there – something is wrong. "Who was it?" I whisper because I can't ask the question out loud. My voice won't let me make it any higher, my body can't push the sound out with any more force.

"It was Trevor. The officer in the other car was Trevor."

"But he's off-duty today," I argue, not believing what he's telling me.

"He was approaching from the opposite direction. They hit head on. When I left they were extricating him from the truck. We need to go to the hospital in Birmingham. That's where they'll take him."

"To identify the body?" I whimper, trembling in his arms.

"Princess look at me," he grabs my chin. "He's not dead. He's not good, I won't lie about that, and I don't know what he's facing, but when I left he wasn't dead. Dry those tears up, and let's get your mom. We have a lot of praying to do."

CHAPTER THIRTY-FOUR
RENEGADE

I GRIP Whitney's hand as we drive silently to the hospital. I don't think I've ever had a more somber ride in my life. If this was under a different set of circumstances, I would make a joke about their mom sitting in the back of the police car. Today though, that joke isn't there. She's quietly crying into a napkin, her phone shaking as she texts her husband updates.

"Will he meet us there, Mona?" I finally find my voice, still shocked at how raw it sounds.

She nods, tears spilling down her face. "He's gettin' someone to drive him. I think he's more shook up than he was letting on when I called him. He'll probably be about thirty minutes behind us, because they were out towards the gulf. Knowin' him though, he'll make them speed and pay for the ticket if they get pulled over.

"He's gonna be okay, right?" Whitney asks from beside me.

I'm not sure who she's asking, not sure any of us truly know the answer to the question. It's a hard one. I saw him, saw how he was gasping for breath, how hard it was for him to make his lungs work. The tips of my fingers felt the weakness of his pulse, and try as I might, I can't get rid of the picture I now have in my head. Trevor pale white with blood dotting his face. None of us know the answer.

"I don't know, Princess," I bring her hand up to my lips in a show of affection I normally don't allow her family to see.

We've been closed off when they've been around, almost scared to show them how into one another we are. Today, I think I need the affection more than her. I could purr when she flips her palm over and cups the side of my jaw, rubbing against the growth of stubble. Was it seriously only a few hours ago she was telling me not to shave? It seems a lifetime ago. I feel like I've aged a thousand years since this morning.

"This is where we've got to give it over to God, Whitney," her mom says from the backseat and I get mysteriously angry.

My jaw clenches and I grit my teeth. There's a part of me that wants to ask what God has to do with all of this. If God were the type of person to care, he would have put Brooks in the back of that ambulance. Trevor is a good man, a great friend, and an amazing human being. He served his country with honor, and he's done things asked of him that no other person probably would have done. For him to end up on the side of the road broken the way he did, at one of his favorite spots, is a travesty, and fuck it all if I'm not angry. I want to shout and rage, scream at the injustice of it all. I can't understand why the fuck Brooks walked away from the wreck and Trevor rode away in an ambulance. How does any of that make sense? Trevor wasn't breaking the law, he wasn't running from responsibility. He was enjoying his damn day off.

"I'll try, Mama," she answers softly, but we share a look, and in that moment I know she feels the same way I do.

The silence blankets us again and I do my best to focus on the hand holding mine. My mind zeroes in on the way Whitney's fingers caress my palm. It's a slow glide of her fingernail against my flesh, but it gives me something to think about. It's a center that allows me to block out all the noise I've been hearing since we came upon the wreck.

There's a ringing in my ears and it only gets louder the more I try to drown it out. Her soft touch is the only thing making it go away, the only thing keeping me sane right now. I focus on it instead. The one bright spot of my day – hell, she's my bright spot of every day.

The drive to Birmingham feels like it takes days, but finally I see the exit for the hospital. I won't lie, when they mentioned taking Trevor to the nearest trauma unit, I about lost it. That has serious repercussions. To be airlifted to a trauma center tells me things are bad.

As we pull into the parking structure, all of us gasp at the amount of police cars already parked there. One of the guys from Laurel Springs is directing traffic, and once he sees us, he directs us to a spot close to the elevator on the bottom floor.

As we get out, he jogs over to Mona and takes off his hat. "We're thinking about you, Mrs. Trumbolt. Anything you need, you let us know."

She doesn't answer, but she grabs his hand and holds on tight. Overcome with emotion, she nods as Whitney puts her arm around her mom.

"C'mon, Mama, let's go find out what's going on."

"What floor do we need to go to?" I ask him.

"Eighth, that's where Holden's directed everybody so far."

We make our way to the elevator as fast as Whitney allows us to. She's being a trooper, walking as quickly as she can. I have my arm around her, holding her up as we move closer. Just as we're about to enter the sliding doors, I hear a loud voice.

"Mona! Whitney!"

Mona lets out a wail as she sees her husband. Stanley Trumbolt has always been a larger than life man, but he looks like the world has beat him down today. I don't think in all my years that I've known the family he's ever looked so scared. I'm reminded of the last time I saw him. It was just a few weeks ago when we cleaned Whitney's gutters and did her yard. Damn, was it really only a few weeks? It seems like a lifetime right now. As he reaches Mona, she falls into his arms, finally letting go of the sobs go she's held back this entire time.

Stanley and I lock eyes and judging by the look in his, I know they need a minute. "Y'all come on up when you're ready. I got Whitney."

We quietly enter the elevator and when the doors close, she collapses against me. The fight's gone from her. I feel the wetness against my neck, where she's buried her head.

"I know, Whit, I know," I soothe her, running my hands up and down her back. "Let it out, it's a shock. Let it out before we get up there."

"I don't know if I can put it back in," she breathes heavily, wiping at her eyes as she moves away. "He's always been my baby, ya know? I was ten when he was born, I drug him around like he was my real-life baby doll. Dressed him up and made him do things that most boys would have beat me up for. Damn, Ryan, he's gotta make it through this."

I clear my throat roughly against the way it closes. "I know, and he's going to. We have to believe that."

But I'm not sure if I can let myself just yet.

ONCE WE'RE on the floor, I see a ton of county, city, and state personnel. Other county departments have shown up and most everyone knows who we are, so they make room and point us in the right direction. I can't let go of Whitney's hand as we thread our way through the crowd, everyone motioning us to a waiting area off to the side. When we get there, I see the members of the team, standing around, and Blaze sitting on the couch, her arms folded against her stomach.

"What do we know?" I announce our presence. "Mona and Stanley need a minute before they come up, we'll brief them when they get here."

Holden directs a glance at Blaze. "Layman's terms, just like you did for us."

She takes what looks like a fortifying breath. "Broken leg, sprained wrist, multiple cuts and bruises, concussion, and what they believe is a collapsed lung. He's in surgery right now for the leg and lung."

That's more than I was prepared for. "Son of a bitch. What about Brooks?"

"Treated and released into custody. Already lawyered the fuck up, but he will be held, since we aren't sure of Tank's outcome yet," Holden speaks quietly.

The implication hangs in the air. He might not make it out of this. "Have they given a prognosis?"

Blaze speaks up again. "There's internal bleeding from somewhere, possibly the spleen. The surgeon didn't want to give us false hope."

Whitney lets go of my hand and walks over to the other woman. "I know they call you Blaze, but I also know that's not your real name. Trevor's talked to me about you before. He wouldn't want you sitting here all by yourself. I don't know about you but I need a decaf coffee, since that's all I'm allowed. Why don't you come with me and get away from all this testosterone for a while."

I watch as Blaze looks up at Whitney, surprise written across her face. Hell, we're surprised, none of us knew that Blaze wasn't her real name.

"I'd like that," she smiles. It's small, but it's a smile.

"C'mon, let's go."

Whitney leans in, kissing my cheek. "If there's news, call me."

I watch as they leave, surprised by the turn of events.

"I'll be damned," Holden lets out a whistle from where he stands.

I have to agree. Nothing ever ceases to amaze me.

CHAPTER THIRTY-FIVE

WHITNEY

I WALK beside this girl who I know because of a few conversations with my brother when he's feeling low. As soon as I saw her sitting there, I knew who she was.

"Trevor's told you about me?" She questions as we wait for the elevator.

I nod, grinning as I wrap my arms around myself, rubbing my biceps. Now that we're away from the group of people, I'm cold. "Yeah, he doesn't talk about a lot, and he talks even less about the women he's interested in, but you he's told me about a couple of times. He cares a lot about you."

I don't know if I should break his confidence. What if he doesn't make it out of this alive and she's stuck wondering what he thought of her. Given the fact I haven't been honest with Ryan, maybe I'm not the right person to ask.

"I care a lot about him," she affirms quietly. "It's just like we could never make it work."

"Trevor's stubborn."

She smiles. "So am I. Neither one of us wanted to be the person to give. Both of us wanted to take."

"He hasn't told me what happened with the two of you," I caution her, because I don't want her to feel like I know and inadvertently tell me something she wouldn't normally. "I just know he regrets it."

"I regret it, too," she steps onto the elevator and we pick the lobby. "You always think you have so much time. I mean the last few times we've seen each other, we've flirted and he's texted me, but I never wanted to give in. I never wanted to admit I was the one willing to give in," she kicks the ground with her black boot. "He wants me to give up my job," she says, surprising the hell out of me.

"He what?"

She shoots me a look with a sarcastic smile. "Yeah. The cop wants me to give up my job."

There's got to be a reason behind this, but I don't want to be nosey. She's trusted me enough to come this far.

The elevator comes to the lobby floor and we exit, walking to the coffee shop. As we stand, waiting to place our orders, I take a good look at her. It's her hair that bestowed her nickname; the red is blazing and tattoos cover her arms. On some people they could be trashy, but on her, they belong. She's small – probably five-three to my five-seven. She looks young, but if I were to hazard a guess, she's probably the same age as Trevor and Ryan. When she glances back at me, I'm struck by her green eyes. I can see why my brother has been a goner for this girl.

"Want to sit over here?" I ask after I order. "We can drink our coffee and then head back up."

"Sounds good."

We sit down and there's another silence. It's not uncomfortable, but I get the feeling both of us are trying to be nice to one another and not delve too deep. I desperately want to know why he wanted her to quit her job, but I won't ask.

"Everybody around town seems to know your story," she starts as she takes a drink of her coffee. "I guess it's only fair I give you mine. I can't believe Trevor and I have been able to keep it a secret."

Neither have I, but I don't say the words out loud. "You tell me whatever you want to tell me. Don't think you owe me anything because I'm the topic of the town gossip mill right now."

"A year ago I was on a call. The person we were helping was having a mental episode. He pulled a gun and held it to my head. Trevor responded to the scene that day," she starts mixing her coffee together before taking another drink. "At that point, we'd been together a few months, ya know just kinda messing around. We'd slept together, but there hadn't been any promises or talk of us being exclusive."

I put a hand on my stomach and rub gently. "I know exactly what you mean."

"Long story short, I got out of the situation, obviously, but Trevor told me if I wanted to be with him, I'd need to get another job. He couldn't stand that I was in danger," she sighs. "I think it reminded him of Iraq and something that happened over there, but he'd never talk about it."

Trevor had definitely come back a different person, as had a lot of the people who went over there with him, but he flat-out refused to talk about it.

"So that's it? The two of you stopped seeing each other?"

Her cheeks heat and turn pink. "We tried, but there's like this invisible rope that constantly pulls at us, bringing us together. Every time though, he asks me to quit, but I love what I do," she shrugs. "I was born to do this."

"Just like he was born to do what he does."

"Exactly," she nods. "But now with this? How do I live with myself if something happens to him and I was too stubborn to spend what could have been the most amazing year of my life with him?"

I have no answers, so I just reach over and grab her hand. If Trevor doesn't pull through this we'll all have regrets, and I can only hope that's not all we're left with in the end.

More than anything, I just want to hug my brother and tell him I love him again. Two small acts in everyday life that mean everything when someone's life hangs in the balance.

CHAPTER THIRTY-SIX
WHITNEY

THERE ARE moments in life you don't expect. I've experienced quite a few in my life. Sleeping with Ryan, finding out that I'm pregnant, thinking Ryan was the officer killed only to find out it was Trevor and he was badly hurt. Most of the time you're unprepared for the emotions and the repercussions these moments bring to you. That's where I am right now. Sitting beside Ryan in the surgical waiting room, holding my breath to see what they say about my brother.

In the corner sits my parents. Married almost forty years, and they've never had to sit at the hospital for either of us, or themselves before. In the opposite corner, Blaze sits next to her partner but both of them have vacant eyes as they stare unseeingly at the room of gathered people. Me? I sit here next to Ryan, my heart bursting.

In the middle of this impossible situation, whether it be appropriate or not, I need to tell him how much he means to me. For once, I have to let go of the fear, and let the truth fly. If there's ever been a time in my life to stop letting fear rule my life, it's now.

"Can we go for a walk?" I ask Ryan quietly.

I want to get up from the uncomfortable chairs, they're killing my back and hip, but at the same time, I also want to speak to him privately. What I have to say is emotional for me, and I don't necessarily want or need an audience.

"Sure," he stands up from the chair, reaching for my hand. I barely listen as he tells a few people we're leaving but will be back.

Everyone watches with sad eyes as we leave. Almost like they can tell I'm at the end of my rope and can't take much more.

We're quiet as we walk along the corridor. In this part of the hospital, it's a weird type of silence. Most of the people in these rooms are waiting to hear about the fate of a loved one. How they live the rest of their lives hangs in the balance of the outcome of the surgery going on upstairs. This is the club nobody wants to be a part of, and when you are, you're devastated.

Needing to ground myself, I grab Ryan's hand, curling my fingers around his. His middle finger rubs my ring finger, where a wedding band would be if I would let it.

"Where do you want to go?" he finally asks as we make our way down the maze of hallways.

"The Chapel," I answer without hesitation. No matter how angry I am with the way things have played out today, something about being in a place of worship gives me peace.

"He's gonna be okay, ya know," Ryan assures me as we walk.

"He's stubborn," I agree.

"The most stubborn person I've ever met besides you."

The smile he gives me as I shoot him a side-eye is brilliant.

"You know I'm right," he squeezes my hand. "You're the only other person I'm reluctant to go head-to-head with besides him and the two of you together? Jesus...."

I laugh, because it's either that or cry. "He's always been my biggest supporter," I admit, feeling the tears pool again.

When we get to the Chapel, he pushes the door open slowly. We enter and I'm glad we're alone. This time, I take control of our direction and pull him to a pew in the back.

Together we have a seat. "We gonna pray for Tank's salvation?" He quirks a brow at me. "I'm pretty sure God's gonna have to forgive him for as much as he'd have to forgive me."

"No," I whisper. "The only reason I wanted to come here was so you and I could be alone. I wanted to say what I needed to without the prying eyes of our friends and family."

I can tell by the way he curls his body towards mine, I have his full attention.

"When people came in The Café saying a police officer had been killed, I was scared to death that it was you."

"Princess," he interrupts. "I'm not going anywhere. You know this."

I reach up, putting my fingertip over his lips. "No, Ryan. Life isn't guaranteed, I think we all learned that today."

He starts to speak, but I stop him.

"Let me finish," I put my hands around his cheeks, forcing his eyes to meet mine. They're a pool of emotion, darker today than normal, and I can't read everything there, but I can sense the underlying turmoil all of us are living with today. I grasp his cheeks in my palms, making sure our eyes meet before I speak again.

"Today was the scariest day of my life even before I knew it was Trevor in the wreck. As soon as people started coming in saying a police officer was dead, I thought it was you. And ya know..." I stop to compose myself, to take a breath and wet my dry lips. "I freaked out. But I didn't freak out the most because the father of my child might very well be dead. I freaked out more than anything because I thought you died..." I have to stop and duck my head, push the tears back, clear my throat, and march on. This time my voice is hoarse as I speak. "I thought you died without me ever telling you I love you."

He inhales deeply and clamps his mouth shut. I can see the rigidity of his body, and I know it's not because he's rejecting me and my feelings. It's because he's feeling too much and trying not to lose his shit.

"I do, I love you more than I thought I could love anyone," I speak again, this time tears pouring down my face and my voice strong. "My life was fine, I was set to spend it alone, and have a hookup once in a while. You blew the lid off my life Renegade. *Pew Pew*."

We laugh hysterically as we remember the night I was drunk and made the joke. I think we're both laughing and crying as he leans his forehead into mine, cupping my cheeks the same way that I'm cupping his.

"I love you, too," he brushes his lips across my forehead.

I sob harder. "I know. It's in every touch, every smile, every laugh, every word you speak to me. You show me every day, and I've held back from you because of my own fear," I shake my head. "That fear won't hold me back any more."

He pushes my hair back from my face. "I won't let you down."

"You've never let me down, I have trusted you with every part of me, and it's time I start showing that I do."

We're wrapped up in our own thoughts for what feels like hours. Each whispering words to one another, placing soft kisses on each other's cheeks and foreheads. We're in our own little world when someone pushes open the door to the chapel.

We don't jump apart like I would have done in the past. Instead, I let whoever it is see me cling to him, I allow them to see how I feel about the man in my life.

It's Holden and the look on his face is one of relief. "He's out of surgery and he's stable. Now we wait for him to wake up."

We turn back and smile at each other. Trevor made it through and we're no longer hiding our feelings. What could have been the worst day of our lives hasn't turned out nearly as bad as it could have been.

CHAPTER THIRTY-SEVEN

WHITNEY

THE HOSPITAL IS quiet this morning as I carry the food and my purse through the hallways before I hit the elevator. Ryan had barely stirred this morning when I left the bed, which says a lot about how tired he is. We've all been stressed about Trevor, but yesterday they'd downgraded him and moved him to a private room on a regular floor. To say we're all relieved is an understatement.

If you ask everyone in my family, I can almost guarantee that we all slept better last night than we have since the wreck. I struggle with believing it's only been a few days.

The elevator dings and I hop on, not surprised it's empty. Not many people want to spend their Thanksgiving morning in a hospital, but it's tradition for Trevor and I have to have breakfast before we go over to mom and dad's for a late lunch/early dinner. I can't bring myself to stop the tradition just because he's in the hospital. If anything, it makes me want to keep it going.

When the doors open on the appropriate floor, I step off, smiling at the staff. They've come to know me in the past few days. I hate they have to spend their holiday here, but I'm very thankful for it.

"I brought y'all some donuts and muffins. I know it's not much," I put the bakery box down on the nurses station counter. "But it was the easiest thing I could think of to say thank you for taking care of Trevor."

They're appreciative and tell me so before I make my way down to where Trevor's been moved. The door's closed, so I knock softly.

"C'mon in."

It's the most amazing thing to hear his voice. I never knew how much I love to hear him talk until I wasn't sure if I'd ever hear it again. "Happy Thanksgiving," I grin as I walk into the room.

I'm surprised not to see Blaze, but I don't say anything.

"She went home for the morning," he answers, when he sees me looking over at the cot she's been sleeping on. "I told her I hoped you'd be here."

I lift up the bag I have in my hand. "We haven't missed a Thanksgiving morning unless you were overseas since you were sixteen," I grab his table and start setting up the pancakes and bacon I brought. "You can have this, right?"

"Yeah, they're about to kill me with the liquid shit they had me on," he sits further up in the bed, raising his leg. "I feel like I've lost twenty pounds."

He looks it too. That's one thing I can't get over, he looks sick and I can't stand to see it. I keep reminding myself he's okay, he'll be fine. It's going to be a bit of a tough climb back, but overall, Trevor will be okay.

"We'll fatten you back up in no time, especially with the way I'm eating now."

His bruised face looks over at me. "How are you feeling? Blaze told me you'd had some contractions?"

"It's okay, it's just the shock of everything. Nothing for anyone to worry about, I promise," I take a bite of my own pancake, moaning when the syrup explodes against my tongue. Lately I love pancakes.

"I wish I enjoyed food as much as you do right now," he laughs.

"Ryan says the same thing sometimes."

We're quiet for a few minutes and I'm content to sit with him, to enjoy his company. "Has everybody been to visit you?"

"Yeah," he takes a drink of his orange juice. "The guys were here yesterday and some other friends of ours showed up the day before. I'm just ready to get home, get started on PT, and put this behind me."

I reach over and grab his hand. "We all are, but make sure you take care of you, Trev. What you went through was pretty traumatic."

He swallows so hard I see his Adam's apple move. "I'm more worried about what Ryan and Blaze saw, to be honest. I hardly remember any of it. I do remember coming to, I guess in the ER, because I was trying to pull the tube in my chest out and they had to hold me down. Other than that, it's a haze of pain and drugs."

I set my fork down, my appetite dying a little. "It was hard to watch, Trevor. Seeing you how you were right after? It was very difficult. Blaze and Ryan saved your life, but neither one of them talk about it. I figure at some point both of them will, but we need to let them do it in their own time."

"I'm just glad I get to see my niece be born," he grins, reaching over to grab my hand.

I grab his tightly. "You have no idea how scared I was you wouldn't make it to her due date. I don't want her to grow up without you Trev, please take care of yourself."

In my head I add, *We all need you so much. You're the heart of this family. Please don't ever let us lose you.*

"Thanks for bringing me breakfast."

I do my best to smile at him, even though tears swim in my eyes. "Can't break tradition. Nothing could keep me away."

And that's the truth. The only thing that's ever kept me away was an ocean, and even then if I could have, I would have swum it just to see him on Thanksgiving morning.

Renegade

My heartbeat returns to a normal rhythm when I hear Whitney's SUV pull into the driveway. I have this irrational fear now that she's going to wreck and end up in the same hospital as Tank. I know from my time in the military I'll get over it. It's a form of PTSD, more than likely originating from witnessing Tank's wreck.

God I miss the asshole. I'm riding with Ace now that Tank's been hurt, and I realize now how much I enjoyed our time together. The door opens and I go to meet Whitney in the kitchen.

"Hey, Mama," I greet her, letting her fall into my arms. She still looks exhausted, even though I know she got more rest last night than she's been getting. "You need to take a nap?"

"Maybe," she answers, curling into me. "I hate seeing him in that hospital bed, even if he does look better and they're talking about letting him go home soon. It makes my heart hurt."

"Mine too," I cup her cheeks, and push her chin up so I can look into her pretty eyes. "How are you feeling today?"

"I've had some contractions," she bites her bottom lip as she tells me. "But as the doctor said yesterday, this whole situation has been stressful and I'm measuring early anyway. I'm ready for her to come any time. It doesn't matter if it's early or not. She's the perfect size. She could come tomorrow and I'd be happy."

That's my girl, always a fighter, always ready for whatever else she may have to take on. "I love you, Princess," I lean down, brushing my lips against hers. "Now let's go lie down before you fall down."

"I love you, too," the way she says it never gets old, and I doubt it ever will. I waited so long to hear those damn words that I want to put them in my pocket every time she lets them slip past her lips. "Don't let me sleep too late, we still have to go to my parents' house for Thanksgiving."

It's on the tip of my tongue to tell her not to worry about that. Her parents are probably just as tired, if not more so, than the rest of us, but then I realize maybe she needs to be with them. Maybe that's how she finds her comfort, with her parents, and who am I to hold that back from her.

We enter the bedroom, and she takes off her confining clothes, slipping naked in between the sheets. Lately that's the way she loves to sleep, foregoing clothing because it's too tight on her skin. "Lie down with me and hold me."

It's a request I can't say no to. I get naked too, lying down next to her, curling my body around hers, and holding her tightly in my shield of protection. "How was he?"

"Tired and in a little bit of pain, but today he's got some of his color back and a little bit of the humor I love," she's quiet for a minute. "Blaze came in right as I was leaving."

"Those two have a very long road ahead of them if they want to make their relationship work," I move the hair out of her face as I nuzzle against her skin.

"We did, and look where we are now," her sleepy voice whispers.

As she drifts off I hear her voice in my head. Look where we are now.

CHAPTER THIRTY-EIGHT

WHITNEY

TODAY HAS BEEN A SHIT DAY. I couldn't get into my favorite sandals because my feet have swollen so much and even though it's damn December, it's still hot in Alabama. The shirt I wanted to wear didn't cover my stomach, and I have the worst craving I've ever had for sweet tea.

I haven't even had a sweet tea since I found out I was pregnant, but today, my mouth waters as I think about drinking one.

Checking the clock on my SUV, I see I have thirty minutes before I have to meet my next appointment. If I swing into the Sonic drive-thru, I should still make it in plenty of time. As I pull into their parking lot, I go around the building to take my place in line, instead of blocking traffic by pulling sideways into the drive-thru. That's a pet peeve of mine, and I always make sure not to do it.

I text the bride I'm meeting, letting her know I'll be there in a few minutes, and then watch as an older gentleman in a Range Rover pulls into the drive, blocking traffic just like I chose not to do. He gives me a wave, motioning for me to let him in line in front of me.

Oh hell no. I put my finger up and shake it 'no' at him.

"No sir, you will not be getting in line in front of me, because you didn't follow proper protocol," I say to myself. "Plus I want this sweet tea like I want a kiss from my man, and there's no way you're going to delay it for me."

As the cars move up, I go to move up and he honks at me. I honk right back, giving him a wave and a pretty smile. I roll down the window. "Sorry, but I'm pregnant, and I need this sweet tea way more than whatever it is you think you need."

I roll the window up as he flips me off and guns his SUV, driving around the building. I let out the breath I'm holding, glad I stood up for myself. The last few weeks have been stressful and I'll be damned if I let someone walk all over me.

Ordering my drink, I wait in line, seeing the man is at least four cars behind me. If he had followed what everyone else did, he would have been directly behind me and not just now placing his own order. When they bring me out my white Styrofoam cup, I grip it with both hands and drink it down. Nothing in the world has ever tasted as good as that sugary drink.

Fifteen minutes later, I know I've done a bad thing when I feel Stella practicing her gymnastics routine in my stomach. Laughing, I reach over and grab my cell phone, taking a video for Ryan.

When I send it to him, I do it with a huge smile on my face.

"DO YOU THINK THIS WILL WORK?" Ryan asks as he holds up a shower curtain to me.

We accidentally broke the one in the bathroom the other night, and while we're getting a few other things, I reminded him we need a new one. I wrinkle my nose as he holds up a lavender one.

"I liked the gray one a lot better," I admit, putting my hand on my stomach as I feel Stella kick. Since my sweet tea this afternoon, she's been crazy.

"I can go grab that one, I know you've had a rough day."

He's such an amazing man. "Please do, I don't like the purple and it won't go with anything else in there."

"Be right back," he kisses me on the cheek as I look for a lane to start checking out.

When I find one that doesn't have very many people in it, I go to the end of the cart and start putting our stuff on the conveyor belt. There's a throat clearing in front of me, and I look up to face someone I haven't seen in a very long time. Who would have thought I'd see my ex-husband in the checkout lane at Target?

"Whitney," Stephen nods towards me.

Manners and politeness that have been instilled in me since I was a little girl wins out as I nod back at him. "Stephen."

We're quiet as we look at one another, neither one of us sure what to say.

"I see you're doing well, finally saved up enough money to get that in vitro," he indicates my stomach.

For a second I think about minimizing my life to him, but then I realize that's what I did the entire time we were married. Why should I hide my feelings to make someone who didn't give a shit about me feel better? "Actually, I'm very happy. Happier than I've ever been in my life."

He gives me a bemused grin. "You should be. Spending that much money to make a dream come true? I mean, you'd have to be really crazy to want to make yourself that happy."

"Got it," Ryan puts the shower curtain down on the conveyor belt, and I turn to face him. He gazes over my shoulder and I can tell the minute he recognizes Stephen. Turning me around, he steps up behind me, putting his arms around my waist, hands caressing my stomach.

"Stephen thinks I'm crazy for spending all the money I did on the fertility treatments for this baby," I lean my head back at Ryan, kissing him softly when he dips his head to mine.

A smile spreads across his face. "Right? That bottle of wine you drank and the two beers I drank were so damn expensive."

I giggle, biting my lip. "They sure were."

It looks like Stephen's a little confused, and before I can clarify, I hear Ryan speaking. "In case you missed it dickhead, all we did was make passionate love. Looks like you were the problem all along, and I managed to do the one thing you couldn't do. My swimmers are fucking perfect, as is our daughter. Her mom though," he leans down, kissing my neck. "Most amazing woman I've ever met. Thanks for fuckin' up."

Stick that up your pipe and smoke it.

"Since I don't see a ring on your finger, I have to assume you'll be a single mom. Such a statistic."

"Her fingers are swollen. You know that happens when you get knocked up? Or maybe you don't know. Either way. We're very happy and we're very much together," Ryan continues, grasping our fingers together. "Any more questions?"

He's speechless, face burning red. He doesn't say another word to us. He pays for his purchases and walks out like the hounds of hell are nipping at his heels.

I can't help it, I laugh hysterically as Ryan joins in. It's one of the best feelings I've ever had. Some of that confidence I never thought I would get back – I got it back in spades tonight.

CHAPTER THIRTY-NINE
RENEGADE

"YOU'RE NOT LOOKING SO hot this morning, Princess."

Yesterday she was like the energizer bunny, cleaning the house like the devil himself was nipping at her heels. Today, it looks like she almost can't get out of bed.

"I think I overdid it," she admits as she tries to sit up. "I'm sick to my stomach, and I haven't been sick to my stomach in months."

"You want me to call into work? You think I need to take you to get checked out?"

It's so hard to know with her, hard to gauge how she feels and what she's thinking. For so long, Whitney's done things her way, but over the course of the last few days she's started to hand some things over. Addison's taking care of the business while Whitney takes a short maternity leave, and her mom is organizing the care for Trevor.

Whitney had wanted to do all of those things because that's what she's always done, but judging by the way she looks right now, it's gonna be a miracle if she can get out of bed today. "Babe, you're kinda scaring me."

"Yeah, I think you do need to call into work," she rests her hand on her stomach as she blows out a breath. "I'm having contractions just like I've been having since Trevor's wreck, but today they feel different."

"Should we start timing them?"

"What do you think?" She asks, her face pained.

"You're older and wiser, babe."

She shoots me the meanest, most hostile look I think I've ever seen her give anyone.

"Ryan," she breathes. "Now isn't the time for that shit."

"Did you just have a contraction?" I ask because she's gone white as a toga sheet.

"Yes, they're coming quicker."

Making the decision for us, I walk over to the bed and move the covers back. "C'mon, we're going to the doctor. Lean on me if you have to, but I'm not letting you have our baby at home. I don't know that I'm strong enough to help you deliver it. I don't wanna see you in that much pain without at least drugs for me."

She leans up, kissing me as she grabs my ear with her fingers.

"Fucking ouch, woman."

"Don't joke about this, I'm scared to death."

Looking at her, I can see she's telling me the truth and I feel bad. "Don't be, Princess. We're in this together. God willing and if the creeks don't rise, hopefully tonight we'll have Stella in our arms."

At least that's the prayer I shoot up because I don't know if either one of us could take a longer than twelve-hour labor.

Whitney

God I'm not going to make it through this. People who told me childbirth wasn't that big of a deal fucking lied. They lied like crazy.

"You're doing great, babe," Ryan offers me encouragement from where he sits beside my head.

Pain hits me again. "Tell me a lie, please tell me a beautiful lie. I don't care when it's from, just help me escape."

He closes his eyes for a minute, and I wonder if he's going to do what I asked him to. "We're on a beach in Bora Bora, it's nighttime and we're walking there, holding hands as the waves lap at our feet."

"Are we by ourselves?"

"Totally by ourselves. Your mom and dad have taken Stella back to our hotel, and we're having some adult time," he continues.

There aren't any nurses in here right now, and I wonder where this is going to go.

"Have you ever fucked on the beach Whitney?"

My breathing calms as the contraction dies down. I'm able to be with him in the scene he's setting. "No," I grab hold of his hand, threading our fingers together. "But I would with you, I'd do anything with you."

"Then that's what we're doing. It's nice and slow, passionate, the way you like it. I'm holding you in my arms and whispering all those things you like to hear me say."

I can hear it, can hear him tell me he loves me, that everything will be okay, that I'm the only person he's ever been able to give his heart to. All the little things Ryan says when I'm in his arms and there's nothing else between us.

"You okay?" he bends down, kissing me on the forehead.

"Thanks for taking my mind off the pain."

"I'll always take you out of any situation that's too much for you. Always remember that."

He leans in, letting me wrap my arms around his neck. We're breaking apart as there is a soft knock at the door before it opens. They wait respectfully at the curtain until Ryan gets up and walks over.

"Oh man, it's so good to see you."

I wonder who he's talking to, and as he pulls the curtain back, enveloping the person in a huge hug. I see it's Trevor. On crutches and obviously hurting but he made it. The one person I'd wanted to be here that I wasn't sure would be. Blaze is at his side, helping as he slowly moves into the room.

"Trev, you've been out of the hospital for a short time, you didn't have to come back," I reach out to touch him as he maneuvers his way over.

Blaze moves a seat closer so he can sit on it and then offers me a smile before she moves to the couch in the room. "I wouldn't miss this for the world. I know mom and dad said to let them know when it gets closer to time, but I've never let you go through something on your own before. Just like you didn't let me spend Thanksgiving by myself," he reaches over and grabs my hand.

"I love you, Trev."

"I love you too, Sis, but fair warning, if they open up your hoo ha and I even get a glimpse, I'm out. Blaze might have to carry me out at that point, but I am totally out if it comes to that."

I laugh loudly, loving the fact he's here. "Completely understood. I'm so glad you're here. For a while there, I wasn't sure whether you would get to see this or not."

He's quiet for a few minutes, his eyes un-focusing before he clears his throat. "I wasn't sure I would either, but now that I am, nothing's going to tear me away."

"So, I think Alabama is playing. Should I turn it on?" Ryan asks, breaking the silence.

It's agreed, and just like that, I'm taken back to my birthday weekend.

"FUCK THIS IS PAINFUL," I yell as I hold my legs back, pushing for the doctor.

"C'mon Whitney, you got this," Trevor encourages from where he sits to my side, as far away from my lower half as he can get. Blaze left a little while ago to give us some time as a family, and I'm pretty sure my screaming and yelling is keeping my parents as far away as possible.

"I don't have it," I tell him. I'm losing my nerve and my energy.

"You're close, babe," Ryan tells me. "I love you so much and I know you've got this, don't you want to meet Stella?"

I do, but God the pain and I'm so exhausted. I don't know how to explain it to them. "I do," I pant, holding my mouth open for more ice chips.

"With the next contraction, I want you to push, Whitney. Push against the contraction and we'll get this baby out," the doctor says from where she sits.

I'm still not sure I can do it, but I hear the clapping in the fourth quarter of the Alabama game start. Trevor starts clapping and I want to tell him to shut the fuck up, but something happens. I can feel my adrenaline start to race; it's almost like I'm back at that game. It's giving me energy I didn't have before.

I can feel the next contraction coming as the crowd starts to sing along to "Dixieland Delight" and I scream as I push. My eyes meet Ryan's and I can feel him giving me his strength, I can feel him encouraging me. Looking into those brown depths, I know if he could take this job and do it for me he would – that's the thing that gives me the last bit of courage and strength I need.

Just as the crowd says "and Tennessee too," Stella makes her screaming entrance into the world.

"She would," Ryan laughs as he leans in, giving me a kiss. "She would come into the world right as they said Tennessee, she loved that game."

Tears stream down my face and I can't hold them back anymore. "Give her to me," I beg them as I watch the medical staff clean her off before they lay her on my stomach.

Through blurry eyes, I count ten fingers, ten toes, I see a dark helmet of hair, thanks to her daddy, and only then do I let myself lean back and relax. She's screaming, upset that she's had to leave her comfort, but she's here and she's perfect.

"You did it, Mama," Ryan mumbles in my ear, reaching out to touch her face. "She's gorgeous," he kisses my temple and I can tell by the tone of his voice, he's as tired as I am.

"No, we did it," I close my eyes, letting the moment wash over me, letting the emotions seep out of me. When I've had my cry and I'm cradling my daughter, I look over at my brother.

The ten years younger brother, who wasn't planned, and has always been my protector. "Come meet your niece, Trevor. I want her to know what a badass uncle she has to go along with her badass dad."

Trevor stands with difficulty, but walks over on his own. Leaning down, he gives me a kiss on the cheek.

"Ain't nobody more badass than her mom, and I think we'll all agree to that."

The tears that I thought I was holding back? They're there again and this time I'm not sure they're gonna stop.

EPILOGUE
WHITNEY

"SHOULD we put Santa gifts out for her?" I whisper as I reach over to lie Stella down in her crib.

Ryan gives me a look, motioning us out of the nursery. When we close the door partway and walk down the hallway, he turns to me. "Whit, she's ten days old. She's not going to even wonder when she gets older if we did anything for her first Christmas."

"Logically I know that, but what if when she's older, she asks for pictures?"

"Then she'll have them of all of us with her at her grandparents' opening gifts. Babe, don't overthink this. Let's just go to the living room, make sure everything is turned off, and sleep while she does. You know as well as I do she'll be up in a few hours and we'll be dragging ass tomorrow."

He's right. We're still trying to get on a schedule and it's been harder than I imagined it would be. "Sounds like a great plan to me."

I almost don't want to go any further down the hall than our bedroom. There's a part of me that wants to ask Ryan to make sure everything is shut down and put away, but I know that's unfair to him. He goes back to work in a couple of days, and we definitely need to be on some sort of routine before he does. I don't want him tired, out there trying to take care of the public.

My foot hits the living room carpet and I glance at our tree. There's a table sitting in front of it that wasn't there earlier. "What's that?" I give Ryan a look.

"Not sure," he shrugs. "Why don't you go check it out?"

I shoot a look over my shoulder as I walk over to the small table. On it is a box that says "open me". I do as it asks, seeing a piece of paper inside the box that instructs me to "turn around".

I do and immediately I gasp and my hand covers my mouth. Ryan is there, on one knee with a ring in his hand, extended towards me. I feel the emotion, the tears already at the surface. There is zero chance of me keeping my shit together.

"I don't have anything earth-shattering to say to you, babe. Nothing I haven't already showed you with how I treat you, and nothing that can mean more than me telling you I love you," he starts, before he takes a breath. "I just wanna spend the rest of my life sleeping next to you, sharing truths and lies, and hearing you laugh so hard you snort."

The laugh I let loose now is a watery one, and I'm overcome with emotion for this amazingly perfect man that chose me.

"It's not gonna matter when I'm forty-five and you're thirty-five?"

He grabs my hands, kissing the back of both of them before he looks at me, his eyes as dark as I've ever seen them. "I'm not going to give a fuck when you're one hundred and five, and I'm ninety-five. It will never matter to me."

I believe him with everything I have. Somewhere in the middle of this ordinary life we've been sharing, our fairytale started. It wasn't with a glass slipper, or some extremely monumental event in our lives.

"Yes, I'll marry you."

He leaps off the floor and folds me in his arms. Those arms are the strongest I've ever felt, my favorite place to be. As he slips the ring onto my finger. I realize our happily ever after started with too much wine and a drunken *pew pew*.

TANK - BOOK II

BLURB

Blurb:

Life isn't promised, love isn't easy, and relationships aren't always clean, but everyone has their soulmate who is willing to forgive when it would be better to forget.

Trevor "Tank" Trumbolt

I never thought in the blink of an eye my life could change, but it did. Cresting a hill driving to my favorite fishing spot, I was hit head-on by a teenager with no regard for anyone's life but his own.

The recovery process has been hard, painful, and damn near beating me down.

The bright spot? Blaze.

Surviving the wreck has given me a second chance to make a life with her. Not knowing if I'll ever be able to rejoin the Moonshine Task Force again has brought my world into focus. It's made me realize what's important.

Blaze. Stella. My brothers. My sister.

The ego that ran Blaze away before isn't here any longer. What's left is a man who's holding his heart in his hands and a burning hope that once I'm healed she'll still be around.

Daphne "Blaze" Coleman

There's only been one person in the world who's accepted me for who I am - from the fiery red of my hair and vibrant tattoos covering parts of my body to the smartness of my mouth and my desire to be matched in the bedroom.

That man is Trevor Trumbolt. When he asked me to give up my job as an EMT because he saw the dangers I face one scary afternoon, it spelled the end for us.

Now that he's been injured, he needs my help and my love. I failed once before when someone close needed me. I won't make that mistake again. For Trevor, I'll give it all freely, but in the end I'm gonna need him to understand one thing about relationships - the give and take, love and sadness, pleasure and pain is a two-way street. He's either in this with me or he's not, but at the end of the day, I won't let him boss me around.

If there's anything that can handle the steel of a tank – it's the heat of a blaze.

CHAPTER ONE

Blaze

"DISPATCH, this is thirty-two, thirty-two show us en route to the call for the vehicle collision at the bottoms," I notify our intent to respond as my partner Logan and I make our way to the call that came over the radio moments before. We're not far away, five minutes on the curvy backroads. I hang on as Logan hits a pothole that's gotten worse after the brutally hot summer we had.

"Damn county needs to fix these roads," I gripe as I brace my hand above my head to keep from hitting the roof of the ambulance.

The radio cackles as dispatch comes through with more information about the scene we're headed toward. "Be advised we're hearing now it's an officer who's been involved in the collision. They've requested the fire department bring in the jaws of life."

Thank God, Trevor isn't working today. He texted me earlier telling me he was going fishing, so the fear I feel isn't as bad as it would be if I were wondering where he is. Going over the list of the guys I know in my head, I hope like hell it's not Ryan because he and Trevor's sister are having a baby. Whatever the officer is facing, it'll be a tough road if they're trying to raise a newborn while recovering. I pull my phone out of my pocket, firing off a quick text to Trevor, letting him know about the accident. Depending on how deep he's gone into the woods will determine if he can hear the emergency vehicles responding or not. We haven't texted in a while, but it still feels right to give him a heads up.

B: Hey, there's been a bad accident at the bottoms. Best to

stay where you are instead of trying to come out. I'll text you and let you know when it's been cleaned up. Maybe we can go have dinner?

That last part is added as almost an afterthought. We left things weird last time we talked, and I haven't felt comfortable answering the messages he's left me in the past few months. Immature of me, I know, but when he asked me to give up my job, it pissed me off. I have to keep reminding myself he doesn't know the specifics of my past and why my job is so important to me. Hardly anyone does. Trevor questioning my chosen profession pissed off an elemental part of my personality that he wasn't even aware existed, and I need to stop punishing him until I can tell him the whole story.

"The bottoms are a damn bad place to wreck," Logan sighs as he navigates the sharp turns and blind spots of the Montgomery County roads that surround Laurel Springs. We're both natives who've lived here our entire lives, and we respect the fact that sometimes these asphalt snakes bite.

"It's always been an accident waiting to happen; no one pays attention to what they're doing. That one curve has such a blind spot, even if you are paying attention, you can't control what the person coming from the other direction is doing. One little turn of a wheel, one second you take your eyes off the road, and you're done. There's no room for mistakes there, no matter how small. Maybe this will make the county pay to have it fixed."

Every time we respond to a wreck at what's becoming something of a landmark around the county, it's my hope they realize how dangerous it is. But three fatals in the past three years, maybe a fourth today, and they still haven't done shit about it. My adrenaline ramps up as I see blue lights flashing in the distance. I'm checking the number on the patrol car, but this is one I don't recognize.

There are two trucks sitting on opposite sides of the road from one another, facing opposite directions – neither one baring the markings of either the city or county police department. "I thought they said it was an officer?" Already I've got a sinking feeling in the pit of my stomach. The premonition you have when you're about to get bad news. No one can ever put their finger on how they know, why they get it, or even what it's trying to tell you. Bottom line is it's bad.

"Me too." Logan grabs his go bag as I grab mine, and we get out of the ambulance just as the fire truck comes to a stop beside us. It's in our best interest to let the fire guys do what they need to do in order to save the person in the wreckage. As soon as we're given the okay, we'll move in.

Taking in the scene before me, I recognize a member of the Moonshine Task Force. Ace is something of an adrenaline junkie, and we've bonded over the fact that both of us have jumped out of planes willingly in our lifetimes. I jog over to him, my bag bouncing against my leg. "I thought it was an officer."

The words barely make it past my throat. The feeling I had earlier is coming back with a vengeance, making me dizzy and my ears start to ring.

His gaze refuses to meet mine as his eyes dart back and forth, focusing on any point other than my face. Finally he sighs. "It is," he nods to the truck on the other side of the road. "Tank," his voice is clipped, like he can't bear to say more words than he has to. That alone indicates how much he's affected by seeing the smoking wreckage. "He was off today."

There's a ringing in my ears as I hear his name. The fear makes me drop to my knees in the middle of the road. As I make contact with the asphalt, the thud of my bones is loud, but nothing like the pounding of the blood through my veins. My heart is scary fast as I try to inhale a full breath of air. If anyone knows what injuries someone could have, it's me. Now I'm more scared than I've ever been in my life.

Tears prick the backs of my eyes, and I do my best to keep my shit together. There's no way that's Trevor in there, no way he was enjoying a day off and he's ended up in this mess. Trevor can't be in the mangled carnage that was once a truck, he surely can't be alive if he is. I watch as Ryan shimmies his way out from under the truck. I'm hoping maybe he'll tell me everybody's wrong and it's not Trevor. Maybe someone else was driving his truck. Which I know is bullshit, because the only other person who's ever driven that vehicle is me. My ears ring louder, my vision tunnels, and I shake my head. Both against the thought I have that I might black out and the fact that the man I love is possibly injured badly. Even after all these months of no communication with one another, the love I feel for him never went away. That itself tells me I should have been making more of an effort.

Our eyes meet, and I know by the white pallor of his skin, it's true. There's no way Ryan would look like death if it wasn't his best friend.

"It's Trevor?" My voice is weak, my hands shaking as I press them against the pavement. Little rocks dig into my palms, but the pain is a reminder that I'm still here, that I can help him. If I can pick myself up off the road. I try, but my legs give out from under me, and I fall again.

Ace comes over, grabbing me by the arm, lifting me up, holding me while I try to center myself. It's a struggle to find my balance when every memory Trevor and I have ever shared is flowing through my mind like a highlight reel of a college football game.

His full lips smiling at me, moving in for the kisses I always wanted to give him. His strong arms holding me when I tried to pull away. Relaxing in hot water, while I washed his hair and he told me his dreams. The way only he can make me ache and scream.

What the fuck were we thinking to let it all go?

That we had all the time in the world, like anyone else thinks.

"It's Trevor," he nods, his voice barely loud enough for me to hear it, devastation written all over his face. It's hard for me to look at him, because I think what I'm seeing is reflected right back. "Get our boy safely to the hospital and give him a fighting chance. I have to go notify his family."

Immediately I worry about his sister, Whitney, who is heavily pregnant. They're close, and as far as I know, she's the only family member he told about our relationship. He looks up to her so much, and he's beyond excited about the baby girl she's expecting. I can tell by the way Ryan speaks that he's unsure if Trevor will have a fighting chance. The thought scares me, and my brain immediately goes to anything and everything that could be wrong with him. I think of him alone, inside the truck. He's probably hanging by a thread right now. Just the thought of it breaks my heart.

When the firefighters crack the door open and motion us over, I hesitate. For the first time in my career I hesitate and I don't know if I can look at this man I love, but can't seem to make a relationship work with. What if this is the last time I see him? What if the last memories he has of me is not answering one of his texts. Because now I know he didn't get the one I sent minutes before, warning him. The first one I've sent him in months, and he never got it.

This instant, I say a promise. If he texts again, I'll answer. If he calls, I'll call him back. No more of this back and forth teenage bullshit we've been pulling on one another. It's time to be adults and admit how we feel. And if he's willing to give me a chance when he wakes up from this – fuck who was right and who was wrong – we face it head on and both apologize.

"C'mon, Blaze," Logan grabs my arm, pulling me to the smoking carcass of the vehicle. "He needs us. He needs you."

My feet move, but it's like they're being held down by a bunch of boulders and I'm drowning in a sea I can't swim my way out of. I'm fighting against a riptide of emotion and it's threatening to pull me under. When I finally get to the truck, I look in, unprepared for what I see. Trevor looks dead. He's gray, his head lists to the side, and I can't make out his chest moving underneath the thin material of his t-shirt. I'm scared to see what's under the mangled dashboard – at the very least he's got a sprain, but given the angle of his leg, I'm willing to bet he has a compound fracture. His chest looks like it took the brunt of some of the force too; airbags are deployed, taking up space in the cab of the truck. No doubt about it, those airbags saved his life.

"He's breathing," Logan is taking his vitals, putting a c-collar around his neck, and preparing to get him on a board. "But it's not regular. Snap the fuck out of it, Blaze. Get it together and let's get him help."

It's then that Trevor makes a pitiful noise in his throat. The noise cuts me to the bone and pulls a moan from my throat. He must be in so much damn pain. The noise spurs me on, makes me run back to the ambulance and get the board we'll need to transport him. It's a blur as we get him on the board and in the back of the ambulance. Logan looks at me. "You want to drive or sit back here with him?"

"With him, I wouldn't be good driving. I wanna be back here, making sure he's comfortable until we hand his care over."

Logan nods, and we race like hell for the helipad where the air evac will meet us to take him to the nearest trauma center an hour away. I administer anything and everything I can to make him more comfortable, watching his low blood pressure and heart rate with a critical eye. My gaze runs down his broken and bloodied face with tears streaming down my own. I always joke about how pretty he is. With blood oozing from above his eye, running down a now slightly crooked nose, and stopping at his beard, he looks like an MMA fighter. One that's gone four rounds with the baddest motherfucker out there. I want to take this pain away from him, to make him sit up in this bed and bitch me out for not answering his texts.

The way Trevor and I left our relationship wasn't good. We had unfinished business, and I swore we'd get around to it, but lately I've ignored his texts because I know he doesn't understand. In this instant, I blame myself for the misunderstanding. It would have been easy for me to lay everything out for him and just be honest. Instead, I've been playing a game, hoping he'll decide I'm worth all the trouble when I decide to give him a chance again. I keep saying it's not fair of him to ask me to give up my job, but it's also not fair of me to not be straightforward with him. I've never wanted a man who insisted I stay at home, but fuck it, I would for Trevor. I truly think I would for him.

We loved each other, and I took it for granted, imagined we had all the time in the world. With my past, I should have known - accidents happen. Time isn't always on our side, I should've known.

It's the biggest regret I've ever had right now. Giving my report to the air evac nurse over the radio, I see I have two minutes left with him. Two minutes to make him want to fight, to let him know exactly how I feel about him. Wiping the tears off my face and clearing my throat, I lean down to his ear, hoping like hell he can hear me. If there's any time for me to be honest with him and lay my heart bare, it's right now.

"Trevor, you fight. You fight for me, your mom and dad, your sister, your niece, and you fight for what we tried to throw away. I didn't want to listen before, but I'm listening now," my voice falters and cracks. "I love you, and I want a chance to make this work. Please don't give up on me. Don't give up on us." I lean down, kissing him on the forehead, pushing his sweaty hair back, knowing how badly he'd be irritated that the curly link had escaped and was now in his face.

The ambulance comes to a stop and it's the worst feeling to hand his care over to someone else. Even if I do know the nurse and she assures me she'll do the best she can to get him to the hospital with the greatest chance of survival.

Standing as close as they'll let me, I fight against the wind, pushing my hair back from my face as the helicopter takes off. I watch until I can no longer see it's rotating blades in the dying sun.

With startling clarity, I know I can't sit here and wait for someone to give me word on his condition. There's no way in hell I'll be able to sit in our station and be updated when people remember to call us. I need to be with him, need to be there in case he doesn't make it out of this alive. "Take me back to the station, back to my car, Logan. I'm heading to Birmingham."

"Fuck that," he shakes his head, his dark eyes flashing with sympathy. "You're in no shape to be driving. I'll take you. We'll find out what's going on with him together."

I nod my okay, because it's all I can do. Either I go with him or I don't, and if I don't, I'm not positive I won't jump out of my own skin trying to make it there.

I have no idea how that trip to Birmingham will end up changing my life.

CHAPTER TWO

Tank

EVERYTHING FUCKING HURTS. I've never felt this kind of pain before in my life, not even when I was in the military. What's worse is I don't remember what I've done to cause myself to be in this agony.

The last thing I can recall is driving to the bottoms with my windows cracked, hard rock playing as loud as I could handle it, and my thoughts on the red-head spitfire who's been ignoring me for months. I was formulating a plan to get back in her good graces, to let her know her job didn't mean jack shit, if it meant my ultimatum kept her away from me. She called my bluff and when I got to my fishing spot, I was going to text her, let her know I'd deal with her job because fuck – I missed her.

After that all I remember is pain.

"Trevor, can you hear me?"

I'm trying to tell this woman who keeps screaming at me that I can indeed, fucking hear her. She's shoving something into my side near my lung and it's killing me.

I go to grab for it, feeling plastic. Maybe it's a tube. What the fuck is going on?

"No, don't be pulling on that!"

More noise, more bustling.

"Can someone get his hands? He's going to yank the tube out before we can get the collapsed lung taken care of. He might be out of it, but he's strong."

Collapsed lung? Now I'm starting to freak out and jerk my head from side to side until someone steadies it with their hands.

"Stop, Trevor, you're going to hurt yourself."

I want to scream at the person speaking to me like I'm a child that I'm already fuckin' hurt. If I'm in the back of an ambulance or at a hospital there's only one person I want, one person who I feel comfortable enough to hand my care over to.

"Blaze," I whisper, wetting what feels like cracked lips with the edge of my tongue.

There's the metallic taste of blood and the indention where my lip has been split. Has someone beat the shit out of me? If they did, I'd hate to see the other guy because I know I wouldn't have gone down without a fight. If I'm fucked up this bad, they probably aren't living right now.

"Blaze," I try again, this time my voice is a little stronger, because I can hear it in my ears.

"What are you saying, Trevor?"

I can feel someone lean down so they're next to my lips. "Blaze," I try again. "I want Blaze."

"Can someone go out there and find out who Blaze is?"

With the knowledge they're going to go get the one person I want to see, I slip back into the blessed darkness where I don't feel anything.

THE NEXT TIME I come to, instinctively I know it's been a while and I know it's late at night. Fighting to open my eyes, I take in my surroundings, waiting for my vision to adjust. The room I'm in is one of the darkest I've ever been in, including some of the hellholes I was in while I was in the service.

Everything hurts again, more than it did last time. I attempt to move my leg, but it's fucking heavy. My arm is heavier than normal, too. I force my eyes to open wider and see an IV in my hand, limiting my range of motion. What the fuck is going on?

A noise, I can't tell if it's a sigh or a moan, comes from my left. The shadows and the sliver of light given off by the machines I'm hooked up to allow me to figure out someone sits in a chair not far from me. Because of the darkness, I can't quite make out who it is. With my teeth gritted, I lift my hand to show them I'm alive, and promptly let out a barely audible *fuck me* as I let it drop back down beside me. The one little movement took a lot out of me, but I'm glad I was able to manage. It feels like a major accomplishment.

The person in the chair jerks awake at my noise, or my words, puts their feet on the floor, and moves quickly toward me. Once they're in the dim light, I see it's Blaze.

"Damn I love you, I've wanted to see you all day, after I came to when they were putting a tube in my chest," I close my eyes as I feel her hands on me. The words are hard to force through my throat. My voice is scratchy, everything feels swollen, bearing the evidence of the hard day I've had. I'm so fucking tired.

"I love you, too," tears slip down her face. "God Trevor, you have no idea how scared I've been."

My mind is going a hundred miles an hour. There's only one thought repeating back and forth in my head. I croak out the question I've been dying to know the answer to. "What the fuck happened to me? What day is it?"

"You were in an accident. Brooks Strather hit your truck head on going almost ninety miles an hour at the bottoms. You've been in and out of consciousness for two days. You had surgery and a collapsed lung. You're lucky as hell you're still alive Trevor."

Two days, I've lost two days of my life. I hear something in her voice, a monotone that sometimes we use when we're delivering bad news to families. It's a way to keep our emotions out of it and do the job we've been hired to do. I dread asking her the question, because I think I know the answer.

"Babe," it kills me to ask, it hurts me because I know it hurt her. "Did you respond to the call?"

Her green eyes show an anguish I'm not sure I can ever understand. She deflates right in front of me, this woman who's always such a badass. She's usually so strong and full of life with the colors of the tattoos she sports running down her arms, but right now that woman is nowhere to be found. I watch her completely draw within herself. I watch as she leans back, grabbing the chair, sitting down before she obviously falls down. Blaze collapses in it, putting her face in her hands for a long minute. She takes what appears to be a fortifying breath and then answers my question.

"Yeah, Ryan and Ace responded first, but Logan and I were the closest medics available," she bites her bottom lip, holding something in.

Fuck me....guilt eats at me. My best friend and my girl both saw me in the worst shape I've ever been in. I can't fathom how I looked in the truck and what I'm sure I must look like laying in this bed, but I need her to be honest with me. If there's anything we need at this juncture of our relationship, it's honesty.

"Baby, tell me about it, let it out. It's okay." I know from my own experiences that you should talk about it, even if it's with the person you're trying most not to let in.

"I wasn't worried, ya know?" she starts, grabbing my fingers in between hers. Hers are freezing, and I have the fleeting thought maybe she's in shock. She plays with the tips of them, rubbing at my fingernails. "I knew you weren't on shift, because you'd texted me the night before, asking if we could talk. But I ignored you, because I didn't know how to talk to you, to face you after what all we said to each other the last time we argued. I was one thousand percent positive you weren't on shift though, it never even crossed my mind it was you. I even sent you a text, warning you of the wreck, telling you to stay where you were. I said maybe we could have dinner, because sometime over the past few months, I realized the argument we had wasn't just me or you, it was me *and* you," she stops to take a breath. "I've been worried I'd never be able to say those words to you. As much as I was pissed at you, us breaking up was partly my fault too. I'm willing to take the blame with you."

I hate hearing the pain in her voice. Feeling the aches I do, I know it was bad when they came on the scene. I feel like I've gone fifteen rounds with a pro boxer and then tumbled around in a washer spin cycle. Everything on my body hurts and aches, including my teeth. I don't even want to think how I'd feel if I wasn't on the pain meds I know they've given me.

"When I got to the scene, I saw two regular pickups. So I yelled to Ace saying it had come over the radio that there was an officer involved. When he told me it was you, I felt like my life was over. I fell to my knees in the middle of the road, and for the first time in my life, I didn't know what to do to help someone. Ryan came crawling out from under the back of your truck looking like he'd seen the devil himself. He was so pale I thought he was going to pass out, covered in mud, probably shit, and your blood."

She continues playing with my fingertips and I welcome the connection. It makes me feel alive, and I need that right now. I need her warmth and the vibrancy of life she carries with her on a daily basis.

"We waited for the jaws to cut you out, and then they told us we could go over. I've never seen you like that before, and hand to God, the way you looked was in the top five of bad patients I've ever seen. I fought like hell to keep you alive until we got to the air evac."

So I'd been helicoptered to Birmingham. It's all kind of starting to click. My receptors are coming back online after being off for so long.

"Logan drove me, and I haven't left. Your sister brought me some clothes and we've talked every time she's come in here. She loves you a lot and she's one tough chick," her words are strained, and I can hear her trying to keep the tears in check. It's killing her, it's killing me.

"Whitney is badass. How's the baby?"

"She's had some contractions, but the doctor said it's not unusual with the shock you gave all of us."

We're quiet for a minute. I can't take my eyes off her, can't stop trying to map the contours of her face. I watch her breaking in front of me. See her chin trembling, her teeth holding on tightly to that bottom lip to keep the seam of her frown together, and the spot between her eyes pulled tight to keep the tears from falling.

Then there's a kink in the armor as one tear slides down her cheek. Her shoulders jerk with the effort she's exerting to hold it all in. I do the only thing I can.

"Blaze, help me sit this bed up and crawl in here with me. I don't care if it hurts; I have to have you beside me, right where you fucking belong."

She reaches over, tears dropping onto my skin as she moves the bed so that I'm elevated.

"Lower the railing and climb in next to me, I need to feel you against me. I can't take away what you saw and erase it from your memory, but I can be here."

Doing what I ask her to, I allow her to cuddle up next to me, and it's the best medicine in the world even if it does hurt like hell. Somehow I manage to reach over with my IV hand and curl it around the nape of her neck, letting her bury her head against my shoulder. Gingerly and biting back a groan, I lean down, kissing her hair.

"Let it out and let it go, because I'm gonna need you babe, more than I've ever needed you before. If you're serious about us being together, then I'm going to want you with me every step of the goddamn way, and there's gonna be a lot of steps. A lot of long days. If you're in this for the long haul, I need you to be all in."

She sobs against me nodding as I talk to her, holding my hospital gown tightly between her fingers, and when my voice breaks too much I can't speak anymore. I let the tears fall too, because damn if I haven't realized just how close I've come to dying.

And I haven't done half the shit I want to do yet. It's most definitely not my time, and I'll never waste another second of what I do have with this redhead lying next to me.

CHAPTER THREE

Blaze

"WITH HIM, *I wouldn't be good driving. I wanna be back here, making sure he's comfortable until we hand his care over."*

Logan nods, and we race like hell for the helipad where the air evac will meet us to take him to the nearest trauma center an hour away. I administer anything and everything I can to make him more comfortable, watching his low blood pressure and heart rate with a critical eye.

Suddenly his already low pressure begins dropping. "Trevor!" My hands shake, and for the first time, I don't know what to do. My normally instinctual training is gone and I'm scared to death. "Don't do this to me," I look around in the back of the ambulance, everything looking foreign to me.

His blood pressure drops further, beeps going off everywhere and I'm lost. Tears are streaming down my face and I'm hyperventilating, unsure of what to do to help him. He's dying in front of me, and I can't help him.

I gasp, jerking awake so hard that I fall off the cot I've been sleeping on the past few days here in the hospital. As my body connects with the hard floor, I cry out, hopefully not loud enough for Trevor to hear, but it's enough to get me out of the nightmare I was living in my dream world. Exhausted, I glance at the clock, seeing it's six am. I've gotten maybe four hours of sleep, but I know I won't be able to drift back.

Leaning over Trevor, I check to make sure he's breathing and alive before I grab my purse and head downstairs. After the nightmare I just had, I don't trust the machines. Coffee sounds really good right about now.

I'M SITTING outside Trevor's hospital room, my knees drawn up to my chest, head down, and crying. I'm not sure why I'm crying. Maybe it's from relief that Trevor is going to be okay, stress from everything we've been through since the call went out, or just the emotional release I need after being at his side for the past few days.

Today, he gets to come home. Surprising everyone, he's healing quicker than any of us imagined he would. Proof of how stubborn he is.

Getting up and moving away from the door, I walk down the hallway to where there's a glass window spanning from floor to ceiling. Whoever wants to can look out over the Birmingham skyline. It's peaceful. Up here, I can't hear the bustling of the street, the roar of the cars, or the impatient honking horns of the drivers. It makes the noise in my head louder, letting the memories of what I saw when I got to Trevor's truck force their way into my awake hours. The silence rings loudly between my ears and I want to scream at it to go away.

Try as I might, I can't get the image of Trevor's face when I first saw him at the crash site out of my mind. I can sleep for a few hours every night, but sometime during the slumber the vision comes to me and the ending to the story changes dramatically. I jerk awake quickly and then have to look at him for myself, just to make sure he's okay.

When he was first brought to the trauma center, I wasn't sure if he'd make it home, but like everything Trevor does, he's excelled. Being in good shape helped, being stubborn definitely helped, but last night he told me I helped more than anything.

The strength of our feelings scares the hell out of me. When you're faced with the possible death of the person you love most in this world, you realize what you have and what you value. It's thrown into your face with the velocity of a major league pitcher's fast ball, and you either duck out of the way or you take the hit head on. We're both taking the hit head on, and we both want this second chance, me more than anything. I messed up once with someone in my life, I don't want to mess up again, but I need him to see me for the woman I am. I need him to really look and accept me for who I am. I'm scared I'll have to go into a dangerous situation again and then we'll be back to square one. We both want it to work, but is it that simple? Can we both put aside thought patterns ingrained in us for years? I guess we'll have to find out together.

"Blaze!"

I turn around and look down the hallway, seeing Whitney walking toward me. Actually it's more like a waddle, but she's making it. She's been a trooper through this whole ordeal, coming to the hospital every day and staying until Ryan forces her to go home at night. I meet her halfway so she doesn't have to make the entire length by herself.

"Hey," I greet her with a hug. I may not have known her before all this started, but she's become one of my favorite people in a short amount of time. She listens when I talk – whether I want to vent, remember, or cry – and she doesn't judge me for what happened with Trevor before the wreck.

"So, he gets to go home today, huh?" She smiles at me, positively glowing.

"He does, I can't believe he's made so much progress. The doctors are surprised too, but he's strong and he's stubborn. That's half the battle right there."

Whitney bites her bottom lip, and gets this look on her face that says she wants to maybe ask me something.

"Are you okay?"

She runs a hand through her blonde locks, so like Trevor's, before she clasps her hands in front of her very pregnant belly. "I have a favor to ask, actually we, as a family, have a favor to ask."

My palms sweat because I'm not sure what they're going to ask. What if they want me to stay away from Trevor while he's recuperating? What if I've overstepped staying at the hospital and spending every waking minute with him? I mean it's not like I have a ring on my finger. Hell I don't even have a toothbrush at his place – at least I don't think I do anymore. Pretty sure he probably threw that out when I told him to take his high-handed archaic attitude and go to hell. I regret that sentiment now, not the fact I said the words. They needed to be said, but I wouldn't have told him to go to hell. I would have been mature, and we would have sat down; talked things out like adults.

It's a super human effort, but I manage not to fold my arms across my chest to close myself off from her. She and her family have been nothing but nice to me, and I remind myself, not everyone has an ulterior motive. "I'm listening."

"The thing is, all of us have a lot going on with the baby coming. Ryan's going to have to do overtime now that Trevor's hurt. Mom's going to be helping me with the business, and Dad's working down on the Gulf. He won't be able to make trips back except for the weekends, but someone needs to stay with Trev," she starts, her blue eyes showing the exhaustion of the past few days.

"I totally agree, he doesn't need to be by himself. If you want, I can call around and see about some Home Health nurses. I know some of the best in the business. It's not a problem for me to do that, just tell me what you want me to ask about."

She's struggling, she's gripping her fingers in front of her, twisting them so tightly I'm afraid she'll break them off. "That's not it, exactly."

Then I'm lost, because I thought it was pretty clear what she was asking me. "Maybe you better tell me, because now I'm a little confused."

Taking a deep breath, she walks over and grabs the handrail before turning around, bracing her back against it. "I think you should be the one to help Trevor. He cares about you, and he'll do things for you he won't do for other people. There's not one other person in the world who will push him the way you will, but you'll make sure he doesn't hurt himself."

"I have a job," I remind her. "One that requires I work long hours."

"Don't you have leave?" she pleads. "I know it's a lot to ask, but you have the medical experience and you know Trevor. You want to be with him, I can see it every time I'm with the two of you. You both want to be together. What better way to figure out if you *can* be together than in the hardest of times? Seeing your way through this together? Might make the two of you realize how much your professions don't matter in the grand scheme of things."

I'm speechless, but I understand where she's coming from. And she's right. If I want to prove to Trevor how important my job is, I have to show him. Doing it for him is the best way to do that.

"I do have leave," I shrug, starting to weaken. "But what if it all blows up in our faces?"

Whitney takes my hand. "Then you'll at least know you tried, and if something like that ever happens again, you'll know you don't have regrets."

In Trevor's job there's a damn good chance something like this could happen again, and the no regrets thing sounds tempting.

"Okay, I'll give it a week. If we're doing good at the end of the week, I'll extend it until he doesn't need me anymore," I hold my hand up. "But Trevor's got to agree to it."

"Already taken care of," she winks at me and gives me the brightest smile ever.

I wonder how in the hell she managed that, then my mind flashes back to Thanksgiving morning, I left the two of them alone so they could enjoy their breakfast. She's already turned and is walking back down the hallway as I shake my head.

Those Trumbolt siblings are slick and nothing but trouble. Trevor though, he's the kind of trouble I like to get into.

CHAPTER FOUR

Tank

A FEW DAYS home and I'm wishing like hell I was back in the hospital. It's not like I actually enjoyed being in the place, but there was a sense of safety I felt. Nurses were around at all times, if I needed it, there was an IV of medication that could knock me out of my misery for a few hours. No one questioned when I asked for it. There the pain wasn't so all-consuming. Doctors and nurses came in at all hours of the goddamn day and night, it gave me something else to concentrate on. In my home I can't get away from my pain, can't get away from the thoughts running through my head, can't get away from Blaze's hot body always so close to mine. I know part of the problem is I won't take the painkillers, but I hate the way they make me feel. And I can't physically take Blaze, because that's just work I can't do quite yet.

"Trevor, where are you?"

My stomach clenches as I hear the voice of the woman-turned-angel who's overseeing my care. Having Blaze fulfill every need I have is both amazingly sweet of her, but at the same time incredibly frustrating. We're stuck in close quarters, and we're so fucking careful with one another, I almost want to antagonize her into an argument to see those green eyes flash with fire and annoyance.

"Back here in the den," I yell so she can hear me. It seriously sucks trying to get up right now, but an ingrained part of my manhood can't help but ask. "Do you need help?"

Her tone of voice is a warning. "Don't even think about it, Trev."

But I do think about it, and she's been gone for a few hours, getting stuff I need around here. A tightness settles in my gut. I'm used to doing things for myself, and knowing she's had to do those errands kills a portion of my pride. Thankful I was given the okay to use crutches, I force my body upright and off the couch. It takes me almost a full sixty seconds to grit through the pain. Every time my leg isn't elevated, it fucking kills me. Something about the blood rushing down to where the hardware they've used to put it back together is located. My arms ache when I test putting my two hundred and twenty pounds on them to swing myself forward, but I grit though that shit, too. Nothing's ever been handed to me, and I don't think this recovery is going to be easy. Not by a long shot.

She glances up at me as I hobble into the kitchen, exasperation on her face. "I told you to stay in there."

The fire and annoyance I wanted earlier? It rages in her eyes and I can't help the smile I direct her way. "When have I ever been good at following directions?"

She laughs, the sound deep and throaty, going straight to my dick. Good, because I haven't felt anything there in a while and I was a little worried. Unfortunately, the only thing I can do is lean against the kitchen cabinets and watch her unload the groceries she's bought.

Blaze is gorgeous today, wearing a pair of cut off jean shorts with an old Brantley Gilbert concert t-shirt. It always amazes people she likes him, but if you ask her, she'll sit and give you a run-down of the twenty plus times she's seen him. She bought his first CD online from a boot store in Georgia – she's a legit fan – and don't try to say she's not. Them's fightin' words.

"Why don't you go over there and have a seat. I'll make us some lunch and you can take a pain pill," she directs that sharp gaze at me.

We've fought over the pain pill issue since I came home. I saw so many guys get addicted to them. They used them to block the pain both physical and emotional, and then they couldn't live without them. I don't ever want that to be me. I already know from having a taste of Blaze, I have a fucking addictive personality. Even though I went on dates with other women while we were broken up, I did it to make her jealous in hopes it would show her she missed me. The truth? Since the moment I met her, there's never been anyone else for me except her.

"Wow," she turns her back to me, putting the bread on a shelf where she can reach it, as I have a seat, propping my crutches against the back of the chair, as I turn my body around. "The fact you didn't argue says a lot about the pain you're really in."

I shrug, reaching over to pull up another chair, thankful for my long arms as I prop my leg up. If I'm honest it hurts like a bitch. "I might be willing to take one."

Blaze

To say I'm amazed at the words coming out of Trevor's mouth is an understatement. He's fought me tooth and nail about the pain pill issue. I've watched him be in agony for days and the only thing he does is grit his teeth and bear it. Watching it is hard, almost as hard as him being in the hospital when I know there's something he could do for it. I understand his reservations, but I come from the school of helping people and when it's as simple as taking a pill; you just do it.

"You'll finally get a good sleep if you do," I gently persuade him. "I know what you're afraid of and I'm here to make sure you don't depend on them."

He sighs when I mention them again. His annoyance is an elephant in the room. He's been on edge since he came home and I think it's because he hasn't let himself completely rest. I think he's scared to allow it. But now I'm saying enough, he's never going to get well if he doesn't.

I turn around and suck in a breath, struck dumb by the long, lean body in front of me. While he tilts his head back, I let my gaze travel along the picture he makes in front of me. Because he's hurting, he's sweating more than normal, which means he's been going around with no shirt on. Right or wrong, I've been giving a thanks to the Heavens above. Trevor Trumbolt is a tall drink of water, as my mom would say.

His biceps bulge where he's got his arms crossed in front of a chest that's broad thanks to hard work in the gym. I've watched him before; he lifts heavy and runs long distances, which definitely helps his stamina, if you know what I mean. It allows him to be strong, but lean and not

overly muscled.

His chest is smooth and most of the hair Trevor sports is on his head and his face. I've never seen him without at least a goatee, but since he's been laid up, he's let the beard grow, allowing what he already had in place to thicken.

He's still not paying attention to me, so I allow my gaze to continue down to his flat stomach. Ridges and dips of flesh paint shadows along his skin. Those v-dips? I've licked them. Not ashamed to say it. I've thought about them more often than I should have, and I've caught myself being mesmerized by them a time or two the last forty-eight hours. Specifically, when he's struggling to get up and he relies strictly on his core. *Dayum* that core is strong.

Sweatpants stop my journey. Just below the v-dips he's got fleece on and even though they ride low on his hips, I don't think they'll be coming off anytime soon. Before I realize it, my gaze has drifted down to the bulge I can see so prominently pressing against the soft material.

Shaking myself, I pull my gaze back up to his head. The longish blonde hair is up in a manbun, which I used to call ridiculous. Now, it gives him a manlier appearance if that's even possible. The days in the hospital have leaned him out further, causing his jawbone to form a sharper line and giving him a more dangerous edge.

His eyes open and he rolls his head to the side, blue eyes glowing so dark they're almost black. "Do I pass inspection?" His tone is both amused and sarcastic - the smirk on his face complete smartass.

I give him my own smirk as I clear my throat and shake off the arousal flowing through my body. "You know I think you're a very good looking man, Trev. Attraction was never the issue between us."

He's quiet as I go about throwing away the grocery bags and cleaning off the counters. I wonder what's going through his head, he never tells me, and if there's one thing I want, it's him to confide in me.

He opens his mouth, but instead of what I want to hear, he asks a question. "What's for lunch?"

"How hungry are you?"

He runs a hand down his stomach, calling attention to the smooth expanse of skin. "If I'm going to take a pill, I need carbs to help me absorb it. I don't want to feel fucked up, Blaze. You know I don't like it."

If there's one thing Trevor hates, it's feeling out of control.

"How about I make us both a baked potato and some grilled chicken to put on top? Then you can take your pain pill and lie down."

He seems to consider what I've asked for a moment, but then a mischievous grin spreads across his face. "Will you lie down with me?"

I'm asking for trouble if I do, and I know it. The problem is, it's always been hard for me to say no to Trevor - about anything. He rests better with me next to him. This is a fact since he's been hurt.

Truthfully, since we've been home, I miss him. He's not as accessible as he was in the hospital. There he was vulnerable, willing to let himself accept help. Here he's not so easy to read. He sure as hell doesn't accept or ask for help the way he did in Birmingham and if I'm honest...I'm tired.

"I'll lie down with you, but I want you to sleep."

He crosses his heart with his finger. "Promise babe, that's exactly what I'll do."

Grabbing some potatoes, I poke holes in them and put them in the microwave to cook. While that's heating, I grab the leftover chicken we had last night, and get it ready to nuke. This is not fancy, but Trevor seems to appreciate anything I do for him. In those aspects, he's a good patient. Telling me his pain level truthfully and taking care of himself? He fucking sucks at that.

"How's your leg?" I wash my hands, going to stand beside him.

"It hurts today," he admits grimacing slightly as he moves it to try and get more comfortable.

"Trev, you can't overdo it." I wish they'd put him in a brace instead of a plaster cast, but with the hardware he received it was necessary to make sure his leg heals correctly. Part of that is going to be Trevor allowing his body time to heal itself. I walk over to him, running my hands down his face, kissing his forehead. "You aren't Superman, you've got to take it easy."

He leans into my caress, allowing himself a few moments of quiet. "You're fuckin' right I'm not Superman," he mumbles. "If anything, I'm Batman, he's way more badass."

I giggle as I make my way over to the microwave, which has beeped. Within minutes, I have our food and drinks ready, setting them on the table, so we both have access.

"You take one this afternoon and if it works, you take one tonight," I say as I hand Trevor a white pill. "You have to rest."

"You'll be with me?"

Only I know the depth of that question, what it costs him to ask it and how much it means that he did. Reaching over, I grab his hand.

"I'll be with you no matter what you need."

CHAPTER FIVE

Tank

I FUCKING HATE PAINKILLERS. I hate the way they make me feel like I'm flying, the dry mouth I get, the weird ass dreams I have. I hate it all, but I've also learned my body needs to rest. And fuck, I'm tired. More than anything, I'm tired – exhausted even.

"Want to take the sweatpants off?" Blaze asks as she follows me into the bedroom.

"Yeah, I'm gonna get hot. I do every time I take these damn things. They make me sweat like a meth addict."

We've cut the legs off this pair to make them into shorts, but it still takes both of us working to get them down my legs, past my cast, and off my feet. I grab onto the waistline of the boxers I wear to keep them from going with them. Laying down, I help her as best I can by adjusting my leg so that it's propped up.

"You comfortable?"

"I'm fucking tired," I yawn, putting my arm up over my eyes. "Tired, sore, and damn sorry you have to wait on me hand and foot."

That's the crux of this whole situation. When I was in the hospital, I was so thankful to be alive, I didn't think about being an almost invalid when I got out. I know I'm being overly dramatic too, but the first day, it was a hard thing for me to go take a piss by myself. For someone who prides themselves on being independent, this has been a shock.

"Hey," Blaze covers me up with a sheet. It's all I've been able to tolerate.

"I'll not have you talking about the man I love like that. I know you're in a bad mood, but I'm hoping a nap will knock you right out of it."

My mouth goes dry when she tells me she loves me. I don't think I'll ever get sick of hearing it. Knowing she does is what got me through everything going on while I was in the hospital, but it's hard to be grateful for things out here when I'm so frustrated.

"C'mon in here with me," I pull her down for a kiss. When she bends over, her shirt dips, allowing me to see the lacy bra she wears underneath it. My finger catches in the material as she makes to straighten up.

"Trevor," her voice is a warning.

"I need to feel you next to me," I admit, costing me some of my male pride. "Take off the clothes and cuddle up," I give her my best puppy dog look. "Please."

She looks like she wants to say no, but she doesn't. Instead she gets rid of everything but the scrap of panties she prefers to wear and crawls in next to me.

"I don't know how you stand just a sheet," she shivers as she arranges herself beside me, thankfully on the opposite side of my bum leg.

"C'mere, I'll warm you up."

Using my arm, I pull her closer, resting her head on my shoulder, cheek on my pec. Her arm goes around my waist, caressing the bruises that are now starting to change color.

"Do these still hurt? We can ice them if you need to."

"No," I trap her hand in mine, entwining our fingers together before bringing them up to my lips for a kiss. "You've taken excellent care of me, and I love you for it."

The deep sigh she makes every time I tell her I love her makes me feel like a bastard. I didn't know what I had before. Obviously I didn't know what the fuck I was giving up.

My eyes are getting heavy and I can feel the effects of the medication as I try to fight against it. I don't want to lose more days in a drug-induced fog, but I also don't want to increase my downtime, which I know I'm in danger of doing if I don't get my shit together.

"Go to sleep," she kisses my jawline, snuggling in deeper, and then I don't remember anything as blessed darkness takes over.

Blaze

I can tell the second Trevor succumbs to the drug-induced sleep. His body, which has been tense for days finally relaxes and goes completely loose. His jaw, which has been clenched, releases and his breathing evens out. It's not the quick pants of someone trying to measure breaths to keep from hurting themselves either. It's long, easy breaths of someone who's sleeping deeply.

The tension lines in his face are gone, making him look all of eighteen years old. The only thing proving he's older is the leanness of his face, the dense muscle packed onto his frame, and the maturity of his beard.

I try to keep the yawn I feel coming on from cracking my jaw, but it does and I realize quickly just how tired I am. Part of me has been scared to death since we came home, and the other part wants to make things as perfect for him as they can be. In the end, I've all but run myself ragged. Not because he's asked me to, but because I've wanted to.

And that's the most honest I've been with myself in a long time.

I'M NOT sure what time it is when I open my eyes again. It takes me a minute to adjust to the darkness of the room and I wonder how long Trevor and I have slept. I can see him slightly in the waning light, so it must be close to evening.

Beside me, he's lightly snoring, his face turned toward me, mouth slightly open. He was right about only needing a sheet, the amount of body heat he's throwing off is enough to keep us warm in a snow storm. Light sweat has broken out on his chest and I take a moment to lazily map the skin with the tips of my fingers.

Trevor Trumbolt has always been the hottest man I've ever seen. The first thing that attracted me to him were his eyes, then it was the sensual curve of his mouth. Those almost too-red lips always look like he's spent a lot of time kissing a woman senseless. Moving my eyes from his mouth, I take in the rest of what he has to offer. Earlier I couldn't peruse my fill without him seeing. Now his body is a visual buffet and the motherfucker is all you can eat.

Like most of the guys our age, he's got tattoos. In fact he's got an impressive chest piece of an eagle. One night when he'd been drunk, he'd admitted he got it right before he went to war. Something they could identify him by if things went tits up. I'd wanted to tell him that's what his dog tags were for, but he'd been so serious about it, I didn't want to break his heart.

Not to say that I don't like it. It's one of the hottest things about him. The way he wears it like a badge of honor. When he's shirtless, like he is now, like he has been for days, I want to lick it and claim it as mine.

Down girl, I caution myself, but it's hard to be good when the one man who can rock your world six ways to Sunday is right at your fingertips with two pairs of underwear as the only things separating you.

Sex has always been the one thing Trevor and I have done well. It's been six long, dry months since we decided to indulge in that favorite past time. Maybe I'm the one who took the drugs, or needs to take a pill to calm myself down, but right now I want to touch him. I want to make him feel good, forget all the shit he's been through, everything I've been through.

Trailing my hand down his stomach, I can feel his muscles clench. Looking back up at his face, I can see he's still asleep, although his breaths are coming a little faster and more frequent than they had been before.

Resuming my path down his happy trail, I encounter the elastic waistband of his boxers and wonder if I want to sneak attack inside, or see if he's ready for this yet. But God I'm ready for it. My nipples, which have been against his bare skin since we laid down have peaked, rubbing against his flesh to get a little bit of relief. I can't wait until his mouth wraps around them, tugging on the barbell each one has through the middle. The only person who knows I have pierced nipples is the man in bed with me.

My hand continues to skate down, bypassing the band for now, and moving with conviction over the bulge in his boxers. He's rock hard against the palm of my hand. Encouraged, I lift my hand up to the waistband, pushing it down slightly, before I stick my fingers in between cloth and flesh. I know the minute he wakes up, because I hear his sharp intake of air as I grab his length.

CHAPTER SIX

Tank

GODDAMN, I'm having the best dream ever. Blaze's hand is on my boxers, cupping my dick with her small hand. It hasn't seen action since the last time she and I were together six months ago, so it's got a mind of its own.

Not to say I haven't jerked it. I have, but there's no one who can get me off the way she does. Blaze isn't one of those *let's do it in the dark with the lights off on days that start in T* kind of women. She's very sexually aware and knows exactly what she wants. No playing coy with her, she'd much rather grab you by the balls and stick her finger up your ass to make sure you get off hard.

Which is why, when I realize this isn't a dream and her hand is actually down my boxers wrapped around my cock, I have to put my own hand down there and grip the base to keep from coming.

"Holy shit," the oath is ripped from my throat as I groan, forcing my eyes open against the lingering effects of the painkillers. "Blaze, I'm gonna come," I grit my teeth against the need to explode all over the both of us.

I've been on edge too long, wound way too fuckin' tight, trying to figure out what the hell is going on in my life for far too long.

She laughs, deep and throaty. The sound goes straight to my dick, making it throb. "Only thing stopping you from coming is yourself, Trevor."

"How long have you been touching me?" I inhale deeply, turning my head toward her, catching the scent that's always hers. Coconut and ocean water. This girl belongs on a beach all day, every day. "Please tell me it was longer than five minutes."

"Probably seven," she gives me a saucy smile. "Let me finish," she slides her hand down to where mine is gripping and then back up, collecting the fluid at the tip to lubricate her way.

I close my eyes, rolling my head around on the pillow. I'm not the type of guy that blows seven minutes into a fucking hand job.

"It's the medicine," she whispers in my ear. "It makes some people incredibly horny and puts them on a hair trigger. If it feels good," she licks my ear with the tip of her tongue and goosebumps appear along my arms. "Let it go."

I reluctantly let my hand stop gripping the base of my cock, but instead I bury my fingers in her hair, bringing her mouth to mine. "Finish me then, but know while it feels good for a second, it's nothing like when I go balls deep inside you. I wanna fuck you," I catch her lips with mine, thrusting my tongue into her mouth, owning it as much as I can from my prone position.

"I know you don't like giving me the upper hand, but let me take care of you."

She's right, I don't like to let her pleasure me without reciprocating. It's so empty. With her, I love to be in the moment, thrusting hard and deep. I love to see her eyes light up, the green turn hazel, and the way her lips quirk into the sexiest fucking grin as she's about to come. I love to hear the cry of ecstasy that she always tries to hold back, and I ache to feel the rake of her nails down my back.

"Let it go, Trev," she sucks my lobe into her mouth, yanking tightly on it as she uses her hand to move up and down my length.

"Oh fuck," I moan, I can feel it gathering at the base of my spine, my entire body tightens as she increases her speed. "I want to come inside you so bad," I grasp her hair tightly in between my fingers, shoving her mouth into my neck. "Own me, Blaze, fucking own me," I beg her.

Her teeth bite into the side of my throat and her hand increases speed, pumping me so fast I can hear her beating against my stomach. Hard strokes designed to get me off. Using my free hand, I reach down, cupping my balls, groaning at how tightly they've pulled against my body. "Yes," I groan as I feel myself break the wall. Stabbing my head into the pillow, I close my eyes, throwing my head back. "Yes, oh God, yes. Fuck," I grasp her hand in mine, jacking my cock together, increasing the speed as I feel her bite my neck again. "Goddamn," letting go of her hair, I reach up, grasping the metal rail of the headboard as I feel the evidence of my release spill over our entwined hands and onto my stomach.

I'm shaking, panting, praying to God I will always know what this feels like and hoping my pounding heart doesn't mean a heart attack is imminent.

"Jesus Christ," I try to regulate my breathing. "I haven't come that hard from a hand job since I was fourteen years old."

She giggles beside me, burying her head in my neck. "At least you're not as tense as you were. Maybe you'll be more agreeable from now on."

I make a non-committal sound in my throat, because if this woman thinks she's going to blow my mind like this and not feel the same kind of pleasure, especially when she's in my bed, then she's all kinds of mistaken.

Broken leg be damned. If there's one thing I know how to do, it's problem solve. This is a problem I definitely don't mind solving.

Blaze

I'm clamping my thighs together, trying to ease the clenching ache after the hottest hand job session I've ever participated in, in my life. Running my hands along my stomach, I let out what I hope is a calming breath, trying to bring my arousal down from its roaring high.

Newsflash. It's not. Trevor Trumbolt burns me up with how hot he is. There aren't many men who've been able to handle me. I know what I want in bed, and I'm not scared to say it. If it's about my pleasure, I'm vocal. Trevor is one of the only men I've ever been with who doesn't try to suppress it. His manhood isn't wrapped up in being the dominant one in the bedroom. We share and alternate that privilege.

"I think my brain shot through my dick," he's panting, wincing when he inhales a little too deeply.

"You okay?"

The question is a reaction I can't temper. My whole life is spent making sure people are okay.

"Blaze, if I wasn't, I would tell you. But hand to God, if you don't come straddle my face right now, you're gonna be sorry."

His blue eyes are on the verge of black, tumultuous with the onslaught of emotion and arousal shining there.

"I don't think it's a good idea," I shake my head. "I don't want to hurt you."

"You're not gonna hurt me. Trust me enough to tell you if you do, but right now I'm hungry," his nose nuzzles my cheek and even that touch is enough to make my nipples harden further. "Hungry for my face to be between those luscious thighs of yours. C'mon Blaze, I can fucking smell you," he scores my jaw with his teeth. "Have some fun."

"Bad idea," I moan, before he surprises me by latching his hand onto my thigh, denting my skin with his fingers, and physically lifts me up onto his face. I have no other option than to straddle him.

His voice is deep as he noses my clit. "Hang onto the headboard, baby. I'm about to rock your world."

Everything he does rocks my world, but I don't like for him to get too cocky. A gasp of air is all I'm able to suck into my lungs when I feel his tongue flick against my needy clit. Twining my fingers around the metal bars of Trevor's head board, I moan. "Don't ease in, Trev. Give it to me, you know how I like it."

When he closes his lips around my clit and sucks, I realize he does know exactly how I like it. He doesn't let up as I feel him bring his arms up behind my thighs, then I feel his palms slap against the skin of my ass.

"Fuck!" My head falls against my hands resting on the metal, I close my eyes, and let myself feel.

Trevor's always been able to push me over the edge faster than any man I've ever been with. It's like he has a step-by-step instructional booklet and he's a straight-A student.

I lose every bit of resolve I have to make sure he's okay when I feel the fingers from one hand sneak from behind and thrust into me, working in tandem with his tongue and mouth.

"Oh God," I cry out, throwing my head back.

He goes after me hard, not letting up when I try to flex my thighs to put some space between us. He slaps my ass again and shoves me further down on his face.

That's all it takes as I undulate my hips against him, riding the tip of his tongue, riding this orgasm I've wanted since I felt him come against my hand. "*Shit*," I let my head tilt, feel my long hair brushing the edges of my back, and give myself over to the emotions of release.

No other man has ever made me feel the way Trevor does, and I vow never to take that for granted again. I almost lost it once, I won't make that same mistake more than once.

I pull my legs from around his face and snuggle next to him. He grabs my hand in his, his thumb caressing my palm in a slow soft stroke. Eventually I hear the even sound of his breathing, letting it lull me back to sleep.

CHAPTER SEVEN

Tank

"HOW ARE YOU REALLY DOING?"

I fight not to roll my eyes at my older sister. She's my second mother, has been since the day I was born. I remember her dressing me up and showing me off to her friends when I was little. I'm glad there aren't any pictures because I looked like a horrible Cabbage Patch Doll reject if I recall correctly. It never bothered me, but sometimes her need to mother me is suffocating, especially as I got older and started living my own life. It's never cool to have two moms breathing down your neck, and that's exactly what I have some days.

"Save all your motherly concerns for my niece. She should be here very soon," I give her a slight grin, adjusting my leg on the couch in the den. I hope the grin softens the blow of my tone. I'm not in the mood for it today. If I'm honest, I'm not even in the mood for my own company. Given carte blanche, I'd probably tell them all to get out.

I hate sitting here, almost like I'm holding court. Blaze sits in the recliner, while Whitney and Renegade sit on the love seat opposite me while we watch some garbage on TV. I do my best not to pay attention when my best friend caresses my sister's stomach and they share a sickening sweet look with one another.

It's still a little shocking they're going to have a child together. It's taken us all a little time to wrap our heads around it. "Dude, stop fondling my sister."

"Stop being a dick," he fires back at me.

That's a fair assessment. I'm not in the greatest of moods today. I have my first round of physical therapy this afternoon and I'm not looking forward to it. The unknown is driving me nuts, and if this was a few weeks ago, I'd go for a run to get rid of the anxiety I have coursing through me right now. But this isn't a few weeks ago, and I'm dealing with the hand I've been dealt.

Whitney sits up straighter, dislodging his arm from around her shoulders, and I seriously do feel like a dick. If there's anyone who deserves to be happy, it's her. Even Blaze is looking at me with barely restrained anger in her eyes.

"Sorry, I'm a little on edge today. I start my physical therapy this afternoon."

I hope my explanation is enough, because I don't want to look too deeply into why I'm being an ass.

Whitney lets out a little noise from where she sits. "Trev, it's going to be fine. Do you want me to come with you?"

"I'm going," Blaze speaks up, not moving her eyes from the TV screen. "So I know what he has to do daily, even when he doesn't have an appointment."

I smile, showing my teeth to her. "She can be my warden."

"So we can get you better," she retorts, not taking my shit. It's one of the things I love about her, but also one of the things that's pissing me off today.

"I want something to drink," Whitney stands up, caressing her stomach when she does so. "Blaze, wanna come?"

She stands up as well. "Sure, there's a lot of hot air in this room."

I fight not to flip her back off as she leaves. God, I'm in a mood today. The only person willing to put up with me is Ryan, who's seen me through the absolute worst times of my life. When I drag my gaze over to him, I see that he's in complete Renegade mode and he's ready to do battle.

"What the fuck do you want?" I snarl. Fuck I want to run, pound a bag, do anything rather than sit here and deal with this anger.

"To know why you're being an ass to the people who care about you. What the fuck's going on in that head of yours?"

If there's one person I can be completely honest with, it's him. He and I have seen and done things together that we'll take to our graves, things we'll never speak of again that got us out of really shitty situations in the war zone in Iraq. If anyone understands, it's him, and if I know Whitney and Blaze, they're giving us a chance to talk.

"I'm scared, really fuckin' scared."

"That's it's gonna hurt?" Ryan shakes his head. "Of course it's gonna hurt, it's physical therapy and you have screws and plates in your leg. But you have to move it. You can't get a blood clot or let the muscles atrophy."

I hold up my hand, stopping his rant. "I'm scared I'll never be the same again. What if I can't make the five-mile run in twenty-five minutes anymore? What if I have a limp? I'm not disabled discharging from this bullshit," I hiss through clenched teeth. It hasn't hit me until today that physical therapy may not work.

Realization washes over his face, and I see him let out a deep breath. "Damn brother, I never questioned whether you would come back from this. Besides the PT they're giving you now is just going to keep your strength up, it's going to have nothing to do with your leg until you get the okay to use it.

I punch my hand against my chest. I ignore the annoying comment and talk about the one that's bothering me. What if I can't come back? "I have; I am - and it's freaking me the fuck out."

"Have you talked to Blaze or the department-appointed shrink about this?"

I shake my head. "Haven't seen the shrink yet, and I'm not laying this on Blaze. She's got enough shit to go through because of me."

Ryan moves forward, resting his elbows on his knees. "Blaze also loves you, and when you love someone, you don't get to pick what you let them go through with you. They're your partner. If you don't treat her like one, you're going to lose her the same way you did before, you stubborn fuck."

I hear what he's saying, but it doesn't help the anxiety I have in my chest, or the dread that's settled into my stomach. The girls come back in and I can't say anything else, instead I spend the rest of their visit brooding in my own head.

"YOU DON'T HAVE to come in with me," I relieve Blaze of her babysitting duties. My tone is clipped as I spit the words past my lips like sunflower seeds on a long road trip.

"I might not have to, but I want to," she fumes as she finds a parking spot.

"What, no letting me out at the front door? I'm an invalid, didn't you know?" I gesture to my leg.

"You're not an invalid, and I don't know why the hell you're acting like this, Trevor. I've never known you to be such an asshole. Your heavily pregnant sister came to see you to make sure you're okay. I'm doing my best to help you out, and you've been nothing but an asshole to me today. I can see you're pissed, but it doesn't excuse the way you're treating people," she slams her SUV in park. "So no, I'm not coddling you and parking at the drop off. You're so fucking determined to do things on your own? Get your own damn crutches. I'll see you inside."

She gets out, slamming the door so hard it jars the vehicle, making it sway slightly. I watch as she stomps off for the front of the medical building. She doesn't even look back to check on me. If I'm being honest, I totally deserve this. Reaching behind me, I snag one of the crutches, but it's too big for me to pull around me. Shit, this just pisses me off more. Opening the door, I lean on the seat as I fight with the piece of metal, almost shoving it through the windshield before I get it out. It's much quicker getting the next one out, but I'm sweating as I make my way up to the front of the building, breathing hard and flat out needing a rest. When I notice Blaze looking at me through the window, I grit my teeth and move on. I'll be damned if she sees me struggling.

"Are you okay?" She asks when I make my way inside, thankful for the air conditioning, even in December. Alabama hasn't gotten the memo that it's winter. Her tone and eyes tell me she's only asking because it's what she's taught to do for a patient. Blaze is still fully pissed at me, and it's probably not going to go away for a while.

I shoot her an annoyed look. "I'm good. Which way do I need to go?"

"We have a follow-up appointment with the surgeon first and he'll recommend the physical therapy, then we'll move down to that part of the building."

I'm already tired thinking about it, but I motion with my crutch for her to lead the way.

CHAPTER EIGHT

Tank

Hearing the surgeon speak isn't making me feel much better. If anything, it's making me feel worse. This is a longer recovery than I thought it would be.

"Six weeks before I can bear weight on it?" I question to make sure I've heard him correctly. Fuck me running.

He nods. "That's right, Trevor, could be sooner though, everyone heals different. I'm giving you worst-case scenario. Keep in mind your six weeks started while you were in the hospital. You've already survived a portion of it. At six weeks we'll make a decision if we can take off the cast and outfit you with a brace. Provided everything is going well, you'll be able to bear weight, as long as it all looks good, and along the way we'll work on getting strength back with the physical therapy. All in all, if things go well, I'm looking to get you back to work in twelve weeks. You're strong and in good shape, we may be able to move that time frame up."

Motherfucker. Twelve weeks before I can get back to work? Three months before I know if I'm going to have to change my profession? What the hell am I going to do for three months? Sit on my couch and eat Cheetos?

"I know this isn't what you wanted to hear," he makes a note on his pad of paper. "But your leg is an important part of your job. We have to make sure it's not only healed, but healed correctly. Do you want to ride a desk the rest of your career?"

"Fuck no," I answer quietly, shaking my hand away from Blaze's. She's tried to grasp it and give me comfort, but right now I don't want the comfort from her or anyone else. I want the biting pain of physical exertion.

"That's my recommendation and it's what I'll be sending it to your boss, Holden. Follow your prescribed PT, and it'll be like you never left. I caution you to not be lazy, but to also not push yourself too hard. Your body will let you know what it can take, listen to it. As I said, we can adjust the timeline, but I won't rush you, Trevor. That's not what I'm here for. I'm here to make sure you heal correctly."

Easy for him to say. I tune out everything else as he talks to Blaze about my daily routine. It amazes me, the first couple of days home from the hospital I'd been thankful I made it through, beyond thankful I made it out of my truck alive. Today, I'm angry as fuck I was put in this situation. Probably one of the signs I need to make an appointment with the shrink. I've obviously got some feelings I need help separating out.

"You ready?" Blaze asks from beside me. I hate the way it sounds like she's talking to a skittish animal, but then again I've given her a lot of shit today.

I shake my head to clear it, obviously I missed out on a part of the meeting, but instead I nod. "As I'll ever be."

She doesn't help me as I get up, and I can admit I miss her reassuring hand on my back as I steady myself. I'm also man enough to admit I've fucked up today. When we get home, I'll make it up to her.

We slowly make our way down to the Physical Therapy room, where I'm introduced to an overly excited guy by the name of Randall, who promises he's going to whip me into shape. Judging by the gleam in his eye - I'm more scared now than I ever have been. But if it's pain I wanted, it's pain I'm going to get.

Blaze

I sit to the side, watching as Trevor goes through the motions of PT. He's putting the work in; I can tell by the way sweat dots the front of his shirt, the way his arms shake as he supports his weight. As much as he's been on edge today, he's given this his all. It makes me extremely proud of him, but I wish like hell he would have been honest with me and stopped brooding for most of the day.

My cell phone lights up beside me with a text from Whitney.

W: What did the doctor say? Has he gotten any nicer? I'm sorry you're having to deal with him, but at the same time I'm thankful he has you.

B: Twelve weeks before he goes back to work. Six in a cast, then a few more in a brace, with physical therapy. It's gonna be a long three months.

W: Oh honey, I know I'm knocked up and all, but if you ever need someone to talk to, I'm here.

It's a nice offer for her to make, and I've grown very close to her in the past - God has it only been two weeks since Trevor wrecked? Feels like a lifetime ago, but if I'm in it for the long haul with him, then I'm all in.

His bad mood today doesn't scare me. Piss me off? Yes. Scare me? No. I can still remember him telling me in the hospital this was going to be a long recovery and I'd have to be patient with him. I don't plan on letting him go this time, no matter how hard he fights my hold. Everybody deserves a bad day, and he probably does more than anyone I know. The fact he's kept his attitude in check for this long says a lot about the man he is.

B: Thanks! I'll let you know if I need some girl time. I'll keep you posted if anything changes with him.

Putting my phone facedown beside me, I watch him again, taking note of the lines of pain near his eyes, the hard line his plump lips have formed while he lifts the weight the therapist has put in his hands. I watch him lift it, hear the count as he brings it back down, and again as he repeats the motion.

No one realizes until they're hurt how quickly your conditioning goes away. It's important to keep him strong. If we do, he'll transition back into his day job with no problems. Glancing at my watch, I see our hour is almost over.

Deciding I want to be nicer when we leave than when we arrived, maybe it'll make him nicer, I grab my purse and carefully make my way out of the room. Leaving the lobby, I notice a vending machine that has water and snacks. Reaching into my wallet, I grab out a couple of dollar bills, purchasing a cold bottle of water and a package of nuts. Exiting the building into the blazing sunlight of the Alabama afternoon, I put my aviators down over my eyes and go in search of my SUV.

I feel bad, having made him walk. It was a rookie move on my part, and I won't make him walk again. Getting in, I crank the air, noticing my temp gauge reads almost eighty. Weeks from Christmas and it's almost eighty? Welcome to the South.

Pulling my SUV up, I leave it running in the drop off area, walking inside. I'm met with the therapist and Trevor.

"We'll see him again on Thursday," he tells me, handing me an appointment card. "We'll do two days a week until he can handle three."

"Got it," I stuff the card in the back pocket of my jeans.

When he walks off, I put my hand at Trevor's back, noticing for the first time, he rests against me. Our fight seems to be gone, and now we're the same vulnerable people who've been dealing with these injuries together. "I pulled up, you don't have to make it across the parking lot."

He breathes deeply, a sigh of relief. I feel petty for making him walk earlier, but I can't change the past. I can only try and make the future better.

We slowly make our way to where I'm parked. I almost suggest we grab a wheelchair, but I know he'll refuse. "Not too much further," I encourage as we exit the building.

It takes a few more minutes for him to get comfortable in the passenger seat. Then I stow the crutches before taking my spot in the driver's seat. "That's for you," I point to the bottle of water and the bag of peanuts.

His head is laying back against the seat, his eyes closed.

"Trev, drink some of the water," I reach down, open the bottle, and give it to him.

He drains it in two drinks. I'm not ashamed to say I'm mesmerized by the way his Adam's apple pushes the water down his throat. "Do you need another bottle?"

He shakes his head, lifting his shirt up to clean his face off. His abs are truly a thing of beauty and I find myself licking my lips. Such an inappropriate line of thinking right now.

"I just wanna get home and take a pain pill. Fuck - everything he made me do hurt like a son of a bitch."

I can hear the pain in his voice. "Then that's what we'll do. You look tired," I take in the paleness of his skin, the sweat still rolling from his temple, and the redness of his lips, no doubt from where he bit them in pain.

"Exhausted. It's not even half of what I used to do in my two-a-day workouts."

"You'll get there, Trev," I reach my hand over and put it on his thigh.

Finally after the day we've had, he grabs hold, pushing our fingers together. "Will I? Today I feel like I'm never gonna get there," his voice is hoarse with emotion. "It seems like an uphill challenge that I'll never be able to overcome."

"Today's day one of a long recovery, Trev. It's going to get better."

We're quiet for a few minutes, each lost in our own thoughts. His mood is different than it's been all day and I'm not sure how to deal with it, so I enjoy us not arguing.

"I owe you an apology," he traces the pattern of lines on my palm with the tip of his finger. "I've been a jackass today, and none of it had to do with you. I was scared about what the doctor would say, scared of the pain of the physical therapy. I didn't know how to deal with it, and it was easier to lash out. I'm sorry, and I'll apologize to Whitney, as well. I'm sure she's blown up your phone talking shit about me."

"No," I grasp his fingertip with my palm. "Both of us knew you were having a hard time with it. People deal with stress and injury differently, Trevor. You're going to have some hard days. Nothing is written in a manual about how you're supposed to deal with it," I shrug as I take back my hand and make a turn so that we're on the interstate heading north to Laurel Springs. "You deal with it how you can. Truth is, you've been dealt a shitty hand. You're going through all this while Brooks sits in jail."

"I still can't believe all he got was a gash on the forehead," he growls his annoyance.

"He'll serve time. You and I both know that."

It's another ten miles down the road before I get the guts to apologize for my part. "I shouldn't have made you do that parking lot, no matter how pissed off I was at the way you were acting. I'm sorry, too," I reach over and grab his hand, kissing his palm. "That was juvenile and I knew better. You would think after fucking up already, we'd be over this shit," I glance over at his strong profile, looking out the passenger side window.

"Maybe we just like to test one another. Sometimes I think it's a form of foreplay for us."

I giggle because he's right. I love to test his patience just to see how much it takes for him to lose it.

"Keep giggling, I like that better than the look of death you gave me earlier," he smiles over at me.

"Keep smiling, those dimples are much cuter than the scowl you've been wearing all day."

As we drive north, I think we'll be okay, as long as we can stay honest with one another. This isn't going to be easy, but nothing worth having ever is. I glance over at Trevor one more time, smiling softly as I see him knocked out, his head against the window, and his arms crossed tightly in front of him.

No matter the difficulties in life, I'll never change anything we have and I know now I'll never give it up.

CHAPTER NINE

Tank

I'M sore from the physical therapy session I had yesterday. I'm ashamed to say I haven't really moved from the couch and it's nearly mid-morning.

"Do you want another pain pill today or just an over-the-counter medication?" Blaze asks as she brings me some toast.

"Over the counter is fine. I'm sore, but it's nothing I can't deal with. I'm going to have to learn to deal with some pain."

She leans down, kissing me on the cheek. "You do better with pain than a lot of other people, give yourself some credit."

I didn't eat last night and the toast is making my mouth water. After coming home from the PT session, Blaze helped me shower, and when I fell into bed, I slept for the rest of the night. Now my stomach is clenching with hunger pains. I inhale one piece in two bites.

"Do you need something else to eat, Trev?" she shoots me a look as she watches me.

I've been trying to eat light, because when pain hits me, it can make me nauseous and I've already puked twice. This morning though, I feel like I have my old appetite back. I think for a minute before smiling up at her. "Scrambled eggs."

She giggles, straight up giggles, and the sound goes to my chest. We haven't had much to laugh about lately. Seeing her throw her head back revealing the curve of her throat, seeing her Adam's apple bob up and down with the force of her laugh - it warms a spot in my heart.

"Then scrambled eggs you will have."

I sit up straighter on the couch. "You know how I like 'em, right?"

"Spinach, onions, garlic powder, and hot sauce. I got this, Trev," she winks as she turns, walking toward the kitchen with a little sway to her ass.

I lay my head back against the arm of the couch and close my eyes, letting them rest for a minute. The extra food will help the pain killers from last night, leave my system, and I hope that I don't have to take anymore today.

I must doze, because the next thing I know, Blaze is handing me a paper plate. "Here ya go; you'll feel more awake when you get this in your stomach."

She sits on the opposite side of the couch, dragging my feet into her lap. It's nice to sit here with her like this.

"You seriously make the best scrambled eggs. They're always fluffy. Mine are almost hard when I'm done cooking them. One day you'll have to teach me all your secrets," I groan as I take my last bite, laying my hands on my stomach.

"I can't share all my secrets," she teases. "Then you won't want me to hang around."

I reach down, grabbing her hand that's resting on my thigh. "I'll always want you around. If anything, it's the most important thing I've learned since Thanksgiving."

"I definitely always want to be around."

We're interrupted as my cell buzzes beside me. It's been quiet since I got out of the hospital for the most part, most people just stop by.

I grab it, flipping it over, seeing a text from Ryan.

R: I'm with your sister at the hospital. This isn't a false alarm. We're having a baby today.

Holy shit!

T: Do you want me to come up or is this something the two of you want to remain private?

I don't want to overstep my boundaries with them. I'll be okay with whatever he tells me.

"Whitney's in labor," I glance over at Blaze, not able to help the smile of excitement that's spread across my face.

"Oh my God! Are you going?"

"I asked what they want me to do. If they want this to be a private thing, I don't want to go barging in there."

She nods in understanding. "Yeah, that's kind of a private thing. Women are usually all spread out," she grins. "You don't want see your sister's stuff."

"Oh hell no, but if she wants me there, I'll be there."

My cell chimes beside me again.

R: Please come up here, I think we both need you. I'm nervous as fuck man. I'm gonna be a dad.

I laugh as I see Ryan's message. I can just imagine what he looks like right now. His eyes are probably bugged out and he's more than likely got a vein popped on his neck.

"C'mon, we're having a niece today," I'm already struggling to get up.

"Are we?" she asks, holding my hand tightly.

The question is there in her eyes and I know what she's asking me. "We are," I tuck one of the crutches under my arm to give me a free hand, cupping her jaw with my palm. "Don't you know I want you in every part of my life? The minute I woke up in that hospital room, my life came into clear view. I don't want to live it without you anymore."

She nods, closing her eyes. I take the opportunity to tilt her chin up, capturing her lips with mine. "One day we'll make it official, Blaze, just know that's where I'm headed. I hope you're headed there too."

"I am, but I also know we have a lot to work out."

I lean in, kissing her forehead. "We'll work it out, all I need to know is we're headed in the same direction."

"We are."

I HAVEN'T BEEN in an actual hospital since I was released, and I'm not prepared for the anxiety I feel as we go toward the room I've been told my sister is in. At the waiting room, we saw Mom and Dad. Neither one of them wanted to be in the room - said they couldn't deal with it. Perfectly fine, Whitney and I have kinda been each other's cheerleader our whole lives.

Not to say our parents haven't been supportive, but Mom wanted Whitney to do pageants and marry a rich guy. Dad wanted me to go work with him on the oil rigs in the Gulf. Whitney supported me and I supported her. We're close.

As we get to the room, I knock on the door, not wanting to see something brain bleach won't scrub from my subconscious.

"Man, it's good to see you," Ryan greets me as he pulls back the privacy curtain.

We embrace and I can feel the anxiety and fear radiating off him. "You got this my man, this is everything you've always wanted. It's all good," I clap him on the back.

He doesn't say anything as he steps back and lets me in. In my peripheral vision I see him hugging Blaze, but my attention is captured by my sister.

I've never seen her look more vulnerable in her life. Not even when she came to me the night she left her husband. She's sitting up in bed, face devoid of makeup, hair up in a ponytail. She fucking looks younger than Ryan and I both.

“How you doin’, mama?” I grin as I carefully use my crutches to get over to her side.

“Really glad you’re here.” The smile she gives me is one of relief and excitement.

"Trev, you just got out of the hospital, you didn't have to come back," She tells me as she reaches out to touch me when I maneuver my way over.

I lean down, letting her hug my neck. Even though she’s the older of us, I’ve always been her protector. I beat the shit out of her asshole husband when I learned what he did to her. That’s a secret the two of us will take to our graves.

Blaze moves a chair closer so I can have a seat and then offers Whitney a smile before she moves to the couch in the room. "I wouldn't miss this for the world. I know Mom and Dad said to let them know when it gets closer to time, but I've never let you go through something on your own before. Just like you didn't let me spend Thanksgiving by myself," I give her hand a squeeze.

"I love you, Trev."

"I love you too, Sis, but fair warning, if they open up your hoo ha and I even get a glimpse, I'm out. Blaze might have to carry me, out at that point."

She laughs loudly. "Completely understood. I'm so glad you're here. For a while there, I wasn't sure whether you would get to see this or not."

I’m quiet for a few minutes, going back to the days following the wreck. My eyes become unfocused as I remember laying in the hospital bed, wondering if I’d be here for this. Clearing my throat, I lay some truth down on her. "I wasn't sure I would either, but now that I am, nothing's going to tear me away."

"So, I think Alabama is playing. Should I turn it on?" Ryan asks, breaking the silence.

BLAZE HAS ABANDONED us to go sit with my parents, but I think it’s because she knew Whitney was close. I’m watching this with complete awe and fear as I sit at my sister’s bedside. I can see her pushing so hard, straining against her contractions as she pushes like the doctor told her to. Ryan stands beside her, offering support, kissing her temple, wiping her forehead down. I’ve never seen either one of them like this, and more than anything, it drives home the fact they temper their PDA in front of me. These two love each other more than I even thought.

“With the next contraction, I want you to push, Whitney. Push against the contraction and we’ll get this baby out,” the doctor says from where she sits.

I’m on the edge of my seat. This is more nail biting than an Alabama football game, which I can hear in the background. We turned it on a while ago, and they’re now in the fourth quarter. I can hear “Dixieland Delight” when Whitney starts screaming and pushing for all she’s worth.

"C'mon Princess," I can hear Ryan encourage her. He puts his mouth at her ear, whispering words of encouragement to her. I can see his lips moving, but can't hear the words he's saying. Whatever it is, it makes her grit her teeth and bear down hard.

In the next moment, I hear the baby drop before anything else. Then the most amazing sound I've ever heard in my life happens when the loud cries of a pissed off child is heard. I'm not sure there's a dry eye in the room as I wipe at my own.

I watch as they put my niece on Whitney's stomach. Ryan looks like he's about to pass out as they ask him to cut the cord. He moves over to my side, and I stand, putting my hand on his shoulder to offer my support to him. It's hard to keep my balance without the crutches, but I do it, because I want to be there for three of the most important people in my life.

We share a look, one that holds so much meaning for the both of us. The man in front of me has laid his demons down and found happiness. In the look, he's telling me to go do the same thing.

I'm fascinated as I watch them clean her up and put her on Whitney's chest. She calms almost immediately as she hears her mom's heartbeat. Ryan and Whitney glance at each other with a love so pure it almost makes me jealous.

I'm about to leave, to give them some privacy when Whitney reaches her hand out to me. "Come meet your niece, Trevor. I want her to know what a badass uncle she has to go along with her badass dad."

I take her hand and let her pull me forward, Ryan's steadying me on my other side. She moves the blanket so I can see the baby's face.

My eyes meet Whitney's and for the second time today, tears are rolling down my cheeks, getting caught in my beard. I use my finger to caress Stella's face. She's the perfect mix of the two of them. I can tell immediately she'll more than likely have the same type of hair I do, and it makes my heart beat a little faster. "She's gorgeous."

"She is," Ryan agrees.

Out of nowhere, her little hand reaches up and grabs my finger. With one tiny finger grab, this girl has my heart, and I swear she kind of smiles. Today, is the best day ever, and I tilt my head back, thanking God I'm here to witness it.

CHAPTER TEN

Blaze

TEN DAYS **Later**

"You're sure it's okay for me to put myself back on the rotation for next week?" I ask Trevor as I sit on his bed, watching him get ready for the day.

"I think it'll be all good," he says as he sets his crutch to the side, working to put his shirt on one arm and then the other before pulling it over his head.

I'm pensive when I maybe shouldn't be. It's been a month since he wrecked, almost three weeks since he was released from the hospital, but I worry he's overdoing it. Fact of the matter is Trevor's starting to look and act more like his old self. Two more weeks with the no weight-bearing and then he'll be able to walk on his own. He won't need me, and I'll have to get back to work. I can't keep hovering over him like some den mother. Today for instance, he's dressing himself and not sweating like a stuck pig. He truly is getting better.

"Then I'll call and have them put me back on rotation. Hopefully Logan's still free."

He shoots me an almost bored look. "You're Logan's partner, it's not like he's going to find a new one while you're gone. Just like Ryan's not going to ride with Ace forever. I get texts every day about how much he misses me. It's sweet really," he wipes at a nonexistent tear.

"What you seriously need is to be taken down a notch, Trevor Trumbolt," I fix him with a glare.

"And you're the woman to do that?" he taunts as he has a seat next to me, pulling the sweatpants on he's wearing today.

I lean in, kissing him hard before grabbing his bottom lip in between my teeth and tugging. "I'm the *only* woman."

He reaches around, digging his fingers in my hair, holding me tightly to him. His blue eyes stare in my green, and the seriousness with which he looks at me makes me want to look away. I can't, I don't want to ignore the pull between us ever again.

"You are," his throat is gravelly. "The only person who totally gets me and loves me no matter what. You're my person," he tugs my mouth to his.

I give in as he owns the kiss he's giving me, tilting my head to the side to accommodate the slide of his tongue against mine. My fingers dig in his hair, disrupting the way he's pulled it back out of his face. God I love his hair; it's silky, way too pretty for a man to have, and the slightest bit curly. I wonder what Stella's hair will look like when it grows out. Will she get this from their side of the family? If Trevor and I ever get our shit together and have kids, will they have this wavy, blonde mass? I pull back from the kiss because I'm too deep in my feelings, letting too many emotions take me out of the pleasure that is Trevor's mouth.

His voice is deep and rough as he speaks. "As much as I would love to keep going and spend the day in bed with you, Whit's gonna be here in a few minutes."

They're having an outing, one I'm not allowed to know about. Days before Christmas, I can guess it's probably to get a present for me.

"And I need to go call into the station. See what kind of shift I can get on where I can still be there for your physical therapy."

His fingers tangle with mine, pulling me down to sit on his good thigh. "I love you," he whispers as he pushes the hair back from my face.

Those words never get old, and I have a feeling they never will. "I love you, too."

Tank

"Thanks for agreeing to take me. I know you had a baby like a week ago and you could have told me to kiss your ass," I grin over at my older sister as I get situated in the passenger seat of her SUV.

"Be thankful to our mom. She's at home with Ryan to make sure nothing awful happens. He was so nervous," she laughs as she backs out of my drive.

"I can only imagine. He's stone-cold when it comes to work, but the personal stuff is sometimes where he draws the line."

She snorts slightly. "He asked me what if she won't stop crying? I had to break it to him that sometimes at night, when he's snoring, she's crying the entire time. It's not like because I'm her mom I can make her stop. I'm as clueless as he is."

"But you're in it together," I remind her. "And that's probably the coolest thing ever. I'm sorry for the way I reacted when I found out," I glance over at her, gauging her reaction. "It's one of the biggest embarrassments and regrets I had while I lay in the hospital. I can't even put my finger on why it bothered me so much."

Early morning traffic a few days before Christmas isn't nearly as bad as I thought it would be, and I think for a minute, Whitney's not going to answer me. When we stop at a red light, she turns to look at me.

"I think it bothered you so much, Trevor, because you want it but you're scared of it. You're also overbearing when it comes to Blaze, which I think is ridiculous after you saw what I went through."

Dayum, sometimes I hate how well she knows me. Not like I didn't already realize it, but fuck my sister is a ballbreaker. "Blaze talked to you about our big argument, huh?"

"She didn't talk to me about it, but she did tell me you asked her to give up her job," she fixes me with a glare. "And since you're alive and well, I can say what I've wanted to say since I found out. What the fuck were you thinking when you asked her to give up her job?"

How do I explain to her how scary it was to see the gun sitting next to Blaze's head? To take note of the shaking hand of the mentally unstable man who held my world in the balance of his breakdown. How fucking helpless I felt while I stood there, knowing I could take him out with my past as a sniper. Yet they made me wait, made me watch everything happen with my own two eyes. So I tell her all of that.

She's quiet for a few minutes before she shoots a pointed glance my way. "The same way she had to respond to your wreck and wonder if you'd even make it to the hospital? Your job is just as dangerous as anyone else's Trevor, even more so. You and Ryan go through life thinking nothing bad is going to happen to you, but more than anything, this should show you how incorrect that is. Trev, you weren't even working, you were enjoying your day off and you could have died. It had nothing to do with your job. It was you living day-to-day."

"I know," I nod, knowing she's telling me the truth. "Trust me, I know. I've thought about it a lot. It's been on my mind more than you can imagine. I still can't get over the picture I have of her in my mind. The asshole was holding a gun to her head, and she tried to be so brave. At first she wasn't shaking, she was crying, but I knew how scared she was. I could see it, I know this woman better than anyone else who responded that day. Her eyes said it all. She was fucking scared to death, and I worried I was going to let her down. What if my co-workers and I couldn't convince this guy to let her go? What if my life ends as I see her brains splattered across the concrete? It was enough to make me sick, and after he pushed her away and we made sure she was okay, I went out back behind the house and puked twice. Ryan found me, and immediately knew what was going on in my head. I couldn't take the fear."

Even now my palms are sweating and I have to rub them against my thighs to dry them off. I take a steadying breath to remind myself I'm not in that moment any longer.

"It's a fear, Whit, a fear I'm not sure I can cope with," I do my best to explain.

She gets onto the interstate, taking us a few towns away so our shopping selection is better. I watch as she checks her blind spot and then sets her cruise control. "You think I don't have fear? Trev, you and Ryan are my life besides Stella. Every damn day I start the morning out with a prayer that you two make it home. If I dwelled on it all the time, if I focused on it, I'd never be able to live my life. I have to trust that the two of you know what you're doing, that you won't take unnecessary chances, and that the people you're with will also do the job they're supposed to. I'm scared almost every day of my life. But you have to realize," she glances over at me, her bottom lip trembling almost imperceptivity. "There's only been one day that fear came true, and that was the day you had your wreck."

"And the bitch of it all was I wasn't even working," I finish for her.

"Yeah," she stiffens her chin. "You weren't even working. If you had been, to be honest, it may have been easier," she admits on a whisper.

I'm intrigued, but she doesn't keep speaking. "How would it have been easier?"

"Because then I would know you got hurt doing what you love. People have to do your job, Trev. If people didn't do your job this world would be a very dangerous place to live. Kids couldn't walk down the street, we wouldn't have the freedom of going to the mall a couple of days before Christmas, and in another world, I may be stoned to death for loving Ryan. The fact of the matter is, it takes all kinds to make this world go round, and if it wasn't you doing this, it would be someone else. I'm comfortable with your choices because I'd never want you to be unhappy. Everyone is the love of someone's life," she shrugs.

"So, you're saying you'd rather be scared and have us be happy?" I'm trying to follow along because I truly want to understand this. I want Blaze and me to be able to make a relationship work, I don't want to be at odds with her, and I never want anything else to hold us back.

"Life is too short, you should know it better than anyone after what you've just gone through. If you really think about it, Trev, I think you'll understand you want the people you love to do things that make them happy, even if they die doing it. At least you'll know they died with a smile on their face, doing what they were called to do," she gestures to her chest. "Because me? I know you and Ryan were born to do what you do. The two of you wear authority the same way you wear your bulletproof vests. You don't hesitate for a second to put them on and get out in the middle of a disturbance, a firefight, in between two people arguing with one another – you *never* hesitate. And you don't hesitate because you're trained well, you know what you're doing, and you're confident in your abilities. I trust you to make good decisions, and I think if you were to sit back and watch Blaze on her home turf, doing what she does, you'd see she's the same as you. And if she's called to do that job, how can you try and make her choose? You and it are both her heart."

I'm quiet for a few minutes, letting what she says sink in. I try to think back to times I've seen Blaze do her job, hell she's done it on me a few times, and there's no doubt she's good at it. She's confident and never second-guesses herself. I would trust her with the care of anyone I love.

"Let me put it to you another way," my sister turns into the mall parking lot. "If you force her to choose again, do you know the decision she'll make?"

The answer hits me with clarity. "I don't know her decision. I'm not sure whether she'd choose me or not."

"Then is that something you want to force her to do? Do you want to live the rest of your life wondering 'what might have been' with her? You've got to come to peace with what she does, Trev. If not, you're going to lose her again, and I'm not sure if you'll be able to get her back this time."

"I did before," my voice is strong, confident, daring her to tell me I'll lose the woman I love again.

"But this time she's been faced with the harsh reality of what your job can do to you – even if it was off duty. If you're not ready to face hers head on – why in the hell are you going to ask her to face yours? That's not love, brother, that's controlling the situation. Do you really want to be that asshole?"

CHAPTER ELEVEN

Blaze

I'M bored without Trevor here, although I have to admit this is the first time I've been alone in his house since I came to stay with him weeks ago. I've gone back to my apartment a few times to pick up clothing, check the mail, and make sure no one has broken in, but since he got out of the hospital I've been here with him night and day. It's weird not to have him here, odd not to have him to take care of. I'm used to listening for him, trying to determine if he needs my help or if he's trying to be stubborn and do things on his own.

This morning, when I watched him doing things more easily, it shot a pain through my chest. He's not going to need me much longer, especially when he gets the okay to bear weight. It'll be time for me to go back to my own home, and I have to admit, I'm scared. Will we go back to ignoring each other the way we were before or are we really going to try and make this work?

Times of great stress tend to bring people closer together, and it's done exactly that to us. The emotions I feel for him are many times more acute and stronger than they were before Thanksgiving. With clarity, I realize I've broken my life into two sections. Before Thanksgiving and after Thanksgiving. It's the benchmark I've used instead of saying before Trevor's wreck and after Trevor's wreck. Thinking of it as Thanksgiving doesn't make my head and chest hurt, it doesn't flash me back to the way Trevor looked inside that truck as we got there. Sometimes I wake up, haunted by the vision of how his head was cocked to the side, even after Ryan told me he was breathing, how I still thought he may have had a broken neck and Ryan was wrong. I don't wake up as much as I did when he was in the hospital, but every once in a while, I can feel my heart pounding, my breath coming faster, and a panic attack coming on. It's part of what you live with every day thanks to the job.

I can't stay inside this house right now, because the walls are closing in. My breath is coming fast, and I need some fresh air. Grabbing my phone and a bottle of water, I walk out onto Trevor's back porch. Inhaling, I do my best to regulate my heartbeat and wait for the sweating to go away. One day I'm going to have to cry about what I saw, but today won't be that day.

Closing my eyes, I focus on my breathing, letting it take me out of my panic. When my hands have stopped shaking and my ears have stopped ringing, I open my eyes and take in the serenity of Trevor's fenced-in backyard. Even though it's December, the grass is green because of the rain and warm temperatures we've had. A fire pit sits in the furthest left corner, a hammock in the back right. As soon as he moved in, his mom planted flowerbeds and they're blooming right now because of the warmth, dashes of color against the greenery of the yard. With a critical eye taught to me by my own mother, I see one of them is being overtaken by weeds. My upbringing won't allow me to let that happen. Mommy dearest didn't like weeds in her garden, as soon as one sprouted up, she'd get the gardener on that ASAP. Or the pool boy, whoever she had on speed-dial that day. Grabbing my bottle of water again, I march out, sink to my knees, and use all my pent-up energy to yank the fucking weeds out by their roots. Ugly things don't belong here, and I'll be damned if I let them stay.

Tank

"Do you know where you want to go first?" Whitney asks as she holds the door to the mall open for me.

I breathe a sigh of relief as I see the mall isn't busy this time of morning. I'd been scared it would be hard for me to maneuver on my crutches and I might have to ask my sister to push me around in a wheelchair. "I do. The first place I want to stop is the jewelry store up on the right," I motion with my head.

She claps her hands with a grin.

"Don't get that kind of an idea," I warn her. "Blaze and I aren't anywhere near ready to make anything official, but there is something I've been eyeing for a while, for her. I've seen her eye it too, but she refuses to buy it because it's expensive.'

Whitney raises an eyebrow at me. "With the money she comes from?"

Not many people know about Blaze's family life, and she prefers not to make it a focus of her day-to-day, but even I have to laugh at Whitney's question. "She doesn't live off her family money, it stays in a trust."

Whitney whistles through her teeth. "The Coleman money is a lot of damn money to let sit in a trust. I think I'd have to dip in, even if to just take a trip to I don't know, the Maldives. Because with money like that, she can afford it."

"Right?" I answer, because I've thought about asking her before if we could take a truly ostentatious trip.

Blaze's family, once you know her real name, is one of the most affluent in this part of Alabama, the entire state if we want to get technical. She comes from old money, and if it were up to her family, they'd have a daughter like Whitney. One that wears her pearls, knows exactly how to act in polite company, and wants nothing more than to be the belle of the ball. Instead, they got the rebellious spitfire that is Blaze.

"Did I tell you I'm going to her parents' house this weekend for their annual Christmas party?" I make small talk because it helps me with the physical exertion of using the crutches.

"Trev, are you for real? Please tell me you have something nice to wear. That's like *the* party of the year. Even though I don't do events, do you know what a feather in my cap it would be to plan that event? Just one time."

"Stop salivating," I shoot her a look. "Yes, I do have a suit to wear. I'm hoping at my final physical therapy appointment this week they'll give me the okay to bear weight."

"Wouldn't that be early?" Her eyebrows come together, worry in the middle.

"We're only looking at a few days early in the grand scheme of things."

"Days that add up to a couple of weeks," she points out, already acting like the mother she's been for only a short time.

"They told me I'm doing well, and we started a little at my last appointment. They took x-rays to see how the bone is healing, and if it's healed enough, I'll get a new cast, which is actually a brace, be able to bear weight and start doing some pool exercises which will help me build muscle up quicker and have much less impact. I'm doing good, sis."

She pats me on the back before she leans over and kisses me on the cheek. "You are, and I'm more proud of you than I could ever let you know."

My chest puffs out with that pride. There are few people in my life I worry about impressing and she's one of them. "That means a lot."

We don't say anything else as we make our way into the jewelry store.

"Do you know what you want to get her?" she asks as we enter and say hi to the two associates working behind the counters.

"Sure do," I go directly to the watch case. "She's been eyeing this G-shock for a while. It's got everything anybody doing her job needs, and she broke her other watch last week. Win-win for me." It's navy blue and hot pink, water resistant, shock resistant, and has the second hand, which she uses when she's checking someone's pulse.

I make my purchase, handing the bag to Whitney, super proud of myself.

It's both practical and feminine, which I know she doesn't get to display very often. In her line of work, the only people who notice she's a woman are the drunks who hit on her when they're looking for a pretty face.

"Is this all you're getting her?" Whitney asks when we exit the jewelry store.

As hard as I try, I can't help the blood red I know my face turns. The curse of being a blond. "No, it's not all I'm getting her. I have to go over here," I point to a lingerie store.

Whitney laughs. "You want me to let you do this on your own, Trev? There's a children's store right up there and I'd love to get Stella a Christmas dress."

"I'll come find you," I promise as I watch her walk away.

Heading into the store, I have a smirk on my face. If there's one thing Blaze loves, even though she's not girlie, it's to wear lingerie, and I have to say, I love seeing her in it. Usually she picks it out and surprises me with it. This time I'm going to get her exactly what I've been dying for her to wear. High-handed? Maybe, but I do love a woman who is sexually aware, and nobody is more sexually aware than my Blaze.

CHAPTER TWELVE

Blaze

"DID YOU GET EVERYTHING YOU NEED?" I question as Trevor comes in with Whitney behind him, carrying wrapped gifts.

"I did," he greets me with a smile and a kiss, before he turns back to his sister. "Thanks for taking me again, Whit. We'll be over sometime this week to see Stella, if that's cool?"

"Just text to make sure she's not asleep. Do you need anything else?"

She looks like she's about to drop, and I pull her into my arms. If there's one thing I know after seeing many new moms, it's sometimes they need a hug. "Anything else he needs, I have. Take care of yourself and be sure to get as much rest as you can."

"I'm doing my best," she closes her eyes as she sighs. "It's hard, though. Hopefully, soon she'll realize what sleeping for longer than three hours at a time is." Her grin is rueful, and I know she wouldn't give any of it up for the world.

"She will," I assure her. "Not that I'm a mother or anything, but you do learn a few things when you work in the healthcare industry. Do your best to get her on a schedule."

"We're working on it," she reaches in and hugs Trevor as he comes back into the room. "Will I see you all at Mom's on Christmas morning?"

My eyes meet Trevor's. I want to be there, but he hasn't asked me to come. When my parents do their holiday party, it's not like we sit around a tree and open gifts, it's never been like that. At least not that I can remember.

"Yeah, we'll be there," he answers. "Eight in the morning for breakfast, right?"

"Yup, I plan on getting there a little early to help," a yawn slips from her mouth before she can cover it up.

I find myself speaking up. "Then we'll get there a little early, too. You just had a baby, no reason I can't help."

We say our goodbyes, Trevor and I watching as she backs out onto the street and speeds away with a wave. It's easy for me to believe this is the type of life I can have with him, but I know I can't make plans, not until we deal with our issues. Those issues seem to have been put to the side while he recovers and I'm okay with it, but I'm not stupid either. Not talking about it doesn't automatically fix anything.

"I'm sorry if she put you on the spot," he holds the door open for me with his crutch as I step inside, in turn holding it open for him.

"On the spot for what?" My eyebrows come together in question. I'm truly confused as to why he's apologizing.

"Christmas morning at my parents'. I mean I know I'm going with you to your parents' big party, but there's a huge difference in attending a holiday party and a family Christmas. If you don't feel comfortable, please tell me."

There's a struggle with what I want to tell him and what I should tell him. Being transparent would probably the smart thing to do, but he and I have never really been smart and we've never really been transparent. Maybe right now is a good time to start. Nothing will change until one of us takes the first step.

"The holiday party with my family? It's like Christmas morning with yours. Mine have never been big on the quaint family life, though. They'd much rather get together and show off how much money they have."

He leans against the living room wall, letting the drywall take his weight instead of his arms and crutches. "You mean to tell me y'all don't open gifts in front of the tree? You do nothing privately?"

"Olivia Prescott Coleman – Prescott with two t's," I flash him a smart grin before continuing on, "never does anything privately, Trevor. Everything she does is manipulated and manufactured to further whatever agenda it is she's working on at the moment. If it doesn't further it, then at least she gets attention from it. All in all, it's a win for her," I stand in front of him, letting my fingers play with the thin material of his t-shirt. "Damon Coleman? Well, Daddy just likes his expensive scotch, cigars, and young secretaries who can keep their lips closed while keeping their legs open at the same time. It's not exactly *A Christmas Story* at the Coleman mansion."

"Goddamn," he makes a noise in his throat. "And you want to take me to this party?"

I shrug. "I wanna take you wherever it is you wanna go with me," I fight the smile tugging at the corners of my mouth.

"Look at you, being cute and flirting with me."

Tangling my fingers tighter in his t-shirt, I tug against it, pulling him so he lowers his head toward mine. Our mouths are mere centimeters apart when he closes the gap, but I grin against the butterflies in my stomach, letting his lips chase mine. I hear one of his crutches fall to the floor as his hand snakes around my neck, holding me in place. When his lips capture mine – and make no mistake, it is a capture – my damn knees go weak.

My fingers hold tightly to his shirt as he thoroughly kisses me. His tongue invades, swiping against mine as our noses rub against one another. I hear the other crutch fall to the floor as he brings me into his body, every part of us is touching. The whiskers of his beard rub against my chin as he breaks our kiss. His fingers tug the hair at the nape of my neck, forcing me to tilt back against my shoulders and expose all the space below my chin to him.

"Trev, we shouldn't be doing this," I gasp as he nips at the pulse point of my throat. "Your leg," I try again, digging my nails into the covered flesh of his amazing abs.

"Is fucking fine," he growls against me.

But I worry. He's a month out from a traumatic situation, and even though he's talking to the doctor about putting him in a boot when he goes tomorrow, I hope he's not rushing his recovery.

"I'm fine, Blaze," he assures me again as he laps at the tendons before smearing his kiss along the side and moving his lips up to my ear. "I've always been a fast healer."

"Batman," I gasp. "Right?"

His chuckle is dark and deep in my ear. "So you do listen to me sometimes."

"I listen to you all the time," I dig my fingers in his hair, yanking out the band he's used to pull it back today. "Following the directions you give me? That's a different story."

The palm of his free hand snakes under my shirt, moving up along my stomach until it encounters the edge of my bra. Just when his fingers squeeze the satin and flesh rising above it, his doorbell rings.

"Trevor honey, it's me."

We jump apart, the intrusion scaring us to death.

"Son of a bitch," Trevor groans as he leans his head back against the wall with a thud. "I'll be right there, Mom!"

I giggle as he adjusts the front of his pants, bending down to get his crutches. His flat palm smacks the curve of my ass as I reach to get his right one, making me gasp.

"Remember how that felt, because when I can, I'm making you pay for that giggle."

"I'll be looking forward to it," I wink, licking my lips as I strut over to open the door for his mom.

Two can definitely play at this game.

CHAPTER THIRTEEN

Tank

SITTING IN WAITING ROOMS OF DOCTORS' offices has become my least favorite thing in the world, and today I'm all by myself. Blaze had to go and meet with her supervisor to get put back on rotation. She insisted on making sure she's available for me whenever I need her, but I'm hoping after today, I can become much more self-sufficient.

That thought hits me in the gut, because I don't necessarily want her to go. I like having her around, love waking up to her every morning, and look forward to the breakfast she always has waiting for me after I drag my ass out of bed. Running a hand through my hair, I realize how much I depend on her – not to take care of me – but to be my partner. What if she decides she's done?

"Trevor, you can come on back."

I didn't even notice the nurse standing in front of me until she spoke. Blaze leaving my home, and possibly my life, is the scariest thing in the world for me right now. There is one thing I do know, and it's after what happened with the gunman, I've got to be honest with her. No matter what happens here today, we'll figure it out.

"How are you doing?" the nurse smiles at me as she holds the door open. I don't miss the way her eyes rake down my body. Sounds egotistical, but I'm used to it and it doesn't even affect me anymore. The only thing that affects me now are Blaze's eyes running down my body, her hands touching my flesh. It's enough to cause a reaction just thinking about it.

"I'm good, ready to see if I can get this cast off and into a boot."

"Kinda early, huh?" she makes small talk.

I shrug because I don't really want to do the small talk dance with her. More than anything, I want this appointment over so I can figure out what my next few weeks look like.

She escorts me to another room and I have a seat on an examination table, waiting impatiently for the doctor to come in. I've done some reading online, so I know there's a chance, if my break has healed enough, I can get the cast off today. I was very fortunate about where Brooks hit me because most of the impact was on the front passenger side, and I'm hoping that's what allows me to get out of this cast today. I want to take a shower, to walk without the crutches digging into my armpits, to get back to work, and to make love to Blaze the way I want to. I wasn't lying when I told Blaze I'm a fast healer, either. I always have been, plus I'm stubborn as fuck.

"Morning, Trevor," the doctor greets me as he comes in.

There are no pleasantries from me. "How did that x-ray look?"

The older man laughs slightly as he shakes his head at me. "I don't know that I've ever met someone who's more anxious to get back to work than you. The state of Alabama is lucky to have you."

I don't need someone to kiss my ass and tell me how great I am. I'm fully aware that I'm only four weeks out from a wreck that could have killed me, but I also know that I have been feeling better the last couple of days. Stronger, more aware of my surroundings, there's been a lot less pain and I've not had to take any pain killers since that first physical therapy appointment. More than anything, I just want my life back. I'm aware it won't be the same way it was before the wreck, there might be things I have to account for and accommodations I have to make. I'm good with that, but I'm not good at sitting around.

He pulls out a piece of paper before he puts his glasses on, reading what looks like a report. "I have to say I'm a little surprised, but I've seen the human body do amazing things. Looking at the x-ray, the report, and talking to your physical therapist, I'm going to say we can take this cast off. You'll still have to be careful, but we can get you in the pool next week. There will be absolutely no running on it yet and you'll probably walk with a limp until you're completely healed. Your physical therapist will help you with that. I'm going to send a note over to Holden letting him know that right now we'll keep your return to work week-to-week provided you do everything else you're supposed to."

Happiness explodes in my chest. "I'm so ready."

As he leaves the room, my phone pings and my smile falters for the first time.

Holden: Excited for you to get that cast off brother, but you better be making your appointment with the shrink. We just

need her to sign off on you – as soon as that's done, you do the physical course and you're back.

Fuck me. I've been putting it off, but I won't be able to any longer. So far I haven't been able to remember shit about the wreck, and I'm scared if the departments shrink starts digging, I will remember. I don't want and don't need that fear in my life. But the writing is on the wall - I'm going to have to face whatever it is, because I won't be able to go back to my job until I do.

Tank: Got it, I'll make my appointment tomorrow and I'll keep you up to date on all progress. Can't wait to get back.

Ignoring the nagging in my gut, I text Blaze, letting her know I'm getting the cast off, and they'll be giving me a boot. I sigh deeply, feeling like one obstacle that's been standing in my way be lifted.

"LOOK AT YOU, WALKING BY YOURSELF," Blaze grins as she watches me approach her SUV at the drop off area.

"I know, right? I can't even begin to tell you how nice this is," I get inside, shutting the door.

"I'm excited that your boot goes with your tux pants," she looks down at it.

"I requested black, for the suit pants and because Batman," I wink at her as she laughs.

"You're in a really good mood."

She's right - I am. I hadn't realized how grumpy I've been, even though I'm thankful I wasn't hurt worse in the wreck. I've still been on edge, because I haven't known what the future will bring for me and while that's true of everyone, I can admit now how damn scared I was. When they took the cast off, put the boot on, and then told me to walk – that was potentially the scariest moment of my life. But I did it, and guess what? While it hurt a little, and definitely felt weird, it's freeing to know I won't be held back as much anymore.

"I am, and I'm sorry I've been kind of a pain in the ass lately. I've been worried, scared to death actually, that I wouldn't be able to be the same kind of cop, same kind of man, I was before. You know how much physical activity and my job mean to me. I want to be able to get out and do things with you, with Stella when she's old enough. It means the world to me."

Reaching over, she grabs my hand. "I get it, I totally do, and you haven't been awful. None of us know how we'd react if we were in your situation."

"I don't know how you've handled it so well, Blaze, I mean what you saw and what you did, was amazing."

"It was my job."

"That's bullshit and you know it, babe. It was my job that day I saw that guy hold the gun to your head, but it didn't make it any easier. I felt more out of control that day than I ever have in my life. My emotions were in a blender, and I wasn't sure I'd be able to make a rational decision. I have no idea how you administered medical care to me and kept it together." And that's the realest I've ever been with her. If we want to face things and start repairing the relationship we fucked up, we have to start somewhere.

She swallows so hard I can see her throat move. "I didn't want anyone else touching you," her voice is low as she drives us back to Laurel Springs. "In my mind, no one cares for you like I do, so I wasn't sure if anyone else could give you the kind of attention I could. While it hurt to see you lying there, see the blood pouring from the cut over your eye, see the swelling that was already happening on your face, and hear you gasping for air, I knew I could keep you going. I knew what to do to make it better, and I was going to be damned if I let anyone else touch you. No one else knew you physically and emotionally like I did, and in my heart I knew I'd provide the best care."

There's a clarity to her voice and a clarity to the feelings that hit me square in the chest. She's damn right, no one does care for me better than she does. Not even my sister or my mom. Blaze cares with her whole heart and her whole body. It reminds me that we have a lot of work to do, and now that I feel like a whole man, we're gonna be putting in a huge amount of time to make it work.

CHAPTER FOURTEEN

Blaze

SOMETIMES WHEN I dress up for these parties, I don't even recognize the person staring back at me in the mirror. No, that's a lie; I do recognize myself, but the me I see is the one who let everyone else control her life. It's the sixteen-year-old girl who was being groomed to marry a rich man and become a society maven. If I close my eyes and think hard, I can still see her. With her platinum blonde hair, wearing her pearls like a southern debutante does, clear eyes innocent as hell only wanting to please her parents.

I can remember her very clearly. She wore pink lipstick and looked at men underneath long eye-lashes, and she giggled when a boy with proper family lineage would pay attention to her. Daphne would shrink into the crowd, smile prettily, curtsy, and be the envy of every other southern debutante in the room.

The memories aren't happy and I don't like reliving a past that's painful. Squaring my shoulders, I lean closer to the mirror, making sure the fake lashes I'm applying are even. "Nice," I grin at myself, running my tongue over my teeth to make sure my bright red lipstick isn't on the white enamel. The little black dress I'm wearing covers the tattoos on my arms, and for one night, I look like what my parents truly want their daughter to look like. As I turn in the mirror to look behind me, making sure my ass is covered, one of the waves I've curled my hair into escapes from my updo. It's an easy fix before I put earrings in my ears and a bracelet on my wrist. One last time, I give myself a once-over before spritzing perfume on my pulse points and leave Trevor's bathroom.

Entering the bedroom I hear a wolf-whistle. He's standing in the doorway, actually standing there, with his hands above his head braced against the frame. He takes my breath away for a moment, because he's so damn fine. I mean *dayum*, I'm going home with that tonight. As usual, he's oblivious to how hot he is.

I've only seen Trevor in a tux once before, at a work associate's wedding. I'd been a guest and Trevor had been in the wedding party. Back then we hadn't been together, and all I wanted to do was go up to him, push the jacket off his broad shoulders, and throw my arms around his neck. Tonight, that's what I want to do, too.

Instead, I know I need to get my head in the game. We have appearances to make. It's so good to see him without crutches, but I'm worried he's pushing himself too hard. "You okay?"

"Am I okay?" he raises an eyebrow, watching as I put my feet into a pair of Louboutins – one of the only extravagant purchases I've allowed my mom to make for me in the last few years. There are certain things I'll skimp on, but one thing I do love are a pair of fuck-me pumps with the red sole. "Woman, are *you* okay? You fell down from Heaven and landed in my house. *Fuck me*," he winks at me.

"Did you really just feed me that bullshit pick-up line?"

"I'm hoping it helps me get lucky later on tonight," he pushes off the door frame and slowly makes his way over to me.

Since he's been laid up with his injury, he's lost weight, but it looks good on him. Just like it'll look good on him when he gains it back. Trevor has the type of body that can carry some muscle and be lean as fuck. He's hot both ways. My hands itch to curl around his midsection as he approaches me. There's a small hitch in his stride, but if I weren't looking for it, I wouldn't even notice it.

"You look beautiful," he whispers as he finally gets within touching distance. Grabbing me around the waist, he adjusts his stance so we're eye level.

I smile slowly, averting my eyes downward. When I look this way and he looks at me the way he is now, it makes me shy. Right now, I'm all Daphne. A part of me wants to bury my face in his neck until I come back out like Blaze. "You think?" He knows I'm not fishing for compliments. What I'm wearing, what I'm portraying, just isn't *me*.

His finger slides under my chin, tilting it so that I'm looking into his blue eyes, clear as the water bordering the Bahamas. "I've never lied to you before, why would I lie to you now?" He reaches in, kissing me softly but powerfully. As he pulls away, he licks his lips before breathing out a harsh breath. "And I'm one of the only people in the world who knows what you have hiding under that dress covering you completely up. Do you know how hot that is? You know what a lucky bastard I am?"

"About as lucky as I am," I go in for the kill, curling my arms around his midsection, pulling him close. "You look good enough to eat in this tux."

He leans in, his breath hot on my ear, his voice deep and sexy when he speaks. "If you're hungry later, then please, let me be your main course."

God, I love this man. He matches me in everything I do, and I never shock him. In fact, sometimes he shocks me. I've never in that kind of relationship before and now I'm letting him meet my parents.

"Why'd you get so quiet?" he questions, his eyes searching mine.

"Are you ready to meet the parents? Like truly, are we at this point in our relationship?"

Trevor pulls me so our bodies touch, his palms cupping my ass. "We're whatever you need me to be. You've done everything you can to help me over these past few weeks, you've stuck by me when other people would have run. If you're ready for me to meet your parents, then I'm proud to stand by your side and be the man you need me to be."

Unexpected tears clog my throat and pool behind my fake eyelashes. Trevor's a sweet guy, but he's also sweet in his gestures. He's not always the most talkative, so for him to say these words to me and mean them - it makes me love him even more. My parents have scared away more than one of my boyfriends. Knowing that he'll be with me no matter what is one of the most freeing feelings I've ever had.

"You ready?" he asks, checking the chunky, black watch he wears on his wrist.

I know from experience the watch is what he likes to wear because it's practical, but it's also the sexiest watch I've ever seen in my life. Hell, maybe it's everything Trevor is and does that's sexy. If anyone asked me, I probably wouldn't be able to explain it.

"I am," I answer, leaning up to kiss him on the cheek.

"Your lipstick doesn't smear when you kiss me," he comments, running the pad of his thumb along my lower lip.

"Nope, it's a stain. It'll stay for a few hours at least," I playfully nip at his thump, sucking the nail up to the knuckle and running my tongue around the tip. "See, didn't smudge at all."

A flame lights in his eyes and I can almost guess what he's thinking. "Interesting," he lets me go. "Is my hair okay? Did you want me to wear it down?"

It's up in its normal man bun, and surprisingly he looks well-kept with it up like it is. "No, keep it, I like it."

"I trimmed the beard up for you," he runs a hand along the tamed hairs on his chin.

"Thank you, but you know more than anyone, I love you just the way you are."

He pulls on my hand. "If you had to button up and look presentable, the least I can do is the same."

"You look way more than presentable, Mr. Trumbolt. You look edible."

He groans deep in his throat as I turn, swaying my hips as I walk out of the bedroom. I can feel his eyes on me, so I make an even bigger curve with my hips, swiveling them as I turn around to face him.

"So do you, Ms. Coleman. I'll have a lot of fun eating you later on tonight."

I can feel my face blush and I'm positive it's crimson in color. "You be good," I warn him.

The smartass grin he gives me tells me he's not going to be good. It tells me we're going to tempt fate, and we're going to do things in my parents' home that my dad's only done with his mistresses. "I always give it to you good, baby. This time won't be any different."

I close my eyes, sighing deeply. Let the man off his crutches, put him in a boot, and he's already making promises about his sexual prowess. Only thing is, I know better than anyone, Trevor's not making promises he can't fulfill.

He'll make good on every single one.

CHAPTER FIFTEEN

Trevor

I'VE NEVER RIDDEN in the back of a limo before. Not even for my high school prom like so many have done. Blaze told me we would have a ride. Silly me, I figured it would be a friend or a family member picking us up. I never expected to see a stretch limo pull into my drive.

"When you said we'd have a ride, this wasn't exactly what I imagined," I take a drink of the beer I got out of the fully stocked bar.

She takes a drink of her wine. "Yeah, well my family spares no expense - ever. Especially when they like to show me what I'm missing."

The way she says the words makes me wonder if she does miss it. There's a catch in my gut. "Do you miss it? They can give you a lot of luxuries I'll never be able to give you."

She's quiet for a heartbeat, and mine almost stops. "No, none of those things have ever been important to me. You know I don't touch the money in my trust unless there's something I really want. I've never missed this stuffy-as-fuck life. I mean look at me tonight." She waves her hand around her face and down her body, as she wrinkles her nose.

I do look at her, and while I like what I see, I know it's not the true woman I love. Leaning over, I run my thumb over her bottom lip. "While you are gorgeous with this suck-my-dick red lipstick, you're right. This isn't the everyday you, but this you is one I can definitely appreciate."

Her pulse is visible at her throat, her chest rising and falling with the intensity of her breathing. "You can?" she takes a drink of her wine, a smirk on her face.

"Who wouldn't appreciate the tightness of that dress? Get the fuck outta here, you know you're hot as hell."

A blush covers her cheeks, making them a pretty pink. "C'mon babe, you've never been shy before."

It's as if I've thrown down a challenge. I see her shoulders square, and she sets down the glass of wine she's been drinking. Her eyes cut over to the raised partition separating us from the driver.

"What are you thinking?"

The smile she gives me is one hundred percent sin. It's the type of smile women have used since the beginning of time to tempt a man - and fuck if I'm not tempted. I've had a semi since I saw the fuck-me heels. I've been a good guy while I've been recovering. I haven't pressed either of us to get physical, because I wasn't sure how much my body could take. Now that the cast is off and I feel ninety-five percent like my old self, I'm ready to shed this celibate skin I've been living. I miss Blaze and the hot sex we had. I'm ready to reclaim that part of our relationship.

"Why don't you use those Lolita-red lips to suck my cock? Give me a real-life demo on how it's smudge resistant."

She makes a noise deep in her throat. Behind the zipper of my tux pants, my cock jumps from its neglected state. The skin covering the hardness is tight and more than anything, I want to feel the heat of her mouth wrap around the length.

"For tonight, your wish is my command," her voice is soft in the quietness of the limo.

Quicker than I imagined, she's sliding out of the seat, onto the carpeted floor. As she gets situated, I help her out by unbuttoning, unzipping, and slipping my pants and boxers down far enough to pull my cock out.

"Are you sure?" she quirks a brow at me. "I don't wanna hurt you."

That sound deep in my throat is back. "The only way you're gonna hurt me is by not taking my cock all the way down your throat. If it's possible for someone to die from a case of blue balls, that'll be me. Being around you, living with you but not touching you for the past few weeks has been torture. Do you know how many times I wanted to throw my crutches to the side and just fuck you?" I stop, cupping her cheek in the palm of my hand, biting my bottom lip, because I can't fucking wait for her lips to wrap around me. "A million. Unless you want me to meet your parents with your mouth wrapped around me, taking it down the throat, you better get to sucking, babe."

She breathes heavily through her nose before she leans forward, wrapping her hand around my length.

"No," I grab her hand in mine, setting both of them on my thigh, fingers entwined. "Just use this gorgeous mouth of yours to get me off."

Her eyes meet mine and the heat there is enough to make me spontaneously combust or come. Right now I'm not sure which I'm closer to. "I'm waiting, Blaze."

The minx winks at me before opening that mouth and taking me deep in one smooth glide.

"Son of a bitch," I grit out between clenched teeth. My fingers ache to thrust into her hair and direct her on which way I want her to go, allow how shallow and how deep she takes me. I stop myself, because I know it took her a long time to fix her hair, and if she walks in looking like she's just been fucked, everyone will know what we've done. Instead, I save my thrusting for my hips, pushing my hard dick as deep as she'll take it. "That's it," I encourage her, letting my head fall back against the leather of the seat. Normally I'm the type of man who enjoys the show, loves to participate, and loves directing her when she's sucking me down. Tonight, I'm enjoying the hot warmth of her mouth too much.

My hand lets go of hers, and I growl deep, feeling it in my chest, as she digs her fingernails into my thighs. Through the material of my tux pants, I can feel the bite of her nails, the desperation with which she's clinging to me. The tight heat of her mouth is the most amazing thing I've ever felt, especially when she comes up higher on her knees, so she leans over and takes me directly down her throat. I feel her gag reflex, and then she swallows roughly, using her tongue to lick against the underside of my length. "God, Blaze, that feels fucking amazing."

She hums as she lets up before moving down again. My fingers curl against the seat until they ache. I flex them, testing the skin I feel tightening all over my body. Pulling my head from where it's resting, I look down at her, our eyes meeting. She's got tears at the corners. I reach down, cupping her cheeks as she hollows them out, sucking me deeper. The pads of my thumbs brush those tears away. I'm breathing harshly through my mouth, thrusting against her tongue, when I feel her hand reach down to cup my balls. Her gaze becomes more intense as we look at one another, and I can see her desire, can feel how much she wants me. If she were calling the shots right now, she'd pry her mouth off my cock, straddle me, and shove me home. It would only take that one stroke and I'd be letting loose deep inside her body. I know that for a fact.

Her tongue does something I've never felt it do before, and *Jesus* it's like a nuclear bomb goes off inside my body, concentrating right on my dick. I lose my rhythm as I spill down her throat. "Oh fuck, Blaze, take it all," I arch off the seat as she swallows against my length.

My heart is pounding and my hands are shaking as she cleans me up, tucking me back into the dress pants. A smirk covers her face, and I know she's proud of herself. If I were her, I'd be proud of myself, too. Snagging her around the waist, I pull her onto my lap, forcing her to straddle me, fixing my mouth at her ear.

"I want nothing more than to push my pants and boxers back down, move your panties to the side, and slide home. I'm dying to feel the scrape of your nails against my back, the heat of your breath against my throat, and more than anything, the grip of your pussy against my cock. It won't be long." The promise is in my voice and sooner, rather than later, I'm going to make damn good on that promise.

Blaze

I ache, dear God, I ache so much. I'm straddling his lap, pressing myself as close to him as I can, but it does nothing to soothe the burn. I've missed him, missed us coming together as one. It feels like an eternity since he's sated himself in my body. I know we're close to arriving at my parents' house, but I can't bring myself to break away from him. My arms wrap around his neck, holding on tightly while I curve my head into where he's speaking to me in that deep voice, laced with authority, that I love so much. He's saying something about my pussy gripping his cock, and I can't help it, I clench on air, moaning in my frustration. I need something, *anything*.

"You'll have to take this," he whispers, before I realize I've said those words aloud.

His mouth attaches itself to my neck, tugging on the skin before he soothes the burn with his tongue. I grab his head, holding it tightly to my flesh as he all but makes love to my neck. His palms slap onto my thighs while his fingers inch up to the hem of my little black dress. He's inches away from the lace of my panties, and I'm dying. Fucking dying. Because I want him to go under the wet panel, I want him to use those fingers to pleasure me, to take the edge off this ache I feel. I want desperately for us to be Tank and Blaze again. It's one of the two missing pieces of our puzzle. We've done everything but have sex and talk about his issues with my job. Right now I'd literally say *fuck me and the job*, if I only knew we had enough time.

"Those little noises you make in the back of your throat, babe," he mumbles as he pulls back, taking my ear into his mouth, tugging on the diamonds I have in tonight. "They're gonna get me hard again."

I can feel him stirring against me with renewed interest. What I wouldn't give to tell this limo driver to turn around and take us home. I don't even care about appearances, not sure why I care enough to make this one for my family. I'm in a dream world where the music playing is the panting of my breath and Trevor's the conductor of the symphony when I feel the limo stop.

My eyes are blurry as I try to focus on what's outside the tinted windows.

"We here?" he's reluctantly letting go of my skin, pulling his hands from under the skirt of my dress and trying to set us both back to right.

"Yeah," I reach up to my lips, wiping the moisture I can feel coating them off.

"Huh," he grunts as he situates his pants.

"What?"

"You were right about that lipstick," he captures my jaw in his palm, turning me left and right so he can get a good look. "Nothing we did smeared it."

I smirk, leaning in to kiss him softly on the cheek. "See? It's blowjob approved."

He chuckles as the limo door opens and I grab his hand in mine. It's show time.

CHAPTER SIXTEEN

Blaze

THE OVER-THE-TOP OPULENCE in this house is enough to make me want to puke. It's exactly why I ran as quickly as I could as soon as I turned eighteen. I'm sipping on a glass of champagne as I hear my dad talking to Trevor about how he *supports our armed forces*. It would be childish of me to say my dad supports them by writing a check and wearing a flag lapel pin on Veteran's Day. I'm sure that counts in the "better than nothing" category.

Trevor's holding his own, though - I have to give it to him. The look my dad gave him when they were introduced wasn't pleasant. If Trevor had been a bug and dad had been the shoe, he would have crushed him. But Trevor gave him the firmest handshake I think ol' pops has ever gotten in his life. That alone puts him on a level of respect for Damon Coleman.

"I've been trying to talk Daphne into giving up that little job she has," he flashes a smile over my way, winking at Trevor.

If only they'd known each other a year ago, daddy would have had a firm ally in his mission to make me quit being an EMT. "I'm not gonna quit, no matter how many times you ask me to."

Trevor takes a drink of his beer. "She's right. I asked her to quit, have asked her to quit a couple dozen times, and she always turns me down."

"Perhaps you should put a ring on her finger. Ya know? Keep her barefoot and pregnant," he laughs obnoxiously. "That's the way to teach these women a lesson who want their own life."

I'm shocked actually, if anything could ever shock me about my family, it's that he's said this to Trevor. "Is that what you thought about mama?" I quip as I take a long drink of my champagne.

He turns on me, his eyes flashing. "Tried to, but the bitch took birth control without me knowing. The number one reason you're an only child."

"My rebellious nature was too much for her?" I snark back, pissed because I've never been an only child and they know it.

He sighs. "Daphne, you were given every opportunity to succeed in this life, yet you work a servant's job, baby. Your mom and I, we just don't understand it."

That's fucking it. I drain my glass, grab Trevor's hand, and go off in search of a quiet room. I need to get the fuck outta here, and fast.

Trevor

If this is how rich people act, I'm counting my damn blessings we were middle class. Holy shit, I don't think I've ever heard a father completely disrespect his daughter the way Blaze's father has – and in front of company at that. It took everything I had not to tell the guy where he could shove his attitude. After witnessing this bullshit, I'm sorry I ever asked Blaze to give up her job.

"Was I as much of an asshole as him when I asked you to give up the EMT gig?" I question as she leads us through a maze of hallways.

"No," she shakes her head.

We're stopped by various people here and there - they want to talk to her, to see how she's been doing. The answers she gives are clipped and totally rude compared to the woman I know her to be. I nod my head and smile when appropriate, saying the only word required of me – Trevor – when asked. I'm as anxious to get wherever it is she wants to go as she is.

"I don't want to hurt you so if we need to slow down, please let me know," she says over her shoulder, maneuvering us through another group of people.

"I'm good, babe, I promise. You aren't hurting me at all."

With those words, she picks up the pace. If I even wanted to get myself out of this place, there's no way in hell I'd be able to. This is possibly the biggest house I've seen in my life. We come to a door, which she opens, glances around to make sure no one is looking, and then pulls me through it. She engages the lock before walking to the other side, leaning against the wall. The breath she lets out is one of relief.

"Where are we?" I slowly make my way to her, hoping not to spook her. She's had a rough night, I can see it in the way she's trying hard to be brave. Obviously her family brings out all the insecurities I never thought my strong girl even had.

Giving me a small grin, she bites her lip. "My childhood bedroom."

"Oh really?" I quirk a brow as I continue walking toward her. "Ever had a guy in here before?"

She shakes her head. "No, the Daphne of my teenage years is way different than the Blaze I am now. For a time, I could have been Whitney's twin, believe it or not."

I'm chuckling in my throat. There's no way this woman could have been like my sister. I don't believe it for a second. "No fuckin' way."

"Yeah," she winks. "For a while I wanted my parents to be proud of me, and I wanted them brag to everyone about me, but I wasn't happy. Daphne has *never* been me. I'm not happy being the girl who smiles to keep up appearances. I don't like to sweep things under the carpet or tiptoe around uncomfortable topics."

When I reach her, I put one hand over her head, bracing it against the wall. With my other, I curl it around her hip, palming her waist. "What kind of a woman are you?"

Her green eyes burn bright in the muted light of the room. Someone has left on a bedside lamp, but it's not enough light to actively see. Instead it casts an almost romantic glow over the room. I wonder if the comforter covering the bed was the one she slept under? The feminine color doesn't match the Blaze I know today, but I'm beginning to get the idea that it would have matched Daphne well. My eyes follow her tongue as it swipes against her bottom lip.

"The kind of woman who desperately wants to know what it's like to get fucked by her boyfriend in her childhood bedroom."

I'm speechless – something that never happens. The words hit me deep in the gut, and the breath I inhale is sharp. "That a fact?"

"The truest statement I've spoken in my life," she puts her arms around my waist, leaning against the wall for support. "Consider it a dare if you have to."

"I don't need a dare, all I need is to know for sure this is what you want to do," I grip her hip hard, almost like my hand there can stop the explosion that's about to happen between us.

It's been building – this moment – since she came back into my life on the side of the road. I obviously didn't know it then, because I was unconscious, but she's been my savoir – the eye of the hurricane surrounding me, the anchor to my ship that's been restlessly floating on the sea. There's a part of me that wants this moment to be perfect, romantic as fuck, candles, champagne, the whole nine yards. There's another part of me that argues this right here is the perfect moment. Anytime I can give Blaze what she wants is perfect. It might not be what I envision in my head, but I realize with startling clarity if I hadn't made it out of the wreck, we wouldn't be here right now. I'd be six feet in the ground, and God knows where she'd be. I hope she'd be finding her happiness, but it kills me to think about it being with another man.

That thought at the forefront of my mind, I lean in and press my lips to hers. She wants to know what it's like to fuck her boyfriend in her childhood bedroom? I'll give her the best time of her life. I have something to prove tonight, not to her, but to myself. It's time to realize once and for all I'm alive. I didn't die in that wreck, and I need to embrace this second chance I've been given. So many people don't get one, and I've been blessed. I need to show this woman what she means to me, and I need to do it starting right this minute.

"Hang on, baby," I whisper against her lips. "I'm about to give you the ride of your life. Nod your head if you understand."

Her breath comes in gusts against my lips. She likes it when I take control. Her head nods, and I smile against her mouth. "Good girl," I pull our lips apart, before I turn her around so she faces the wall. "You ready?"

"Yes," her voice is breathless. "Take me, Trevor," the words muffled by the wall, she's buried her forehead in, but I hear what she's saying loud and clear. Every fucking part of me hears it loud and clear.

CHAPTER SEVENTEEN

Blaze

I'M WAITING for the moment he makes his move. Every part of my body is on alert. My nipples push against the lace of my bra, my fingers clench against the wall in front of me, and between my legs I ache more than I've ever ached before. My breathing is labored as I wait, eyes closed, forehead leaning against the solid surface, dying to see what he does, where he touches me first.

"You've never had another man in here? What about some horny teenage boy?" he breathes close to my ear.

Trevor comes up so close behind me I can feel the heat pouring off his body. Flattening my palms, I push myself back far enough so we touch. It's a whisper of one, but it's enough for now. Tilting my head, I can feel the hair of his beard tickling against my neck. Tucking my chin down, I try to nuzzle against him. I shake my head. "No, never had a man before you, or a boy either. You're the first, the only."

"Better fuckin' well be the last."

I open my mouth to tell him he's it for me, but he picks that moment to touch me. His arms come around my body, his fingers hook into the top of my dress, pulling the clingy material down far enough so my tits rest atop the edge. Once he's secured the fabric so it's no longer in his way, his palms move back up, cupping my flesh. He squeezes roughly, making the lace enclosure gap, giving room for his fingers to sneak inside.

His voice is hoarse, deep, and the sexiest damn thing I've ever heard in my life. "Was this expensive?"

"You know my lingerie is always expensive," I press my thighs together, bending my knees to give a little relief. Besides my shoes, it's the only other thing I splurge on.

"I'll buy you more."

With those words, he reaches completely into the cups, grabs hold of the fabric, and rips it off my body. It hangs loose, flapping as my breathing speeds up again. "You just ripped my bra," I turn my head so I can see his blue eyes in soft glow of the room.

"I did," he confirms as he captures my lips the same way his palms capture my freed tits. It's rough and out of control as our tongues duel for the dominant position. He wins, but only because I concede the victory.

Using the pads of his thumb and pointer fingers, he worries the hard nub decorated with a barbell, causing me to pull my mouth from his. I face forward, tilting my head back onto his shoulder, thrusting my chest into his hands. "Please, Trevor," I beg, wanting to feel what I've been missing for so long.

"Lift your dress up for me."

I shiver as he mouths the side of my neck, his breath hot as he speaks against my skin. My hands shake as I remove them from the wall. His biceps tighten as he catches my weight against his palms.

"Your leg," I bite my bottom lip as I reach down, pulling the edge of my dress up past my thighs, settling the material against my hips.

"The mother fucking leg is fine, Blaze. Higher," he growls against me.

I'm totally confused. "What?"

"Pull it higher. Give me enough god damn room to work."

The tension between us is about to break, and I wonder what it'll take to snap.

I yank the material higher, like he instructed. "That enough room for you to work?"

Moving his hands down to my hips, he pulls my panties down before he smacks me hard against the left ass cheek.

"That's for your smart mouth."

I smirk because I know deep down he loves it just as much as I do.

"Hands on the wall."

Slapping them back where they started, I push against the wall, sticking my ass out at angle. He's fumbling with a condom; I can hear the paper crinkling in the stillness of the room right before I feel it float to the ground next to my foot. Precious seconds are wasted as he suits up before *fucking finally* he again wraps his hands around my hips. There's a slight tilt, a push against my back to angle me, and then there's a thrust. That thrust is the best thing I have ever felt in my damn life. "Jesus," I groan as he withdraws, thrusting back home. Letting the wall take my forehead, I become a ragdoll as I enjoy the way this man plays my body.

Trevor

God this feels good, so fucking good. Blaze and I have always been able to heat up the sheets, no pun intended. If there's one thing we've done well from the beginning, it's this. And to be without her for as long as I've been? It's been torture. What we're doing right now? The fact she's invited me back into her body? Fucking dream come true.

Taking my hands off her hips, I run them down her arms. I stretch out from behind her, curling my fingers in between hers, as I hold her against the wall with my weight.

"Fuck me, Trevor," she sighs as I thrust so hard, I life her up off her feet.

Feet encased in the sexiest shoes I've ever seen in my life. My hips have a mind of their own, pushing, pulling, the plunge, the withdrawal. I'm on autopilot as I work against her body.

"You feel so good," I whisper against her neck, sucking the flesh as I thrust deeper, hold there for a few heartbeats, and then withdraw again.

"Ohmigod," she moans, the sound echoing off the surface in front of her. "Make me come, Trevor," she begs. "Please make me come."

I take one of my hands from hers, bringing it back to her hair, fisting it with my fingers. "You've been a good girl, Blaze," I pull her mouth around, fusing our lips together. "What do you need? Take your hand off the wall and show me what you need."

Reaching around my back, she grabs my free hand, bringing both our hands down to her core. With both our index fingers, we flick her clit, working in tandem to get her off.

"Yes!" She thrusts against our hands and then back against my cock in time with me.

My legs are shaking with the effort to hold back, but more than anything, I want to feel her come. I need to feel her pussy clench around me, have to hear the little noise she makes in her throat as she gets hers. There's more lubrication, helping our digits slide against each other and her.

"Come on, baby, come for me," I encourage her, because I know I'm going to blow, even though I already came once tonight.

"I'm so close," she leans her head back against my shoulder.

Taking my other hand off the wall, I go to work at her tits again. Roughly grabbing, twisting the nipple, wishing like fuck I could turn her around and lick it with my tongue. I miss it, my mouth waters at the thought of holding the piece of flesh there. But this isn't about me, it's about her. Letting go, I lick the pads of my fingers before moving them back to her nipple, squeezing the way I know she likes it.

We're both sweating, breathing heavily, grinding against one another. We're both so damn close it's almost a live thing between us. I'm clenching my teeth, wanting her to go before me, because I'll be damned if I come before her. To wait this long and be a two pump chump? No fucking way.

Her palm comes off the wall, and she grabs her other breast, going to work on the erect flesh. "Yeah, yeah," she's chanting in time with my thrusts. Her body is getting slammed into the wall by mine, but she doesn't care, and if she doesn't care then I don't care. Can't bring myself to. Only thing I want to do right now is come and feel her come.

"Feel good? You there, babe?" I bite down on her shoulder just as she clenches on my dick.

"Yes! Fuck yes!" She moans, thrusting back against me. It's like she's broken through a brick wall and she's on the other side, breathing heavily, now lazily stroking her clit, and putting her hand back on the wall.

It's all I need. I push home, let myself go, and groan deeply in her ear as I pour myself into the thin piece of rubber that separates our bodies. And finally, fucking finally, I feel like I got a piece of myself back tonight.

Maybe, just maybe Trevor Trumbolt can start to put himself back together.

CHAPTER EIGHTEEN

Blaze

GLANCING at my reflection in the mirror, I again don't recognize the woman staring back at me. Instead of someone with a polished updo and perfect makeup, I look alive. More alive than I have in months. Turning my head from side to side, I see my neck bears the evidence of what happened a few minutes ago with Trevor.

Reaching up, I run my fingers along the already purpling bruises and finish taking down the hair he wrecked with his fingers.

Luckily for me, I curled it before I put it up. Using my fingers and a comb I found in one of the drawers in the bathroom, I go to work, trying to make it look less "just been fucked" and more "beachy waves". Once the hair is as good as it's going to get, I take in my face with a critical eye. My lipstick, true to my words earlier, still hasn't smeared. My mascara is a different story, it's smudged under my eyes. A quick dab of water-softened toilet paper and I've fixed it as much as I can.

This is as good as it's going to get. Opening the door, I spot Trevor sitting on what was my childhood bed.

"If I had come out of my bathroom as a teenager and you'd been sitting there, I'd probably think I had died and gone to Heaven," I tease.

He's fixed his pants, tux jacket, and looks like he's run his hands through his hair, just like I did.

"If you had come out of the bathroom looking like you do right now, teenage me would have come in his pants," his voice is deep, pitched low with arousal I'd thought we'd already taken care of.

"And what does mid-twenties you think?"

I can't help asking the question because I love knowing he's affected as much as I am. Most of the time I'm completely comfortable in my skin and one hundred percent sure of who I am, but there's still a part of me that likes to hear it.

He reaches out from where he still sits, bringing me into the circle of his arms and his spread legs.

"Mid-twenties me is contemplating staying here with you in this room for at least a few more hours and not letting you go until we've made up for lost time."

I bury my head in his neck. "Mmmmmm I can't say I'd disagree with that, but I already have marks on my neck I've had to conceal."

"It'd be your fucking dress next, Blaze. I'd have to get you out of it, and it might not make it in one piece."

My pussy clenches at the visual his words conjure. I've never been with a man like Trevor before, and God-willing I won't know anyone except him the rest of my life. He makes no excuses for how he likes things to go in the bedroom and he allows me to play. I have absolutely no complaints either way.

"I'm not going to lie, I'd love to see how many pieces you can rip this dress into. We could hole up in here for the weekend and forget these last few months where I was stupid not to answer your texts. But..." I grab hold of his lapels, pulling myself closer. "Tomorrow is Christmas and I think your family would miss it."

"Tempted to say fuck the family, but I really want to see Stella," he cups my face in the palms of his hands. "I didn't hurt you, did I?"

"Hurt me? No, I loved it. I'm kind of sore because it'd been a while, obviously."

A noise in the back of his throat makes me not only laugh, but goosebumps to rise on my arms.

"I'm glad there was no one while we were apart," he nuzzles my ear. "At least I didn't fuck it up that much."

"It wasn't just you, Trev," I nuzzle him back, melting into his arms. "We both said and did things that weren't mature."

He grunts. "But I started it."

I won't argue; he's telling the truth. Had it not been for him giving me an ultimatum, I wouldn't have left, but honestly I could have handled it better.

I lean in, kissing him on the lips, softly and slowly. "C'mon, we gotta go make an appearance."

He groans, kissing me softly on the neck. "Alright baby, let's go make an appearance."

I'M nervous as we snake our way through the friends, family, and strangers who have gathered in my parents' home to celebrate the holiday. Drinks are flowing, finger foods are being eaten, and I'm sure deals are being made in my daddy's office. There the expensive scotch has been brought out, as well as the Cuban cigars. He's more than likely closed on something that'll make him another couple hundred thousand dollars. Mom's working the room; I can see her from where I stand, flittering from one group of ladies to another. This right here is everything I hate and everything she loves. Whitney would have been the perfect daughter for her.

"Daphne dear," her voice is like nails on a chalkboard. Tightening my fingers around Trevor's, I pull him in her direction.

"Hi, Mom."

She leans forward, kissing me on both cheeks. "Daphne honey, it's so good to see you."

I can feel Trevor vibrating at my side. He always laughs when he hears anyone call me by my real name.

"Mother, I'd like you to meet my boyfriend, Trevor Trumbolt."

With assessing green eyes, so much like mine, I watch her rake his body from his toes to the top of his head. She appreciates good looking men, and I can tell by the way her eyes light up, she appreciates the man on my arm. I want to hop up, wrap my legs around his waist, fuse our mouths together, and fucking lay claim to him. It wouldn't be the first time mommy dearest flirted with one of my boyfriends since I turned eighteen.

"Trumbolt," she puts her hand out, fluttering her eyebrows as he politely takes her hand. "Any relation to the party planner, Whitney? Her name has been thrown around to possibly do our annual fundraiser in April."

My stomach clenches in both excitement and dread for Whitney.

"Yes, ma'am," he answers. "She's my older sister."

"Oh honey, call me Olivia. Any friend of my daughter's is a friend of mine."

I cover my snort up by coughing.

"Thank you, ma'am, but my mother raised me to respect my elders."

Mom sniffs, shooting him a glare. There's a flare of irritation in her eyes that she isn't the recipient of his attention.

Dear Lord, but I do love when Trevor throws those manners out the window and takes me exactly how I want him to.

My mom takes a drink from the champagne glass in her hand. "Thank you, at least, for dressing decently, Daphne."

I open my mouth to tell her your welcome, but she continues.

"Now have you decided you're going to give up that servant's job you insist on keeping? Perhaps Trevor here can convince you to stop doing things beneath your station in life."

And just like that, she's managed to piss me off. "No Mom, in fact Trevor's a cop."

She gives him a slick smile. "I would imagine a man would have to be strong to take another man down."

I want to fucking pee on his leg so she gets the hint. "He was actually injured in the line of duty," I say between clenched teeth. "So we'll probably be leaving soon."

She turns to me, mouth in a line and shrewd. "Thank you for gracing us with your presence Daphne, but next time, please do wear your hair up. It's the respectable thing to do."

I've had about all I can take of this whole situation and I'm feeling a little ornery. Letting go of Trevor's hand, I pull my curls up into a ponytail. "Like this? So everyone here can see the love bites on my neck? By the way, I got those less than an hour ago in my childhood bedroom. If you happen to find an empty condom wrapper up there - no need to worry about daddy - it was ours," I point to Trevor. "And thanks to the workout he gave me, I'm tired and I think we'll be going. Merry Christmas."

When I turn around, my mom's jaw is hanging open so wide she could catch flies with it. "C'mon, let's get the fuck outta here."

I drag him through the crowd and out into the fresh air of the semi-cool night. The air helps to ground me, and I thank God I don't have to do this more than a few times a year.

The car that brought us is waiting and we get in without looking back. As it pulls away, I give him a grin. "Sorry, it pissed me off how she kept hitting on you."

He chuckles, pulling me to him with an arm around my neck. "Don't be, it was fucking hot, and I think now I see why you resisted me asking you to quit so much."

As we make the drive back to Trevor's house, I can finally feel myself beginning to relax. I'm nothing like those people I just left, and as long as I stay true to myself, I never will be. At least I hope not.

CHAPTER NINETEEN

Trevor

"SIT RIGHT THERE and I'll bring you a drink."

I kinda love how my mom still assumes I can't fend for myself. On the other hand, I'm a grown man who's lucky to still have the use of his body after everything I went through. "I got it, Mom."

"Let me take care of you, Trevor," she leans in giving me a hug. "Let me enjoy the fact you're still with us."

Hardly anything anyone else has said hit me the way these words from my mom hits me. I have to bite back the wave of emotion those simple words bring forth. I'm not even sure why this affects me more with such a punch in the gut. I watch as she goes into the kitchen before I turn my attention to my best friend, Renegade.

"How are you?"

He looks up from where he's rocking the carrier my niece is sleeping in with his foot. Dark circles form half-moons under his eyes, and I'm pretty sure he hasn't seen a razor in a week. "Tired as fuck," he admits. "But I've never been happier in my life."

I can tell, even with the haggard appearance, he has an easy smile and relaxed body language. "How much sleep are you running on right now?"

He tilts his head back, doing calculations in his head. "About three hours, which isn't bad, but it's like the fourth day of it. I let Whit sleep last night since I knew your mom would need help."

I nod, proud of him, proud of the man he's become, and hope like hell I can be the same kind of man. Maybe one day I can be the same kind of partner he is, sharing in the care of my own child. It's something I've been thinking about since Stella was born mere days ago. Part of me wonders if I'm still too selfish, the other part would love to talk to Blaze about it. Either way, I know it'll all come in its own time. Forcing things has never worked for me.

"How's the leg?" he gestures to the brace.

"Good actually," a grin spreads across my face. "I gave it a good workout last night. It was a little sore this morning, but feels good. The physical therapist told me one day it would all click and I would feel close to a hundred percent because the bone would be healing. I think I've gotten to that point."

"Wipe that fuckin' smug ass smile off your face," Renegade throws a pillow at me. "I can tell by one look at you how you tired it out. You're getting your rocks off and I'm grabbing a cat nap."

I laugh, grabbing the pillow with one hand before it hits my face. "You wouldn't change it, so don't be a hater."

At that moment, Stella starts screaming, a loud noise I'm not sure should be coming from such a little baby.

"Right on time," Renegade reaches over, grabbing the diaper bag they brought in with them. "You wanna pick her up?" he raises an eyebrow at me. "She'll scream until she gets this bottle."

No time like the present to learn how to be an uncle, I guess. Getting up off the couch, I go sit over next to him as he rifles through the bag, pulling out a container, a bottle of water, and an empty bottle.

Pulling the carrier over next to me, I look at my niece. Her face is scrunched up and red, her blue eyes filled with water, and she's screaming bloody murder. I reach down, picking her up out of the carrier. "Hey Stella," I soothe, supporting her head and bouncing her in my arms. She's so fucking small, I'm scared to death I'll either drop her or crush her with what bulk I still have. "Why would a pretty girl like you make such an ugly face?" I tease, reaching out to wipe away some of her tears. She stops crying, glancing up at me as I continue to bounce her. "Remember me?" She tilts her head to the side, almost as if she's contemplating whether she does or not.

Ryan's shaking up the bottle, holding his finger over the nipple when all three women come running into the living room. I glance up, a grin on my face. "We got this, y'all can go back in there."

Whitney leans against the doorframe, holding her phone out as I assume she takes a picture, a look on her face I'm well acquainted with. "Don't start crying, sis."

Ryan taps my bicep, handing me the bottle. "Go for it, just watch her head and she'll do the rest."

I put the nipple to her mouth, and just like Ryan said, she does the rest.

Glancing up, I see all three sets of eyes from the women on me. "Why are you looking at me like I'm the first man to ever feed a baby?"

"I think we all have different reasons why," mom says, her voice clogged with emotion. "Me, I worried I might never see you sitting in my living room again and to watch you doing that? It makes my heart so full, Trevor. Nobody had to get me a damn thing for Christmas this year, just seeing you alive and walking around is enough for me." She turns around and walks back to the kitchen, wiping her eyes.

Blaze gives me a saucy smirk, hitching her hip out to the side. "Me? I just think you look hot with a baby in your arms. I mean not like we need one, but we can totally borrow her, right? Because you with your hair, your beard, your muscles, and the cutest baby ever? Total ovary exploding moment right here," she blows me a kiss as I do my best not to listen to the chuckles coming from Ryan.

With expectant eyes, I glance at my sister. "Do you wanna give me your take on this?"

She walks closer to us. "You need to burp her if she's slowing down. Ryan, hand him a towel just in case she spits up." Once she's close enough, she pulls Stella up, sits her on my thigh, and holds her head, instructing me on how to pat her back.

"My take on this? It's one of the most emotional moments of my life and why I had to take a picture. Not only did I worry you'd never get to meet her because of the wreck, but I also think about all the times I cried to you about wanting a baby. I think of the night you saved my life with Stephen, and I think of what an amazing brother you've been to me. It's just emotional, and you're gonna have to let me have my emotions, Trev."

She leans down, kissing me on the cheek, before she runs a hand over Stella's forehead. "Love you, bro."

"I love you, too," I watch as she goes back into the kitchen, and it's then I notice Ryan watching me. "Not you too?"

"I have to admit, I worried you wouldn't be here for these parts of life too. For half the pregnancy, I was worried you'd be pissed because of what Whitney and I did. Then when I saw you in that truck, Tank," he stops, shaking his head. "If anyone had asked me, I would have said you were dead. I worried about it, checked your breathing, and lost a few years off my life. It's a monumental moment for you to be sitting here, burping my daughter."

I'm quiet as I continue the job at hand, taking in how much everyone was affected by the wreck, and realizing for the first time that as I put myself back together, my family is doing the same.

Today is a damn good day.

CHAPTER TWENTY

Blaze

"I'M SO TIRED," I sigh as I take my shoes off, sinking my toes into the plush carpet in Trevor's living room. My feet still hurt from wearing the heels I did last night.

"I am, too," he yawns as he takes his wallet out of his back pocket, putting it on the table next to the door. "It's been a long couple of days."

I collapse on the couch, snuggling into the blanket I left last time I'd laid there watching TV. Yawning, I glance up at Trevor. "Why don't you come watch mindless TV with me? We can fall asleep in front of the Christmas tree like an old married couple."

He laughs, the sound deep and rich. I love when he laughs like that. I'm thankful every time I hear it. I must close my eyes and doze off slightly, because the next thing I know, I jerk awake. Trevor is sitting on the other end of the couch with my feet in his lap, massaging the hard knot I have located in the ball of my foot from wearing those shoes last night.

"Oh dear God, that feels amazing, please don't stop," I moan, flexing against his fingers.

"It never disappoints me, hearing you say those words. It amazes me how many ways I can get you to say them though," his tone is amused as his fingers continue to work against the hard spot.

"Now isn't the time for you to make sex jokes, this feels so good. Merry Christmas to me."

He drops my foot and I moan at the loss of the pressure. "Speaking of Merry Christmas, I have a gift to give you."

"I have a gift to give you, too," I smile over at him. "Let me go grab it," I swing my legs over the edge of the couch and get up with a grimace as I put weight on my feet.

We meet back in the living room, sitting down together in front of the tree. Trevor's legs are stretched out in front of him, before he leans over, cupping the palm of my cheek in his hand. He turns my face from side to side tilting my chin so he can inspect my neck. "I did good, huh?"

A saucy grin spreads across my face as I reach over and cup his dick in my hand through his pants. "I did good, too."

He clears his throat loudly as he adjusts and hands me one of the wrapped gifts sitting next to him. "This is an apology for what I did last night."

I'm intrigued with the way he's phrased the words. As far as I'm concerned, there was nothing at all for him to apologize for. What we did last night was everything I wanted and more. "You know you don't have to apologize, I loved last night."

"You'll love this too," he assures me as he motions for me to open the gift.

Wrapped in Christmas themed tissue paper is some of the skimpiest, but also most beautiful lingerie I've ever seen in my life. It's in colors I never would have gone for. I'm more of a black lace type of girl, but what he's purchased runs the gamut. From virginal white to the most beautiful lilac color I've ever seen to bright yellow, and even a hot pink. Apparently my man has an affinity for this stuff, and he likes to have a shit ton of options.

"I don't even know what to say about all of this," my mouth hangs open as I continue to pull pieces from the never ending box of color.

"You don't have to say anything," he gives me a sexy smile. "All I want you to do it is wear it. I love that when you're with me you're a girlie girl. When you're with the guys you work with, you adapt your personality to be able to hang with them. While that's cool, I get to see a side of you that no one else gets to see. It's special to me, and I always want to nurture that part of you. I never want to make you feel like you have to hide that part of yourself. With me you can be anyone you want to be, you can show me whatever part of you, you need to. That's what makes me love you so much. You're vulnerable with me."

This man sees things in me that I never see in myself. He gives me the courage to be who I am without sacrificing my integrity. He encourages me to be sexy when other men have tried to dial me back. I will love this man forever, and I know I will. "I want to be vulnerable with you because I know you'll put me back together again if I fall apart," I whisper as I get up on my knees, walking over to him.

In the back of my head, I tell myself I should be honest about everything. I should let him know about the past I keep hidden. If I let him completely in nothing would stop us as a couple. He hands me a smaller box, this one from a jewelry store I like in the mall. I know without a doubt this isn't an engagement ring or anything of the sort, the box is too big for that. "What did you do here?"

He surges up, fusing our lips together, before he pulls away. "Why don't you open it and find out?"

Opening the box, I spy the watch I've had my eye on for months. It's not super expensive, but I couldn't bring myself to throw away the cheap watch I got at Walmart when I very first got out of school and buy this one. I felt like that move was something the old Daphne would have done, and the new Blaze wasn't that caught up in name brand things. This though – Trevor giving me a gift is the most awesome thing in the world.

"I love it!"

"I know you do, you'd look at the thing every time we'd walk by it. Whatever your reasons are for not buying it for yourself, they're yours. But now you have what you need and want."

I lean down, kissing him hard again because this man knows me. "You pay attention to me, you listen to me."

"I wonder why I couldn't do that with Whitney," he mumbles as he purses his lips. "Renegade told the family we listened, but we never paid attention."

Tilting my head to the side, I give it some thought. "Maybe it's because with the people we fall in love with, we pay *more* attention. We want to be everything they need us to be, everything they want us to be. We're willing to let certain parts of ourselves go in order to converge into one unit with them, so we want to make sure they're happy. Knowing their happiness doesn't take any more than truly listening to what they're saying."

"Maybe you're right, but you know more than anything I want my sister to be happy."

"You do," I agree. "But you want her to be happy by fixing her problems, not listening to them."

The way he's quiet, I can tell I've struck a nerve, and maybe he truly gets what I'm saying. It's making me nervous. I'm throwing down some truth, when I'm not sure if he's going to like the Christmas gift I got him. "I hope you like this."

He gives me a look. "I love everything you've ever given me, why wouldn't I love this?"

I have to be honest. "It took me a long time to figure out what I wanted to get you. Nothing seemed like it fit right, if that makes sense. I didn't want to be too romantic, and not romantic enough, but I wanted it to mean something."

"I'd venture to say anything the two of us say or do with one another means more post-Thanksgiving than it ever has," he glances up at me as he unwraps the gift. "Words, sounds, gestures – they've taken on a whole new meaning when you aren't sure if you'll ever be able to do them or have them done to you again."

I watch as he opens the box, wondering if I've made the right decision in what I got him. My heart beats heavily against my chest, thudding hard against my ribs. When he pushes the tissue paper back, I stop breathing all together. "Is this what I think it is?"

Even though he's not looking at me, I nod.

"This was taken at the cookout," he looks over at me, grinning.

It's the very first picture that was ever taken of us. We didn't know it was being taken, and we'd only just met hours before, but looking at the two of us, even then, you can see the chemistry there. "Holden gave it to me while you were in the hospital, and at the risk of sounding assuming, I thought you might like to have a copy, too," my words are strained as I speak around my tight throat. "To remind us of where we started. The people in that picture had an attraction and quick smiles for each other, they laughed all night long while they talked about stupid shit, and then they exchanged numbers at the end of the night with no preconceived notions about one another. Sometimes we get caught up in the stupidest shit that doesn't make a difference at the end of the day. Trevor, let's never forget how we felt that night."

He puts the picture down banding his arms around my body, crushing his mouth to mine. "I never want to forget it again, or how we feel this night. I don't think I've ever felt so close to another human being, I know I've never felt so close to you before. I don't want to lose this. Whatever we have to do, to make it work, let's put the work in, let's do the job. The only people who can fuck this up are us."

And I know more than anything he's right, and right here, on Christmas in front of the Christmas Tree, I decide once and for all – I'm fighting for what we have, I'm never letting it go, and even if it kills me, I'm going to tell him the truth about my past.

Not tonight, but soon, because nothing is going to ever stand in our way again.

CHAPTER TWENTY-ONE

Trevor

I'M TREADING WATER, waiting for Blaze to come out of the women's section of the locker room. She just got off work, and I'm doing one of my last physical therapy sessions before they'll be releasing me. The month of January is flying by, but I can't wait to know what my game plan is for the rest of my career, and truthfully, the rest of my life. I have an appointment with the shrink tomorrow, and I just need to make it through this workout.

We're the only ones here, and since it's near closing time, I think we'll probably be the last ones to show up. Luckily for me, I know the owner and we have a key. I love working out in the pool because there's little impact on my joints, and right now, they do hurt if I abuse them. The physical therapist told me in the next few weeks that should go away and then I'll be able to rejoin my guys in the Moonshine Task Force. Truth of the matter is, I'm so ready. Sitting around is definitely not the life for me, I can't fucking stand it. I hear the door open and turn around, whistling loudly as I see Blaze headed toward the pool dressed in a white bikini. The white shows off her hair, her skin color, and her tattoos. Damn, she looks smoking.

"I can't wait until this summer at my parents' house," I wink at her. "I'm gonna do things to you in that pool I've always fantasized about."

She gives me a look as she sinks into the water, shrieking at the temperature. I'd had to do a deep intake of breath when I entered the pool as well, maybe I should have warned her.

"It takes a minute to get used to."

I swim over to her, gathering her up in my arms. I can't help but notice her hard nipples rubbing against my chest. It puts thoughts of those fantasies back into my head.

"I'm all for doing sexually adventurous stuff, Trev, but it seems wrong to joke about doing it at your parents'," she curls her arms around my neck.

"So much more exciting though, and need I remind you, we did it at yours" I tease and remind her, thinking about all the pervy situations I'd gotten into as a teen. There was something much more exciting about doing all those things with her.

As my eyes land on her tits, she smacks my bicep. "Get you mind out of the gutter, you're supposed to be doing your laps."

God, I hate laps. They help to build up the strength in my leg and it's making a huge difference, but damn do I hate them.

"I'll be here waiting on you at the end," she blows me a kiss.

"Alright, let's do this."

The entire time I do the laps, I focus on my movement; one arm in front of the other, kick the way I need to, use my core to help offset the less muscle in my leg. Repeat over and over again until I count off the one hundred laps I've been told to do. Once I come up, panting from exertion, I see Blaze hanging out on the side of the pool. She's holding a beach ball in her hands.

"You ready?" She bounces it from one hand to the other. In the shallow end, she can stand up straight and the water goes up to her shoulders, on me it'll be at my chest.

"I'm always ready." The cocky part of my personality shines bright sometimes.

As I'm walking to her, she rears back and throws the ball slightly to the left of me. I have to plant my feet and lean to catch it. Last time I did this, it knocked me off balance and I'd face planted in the water. This time I catch it – a little wobbly, but I make it.

"Good job, Trev! Now throw it back."

I do as she asks. This exercise helps me become more flexible and tolerate standing. I can't wait until they allow me to run on my leg. Hopefully next week, and damn am I ready. "Thanks for coming to hang out with me."

She gives me a look, the ends of her lips tilting up in a pleased smile. She throws the ball, this time with a little more force behind it. "I'm sorry I haven't been around as much. It's hard getting back into the swing of things and obviously I don't plan on working late, but sometimes emergencies happen when we're about to go off shift."

I raise an eyebrow. "Babe," I throw it back at her. "I think I understand that better than probably anyone. I've been able to drive myself with no problems. More than anything, I want my life to go back to normal, and while I know you want to be with me at everything, I kinda like doing a few things for myself."

I wince, because I'm afraid I'll offend her by what I just said.

She laughs loudly, stopping our volleying of the ball as she giggles. "You should see the look on your face. You didn't offend me."

"Good! I don't want to. Just because I'm doing things on my own doesn't mean I don't want you around. I want you around, all the time. I'm used to you being around."

This hadn't been planned, but I'd been thinking about it a lot lately. I don't want Blaze to go back to her apartment, I want her to stay full-time with me, in my house.

"Are you asking me to move in with you?"

"I guess I am," I throw the ball behind my shoulder and swim toward her. "It wasn't planned, but I've been thinking about it for a while. I don't want to live without you now that I have you. We'll go slow. I know we're still learning things about one another, and we obviously aren't at the same point that Ryan and Whitney are. But I also want you to know that's where I'm heading. If the wreck taught me anything, it's that I want you in my life forever. No one else can take care of me the way you do, and no one makes me feel more loved than you do. If something were to ever happen to you, I know I would be the same way."

She's quiet, and I'm scared I've overstepped and possibly shocked the hell out of her. "You don't have to answer right now, I know that wasn't the most romantic way for me to ask. But real talk, I felt it and wanted to ask. I don't regret it."

"Neither do I," she launches herself at me, and at that moment, I know my leg's okay, because it doesn't give out as I catch her against me. "I'd be super excited to move in with you."

My heart starts beating again as I hear the words leave her mouth. "I love you, and thank you for being everything I've needed throughout this crazy process. We'll get you moved in as soon as we can. I don't want to spend a night without you."

She squeals as I pick her up, putting her legs around my waist.

Here in this pool, with the woman I love hanging onto me, is the happiest I've been in months. With everything I have, I know I'm going to do whatever it takes to keep making this happen.

Blaze

"YOU SURE THIS isn't too much?" I ask as I look around at the boxes that have invaded Trevor's home.

I'm still unsure what I'm going to do with my apartment. There are certain furniture pieces I have that I love, and I don't necessarily want to part with. I'll figure it out as I have more time, but everything that matters to me in the world is here with me right now.

"Not at all, we'll figure out where to put everything," he pulls me into a hug, wrapping his arm around my neck. "The most important thing is you're here with me, and you'll be here with me for the foreseeable future."

I grin up at him, because I like the sound of that. "Thanks for helping me," I throw Ace a fifth of Jim Beam, his payment for helping me move today. "I think I remember this is your favorite."

He grabs the bottle out of the air and grins at me. "It is. I'll have fun drinkin' this on the lake next weekend."

"You're already going out to the lake?" Trevor questions, as he has a seat, pulling me down in his lap. "Little early for that, isn't it?"

Ace rolls his eyes. "This is Alabama, it's eighty in February. It's never too early for the lake."

I have to laugh because he's right, in our part of the state, it's always hot. "Either way, thanks for helping today."

"Yeah," Trevor holds out his hand for his friend to shake. "I appreciate you doing the heavy lifting."

"I'm sure you're healed up nicely, but there's no sense in testing it out. I was happy to help," he grabs his wallet. "But if you don't need me anymore, I'm out. I got shit to do tonight."

"Thank you again," I get up off Trevor's lap and hug the man who saw me at my worst. Ace was the only person who saw me hit my knees that day on the road as I realized it was Trevor in the wreckage. We've never spoken about it, but as he hugs me, he offers me a little squeeze.

"Cherish it, every day," he whispers.

"I will," I whisper back.

And like that, we've said all we're going to. I go back to Trevor's lap, and the world keeps spinning.

CHAPTER TWENTY-TWO

Blaze

I'M nervous as Logan lets me out at the front of the Medical Arts Building in Laurel Springs. I check my watch to make sure I'm on time and see that I have about five minutes to spare. Today's the day Trevor has to do his psych evaluation and they've asked me to be there. Part of me is extremely nervous. I don't know what he remembers, if he remembers anything. Another part of me wonders what else might get brought up in this session. Counselors in our professions are very quick to tell when something is off, and the fact I haven't come clean with Trevor yet rubs me the wrong way. I'm going to have to make it a point to sit down and talk to him.

I enter the building and hit the elevator for the fifth floor. My hands shake as I wait for the doors to open. This isn't my evaluation and I have to wonder why I'm so damn nervous. Exiting the elevator, I walk into the lobby, spotting Trevor immediately. He's sitting in the back, filling out paperwork. There are two women sitting not far from him, eyeing him up and down as he reads the papers he's signing.

God he looks hot as his eyebrows come together, studying the words he's reading before he signs his name with a flourish. His hands look huge as they hold the small pen. I know exactly what those hands can do, and they can play my body like a damn violin.

"Hey," I whisper as I make my way over to him. "I hope I'm not late."

He smiles up at me, standing to give me a kiss in greeting. I can't help it, I turn to those women who had been checking him out and give them a huge smile. They turn their noses up at me and turn around in their seats. That's right ladies, he's mine. "Nope, you're right on time. Let me just take these papers to the desk, and they should be calling us back shortly."

I stand where he leaves me, dumbfounded as I watch him walk to the front desk. The pants he wears today hug his ass perfectly and I can't help but lick my lips as I watch him. "C'mon babe," he motions to me, and I have to shake my head to clear my thoughts.

He holds his hand out, grasping mine as we head to the back, where the offices are. We're pointed to a room where there's a couch and a couple of chairs. They shut the door and tell us the doctor will be in soon.

"Which doctor are you seeing?" I ask as I have a seat next to him, crossing my legs and getting as comfortable as possible.

"Doctor Cole," he glances at his piece of paper. "I've heard of her before. Some of the other guys in the department have seen her."

The last words leave his mouth when the door opens and in walks a middle-age woman who could pass for early thirties. I hope I look as good as her when I get that old.

"Trevor?" she glances at him, holding her hand for him to shake.

"Yes ma'am, and this is my girlfriend, Blaze," he introduces me.

Damn his manners are sexy. He's such a good southern boy.

"The hair, right?" she grins at me, reaching out to shake my hand as well.

I grin back. "It's always a good conversation starter."

We get through the getting to know you portion of the sit down, where we verify what Trevor went through and why we're there. Finally Doc Cole starts asking her questions.

"What do you remember about the wreck, Trevor?"

He shakes his head. "Absolutely nothing. I still don't even remember Brooks coming over the hill. I don't know at what point I saw him or even if I did. The only thing I can remember before I woke up two days later was a moment in the ER when they were putting a tube in my chest. I came to and asked them for Blaze. The next thing I know, I'm waking up in the hospital and Blaze is asleep in my room. Nothing between me leaving The Café after talking with Whitney that morning and listening to hard rock music until the ER and me waking up remains. I can't tell you anything."

I've often wondered if he's telling the truth when he says those words. Three times since the accident I've slipped into conversations ways to find out if he's been fucked up by what happened to him, but every time he says he doesn't remember anything. Maybe it's time to believe him.

"Is there anything you're having issues with you'd like to talk about? We have an hour and if you have no thoughts about the incident that put you here, maybe you'd like to talk about something else? Are you angry with Brooks Strather?"

"I wouldn't say so much angry as hopeful the system works and makes him pay for what he did. He's a kid who's never had to face consequences, and until the system makes him do so, nothing I do is going to change that. I'm angry I've been laid up all this time, had to take a leave from my job, and had to worry my family, but I'm also thankful."

I think I know where this is going so I reach over and grab his hand. I want to get over this part of our lives too, and if we need to do it here, in front of a shrink, we will.

"Why are you thankful?"

He glances over at me. "The two of us weren't talking to each other at the time of the accident. We'd broken up and hadn't spoken in months."

"Did she respond to the call?" she asks, staring at my uniform.

"I did," I clear my throat. "It was the hardest thing I ever had to do, and if either one of us has had some sleepless nights about this incident, it's been me. I'm good now though, I haven't had a nightmare since a couple of nights after he came home. I think it was just the shock of everything, to be completely honest with you."

"Why had the two of you stopped talking to one another?"

Immediately I kind of feel like we've gone from work territory to personal territory, but if this helps us get where we need to be, I'll do it.

"She was held at gunpoint by a mentally unstable man and my unit responded. I asked her to quit her job because I thought it was too dangerous, she refused and we said some very hurtful things to one another."

"But the accident helped all that?" She makes some notes in her notebook.

"It made us realize what was important," I answer for the both of us.

She continues writing, nodding, before she stops and gazes at first me, then him. "You realized what was important, but have you yet talked about the situation?"

We both swallow loudly. "We haven't," my tone is clipped. "We've been too busy getting him well enough to return to work."

"Well, here's my recommendation that he go back," she hands Trevor a piece of paper. "And then off the record, my recommendation to the two of you? Sooner, rather than later, you need to talk about what happened. The type of job you're in, it's a ticking time bomb for someone else to put either of you in harm's way. Until you start being honest with each other, no matter how much you love one another, it's not going to automatically fix itself."

I know what she says is true, and as the two of us get up, leaving her office, we're somber. I don't think either of us realizes how long it will actually be before we talk about what lead us down our dark path.

CHAPTER TWENTY-THREE

Blaze

"YOU'RE sure you're okay with watching her?" Whitney asks as Ryan tries to herd her out the door. "It's Valentine's, maybe the two of you had plans," she tries again, looking between Trevor and me.

"Our plans are right here, with her," I give her a reassuring grin. These two obviously want some time alone, and it looks like it's going to be difficult to get Whitney out the door. "Stella will be fine. You two go out and have a nice night. You deserve it."

She looks like she wants to say no and argue with all of us, but Ryan clamps a hand over her mouth.

"We totally appreciate the two of you forfeiting your Valentine's Day so we can go out. We'll be home no later than midnight."

Trevor tsks from where he stands behind me. "No sir, you will have her home no later than eleven thirty. It's a work night and she has a curfew."

I laugh at the two of them when Ryan lifts a middle finger in Trevor's direction. "Don't tempt me, we'll stay out all night."

Whitney shakes her head behind the palm of his hand, making muffled words and gestures with her hands, eyes wide.

"Would you two stop? That way they can leave."

Ryan ushers her out the door, throwing back a "Don't do anything I wouldn't do," before they're gone.

"I never thought they were going to leave. They act like neither one of us have jobs where we have to be around kids," Trevor shakes his head as he grabs a slice of the heart-shaped pizza we brought over.

He's doing well since he's gone back to half-days, mostly doing paperwork. I'm pretty impressed with how he's handling everything. I know he wants to be out on calls and things like that, but he's doing almost everything but.

"They're new parents, give them a break," I take a bite of the pizza he puts to my mouth. "What are they doing tonight anyway?"

He quirks an eyebrow at me. "Knowing Renegade? He probably got them room service and an empty bed for the night. Being romantic with your lady with no interruptions? That would be number one on my list if we were parents to an infant."

"Well, hopefully he's a little smoother than you."

"I'm smooth like butter, baby," he lifts his shirt up, showing his abs. "When was the last time you said no to this?" He uses his hand to indicate the entire expanse of his torso and mid-section.

I try to think back and realize he's right. I've never said no to him. Truthfully there's a problem there, I should probably make him work harder than I do, but he knows me so well. "Never."

He leans in, giving me a kiss. "Exactly."

We grab our paper plates and our bottles of beer to take into the living room. Stella is in her vibrating seat, paying attention to what's playing on TV. "She's acting so mesmerized by the shopping channel," I laugh when she makes a noise as they show a diamond ring. "Yes honey, you tell him that's what you want."

Trevor tilts his head to the side. "I wouldn't have pictured you for a diamond girl. Is that what you'd want?"

This conversation feels heavy to me, one I hadn't planned on having with him tonight. "In so many ways I'm not the norm, but I think if this came up in a conversation, I would have to say I'm pretty traditional when it comes to things like this."

He sets his plate down, pulling his phone out. "What are you doing?"

"Taking notes for when we decide the time's right for us. I want to blow you away, and I'd be stupid not to give you what you want and deserve."

This man has no idea how much he affects me, how much it means to me that he listens to what I want. I don't even know what to say. "Quit joking around, Trev."

"I'm one thousand percent serious. I've told you before this thing we've got going on is headed toward an altar, and I mean that. Do I think we're ready for it now? No, but it's heavy on my mind."

Stella picks that moment to start crying. As a team, we work to get her bottle ready, and a piece of me melts as I watch Trevor pick her up in his arms, giving her the bottle. "You're a natural with her."

He shrugs. "I babysat as a teenager. Not really the coolest thing for a guy to do, but there was a family that lived about five miles from us with three kids and they couldn't afford a daycare. I started watching them the year I turned thirteen," he repositions her on his legs and continues giving her the bottle. "Ya know back then there wasn't this call to arms about everyone being trained in CPR and all of that before you could watch kids. All of them were boys, so we basically spent our summers playing kickball and baseball. The youngest was two and he still took a bottle and had diapers. Not to stay I changed and fed him all the time. His brothers helped a lot, but I learned the basics and they kind of stuck with me."

He hands her to me as she gets done with the bottle, letting me burp her as he goes and takes care of what we've dirtied up. "You never cease to amaze me, Trevor. I mean, I think I know everything about you, and you surprise me with something like this."

He comes back into the living room holding a piece of chocolate cake with ice cream on it. "Our dessert," he sets it down on the TV tray in between us. "And I hope I never stop surprising you. I love surprising you. There's something I never told you, but when we met, I was on a dark path. I didn't necessarily do things for the right reasons. I joined the military and the Moonshine Task Force because of Renegade. I never wanted him to move on without me, but that night I met you, I started really think about my life," he grabs Stella from me before feeding me a piece of the cake.

It's the best kind of cake, full of flavor with just the right amount of moisture. "What did you start to think about?"

"How to get you to go out with me. Some of the stuff I was doing, I knew you wouldn't have anything to do with me."

Stella grabs for his fork, but he keeps it out of her reach. "What exactly were you doing?"

Now I'm curious. It occurs to me I don't know a ton about Trevor's past, and while that's okay, I'm interested now.

"Drinkin' too much, staying out too late, seeing multiple women at once, and then not calling back the ones who would have been good for me after I got what I wanted. I went a little crazy after I came back from overseas. It's a shock to reacclimate," he feeds me another piece of cake.

I speak around the food, "I imagine, and it must be difficult when not everyone comes back with you."

I remember one of our units lost a couple of men on the last tour Trevor and Ryan had done together.

"Yeah," he gets a faraway look in his eyes. "You wonder what they would be doing today. Would they be married to the girls they were dating? Would they be dads? Hell, one of them might have my spot on the Moonshine Task Force. There's so many unknowns, and it's hard to live with. At least for me it was.

Renegade didn't have the problems I had, probably because he had such a shitty childhood."

"What changed?" I grab Stella, snuggling her close to me. The innocent scent of talcum powder and formula is one of my favorites. It grounds me in this conversation we're having.

"I met you," he reaches out, rubbing Stella's back. "I met you by chance at that damn cookout Holden dragged us to so we could meet our EMT counterparts," he rolls his eyes. "Holden still tells me how much I owe him, he probably will until the end of time. Even when we'd broken up, he would leave little notes in the squad car about how I should tell him thank you. Without him, I'd never have at least known the love of a good woman."

I laugh as he makes a face. "Remind me to thank Holden next time I see him."

"Oh hell no, he'll keep at it." He stops laughing along with me, before he reaches over and grabs my hand. "Truthfully, when I met you, things didn't look so bleak anymore. I felt like I had a purpose. I wanted a date with you, even though it took six weeks."

"I thought you were joking with me, I mean look at you."

He blushes a bright red. "Babe, look at *you*. You're totally outta my league."

"Somehow we both managed to compromise our values and find one another," I move a now sleeping Stella back into her seat. "Amazing how that works, isn't it?"

Trevor moves quickly and before I know it, I'm on my back on the couch, his big body has covered mine, and he's dipping his lips down to capture mine. "What do you say we do exactly what Renegade would do?"

"Right here?" I smirk, keeping my voice low as not to wake up the baby we just put down. "This is kinda low-key teenage making out."

"Baby, I'll show you just how much I'm a man. Lay on back and relax."

My belly clenches as I feel his palm moving up, pushing my shirt to bare my flesh. He places a soft kiss on my skin, before he starts pulling the skirt I'm wearing down. I hadn't really been thinking easy access when I'd put it on, I'd been thinking comfort, but now I'm totally glad I decided to wear it.

"Happy Valentine's Day to me," I moan as I feel his fingers slip beneath the lace of my panties.

He glances up at me, our eyes meeting. "Nah babe, Happy Valentine's Day to us."

Considering a few months ago I worried we'd never have one again. I'm going to do everything I can to be present and enjoy the hell out of this.

CHAPTER TWENTY-FOUR

Tank

"I THINK she's grown like three feet and nine pounds since the last time we saw her a week ago," I observe Stella sleeping in her carrier.

There was a time when I hated coming to my sister's. I wasn't ever sure what kind of a mood she and Stephen would be in, and I didn't like holding my tongue when it came to her ex-husband. If it had been up to me, the night I showed him how I really felt about him, I'd have killed him and buried his body in the damn woods.

"She's growing like a weed," Whitney confirms as she hands me a drink and has a seat next to Renegade on the loveseat they're sharing.

She lies down, putting her feet in his lap. Not missing a beat, he grabs her legs and lazily starts stroking them up and down. I have to say back when they first told me about their relationship I acted like an ass, and that's totally my fault. I couldn't see how they would be able to love each other after the past the two of them shared. I'm happy and proud to say I was dead wrong. They love each other with an intensity I hope Blaze and I share.

"How's work?" I ask Renegade. Not being able to patrol alongside my brothers in blue is starting to get to me, but I hope to be back on the schedule in the next few weeks.

"Not bad," he yawns. They're pulling more overtime with me off than they have in a while. "The Strather's are ramping up again. Speaking of, have you heard anything about Brooks and the charges they're bringing against him?"

"I got a call from the state prosecutor early this week. They're going for the maximum penalty on him. I heard through the grapevine that even though he's out on bail, they caught him over in Oldham County speeding the other day. I hope they lock the kid up and throw away the key. He didn't succeed in killing me, but he's not going to stop until he kills someone – probably himself. It's scary he has no regard for human life."

Blaze snuggles next to me. "Yeah but look at the family he was raised with. None of them consider anyone important besides themselves. Trust me. When you're raised with family like that, it's hard to care about others," she shrugs. "I'm not making excuses for him, but I do kind of understand where he gets his apathy. He's in for a rude awakening though, because the rest of the world wasn't raised like that."

We're quiet as we settle back in to watch a movie Renegade's rented for us. I think we're watching it just because he wants to sleep, and this is the easiest way for him to get away with a quiet weekend afternoon. Either way, we're all kind of lethargic, and I'm positive we're all about five minutes from going to sleep when Stella's loud cries scare us all to death.

"Holy shit, she about gave me a heart attack," I jump up, dislodging Blaze from where she was nearly asleep against my shoulder.

"She's really good at doing that," Whitney yawns and blearily reaches down to grab the bottle they already have prepared. "It's like she's on a timer and knows when we're about to doze off. But she's also been so congested lately," she lifts Stella up, putting her in her arms so she can feed her.

"This weather has all kinds of kids sick," Blaze confirms. "RSV is at the highest level they've seen it in a few years in this area. We've had more than a few runs the past couple of days where kids are in distress."

"I was worried about that the other night," Ryan sits up straighter, rubbing his eyes. "She's too little to really get the congestion out of her."

"Yeah," Blaze nods. "That's the biggest problem. Do you have a suction bulb? That's the easiest way to do it."

He reaches into the diaper bag on the floor and fishes one out. "Before I leave, I'll show you guys what you need to do."

We're all quiet again as we settle back into the movie. I'm not even sure where it left off, all I know is I'm enjoying this quiet day with my family. It's amazing how different our are lives now than they were back right before Thanksgiving. If this was before the wreck, I might have decided to go do something else, but now I understand how important family time is.

Blaze is running her hand along my leg and she's laughing as I situate myself deeper in the couch. "Don't get too comfortable," she teases.

It happens in the blink of an eye. Whitney drops the bottle and we hear Stella coughing violently, gasping and wheezing, trying to take in a breath. "Oh my God, Stella," the fear in her voice is nothing like I've ever heard before.

The rest of us look to be on the edge of a freak out, when calm as she ever is,

Blaze gets up from her position on the couch, walks over, picks Stella up and walks back over to the couch we were sitting on. Stella is trying to breathe, we can all hear it, the gasp for breath is the scariest sound I've ever heard in my life. Her little throat muscles are working hard as her chest pumps up and down in small little pants, trying desperately to take in air.

Blaze sits down next to me, turns our niece over on her forearm before she begins tapping her between the shoulder blades with the heel of her hand. As she works, she says in another calm voice. "Trevor, do me a favor and call nine-one-one and put them on speaker phone."

My hands shake as I do as she's asked. I glance over seeing Renegade and Whitney both white with shock. I count the loud thuds Blaze makes as she slaps Stella on the back. When nine-one-one picks up, I hear Blaze talking but I have no idea what she's saying. If someone asked me later on what was said, I would never be able to repeat one word from the conversation.

"Hang up the phone, Trev, they're on their way."

She's still thumping her back, and I'm praying with everything I have to hear her cry - if she cries that means she can breathe. After what feels like an eternity, Stella violently expels a mouthful of formula all over Blaze.

The entire group collectively makes a noise as we hear Stella make a noise.

"She's okay, she's okay," Blaze turns her over, checking her out. "Her color's good, and I don't hear any laboring."

Right then we hear the wail of the ambulance, and I jump up to let them in. It's a whirlwind as they check Stella, making sure everything is okay. I watch as they put a little oxygen mask on her as a precaution; they won't be taking her to the hospital. Blaze excuses herself to go clean up in the bathroom while mom and dad dote over their baby.

I follow Blaze, I need to be close to her after what's happened. But I'm too slow, she's shut the door to the bathroom. "Blaze, let me in," I try the knob, and it turns easily.

When I open the door and she looks up from where she's sitting on the ledge of the bathtub, my heart breaks for her. She's got tears streaming down her face and her hands are shaking. "I just need to get washed up," she stands and walks over to the sink, soaping up her hands, and using a washcloth to clean her clothing.

I shut the door softly behind me. "It's okay if you were affected by that, I think we all were."

She stops what she's doing and braces her hands against the counter, letting her head fall between her shoulders. "It's so damn hard to see a baby fight for breath like that," she cries, her shoulders shaking. "And I was scared to death, what if I couldn't get the airway unobstructed? How would I be able to look at myself again? How would you be able to ever look at me again."

Walking over, I take her in my arms, putting my chin on top of her head. "I never doubted you, babe, because I know you're damn good at your job. We were all fucking scared out there. You were the one though who handled it like a champ. You grabbed her up, did your thing, and made sure she was breathing. That takes skill and guts."

"That's the hardest part of my job, knowing what to do, but not being in control of everything. We can sometimes do all the right things and the patient still doesn't make it. I worried about that with her, especially after the first few times she didn't respond."

I turn her around, folding her in my arms. Like they have their own honing beacon, my lips find hers and I kiss her hard. There's no passion, which is so unlike us. Instead it's a relief that we both feel. "Thank you for being there when our family needed you," he breathes heavily. "Thank you for being the person who stood up, kept a level head and did the most badass thing I've ever seen in my life. I don't think I could have done it, I know I couldn't have done it. Thank you for being with me."

She giggles, disrupting the flow of the tears down her cheeks. "I'll gladly stand next to my Batman."

"Fuck that, your Batman will gladly stand next to you."

Blaze

I'm shaken when we get home, terrified of what I just did and who I saved. It feels like it did the afternoon I saved Trevor. My teeth are chattering as he pulls us into his drive.

"Are you okay?"

I nod. "I think it's delayed shock to be honest with you. It's been a long time since I've been that scared. To see someone you love going through something and you aren't sure whether you can do anything about it. It affects you."

His blue eyes flash with annoyance, and it takes me by surprise. "You're really gonna go there, Blaze?"

I watch as he opens the door to the truck and stalks into what's now our house. "What did you mean am I going to go there?" I burst through the back door, following him. He's already at the fridge with a beer out, taking a large drink of it.

"Let's talk about the elephant in the room, sweetheart. Let's talk about how I was affected by what I saw *you* go through."

I'm speechless because I know at the end of listening to him tell me his story, I'm going to have to tell him mine.

CHAPTER TWENTY-FIVE

Tank

I TURN AROUND, ready to face whatever this fight is going to be. "So this is it, huh?" She questions, hands on her hips, lips pressed into a firm line. Blaze is fucking pissed, and I can't say that I blame her. "We're gonna have it out now? After all these months of walking on eggshells with each other, you're finally going to let me have it?"

"Do you *really want it*?" I take a pull off the beer in front of me. "Be careful what you're askin' for, sweetheart. Make sure you can handle it."

"I think I saved Stella today and I showed you how important my job is for the world at large. That should count for something."

She's right, it does count for a lot, but there's always going to be a fear I have after seeing what I saw. "You didn't see what I did," I argue.

Blaze gets in my face. "And you didn't see what I did when you were in that truck, Trevor. The difference between us? I told you after it happened, I told you how scared I was, I shared my feelings. You've been tight-lipped about everything when it comes to the day you got smacked in the face with how real my job actually is. It's not fair to me, it's not fair to us, and it's going to fucking ruin our relationship. Is that what you want?"

My leg bounces up and down with barely restrained anger and I'm doing my best not to take everything out on her, but fuck if I'm not pissed. "No it's not what I want, but I want you to get it through your thick head you could have died!"

"Same with you!" Her voice is high-pitched before she bites her lip and blows out a calming deep breath. When she speaks again, she's more in control of her emotions. "Help me understand, Trev. You know what I saw, because I told you. To be completely honest, I don't remember a whole lot about that day," she grabs my beer and takes a drink. "All I knew was I didn't want to die, and I was praying to God to let me go home that night."

She's asking me for something I don't know that I can give her. I've tried with everything in me to forget that day, but somehow if I close my eyes, I can take myself back to those mind-numbing moments like they were yesterday.

"You were wearing the uniform you hate. The one you accidentally shrunk a little in the chest when you washed it. You know, the one that gapes at the buttons. Your hair was curly and you had a braid going from the left side in the front to where it ended on the right at your shoulder. That day you'd lined your eyes with that black shit you like to use, and it made the green in them pop," I speak almost robotically. "I know because I looked into your eyes the *entire fucking time* I stood to the side and let someone else save you because they had the hostage negotiation training," I turn around so I'm not facing her anymore, putting my hands on my hips. "When all I really wanted to do was un-holster my gun and put one right between his fucking eyes for putting the fear in yours."

I shove my fingers through my hair and hold the back of my scalp as the memory hits me like a brick in the chest.

Holden's voice comes over the radio. "There's a domestic situation at 1345 Main Street. EMS is on scene trying to administer to a patient having an episode. Call just came in that the man has taken a female medic hostage. Sources at the scene say there is a gun involved. Whoever can respond, please do so with extreme care in mind. Myself and a negotiator are in route."

My pulse pounds in my throat as Ryan and I glance at one another.

"It wouldn't be Blaze, would it?" He questions, holding on as I take a turn a little too fast.

"Could be," I answer between clenched teeth. "She's on shift today, and when I texted her about thirty minutes ago, she didn't answer. Normally when she doesn't answer, she's busy."

We're both quiet as we take in the fact one of our own could be in danger. We work at lot with EMS, and they work a lot with us. In our occupations, you watch out for one another, and we're all incredibly close when it comes down to it. None of us wants the others to hurt, and those EMS men and women are there for us in some of our darkest hours. This job isn't easy, and every once in a while, someone gets hurt. It's up to them to put us back together or to keep us calm until we can get to the hospital. I imagine it isn't easy for them to administer to us, but they do, and I have the utmost respect for them.

But what I have right now is the worst fear I've ever felt in my heart for my girlfriend. We made it official a few weeks ago. I let a small smile spread across my face. I haven't had a girlfriend in fucking years, but there's something about Blaze, she gets me like no one else ever has. I've kept quiet about it for the most part because I'm scared to jinx it. The only people who truly know what's going on between us are my sister and my best friend.

As I pull our squad car up to the house, I see where the ambulance has parked. Logan, Blaze's partner, is standing next to the open back doors of the bus, talking to someone. They're blocked by the angle it's sitting. Both Ryan and I make sure we have our vests on before we try to make contact. It's then I see the department's hostage negotiator, sitting his gun down on the pavement. As we get closer, I can make out his words.

"Leonard, you don't need this woman. Let her go and we can talk about whatever it is you need to talk about. But we can do that without her."

My blood goes cold and immediately the adrenaline flows through my body. I'm not sure what I thought when I didn't see Blaze. Maybe she was in the back, tending to another patient or sitting in the driver's seat, getting ready for them to take off? I move closer to get a look at what's going on, and my heart stops.

There's the woman I made love to not twelve hours ago, standing on the sidewalk with an arm wrapped around her neck, a man holding her back to his front and the barrel of his gun resting against her temple. I lose my breath and damn near almost lose my mind. Ryan grabs my vest as I make a move to go toward her.

"Don't even think about it. He'll put her down before you can get there." His voice is low in the tense atmosphere.

"How am I supposed to sit here and watch this?" I can hear the pain, the frustration in my voice. "I was a goddamn sniper. They need to let me take this guy out."

"If this can be resolved peacefully, that's what needs to happen," Ryan argues, playing devil's advocate.

I hold back what I want to tell him. Starts with kiss and ends with my ass. He isn't in my position, doesn't know how I feel, and can't even begin to fathom it right now. I'm trying very hard to keep my shit together, but it won't take much for me to explode.

"Calm down," Ryan crowds me, making it so I can't see Blaze anymore. "Take some deep breathes and calm the fuck down. You can't let this guy see you this worked up. He sees it? He's going to use it. You have to stay calm and know your lady knows what she's doing – she has training just like we do. Trust our team and know they won't let anything happen to one of ours."

I walk away because I know he's right. Hardest fucking thing I've ever done in my life. Walking away and letting her stay on that sidewalk with him. The sun is beating down on this hot ass, Alabama day. I almost wish it were overcast and raining, at least then the sun wouldn't be in our eyes and we'd all have a better chance of having a visual. The hotter this guy gets, the more apt he'll be to go off book from how we think he'll proceed.

"Is there anything you need, Leonard?" I hear the negotiator ask.

"Don't wanna go back to that hospital," he cries.

I can hear the despair and fear in his voice, and for a split-second I feel sorry for him. He's been dealt an obviously shitty life card. He has an illness, one that needs treatment, but the illness doesn't allow him to admit it.

"They won't keep you Leonard, they'll make you feel better."

He shouts again, this time anger fills his voice. "They'll give me those pills and I won't feel like myself. I don't like it when I don't feel like myself. I walk around in a haze and days go by before I realize what's going on."

"You and I both know it'll happen in the beginning, but after a few weeks you'll be able to go back to your job at the Quick Stop. Don't you miss your friends there?"

Everyone stops talking, and I let out the breath I've been holding before I turn around and look at the scene again. This time I'm as calm and composed as I can be – as I'll get. My eyes focus on Blaze and my heart rips out of my chest. Anyone who doesn't know her will think she's got this together. Her façade appears unaffected, but me, I see it. Her bottom lip is slightly trembling. She's got her hands formed into fists, gripping the uniform material at her thighs. And that's when I make my biggest mistake of all – I let myself look into her eyes.

It's like a scene out of a movie. Between people, distance, and the intensity in the air, the two of us lock gazes. My stomach drops like it does on the first hill of a roller coaster, it's somewhere down at my feet as I see the fear in her eyes. Tears are pooled behind the black stuff she uses to make her green eyes pop, and I want so badly to reach out to her and take her in my arms. Tell her this is all gonna be okay. I mouth to her I LOVE YOU, because I want her to know. We've been saying it a little here and there, it wasn't this grand declaration of feelings. Nothing with us ever is. It was organic, and to be honest, I can't even remember the first time I told her. All I know is one day she kissed me on the cheek as I left, told me she loved me, and I said it back. Everything with our relationship has been easy. Until today. Today I feel as if someone's dropped an anvil on my head and it woke me the fuck up. We can't continue to live in our bubble. Neither one of us have jobs that will allow us to.

Blaze nods, her bottom lip sticking a bit further out and I see her trying to keep the tears from rolling down her cheeks. She's a proud woman, and the most beautiful one I've ever seen in my life.

"It's okay," I say. "You're gonna be fine, babe."

People look at me, I can feel their eyes on me, but the only person I care about it is the redhead with the green eyes, looking at me like I'm a superhero for giving her a little bit of hope.

"Don't do that," Ryan warns me. "Don't turn his attention on you."

I would gladly take every bit of his attention. I'd trade places with her in a nanosecond. I rest my hand on the butt of my gun, ready to pull it if I need to. God, I want to. As a sniper, I had kills that I can never talk about, ones that left me upset for days, but this one – to save her – I would do it without any kind of hesitation.

Our hostage negotiator is talking to him again. "Leonard, aren't you hot? It's a hot day, let us bring you some water. If not you, let us bring the lady some."

His hand shakes uncontrollably as he holds the gun to her head. I watch a trail of sweat as it runs from his forehead, down his cheek, and pools at his neck, getting soaked up by the cotton of his shirt. Damn right he's hot, he's tired, and he's scared. He's probably got the most amazing adrenaline high of his life, which means he's the most dangerous motherfucker on the planet right now.

"I wanna go inside," he announces. "There's air conditioning, and she'll be comfortable," he runs a hand down Blaze's neck, caressing the column, before he closes his palm around her throat. I almost roar with anger. Nobody touches her but me, not like that, not the way he is. I make another move, and this time Ryan loops an arm around my waist from behind, using his body weight to keep me from going at them.

"Take it down a notch, bro. You can't do what you want to. I get it though, I get it," he's telling me, trying to calm me down. "The best thing you can do right now is cool off. If Holden sees this, he will pull you outta here so fast, your head will spin. Get your shit together."

It's easier said than done, but I regulate my breathing, slow my heart rate down, and try to take stock of the situation in front of us. My girl is holding on like a champ. The only one who can tell she's freaking out is me, and it's because I know her so well. She seems like she has it all together; I send her every bit of good energy I have. Until my heart drops in my feet again as he starts pulling her back toward the house.

"No!" Everyone yells, me included.

"Leonard, you can't take her inside. You take her inside, we will come get her out," the negotiator threatens.

I wonder at that moment if it's smart to be threatening this man. He's crying now, his moods are shifting quickly.

"I just want a friend, and she can be my friend," he tightens his grip on her throat. I can tell by the way she grimaces.

"I can be your friend," Holden steps up from where he's been standing to the side, putting his gun down on the ground, holding his hands up. "Let her come out here, and I can be your friend. You can take me and do whatever you want with me. She's tired, Leonard. Aren't you tired? She's just as tired as you are."

"But she tried to help me," he argues. "She told me things were going to be fine, and she'd make sure of it."

"She did try to help you buddy, and you put a gun to her head. How can she trust you?"

"How can I trust her?" He shifts again.

This is bad, his shifting moods. He's hot, he's irritated, and he's got a gun to the woman I love's head. Right now I'm not even interested in how this ends. All I want is my arms around her. I want to feel her heartbeat against mine. More than anything I want to tuck her head under my chin and feel the bite of her nails around my waist. When Blaze hugs, she hugs for all she's worth. I need that hug right now, I want to give one back in return.

It's then I see someone approaching from behind. Leonard can't see Mason, the quietest member of our team, who goes by the name of Mace because basically because he gets in, gets the job done, and does it with the quickest efficiency any of us have ever seen. We joke it's because he's a single dad, and has to jerk it fast. Today I'm not joking, and my heart is in my throat as I see him get closer to the two standing on the sidewalk.

I can't even hear anymore what's being said, I'm not even paying attention to it. My eyes are again locked with Blaze's and I'm trying to communicate to her to wait, we're coming. Quick as a cobra, Mace puts his arms around Leonard, takes the gun, subdues him, and has him on the ground. Literally it was in the blink of an eye.

Blaze's knees give out as I run to her, gathering her up as she collapses. We crumble in a heap against the hot concrete. She's shaking and crying, burying her head in my chest. Her tears wet the piece of skin that's not covered by my vest and I want to rage again for the fact someone's upset her this much.

"I got you babe, I got you," I'm breathing like I've run a marathon. Pulling back, I frame her face with my hands, running them over her, making sure she's still in one piece.

"I know," she nods, swallowing those tears. "I know, but oh my God, I was so scared. I've never been that scared before."

Neither have I, and it's hard to keep my own hands and body from shaking. The adrenaline is coursing through me, making it hard for me to take in anything going on around us except for Blaze. I capture her lips with mine, not caring who sees. We've tried to keep our relationship on the quiet side just because we didn't want any of the usual teasing our friends are capable of, but right now I couldn't give two fucks.

"Sorry you two, but Blaze, they say I have to check you out," Logan interrupts us, the look on his face one of regret. "I told them we could wait a minute, but all the supervisors want to make sure you're okay."

She looks at me, almost as if she's asking for permission, which is nothing like her. She's more of the ask forgiveness rather than permission sort. That alone tells me how much this has affected her. "Go on," I push her toward Logan. "Put everybody's mind at ease, I'll come get you in a minute."

She leans into me, wrapping her arms around my neck. "I love you, Trevor."

The broken tone of her voice does me in. "Love you, too," I whisper as I kiss her forehead. We stand up, and I help her to the ambulance, before I go to find a moment alone.

Once I'm around the back of the house, I lean into the brick wall, bracing myself with my hand. It doesn't take much until everything I've eaten all day comes up. I try to tell myself I'm okay, it's just reaction and it won't be so bad in a few hours, but I know that's kind of a lie. I'm not sure I'll ever be okay again.

"And now I have to be okay, because I've seen you save people we care about. I see the joy it brings you and the safety and security it brings to the people around you," he reaches in, grabbing hold of my waist. "It's scary, sharing you with the world."

"If I explain to you why I do what I do, why I have to do it, will you listen? Will you try to understand?"

Her voice is thick, strained, and so full of emotion I can't help but agree to it. In this moment, she's the most vulnerable I've ever seen her, and I know if I don't meet her in the middle, she's going to eventually run.

"Please," I grasp her chin, pulling her to me for a forceful kiss, one of ownership, but also one of a desperate man trying to hold onto the most important thing in his life. "Let me in."

CHAPTER TWENTY-SIX

Blaze

"YOU ASKED me once why I do what I do and I told you it was because I just like to help people. I haven't been totally honest with you, and I feel like I need to be. If we're going to go headlong into this 'new' relationship of ours, then it needs to be with the truth being shared between the two of us."

I have his attention now. "Nothing's going to change how I feel about you. I understand why you love your profession and I support you totally in it. This isn't going to be a problem between us again, Blaze. I swear."

I take his hand in mine, relishing the energy and comfort I take from the simple touch. "No, I know, but I still want to be completely honest and more than anything I feel like it's time. I've never told another person this story," I admit. I do my best not to think about this part of my life.

"Now you're starting to scare me," he lets go of my hand and palms the back of my neck, bringing my gaze level with his. "But if I'm the person you've decided to trust with this secret of yours, I'm honored. We've come too far to let things come between us, Blaze. So you go ahead and tell me what you need to. I can say with one hundred percent certainty, it's not going to change the way I feel about you."

I want to cry as soon as I hear those words come out of his mouth. I've never opened myself up about this to anyone, and it's almost as if proof and memories were wiped away. It fucking hurts to remember. I swallow harshly against the swelling in my throat as I open this wound.

"I didn't necessarily become a paramedic because I wanted to help people.

It's way more personal than that." I'm already crying, I can feel the wetness of the tears streaking their way down my face. This may be the hardest thing I've ever done. For minutes I struggle with what to say next. Countless times I open and close my lips, but no sound comes from between them.

"Babe, you do what you need to in order to tell me this. Obviously it's painful for you."

Grabbing my phone, I do the one thing I can do. Going into my pictures, I pull up the most coveted I have there. It's a fifteen-year-old me, laughing with the person she looked up to most in the world. I trace her face for a second with my fingertip before I turn the screen so Trevor can look at the image.

"She looks like you, who is she?"

I bite my bottom lip and quirk my eyebrow as I push the words past my tight throat. "My sister."

The shock is apparent on his face. "I never knew you had a sister."

I laugh, but it's harsh and filled with so much hurt that even I can hear it. "My parents would love it if no one remembered her," I stop and take a fortifying breath. "But I do, every day I remember her."

He leans in, kissing my lips softly, taking some of the salty tears that have flowed past those speed bumps while the rest of them roll down my chin and neck, gathering in the spot where my clavicles meet. "Tell me about her, baby. Let it all out."

"Annabelle was sixteen years older than me. Mom and Dad had a teenage pregnancy that they tried to pass off as a honeymoon baby. They tell everyone they got married when they were seventeen, but the truth is they got married when they were twenty - money can change any fact and hide so many secrets," I give him a mirthful smile. "It's exactly why I don't care to ever have the type of money I grew up with."

I take a minute, trying to figure out how I want to go into this story, how I want to portray my sister. Over the years I've come to learn some hard truths, but I don't want to taint her memory in any way and I don't want Trevor to get the wrong idea about her.

"Annabelle was different. She marched to the beat of her own drummer, danced to songs only she heard, and tried to live her life the best way she knew how," I finally decide that's the very best way to explain her. "She tried to be everything my parents wanted her to be and she was my hero. When the pressure got to be too much, I could always go to her little apartment, crawl in bed with her, and she'd tell me a funny story. Somewhere around her twenty-fifth birthday, things started to change a little. At first I think I'm the only one who noticed it."

Immediately I get a flashback of her overexcited behavior about a pair of shoes being on sale, which had been so unlike her months before.

"She would get really excited about an idea, over-the-top excited, and she'd put everything she had in her toward it, but then it would crash. She'd not get out of bed for days at a time, she'd cry, talk about how much of a failure she was, and how she couldn't do anything right. It was this never-ending cycle."

I get up to pace, because I can't take Trevor's eyes on me anymore, can't stand the way he's looking at me with pity.

"Around that time, my parents decided she was too old be single. For the next three years, they pushed men at her, told her bullshit about men not wanting to be around her because she liked to color her hair. She hated being a blonde, I mean absolutely hated it. Red was her favorite color," I admit, a soft smile on my face.

"Oh babe," he sighs.

"Yeah," I tilt the corners of my mouth up. "She got a tattoo that year and they said at twenty-eight she was too old to be doing that type of thing. But she got it where no one could see it, ya know? On her back so it could be covered unless she was wearing a bikini. While she was at the tattoo parlor, she ran into a friend of our family. Jake was the son of one of my dad's business partners, and he was a lot like her. They both loved to rebel. Neither one of them wanted to be stifled by the lifestyle our parents liked to lead. At twenty-eight years old, my sister fell in love for the first time," I continue to pace, but now I look at Trevor.

"Why do I get the feeling this is the beginning of the end?" He asks.

I want to answer him and tell him it's not. To tell him it was the beginning of an absolutely beautiful relationship that goes on today away from everyone, but I fucking can't.

"Jake was the love of her life, but it didn't stop her weird mood swings. He had them too, actually." I stop for a second. "What Jake did was introduce her to a way of dealing with them. Jake was a hardcore drug user. Within two years of being with him, she lost sixty pounds and was skin and bones. My parents didn't know what to do for her, so they wrote her off. Me? I couldn't," I fight the tears again. "No matter how many times she hurt and disappointed me, I couldn't let her go," I put my hands up on my head, clasping my fingers together.

"That's not unusual, babe. You know as well as I do - it's hard."

"It's impossible if it's your family," I argue with him. "Completely and totally impossible. One day she called me and asked me to come meet her. Mom and Dad had cut her off of the family money, but even at fifteen I had a debit and credit card. My driver picked her up, and we drove to Birmingham where I withdrew two thousand dollars from my account and gave it all to her. After that we went to this horrible neighborhood. She had me wait out in the car. My driver kept asking if I wanted to leave, and I did Trevor, I wanted to leave her there because I was so scared."

"You probably should have."

"What happened next I will never forget in my life. She came out of the house and got back in the car. I told the driver to take us back to Laurel Springs. I felt dirty and knew I'd never be able to do this for her again. I had to stop enabling her, and none of this felt good. We got on I-65 and she was okay for the next twenty minutes or so. She told me, 'It's not working the way I need it to, Daphne. I need more now.' I didn't know what that meant, Trevor, I swear to God."

"Of course not," he's still keeping his distance, almost like he's afraid to come too close. "You had absolutely no idea what it meant."

"I watched her pull out a tourniquet and a syringe. I started screaming, asking her what the hell she was doing, and she said the most horrible things to me. About how I was the favorite child, and she was a throwaway, and the only reason she put up with me was because I gave her money. It was so painful to hear her talk to me that way. And back then, when I got hurt, I hurt the other person back. It's what my parents taught me to do, it's what they did to one another. I told her have fun killing herself then, because that's what would happen."

"Shit," he closes his eyes, devastation written all over his face. Devastation for me, devastation for her, I'm not sure which.

"Yeah," I answer, feeling the fresh wash of shame I always do when I think about that day. "She was shooting up, and I was so mad and hurt, I didn't pay attention at first when I heard the noise. To be fair, I didn't understand what the noise was. When I glanced at her, she was slumped over, her eyes open, stuff coming from her mouth. The syringe was sticking out of her arm still. I didn't know what to do. Back then I had no idea what Narcan was, didn't even learn about how it reverses the effects of an overdose until I was an EMT, I was helpless as I yelled to the driver. Cellphones were a newer thing, and I had one, but the ambulance didn't get there in time. She died in the backseat of that car, with me sitting next to her."

I finally let him take me in his arms, and I cry like I've never cried for Annabelle. I've kept it in for so long, and telling him about the situation releases a dam that's been holding back all these feelings. I sob against his chest as he holds me tightly, promising me it's okay to break down, to feel the way I do. I pull back, mopping up my tears from my face.

"We found out later she was bipolar, and she wasn't medicated. My parents knew it, and they encouraged her to not be medicated - they didn't want anyone to know. How crazy is that? They'd rather her be a drug addict than have a mental illness. To this day, I'm not sure I've ever forgiven them. I went through life in a haze for the next year, until something clicked. They acted like Annabelle had never even been in our lives, and I wanted them to see her every time they looked at me. I wanted them to be reminded of what they did to her. If they had pushed her to get help and treatment, she'd probably still be alive today."

"What happened to Jake?" he asks, pushing my hair back from my face.

"Died the same way she did, except he was alone in the bed they shared. I swore to myself I'd be able to help the next person I saw who needed it. It's one hundred percent why I became a paramedic, why I don't take my tests to get out of the bus. It would take a lot for me not to do it anymore, Trevor. It's so personal to me, and when you asked me to quit, I just couldn't. I can't."

"I understand that now," he pulls me into his arms, rocking me against his chest. "I saw that tonight as you helped Stella, and now I understand it so much better. I wish you would've told me this before, but I know it hurts and it's hard."

"So hard," I feel fresh tears. "I'm gonna go through all these events in my life she's never going to have. I'm going to get married, have children, and she's never going to see it, she never got to experience it. There are some days I feel so damn guilty," I break off, shaking my head.

"You're living the life she couldn't. I have no doubt if your moods started swinging, you'd get help. You'd ask why."

"But I would ask why because of her. Nobody would help her," she protests.

"Ten years ago, we didn't understand mental illness the way we do now, Blaze. It's a sad but true statement, and you have enough people in your life that recognize the symptoms. You wouldn't be left alone, baby. I promise you that. I'd go to the ends of the earth to help and save you. I know it doesn't seem like it after I was such an asshole about your job, but I promise you I've changed."

"I know you have. We're both to blame for that," she admits. "You for not understanding, but me too for not explaining. We're on a clean slate now, right?" I want this man to be in my life forever, and if that means being more honest with him than I've ever been with anyone else, I'll do it. I love Trevor Trumbolt with every piece of me, and I will lay myself bare before him - completely broken and I know he'll put me back together again.

"Yeah, we're in this together," he clasps our fingers together. "No one can break this bond."

And finally, for the first time in my life, I feel like I can breathe without the guilt of my sister's death on my conscience. That weight has finally been lifted, and it feels better than I ever imagined it could.

"I wanna go to her grave together, if we can, I want to introduce you to her," I tell Trevor. "I know that sounds weird, but when I need to talk to her, I go to her grave."

"We can do whatever you need to. I'll do anything you need me to. We're in this together, Blaze. You never have to deal with anything on your own again."

I slump against him then, suddenly so tired. He picks me up and carries me to the bed we've been sharing since he came home from the hospital. Together we lie down, and when I close my eyes, I go into the deepest sleep I think I've ever had.

CHAPTER TWENTY-SEVEN

Tank

THE NEXT MORNING, we both wake up somber and apologetic toward each other. "I'm sorry about how everything played out yesterday," I hold Blaze's head on my chest, running my fingers through her soft hair. "What happened was not at all how I meant for things to go, but if it got everything out in the open for us, then I'm willing to be thankful."

She's quiet for a few moments before she kisses my bicep, then raises her eyes to meet mine. "I regret us regressing back to saying mean words to one another. We could've had a peaceful discussion if we wouldn't have been so hot-headed, but like you, I'm glad it's all out in the open. I've wanted to tell you about Annabelle for a long time, but I didn't know how to approach the conversation. With my parents acting like she never existed and I'm an only child, I never know how to tell anyone about her."

"Do you want to tell people about her?" I ask. I've been up for a long time watching her sleep, going through the memories of us being together, trying to put together the pieces that make up this woman I love.

Propping herself up on her elbow, she gives me a gorgeous smile and her eyes shine bright. "I'll tell anyone who'll listen about Annabelle, it's just hard for me to talk about her."

I grab her free hand, pulling it up to mine for a kiss. "People say the more you talk about things that are difficult, the easier they get."

"I know, but I'm never sure how to start out the story. I'm never sure how much to divulge. There were so many angles and crevices to her, you could know her your whole life and still not know everything there was to know. I found journals after she died, and some of those journals shed some light on what was going on inside her mind. She had to have been so scared, Trev," she swallows roughly. "To not have any help, to be self-medicating because that's all she knew how to do. Some days I hate myself for not seeing it."

"Babe, even if you did, you wouldn't have known what to do."

There's been one idea in the back of my mind since I woke up early this morning. It woke me up from a dead sleep and I kind of feel like it's Annabelle's way of making sure Blaze does something amazing. "What if you could help people in the same situation?" I ask, carefully, not wanting to step on her toes.

"What do you mean?"

"I mean, what if you use some of the money you hate so much to set up a trust and a program to help young adults whose parents don't understand what they're going through? What if the program helps these young adults become medicated – if they chose to be – and it gets them the counseling they need to deal with the highs and lows of their condition? You have a great foundation in knowing what Annabelle needed, babe, all you need is someone to help you make this work. Hell, I bet Whitney could get you into contact with the right people."

I say it all in rush so I can get all the words out. I don't want her to stop me until she hears my full idea. It's not a full business plan, per se, but hopefully it's enough to help her figure out where she can go with the rest of it. Suddenly there are tears streaming down her face and she's throwing herself at me. "Thank you, Trevor. Thank you for wanting to help me give her a voice. I thought about things like this in the past, but I wasn't sure how to ever make them work. You're right, Whitney is the best person for me to ask."

"And I'll help you as much as I can," I rub my hand up and down her back. "I want to be here for you, through everything. I never want to force you to make a decision again, especially when I don't know the full story. Please don't keep things like this from me. We're a unit," I pull her face back from my shoulder, making her look at me. "Even if it's hard, we have to communicate. I don't ever want what happened to us here, to happen again. We wasted time, baby," my voice is strained as I try to properly convey my feelings. "What if we'd never gotten the time back like we have right now. If it had been you in that truck, and I found out later all this shit was what kept us apart? I wouldn't have been able to live with myself."

Tears streak down her face. "Then you know how I've felt since I saw you in that truck," she sniffs. "It's not been easy, and there've been times where I wanted to tell you, but the subject of my sister is so taboo in my family," she shrugs. "It's just hard."

"She's not taboo between us, Blaze. I can't imagine if something ever happened to Whit, never talking about her again, never acknowledging my love for her. God, it would kill me."

Her voice is pitiful as she squeaks out. "It does, I feel like her memory dies every day that I don't talk about her. But at the same time it's like this whole town has been brainwashed and nobody remembers her."

I sit up, bringing her with me, leaning against the headboard of the bed. "I don't think that's it. I think people who knew her take their cue from your family. How many men in this town have died overseas? Do you know?"

She looks up at me from where she lays against my chest, and I can see her counting in her head. "Five? If I remember correctly, five."

"Twenty," I correct her. "Twenty men who left wives, girlfriends, moms, dads, kids, grandparents, friends and other family. You remember five, because those families talk about their loved ones. They wear the deaths of those men on their cars with their yellow ribbons, some of the grandmothers still wear the pins of those professional soldier portraits they wore while they were deployed. They never took them off so no one forgets the sacrifices they made. Us not talking about the dead lets their memories fade further and further away, Blaze. We have to honor them, make sure they live on in our hearts and minds. If we, the people who knew them best don't, then they will be forgotten. I don't want that for your sister," I entangle our fingers together, bringing them down to rest over my heart so she can feel it beat. It beats for her, and always will. "When we get married and have kids, I want them to know her as well as they know Whitney. It's the right thing to do, and if it means this much to you, it's what I want to make happen for you."

She's sobbing uncontrollably now, and I know the only thing I can do is hold her - let her get out the years of repressed sorrow. I'd be devastated if someone didn't let me mourn my sister, and I think it's past time Blaze was allowed to mourn hers.

Blaze

When I wake up again, Trevor is still laying with his arms wrapped around me, leaning against the headboard. I use my fingertips to trace the ridges of his ab muscles before I move up to the tattoo of the eagle across his chest. When I start circling his nipple with my nail, he grabs hold of my hand, his voice deep with sleep. "Watch what you're playing with there."

I love the way his voice sounds right as he wakes up. It's been one of the best parts of us living together. I give him a soft smile. "You know, I have something I think I want to do today with you."

He smiles back, the motion breaking his face into the laugh lines you can still see above the beard he's sporting. "What is it you want to do with me?"

I'm careful with the next words because I've never spoken them to another human being before. "I want to take you to meet Annabelle."

His sharp intake of breath and the way he squeezes me in his arms is everything I need to know. "Let's go today, let's not put it off. The sooner we do this, the sooner we can move on with one another."

I know he's right. We'll both still have instances where we'll fear for each other. It's inherent with the jobs we have, but I'm with him, I feel like once this is completely all out in the open, we'll be able to move on. I'm so ready to do that with him. "Let's get dressed and go."

WE STOPPED and got Annabelle's favorite flowers. She was a lot like me, didn't give two shits about the money my parents cared so much about. She loved bouquets of wild flowers you could get at any supermarket. Pink, purple, red, and yellow were her favorite colors.

"She's over here," I pull Trevor along through the nice area of the Laurel Springs cemetery. I'm still surprised they paid to have her buried here. Part of me wondered if they would cremate her and then spread her ashes. It killed me to think I wouldn't have a place to come talk to her. The funeral had been held late in the afternoon, only immediate family had been invited, and then we'd moved on like nothing had happened.

Coming to a stop in front of her grave marker is always the worst for me. Seeing her name there is final, and for the longest time I couldn't look at it. Every time I would go visit her, I'd bring something to cover it up with. I hate how my mom and dad put *beloved daughter* on the stone. They don't love anyone but themselves. I drop his hand, reaching in to clean the gathered grass and dirt off the bottom of the stone, before I arrange the flowers in the two vases. "Hey, Anna," I kiss my fingers before putting them to the picture of her at the top of the marker. "Sorry it's been so long since I've been here, but I brought someone to meet you."

Trevor and I have a seat on the grass, both quiet for as we take in the serenity of the spot. "His name's Trevor," I finally continue, my voice breaking. "I love him and I would love for you to actually be here right now to meet him. I think you'd really like him," I wipe at the tears streaming down my face. "He makes me laugh, he loves me like no other person ever has, and he doesn't put up with my shit."

Trevor laughs at that, putting his arm around my neck and pulling me to him. "I put up with your shit about as much as you put up with mine."

"She would have loved you," I whisper. "She loved to laugh and to know you put a smile on my face every day, it would have meant the world to her. It means the world to me. Even when we're upset with one another, I can still think of something you've said or done and smile."

Trevor speaks then, surprising me with his words. "Annabelle, I'm sorry I never got to meet you and I have a feeling you cared more about Blaze than your parents ever did. Your mom is a total piece of work – I've met her."

"Amen to that," I laugh through my tears.

"More than anything, I hope you know I love her, and I'd do anything in the world to make her happy. We've had some rough patches, but we're learning from them and moving on. I want you to know I'll take care of her," he pulls me closer to him. "Not that she really needs anyone to do that, but sometimes she needs a shoulder to lean on. I'll always be there for her, Annabelle. I'm in this with her for as long as she wants me."

I'm crying, feeling so emotional about this whole thing, but at the top of the big pile of emotion is relief. I've finally been able to share one of the most important people in my life with one of the other most important people. There's nothing holding me back now. "I love you, thank you for doing this with me, and thank you for suggesting I keep her memory alive. You're right about that and it's something I'm going to look into."

There, on a warm March afternoon, I realize I'm where I need to be, where I'm supposed to be, and it's the most beautiful thing in the world. I've never felt so safe in my life, and it's because of the arms wrapped around me, and the man at my side.

CHAPTER TWENTY-EIGHT

Tank

MY HEART BEATS a steady rhythm in my chest as I stretch, feeling the pull of muscles at my legs. It feels good, better than I thought it would. I move my neck form side to side, trying to get the tension to loosen. My stomach is tight with nerves, and I'm scared to death I won't be able to pass this final test to get back onto the Moonshine Task Force.

"You ready?" Holden asks.

Am I? I'm not sure. I know I'm not ready to fail, but I'm scared to death I will. Once before I did this, I can do it again.

"I'll be right beside you," I hear, my gaze shifting to the right. Renegade is there, wearing a pair of athletic shorts and a t-shirt, just like me. "We're gonna do this together."

"You don't have to do this," I'm overcome with emotion I didn't know I had.

"I do," he shakes his head. "No man left behind, ever, and you're my brother. It'll be my honor to run this course with you. You're going to make it."

I can't believe how lucky I am to have the people I do in my life. "Thank you."

"Thank you for allowing me to be a part of your family and for trusting me with your sister," he pulls me into a brotherly hug. "Now, let me help you get through this."

"On my mark," Holden holds his phone, using it as a stop watch. "Good luck, and go."

As my feet pound the ground, eating up what will become five miles and an obstacle course, I realize two things. I feel good, and I got this. There's nothing that will keep me from accomplishing my goals ever again.

Blaze

"Why do you keep checking your phone?" Logan asks as I turn my phone over for the tenth time in the last thirty minutes.

"Trevor does the physical test today to see if he's going to be allowed back on the Moonshine Task Force. I'm not sure if he should be done by now or not, so I'm watching to see if he made it."

A part of me had wanted to be there, but he'd assured me he needed to do this on his own and if he failed, he wanted to handle it in his own way. Failure is not an option for him, so I know if he doesn't pass this test, he will be devastated. Which is why I keep impulsively checking my phone for a text message.

"Is he really worried he won't make it?" Logan swings us into a gas station. The radio's been pretty quiet, and we need to get lunch while we can. Sometimes the best you can do is gas station food, although gas stations out here in the country usually carry decent food.

"I don't know that he's worried, but it's a definite concern. I mean, he's been out since Thanksgiving. When he gets reinstated he'll probably start the week of St. Patrick's Day, so that's a long time. I'd be nervous too, if I were him," I shrug as we get out. "I'm gonna go throw this stuff away," I indicate the breakfast trash from where I brought us breakfast wraps. "And then I'll be in there."

"I'm gonna hit the head, so you're good," Logan waves as he runs off.

It's nice to stretch my legs every once in a while. It's a beautiful March day in Alabama, already hot as hell. If I remember correctly it's going to be in the eighties today, but the sun is shining and it looks like Trevor and I are hopefully overcoming a huge hurdle in our relationship. When he gets back to work, then we can begin to repair and build our lives. I'm excited for it, more excited than I've been for anything else in recent memory. The wind is blowing, so when I put my trash in the can, some of it blows out. Running to grab it, I round the building to where some picnic tables are set up for nice days. Pushing my hair out of my face, I see a young woman sitting at one by herself, blood pouring from her nose as she's trying to staunch the flow.

"Are you okay?" I call out as I approach.

When she lifts her head up, I see it's Leighton Strather. "I'm good," she tries to pull into herself, stuffing the tissue up her nose.

"That's not gonna work, why don't you come back to the ambulance and let me take a look at it?" I reach my hand out. She's not much younger than me in age, but she looks scared to death right now. There's a protective side of me that hasn't come out since I had my sister around, and it makes me want to help this girl. I've seen her around a few times, and everyone in this town, hell in the county, knows her family is the main target of the Moonshine Task Force guys.

"I don't have any money," she shrinks away from me again.

Everyone also knows that's a lie. The Strathers have a shit ton socked back from where they've been running moonshine for so long. "This one's on me," I smile at her softly.

She gets up, shouldering a huge bag and picking up another at her feet. Something about this doesn't sit well with me. Why does she have all of these bags with her? "You going somewhere?"

Wild eyes look at me, like I've accused her of a crime, and her semi-relaxed pose is again rigid. "If you don't wanna talk about it, you don't have to, but if you're in trouble, I can get someone to help you."

Leighton shakes her head. "No, I don't want to get anyone else wrapped up in the shit show that's become my life. I got myself into this situation, I'll get myself out of it."

It's on the tip of my tongue to ask what the situation is, but I don't want to scare her off. I can see a couple more cuts on her arms, and there's some bruises forming. If this girl's been abused, I at least want to make sure she's okay and doesn't need to be in a hospital. "Okay, then let's just walk to the bus and get you checked out."

We're quiet as we walk around to the ambulance, and I worry she's going to bolt. I'm surprised when she gets in after I open the back door. I indicate that she can enter before me and watch as she tries to step up, but can't. A sharp intake of breath tells me she's either bruised or broken a rib. "Let me get in before you, and hold you steady as you step up."

She nods, tears at the edges of her eyes. We carefully get her up into the ambulance and situated as comfortably as we can. "I'm going to text my partner, who's inside, my order and I'm going to let him know I have someone out here, that way he doesn't freak out. Is that okay?"

She leans her head back against the wall, nodding. Those tears are now streaming down her face. I feel awful for this girl, she's not in an enviable situation. I fire off a text to Logan and ask him to get one of the Moonshine Task Force guys out here, just to talk to her. I'm scared something bad has happened.

"Wanna tell me what happened?" I ask as I glove up and go to work on her face, cleaning up the dried blood and fixing up a couple other cuts I hadn't seen before.

"No," she slightly shakes her head. "I'd rather just forget who I am."

"You and I both know it doesn't work like that, honey. Anyone who knows me, knows that even underneath the red hair and tattoos I'm a Coleman, right?"

I realize we have a little bit of a common ground there, and I try to play it up. "But just because my parents are snobby doesn't mean I am, ya know? I live my life the way I want to, and if they don't approve of it, then it's their problem not mine. My life and reputation isn't defined by my last name."

Leighton opens eyes that had been closed before. Her brown gaze collides with mine. "Do you truly believe that, have people forgotten you're a Coleman?" She whispers the question, and I can tell she thinks I'm lying.

"It's true, most people don't even know my real name anymore. Everybody calls me Blaze. Sure, my mom, classmates, and people like that call me Daphne, but I've managed to find my own identity. I'm not saying it's easy, Leighton," she hisses as I clean one of the cuts above her eyebrow. "But it's worth it. It's worth it not to have to live under that shadow all the time."

She swallows hard as I start doctoring what I can of her nose. I'm pretty sure it's not broken, but it's going to be sore for the next few days. "I want out from under the shadow so bad," she whispers. "I'm not like them," the tears come again.

"I know you're not. You're a sweet girl who got caught up in a bad situation."

"They got me arrested," she sniffles, rubbing softly against the nose that's still bleeding slightly. "And they didn't even care. I spent a night in jail, over something that I didn't even do. My daddy and brother said they did it to teach me a lesson."

Her eyes widen as she glances at the back of the ambulance. Holden's standing there, his big arms folded over his chest.

"Before you freak out on me," I speak softly and calmly to her. "I called him because I know you need help, and if there's anyone that can help you, honey, it's Holden."

"But he's the one who arrested me."

He grunts as he enters the back of the ambulance and stalks over to us. He slightly pushes me out of the way as he grasps Leighton by the chin, turning her face to the left and right, taking in the bruises and cuts. His voice is gruff when he speaks. "Not because I wanted to. Did your dad do this to you?"

She nods, biting a trembling bottom lip between her teeth. "I told him I want out – completely. He didn't like that much."

His eyes take in the duffle bags laying at her feet. "So you're running, that's your grand plan?"

"Best one I had," her eyes flash and I'm so glad to see irritation amongst the sadness. She's got some fire in her. "Do you have a better one?"

"Blaze is cleaning you up, and then you're comin' with me." There's no room for argument with his words.

"Are you okay with that? If you're not, I have an apartment that's empty," I have to give her another option, strong-arming her is acting just like her family.

"She won't be safe there, and you know it, Blaze. They're going to come after her. Once they realize she's truly gone, they'll come. You know secrets that no one else does," he locks eyes with Leighton again. "You're worth a lot to them."

"What am I worth to you?" She smarts off again, and I can't help the grin escaping from my lips.

"More than you can probably imagine."

It feels like an intimate moment between the two of them, and I'm the third wheel. I don't know how well they know one another, but they obviously have a little bit of a past. I finish cleaning her up and then leave, so they can hash out whatever it is they need to. As I jump out of the back of the ambulance, I see Trevor leaning against a squad car, dressed in his uniform. Which he looks so *motherfucking fine* in.

"Ahhhh!" I scream as I run toward him. "You did it?"

He picks me up, spinning me around as I laugh, so happy and excited for him, even before I know this answer. He's in uniform – what's not happy about this situation?

"I did it!"

His voice sounds so happy, so relieved. I'm happy for him. "So you're back on shift already?" It seems fast to me.

"Holden told me he was driving out here to meet you and Leighton. When he said your name, I was ready to go."

I frown. "Leighton's got a long way to go, and I hope you all can help her."

"I hope we can, too," he leans down, kissing me softly before straightening up. His gaze is locked where the ambulance is parked, which lets me know the two of them are probably exiting.

I turn, seeing them walking our way.

"Is there anything you can give her for pain?" Holden holds onto her side as they slowly walk across the parking lot.

"I can't, but I can place a call to Doc Miller, if you give me a few minutes. She can get you some pain meds and some antibiotics. I don't think you'd develop an infection from those cuts, but some of them were dirty. It's better to be safe than sorry."

"I'd appreciate it," he directs her to the back of the squad car, putting her stuff in the trunk.

"Will do, I'll text you the pickup time Doc Miller gives, if that's okay with you."

Trevor leans down, kissing me, before he lets me go, smacking me on the ass. "I'll see ya at home?"

"You most definitely will."

As I watch the car full of people take off, I realize I still haven't had lunch, and I realize exactly how worried I am about Leighton. I hope she can be helped, and I really hope her family doesn't screw it up for her.

CHAPTER TWENTY-NINE

Tank

"CONGRATULATIONS," I hear as soon as Blaze comes through the front door.

My heart explodes with happiness as she runs to me, hopping up in my arms. "Thanks babe, I can't tell you how excited I am."

"When do you get to start?"

"Tomorrow," I put her down, smacking my hand against her ass. "I filled out all my paperwork today. I'm good to go back on rotation tomorrow. Renegade and Tank will be burning up those backroads at zero nine hundred. So your lead foot better watch out."

"Fuckin' speed trap artist," she grumbles as she stands on her tiptoe, kissing me on my jawline.

"If you'd obey the speed limit, there wouldn't be a problem."

She knows I'm right, but she shakes her head anyway. "I'm gonna go change out of this uniform. It was hot today," she fans her hand in front of her face.

It *was* hot today, but I honestly didn't care. I was too excited to be back in a police car, even if I did have to transport Leighton with Holden. That situation is really odd, and if I had to make a guess – our fearless leader might care a little too much about what happens to the moonshine girl. However that's totally none of my business. My business is Brooks. I got a letter today asking me to be present at the trial. I know they won't call me to testify because I remember nothing, but it's a tactic prosecutors like to use; have the victim in the court room for the jury to put a face with the injury.

Going over to the fridge, I open it, looking for something easy to have for dinner. It's a nice night, and grilling doesn't sound horrible. "Babe, what do you want for dinner?"

A throat clears behind me and I turn around, wondering if Blaze needs something. When I do, my jaw falls open. She's standing in front of me wearing nothing but a pair of the skimpy panties I got her for Christmas, her nipple rings, and a smile. Her wet hair is hanging over her shoulders, teasing by barely covering those pierced nipples, and her belly is going concave with the depth of her breath. "How about we feast on one another?"

Immediate erection. Like totally involved. It's been a long time since we've been intimate with nothing between us. No cast, no boot, no secrets, and now I need this more than I need the next beat of my heart. "What brought this on?" I ask as I walk across the kitchen, pushing at the athletic shorts I'm wearing.

"You passed, I'm horny, and you looked delectable in this faded t-shirt. It sculpts everything," she runs her hands down my pecs, scratching the ridges of my abdomen hiding behind the soft jersey material of the t-shirt I wear. "Plus, I haven't been able to wear any of my Christmas presents yet. I thought, why not?"

"Why not is as good a reason as any for me," I drop to my knees in front of her, pushing her back against the wall in the hallway as she stumbles. Putting my hands around her hips, I kiss along the edge of the panties before moving my mouth up her stomach, appreciating the hard strength she has there as well. Blaze is a strong woman who works out to keep strong and fit, her body is one of the best I've ever seen.

"Trev," she sighs as she leans her head back against the wall, gripping her fingers in my hair. I love the sigh, love the way she grabs hold of my head and shows me what she wants. When I get as far as I can in my position, she grabs my hand, dragging it up to her tit. And Lord does she have a set of those. "I want your mouth where I'm putting your fingers," she whines, spreading her thighs wider.

"Too fuckin' bad," I tell her as I grasp the nipple roughly, before I use my other hand to pull down the slip of lace, exposing her body to my gaze. Taking two fingers of my free hand, I move them up to her mouth. "Open for me and get them wet."

My cock stands at attention as I feel her tongue swirl around my digits, prepping them to go inside her body. With concentrated effort, I pull my fingers out of her mouth, before rubbing them along the edges of her pussy. She's trembling, bending her knees, silent signs that she's dying for me to take what I want. Using those two fingers, I glide inside her core before I lick my lips and lean forward, burying my face between her thighs.

"Oh fuck," she lifts up on her tiptoes, trying to put me in a better position or get away from the sensation, which I'm not sure, but I take the opportunity to shove my shoulders under thighs and hold her weight against the wall.

"Trevor," she whines loudly. I can feel her fingers fighting with mine at her tit grasping her nipples roughly, pulling on the rings she's got there.

"Hmmm?" I hum against her pussy causing her legs to shake. "You need something, babe?" I wrench myself away so I can speak.

"You in bed with me, I ache for your cock," she's running her hands from her waist up to her breasts, grasping her nipples and then running them back down again, making a track of pleasure on her entire body. "It's been a while since we've been able to do it right."

As much as I'm enjoying my feast, I know she's right. We haven't been able to do it the way we like in far too long. Standing up, I use my core to lift her and carry her back to what's now our room. Throwing her down on the bed, I reach behind me, gathering my shirt up and over my head, before I cover her body with my own.

"This what you wanted?" I bury my face in her neck as I feel her legs climb up my back, her heels digging into my waist. Her nails scratch along my neck as I nip at her throat, leaving marks that I know other people will be able to see unless she covers them up. This is one of the things I love about her. She matches me in the bedroom, she's not shy, she asks for what she wants and does what will get her off. I never have to wonder with Blaze, she lets me know exactly what she needs.

"Yes," she moans, widening her thighs, allowing mine to rest in the cradle of hers. With a thrust up, she seats me heavily inside her. My brain is screaming to my dick reminding me I don't even have a fuckin' rubber on yet.

"Goddamn this feels good," I reach up with my hands, grasping hold of her arms as I put my feet on the floor, to give me leverage. "You're so hot and tight, and your piercings are rubbing against my chest," I shiver as her hard nipple catches mine. "It's the hottest thing in the world, but I gotta get a condom," I warn her.

She doesn't release her feet from around my back and I can't stop the motion of my hips against her, it feels too good. I've wanted her this way, face to face, for far too long.

"Trevor, grind against me, please. I need the friction," she gasps as I do what she asks, pushing my hips against hers, able to use both my feet to stabilize us.

"This what you need babe? Me to fuck you hard?" I grunt as I withdraw and then plunge back in.

"Yes," she rakes her nails down my back until she gets to my ass, gripping it hard in her hands.

I return the favor, letting go of one of her hands to move mine down to grip her ass, so I can go even deeper. We're grunting and thrusting against each other, and I can feel her opening, can feel her getting wetter, tightening against me. "You coming, Blaze?"

She nods as I latch my mouth onto one of her nipple rings and pull sharply with my teeth, it's one of the moves she loves. Her scream is in my ear as she grinds hard against my body. Reaching down in between us, I feel her hand on my cock, jacking me while I'm still inside her.

Fuck that feels amazing, I love the way her hand caresses me anytime she touches me. I'm still pumping inside her as she helps me pump my cock. She's breathing heavily, her breath tickling the hair that's sticking on my face.

"Come for me, Trev."

"Where?" I groan. "Where can I come?"

"All over me," she releases me with her feet and I pull out with super human effort. She jacks my cock while I thumb her nipple. Something about the way her eyes get dark, her mouth hangs open, and her nipple responds gets me every time.

"Shit, shit, shit," I throw my head back as I chant in time with her hand on my length and then I feel myself let go, coming against the smooth skin of her stomach.

It seems to go on forever, but I know in reality it's only a few seconds. Sweat pours down my body and my chest heaves as I try to slow my heartbeat and breathing down. Getting on my feet, I somehow make my way into the bathroom and return with a towel for her before collapsing face down beside her.

She giggles as she taps my shoulder. I sleepily move my face to the side so I can see her gorgeous smile.

"Hey," she smirks. "Congrats."

"If that's the way you congratulate me? I'm gonna do something amazing every fucking day."

She laughs again as she snuggles against me. Closing my eyes for a few seconds, I realize this right here? It doesn't get much better.

CHAPTER THIRTY

Tank

"SO HOW DOES IT FEEL?"

I look over at Renegade, not able to keep the smile from spreading across my face, or the joy out of my voice as I answer. "To be back? It feels fucking amazing."

He laughs as he takes a drink from his to-go mug of coffee. "It's awesome to have you back. I like Ace, but you're my best friend."

I'm letting Renegade drive, which is totally unlike me, but they've all asked me to be honest with them, and I admitted to Holden it would be best for me to wait a few weeks. I need to do a couple of pass-through's on the bottoms before I'm ready to drive the road myself. It's nothing like PTSD, but there's a nervousness I can't explain, even though I've tried. Everyone seems to understand and for that I'm grateful.

"I know, I love Blaze, don't get me wrong," I stretch my leg out, pleased at how it feels. "But I'm glad to have someone else's company for a while."

He nods in agreement. "Same. I love Whit and Stella, they are my life, but I enjoy coming to work and hanging out with the guys."

"Y'all set a date yet?" I ask as I take a drink of my coffee.

This right here, riding the backroads of Laurel Springs and talking with my best friend is what I've missed more than anything. It's just not the same, texting.

"We're talking about it," he stops at an intersection and looks both ways before he eases through. "I think it'd be fun to have a destination wedding this summer."

"Dude, who the fuck are you? How do you even know what a destination wedding is?" I'm this close to revoking his man card.

"I live with a damn wedding planner, man. The question is how do *you* not know what it is?"

I shoot him a look. "I'm sorry, you're the one who figured out she wanted to actually go to an Alabama game for her birthday, after she tried to tell us for years. I think that should tell you how well I'm able to comprehend shit my sister talks about."

We're interrupted as the biggest boom I've heard on this side of the world rocks the silence, and the ground surrounding us trembles.

"Either we just had an earthquake, a bomb went off somewhere, or a fuckin' still just exploded," Renegade stops the car and both of us get out to look along the tree line.

"Over there, near the Strather's place," I point to dark smoke billowing above the trees.

We jump back in the car as I radio in our position and let dispatch know we're responding. Seems like everyone else is also responding and as we come to a screeching halt at the access road, we all get out of our cars. The team can see the flames from where we stand, we'll have to wait for the fire department to do their thing before we can move in.

"Alcohol vapor?" I question as we stand around in a circle.

Ace nods, rolling around a toothpick in his mouth. "Or it overheated. Either way, it's enough to make it go boom. Highly concentrated, whatever it was."

"Think we'll find a body in there?" Renegade asks, as he wipes the sweat from his brow. This fire is hot as hell.

The roar from the fire trucks drown us out until they get set up. All of us stand a respectable distance away, letting them do what they need to.

"To answer your question," Holden looks at Renegade. "I don't think we'll find a body. I think they've started to automate the process."

"You figure that out, or did Leighton tell you that?" The words are out of my mouth before I can take them back. I'm not sure if everyone knows he took her home with him or not, and to be honest, it's not my place either.

Luckily he doesn't hand me my balls, but from the look on his face, I know not to push my luck again.

"To be honest," Holden meets my gaze. "I think this is to send Leighton a message. They know she's staying with me because they aren't fuckin' slick about snooping around my property. They've been watching me, and I've been watching them. I think they're afraid Leighton will talk so they're getting rid of evidence and moving operations."

"Has Leighton said anything?" Renegade asks as we watch the fire department go to work.

There's a stormy look on Holden's face, one I'd never like to be on the receiving end of. "She doesn't talk much about them, and I can't say as I can blame her. If she talks about them and incriminates herself, she's probably afraid I'll take her in."

"You have before," I point out. "It's a valid concern."

"Yeah," Renegade laughs softly. "Unless you're married. Then you can invoke your right to silence, but who'd get married to someone they don't love."

"Somebody who's scared to death," I answer for them. "I saw her that day, she was scared to death. Hell, *I'm* scared thinking what may have happened to her had her path not crossed with Blaze. None of us truly know what she's been living with in her family."

Holden's eyes darken and his face becomes a mask. I think for the first time, maybe he does know some of the things she went through, maybe Leighton's confided in him. But my gut tells me if she has confided, she's not told him everything. I don't think she trusts anyone that much. "He's right, she is scared to death of them, and this is definitely something they would do."

"Probably because the trial is in a couple days," I remind him. "Are you all going to be there?"

"Damn right we're all going to be there. We have a couple of guys from Birmingham coming in to cover shifts while we're all at the court house. We want to see Brooks get what's coming to him. He deserves that and more after what he did to you," Holden and Renegade both agree.

"You know it's not in our hands. It's in the hands of the judge and jury, so we'll have to respect whatever happens."

It's hard to have that mindset about the trial, though. I want badly to know exactly what the fuck's going to happen to the kid who tried to ruin my life and the bitch of it is, I have no say in the matter. Other people do, and they have the option to either make him pay or let him walk free. Neither option feels great to me, because I think above all, he should learn a lesson.

I just hope like the hell the judge does the right damn thing.

CHAPTER THIRTY-ONE

Tank

I TUG at the collar of my dress shirt as I stand outside the courthouse, surrounded by friends, family, and coworkers. There's a part of me that doesn't want to be here, but there's also another part of me that knows I need to be here. I have to see justice be served. More than anything, I deserve to see justice served.

"You doing alright?" Blaze asks as she stands next to me, her hand on my arm.

Glancing down at her, I take in the dress she's wearing. Conservative, not her normal wear, and she has her hair pulled back in a pile of curls on her head. She looks nothing, if not sophisticated. Beside her my family stands, and then the guys from the Moonshine Task Force.

"I'm good," I clear my throat. "Want this over with so we can truly move forward."

"It does feel like there's a dark cloud hanging over us in the form of Brooks, doesn't it?" she puts her arm around me, leaning into my chest.

"Yeah," I answer truthfully. "It's the unknown. I don't want to ruin the kid's life, but he also deserves to pay for what he did to me. I could have died, at the same time, I'm almost thankful because it brought us back together. I'm conflicted as hell. He's lucky he didn't kill someone."

She nods her agreement as I see Holden ascending the stairs with Leighton on his arm. She looks pale, but that's nothing unusual; her dark hair gives her the look of a modern-day Snow White every time I see her. "Thanks for coming," I put my hand out for Holden to shake it, and then give Leighton a quick hug.

"I never apologized to you for what my brother did. I'm really sorry," Leighton tucks a curl behind her ear. "He wasn't ever taught better and didn't care to learn, either. I hope he'll still have some life left if they decide to let him out."

"My wish isn't for them to lock him up forever, it's that he learns there are consequences to actions, and not all of those consequences involve paying off someone," I shake my head, pissed off because that's normally what the family does. "No disrespect meant to you."

"None taken," she smiles sadly. "All of us have to learn in our own ways."

The state prosecutor comes over to our group, pulling myself and my family to the side. "This morning there was a meeting for a possible plea bargain and I refused to play ball. I've got this little bastard dead to rights traveling in excess of ninety-five miles an hour on a curvy backroad where the speed limit is thirty-five. I'm gonna nail his ass to the wall, but if you, as the injured party in the attempted vehicular manslaughter charge, want me to work with his lawyer I will. He'll still go to jail for his reckless driving, felony reckless driving, and driving on a suspended license. You tell me what you want, Trevor," she looks at me, her lips pursed.

To be honest, she scares me and I'd hate to face her in a court of law. I think she could probably take a man's balls and pull them over his head if given the chance. I realize I can't make it easy on Brooks, none of this was easy for me. I had to recover, had to prove my physical fitness to get my job back, and I'm the one having to deal with the sweaty palms every time we drive that stretch of road. I have my consequences just like he's going to have his.

"No deal, let him get what's coming to him."

Everyone with me seems to breathe a sigh of relief as they hear what I say. I have to admit, I do too, but now all I want to do is get this whole situation over with.

THE WHOLE TRIAL passes in a blur, I try not to pay attention too much. For me, the less I know, the better off I am. I have no recollection of the wreck, and if I can keep it that way, I think I'm better off. For the two hours we're there, and while the prosecutor presents her case, I keep my gaze on Blaze, watch at points where her face pales, and then I see tears pool in her eyes. Only then do I glance up to see they're showing pictures of my truck and pictures of me from what must have been the first day I was in the hospital. They turn my stomach and I decide to again focus my attention on the beautiful woman sitting next to me. On the other side of me, my mom grabs my other hand, holding on tightly.

At one point, Renegade leans forward from behind me, claps his hands on my shoulders and quietly tells me, "This fucker is going down for good."

I know without a doubt he will, but I can't let myself get fucked about it. It happened, and I'm moving on.

"Do you have any remorse for what you did, Mr. Strather? The man you hit is a respected officer, a member of the Moonshine Task Force, a boyfriend, a son, a brother, an uncle, and a loved friend to many of the people in this court room and in this entire community. Do you understand what you could've done?"

Only then do I let my eyes meet his. I want him to look at me as he says whatever it is he's going to say.

He smiles, and it's cocky as hell. "When it's your time, it's your time. Regardless of who or what causes it, ma'am, the good Lord chooses, not me and my lead foot."

"Son of a bitch," I gnash my teeth together, shaking my head. I have to take my arm out from behind Blaze and shake my momma's hand out of mine. Anger courses through me like nothing I've ever felt before. Scooting forward, I put my elbows on my knees and stare straight ahead at this piece of shit. He's going to talk about me and my time to die? He can damn well look at me while he does it.

Blaze scoots beside me, talking in my ear. "He's young, babe, he doesn't get it and look where he comes from. He doesn't know any better."

I'm trying like hell to remember she's right. He's a product of his environment, but it doesn't make it right. I let out a deep breath and try to calm the adrenaline flowing through my body. Getting pissed won't do any good to anyone. Finally I calm down and sit back against the bench again. My mom grabs my hand, quietly soothing me.

When the verdict comes in, I feel vindicated when they give him twenty-five years with the possibility of parole in fifteen. Chances are he'll get out earlier because of overcrowding and good behavior, but it's a lot more than a slap on the wrist.

We're all getting up to leave when Leighton's dad, Jefferson, walks over to our group. He singles her out, ignoring the rest of us. "I see you're sittin' with the enemy. You think I'm not watching you? You think I don't know the things you've probably told these people, Leighton?"

She doesn't back down, but I can see her shaking. "What are you gonna do? Beat me? Already did that."

He steps closer to her. "If I find out you've betrayed your family, little girl, I'll kill you."

Holden picks that moment to step in between them, putting his body in front of hers, and it's then that anyone who's never seen him work figures out why we call him Havoc. He's able to ruin someone with one punch, one well-placed word. "To get to her, you're gonna have to get through me. Bring it on, I'll rain down hell on you."

Bailiffs rush over to separate everyone, and I grasp Holden around the waist. "C'mon, not here."

And I know without a doubt the Moonshine Task Force isn't done with the Strather family. I have a feeling we're only just beginning. I glance at Whitney, our eyes meeting over the fray. If there's one thing I do understand, it's sometimes choosing family and love over the long arm of the law.

CHAPTER THIRTY-TWO

Blaze

"IT'S TOO cold to get in that pool," Whitney and Trevor's mom, Mona, yells at Ryan as he dips his feet in the shallow end of the pool in their backyard.

It's been hot all day, but as night falls this time of year, it usually gets cold.

"He's gonna catch his death of cold," she mumbles as she watches him not heed her warning.

"Whatever, it got up to ninety today and it's almost April. Hell," he takes a drink of the beer in his hand. "It's damn near summer."

I glance at Whitney, who shakes her head laughing when she sees Trevor making his way over to Ryan, sticking his feet in the pool too. I'm not sure what the two of them are talking about, but we're rewarded with their deep laughs as they both throw their heads back. I love their friendship.

I'm holding Stella in my lap, facing outward so she can see all the goings on. In the past few weeks, she's started to become more animated and to show a little bit of personality. She smiled at me the other day and I thought I'd break my face smiling back.

"Those two are always getting into trouble together," Whitney looks back at her mom. "Do you want me to help you?"

"No, it means a lot that all of you came over for dinner tonight. I hate being here by myself when your dad's workin' through the week," Mona sighs as she sets a platter of deviled eggs and a bowl of baked beans on the table in front of us. Those join a salad and what looks to be enough potato salad to feed all the guys at the EMS station and every member of the Moonshine Task Force.

"I'm ready for either one of you to grill," she yells to the guys.

"I got this," Trevor hops up, carrying his bottle of beer with him. Sitting it down on the table in front of me, he bends over to give first Stella a kiss on the cheek and then me a kiss on the lips. "Watch this Stell Bell, I'm gonna show your daddy how to cook a steak," he tickles her stomach, smiling when she laughs back at him.

"Why don't you hurry up? The rest of us are hungry," I smack his ass as he makes his way around me.

"Perfection can't be rushed," he yells back. "Mom, is everything over here?"

"No, the steaks are marinating in the house, let me go get 'em for you."

"You stay there," he's already jogging for the house. "You did all this for us, let us do the rest."

We all watch as he takes his place at the grill. I'm bouncing Stella on my knee, but I notice the rest of us are deep in thought. There's something weighing heavy on my heart, and I have to tell these women what I'm thinking.

"Thank you for inviting us. I never had anything like this with my family," I smile over at Mona. "It's so weird for a kid like me, who basically grew up with servants making sure she had a little bit of love, to be in a situation like this. It used to make me uncomfortable, but you all make me feel kind of like I'm home," I finish, praying I haven't overstepped my boundaries with these friends of mine.

Whitney and her mom exchange a look, and it makes me even more nervous so I keep playing with Stella, trying to make it seem like their non-answer doesn't hurt.

When I hear Mona talking, I glance up, shaken by what she says.

"You are family, honey. If Trevor loves you, that's the only thing that matters to me. He's a great judge of character," she reaches over, grabbing my hand. "Not many women your age would have stuck by him when they saw what you did at the crash site. So many people nowadays are selfish, and they immediately think how much an injury like what he had would inconvenience them. You never did that. Geeze Pete, you took time off from your job to help him recover. I couldn't think of a better woman for my son."

I'm trying to push back tears. I had absolutely no idea Mona felt this way about me, and it touches a place deep inside that's never been touched. Burying my face in Stella's head, I surround myself with the scent of baby. "Thank you."

Those are the only words I can push past my tight throat, and I can't help but think I've finally found the place I belong.

Tank

"You okay?"

Blaze and I are cuddled up on one of the pool loungers, both full from the food we ate. The night has turned off a bit chilly, and I curl a blanket around us that Renegade brought over not too long ago. She's been quiet for a while, and I'm worried someone's upset her.

"I'm good," she gives me a sleepy smile.

"You've been quiet since I started grilling. Was my food not good?" I tilt her chin with my index finger, forcing her eyes to meet mine.

She stretches against me, shaking her head. "No, everything was great. Your mom said something to me and it kind of shocked me. She welcomed me to the family."

I love my mom, she always knows the right things to say. "That means she likes you, and she's right. You're totally a part of this family now."

"It felt good, but weird at the same time. You saw how my mom is and what my life was like. Your mom is amazing and to know she approves of me in your life gave me a sense of belonging I didn't know I needed."

I lean in, pouring every bit of feeling, of love, of how much I need this woman into the kiss I give her. Coaxing open her lips, I kiss her with an unrestrained passion I'd normally save for behind closed doors, but it's a must right now. Pulling away, I press my forehead against hers, enclosing us in our own cocoon. My voice is just above a whisper. "Don't you know, Blaze? You've belonged to me since the first moment I saw you. You've owned me from the first moment I tasted you."

She hugs me tightly, and for the longest time I think she's not going to say anything, but then she pulls back. "I've always been scared to completely let my emotional walls down with you, Trevor. I can be sexual any day of the week, and I know you're good with that, but sometimes I do that to hide how I feel. After telling you about Annabelle, I think I've started to let go of some of the walls and guards I've had up."

"You never have to hide your true self from me, if there's one thing you should know about me by now it's I love all of you. Not just the good and easy parts, but the ones that force me to dig a little deeper. I lost you once, Blaze, I'm not going to be a dumbass and lose you again," I frame her face with my hands. "No one else would have taken care of me the way you do, no one else would have put their lives on hold to be by my side. You saved me, and you changed me. I love you more than I could ever tell you, express to you, or show you. So I'll just spend the rest of my life trying to become worthy."

She sniffles, her green eyes wet, eyelashes incredibly long with tears spiking the ends. "I'll spend the rest of my life trying to become worthy of you, because everything you said, is exactly how I feel, too."

There, underneath a clear Alabama sky, holding the woman who changed my life, I'm not worried about the future, because I know we're gonna make it.

CHAPTER THIRTY-THREE

Blaze

TWO MONTHS Later

I enter The Café with a huge smile on my face. Today's been a great day. In what's become our regular booth, I see Trevor waiting for me, wearing his hot as fuck white t-shirt with his bullet proof vest over the top. It's too hot for them to wear their button-down shirts and this is what most of the guys look like around these parts right now.

"I'll be right with ya, Blaze. He already ordered your drink," Leighton tells me as she gives me a grin.

Not long ago she started waitressing here, and she seems to have acclimated well. "Sounds good."

As I approach the booth, Trevor stands up, grabbing hold of my hand and bringing me in for a kiss. "Hey, hot stuff," he whistles between his teeth as he sees the dress I wear with my Louboutins. "Look at you, how did your meeting go?"

"Hey, handsome," I kiss him, gripping him around the waist as he motions for me to sit in the booth. We're same-side sitters and everybody makes fun of us, but I love being pressed up against his hard body. I curl my hand around his bicep, grabbing for my drink. "It went well, they approved me!"

"I'm so damn proud of you, and I know Annabelle is, too."

He hugs me to him with his arm around my neck, and I revel in the scent of his cologne. Nothing makes me feel more at home than that smell and the scratch of his beard on my forehead. "I'm proud of myself," I admit. "I wasn't sure if the bank would go for it, if they'd be willing to release my trust fund to me. Ya know so I could turn around and basically give it away."

"You're gonna change people's lives, Blaze. I mean completely change them. People who weren't sure if they were ever going to have a chance will have one now, because of you."

I duck my head because it's embarrassing to get this much praise. All I want, more than anything, is for someone besides me to have a memory of my sister, and I know the Annabelle Coleman Foundation will do just that for so many people. My goal is to give anyone with a mental illness the chance to get help, regardless of age, race, or creed. I want to make it readily available in our community. "I'm talking to the attorney tomorrow about finishing up the paperwork to make everything legal, and I'm looking at the building down the street from the EMS station for a possible office space. I'm excited Trevor, more excited about this than I have been for anything in a long time - I feel like I'm making a difference. We should be able to start talking to groups next month!"

"You are, babe, you're changing the world, one day at a time. Hell, you changed mine just by being in it, imagine what you're going to do when you set your mind to it."

His unwavering faith is all I need, and it's everything I'll ever want in this life. No matter the trials I've gone through, I'm damn lucky to be where I am now.

Tank

I head back to work with a smile on my face, I'm so damn proud of Blaze. She's taken a situation many people wouldn't have been able to understand and is turning it into a platform to help others in the same situation. Not many people in this world would give away their money like this, but the woman I love? She's amazing like that.

As I head up the steps to the station, Holden comes barreling out the door. "You okay?" His face is a mask of anger and what appears to be frustration.

He motions for me to follow him behind the building. "We got a threat at the house last night and I'm trying to track who's doing it without Leighton finding out."

"Gotta be her family, man. They're scared to death she's going to give them up."

Holden turns around, putting his hands on his hips and looking up at the sky. "The shitty part about this whole situation? She's not giving them up, she refuses to talk about it, but you and I both know her family won't believe that, ever. The only way I'll get them away from her is to either arrest them all, or beat the shit out of them," he shakes his head, chuckling darkly. "That's somethin', ain't it? A man who's sworn to uphold the law, looking to beat the shit out of another human being."

"No," I answer quickly. "It's not. Sometimes it's the only thing you *can* do." Immediately my mind goes back to the night I confronted my sister's ex-husband, Stephen.

"I saw her face, you motherfucker. I saw what you did to her. Did you think I'd let that shit go? You think I'd not listen to her?"

I advance on him, grabbing him by the collar of his shirt, lifting him off his feet, and shoving him into the nearest wall.

"Trevor, aren't you sworn to uphold the law, not break it?" he taunts me.

"I'd give it all up for her, and you know it. You think it's fun to beat on someone smaller than you? Does it make you feel like a man? How about you beat on someone closer to your own size. You get one free shot, and then I'm going to tear your ass up."

A part of me half expects him to not do it, he's a lot of all talk and not much action. I'm surprised when I feel his fist connect with my cheek. When it does, I feel my rage explode and I go to town on him. As I feel his skin break and his bones crack, I think of my sister's black eye, the wounded look on her face, and the way she's changed since she married him.

I know this asshole is to blame and he's going to pay tonight. Luckily not with his life, but maybe by the time I'm done, he'll wish he had. For once I'm going to let the control I normally have over my anger and emotions go, and he'll wish he'd never met my family.

"So what do you suggest?" Holden's voice brings me back from my memory.

"You protect her," it's as easy as that for me. "Anyway you can, whatever you have to do, you protect her. If there's anything I've learned in the past few months, it's that we as humans are capable of amazing things, especially when we're pushed to the edge. Ask yourself what you're willing to do for her, because I know exactly what I'm willing to do for Blaze."

"You love Blaze," he reminds me.

I lean in close, because I respect the man in front of me. He's my boss, but he's also my friend. "Holden, don't kid yourself. You'd do whatever it takes to keep her safe. You and I both know that."

I give him a wave as I go into the office, ready to finish out my shift and get home to the love of my life.

EPILOGUE

Tank

AUGUST

"I didn't expect to see you here today," I lean over kissing Blaze, who looks gorgeous in her sundress and sandals. The turquoise color she's picked makes her look like The Little Mermaid with her red hair.

"I gave a talk at the high school about mental health awareness," she explains, putting a bag on my desk. "Then I went and got a piece of pie from The Café, because when your arms aren't available, chocolate and coconut make it all better."

I get up from my seat, enveloping her in my arms. "Why have chocolate and coconut when my arms are yours whenever you need them?"

She burrows her head into my chest, and like always, it makes me feel like I'm the strongest man in the world. To know this woman counts on me to be her anchor in the storm that's sometimes our lives is the biggest blessing I've ever received. "You okay?" I kiss her on the forehead.

"Yeah," she whispers. "Sometimes it's hard to talk about her, but I'm really proud of the work I've been doing in the past few months."

I'm proud of her too, more than proud of her. She took something that would have broken a lesser person and is making a difference in the community. There are open forums now on mental health, where people who are suffering can come to speak to counselors without fear of repercussions. She's being the change when before she didn't know how to be. "You're doing amazing things, and I'm beyond proud to call you my girlfriend."

"Anyway," she runs a hand over her face. "I stopped by The Café to get my pie and figured you and Ryan might like some lunch."

"You're going for girlfriend of the year. Did you bring us pie, too?" I start rifling through the bag she's put on my desk.

"Did I hear pie?" Ryan asks, rubbing his stomach as he makes his way into the squad room.

"You did, I brought you two lunch and pie."

We sit down to have lunch with her. I enjoy my time with her now more than I ever have. We've been through a lot, she and I. Finding our way back to each other, living through a medical emergency, and doubts that could have torn us apart. We've thrived through all of it, after that first hiccup. She's stuck by me and I've stuck by her. One day soon I'm going to give her my last name and make it legal, but for now I love the life we have. It's got to be right for the both of us, and it's not right for her yet. She has work to do, people to save.

More than anything I realize now, that's what Blaze was put on this earth to do - to save people. Regardless of whether it's from the back of an ambulance, my sister's living room, or giving a speech to a high school gymnasium full of kids. She's got a calling, and she's fulfilling that calling like the amazing woman she is.

"I'll see you at home tonight?" I ask as I finish eating my last bite of pie, rubbing my stomach as I groan. "Damn, that was good."

"Yup, I don't have to go in tonight. I switched with the new recruit out of Birmingham. She wants to get a few more hours in. I think she wants a few more hours with Logan, but that's just me," she gives me a grin.

"You think so?"

"Ohh yeah," she nods, standing up to hug me bye.

As we're breaking apart, Leighton strolls into the squad room, her eyes connecting with Holden's. Without a word they go into his office, shutting the door.

"Wonder what that's about?" Renegade asks as he looks at me.

I know exactly what it's probably about, but I don't say anything because it's not my place. "Who knows with those two, all I know is he'll do anything to protect her, and none of us knows how far he'll go."

Since Blaze and I got together, we've somehow escaped the Laurel Springs rumor mill and they've moved on to Holden and Leighton. No one knows for sure what's going on, because they're both tight-lipped about it.

"I'm gonna go, glad you guys enjoyed your food," she leans in, kissing me on the cheek before she gives Renegade a hug. "We'll be over to see Stella this weekend."

"Maybe I can talk you into letting me and her mom have a date night?" he gives her the smile he uses when he wants to get his way.

"I think that could be arranged as long as Trevor's okay with it."

I'll do anything for my sister, and they both know that. "Order us a pizza and you've got yourself a deal."

Blaze leans in for another kiss, and I take the opportunity to grab her ass, pulling her closer to me. Have I mentioned how much I love it when she wears dresses. I'm leaning against my desk, laughing as she keeps trying to leave, but I keep pulling her back in. If anyone had told me a year ago this would be my life, I would have said they were crazy.

But my Blaze has shown me more than I ever imagined. I've pushed her away, loved her, worried her, and said some things along the way I didn't mean. She never let any of it get to her, never believed anything other than the truth that we should be together.

When I grasp her around the waist one more time, whispering in her ear, Holden's office door opens. Every eye in the room goes to where he and Leighton stand. He's wearing a suit, and she's wearing a white sundress. None of us know where they're going, but she's carrying flowers and he's got a ring box in his hand. Mouths hang open as we watch them leave, neither one of them saying a word.

"Did that just happen?" Blaze asks, looking up at me like she's seen an apparition.

"I think so, don't ask me what it was, but I think that just happened," I move my lips down to her ear. "That'll be us soon."

"Only if you can keep putting up with me," she fires back, sass in her voice.

"We do pretty well putting up with each other," I clasp our fingers together, bringing our hands up to my mouth, kissing her fingers. "I wouldn't be here if it wasn't for you, and I think you know that. You're everything to me, Blaze."

"Right back at ya," she leans her forehead against my chest.

And just like that, right in the middle of the squad room, I'm at home and at peace because she's with me. She never gave up, and she never let me down. Because if there's anything that can handle the steel of a tank – it's the heat of a blaze.

The End

HAVOC - BOOK III

BLURB

When a marriage of convenience turns into the passion of a lifetime...

Holden "Havoc" Thompson

My job as the leader of the Moonshine Task Force is my life. I eat, breathe, and sleep it. The men under my command mean the world to me. Knowing they count on my guidance has kept my demons at bay for longer than I care to admit.

The control I have over myself is an iron fist that sometimes threatens to squeeze the life out of me. What I want more than anything is to live again – someone to show me the light when all we have in our line of work is darkness.

I don't expect it to come in the form of a Moonshiner's daughter needing my protection.

Leighton Strather

My whole life has been defined by who my family is. In the state of Alabama, we're number one with a target on our backs. The danger and prestige isn't for me. I don't care about the money, and I care too much about the families we've ruined.

My brother and my dad are proud of it. They wear their arrest records like a badge of honor. Me? I want as far away from the lifestyle as I can get.

It's the *only* reason I ask Holden to marry me. At least that's what I tell myself.

I never expect his whispered yes to cause such upheaval in my life. Even though I resist, I learn some havoc is good – and this one? It's a whirlwind of lust, hope, and love and all I can do is let it sweep me away.

PROLOGUE

Havoc

SIX MONTHS **Earlier**

"Holden, do you take this woman to be your lawfully wedded wife? To have and to hold, from this day forward, for better, for worse, for richer, for poorer, in sickness and health, until death do you part?"

It's hard to swallow against the lump in my throat. I worry that I'm doing the wrong thing here. Making this young girl trade in one life she didn't want to live for another. But as I look at her, I see a future for me. One I'd never thought possible. As a rule, I don't trust women, but I have trusted her since I met her.

For six months I've lived with her, learning the type of person she is, knowing without a shadow of a doubt that she has a good heart. In some ways she's a product of her environment, in other's she's risen above and beyond. I want to be the person who helps her realize her destiny, the future she can have. I've come to care for her, come to be her friend, and I know there's nothing I won't do for her. Somehow, she's wormed her way beyond my defenses and I'm willing to do whatever it takes to not only make her happy, but keep her safe.

"I do," I answer, and mean it.

I take a moment to look at her. The brown hair that shines black in certain lights, hangs in curls and a braid around her face. Her white dress is a lace number that stops at the top of her thighs. Maybe a little too risqué for wedding? Probably, but it shows off her amazing legs. She wears pearls in her ears, like any good southern woman on a special occasion, and there's a small pendant at her throat that I can't quite make out. I want to lean forward and study it, discover all her secrets, all her desires.

I'm brought out of my daydream as the man in front of us starts speaking again. The Justice of the Peace asks her the same question. Looking into those brown eyes of hers, I search for hesitation, for fear, but my girl? She has none. As I prepare to slide the ring on her finger, I'm reminded that for now, she is mine, and I'll do whatever it takes to keep her. My life is more vibrant with her in it, and maybe it's exactly what I've needed.

Leighton

"Leighton, do you take this man to be your lawfully wedded husband? To have and to hold, from this day forward, for better, for worse, for richer, for poorer, in sickness and health, until death do you part?"

I stand next to the man who's protected me since he picked me up from the back of Blaze Coleman's ambulance, and I give him the same thing I started with – my trust and my acceptance. Over the past few months, I've wanted to give him more, but he isn't receptive yet. I'm hopeful that the ring he's about to place on my finger and the one I'm about to place on his will change things. Maybe they will, maybe they won't, but there's no denying I'm happier now than I've ever been in my life.

"I do," I whisper, feeling the impact of these two words. I know exactly what they mean now and what they will mean in the future.

We repeat more words, make a few more promises, and my heart pounds as I realize it's time for the kiss. We've done this once before, not that anyone knows it, but *that* kiss? It had been out of control, two people with no pasts not sure of their future. I wonder how he'll kiss me this time? Will he let me start with the control again, or will he take control from the moment our lips touch? Will he grasp the strands of my hair in his fingers and tug me in the direction he wants me to go?

I lean up, grasping at the front of the white button-down shirt he wears. My fingers tug on the material and I tilt my head to the side, leaving it open, leaving it up to him. My heart pounds in my chest as his face gets closer to mine. The smattering of a slight beard, the pink-red hue of those full lips, the long eyelashes that feather against the freckles he has on his cheeks – I see it all as he bends me to his will. He wraps his arms around my waist; I in turn wrap mine around his neck, pulling him down as he tugs me close. He pauses, his eyes searching mine, before he takes the kiss that now belongs to him. This kiss is different than our last; chaste in the way he takes my lips, and disappointing in the way he doesn't take my tongue.

When he ends it quickly, I all but stumble back, because I was all-in with giving myself over to him. He holds me tightly, a smirk twitching the corner of his lips.

"Congratulations, Holden and Leighton."

We both turn to the man who officiated our wedding, thanking him. Holden puts his hand on the small of my back and leads me out of the room. I hold our certificate in our hands as I watch the next couple enter the room. So that was it, huh? I'm now a married woman. Something told me I'd feel different, and right now, I don't.

Holden's got his cell phone out, texting to someone. Then he puts it back in his pocket, loosening the tie he's wearing. "So you want to go grab some dinner? We can head to Birmingham, to someplace nice."

"Sure," I agree. I'm a little shell-shocked and not sure how to respond. This had definitely been our plan for the day, but at the same time, I wasn't sure whether we'd go through with it.

When we get to his truck, he opens the door and helps me up so that I don't flash everyone on the street. When he goes to help me buckle around the bouquet of flowers I'm holding, he grasps my chin between his thumb and forefinger, bringing it down, forcing our eyes to meet.

"Change your last name as soon as possible, Leigh. The quicker we can get you away from anything having to do with Strather, the better off you'll be."

"People in this town aren't going to forget where I came from," I remind him, letting myself drown for just a moment in those eyes of his.

"If I have anything to say about it, they will. You let me worry for the both of us."

He leans in, kissing my cheek, before he lets go to make his way around the front of the truck. I close my eyes and take a deep breath. Life as I have always known it has just changed in a big way.

An over six-foot, two-hundred pound, heavily tattooed kinda way.

CHAPTER ONE

Leighton

PRESENT DAY

Sometimes I wonder what would have happened if I had never met Holden Thompson in a capacity other than an official one having to do with his job. Our civilian introduction is kind of a funny story. It involves a shot of whiskey and my first game of truth or dare. In this small town, my last name is synonymous with Moonshine, anything illegal, and now the accident that injured Trevor Trumbolt.

A year and a half ago though, right before Whitney Trumbolt and Ryan Kepler became an item, I'd stood up to my family and had gone to Birmingham for one semester of college. It was the first time I rebelled against them all. I said fuck my last name, my family, and their reputation. I was going to make my own way. Ultimately, I paid for it by being arrested for them. But the night I truly met Holden Thompson is forever ingrained in my brain.

"C'mon Leighton! You mean to tell me you've never done anything reckless?"

I swallow the drink of beer I sucked down hard. Reckless? My whole family is reckless, but me? I like to stay on the fringes, obey the law, and do my absolute best to be a good person. Growing up I was lucky if I was able to ride on a different seat on the school bus without someone telling my dad. He believed in keeping a tight leash on who many dubbed the Princess of Moonshine. I figure maybe a half-truth is better than an out-right lie. "Depends on what you mean by reckless."

One of the other girls we're sitting with does the shot in front of her, hands me one, and grins at me. "The next man to walk through that door," she points to the entrance, "is gonna be kissed by you tonight."

I've never played "truth or dare" or any of those games most girls played at sleepovers; truth is, I was never invited. Everyone was scared of my family. This is my shot, in some ways, to experience the pieces of life I've never been able to. If that means taking the shot of alcohol in front of me and kissing the next man who walks through that door – no matter how not my type he is, I'll do it. Even if it's only to say I'm part of this group.

Tipping my head back, I put the rim of the glass up to my lips and let the heat of the alcohol travel down my throat into my stomach. I can hold my liquor, it'd be an embarrassment to my family if I couldn't, but even I'm starting to feel the effects of the amount we've been partaking in tonight. Hopping down from the bar top table we've been occupying, I lick my numb lips and wait to see who fate is going to put in my path.

The door opens and over the bass thumping in the background, I can hear a couple of guys talking to one another. The first one steps forward and my mouth hangs at the jaw. Holden Thompson, commander of The Moonshine Task Force stands in front of me.

I've always thought he was one of the hottest men I've ever seen in my life. And make no mistake about it – he's a man. If I had to hazard a guess, he's probably fifteen years my senior, but he's never treated me like a little girl when he's come to our house to question any of the family members who are in trouble. Last time he talked to me like I was almost an equal.

"Leighton?" Those plump, pink-red lips question, an eyebrow raised. That's when I realize my eyes have gone right to his mouth. Truth be known, I've wondered what those lips feel like. They look soft, a softness I've never experienced before. The kisses I've had before were stolen and rough, leaving me wondering what everyone else went on raving about.

I realize I've been glued to the floor for a long time. He's still got his eyebrow raised, wondering what I'm doing standing in front of him. I take my time walking closer to him, because more than anything, I want to remember this one reckless moment when it doesn't matter who I am, who he is. No, walking isn't the correct term. For the first time in my life, I strut; I want a man's eyes on me, and I want him to appreciate what he's seeing.

His hair is buzzed, not long like Trevor Trumbolt's, or full like Ryan Kepler's. Holden is his own man with his own set of likes and dislikes. His dark, brown eyes look at me, asking the same question his mouth did just a few seconds before. He's wearing a gray tank top on this hot night; almost summer and sweat is already visible on his biceps. It makes the tattoos he has inked there stand out in stark relief against his tan skin. The lights of the bar reflect off the smooth ridges and planes of his body, casting shadows on parts I'd like to explore.

My hands shake as I shove them to his waist, gripping the cotton of the tank top he wears, dragging him to me. I take him by surprise, but he quickly recovers and takes me the same way. One of my hands leaves his stomach, traveling up to his neck, pulling him down to my level so my lips can capture his. He's got to be at least six-two to my five-four.

They're soft and hard at the same time, surprised and demanding as I melt against him, a five o-clock shadow rasping against my smooth face. The kiss I initiated, he takes control of as he digs a hand through my hair cupping the back of my head in his palm.

I don't know for how long we stand there kissing, making out like teenagers, but I become aware of the hard length of him pressing against my stomach and the tips of my hard nipples rubbing against his chest. I tell myself I have to stop this, it wasn't supposed to go this far. The dare was one little kiss, not a make-out session capable of landing us in lock up for public indecency.

Pulling back, he chases me, his lips following mine as I retreat. We're breathing heavily, taking up space between each other's lips. "I can't do this," I whisper.

"You already did," he reminds me. "But if you have to run, know at some point I'll chase you. Kisses like this don't happen every day."

My stomach clenches at his words, and I grip his waist again, steadying myself before I do just as he said. I shoot past him, run away from the way he's made me feel, the passion he awakened, and the safety I felt in his arms. What was probably five minutes out of a whole lifetime has opened my eyes and kindled a fire I never even knew I had.

As I fumble with my phone, calling a cab, I wipe my lips, acutely aware that I can still taste him on my tongue and I can smell him on my clothes. Can still feel his lips imprinted on mine, my chin itches from the burn of his whiskers.

Something tells me this could be the biggest mistake I've ever made.

Pulling myself out of my memory, I look down at my left hand as I have a seat, lining up the ketchup bottles for The Café. Filling them isn't necessarily my job, but it's also not my job, and I'll do anything to keep myself busy. In the late afternoon sun, the diamond engagement and wedding set catches the light, twinkling against the leather seat of the booth I'm sitting in.

At the time, I'd thought that was the biggest mistake I could ever make. Oh how wrong I was, I can't help but laugh softly at myself. The kiss was the second biggest mistake I ever made, because in the end I married Holden, and Lord knows that's going to end up completely breaking my heart.

CHAPTER TWO

Havoc

"**S**ORRY I'M LATE GETTING HERE," I call to my guys. "I was in the middle of the mother of all traffic stops. I got a car transporting fifty fucking pounds of marijuana, and I had to hand that shit off to another officer," I grumble, throwing my MTF uniform on.

"Oh, quit your bitchin'," Tank throws over his shoulder as he's putting his gear on too. "I was having lunch with Blaze."

"And I was in the middle of naptime with Stella," Renegade throws in his two cents. "We're all making sacrifices for what we do."

"But my picture could have been on the State of Alabama Facebook page for the biggest marijuana bust in these parts in years," I argue, a grin on my face that they can't see.

"It don't matter who likes your ugly mug now, Havoc," Menace, the oldest of my guys, besides me, pipes in with his response. "You're married, you don't need the notoriety."

"Yeah." Ace grins at me as I turn around to face them. "Menace here has been celibate since Caleb was like four, more than likely. He needs to get laid so much more than you do."

Poor Menace, being the single dad of the group gets him picked on every time. I laugh at them, happy that they're this relaxed before we move out, but I know I have to rein it in. "Ace, do you have the intel for me?"

"CI's that Menace and I picked up earlier today said they saw a load of moonshine being transported into Laurel Springs from Stewart County."

My brain is working quickly. Stewart County is the next county over and they're beginning to have the same types of problems we are. Before I continue getting ready, I pull my cell phone out of my pocket and fire off a quick text to Leighton.

H: *I've been called out with the MTF. I might be late getting home.*

Immediately she responds, something that always makes me smile.

L: *Please be careful. Get home whenever you can, but get home in one piece.*

The words put a warmness in my chest I never had before she came along. I hold it tightly and close to me, not ever wanting to let it go.

"You think that's where all the moonshine is coming from?" Renegade asks as he arms himself with weapons for possible hand-to-hand. "The field parties we've been breaking up lately," he points to Tank, "have glass bottles littered everywhere, but we can't make heads or tails of whose still they're coming from. Not with the Strathers out of business."

"I don't think they're out of business." I strap on my gloves that help me keep hold of my weapon, even when adrenaline makes me sweat. "I think the explosion interrupted production, but I think they're purchasing from Stewart County and passing it off as their own, until they can get back up and running. They're not going to let go of the stranglehold they have on this territory."

"Is that what your wife told you?" Ace raises a brow at me.

"Nope, that's what my guts telling me." I ignore the way he's slightly questioning where my loyalties lie. It's been a common occurrence since I moved her in and got married. One I figured on, and one I'm dealing with.

He rolls his head around on his neck, chomping on a piece of gum. "That's good enough for me then, bro."

"So where are we hitting? Where did your CIs see this truck coming from?"

Ace motions me over, grabs his phone, and pulls up the map program we use. It's a small road on the Stewart and Laurel County line. We have jurisdiction for the whole state as long as we're chasing 'shine. "Then let's get this show on the road."

We're quiet as our transportation takes us across the county line, and I can feel my heart rate kick up. This isn't our normal territory, and I'm totally unsure at what we could face. We're acting on the tip we've been given and normal recon isn't available. Basically, we're flying blind. Something I don't like to do.

My mind is quiet as I focus on the job at hand, chomping on the gum in my mouth, and try to keep my mind off the woman who makes me want to believe in happily ever after. If I go into this distracted, I may not make it out, and I don't want to leave her unprotected – ever.

"Alright, guys," our transport driver yells back to us. "Time to bail!"

As I hit the ground, the thud of my well-worn combat boots makes a welcomed sound. It's the indication that I have a job to do and I'm ready to kick some ass. We're quiet as we move through the dirt and tall grass that's allowing us to sneak up, undetected. As we broach the perimeter, I can see a makeshift still. It's not the most sophisticated operation I've ever seen, but I have no doubt it can get the job done.

I motion for the guys to fan out. They know their jobs – take pictures, check for stragglers, and see if we can find any illegal product. "Keep alert," I yell out, because something doesn't feel right about this. Normally I'd keep quiet, but I'm willing to give up my position to protect my guys.

My gaze is sweeping the perimeter where we came from when I catch a glint of metal, and before I can yell at everyone to take cover, the bullet catches me right in the chest. I'm knocked down and the breath has been taken from me, but it was taken by the impact of the bullet piercing my vest, and not my skin. I struggle to catch a breath, already wondering what the bruise is going to look like, already thankful I get to go home and see Leighton in a few hours.

Thank God, because I wasn't ready to die today.

"DO y'all need anything else before I head out?" I ask my guys as they sit at their laptops, finishing their reports. None of us had planned on doing anything with the MTF today, but when the State of Alabama calls, we answer.

It's been a long fucking day. Hell, it's been a long six months since the explosion and the wedding. Looking down at my left hand, I catch a glimpse of the black band of silicone resting against the skin. It proclaims me a married man, and I took my vows seriously when I spoke them, but it still feels foreign to me. Especially because I go back and forth between this silicone band, and the metal one I wear when I'm not working or working out. The guys gave me so much shit when I ordered one I could wear at work, but what can you do when the symbol of a connection to the woman you're married to grounds you?

"You sure you don't want me to call Blaze and have her come check you out?" Tank asks as he glances up from his laptop, concern written on what's usually a smiling face. If there's one thing we do well in this unit, it's take care of one another.

I roll my shoulder back, feeling the tightness in my chest where the bullet hit me square in the vest this afternoon. I've been hit before, and I know it'll be a few days of soreness and eventually it goes away. I refuse to take the vest off, because I don't want the guys to see how bad it possibly is right now. "I'm good, I'll see y'all tomorrow."

When I breach the door of the Moonshine Task Force Headquarters, I let my shoulders slump and give into the absolute agony I feel along my chest wall. Looking back, I make sure no one is watching as I go out to my truck, before I open the door and pull myself into the driver's seat.

I sigh, bracing myself as I unclip the vest, and painfully pull it over my head. Breathing hurts slightly, but I'm ninety-nine percent sure I'm good. Resting my shoulders back against the leather of the seat, I give myself a few minutes to get my shit together. In the cup holder, my cell buzzes.

L: *Roles seem to be reversed...LOL! Just letting you know, I'm gonna be late tonight. I'm going to take Caleb home for Mason and then swing by the grocery. You need anything? I'll pick up something to cook for dinner.*

Menace will appreciate that she's going above and beyond to help him out, and I can't help the little smile that spreads across my face. Leighton's stepped into her role as my wife better than I could have imagined. She cares about my guys as much as I do, and all of us notice it.

Rolling my head around on my neck, I work my shoulders to try and loosen some of the tightness in them. A hot shower is going to be the only way I'll be able to move tomorrow.

H: *Whatever you get is good with me. It's been a fuckin' long day. See you at home. Be safe.*

Saying be safe is the only way I can let her know that I care without saying it to her. She deserves a man who loves her, who worships the ground she walks on, and in the past year I've come to care about her a great deal. There are times when the depth of my feelings surprise me, but I'm not sure I'm the type of man who can fall so selfishly in love with a woman. Not after my past. I'm giving her pieces of myself I can stand to give her, but in a way I feel sorry for her; she married me and not a man who's romantic enough to bring her flowers on a random Tuesday. Maybe one day I'll be that man, but right now I'm the furthest thing from it. Starting my truck, I drive off into the late-evening sun, looking down at my wedding ring again.

Marriage. Before Leighton Strather came into my life, I'd never given the word a thought – whether it be for convenience or love. It wasn't an institution I was interested in, not when I'd seen so many of my friends attempt it and have it backfire. Granted, all of those instances happened in a war zone, but the one time I had a girl back home, she did the same shit to me. Broke my fucking heart, but there was something about Leighton Strather I've never been able to get out of my head.

I became interested the day she kissed me in a bar, but was able to push it out of my mind. At least that's what I've tried to tell myself. That shit changed the day I saw a darkening bruise on Leighton's chin and a slightly crooked tilt to her nose in the back of an ambulance.

For most of my life I've been in charge of people, I've been given the absolute honor of protecting eighty percent of the men and women I come into contact with. Very few times I've failed in that protection, and I know without a doubt I won't fail this woman. Whether I admit it to anyone or not, she's got a piece of me that I never want to take back. She's had it since she glanced up at me, her brown eyes dark with fear, asking me what would happen to her if her family got hold of her again. I couldn't stand the wobble of her chin, the puffiness of her bottom lip from where she'd taken it between her teeth in fear, or the tears pooling in her eyes. I've always been the type of man to take action when it's something I can help with.

This, I can help her with, and the day in the back of the ambulance? When I saw her sitting there so small, so closed off to everything around her, I made a decision that has effectively changed not only our lives, but also the course of our future. That was the moment I decided to give her my last name, and I always take care of what's mine. Even if it costs me everything, including the beat of my heart and the air I breathe.

I don't even remember getting home; just realize I've pulled into the driveway when I notice the house in front of me. The house is my pride and joy. It was the first thing I bought when I came back from my tour and decided to stay in my hometown.

My reasons for joining the military were simple. Pussy and getting out of what had been a three-stoplight speck on the Alabama state map. Funny how life changes in the course of almost fifteen years. Laurel Springs now has over thirty stoplights, as well as a parkway and interstate connection, and as of this moment, there's only one pussy I want. The one I can't have. Even if she does wear my ring and have my last name.

I shake my head, trying to clear my thoughts. The hit to the vest must have taken more out of me than I thought. I put the truck in park and turn it off, before taking a minute to collect myself. I'm tired as hell. So damn tired. And so mother fucking frustrated I could scream.

That's what happens when you feel like you live a lie every day of your life. It's a pressure beating down on your shoulders, pressing on the lean tissue, causing you to hunch over. Eating away at the muscle and strength, but you have to decide if you're going to let it.

That's not me though; I stand tall no matter what. It's what was taught to me as a kid and then added onto when I joined the military. Now I command my own unit for the State of Alabama. I take my responsibilities very seriously. And right now, those responsibilities are my guys in the Moonshine Task Force and the woman wearing my wedding ring, signing my last name after her first.

Gathering the last bit of energy I have, I open the door; turn in the driver's seat and gingerly drop to the ground, enjoying the crunch of gravel under my feet as I do so.

Reaching in, I grimace as I grab my gear, strolling tall to the house. On the walk to the porch, I give no indication I'm hurting. If anyone is watching the place, and I know they are, they'll see me just like I want them to see me. Someone not to be fucked with.

Once I'm inside, I let my shoulders fall, throw my stuff down, and head straight for the shower.

CHAPTER THREE

Leighton

"THANKS FOR PICKING me up and dropping me off."

I glance over at Caleb, giving him a soft smile. He looks older than his fifteen years, but he's had to grow up quick, just like I did. From what I've been able to gather, Mason's been a single dad for at least the past thirteen years, and I'm not sure if Caleb's mom is alive or not. They don't talk about her much; no one talks about her at all, to be honest.

"Not a problem. You know I don't mind helping out if you need it. Do you work tomorrow?"

I waitress at The Café, and Caleb helps in the kitchen and busses the tables. It's not much work, but he does it, and does it well. Mason's instilling a good work ethic in the kid, and I can't help but admire it. I wish I had come by my own work ethic the way he is, and not by helping out with the family business as a teenager.

He nods, a yawn cracking his jaw. "Yeah, I'm gonna be there after football practice. So I'll be working later than you will be," he explains as he grabs his bag, reaching for the handle on the door to let himself out of the car.

"Still," I say, reaching into my pocket and give him a portion of my tips. My way of thanking him for keeping my tables clean and honestly just to help him out because I know he's living a difficult life right now. "If you need someone to drive you, either I or Holden will help."

"My dad won't get in trouble?" he asks quietly, mentioning Mason. "I hate asking his boss for a ride. It doesn't seem like something most bosses would do for the people who work for them. I don't want charity and I don't want to inconvenience anyone." His voice is strong as he says those words, and I wonder just how much he thinks he's a burden to other people, how much that weighs on him. It's weighed on me for most of my life, and I'm not the person to be helping someone else get rid of that weight, but I want to at least try and make it easier on him.

"We're here to help," I explain, like I always do to this teenager who's got the weight of the world on his shoulders. "Everybody's here to help. All you have to do is ask. The same way we'd ask you or your dad if we needed help. It's what families, whether they're blood or by choice, do."

I don't want the weight he has on his shoulders to crush him. Don't want him to end up in the same situation I was in before Holden rescued me. Not that he has a family making moonshine, but it's important for me to let him know he's cared about.

He reluctantly takes the tip out I hand him, before getting out of the car. "I know," he says with a grin. This kid will be a heartbreaker one day soon, and I can't help but smile back.

"See ya around, Caleb."

He gives me a wave as I pull out of the driveway and turn my car, heading for the grocery store.

AS I PUSH the cart through the aisles, I glance at the shelves wondering what in the world I'm going to cook tonight. Sometimes I wish Holden would give me an idea, but he never asks for anything different than what I make. He never questions, and he never makes demands in everyday life either. I truly get the feeling he's happy with the little life we've carved out for ourselves, but every once in a while I wonder, what would it be like to live with a man who can't keep his hands off of me? What would it be like to go to bed with someone who spooned me from behind because he couldn't stand not to touch me? What do Holden's lips taste like first thing in the morning? These are all questions I want the answers to, but I know we aren't there yet, maybe never will be, but I'm holding out hope. If he cared enough to marry me because of some sense of obligation to protect me, there has to be feelings there. And honestly, how do I expect him to feel things for me, when I don't even know what the feelings I have for him are?

All I know is I like it when he's around and I like it even more when he looks at me like I'm the center of his universe. Which is something I'll never admit to anyone.

As I pass the alcohol aisle, I glance at the six packs of beer, the bottles of amber liquid, the taller containers of wine, and I wonder what he likes. Things have been tense with us lately, and I'm unsure why.

Maybe it's because I'm not good at ignoring him anymore. I haven't been for months now. It used to be I could look objectively at the hot man with whom I share a house.

That changed one day when I came home from work early and caught him masturbating in the shower. He doesn't know. It would mortify me if he knew, but the way he'd groaned my name had me bracing my hand against the bathroom wall and fighting not to open the shower door.

I've woken up countless times since then, my hand between my thighs and his name on my lips as I explode, hoping like hell I haven't woken him up, since we sleep in the same bed. The orgasm? It's empty. As empty as I feel our life together is most of the time. The hardest part about the emptiness is the little glimpses I get every once in a while that show me how full it could be if we'd both just let our guards down.

"Leighton!"

I steel myself as I hear the sound of Mable Hall – sounds like an eighty-year-old grandma, right? Wrong. She's a forty-year-old divorcee who wants my husband. She's told me so (in not so many words) on numerous occasions. Newsflash – I wear his ring, and one day I'll know what it feels like for him to be inside of me as he loses control. God as my witness, I will make that man lose control.

Reaching over, I grab a pack of the Corona bottles and drop them in my cart, as I try to get away from Mable. I pretend like I can't hear her and keep moving my cart up the aisle, farther away from her.

"Leighton, do you not hear me talking to you?" Her voice is high-pitched and like nails on a chalk board to my ears.

Gritting my teeth, I turn around, fake smile on my face, false apologetic tone to my voice. "Sorry, I'm just in a hurry to get home and get dinner done. It's been a long day, and I like to spend my evenings with my husband." I twirl my wedding ring around on my finger, hoping she takes the hint. My husband, not her piece of ass to mess around with.

Her eyes drop to the diamond on my finger, and if I'm not mistaken, I see a glimmer of unease in her eyes.

"I was just wondering if you could give Holden a message for me? He came and spoke to our pre-school class earlier this week, and I had a few things I wanted to verify. Can you have him call me? I didn't think to get his number in case any of the children needed to know more."

I grit my teeth, a flush working its way up my neck and chest. I can feel it, and I wish to God my emotions and thoughts weren't always written all over my face. This isn't just embarrassing for me, but also for her. She wants a man she's never going to have. We've made it to the checkout lanes, and I start unloading my cart.

"The best thing to do, Mable, would probably be to call the station. Off-duty is time for family and friends. He doesn't really like to take work home with him, if you know what I mean."

I'm feeling awfully proud of myself for standing up to her, when she glances at me from head to toe, sniffing in distaste.

She laughs, the tone downright ugly. "You should know better than anyone he takes his work home with him. After all, honey," the word is dripping with sarcasm, "he married you."

She waves her fingers in my direction before she turns and walks off. I try like hell not to throw my purchases on the conveyer belt, but I fail when I think of her standing in the community, how much closer she and Holden are in age, and honestly how much bigger her tits probably are than mine. It's a hard realization that Holden made a big mistake in marrying me, and more than likely he can't wait until we he can correct that mistake.

CHAPTER FOUR

Havoc

THE HOT SPRAY of water beating down on my shoulders is doing its best to loosen the tension I have weighing there, but I have tension in other places too. Namely the space between my legs where I'm hard as a fucking rock. The tension has been there for weeks, and I can't help but try to relieve the frustration. Grasping my cock, I play for a few seconds, stroking it up and down, dragging my hand along the length. I know it'll never fully be gone until I can bury myself balls deep into the woman who teases me every day, but until then, this is the best I can do.

I grunt harshly as I curl the fingers of my free hand into a fist, beating it against the tile of the shower. Sometimes a little bit of pain makes the pleasure sharper. The hand holding my cock picks up speed and I grip the base a little harder on each down stroke, curling my palm around the head on every upstroke. I'm sensitive and so fucking ready to blow, but I hold off, knowing the orgasm will be stronger if I can edge it out just a little bit longer.

My chest is screaming with agony as I beat myself off, but the shower is the only place I can get any relief. Being near Leighton, sleeping with her every night, and listening to her moan as she experiences whatever she does during her dreams is enough to drive a man insane. I can't even begin to tell you how many times I've wanted to say *fuck it,* position myself between her thighs, and wake her up to the best ride of her life.

Take last night, for example. She moaned like she was having the most intense orgasm of her life. Her legs fucking shook. The thing is, I know she's asleep. Every time I have to fight with myself – do I want to wake her up and offer to ease the ache, or do I lie there and deal with my own ache? I can't make the decision. Which is why I'm jerking off in the shower.

I close my eyes tightly, picturing her in my mind. She has the most expressive eyes, and her body is so damn responsive. I bet she has absolutely no idea how often her nipples harden against those thin t-shirts she likes to wear. If she knew how I walked around this house in a state of half-arousal every single day she'd probably call me a pervert. But hey, I'm a red-blooded man and I appreciate her body. Immediately my mind goes to my favorite fantasy staring the two of us.

In my head, I can hear the bathroom door open; I can feel her eyes on me, even through the cloudiness of the shower door. My skin breaks out in awareness as I hear her coming closer.

"Holden?" Her voice is hesitant, but soft and husky with the slightest hint of arousal. Like maybe she wants this as much as I do.

Reluctantly, I let go of my cock and force the door to the shower open. I turn to face her, letting her see my own arousal, inviting her with the tilt of my head to join me if she so chooses. The sharp intake of her breath and the flaring of her nostrils is enough to tell me what I want to know. She's interested, but I can also tell she's unsure. Maybe she's scared of where escalating this attraction will take us, maybe she's afraid I won't pleasure her, or she won't pleasure me. Those thoughts have never crossed my mind, and now it's time for me to man up and take fucking control of the situation.

I step out, not caring about the water I'm tracking all over the tile floor. My focus is on one thing in the room, and that object is the woman who's been driving me nuts since she moved in with me almost a year ago. Putting a ring on her finger didn't help anything either, possibly made it worse, because I have a claim on her I'm not sure I can ever act on. When I look down at that piece of metal and diamond on her finger, it's a struggle to not beat my chest and tell the whole world she's mine.

Because she's not really. I'm kind of borrowing her until it's safe for her to live the life she wants.

"Holden?" she questions as she inches back toward the vanity, gripping the edges of the sink as it stops her from traveling any farther away from me. I don't know if she's running away from me, or her feelings. I've noticed she does both.

"Leigh." My voice is full of gravel and lust, harsh and seductive in its tone. I feel like I'm about to lose control and I haven't even touched her yet. In my mind, I tell her I want her, but what comes out of my mouth in this dream sequence is something cruder than I intend for it to be. "Let me fuck you. Let me bury this hard cock inside what's undoubtedly a sweet pussy and show you just how good it can be for us."

She closes her eyes and pulls her bottom lip in between her teeth. Those responsive nipples pebble against the material of the t-shirt she's wearing, and I decide I'm going for it, consequences be damned. Maybe I'll never have another shot like this again, and I'm not okay with not taking it.

Shoving the fingers of one hand through her brown locks that she's curled today, I use my palm to maneuver her mouth to my liking. Tilting it to the side so that we're almost sharing the same breath, yet not touching her lips. I show her what a tease I can be, trying to give her a little of the tease she's given me. With my other hand, I grab her hip, pulling her fully into my body. I groan as I realize she's still wearing clothes and I can't feel her naked body against mine.

My mouth can no longer wait for a taste and it has a mind of its own as I once more adjust the tilt of her head and dive in for a kiss. The first one we've had since we got married. The first real one we've had since that night in the bar so long ago. It's not so much a kiss as it's a possession. My lips take control, my tongue tangles with hers, and she leans back at the ferocity of it for a split second, seeming to gather herself before she springs into action.

In the span of five seconds, she's climbing me. Her fingers are gripping my waist, nails digging into my flesh and she's trying to hook her legs around me. I hear a moan, a sound of frustration from her throat, and it's enough to make my cock jump where it's resting against her belly. I feel the same goddamn frustration, have felt it for months. I'm glad we're on the same page, finally. The hand on her hip snakes down to the globe of her ass where I palm it and lift, encouraging her to wrap her legs around my waist before turning us around and taking us back into the shower.

Once there, I crowd us into the wall, loving the feel of her bare feet digging into my ass. The water saturates her shirt, giving me a glimpse of everything I've always wanted to see without having to take her shirt off. It molds to her skin, giving me an erotic view of both everything and nothing at the same time. I don't think I've ever been as hot for another woman in my life, as I am for her.

"Holden, here," she gasps as she grabs my head in her hands, pushing it toward her tits. "I need you here."

I don't require any more encouragement as I lift her higher, putting her rack even with my mouth. My lips grab hold of the puckered flesh through the clothing and I pull tightly against the cotton, using my tongue to swirl around the hard nub. The smooth material against the abrasiveness of my tongue is a turn on all by itself, and I can only imagine how she's feeling right now.

"Yes!" she arches in my arms, pushing her chest deeper into my mouth and pressing her middle harder into my cock.

As she begins to writhe against me, I begin to grind on her, letting her feel the evidence of my desire. The hard length presses into her and I groan loudly when she lets go of my head, reaches down and grasps my girth in her small hand, squeezing slightly. Closing my eyes against the pleasure, I ride along the edge for a few seconds, before I realize if I want her to do anything else I need to tell her.

"Holy fuck," I ground out against the clenched teeth at her tit. "Fist it harder, rougher."

My chest is heaving, panting like I've run five miles and done the obstacle course. Already feeling like I could come if a gust of wind hit me the right way.

Her small hand jacks me up and down, covering the head and squeezing the base, just the way I like it. I don't know how she knows this about me, but fuck it feels good. Maybe it's kismet, she knew me in another life and I've just found her again. We all think that sometimes, huh? The whole soulmate situation. The verdict on whether it's true or not is still out, at least for me.

I can feel a tightening at my spine, and I'm thrusting against the tight ring of her hand. Biting down roughly on the nipple in my mouth, she makes a crying noise of pleasure and that's all it takes for me to come all over the hand grasping my cock. "Leigh! Fuck, don't stop!"

When I open my eyes, I'm back in the shower by myself, coming against the tile wall, biting my knuckle as I squeeze my flesh tightly in my hand. "Shit," I breathe slowly, trying to settle my breathing down, and escape the ringing in my ears. If Leighton and I ever do get naked, alone, and willing, it's going to blow my mind. My heart is pounding against my sore chest, and I'm trying to shake away the stars I see behind my eyelids.

"Holden, are you home?" I hear the voice of the woman I just jacked off fantasizing about as she makes her way through the house.

Damn, I hope I wasn't loud. It's not like I don't necessarily want her to know what I was doing; my hope is one day she joins me, but it makes me feel a little skeevy. Especially since she wasn't home, and I knew it. "Yeah, almost done in the shower. Be out in a minute."

I finish this shower quicker than ever before. As I get out and dry off, I realize I only brought a pair of shorts with me, and no shirt. I hadn't really wanted her to see the bruise on my chest, but I guess there's no way around it, considering I'll have to walk through the kitchen to get back to the bedroom.

Opening the door, I brace myself as I prepare to see the woman I just blew my load to the thought of.

CHAPTER FIVE

Leighton

"HOLDEN, ARE YOU HOME?"

I hear him answer me from the bathroom, at the same time I hear the water in the shower. Good, that lets me know I have a couple of minutes before he gets done. Quickly, I take the few bags I have, put them on the counter, and then head back to the bedroom to change into a tank top and a pair of shorts. When I bend over, the shorts almost show the curve of my ass – I know because I've looked. Fair? Probably not, but I'm learning as a woman you have to sometimes play the game to get what you want. If I'm honest with myself, I wear these clothes because I want Holden to notice me, yet I'm not sure he does.

"How does hamburgers on the grill sound to you?" I ask, bending over to get the lettuce, tomato, and cheese out of the bottom of our fridge.

"Sounds good. I can grill them for us as long as you take care of the sides."

His voice surprises me, closer than I anticipated it would be. It makes the hair on the back of my neck stand on end and goosebumps to appear all over my body, in the most pleasurable of ways. Holden's voice is one of the sexiest things about him. I love when he calls me on the phone instead of texting me. It's a privacy I enjoy, a little thrill no one else knows I get except me. Regardless of whether it's on the phone or not, I love talking to him and the intelligent conversations we have with one another.

Purposely, I shake my ass before lifting up from my bent-over position. Making a bit of a show of it, I place the stuff I got out of the fridge onto the counter. That's when I get my first good look at him. A dark bruise covers almost his entire pec, and I immediately get a sinking feeling in my stomach. It's hard to discern from the tattoos he has covering his body, but I can make it out, looking like a bullseye, right over his heart. I hope my family had nothing to do with this. I'll never forgive myself if they have. "Oh my God, Holden! What happened to your chest?"

He rubs his hand across his pec, drawing attention not only to the already purpling bruise, but the solid strength there. He grimaces slightly, but I don't know if it's from the movement or the pressure he puts on the skin. Sometimes when I'm tired of fighting the fact I'm attracted to this man, I let myself rest against his bare skin, and knowing he's hurt right now hurts me. Reaching for the beer I put on the counter, he pops the seal with his big hand.

"I'm okay," he assures me, taking a drink of one of the Coronas I picked up at the store. "A bullet got me, but my vest stopped it – the exact way it's supposed to. It did its job, just like I did mine."

I freeze, stop everything I'm doing and look at him. How can he be so collected and calm about this? Obviously if there hadn't been a vest there, he would have taken a bullet to the chest. He very well could have died. I don't know why, but I've never thought of it that way before, never imagined what he did had him truly in danger. I guess in my mind, I thought he sent other people out instead of himself, but that's not really Holden Thompson, is it? That's not the kind of man he is. "So, you got shot at?" I ask carefully.

"Kinda part of what I do, sweetheart." He takes a drink of the beer and levels me with a gaze, the side of his mouth tilting up.

The gaze is enough to stop my heart, the intensity in his eyes cause butterflies in my stomach, something I've never felt before. In the blink of an eye, I realize how much I've come to count on that gaze, and something else hits me like a ton of bricks.

Today is the day I truly realize just how dangerous Holden's job really is.

CHAPTER SIX

Havoc

LEIGHTON'S FACE has gone as white as the walls of the kitchen, and she's looking at me like I just told her Santa Claus isn't real. I hand her the beer I've been drinking, encouraging her to take a drink of it with a flick of my wrist. I'm glancing for clues that she's not gonna pass out on me, but I'm not feeling overly confident about the situation. "You okay, sweetheart?"

I watch as her lips wrap around the head of the bottle right where mine were, touching the same glass I did. She tilts her head back and drains half of it, and I can't help but groan when I watch her push the liquid down with the motion of her throat. I can imagine her on her knees in front of me swallowing down my cock, her throat pushing against my length. It's hot as hell when she finishes, sets the bottle down, and laps up the remaining moisture lingering on her bottom lip with a swipe of her tongue.

As I watch her pink tongue swipe at her red lips, I have to move behind the island so that my body is concealed from her view. Reaching down, I adjust the rapidly rising evidence of how much I want her. Inevitably, questions will come if she knows how many hours a day I think about the two of us naked, and those are answers I don't have yet. Maybe I should have taken a bit longer in the shower. "That bother you?" I ask her, because I do wonder. "Me taking a bullet to the vest?" How would she feel if something happened to me? Does it make her stomach hurt the way it makes mine hurt when I think of danger coming to her door?

She looks away from me, one of her dark curls concealing her face from my gaze. It pisses me off; I want to see the truth in her eyes, the emotion on her face. She's expressive as hell, and right now I need to see it all. "Of course it bothers me." She clears her throat before she turns back to me, her eyes taking in the bruise on my torso again. Her voice is quiet as she speaks the next words, "You're a very important part of my life. You're basically all I have. If something happened to you, I don't know what I would do."

The way she speaks lets me know she's laying the truth out for me. I'm not sure how to react. On one hand, I want to be the person she leans on, on the other I don't want it to be because she has no other options. It's a stroke and blow to my ego all in the same sentence. "You're a strong woman and an incredibly intelligent person, you'd figure it out, Leigh." Then I realize that since she's been real with me, I need to be real with her, too. "But I don't want you to ever have to figure it out on your own. I want to be the person you call if shit ever goes sideways, and I'll protect you until my last breath. I don't let anybody fuck with what's mine and don't ever doubt you aren't mine."

Her chest is pumping up and down as she takes in my words. "I know, it's why I trusted you when you asked me to move in with you. It's why I said yes when you said we should get married. I've never trusted anyone as much as you," she whispers. I notice she puts her arms in front of her chest, hugging herself, in a protective gesture. If I were any kind of man I'd give it up and go over there, take her in my arms, let her know everything's okay. But I'm raw right now; we're talking more today than we ever have, all because of a bruise on my chest. Tank and Blaze admitted their feelings because of a wreck – maybe it is true what they say, certain situations put life into perspective. She's still speaking, so I give her my full attention. "That may make me the stupidest person ever, but I trust you with everything."

I shake my head. "Doesn't make you stupid, sweetheart. I trust you with everything too, and I'm fully aware it puts us both at risk."

She nods almost imperceptivity. "Is that risk the reason you're bruised right now?" I know what she's asking. She wants to know if her family had anything to do with me getting hurt. It annoys me, that she even has to worry about that shit.

I clear my throat. "Nope, this was something else entirely, and you know it's never mattered to me what stock you came from. What matters to me is the type of person you are."

I realize then how true those words are, as I grab the hamburger patties and head out to the deck, snagging another beer on my way. Sometimes you need to let loose, and maybe I'm gonna do that by having a couple of beers tonight. Otherwise, I might do something I could totally regret.

CHAPTER SEVEN

Leighton

I'M DOING my best not to let my emotions show as I watch his incredibly toned back walk out of the kitchen I now call ours, onto the deck. Once he's there, I watch as he gets the grill started, and it's only when I turn away from the window do I let myself feel. Tears silently stream down my face as I let the impact of the words he spoke wash over me. I never knew how much it truly mattered to me, his opinion, until he uttered the words it didn't matter what stock you came from.

This afternoon, here in our kitchen, after almost a year of living together and six months of marriage has been an absolute game changer. One I never saw coming, but at the same time, one I'm absolutely grateful for. I try to take a breath, but let out a sob instead, not sure how to handle this onslaught of emotion. It's never much mattered to me what others thought, because I couldn't change the way they perceived my family. I knew at a very early age I was an extension of what others believed of my family and I was included in those assumptions. Looking back, I never had a chance, and damned if I haven't gotten one now because of the man standing on the back deck, making me a hamburger. I'll make him proud, no matter what I have to do. He's the only person in my almost twenty-four years that's ever taken any kind of chance on me, and I won't let him down.

Cleaning the tear tracks off my face, I go about making some macaroni and cheese, along with the steamed vegetables Holden likes to have at every meal.

Letting my gaze travel back out to the deck again, I let it roam over his body.

Truly, he's a magnificent piece of work, all lines and dark ink, everywhere the eye can see. He's cut and lean, muscular and amazingly athletic, yet gentle when he has to be. I've been witness to the hard work he puts in to maintain the six percent body fat I've heard the other guys give him shit about. Therefore, I want to help him as much as I can. I've also been witness to the tender side of him, the one that'll help a little old lady across the street when we're having a festival downtown and cars don't want to stop. It was panty-melting, not even gonna lie, when he took June Sutter's small hand in his and walked her straight across Main Street, daring the drivers he held up to defy him by going until she'd made it safely to the other side. I imagine the way she gazed up at him with awe in her eyes is the same way I gaze up at him.

Holden Thompson is an enigma with lots of twists and turns, secrets and hidden doors. I want to navigate them all, know them all, and not stop until there's absolutely nothing between us. He's done all he can to help me, and I'll do anything in my power to help him. Regardless of whether we wanted to be, we're a team, and right now it's kinda us against the world.

"YOU GET to pick the movie tonight," I remind Holden, glancing over as we load the dishwasher with our dinner dishes.

He laughs, throwing his head back. I love when he does that, his face completely changes and the way his Adam's apple moves up and down is incredibly sexy. He tilts his head forward, still chuckling as he looks at me. "That side-eye you just gave me says you get to pick, but don't pick anything you really like because I hate everything you love."

A small smile spreads across my face as I nod slowly, willing to admit to his criticism. "I do hate everything you love when it comes to movies. Why can't you like a good comedy or an action movie? Why do we always have to watch the ones that scare me a little bit?"

"First of all, there's no such thing as a good comedy, not really. And please, a little bit?" He raises an eyebrow in disbelief, a pure bad boy smile making its way across his face. It's that smile I love the most, when he lets go and shows me every bit of his personality. "The way you jump into my arms sometimes says you're more than a *little* scared."

My face burns with embarrassment and I roll my eyes in annoyance. I'm convinced he does this to see my face turn red. I've never been good at movies where people jump out at others, never, not even when I was a kid and I didn't know all the dangers lurking in the dark. "Total girly reaction, what can I say?"

He leans back against the granite counter, arms folded across his bare chest, the dimples I hardly ever see popping against the darkness of his five o'clock shadow, and the smart ass smile still on his face. "It's okay if you're scared, I'll protect you," his voice deep, his tone teasing as he continues. "We'll even leave the lamp on if you need to, Leigh."

I throw the nearest dishtowel at his head, scowling when he catches it with a quick flick of his wrist. "A scary flick it is."

Twenty minutes later we're sitting on the couch, in what's become our usual nighttime routine when he's home. After dinner we watch a movie. Twice we've ended up in each other's arms, without necessarily meaning to. Tonight though, I want to be there. I want to feel his heart beat, want to feel the warmth of his skin next to mine. I'm finding more often than not during the day I miss him. Whether it's just to have him next to me, or to share a quick word. He's become my friend, and he's becoming the type of family I've never had.

If I'm being honest, this movie isn't one of the scariest we've ever watched, and I'm laying my fear on a little thick. Holden laughs softly as he reaches out with his thick arm when I hide my eyes behind my hand, pulling the pillow tighter to my chest.

"C'mon in here." He pulls me against his side, his arm resting against my shoulders, curling around my neck. The weight of his muscles is enough to make me melt into the curve of his body. If I explained our situation to other people, they'd think we were crazy, but I've always been comfortable with him. From the first night I stayed here, we've been snugglers and touchers. So far, it's never gone further than that, but tonight I'm feeling a comfort from him. It's a comfort I haven't felt in a long time, maybe even never.

Just like that, I'm right where I want to be, feeling the warmth of his skin beneath me and the strong beat of his heart. It could quickly become my favorite place to be, and it scares me more than the movies we normally watch and my family combined.

CHAPTER EIGHT

Havoc

I PURPOSELY PICKED this movie because I knew it would make her want to curl up next to me. Apparently, I'm a glutton for punishment, but I need this. After my day, I need to hold her in my arms, smell the strawberry scent of the shower gel and lotion she uses, and feel her soft skin against mine. Maybe I need it more than she does, because today, regardless of what that bullet hit, I'm feeling my own mortality and I need her next to me probably as much as she needs me next to her. I'm not stupid, and I know she cares for me in her own way. There's no way she would have married me otherwise, and I'm not stupid enough to question it. Tonight, I'm willing to give into my wants, give into the way I know she can make me feel if I allow her to. Maybe tonight I wanna play with fire, and I'm willing to get a little singed by the flame.

She gasps at the current scene as someone jumps out and scares the main female character. It causes her to hold onto the forearm I've looped around her neck with the tips of her fingers, slightly digging her nails into my flesh. It's a turn on, because around her I feel like I'm a teenage boy.

"Don't be scared," I whisper into her ear, soothing her, trying to get her to relax against me.

"Never, at least not with your arms around me," she answers as she turns her head into me. The seductive tone of her voice is one I've only heard once before. The night she kissed me in that bar. I swallow roughly against the memory of that night.

"What did you think about me? The night when I kissed you at the bar?"

It's like we share the same brain sometimes. I clear my throat and try to put my thoughts into words. "It side-swiped me like a car not stopping at an intersection. I'd seen you around, I know you noticed it."

"I did," she shrugs in response. "Every once in a while when you would come to the house, your eyes would linger on me, and I'd wonder what you were thinking."

"For the longest time I felt so goddamn sorry for you, that you were brought up in that bullshit, knowing you had nowhere to go. Then that summer, I heard you'd convinced them to let you go to Birmingham. I thought this is her chance, her one shot to get out from under the thumb of her family and do something for her." I rub my hands up and down her arms. "I never expected you to be in that bar when I walked through the door."

I close my eyes against the memory, living in it again. I know what I want to say, and I'm chalking it up to that mortality shit. "You were beautiful that night." Quickly I amend my words, "Not that you aren't beautiful all the time." She laughs softly. "But that night you had a confidence about you, like you were ready to take on the world and strangle it with your bare hands."

For a minute I stop, open my eyes, and wonder how far I want to take this, do I tell her everything? The flinch of a muscle spasm in my chest wall tells me I should. What if we don't have tomorrow? "You blew my mind when you kissed me." I bring my hand up to my lips, remembering the moments. "Your taste was something I couldn't get out of my mouth for weeks. Rubbed a couple out thinking about you, not gonna lie."

"You still do that now?" she asks softly.

She turns in my arms, facing me, her eyes sweeping across my face. I can tell what she wants by the increased level of breathing and the way her eyes dilate. It's important to me she initiate this though; I don't want her thinking later on that I took advantage of her. Anything that happens between us, I want to be because she wants it and is feeling it – not because I pressure her.

"Take it, Leigh," I whisper, challenging her. "You weren't scared to take it in that bar."

She licks her lips, leaning in farther. Our faces are centimeters apart, and it wouldn't take much for either one of us to make our lips connect. "Now it's so much different, it seems like everything is magnified. Our actions are so much more important."

"It is; they are," I agree with her, entwining my fingers in her hair. I hold her loosely against the palm of my hand, not wanting to influence the final move she makes. I want it to be entirely her decision. "It means more because we've made a commitment."

"But are we supposed to keep this commitment forever?" she asks, her breath hot on my lips.

The fucking question of the century as far as I'm concerned. Perhaps neither one of us wants to be the person who says yes, but I want her to know it's an option.

"We'll keep it as long as we need to, and then as long as we want to."

I don't know if that's the right or wrong answer, I'm unsure of what the future holds for us, but I do know this woman makes me want to be a better person. She pushes me to want more in the future, like what everyone else wants. And her? I want her to know what she wants, what she says, matters, I want her to know she can be somebody's forever and it doesn't matter how she started out. I want her to feel cherished, treasured, and appreciated.

"Take what you want, Leigh," I prompt her again, encouraging her to make the decision for herself. I'm against the arm of the couch, half-sitting, trying to look as if this woman doesn't blow my mind.

And she does. She launches herself at me, straddling my hips. I hold on tightly as she fuses our lips together, shoving her tongue in my mouth. We lap and eat at each other like dogs in heat as we try to get closer to one another. The clothes we both wear make it difficult, but I know I don't want to go that far with her, at least not yet. I don't want to make it more awkward than it's already going to be. Hell, I know I could have her, but it doesn't seem like it would be fair to either one of us, not when we've both had a day like we have. And not when our feelings and actions on those emotions are so new.

She pulls back, and I chase her slightly, catching her bottom lip between my teeth, nipping hard enough that it makes her nipples pebble against the cloth of her tank top.

"I know how you feel," I moan as I settle her between my thighs, against my cock. "I can tell every time you're turned on, because these nipples pucker. They fucking poke against whatever piece of material you're wearing, and every time I want to take them into my mouth." I reach up, cupping them with my palms, worrying the tight skin with my fingers. "I wanna take them into my mouth," I keep talking, letting my voice stay low and seductive – I don't want this web of eroticism to leave us yet, "and tug hard against the tightness, I want to feel you pull away, make the bite of pain a little more intense. I want to tongue the ache and feel you thrust against me, the way you're doing now," I moan against her throat as I pull her closer to my body.

We're moaning, thrusting, and dry humping on the couch with some horror movie playing in the background. I want to slow us down, but there's no slowing down when you're this close to the edge.

Pushing my hand up to her face, I put my index and middle finger into her mouth. The way she swirls around the tips of them gets my cock harder than ever. Inside my boxers I'm wet, needy, hard, and fucking frustrated.

When I've had as much as I can take of her tongue, I withdraw and move that hand down her body, beneath the elastic bands of the shorts and panties she wears. "You want it?" My mouth still rests against her throat, but I can feel her nod of permission.

As I begin the press into her body with my fingers, she moans, pushing against them, opening wider to me. Her hand is grasping in the dark, and when she makes contact with my hard length, I nip at the tendons of her neck. I want to fuck her, show her everything I can make her feel, but I know right now isn't the time. Instead, I go to work hard on her clit with my thumb, pushing and pulling my fingers into and out of her warmth.

"Holden," she moans as she sneaks the questing hand between my clothing and skin, taking me into her palm. Cupping her hand, she uses her thumb to glide over the head of my thickness, coating it with the moisture of my desire. We're straining against each other in a way I haven't done since I was making out on a friend's couch in high school. That doesn't seem to matter though, I can feel it coming, can feel completion beating down on me for the second time tonight. This one, though, is going to be so much sweeter.

"Fuck, Leigh," I groan, crushing her flesh in between my teeth, marking her so that anyone else who sees her knows she's mine. I've never been this type of guy, one who's so into making others know my woman is taken. But this one, I want her with everything I have, and when I feel her tighten around my fingers and I hear her sharp intake of breath? I'm the baddest motherfucker on the planet because I did that to her. Even as I lose my battle and my release covers the both of us in the end.

Leighton Thompson is a danger because she makes me feel, but she's a danger I'll sign up for every time, if given the chance.

CHAPTER NINE

Havoc

I'VE BEEN UP HALF the night thinking about what could have happened on the couch last night, wishing like hell I had let it happen. It wouldn't have taken much for me to have her clothes off, legs open, and my still-hard cock buried deep inside her body. I wanted it so bad I could taste it, can still taste it this morning. However, I know if I had sampled it, I'd have a foul taste in my mouth on what would be the morning after. I wouldn't respect myself very much, and I've worked hard to be a guy I can at least respect. When the two of us finally seal the deal, I want it to be because we're crazy with passion and feelings, not because I've had a close call and she's reacting to the clues I'm giving her. I want it to be organic. Hell, maybe last night was organic, I don't know, but I don't want her to ever feel pressured.

Unfortunately, the part of my personality that was a good guy last night and is trying to talk the bastard I feel like this morning down, is super pissed off at himself right now. I've tossed and turned, seen every hour on the clock, and I'm cursing my good guy self right now for not being the selfish asshole I wanted to be last night.

Rolling over, I face Leighton, looking at her in a way I only ever get to when she's asleep. I spend a good portion of my time watching her when she doesn't think I am. Kinda makes me feel like a creeper, but she makes me feel too much shit. Emotions I thought I had a lock on, things I never thought I'd feel again. I'm not comfortable letting her in on those feelings yet, because I'm not sure of the future.

Whoever is sure of the future? That's what you're thinking, I know, but I'd like to know we have one before I go completely all in with her. There's still a chance I could be a fucking chump and she could stab me in the back. She's still not been honest with me about what her family's done. Can't say that I blame her, but one day she'll trust me enough to tell me, and then I'll have to decide what I want to do; betray her or the job. I'm not anxious for that day to come.

Instead, I let my eyes take her in again and forget all the fucked-up parts of the lives we're living right now.

In sleep, she has the innocence of a teenager. The things she's seen don't cloud her eyes and they don't make her frown or grimace with some unknown memory plaguing her. She doesn't turn a corner to avoid a family member at the grocery. In sleep, she has no worries, is beautiful in her tranquility. It's the kind of serenity I want to put on her face, the level of comfort I want her to have with me.

I roll over onto my back and close my eyes, hoping and praying that someday what we have can be the real thing, not because it benefits us both and not because she's scared of her family. But because we both want it so bad we can no longer deny the feelings between us. What I want is real, and I think she does too, but we've gotta cut through the shit first.

CHAPTER TEN

Leighton

IT'S a slow day at The Café. After the lunch rush, we haven't had any of the stragglers we normally have. They usually help pass the time, but today there's only been one or two customers. Given that it's a rainy Wednesday, I can't say I blame everyone for wanting to stay at home and take a nap. If I was given an option, I'd probably do the same thing.

Since it's slow and I've already taken care of what I need to, I sit down at the bar and pull my laptop from the bag I carry with me everywhere.

"What are you doing?" Violet, a waitress newer than me, asks as I wait for my MacBook to boot up. She's a little older than me, maybe by a couple of years, but I think we could be friends if given time. There's a kinship you can instantly recognize with people who seem to have had hard lives, and I recognize it within her. It's the dark moons that mar the space below her eyes, the way her eyes dart back and forth when the bell rings, and the way she looks up when anyone new comes into the building. I'm not sure who she's looking for, but I have a feeling I'll know the minute they walk through the door.

"Taking online classes." I crack my knuckles, before I put in my password and connect to The Café's Wi-Fi. "I can't make it down to Birmingham to go to classes on campus, but I've been able to sign up for their online program. I think it's going to take me a little more time, but it's important to me to have an education."

She glances at me, a hesitant look on her face. "Your husband doesn't care?"

The question catches me off-guard. Why wouldn't someone's significant other want them to improve themselves? It was never a question for me. "He supports it completely. He knows how important it is to me."

In fact, it had been Holden's idea for me to start the online classes. One of the first things he'd helped me sign up for after we'd gotten married, since there was a tuition reimbursement program through the department.

He'd sat down with me and we'd filled the paperwork out together. I'd thought it odd, but I didn't really have any kind of experience with which to gauge it by. Looking at her face, I think I kind of see how odd and endearing it is.

"That's amazing." She smiles slightly, grimacing as she eases herself into a sitting position on the stool next to me.

"Are you okay?" I ask as I watch her take a careful breath. Kind of like I did when my ribs were sore from the last time I left my family and they'd made sure I'd feel it for a couple of days.

Her eyes don't meet mine, and she doesn't answer the question.

"That's got to be expensive, right?"

I can't tell if she's genuinely interested or she's making sure I don't ask any more questions about why she's having a hard time sitting. Either way, I indulge her.

"There's a tuition reimbursement program through the department, and since I'm Holden's wife, I'm included," I answer, catching on to the fact this is obviously something she wants to do when I see her eyes flair at the tuition reimbursement. "If you could go to school, what would you study?"

"I want to be a lawyer." Her answer is swift and precise, and completely to the point. "I want to help women who can't help themselves. I would do a ton of pro bono work to get women out of dangerous situations," her voice is soft as she shares.

"That's commendable." I'm careful with what I say, because maybe I'm reading between the lines, but it seems as if she's telling me something without really telling me. "There are a ton of women who need help getting out of situations that seem helpless."

"And there's not a whole lot of people who will help if it doesn't concern them." She takes a drink of the Coke in front of her.

There are a ton of questions on the tip of my tongue. I have a feeling the reason she's grimacing and asking these questions is because she's in a hopeless situation. I want to help her, but I don't know how.

"What are you going to school for?" She turns the conversation back to me.

Now this is a question I can answer. "Accounting. I know it's kind of boring, but I want to go into forensic accounting."

"What is that?"

"Where you find out how people are stealing money. You can notice patterns of fraud and figure out where they're filtering the money to." I shrug.

"I hate people who steal from others; it's a pet peeve of mine. Plus, I find it fascinating, and I always did the books at my family's business."

Immediately I close my mouth. I probably shouldn't have said that, but Violet didn't grow up here, she doesn't know my family. "I never had any formal training with it, and I'd like to be able to work from home. A lot of this is just companies emailing you files and you combing through it, looking for something out of the ordinary."

"Yeah, sometimes working with the public isn't my cup of tea." Violet rolls her eyes at me as we share a smile. Both of us have had some unwanted attention, no matter how much we try to make it go away.

Earlier in the day, she had someone who was passing through hit on her. I know what she means, but most everyone knows I'm married and leaves me alone. Unless it's someone from out of town, then I have to go through a spiel of showing my wedding ring and letting them know my husband is a cop.

Just as I'm figuring out which assignment I have to do for this week, the bell chimes, signaling we have customers for the first time in over an hour.

"I'll get them, I could use the tips." Violet scoots off the stool, hissing slightly as her feet hit the floor. My heart hurts for her, it sucks not having anyone to go to, but I know it's not my place to help her. She has to come to that conclusion on her own, and be willing to accept the help.

I glance over my shoulder, trying to see who came in on this nasty day. I grin when I notice Ace and Menace from the Task Force taking a seat at one of the empty tables. I give them a wave, watching as Mason gets up to walk over.

My attention for a minute, however is on Ace and Violet. Ace isn't the kind of guy who knows how to keep his voice down.

"Hey gorgeous," he greets her. "I don't think we've been introduced, but I've seen you around here. I'm Ace."

"Violet." She doesn't hold out her hand the way he does. If anything, she shrinks back into herself. Ace is like all the other members of the MTF and notices everything. He shoves the lame hand through his hair and rattles off a drink order for her to take down.

I notice his eyes follow her as she moves back to where we keep the fountain. By this time, Mason has made his way over.

"Hey," I greet him. It's still hard for me to believe this man, who's younger than Holden, has a fifteen-year-old son.

"I wanted to thank you for taking Caleb home for me the past few weeks. I've been working some security in Birmingham, saving up for the college prep exams he'll need to take and the application fees for college in the next year or so. I know it's a little out of your way, but I appreciate it," Mason thanks me, running a hand over his neck, possibly with the air of embarrassment. Again, I want to ask about where Caleb's mom is, but I know it's not my business. If

Mason is working this hard to give his son everything he needs to be a success, who am I to question him?

"It's not a problem, he's a really good kid, and I don't mind helping. I kind of understand how he feels, to be honest. As a teenager, you never want to be a problem for your parents. He's in that awkward stage where he can't drive because he doesn't have a license and he'd rather not walk or take the school bus." I shrug, letting him know it doesn't bother me.

"Either way, you've been really good to him, and I know it's not easy. Sometimes he's got a smart mouth." He hooks his thumbs in the belt loops of his pants and rocks forward on his boots. "If he gets out of line, please let me know."

I laugh, because Caleb has never, not once, gotten out of line. Mason obviously doesn't know what kind of a young man he's raised. "No smarter than what I grew up with or what I live with on a daily basis. He's a good kid, and I'll help him anytime I can."

He laughs along with me. "So true, and probably why you handle him so well. Probably nothing you've never heard before, huh?"

"No, and if he ever got out of hand, I would handle it and let you know. He hasn't though; he's a good kid who works hard. You should be proud of him."

Mason doesn't say anything and I can tell I've touched him by the way his face takes on a different shade of red. The earnest tone of his voice gives emotion to the words. "I try hard with him."

Reaching over, I put my hand on his shoulder. "Trust me; you're doing a great job."

He sighs, seeming to take in my praise before he gives me a quick smile. "That means a lot, Leighton, he's lucky to have a friend like you. Anyway, I just wanted to say thank you. No one's ever gone out of their way to help us until I came to town to be a part of this unit."

"I know how much the MTF means to Holden," I explain, and in my own way of helping them means I help my husband, which makes me feel good. "I'll do whatever I can to help. It's a type of family I've never been a part of before."

He chuckles. "Me and you both. I didn't know there were people like this in the world, but this group of guys constantly amazes me."

"You aren't the only one," I laugh along with him.

He tips his head and goes back over to the table when the bell above the door rings again, this time bringing in the man who makes my heart beat ten times faster.

My eyes meet Holden's as soon as he walks into The Café; it's like we're drawn to one another. He's walking next to Ryan Kepler, deep in conversation, but the minute he catches my gaze, he stops and gives me a grin.

I can't help it, I grin back at him, especially when he says something to Ryan and then heads my way.

"Still raining out there?" I ask as I take in the damp appearance of the dark button-down officer's shirt he wears today. Usually it's a dark blue, but it looks black in the dim lighting of The Café. His long eyelashes are spiked with water, and I can see moisture dripping from his neck.

"You could say that," he says as he leans in, not touching me, as he lands a soft kiss on my lips. I don't miss the way his eyes go to my neck, where I spent a lot of time this morning applying concealer and foundation to camouflage the huge hickey I have. "There was a wreck out on 101, and we were directing traffic while EMS did their thing. I didn't have my hat with me and got a little water-logged. All of us responded and missed lunch, so here we are."

"Sounds like you've had a busy day."

He glances around. "Looks like you've had a slow one, why don't you and Violet join us while we grab a bite?"

I think he's flirting with me, but I have absolutely no basis for comparison. Guys have never flirted with me; they've always been too scared of my family. After last night, I can see why he would flirt, but it still confuses me. "I guess we could, not like we've done a whole lot today."

"I mean if we aren't intruding on your busy schedule."

I giggle. "Holden Thompson, did you just make a joke?"

He leans in, this time pressing his wet chest to mine. "I do know how to have a little fun every now and then."

Deciding I want to flirt a little too, I duck my eyes, looking up at him past my eyelashes. "I can't wait for you to show me what you think is fun."

The grunt I hear from behind his closed lips is worth the flirt, and totally worth the way his eyes scorch me with a look. "One day, little Leighton, you're gonna find out."

And I can't wait for that day to be here.

CHAPTER ELEVEN

Havoc

I'M A GLUTTON FOR PUNISHMENT. I think I've said those words before, but they've never been truer as I sit here tucked into a booth with Leighton's body pressed so far up against me that I've had to turn sideways and wrap my arm around her shoulders. These booths were obviously not made for grown men and women. She's sharing my hamburger and fries with me, so I can't complain.

"How's Stella doing?" she asks Renegade, unknowingly opening up a can of worms the rest of us had effectively closed shut earlier in the day.

"Aww hell." Ace throws his burger down on his plate. A look of resigned disgust on his face. "Here we go again."

Ryan beams as he looks at Leighton, already moving so that he can stuff his hand into his pocket, to grab his cell phone. "She got pictures made the other day, wanna see?"

"Say no, for the love of God, say no," I tell her, holding her closer to me. "You're gonna go down a rabbit hole of the cutest pictures of a toddler you've ever seen in your life, and you're gonna find yourself talking about how cute the pink ribbon is in her hair, the small pearls are around her neck, and then you're gonna hand over your man card because you're noticing all this shit. So do yourself a favor and just don't look."

She grabs the phone from Ryan. "I don't have a man card, so I can look all I want." She winks at me, and fuck if I'm not floored.

I take a drink of my Coke, swallowing it slowly as I watch her start to scroll through the pictures. "I guess you don't have a man card," I speak softly in her ear, making sure only we can hear what's being said between us. "You're all woman to me."

Her finger stops scrolling, before she glances up at me with big eyes. "Sometimes I don't think you notice."

"Trust me, I definitely notice."

The blush I see covering her cheeks is payment enough for the praise I've given her. Knowing that I'm the person who made her blush? Priceless to me. I would do it every day if I could.

"Oh my God!" she squeals as she sees a picture of Stella that she obviously likes on the phone. "She was wearing this shirt in here the other day."

Renegade leans over the table, grinning when he sees his daughter wearing a shirt that says *I wear bows and daddy wears a badge*. "Tank got her that one; it's probably my favorite so far."

"Wait." I hold my hand out to stop the conversation, trying not to laugh. "*Tank* bought that shirt for her?"

Renegade raises a brow. "There's not much you don't give the little girl that's the center of your universe. And lucky for Stella, she's the center of a lot of universes. You just wait." He takes a bit of his hamburger. "It'll happen to you, too."

Leighton and I share a look. Not many people really know what's going on between us, because we want to make it seem as real as possible. The less our marriage is questioned; the better off it is for the both of us. "We'll see," she shrugs, flashing him a smile. She takes a drink of her Coke before she hands Renegade his phone back.

"I watched her the other day, actually."

"Stella?" he asks, all ears when it comes to talk about his daughter.

"Yeah." She scoots closer into my body, and even though I'm still damp and should be cold, I feel a warmth where we touch. "Mona was supposed to meet Whitney here, but it was the day that grain truck overturned out at the Bottoms, and obviously she didn't trust going through there."

I notice that Leighton stops. "Nobody blames you for what happened with Trevor," I remind her.

"I know, but it doesn't mean I don't sometimes blame myself." She sets down her fry and puts a smile on her face. "Anyway, your soon-to-be-mother-in-law couldn't make it, and I was about to take a break, so I watched her for Whitney. We went to the park down the street. She's definitely got the walking thing down."

"Yeah," Renegade agrees. "Now it's just trying to get her to feed herself. She's trying, but it's messy. We weren't going to push it, but she likes being independent."

"Wonder where she gets that from?" Ace finally speaks from where he sits.

"Definitely her mother." Renegade throws us all a bashful grin. "Thanks for helping Whit out. Her and Addie are gonna have to hire someone soon. The two of them are basically dying with the amount of planning they've got going on."

"Didn't they take on Blaze's parent's big shindig for St. Patrick's Day?" I offer Leighton the last bite of my burger. When she doesn't take it, I shrug and scarf it down in one swallow.

"Against everyone's better judgement. I'm telling you, her parents would turn a saint into a sinner. Like I didn't realize how many dirty words my woman knew until she came home from meeting with Olivia Prescott Coleman, with two t's."

Beside me, Leighton giggles. "It cracks me up how everyone in this group makes that distinction every time they say her name."

"Have you met her?" Ace levels her with his gaze.

"No," she shakes her head as she answers. "Somehow I've been able to avoid it."

"We have." He points to all the guys. "And the way she looks at us like we're strippers about to give her a lap dance really pisses me off. If I'm gonna give somebody a lap dance while in uniform, she needs to at least be able to make some sort of expression. Her mom's had so much goddamn Botox, she can't even frown. That's not sexy to me. Show me your feelings, if you can't, you might as well be a blow-up doll."

I run my thumb along Leighton's jawbone, while I formulate my plan. I love to make Ace annoyed, love to see his ass get riled up. "Blow-up doll, huh? You have a lot of experience with those?"

"As much as you do, asshole." He throws his wadded up napkin in my direction.

"That's *Sir* Asshole to you, since I'm your superior." I live for this shit.

"Do you make her call you Sir?" He points at Leighton, and I feel a possessiveness clamp down on my body, a ribbon of tension that chaps my ass since he's just playing around and I know it. To be honest, though, it seems disrespectful to me, and I don't handle disrespect well when it comes to her.

"What my wife calls me is none of your business."

Judging by the way he leans away from the table in reaction to the tone of my voice, I think he knows he crossed a line. There aren't many times I have to get stern with my guys; they tend to know what sets me off and what doesn't. But this...it's a whole new ballgame, because Leighton's an unknown. Even after being married to her for the past six months, I'm still unsure how deep our feelings go, how deep they *can* go based on the factors as to why we got married. Hell, the guys have no idea I'm not getting any. For all intents and purposes, they think this marriage is legit.

My conscience says *isn't it?* You treat her, for the most part, like she's your wife. You protect her, you provide for her, and you do your best to make her life easier. The only things you don't have are the physical and emotional aspects of a real relationship.

"Sorry," Ace is saying. "Didn't mean to piss you off or disrespect Leighton. It was just a joke, man, but I can see where it wasn't appropriate." He pushes back from the table. "I'm gonna go see what pie is up there for dessert today."

"Dessert sounds damn good to me, too." Renegade makes off like his boots are on fire.

"Well that's one way to get them out of here." She turns to face me, her dark eyes glancing up at mine. "He was just joking."

"I know." I'm slightly uncomfortable at her perusal. "I just don't like when people joke about you. What we have may not be traditional and even to us it's weird sometimes, but it's ours."

Her eyes flash as I say the words *it's ours*, and I think maybe I've done something good in this moment. Maybe for once I've said the right thing, done the right thing, when usually I'm winging it and failing miserably.

"You're right," she says as she grabs hold of my hand, tracing my wedding ring with her finger. "Whatever this crazy situation we have going on with each other is, no matter what, it's ours and we don't have to explain ourselves to anyone."

"Nope, we don't."

The moment seems heavier than it should, and I wonder what's happened here in the span of ten minutes. Leighton's looking at me like I hung the moon, and I'm not comfortable with the adoration in her eyes. I'm not that type of guy, I don't do things for adoration, I do them because they're practical, or it's imperative to keep my family safe. I don't want her hero worship; I've done too many awful things in my life to deserve it.

"I guess I should get back to work," she licks her lips, obviously unsure of where we stand. These moments are getting more and more prevalent. At some point we'll need to make a decision, but today won't be that day.

"I'll see you at the house?" I lean down, giving her a chaste kiss on the lips, when really what I want to do is devour her the way I did last night.

"I'll be there, with bells on." She relaxes against me, somewhat back to her old self. "Picking out a much better movie than you did last night. I won't have nightmares, or have to hide my eyes."

I tap her on the thigh, signaling for her to move so that I can get out of the booth, and when she does, I sit at the end, opening my legs, and bringing her between them. With a murmur of surprise, she twines her arms around my neck and settles where I want her to, bringing us together so that our foreheads touch. Her hair falls in a curtain around us, effectively shutting everyone else out from our conversation.

"If what you've been having is nightmares, moaning and thrashing the way you do, I want to have a damn nightmare every night," I tell her, feeling a little brazen. "Maybe next time you have a *nightmare* I'll be sure and wake you up from it, and we'll see just how scared you really are." I move my hands down to her waist, pulling her even closer. "Both of us know you aren't waking up gasping because you're scared, baby. You're waking up because you're dripping wet and coming."

She's closed her eyes, and her mouth is hanging open. I give her ass a tap before I move her back from me, and yell to Renegade, telling him to come on.

"See ya at home," I give her a wink as me and the boys leave. A huge grin's on my face the rest of the day, because now I know I've given her something to think about.

CHAPTER TWELVE

Leighton

MY FACE BURNS as I watch Holden and the rest of the MTF guys leave The Café. I guess I've been naïve thinking he doesn't know how I've been waking up ninety percent of the time.

It messes with me, since I've never really been a sexual person. But Holden? He brings out every carnal thought I've ever had as a woman and completely makes me wonder if I even know myself.

"They're nice." Violet has a seat next to me at the counter again.

I chew the tip of the pen I have in my hand, a nervous habit I've developed over the past few months. "Yeah, they are. One of the best group of guys I've ever met in my life."

"How did you meet your husband?" She asks out of the blue.

It throws me off guard that she doesn't know, but then I remember she's new to town, and not everyone is privy to the history of Laurel Springs. I shift in my seat. "My maiden name is Strather, and he's spent the last few years arresting various male members of my family for making moonshine."

Her eyes are wide. "You're related to the Strathers?"

Now I'm uncomfortable and borderline sorry I said anything. Trying to be honest sometimes works for me, other times it gets me into situations like this. "Yeah, my grandfather is Merle, my brother is Brooks." I purposely leave my dad's name out. Our relationship has never been good, and I don't want other people to think I *belong* to him.

"The one that hit the officer?"

Again I feel the weight of my family on my shoulders and wonder how in the hell Holden and I will ever be able to forget the past and move forward. "Yeah." I twist my hair around my finger. "He's paying the price." I feel the need to stand up for my younger brother. If anything, he had even less of a chance than I did to get out of our family business. He'd been groomed for it since he could walk.

"I'm sorry," she says as she puts her hand over her mouth. "I'm just in shock; you seem so normal and sweet. You and Holden seem to have such a great marriage."

"I know." I grin ruefully. "It's weird, huh? The head of the Moonshine Task Force marrying a moonshiner's daughter?"

I let that sink in for a second, reminding myself exactly who we are and why all of this is a bad idea.

"Yeah." She nods. "But the two of you seem so happy, and you can tell you care for another when you're together. Maybe you're kinda like Romeo and Juliet."

This is news to me, no one's ever made commentary on mine and Holden's relationship. "Do we?" I'm dying to know what it looks like from the outside to someone else. And I don't bother to tell her that Romeo and Juliet died.

She grins, resting her chin on her hand as she looks at me. "Yeah, you do. As soon as he walked through the door, you couldn't keep your eyes off him. Then after he convinced you to sit in the booth with him, he couldn't keep his hands off you. It's sweet, and the chemistry between you is so explosive you can see it just looking at you two."

For the first time, in possibly ever, I'm going to allow myself to be the woman I've never allowed myself to be when it comes to my husband. Since Violet doesn't know much about my past, only what I've told her, and she came to town after we got married, I'm going to gush. I'm going to be *that* girl. "My husband is a very good-looking man, and I'm lucky he chose me to marry."

"It's the tattoos." She giggles.

I giggle right back. "No, it's the tattoos, the air of authority, the dark intensity of his eyes, and honestly just the way he carries himself." I keep going, because now I can't stop. I've lifted the gate on keeping my mouth shut, and now I have to share all the amazing attributes of the man I married with *someone*. "The guys give him a hard time because he's so cut, and he's in such good shape." I lean in, lifting my eyebrows suggestively. "But I get to watch him work out, and oh my God," I fan my face, "I've never seen anyone as intense as he is when he's focusing on his form and core for an average of forty-five minutes a day."

"You're a lucky woman, Leighton," she sighs. "He's hot, he's a genuinely good man, and the way he looks at you says he wants to eat you up every second of every day. Pretty sure if you two were alone much longer over there in that booth, you would have spontaneously combusted. A lot of women would kill for a love like that." She grins ruefully before she gets up from the stool and walks behind the counter, starting on the last of what we have to do before the next shift comes in.

Does Holden look at me like that? Am I oblivious to it? And why haven't we been acting like a normal married couple? We've never been out on a date, never gone to restaurant together, except on our wedding day. Either we stay in and cook or one of us brings something home. Deep down I know I've been scared of running into my family, but I'm beginning to rethink my position on that now. Maybe I want us to have a more traditional relationship, and I know if that's the case, the person who initiates it is going to have to be me. It's time to pull up my big girl panties and let my husband know what the hell I want.

Decision made, I hop off the stool, and start cleaning off all the tables, grinning to myself as I clean the one I sat at not two hours ago. I can still smell Holden on my clothes, and I realize with a startling clarity how happy it makes me.

Can this be more than a marriage of convenience? I'm not sure, but there's only one way to find out.

CHAPTER THIRTEEN

Havoc

I'M TIRED, and still a little soggy as Renegade and I head back into the station, almost three hours after we had our lunch. The amount of rain that's fallen on the county in the last few days has caused so many traffic accidents, we're all working overtime in our main capacity as officers of Laurel Springs instead of the Moonshine Task Force. I don't mind either way, but I don't like when we get too far away from the MTF side of things, it starts making me nervous for Leighton.

"How are the roads?" Ace asks from where he sits at his desk, laptop open in front of him. He came on shift a few hours after Renegade and I did, so he's got a few more hours to go.

"Not bad." I tiredly sink into the chair at my own desk. "Most of the water is starting to recede. It hasn't rained since this afternoon, but they're calling for more overnight. It's going to be up in the air, depending on how many people are out on the roads tonight." I pull the forecast up on my phone. "And temps are falling down into the thirties, so it's gonna be a chilly one. Hopefully that rain doesn't freeze, cause nobody knows how to drive on ice around here. Throw in black ice and we could be fucked."

"Leave it to us," Ace shakes his head, "to have one of the coldest days of the winter on the night when we get the most rainfall we've seen in months."

"Shit happens," I remind him. "And it always happens to us."

I take a look around the squad room, noticing the shift change is starting to take place. I'm ready to be off. Today's been a long fucking day, and all I want to do is go home, sit in front of the fireplace in my house, and cuddle with my wife. I'm chilled to the bone after having been out in the rain earlier and haven't been able to get warm ever since. When I see my replacement, I give him a nod and grab my stuff.

"I'm out, see you tomorrow afternoon."

Ace gives me a wave, as I exit the squad room like I have the hounds of hell at my back. Walking out into what's now the night air, I shiver, seeing my breath as I make my way over to my truck. Typically during the winter months, we have a cold spell or two, but we haven't had one yet this year. With March fast approaching, I figured it was time, but I didn't think it would be this damn cold.

The leather of the driver's seat creaks as I pull myself up into it, grimacing as it puts a strain on my chest wall. So far today it hasn't hurt as much as I thought it would, but now that I'm allowing myself to relax as I wait for my truck to heat up, I'm feeling all the aches and pains. Fatigue sets in after the adrenaline of being "on" all the time fades from my body. This is the moment I allow myself every day where I let go.

My back hurts as I shiver, my legs ache, fuck even my knees ache. It's unusual for me – normally the cold doesn't affect me like this. My head falls back against the seat, and I crank the heat up higher. I feel fucking beat up, and maybe that's an honest description of my life right now. I'm bruised, cold, tired, and wondering all the fucking time where I stand with my wife.

Leighton. It was nice to see her in the middle of a workday, nice to hold her against me for a few minutes and let her warmth infuse my body. I look forward to seeing her all the time, whether I want to be honest about it or not. She makes everything a little more tolerable, puts a smile on my face whenever I see her, whenever I think about her.

I've never wanted to look too deeply into it. Since the day I met her at her grandfather's house standing in the back of the living room while I questioned the men in her family, I've been intrigued by her. The dark hair, the big eyes, the hot body (if I'm completely honest), and the way she carries herself. There aren't many women who have the air of regality she does, and even if she's a Moonshine princess, it doesn't seem to matter.

A part of me wishes we could have met in a different time where both of us have different lives. I know more than anyone, though, life doesn't give us the circumstances we want. We're dealt a finite number of moments and we're supposed to turn those moments into memories and life-changing situations. I didn't know seeing her standing there, as a barely nineteen-year-old kid would change my life. Looking back on it now, I know it did. We were put into each other's life paths for a reason and instead of fighting it, I'm beginning to think we need to figure out why that was.

I liked being next to her today, enjoyed kissing her in public, and not tempering my affection. Out of nowhere, I realize today was the first day we've actually been in public together since we got married. The first time I shared a meal with her and let other people see us together here in our hometown. Any other time we've done anything, it's been in Birmingham. I know part of that has been to protect her, but maybe the other part of it has been to protect me.

I have a fear that as soon as she doesn't need me for protection anymore, she'll be gone. The only thing I can do to prevent that from happening is prove to her what kind of a life we'll have together if she stays. Why haven't I thought of this before?

Fuck, I'm getting soft and I'm getting old. Thirty-six is making me feel like an old-timer. Or making me think about my own mortality, not exactly sure which. Either way, I know I have to get on the road, because if I sit here any longer, I'm going to fall asleep in the station parking lot. That won't look good for anyone involved.

I put the truck in gear and make my way home.

CHAPTER FOURTEEN

Leighton

IT'S FREEZING COLD TONIGHT, temps dropping low enough that it's gotten chilly in the house. I just checked the thermostat and it reads fifty-nine. Which wouldn't be so bad if I knew how to work the heat.

Central heat wasn't something we had at my house. Everyone assumes moonshiners are rich, and to an extent they are, but most of them are greedy, too. And instead of doing things like giving your kids central heat, you go out and purchase a sixty-thousand-dollar truck for a teenage kid who doesn't understand responsibility and gets put in jail a year after getting it. None of my family has a sensible bone in their body, and they suffer for it.

My grandpa yells to anyone who'll listen that he makes moonshine because his social security isn't enough for him to live on, when the fact of the matter is, the man's never learned to budget a day in his life. He has no savings, and he wouldn't know what to do with it, if he did. Same goes with my dad and brother.

I'm not really sure where I get my sensible thoughts from. Maybe my mom?

I shiver, running through the house to find some warmer clothes to wear and to get my mind off of thinking about my mother. That's a place I haven't wanted to go for years, and definitely a place I don't want to go tonight. Glancing through my chest of drawers, I see I have nothing to keep me warm for temperatures like this. A testament to how few nights we have this cold.

"I guess that's what I have a husband for." I shrug as I go over to his closet and open the door.

It's not very often I go in here, basically only when I'm putting up his laundry or helping him get dressed for the day. The scent of his cologne that lingers on everything is prevalent here, and I like to take a second to let it wash over me. I'll always, for the rest of my life, associate this smell with my husband. Snapping out of it, I rifle through the stuff he has there, before I find a hoodie and a pair of sweatpants.

I'm shivering as I take my clothes off, leaving my socks on, and do a quick switch out of my outfit for his. Putting the hood of the sweatshirt up over my head, I sigh, finally encased by warmth. Tiptoeing back out to the living room, I take another look at the thermostat, trying to figure out how to turn the heat on. I feel inadequate, not knowing how to do this, when so many others probably do. Just another time where my upbringing failed me.

I hear boots on the porch and make a small sound of joy in my throat that Holden's home. The door opens, with it spilling in the cold air. I clasp my arms across my chest to ward off the chill, thankful when he shuts the door.

The moment Holden turns around to look at me, I see a hunger in his eyes I've never seen before. I want to ask what it is, but my tongue is stuck to the roof of my mouth and I'm frozen in the spot I stand.

"What?" I finally ask, self-conscious as hell.

"My clothes look better on you than they do on me. You look really fuckin' good in my shirt," he answers, his voice rough.

For the first time I get a good look at him; he's a little pale and shivering himself. "I was cold and couldn't figure out how to turn the heat on," I explain. His eyes are a bit glassy, and I'm a little worried. "Are you okay? You don't look so hot."

"The house doesn't have central heat because it's an older one. I have gas logs in the fireplace, and when you crank it up, it'll get the whole house warm," he explains, making me feel better about not being able to figure it out.

"I'll turn it on for us, because I'm freezing, too."

I walk over to him, watching as he squats and opens the glass barrier of the fireplace and turns a few knobs, cranking up the heat. Immediately I can feel warmth coming from the area. "You'll have to show me how to do that, so I can warm the house up before you come home if this happens again."

"Tomorrow," he hangs his head. "Tonight, I don't feel like it."

He's shivering as he stands up, teeth chattering with the cold. "Holden, are you okay?" I ask again.

"I feel a little like shit," he admits, leaning against the wall. I can't tell if he's doing it because he's tired, or if it's for support.

Reaching out, I grab hold of his waist and gasp. He isn't freezing, he's burning up. "You're on fire." I immediately take my hand and put it to his forehead, feeling the hot skin.

"I'm fine." He tries to shake me off, but stumbles as he leaves the firm support of the wall.

"You're not fine, and you may have dealt with this yourself before, but I'll remind you, you have me now. If you're sick, I'll take care of you."

His dark eyes run over my face, and like normal, I can't tell what he's thinking, completely unsure of what's running through his head. When I almost give up hope he's going to take my help, he reaches out and grabs my hand. "I'm so cold, I feel awful, and all I want is a shower."

Given the way he's swaying without the support of the wall, I know he's telling me because he's going to need my help. I swallow roughly against the dryness that's crept into my throat. "If that's what you want, then I'll help you get it, but first we need to take your temperature and get some medicine in you. It's probably from when you stood out in that cold rain today without a hat on."

He says nothing as I pull him toward the island in the kitchen. "Where's your thermometer?"

He leans heavily against the granite countertop, crossing his arms over his broad chest. He coughs slightly, grimacing, before pointing up to a cabinet. "Anything for sickness is up there."

In the time I've lived here, I can't believe I didn't know that. Neither one of us has been sick, so I guess it makes sense, but it also makes me wonder what else I don't know about my home, about my husband. As I'm fumbling through the basket of medicine, looking for the thermometer, I realize I want to know everything. I'm not content with the way we've been going anymore. After talking with Violet and getting a small taste of the intense man last night, I want more – I want it all.

At the same time, I know I'm going to have to initiate it. And given the opportunity, I will, I'll initiate until we're naked in our bed with our bodies rubbing together. I suck a breath in, amazed at the thoughts running through my head. But I know immediately this is what I want, it's what I've *wanted* and today gave me the courage to go after it. But first, I need to take care of my man.

Thermometer finally in hand, I turn to face him. "Open your mouth and hold it under your tongue."

He opens his mouth and lets me press the plastic instrument in there, holding it with his hand.

"Have you been feeling bad since this afternoon?" I ask, knowing he can't answer me because he's got his mouth full.

He shakes his head and mumbles something around the stem of the thermometer. "Since you left to come home?" I ask, almost positive that's what he said.

A nod this time. The thermometer beeps and he removes it from his mouth, handing it to me. "Hit me like a ton of bricks as I left the station."

I glance at the digital readout and whistle between my teeth. "One hundred and two. Did you get a flu shot?" I glance at him with an eyebrow raised.

"It's required of everyone in the department."

Hopefully the flu shot is still working then, but I have a feeling the next few days aren't going to be fun. "Well let's get some medicine in you, and then we'll see about getting you a shower."

The fact he doesn't protest speaks volumes to just how badly he feels. A few minutes later, I've gotten him to swallow down a fever reducer, a pain reliever, and a few sips of orange juice as we make our way toward the bathroom.

"You don't have to do this," he says over his shoulder.

"I don't, but I can't let you possibly fall and hurt yourself either. We're adults; we can handle seeing each other's naked bodies."

At least I hope we can.

CHAPTER FIFTEEN

Havoc

I'M CALLING myself a ton of words, none of them good, as I all but agree to her plan. I'm not disagreeing, but maybe that's worse. If I were disagreeing, at least I would be putting up a fight and not just letting this happen. I've wanted her for too long, and I'm starting to lose the fight.

Fact of the matter is though, I feel awful, and if the only way she's going to let me take a shower is with her, then I'll do what needs to be done. I'm sore, tired, achy, and perpetually horny. Any one of those things would be enough to put someone in a bad mood, but all of them at once? Shit, I'm gonna need the patience of a saint.

Another cough rattles my chest, pulling against the not-yet-healed bruised tissue. It might be time to face the music and admit that I'm sick. Sick isn't a word I have in my vocabulary – I don't have time for that. But when it happens, it's awful and it takes the wind out of all my sails. I don't suffer from man flu like some of my friends do; when I'm sick, it's bad. And this right here? Feels *really fucking* bad.

"Are you okay?" Leighton asks as she puts an arm around my waist.

Apparently I stumbled. Knowing she won't be able to handle my weight on her own, I put the palm of my hand against the wall and do my best to help her. I'm not used to being an invalid, and this fucking sucks.

"I'm fine." I try to nod, but the room swims in my vision.

"Holden, you're shivering, are you sure you want a shower? Do you want to lie down instead?"

"Shower," I croak out. I want it so bad, because I know the warm water will feel amazing on my aching body. "Need to." My teeth chatter as she helps me into the bathroom.

As we enter the room, she points to the toilet, and I gratefully sink onto the closed lid. Leaning forward, I put my elbows on my knees, and close my eyes. The room spins and I feel hungover. Fuck, I haven't felt hungover in at least the last two years. I've been a damn boy scout, doing what I'm supposed to do, taking care of my guys, and living the life of a monk. My mind wanders, and I wish like hell I didn't take responsibility so seriously. If I didn't, I wouldn't be carrying around this second ache in my pants. With my eyes closed, my hearing overcompensates. Leighton is moving around, cranking the water on. Hot because I can feel the steam starting to come from the shower. That's when the nightmare really starts. She's now taking her clothes off, and even in the state I'm in, I notice the sound her shirt makes as it goes over her head.

"Stand up, Holden." She places her hands under my underarms and helps me stand. "Let's get these clothes off you," she mumbles pushing her hands underneath my shirt. I can feel her palms against my skin, her touch warm and caressing, against my aching muscles.

With quick efficiency, she strips me, and I'm standing naked in front of her. Finally, I barely open my eyes, inhaling deeply when I see she's as naked as I am. My eyes travel from her feet, straight up to the top of her head, and then I go back to her face. It's pink, with either embarrassment or the heat from the shower. I'm not sure which. I close my eyes and let my head tilt to the side on my neck. When I lift my lids, I can't help but stare openly at her chest. There's a little more than a handful there, the tips tight against the cool air in the shower, and they look like they're swelling for my touch.

"You're gorgeous." The words slip from my lips before I can stop them.

She laughs softly, ducking her head. "You're feverish."

I lick my dry lips and lean in, grasping her hips with my hands. "Maybe for the first time with you, I'm being one-hundred percent honest."

Leighton

Dear God, why does a sick and feverish Holden have to be so damn irresistible? His eyes are glassy, his face is flushed, and I've watched him stumble his way to the bathroom with my arms wrapped around his waist. I know he's not faking the sickness, but who's to say he realizes what he's saying right now.

Even as I touch his skin, it's burning up. He's definitely spiked a high fever, and I'm waiting for the spray from the shower to cool down a bit. I don't want to shock his system, lukewarm will hopefully bring his core temperature down. Instead, as I glance over his naked body, mine's heating up.

"C'mon, Holden." I lead us into the shower, turning him around so that the water is flowing over his neck and back muscles. I watch as he lifts his face up, tilting his head back, letting it wash over him. Rivulets of water snake down his head, past the short beard, making a track through the dark ink on his chest, to where I can't see anymore. "You okay?" I grab his shoulders, holding on tight.

He sways slightly as he brings his head back forward, regarding me with those dark eyes. "I hurt so bad," he admits, rolling his head around on his neck. He wipes a hand over his face to remove some of the water. "I feel like shit."

Bringing him in for a hug, because that's what I need most in this world when I feel like shit, I bury his face in my neck. We haven't ever been this vulnerable with one another, and I let my hands travel over the buzzcut on his head, before moving down to grasp his shoulder with one hand, his waist with the other. After what I think is an eternity, he lets his body relax and wraps his arms around my waist. Closing my eyes, I let myself enjoy the complete satisfaction I get from the two of us being wrapped up in one another.

"You smell good," I mumble against his shoulder, kissing the wet skin on a whim. Every inch of our bodies is touching, and I would give my life to push us toward the bedroom right now, let him lay me down, and have his way with me. Holden is all man and would show me what I've been missing in that department, I'm sure.

He grunts deep in his throat, the sound made even more manly by the scratchiness I heard there earlier. "You always smell fucking delectable. I don't know what it is you wear, but I smell that shit in my dreams at night."

Those words please me to no end, and when he turns his head further into my neck, dropping a kiss, the same way I did, I'm done for. I want to do a fist pump, give a shout, and maybe dance a jig. But I can't, I can't let Holden know how much he affects me, how often I daydream about us being truly together and where our future may take us. Right now though, I can enjoy the hell out of this.

Tilting my head to the side to give him better access, I bite my bottom lip, releasing a pleased moan, as he uses his tongue along my jawline before he dips down and takes a nip at my flesh. "Havoc," I breathe out, unsure of why I choose this moment to use his call sign.

"What'd you say?" He stops, grasping my chin between his thumb and forefinger, leveling our gazes at one another. His eyes burn hot, darker than I've ever seen them before. Arousal rides high on his cheeks, and I wonder if I've done something good or bad.

"I called you Havoc, I'm sorry." Why I'm apologizing I'm not sure, but I feel like I need to. He stares at me for an eternity before he shakes his head.

"No, don't apologize. I've never heard a woman say that name before. At least not in that breathy, aroused voice you just used." He takes my hand in his and lazily moves it down to what I've been trying to ignore. "Can't you feel how hard it got me?"

It did get him hard, and that's a good thing to know in the back of my mind. He moans as I grasp him in my hand, using my fingers to caress the hard length. "We shouldn't be doing this," I whisper in his ear before I take the lobe in between my teeth, running my tongue along the diamond earring he wears. I can't seem to help myself. Now that I've started, I don't ever want to stop. The ring he wears on his left hand gives me rights, ones I've never used before, and even as I'm saying we shouldn't, I fucking really want to.

"Why?" he uses his weight to push me back against the tile, to hold me while he moves one hand up to the curve of my breast, then sneaks his thumb to the peak of my nipple. He's not pressing hard though, I know what it's like to be crushed to this man. The way he's moving me around is almost tender. "Why shouldn't we do this?" His voice is strained, deep, and needy. I'm sure mine sounds the same way. My body is humming, skin tight from where he's been touching me, and I want nothing more than to try out the shower sex that I've heard people talking about, but my conscious is telling my body to slow down.

He teeters again, and I drop his cock to help him get his balance. "That's exactly why – you're sick."

"Not dead." He shoves his mouth into my neck again, having already figured out that's an extremely erogenous zone for me. "Maybe not in tiptop shape."

I forcibly remove his mouth from my neck, meeting his eyes with mine. "Maybe I want you in tiptop shape, and maybe I want to make sure you aren't going to pass out on me."

"Trust me; I've wanted you long enough not to pass out. At night I lie in bed thinking about this, wondering how long we're going to be able to hold back from one another. It's so thick between us; you can cut it with a knife. These feelings aren't going anywhere, Leigh."

Suddenly, I feel like I've stepped into another dimension. I'm not sure how we got from where we were this afternoon to here. Part of me knows it's mutual sexual attraction between us, the other part of me wonders if we're just sick of fighting it. Lord, I've been fighting it for so long, and I don't want to give in, just to have our relationship be over. "No they aren't, and if that's the case, I think we should finish the shower and get you in bed."

And those are the hardest words I've ever spoken in my life. *Please don't pull away from me*, I beg in my head. I like this Holden, like that he's willing to show me a part of himself he never has before. Sitting with him in the booth earlier today and being with him tonight have made this whole situation I've been thrown into almost worth it.

He clears his throat. "Maybe you're right."

The coldness I feel when he leaves me is like the frigid temperature of Antarctica, and this time my teeth begin to chatter. Gone is the warm fuzzy feeling I'd had a few minutes ago, and in its place is the coolness I've felt most of my life. I know he doesn't mean it, but it's like we've thrown ice-cold water on one another.

Without any of the playfulness we'd had minutes ago, we finish the shower, and I help him dry off and get dressed. In the end, his eyes are droopy and I know it was for the best that I called off whatever was going to happen between us. He's done for, and I think we both know it.

"Are you going to lie down with me?" he asks quietly as we walk into the bedroom we've shared since I moved in. Tonight, I'm wondering how in the hell we've kept our hands off one another every night. How have we been so successful in avoiding the way both of us feel? What changed? Maybe that's the question I should be asking. What the hell changed? Why do I feel so close to him tonight?

"Do you want me to?"

I don't want to pressure him, especially after what happened in the bathroom. Neither one of us needs the temptation or honestly the frustration.

"I hate being alone when I'm sick," he admits.

"Which is totally different from how you are all the rest of the time." I wink.

"It's true, normally I love my alone time. I've always been a bit of a loner, but when I'm sick," he shakes his head as if to say *I am who I am*, "I like to have company."

"Then you'll have company, just let me go make sure everything is turned off and the doors are locked."

I quickly pad back into the living room, make sure everything is taken care of, and get back to him for the night. At the doorway to our bedroom, I stop quickly. He's lying on the bed, propped up by some pillows, looking so much like a little kid. Holden barely lets his guard down with anyone, and right now there is nothing in between us. I'll hold onto this memory forever. It doesn't take me long to get ready and hop in next to him.

"It's your turn to the pick the movie," he tells me as I come back into the room. He's already got the TV on, Netflix queued up on the screen.

"You sure? You're sick, maybe I should let you pick it."

"I can almost guarantee I'll be out before this movie is an hour in. You pick what you want."

On impulse, I pick a love story. One I've seen a million times. "I always wanted someone to dance with me like this." I snuggle in next to him, allowing him to wrap me in his arms.

As he watches Patrick Swayze shake his hips on the screen, he snorts. "I'm not your dance partner if that's the kind of dancing you want."

"We could take lessons," I suggest, turning my face so that ours are inches apart in the darkness of the room. Only the TV lights the way for us to see one another.

"You want me to take dance lessons with you?"

"I'm sure they offer them in Birmingham." I'm quick to make a suggestion. The confession had been uttered before I realized what I was saying, and then the invitation to take lessons hadn't been thought through either.

We're quiet for a long time, and I wonder if he's not even going to give me an answer. Maybe this is the time I've overstepped my boundaries and I've asked too much of him.

"Does it mean something to you?" His question is whispered in the relative silence of the room.

I shrug. "Just something I always wanted to do."

I'm downplaying it, and I think he knows.

"Leigh, if we want this to work, you have to be honest with me. There's no other way we can make it if you're not."

He's already done so much for me, I hate to lay this on him as well, but I brought it up, and he's asking, so I'm going to give him the whole spiel. Doesn't matter in the end anyway, because I don't know if this marriage is forever or not anyway.

"When I was ten, I saw that movie for the first time."

He interrupts me. "Are you shitting me? That's a sexual movie for a ten-year-old."

"Remember what family I come from." I raise an eyebrow and he motions for me to continue. "From that point on, I had it in my head that on my wedding day, my husband and I would do a portion of that last dance, including the lift," I laugh as I say it now. "Never in my life have I trusted anyone to hold me up like that, and without a doubt, I knew even then that the man I married would have my trust. I'd trust him enough not to drop me, for me to let go, and spread my wings as far as I could."

I stop, biting my lip, not going any further. I glance at him, giving him a tilt of my mouth. "Stupid, huh?"

"Not stupid." He grabs my hand in his. "Am I the man to have that trust?" His brown eyes search mine, looking for something I'm not sure I'm ready to give.

"It doesn't matter why we got married, Holden," I whisper, because it's the only way I can get through this. I'm about to lay some truth out, and hope he hears it loud and clear. "I wouldn't have married you if I didn't trust you."

He makes a sound in his throat, one I'm not sure of what origin, but I squeal happily as he pulls me into his chest. "Thank you for that gift."

"Thank you for keeping me safe."

As we're both drifting off, I can feel him push my hair back from my forehead, and in that hoarse voice I can hear him speak. "If keeping you safe is the only reason you think I married you, Leigh, you aren't lookin' hard enough at what I'm trying to show you."

CHAPTER SIXTEEN

Leighton

"NO! GET BACK FROM THE WALL!"

I'm having the weirdest dream. Holden is telling me to get back from some wall, and screaming at me to take cover. I feel a huge weight on top of me, strangling the breath out of my lungs. My eyes pop open and I realize quickly I'm not having the dream, Holden is.

It's a nightmare. He's on top of me, his hands on my head, protecting me from some unknown flying object he's seeing in his dream. I try to get up.

"Stay the fuck down, we don't know when they'll come back around. We've got to radio in and let them know we're under attack."

"We're good, Havoc." I purposely use his call sign. "We're good." I grab hold of his hand. "They won't be coming back around tonight."

He opens his eyes, but he's not seeing me. They aren't focused, and he's not locked in on my face. "How do you know?" There's a tremor in his voice, and his face is pale, white with the flush of fever and fear.

This man needs me, and by God, I'm going to be the person he needs. He's always there for me, has made a ton of sacrifices since he invited me into his home. If I can sacrifice sleep one night for him, I'll do it. "Because they're out of fuel," I make something up off the top of my head.

"Makes sense." He nods. "That tanker never made it here. No tellin' how much they had and now how much they have. Think we're good to go?"

"Yeah." I grab his hands, pulling him closer to me. "But first, I think we need to rest, you've had a rough day."

"I'm so tired," he admits, resting his head against my chest. "So damn tired."

Wrapping my arms around his body, I hold him to me, running my hand over the fade he still keeps. I shush him and quietly hum until I can feel his body relax and can hear the heavy breathing of someone in a deep sleep.

It's only then, that I allow myself to go to sleep too.

WHEN I WAKE UP AGAIN, it's later than I anticipated, judging from the way the sun is shining through the window. Reaching over, I grab my cell, squinting to read that it's almost nine-thirty in the morning. *Shit!* Both Holden and I are late for work.

Taking stock of everything going on, I close my eyes for a moment. Holden isn't radiating as much heat off his body as he was last night. I let my hand lightly rest on his forearm and breathe easier at the clammy feel of his skin. Sometime over the night, he broke his fever. He still shouldn't be at work today, and he shouldn't be alone, either. Tiptoeing over to his side of the bed, I swipe his phone and quietly make my way out of the bedroom, shutting the door, and down the hallway.

I have five missed calls on mine, all from Ernie and Violet, along with a text message from Caleb trying to reach me for his dad. Quickly re-dialing the last number that called me, I wait impatiently while the number rings.

"The Café, Ernie speaking, and this damn well better be Leighton."

"Hi." I run a hand through my hair, nervous at the gruff tone of his voice. "It's me."

"Girl, I have been scared to death. No one's heard from you and Holden today. Some of the MTF left here for your house about ten minutes ago; we've all been worried sick."

It never occurred to me that people would worry about me. No one did when I was just a Strather. "I'm so sorry," I apologize. "Holden was sick last night, running a high temperature and we had a rough night. Neither one of us set our alarms when we went to sleep, and I just now woke up. He's still asleep, but I think he broke his fever," I explain quickly. "I can be there as soon as I get him settled," I offer, not wanting to upset Ernie any further because he's been so good to me.

"No need, honey, and I'm sorry if I was rough earlier. We were afraid something happened with your family." His voice is quieter now, like he's keeping that between the two of us.

"We're fine as far as that goes," I reassure him. "I just hope y'all aren't too busy."

He chuckles. "You must not have even looked outside yet. We got ice all over everything. Not many people are getting out of their beds to go anywhere, but I was still worried when I didn't hear from you. School's closed and Caleb got dropped off before his Dad went out to help."

"Ice?" I can't remember the last time it got cold enough for ice to form or for it to snow for that matter. Maybe when I was in middle school?

"Yeah, damn miracle. Should melt today though, as it warms. Everybody says it'll get up into the forties."

I have to cut him off, Ernie will talk forever. "Okay, thanks, I'll plan on being at work tomorrow."

"Even if you're not, honey, just call me and let me know. Don't make an old man worry."

I smile, despite myself. "I won't, I promise."

After we hang up, I grab Holden's phone and swipe my finger across the bottom. Chances are it's locked, but if it isn't, hopefully I'll be able to cut the guys off at the pass before they make it all the way out here. I'm not surprised when there's a pass code. On impulse, I pick our wedding date, which he knows I would know. The phone unlocks, and a warmth spreads across my chest and through my stomach. Maybe there's a trust between us I don't realize, and it makes me smile.

Sifting through his contacts, I find one that I'm somewhat familiar with. Ryan. Clicking the button, I walk over to the kitchen window and push back the curtain. The coolness coming through the pane takes my breath away as I see the ice glistening off the trees around the house. They hang low, brushing the power lines, making me hope they don't break, and cause a power outage.

"Havoc, we've been worried sick about you and Leighton. We're on our way."

He doesn't even say *hi* as he answers, causing me to have to wait until he's done before I can speak.

"This is Leighton," I explain, hoping they believe me. "Holden's really sick, he ran a fever all night last night – still has a small one this morning. We both overslept and I had no idea about the ice storm," I finish in a quick breath.

"But the two of you are okay?"

I nod before realizing he can't see me. "We're fine, I promise."

There are voices in the background before he comes back to the phone. "We're ten minutes out, tops. We'll come salt the porch and make sure there's nothing on the power lines, since we've already come this far."

Immediately my stomach drops and tears come to my eyes. I'm used to not being believed, and it hurts to know these guys don't believe me. After all I'm the daughter of a criminal. "Okay." My voice is soft, wounded, scared to even my own ears.

"Hey, I believe you." Ryan seems to be able to understand what I'm feeling. "Nobody blames you for your family, Leighton; we just want to make sure the two of you are okay and taken care of. It's kinda what we do."

Furiously, I scrub at the tears leaking from my eyes. Why I let my doubts get to me, I can't explain and I hate it. Hate it almost as much as I hate the stock I came from, but it's another thing I can't seem to be able to change.

"See you in a few minutes."

C'mon Leighton, it's time to get it together. But I'm cold, and I don't know how to light this gas heat. A part of me wants to wake Holden up, but the other part wants to be able to figure out this problem on my own, or maybe ask the guys when they get here. Quickly, I quietly go back to the bedroom, put on a pair of sweatpants, boots, and grab a huge hoodie of Holden's.

As I walk out onto the porch, a truck carrying Ryan, Trevor, and Caleb are headed my way. I at least had the presence of mind to put my hair up; I don't look like a complete homeless person. "Hi," I greet them, still embarrassed with the way I acted on the phone.

"Hey," Ryan waves a hand at me. "We're not here to judge, promise." He gives me a small smile.

"I know, and I'm sorry."

He grabs a bag of salt from the back of the truck and walks toward me. When he gets close enough, he drops his head and voice enough so only the two of us can hear. "My parents weren't the best in the world, Leighton, and I know what it's like to carry that shit around with you. But if there's anything I've learned in the last couple of years, being a part of this team, it's that where you come from doesn't mean shit. It's your heart and how you act." He stops, giving me another smile, probably the one that got him into Whitney's bed. "Your heart is amazing, I hear about how you make time for Stella when Whitney has meetings at The Café, and you've been nothing but nice to the rest of us. You don't ever have to worry we think you have ulterior motives, because that's so not the case." He nods to Trevor and Caleb, who are inspecting a low-lying branch. "We deeply respect Holden, and he'd be out here doing this for us if the shoe were on the other foot. Now just let us help, and then we'll be on our way."

I step back. "Got it, let you help," I laugh. "More than anything, it's freezing in the house and I'm not sure how to work the gas logs," I admit.

"You're in luck, Tank has those same logs at his house. Tank!" he yells across the driveway, "you need to show her how to start those logs, they don't have heat right now."

He flashes a thumbs up at his friend, looks like he gives Caleb some instructions before he carefully makes his way across the gravel. "Same one as my house, right?" His breath flashes white in the cold air, crystals forming on his beard as he questions Ryan.

"Exact same."

Trevor looks at me, and I'm slightly mesmerized by his gaze. Are all these guys so damn good looking?

"Alright then, let's go." He turns back, lifting his eyebrows in my direction. "Let's get the house warm, then we'll work on the outside."

"O-O-kay," I stumble over my answer. I've never really been alone with these guys before, and obviously I don't know how to speak any longer.

As we climb the steps of the porch, he lets me step in front of him to open the door. "You know I don't bite," he teases, coming inside and taking his gloves off.

"I know." I blow out a breath. "I'm just never sure how to act with you, how to talk to you. I feel so damn guilty about what happened to you," I explain, for the first time opening up to Trevor. Usually I make sure we never even have to speak to one another.

"What your brother did, isn't what you did, Leighton. Holden wouldn't have married you if he thought you were anything like your family. I can't speak for what your marriage is like behind closed doors, but Holden seems happy, and that's all any of us care about."

Speechlessness doesn't happen to me very often, but it happens right now. "Thank you," I whisper because it's all I can say, all I can do.

"Let me show you how to light this thing so we can get it warm in here."

I nod, watching as he squats next to the logs and proceeds to show me what to do. I'm thankful for his patience and his instruction when I feel the warmth start flowing through the house.

"Alright, let's go see if the other two need some help."

Less than an hour later, all of them are loading back up in the truck, waving as they pull away from the house. I wave back, before I re-enter the house, surprised to see Holden standing in the hallway, a blanket wrapped around his body. I cross my arms over myself as his eyes travel up and down the length of me. Our eyes meet across the room, the air getting sucked out of the space. I wait, wondering what he'll say to me. Wondering what in the hell he remembers from last night.

His voice, when he finally speaks is deep, scratchy, and washes over me like warm whiskey. "You look even better in my clothes this morning."

Heat warms my cheeks as I take in what he's said. It's not at all what I expected, but it feels better than anything he's ever said to me before.

CHAPTER SEVENTEEN

Havoc

"YOU LOOK EVEN BETTER in my clothes this morning."

Lame. The words I spoke were so lame. Usually I'm much smoother than this. When I woke up, I'd been disoriented, wondering why I was still in bed with it being so light outside. Then bits and pieces of the night before had come back to me, and then I'd made the mistake of trying to swallow and almost come off the bed. Right now, it feels as if there are shards of glass working their way out of my throat and tonsils. Leaning against the wall, I cross my arms over my t-shirt covered chest, surprised at how warm it is in here.

"Sorry." She ducks her head. "It's cold out there, and I've been helping Ryan salt the porch."

"Renegade?" I'm more confused than ever. How fucking long was I out for? And why in God's name are they salting the front porch?

She nods. "Yeah," she replies, before she reaches down to take her boots off. "Why don't you come to the kitchen and I'll fix you something to eat? We need to get some more medicine in you and you need something in your stomach."

"My throat is killing me," I admit.

"You were running a fever last night." She walks over to me, stands on her tiptoes, and puts her palm against my forehead. "You're still a little warm. How are you feeling? Did you sleep okay after you woke up?"

"I woke up? I don't remember, why do you ask?" Something in her tone and the lack of eye contact makes me wonder what the hell I did.

"You had a nightmare," she admits quietly.

I capture her hand in mine as she tries to pull away. "The nightmares sometimes happen when I'm sick. They aren't of one incident that happened while I was over there, it all melds together. When I've worn myself out and I've had some stressful situations going on, they happen. I'm sorry you had to see it. You take care of me?"

She grins. "As much as you let anyone take care of you. You were a little out of it last night, though. You needed someone to take care of you."

Rolling her hand around in mine, I finish so that she's palm up and I'm tracing the lines with the tip of my finger. Maybe it's the fever, maybe it's the fact she looks so damn cute and sexy in my shirt, or hell – maybe it's been building for a while, but I can't stop the words from coming out of my mouth. "I like it when you take care of me."

Her eyes meet mine, before they pull away and she bites her bottom lip, looking pensive and unsure. "I like taking care of you," she reaches up, hugging me around the neck, "and I like when you, in turn, take care of me."

A slow smile spreads across my face, as I push her slightly away from my body. I'm still not feeling great and I don't want her to get sick, but I also don't want her too far away from me. "Why don't we go to the kitchen where we can find something we can both eat, and you tell me why in the hell Ryan and the guys were here?"

She looks pleased at what I've suggested and I want to reach around, pat myself on the back. There's been so little for her to be happy about, and for me to put a smile on her face? Right now it kinda means everything to me.

No woman has ever taken care of me, except my mom. There's never been anyone in my life who stuck around that long, lived with me, or worried when I had a fever. The one woman I'd thought would, left me while I was in a war zone a million miles away. Knowing that Leighton stayed with me last night, obviously stayed with me this morning, does things to me that I don't want to investigate too closely.

She motions for me to have a seat at the counter while she grabs stuff to cook and medicine for me. Opening the kitchen curtain wider, she points outside. "This is why they came over. Well that, and the fact no one could get hold of either of us. Apparently Ernie had already gotten himself into a tizzy, thinking my family had gotten to us."

I shake my head. "Well if this doesn't prove to you that you have made friends that care about you, regardless of what your family has done, Leigh, I don't know what will. Ernie was worried, and he got people to come check on us."

The way she pulls her bottom lip between her teeth and holds it there, makes me wonder if she's going to cry. "It was very nice of them." She forces out in a tone that tells me she might cry.

"Don't let that make you cry, they care about you."

She turns around to look at me, truth in her eyes. I get the feeling she doesn't want to say exactly what she's thinking, but silently I encourage her. I want to know everything that goes on behind her eyes, in her head, that she keeps to herself. "It's been a long time since anybody's cared about me."

Right now, it's time for me to man up. This woman has been my wife for months, and she doesn't think anybody cares for her. Fuck the sickness, fuck the scratchy throat, and fuck self-preservation. Maybe I've been holding back, but over the last twenty-four hours she's shown me how much I mean to her, and I can't let it go unnoticed. "I care about you, Leigh. Please know, I care a whole hell of a lot about you. I'm beginning to think I haven't been good in showing you that."

"That goes both ways, tough guy."

Shuffling over to where she stands, I circle my hands around her waist, bend with my knees, and put her on the counter. When she spreads her knees, I step in between them. Turning my head, I cough, while she giggles. "Romantic, huh?"

She shrugs. "Everything with us has happened in such an odd way, Holden, that I figure it's all going to be ass-backward. Besides, I'm glad to hear you coughing after the way you were wheezing last night. We still need to get you some medicine."

Making a move to jump down and grab me that medicine, causes me to put my hands on her knees, tightening the grip. "Medicine can wait." I reach up, caressing her jawline with the palms of my hands. "I care about you, I care so much about you, and I'm willing to do whatever it takes to protect you."

"Protection and love are two different things," she whispers, and I can finally see her dilemma. She wants to be loved. Don't we all?

"Love comes naturally, and in its own time, Leigh. Like you said, we've done things completely ass-backward. I've never loved anyone besides my family before, but I can say with certainty I love my brothers in the MTF. I know without a shadow of a doubt I care very deeply for you." She blows out a breath. "Probably shouldn't even admit to that. We don't know where we're going with this, do we?"

"No," she loops her arms around my neck, "we don't, but I know where we've been. And we're light years away from where we started. Whether we want to admit it or not, Holden, I think we're both in a bit deeper than we ever meant to be."

"I think you're right about that, so from this moment on, I want you to know something." I lean in, so that our foreheads are touching and brace myself for being one hundred percent, totally honest. "When I married you, it was for real, it was for life, and I didn't plan on it being anything different. Maybe it's time I start treating you like my wife."

Her deep inhale of breath gets me, because I'm unsure what it means. "I've always been the kind of woman who only wanted to be married once," she admits softly.

My mouth hitches up in a smile. "Then I think we do know where we're going. We just have to let life take us there, and not impede what's happening naturally. No one is here to judge us, because no one lives our lives but us, Leigh. We don't have to answer to anyone except God and each other."

"Okay." She leans in, kissing me on the cheek.

"Okay?" I tilt her head up so that I can see her eyes. So she can look straight into mine as she speaks. "I wanna act how I want to act with you; I don't want to temper my words, touches, or actions. Whatever happens from this moment forward, know I do it because I want to, not because I feel fucking obligated by a piece of paper and a ring on your finger."

"Same here." She tightens her legs around my waist. "I've wanted to do this for a really long time, the cold you have be damned."

And I'm speechless as she pulls me tighter into the circle of her legs, grabs my shirt and hauls me up to her mouth. She kisses me like she did that night in the bar – there is no shyness, no trying to pretend like she doesn't enjoy it. All I can feel and taste are want and the sweetness of her. Her tongue tangles with mine and I feel a tickle in my throat as I pull away. "Gotta cough."

She laughs as I turn away from her. "Let me get you some medicine, for real this time. I'm not doing it because I want to avoid a conversation. You really need it."

I don't fight or argue with her as she goes about pouring me some orange juice and putting some pills on the counter. "It's going to take a while for everything to defrost. How about we stay here? Curled up on the couch?"

I hope like hell she says yes.

"Sounds like a damn good idea to me. Let me fix us some food, then you and I have a date with some Netflix, the couch, and a blanket. Naps today are going to be a priority."

Nothing in the world has ever sounded so good to me.

CHAPTER EIGHTEEN

Leighton

AFTER HOLDEN GOT SICK, things changed between us. I count myself lucky to have not gotten whatever it was he had. I smile to myself as I think how the past few weeks have gone. I've stopped hiding behind the fear I had he was going to leave when things seemed to straighten out for me, and I think he's starting to smile more. One thing I do know is we're starting to touch more, becoming comfortable with each other in a way we've never been before.

Take now, for instance. We're on separate shifts for the next few days, and have been for the last couple. I'm getting up as he's entering the part of sleep where he's the deepest, and he's not even at home at night when I'm going to sleep. I've started something this week though, that's totally making me go to work with a smile on my face every morning.

A couple of days ago, when I woke up, Holden reached his hand out to me, clasping our fingers together, pulling me to him in his sleep. At first, I assumed he was awake, but I realized when I looked at him and his eyes were closed, eyelashes brushing those freckled cheeks, that he was gone to the world. Because he pulled me so hard, I ended up straddling his waist, and I couldn't help but to lean down and nuzzle against him. He rearranged his body, and took hold of my hips so that I sat more comfortably, and then turned his head so that we could kiss. And when I say kiss, I mean there was tongue involved, and I trailed a path to his neck, where he opened up to me so I could get a few licks in.

Then as quickly as it happened, it ended, and he tapped me on the ass before sending me on my way. After I got up and wondered if I'd imagined the small moment we had together, he smirked in his sleep, and then turned over, grabbing hold of my pillow.

Since then, it's been a ritual. One I'm absolutely loving.

WEEKEND BREAKFAST RUSH is over and lunch rush is still an hour or so from getting started, as I glance around The Café and see that all the work I need to do is done. "I'm gonna go over there and get some work done," I tell Violet as I nod to the booth in the back.

"Go for it, if someone comes in, I got them."

She doesn't say it, but I can hear the unspoken *I could definitely use the money*. I wonder what she's doing with all the money she makes here. I've seen the trailer she and her husband live in. Only once, though, when I went to pick her up so she wouldn't be late. I wouldn't say it's the worst place I've ever seen, but it's not the best, and for the life of me, I can't imagine her living there. It's not a subject I'm willing to broach with her, because every time I mention her husband, she clams up.

"I'm going to run this down to the station." Caleb holds up a pie. "Ernie said he hasn't sent one down lately, and I wanna see my dad. You want me to tell Holden anything for you?"

"No." I grin at the kid. "He's on nights this week. He's at home asleep right now."

"That must suck." Caleb looks like he sucked on something sour. "I mean I know it sucks when I can't see my dad all the time, so when you're as close as a married couple, that must be hard."

"Just wait until you've been married for years, kid." Violet shoots him a wink. "You'll be wishing you got some time to yourself every once and a while."

Caleb wisely decides not to comment before he heads out the door. While my laptop boots up, I take a good look at Violet. "How old are you?" I ask before I can stop it. Sometimes I think we're close to the same age, other days I think she's way older than me. It seems to depend on how she and her husband are getting along.

"Twenty-eight," she sighs as she has a seat at the table across from the booth I'm sitting in. "Somedays I feel like I'm ninety."

It's on the tip of my tongue to ask her why, but just as I'm about to try and have the conversation I've wanted to have with her for a while, the door opens and in walk two women. When I see it's Whitney and Blaze, along with Stella, I throw them a grin and a wave.

"Hey!" I smile when Stella's feet kick as she recognizes me.

"Leigh!"

It warms my heart when this little girl says my name. Never in my life have I thought I was maternal, probably because I had no basis for it, but this little girl? With her dark hair turning blonde and her complexion reminiscent of her dad, she makes me want things I've never wanted before.

"You mind if we join you?" Whitney asks as they approach my booth.

Even though I've just spread my stuff out and booted up my laptop, I make room for them. I've never been one to have many friends, so the fact these women have invited me into their circle will never be lost on me. "What are you three out doing?"

Whitney grins as she elbows Blaze. "Blaze needs some hardware, so she asked us to come with her."

"Hardware?" I'm so confused.

Blaze is blushing a color as red as the hair on her head, shushing Whitney. She busies herself handing Stella a piece of paper and some crayons we have sitting on the tables for kids, focusing all her attention on the little girl, who's perfectly happy and content to be coloring.

"Nobody is even in here, Blaze. C'mon, she's our friend, you can tell her what happened. Stop using my daughter to deflect the focus from you."

Blaze shoots a glare at Whitney. "I never should have told you. I wouldn't have if I'd known you'd hold it over my head," she grumbles, before she turns to me. "I need hardware to fix the bed. Trevor and I broke the bed."

I giggle loudly, holding my hand in front of my mouth. "You did *what*?! I knew Trevor was intense, but..." my shoulders shake as I watch the woman in front of me. She looks like she could let this booth engulf her and not let her go until we're gone and have forgotten about the info I've just learned.

She clears her throat, a smile playing across her lips. "He's definitely," she licks her lips and lets the smile loose, "intense, but I never thought that would happen. It's been making a noise, it's metal, and we didn't think anything about it."

Whitney snorts. "Until she ended up being pitched into the wall and sporting a knot on the head, if you know where to look. The best part is what Trevor said to her when the bed broke, even if he is my brother."

"What did he say?" I can't help but ask.

Blaze obviously isn't going to answer, but Whitney does instead. "He smacked her ass, told her to get on all fours on the floor because they were going to finish now and worry about the bed later."

We're howling like teenage girls at a slumber party.

"Would you *stahp*???" Blaze draws the word out, putting her face in her hands, but winces.

When she pulls back, I can see a darkening bruise on her forehead. "Oh my word, you did hit the wall." I get up and walk over to the counter, grabbing a piece of pie before I come back over to my friends. "I think we deserve a piece of pie to commemorate this situation."

Whitney grabs her fork, and holds it up as a salute, a saucy smile on her face. "We do, but I also think, Leighton, that you and I need to make it our duties as of today to also break our own beds."

I choke on what I have in my mouth. How do I even tell them that Holden and I haven't done the deed yet? And it's been bothering me, to be honest, but I have no one to talk to about it. I finally get the piece of pie down, and take a long drink of the water I have sitting in front of me. They look at me, wondering what the hell just happened, and I wonder if I should tell them. I've never before had women to talk to. Deciding to rip it off like a band aid, I blurt out. "Holden and I have never had sex."

Both of them stop what they're doing, and it's actually pretty comical. The forks come to a stop half-way to their mouths and they glance at one another, and then at me, with eyebrows raised.

"I'm sorry," Whitney sets the fork down on her plate, "you're living with that hot specimen of man and you haven't sampled the goods yet?"

Both Blaze and I give her an incredulous look.

"What? It's not like I don't notice other hot guys. Just because I'm with Ryan and he's like sex on a stick doesn't mean I can't appreciate other men who are also good looking. And Leighton, baby doll, he's good looking."

Blaze agrees. "Yeah, if I hadn't met Trevor first, Holden would totally be my type of guy. Dark eyes, dark looks, tattoos and muscles for fucking days..." she trails off. "What?" She glances at us. "I'm making a point for *her*." She gestures at me. "Wait," Blaze stops and tilts her head, "I know what I saw in the back of that ambulance the day he came to get you. You mean to tell me you've never done the deed, because the chemistry was flowing off the two of you that day? I thought you'd been lovers for a while," she admits.

I'm uncomfortable under this scrutiny, so when Stella reaches for me, I allow her to come into my lap, holding her in front of me like a shield. "No, we're very attracted to one another, and we've done all the other stuff, but we've never sealed the deal, so to speak."

"Oh but the other stuff can be *so good*." Whitney flashes me a wink. "Sometimes the other stuff means more, ya know? Like he takes the time to make sure you get there before he does. Holden does that for you, right?"

I think back to the times we've been together, and I know he's always made sure I'm taken care of – in every aspect of our lives together. "Yeah, he does, but I want more."

"Then tell him," Blaze says it like it's that simple.

"I'm scared to, I've never been the type of girl to go for what I want. I mean most of my life I was surrounded by men who didn't give two shits about me, they just wanted the things I could do." I realize quickly how that sounds. "I don't mean sexually, I mean I'm smart with books and numbers. I know how to keep track of things, and I can normally talk someone into doing something they don't want to do. Not really proud of that, but I can be persuasive."

"Then be persuasive with your husband." Whitney takes another bite of the pie I seem to have completely forgotten.

"I'm scared to be. What if I throw it out there and in the heat of the moment he doesn't want it?" Rejection is a huge fear of mine. My dad and grandfather always rejected me. If I get the same thing from Holden, I might as well die.

Whitney rolls her eyes. "You've got to be kidding me. He isn't going to reject you, Leighton. You're beautiful. Plus he wouldn't have married you unless he wanted to. There's nothing for you to worry about."

There's everything for me to worry about my brain says. But these women aren't going to understand because they didn't grow up in the same kind of situation I grew up in.

"Leighton," Whitney reaches over and grabs my hand, "what happened to your mom?"

The question catches me off guard. No one ever asks me about her anymore, and it's been a long time since I talked about her. I think about her almost every day, but talking about her is a different situation altogether.

"If I overstepped, please tell me. You don't have to talk if you don't want to, but I get the feeling her not being around is affecting you when it comes to your husband."

For a long time, I think about what I want to tell them. Should I make it sound less harsh than it really is? Should I play it off like it doesn't matter? Then I realize it does matter. Rejection has been a part of my life for a long time, starting with her.

"She left one day to go to the grocery store and never came back," I whisper, licking my suddenly dry lips. "I was eight, and Brooks was two. She told me she was bringing home ice cream." I give them a sad smile. "So I sat by that door waiting on her, I could taste every flavor of the Neapolitan, because it was my favorite. It was the one she always brought home. It was a hot, summer day, and I was looking forward to it. She left when the sun was high, and I sat there until the sun went down and my dad came home. I asked him where mom was, and he told me she left us because we'd been bad. We were told to never speak of her again, and now everything she'd done was my responsibility. I never saw her again." I finish the rest of my story with a whisper.

Blaze wipes tears away from under her eyes. "Where do you think she is?"

"I don't know," I answer truthfully. "Part of me hopes she's dead, because I don't know how a mom could leave us with my dad and grandfather, knowing what they do, and not look back. Another part hopes she got out and lived the life she wanted to. My dad has never been a soft man."

I can't even cry anymore, because I've spent most of my life crying about it. Usually late at night when I know others can't hear me, but it's a hole I have that I'm not sure will ever be filled. I lean down, kissing Stella on the head, sniffing at the smell of her shampoo, and letting it center me. I know Whitney will *never* leave her daughter.

"Because of that, I've lived with this fear of rejection, because that's what it felt like when she left a big, fucking, rejection. The next morning, I was expected to run a household, and I did it, but sometimes I didn't do it right, or I had lessons to learn." I hold my chin high. "It was hard, but I did it, and at this point in my life, I can't take anymore rejection. Especially not from the person I want to be accepted by so much."

The table is quiet and I wonder if I've shared too much, until Whitney squeezes the hand she still holds. "I'm sorry you had to live through that, and now that I'm a mother, I can tell you without a doubt, she didn't leave you. Something prevented her from coming back. And I can also tell you, Holden will never reject you."

I want to believe her, want to believe Holden and I are the real deal and we will be forever. As I open my mouth, someone comes into The Café, looking around. "I'm looking for a Leighton Thompson."

"Tha...that's me." I hold up my hand. Surprised when I see what the man carries.

"I have a delivery for you. I just need you to sign here." He sets a bouquet of flowers down on the table in front of me. Fumbling, I take the pen he pushes in my direction and sign my name quickly. Just like that, he's gone, and I'm left staring at the gorgeous arrangement now blocking Whitney's face.

"Hand her over, so you can open the card." She reaches for Stella.

My hands shake as I open the card attached to the fresh flowers. They smell absolutely amazing. In handwriting I've come to recognize as Holden's there's a message.

I know it's been a few weeks.
Thank you so much for taking care of me!
It's been a long time since anyone did.
Here's a thank you for it.
I hope you love it!
Holden

"They're from Holden." My captive audience is hanging on my every word. I shuffle through the envelope and let loose with a small shriek when I see what else is included. He remembered what we talked about, the movie we watched. He got us dance lessons.

I pull out my phone, hands shaking as I text him.

L: *I can't believe you did this. Thank you for the flowers, for the lessons...*

H: *Thank you for taking care of me, and just remember...those lessons are one night only.*

I laugh loudly, holding the vouchers up for the girls to see.

"Girl," Blaze levels me with a look, "I don't know who's got it worse...you or him. But you've both got it bad."

Do we? I can't think about it right now. Disappointment would ruin this moment. All I want for now is excitement, and as I look at the date on the lessons and realize they're in a couple of nights. Excitement is all I can feel.

MY SHIFT IS over in fifteen minutes, and I'm doing the last of my cleanup, getting the last of my papers together. Today I want to clock out quickly, because I'm so excited about the gift Holden gave me. Just as I finish sweeping up my section, the door opens and in walks Ace.

"Hey." He hitches his chin at me.

"Hey." I smile back, but on the inside cringing when he sits in my section.

"Is this yours or Violet's?" He asks quietly as he grabs a menu.

"The section?" I ask, to make sure I understand what he's saying.

"Yeah."

"This one's mine, if you want hers, you need to sit over there." I point to two booths over.

Without a second glance, he puts the menu up and strolls over, having a seat in the booth. I tilt my head, studying him. "You know she's married?"

"I know," he nods, "I also know she deserves better."

I wonder how he knows that, but I don't have time to ask as Violet comes out from the back. She stops in her tracks as she spots Ace.

"I can get him if you want me to," I offer. I get the feeling Violet has enough trouble at home.

"No," she clears her throat, voice strong, "I've got it. You can clock out."

Ace is someone I trust, so I do, but I have to wonder just what in the hell those two are doing. Even if it is none of my business.

CHAPTER NINETEEN

Havoc

GLANCING at the cell phone I hold in my hand, I check the time again. "Leigh, we gotta go if we're gonna make it."

I hate to rush her, but these lessons weren't cheap, and I know she wants to do them. With a drive to Birmingham tonight, we're going to cut it close if we don't leave soon.

"I'm coming," she yells from the bedroom. "Do you think this is okay?"

I look up from where I was texting with Mason and let out a wolf whistle. I can't help it, it's just a natural reaction to what's standing in front of me. Her long, dark hair is in soft curls, framing her face. Her makeup is more dramatic than I've ever seen it, causing her eyes to look huge, brighter than they ever have before. The dress she's put over her body is showing curves that I rarely get a chance to look at openly. It's low-cut up top and comes to a stop around her knees, a burgundy color, showing off the tan most of us keep year-round down here. On her feet are flats, thank God, because I don't want to worry about her breaking an ankle doing this. For a few long minutes, I can't find my voice. All I can do is take her in and realize this woman is mine. For as long as I want her, she's fucking mine. A lightbulb clicks in my head and it's clear as day how lucky I am, and how much I want her forever.

Getting up from the couch, I stalk over to her, admiring the way she fills out the clothing she's wearing, loving the way she takes a bit of a step back when I get into her space. It's not a step back because I'm invading, it's an inviting step. She grabs hold of my button-down and holds me close to her. Tilting her head back so she can see me, we look at each other for what feels like hours, until I angle her chin just right and lean in, sampling a taste of the dark red lips in front of me. A hint of her flavor and I'm like a crack addict taking a hit, immediately the need floods into my body and I run my hands down, stopping at her hips. Curling my hands around her waist, I push her back against the wall, before I move them down to the hem of her dress, pushing it up her thighs.

"Holden," she pants, pulling our mouths apart from one another. There's so much emotion in the way she says my name.

"I know." I move my mouth down her neck, connecting with the flesh there. "We gotta go."

"I'm almost ready to say fuck the class." She closes her eyes and slams her head back against the wall.

"Me too, sweetheart, but this has been something I think you've wanted to do for a while, and I don't want to be the person to keep you from it."

I lean in so that our foreheads touch and take a fortifying breath. "But to answer your question, you look amazing. I think it's perfect."

She gives me a smile, one that shoots straight down to where my dick is hard. "Glad you like it."

"Love it," I amend. "I love it. You look like some nymph, ready to tempt me into anything."

"If only it were that easy." She runs her hand down my chest, hooking her fingers into the belt holding my jeans up.

"It is that easy," I breathe into her ear. "You can talk me into whatever you want." Maybe that wasn't the smartest thing to tell the woman who could hurt me more than any other, but what's this life without honesty between us.

"Let's go," she whispers, pulling that full bottom lip between her teeth.

I push off from the wall, holding my hand out to hers. "C'mon."

"WE'RE the youngest here by like thirty years," she giggles into my ear as we wait for the instructor of the class to tell us what to do.

"Maybe thirty years for you, more like twenty for me," I laugh back with her.

It feels good to be here in this setting. She's standing next to me, my arm around her, holding her close. I kiss the top of her head, just because I want to. I don't know what it is about being out of Laurel Springs, but I feel like I can be free with her here, that if anyone sees us there's no judgement. I think that's more for her than for me though, to be honest.

"How long have you two been married?" One of the older women asks as we wait for our next instructions.

"About seven months," Leighton answers for us.

"Still newlyweds! Did you dance at your wedding?"

"No ma'am," I answer. "We had a shotgun wedding." I give her a smile.

"Doesn't look like it was too much of a shotgun, otherwise you'd be holding a baby right now, or she'd look like she's about to pop."

Leighton grins up at me. "It was more a family situation. Think Romeo and Juliet." She laughs as she grabs hold of my hand and pulls it around her waist. "Holden is a cop, and let's just say my family is not always on the right side of the law."

"Oh, how romantic!" She puts her wrinkled hand on Leighton's and looks up into Leighton's face. "I bet the two of you were sneaking off, away from your families, enjoying your little trysts on your own. How does it feel not to have to hide it anymore?"

"It feels good." I lock my gaze with Leighton's. "Not having to pretend like I don't care for her, not having to worry who sees us kiss. It's all a new kind of freedom we've never had before. We're still not sure how to deal with it."

Which is totally the truth. We're all over each other one minute, the next we're shy. I hope that gets better the more comfortable we are in our new roles.

"You kiss her every chance you get, you tell her you love her every day, and always make time to make sure she's okay," the older woman says slowly. "And you, my dear," she looks at Leighton, "try to dress up for him once in a while, ask him how his day has gone, and don't make him ask you for a blowjob. Offer it, and do it better every time."

Leighton gasps and turns her face into my chest. I bet hers is just as red as mine is. "Thank you for the advice." I chuckle, as I run my fingers through her hair, soothing her as the older couple walks off.

"Oh my God," she looks up, her chin against my chest, "did she really just say that?"

"She did," I laugh into her hair. "And ya know, I wouldn't be opposed to the idea, if you felt like it was something you needed to do."

She smacks me in the stomach. "Of course you wouldn't."

The instructor reels us back in, and we stand there listening. "What I want you to do is listen to the music, let it move you, let it show you the way you want to go. There's no right or wrong here. Dance a salsa, do a tango, or just sway in your lover's arms, however you feel comfortable."

A slow song comes over the studio speakers. "I don't think I'm good enough to do a salsa, or a tango, but I would love to have you sway in my arms," I tell her the truth.

"I think I'd like that a lot." She slides her arms around my neck and we sway like two teenagers at a middle-school dance. I cherish this, these stolen moments we have. It what we have because we didn't get to date, didn't get to have memories made with each other in them. As we live our day-to-day now, those are the memories. And this is one I want to remember forever.

CHAPTER TWENTY

Leighton

I'M DRAGGING ASS this morning, after Holden and I were out late last night at the class he arranged for us. I would do it again though, in a nanosecond. If I could just get myself to wake up.

"I can't believe I agreed to a shift this early on a Saturday," Caleb complains as he enters my car on the passenger side.

"Totally agree, but look at it this way, you can come home after you're done and take a nap. It'll be so early in the day you'll be able to go do something after you wake up."

"Kinda like having a two-a-day." He grins at me.

This morning I'm starting to see the man he's growing into, and he's going to be a heartbreaker, especially with a dad like Mason. He has a little bit of peach fuzz on his angular jaw and I don't think he brushed his hair. As a football player, he's building up his muscles, and I'm pretty sure that within the next six months he'll be able to get any girl he wants.

"Yeah, like a two-a-day," I agree.

At the end of the driveway, I stop to let a truck pass before I pull out onto the main highway. When I get a glance at the driver, the hair on the back of my neck stands up. It's my dad. He offers me a wave that I don't return. Instead, I turn to check the blind spots on both sides before I take the road to town.

"Who was that?"

Caleb has the instincts of a cop. If this football thing doesn't work out for him, he'd be a welcome addition to the force – I'm sure of it. My dad isn't someone I like to talk about, but I feel like Caleb and I have gotten close. We've become very good friends in the short time we've been working together, and I always want to treat him like an adult.

"My dad."

He picks at a string hanging on his athletic shorts. "Ya know, sometimes I wonder what it would be like to have to choose between a mom or a dad. Like my mom left, and I never knew her, but as much as my dad gets on my nerves, I don't know what I would do without him." His deepening voice is getting contemplative this morning.

"You'd learn to live, kid. That's all you can do."

"Is that what you've done? I notice you don't have a relationship with your dad."

"It's what I had to do. My dad wasn't like yours. He wasn't on the right side of the law. He broke it every chance he got, and it was dangerous."

This is the first time I've really talked about my home life, and it doesn't escape me that I'm talking about it to Caleb. No matter how young he is, we share a piece of our lives that no one else should ever have to share.

"Is your mom alive?" I ask, because it's been bothering me for a while.

His jaw hardens, a tick appearing against the strong line. "Dad doesn't talk about it. I don't know," he finally admits. "I stopped asking, I get the feeling she couldn't handle life with a kid."

"If she knew what an amazing kid you are, she'd be kicking herself for ever leaving you." I grab his hand.

"Problem is, she'll never know."

"Maybe one day she will," although I don't exactly believe my words, "maybe you'll be the one in a million whose mom decides to come back and find out what you've been doing with your life."

He glances over at me, that young face so serious. "I don't know if I'd welcome her back."

I'm not sure I blame him.

Havoc

This morning, I'm sucking down the damn coffee. I wish I would have looked at the dates of that dance class a little better. This was my early morning and I was thirty minutes late.

L: *I need so much more sleep. The caffeine isn't working.*

I grin as I read the text message from Leighton.

H: *I totally agree with you. Take a nap when you get home from work.*

L: *I have a paper due :(*

She's so dedicated to what she wants to do. Makes me so fucking proud of her.

***H:** Write your paper, I'll bring something home for dinner, and we can crash early.*

***L:** We're sounding like one of those old, married couples. I'm not taking that woman's advice. What if you leave me for a more exciting wife?*

I chuckle, smiling wide as I remember the advice of the older woman last night to give me blow jobs.

***H:** I'm so tired that I'm not sure I could even get it up if you had that kind of an idea for me. Tonight, we sleep.*

***L:** I think I love you, that's exactly what I wanted to hear.*

The *love* throws me off, but I imagine it's just an expression and she didn't mean it the way my fluttering heart took it.

***H:** Have a good day, sweetheart. See you tonight.*

I don't even know why I put the sweetheart in there, it just felt right. Calling myself three kinds of an idiot, I put my phone in my pocket and go to pick up the paperwork for my shift.

"Riding with you today," I tell Mason as I look through the information that's been left for me. "Let me grab some more coffee and we'll be ready to go." I haven't ridden with Menace in a while, and since the two of us are close to the same age, we tend to have more to talk about than the other guys. I quickly refill my cup, let dispatch know where I'm going to be, and then we head out to the cars.

"How are things going?" I ask him as we start making our designated route through the town, up and down the one-way streets before we patrol the backroads.

"They're good," he answers, stopping at a stoplight and then accelerating to make a left-hand turn. "Been working a lot in Birmingham doing some security gigs."

"I noticed you hadn't been volunteering for overtime as much anymore, are we about to lose you to the bigger city?" I'd hate to lose him; he's a good officer, was a decorated member of the Marine Corps, and has done well at every post he's been assigned to. If we're holding him back, I want to let him know to go for it.

He shakes his head. "No, this is the only place where Caleb has ever felt like a part of something. He has football, Leighton, The Café, you all. I won't take it away from him."

"I love how you add my wife into that equation."

"I don't mean to disrespect you, but he cares a lot for her. I feel like he's a better person because she's come into his life. He needed someone like her."

"Didn't we all?" I ask softly. Hearing him describe what a better person his son is for having Leighton in his life is affecting me, because I know I'm better for having her in my own. "I get it, and I'm happy to share her with him if need be. Those two kinda have a kinship, both not having mothers."

"They do," Menace agrees. "And right now, he needs all the friends he can get. He's having a hard time."

"With what?"

If my guys are having problems, I want to know. I want to be a part of the solution, because that's what a good leader does. Not to mention these guys are my family, and my responsibility. I need to know if their heads aren't completely in the game.

"School," Menace spits the word out like it's got a bad taste. "He's got this teacher who seems to think he's not giving his all, and I just don't know what to tell her."

"They only have a few weeks left, right?"

"Yeah, but I've heard through the grapevine she's moving up a grade next year, so he'll have her again."

I take a drink of my coffee. "Is the teacher right? Is he not giving his all?"

"Hell, I don't know. It's some sort of math bullshit that I can't even understand. I went overseas and kept people safe, Havoc, and I can't figure this shit out. Do they want these kids to be rocket scientists?" He runs a hand through his hair. "Either way, I don't know what to tell her. I can talk to him until I'm blue in the face, and he'll tell me what I want to hear, but I can't force him to do what she wants him to do. Fuck, I don't even know if he can."

"Caleb's a good kid," I reiterate. I think Menace needs to hear that right now.

"He is, but I'm worried if we keep harping on him, asking for more than he's giving, it's gonna make him rebellious. Right now, I leave him at home at all hours by himself and I don't have to worry where he is. He's never lied to me, never had people over when he shouldn't, always calls me when he's leaving. I'm his dad, but he's also my best friend. We've grown up together. He knows not to lie to me." Menace seems to have a hard time putting into words what he wants to say. "But at the same time, I don't want to put too much pressure on him, because I want him to have a choice, ya know?"

"You don't want him to have to go into the military like we did?"

He slaps his hand on the steering wheel. "Exactly! It was either that or get a fuckin' factory job where most of the people who work there are on uppers and downers, or get stuck going to community college hoping to one day have enough credits to transfer. I want better for him."

He's a good dad. I hope I'm the type of dad Menace is if Leighton and I ever decide to have kids.

"He'll have better because you do whatever it takes to give him better. And what if you make an appointment with this teacher? Ya know, talk to her about your fears when it comes to pushing him? Don't they have conferences or something like that?"

"They do," he confirms. "I just always get a look when I go in there. People look at me and they go oh my God, you have a fifteen-year-old son? Is he adopted? Are there extenuating circumstances? They whisper it like it's some secret. I mean, imagine how they look at me when I'm like no, I was having sex at sixteen, had a baby at seventeen, and became a single-dad at nineteen. I'm thirty-two now, do you have any more questions?"

"Are they really that invasive?"

"Fuck yes," he breathes out harshly. "And ya know – I get that they wanna help me, that they want to make things better – but where the hell were those people when I was serving my country and my mom had to move in to help me?"

"Nobody ever thinks about the sacrifice, brother."

"I missed a lot of shit I'll never get back, but I've done it to give him a better life, and I'm scared to death that the pushiness of a society that always preaches *you can do better* is going to ruin it all."

This is some heavy heart-to-heart stuff, and I wonder how long Menace has needed to talk. How long has he been dealing with this on his own? I feel like he should have come to me before it got this bad. "Next time you need to talk, you come to me. If you don't want to do it at the station in front of people, come to the house. Bring Caleb with you, don't hide what's going on from him. He's old enough to know what's going on."

"I didn't mean to lay this all on you, boss, it's just been heavy on me lately."

"You lay whatever you need to on me, I've got big shoulders. I can take it."

I can handle anything that anyone throws at me, as long as I know my team and my family are good.

CHAPTER TWENTY-ONE

Leighton

"WHY WON'T THIS THING SAVE?" I beat the keys on the laptop harder than necessary. I growl at it, hoping that it feels my wrath by the way I'm shooting daggers at the screen.

"Be nice to it, and maybe it'll do what you want it to," Holden jokes as he comes through the front door, carrying a pizza.

"How long have you been standing there?"

"Long enough to hear you call it some not so flattering words and see you try to beat it to death. C'mon, take a break and eat dinner with me. I'll leave you along to finish when we're done."

He hardly ever leaves me alone when we're at the house together, and it makes me feel good, because I know it's because he wants to be with me, not because he's worried I'll do something he doesn't like. "What are you going to go do while I work on this?"

"Probably work out," he answers tiredly. "Even though I don't want to, but it's been a couple of days."

I get up from where I'm sitting and join him at the kitchen table, taking the paper plate he's offering me. "I wish I had your dedication."

"You do." He takes a huge bite of the piece of pizza in front of him. "You work on homework all the time, and you work a job at The Café you know you don't need. That's dedication."

"Different kind of dedication."

He agrees as he makes a noise in his throat. "But still dedication nonetheless. I tell people when they talk about criminals, that they are the most dedicated people I've ever seen in my life."

I have to agree with him. I push out an amused breath. "Yeah, no shit. Like who else would spend that much time trying to hide a part of their lives, just for the sake of it. I always used to ask my dad, what's the point? We weren't living rich, hell sometimes we weren't even living good, yet he went to all that trouble."

"How did you live, Leigh?" He asks softly, and for the first time I feel like it's non-judgmental. I feel like it's my husband asking me, rather than an officer asking me.

"It was hard." I'm honest with him. "There were sometimes when there wasn't money for food because he'd put all of it into the business. At least until I figured out what I was doing." I clamp my mouth shut, not believing I just said what I did.

"No, don't stop now, what do you mean?"

Damn me and my trusting mouth with him. I realize I've got to tell him, it's the right thing to do. If there's anyone I can trust, it's Holden. "I'm good with numbers. It's why I want to go to school for accounting. Back when my dad had me doing the books, I started messing with them, so that Brooks and I would have enough money for food. Or maybe I could find enough money to get Brooks a birthday gift. Something like that."

"Damn, Leigh." His face shows more emotion than I've ever seen. It's like admitting this to him shows him how desperate I was. "No kid should ever have to do that."

"No," I agree. "But they do. There are plenty of kids in this country, in this county, in your town who do this because they have to. If I hadn't done what I did, there were times Brooks and I may not have survived. That's why it killed me when he went to jail. I tried so hard to teach him better, it's why I take Caleb under my wing like I do. I failed Brooks." I let tears that have gathered behind my eyes fall. "I wanted him to be different; I wanted him to have options and choices. But life took that away from us. I want Caleb to know he doesn't have to be the status quo. Just because he's only had one parent his whole life doesn't mean he can't be amazing. I worry about him, because I think he takes things too seriously. Brooks did too, and we see where he ended up."

Havoc

"It's not your fault that Brooks is in jail." I grab her hand, pushing my pizza away. Frankly, I've lost my appetite.

"But it feels like it. Someone had to be responsible for him."

"That wasn't you," I argue.

"It was," she argues back. "I took responsibility and then I failed him. He should have respected the police, should have respected the road."

"Leighton, listen to me. When he hit Trevor, he was an adult. You can't take the blame for that. He knew right from wrong."

She's listening to me, but I'm not sure I'm getting through.

"He knew right from wrong." I try again. "He chose to do wrong."

She sobs, something breaking apart inside of her. She's been so strong this entire time she's been with me. I've never truly seen her lose it, never seen her mourn the loss of her family, of a brother she so obviously loves. "This hurts so much." Her bottom lip quivers as she puts her face in her hands, her shoulders shaking.

"What does? You gotta let it out." I soothe her as I walk over to the chair she's sitting in, lift her up and settle her in my lap. This strong woman is sobbing into my shoulder, a dam breaking that I'm not sure she knew she had. It's the worst sound I've heard in my life, like a wild animal who's had their child torn from their hands.

"He's my family." She rubs at the tears still coming from her eyes. "I wanted him here for every part of my life. I had dreams, ya know?"

"Tell me about them, baby. I'll make every one of them come true."

And in this moment, I know I'm telling her the truth. I never want to see this look on her face again, never want to feel the devastation I feel watching her face screw up in obvious pain and turmoil as I am right now. This hurts me as much as it hurts her, if not more because I don't know how to make it better. "Talk to me," my voice begs. Unless I know how to, I can't help, and fuck I want to right now. My mission in life is to help. When it comes to her, my mission is whatever she needs it to be.

"My dream was to always have a family," she breathes out of her mouth, using her palm to wipe at the tip of her nose, "to have someone who cared about me, unconditionally. My dad found out I was skimming from the top. That's what started the fight the day I left. I'd been saving money to do just that, to get out of here and go build a life for myself. He found the money I'd hidden, and he wanted to make me pay for what I had done."

"God, Leigh. I wish you had come to me," I whisper as I cradle her against my frame, hunching over to protect her from the harsh realities of the world. "I would've done anything to protect you." I push her hair up from her face, making her look at me.

She's never been more gorgeous to me right now. Face red, tears streaming down her face, lips chapped where she's been continuously licking them, nose red and running. This is the woman I want for the rest of my life. This is the woman I want to have my kids one day, sleep with me every night, and wake up to every morning. "Do you know since the night you kissed me in Birmingham – I haven't been out on a date with another woman? I haven't kissed anyone, I haven't hugged anyone, haven't even texted anyone in any kind of manner that could be construed as me flirting?"

Her intake of breath is sharp, and I can tell I've shocked her. "Goddamn woman, you blew my world apart when you swept up to me in that bar, and I've been trying to hold you at arm's length ever since, because I'm scared to death to let you get too close. I don't want you to run." My voice is gravelly as I'm laying this down for her. "I don't want to scare you, because of how I feel about you."

"What do you feel?" she whispers, her voice soft, her small fingers digging into the material of my shirt.

"Everything," I crush her to me. "Everything you can ever imagine I feel for you, and if that scares you then fuck it, because I'm sick of pretending. I can't do that anymore."

She makes a noise deep in her throat as I pick her up and carry her to the bedroom. When I take us both down onto the mattress, wrapping her in my arms, she comes with me easily, putting her head on my chest, circling her arm around my waist. Our legs entangle and we watch the sun go down together, and it's the best night I've ever had in my life, because I'm done hiding and I'm done running.

And I hope like hell she is, too.

CHAPTER TWENTY- TWO

Leighton

THE NIGHT I told Holden what happened with my dad, why he did what he did and cast me out, proved to be a turning point for us, and two weeks later, things are better than they have ever been between us.

Oh there's still tension, lots of tension, but it's the good, sexy kind. Not the *neither of us knowing if we're in this for the right reasons* kind. Which leads me to my stress for tonight.

This has been deemed something I've never done before: date night.

It's never been something I've really ever experienced, but I'm excited for it to happen. Holden called me on my way home from work, telling me we're meeting a couple of the guys he works with and their significant others for drinks. While I'm pretty sure I know who he's talking about and I'm comfortable with them, I'm immediately nervous.

What if they don't like me outside of The Café? What if I slip up and do something stupid? What if I embarrass Holden? What if I embarrass myself? I'm not sure I've ever worked myself up into such a tizzy in this short amount of time. Glancing at the clock, I see I have about an hour before he gets here. That hour has to count.

It's almost as if I'm running a marathon as I quickly go into the bathroom and start the shower. I probably take the quickest one known to man, before I'm getting out and wrapping a towel around my body. Even though I've lived in Laurel Springs all but six months of my life, I've never set foot in any of the date-night establishments, so I have no idea how people around here dress. And why this is slipping me up, I have no idea. I've never given a damn what people thought of me because of my family. Why am I even worrying about it now?

"Because you want Holden to look at you and want you."

It's what I've wanted since the day he came to help me. Maybe tonight is the night he sees me as someone worth it and worthy of him. Maybe tonight is the night we finally can't keep our hands off each other and we do what we've both wanted to for so long. I know we both want it, we've come close so many times. Deciding not to worry about the clothes, I stand in front of the mirror, putting makeup on. It makes me feel weird; I normally don't wear anything other than lip gloss and mascara most days because I bust ass waitressing. Nobody wants to see a waitress with eyeliner running down her face and smudged foundation caking her cheeks.

"Let's see if I remember how to do this," I say to my reflection.

I dig through my makeup bag, hoping I haven't lost my touch. One day, not too long ago, I was really good at this. I could make myself look older than I was, and could have a man bowing at my feet. Hoping the makeup gods are with me tonight, I pull out everything I'll need and go to work on my face.

In the end, I decide to forego the intricate looks I've had over the years, and stop before I hit the showgirl category. Inspecting myself in the mirror, I smile, amazed by how much I look like an adult. The past year has changed me, made me grow more than anything else ever has. I see it in my eyes, even in the bone structure of my face. Finally, I'm becoming the woman I've always wanted to be.

Grabbing the curling wand I plugged in earlier, I randomly curl a few pieces of hair here and there, giving it a bouncy wave. Thinking back, I try to remember the last time I fixed my hair in some other way besides a ponytail for work, or just leaving it down when I'm at the house. Maybe the wedding? God, no wonder Holden doesn't ever look at me like he wants to rip my clothes off; we never had that *getting to know you* period. And I sure haven't put that old lady's advice to use yet.

There was never the rush of feelings, trying my best to impress him, never the butterflies in my stomach when he came and picked me up for a date. Simply because that wasn't our situation. The day he got me out of the back of the ambulance was the day we started living together.

He's seen me at my worst from day one, and there's nothing I can do to change the beginning, but fuck it, I can change the middle and the ending. It won't take much for me to care a little more about what I look like, and hopefully he'll appreciate it.

With hair and makeup done, I feel like a totally different person. I pick up my cell phone, checking the time. I have about twenty minutes before he should be here to pick me up. Just enough time.

Early April has turned a little cool at night this year, even though last year it was already sweltering. I opt for a pair of jeans with a designer rip in the thigh, my riding boots, and a long-sleeve, body hugging shirt. Just because I don't usually show it off anymore doesn't mean I don't have what some have referred to as a bangin' body.

Fifteen minutes later, I have earrings in, jewelry on, and perfume spritzed at all the points Holden might be smelling me tonight (with any luck). Operation *Seduce My Husband* is in full effect.

My hands are shaking as I wait for Holden to get home, and my hearing is superhuman as I listen for his truck in the driveway. I have a very distinct feeling that when I look back at my marriage it will be split into two categories. Before tonight, and after tonight.

And when I hear the crunching of the gravel, I know my time has come. I realize with great clarity that the only person who can change my marriage and what I want in it, is myself. Do I want this marriage to be merely a piece of paper; do I want him only as a protector? No, I don't think so. I want him to be my lover; I want him to be my best friend, to be the person he turns to in the middle of the night when he's having a bad dream. Desperately, I want to be the person he wakes up when he has a hard-on that just won't go away. I want to be the reason Holden smiles in the morning and the person he holds at night. I want to be the person he kisses on the neck when he spoons me from behind and the one hug that can make his day better. I vow right here and now, I will be this person. There won't be anything that stands in our way. If there is, we'll go through it, over it, beside it, or jump that motherfucker like it's a canyon.

Together we'll make it, and it'll be because we wanted to, not because we had to.

Havoc

To say I'm a little nervous is an understatement. When the guys asked me if Leighton and I wanted to go out, I'd balked, but then I realized I want to. I want to be seen with her, I'm sick of hiding at our house like we've done something wrong. Nothing about me wanting to protect her was ever wrong, and I'm getting the feeling that my trying to protect her has maybe given her the idea I'm not proud to be with her. I am. There's something about putting my wedding ring on every day, about knowing I'm coming home to her at night, and knowing without a shadow of a doubt I'm waking up next to her in the morning.

I never thought this would be me. In a million years, I never imagined I'd be the guy who got so caught up in a woman. But yet, here I am, dying to get inside the house to see if she's fixed herself up for our night out.

When I unlock the door and step through the threshold, I'm completely unprepared for the woman who meets me. I've seen her before, but not in a long time. Immediately my mind goes back to one hot night in Birmingham, where Leighton Strather blew my mind and made me aware of her in a way I haven't been able to forget since.

She's got on these boots that I jokingly call basic bitch, white-girl boots when I typically see women wearing them, but on her, they look amazing. They frame her legs in a way that immediately gets me hard. Same with the tight jeans and tight long-sleeve shirt she's wearing. It hugs all the right places, and rides high on her body, brushing the waistband of the faded jeans. I knew she had a body this bangin' underneath her clothes, I've inspected it, but damn there's something intimately sexy seeing it covered the way it is tonight. She's done something to her face, too. Those eyes of hers pop impossibly bright, like the night we took our dance lesson, making me want to stare into them for the rest of my damn life. Her hair? Shiny as hell and I have to curl my fingers into the palms of my hands to keep from reaching out and touching the waves.

"Wow!" I try to inhale, to feel my lungs with life-giving oxygen, but she's literally rendered me breathless and speechless.

"Too much for where we're going?" She frowns as she runs her fingers through her hair, doing something to the curls she's arranged.

"No," I push my arm out, grabbing her hand to stop her, "not at all," I swallow roughly against the knot that's formed in my throat. She's so fucking beautiful it hurts. "Completely perfect." I entwine our fingers together, bringing them up to my lips. "Don't change a thing about yourself."

She gives me this smile. It's equal parts sexy, sweet, unsure, and totally quirky. All in that ten second exchange, I do what I once believed to be the impossible for me with any woman.

That guy who got his heart broken while he was fighting a war, watched all his friends move on, in one way or another. That guy who's watched his guys on the MTF find love and become comfortable in their skin? In this moment, that guy falls head over heels in love with his wife.

I put my hand to my chest to make sure my heart is still beating, because fuck what a breath-stealing moment it is.

CHAPTER TWENTY-THREE

Havoc

IT'S BEEN a little strained between the two of us since we got to the bar, and I blame myself for that. I haven't been able to get the way she looks out of my mind. It's odd, I spend countless hours with her a day and I've always found her attractive, but tonight I realize just how hot she is.

"You okay?" She leans in, speaking against the outer shell of my ear.

The one little act sends shivers down my body and hardens my erection to mass critical levels. I've been sporting a semi since I picked her up, and now thanks to her hot breath against the sensitive skin of my ear, everybody in the free world can tell I want my wife.

"Good." I nod, glancing at the two couples we're sitting with.

Renegade, Tank, Whitney, and Blaze are all looking at us like they're watching monkeys at the zoo. Maybe that's an apt description. This woman has got me all kinds of flustered, and I'm unsure if I'll ever be able to be normal again.

"Leighton, you wanna go play pool?" Whitney asks, breaking the uncomfortable silence. "Blaze and I have a little wager to settle and we wouldn't mind if you played with us."

"A wager?" Renegade asks, taking a drink off his beer bottle. "Do tell."

Whitney turns to her fiancée and winks. "It's something private between the two of us. You know I don't normally keep secrets, but this is in my girl vault."

"Fuckin' girl vault," he complains.

"Yeah," Leighton stands up, my eyes going immediately to her tight ass, "I'd love to join the two of you, even though I don't know how to play." She looks down at me, her eyebrow raised.

"Go on, have fun." I take a drink from my own beer bottle as I watch the trio walk away.

I'm still staring at her ass when I feel the palm of someone's hand make contact with the back of my head. "Son of a bitch!" I wince as my tooth makes contact with the rim of the bottle.

"Are you deaf, blind, and stupid?" Tank gives me a look.

"Something tells me you don't really want me to answer that." I shrug, wondering what the fuck he's getting at.

"Christ almighty," he breathes, rolling his eyes. "Y'all say I'm the one that has no clue." He looks pointedly at Renegade before he turns to me. "She told you she didn't know how to play pool so you'd go teach her, you dumb shit."

"What?" I shake my head. "That's what Whitney and Blaze are there for."

He looks at Renegade and sighs, before he cuts his eyes back over at me. "Help him," he pleads with his soon to be brother-in-law and best friend. "For the love of God, help him."

Ryan shakes his head as he leans in so I can hear over the loudness of the bar. "Why do you think your wife dressed for sin tonight? Normally whenever we see her, she's wearing a baggy t-shirt and a pair of leggings. The shirt she's wearing tonight is so tight you can see the outline of her bra. She fixed her hair, she fixed her makeup."

"How the fuck did you notice all this shit?" I ask him, getting a little pissed.

"Because I'm getting married for real soon, I'm supposed to notice all this shit."

That hits a nerve. "We're married for real," I argue.

"Are you? Because I can guarantee you, the first night I went out with Whitney? I couldn't keep my goddamn hands off her, and she sure as fuck wouldn't be bending over a pool table shaking her ass for every horny guy in the place. I'd be right up behind her, letting her shake that ass on my cock, and copping a feel while doing it." He glances over at Tank. "No offense."

"None taken – desperate times call for desperate measures. I got you." They give each other a high-five, and I'm tempted to roll my eyes at them this time.

But then it happens. I turn to where the girls are playing pool, watching as Whitney and Blaze truly are playing a heated game, but my gaze travels over to where Leighton is bending over an empty pool table. She's testing the cue in her hands and watching the girls, before she bends over and tries to break, missing terribly. I watch as she laughs at herself, before she moves to get the cue ball and again try to break. There are men watching her from every corner of this bar – some from the sidelines, some looking like they're about to make their move.

"Fuck this." I grab my beer and drain it, as I stand up and walk over to what's fucking mine.

"Yeah, man." I hear the guys encourage me, as I grab another beer off of a waitress's tray. When I get to where Leighton is standing, eyeing that cue ball, another guy is headed the same way. Over her head I make eye contact, giving him a warning with my glare. He quickly turns, walking the other way, which gives my ego the stroke it needs.

"Hey, babe." I lean in, kissing her on the cheek as I grab her hip. "Sorry I took so long to get over here."

She's obviously confused, because she's looking at me like I've grown another head. I clarify quickly. "You wanna learn how to play pool? I'll teach you."

"And we'll help," Renegade and Tank add as they make their way over to us, all holding fresh beers. Apparently they didn't want their women to be without them either.

"Did you see me fail miserably earlier?" She buries her face in her hands.

"Yeah." I can't help the chuckle that comes from deep within my body. "That's okay though, we can work it out. We'll have you actually hitting the balls before we leave here."

She laughs, an adorable snort making its way past her hand, as I set my beer bottle down on the edge of the pool table. "Alright, first things first, you need to learn how to hold the stick."

Immediately I realize just how sexual this whole situation is going to be, and I find myself hoping it leads to other things before the night ends. Otherwise, I'm a damn glutton for punishment.

"How do I hold it?" She asks, running her hand up and down the shaft.

"Like a cock" is out of my mouth before I can stop the words.

"Oh yeah?" She shoots me a heated grin. "You sure that's not your wishful thinking?"

I step closer to her, planting my feet wide on the concrete floor of the bar, putting my arms around her waist. I push her back against the pool table, pressing my body into hers, feeling like a flirtatious husband for the first time in my marriage.

Maybe I've had more alcohol than I thought, because I'm feeling a little buzzed as I wrap my arms around her waist. With hands that I wish were more familiar with her body, I run them down her lower back, until they cup the curve of her ass, tilting her deeper into my body. If I'm not mistaken those dark eyes flair with a recognition of arousal and desire. I lean in, whispering against her ear.

"One day soon I hope to find out."

"Teach me how to shoot pool and you just might."

I have to take a step back, get myself together before I put my hand over hers on the pool stick. I gently take it from her grip and turn her around in front of me. "You want to bend over and hold it like this," I say as I lean over her back, positioning the cue where she can easily hold it. "You want to line up your shot like this." I show her how to option her hand to hold the cue steady, and together we push the end of it to the cue ball.

She shrieks as we make a clean break. "I did it!" She turns in my arms, throwing hers around my neck. I'm so surprised at the way she's thrown herself at me, it takes me longer than I care to admit, to respond.

"C'mon, let's shoot the rest of them." She's genuinely excited to finish the job.

AN HOUR AND A HALF LATER, I'm seriously in hell. Leighton's continued drinking as we've been playing, and she's getting much friendlier with her movements, more brazen with her touches.

"Am I doing it right?" She bends over, pushing her ass into my crotch, and wiggling it around. Her shot is a little sloppy, but she hits the ball into the pocket and does a little victory dance.

"You're doing it all right," I tell her as she leans in, kissing the hollow of my throat.

I moan, fisting some of her hair in the palm of my hand and tilting her head back. She laughs deep in her throat, and I'm fully aware of my guys watching us. Hell, the whole bar is probably watching us at this point.

"I have to hit the ladies room," she whispers into my ear.

Her breath is hot against my skin as I let my hand travel down her backside again. "C'mon, I'll walk you."

"Such a gentleman," she giggles as I take her hand, leading her down the hall to the bathrooms.

"Be right back." She waves as she goes through the door.

The entire time she's gone, I berate myself for being ten kinds of an asshole, thinking I could ignore the way I react to this woman, to try and tell myself she doesn't make me feel things I've never felt, to try and tell myself I'm ever going to be able to let her go.

She comes out of the ladies room with her head down. "Can we step outside for a minute? I'm so hot."

I take a good look at her, and sure enough she's flushed. "You gonna puke on me?"

"Not if I can get some fresh air."

I direct her out the back door and immediately we're in the warm air of what's going to be an early summer. There's a soft glow from a light above the door, and I turn her to face me. "You okay?"

"Yeah." She nods. "Just got a little hot in there, in more ways than one."

Even though her eyes are glassy, I know what she means. "You're damn right about that. What is it about tonight, sweetheart? Why are you testing me?" I push her up against the wall, tilting her head back so we can look at each other. She tries to lower her head, but I grasp her at the chin and force her eyes to meet mine. "What's gotten into you?"

"I want you," she admits, running her tongue along her plump bottom lip. "I've wanted you since that night in Birmingham."

She gave me a truth, so I'll give her one, too. "Same, and it's hell not being able to take something that should rightfully be yours. You changed your last name, you wear my ring on your finger, and you curl up to me every night. You try my patience more than any woman I've ever met, and I'm not sure how much a man should be able to take."

She puts her hands on my hips, pulling me closer to her. "I know how much I can take, and I can't take any more, Holden. I want just a little taste, just a piece. Can I have that?" she breathes against my neck, where she's buried her head into my skin. "Can you give me a little taste?"

"Right here? Right now?" I question, looking around, wondering if I can give her what she needs here. Better yet, wondering if I can't not give her what she needs here. Leighton doesn't ask me for much, so when she does, I want to make things happen for her.

"C'mere." I pull her around the building, leaning back against the brick wall. Turning her around so that her ass grinds against my front. "People are coming and going, keep it quiet." We can hear groups of people leaving the bar.

She looks over her shoulder, her eyes smoldering as they meet mine. "Make me feel good, Holden."

I lean back against the building, bending my knees and pull her ass into the seat I've created with the angle of my body. My lips meet her neck, lightly at first, but when she grinds hard against my cock, I suction my lips against her skin, pulling harshly against the resistance it offers me. With one arm, I wrap it around her chest, palming her tit, cupping it in my hand. She thrusts her upper body out, punching her hard nipple into my skin.

"Holden," she whines as I grasp her nipple between my middle and index finger, squeezing hard, causing her knees to weaken. Using my other arm, I snake it around her hips, palming her stomach as my fingers catch on the button of her jeans. I unfasten it, slipping my hand into her panties. With some maneuvering, I get my middle finger over her clit and immediately begin strumming the hard nub.

"Oh my God." She bucks against my touch.

"Yeah, you're wet and fuckin' primed for me, aren't you?" I whisper in her ear, pulling her further into the cradle of my body. "You flirting with me has turned you on. Hasn't it, baby girl?"

I don't know where that nickname or term of endearment comes from, but it sounds good rolling off my tongue. "Yes," she moans, pushing against my finger.

Her pussy is wet as I move the tip of my middle finger up and down her swollen nub. "You're so goddamn wet," I groan, wishing to hell I could push my jeans down, pull my cock out, and shove it deeply into that wet heat.

Attaching my lips back to her neck, I inhale deeply. "God, you smell so damn good," I moan as I nip at the flesh with my teeth.

"I wanted to smell good for you," she admits, pushing against my hand. "I wanted to look good for you, to entice you to lose control."

"You've got me there, baby. I'm losing complete fucking control when it comes to you," I growl out between gritted teeth.

"Me too," she growls out, gasping as I move my hand further down, using two fingers to push inside her tight tunnel. A loud moan erupts from her throat as another group of people exit the bar.

"Shhh." I take my hand off her tit and move it up to her mouth, flattening my palm against her lips as she lets out another loud moan.

She's talking as she thrusts against my fingers, dragging her clit along my thumb. The words are muffled against my skin and I can feel her tightening against me. "C'mon baby girl," I whisper into her ear. "Give me what I want, and in case you aren't sure what that is, it's you coming against my hand."

Another muffled scream and I feel her tighten against me, feel her come, and then collapse against me as her knees give out. Tightening my arm around her waist, I hold her up, as she tries to catch her breath.

"You okay?"

Her head rolls against my shoulder, as she continues to try and catch her breath.

"Jesus Christ, Holden. I think you blew my mind," she laughs, running her hands along her body.

My laugh is strangled. "You're lucky I didn't blow my load in my jeans." I pull her face around, kissing her soundly on the lips, giving her a taste of my tongue.

"Why don't we go home and you can blow your load inside me?" Her voice is throaty and deep.

I freeze. "Are you serious?"

She turns to face me, boxing me in with her hands on either side of my body. "I've never been more serious about anything in my life. I'm ready, Holden."

I inhale deeply. "Then let's go."

CHAPTER TWENTY-FOUR

Leighton

I CAN'T BELIEVE I just said what I did. Telling him we can go home and he can blow his load inside of me. I've never been so brazen before, never let this part of my personality out to play. The things this man does to me should be illegal in all fifty states and the damn District of Columbia.

"Should we have gone in and said goodbye to everyone?" I ask as we drive along the backroads toward our home.

He sets the cruise, then braces his feet on the floorboard of the truck, lifting up as he pulls at the crotch of his jeans. He groans when I suspect he gets a little breathing room in the tightness of the fabric. "Trust me, the way we were all over each other in there, I'm pretty sure they understand where we've gone and why."

"Were we that bad?" I ask, embarrassed with the way I acted in public, behind a bar. I've never been that out of control before, never had a man make me feel the way he made me feel in those crazy moments of abandon. I can't even blame it on the alcohol I've consumed. I wanted him, wanted him to do what he did to me, wanted to do what I did to him.

His dark eyes glow in the light thrown at us from the dashboard of the truck as he looks at me. His gaze is feral, turned on, dangerous. Holy hell it's a danger I want to be a part of. When he speaks, his voice is ragged against vocal chords that sound shredded. "I can taste you, I can smell you, and I can still feel your body against mine. That started over two hours ago, Leigh. Everybody in that bar knows exactly what we're going home to do."

I glance over at the man who just had his fingers inside me, who made me come apart in his arms. No one has ever made me feel the way he does. I've always held myself tight and strong, never allowing anyone to see the real me beneath the skin. The one who feels, wants, and desires the things normal women do. For so long I've had to hide who I really am. It feels good to know with this man, I can truly be me. And he appreciates me for who I am.

"Are we really going to do this when we get to the house?" he asks, gripping the steering wheel. "Once we take this step, Leigh, we can't go back from it. I know myself," he reaches over, grasping my hand in his, "once I've had a taste, I'm not letting you go."

"Perfect." I shoot him what I hope is a sexy-as-sin grin. I'm not playing a part; I want this, but I've never been the type of girl to ever get what I want. Knowing I can finally have this? It's a fear and a mind-blowing moment at the same time. One I've never known, one I never hoped for. "Once I have a taste of you, I'm not letting you go, either."

It's important to me to make a claim on him. Somewhere in the middle of this crazy life we've been living, I've come to crave him. I've come to live my life for him, with him, and I can't see myself letting him go. If I have to, I'm not sure I'll ever get over it. It will completely wreck and destroy me, and I've had enough of that to last a lifetime.

As he pulls into our driveway and parks, he shuts the truck off. I run my hands against my thighs, shivering as my skin responds, still hyper stimulated from the bar.

"You sure you want to do this?" he asks one last time, his eyes boring into mine. He keeps his hands on the steering wheel and I can see the whiteness of his knuckles, showing me the superhuman grip he has on his control.

"I've never been more sure about anything in my life. I want to be with you, have wanted to be with you since the first moment I saw you."

He glances over at me. "You mean when you kissed the shit out of me in Birmingham?"

"No," I grin, shaking my head, "the first time you ever came to my house and questioned my dad and grandfather. I stood there, in the corner, watching as you did your best to treat them with respect, even though they were being assholes to you. You were one of the best looking men I'd ever seen in my life, but I knew I was too young. I'm not sure why we've come to be in each other's lives the way we are. There's a part of me, though, that wonders if it wasn't meant to happen this way."

He's quiet for a long moment, and I wonder if I've said too much.

"Ya know, I've wondered that too." He plays with his keyring. "We've consistently been put in each other's path, or in each other's lives for years. I'm not sorry I made the decision to marry you."

My heart flutters in a way I never imagined possible, because I never thought I'd have this with any man, much less the one I wanted. It's not a declaration of love, but it's the closest I've ever gotten. Smiling at him, I echo his sentiments. "Best decision I ever made, too."

HE HELPS me out of the truck and as soon as I'm in his arms, we're all over each other. We trip against each other's feet as we try to make our way across the gravel drive, laughing and giggling when we both almost fall. His strong arms hold me tighter as his mouth takes mine. Up the steps and into the house we go. The minute he slams the door shut, we're all over each other again. Even more than when we were at the bar. I'm pressed up against the wall, and my hands are working Holden's jeans down his hips, the same as he's pushing my jeans down my hips. Once we're both naked from the waist down, I know this isn't a game. Neither one of us seem to be able to wait any longer. His hands cup my thighs, coming around my ass to pick me up and hold me against the wall.

He spreads my legs wider, nestling in between them. He coats his cock with my wetness and he's at my entrance, pressing in, before I know it. I'm opening to him, dying to feel the stretch of his girth, his length. Right as he's about to press inside, there's a knock at the door.

"Havoc, I need to talk to you."

"What?" I'm breathing harshly, trying to pull myself out of the haze of passion. "Who is that?"

He groans, throwing his head back on his shoulders, before bringing it forward and letting it hit the wall with a thud. "Fucking Ace, and if he's here, there's a problem," he assures me. "I've got to take care of this."

I'm disappointed but trying not to let it show. "You do what you have to. I'll go in the bedroom so you two can have some privacy."

"We're coming back to this," he promises. "Maybe not tonight, but we've come too far now to ever turn back." He leans in, giving me a harsh kiss before we both go about putting our clothes back on.

"Be there in a sec," he yells to Ace.

And I know without a doubt, my night is over.

Havoc

"This better be good. You have no idea what you fucking interrupted in there," I grumble as I walk out onto the porch, leaving my shirt untucked. No reason for my guy to see what he interrupted. Make no mistake, it's very obvious.

"I know, I called the guys at the bar to see if you were still there with them.

They told me that you and Leighton left together. I'm sorry, but we have a situation."

This is my job, it's everything I have to deal with on a daily basis and none of the crimes committed or the emergencies care that I'm about to get laid. "Lay it on me." I walk with him out to his truck. "What we got?"

"There was a field party out on Cooper's Creek tonight, and we busted it up."

"Damn," I shake my head. "School just got out last week, they already having field parties?"

"You and I both know it's the only thing to do around here, but that's not why I'm here. We found 'shine."

I curse under my breath. "So they're back up and running."

"I'm assuming they are. One more thing that's going to make your night fucking a-maz-ing. When we broke it up, a couple of kids were worried about a couple who'd gone to get some alone time. They called the K-9 unit because it's obviously dark as shit out there. The dog hit on a spot in the woods. There's a grave, with a body."

"Son of a bitch," I sigh. Can this night get any worse? "How old?"

"Won't know until they get all the tests back, but they'll have to send off for dental records. That's how old it is. CSI was out there, as well as the Alabama Bureau of Investigation. Some were putting time of death due to decomp at fifteen plus years."

Well that makes my life a little better. It's an older one, which means I have time, because the initial forensics won't get back for months. "Alright, let me go in and approve all the shit you're gonna need to finish up your shift tonight. I'm off tomorrow, so we'll reconvene when I get back, unless you need to talk about something right now?"

"I'm straight, and I'm really sorry I interrupted you."

"Hey, it's what I get for making the big bucks." I shoot him a grin.

As I watch Ace leave, I shake my head. Fucking 'shine, a dead body, and a field party. So much for wanting to have a date night with my wife. I go back inside the house, seeing Leighton sitting on the couch, looking up at me with those big eyes of hers. "Why don't you go to sleep, I gotta go to the station, and you look like you need to sleep the shots off a little."

"Sounds like a good idea," she agrees. "But I'm gonna miss you." She wraps her arms around my neck as I pick her up and carry her to bed.

As I tuck her in, kissing her forehead, I sigh at the turn this night took. Definitely not what I was planning on.

CHAPTER TWENTY-FIVE

Havoc

FRUSTRATION EATS AT ME HARDCORE, especially after the many close calls Leighton and I have had. Namely last night. I groan loudly – I can still feel her heat on the tip of my dick – the wetness coating it as I almost slipped inside her. Fucking Ace. I could have killed him, could *still* kill him, for interrupting that moment. I woke up with her on my mind, wanting to pick up where we left off, but realized she had to work today when I found her side of the bed empty. Since then, I've been in a foul mood, ready to rip my skin off my muscle.

I almost went to work today, even though it's my day off, just to give me something to do. Maybe arrest a few people and get rid of this irritation and frustration riding high in me, tensing my body. I don't have that release today though, haven't had that sexual release in almost two years. Remembering the way she trembled in my arms, how she arched for my touch, how she moaned when my mouth connected with the tightness of her nipple has me growling. There's only one thing for me to do; I'm gonna have to work out until I drop. Go until there's no more go in me left and I'm collapsing because I've given it everything I have.

Rolling my shoulders, I strip off the shirt that's feeling way too restrictive and push my athletic shorts a little further down on my hips. Even though they're loose, they aren't doing anything for the erection still there from last night.

Heading out to the garage where I have some equipment, I open the bay doors and do a few stretches, limbering myself up. Thinking better of it, I stop and turn on a few of the oscillating fans I keep out here. Temps in the low-eighties mean it'll be almost unbearable in here by the time I'm done. When I'm sufficiently warmed up, I use the code to unlock my cell phone, connecting it to the Bluetooth speaker I keep there for just this purpose. The sounds of my playlist – Metallica, Five Finger Death Punch, Avenged Sevenfold, and any other angry rock I could find – fill the empty space. I let the first loud beats roll through my body and then I hit the treadmill hard.

Doing my best to control my breathing and hold my form, I run. I run away from the feelings my wife evokes in me. Run like hell from the way I want her, the way my body craves her. It's driving me crazy, making me insane, and I'm scared to death it's going to cause me to make a stupid decision.

One mile goes by, then two, and three. Still I'm wound up; I'm not relaxing at all. If anything, I'm hornier than when I started. Probably all the adrenaline flowing through my body along with the testosterone.

Panting, I bend at the waist and spy my pull-up bar. Stepping off the treadmill, I make my way over to it, grasp the metal, and start pulling my weight up. When that still doesn't work, I stop, strap some weight around my waist, and then go back to work.

I concentrate on my breathing, hold my legs tight, pull up with my arms, hold it, and then control my descent back down again. I don't know for how long I do this, how many reps I do – all I know is when I'm done, my arms are jelly. I'm breathing heavy and I'm tired, but the need for her persists.

I still can't get Leighton out of my head.

My skin prickles with awareness for the first time since I came out here. Turning to face the doors, I see the object of my desire, basically my obsession, looking at me like she could eat me alive.

Interesting, because that's exactly what I want to do to her. I'm trying to catch my breath when she starts strutting toward me, and make no mistake about it, it's a strut. It's like I've conjured her from all my impure thoughts, and she's here to do everything I've been thinking about since before I put a ring on her finger. Her purse drops to her side, the contents spilling out across the concrete floor, but neither one of us seem to care.

Her hips are swaying, her ass is probably shaking, and she's got this look in her eyes I've never seen before. It's hunger, desire, and need all in one.

"I thought you were at work," my voice is gruff as I speak to her.

The walk to me seems like it's a million miles, because she's still making her way across the garage. I move my eyes from her face, take in the flush of her chest, those fucking hard nipples that always give her away, and the way her hands are gripped at her sides.

"Left early." She finally gets close enough to me that I can touch her. "I missed you."

Those words are a punch to my gut and I know without a doubt, this is it. The moment we've been waiting for, the piece of time we've been skirting. I'll be damned if anyone stops me now.

Leighton

"I missed you."

When I finally get to him, I put my hands on his sweaty stomach, caress the firm ridges there, and lick my lips. He's a feast I want to partake in, an ice cream sundae on a hot day, and I've been given permission to have it before my main course. After last night, I'm ready to be honest, I'm ready to stop messing around.

"I want you, need you, crave you, and if I don't have you, Holden, I'm going to go insane."

He makes this sound in his throat, the sexiest sound I've ever heard in my life, as his hands cup my jaw and bring my mouth to his.

This kiss...

Is nothing like I've ever felt before. It's one without restraint, without censure, and it's out of control from the moment his lips touch mine. Shoving his hands into my hair, he adjusts my mouth to his liking, jerking me to the side, so that he can step further into my personal space.

With over two-hundred pounds of muscle coming down on me, I grab hold of him around the waist, pulling our bodies together. Moving my hands up his slippery back, I grasp at his muscles, holding on tightly as his tongue slips between my lips claiming every inch of real estate for himself. He's marking me so that no one else can ever stand a chance. Ruining me because he's so good at what he does. When he pulls back, nipping at me, I open my eyes and am hit with a punch by the desire I see in his.

"Fuck I want you, and I don't wanna stop this time. But goddamn I don't have a condom out here." His voice is low, deep with arousal, and the hottest thing I've ever heard in my life.

Fuck fighting anything anymore. We've fought it the whole time. Let's just give in and see where that gets us. "You're good, we're covered, I'm not stopping either."

I reach down, pushing his shorts and boxers off his hip bones. He groans when I take hold of his hard cock in between my hands. "Leigh." He buries his face in my neck, the rasp of his short beard scoring my flesh. It's the hottest thing I've ever felt in my life.

"Don't stop me, Havoc," I breathe into his ear, grabbing the lobe and pulling at the earring. "I want this, want you, need to feel you inside me."

"Here?" He questions, his fingers denting my flesh with their rough grip.

"Here," I confirm. "We've gotten a taste of each other, and I'm sick of the taste. I want the whole fuckin' sundae, not just the whipped cream topping."

He pulls back, grinning at me, before he moves his hands down, gripping the edges of my t-shirt before pulling it off my body. Again, I pitch backward as he presses against me until my back hits the wall of the garage.

"Sure you don't wanna go inside? Get a comfortable bed and let me lay you down." He smears his lips against my neck. "Let me ravage you."

"You can ravage me just as well here." I reach down, pulling the cup of my bra down, exposing my flesh to his gaze. "Please ravage me, show me what I've been dreaming about isn't a dream.

He leans down, capturing my nipple in his mouth, tugging on the tight flesh before he swirls it with his tongue, soothing the pinch. My arms tighten around his neck, holding him closer, arching up to his mouth, wanting his touch.

"God you feel so good," I moan, spreading my legs wider, giving him more room. I can feel his hard cock, pressing against my core, but I still have clothes on and it's frustrating me.

"Need to get these leggings off," he growls as I push up into his hard length.

Trying to get them off while I'm pressed against the wall proves impossible. It's then that I hear a growl and then hear a rip, I look down, seeing the hottest thing ever. He literally ripped the clothes from my body. "Jesus," I gasp for air, before he covers my mouth with his again.

Anchoring my thighs to the wall with his hips, I feel his fingers run through my core and both of us moan at the moisture there.

"Always so goddamned wet for me." He smears it up and down his cock, which right now is the second hottest thing he's ever done, and then moves my panties as he shoves home.

I realize quickly that sex with Holden isn't hearts and flowers. It's ripped clothes, slick skin, grunting, groaning, and slapping flesh. It's amazing.

My legs tighten around his waist, my feet dig into his ass, and I try to push my back against the wall to give me purchase as he slides in and out of my body. Pushing up, pulling out; it's a dance we'll perfect if there's anything I have to say about it.

Closing my eyes, I let my head fall back against the wall, let my shoulders take the weight, and then I feel his lips on my neck. His teeth nip at the tendons before his tongue soothes the bite and then his mouth sucks harshly against the flesh. I'll wear the badges of this coupling for weeks, I'm positive, but I'll wear them with pride.

"Yes," he grunts as he pushes deeper into my body, hitching my legs higher, bottoming out, and rubbing against my nipples in the best of ways. Every single part of my body is turned on, on fire, and ready for what he's doing to me.

When he picks up the pace and reaches down to put a thumb at my clit, I'm done for. There's not much more I can take. I force my eyes open and watch as his thrusts become less calculated, more frenzied, and he closes his eyes, pushing his head back on his shoulders. The strong tendons of his neck pop out as he strains for the finish. I lean in, grabbing hold of his earlobe between my teeth, something I learned in one of our make out sessions that he loves.

"Fuck yeah, Leigh, what do you need?" he pants, his body going rigid, harder as he thrusts into me and we work toward the end together.

"Hard, faster," I pant. And he gives me everything I want. The only sounds in the garage are that of fucking. The slapping of flesh, the moans, the groans, the sounds he makes as he withdraws and then pushes back in, my sharp intake of breath when he hits all the way so that he pushes against the finger on my clit.

"Can't hold back much longer," Holden moans.

"Let it go, Havoc," I groan. "I'm with you, take me with you."

Our bodies slap against each other, wanting the orgasm we each crave, that we've denied each other for so long. My flesh is swollen and needy, ready to take what he wants to give me. And give me he does.

With one last guttural groan, he thrusts into my pussy and his body tightens, holds still as he comes, collapsing against me, his mouth open against my neck. His hot breath on my flesh and the feel of his jerking cock is all I need as I writhe against his thumb.

"*Fuck me*," he moans, slightly pushing in and pulling out as aftershocks wrack our bodies.

We're both quiet, trying to figure out what to say to each other. But when our gazes meet, I giggle. I can't believe I just had sex with him outside, with the doors to the garage open where anyone can see.

"I've never done it outside before," I laugh, holding his body close to mine.

"Me neither. Thank God we live out here, and no one could see you. If we lived close enough to have neighbors, I never would have chanced someone seeing you like this besides me," he admits, kissing me softly. "Guess that's one to scratch off the bucket list."

We're quiet for a few minutes as we try to clean up and he helps me get my footing underneath me. Neither one of us seems to know what to say to one another, but I catch him looking at me. Looking at me with passion and desire, and it heats me back up again.

"How would you feel about knocking something else off the bucket list?"

He gives me the sexiest grin. "I say I'll meet you inside, wife of mine, and we'll see what we can do."

I giggle as I run into the house. Finally, I'm getting to the best parts of being married, and I'm hoping like hell he's letting his guard down enough to let me in.

CHAPTER TWENTY-SIX

Havoc

IT'S unusual for most of us to have the night off together, but the scheduling gods have shined down and the five of us sit at a table, each nursing our own beers. Laurel Springs has one bar, Hooligan's, and I think all of us, except for Mason who didn't grow up here, have been kicked out once for underage drinking. It's nice to be back and not have to worry.

"How's Caleb? Had a chance to talk to the teacher?" It's important for me to know what's going on in my guys' lives, what could distract them from the job at hand. It's a dangerous one, and knowing what they're going through helps me, and talking about it can help them too.

"He's good," he chuckles. "I haven't heard much about the teacher, and I have a conference scheduled with her. There's one thing I do know, though he's half in love with your wife."

I take a long drink off my bottle, grinning over the top at him. "I know."

"Does she?"

"Oh hell no, she has no idea," I laugh along with him. "It's good though, if she did, she'd probably make it awkward. You know how it is to be a teenage boy in love with an older woman, don't you, Renegade," I tease the youngest member of our team.

He answers with a middle finger pointed in my direction. "I also know what it's like to be the man she loves in return. If I were you, boss man, I'd watch myself," he teases me right back.

Taking another drink off my beer, I smirk. "I ain't worried."

"What's the deal with you two anyway?" Tank interjects in our conversation. "Sometimes looking at the two of you, like the other night, and I think you two are madly in love. But then I know how it started, we all do. What's going on?"

I swallow roughly, because I don't know what to say to him. "It is real, but life has a way of making what should be the simplest of emotions and situations...complicated."

Maybe that's the easiest way to put it. She's the most important person in my life, and I feel things for her I never thought I'd feel for another woman. But it's a vulnerability I can't allow myself, not after the young kid with the huge heart had it broken by a girl who couldn't deal. I take another drink, draining the amber bottle I'm drinking from, and realize it was a girl who broke my heart, not a woman. Maybe I had been wrong to expect her to deal. Hell, sometimes I can't even deal with the nightmares I have, the flashbacks I get at the weirdest times. I'm lucky I came back a whole man physically, and mostly a whole man mentally. It's time I realized that.

"Well *un*complicate things." Tank throws a glare in my direction. "You're lookin' at the fuckin' poster boy for getting off your ass and making sure the person you love knows how you feel. Don't end up in a situation like Blaze and I did, man. I'm telling you, it's not worth it."

"Nobody said anything about love." I shake my head at him, gazing at him over my own bottle.

"Nut the fuck up, dude. It's not that hard."

Easy for Tank to say. He had a life or death situation to spur him on. It was either he had to figure it out, or they were going to lose everything they had. My situation, though, differs so much from his, and it's hard to explain. She wears my ring, and I don't think I'm ever going to let her go. I enjoy our life together too much.

And the realization floors me. Grabbing my beer, I take another drink.

Tank glances at me. "Love is love, and you can try to cut it every other way, but it is what it is. But it's not fair for you to keep her now if you aren't going to keep her later."

"I'm protecting her," I argue.

Every man sitting around the table laughs at me.

"Yeah okay." Ace claps me on the shoulder. "You keep telling yourself that, and maybe you'll believe it."

I stretch my leg out when my phone starts vibrating so that I'm able to reach down into my pocket to retrieve it. Pulling it out, I see Leighton's smiling picture and name flashing.

"Guy's this is Leigh, I gotta take it." I'm already up and walking toward the entrance.

I don't miss Renegade talking shit as I get up. "He doesn't love her, but she's got a nickname and he makes it a point to take her call on guy's night."

I flip him a finger and continue out to where it's quiet enough so that I'm able to hear her. I never told them I don't love her, but that's my business to keep. She needs to be told before I tell them.

Leighton

"Have a good night, Caleb, and if you need anything call me. I know your dad's out tonight."

He smiles over at me, looking too much like a grown man. "Leighton, I've been staying by myself in one way or another since I was twelve. I think I got this."

"Still," I give him a look, "if you need anything, I'm around."

"If *you* need anything I'm around," he argues, making me laugh.

I wave and watch for him to get into his house before I pull away, heading toward my own. Truth be told, I hate driving late at night. Astigmatism makes it hard for me to see and reminds me of having grandmother eyes, no matter how young I am. Typically, I try to be home before it gets too late, but tonight Holden's out with the guys and we had a party at The Café for one of Whitney's clients. Cleaning up took longer than we thought, and here it is, after ten pm and I'm just now headed home.

Slowly, I make my way along the back roads, creeping along because it doesn't matter if it's deer season or not, they like to run across the road. And the one who runs right in front of me proves my thought as I throw on my brakes to miss it, while jerking the car to the left. When I do, I feel my passenger tire blow.

"Shit."

When the car stops, I'm shaking because I don't have much experience with things like this. I'm not sure what to do, although I know I can't change the tire myself. Nobody ever taught me how.

Getting out, I walk around, using my cell phone as a flashlight so I can see how bad it is. Maybe I can drive the twelve remaining miles home without too much trouble.

As soon as I see the condition, I know without a doubt, I can't. Immediately I'm scared. Out in the dark by myself, with no idea how to change a tire, and it being so late at night.

"Think Leighton, what to do?"

Glancing down at my hand, my wedding ring shines against the cell phone turned flashlight. This is what a husband is supposed to do, right? Part of me hates interrupting him on his night with the guys though, he has so few of those. The other part of me is just too scared about being out here in the dark by myself.

Mind made up, I flip my phone over and dial my husband. There's very little hope that he'll pick up, so imagine my surprise when he answers on the third ring.

"Let me get outside so I can hear ya," he yells into the phone, and I almost want to cry with relief when I hear his deep voice.

The background noise gets quieter, but I can still hear him calling out hellos to people. When you're the head of a taskforce in a small town like he is, everyone knows you and wants to talk to you. Finally, it's blessedly quiet and I hear his taut tone over the phone. "You okay, babe?"

Babe is new since the afternoon in the garage, and I have to admit, it makes me grin every time I hear it. Which proves just how bad I'm starting to have it when it comes to my husband. "Hey, a deer ran out in front of me on Copper's Creek Road," I start.

"Are you okay? Did you hit it?" I can hear the worry in his voice and can just imagine the look on his face.

"I'm fine, and I didn't hit it, but I blew a tire when I was swerving out of the way."

He curses in the voice that sends goosebumps down my arms. "Probably where they're doing construction on the Foster Farm. We've been after them to clean the shit up those trucks throw behind them, but obviously they aren't paying attention. Give me twenty to thirty minutes and I'll be there."

Even though it gives me a warm fuzzy that he's willing to cut his night out with the guys short, I feel guilty. "You don't have to come. If you could call me a wrecker, I'd be grateful. I didn't know what to do, or who to call. I don't know how to change a tire," I admit.

"I'm not leaving you on the side of the road while I hang out with my boys. Trust me, it's not that big a deal. I won't be able to change your tire tonight, but we can lock everything up, I'll drive you home, and we can head back out tomorrow for your car."

I bite my lip, second guessing my decision now, because I'm never sure where I stand with him, where we stand together. "I didn't know who else to call."

"No, you did the right thing calling me. Me. You always call me. No matter what it is. You have a good day, a bad day, blow a tire, need a hug, need to get laid. You need someone, for anything? You call me; I'll take care of it. You feel me?"

Frustration eats at me, and even though my heart dances a jig at what he's saying, I still hate bothering him. "I feel like you're always taking care of my messes and cleaning up after my mistakes."

He sighs heavily into the phone. "I don't do this for everybody, Leigh. In fact, I don't do it for anybody else."

"Why?" I have to know why he's picked me to be his charity case. "You don't know any other damsels in distress?"

For a few moments, I think he's not going to answer. "The truth?"

"Always the truth, Holden. You're the one person in my life who doesn't lie to me. I wanna keep it that way."

His voice drops an octave, and it causes a reaction in me I'm not prepared for. Since the afternoon in the garage, everything he does not only turns me on, but makes my heart flutter faster. "There's nobody else I care about like I care about you."

I'm speechless. Holden is a man of few words, but holy shit when he says them, he makes them count. It gives me a feeling in my stomach that I can't name. No one, not even the social workers who were called on my dad, gave a shit about me. They looked at him, took the money he handed off in their direction, and left a young girl in a house full of men who didn't know what to do with her. None of them knew what to tell me when I started my period. When I had questions about how to do my makeup, my hair, or what was the appropriate way to act on a date, there were no answers. There wasn't even any trying to understand what I was going through. Looking back now, I realize they didn't give a shit. Instead, I had to ask other women, not related to me, how to use tampons, to help me make an appointment at an OBGYN's office to get birth control. My whole life, I begged for help and it was never given to me.

But this man, this thoughtful amazing man, took me in, and he's teaching me that I can count on someone besides myself. I can open myself up to another person and not always be fucking disappointed.

"Thank you for caring, Holden."

He clears his throat, maybe uncomfortable with what he's shared. "Get in your car and lock it until I get there. I don't think anybody will be traveling that stretch of road this late at night, but if they are – they're up to no good."

"Got it. Thank you," I whisper.

"Be there as soon as I can."

CHAPTER TWENTY-SEVEN

Leighton

I NEVER REALIZED how dark it is at night, especially out in the country, until I'm stuck in it. At my childhood home, I never went outside at night by myself. I wasn't one of those kids who liked to catch lightening bugs. The dark has always scared me. Usually when I'm at home with Holden, we're inside or we're outside together. I have to admit I'm spooked to be waiting on him. I can hear all the sounds of the wilderness and my imagination starts running wild. Nobody escaped from jail recently, did they? Or maybe there's some weird serial killer in the woods looking for their next victim.

"You're prime pickin' for them if they are, Leighton," I whisper as I turn the car back on, turn up the radio, and hope to drown out the sound of my own thoughts. Hoping like hell Sam Hunt can lure me into a sense of safety, I sing along to every song I know.

I freeze when I see headlights in the distance. Glancing at the clock, I know Holden hasn't had time to make it over here, not unless he was speeding and had blue lights flashing. Since I see no flashing lights, I'm pretty positive this is someone else, and immediately I'm nervous. I don't know where these nerves come from, I'm unsure why my stomach is tightening and I get a thickening in my throat. I'm working myself up to a damn panic attack. Gripping my steering wheel, I hope like hell they're gonna drive right by, but they don't. Instead they park in front of me, and as the person gets out, my breath catches. It's the last person I want to see, the last person I expect to see. My dad.

He's walking to the car, the same way he does everything else, without a care in the world. I reach down to make sure the locks are engaged and try to tell myself he wouldn't hurt his own daughter. I'm aware of how much a lie that is, though. He's tough. He sent me to jail once and I'm sure he can make it where nobody would ever be able to find my body, if he chose to do so.

"You need help, girl?" he calls out as he makes his way over to me.

I've rolled my window down just enough to hear him. "No, my husband is on his way."

He rolls his eyes, putting his hands in the pockets of his jeans. "Your husband?"

"Yeah, I know you heard we got married. It's been the talk of the town since it happened."

Once he reaches the driver's side door, he puts his hands on the top of the car and leans down. For the first time in over a year, I get a good look at his face. Jefferson Strather has aged years in that time. Dad's always been a good-looking guy, it's where Brooks got his looks from, and he's always used it to his advantage. But from where I'm sitting, those looks are gone. He's got lines on his face, and a deadness to his gaze. "I can help you, I'm your dad."

I've been taken in by that excuse so many times I can't even laugh about it anymore. Most girls would call their dad, they'd call him and ask him to come help and nothing would be expected in return. Not mine. He'd want me to do something to hurt Holden, and I won't do that. Lately I've been starting to think of our marriage as real. I've been feeling things for him, I've never felt before. Even if I'm unsure of it, I know I'll never betray him for my dad. "I don't need it; my husband will be here in a few minutes."

That pisses him off.

"As fucking stuck up as your mother. Never wanting to take the help that's thrown your way. You've always been like her, never wanted to have anything to do with me," he sneers.

My hands shake, so I keep them on the steering wheel, gripping it tightly so he can't see in the dim lights of the dashboard. "Stop talking about her like that."

"You never knew her, Leighton. Why does it bother you how I talk about her?"

I've never talked back to him, not really, and I've never expressed how I feel when it comes to what he's said to me. I'm nervous, scared as hell he's going to strike out at me before Holden can get here, but I also know I'm sick to death of not standing up for myself. "Because she's not here to defend herself."

"That's right, she's not, and you know why?"

Setting my jaw, I'm determined not to rise to his bait. He does this to me every time.

"Because of you Leighton, she couldn't deal because of you. You and Brooks were such bad kids she had to go away, and she never came back. How do you even live with yourself, little girl? Don't you have any guilt that you broke up a happy family?"

All my life I've heard this, and I've tried to be a good daughter – I have. I've done everything this man and my grandfather have asked me to do. Purposely I've never caused any trouble. The only things I've ever done that went against their wishes or surprised the hell out of them was go to college one semester and marry Holden. I'll never take any of that back either, I swear to God I'll never take it back. Marrying Holden was the best decision I ever made. Listening to this man, I'm reminded quickly of why I wanted to get out so badly.

"It wasn't me," I fight back, feeling the backbone Holden's helped me find. In the time we've been together he's shown me how to stand up for myself, how to not back down when I know I'm right. "It couldn't have been me," I argue. "I found her diary, Dad, and my baby book. Before I left for Birmingham. She *wanted* us. She *loved* us. What she didn't love was how you treated her. What she wanted more than me was to get out from under your thumb and the stigma of being a part of the family. If anything, you snuffed her out."

"You didn't know her!" he screams at me.

"Because you ran her off before I got a chance to!" I scream back at him. Tears are pooling behind my lids because this is what happens when I get upset. My emotions come out, and I cry. "If anyone is to blame for the things that have happened to our family, it's you. Brooks is in jail because you didn't raise him to respect authority and to care about anyone other than himself. Grandpa is frail and sick because you didn't think it was worth it to make sure he saw doctors and have good food on a regular basis. I'm gone because you couldn't keep your fists off me. Look around you, Jefferson." I call him by his first name, hoping it strikes a blow. When I see that it does, I'm happy and I try not to realize how much that makes me like him. "You're alone because you're a miserable excuse for a human being, and you have no one to blame for that but yourself."

I'm breathing heavily, like I've run a marathon. I've never stood up to him like this before, never felt like I had the courage to. This is what Holden does for me, this is the woman he makes me.

He rages loudly, shouting as he tries to open my door. The handle doesn't allow him too, because I've locked it. Immediately I'm trying to calculate how far I can go on a blown tire, how badly I'll hurt my car, and maybe how much time I have to stall until Holden can get here. It's then I see more headlights in the distance of my rearview. I pray to God it's Holden.

"You wait until they pass by. Once they do, I'm going to show you what happens to smart mouth little bitches like you."

I shiver and mentally start taking inventory of what's in this car. What can I use as a weapon? What can I defend myself with? He's bigger than me, and I know he'll take me easily if he wants to. When the lights pull in behind me, I thank God, and I want to cry because I'm so relieved.

"Can I help you, Jefferson?"

I hear my husband's voice and I want to shout a hallelujah to the sky.

"Just stopping to see if my daughter needed any help. Noticed she was parked on the side of the road as I drove by." Dad sticks his hands in his pockets, rocking back on his boots.

"I suggest you put your hands where I can see them unless you want me to fire a warning shot."

"You'd shoot an unarmed man, officer?" Dad cajoles him, in the snarky way he hates for others to do to him.

"I'd shoot any man I thought would hurt me or mine, and what's in that car is mine, make no mistake about it."

I'm looking back in my rearview, seeing Holden with a gun trained on my dad. Holden's hand doesn't waver, it doesn't shake, and he doesn't look at all scared by the man standing in front of him.

"I think you should leave."

Dad takes one look at him, and then another look at me before he holds his hands up in mock surrender. He backs away to his truck, gets in, and kicks up gravel and dust as he leaves. Holden and I both wait a good five minutes before he holsters his gun, has me unlock the doors, and gets me out of the car.

"Are you okay?" He puts his arms out and I collapse into them.

Since the day I left home, I've been scared to death I would come face-to-face with my dad, and I never wanted it to be on a dimly lit backroad with no one around to help me. "I'm good now. He scared me."

Using his hands, he cups my jaw, tilting my face up so he can look at me. "What did he say to you? Did he threaten you?"

Right now, all I want is to go home and sleep in his arms, forget what's turned into a shitty night, but I know he won't let me. "It's the same old stuff he always says to me. I made Mom leave, and I'm a horrible person. It just upsets me. I think more than anything, he thinks I've told people about what he's doing."

That's a spot of contention between us; I refuse to talk about my dad's operation with Holden. I guess I feel like I'm protecting Holden for once. If he doesn't know, he can't be hurt. I realize it's also flawed logic, because what he doesn't know could probably kill him, but I have to do what I see as best.

"C'mon, let's get you in the truck and lock up the car. I don't like being out in the open like this."

I agree, I hate being out in the open as well, and I notice he's taken his gun back out. I let him drag me away from the car and put me in his truck. Before he closes the door, he pulls me close. "There's another small gun in the console.

Anything happens, take it out and fire it. Don't ask questions, those can come later. This place has got me feeling on edge."

It has me feeling on edge too, but I don't say anything. I only nod, trying to look out into the darkness as he makes his way back to my car. I watch as he gets my purse and keys out. Locking it up, he jogs back to his truck and quickly gets in.

Once we're both inside the cab, I can breathe again. "Let's go home." I entwine his fingers with mine, as he heads for our house.

Neither one of us talk anymore about what happened, but when we go to bed, I migrate over to his side and fall asleep with his arms wrapped tightly around me. For once I'm not sure if it's for his sake, or mine.

CHAPTER TWENTY-EIGHT

Leighton

I'VE STRUGGLED with doing this for months, not sure if I should, but scared of what happens to me as a person if I don't. It's been almost a year since Brooks was put behind bars. A year since I've seen the person I once considered my best friend. This has been heavy on my heart though since I saw my dad on the side of the road.

I've missed him more than I can say. I don't miss the Brooks who hit Trevor, I miss the brother I know, the one no one else got to see. He was kind to me, even when he was an asshole to others. He supported me going to Birmingham, and there were nights we'd talk about what we'd do if we ever got away from our Dad. That's the Brooks I miss. When I see Trevor and Whitney together, I miss the relationship I had with him before everything went sour. Before my dad got hold of him and turned him into the person he is now.

"I'm here to see Brooks Strather," I say quietly to the person behind the sign in desk at the state penitentiary where my brother is being held. Holden has pulled some strings for me, and I'll be allowed to actually be in a room with him.

"Name and ID," the receptionist holds out her hand.

"Leighton Thompson. I'm his sister."

I'm nervous as I wait for her to make a copy of my ID, run my name, and then finally hand me a badge. "Go to that door," she points down the hall to the left. "The officer will take you to the room, and they'll bring the prisoner to you."

I flinch as I hear the term prisoner. It still bothers me that's the term my brother will be known by for the rest of his life. No matter what he does, he'll always be the guy who almost killed Trevor Trumbolt and showed no remorse. My heart hurts because I know that isn't him; he's been colored by his environment and wasn't able to shake the influence. In a way, I feel as if I've failed him. If I had been a better sister, maybe I could have helped him. I could have given him the female influence he so desperately needed after our mother left. I so wish I could go back and change things. He deserved a chance at a better life; he should be at college right now, living it up as a frat boy.

"Hello, Mrs. Thompson, I'll take you to your brother."

My thoughts are running so deep, I didn't even realize I'd made it to the door. "Thank you."

As he leads me into another room, my hands shake and my stomach has butterflies. After all this time, I'm not sure how Brooks will react to seeing me. I hope like hell he doesn't send me home.

"Have a seat, and we'll bring him in. Just a warning – you won't be allowed to touch him."

So I can't hug him. God, I'd wanted to hug him so tightly. "I understand," I whisper as I play with the badge they've given me. I'm nervous and I need something to do with my hands.

I hear sounds and clicks, noises I'm not used to, but I remember from my one night in jail. When the door opens and I see my brother for the first time in almost a year, my breath is taken away from me.

"You're who wanted to see me, huh?" There isn't any happiness in his voice, or any disappointment. It's emotionally dead, and I worry that's where he is at this point in his life that he has no emotions.

I smile at him. "Yeah, it was me. I'm so glad to see you, Brooks."

"You come to brag about how you married a member of law enforcement? About how you're better than me?" This is our dad talking, and I know it, but it still hurts. It hurts more than I can say.

"No, I came to see my brother, you know the one I held when he cried at night after Mom left. The one who stood up to Dad for me when I was little."

I'm hoping that a reminder of who we used to be to one another will break through this wall he's built around himself.

"Got my ass beat a million times for you, Lee Lee."

Hearing the nickname makes me want to cry. "And I've never forgotten any of them." My throat closes as I speak to him. "So I hope you understand I had to marry the man I did to save my life."

"Bullshit, Lee Lee. You should have run like Mom did. Gotten on 65, drove until your tank of gas was empty, and never looked the fuck back. Being in the same county as our old man is just as bad as being under his roof."

"Holden's kept me safe so far." I give him a small smile, hoping the love I feel for him doesn't show on my face. It would be something that people would use as ammunition between the two of us.

"I've heard a lot about him since I've been in here. He doesn't seem like a dick."

I snort. "Sometimes he's an ass, not gonna lie, but for the most part, he's a really good guy, Brooks."

He folds his hands in front of him. "Do you care for him? Are you happy?"

Conveniently, I skip the care question. "I'm happier than I've ever been. The only thing that would make me happier would be if you were with me. I'm working at The Café and doing online school through the University of Alabama at Birmingham. I'll graduate earlier than I expected if I keep it up. Holden approves of my goals and he's done everything he can to help me achieve them. Regardless of how our lives end up, I'm glad to have had this time with him."

"I'm happy for you, Lee Lee. One of us should have been able to get out of that fuckin' hell hole and live a good life." His voice is almost inaudible, but I can hear the happiness for me in the inflection. There's emotion left in him, he has a shot at being a good man. I know it with everything I have in me.

My stomach hurts because it's so obvious he doesn't think he deserves a good life. I can see it in the set of his shoulders, in the way his face has lines that no person his age should have. His eyes? They're dead, completely devoid of emotion, and I want so desperately to put a spark of life back into them. "You've gotta fight for your life, Brooks. No one else will fight for you."

"Fight for it?" He clenches his jaw. "You have no idea what I go through in here, every day. Fuck, every night. We thought living with Dad was bad?" He gives me a dark chuckle. "I would go back any day of the week."

"I'm sorry," I whisper, my heart aching for him in a way I can't explain.

"You're sorry?" He slams his fist down on the table. "Lee, they stuck me in here with fucking murders, rapists, and child molesters. I made a mistake by not respecting the law and not slowing down, and then I was a jackass about it at the trial. I know that now, but I'm not the type of person who deserves to be here. This place is hell."

I'm calculating dates in my brain, trying to make him see it's not as bad as he thinks. "Two years, Brooks, they said you can get out in two years with good behavior."

His eyes meet mine, and again there's that crater of blankness, a canvas with no emotion. "Lee Lee," he swallows roughly, "I'm not gonna make it that long in here."

A coldness washes over me. A bone-deep frigid blast of arctic air like I felt the day of the ice storm. He's given up, and I'm not going to be able to convince him to hope for a chance. To hope for the life he could have when he gets out of here. He's already decided he's never getting out and even if he does, he's never going to have what he wants. "Please don't give up." I reach across the table, grabbing his hand. Desperately I want to offer him some sort of comfort, let him know he's not alone, and I'm not abandoning him the way our family has done to both of us over the years. "Please try and make it. I need you in my life."

"Let him go," one of the guards from across the room directs me, and I realize I've done something I shouldn't have done. Reluctantly I let the connection between us drop.

"No one else does, Lee. And what happens when I get out of here? You think your law enforcement husband is going to welcome me into the family you've made, welcome me into your home? I almost killed one of his officers. He's never going to forgive me." He rubs at his cheeks. "Fuck, I'm not sure I can forgive myself."

There's the little boy I knew who cried when he fell down, who begged me to read him a story at night after our mom left so he could fall asleep. He's in there, I know he is. "You're right, you did make a mistake, and you're paying for it. I don't think the people we live with will banish you forever, but I think *when* you get out of here." I put an emphasis on it. "You've got to prove you've changed."

He leans his chin down into his chest. "What if I can't change? What if I'm the same man, no matter what I do?"

"You can, I know you can, and I'm going to promise you here and now, if you need me to come visit you every week, Brooks, I'll do it. Even if I'm your only source of support, I'll be there no matter what. We've always stuck together. And if there's one thing I know about Trevor Trumbolt? He loves his sister more than anything in the world. He understands the bonds between siblings. The most important thing is to not let your ego get in front of what makes you humble. Use this opportunity to become the person you've always wanted to be, not the person our family tried to make you be."

I get up from the table, because I can't take anymore. I can't stand to see him look at me this, can't stay here and know that I'm going to walk out of the jail without him. I want to take him home and show him what kind of a life we can have together, that not everything our family put us through was right with the world. There are different types of people, and there are different types of families. But I know he's not ready for it yet.

The guard comes to stand beside me, directing me toward the door. Another guard directs him toward his door, opposite of mine.

"Will you?" He stops me as I fully turn my back to him.

"Will I what?" My heart pounds in my throat. He's extending an olive branch and I want to grasp it tightly in my hands. I glance over my shoulder, giving him my attention.

"Come see me?" He's almost shy with his request. "Not forget about me in here."

"Never." I give him a smile. "You want me to come every week?"

He shrugs. "Whenever you feel like it. I can't make demands on your time when I didn't give a shit about time for other people."

"I'll see ya around." I wave at him as he's taken back behind the door, and I walk out of my own. Whether he knows it or not, he's started his redemption in my eyes, and he's on a path without the influence of our family. I hope and pray it continues, because once I have him out of here, I don't ever want to lose him again.

CHAPTER TWENTY-NINE

Havoc

"YOU READY?" I yell through the house, hoping it makes Leighton hurry up. We were supposed to leave twenty minutes ago, but she wasn't sure what she wanted to wear. Luckily I'm not working today, so I don't necessarily have a time I actually need to be at the Founder's Festival, but I'd like to get there before all the carnival food is taken.

"Sorry." She runs into the living room, looking cute and sexy at the same time. "Do you think this will be fine?"

She looks like any other twenty-something girl in the South on a hot summer day. Low-top Converse cover her feet, sans socks, a pair of cut-off blue-jean shorts encase the ass that I'm now well-acquainted with, and a tank top covers what looks like a bikini top on the upper-half of her body. The long hair I love to bury my face in is in some sort of intricate looking braid on her head. "I think I'm gonna have a hard time not looking at your body all day," I admit as I pull her into me, kissing her fully on the lips.

The smile she gives me is enough to make my chest warm, to increase my heartbeat and blood pressure. I'm not sure when the change occurred, but we're acting much more like a couple in the last month. Maybe it's because we've continued heating up the sheets whenever we can, and there's no unresolved sexual tension between us any longer. Maybe it's the fact we got sick of pretending we didn't mean anything to each other. Regardless of the cause, I'm really happy with the effect and the way we're living our lives right now.

"And I'm not going to have a hard time looking at you?" She smiles up at me, putting her hands around my waist, fisting the worn cotton of my t-shirt in her hands as she puts her lips on mine.

I allow myself a moment to let my own palms skate down her back and cup her ass, rocking her into the body that's always hard for her. "I'm nothing special, Leigh. Just a thirty-six-year-old guy who got lucky as fuck to have you with him every day."

Her eyes meet mine and the way they shine make me want to take a picture of this moment. They've been coming more and more often lately, the moments that I want to remember forever. "I think I'm the one who got lucky. You don't know where I could be right now, Holden. In another city, on the side of the road dead somewhere."

"Don't say that," I move my hands up to cup her cheeks, bringing her in for another kiss. "Please don't even joke about that possibility."

"It's true." She squeezes my shirt in her hands. "None of us know the paths we don't take, but I do know my path was on a downward spiral and I'm scared to know where it would have ended up had Blaze not done what she did and had you not come and saved me. I owe everything I have to the two of you."

Maybe it's time for some more truth for her. "I owe the man I am right now to you." I lean so our foreheads are touching. "I was alive before, but I wasn't living. Mired so deep in what I thought was my journey in life, I didn't know how to push my past and work aside to live. You've taught me that. You taught me how to laugh, and not be so serious."

"You've got a great laugh." She leans up, pecking my lips with a kiss. "But I love your serious expression too, like when you're about to get down and dirty with my body. You have this way your eyes darken and your forehead pulls. It causes a wrinkle between your eyes, but instead of making you look older, it makes you look more distinguished."

I strangle out a laugh at her. "Well thank God I don't look older." I lean down kissing her on the neck. "Regardless of how it's said, Leigh. You've changed my life, tilted the axis on what I thought was normal and completely blew my mind in the process. If either of us needs to thank someone for saving them, it's me thanking you. My existence was just that, an existence before you came into it."

"Learn how to take a compliment, old man," she jokes, as she buries her head in my chest.

"Same back to you. I'm not saying these things because I want to be romantic. I do, but I feel like you need to hear them. You grew up with some preconceived notions about yourself, Leigh, and I'm here to tell you, most of them are fucking wrong. You're a good woman, a damn good wife, and an amazing friend. Don't let what you heard affect you. I'm happy with you, and I'm thankful to have you in my life."

When I look at her this time, there are tears in her eyes, and I can tell

I've touched on a subject she doesn't necessarily want to get into. But she needed to know. I kiss her nose and clap my hand on her ass cheek. "Grab your bag and let's go. We wait any longer and all the good carnie food will be gone."

She takes a minute, seeming to get hold of her emotions, and I allow her the time. Truth be told, I need a minute too. I'm not used to opening myself up the way I open to her, but if it'll make her stay here, with me, I'll do whatever it takes. With a wink, she turns, grabbing the bag she's packed for the day with sunscreen, water, and no telling what else, before we head out the front door and to the truck.

"If you like stuff like this, with people around and fun," I tell her as we get inside, "I'll have to get Ace to take us out on his boat."

"He has a boat?"

"Yeah, he's an adrenaline junkie. He tubes, and skis, and he's even been known to dive out of planes."

Her gaze is on me, I can feel it moving across my body. "He likes Violet, ya know? He came in The Café the other day to get lunch, tried to talk to her and she ran away."

I nod. "He's mentioned something to me about it, in confidence, but since you brought it up. I guess it's okay to talk about. You forget, there's a huge thing holding them back. She's married."

"I hope he gets her away from her husband. He doesn't seem like a nice man."

Reaching over, I grasp her hand in mine. "Anything we should know about?"

She's quiet for so long, I wonder if she's clammed up and won't tell me. When she speaks, her voice is soft and small. "She doesn't really tell me much, but I get the feeling she's scared of him. I don't think there's much love there."

"What makes you say that?"

"She saw me taking my computer classes, and she asked if you were supportive. When I told her you were, she said it would be nice for her to have a husband that's as supportive as mine is. I get the feeling he doesn't want her doing anything that would take away from him."

I need her to be completely honest with me. If she's worried for her friend, we need to get this taken care of, and suddenly I'm worried for the both of them. If he's a volatile character, it could mean Leighton's in danger, as well. Men like that fly off the edge and usually take everything within a certain distance down with them. I don't want that to happen to her. "Be specific, babe. I want to help her if I can."

It takes a few stops and starts, but suddenly she begins to talk and I can feel the anxiety ramp up in my chest as I listen to the words. "Some days she wears more makeup than others. There's been weeks where it's been hard for her to sit at the counter. She had trouble getting up and down into a chair. She says he calls her at random times just to check on her."

"But you don't think that?"

"No," she shakes her head, "I think he's checking to make sure she's there. If she doesn't answer her cell, he'll call the business phone, and I've noticed if we're in a rush and Ernie doesn't answer the business phone, he'll drive by."

Now I'm worried. More worried than I've been in a long time. The things she's telling me aren't setting my mind at ease in any kind of way. While I thought she was maybe overreacting, now I'm not so sure she isn't under-reacting. She should have told me about this the minute it began. "How do you know it's him?" I need to know what kind of a vehicle this asshole drives, because I need to pay him a visit and make sure he knows my wife has nothing to do with this irrational need he has to control his own wife.

"He works for Strait Edge Lawn Care," she tells me, glancing over at my profile. "He's usually driving one of their trucks."

I know the owner, and I know who I'll be stopping to talk to as soon as I'm back on shift. I won't let this go for very long. "Wonder if the owner knows his employee is using a work truck to stalk his wife during the day?"

"I don't want to get anyone in trouble, Holden." She bites her lip as she looks over at me.

"Babe, trouble or not, you break the fucking law, you're gonna feel my wrath. You mess with what's mine, you're gonna feel my wrath. And let me tell you something, the ring on your finger, makes you mine. He's not going to mess with what's mine. If you're telling me about any of this stuff, it's making you uncomfortable, and if it makes you uncomfortable, then it's up to me to take care of it." I reach over, pushing her hair back from her face. "That's what I signed up for, to protect you from the dangers of life."

"You don't always have to take that so literally." She gives me a smile.

"I'm beginning to learn something important about you and my life. You're the part that makes it worth living. I want to keep you around and safe for as long as I can."

And those are the truest words I've ever spoken.

"I GUESS it pays to be married to the leader of the Moonshine Task Force," Leighton teases me as she gets her second free fresh-squeezed lemonade of the day. Everyone keeps telling her in honor of my service she can have whatever she wants.

"If you would've known about all these perks before, maybe we could have moved the wedding date up about a year," I tease her back as I sling my arm around her shoulders.

We're walking along the main thoroughfare downtown that's been turned into a midway for the carnival atmosphere we're in right now. "I don't know if I could have handled all this sexiness then." She shoots me a grin with an eyebrow raised over the sunglasses she wears.

"You would have totally figured it out," I laugh, pulling her forehead down close enough that I can kiss her.

"I definitely would have been up to the challenge."

"Holden!" We hear a woman's voice yell at him as we fight the crowd along the midway.

When I turn to see who's trying to get my attention, Leighton curses loudly. Mable Hall is walking quickly to catch up with us.

Leighton grasps my bicep tighter in her hand, holding me to her. "This woman is ballsy," she whispers as Mable finally makes her way to us.

"I'm so glad I caught you, Holden. You haven't answered any of the messages I've left at the station." She shoots her gaze to Leighton. "And I'd asked Leighton to relay a message or give me your cell phone number. I'd like to see about getting you to come and talk to the class again, either for summer school or the next school year."

Leighton's nails are digging into my skin, and I'm not appreciating the way this woman is looking me up and down like a damn piece of meat. I also don't appreciate the way she seems to think it's my wife's job to pass along information to me.

"I'm sorry to have neglected the messages you've left at the station, but most of those requests go through the post. Usually they're routed that way, and I'm not obligated to answer them," I explain. "Your best bet is to place a call to the main office." I pull Leighton closer to me, dropping a kiss on her head. "As for my wife, it's not her job to tell me what others tell her. Don't use her as your messaging service again. Time with her is precious, and I sure as hell don't want to spend it talking about you." I give her one of my best smiles. "Have a great day."

At my side, Leighton is trying to keep her laughter in, but failing miserably as Mable leaves without a word.

"That was awesome." She leans up, grasping my ear in between her teeth and giving me a little lick. If that's how she wants to repay me, I'll put someone in their place, every day of the week.

"There's some of the guys." I point to some of my team who's congregating under a food tent. Out of the sun it's at least fifteen degrees cooler.

"What are y'all doing?" I ask as we walk over to where they've commandeered three picnic tables.

"Trying to decide what we want for lunch." Renegade takes his daughter off his shoulders and sits her down on the table in front of him.

"She's gonna need some more sunscreen." Whitney checks Stella for redness. "And I think she's thirsty. She finished that bottle of water."

Leighton has a seat next to Ryan, before leaning in and tickling Stella on the stomach. These two are well-acquainted with each other and she willingly goes to Leighton. "What's up, buttercup?"

"Leigh!"

I watch as Stella grabs hold of her friend and gives her an excited hug. Stella can say a few words, but she's obviously not at the point where she can make full sentences. "You having fun?" Leighton asks her.

Stella nods and reaches for Leighton's cup of lemonade. "Drink?"

"Is it okay for her to have Lemonade?" she asks Ryan before she hands the cup to Stella.

"Yeah, I'm gonna go get her some more water, what'd you want?" He asks Whitney as I watch my wife with Stella.

I've always known that Leighton has a soft heart, and a good soul, but I've never really seen it until this scene in front of me. Lots of people tell me how they hang out when Whitney comes to The Café to do her business meetings, but I've never been able to be there when it happens, so I've never seen them together. Right now, what I'm watching is something amazing. Stella is yammering on in the way she tries to talk and Leighton is listening with rapt attention, tying Stella's shoe that's come undone, fixing the bow that's become crooked in her hair, and taking a baby wipe handed to her by Whitney as she wipes off the toddler's face. She does it all with a smile and a genuine affection for the kid in front of her.

When Stella hands back the cup of lemonade telling Leighton "All gone," I want to laugh. She let her have every bit of the drink she just got.

"You want another?" I ask her with a chuckle.

"If you don't mind? And I'd like some food, too."

After the way my eyes have been opened to this woman today, I'll get her whatever she wants. Anything she asks for is hers, and for the first time I pray that I'll never have to know what my life is like without her in it. She's ingrained herself into not only my life, but the lives of my guys, the people who mean the most to me. They like her, care for her, and count on her, even if they didn't want to before. She's become a part of a team that she and I are together, and I'm never going to give it up.

"Be right back."

The scene in front of me is mesmerizing and filling me full of hope. It's making me want things I never thought I wanted. A family, kids, a lifetime of memories that no one can ever take away from you. Suddenly I'm seeing those memories as good ones, not ones tainted by a war and a girl who couldn't hang. They're being replaced. And while it scares me to admit it to anyone, including myself, it feels good at the same time. Maybe I'm not as damaged as I always thought I was.

CHAPTER THIRTY

Havoc

"YOU WANNA GO?" I ask Leighton as we eye the Ferris wheel. It's one of the few rides we're still allowed to have at the Festival. The sun is starting to set and there'll be a fireworks show once it gets dark enough. One of the perks of living in Small Town, USA. I can't wait to see her hair under the colored lights. Today has been an affirmation of how happy she's made me. This woman gets me, and I get her. Every day she makes my life better, in a big fucking way.

She grins up at me hard, so hard I see the barest hint of a dimple in her right cheek. "If you do. Just know I'm kinda scared of heights, but if you go, I'll go."

Her grin gets my stomach shaky. It's not the first time it's happened, but it's the first time I've truly admitted it. I put my arm around her neck and pull her in, feeling like I'm the luckiest guy in the world when she loops her arms around my waist and slides up next to me in line. I lean in, kissing her forehead, taking my sunglasses off so I can see her better. Hooking them in my t-shirt, I use my other hand to tilt her chin up. Those eyes of hers are amazing in the waning light of the night. They sparkle, and she looks at me like I made her life, hung the moon, and gave her the very best gift ever. I can't help it, I have to duck in and get a taste of those lips. When we break apart, I smile back at her. "You'll be safe with me, Leigh. Never, ever gonna let anything happen to you."

Here under the brilliant colors of a setting sun on a June night, I realize just how serious I am. Whoever tries to take her out of my arms will have a fight on their hands. Like I told her dad back in that fucking courtroom, I will rain down hell on anyone who messes with her. Tightening my arm around her, I hold her fiercely at my side. She's exactly where she's supposed to be, and I'll be damned if I ever let her go.

"Two?" the person taking the tickets asks as we step up to our turn in line.

"Two," I confirm, pulling the tickets out of my pocket and handing them over. "You ready?" I ask her when he opens our bucket.

"As I'll ever be, I may have to hold on tight." She sits as close to me as she can in the middle. "Told you I'm scared of heights." She jumps when he closes the door and we move up slightly. The shriek in her voice makes me laugh. I can't remember when the last time was I smiled so much.

"And I told you I'll keep you safe. There's no place in the world more peaceful than up here, in our own little haven," I explain, turning the tone of my voice deep and low, hoping it lulls her into a sense of security.

"Ohhh you're good," she accuses, kissing me on the nose before she looks out in front of us.

"I have some practice," I admit.

"Do tell, we have no place to be." She indicates how we've stopped as they let people on and off the ride.

I tilt my head back, looking up at the stars that are starting to make their presence known. A part of me wishes we were down on the Gulf with the waves crashing so closely we could hear it. I can almost smell the salt of the ocean air and feel the heat rolling off the sand and blacktop. It hits me immediately that I want to take her there. I want to experience *everything* with her. "I was a confident, cocky, young guy." I'm interrupted by a throaty laugh.

"You? Never, like, I don't see it at all." She rolls her eyes and turns her face away from me, hitting my cheek with her braid.

"I know, I hide it well." I manage to keep a straight face as I talk to her for all of two seconds, letting the laugh escape. My fingers inch along the back of the bucket, before I grasp the end of her braid, playing with the hair there. "Anyway, my thing was getting girls I was interested in on here. They'd inevitably get scared at the top, and I'd have to calm them down."

She's quiet for a few minutes as we move up to almost the very top. Soon we'll do a few loops, when it's been completely refilled, but right now I'm enjoying spending time with my wife. "If I were scared right now, how would you *calm me down*?"

Her eyes are hooded when she turns her face to me. Almost as if she knows what action I'm going to take. I watch as her tongue sneaks out from between her lips and swipes against the dry skin. In its wake, the moisture allows the lights to mirror off the pink tint of her lip gloss. It's all the invitation I need. I lean in whispering "I'd do a little something like this" before I go in for the kill.

This kiss we share is different from any of the others we've shared. There's a spark of teenage love in the air as we make out on the Ferris wheel at the

Founder's Festival. Admittedly, I haven't done this since I was a teenager. There's not much difference, though; I still can't move much, and I'm just as frustrated as I was back then. My fingers play with the braid that's driven me crazy all day. Not being able to take control is a problem, so I use the only thing I do have control of, my mouth and hers.

I deepen the kiss, close to eating her up, here in front of the whole town, but I can't seem to stop myself. My breathing is ragged when I pull back for a split second, before going back in, my tongue sweeping against hers, tasting the lemonade and strawberry sundae she had earlier. I'm drunk on the taste of Leighton. No one I know has ever enveloped my life the way she has – her smell, her taste – everything about her turns me on.

"Holden," she whispers as she's able to pull back, giving me little nips before I manage to disentangle my fingers from her braid and then use my palm on the back of her head to press our lips harder and closer together. "We're in public," she manages before I leave her breathless again.

"I'm the police, what are they gonna do? Arrest me?"

She giggles deep in her throat as I continue to own her mouth, loving the silky feel of her tongue against mine, the way she's gripping my shorts with her fingers, the way she's leaning into me. Fuck if I could get one leg on the bench seat, I'd have her laying over me. We'd really start rocking this bucket.

"Holden Thompson! Knock it off or I'll turn the water hose on you again!" I hear the voice of one of my old teachers from high school. Mrs. Bennett, if I'm not mistaken. She taught history and always caught me at my worst.

Knowing she's not lying, I finally end the kiss with Leighton, wiping the gloss off my mouth as I turn to her. We've stopped at the bottom and neither one of us noticed it. We were too far gone with each other. "No problem, Mrs. Bennett." I pull the shorts I'm wearing discreetly at the crotch so I'm not giving everyone a show when I get up from here, and we exit our bucket.

Leighton holds my hand as we travel down the ramp, barely holding in a laugh. When we're finally out of the earshot of everyone else, she lets loose. "She got you with a water hose once before?"

"Not one of my finer moments." I grimace as I lean into her, hiding the front of my body from passersby. "I will tell you this though, baby girl. I sure as shit didn't have a fucking hard-on like this with the girl she caught me with in high school." I cup her cheek in my hand, forcing our foreheads together. "I don't know what it is about you, but you affect me in ways I never imagined."

"You affect me too," she breathes against my nose. "I try not to let you. I'm scared one day you'll decide it's time for me to go and my heart will be broken, but I'm losing the battle."

"Lose the battle with me, Leigh."

"It's crazy." She shakes her head, and I can feel her anxiety ramping up.

"It's not, but even if it is, Leigh...baby, be crazy."

I can feel the way she's fighting against this, the inner struggle she's having. The Holden I've always been wants to make the decision for her, force her to see what we can have together, make her understand what she means to me. But this Holden, the one who cares for her, and wants what's best for her, knows I have to let her make her own decision. If she in any way feels like I've forced her into something, she'll rebel, and I'll be no different than her dad. I refuse to be that man.

"I need time," she whispers, her voice teary.

"I'm not goin' anywhere," I remind her. "Take all the time you need." I give her another kiss. This one chaste, tame, taking down our arousal a few notches. "In the meantime, enjoy me worshipping your body, because that's one thing I don't plan on stopping."

"Please don't ever stop."

And those words give me hope. Hope that she feels the same way about me that I do about her. My past won't allow me to say the words without being sure, but I know deep in my heart – there is absolutely no one else for me, and there never will be.

Leighton

This man undoes me with every word he says, every way he touches me, and every look he sends my way. He's perfect, but that's my problem. I've been raised to believe that no one is perfect, and if they are, then they want something from you.

I'm trying really hard to change that way of thinking, but it's hard, especially when you've been conditioned to think that way. If there's anything I am, it's conditioned to believe everything I've been taught since I was a kid. I'm trying very hard to change, but it's a slow process. Slower than I even want to admit to myself.

Wanting to bring the fun times back around again, I grab his hand and start walking over to where people are setting up lawn chairs and blankets. "Let's go watch the fireworks."

"This is my favorite part of the night," he admits, holding me close to his side.

There's one thing about Holden, he always needs to be touching me. At first it was disconcerting, but now I love it. I feel like he's mad at me if he's not touching me. Amazing how the human body adapts to those types of conditions so quickly. "I've never been able to watch the fireworks," I admit softly as we go join the group of MTF guys and their significant others.

"Why not?"

I clamp my mouth shut on reflex. I hadn't meant to let those words slip past my lips, but now that I have, I have to let him know I trust him. Our eyes meet, and I hope he realizes how much it costs me to give him this bit of information. I hope it goes a long way in him believing I'm not playing him.

"You about to tell me some deep, dark secret, babe?"

He's joking, but he doesn't know how important what I'm about to tell him is. I'm betraying the only family I've ever known, and no matter how shitty they've been to me, they are my family.

"The Founder's Festival always has everyone at it, including a shit ton of police to help with crowd enforcement. How do you think all that 'shine gets moved, Holden? When nobody's watching."

His face is pale in the darkness as it clicks with him what I'm saying. "Leigh, did you just tell me what I think you told me?"

I nod, swallowing roughly against the lump in my throat. Hurting family is hard, regardless of how it happens. He's immediately grabbing his phone out of his pocket and I'm reaching around, picking up our stuff. "What are you doing?" he asks, as he holds the phone to his ear.

"Aren't you going to go?"

His eyes flash with something I've never seen before. "After everybody's seen me here with you today? I'd be signing your death warrant, sweetheart."

Whoever's on the other line picks up, and I listen to his deep voice in the darkness of the warm night. "Have Ace and Menace go check out," he looks at me for verification.

"Old Chapel Hill Road."

His eyebrows shoot up, because we both know that's a location none of them knew about before this moment.

"Old Chapel Hill Road," he relays to whomever he's talking to. "Have them take some uniforms. If they see something, have them observe and take pictures. We don't want an arrest; we want probable cause for a search warrant."

He swipes his thumb over the phone, ending the call. Taking a deep breath as he looks at me, his nostrils flare before he gathers me in his arms and pulls me deep into his chest. "You're safe with me."

The tears escape before I can hold them back. "I know," I whisper, although right now, I'm really not sure I am. They'll come now. This will make them come for me.

CHAPTER THIRTY-ONE

Havoc

I'M DRAGGIN' ass on this hot night. We were prepared for moonshine to move tonight, thanks to the tip from Leighton and some other intel we picked up. Spoiler alert, it didn't. Instead we sat in the woods, sweating our balls off. Nothing happened and the heat zapped us all. I hate when a plan doesn't come together, and it's not very often that mine don't. Failure for me is a hard pill to swallow.

I park my truck in the driveway, grabbing my stuff as I groan. My shirt's wet, and my pants are rubbing against my legs in the most uncomfortable way. I want to get in the house, take a shower, and sleep with Leighton curled against me.

We've been missing each other the past few nights. She's had a paper due, and I've obviously had work to do. I'm pissed that those nights I've spent away from her have been for nothing. Coming up empty-handed is not my idea of a damn good time.

I've grabbed my stuff, and I'm fixing to head to the house when I happen to look at the garage and see there's something on the door. It gives me a weird feeling, like when you know a rifle scope is pinned on you. I place my stuff back in my truck and grab my gun from where I have it holstered, holding it in my hand as I make my way across the driveway. It's hard not to show fear, because it's there. My heart pounds, sweat pours down my back and face, and I'd be lying if I said my hands didn't shake when I grab the piece of paper that's been taped to the door.

Neither of you are safe. Don't drop your guard. We're still coming for you.

"Son of a bitch." I know it's from her dad. He's still pissed she told us about the still over off Old Chapel Hill Road. We thought it would disrupt the flow, and it doesn't seem to have done so, but maybe we did disrupt something. Looks as if we possibly put a kink in a part of their operation. Otherwise, they wouldn't be trying to scare me away.

I grab the piece of paper, put it in my pants pocket, and head back to my truck. In reality, I need a minute to let all of this sink in, but I know leaving myself out in the open like this isn't smart. Picking up my stuff, I don't waste any time getting into the house.

"Leighton? You here?"

When I initially don't hear anything my heart drops. Then, I hear her off-key singing in the kitchen, and I can breathe again.

"Right here," she yells as I enter into that part of the house. "How was it tonight?" she asks, looking at me.

"Shitty. I'm tired, I want to take a shower, and go to bed."

She comes over and wrinkles her nose at me. "You do stink a little."

"I stink a lot," I laugh. "I can smell myself. Cute of you to act like I don't smell so bad, though." I lean in, giving her a kiss without touching her, glad to know she's okay. "How was your night?"

"Same old, same old. Did some homework, cooked dinner for just me." She throws her bottom lip out, and I reach in, catching it with my teeth.

"I hated being away from you, too. Hopefully not much longer."

She makes a noise of protest in her throat, as I pull far enough away she can't try to haul me towards her. "Let me go take a shower."

I take one in record time, sighing heavily as I appreciate the feel of clean skin. I never realized how much I needed it until I was stuck in the sand for a year. Now? A shower can sometimes be my favorite thing. Putting on a pair of boxers, I tiptoe through the house, checking the locks, the windows, and arming the alarm system. I'm still on edge from the note I found.

Do I think they might make a play for her or me? Maybe – depending on if Jefferson can get anyone to make the play with him. I'm not scared, and I'll kill him before he can hurt either one of us. I'm beyond sure of that.

When I enter the bedroom, Leighton is on her side, facing away from me. Her eyes are closed, and her breathing is even. Turning off the TV and the lamp, I climb in behind her, but tonight I want to be close to her. I reach over, pulling her against my chest. When she situates herself, her tit falls into the palm of my hand and that's all it takes for my dick to take notice.

We've been passing ships lately, and I've missed the fuck out of her. Dropping my mouth to her neck, I lightly kiss the flesh as I squeeze her breast in my hand, rubbing my palm against the hard nipple. I'm making no demands; it's a lazy seduction, one I hadn't planned when I laid down behind her and brought her into my arms, but I want her. I want her body sliding against mine, her nails trailing down my back, and the heat of her pussy wrapped around my cock. I shift around, pushing my boxers down to my knees, kicking them off with my feet, as I turn Leighton over onto her back.

"Holden," she moans, her eyes closed, her legs widening for me.

I brace my knees against her thighs, pushing her shirt up and over her head, leaning down to capture a nipple in my mouth. I bathe it with my tongue, growling when I feel her nails digging into my shoulders, the sharp intake of breath that tells me she's awake. "Shit," she pushes her head to the side, thrusting her chest deeper into my mouth.

"Feel good?" I moan as I nip at her skin, sliding down her body until her thighs bracket my shoulders.

"Holden," she whimpers when I take two fingers, testing out how ready she is.

"Yeah?" I glance up, my eyes on hers in the dim light of our room.

"I don't know if I can handle it."

I flash her a grin, accompanied by a wink. "Then you better hang on, baby."

She's not ready when I push those two fingers into her, at the same time as I use my mouth to suck on her clit. My tongue worries the piece of flesh, before I pull slightly; pushing my fingers in before pulling them out, making sure she's ready for this. Making sure she's ready for me. Her fingers push my head down, as she opens her thighs wide to my body.

"I want you inside me, Holden, not your fingers."

That's all the nudge I need. Dragging myself up her body, I spread her thighs further apart and push myself home, moaning as she grips me.

"Feels so good," she breathes into my neck as I put my hands on either side of her head, in a push up. We slide along the sheets, but when she grasps hold of my ass, I know she's right there with me. "Harder," she begs.

"Whatever you need, love."

"You mean that?" Her eyes are dark as they look into mine. Her face is pleading, when she hooks her legs around my waist.

"I love you, Leigh. I've tried so hard to not make things complicated for you, tried to keep my feelings out of every equation because I didn't want it to cloud any judgement. But I love you." I bury my head in her neck. "You mean the fucking world to me."

"I love you, too." Her voice is strong and soft at the same time, it's everything I need to push us both to the end.

She screams, I moan, and we wrap our arms around each other, holding tightly to one another.

"I've loved you for a long time," she whispers. "I just didn't know if you wanted to hear it or not."

"Probably wouldn't have listened," I pant, pulling her against me. "I'm listening now."

Minutes of silence pass before I hear her whisper.

"Can I ask you a question?"

I'm surprised when her voice cuts through the dark, I thought she'd gone to sleep. "Yeah, you can ask me anything you want."

"Why hasn't anyone snapped you up by now? Seriously Holden, you're a great guy."

I situate her beside me, running my fingers through her hair as I pull her closer. "I didn't want it," I admit, blowing a breath out that moves her hair. "When I was in the military, I had a girlfriend who wrote me a Dear John letter while I was over there."

"Are you kidding me?"

"No." I shake my head, entwining our fingers, pressing our palms together. "It's a common occurrence, believe it or not. It's hard to deal with, on both sides, and I guess now, being older, I understand more than I did then. I get why she couldn't live with the unknown. But it broke my heart, and I never wanted to open myself up to that again." I twist so that we're face-to-face.

"You never wanted a relationship?"

"Not at first. I came back, did what it took to get back into civilian life, watched my parents retire and move to Gulf Shores, and by that time the job with the MTF came up. I just never had the time, ya know? Never made it a priority. I was good with having a few one night stands here and there, but then I walked into a bar in Birmingham one night, and my mind was blown by the kiss I got unexpectedly."

She laughs, putting her arms around my neck and pulling us deeper together, hooking one leg at my side. "Best dare I ever took."

"I can't tell you how happy I am that you took that dare."

We're quiet for a long time this time, but there's still an adrenaline rush coursing through my body. "Can I ask you something this time?"

She nods, her sleepy voice answering. "Of course, you can ask me anything."

"Promise me you'll keep your cell with you in the house at all times, and you'll keep the alarm armed at all times. Please don't ask me to tell you why – just trust me. I'm asking for your trust."

She stills in the moonlight. "You've got it, and I promise."

She makes a noise in her throat, kisses my chin, and we fall asleep wrapped in each other's arms. It's where we both belong.

And from here on out, every time we're in the house, the alarm is set.

CHAPTER THIRTY-TWO

Leighton

"THANK GOD IT'S CALMED DOWN," I sigh as I sit down in a booth, hoping to catch my breath for a few minutes. I'm a little sore after the way Holden woke me up last night, and I hadn't been fully prepared for the way we've had to work this morning. "That breakfast rush was insanity. It hasn't been that busy in a while."

Ernie has a seat across from me, sighing with relief as he puts his own feet up. "I heard from someone during one of the heavier rushes that a transformer blew out on Mill Creek, and most of these folks were without power."

Now that I can understand. "No wonder we sold so much coffee." I lean my head back against the plate glass window.

Violet is holding a cold Coke in her hand and sinks into a chair facing us, putting her feet up in one she's drug over. "Can we lock the door for twenty minutes?"

I laugh, because I thought the same thing. I don't want to worry about moving for the next hour, if my opinion counts. "The only way we'll open it is if my husband is knocking on the door." I wink. "Or Whitney with cute, little Stella."

They nod in agreement. I take a moment to close my eyes, thinking about what all I need to do when I get home. There's a paper due next week, and I'm supposed to have a girl's night out on Friday. Which means I'm already freaking out about what I'm wearing. I've come a long way from where I started, as a young girl not knowing her way around relationships, but I still have a long way to go. I'm not sure if the anxiety will ever fully go away, but I'm willing to give it all a shot. Anything that will make it appear as if I grew up as a regular little girl, with a mom who cared to teach her all this shit.

I hear the bell ring that hangs over the door and groan. I'm gonna have to open my eyes and see if there's a customer to wait on. As soon as I pry them open, I see a man running toward Violet, who has her head down on her arms. Ernie's also struggling to be alert.

"Look out!" I yell as I see him ball his hand into a fist and cold-cock her across the face. Her head whips around and she falls immediately to the floor.

"You dumb bitch!" he yells as Violet screams when he reaches down and grabs her by the hair, yanking her up. "Thinking you can go behind my back, take those classes you're always harping about. You think you're so much goddamn smarter than I am."

I flinch, closing my eyes as I hear him continue to hit her, the sound of flesh on flesh is sickening as I hear a bone crack. Ernie is still sitting there shocked. I fumble with my phone, dialing nine-one-one.

"What's your emergency."

"I'm Holden Thompson's wife, and we've got an assault happening at The Café. The other waitress' husband is beating the holy hell out of her."

"Ma'am, do not try to step in the middle of this," she tells me, as I'm already starting to scoot down the booth.

"I can't help to not get involved. Please send help."

I disconnect the call and spring into action, looking around for something I can use. Not seeing anything, I take a napkin holder, throwing it as his head, followed by salt and pepper shakers. Anything to dislodge the hold he has on her. Blood is pouring from her face, and the sound is a wheeze as she tries to breathe through her nose. I'm scared she's dead, because of how limp she is. I continue throwing anything and everything I can find, and when he's finally done with her, he turns on me.

"My husband will murder you."

"Or I will before you even get a chance to get to her." I hear Ace's voice, and I want to weep with joy. The police have finally arrived.

Havoc

"What the fuck is happening on that radio?" I question as I enter the squad room, listening to the radio I have in my hand.

"Something at The Café," Renegade says from where he sits. "It was called in a minute or two ago."

"Anybody responding?"

Leighton is over there and hearing she may be in danger has my blood pressure immediately rising. "Ace is on his way, but he's riding by himself today," Renegade says as he puts on his vest. "Tank's on his way, but I'm thinking we won't be able to wait on him. He got stopped at the tracks by a train."

"C'mon," I tag him on the chest, "we'll ride together, something about this doesn't feel good to me."

"Me neither." He's tapping the button on the radio, letting everyone else know we're responding and informing Tank on where to meet us at.

My heart pounds as we approach The Café. Not much is being said over the radio, and what I'm hearing, I don't like.

"Be advised, there's a Strait Edge Lawn Care truck out in front of the business. Witnesses say our alleged attacker was in that truck," Ace radios and immediately my stomach drops.

"Son of a bitch. I told Leighton to let me have a talk with that fuck face." I beat the heel of my hand against the steering wheel.

"What fuck face?"

"The other waitress there has a dick for a husband, and some things weren't adding up. I wanted to have a talk with him, but got busy, and then Leighton never mentioned it again. She's really good at that shit. Motherfucker," I growl as we make our way through downtown.

It takes us minutes, but we make it to The Café, noticing Ace's squad car, parked adjacent to the front door of the building. He's not at the car, so we know he's inside. "Ace, Leigh," I yell as I enter the building, gun at the ready.

Renegade's at my point, and I take in the scene in front of me. Ace is in hand-to-hand with this guy, and the guy has apparently had the upper hand, because blood is running down Ace's forehead and his lip is split. I cringe as I hear skin slapping against skin, the thud telling me Ace may now have a broken nose.

"C'mon pussy, come at me," the other guy is taunting Ace.

Looking at him, I can tell he's on some kind of narcotics. He's got superhuman strength, because I know Ace. He's one of the guys I'd want by my side in a fight. Coming up behind the attacker, I grab him around the throat in a chokehold and start to bring him down before he starts throwing his elbows. "You're under arrest, down on your knees," I shout at him. He doesn't hear me, he's fighting and it takes all three of us to get him down. None of us are small guys, and once he's handcuffed (still kicking and yelling I might add), we all take a minute to catch our breath. I pant out my question. "Why were you called here?"

Ace indicates where Leighton sits in a booth, holding Violet in her lap. The other woman has had the absolute shit beat out of her; she appears to be unconscious, and I wonder briefly if she's not dead.

"Leigh called, because he was beating the shit out of her."

There are a ton of questions on my lips, but we're interrupted by both Blaze and Tank. "Sorry I missed it." Tank takes a look around the place. I can imagine what he sees. It looks like a tornado came through here.

"It's okay, wouldn't want to ruin that pretty face of yours," I tease as I wipe the blood off my nose where Violet's husband's elbow got me.

I watch as they get Violet out of the seat and onto a gurney. Ace follows closely behind, answering the questions Blaze asks. When things calm for a moment, my eyes meet Leighton's and I see tears in hers. She turns in the booth, putting her arms on the table and burying her face in them. When I see the shake of her shoulders, I know it's affected her on a deep level. I hand over the scene to another officer with a rank comparable to mine and stick my gun back in its holster, walking slowly over to my wife.

Taking a seat beside her, I put my arm around her shoulders and pull her trembling body against mine. "You okay?" I whisper, trying not to spook her. What she's seen here today has scared her.

"No," she cries, her bottom lip sticking out as she wrinkles her nose up to stop the flow of tears. "Not at all. He just kept beating her, Holden. Even after I called nine-one-one and told him y'all were on the way, he said he didn't care. She had to be taught a lesson."

"A real man would never hit a woman," I remind her. I have a feeling some of this is going back to her childhood and the years she spent as an adult before she moved in and married me.

"I know that in my head, like without a doubt," she wipes the tears out from under her eyes. "I know that, my head knows it and my heart knows it, but there's a part of me that's still in the mindset that it's expected. I don't wanna be that way, she didn't deserve what happened to her here today."

I nod my head. I agree with her, but neither one of us have a psych degree and we don't know for sure what was going through his head. "Was he on drugs?" I question her. "He was superhuman strong. I mean we're three big guys, and it took all of us to pull him down. It wasn't easy."

"He had the look of someone who was high. His eyes were glassy and he just wouldn't listen to her, he just kept screaming." She runs her hands through her hair, before she turns her eyes up to me.

My superior comes over with a notebook, giving my hand a shake. "I understand Leighton was here today."

"Yeah," she answers as she eyes the notebook. Chances are, she's seen those notebooks lots in her life, especially when people came to her dad's house. The notebook is the cops most trusted weapon besides our guns.

"If you wouldn't mind, I want you to take me back through everything that happened here. I want to make sure this piece of dirt gets everything he deserves, and I can't do that unless I know what he did. I want justice for your friend."

And if there's one thing she wants, it is justice. It's the only thing any of us want. She takes a deep breath, and I tighten my arm around her. "I'll be right here until you're done, babe. Just tell him what happened. Start at the beginning and tell the whole story. I love you," I whisper as I lean in and kiss her on the forehead.

That seems to give her the courage she needs. "Okay." She nods, before she starts and I hope she never has to do this ever again.

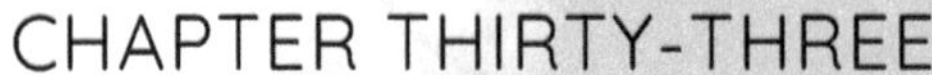

CHAPTER THIRTY-THREE

Leighton

"YOUR PHONE HAS BEEN BUZZING since you got up to go to the bathroom," I tell my husband as he comes back, having a seat across from me.

"Must be something big, everybody knows I'm off tonight and it's date night." He flips the phone over and I raise my eyebrows at the five missed calls.

"Told you it went crazy while you were gone." I was so hoping we'd have a nice night tonight. Violet's not back at work yet; she's recovering while Caleb and I have been picking up the slack. But Ernie closed early tonight to give us some time off. I had grand plans on taking my husband back to our house and showing him how much I love what he's wearing.

His jaw tightens as he situates himself in his chair, pressing a button on the phone. "I got a bad feeling about this." He presses his fingers against the bridge of his nose, pinching it in a way that tells me this may be a long night.

Something in the way he says the words puts me on edge as well. Our food hasn't gotten to us yet, and I've already lost my appetite. Listening as the person on the other end of the phone answers, I try to make sense of what Holden is saying.

"I know you wouldn't call unless something big is going on. Tell me."

My heart beats faster and may palms get sweaty as I see his face pale.

"How many, and where? Have you called the ambulance yet?"

Now I'm really paying attention, trying to figure out what the hell is going on, and who it's happening to. "Don't," he slaps his hand against the table. "I'll be there ASAP."

I watch with wide eyes as he slams the phone on the table with barely leashed restraint. His jaw is ticking double-time and I don't recognize the man sitting across from me. For the most part, Holden is completely in control of his emotions, his anger rarely gets the best of him when I'm around, but I have a feeling right now I'm about to learn what the nickname Havoc means. He pulls his wallet out, throwing down a couple of bills across the table as he stands up. "Let's go."

He drags me out of the building, on high alert, watching the scenery as we make our way to the truck. I imagine this is what he looks like doing his day job, how he makes sure he and his guys come home safe and sound every night. It never occurs to me to ask where we're going, what we're doing. His eyes are wide and wild; they're haunted by something I haven't been a part of. As we run to the truck, and I get in, he flips on lights I've never seen him use. "Buckle up and hold on," he instructs before he puts it in gear, and we take off like a damn rocket.

I'm hanging on as tightly as I can as we take turns at speeds that can't be safe. I'm scared, no denying it, but if he's this upset and worried, there's a reason. "What are we going to?" I finally ask when the curiosity gets the best of me.

He doesn't answer for what feels like the longest time. Sparing a glance in his direction, I see the firm set of his jaw, the way his teeth are clenching and the panting breaths he's taking, evidenced by the flaring of his nostrils. "When we get there, I want you to stay beside me," he growls as someone doesn't get far enough out of his way. "C'mon!" he beats the steering wheel with the heel of his hand, frustration making his body tighten into a string that I'm scared is going to break.

"Where is there?"

"There's a barn party out in the county," his words are clipped, terse, like he's trying desperately to keep his emotions out of this.

"That's not unusual, right? I remember kids doing it back when I was in high school. What's different about this one, babe?" I ask, putting my hand on his knee, trying to offer him some sort of comfort.

"This one includes Caleb. Menace is the one who called me. It's bad, Leighton."

I don't know why, but the tone of his voice sends shivers up and down my arms. I'm worried, but I'm not completely sure what I'm worried about. The quietness in the truck lets me know we both are.

A half-mile from the scene, I can see the lights against the canopy of the trees. There are a ton of vehicles there, ranging from fire, to ambulance, to cops. As we come to a screeching halt, Holden bails out of the truck. For a few minutes I sit there, taking everything in. I see three stretchers with paramedics attending to what look like teenagers laying on them. One of the stretchers has a tarp covering one of the bodies, and I know without a doubt that person is dead. There's another three or four being surrounded by law enforcement, they're all bent over at the waist. As I slowly unbuckle my seatbelt and open the door, one thing sticks out to me. There's blood everywhere.

I see Blaze, who's standing behind one of the ambulances, with her rubber-gloved hand covered in blood braced against the metal, her head hanging low on her shoulders. Carefully I walk over to her. "Are you okay?" I whisper as I approach.

She turns quickly, not able to wipe the tears from her eyes, as her hands are still covered in blood. Slowly she takes the gloves off and throws them on the ground. "No, and Trevor can't be over here right now because he's working."

"I can be, do you need a hug?" I ask her softly.

Her bottom lip trembles and I can hear her sniffle, trying to keep it in. "Yes, yes I do."

I throw my arms around her, holding her as her shoulders shake against me, as she sobs. Desperately I want to know what's happened, I want to make sure the person under that tarp isn't Caleb, but I'm scared to ask the question. "It isn't Caleb," she finally says.

"Thank God," I breathe out. "I was worried."

"Me too," she nods, pulling back as she wipes her hands over her face. "When we got the call, I knew this was the type of thing he'd be at, at his age. I didn't expect what we found."

Looking around again, I try to figure out where all the blood came from. I don't see anyone with a weapon, or one that's been discarded. Trevor and Holden are walking toward us, each wearing their vests with their badges proudly displayed. MTF in yellow letters glow in the darkness of the night as they approach.

"I need your help, Leigh," Holden tells me when they come to a stop in front of us.

"*My* help?" Now I'm really confused. How in the world am I going to be able to help with this? But I know without a doubt I'll do anything for this man. Putting my hands in the back pockets of my jeans, I rock back on my feet. "Whatever you need, you know I'll give you."

He's carrying a bag, and he pulls a jug out of it, showing it to me. "Is this your family's?"

I examine the jug. Ours don't proclaim them to be ours in many ways. They're usually clear glass, without what looks to be any identifying marks, but they're there. You just have to know where to look for them. I flip it over, looking for the etching. I gasp when I find what I'm looking for, my eyes meeting Holden's. "Did they *drink* this?"

"Yeah." He nods, his face grim as his eyes search mine.

"Oh my God." Immediately tears come to my eyes and I curse my dad. "What the fuck was he thinking?"

"Tell me what it means, baby girl." His tone is light, like he's scared I'm going to leave. Honestly, there's a loving lilt to it that I'm not sure I deserve.

My hands shake as I bring it over to him. "This right here," I show him one of the markings, "says it's our brand, our batch." My voice is low and I clear my throat as I try to get out the rest of the words. God this hurts to know my family doesn't care a thing about the people's lives they destroy, about the kid they killed here tonight. "This marking," I close my eyes and let the tears fall, "says it's a bad batch."

"So what are we dealing with?" Tank asks quietly.

"More than likely Methanol Poisoning."

"Fucking son of a bitch," Tank fumes from where he stands beside of me. "So they knew it was a bad batch, and gave it out anyway."

I nod. "Probably at a discount, so these kids thought they were going to get wasted for less money than they can go buy a keg for. They had no idea, they couldn't have." Immediately a thought occurs to me. "Oh my God! Did Caleb drink any of this?"

"No." Holden puts his arms around me, bringing me into his chest. "No, Caleb stuck to beer and called us when things started getting out of hand."

Blaze joins us as Tank quietly tells her what I've told him. "Explains why they were puking up so much blood," she sighs. "As young and small as they are, as much as they normally drink, it probably ate through their stomach lining."

"One of the reasons the old-timers call it rotgut," Holden curses as he rubs a hand over my hair. "You didn't do this, you know."

"But I didn't stop it, either," I fire back. "When is enough, enough for them? You've gotta arrest him."

Holden's eyes flash. "I arrest him, he knows you told me. You're already on their radar for telling me what you did at the Founder's Festival. You know that, right?"

"What's my life for that kid over there?" I point to the stretcher with the tarp still covering it.

His eyes are hard when they meet mine this time. "*You* are my life. We will figure this out." The promise is there in his voice, and I have to wonder what he's willing to do to protect me and keep me with him forever. At some point my family has to pay for what they've done, and I don't know how much longer I can sit by and watch lives get destroyed while I live the happiest one I've ever known. Glancing around, I see Caleb, and I know I have to go to him.

"How are you doing?" I ask quietly as I approach Caleb. He's sitting off to the side, watching the guys work, taking in the cleanup the paramedics are doing. I've watched him for what feels like hours, but I know it's been less than that. His eyes are glazed over, and his stare is remote.

"How the fuck you think I'm doing, Leighton?"

I'm taken aback by the harsh tone of his voice. He's never spoken to me like this. In the moment, he's more of an adult than he's ever been. What I'm seeing is the man he's going to turn into, and I'm scared at the rage and anger in his eyes. "It's okay to be upset."

"Upset? The kid over there on that stretcher with a tarp over his body? He was my teammate. He was the first person to come up to me at my first practice and introduce himself. He let me eat with him at lunch for a week until I made new friends. He never made me feel like the new kid, even though he was a senior. He was a good guy, had a scholarship to go play in the fall, and now look at him. He's got nothing." There are tears leaking out of his eyes, and I want to give him comfort.

Instinctively I know it's not something he gets most of the time. We've both lived without mothers, there's something about the way they take you into their arms and hold you close, neither one of us have had. "Do you want me to go get your dad?"

"No," he sobs. "I don't want him to see me like this, he's working. God, I wish I'd never have fuckin' called him. But I got scared when they started puking blood. I knew something was wrong." He wipes his nose on his arm. "Dad screamed at me over the phone, asked what I thought I was doing. I tried to tell him, being normal for once. Not worrying about being the good kid, blowing off a little steam." He puts his face in his hands. "I met a girl out here," he shares with me.

"Is she one you like?" I try to get his mind on something else besides the blue tarp.

"I've been trying to get her to talk to me for months. She texted me this address and asked me to come out. She and I stuck to beer," he reveals his actions. "Because neither one of us likes to get fucked up. We were behind the barn, she was on her knees giving me a blow job while my friend over there was dying."

I'm speechless. Beyond speechless at what he's telling me.

"I was getting off, while he was dying," his voice breaks as he continues to sob. I can't take it anymore as I pull him into my arms, holding him tightly against me.

"It's okay, Caleb. It's okay."

He doesn't say anything as he buries his face in my neck, his shoulders shaking. I can't hold back the tears either, as I rub his back, hoping to offer him a little bit of comfort for this shitty situation. Across the field, my eyes meet both Holden's and Mason's. Both of their faces are wrecked, their eyes haunted, and I wonder how this community is ever going to come back from this. How is Caleb ever going to get over this? I know he will, we all figure out how to move past the pain of circumstances in our lives, but this is something I never would have wished on my worst enemy.

CHAPTER THIRTY-FOUR

Havoc

"WHEN DOES THIS END?" she questions as we lie in bed a few days later. I've had to report my findings to the state, and while I want to keep her name out of it, I have to figure out a way to do so. We haven't come this damn far in our relationship for me to have to lose her over something like this. "When are we allowed to be happy?"

"We are happy," I remind her, pushing her hair out of her face as she leans against my chest. "It's the other bullshit we could do without. The outside influences, and the people who want to make things difficult for us."

"My dad," she sighs. "It's always going to come back to him. He'll always want me under his thumb, under his control. Until he's out of the equation, we'll never be able to let our guard down, Holden."

I know she speaks the truth, but I have a plan. One I happen to think is foolproof and will get this bastard away from us for the rest of not only our lives, but his as well. I'm scared to tell her, afraid that she may still have some loyalty to him. I mean, it's her dad, how could she not? Not to mention I don't want her caught in the middle of this. She's been caught in the middle of too much in her life. This is one thing I want her to be out of.

"We'll get through this," I promise. "I'm working on a way to take your dad down without your name being mentioned."

"How are you going to do that? I'm the one that pointed the finger. I identified the moonshine. When you arrest him it'll be because of me."

"You let me worry about it. I'm telling you, I've got this."

She looks like she doesn't want to believe me, and honestly, that's okay. I'll prove it to her, my plan will work. It has to, because I refuse to live my life without her in it. We've come too far, and she means too damn much to me.

"Go to sleep." I kiss her nose. "Tomorrow is a new day, and we never know what it's going to bring."

She giggles. "Sometimes you're so corny, Holden."

"It's my old man coming out."

"I happen to love that old man," she whispers as she snuggles in next to me.

As I hold her tonight, I hold her with strength and with a hope I haven't had before. A hope we can get out from under this shadow. We have a chance, and I'd be dumb not to take it.

COMING to the state pen isn't my idea of a good time. It especially isn't on my day off when I could be spending it with my wife, but I'm here for a reason today.

"We'll go get him for you, Havoc," the officer working the front desk tells me as I show him the paperwork I have which allows me to talk to a prisoner.

"Can you tell me what room we're going to be in? I want to be there when he comes in."

He points to a room two doors down the hallway on the right. I'm nervous as I go in. Which is odd. Not many things in this life make me nervous, but this means more to me than most things in my life do. As I hear the clangs, beeps, and bangs that signify they're releasing the prisoner into the room, I sit up straight and look ahead. When the door opens, the person throws their head back and laughs.

"Holden Thompson, what the fuck are you doing here?"

Holding out my hand, I indicate the seat in front of me. "Have a seat, Brooks. We have a few things to talk about."

"We don't have shit to talk about," he shakes his head.

"That's where you're wrong – we do."

There's a battle of wills that ensues between the two of us. We stare one another down, and I can see Brooks trying to piece together why I'm here. I know Leigh's come to see him before, but I've never stepped foot in here to see him. As far as I know, no one else besides her has either.

"You've got five minutes before I ask them to take me back to my cell."

"Five minutes is all I need." I have a bag at my feet, but I won't put it on the table until I'm ready. "Do you love Leighton?"

"What the fuck kinda question is that? She's my sister. Of course I love her."

"Then I need you to listen to me closely. I need you to man up and be the person you should have been for her, her whole life. I need you to stop being selfish, and I need you to want to be a better person. Want something else for yourself, want something else for her. If she and I have kids, I want you to be able to see them as babies, and not in here like this."

"What's your fuckin' point?" he interrupts me.

I lean forward, so we can look each other straight in the face. "I can get your time reduced."

"What do you want from me? That shit doesn't come for free."

Now I seem to have his attention. "Leighton clued me in to something, and I know you can clue me in, too. I need someone to testify for the DA and it's sure as fuck not going to be my wife. She's not going to have that bull's eye on her back. I want you to share some knowledge with me. And if you do, I'll make sure you're out of here in two years tops. Trevor Trumbolt agrees with this. You being honest with us will get a lot more off the street than just your dad; it'll shut down the entire Strather operation."

"What about my grandfather?"

I know he asks this question because he's worried about the old man. But Merle is stubborn – he'll hold on to the old ways until he's dead and buried.

"He's not up to me. And he's not up to you. He's picked the life he's wanted to live for the past seventy-five plus years, Brooks. You have your whole life ahead of you, and so does Leighton. Want to live it? Help me."

I let my speech sink in and hope Brooks has some common sense left in his head. "I know you hate it in here, I hear things. Let me help you, by helping me."

Eventually I see him close his eyes, mouth the word *fuck*. And I know I have him.

"What can I do?"

It's the most grown-up question he's ever asked, and believe me, I know what it cost him to ask. Reaching over, I pull the jug out of the bag and set it on the table. "Two things – how do I know who's that is and what batch it is."

Watching as he flipped it over the same way Leighton did, I see the minute he recognizes what he has in his hands.

"Did he sell this?"

"Yeah," the laugh I left out is harsh and dark, "to a bunch of high school kids having a field party. Two are still in the hospital, one is dead, and a class of incoming seniors won't be graduating with someone they've been going to school with since kindergarten. It's a fucked-up situation that could have been prevented had your dad not sold a bad batch." I lean forward. "I want him on this, but I don't want it to come back to Leighton. You feel me?"

He knows as well as I do how much trouble she would be in, how big of a betrayal it would be if anyone knew she talked to me.

"For one time in your life, Brooks, do the right thing and protect her. She's spent her whole life trying to protect you. You do this, and I promise I'll get you out of here; I'll help you when you get home, and I'll show you that you can change. This doesn't end you, man. Lots of people come back from shitty situations, but help me put an end to Jefferson."

"It's this." He points to the two etchings Leighton showed me. "This one means it's the Strather brand, and this one means it was a bad batch. We mark it so we don't get them mixed up. Because of the methanol they have to be dumped. And we don't want to dump good batches."

"He knew exactly what he was doing?"

"Exactly what he was doing," he confirms. "He didn't want to waste any money. Times must be hard."

"Yeah, I imagine they are."

I can't help the feeling of triumph I get from knowing I've made it hard on them. Good. They've ruined everyone's lives they've touched. Including the one sitting in front of me and the one who sleeps in my bed every night.

"I'm gonna take them down, Brooks."

For the first time, the kid looks like a man to me, with the harsh set of his jaw, the growth of beard on his face, and the experience in his eyes.

"I know, and I'm glad to have helped you. Now don't fuck me over."

I put my hand out to his for a shake. "I'll send the DA here with the deal and to talk to you about testifying. Please don't share this with Leighton if she comes to see you. I don't want her to know until it's done. I don't want her in danger. Right now I'm going to get the warrant to take your daddy down."

He nods and gets up, his shackles clanging as he makes his way back to where he's been destined to live for now. But he helped me, and I'll gladly help him. Tapping my knuckles on the table, I get up with a spring in my step.

I've promised Jefferson that I will rain down hell, and that's exactly what I'm about to do.

CHAPTER THIRTY-FIVE

Leighton

"DID you hear about the barn party?" I ask Brooks as we sit in the same room we occupied the first time I came here.

"Yeah." His voice is devoid of emotion. "It was Dad, wasn't it?"

I nod, I can't put it into words. Not here, not now, not when I feel like I'm failing everyone by not being able to put the man who raised me behind bars. That's mostly Holden's doing though, and not mine. He doesn't want me involved, but I don't see how he's going to prevent it.

"It's not our fault," Brooks' voice is strong in his conviction. "I've done a lot of things that are my fault, and a ton of shit I'm not proud of, but this, Lee Lee, isn't us. It's time Dad takes responsibility for the lives he's wrecked, just like I have."

The phrase is jarring coming from him, and I realize he's right.

"It's not going to be easy." I push my hair back behind my ears, in a gesture that's more nerves than anything.

"Nothing we've ever done is," he reminds me. "But I suggest you listen to your husband."

My head snaps up. "Have you talked to Holden?"

"All I'm telling you is let him handle it. We're going to see the light at the end of this tunnel. Both of us are." He stops, twisting his fingers together. "Holden's a decent guy, and I'm glad he's taking care of you when I can't."

"He's the *best* guy," I amend.

Brooks smiles at me, looking younger than he did the last time I was here. "And you deserve nothing but the best."

AS I PULL my car into the driveway, I see that Holden's not home yet, and it makes me a little sad. I've counted on him more lately than I ever have. He's been a rock for me, and we've been closer since the barn party. Caleb's having a rough time, but we're talking, and I know he's going to pull through this.

Standing in front of the fridge, looking for something for dinner, I hear Holden stomping up the front porch.

"Hey babe," he yells as he comes into the house.

"I'm in the kitchen."

Turning to brace my hands on the island and watch as he crosses the threshold, I inhale sharply at the look of the man before me. Normally before he enters the house, he disarms, takes off most of his work stuff and stores it in his truck, but today he hasn't done that. He's standing in front of me, wearing his bulletproof vest, badge, and cuffs. I'm not sure where the gun is, and I can't bring myself to care. My eyes flitter down to the cuffs hooked at his side.

"Something wrong?" he questions, raising a brow.

I debate for a full minute if I should say what's running through my head. But the two of us? We've made huge strides in being honest with each other, and this is just another form. "The day you arrested me." I tilt my head, eyes focused on those cuffs, bottom lip between my teeth before I let it go. My fingers are caressing the countertop, as they slide to the edge, gripping it. "I wondered what it would be like for you to use those cuffs in a sexual manner."

"In a sexual manner?" his eyes widen with surprise.

"Yeah, like you cuffing my hands behind my back." I stop. It's hot as hell in here.

When he looks at me this time, his eyes are hazy, lids heavy with desire. "And fucking you from behind?" he finishes for me.

"Just. Like. That."

A smirk lifts at the edges of his mouth, those lips of his I love curving into a bad boy smile, as he comes around the island to stand behind me. "Want me to do it right?" He asks as he leans in to whisper in my ear.

Immediately my body tightens, every single piece of flesh, every bit of muscle. I nod, not trusting my voice.

"Alright baby, first I'll have to frisk you, ya know? Make sure you don't have anything that can hurt me."

The heat in the kitchen goes up a thousand degrees as I stand there. Waiting. Anticipating. Literally dying inside. Wondering what the hell he's going to do next. The palms of his hands move down my tank-top, pulling it up and over my head. The noise is loud in the room as he drops it to the floor.

"The bra I'll deal with." He's back in my ear again.

Standing in front of him with bare feet and him in the combat boots he wears most days increases the difference in our heights exponentially. I feel small and dwarfed by him, but I think that's more the point than anything. Using his feet, he kicks mine apart, widening my stance.

"Hands on the counter, Leighton." His voice is sharper, more forceful than he normally uses with me. It causes my hair to stand on end, my body to respond to the tone.

I press them harder against the cool surface, spreading my legs, and sticking my ass out, because I think that's what he wants. As he runs his hands down my body, cupping my tits, and then pushing his palms down my stomach, before running them along my thighs, I almost lose my footing. Just when I think I can breathe again, he puts his hands over the top of mine, and pulls them behind my back, clicking the cuffs in place.

Pulling me back with his hands on the metal, my body brushes against his, letting me know just how turned on he is. Leaning down, he kisses me on the neck, before moving that sinful mouth of his up to my ear. "Is it too tight? I don't want to hurt you."

I test my bonds. "No, it's good."

"I have to know before we get going. What do you want?"

I lower my head, letting my chin touch my chest. "I don't want sweet. I don't want you to hold back. That night you arrested me I was pissed off, and I wanted to tear your clothes off because all I could think about was how hot you were."

He inhales sharply. I can imagine the look on his face, the flare of his nose. He pulls my hair up in his hands, licking the back of my neck before he lets it fall and grabs hold of the metal holding the cuffs together. He pushes, but not hard enough for me to fall, just enough so that I feel myself teetering, directing me to the bedroom.

Just before I reach the bed, he stops us, standing there, but not touching me yet. I'm dying for the touch, want to feel his hands on my flesh. "Touch me, please," I beg.

With those words, he pulls us so that we're crowded against each other, running both his hands up and down my body. His palms roughly cup my breasts, pressing against the tight skin. They feel heavy as he pushes the lace down, gripping my nipples in between his thumbs and forefingers, working them rough and hard. I'm pressing back against his length, grinding against the hardness. "Fuck me, Havoc." The words are out of my mouth before I can stop them.

One of his hands leaves my body; I can feel him unbuttoning his pants, pushing them down around his hips. The other hand, moves down mine, doing the same for me. I reach back with my still cuffed hands and cup his erection the best I can. The guttural groan I'm rewarded with is enough for me to lean forward, pressing my cheek to the bed, arching so we can connect.

He lifts me with his hands around my waist, pushes me toward the pillows, helping me get one under my face before he layers his front over my back, sticks a hand around my hip, flicks my clit, and then presses against me. I can't grasp for anything, can only lie there as he pushes in, pulls out, and it's the best sex I've ever had. I'm able to give my body completely over to him. I can feel Holden losing control as he roughly grabs hold of my hip and slams deep.

"Don't hold back, let me feel what you feel," I throw back over my shoulder. "Oh God," I groan as he does just what I've asked him to do.

Minutes pass, or it could be hours, as he plays my body like an instrument. The orgasm, when it hits me is unexpected, as is the feeling when he withdraws, coming all over my back.

As I lay face down, him beside me, I realize I can't feel my arms anymore, but at the same time it's the best thing in the world. I start giggling, turning my face over so I can see him. When our eyes meet, his are warm with love and worry.

"Don't worry," I assure him as he goes to get the keys to the cuffs. "I loved this as much as I love you."

Havoc

"Last night was fun," I growl into Leighton's ear as she stands at the counter, grabbing coffee this morning.

"It was fun," she agrees, turning around to put her arms around my neck.

I hold her there for a long time.

"Maybe we could do that again? You know that putting my hands behind my back with your cuffs?" Her face is red as she buries it in my chest.

"You like that?"

"I did." Her voice is muffled.

"Fuck." The word is ripped from my throat. "I'm going to think about that all day today."

"Trust me," her brown eyes glance up at me, "I'm going to be thinking about it, too."

CHAPTER THIRTY-SIX

Leighton

STELLA and I are slowly making our way up main street from where we've been playing at the park. Whitney had a meeting, and asked me to watch her. Violet's been working half-shifts the past couple of days, and sent me off with an encouraging smile, telling me she had to watch the place by herself at some point. Which leads me to where we are right now.

"You thirsty?" I ask her. It's still a mile before we get back to The Café, and it's a scorcher today. We'd taken some bottles of water with us, but we'd drank them dry about thirty minutes ago. I know if I'm thirsty, she probably is too.

"So hot," she pushes her hair out of her face from where she stands next to me, as she nods.

"I know, Stellbelle," I pull us into the shade of a building's awning, reaching into her diaper bag to see what I can find. "Oh yeah, here we go," I grab out a hairbrush and a ponytail holder. Having a seat on the sidewalk, I motion for her to stand in front of me. "Let's get that hair up off your neck, you'll feel better."

She turns her back to me, patiently waiting while I pull her thick, darkening hair up into a ponytail and secure it with the holder I found. "Better?" I stick the stuff back in the diaper bag and stand up, placing her on my hip. She likes to walk on her own, but we'll get to the store sooner if I carry her.

"Yeah," she nods, hugging her arms around my neck, laying her red cheek against my shoulder.

"Let's get out of this heat," I hoof it quicker.

Within minutes we're in the Quick Mart, and I'm thanking sweet baby

Jesus for air conditioning. "Hey Myra," I wave to the older lady behind the counter. She's a regular in The Café.

"Hey Leigh, what are you and Stella doing?"

"Dying in this heat. We need some water," I joke as I put Stella down on the ground and watch as she runs back to the water and juices. She grabs a bottle of water, and her favorite juice out of the cooler, jerking the bottle open, sitting down in the aisle and drinking it dry.

"I think she was thirsty," Myra laughs, as we watch her going into the cooler and grab another one.

"I think so too," I laugh along with her.

Walking back to where she sits against the cooler, I bend down. "That bottle of water for me?"

She nods, still sucking on the juice. I reach down, grabbing, and popping the seal on it. Just like she did, I drain the bottle, before reaching in and getting another. As she and I are enjoying our drinking party, the bell above the door rings. I get a weird feeling when I see Myra's ex-husband, Dale walk in.

"What are you doing here?" Myra stands up straighter behind the counter, glaring at him.

"It's hot, in case you haven't noticed, and I'm thirsty," he walks to the opposite side of the cooler from where we sit, grabbing a six-pack out. From where I stand, I can smell the alcohol coming off him.

"I'm not selling you that, Dale," she threatens.

"Didn't say I was buying it. I figure since you got this place in the divorce, you can afford to give it to me."

"You can't steal it!"

"I can, honey bunches," he taunts her. "Just watch me," he nods at me and Stella as he gets a bag of chips, some donuts, and a package of toilet paper. "At least allow me the decency of being able to wipe my ass," he holds up the package at her.

A smile plays against my lips as I watch this, but I can see Myra is starting to fume.

"I'll call the cops, Dale."

"Go ahead, I don't care," he shrugs as he continues filling the basket he'd grabbed on his way in.

I pick Stella up and we walk over to where Myra has a few tables set up for some of the old timers who like to play the lottery and drink gas station coffee. No matter what happens, I want us to stay out of the way. As I see Myra with her cell phone to her ear, I have a feeling we're going to be here for a little while longer.

"The police are on their way, Dale. Put the stuff back and get out of here."

"You're gonna call the police on me for taking a few items, that rightfully should be mine? I put up the money for it, added on that addition with my own bare hands. If I wanna take some beer and some toilet paper to wipe my ass, I should be able to do that."

"The divorce settlement says you can't," she fires back at him.

I hear police sirens in the distance, and breathe a sigh of relief. The car parks at the front door, and Lord help my heart when Holden hops out, wearing his authority, his uniform, and his badge. I reach in, grab that bottle of water, and drink it down. This situation just got a lot hotter and I'm watching with rapt attention.

Havoc

I'm riding by myself today, which I haven't done since Tank was injured. My mind keeps going back to what happened last night with me and Leighton. I don't think I'll ever forget it, the way she gave herself to me, the way she trusted me with those cuffs. Fuck, I'm hard thinking about it right now.

"Holden, we have a nine-one-one call from the Quick Mart."

Shit. "Myra and Dale?"

"Affirmative. You wanna take it? You're the closest," dispatch shares with me. This couple will never stop arguing over anything. "Yeah, show me as responding. Mark me as arriving, I can see the Quick Mart from where I am."

I see Dale inside, as soon as I park the squad car. Walking inside, I take stock of my surroundings, seeing Leighton and Stella sitting back at the table area. They seem to be comfortable and not scared. I offer my wife a smile, waving at Stella.

"Daddy!" She squeals, and that word kicks me in the gut. She knows her Dad wears clothing like this, and from far away, it's probably kind of confusing to her. But there's a piece of me that wants to explore that word at some point. Never before have I wanted to do that.

I watch Leighton grab her as she tries to run towards me. Leaning down, she says something in Stella's ear, causing her to giggle and bury her face in Leighton's shoulder. Turning my attention back to the problem at hand, I question Myra.

"What's going on?"

"He's stealing stuff and won't leave," Myra points at him.

"She won't let me have my beer and my toilet paper. You know she stuck it to me in the divorce, I should be able to come in here and get what I want, since I have no more income," he argues.

While I kind of agree with him, that's not what the law states. "Dale, you and I both know that's theft."

"Bullshit, Holden."

"Put it back, and you can leave with a citation. Will that be acceptable to you?" I ask Myra.

"I want a no contact order with this place," she starts. "But I won't press charges for theft if he puts it back."

"No contact?" He starts to spout off.

I put my hand up in front of him. "You'll need to go down to the station and go before the judge on that. I'm not getting in the middle of it. Dale, put the shit back, and get out of here."

"The hell I will, Holden."

Fuck me, he's gonna make me arrest him. "I'm giving you two minutes to put it back, Dale. If not, I'm taking you into custody."

"I wanna talk to the supervisor, Holden."

Placing my feet further apart on the floor, I put my hand on my gun, rolling my eyes. "Dale, you now *I'm* the damn supervisor. Put the merchandise back, or I *will* arrest you."

"Good luck," he gives me a flippant wave as he turns to leave.

I've had enough. Grabbing him around the collar of the shirt, I drag him around, knocking the merchandise basket to the ground, pushing him up against the counter. "Hands on the counter, Dale. You're under arrest," I put my leg in between his, kicking his feet out, as I search him for weapons.

"You got anything on you?"

"Fuck you, Holden, this is uncalled for. You know I don't have anything."

Ignoring him, I start reading him his rights, snapping the cuffs at his back. Turning my head, I see Leighton watching me with interest in her eyes. "See you at home tonight, gorgeous, maybe we can have a repeat of last," I wink as I push Dale through the door and load him into my police car.

Our eyes meet as I look back through the plate glass of the store, seeing her and Stella sitting there. She mouths *I love you* to me, and I know no matter what I have to do with my job, what she and I have is completely solid. It's the best feeling in the world, because I know the day is coming when I'll be taking her dad down, and I know now, she'll understand.

CHAPTER THIRTY-SEVEN

Leighton

"I'M SO EXCITED!" Blaze literally bounces in the seat next to me as I navigate Holden's truck through traffic. Normally I hate driving it, but tonight I'll make an exception.

"Me too," I mumble as I try to jockey for position in the VIP entrance line.

Holden and Tank surprised us two days ago with tickets to a Brantley Gilbert concert. Both of us had been under the impression it was sold out, but the guys had been tapped to work, and had gotten free tickets for their service.

"This guy's going to let you over," Blaze waved back at the person behind them, flashing them a smile and the horns.

"Thank you!" I yell through the window, appreciating someone not being a douchebag.

The person directing traffic at this portion of the parking lot sees the pass Holden hung on his mirror before he and Tank left, and motioned me to another line, that was less crowded. "Holy shit," I sigh. "This is worse than driving in rush hour in Birmingham."

"People wanna see *the man*," Blaze takes a drink of her water, winking. "I mean who doesn't wanna see *the man*?"

"He is pretty hot," I agree, but then my gaze recognizes someone standing a few feet away from us, checking ID's and waving cars through. "But fuck if my husband isn't a little hotter when he's dressed in uniform."

Holden and Tank stand with another man, waiting for what looks to be a large tour bus go through. Tank must say something funny because Holden and the other guy laugh. And it's the laugh of Holden's that I love. He throws his head back, his Adam's apple bobbing up and down.

"They are pretty hot, aren't they?" Blaze whistles through her teeth as she gazes at our guys.

Hot doesn't even begin to describe it. My perusal starts at the bottom of his booted feet, past the black cargo pants that hug his legs just right. He folds his arms over his chest, which pulls his shirt up slightly at the waist. I want that shirt to rise up further, to see the ridges of his abdomen, the lean muscle of his torso, but the bulletproof vest he wears with Security on it stops the upward climb of the material. Sunglasses cover his eyes and a hat turned backwards on his head, makes him look like the twenty-something bad boy he probably was at that time in his life. He brings his hand up to his chin, rubbing at his beard, as he turns to his left, seeing us. The moment he sees us, his smile spreads across his face, he hitches his chin at Tank, pointing towards us, and begins a loose-legged swagger-filled strut over to his truck.

"Hey babe," he steps onto the running board and leans in my rolled-down window, giving me a chaste kiss. "Y'all got here just in time. Saved a spot for you."

His freckles are brighter than normal, thanks to the sun he's been in for most of the afternoon. My gaze follows where he's pointing, I look back at him, disbelief on my face. "I can't park this truck there, you know I can barely park it in a fucking field – in between two equally big trucks – you've gotta be kidding me."

The smile widens. "You want me to do it for you?"

Putting it in park, I motion for him to jump down so I can open the door. Unbuckling my seatbelt, I turn so that my legs swing over the edge. Holden, being who he is, takes advantage and steps in between them, taking a moment to cup my neck in his hands pulling me so our lips touch. Compared to the rest of the kisses we've shared, this one is on the chaste side. Tapping my thigh, he grabs me around the waist, and sets me down on the ground. I watch as he hitches himself up into the driver's seat and shuts the door. He says something to Blaze that makes her laugh, and then pulls into the damn parking spot like a glove. Sometimes he's so good at everything, it pisses me off.

Tank come to stand beside me, as we watch our significant others get out of the truck. "We'll be done about thirty minutes into the show, so we'll get to come watch the rest of it with y'all."

"That'll be fun for you two," I give him a grin. "I mean watching us drool over a celebrity."

"Y'all were drooling pretty hard when you were looking at us earlier, so I'm not worried."

He's got me there. As Blaze hops down and comes around the tailgate, Tank gets his first good look at her.

"Coleman," he calls to her, his voice a bit deeper than it was when he was talking to me. "Those shorts don't pass inspection," he sticks his hands in his pockets, rocking back on his heels. "I think I can see the curve of your ass."

"I don't remember asking your permission for what to wear, Trumbolt," she fires back at him.

Holden slings his arms around my neck, pulling me close as we watch the two of them.

"Y'all see what I deal with? This smart mouth she's got on her."

She plasters herself against his chest, throwing her arms around his neck. "You love this mouth and everything it does for you and to you."

I smirk. "Especially when it tends to break furniture."

Tank's face immediately turns blood red while Holden laughs. "Do I even want to know?"

"No," Blaze shakes her head. "You don't want to know, I'd rather not go through that again."

"Don't deny you didn't have fun."

"Oh I did, until I almost knocked myself out."

They continue playfully arguing back and forth, giving me the opportunity to take a minute with my husband. "You gonna be able to come watch the concert with us when you get done here?" I verify, excited to share this experience with him.

"Yeah, be careful until we get there. You ladies drinking?

"Since we're not driving, I know I'll at least have a drink or two, figure Blaze will do the same," I lean in, giving him a soft kiss on the neck.

"I gotta get back to work, but I'll catch up with you later," he taps me on the ass, and yells at Tank. They walk with us until we get to their post, and then let us go.

"WHY DOES BEER ALWAYS TASTE BETTER at concerts?" Blaze takes a large gulp of hers.

"Because it costs like ten bucks a pop?"

We're quiet for a few minutes as we wait for the roadies to change the stage over.

"Thanks for coming with me tonight," I take another sip of mine, before I sit it in the cup holder, and place my hair in a topknot. It's hot as hell, and I have no doubt that as soon as *the man* takes the stage it'll be even hotter.

"No way, thanks for coming with me. Whitney will be sorry she missed this," Blaze does the same with her hair.

I glance down at myself, wearing a Brantley tank top, and then over at

Blaze who wears one that reads *Bottoms Up*. "Whitney may be a little refined for this," I giggle.

"Unless it's Bama football, she's a southern lady all the way," she agrees. "You and Holden seem to be getting along well."

"We finally did the deed," I blurt out, face on fire.

"Yes girl! How was it?"

I've never had this kind of relationship with anyone, but I find myself wanting to tell her. "So good, I never knew it could be like that."

"There's something to be said for these guys and their stamina," Blaze gives me a high-five.

Before we discuss any further, the house lights drop and he takes the stage.

"We're so close!" Blaze screams to be heard.

And she's right, we're so close, you can reach out and touch him. Our men take really good care of us. "Let's take a selfie," I yell back at her.

She understands what I'm saying, turns us and positions her phone so that he's in the picture with us. "I'm tagging Whitney in this, so she knows what the hell she's missing."

I giggle, singing along to the words of the song. We scream and yell, dance, and finish our beers. Four songs in, I feel strong arms wrap around my waist, and I lean back into the chest of my husband. His mouth finds a spot on my neck, kissing and nipping at the tendons. "Thanks for exposing that neck for me," he growls in my ear.

"My pleasure," I turn around in his arms, giving him a hug, before I turn back around.

I missed him today, and while I'm happy to be at the concert, I'm also happy to be with him. My phone is in my hands, to record my favorite parts and to get the pics I plan to put on my social media later. Holding the phone out, I turn the camera around. Holden and I don't have many pics together, and I'm not going to waste an opportunity.

"Smile for me." He gives me a wide one, showing off the dimples I hardly ever get to see.

As I look at the picture I've captured, I realize this is going to be my favorite one ever.

"We got any good girls here who like bad boys?" The man on stage asks.

Blaze and I scream so loud I'm pretty sure we've busted out our own eardrums. The crowd participation is insane until he launches into the next song.

Holden leans into my body, surprising the hell out of me as he sings, clearly and beautifully into my ear. I turn around, my mouth hanging open. "You can sing?"

The words are spoken louder than I mean for them to and Tank hears me.

"Wait, you don't know who you're related to by marriage now?" He shoots Holden a look.

"I keep it quiet," Holden answers. "And we haven't had a family reunion yet. They're so busy we have them every two years. I was going to explain before we went," he looks down at me. "My cousin, is Garrett Thompson."

The name rings a bell, but I can't place it. "Why should I know that name?"

Blaze looks intrigued as she watches us. "Yeah, who is that?"

"He's a rocker married to a country music star. They're both *very* popular."

Blaze squeals beside me. "Oh my God! It's Reaper!"

It's then that it dawns on me. I'm related to Reaper from Black Friday, oh my God. "I always thought you two looked alike," I grab hold of his shirt, putting my hands up under the material.

"We do have some of the same features," he admits. "But I keep it quiet, mostly for his safety. You'll definitely get an introduction. I promise."

"I can't wait," I grab hold of his arms, pulling them around my body. "But if anybody had to ask me who my favorite Thompson is? That's always gonna be you hot stuff, always you."

Using the hands I've pulled around my body, he cups my tits for a brief moment while the lights are low. "Those words, Leigh, will get you the orgasm of your life in the next few hours."

There's a smirk on my face as I lean back. "I'll hold you to that, hot stuff."

And when I get to actually touch the singer on stage? All of it combines into one of the best nights of my life.

CHAPTER THIRTY-EIGHT

Havoc

H: *Do me a favor, babe. Whatever you hear through the grapevine today, give me a chance to explain when I get home.*

I wish I had been able to tell her what's going down, what's going to happen now that I've spoken with Brooks and gotten approval from the state. I wish I could have let her in on all of this, but I couldn't. I couldn't make her keep a secret, couldn't let her feel any more guilty than she already does. I promised her I would take care of Jefferson, and that's exactly what I'm going to do. This man will never have a hold over us anymore.

L: *That makes me nervous, Holden. Please don't do anything stupid.*

H: *I'm doing my job, Leigh, just don't worry. I love you, no matter what you hear, I love you.*

L: *Doesn't make me feel better, but I love you, too. I trust you with everything.*

H: *That's all I ask. I'll be home as soon as I can.*

"We ready to do this?" Tank asks as the group of us suit up.

Normally it wouldn't take all of us to go arrest someone, but you never know with Jefferson Strather. Especially since we're about to take him into custody. I'm leaving nothing to chance. "I'm ready."

The five of us break into three cars. I'm driving on my own because I need to be alone with my thoughts, need to calm myself down so I don't hurt this guy the minute I see him. As we pull up to Leighton's childhood home that we've visited so many times before, I get a sense of satisfaction. This is something I could do for her that she could never do for herself. Make him pay for the misery he put so many people through.

As we park and sort everything out, we each climb the steps of the older home. I knock on the door with authority.

"Jefferson Strather! It's the police! Open up."

I wonder for a few minutes if he's going to. Or maybe if he's going to come out with guns firing. That's been a fear of mine since the warrant came through, but it's why I wear a vest, and why I have these guys with me to protect me.

There's noise inside the house, and I stand tall, ready to do whatever it takes to get this guy off the street and out of my life. He opens the door, surprised to see us all standing there, but he plays it off well.

"Son-in-law, what can I do for you?"

That pisses me off. "You can start by shutting the fuck up and coming out here. We have a warrant for your arrest."

He opens the door, shock on his face. "What do you mean?"

I turn him around, slapping cuffs on his wrists, tightening them. "Jefferson Strather, you're under arrest for the distribution of illegal moonshine with the intent to distribute a deadly product, second degree murder for selling a bad batch of moonshine, and tampering with physical evidence. You have the right to remain silent..."

It feels good as I shove him in the back of my squad car. He's yelling to Merle to call his lawyer, but I think I kind of see relief in Merle's eyes. Maybe he's sick of the business, too.

"You think you can fuck me the same way you fuck my daughter?" he screams at me through the window of the car.

I walk over to it, open the door and lean in. "I told you more than once that I protect what's mine and I'd rain down hell on you, motherfucker. You gave me enough rope to hang yourself. You should've left her alone, you should've left this alone when that still blew, and you sure as fuck should have buried that body a lot better than you did."

He looks at me with wide eyes. "What are you talking about?"

"I don't have enough proof yet, besides my gut, but damn my gut has never steered me wrong yet. The crime lab won't have my results back for three more months, thanks to a motherfucking back log of assholes like you. But Jefferson, I know that body we found in the woods is Leighton's mother, and I know you're the son of a bitch who killed her. You bet your ass as soon as we get those fucking dental records back, I'm sticking that charge on you. And then I'll tell your daughter you killed her mom, but made her think she left her, her whole life. How do you think she's gonna react to that?"

"I'd like to see you try," he snarls at me.

"You didn't think I could do this." I grin at him.

"Ain't like it'll ever stick since you got information from your wife," he spits the words out.

"See, that's where you're wrong, Jefferson. Both your kids hate your guts. The reason Brooks is behind bars is because you were a shitty example for a parent and he actually wants to make something of himself. You made this easy because you're such a piece of shit. This is a good arrest, and I think the boys in the pen will definitely have something to say to you. Especially when it all comes out about Leighton's mom. They don't take well to men who kill women."

He's finally speechless as I slam the door in his face. Fuck that felt good.

"I'll drive him over." Ace grabs my keys from my hands.

"Thanks, I'd rather not. I'm gonna go see Leigh, let her know what's happened."

As I watch my guys leave, I turn my attention to the most important person in my life. A life we can now live without the fear of retribution coming back at us. There will always be people making moonshine, there will always be people who tiptoe around the law, but I won't have to worry about Leighton anymore.

Leighton

I'm nervous as I wait for Holden. He asked me to let him explain what was going on, if I heard what happened. Holy hell did I hear what happened. My dad's arrest was the talk of the town this afternoon. Everyone wanted to know if I knew it was coming, did I have a hand in it? I had to admit to all of them I had no idea it was happening.

"Are you mad?" he asks as he walks into the house.

I didn't even hear his truck, which tells me just how out of it I was. "No." I shake my head. "I always knew he'd slip up. It was only a matter of time. Will I have to testify since I'm the one who identified the bottles?"

"No." He sits down next to me, pushing the palm of his hand against my jaw. "Your brother will be the one testifying because he also identified them. He's doing this to get a lesser sentence and to save you."

My heart drops when I hear Brooks is doing this. "How?"

"I went to visit him, explained to him I could help get the sentence reduced, and told him I wanted you as far away from this as you could be. We talked. He understood, and he agreed. Your brother isn't all bad. He cares about you."

Tears spring to my eyes as I listen to what he's said. As I think about the reasons we've been together, I feel a dropping of my stomach. "What about us?" I ask, because even though we've shared words of love, I've known my whole life to never count on anything as fact.

"What do you mean what about us?" he questions, pulling me so that I'm sitting in his lap.

I hold up my hand, showing him my wedding ring. "You did this to protect me."

"I did that to have a claim on you with hopes you'd fall madly in love with me while we were pretending. I thought you knew that." He kisses my jaw softly, his whiskers leaving behind a slight mark I can feel.

"I do, I just needed to hear you say it again."

I feel him smile against me. "I'll say it every day as long as you say it back."

"I love you, Holden, and I don't think I can ever imagine my life without you. Thank you for giving me everything. A family, a sense of security, love, and a home I never thought I'd have."

He enfolds his arms around me, holding me tight. "Thank you for giving me hope I'd lost, Leigh. Without you, I'd just be a guy going through the motions. You make me hope for a future, and I'm excited to be sharing it with you."

"I have a secret," I whisper, putting my forehead to his. "I'm not scared anymore." I run my hand over his buzz cut.

He pulls back and smiles at me, the dimples showing, the eyes shining. "I'm not, either."

And in a relationship that started based on secrets, that's the best one we've ever shared.

EPILOGUE

Havoc

"YOU READY TO GO, BABE?" I watch as she grabs her purse, before waving a goodbye to Ernie.

"Yeah, I'm ready to spend the week, just with you," she gives me a gorgeous smile, "then watch our friends get married."

We never really got a honeymoon. I try to think back now to why, but I know a part of me worried that trying to make it look too official would somehow jinx us. Today, a year and a half later, I'm no longer worried about that. We're solid, and I know we're solid. Doesn't mean there isn't a part of me that worries her grandfather won't manage to reignite the family business on his own, but knowing that Jefferson is behind bars lets me sleep at night.

For the first time since we got married, we're planning, making a future a huge possibility. I want the whole nine yards with her – kids, growing old, grandkids later on down the road. Our lives are open, and there is no damn expiration date on anything.

"We'll see you down there?" I yell to Ace, watching as he stands next to Violet.

No one is at all sure what's going on with them, but I know from where he calls in his position every night, he sits outside her home when he doesn't have anything else going on. He watches over her and I know he helps her sleep at night knowing he's there.

"Yup, some of us weren't able to get the whole fuckin' week before the wedding off to enjoy the beaches."

I take his ribbing in stride. "I had vacation time, and we never got a honeymoon. A week at Gulf Shores before the long-awaited wedding of Whitney and Renegade is exactly what I need."

He gives me a shake of his head. "Handing over your man card."

"She controls it," I jerk my thumb back at Leighton, "and I have no problem with that. So don't expect me to answer any phone calls the minute I walk out of that door." I point to the front door of The Café. "It's officially vacation, as soon as these feet step over that threshold." I point down to the feet encased in flip flops.

"And I don't know about him, but I'm anxious to start it," Leighton grabs hold of my hand. "We'll see you?" She looks at Violet.

The two of them stare at each other for long moments. I have a feeling they are sharing a silent conversation that only victims of abuse can. "Yeah," Violet offers her a small smile. "Anthony is bringing me as his plus one." She averts her eyes to Ace.

"Awesome! I'm glad you're joining the crew."

Violet opens her mouth and I'm sure she's going to tell my wife that she isn't joining the crew, but Ace puts a hand on her shoulder. "Just let Leighton think what she wants."

Leighton gives him a glare, and then pulls me toward the door. As we walk out the door and toward my truck, she leans in, kissing me right beside my ear. "A beach destination wedding is the perfect place for them to fall in love, Holden."

I clasp our hands together, entwining our fingers, before I bring her hand up to my lips. When we get to the truck, I open the door and pick her up, putting her on the passenger seat as I step in between her legs. "Know what else it is?" I ask her, putting my hands on her thighs, caressing them softly.

"What?"

"The perfect place for us to fall deeper in love."

She sighs, giving me this look she reserves only for me. It's a softening in her eyes, a tilt to her head, and a quirking of her smile. Grabbing my hands, she pulls them around her waist, leaning in to put her mouth to my ear again. The whispered words aren't what I'm expecting at all, but it's enough to make my heart race. "Or for us to get started on that baby we've been talking about lately."

I'm speechless as I pull back and look into her eyes, searching them for the truth in her words.

"I stopped my birth control last month, Holden. I'm ready," she whispers. "I'm ready to trust you with forever."

Those are the best words I've ever heard in my life, and as I lean forward to take her lips with mine, I hope like hell the rest of my guys find this happiness I've found.

Doesn't matter where it begins, it only matters how it ends. And ours is going to end fifty years from now when we both fall asleep together and never wake up. Because I know without a doubt, I can't ever imagine my life without her in it.

She is mine.

I am hers.

And together, we are an unbreakable force that learned how to overcome every obstacle thrown our way. We are the love story that everyone wants, and I know we'll never let that love go.

Continue the MTF with Ace!

ACE - BOOK IV

SUMMARY

Anthony "Ace" Bailey

I'm not a rules kinda guy.
Department Policy? Kinda sucks.
Playing it safe? Not my thing.

Married? Not a deal breaker when I know she's unhappy, scared, and not with the right man.

I'm one of *those* guys – a sniper in the military, a little bit of an adrenaline junkie, and a member for the Moonshine Task Force. I've lived through some shit.

My gut has never failed me. It's my sixth sense. Warning me of a gunshot coming my way, of a traffic stop being potentially deadly, or the tingling in the back of neck when I go to sleep telling me I'll be woken up by a call in the middle of the night. My gut has always kept me honest and safe.

Like the day I walked into The Café and saw the new waitress. There was a ring on her left hand, but I didn't care. One look in her eyes told me everything I needed to know. Her marriage wasn't one made of love and respect. It was one made of fear and doubt.

It's why I ignored that ring, why I arrested her husband, and the reason I'm willing to take my time. Patience is a virtue, and with this woman, I have it in spades.

Violet Miller

Meeting Anthony Bailey changed my life. He did things that no one else has ever done for me.

Feeling safe? Never happened before.
Feeling wanted? It's been years.
Being independent? I'm learning.

It's foreign, not having someone question my every move, being able to eat what I want for dinner, and sitting out on my front porch talking to Anthony every night while we share a couple beers.

I try to tell myself he's just being nice, that he's doing his job and working within the community. The problem? The night he takes the kiss we both want, everything changes, and I can no longer deny what I feel. But it doesn't stop me from trying, and I learn quickly that Ace knows me better than anyone else ever has – including myself.

All I can do is hang on as he takes me on the scariest journey of my life. The one that bends us until we almost break and ends with a happily ever after I never thought I would get.

PART 1

RECOVERY

CHAPTER ONE
VIOLET

"MRS. MILLER, is there someone who can come get you?"

The voice speaking to me is careful. Almost as if she's scared to use her normal tone. Everyone who's walked through the door since I got here, has treated me as if I'm about to break. Truthfully, I think I am.

My eyes travel along my blanket covered legs, past the IV in my arm, over the identification bracelet on my wrist, and then up to the face of the nurse asking me the question. She's been the one taking care of me for the last few days. Everyday she's looked at me with pity in her eyes, and I can't say that I'm not looking forward to getting away from her knowing gaze. All I want right now is to go home, lick my wounds, and try to gather the pieces of my tattered pride. Try to make a life out of the smoldering wreckage left behind after the beating. I realize with great clarity my life has now been split into two parts – before the beating and after the beating.

The beeping of the monitors have been comforting while I've laid here; a part of me has focused on their beeping, proving I'm alive. They were the first indication that I'd made it when I came out of the darkness that'd encompassed me after Brent had attacked me.

"You're going to be released as soon as the paperwork is signed, and you'll need someone to drive you home, honey. With the amount of pain medication you've been given, you can't drive yourself."

I nod to show my understanding, strengthen my reserves, and manage to push out the word "cab" on a whisper. Pain radiates through my jaw with that one little word, and I wonder how I'm going to survive the next couple of days – forget the next few weeks, months, or even years.

The disapproval is in her eyes, but honestly there's nothing else I can do. They took my husband to jail for doing this to me, and I'm not willing to involve any of the friends I've made since I came to Laurel Springs in this mess. She doesn't want to call a cab, but I have no choice. Story of my damn life.

She opens her mouth to speak to me again, when I hear a voice at the doorway of my room. Since the first day I heard it - the deep timbre, the accent - it's always been the voice of an angel. The one thing I could cling to in the darkness of the life I was living.

"I'll be taking her home."

Surprise grips my stomach, but it really shouldn't. Anthony "Ace" Bailey has been around since the first day I hit town. From the moment he walked into The Café, he's had my attention, and I know I've had his. Every day he's always had a gorgeous smile for me, a kind word, and a little bit of hope that life will change. Never did I expect the life-changing moment would be me getting the holy hell beat out of me and him arresting my husband.

While I've been here in the hospital, I know he's visited me – I've felt him, but it's always been when I was deeply sedated, or just too weary to pry my eyes open. A couple of times I even had dreams about him. What would happen if I'd let him sweep me away like he'd joked about once or twice. But not once when he came did I acknowledge his presence. Luckily he doesn't seem to have taken offense to it.

Today? I gobble up the sight of him, and my heart pounds as I see him standing there, a bag in his hand. He wears a bruise across his nose and slightly under his eyes. My memory vaguely unlocks a moment during the struggle, where I heard Anthony cry out. Brent must have gotten him with an elbow as they fought over control of my body, which at the moment had been flung around like a ragdoll. I flex my fingers against the blanket covering my body. I want to reach out, grab his hand, feel the warmth of his touch. Looking back down at the bag he's carrying, I notice it's from a department store in the mall that I like. Leighton and I have gone shopping there for her, but I've never bought myself anything, because Brent kept such a tight rein on the finances. He lifts the bag up. "Brought you some new clothes."

The clothes I'd been wearing at The Café had been smeared with blood and cut off of me. Since they were my regular work clothes, chances are they smelled like grease too. No way I'd be wearing them home. I'm not even sure I can handle that smell anymore. I feel as if the first time the stench hits me, I might be sent back to that day when I was minding my own business, my head down and unaware. Shaking my head, I go back to thinking about the clothes. Those are safer, and there's no emotional attachment in them. Honestly, I'd figured they'd give me some scrubs, at least that's what I've seen on TV shows.

"Please let me take you home, make sure you're good. You've been through hell, Vi, and you need someone to take care of you. Doesn't make you weak."

He winks as he enters the room and has a seat on the chair. He looks like he always does, like he doesn't have a care in the world. But as his green eyes rake over my body, I get the feeling he does have a care, and that care is *me*.

"You realize it'll be up to her, if she goes home with you." The nurse is oddly protective of me. It's obvious she's not going to let me go if I don't want to go. I have a feeling if I can't figure out how to get home, she'll drive me herself; rules be damned.

"I respect your protectiveness of her, but I'm a cop, I'll keep her safe. There's absolutely no pressure. If she doesn't want me, I'll call our friend, Leighton to come get her," he turns back to me, an expression on his face indicating not to argue with him. "It's not a big deal for any of us, but I'll be damned if you take a cab home after the ordeal you've been through. Not when you've got people who care about you."

I weigh my options. I don't want to bother Leighton, but I don't want to be a burden on Anthony either. That's my damage, no one else's. I realize quickly they're waiting for me to respond.

"Go with you," I whisper out, letting my jaw open as much as I can. The pain is still excruciating, and I'm mentally calculating how long it is until they'll let me have another pain pill.

The pleased smile on his face hits me in the gut. He's genuinely happy to help me, and I can honestly say a few things about this man. He's my hero, a savior, I really don't think he set out to be. In all the time I've been dealing with my husband and his fists, no one's ever saved me, they've never made me feel safe, and none have ever made me wonder what it would be like to have a different man in my life.

Anthony Bailey, in the small amount of time I've known him, has saved me, made me feel safe, and kept me awake at night wondering what it would be like to be his.

And honestly – after the way I've been treated – I can't even feel guilty about it.

"C'MON HONEY, let me help you put these leggings on." The nice nurse takes them out of the bag, and holds them open for me.

"Wish I could do it myself." Tears are pooled behind my eyes. This is a new kind of humiliation, one I'd never imagined myself having to deal with. I'm sure the embarrassment is written across my face.

"My sister had a husband like yours and was killed a few years ago." She smiles sadly. "She didn't get a chance to be embarrassed. I would give years of my life to be able to help her put her leggings on if it meant she were still here."

I can't meet her gaze as I pull them up over my stomach and slowly pull the shirt over my head. Lucky isn't something I would have described myself as until I listened to this woman's story. "Sorry for you." I lick my dry, cracked lips.

"It's why I take care of the domestic violence victims. The next weeks, months, and years will be hard on you, Violet. You might remember things that give you pause, have nightmares, and wonder where you go from here. Just remember you're alive, you've got friends, you've got a man who seems to care about you, and you're strong enough to come out on the other side of this."

"I know." My voice is quiet as I let some of the tears fall.

"Now, get out of here and take care of yourself."

As I have a seat in the wheelchair so that I can exit the hospital, I can't help but wonder where exactly life is going to take me. I can't say I'm excited at this moment, but I'm resigned, and that's better than I have been.

Ace

She's not speaking, and while I know her jaw was this close to being wired shut, it's still worrying me. I'm not sure if the silence is because of the physical or the emotional pain she's been through. Being stuck in your head, after a situation like what's she's been through is the most dangerous detriment to her recovery.

"The clothes fit okay?" I question as I turn my truck onto the main road.

A noise in her throat is the only answer I get, but I can tell it's affirmative. Hell, anyone with two eyes can see that they fit, but I still feel the need to ask her, to make sure I haven't overstepped my boundaries. Her eyes roam the passing scenery as I drive away from the hospital and toward the area we both live in. I'm undecided about where I want to take her. She wants to be alone, that much is obvious from the way she's tucked into herself on her side of the truck, not looking at me, not paying attention to what I'm doing, or even really acknowledging my presence. However, the public servant, the man who cares for her, and the person who has a little bit of first-aid training thanks to the military wants to keep her as close as possible. When I come to the intersection that will lead to either my duplex or the trailer she lives in, I come to a stop and don't indicate which way I'm going to go.

"It's up to you, Violet. Which way am I going?"

I wait for her to answer.

"Why do you have a truck now? You used to have a sports car."

The question catches me off-guard, as well as the change of subject. She paid attention to me, and I never even knew it. "I have a boat, I got sick of asking others to help me transport it, and after Tank's wreck, I decided to slow down. I don't do a lot of the crazy stuff I used to. I realized with great clarity you have one life, and once it's gone, it's gone. Now, which way am I going? You coming home with me, or am I taking you to your place?"

Her head whips around to me. Struggling, she pushes out. "What? Take me home."

"I'd rather take you to my home," I argue, softly. Maybe this was something I should have discussed with her before we'd gotten into the truck. "You don't need to be by yourself. What if you need help during the night? What if something frightens you?"

"He's in jail." She puts her hands between her legs, squeezing them between her thighs. Almost as if she's trying to ground herself in what must be a twinge of pain.

It doesn't escape me that she's gotten right to the heart of the matter. I didn't mention him, didn't say she might be frightened of him. But something tells me she's lived her whole life trying to figure out how much to tell people and how much to keep to herself.

"Doesn't mean you're not going to need help. You've been through a lot." I try to reason with her. "Getting scared will be normal. You've been through a trauma, lived through something a lot of people have never had to live through. Most don't ever think about it. There's nothing wrong if you do get scared."

Her dark eyes cut over to mine, no longer warm and thankful that I came to get her. Now the brown pools are hard, tough, and unrelenting. "I don't ever get scared, Anthony," she stops, and by the way she grabs her jaw, a pain must shoot through the bone. Angry tears threaten to spill over her lids, as she fights to open her mouth again. I wish we could communicate easier, but she keeps the bravado up as she pushes out the final words. "It's never done me any good to get scared."

Which I know is a lie, but if she needs to believe this about herself, I'll let her. Encourage her, even. Show her that I trust her. Doesn't mean I'm not scared for her. And not only physically, but emotionally too. There's many pieces that will reveal themselves as she begins the recovery process to put herself back together again.

I want to be there for her, to be the person she turns to when she's dealing with things that might break the façade she's maintaining. There will be a chance for me, I'm optimistic about it, but I know I can't pressure her. Letting her come to me or meeting in the middle will be the hardest thing I've ever done, but it's a must in this situation.

Many would ask me what makes her different. Truth is I can't put my finger on any *one* thing. It's a combination of everything about her. Her stoic strength, the vulnerability that lingers just below the surface, the passion I've seen spark in her eyes once or twice. When Violet unleashes all of this, and allows the world to see what she's hiding under the exterior, everyone will realize exactly why I want this woman.

One thing I do know is the decision is hers, and if I try to talk her out of it or assert any kind of authority over her, I'll be met with rebellion. I'm better than her husband, and I have to prove to her I am. Taking care of her won't be easy, but I'll do it in a way that's non-threatening to her. Against my better judgement, I turn the truck in the direction to her trailer.

"Then home is where you'll go."

CHAPTER TWO
VIOLET

ALONE.

It's an emotion I've felt for years, but it's never consumed me until this moment. Fact is, even when I've felt alone in this home, I've been here with Brent, and the loneliness was figurative, not literal.

This afternoon it's literal. The clock on the wall ticks loudly in the silence. He's not sitting in his favorite recliner, watching some game on TV, drinking a beer, and smugly asking me when lunch will be served. I don't have to stand at the stove with my back to him, every retort running through my head to the foulness he speaks. My back doesn't have to stiffen when I hear him get up and feel him come behind me. I don't have to cringe as he touches me, pretend to enjoy the way his hands caress my body. Never again will I have to zone out as he finds pleasure in an act I haven't found pleasurable for years.

But the silence - the being alone –gets to me.

Truly, I can't remember the last time I was alone in this home physically. Brent never allowed me to be here by myself. The only time I got a reprieve was when I was at work. Somehow he made his work schedule fit mine. Sneaking away to night classes was hard and probably why I only managed it for a few weeks before he found out. Maybe he thought that if I was left to myself, I'd pack my shit and hit the road. It would have been the smart thing to do, but I'd never been strong enough to do it. The huge task of starting over always exhausted me, always frightened me more than staying with him did. I'm weak, a really fucking weak person. Maybe that's why I'm so attracted to Anthony; he seems to have zero fear and he seems strong enough to do anything.

My eyes take in the threadbare carpet, the yellowing of the walls. Even though I cleaned them every week, he continued to smoke inside, so they were never clean enough. I can still smell the stale cigarettes. God, I hated that he smoked, begged him to give it up because it gave me headaches. His response? He needed something to tackle the stress I gave him. Often I wondered if he were on other things. Money disappeared pretty regularly from our account, and it wasn't unusual for the threatening notice of our electricity being shut off to be hung on the front door. One more thing I guess I'll never know. I don't plan on ever speaking to him again to ask.

Running my hand along the faded countertop, noticing the scars in the cheap laminate that have been there since we moved in, I tap my fingernails, listening to the sound echo in the emptiness of the space. No pictures on those yellowed walls to absorb the sound. No cute little rug in front of the sink to offset the cold vinyl of the floor in the winter. The fridge kicks on, as does the air conditioner, on this hot day. I close my eyes against the sounds, and immediately I'm taken back to that day.

I hear the bell ring that hangs over the door and situate myself on the table. I should really lift my head up and wait on this customer. As always, I need the tips more than Leighton does. Before I can lift my head, I hear Leighton's voice screaming at me.

"Look out!" she yells, just as I get myself out of the fog I'm in.

When I lift up, it happens in slow motion. His hand balls into a fist and cold-cocks me across the face. The force causes me to grunt, and I can taste the blood as my head whips around and I fall immediately to the floor.

"You dumb bitch!" His voice sounds like it's coming from a million miles away as it reverberates through my head. I scream when he reaches down and grabs me by the hair, yanking me up. "Thinking you can go behind my back, take those classes you're always harping about. You think you're so much goddamn smarter than I am."

Lifting my arms up, I try to grab at his fingers, desperate to get him to let go of the hair he holds in a vice-like grip. Desperate to save myself from whatever this ends up being. I have no illusions, he's done this before, and I was stupid to think I could take these classes without him finding out. His fingers loosen, and he allows me to drop a few inches until my feet touch the ground. I reach out to the table, to try and steady myself, and when I do he pushes my head forward, causing it to hit the table. Stars bounce around my skull and I can almost swear I can hear birds chirping. All of a sudden I'm ripped from his clutches and pulled over to where Leighton sits. She's speaking softly to me, and I get a glimpse of Ace approaching Brent, gun drawn. It's then that I start to go in and out of conscious.

Inhaling air, I fight to get it into my tight lungs, I try to calm myself down, try to prevent the panic attack that's threatening to take hold of not only my body, but also my mind. Looking around the trailer, I want something to ground me, but all I can see are reminders of Brent everywhere. There's the paper he insists on reading every morning. His three pairs of work boots, when I'm only allowed to have one pair of shoes for my job. The side table sitting next to his recliner, so he never had to reach too far for anything. It's painfully obvious how easy his life was made, while mine didn't matter.

Painfully reaching up into the cabinet, I angrily grab a trash bag and open it up. Ignoring the searing heat in my ribs and general soreness of my body, I eradicate every piece of evidence that Brent Miller lived here with me. Struggling, I open the front door, throwing the bags out.

As fast as I'm able to, I run out and stumble down the porch. Trying to get breath between my lips that can barely open. Putting my head in my hands and threading my hair through my fingers, I pull slightly, letting the pinch of pain bring me back to the present. It reminds me that I'm here, I'm alive, and I've made it through an ordeal I wasn't sure I would.

"Get your shit together, Violet." I let the tears come to my eyes, taking in my situation for the first time.

My eyes roam the trailer that's been our home since we came here. I see the rusted roof, the fading chipped paint, the porch that's a few strong gusts from tipping over. My car is a car; it's a few years old, but well-maintained, not something I'm ashamed of other people seeing. My home? I'm devastated and embarrassed that Anthony brought me here, that he saw what I've been living in. Even though the inside is impeccably clean, the outside looks like a den for a meth operation. I want something better. I always have, but for once in my life, I'm going to make it happen.

Brent's voice in my head taunts me. "How ya gonna do that, Violet? You're a waitress who's borrowed money to go to school. How in the hell will you make all your bills and still be able to eat? You need me. I'm the only thing keeping you off the street."

For the first time, I let the rage go, I don't push it back and pretend I'm fine. A loud scream sounds from my throat. A purge of all the bullshit I've put up with over the years. I let the anger flow through. Not only the anger for what's been done to me on this particular occasion, but what's been happening for years. It's a heat that takes hold, washes over me, and makes me curl my hands into fists. He's beaten me down too long. A part of my personality I didn't realize was there is pushing itself to the surface. I feel strong, and I feel like I could kill Brent if he were standing directly in front of me. "Shut the fuck up," I tell that voice of reason. "You've held me back for far too long. I'm going to heal, and then I'm going to make a plan."

With the declaration said aloud, I go back into the trailer, unearthing the used laptop I had Leighton buy me. It had been hard to keep it hidden, but worth it when I went "grocery shopping" or to "run a few errands" to get him things he needed. Those little reprieves from my life allowed me to do school work, to attend the classes, and to hope for something better. They showed me what could happen if I ever got out from under his thumb.

In those classes, there were truly no right or wrong answers. There were discussions and respect from both sides, even if we didn't always totally agree. At the library, there were people to help. They never made me feel stupid, and they'd always point me in the right direction. A true north, if you will, allowing me to find my way out of whatever situation I couldn't find the answer to.

Maybe that *is* the answer. This laptop, Anthony, this whole situation – it's my wakeup call to be a better person. It's my defining moment to learn to believe in myself. My one shot that I don't want to blow. This right here is the true north I've been searching for this whole time.

MY RESOLVE LASTS until I go to bed that night in the once again quiet home. I've done all my homework that I missed while I was in the hospital, and I've worked ahead for the week. Turning over onto my side, I grimace when a stab of pain shoots through my ribs. The remote for the TV is on the nightstand, and I reach over, grimacing when I feel the pull of my sore ribs. Heaving a sigh once I have the remote in my hand, I turn it onto Netflix, searching for any show that's long enough to get me through the night. Leighton had offered to let me stay with her and Holden, but I don't want to impose on anyone. I need to face facts, to realize I'm on my own now. I'll never be with Brent again. Beside me, my phone dings with an incoming text message.

I unlock the screen and can't help the little flutter in my stomach when I see that it's from Anthony. I had no idea I had his cell number or he had mine, but this message is a beacon of light in a very dark night for me.

A: Don't think this is creepy, but I figured you might be feeling a little alone. I have some paperwork to do, so I'm parked in your driveway. Nobody's going to bother you as long as I'm here. You want me to leave, just tell me.

My hands shake as I push the covers off my legs and slowly inch my way over to the window that faces the driveway. Slightly, I pull back the curtain, and breathe easier when I see Anthony's squad car. Knowing he's so close makes me feel safer, knowing he'll be here if anything happens gives me a peace I haven't had in such a long time. It brings tears to my eyes and makes my throat close. How he knew I would need this, I'm not sure, but I respect the way he's going about helping me. The only thing I can text back, are two very simple words which fail to convey the depth of my gratitude. Right now, though, they are all I can manage.

V: Thank you.

A: Sleep well, sweetheart. I got your back.

Shuffling back to the bed, I lie down, pull the covers up around my face. Instead of lying there for hours wondering what I'm going to do with my life, worrying about what happens if Brent finds out about the classes, or wishing I were anywhere but here, I relax. And for the first time in a long time, I fall asleep with a smile on my face. There's still worry and fear, but it's not crippling the way it's been in the past. Somehow, I force myself to believe this is the beginning, not the end.

With what remains of my tattered pride, I'll show Brent that he didn't break me. He hurt me, and he damaged me, but he didn't break me. No one has, and no one ever will.

CHAPTER THREE

VIOLET

IT'S BEEN a week since I got out of the hospital, and I'm settling into a new routine, a new normal for me. Part of that new normal is having Anthony parked in front of my house almost every night. The other day he even did it in his own personal vehicle.

I've taken to texting him when he arrives, to thank him for being out there, but we haven't really had a conversation since he brought me home. I have a feeling that's more my doing than his, and he's waiting for me to give him an opening. Tonight, I'm trying to create that opening.

Taking the hamburger off the grill pan I've cooked it on, I plate it on a bun with the ketchup, mustard, mayo, and relish I know he likes. Every time he comes into The Café, it's how he orders his. I have one for myself too; eating is still a little difficult, but not as much as it had been when I first came home. Grabbing both of the plates and a bag with drinks and chips, I take a deep breath and head out my front door, toward the squad car he's parked in.

"Vi? Everything good?"

"Yeah." I offer him a small smile. "Just thought maybe you'd like a home-cooked meal and maybe you'd like to share it with me?"

The smile that spreads across his face is so bright, it's almost as if I just gave him the key to the city. He opens the car door and sits on the hood, motioning for me to do the same. Taking the plates from me, he puts them down and helps me as I get my balance. "I'd love to have dinner with a beautiful woman."

His stomach growls and we both laugh. We hardly talk while we eat, but being around another person is nice and I'm thankful there's no anxiety. Maybe, just maybe I can find a way to live my life without looking over my shoulder or behind my back. If anyone can teach me, I know it's the guy beside me eating a hamburger in all of three bites.

"Hungry?"

He looks a little chagrined. "Starving. This was perfect."

And I find that as I'm finishing up my burger, and sharing the bag of chips with him – it truly is.

"I gotta go." He wipes his mouth, patting his stomach. "I have to do my normal rounds. I'll check in again tonight before I go off-shift though."

A part of me is disappointed he's leaving. I've come to enjoy knowing he's here. "Thanks for checking on me."

His hand moves toward my face, knuckles out. On instinct I jerk back, and his hand freezes in mid-air.

"Sorry," we both say the word at the same time.

"Shouldn't have done that," he runs the hand through his hair.

Against my better judgement, I ask the question running through my mind. "What were you going to do?"

Slowly he turns towards me, his knees slightly touching mine. I close my eyes and force myself to relax.

"Open those eyes, Vi. I want you to know what's going to happen, I don't want you to tense up in fear. Open eyes here, sweetheart. You're gonna see what's coming at you with me."

My eyes open and I pull my bottom lip in between my teeth, biting so that I feel a little sting. To remind myself I'm in control. Following his hand with my gaze, I watch as his long finger extends from his fisted hand, and then crooks before he places it under my chin. He lifts my face, silently asking me to meet his eyes. When I do, I see no anger, no hostility. There's concern, and compassion. Finally, he speaks.

"There's no one else I'd rather be checking up on. It's truly my pleasure. I wouldn't be doing this if I didn't want to be."

So many thoughts swirl in my head, and before I can stop it, another question pushes past my lips. "Why me?"

"Why not you?" He grins, his sense of humor and playfulness coming through.

There's a smile on my face, and a laugh on my breath. Two things I haven't experienced in a long time. "Seriously, Anthony."

"Everything, Violet. You're everything."

I shake my head, the tears coming quickly, like they do so often lately. "I'm nothing."

He takes a chance, removing the finger from under my chin and placing his palm on my cheek, cupping it with gentle pressure. "To him you were nothing, to me you're everything. Sooner or later, you'll figure out I'm not him. You'll figure out I'm a patient man, and realize how great love can be. It doesn't have to hurt, Vi. Sometimes it can be great."

Opening my mouth, I want to refute everything he's said to me, but his radio makes a loud noise, and he's jumping off the hood of his car. Reaching up, he helps me down, and before I know it, he's gone, blue and white's swirling atop the cruiser.

As I watch his taillights fade in the distance, I ask for one more miracle to happen. Not like I deserve it, but I want it either way.

Maybe one day, I'll see myself the way he sees me.

"VIOLET MILLER."

Another part of my new normal? Visiting a therapist. It hadn't even been on my radar. Not until Whitney showed up at my door, demanding to know if I was okay. Apparently the group had put her in charge because of her past, and she had given me her best advice. Talk to someone, she'd said, and after last night, I feel like she was probably right.

Standing up, I tug the shoulder strap of my purse up and try to walk with my head held high through the waiting room. It's a blur, as they take my information, and then leave me to presumably wait for the doctor. I'm playing on my phone, to keep myself from going crazy.

A: Have a good day today. I'm sorry if I overstepped a boundary last night, but it needed to be said.

V: I'm seeing a therapist today, only because I truly want to believe the things you tell me.

Why is it so much easier to say things over text with him? Lord, I wish I could talk to him as easily as I could text him. My phone dings with a response from him right as the door opens.

"Violet?"

"That's me," I put my phone back in my purse, and give my full attention to the situation I'm in.

A woman looking a little older than me enters. "I'm Dr. Whitmer, nice to meet you." She has a seat, before leaning in to offer me her hand. The grip is firm, and in that moment, I decide the next person I meet I will have enough confidence in myself to give them a handshake like the one she gave me.

"You wanna tell me a little bit about why you're here?" She crosses her legs, sitting back in her chair, as she holds her pen at the ready.

Like diarrhea of the mouth my whole story flows without stopping. I speak so long that my jaw begins to ache, and when I'm done, I feel as if I've gone ten rounds with a boxing champ.

"Jesus." She takes her glasses off, setting them down on her lap with the notebook she's been writing in. "After all that's happened to you, what do you want for *you*?"

Not many people have ever asked me that question. Brent never did, that's for damn sure. Immediately, last night flashes back to me, and I know without a doubt what I want, who I want to be.

"I want to be a woman strong enough to believe a man loves her, not because he wants to control her, but because he wants to be her partner. I want to be strong enough and confident enough to be that partner for another man."

A smile spreads across her face. "Then that's what you'll be, Violet." She leans forward, a piece of notebook paper in her hand. "And this is how we're going to get you there. We'll see each other a few times a month until you feel like you don't need me anymore."

Looking at the plan she's laid out, I feel some things I haven't in a long time. Excitement and hope – like I just might make it through this after all.

CHAPTER FOUR

ACE

TWO WEEKS **Later**

"You sure you wanna do this?" I question Violet as we stand outside her trailer. She brought me out a drink to where I'm parked in her driveway. Like I am every other night.

She nods. "I go back to work in two days, and I really want to feel safe when I go there. Trust me, I know this isn't a fix-all, Anthony, but it'll make me feel better."

"You know I'll do whatever it takes to make you feel safe, and if showing you how to fire a gun is going to do that, it's what we'll do."

I've tried to be accommodating with things she's needed, and I completely agree with this request of hers. I believe more than anything, she should be able to protect herself, and if I can help her with that, I'm going to do it. The small can of pepper spray she carries can buy her some time if it ever came to that, but a gun? It could save her life if push came to shove.

"Can't we do it here?" she asks, even as she's getting into my truck.

I shake my head as I start the engine. "Not here, there's too many variables I can't control. If we go to a shooting range, I can make sure you learn how to do it right and have all the tools you need within reach."

She's quiet and I get the feeling she isn't being completely honest with me. "What's really bothering you? Is it going back to work?"

"Will everyone be staring at me? Whispering about what happened to me? That's my biggest fear about going back to work. Will people look at me with pity in their eyes, Anthony?" She pushes back her dark hair, her eyes cutting over to me across the seat. "I don't know if I can take it. Everywhere I've been, people have looked at me with pity in their eyes." She licks her lips. "Everyone but you. You've never looked at me like you could fix me, and I can't tell you how much that means to me."

"You're not broken, Violet. There's nothing to fix." I reach over and grab her hand, entwining our fingers together. When I come to a stop sign, I let my eyes drink in the sight of her, see her face for the first time in weeks without the mar of bruises and the tightness of tension.

The shaky breath she pushes between her lips is the only sound in the cab of the truck. "Thank you," she whispers, silent tears slipping down her cheeks.

Reaching over, I use my thumb to wipe up the moisture. If I could give this woman anything, it would be my vision of how I see her. She doesn't understand what a strong person she is. How she's handled what's been given to her is nothing short of extraordinary. "No thanks necessary. I'll do whatever it takes to make you see what an amazing woman you are."

"I'm not amazing." She keeps her head down, averting my eyes.

Trailing my thumb down her cheek, I sweep it under her chin, tilting it to force her to look at me. "You're everything, and I won't stop until you realize it."

Realization of what she's doing flairs in those eyes of hers, and I think for the first time, I'm getting through. "Please don't stop. Give me hope, Anthony."

"You got it." I lean over, kissing her on the cheek.

One small peck holds our past, our future, and everything in between. Her brown eyes are locked on my green ones, and in this moment, we're on the same wave-length.

The honk of a car horn behind us breaks the moment, but as I continue to the shooting range, I know this has been a game-changer. After everything she's been through, Violet trusts me.

I'll never betray it or abuse it, but I damn well will nurture it. And if she lets me, I'll turn it into the most passionate love she's ever experienced. I've waited to meet her my whole life, and I'll be damned if I let the damage of the man before me wreck what could become the best thing either of us have ever had. I've been patient, I'll continue to be patient and I'll put in the time, because she's worth every bit of the effort.

"KEEP YOUR FORM TIGHT," I tell her as I stand behind her.

"Like this?" she asks as she widens her stance, holding the gun in front of her with both hands.

"Is it okay if I show you?"

Glancing over her shoulder, she nods. "I want to know how to do this correctly. I'm good with pepper spray, but I'd like to have more than that to save me if I need it."

If I have anything to say about it, she'll never have to worry about protecting herself again; that'll be my job. Stepping up close behind her, I tuck her back into my front. Awareness flashes through my body at holding her for the first time. I've wanted to hold her in a million ways since the day she came home from the hospital. If this is the only way she'll let me, I'll take it.

I extend my arms alongside hers, leveling her arms and adjusting her grip on the gun. After I guide her left hand to cradle the butt of the gun, I place her pointer finger alongside the trigger.

I lean in close, trying to ignore the way our bodies fit together. If this had been any other woman, at any other time, I'd press myself completely against her, let her feel the way I react, but I don't want to scare her, and she's tense enough. "Relax. You're too tense, you'll be sore tomorrow if you don't take a breath and loosen up." My voice is quiet, tone is level. "Relax, line up your sights, and focus on your target. When you're ready, move your finger on to the trigger. Take a deep breath and slowly pull. You need to get a feel for how the gun fires."

She pulls the trigger, staggering when the recoil forces her to lose a bit of her stance. Holding her up, I help brace her body as she adjusts her stance and arms and continues to fire until she empties the revolver we're shooting.

"Wanna go again?" I ask, raising my voice so she can hear me above the ear protection. We're alone in the range, having picked a time when I knew hardly anyone else would be around.

"Yeah, this time by myself. I get what you're saying about relaxing, yet being strong."

Taking the revolver she set down, I show her how to load the chambers. Placing it back down, I give her a nod. "It's all yours."

I step back, watching her as she assumes the position, lines up her shot, and fires. Her aim isn't completely accurate, but she's shooting well enough to injure someone if she needed to. When she empties again, she looks over her shoulder to me.

"It's not perfect," she worries her lip between her teeth.

"No, but no one ever starts out perfect. It's just like anything else, you have to practice. Once you practice enough it's muscle memory and you won't have to even think about it. We started you out with a lower caliber gun, and when you're ready, we can practice on something bigger. The most important part is being able to accurately shoot whatever gun you have."

Her brain is working, I can almost see it as she nods. "Do I have to be with you to come here?"

"No, but it helps to have your concealed carry license to rent a firearm and buy ammunition. Plus you'll be able to carry. We can work on getting it, and then you'll be able to do this whenever you want to."

"Good." She carefully lays the gun down and takes a step back. "This is what I want to do." She runs her hands over the back of her jeans, and I try not to pay attention to how well they fit.

Clearing my throat, I start putting our stuff away. "Are you done for the day?"

"Yeah." She gives me a smile. "Yeah, I think I am."

Seeing the little bit of pride she has in herself warms a space within me. Since all this went down, she's been a shell of the girl she was when I first walked into The Café, but today it seems as if she's gotten a little of herself back. The spark that initially intrigued me, is back today. I'm not ready for us to leave one another, I'd like to spend more time with her.

"You hungry?"

"Starving." Her voice is soft again. I've noticed it gets that way when she's answering questions she may not be used to being asked.

"Then let's go get some lunch."

We're leaving the range when she grabs my hand, pulling me to a stop.

"Not at The Café, right?"

Even though that was exactly where we were going, I cover it well. "No, we'll go to my house if that's okay with you."

Again she shows an amazing trust in me. "Sure, sounds good."

And now I have to figure out what the fuck I'm going to feed both of us.

Violet

"I know you weren't planning on feeding me and you probably did think of going to the Café, so thank you for not making a big deal out of it," I speak around the grilled chicken I have in my mouth.

Ace had covered it well when I asked him if we had to go to the scene of the crime, so to speak. But when we got here, I could tell he hadn't been planning on feeding me. We've done a good job as a team, though. He grabbed some chicken out of the fridge, grilling it to perfection with homemade barbecue sauce on it, while I found some sides to go along with it in his cupboards.

He laughs as I call him out.

"Guilty as charged. To tell you the truth, you're dealing with everything so well, I didn't even think about it."

"You think I'm dealing with things well?" I take a drink of the best sweet tea that's ever been placed in front of me. When I'd asked him who made it, he'd said his mom with a wink and a smile. By the end of the lunch, I have a feeling I'm going to be trying to figure out how the hell to get her to make me a week's supply at a time.

"Hell yeah." He takes a bite of his baked potato, blowing out a breath. "Damn, that's hot."

It's comical, him trying to get a drink without spilling it down the front of his shirt, and a giggle breaks its way past my throat. It feels like forever since I've had any cause to laugh, but it feels good. Anthony Bailey gives me hope that things in my life can be different.

For a moment, I let my brain drift back to us at the range, his body pressed up against mine. It had taken everything I had not to show how it affected me, how my hands shook, how my heart pounded, and my breath hitched. I'd done my best to keep it friendly, hoped one day, that things in my life will be different. One day I'll know what it's like to settle in his arms, and not have to pretend like it doesn't affect me.

"Anyway. I'm proud of you." He finally swallows, giving me his attention and directing mine back to him. "You're getting out of your house, even if I have to drag you out. You're facing things head-on. That would be a problem if you weren't. But you're taking things at your own pace."

I give a little nod, showing I'm accepting the praise, and just maybe I'm a little proud of myself.

CHAPTER FIVE

VIOLET

MY HAND SHAKES as I put a portion of my hair in a braid and pull it halfway back into the locks trailing down my shoulders. Half-up/half-down is one of my favorite ways to style my hair. Brent hated when I would play with my hairstyle like this – anything that was playful, fun, or age appropriate, he would sneer his nose up at. He preferred for me to wear it pulled back in a bun style that was so severe, it made me look like I was in my forties. Given the way I never smiled, never met anyone's gaze – I probably did look like I was in my forties. Some miser who hated her life, and for a while I did. But I've come to realize over the past few weeks that's so not me.

Not many people know I'm actually twenty-nine. Much too young to feel this damn old. Isn't that a song or something? Once upon a time, I was someone who loved life, enjoyed pushing limits, and woke up every day looking forward to whatever adventure might be mine. Of all the things he took from me, that's one of the things I miss the most, and probably why I'm so attracted to Anthony. The way he embraces every second of every day really does it for me, if I'm being honest.

"You can do whatever you want to now, Vi." I remind myself. There's no one to tell me yes or no, other than myself. Typically, I don't wear makeup when working because Brent didn't like that either. He didn't want me to encourage what he called unwanted attention. Didn't want another man to hit on me, or make me feel pretty. Just another way he controlled me and kept me afraid.

Flipping my middle finger up to the memory of my husband and the fear he forced me into, I grab the small bag of makeup I allowed myself to have. Rifling through it, I wish like hell this had been the first thing I did when I'd come home. Maybe that means I'm starting to heal, maybe I'm moving on from being the scared person I've been the past few years of my life. Hopefully the Violet I had been before I married Brent is starting to show herself.

Teenage Violet had been strong until one incident made her feel weaker than she'd ever felt – at least until what I've been through now. She'd been searching for something, someone to make sense of a tragedy. To make her feel again.

Funny, adult Violet is doing the same thing.

It's going to take longer than a few weeks, that I'm fully aware of, but just the small glimpse of who I used to be puts a smile on my face. Finishing up my mascara I run the palms of my hands down my jeans and take a fortifying breath. Grabbing my bag, my phone, and my keys, I'm ready to start my first day back at The Café.

As I step onto the front porch, I take in the sun coming up over the horizon and vow to embrace this new day, the new beginning that I'm being given. Stepping off the bottom step and turning to my car, I sigh and let a small smile spread across my face.

Anthony is parked there, leaning against his personal vehicle. This is the man who's quietly been my rock the last few weeks. Between the texts, sitting outside my house, sharing dinner with me, and just being a presence, he's helped me more than anyone or anything else has. In the beginning I worried I was leaning on him too much, but the fact of the matter is, there's no one else I trust like him. For him to know what I need before I ask for it? I'm blessed to have him in my life.

My heart does this little flutter that it hasn't done in a long time. Years, if I'm being honest. His legs are crossed at the ankle, encased in jeans that fit loosely enough to show me a little of what he has underneath them. A fitted gray t-shirt stretches across his chest as he braces his palms against the grill of the truck, pushing off and slowly walking toward me.

"What are you doing here?" My eyes take in his face, covered with stubble, dark circles call attention to the pale green of his eyes, and a sleepiness gives him a sexy laziness as he stops in front of me. "You look tired."

He yawns loudly, the chiseled jaw cracking as he puts a hand over his mouth to hold it back. "I am. I worked the night shift. Got off around midnight. Three hours sleep is rough, but I can handle it. I wanted to see you this morning." He reaches out grasping hold of the end of my braid. "I like your hair like this."

The words please me immensely. I try not to look into the fact that I probably did this, not only for me, but for him too. I hadn't expected him to be here this morning, but I had expected to see him sometime today. "Thank you. Now what are you doing here?"

Reaching into his jeans with his free hand, he pulls his keys out, flipping them into the palm of his hand. "I'm here to take you to work. It'll be a rough day for you, regardless of how ready you are to go back. You may need support, and I wanna be there."

"You've been here a lot." I swallow against the lump that's popped up in my throat. When I think about everything he's done for me, that lump is a constant. Sometimes, I sit back and can't believe the goodness he's brought to my life.

"Only because I've wanted to be." He continues playing with the end of my hair. I want to curl into his caress, purr like a cat, and let him pet me everywhere. It's been too long since a man touched me so softly.

"You're a good man," I whisper as he drops my hair and lets his hand cup my cheek. This time I do curl into his caress, but I keep from purring. That would be a little too weird for both of us.

His head shakes as the side of his mouth tilts up. "I'm just a guy who wants to show you there are good men out there."

"Trust me, Anthony." I lean in, kissing him on the cheek. "You're doing a really good job of it."

"Let's go." He hitches his head toward his truck.

I let my hand fall, grasping his lightly as he helps me step on the running board and take the passenger seat. As he turns to head for town, I look in the side-view mirror, seeing my home in the distance. There could be a metaphor here, me leaving my past behind as I drive toward my future. This is something that would have scared me before, would have given me so much anxiety I would have re-thought the situation and decided to stay where it was comfortable. My fear of change kept me with Brent for so long, I almost didn't live to see my way out. Crazy how things work in life.

Across the console, Anthony reaches over, grabbing my hand. His every action has shown me that he will help me go where it's uncomfortable, he will be by my side when it doesn't feel like I can handle what I've been dealt. I hold onto his fingers for dear life, and I know that with him by my side, I can do anything I put my mind to.

For a moment, I close my eyes, center myself, and realize I'm ready. This may not be easy, but it'll totally be worth it.

"VIOLET!!!"

I hear the high-pitched squeal before I even make it inside the building. There's a small hesitation as I come to the doorway of The Café; I feel a small push of foreboding, a little bit of dread. I know that I must overcome it. If I don't, every time I walk inside, every time I drive down the street, or when I happen to think about it will be a hard moment to overcome. Instead I have to choose happiness. I have to choose excitement, and I need to remember this greeting one of my best friends is giving me. "I'm so glad you're back!"

I've missed Leighton, almost forgetting how contagious her smile and good mood are. When you're around her you can't help but have a good time. She makes sure of it. She runs to me, hugging me tightly around the neck, whispering words of encouragement in my ear. "I'm glad I'm back too." I squeeze her hard. Regret hitting me hardcore that I haven't made time to see her, that I haven't allowed her to be a part of this recovery process. At first I'd thought I needed it to be singular, but now, looking at her, I realize we've all been recovering. "I'm sorry I haven't seen you," I whisper.

"Don't even." She pulls back, shaking her head, not accepting the apology. "Don't even. We all deal with things the way we need to. I've had Ace keeping tabs on you, and he's been assuring me you're fine." She looks over at him, an eyebrow raised as she turns her gaze back to me, looking for confirmation that he hasn't lied to her.

I struggle for what to say. What is there to say? I'm obviously not a hundred percent, but I'm good enough to be here right now. There's not a magic wand I can wave and make everything okay again. If there were, I would have waved it the day I got out of the hospital. Instead, I answer as honestly as I can.

"I'm gettin' there."

And I say the words, I realize I'm telling the truth. Glancing at the table I'd been sitting at when Brent attacked me, I feel nauseous and light-headed, but I tamp it down. He will only have power if I give it to him, and I refuse to give him anything else to use against me. I force myself to look closely at the table. Imagine myself sitting there and run through the memory of what happened that day. It's not easy, but it's necessary. The only person who can force me to face the truth is me.

Looking around the room, I see regulars sitting in their favorite booths. Ernie's come out from behind the grill, a huge smile showing teeth we never see on his face, and it looks like even Caleb has made the trip over before school. He's got a proud smile on his face, and it feels good to know all of these people have come here for me, that in some small way, I've made them proud. If I'm not mistaken, outside, members of the Moonshine Task Force are loitering, drinking coffee, but at the same time keeping an eye on what's going on inside. All of these things combined reiterate the fact that this is home. I've made the right decision in staying here, in allowing these people to be friends, allowing them to be a part of my life.

"You okay?" Anthony asks. His voice is quietly reassuring, giving me the encouragement I need. I can't imagine what he's thinking, if he's wondering that he pushed me too hard, that maybe I should have waited a few more days before I came back here.

Truth be told, I'd almost come back in the dead of the night to face this place, without the prying eyes of friends and community. But that had felt like a coward's way out. I can say with total assurance right now this is the way I was meant to do it, and I'm glad I've been able to push myself this way. I no longer want to hide in the shadows, pretend that things don't bother me, and live my life only turned half-way up. Now, I want to experience it at full volume.

"Everything's good."

And I realize for the first time in a long while it's the truth; I believe those words and I'm ready to live them. The only thing holding me back now is me.

CHAPTER SIX
VIOLET

IN THE LAST TWO MONTHS, things have settled down. I'm in a routine that I can live with. One that allows me to feel safe but also stretches the boundaries of what makes me feel comfortable. The only thing I would change would be my living situation. I hate being out in the middle of nowhere and wish I could afford to move closer town.

I'm wiping down the counter, waiting for The Café to open when Caleb drags himself through the front door. "Morning." I give him a smile.

He gives me a look, scrunching up his nose. "It should be illegal to be getting up this early, especially to be in a good mood about it."

"When you've been through things I've been through, you're glad to be able to wake up in the morning. You're thankful for it."

He raises an eyebrow. "I guess."

"C'mon back here." Ernie motions to the younger boy. "I already got enough dishes for you to run a sink full."

He sighs but puts on an apron and gets to work. It's a Saturday, I guess I can understand why he's upset. He probably has a party to go to tonight. According to Anthony, the kids have been partying it up in the fields and at the barns lately. Although Caleb is a good kid, it doesn't mean he's not out having a good time too.

"I'm going to open the door," I yell back to them, checking the time on my cell as I do. Leighton will be in a little later today, and we've picked up a high school girl who helps fill in the gaps.

As I lift up the blind that covers the plate glass door when we're closed, my breath is taken. The sun is coming up over the horizon, marking the sky with pinks and purples. Stars are still shining in certain spots as a new dawn starts to reclaim the night sky. Taking a deep breath, I realize what I said to Caleb is true. Anytime I can enjoy a sunrise and a sunset, I will mark it as a blessing in my book. Months ago, when I laid in that hospital bed, I worried I'd never see one again.

Pushing the door open, I hold it with my foot as I pull the chalkboard sign out that announces our specials for the day. When the weight is taken off my foot, I glance up. Standing in front of me is a person who sometimes takes my breath away. "Mornin', Violet."

Dressed in his gear, Anthony is a feast for the eyes. "Morning." I take in his appearance, the scruff on his cheeks and chin, the dark circles under his eyes. "Did you work overnight?"

"Yeah, it was unexpected, but Stella's sick enough they had to take her to the ER so I covered for Renegade. Which means I have to be back to work in about eight hours."

"What are you doing here?"

He runs a hand across those abs of his pulling his shirt tight against the muscles. "Hungry as hell, and I wanted to talk to you about something."

Now my interest is piqued. He holds the door open for me as we enter the still empty Café. Ernie sees him from the back and yells out a greeting, telling him his usual will be right up.

"Coffee?" I ask, as I get behind the counter and he has a seat at one of the chairs attached.

"Better not, I've got to go to sleep when I get home. How about some OJ?"

"Coming right up."

Making myself busy, I get him a big glass of OJ and then pick up the food Ernie has already finished for him. Setting it down, I watch as he digs in. "So what is it you wanted to talk to me about?"

"Oh yeah." He takes a drink of his OJ, washing down the huge bite of food he took. "You know I live in a duplex? The other part is now vacant. They were evicted last week, and my landlord hasn't rented it out yet. I told him about you and how you wanted to move closer to town. You should come take a look at it this afternoon."

"There's no way I can afford to live there, Anthony. Thank you for recommending me, but I can guarantee you I can't afford it."

His green eyes meet mine, the dark stubble around his mouth making his lips stand out. "I think you'd be surprised. All you have to do is go check it out and talk to him. He'd be willing to work with you. Besides you aren't stuck in a lease with where you're living. Brent is in jail for the foreseeable future, so sweetheart, you can do whatever the fuck it is you want."

I know with every fiber of my being that I won't be able to afford the duplex, but to make Anthony happy, I'll have a look. "Can you get in touch with him and ask if I can look after I get off work?"

He pulls his cell phone out of his pocket, giving me a heart-fluttering smile. "Sure thing."

AND THAT'S how I ended up here, sitting outside the duplex Anthony lives in waiting for his landlord. I'm assuming Anthony is fast asleep, or just waking up, depending on when he actually has to leave for his shift. I've been here a few times, and each time, I wonder what it would be like to live in a nice place. The outside is brick, the doors to each side face each other with a shared wide porch in the front, and in the back. The doors aren't the cheap kind that my mobile home has. They're solid wood with an actual peephole and a patterned glass situated in the middle. Again, nicer than anything I've ever lived in.

A huge truck pulls up beside my little car, and a man hops down, walking toward me with his hands in his pockets. This must be the landlord. Quickly grabbing my purse, I get out of my car.

"You must be Violet." He holds his hand out for me to shake. "Ace has told me a lot about you. I'm Fulcher."

I just bet he has. "I am, and nice to meet you." I shake his hand confidently. "I'm gonna be real honest with you though, Fulcher. I'm not even a tiny bit sure I can afford what you've got here."

"Let's just take a look at it, and then we'll talk about it."

There's a part of me that doesn't want to get my hopes up, but there's another part of me that desperately wants something good to happen, something that I didn't expect. A beautiful surprise. Dear God, let this be it. We enter, and the clean smell assaults me. No stale cigarette smoke; I still can't get the smell out of the trailer even though Brent's been gone for months. There's newly finished hardwood floor, judging by the way the boards shine. The open concept is appealing, I can see the front door from the sink. There's a nice stove, a dishwasher, and a small pantry.

"It's a one-bedroom," he cautions as we walk down the hall-way. "Ace has two, but I wanted to have options when I built the place."

"One is perfect for me," I assure him as we enter. It's good-sized, bigger than both the bedrooms in my trailer and it looks like they've put in new carpet.

"Because it's only a one bedroom, it's got a walk-in closet that's huge. I've seen other people in my rentals turn them into closets with offices in some of the extra space, it's so big. Ready to see it?"

"Yeah." I grin.

When he opens the door, I gasp. It's huge, gorgeous, and everything a woman would want. There's even a vanity in the back, which is probably why many turn them into offices. We end the tour with a look at a basic bathroom.

"There's a small storage shed on your side. Ace has his own in the backyard. I don't allow pets without a deposit, but if you were to want to get one, the back is completely fenced," he explains as he watches me, looking over the place again.

"What about upkeep?"

"I take care of everything that naturally happens. You bust a hole in my drywall, I charge you for it. A pipe bursts, the washer or dryer goes, the dishwasher takes a shit, that's me. I also take care of yard work, that's included in the lease."

I take a deep breath, ready to ask him the question that's been at the back of my mind since we started this. "How much is it a month?"

"You were honest with me, I'm gonna be honest with you." He sticks his hands in his pockets and leans against the breakfast bar. "I normally rent this place out for seven-fifty a month with a deposit, background check, and credit check."

My face crumbles. I'm paying five hundred for the little trailer, and some months it's hard to come up with that. There's no way I have enough for a deposit or another almost three-hundred bucks a month. "This place is gorgeous, and I wish I could afford it." Embarrassing tears are pricking at the back of my eyes.

"Wait." He holds up a hand. "That's what I normally do, but Ace has told me a lot about you. My niece was in the same sort of situation you were in, and someone helped her. I'd like to pay that forward. This place is paid off so all this is, is income for me, and I served with Ace in the military. He saved me once, and I've owed him a long time. How much do you pay for rent now?" He crosses his legs at the ankle and stares at me.

"Five hundred." I cringe. "Thank you, but there's no way you can give me this place for five hundred, and I understand that."

"Yes, I can." He comes off the bar. "I hear you're in school."

"I am." I nod. "Should be done at the end of next year, when I plan to get a better job."

"How about we do this?" He pulls a piece of paper out of his pocket.

I eye it, it's a folded-up piece of notebook paper, and he's making notes on it in hurried scratches. The writing so undeniably masculine it makes me want to laugh. I watch as he writes what he's saying.

"The first year, you'll pay five hundred a month. If you're still here during the second year, after you've found a new job, you'll pay six hundred, and then if you can afford it and you're still here, we'll raise it to the normal price in the third year. I'm not above working with you, Violet. Like I said, I owe Ace my life, and there were a lot of very nice people who helped my niece. I know you'll pay your rent." He lays the pen down. "The people here before you didn't pay shit for almost six months. They made me evict them. I have a feeling you're honest."

"To a fault," I agree.

"Then let me do this for you. Let me do it for my niece, let me do it for Ace."

My heart is pounding and my head is spinning. "Are you sure I wouldn't put you in a bind?"

He shakes his head, smiling ruefully. "I fucked my knee up on Ace and mine's last mission. I was medically discharged from the military and Uncle Sam pays me a nice pension. I do this because I don't wanna be fucking bored all day long. I can afford to be nice to you, if you'd just let me."

I lean in, take the pen he's set down, and sign my name. "There, sign yours so it's a contract."

He grins. "Awesome, but can I be real honest with you again?"

"I think that's the only way we know how to be, Fulcher." I grin back at him.

"I have a real good feeling you're not gonna be here in a year. That guy next door seems to care about you, and if there's one thing I know about him, he's patient but he's stubborn as fuck."

"We're friends," I argue.

"Friends make the best lovers." He holds up his left hand, showing a wedding ring. "If anyone knows that, it's me."

I'm speechless as I look at him.

"Here's your key." He hands me a set. "They're new locks, so the old tenants can't get in. The utilities are still on; all you have to do is have them transferred. Your first month's rent will be due on the fifteenth of next month. That day good for you?"

In a whirlwind I tell him yes and watch as he walks out of what's now mine. Left alone, I twirl around in a circle. How did I ever get this lucky?

And when my eyes land on the door across the way from mine, I realize it was all when the man living there came into my life. If there ever was a gift from God, Anthony has been mine.

CHAPTER SEVEN
ACE

"WHERE DO YOU WANT THIS?" I groan as I hold tightly onto the box that must hold every pot and pan Violet owns.

"The kitchen," she directs me, as she turns around, pointing to where I need to go.

As she does, I try to force my eyes away from the tight pants she's wearing. If there's one thing Violet has, it's a grade A ass. It's firm, tight, and round, with what looks like enough give I could get a good handful if she'd ever let me touch her. Thankful that the box I'm bringing in is hiding what is now an erection, I focus back on the task at hand. Especially when I hear the other helpers stomping up the steps of the porch.

Renegade and Tank come in behind me, both holding boxes, waiting for her to give them directions.

Whitney comes in, carrying Stella in her arms. "Hey Violet, the couch and chair I was able to get from the warehouse that was going out of business is here. You want me just to have them put it on the porch, then the guys can move it?"

"Yeah," she answers, sounding a little overwhelmed.

Looking over at her, I see she is, in fact, overwhelmed. "Be right back." I glance over at my friends. Grabbing Violet's hand, I pull her out onto the back porch. "You okay?" I ask as I take a drink of bottled water.

"I can't believe everything everyone's done for me, and I'm starting to freak out a little bit." Tears spring to those brown eyes of hers, and she pulls her lip in between her teeth. "What did I do to deserve this?"

"You're you." I reach out, putting my hand around her neck, massaging the tight muscles lightly, hoping to relax her. "These people care about you. If Whitney wanted to spend two hundred bucks getting you a couch and chair, let her. She's been where you are. If Blaze wanted to give you a gift card for groceries to fill this new fridge up with, let her. They don't do anything they don't want to do, Vi, and you're an important part of our lives. Just smile and accept it. One day you'll pay it forward."

Tears slip from those eyes. "It's so much."

"In the grand scheme of things, it's nothing," I insist. "Every day we assist someone in the community, why can't you be one of those people?"

"I don't feel like I deserve it," she whispers. "I got myself into the situation I was in."

"Stop it right now. No one ever asks to be hit, Vi. You and I both know that."

"It's just hard to accept so much charity."

I tilt my head back and take a deep breath, calling on the patience I usually have. "No one is doing this because they feel sorry for you. They're doing it because they want you to succeed. When you do, we'll all celebrate with you. We've all needed help in our lives, all we're doing is paying it forward. When you can, you will. Simple as that. Okay?"

"Okay." She nods.

"Now let's get back in there and get you moved in."

HOURS LATER, I'm lying on the floor of Violet's bedroom, sprawled out on the plush carpet as she hangs up her clothing in the huge closet. If I was a woman, I'd be envious of this closet. It's way bigger than the one I have on my side.

"Are you okay?" she asks, a giggle in her tone.

"I'm dead." I close my eyes, groaning. "I thought working out the way I do kept me in shape, but it's painfully obvious that the gym is no match for physical labor."

"How about I feed you?" she asks as she comes to stand over me. I can feel her presence, and when I open my eyes, I wish like hell she was in a skirt. Guess that teenage boy inside will never fully go away.

"Please do." I roll over, pushing myself up on my arms. "I could probably eat you out of house and home right now," I warn her.

"I've got plenty. C'mon."

Following her into the kitchen, I take in the way the place looks. Since we had Blaze and Whitney with us, they got almost everything put away before they had to leave.

"I wish everyone else had stayed, I could have fed them, too. They did a lot of work for me today."

"They enjoyed it." I have a seat at the breakfast bar. I'm not sure where these stools came from, but at some point, someone set them up. "Now what are you feeding me?"

"You have a couple of options." She holds open the fridge. "I can do a broccoli chicken casserole type dish, burgers, I've got some shrimp that I can make into a shrimp pasta, ummm..." She bends over and I try my best to avert my eyes from her ass that's now in my face. Violet has always been a beautiful woman, and I've always noticed it. "Or I can make you breakfast."

Averting my eyes from her ass, I veto the breakfast. "I get breakfast at The Café all the time. I'll take the broccoli chicken casserole."

"It'll take longer, but I'd love to make it for you." She gives me a smile.

"Then I'd love to eat it."

I try not to let those words go to my groin, but they do. Truth be told, I've had a hard-on for this woman since the first moment I saw her. Clearing my throat, I turn away from where she's prepping the meal and gesture to her TV. "I'll hook up the Firestick I got you, and then we can watch some Netflix while we wait. Sound good?"

"You really didn't have to do that," she reminds me. "It's not like I had cable before, and I was just fine watching Netflix through the TV."

"I know, but it's something you enjoy. Just let me give it to you?"

She agrees and I go to work away from where she tempts me.

Violet

The looks Anthony has given me all afternoon have caused feelings in my body I haven't had in years. Flustered after he told me he'd love to eat what I'm making, I turn away from him and begin going to work on the meal. There's never been so much sexual tension in anything I've ever done. I'm almost positive he feels it too, but I can't go there. He's done too much for me, and I don't want to confuse real feelings with hero worship.

"Do you like biscuits or rolls?"

"I like both," he answers as I hear him flipping through things on my TV.

"Tell me which one you want." I'm feeling slightly anxious. Whenever I would make decisions for Brent, they would be the wrong ones, and for a moment I'm not sure what to do.

"I decided about dinner," his voice is preoccupied. "Your turn."

That answer gives me even more anxiety. Heat rushes up from my stomach to my chest. Inexplicably I feel panic. "Anthony, please just decide." The tension in my voice is palpable, and he's tuned in to the fact something is happening with me.

"Why? What's so wrong with you deciding?" He gets up, coming over to where I am, keeping the breakfast bar in between us.

"I never got to decide, and when I did it was wrong," I push the tears back with an inhumane force. "This feels like a trap."

His voice is tender and low when he speaks. "It's not sweetheart, not a trap at all. You fix what *you* like. It's called compromise, and it's how we're going to have a relationship. I'm not a dickhead who has to control every aspect of your life, Vi. You pick what you want. If I don't like it? I still eat it, and act like I do, because that's what you do for the lady in your life." He gives me a smile.

He turns, goes back in the living room, leaving me to it. Pushing the fear and confusion down, I shake off the melancholy feeling, and take a deep breath.

Grabbing the rolls out of the freezer, I set them down on the counter until I'm ready to put them in the oven. I've mixed everything in the casserole, and when the pre-heat timer beeps, I stick it in and set the alarm on my phone so that I don't let it overcook. With nothing else to do, I walk into the living room and have a seat on the opposite end of the couch from him. I could have sat in the chair, but I'd be lying if I didn't admit I want to be close to him.

"So what is it you like?" He kicks off his shoes and puts his sock-covered feet on my coffee table.

I give him a glare, but he returns it with one of those smiles of his.

"My legs hurt," he explains. "I have to stretch them out. I sustained some muscle damage when Fulcher hurt his knee. It doesn't keep me from everyday life, obviously, but sometimes I have pain."

"Then I guess you can have a free pass."

He's going through the menus and asks me again. "What kind of shows do you like?"

"I like all the comic stuff, almost any of the crime shows, I like to laugh, but I also like to use my brain."

"Good, then let's find a series that's got like a million seasons." He goes through some of the most popular shows. "What about *Supernatural*?"

"I've only ever seen one episode."

He clicks on it. "I saw the first season a long time ago, but I can't even tell you what happened, so it'd be like I was watching it for the first time.

"I'm ready when you are." I grab the blanket someone put on the back of the couch and snuggle in for a nice marathon.

Almost an hour later when the timer goes off on my phone, we pause it and grab food, along with drinks, and the utensils to eat. Anthony pulls the coffee table toward the couch so we have something to sit our plates on.

"Oh my God," he moans as he takes a bite of the casserole. "I haven't had one of these in a really long time. My mom and I love them, but my sister and dad hate them, so it was always a special occasion at my house when I got it. I can't tell you the last time I had one. This one is just as good as my mom's."

The praise makes me feel good, brightens up a dark spot inside my soul. "I'm glad."

He grabs the remote off the table and starts the show back for us as we eat in a companionable silence, only speaking when we make a comment about what's happening on the screen. When we're done, we move our stuff out of the way, and I lie down on my side of the couch.

"You can put your feet in my lap," he offers. "I promise I won't tickle."

There, lying together with full bellies and content spirits, we start what becomes a nightly occurrence for us. We simply enjoy each other's company and friendship. However, I have no idea how this little plot twist in my story will completely alter the ending, how it turns a miserable existence into a happily ever after.

A few hours later, as I'm trying to keep my eyes open and I know I've heard him lightly snoring for the past thirty minutes, he sits up. "I gotta get going, otherwise I'm gonna be your first overnight guest."

The sleepy smile he gives me is lazy and sexy. On a whim, it makes me want to tell him he can stay, but I know I'm not ready for that. "Can you do one thing for me first?" My voice is quiet in the stillness of the room.

Reaching over, he cups my chin. "You know I'll do whatever you need me to, Vi."

"Can you do a walk-through. Make sure everything's locked?"

It's hard to ask this of him, and given the glimpse of compassion in his gaze, this isn't easy for him either. "Yeah, give me just a sec."

Wringing my fingers in my lap, I try to explain. "In the trailer, I knew where all the hiding places were and..."

A well-placed finger to my lips stops me from continuing. "I get it sweetheart, you don't have to explain yourself to me."

And that's the awesome thing about Anthony Bailey; I honestly don't have to explain myself, because he gets me in a way that no one else ever has.

PART 2

REINTEGRATION

CHAPTER EIGHT

ACE

APRIL OF THE FOLLOWING YEAR...

"I'm on vacation, motherfuckers!" I raise my arms in victory as I enter the squad room. My declaration is met with boos and wads of paper being thrown my way. One smacks me across the face, and I shoot the thrower a glare, but I can't blame them. I'm headed for a weekend of fun and sun. They're stuck working a stressful job.

"Shut the fuck up, Ace."

I hear the bitching phrase tossed in my general direction. I can't tell which asshole said it, but I can't be bothered. I deserve this time off as much as anyone else does. The last few months have been some of not only the most stressful, but also enlightening ones of my life. Last time I tried to take a vacation...that shit didn't work out well. I'm beyond excited for this.

"It's not my fault all y'all didn't get invited to the wedding of the decade," I reference the union of Renegade and Whitney. Everybody's only been waiting on it for what seems like forever. They'd tried getting married in October of last year, but almost as soon as the whole crew had gotten down there, a storm had formed in the gulf, and being first responders, we were called back to Laurel Springs. Instead of going to the Justice of the Peace, these two wanted to do it correctly.

Neither one of them seemed to be in that big of a rush, but damn the rest of us have been. April seemed a weird month to get married to me, but it's how it worked out. Regardless, down on the Gulf it's hot as balls, so we can always go into the ocean. Plus it coincides with Caleb, Leighton, and Violet's spring break as well, so I concede there are reasons.

Violet. My pulse speeds up as I think of the woman who's had me turned inside out since the moment I saw her at The Café. Didn't matter to me that she wore a ring on her finger, because I could tell with one glance she wasn't where she wanted to be, wasn't where she *needed* to be. There was a sadness in her eyes, no smile on her face, and lines of worry across her forehead. In my mind, no woman should look like that – especially one who wears a wedding ring. The husband should be making sure his lady is happy and cared for. It didn't take long for me to figure out what kind of a man she was married to and what a loveless marriage they had.

"Numb nuts." One of my fellow officer's smacks me on the back. "Someone has to be here while y'all are on vacay."

"It's not a full week," I argue. I wish it was a full week, but I'll take what I can get. "I'm only going to be there for the weekend."

"Better than what the rest of us are getting."

He's not wrong. I quickly lock up my desk, clean off any last-minute things that need to be done, and then I'm ready to clock out.

"On a serious note, does anyone have anything they need to me do? As soon as I clock out, you can fucking forget it. Last call." I offer one last time, because I'm a team player and I don't expect anyone to have to do anything by themselves when I can help with it.

"Get out of here." The commanding officer on this shift throws his thumb toward the door and gives me a grin. "Go enjoy yourself, Ace. You deserve it."

And with that I'm out the door. I'm ready for a weekend with the lady I've come to care more about than I ever thought possible. In the beginning, I had wanted to help her, not because I felt sorry for her, but because I cared about her. In helping her, I've come to care about her even more. I don't know what my life would be like without her. There's also a part of me that knows if she got spooked she'd be gone without telling me goodbye. Every morning I wake up and look out to see if her car is gone. If it is, I go have breakfast at The Café just to make sure she's still around. If she left, it would break my heart. But I can't tell anyone that, that's my secret to keep.

No one knows how much I want her in my life, by my side, and in my bed every night. Even my best friends think I'm this happy-go-lucky guy who likes living life to the edge with no responsibility.

What would they do if they knew I wanted everything they have, and all the responsibility I can handle?

Violet

"Are you sure you'll be able to make it without both me and Leigh here? I don't know these people that well, so it won't matter if I'm not at the wedding."

Ernie is looking at me like I've grown another head. "They may not care that you're at the wedding, but Anthony will," he references Ace's real name. "He cares a lot about you."

I sigh because I know it's true, but the situation with Anthony, is...well, it's complicated. In so many more ways than I even want to elaborate on. "I'm just offering." I finish filling up my last ketchup bottle. Then go to work filling the sugar packets before I leave.

"No, you're stalling, and there's a huge difference." He comes out from the back where he usually mans the grill. The lunch rush is gone, and it's only us and an elderly couple who's eighty, if they're a day, in one of the booths. "Violet, you're allowed to have fun. Don't let what that son of a bitch did to you ruin your life. You've got someone who'd very much like to be a part of yours if you'd let him."

My brain and memory immediately flash back to August of last year. There's a lot I don't remember, but there's also a lot I do. We'd had a lunch rush that was out of this world, and we'd been relaxing, hoping to get a breather before anyone else came into The Café. I'd had my eyes closed, head down on a table when my husband came through the door and started knocking the holy hell out of me. At first I hadn't realized what was happening, and when I did, I thought I was going to die. Ace had been the responding officer and he'd saved me. It hadn't been the first time my husband had beat me, but it had been the first time somebody had saved me.

"I'm trying, Ernie." And I am, but there's a lot of bullshit to overcome. No one knows the half of it, and I'm not sure they ever well.

"Well keep doin' it, doll. You're looking better these last few weeks, better than I've ever seen you look."

I don't know how to respond, so I don't. "I'll see you in a few days, Ernie."

He gives me a wave as I pull my cross-body bag over my head, securing it on my shoulder. When I step out of The Café, I breathe a sigh of relief. The place is a source of comfort and discomfort for me, but I haven't been able to give it up yet. My phone vibrates in the pocket of my apron. When I notice I have a text from Anthony, I tell myself not to look immediately, but I can't stop.

A: Hey, I'm at the house and I've got my stuff loaded. As soon as you get here and get ready, we can go.

V: I'm on my way.

Ten minutes later I'm pulling in and parking next to his truck. He meets me on the porch, and I have to tell my breath not to catch, my hands not to shake. Anthony is a good-looking man, and I've always thought so even when I shouldn't have.

"Hey," he greets me with a smile that I can't help but answer with one of my own.

"Hey, just let me grab a quick shower and get my bag. Give me thirty minutes or so?"

"Take your time." His eyes run up and down my body, as they always do. He's never seen me naked, but I feel like he undresses me every time those green eyes sweep me from head to toe. Those eyes of his are always so expressive, but I don't know him well enough to know what he's thinking at all times. Maybe one day I will.

"I made some cookies last night if you want to come hang out while I get ready."

One thing Anthony has more than anyone I've ever met in my life, is a sweet tooth. Although looking at him, you would never know it. His body is lean, abs are cut, muscles are solid. He must work out like a goddamn fiend to eat the amount of sugar he does.

"You don't have to ask me twice." He locks up his portion of the duplex and follows me to mine.

Like most women who've lived through the same situation as I have, I do my rituals. First, I unlock the door and deactivate the alarm that was installed for me, but I don't set my purse down until I've done a sweep of the living space. There's absolutely nowhere in my place that anyone can hide; I made sure the first night I was here. Setting my purse down, I reach in and pull out the gun that I'm licensed to carry. When I'm home, I keep it locked up because I have other weapons stashed throughout the house I can use at a moment's notice. It doesn't matter if my husband is still behind bars, there's no way in hell I'll let another person beat me again.

"How's that working for you?" Anthony nods toward the gun.

He'd gone with me to pick it out, took me to get my permit, and spent hours with me at the shooting range so I wouldn't kill myself trying to shoot someone else. It had taken me a little bit to find a gun I liked.

"Good, I went to the range the other day." I reach into my closet, pulling out the sheet from my last session. Nine out of ten shots on this one hit my target.

"Damn, Vi." He whistles between his teeth before giving me a high-five. "That's my girl."

I try not to let his words mean too much, but they warm a place in my chest that's been cold for a long time. "I'm getting there."

"You're there, don't put yourself down. You're making things happen, Violet. Don't think you're not."

"I am." I nod. Although a part of me doesn't believe it. I was told too often how much I didn't matter, all the things I did wrong, and how I'd never be able to do anything right. I'm not sure when I'll stop having these self-loathing thoughts, but at some point it's got to change. Right? "Be right back."

I escape to the bathroom, planning on taking the quickest shower of my life.

Ace

I can't tell if she's uncomfortable with me, or with the praise I give her. I know from my line of work that it could be one or both. From experience I know that if I keep staying the course I have with her for the last eight or nine months things will work out the way they're supposed to.

I'm a patient guy, I had to be when I was a sniper. I literally waited for days sometimes to get my target. This woman in the bathroom enjoying her shower is going to be the ultimate prize for me. She's a target I'm not going to miss. I never missed during my time while in the special forces, I won't miss here.

I just worry that I'll come on too strong for her, that the intense guy I am will push through and the patience will wear off.

"You got this, Anthony," I whisper to myself as I reach forward and grab another cookie, stuffing it in my mouth. I have to have this, because the moment I met this woman I felt a spark. One I've never felt before in my life.

So patience is the word of the day when it comes to this woman, and myself. She's been let down by a lot of people in her life, and I won't be a letdown for her. I'll be the person she can count on and the one who'll lift her up.

CHAPTER NINE

ACE

"YOU EVER BEEN DOWN to the Gulf before the last time we tried to go?" I break the silence that's encompassed us since we left Laurel Springs an hour ago.

You give Violet and me a series on Netflix, a pizza, and a beer, we can talk all night. Apparently, you put us in my truck on a road trip and it's fucking crickets.

"No, this is as far south as I've ever lived, and I've never visited the beach or ocean before."

This is the first I've heard about this being as far south as she's ever lived. We've never talked about things like this. I take the plunge and ask the question. "Where are you from, Violet?"

The windows are down, and within the first thirty minutes she'd pulled her dark hair into a braid. Now she's holding back escaped tendrils with her palm. "Oklahoma," she answers above the whipping of the wind.

"How did you end up in Alabama?"

This drive has loosened my lips and I'm asking all the questions I always wondered about. There's a good chance she won't answer, but all she can do is tell me to fuck off. I've been told that plenty of times in my life – no skin off my back.

She's quiet for a long time, and I wonder if she's going to close up, but then she starts to talk. "Brent..." She stops, seeming to gather what she wants to say before pushing it all out. "Worked in the oil industry. For a while we had good money, but then it fell apart in Oklahoma and he began chasing the next big thing. We came here because he actually wanted to get to the Gulf to try and work on the oil rigs off the coast, but we ran out of money. We were both working to get him there."

"Is that where you wanted to go?"

"Didn't really matter what I wanted." She shrugs. "I was supposed to go with him and support him. That's what I was doing."

I can tell by the tone of her voice that she truly believes she was supposed to be blind in her support of him. Instead of dwelling on the piece of shit, I steer her to talk about herself. "What is it you want to do now?"

This time her words are immediate. "What I'm doing right now. I want to finish my paralegal degree to get my feet wet in the legal industry. Then I'll figure out if I want to commit the time to try and be a lawyer. I'm just not sure if I'm smart enough." That last bit is mentioned on a sigh.

"Fuck that noise, you're one of the smartest people I know." I reach over the console, wrapping my fingers around hers. This is the small amount of contact she'll allow us to have. "You always beat the hell out of me when we go to the sports bar and play trivia. You're a fountain of knowledge."

She snorts. "Yeah, useless knowledge. If you need to know a band's name or lyrics to a song, I'm your woman."

"No knowledge is useless, doll."

I know it won't do well to argue with her; once she has her mind set on something, she's fucking stubborn in changing it. Good thing I'm a patient man.

Violet

I'm still wondering what hell I'm doing here with this man, like who in the world do I think I am?

"Here's the city limits," he announces as I see a sign welcoming us to Gulf Shores.

The windows are still down, the air is warm, and there's a slight smell of salt in the air. There's an electricity that's tangible, I wonder if it's like this in every oceanside town. The lights of the buildings are flashy, neon colors that glow in the darkness of the night, and people are walking on the sidewalks as far as I can see down the main strip. Not a lot of children at almost nine at night, but lots of couples holding hands. Buildings are built on top of each other, and even though it looks like a tourist trap, I hope one day Anthony and I can come back and go through every single one of them.

"How far away from the resort are we?" My memory of the area is vague from the last time, because of how quickly things had happened.

"About five minutes. It's gorgeous, I think you'll love it." He stops at a red light, chancing a look at me. "This time you'll actually get to go in."

I laugh, thinking back to the last time Ryan and Whitney tried to get married. We'd all literally just parked and were getting ready to check in when all the guys were called back to Laurel Springs. "You've been inside before?"

"My little sister got married here," he reveals, sharing a little of his own life to me.

"You've mentioned her once or twice before. How much older are you than her?"

He stretches his neck as the light turns green and we slowly move through the traffic. "I'm twenty-eight, and she just turned twenty-five. She got married when she was twenty-three."

"So young," I comment, even though I got married young too.

"Right? Wasn't sure they'd make it, but they keep on trucking. They had my first nephew last year."

"They must not live around here?"

He turns his turn signal on to merge into the lane that takes us to the resort. Checking his blind spot, he slowly slips in. "She's always looked up to me." He flashes me a smile. "To the point of marrying a man who's going into special forces like I did. They're stationed in North Carolina right now."

"So far away." Then I realize how far away I live from my own family.

"I'm used to it." He shrugs. "I joined up when I was eighteen, and the week after graduation I was shipped out to Fort Benning. From there I was stationed in North Carolina too, deployed, had a trip to sniper school, deployed again, and then came back home. It wasn't until I came back here at twenty-five that I had an address I knew wasn't going to change."

"Your parents must be happy to have you back, since she's gone."

We pull up to the resort I remember from last year, still as breathtaking as I recall it being.

"My parents are excited that I'm not the little shit I was when I left. They're happy I grew up and became a man. I was hell on wheels when I left here at eighteen. One of the reasons I decided to join – I desperately needed the structure it gave me."

We pull up to the valet, which cuts off our conversation. I learned more about him in the last few minutes that I have in the last few months of us hanging out. What we've shared before has been superficial, and I wonder if we haven't done that as a defense mechanism with one another.

We both get out of the truck and enter the lobby of the resort, heading to check into our rooms.

"Anthony Bailey," he says as we're waited on next. "We're with the Kepler wedding party."

We'd actually gotten a code to get rooms cheaper because Whitney is the shit. I barely listen to what's going on until the person at the registration desk asks him if he wants two keycards for the room.

"Wait, there should be two rooms." I interject myself into the conversation. I'd promised to pay Anthony back if he got us two rooms.

"There was a problem with the block they got. When we asked if we could double up two of the occupants, Mr. Kepler assured us that you were okay with getting rid of one of your reservations. Is there a problem?"

"Fuckin' Renegade." I hear under Anthony's breath. "No, it won't be a problem, this will be fine."

I want to argue with him, tell him it won't be fine, but I don't have a credit card and there's no way my debit card will let me rent a room in this place. I have cash at home that I was going to give him when we got back. But if I trust anyone, it's Anthony.

He turns to me, his jaw clenched, teeth working in a grinding motion. "I'm so sorry about this. He didn't ask me, and I hate that he acted like it wasn't a big deal. People think things about us because we spend so much time together."

"It's okay." I do my best to smile, even though I know it's shaky. "I trust you, and I don't want to be a problem. This is supposed to be about having fun, and that's what we'll do."

"Here's your two keycards, Mr. Bailey. We hope you enjoy your stay here."

Our bags have miraculously appeared at our feet and Ace reaches over to grab both of them. "Well let's go see what this room looks like."

IT'S GOT ONE BED. Granted it's a king and it's huge, but it's got one bed. There is a couch, but it's small.

"I can take the couch," he offers before I say anything.

"No way, you're too tall. Hell, I'm too tall. We're adults." I nod to convince myself I'm speaking the truth. "We can handle sharing a bed together in this paradise."

"Are you sure? I don't want to make you uncomfortable."

His phone vibrates in his pocket, and he quickly takes it out, checking the message.

"I'm sure, I trust you."

"That's Renegade, he said they're all downstairs having a drink. We're the last ones to get here since I had to work today. Wanna go join them?"

For the first time in a long time, I feel carefree. This is vacation, I'm here with people I like, why not enjoy it? "Yeah, let's go. Can I just run a brush through my hair first? The drive down did a number on it."

His eyes soften as he looks at me. "Yeah, I need to put some different shoes on." He points to his tennis shoes. "The bar is on the beach, and if you ask me, your hair looks gorgeous. Just like you."

I turn to face him, but he's quickly taking his shoes off and putting on flip flops. I wonder if he meant to say what he did. A few hours, a few hundred miles from home, and lips seem to be looser than they've ever been between us.

Looking into my bag, I grab my brush and go to work on the braid that's completely fallen out. Since Brent has been gone, my hairstyles have been the poster children for fun, flirty, and even sexy if I do say so myself. Because I put it up when my hair was wet, it's got a nice wave to it, and I decide to keep it like this.

"I'm ready if you are, Anthony."

When our eyes meet across the bed, it's an intimate look. One we've never shared, but I've wanted to. Enclosed space has apparently made me more aware of the man standing on the either side of the piece of furniture.

"I'm good to go." I watch him pick up his wallet, put it in his pocket, slip on the shoes he's laid out, pick up his phone, and make sure he has a room keycard. It's all so intimate, the things that a boyfriend and girlfriend or a married couple would share.

It's getting hot in here, and I know I have to get us out of the space. Feelings I've been able to keep in check for months are threatening to spill forth and make me very uncomfortable.

"C'mon Anthony, I can't wait to feel the sand between my toes." It's not a lie, but it's also a way to get us out of the situation we're in.

And as I leave the room, waiting for him outside, I tell myself to calm down. I tell myself we're friends; he only invited me to keep me from staying at home while everyone else was gone and having fun. There's no way he could want a person as fucked up as I am. Not when I'm not even sure who I am anymore. Not sure I ever knew who the hell I was. But one thing is for sure, I will figure out who I am, or I'll die trying.

CHAPTER TEN
ACE

"NO ANTHONY! DON'T YOU DARE!" she screams as I pull her from the dry, sandy beach, toward the crashing waves on the shoreline.

I try not to notice the way her tits shake in the cups of her bikini as we push and pull one another. Try not to notice the beaded nipple against the fabric. It wouldn't take much for me to pull her into my arms and crush her against my chest.

"C'mon, I'll protect you." I grin at her, grabbing hold of her hand and coaxing her to where the waves and beach meet.

"I don't know if I trust you, Ace."

I give her my best grin. "Violet, you trust the fuck outta me. It's why we're sharing a bed."

Her face blushes a pink shade that matches the skin peeking out from beneath the turquoise bikini she's wearing. The very bikini that had made me do a double take when she'd walked out of our bathroom this morning. Even though she and I have been hanging out, it's typically in sweatpants and t-shirts. What's covering her body today isn't leaving much to the imagination.

"Stop teasing her." Leighton throws sand in my direction.

"Shit, that could have gone in my eye." I turn my face away. "And nothing hurts worse than getting a fucking grain of sand in your eye. Not cool, Leigh," I laugh, wiping my palm over my forehead.

"Not cool the way you're dragging her into the ocean." Her point is made with the bite of her tone.

Looking at Violet, I take in that her face does look terrified and she is digging her heels in deeply. It causes me to drop her hand, makes me feel like a piece of shit. "If you don't want to go, you don't have to."

"Do you think I'll like it?" she asks softly as she pushes back hair that's escaped from her braid. The moment that asshole was locked up, this ultra-feminine side of Violet came out, and I fucking approve.

"I think you'll love it. There's nothing more relaxing than just letting the waves take you where they will. It's trusting them to move you in the right direction and not fighting against the current."

"Like finding my true north," she says softly.

"Yeah, exactly like that."

It doesn't escape either of us, what I'm saying to her. Violet's life has been spent fighting against the current, and here I am telling her to go with it. I can tell by the way her head tilts a little to the left. She's wearing mirrored sunglasses and I wish I could see her face, but I'll take the tilting of her head as an indication of what we're sharing.

Slowly we walk out into the water. I wait until she gets acquainted with the first few steps – shrieking when the waves crash into her and runs back – before she starts walking toward me again. Reaching out, I offer my hand to her this time, palm up. No more grabbing hold and pulling her into a place she's not sure she wants to go.

Gradually we make it out far enough that she's up to her hips. She grabs hold of the waistband of my swim trunks, stopping me. "I think this is as far as I want to go."

"Then we won't go any farther." I turn her to face me. "How's it feel?"

"Weird, I can't see the bottom, can't see my feet, so I'm unsure of what I'm stepping on. But it's peaceful, the way it's wrapping around our bodies."

"You're going on blind trust." I put my arms around her waist, holding on tightly. The tits I was eyeing earlier are now definitely pressed against me. I just hope she can't feel the reaction that's sprung up in between us. "I'm proud of you."

She gifts me with the brightest smile I think I've ever seen her give anyone. "Ya know what? I'm proud of me, too. All the changes I've made in the past few months. Honestly though, I wouldn't be where I am without you."

"You should be. It's taken a lot of courage to make those changes, Violet. I know none of this has been easy for you. And you would have done what you had to do, I've done nothing but help facilitate you becoming independent. You did that all on your own."

She's quiet for a few moments, and I'm enjoying being with her. It's almost as if we're sitting back out on the porch, sharing a couple bottles of beer and a container of wings from the BBQ joint we both love. When the next words come out of her mouth, I'm not prepared for them.

"I've filed for divorce, Anthony. I want to be free. I don't want my life tied to what's happened with him the past eight years. It's time for a fresh start. The counselor I saw for the first few months I was back to work told me I'd know when I was ready. I woke up the other day and just knew. It helps knowing he's going to have to serve time for what he did and knowing I have a restraining order for when he does get out, but this is my decision. Like you told me not long ago, our relationship is about compromise, and this is mine."

There's a lump in my throat, and I'm scared to ask the next question. "Is that fresh start gonna be away from Laurel Springs?" I want to take off those damn mirrored sunglasses of hers and see the brown depths that I sometimes get lost in, see for myself how she's feeling, be prepared when she lets me down easy.

She plays with the edges of my swim trunks, she has yet to let go of. I'm not even sure she realizes she's doing it, but I let her because it seems to be soothing her. I hope like hell it'll get her talking to me.

"I've thought a lot about it. Leaving or staying in Laurel Springs – there are pros and cons to both. It's kept me up at night, to be honest with you, but after I filed for divorce, I knew what I had to do."

"What's that, honey?"

She pulls me closer, using the waistband of the swim trunks. For a moment I panic, hoping like fuck my hard dick doesn't appear over the edge. I don't want to stop her, since she seems to be feeling more confident, but motherfuck how much am I supposed to withstand in a day? "I've started to build a life here, with the people who have become my friends. I go to school, I have a job, and I have a home. None of that is thanks to Brent, I've done all those things on my own. With your help of course. You've shown me what it's like to be independent. I've stood on my own two feet. And I've never had that anywhere else, Anthony. If I leave" – she pulls her bottom lip in between her teeth, lifting her shoulder up in the absence of words, before she continues – "I lose two of the best friends I've ever had in you and Leigh. I don't think I can handle that."

My palms cup her face. I have to touch her, have to have some tangible connection to the string of awareness we have with one another. I want to kiss her. I've kept myself from doing it so far, I can wait a little while longer. Little pecks on the cheek have been the name of our game, and we'll keep it that way until I can blow her mind. My voice is rough and choked with emotion when I finally speak. "I'm glad you're staying. I truly don't know what I'd do without you in my life, Vi. You've become a very important part of it."

And those words are no bullshit. They're self-preservation, because I can't lose this woman. She means way too fuckin' much to me.

Violet

"Oh my God, Stella." I giggle as she picks up handfuls of wet sand and throws them over her shoulder.

They land in her hair, tangling it into a knotty, wet mess. "Your mom is going to kill us." I giggle as I glance over at Leigh.

"Nah." Leigh wrinkles her nose. "She'll just make us clean her off, but given the amount of sand this kid has in her hair, that might take a while."

I silently agree as the three of us sit under a huge umbrella on the beach. The rest of our group has gone to parasail. Leaving Leighton, Stella, and myself to hold our spot.

"I know why she didn't go, and I'm scared to death of heights. Why didn't you go?" I ask Leigh as we watch the sky for our group. I can see the boat, a small dot out on the horizon. This is one of those times I wish Anthony's fearlessness would rub off on me.

"This child I'm carrying has to have one parent when my husband falls to his demise in that deathtrap of a parasail." She places her hand over her still flat stomach as she too watches the horizon.

"What????!!!!" I turn to face her. "How did you not tell me? How did I not know?"

"We haven't told anybody." She grins over at me. "You're the first, my friend."

I leap up from my seat, wrapping her in my arms. "I'm so excited for you. I know you all have been trying since October."

She wipes at her eyes. "We have." She nods. "But we'd decided just to forget about it, and go on with our lives. Maybe go to a fertility appointment or look into adoption. We got a little drunk on Valentine's Day, and surprise."

"That's why you aren't showing yet."

"Right, but if you look closely I'm up a damn cup size in my boobs. Like I can't believe how big my tits have gotten. The fact that no one has noticed tells me how small I was before," she huffs as she reaches forward, pushing some sand off Stella's face. "Stell-Belle, you're a mess," she laughs.

"When are you going to tell everyone?" I take a wipe out of Stella's bag and go to work on trying to at least clean her face, as Leighton tries to get the sand out of her hair.

"When we get to twelve weeks, but I've been dying to tell someone, especially you. We work together so closely, and there's been some days where I've had to go out back, puke, and go back to work with a smile on my face. It's not been awful, but I have had some morning sickness."

"I thought you've looked green some days." I think back to a few times when Leighton complained of not feeling well. "How's Holden taking it?"

"Oh my God." She giggles. "He's walking around like he's the only person in the world to ever get a woman pregnant. It's a point of pride with him, and he acts like he's got super sperm. It's embarrassing. We have an ultrasound picture on our bedside table. He'll walk by it and say, 'Look what I did.' Like seriously dude? You didn't do this on your own."

I'm laughing hardcore. If there are two people in the world who are meant to be parents, it's these two. The way they love each other is how I aspire for a man to love me.

"Since you shared a secret with me, I'll share one with you."

"Oh do tell." She leans close, as she pulls Stella's hair into a ponytail. "Have you and Ace done the nasty yet? He's talented with his hips, isn't he?"

"Jesus, woman!"

"I can't help it. I'm one of those women who has gotten incredibly horny since getting pregnant. I think about sex like a teenage boy. Holden is loving life right now, let me tell you. In between puking, we're fucking like rabbits."

I can't even with this girl. She's one of my best friends, but right now, I seriously can't with her. Putting my face in the palm of my hand, I giggle. "TMI, Leigh. So much TMI. But to tell you what's going on with me – I filed for divorce."

"For Ace?" she asks excitedly.

"No." I shake my head. "For me, but Ace is a part of it. If I decide to hop into a relationship with him, I want it to be fair for the both of us. If I'm still married, it's not fair for him. He'll always be the other man, and I don't want that."

"Let's be honest, Violet, he's never been the other man with you, not since he walked into The Café."

Leighton's right. Anthony's the only man and maybe that's what scares me more than anything. He has the power to hurt me more than Brent did. But I've learned something about myself in the last few months. I truly believe in the happily ever after, and I'll be damned if I don't have one for myself. Complete with a hot man, a screaming orgasm, and the settled life I've always wanted to have with a man I love and respect.

CHAPTER ELEVEN

ACE

"DO YOU THINK THIS IS OKAY?" I turn my gaze from where I'm looking out of our glass balcony doors to the sound of Violet's voice. She stands framed in the doorway of our suite, in the most beautiful dress I've ever seen her in. Having the sister I do, I know a thing or two about dresses. She could give Whitney a run for her money in the southern debutante category.

Violet is a vision of a wet dream in this pink/peachy thing with a hem higher in the front to show off her muscular thigh, lower in the back to help showcase the tan she got today. Her arms are on full display and the lace cut outs at the top are playing peak-a-boo with her perfect cleavage. Her long hair is down – I hardly ever see it that way, but it's curly (which I've never seen) and she's got this dark stain on her lips. The stain gives me ideas about how that dark color would look smudged at the corners, or maybe smeared up and down my cock as she goes down on me.

"Anthony?" Her voice is full of uncertainty, and I realize I've been standing like a dumbass just staring at her.

"You look absolutely amazing." I unanchor my feet from the floor and walk toward her as fast as they will carry me.

"You sure?" she questions, pushing her fingers through her locks. "I got this dress at a thrift store and did a little sewing on my own to it."

"It's gorgeous. You're a ten, Vi, don't think you aren't – ever."

The way her lips spread in a smile is worth the compliment, because her unguarded smiles are so few and far between.

"You're not so bad yourself, abs of steel."

I snort as I hear the nickname she's given me. I took my shirt off one night after a few beers and she started calling me that. She doesn't use it all the time, but when she does, it never fails to make me grin. Whatever the reason and whatever the motivation – I'll take it. If we're deep enough into our relationship to have nicknames, it's a damn good sign.

"A pair of khakis and a polo doesn't compare to what you're packin' babe, but at least we'll make a good showing."

I turn around, grabbing my essentials off the dresser. Sunglasses, cell phone, wallet. She makes a sound in her throat, one I've only heard once or twice. The sound sends a shot straight down my spine to my crotch.

"If you could see your ass in those khakis, abs of steel? You'd know that you do a little better than just cleaning up."

My eyebrows raise to my fucking hairline as I hear the words coming out of her mouth. I can count on one hand the number of times Violet's let something like this slip. Most of the time we're completely and totally platonic, by mutual choice. There's no way I want to push her, and rejection doesn't sit well with me.

Presenting her with my elbow as she slips into some shoes, I hold what I really want to say in, and instead joke with her. "Let's go make all these coupled up people jealous by how hot we are."

She giggles, a sound I haven't heard much of from her either. Another sound I love. "Let's do it."

THE DRINKS ARE FLOWING, the laughter is loud, and we're having a great time with our friends. We've even been graced by some music royalty.

"Can you believe that Reaper and Harmony are here?" Violet whispers to me as she glances up to where Holden sits next to his cousin. Together, you can definitely see the family resemblance.

"No." I laugh as I shake my head, taking a drink of my beer. "Last thing I expected, to be honest with you. I knew they were related, but I didn't think they'd come to a random wedding in Alabama."

Holden gets up from his seat, heading over to the bar. In the next few minutes, he's back with a tray of shots, handing them out amongst all of us, before sitting another full bottle down. "If we're gonna enjoy our vacation, let's enjoy our vacation. Sorry, Caleb." He gives him a grin as the rest of us hold our shot glasses up. "I'm obviously not the best man here, but I feel like I have a vested interest in everybody at this table. Some of you are family to me." He tips the glass to Reaper and Harmony. "Others of you are family by my choice." He tips his glass to the rest of us. "Many times the family by choice is closer to me than my real family, because of all the shit we go through together. Which is why I want to do this here."

I'm unsure what Holden's going to say. When he has a few drinks in him, he becomes a sappy bastard. The elder statesmen of the group he truly is, if you will. He waits until he's got everyone's attention.

"This group of guys here are my brothers. We've been through a little bit of everything together, personally and professionally. You've all grown in leaps and bounds over the last few years. We've welcomed girlfriends, wives, kids, and new friendships" – he sends Violet and me a glance – "into the fold. All of these changes have made us better men, better officers, and more compassionate people. I'm fucking honored to be able to share in the step Renegade and Whitney are taking tomorrow. The same way I'm really excited to tell Tank and Blaze congratulations on an engagement that happened this afternoon when none of us were around. Fucker." He points at Tank.

"I didn't want anyone to ruin it." Tank laughs, as Blaze shows everyone her ring.

"I'm almost as proud of Caleb for getting a full ride to the University of Alabama as if I were his dad." He tips the glass to Menace and Caleb, who sit next to each other.

The table goes wild, because none of us knew this before right now. The kid has been through a fuck ton, and for him to be able to do this for himself and his dad is amazing. I watch as Menace pulls his son in with a huge arm, dropping a kiss on his forehead. That may seem weird to some people, but for these two – it's been them against the world since Caleb was a small child. If anyone can be proud of his son, it's Menace.

"And Ace," Holden continues. "My fuckin' crazy-ass daredevil. I bet y'all didn't know he's taking the exam to become a member of the water rescue squad – on top of what he's already doing. That job isn't as glamorous as this one, and when you're called to help the hours are shit, but it takes a talented person to do it. They'll be lucky to share you with us when you make it."

"If I make it." I blush at the attention. Becoming a member is hard, and it's not a guarantee I'll make it.

"*When* you make it," he presses on.

"What about you, boss?" Menace raises his glass to our leader. "What do you have to celebrate?"

Havoc's gaze softens as he glances down to his wife. He and Leighton started in the weirdest of ways, but there's no denying how much these two love each other.

"I do have a little announcement to make." He pulls Leighton up next to him.

Their smiles are contagious, enough to light the beach around us if the tiki torches go out. I wonder what they're going to announce.

"Leigh and I have are so excited to tell you all that Stella isn't going to be the only baby in this place for very much longer."

"We weren't going to tell anyone yet." Leighton tilts her head back, giggling. "We were gonna wait."

The table erupts in excited cheers, including Havoc's cousin, as Reaper jumps up, giving him a huge hug. "You're gonna love it." He pats him on the back. "Kids are fun, and if you have a boy, I have all kinds of shit you can take."

If I remember correctly Reaper and Harmony have two boys. The offer Reaper just gave him highlights why I love the people I share my life with. They go out of their way to help each other, even when they don't have to. Like when someone finds out they're having a baby. Holy fucking shit. Havoc and Leigh are having a kid.

I sit back, watching as the people I care most about in the world congratulate each other. My head pounds with the want and need to be happy for everyone at the table. But my heart, fuck my heart aches because everyone else had personal accomplishments while mine is a professional goal. I'm still in this holding pattern with Violet, not sure of when it'll end. As we all salute and take a shot, I grab the bottle that Holden brought to the table, refilling the glasses as I try to remember that everybody's on their own timeframe. Just because my brothers have found their forevers, doesn't mean I have to be in a hurry to do so. It doesn't mean there's not hope for Violet and me.

But none of that helps the loneliness I feel in my bones, or the want I feel in my groin, or the need I feel to have her wrapped in my arms. And with those thoughts twirling in my head – I pound back another shot.

"ANTHONY, you gotta help me get you in there."

I hear Violet, but it's almost as if her voice is coming from far, far away.

How much did I have to drink? My tongue is heavy, vision is hazy, and even I know I'm not walking in a straight line. "Sorry," I apologize as I try to keep my shit together long enough to help her open the door and push me inside.

"Don't be sorry," she groans under my weight. "You were having a good time, celebrating your friend's good news."

As we get in the room, I'm burning up. Reaching behind me, I fist my shirt and yank it over my head. "No, let me tell you what's fucked up." I fumble with the buttons on my khaki's before I push them down my hips, leaving me in boxers and my shoes. Fuck, my shoes. Plopping down on the bed, I go to work on them, cursing the fact I didn't wear flip flops.

"What's fucked up?" Violet takes my shoes and helps me untie them.

"The whole time I was supposed to be happy for my friends, I was thinking about how pissed off I am at myself."

"Why are you pissed off?" she asks as she gets my shoes off and pulls my pants the rest of the way down.

"Because I want something, and I can't seem to force myself to take it."

Our eyes meet. In the silence of the room, I think she realizes I'm talking about her, about my feelings for her.

"Which is what?" Her voice is barely above a whisper.

She's still kneeling, and I want to be where she is. I slide off the bed, my knees hitting the carpet. Down here I'm not so dizzy, the room doesn't sway, and my tongue doesn't feel so thick. My palms cup her cheeks, before my fingers push into her hair.

"You," I groan as I use my fingers to situate her mouth how I want it. "I want you more than I want to breathe. I want your kiss more than I want to sleep at night. I want your love more than anything else I've ever wanted in my life."

"These are drunken ramblings, abs."

"Fuck drunk ramblings." I pull her closer to me, pushing my erection against her. "Reaction doesn't lie, Violet."

And in that moment, I take the kiss I've wanted to take for months. I push against her walls, knock down a few of them, and burrow my way into her mouth. Hoping against everything stacked against us that the taste of me on her tongue will change it all and point us in the right direction.

CHAPTER TWELVE
VIOLET

ANTHONY HASN'T MENTIONED the kiss from last night, and I haven't either. To be honest, I'm not sure how to bring it up. If he can't remember it or if he did it because he was drunk, and it meant nothing...it will devastate me.

That's not to say it didn't affect me. I went to bed with my lips tingling and spent all night convincing myself not to cuddle up next to his warmth. By not mentioning it, I figure I'm saving us both the embarrassment – him for doing it and me for thinking it might have meant something.

"You look amazing." Anthony's voice is hoarse as his green eyes sweep up and down my body. I can feel it in the fiber of my being. My skin pricks with awareness, and I can feel my breasts swell against the lace of my bra. I didn't start having actual physical reactions to men until this one came into my life.

This dress is the prettiest thing I've ever owned. An aqua blue color with a lace overlay on top, flowers running up and down it. Whitney went through her closet a few weeks ago and invited the ladies over to "shop". When I saw it, I wanted it, and prayed that no one else did. It sat on the couch for an hour, before Blaze stalked over, picked it up, and handed it to me.

"You've been eyeing it since the moment you got here," she told me as she dropped it in my lap. "If you want it, take it."

I'd taken it, but I hadn't tried it on until I'd gotten home. And when I did, I'd spun around like a princess in a cartoon. Hell, I'd even clapped my hands and did a curtsy. In some ways, that moment and this dress signaled the change I needed in my life. I'd been floating by, doing my day-to-day, but I'd stopped challenging myself. After that day, I started to take charge again, I went after things I wanted.

With one exception. Anthony. Because if he rejects me, I'm not sure how I'll handle it.

Now here I am, wearing the dress, staring down the man who gave me the best kiss of my life last night, and my heart is pounding as I wonder what kind of move I've going to make.

"We need to leave if we're going to make it in time." He's slipping on his shoes, and I realize I've waited too long and lost my window.

Instead of being disappointed in myself, I promise myself that next time I won't let the moment pass. There will be another opportunity. I know there will because we've been dancing around each other for months, and I have to believe I can be someone desirable. That my husband didn't ruin me for other people. As soon as the ink dries on the divorce agreement, I'm going to make my move on this man, and he'll either accept me or reject me on my own merit. In some ways, that's worth all the heartache I've gone through. If I can find my true happiness, I'll accept everything that happened before was in preparation to show me what goodness was around the corner. Maybe it taught me how to appreciate a good man. More than anything, I hope I get to experience the kind of happiness the other people in my life are experiencing right now. To know the feeling behind the smiles on their faces? I'd be the luckiest person in the world. The luckiest person who now understands her worth, even if it's hard for me to realize it sometimes.

Grabbing my purse, I give him a smile. "I'm ready when you are." And I realize those words apply to so many areas of my life.

"THEY PINTERESTED the fuck outta this wedding," Anthony whispers as we make our way to the stretch of sand Whitney and Ryan have selected to say their vows on.

I shoot him a glare, but giggle too. "What do you know about that?"

"My sister." He rolls his eyes and sighs heavily. "Did the same with hers, and now I've had to get a motherfuckin' account so I can be added to some damn private board to plan our mom's birthday. Do you know what that does to my masculinity? To know I have the Pinterest app on my phone, and I'm adding shit to it?"

Now my giggle has turned into a full-blown laugh. "Does anyone know this about you?"

"Just you, Vi." He slowly snakes his arm around my shoulders, pulling me closer. "And I'm counting on you to keep my secret."

He doesn't have to worry. As long as he keeps touching me, I'll keep every single secret he chooses to confide in me.

"Oh, son of a bitch." He points to a sign at the back of where the chairs are set up for the guests. "Does she have Renegade's balls in a vice? *With sandy toes and salt-water kisses, we became Mr. and Mrs.*? How fucking lame is that? So lame..."

Putting my hand over my mouth to hide the laughter, I lean into him. "Let them have their fun. You never know, maybe one day you'll think there's a woman worth making a cute little rhyme about."

He gifts me with the sexiest smile I've seen him give anyone. "What? You mean something like, *Oh Vi, you look so fly*?"

Slapping his shoulder, I give him a look. "Stop, don't make fun."

And for some reason it hurts that he's just made up that little rhyme. Like all that optimism I had when we were in the hotel room is gone.

"I'm not making fun." He grabs hold of my chin as we come to a stop in the middle of the aisle. Other guests of the wedding have to go around us to get to their seats, but Anthony doesn't let my chin go, doesn't break his gaze from mine.

"It feels like it," I whisper.

"I'd never make fun of you, and I'd never make fun of the way I feel for you, Violet. A lot of times I'm the one who brings the laughs, and I'm okay with it, but I hope that you of all people can see behind the laughs. You know the pain a smile hides, and I hope if I can ever be myself with anyone, it'll be you."

Finally he breaks our gaze and his hold, ushering us to our seats. My mind is full of turmoil at the words he spoke, twisting around like leaves in an autumn storm. I have a feeling he was trying to tell me something important about himself. But I don't want to make assumptions, and without concrete proof, I have no idea what his words mean.

Ace

The whole crowd gasps with joy when they see Stella making her way up the aisle, throwing petals on the runner covering the sand. She's cute as can be, her chubby legs toddling. When it looks like she might take a tumble, Caleb rushes in from the side, grabbing her hand.

Stella gazes up at him like he's some sort of prince charming, smiling so widely at him you can see a little dimple in her cheek. He smiles back at her, and I realize it's been a long time since any of us saw Caleb freely give one of those. The barn party last year changed us all, but no one more than Caleb. We're all still trying to recover from the shock of losing one of our own in the community.

"C'mon, Stell Belle," he whispers loudly. "Let's get you up there and get your parents married."

He swoops her up in his arms, giving her a little kiss on the cheek that makes her squeal before depositing her next to Blaze, who holds out her hand.

Stella grabs it tightly, while we all stand for Whitney. Reaper and Harmony sing from the left-hand side of the aisle, it looks like another member of Black Friday plays guitar as they sing their number-one duet.

"This is so exciting." Violet beams back at me. Her hair is highlighted by the glow of the setting sun behind us. There's a slight breeze blowing, and if I'm honest, this couldn't be any more perfect. "I've always wanted to see Reaper and Harmony, and this is like a private concert."

I'm ashamed to say I don't know much about either one of them; I just know they're one of the most popular celebrity couples in the world and they had a whirlwind romance. Over the past few weeks, as the girls have prepared for this wedding, they've talked about the sweet love story between these two. I've watched more celebrity gossip shows and YouTube videos about this couple than I've probably watched my entire life.

But if this makes her happy, then there's nothing I want to change about this day. Keeping that all to myself, I give her a little bit of the story as it was told to me.

"Holden mentioned we were all coming down for the wedding to Reaper and they were looking to take a small vacation before Black Friday has to head back into the studio. They knew they wouldn't be bothered here with us, and they offered to sing. I knew you liked them, so what better way for you to see them?"

For just a few moments I feel like the most bad ass guy in the place, because I helped put that look on her face. I didn't give up every time she tried to blow me off. The fluttering in my stomach as she grins at me is worth every time I've wondered if what I was doing was working. Stepping forward, I put my arm around her neck, letting my hand hang down against her chest so she can grasp mine with hers.

She still doesn't trust enough to let all her walls down with me, but it's a start, and a start is all I've ever wanted with Violet.

"She looks gorgeous," Violet whispers as we watch Whitney come to the head of the aisle.

My eyes drift from Whitney to where Renegade stands at the end of the aisle waiting for her. The look on his face is one of complete and total love and devotion. There's a passion I see as he watches her, even a few tears make their way down his cheeks. He's saying something, but I can't tell what it is because he's put his hand over his mouth. I've watched these two friends of mine fall in love, and I'd be lying if I didn't say I've wanted it for a while. Knowing they've been able to have it gives me hope.

As I look down and watch her gaze follow Whitney up the aisle, her tear up as they exchange vows, and the way she puts her free hand over her own mouth when they kiss gives me hope. I have hope she remembers what a happily ever after is and that she allows me to give it to her. Nobody else in this world deserves it more than she does, and nobody else wants to give that happiness to her more than I do.

When the minister pronounces them husband and wife, I close my eyes and send up a little prayer for myself. Renegade waited a long time, and if he did, so can I. With all the crazy shit he's been through, he persevered, same with Whitney.

I open my eyes just in time to see them break apart and lean down, grabbing their daughter. As they make their way down the aisle, after they're pronounced husband and wife, I'm hit with a feeling in my chest I've never felt before. It's the type of emotion that steals your breath, makes you want more than what you have, and to be the best version of yourself you can be.

That shit doesn't happen overnight though, it doesn't strike like lightning. The feeling might, but the reality of it is so much slower than the realization. That shit takes time, it takes understanding, and diligence.

Not to mention all the stars aligning and maybe a little bit of luck. No big deal, right? I got this. When it's supposed to happen, it happens. And I believe right now, more than ever, that Violet and I? We're supposed to happen.

CHAPTER THIRTEEN
VIOLET

THREE WEEKS **Later**

"That's all I have for y'all today." The teacher at the front of the class checks her watch. "I know it's fifteen minutes early, but let's go ahead and cut out. I'm sure we've all had a long day."

When I started night classes, I wasn't sure what to expect since before this I didn't have more than a high school education. There was a fear I wouldn't measure up to the other students, but I learned quickly we all had our own stories. Meeting Karina Holland changed my academic life. She'd tutored Leighton in one of the subjects she needed some help with, and when I told her off-handedly I wanted to go back to school, she'd made it happen. As I put my backpack on my shoulders and pick up my bottle of water, she stops in front of me, a welcoming smile on her face.

"You doin' okay, Violet?"

"I am." And I mean it. The last few months have been difficult, but I'm happy with this life I've carved out for myself. I'm doing better than I ever imagined I would be. Anthony is working tonight, but I don't work tomorrow, so we're getting together for a late dinner when he gets off shift.

"You're tan, I take it your trip to the shore did you well?"

Even though the wedding was three weeks ago, I'm still sporting the color I got while I was there. She's not pressing; she's asking like a friend, and Lord knows I've needed those more times than I've cared to count in my life. "It did, thank you again for letting me miss the class to attend."

"You're one of my brightest students, Violet. If anyone deserves to have a good time, it's you."

The praise embarrasses me, I'm not used to it, and I don't respond to it well typically. My cheeks are red, I can feel the heat in them, and I duck my head, but I manage a soft "Thank you."

"Seriously, Violet, not many people can be out of school as long as you've been, come back, and make it your bitch the way you have. Take the praise, and revel in it. You earned it."

When I learn how to take the praise, I will. Instead I nod at her, sure she knows I'm a fake. I don't have all my shit together, I don't even have a little of my shit together. I'm hanging on by the skin of my teeth and a prayer. Thank God for the man sleeping in the duplex next to me. Without him, I'm not sure where I'd be. Probably at some truck stop in Florida fulfilling my prophecy as a lot lizard. Luckily a hot cop by the name of Anthony Bailey stepped up and helped me out. Before she can embarrass me further, I gather my stuff up and make my way toward the student parking, where my car sits under a light. I'm nothing, if not safe.

I'm five feet away when I hear someone yell my name, or rather a nickname that drives me completely crazy.

"Vi Pie!!!"

Caleb is the only person on this earth who calls me that, and he's lucky I haven't cut his tongue out for giving me such a shitty nickname. The way he's shouted it, makes me turn to him. There's an urgency in his tone, one that makes me worry about him immediately. "Are you okay?"

He's half-way staggering as he strolls up to me. "Am I?"

As he steps into the light, I gasp when I get a good look at him. There's blood dripping from his nose, and his chin is scraped. I gasp, pulling my backpack around and taking a wet wipe out of it. "What happened to you?"

I reach over, grabbing him by the elbow, but he outweighs me by at least fifty pounds and he's not steady on his feet.

"Took a tumble." He laughs, and that's when I smell the liquor on his breath.

"Are you drunk?" The question is unbelievable as I push it past my lips.

He gives me a look. One that's way too adult for the teenager looking at me. "C'mon, Vi Pie, don't act like you're surprised."

The fact is, I am. Very surprised, and I wonder why he's saying these words like I should be able to notice when he's three sheets to the wind. "Let's get you over here." I pull him to my car, leaning him against the hood.

Now that he's fully in the light, I see a purple bruise popping up on his collar bone, some scratches on his neck. Using the wet wipe, I try to get rid of some of the blood caked on his chin. But I have to ask about the other marks on his body.

"Caleb, what else did you do tonight?"

Giving me that same grin he gave me earlier, he purses his lips. "A really fucking hot co-ed, who knew how to ride my dick in ways these high school girls can only dream of."

Holy Jesus. What am I going to do with this kid? "Did she know you're not eighteen?"

"Do I look like I'm not eighteen?" His eyebrow raises as his cocky tone grates against my nerves. Lifting a bottle of Jack from somewhere, I'm not completely sure where it appeared from, he takes a drink. When I reach for it, he holds it over my head.

He looks like he's in his early-twenties with the big body he has and the scruff on his jaw. "You look like shit. Now give me a few minutes, while I figure out what the hell to do with you."

He crosses his arms over his wide chest, his long legs cross at the ankles and shoots me a defiant look, as he takes another drink. One that makes me glad I've never had children, because if this shithead were mine I'd knock the smirk off his face then tell him to cry it out, because it's obvious he's hurting more than any of us know how to deal with.

It makes me sad, and I vow right here and right now, I'm not letting Caleb down. Not the way I've been let down my entire life. Sighing, I grab my phone out of my purse and make a call. He's used to cleaning up my messes, so it should be no surprise that I'm calling him to clean up other people's, too.

Ace

"I didn't know who else to call." Violet's voice is apologetic as she looks at me from where she leans against the car, her arm around Caleb.

"Told her to call my dad, don't give a fuck," Caleb slurs, kicking his long legs out in front of him, trying to stand up straight.

"You do give a fuck." I relieve Violet, taking Caleb's weight on me. "Dude, you're solid," I groan as I help him get situated. "Come over here and sit on the grill of my car." He's done a lot of growing up on us in the last year. Not all of it good. Since the barn party where a classmate died from drinking a bad batch of moonshine, a part of him has become withdrawn. He's not quick to smile, not so quick to joke around. It seems to have affected him more than any of us realized. Maybe we'd all hoped and assumed too much with him getting the scholarship and being affectionate with Stella meant he was okay. Looks like we were very wrong.

"Working out is about the only thing that lets me sleep at night without seeing that body with the tarp over it. And when that doesn't work" – he gives me a grin – "a little bit of Jack Daniels takes care of it." He holds up a bottle I hadn't noticed before.

"I tried to take that from him, but he's taller than me," Violet interjects from where she is.

Which is exactly what I can smell coming off his breath right now. "The problem, Caleb" – I shift him to my other side – "is that you're not old enough to be drinking Jack Daniels."

"Isn't that somethin'?" He laughs hysterically. "The cop's kid, doing something illegal. Guess I'm just a disappointment all the way around." He takes another drink.

"Stop this shit now, Caleb." My patience is thin and wearing thinner as I try to reason with him. There's so many people who care about this kid, and he's pretending like he's stuck by himself with zero help.

"Nah." He shakes his head. "Mom left when I was little, she hasn't given a shit since. Dad can't find a woman who wants to take on him *and* a kid. My buddy poisoned himself while I was getting a blow job not thirty feet away. Fucking girl won't even call me back now. Like I don't need somebody to talk to?" He points to his chest as he gets himself out of my arms and away from me. "Like I don't need somebody to ask me if I'm okay? Like I don't need a goddamn hug every once in a while."

"Is that what you need?" Violet asks softly, speaking for the first time in long minutes. "Because I know what that feels like. And if you need a hug, you don't even have to ask me, Caleb. Just open your arms up and let me give you one."

I'm watching quietly, waiting to see how he'll react, how she'll react. The stubborn set of his jaw indicates he's not going to take the bait, but right as I'm pretty sure he's going to be a fucker, he puts the bottle down, sways, and opens his arms. Without any hesitation, Violet pushes herself toward him, circling her arms around his waist, because she's so much smaller than he is. I watch these two, hugging it out in the parking lot of the community college, and I wonder... does Violet need this as much as he does?

"I don't care if you don't give a fuck." I grab Caleb by the shoulder to steady him as he pulls away from the woman I've grown to care so much about. "I do. I don't want to break your dad's heart by taking you home like this."

He's hugged it out with Violet, and now he's back to being belligerent, much like a drunk. "Maybe my dad should have thought about breaking my heart, ya know, by not having a mother in my life who cared about me. Or maybe he'd like to talk to me, really tell me what happened between them, instead of me speculating."

I know nothing about what happened with Caleb's parents. As far as I know, none of us do. Menace, for the most part, is a very private guy. "I'm not going to pretend like I know how you feel, Caleb, because I don't, but what I can tell you is you're on a path you don't want to be on. None of us want to see you here. The danger of you doing something you can't apologize for is high. You do remember the name Brooks Strather, right?"

He swivels his head to face me. "Now you all want to pretend like you care? Nobody has seen how destroyed I look? I don't sleep, I don't enjoy school anymore, half the time I show up for work drunk, and nobody even notices. The only thing I love is football because it hurts. When a big motherfucker hits me, I feel it. When I make a touchdown, it's pure joy, but it leaves as soon as it comes. There's nothing in my life I can find happiness in anymore."

I put my palm against my neck and let out a deep sigh. I'm not equipped to handle this kid in the shape he's in. He's basically admitting to me he's a depressed, functioning alcoholic at seventeen years old. The horrible truth? None of us noticed it. He's gotten so good at hiding it, we literally didn't notice it.

"Look, I'm not going to pretend like I understand exactly what you're going through. I didn't lose any friends when I was your age, but I lost a lot the year after my nineteenth birthday. Then even more after I turned twenty-one. Did I bury my guilt and sorrow in alcohol and pussy? Yes. No one is faulting you for that Caleb, but it's going to destroy you from the inside out, my man. It will make you a shell of the person you were before and you'll become a bitter guy who takes no pleasure in anything. That alcohol you enjoy now? It'll take a whole lot more to get you drunk. That pussy you like burying yourself in? You won't realize what's truly love and not just ass. Don't ruin the chance you have."

"Fuck a chance." He turns his dark eyes to me. They're fierce with anger, and what looks to be frustration. "Nobody else got a chance. He should be the one making the trip to Tuscaloosa, not me. He was a better player than me, a better everything."

Survivor's guilt is a real thing with Caleb. Irritation grates at my nerves. And his attitude hits a sore spot with me. "You wanna fuck up your life? Go ahead, but I won't be hiding it from your dad anymore after tonight. I'll take you home this one time, but I see you drinking again, I'll arrest you and we'll call Mason to come get you."

His eyes narrow, his face becomes hard, and Violet watches us quietly. The words, when he speaks them, are laced with the same attitude he's had the entire time. "Yes sir."

"Get your ass in the car."

He throws the bottle of alcohol into a nearby trash can defiantly before climbing into the squad car. I sigh when he slams the door shut. I'm used to adults being assholes, but a kid who's hurting emotionally? I'm not sure how to deal with that, and there's a part of me that worries I didn't handle it at all.

"Sorry you had to deal with that." I hitch my thumb to him as I speak to Violet.

"Sorry I dragged you into it. For some reason I thought he might respond better to you than me. Seems like he's an equal opportunity spoiled brat." She offers me a grin.

"He's hurting, and he's surviving the only way he knows how." I make excuses for him now that he can't hear. He's got to learn that leaning on others isn't a weakness and nothing to be ashamed of.

"I'm gonna take him home – maybe we should take a raincheck on dinner. I have a feeling it's going to take me a while to get him situated."

There's disappointment in her gaze, but right now Caleb needs someone to take care of him, and I'm stepping up to be that person – whether he wants me to or not.

I walk her over to her car, open the door, and lean in, giving her a kiss on the cheek. "See you tomorrow." I watch as she gets in, buckles up, and starts the vehicle.

"See ya. Be careful with him, okay? He's not as badass as he wants everyone to think he is."

"I know." My answer is accompanied by a nod. "He's walking a tightrope right now that he may very well fall off of, if we don't give him a net to catch himself."

"I don't want him to fall, abs of steel."

"I don't either, Vi, I don't either."

CHAPTER FOURTEEN
VIOLET

TONIGHT HAS TURNED out to be super long. Rolling my neck around on my shoulders, I reach over to the bedside table and grab my cell phone, checking the time. A little after midnight. It's a good thing I don't have to work tomorrow, because I can't get my brain to shut off. I wonder if Anthony's having the same problem I'm having.

V: Abs of steel, you awake?

Immediately I see the three little dots on my phone, indicating he's awake and typing a message.

A: Yeah, I can't sleep after what went down with Caleb.

V: We're in the same boat.

A: Come over, we can watch TV or something.

Those were the words I wanted to hear. Being stuck here by myself with nothing to distract my brain made me think of everything I could have done differently for the last ten years of my life. Things that have no bearing on my life today are all I can think about. Pushing the covers off my body, I get out of bed. Looking down at myself, I realize I need a pair of sweatpants and a bra under the white shirt I'm wearing.

Too bad Anthony wasn't just lying next to me and I couldn't reach over, grasp his arm, and shake him awake. Those thoughts are coming more often now, even when maybe they shouldn't be. Walking to my kitchen, I grab a plate of the cookies I made when I had been trying to take my mind off what happened. I balance them on my hand and look around for a pair of shoes to wear. Stuffing my feet into a pair of flip flops, I go out my side of the duplex and into his.

"Hey." He yawns as he stands in the kitchen. "I'm fixing me a snack, you want anything?"

"I brought over some cookies I made earlier, if you want."

"You know I've got a sweet tooth and you know I have soft spot for any of the sweets you make."

I do know this; it's one of the things I've learned about him since I moved in next door. Kicking my flip flops off, I collapse onto one end of his couch. He collapses onto the other, laying out a blanket for us to share. This is normal for us, the epitome of how we spend our time together.

Sometimes we talk, sometimes we don't. Over the past few months we've settled into a respectful friendship. A part of me knows that one day it'll go further. We've been on that collision course with each other since we started, I'm just not sure when it will be. What will be the situation that makes us finally stop tip-toeing around one another?

"Do you care what we watch?" he asks as he leans his head back against the arm of the couch.

"No, I just need something to take my mind off Caleb."

He nods, starts something, and we're both quiet for a long time. Even though there's a show playing in the background, I think about why I married Brent. A friend of mine died my senior year of high school too, one of my best friends. Marissa was someone I spent most every weekend with – we went on vacation together, even worked at the same fast food joint. We had plans to go to the same college and room together, but when she passed away in a car accident, my whole life changed. I lost the will to do amazing things with my life. Dropping into a seriously deep depression, it wasn't until I met Brent, who told me everything I *wanted* to hear, that I came out of it. By then he was my saving grace, the one person who seemed to love me above all others. How stupid was that?

"You're thinking awful hard over there." Anthony rubs my leg as he speaks. The touch goes straight through my body, and I'm re-thinking what I told him about waiting until my divorce is final.

"Just remembering what made me turn to Brent in the first place. One of my best friends passed away in a car accident and I floundered. Depression gripped me hardcore, and the person to bring me out of it was Brent. I clung to him like a lifeline. What if the same thing happens to Caleb? What if he's clinging to drinking to save him? To numb the pain so he doesn't have to feel anymore. You see what kind of a road it took me down, I don't want that for him."

"Then maybe you should be honest with him, treat him like an adult and share what you went through. He can listen to us all day long, he can ignore us and back talk, but until he sees something tangible, it's not going to sink in. I can promise you that."

I pull my leg away from his fingers, sitting up on the couch. "You think he'll respond to it? He might just see it as me being an adult trying to tell him how to live his life."

"If you could prevent him from making a dumb decision does it even matter?" he questions, and I know he's right.

Ace

In the glow of the TV, Violet is more beautiful than she's ever been. This is when I like her the most. Relaxed, hair all crazy, free of makeup, and being herself. She's worried about Caleb – we all are, but the way she's pulled her lip in between her teeth has my eyes zoning in on her mouth. I've thought of nothing but our kiss since it happened, and I've wanted nothing more than to take another. What's held me back is her asking to wait until the divorce is final.

There are times, though, times when I look at her and I can almost believe she's undressing me with her eyes. She's imagining what I look like with no clothes on, and she's holding herself back.

Tonight I'm tired, I'm frustrated and I'm tired. I don't want to keep my hands off her, and to be honest, I just want a little bit of pleasure to go with this crazy-ass life I live. Reaching in, I test the water's slightly. I leave the palm of my hand on her cheek for longer than necessary. When she doesn't make a move to retreat from my touch, I lean in with my body. Giving her ample time to back away, I tilt my head and slowly take her lips with mine.

Nipping at her bottom lip, I tease along the edge, wondering if she'll let me in, or if she'll stop me. I'll respect either decision she makes, but when she wraps her arms around my neck and pushes her body against mine, I'm more than surprised.

Pulling back slightly, both of us are breathing deeply. "Are you sure?"

"I shouldn't be, but Ace, I want you."

Ace. She never calls me Ace. The unexpected declaration from her does crazy things to me. Instant fucking hard-on.

"I want you too," I smear my lips down the side of her neck before moving back up to her ear. "Wanted you since the first day I walked into The Café and saw you."

She giggles, tilting her head to the side, giving me permission to suction my mouth to her neck. "Even when I spilled coffee on you."

I chuckle against her skin. "*Especially* when you spilled coffee on me."

Tunneling my fingers through her hair, I pull her closer to me, capturing her lips with mine. Her balance is shaky. To keep it, I lie down with my back against the arm, pulling her over top of me. There's a low growl in my throat when I feel her fingers play with the edge of my shirt, pushing up against the cotton, but inadvertently brushing against my erection. Twisting her hair in my grip, I disengage our lips. "Watch those hands, honey. It won't take much. It's been a long time."

Her brown eyes are almost black with desire. "How long?"

"What?" My brain is not firing on all cylinders. I can't comprehend exactly what she's asking.

"How long has it been for you?"

It dawns on me what she's asking. She settles against me, her body cradled in mine. Pushing her hair back from her face, I lick my lips, close my eyes, and inhale the clean scent that is Violet. "Not since you spilled coffee on me at The Café."

"You're kidding." She pushes up, pressing her lips against mine.

"No." I frame her face with my hands. "If we want to get technical, about a month before I met you. But the day I saw you, looking so beautifully sad, I knew I had to make you happy again."

"Nobody's ever wanted to make me happy," she whispers as she tucks her face into my neck.

Curling my arm around her neck, I press her tightly against me. "I do, I've always wanted to."

Her lips tentatively work against the tendons of my neck. Opening widely against my skin, she suckles, nips, and then soothes with a soft touch of her tongue. Leaning up, her breath is hot against my ear. "I want to make you happy, too."

Turning my head, I capture a kiss from her again. We're straining against each other's body and there's no doubt how much I want her. The sweatpants I wear do nothing to hide my desire. Reaching down, I hook her thigh in my hand, pulling her tighter against me. My other hand trails up under her shirt, stopping when I feel the smooth material of her bra. Palming the flesh, I feel the stab of her nipple. Lightly squeezing, I deepen the kiss and push my body further against her. At some point we've started grinding against one another, and her hand has snuck beneath the waistband of my sweat pants, searching for what I have down below.

As her palm caresses my length, I'm reminded of what she told me before.

"Vi, baby." I pull back from her, holding her chin with my had. "You aren't divorced yet. That was an important point to you when we almost did this before."

She leans her forehead against my chin, seeming to try to calm her breathing, the pounding of her heart. I can feel the hot air rushing against my chest as she tries to regulate herself. "You're right. I wanted to be yours freely before we did this. I'm sorry," she apologizes as she drops a chaste kiss on my chin.

"No reason to be sorry," I assure her.

Glancing down in between us at the tented front of my sweatpants, she licks her lips. My eyes follow her pink tongue as she collects the moisture. "We're just both going to be very frustrated people, huh?"

"Yeah, I'll definitely be taking a cold shower after you leave," I groan, throwing my head back against the couch. "Ninety-nine percent sure I'll be jerking one out, too."

She giggles against me. "This isn't what I had planned on when I came here, I promise."

"I know, Vi, I know. It wasn't even on my radar, and regardless of how frustrated I am right now, I love kissing you." I tilt her head back against my hand at her neck. "I love hearing you moan, feeling you strain against me – it was totally worth it. All totally and completely worth it."

Her voice is husky when she speaks again. "It was worth it for me, too. If nothing, I know now that when we are able to be together freely, it'll be combustive."

"Baby, like a five-alarm fire." I grasp her around the ass again.

"I better go." She kisses me on the cheek.

I'm reluctant to let her up from the couch, but I know she has to leave. To keep our sanity, she's gotta go.

"See you soon, abs of steel."

She slips out of my side of the duplex, and I'm left feeling lonely, horny, and not entirely sure what just happened. We've been so good about not mixing relationship with friendship, but I have a feeling we just crossed a line. One we won't be able to come back from.

And I can't say I'm sorry about it.

CHAPTER FIFTEEN

VIOLET

BREAKFAST RUSH IS OVER, allowing Leighton and I to lazily fill the syrup dispensers and talk about what's been going on in our lives. Since the wedding, I feel like all of us have been balls to the wall. We haven't hung out in forever, and after what happened between Anthony and I a few nights ago, I'm wondering if I want to discuss it with my friend or not.

"You and Ace looked pretty close at the wedding." She hits my elbow with her own as she cuts her eyes at me.

Stupidly I wonder if she can see what happened between us all over my face. I can feel my cheeks heat, and my thoughts are plunged back into how I felt on top of him with his hand caressing my entire body. It would be a lie if I said I have thought about anything other than that particular situation since it happened. Pulling myself out of the memory, I give her a look.

"Just because you're married and pregnant doesn't mean that everyone else has to be too," I joke with her, secretly super happy she and Holden are having a baby. She hasn't gained much weight, but she's glowing. Pregnancy looks good on her.

"Oh yes, pregnancy sex is where it's at." She purses her lips giving me a nod. Her eyes dilating, a far-off look covering her face, it's obvious she's remembering a thing or two herself. "Seriously, favorite thing ever right now."

"TMI, Leigh. TMI!"

She giggles, seeming to enjoy making me uncomfortable. "Seriously, though, what's going on with you and Ace the hottie? I figured after the way the two of you shared a room at the wedding, it wouldn't be long before you had an announcement about being together."

"I thought you were married to Havoc the hottie?" I try to deflect the questions she's asked me.

"Let's be real honest. They're all hot. Stop trying to ignore my question. What's happening with the two of you?"

"We hang out, we eat together, and watch Netflix together all the time, but other than that not much."

My frustration with myself and him is obvious in my tone. I wish I didn't have some sense of loyalty to Brent, wish I didn't still feel like a married woman and could live in sin the way so many other people do. The fact is, I want what Ace and I have to last, it feels wrong for me to start something with him when I'm not entirely free.

"You've never done anything else? You're hot, he's hot. The two of you haven't looked at each other and just like spontaneously combusted before? Because, when I look at the both of you, sometimes I want to spontaneously combust."

My cheeks heat and she appears to understand she's sniffed out a story here. "Why are you blushing? C'mon it's not fair to keep something like this from me, Vi."

Quickly, I decide to give her the bare minimum. Let her think she's got a scoop, and then hopefully we can move on. "We kissed. In Gulf Shores, we kissed," I blurt out, because there's no other way for me to ease her into this.

"Oh my God." She literally vibrates with excitement over this turn of events. "How was it? Have you done it again? Does this mean you're dating?"

"Slow down." I put my hand up in front of her mouth. If I let her keep going, she'll have us married and living next door to her and Holden in five minutes flat. While the idea does have merit, I'm still trying to get used to what we did last night on his couch.

"He kissed me, but he'd been drinking and we haven't really talked about it since. Which is good," I continue, "because I don't want to start anything with him or anyone else until I'm ready."

The lie feels wrong, like I should be telling Leighton the whole story, but the whole story isn't exactly one I'm sure of yet. I don't know where we're going, don't know how it's going to end up. Something tells me Leighton would be as heartbroken as we would be if we didn't work out.

"You've gotta bring it up, Vi. It could be a game changer for your life. Like an epic game changer."

She's telling me nothing I don't already know. I wonder constantly if I'm sabotaging myself by not acting on what we showed each other a few nights ago. That kind of attraction and desire isn't something that comes along all the time. But what if we try and it doesn't work out? That's more than I can take. "I'm trying to save what's left of my wounded pride."

Leigh levels me with a glare. "Tell me what's really going on."

"I have a moral problem. I don't want to start something with Anthony when I'm not divorced, and Brent won't sign the papers."

She's the first person I've told. I found out a week ago. When your husband is in jail, he's not hard to serve, and it's not difficult to get the ball rolling. Particularly when you don't have kids and you didn't own shit together. However, I received them back with a note that said he declined to sign them.

"Why won't he sign them?" she asks the same question I had as soon as I'd opened the packet up with shaky hands. Seeing the note from him devastated me. I'd been doing so well planning the life I could have with Anthony, and then here he was, rearing his ugly head. Brent, miracle of all miracles, can still fuck shit up from behind bars.

"Because he's an asshole?" I shrug. It was the only explanation I'd had. "The ugly truth is if he's unhappy, he wants me to be unhappy too. But my lawyer says I can get a divorce because he's in jail. There are certain avenues we can take to force his hand."

"Is it that important to you, to be divorced before you start living your life?"

It's a hard situation to explain to people, but I don't feel as if I'm free. What if I'm never truly free? What if he gets out of jail and stalks me to the ends of the earth? What if I have children with someone else, and he hurts them? These are thoughts that continuously cycle through my mind. But if there's anyone I can be honest with, it's Leighton.

"It's very important to me. If I think about my life as a whole, I don't feel as if it started yet. There was a small window of time, back when Brent and I first got together, when I was happy. The rest of the time, I've been living in some sort of anxious fear. There were moments where it wasn't paralyzing and I could enjoy aspects of life. There are others when it was paralyzing and I couldn't even get out of bed. I'm using this time to figure out who I am, Leigh. Anthony doesn't deserve half a woman who's unsure of who she really is. And what if there's a problem with the divorce and he wants to move forward, but we can't?"

"Now you're inviting trouble." Leigh tsks me. "Why don't you wait and see where this situation with Ace goes before you start explaining it away. The first thing you need to do is confront him about the kiss the two of you shared."

She will not let this go.

"Do you know how embarrassed I'll be if he says it was a mistake?" And I'm not exactly talking about the kiss, I'm talking about the night on the couch, when we almost let our bodies take control, instead of our good sense.

She turns it around on me. "Do you know how good it will feel if he tells you it's been keeping him awake at night jacking off to the memory?"

"Leighton." I spit out the drink of water I've just taken.

"Oh come on, Vi. Imagine his big body alone in bed, naked. Those ab muscles of his tightened up as he wraps his hand around his length, working it furiously at the memory of your kiss."

Dear God. This woman. "Leighton," I groan. These are things I don't want to think about. "My imagination doesn't need your imagination piled on top of it."

Leighton gives me a smile. "Well, thank God you aren't a nun, and you're at least thinking about the piece of man meat you have at your disposal. Trust me, Vi. I'm sure Ace is thinking about you too. One of you is going to have to make the first move, and maybe he did it when he kissed you. Especially since neither one of you have mentioned it since it happened. How are you going to know?"

For the first time I'm thinking about it in terms that aren't black and white. What if she's right? What if this whole time he's been waiting on me and I've lost my chance? I promise myself I'll talk to my lawyer tomorrow, and I'll get a direct answer from the judge. Suddenly I'm desperate to move on, and Anthony Bailey is definitely the man I want to move on with.

"HOW ARE YOU LADIES DOING?"

We both look up from where we were gossiping to see Caleb, slowly making his way in and going behind the counter.

"You're late." Leighton gives him a hard time. "You were supposed to be here like two hours ago. Where have you been?"

She's grinning at me, and I'm grinning back at her, because we like to joke with him. It's fun to see him get riled up. However, neither one of us are prepared when he whirls around, a mean look on his face.

"What does it matter to you? You don't have to mother me anymore, Leighton. Go be a mom to your own kid."

The hateful tone rubs me the wrong way. "Hey, don't talk to her like that!"

"What, you wanna come at me, too? Your husband didn't teach you not to mess with people bigger than you?"

Another voice enters the conversation, and I sag back down into the chair with relief when I hear Holden.

"Look kid, I don't know what's gotten into you, but you won't speak my wife the way I just heard you speak to her, and you owe Violet an apology, too."

"What? You gonna run and tell my dad?"

I'm trying to figure out what happened to him from Gulf Shores to here. There he seemed to at least be happy, but I'm reminded that I too put on a smiling face for a long time, and no one ever bothered to look beneath it.

"No, you're an adult, you can take responsibility for your own actions," Holden steps up to the counter. "Now apologize to both of them."

"Fuck you." He flicks the dishtowel he'd been about to use in our general direction before turning on his heel and leaving The Café, the door slamming as he takes the sidewalk at a jog.

"I don't know what's gotten into that kid." Holden shakes his head. "But I'd like to bust his ass."

"He's hurting." I watch as he runs out of our sight. "He's hurting so bad he doesn't know how to deal with it, so he's lashing out. Either he's going to come to his senses, or something will force him to."

"You seem to speak from experience."

Nodding, I still remember the scared girl who married a man she thought she was in love with, picked up her entire life, and moved away from her family. It had ended up being the worst mistake of her life, but had brought her the biggest blessing when she came to this town. Hopefully Caleb won't make the same mistakes I did.

CHAPTER SIXTEEN

ACE

"REQUESTING BACK UP at the bottoms, down by the boat ramp."

I can hear Tank's voice on the radio. It seems amused, tired, and inquisitive as he requests another patrol car to come help him. I'm in the area, so I pick up the radio and call in my position. Flipping on my lights, I accelerate so that the police package in my cruiser responds. Carefully, I make my way through the bottoms, and in minutes I'm pulling in behind his car, turning off my siren.

Getting out, I take in what I see in front of me. Tank's got what appears to be a teenage guy and a teenage girl leaning against the back of his patrol car. He doesn't have them cuffed, so I'm assuming it's not that big of a deal, whatever went down, so now I'm wondering why he called for backup.

"What's going on?"

He turns to me so that we face each other, but neither of our backs are to the kids. "I was doing a round down here, making sure nobody was loitering or doing anything they weren't supposed to be doing, when I saw this car." He grins, chuckling. "The damn thing was rockin', I'm not kidding you. So I roll up and get an eye-full of this dude's ass while they're goin' at it." He turns his head, laughing.

"Aww damn, why didn't you just leave 'em alone and let them finish? If they were out here, you know they're trying to get away from parents. You cock-blocker. Are they both eighteen?" I look over at them again, holding the smile back from my face.

"No, they're sixteen, so there's no issue with consent or anything like that. But when I looked in the front seat of the car, I found that." He points to a clear glass container of moonshine sitting on the ground next to the car. "For that, I had to interrupt."

"What are you going to do?" I hook my thumb in my gear belt as I glance over at the two kids, who are doing their best to not touch one another.

"Separate them. I'm almost positive she's drunk. I could smell it, and it was under her seat. Wouldn't surprise me if he brought it for her, but I'm wondering where the hell he got it from."

"You take him? I'll take her?"

Tank nods. "You've got those movie-star good looks, abs of steel," he jokes.

"How the fuck did you know about the nickname?"

"Ole Tank knows everything." He winks and flicks the cotton of his shirt in a swagger-filled move that could only be his.

I fuckin' hate that guy. Sighing I walk over to the girl. "You got your ID on you?"

She nods, silently handing me her license. Jackie Sampson. "So Jackie, what were you doing down here today with him?"

Tears are slightly streaming down her face and her voice is squeaky as she speaks to me. "Winston is my boyfriend and my daddy said I couldn't see him." She rubs a hand over her nose. "But I told my parents I was spending the night with a friend. He picked me up this afternoon about two miles from my house and we went riding around."

"Who had the moonshine? You or him?" I relax my stance, giving her non-verbal cues so that she knows I'm listening and not a threat.

"He did. The first couple of times we've had sex" – her cheeks burn a bright red – "it's hurt a lot." She puts her hand up to her lips. "Because he said I wasn't relaxed enough. He wanted me to be relaxed enough this time."

"How much did you drink?" I eye the bottle sitting at our feet next to the car.

"It was full when he gave it to me."

There's about a fourth of it gone, and not knowing how strong the liquor is inside has me worried. Especially after what happened at the barn party last year. "You feeling sick?"

"A little, but mostly embarrassed and scared you're gonna call my parents."

"Well honey, that's definitely gonna happen. Do you know where he got the moonshine from?"

She shakes her head, looking miserable. "No, but it's all over school. You mention you need some and it just appears the next day in your locker."

That's news to me, and I'm sure it'll be news to the rest of my colleagues. I make a note in my phone. "Okay, wait here. I'm gonna have someone come check you out. A kid died from drinking bad moonshine last year, I'm sure you heard about it."

Her face looks stricken. "You think I could die?"

"I think you don't know what the hell you just put in your body, and we don't know who had that before your boyfriend over there, so I think we should be on the safe side. Don't you?"

She nods as I key the radio on my shoulder and request EMS assistance. "I'm going to give your parents a call, anything else you wanna tell me before I do?"

"No." She folds her arms over her stomach. "Just that the sex so wasn't worth this."

Chuckling, I look over at the boy. Poor guy, he's got a lot to learn. "In a few years, when you meet a guy who's willing to make it *not* hurt for you, you'll see what all the fuss is about. My advice to you right now? Drop this dude like a bad habit. If it's still hurting after a few times, he don't know what he's doing, and dear Lord, please tell me you were safe while you were doing it."

"I'm a cheerleader who has a shot at a scholarship to the University of Alabama next year. I'm on birth control because I don't want to mess it up, and I always made him use a condom."

"You've got a good head on your shoulders, Jackie. You'll get a citation for being drunk in public, but as soon as EMS checks you out, you can be on your way."

Looking over, I see that Tank is done interviewing the boy.

"She said it was his," I tell him as we meet in the middle.

"He confirmed. Said he got it at school."

"That's what she said too. You say you want some and it just appears in your locker. I bet they gotta leave money though." My brain is working overtime. Somebody has to be deeply connected with the school in order to have free rein of the hallways when kids aren't in class. "By the way, I sent for EMS; she drank a lot and I wanna make sure she's okay after what happened last year."

"Good call, I'm going to report in to Havoc."

Adrenaline courses through my body, because after almost a year of nothing, it appears that another supplier has moved in. And he's targeting our most vulnerable, which will never happen on my watch.

Violet

My classmates have already turned in the test we're taking today, but I want to check one last time, make sure my answers are right. I've done well in this class, and I'd like to pull an A.

Glancing at the clock on the wall, I sigh, unsure of one of the answers.

"Take as long as you need, Violet. Just because everyone else rushed through it doesn't mean you have to. Be happy with the answers you've given, and turn it in when you're ready."

I nod, going back to the question that's got me stumped. I've gone back to it three times, and in the end, I decide to go with my gut. Since I trusted my gut to stay in Laurel Springs, things have gone well for me, even if Brent did get put in jail and I had a hospital stay. I'm coming to learn that those were bumps in the road to the happiness I have now.

"Here ya go, Karina." I fumble with my purse as I hand in the test. "Sorry it took me so long."

"No problem." She gives me a smile. "I wish everyone took this as seriously as you do. It's not too late. Do you want to go have a drink at the coffee shop? I have an empty house to go home to, and I just don't want to do it tonight."

I'm kind of thrown off by the invitation, and I wonder for a second if she's hitting on me, but I don't have many friends in town that aren't connected to Leighton or Anthony, so I quickly accept. "Sure, they have a raspberry tea refresher I love."

"I KNOW I probably freaked you out asking you to come for a drink with me, but the truth is, I don't know many people in town," Karina explains as we have a seat in the back of the shop.

I take a drink and make a noise of relation. "I've only been in town a short time myself, but I was lucky to be integrated into the Moonshine Task Force group of friends. They kinda take over your life and then you wonder how in the world you lived without them. So what brought you here?" I ask, I've never heard her story and everyone knows mine, so I'd like to hear hers.

"Oh man." She situates herself in the seat, crossing her legs. "You know those stories where women don't know they've been cheated on until three days before their wedding?"

"I've seen enough Hallmark and Lifetime movies to know what you're talking about."

She raises her hand. "That's me. I came home from the salon, after getting everything waxed and plucked, was packing the *small* bag I had for my honeymoon," she emphasizes small, "when I heard a noise in the spare bedroom of my house. I honestly didn't think about it, but we had a dog so I went to check it out. Imagine my surprise when my best friend and my soon-to-be-husband were fucking without a care in the world. I stood there for a good minute, trying to figure out if what I was seeing was the truth or if I had conjured up some horrible dream. But they didn't even notice me. It wasn't until he came and laid down on his back that he saw me. I don't know why I stood there, but I couldn't move. It was like I was stuck in this trance, and I couldn't knock myself out of it..." she trails off.

"I'm sure it was a shock."

"More than a shock, I felt like my entire world had ended. Every plan I had was altered, every dream I had was gone."

"I'm sure you've heard my story." I take a drink of my tea. "I can relate."

She gives me a small smile.

"How did you end up here?"

"Answered an ad for a high-school teacher, and haven't looked back. When I got here, I started teaching these classes too. I'm originally from Pennsylvania so I don't know how I'm going to handle not having snow for Christmas. It was cool last year, but I have a feeling this year I'm going to miss it."

"But we have biscuits and gravy here." I wink. "And the Moonshine Task Force."

"You do have a point, but I'm lonely," she admits. "I think I'm ready to start dating again, I just don't know how."

"I'm of no help to you; I'm still married and trying desperately not to break my own rule by sleeping with the man who seriously makes my heart skip a beat. I'm a horribly bad influence."

She laughs. "Oh Violet, I signed up for a dating app, I just can't seem to make my profile public."

"Do it!" My smile is bright. "Look, I know this sounds weird, but I'm here to tell you that since I came to town, I've watched three couples come together and I'm waiting on my own chance. Laurel Springs has something magical about it, Karina."

"What if there's no one worth meeting on here?" She holds up her phone.

"Then just keep swiping left until you see your happily ever after. In some way or another it's worked for the rest of us. Why mess with a proven track record?"

Seems as if her decision is made when she looks down, tapping on her phone. After what she's been through, I send up a small prayer that she can find someone who can make her as happy as Anthony makes me.

CHAPTER SEVENTEEN
ACE

IT'S a slow night in Laurel Springs – my kind of night to be honest. When there aren't people acting insane and hell bent on breaking the law. I'm an hour away from going off shift and ready to Netflix and spend some time with Violet. We've been good since our interlude on the couch, but I'm unsure how much longer I'll be able to keep my hands off of her. She's an itch I can't scratch, a temptation I can't give into.

Sitting on the side of the highway, I'm randomly clocking speed while finishing up some of the reports I have lingering from earlier in the night. A few cars have gone by about five over the speed limit, and I've let them go because it's only going to cause me more paperwork. There's something else I want to see tonight rather than a stack of reports. I'm finishing up the last paper to work on when a car goes screaming by me. I glance at the mounted radar, whistling when I see they were easily twenty-five over.

Punching my radio, I call in my position and give the specifics on the car. I can't read the license plate since they got so far in front of me. Gradually, as they slow in the curvy section of road, I tuck in behind them. For a moment I think they're going to take off in the straight-stretch, but instead they pull over. Now that I can see their license plate number, I call it in and exit the vehicle. Approaching, I can see there are four people in the car, and instinctively I call for backup, requesting Renegade and Tank who I know are riding together tonight. Touching the driver's side corner of the trunk, I observe what's going on inside before addressing the driver.

"Is there a problem, Officer?" the teenager asks as I approach the driver's side door. His voice even cracks as I get closer, but I know not to let his age dismiss him. Someone who was driving a car that fast and gives me this sort of feeling? He's got something in there.

"Yeah, you were going eighty in a fifty-five. That's a problem. Let me see your license and registration."

The tension in the car is thick, I can feel it prickling the back of my neck as I watch him reach over to get it. The driver has sweat pouring off his face, down his neck, collecting at the collar of his shirt. When I hear sirens and see blue lights approaching from the opposite direction, I breathe a little easier. Renegade and Tank exit their squad car and hurry to assist me.

"Got four in the car, I can smell marijuana and alcohol," I mumble toward them.

They take points around the vehicle, shining their flashlights in. The darkness makes everything a little bit more dangerous. "Everybody get out of the car, I need to see some identification."

The driver finally hands over his info, and I see that he's seventeen years old. Back when I was seventeen, I wasn't driving a car twenty-five over the limit, with drugs and alcohol inside. What the hell are these kids thinking? "Is this your mom or dad's car?"

"Dad's," he answers, squeezing the steering wheel with his hands.

"Go ahead and get on out."

As we line the group of them along the trunk so that the lights from our cars give us the ability to see, I reach over to collect the IDs. And that's when I notice Caleb. *Son of a bitch, what is this kid doing?*

"What's going on here, Officer?" he asks, smartass grin on his face.

Because I've already had to deal with his attitude once, I give him a glare. "You're with people you shouldn't be with, and I can smell alcohol and marijuana in the car. Not to mention the driver" – I hold the ID out so I can read it – "Mitchell Sanders, was driving fast enough for me to take his license tonight. You got any more questions, son?"

"I ain't your son." He leans back with an arrogance that makes me want to smack the taste out of his mouth.

"You damn right about that." I step closer to him. "If you were, I'd ground your ass and you damn well wouldn't be playing in the game on Friday."

"Right." He folds his arms over his chest, testing me with another grin.

"Call his dad, in fact, let's call all their parents." I walk up to the driver, pointing to flakes of marijuana on his shirt. "He's got marijuana on his shirt. Before I search this car, is there anything else in it?"

All the boys shift in their shoes, glancing down at the ground. No one seems willing to spill.

"I can smell the alcohol, just be honest with me. What's in the car? How many of you are football players? Do you want me to call your coach?"

One of them speaks up. "There's moonshine, another baggie of weed, and a one-hitter where I was sitting in the passenger side door."

"Did you all get this at school?" I go to the car and pull the bottle of moonshine out, holding it up. Since the girl told me they were able to get moonshine at school, it hasn't sat well with me. There's not a lot we can prove, at least not yet, but we will. Eventually everyone fucks up and makes a mistake.

The kid who told me what was in the car nods. "How do you get it? You tell someone? You leave money in your locker, and boom it appears?" I question. "There's some sort of process, and I'd like for you tell me what it is."

He acts like he doesn't want to say anything, but after a few minutes of me uncomfortably staring at him he starts talking again. "There's a box in the janitor's closet. You want something? You go in there and put your locker number in the box. That night you leave the money in an envelope inside, the next day you come to school, you've got moonshine and the money's gone."

"You have any idea who's doing this?"

"None!" He holds up his hands. "All we know is that after the barn party, there wasn't any moonshine for a while. It started showing back up when school started, and eventually we all knew how to get it."

This is all information I have to tell Havoc, and I know he'll be pissed when I do.

"Parents are on their way," Renegade speaks up, sending Caleb a look. "All of them."

My mind isn't on the field sobriety test I'm giving to the driver, I'm thinking about what's going to happen when Menace shows up. Within fifteen minutes, parents arrive, I've written citations, the driver is in the backseat of Renegade and Tank's cruiser. Newsflash, he failed. I can't believe Caleb got in the car with a drunk or high driver. I'm still not sure which it was with him. We've let the dad take the car, and I'm waiting on Menace to show up. I motion for the guys to take the driver as I see another squad car pulling up.

"I got this." I hitch my thumb back to where Caleb is leaning against the trunk of my car. His arms are tight across his chest, the look on his face is thunderous.

Menace parks the car, and I wait as he turns the car off but then sits there for a few minutes. I wonder if he's trying to pull himself together, or if he's trying to decide what he wants to say to his son. Is he embarrassed? Is he scared? Is he pissed?

I'm aware he could be pissed. I've worked with people before who've ripped me a new one because I pulled their kid over. This with Caleb, though? It's different. I care about him, I'm worried about him, and I have a feeling he's not being completely honest with Menace. If I have to be the bad guy, then I will be.

Caleb steals a glance my way, probably wondering what it is I'm going to tell Menace, when the older man finally unfolds himself from his squad car. Truth is I'm not sure what I'm going to say – the truth? Is there really anything else?

"Did you really have to drag him into this?" Caleb hitches his chin to where his dad still sits in the car. "Hasn't he had enough bullshit in his life?"

"I could ask you the same thing. He deserves better than how you've been acting."

Heat rises to his cheeks, the rosy tint they take is visible, even in the darkness of the night around us. Menace finally gets out of the car and ambles over to us. He doesn't say anything as he looks at first Caleb and then me. He's big, and I've never been more intimidated than I am in this moment.

"What's going on?" His voice is quiet as he asks the question to both of us.

I hold back for a moment, trying to see if Caleb will be honest with his dad, if he'll give him at least that much respect. When he doesn't, I'm disappointed and clear my throat.

"Here's his citation." I hand it over. "And to be honest, I think we need to have a talk. This isn't the first time I've caught him with liquor on his breath. The three kids he was with?" I shake my head, running a hand down my face. "Bad kids, he shouldn't be with them."

As I watch Mason's face fall, I know he has no idea what's been going on. He looks like he's been punched in the gut – literally taking a step back from where he's standing. His dark eyes shift over to the son who looks so much like him. Before me, their relationship is changing, and I hope Caleb will be honest for just a few minutes, long enough to let his dad in.

"You told me you were good. Every time I asked, you said you were good. I offered to get you counseling, to go with you, if you needed me to." His eyes are sad, half-way filled with tears, and it's killing me to watch this exchange. "But you looked straight in my eyes, right in my face, and lied to me, Caleb. Why? You've never been a liar, why start now?"

The teenager purses his lips, pulls his arms tighter across his chest, and brings his hands into fists. His forearms flex as it looks as if he's literally holding onto the words by sheer force. Suddenly they break free with a shout. "Like you needed another disappointment in your life – another fuck up – something else that didn't go as planned."

There's a long stretch of silence, until a sniffle is heard. Both Menace and I glance over to Caleb, seeing him double over into himself as the kid sobs like I've never heard anyone sob in my life. Menace almost breaks his neck trying to get to him, wrapping his arms tightly around his son. It's the first crack in the armor that's been around him since the barn party – and I have to wonder – how many more in this community are silently suffering?

How many of them are self-medicating with the moonshine that killed their friend? How many of them don't understand the dangers of what they're doing, and who the hell has brought this shit back into our community? There are more questions than there are answers, but I know once we're on the case, we won't stop until we find the culprit behind this situation. We didn't eradicate it once to have it come back again. And one thing is for sure, this person must be new to town, because they have no idea who the hell they're messing with. But we will find them, and we will make sure justice is served.

CHAPTER EIGHTEEN

VIOLET

YOU KNOW that moment in time when you realize a situation you thought was handled, no longer is? It's a moment that takes your breath away, that makes your hand fan your face as heat rises up your neck. It's the flush of awareness when you realize the man who's been living next door to you is so hot he should be on the cover of a calendar.

Typically when I see Anthony after shift, we've both changed and gotten comfortable. Nine times out of ten, he's knocking on my door wearing a pair of sweatpants and a ratty old t-shirt. Not that he's not a good-looking man when he's dressed for lounging, he's hot then, too.

Tonight though, as he climbs out of his squad car, he looks different. On the one hand he looks dangerous. Like a badass no one would dare to cross. On the other hand, he looks all buttoned-up, too-well put together, and I want to muss the control he seems to have on himself. A bullet-proof vest rests over a black t-shirt, down into a pair of black pants. A thigh-holster wraps around muscle I haven't really paid attention to before, but now that I've seen it, I can't not look at it.

"How's it going?" his southern-tinged voice asks as he reaches into the car, giving me an unobstructed view of a perfectly shaped ass. I never got the aspect of ogling an ass before, but dear Jesus, the way those pants cup the firm cheeks of Anthony's backside? I think I finally understand. Standing up straight, he turns around, lifting an eyebrow. "You okay?"

I realize I never answered his first question. "I'm good, I made us dinner." I clear my throat. "If you want to go get changed...or not, I mean, however you're comfortable."

His eyes narrow as his gaze rakes over my body. I'm sure he can tell what I'm thinking just by looking at me. Since the night at his house, all I've thought about is getting him beneath me again. Or him on top of me – I'll take whatever I can get. "You sure you're okay?"

My eyes have landed at a spot they shouldn't have landed. The paradise where his vest meets his belt buckle, which only emphasizes the bulge hidden beneath the zipper. This time he clears his throat, and my gaze travels up, taking note of the yellow letters on the vest – they read MTF – and I spot his badge hanging around his neck. Speaking of the neck, I get stuck staring again when I encounter his Adam's apple. It's bobbing as he swallows.

"I'm good," I finally squeak out. "Hope you're in the mood for homemade pizza."

The smile that slowly spreads across his face tells me I'm not fooling anyone. He knows exactly what I was looking at. He knows exactly how he's affected me, and if it were up to him, he'd use it to his advantage.

Luckily for me, Anthony isn't the type of man to flaunt much in anyone's face. However, he does like to tease. So as he climbs the steps of the porch, he squats down so that we're eye-level. He dips his voice low, whispery enough that it could be confused with the rumblings of a lover on a dark night, instead of a guy coming home from a long shift.

"I hope you made that pepperoni and pineapple I love."

Clearing my throat again, I answer, "I did."

"Tell me, Vi. Would you prefer I kept the thigh-holster on, or nah?"

I close my eyes, count to ten, and hope that the entire ground opens up and takes me with it. My words stutter the first couple of times I try to say them, but eventually I push them past heavy lips. "Whatever's more comfortable for you."

"Sweatpants with the thigh-holster." He grins as he unlocks his door and ducks in. "Got it – see ya in five."

After he shuts the door, I lean back in my chair, hands over my face, as I allow myself a moment of complete and total embarrassment. "Get it together, Violet," I whisper as I get up and quickly shuffle to my side of the duplex. I'm gonna need to throw some cold water on my cheeks – otherwise I will never be able to face this man again.

Ace

I'd have to be blind not to notice the way Violet was looking at me. She apparently loves the way my thigh holster looks, and I'd be stupid not to use that to my advantage anytime I can. Tonight, however, is not that night. I'm not really in the mood for any kinds of games – especially not after what happened with Caleb. Not to mention I want her too much, and there's only so many times we can stop each other. Quickly, I shower, throw on a pair of sweatpants with a t-shirt, and run over to her side of the duplex.

"God, I can smell that out here," I praise her cooking abilities as I enter her side.

She's bent over the stove, and being the man I am, I take a minute to appreciate the picture she's presenting to me. For a minute I allow myself to imagine I'm coming home to her after shift, that her ass is mine to grab, her lips are mine to take.

"Hope you're hungry." She gives me a smile. "I have cookies too, made them just for you today."

Mother fuck I am, but not for food. Since having a taste of her the other night, I've spent more time than I care to admit imagining what it's like to taste her again. Woken up hard remembering her sleeping beside me in that bed. "Starving." I give her an answering grin.

She pulls the pizza out of the oven, before she carries it over to the table, putting it on a trivet. Within minutes I've gotten us drinks, while she's cut the pizza and served it up on plates.

"How was your night?"

I sigh as I try to lessen the tension in my shoulders. Do I tell her about what happened with Caleb? I mean she knows how upset he's been, she was with me the last time and she cares about him. Maybe she can help steer him in the right direction. Lord knows Menace needs all the help he can get.

"Pretty shitty. I pulled over a car with four teenagers, they had weed, moonshine, paraphernalia, and the driver had been drinking. One of the teenagers was Caleb."

She gasps. "Oh my God, is he okay?"

"He will be." I swallow the bite I've taken. "I think him and Menace are gonna go home and have a long talk. They were both pretty upset when I left, but they were talking. Mason had called in and gotten someone to cover the rest of his shift."

"Caleb's been hurting for a while. I just don't think he has the emotional capability to handle it. He's a kid who didn't have a mom growing up, and now he's lost a friend. It's got to be confusing for him."

If anyone realizes that, it's probably Violet. "I'm thinking the entire community is hurting silently, the way Caleb's been. We need to have an open discussion, if we can. I'm not sure how that could happen, maybe Blaze could help us. We found moonshine in the car too, so that's something else we have to worry about. We think it's coming from inside the high school."

Her eyes soften as she gazes at me, taking a bite of her slice. "You wanting to save the whole town? You're such a good man, Anthony. You wanna fix everybody."

"Nothing like that, I just want everyone to live their fullest life."

"Why is that?" Her eyebrows narrow.

The question hits a little too close to home for me, and I rely on my smile and carefree attitude. "Because what's life if we don't live it to the edge? Push on some boundaries and say that was a crazy ride, but damn we made it?"

I don't think she believes me, not the way she's eyeing me. Maybe I laid it on a little thick. But I can't open myself up to her – not yet, I'm not ready. Not sure when I ever will be, and maybe that makes me a bastard, because I'm trying to get her to open up to me.

Instead of questioning me, she goes back to her pizza.

"YOU SURE YOU don't want to stay and watch a movie?" Violet puts the last of the dishes in the dishwasher before standing up and facing me.

"Nah." I shake my head, exhausted. "I better go, but I appreciate the offer."

She comes to stand beside me, wiping her hands on a dishtowel. "What are your plans tomorrow? I'm off."

"I really wanna go out on the boat. This is gonna be one of the last free weekends we'll have before things start getting crazy with football Friday nights. My turn to work the games starts next week. Then it'll be fall, and then the holidays. Tomorrow, it's supposed to be mid-eighties. I'll invite the crew if you're interested."

"I've heard about this boat of yours, and I hoped you'd invite me over the summer, but we just never seemed to get around to it."

"You did, huh? We were kinda busy living life." On instinct, I lean forward, cupping her chin in my palm, and place a kiss softly on her lips. It's meant to be a peck, a thank you for having me for dinner and agreeing to hang out with me. With one swipe of her tongue, it turns into something much more.

I bend at my knees, lean down, cup her ass in my hands and lift her onto the countertop. Her hands are in my hair, my fingers are tracing up her thighs, cursing the cut-off shorts she's wearing. And then Violet does something that shocks me. The woman who's been so very shy with me? She pulls back, licks her lips, tilts my head slightly, and takes my earlobe in her teeth, nipping enough to make me stand on my tiptoes.

"Vi?" The question is in my tone, a growl pulled from my throat when she smears her lips down to my neck, nipping the tendons there with enough force to leave a bruise.

"I don't want to stop," she whispers heavily against my skin.

And neither do I. But I know I should, because neither one of us wants to do something that will jeopardize how far she's come. "Violet," I gasp to get air into my lungs, as I grab her hands and hold her close to me. "You wanted to wait until the divorce was final. I don't want you to make a snap decision on how you're feeling right now. I don't wanna ruin what we're building."

She's struggling to regain her composure. "You're right." She rests her forehead against mine. "You're absolutely right. When I come to you, I want it to be completely free and clear of him. For once in my life, I wanna do things the right way, not the easy way."

I pull back from her, breathe deeply, and then place a chaste kiss on her cheek. "Then that's what we'll do." But as I'm helping her off the counter, and I turn to leave, I give her a wink. The right way never sucked so bad. "One request? For the love of God, please wear a one-piece tomorrow. I've had a hard-on since the first moment I saw you, and I'm about sick of fighting it."

The way her cheeks redden give me a thrill in my stomach. I wave at her as I make my way across the porch to my part of the duplex. Tonight is going to be a fucking long night.

CHAPTER NINETEEN
VIOLET

THE KNOCK on my door at eight a.m. causes my heart to pound against my breast bone. I know without a doubt that knock is from Anthony. Last night I spent way too much time wondering what it would be like to share a bed with him for real. To give him free reign over my body, and to hand over my pleasure to him.

Today? I'm draggin' ass, but I'm going to do my best, to keep up with him.

"Morning." I give him a bright smile as I pull my door open. There's a smug part of me that's happy with the dark circles under his eyes. Maybe he had as hard of a time as I did going to sleep last night, after what we shared in the kitchen.

"Morning." He hands me a to-go cup of coffee, with a soft smile.

I take a grateful sip of the hot beverage and turn in a circle, feeling his eyes on me. "Do I pass inspection?"

I'm wearing a pair of cut-offs and a t-shirt, but I've lifted the t-shirt so he can see my bathing suit is a one-piece. Even though his eyes are covered by aviators, I can feel his gaze on me. I know it follows every move I make, it catalogues every piece of skin exposed, and I have no doubt he knows just by looking at me once, everything I'm wearing. Seems to be one of those gifts he has from being an officer of the law.

"You'll do." The side of his mouth tilts in a smartass smirk.

"Do I get to inspect you?" I ask, meaning it to be a joke, instead he answers with words that give me pause.

"Anytime you want to."

While I know it's probably the wrong thing to do, I circle my arms around his waist and pull him close. I can feel the firmness of the muscles beneath my fingertips. Lifting his shirt from where it meets his shorts, I eye the v-cut he has and the washboard that is his stomach. His hair is hidden by a hat turned backward, and he's got a small amount of stubble on his face. He didn't shave, and I'll take that any day of the week.

"You'll do, abs of steel, you'll do," I echo what he'd said to me, letting the shirt drop to cover his rock-hard muscles.

"Good, now let's get outta here."

Grabbing his outstretched hand, I let him lead me to his truck. Being the gentleman he's been since the first day we met, he opens the door, waits for me to slide in, and then walks around, taking his spot in the driver's seat. I'm nervous as he fires the engine, a part of me can feel that going on his boat with him means something. What, I'm not sure, but I feel like after today, there's absolutely no turning back.

"HAVE you ever been to the lake before?" Ace asks as we bump along in his truck.

We have the windows down, and when I turn to face him, hair goes into my mouth. Holding it back, in one hand, I answer, "Nope, can't say as I have. No one else I've ever known has been about the lake life."

"Good thing you met me, baby." He flashes me a killer grin. "The only one more interested in the lake life is Tank. Too bad he won't be here today. Somebody's gotta be patrolling the streets."

Meeting Anthony was the first round of luck I've had in my life. Part of me wishes I could tell him that, the other part worries that if I do tell him, I'll give him too much power over me. It's a fear I have after being married to the man I was. Glancing down at my left hand, I see the spot my wedding band used to sit. I took it off last week, and so far no one has noticed. Or if they have, they haven't said anything. Either way, I feel good. I made the decision to take the ring off. He didn't make the decision to take it from me. It's an important distinction that I will continue to make in my mind.

As we pull into the parking lot of the marina, I see a bunch of familiar faces. Caleb and Mason sit on the tailgate of Mason's truck, while Renegade flies a kite with Stella as Whitney watches with Caleb and Mason.

"Full boat today?"

"Not at all, my boat's pretty big."

Something tells me he means that in a way that has nothing to do with his actual boat. I try to hold back the snort, but can't as he pulls to a stop and we get out of his truck.

"Bout time y'all got here." Ryan bends over at the waist. "I've run this kite back and forth so many times, I need a nap."

"If you need somebody younger, Whit, I'm your man," Caleb teases, hopping off the back of the tailgate.

Ryan throws him a glare. "Trust me kid, you don't know how to handle that woman over there."

Whitney blows him a kiss and reaches out to take Stella in her arms. "He's right." She winks at Caleb. "Not many men can handle me, but good luck on your future endeavors with older women."

"Ouch." Caleb grabs his chest. "Anybody see my pride hanging around here anywhere?"

"You're young." Anthony puts his arm around the teenager. In the gesture, I see Caleb accept what's an unspoken apology about last night. He leans into Anthony and listens as he speaks. "You'll get used to getting shot down a lot in life. It builds character."

I take a good look at Caleb. He looks lighter than he has in a while, almost as if he's not carrying the weight of the world like he has been these past few months. None of us have any idea what happened with him and Mason after they were released from the traffic stop last night, but I hope they've talked. I hope Mason was the father I've seen him be. Next time I work with Caleb, I'll be sure to ask him how things are going and today if there's a chance, I definitely want to pull him aside and talk to him.

Anthony grabs my hand. "Daylight's wasting, let's get out on the water."

"COME WITH ME?"

I turn to see Anthony staring at me. I've seen him drive, seen him ride inner tube after inner tube through the water, and seen him take some hits that I was sure broke his neck or his back. But each time he's gotten back onto the boat with the biggest smile on his face. I have yet to go out into the water.

"I don't know, it seems pretty rough. I mean I have to be able to walk tomorrow so I can wait tables."

"They'll take it easy on ya," Whitney promises from where she lies on the deck, soaking up the sun. God I hope I look like her after I have a kid. "You can't come out here and not do it at least once."

"Yeah, go on." Mason points from where he's driving the boat. "You become a true resident of Alabama when you ride around the lake at top speed, screaming your head off and laughing at the same time. It's an important initiation, but if you're scared, I promise to not go full throttle."

"Heaven forbid I don't become a full-fledged member of Alabama society." I reach out, grabbing Anthony's hand. "Please initiate me."

At some point, he's taken off his sunglasses and his green eyes are clear as the day we have. Our gazes lock, and I see the raw need there. "It would be my pleasure to initiate you."

The sexual tension is immediately all through my body, and I wonder if anyone around us can feel it. Clearing my throat, I allow him to help me on to the inner tube, and we hold on for dear life as Mason takes us through the lake.

There in that moment, screaming and laughing with Anthony, I get a glimpse of the future I could have. Of the future and life I desperately want and can seemingly have right at my fingertips.

THE SUN IS SETTING over the tree line as we lazily float on the lake. Many of the boats have docked, families going home for the night, but we're still floating.

"I'm gonna wait a little while, let the dock calm down before I pull in," Anthony explains as he notices me looking. "It'll be insanity if we try to go now. I have a slot at the marina, but we'll just be stuck in the line trying to get there."

Nobody seems to be in a real big hurry to leave. Whitney and Ryan sit on their side of the boat, Stella held in between them, as they put their heads together, whispering to each other. Mason is sitting by himself, looking out over the water, and I sit next to Caleb. This is my chance, the opening I've been waiting on to speak to him.

"I'm not going to pretend like I know how you feel about losing your friend, Caleb, but I do want to tell you about what happened when I lost mine."

He turns, all ears as he pays attention to what I'm saying. "We had plans, she and I, to go to college and make something of ourselves. When she was killed in a car accident, I withdrew from everyone and fell in with a wrong crowd. That's how I met my husband."

"The one who beat the shit outta you?"

"Yeah, that one. It became easier for me to let other people make my decisions. To stop being a leader and to be a follower. It was like when she died, I lost my will to be something better than what I was." I reach out, putting my hand on his forearm. "I'm not saying any of this is what you're going through, but I'm begging you not to let your guilt and hurt put you in a bad situation. Don't allow your feelings to lead you astray. It's okay to be sad, to feel guilt, and to question why it wasn't you; they're all normal reactions, but don't let this change who you are."

He swallows roughly. "I'm drowning, Vi Pie, drowning in this sea of nothingness, and I'm fighting hard to keep my head above water."

"Keep fighting," I encourage him. "Keep treading water, and at some point, the days won't seem so bleak, you won't wonder how to put one foot in front of the other. It'll all be easier."

"God, I hope so. Do you know how embarrassing it was for Ace to pull me over last night? How much of a dick I acted toward him?"

"Kinda like you were with me and Leigh the other day?"

He ducks his head. "I'm sorry, I've not been the easiest person to be around."

"Apology accepted, and no one expects you to be the easiest person, but we do expect you to tell us if you need help."

The moment hangs between us, and I decide to take pity on him.

"I can imagine it was embarrassing, but he didn't tell me anything about how you acted."

"That's because he's a good guy." Caleb laughs. "Anyone else would have taken me to jail, they wouldn't have cared who my dad is."

I glance over to where Anthony is driving the boat. Our eyes catch in the dying sunlight, he crooks his finger at me, motioning me over to where he is. Turning back to Caleb, I mean to ask him if it's okay if I leave, but he's already up, walking over to where Stella is.

Left alone, I get up and make my way to where Anthony sits. "Were you lonely?"

He pulls me down into his lap, both of us not caring who sees, both of us sick of fighting it. He buries his lips in my neck, and I accept the kiss by tilting and giving him room. When he pulls away, he puts his arm around my waist, holding me close. "I'm always lonely when you aren't around."

And those right there are the type of words I've waited to hear my whole life from a man who cares for me. Out on a lake, with friends, and the peacefulness of the day, I realize this was the perfect place, perfect time, and this is the perfect man.

CHAPTER TWENTY
VIOLET

IT'S a dead day at The Café as Caleb and I sit at a booth folding silverware into napkins. It's been a week since the lake, since Caleb got pulled over. I've bided my time, but now I'm interested in how he's doing.

"How are things going?"

His gaze is intense before he shifts it back down to our task at hand. "I know Ace told you about pulling me over, me being drunk, and then calling my dad. That's why you said what you did when we were out on the lake."

"He did, but it hasn't been my place to bring it up."

He's quiet for a few minutes, and I wonder if he's going to speak about any of it to me. Blowing out a deep breath, he scratches a cheek that looks as if it has some stubble on it. When did Caleb start growing up on us? Eventually he shifts in the seat and begins to speak. "Dad and I had a really long talk."

"How did that go?" I can just imagine what Mason had to say to his son.

"Awkward as fuck, but he said some things I've needed to hear, I guess." He shrugs as he continues rolling the silverware. "I've been struggling since the party, pissed off that so many of us lived through what happened while we lost a friend. It's been a guilt thing, I guess. He made me talk to Blaze, and Blaze is setting up counseling for the school through her program. I think a lot of us need it." He runs his hand through his hair and then down his face. "I know I do."

"There's no shame in it, Caleb. I've talked to someone a time or two about what happened to me here." I look around the Cafe. Sometimes I can glance around and it doesn't bother me, other times, I can still see Brent coming at me, a look or rage on his face.

"Does it help?" His voice is doubtful and hopeful all at the same time.

"It does, but you've got to be willing to let it help you. Be open to it, work the program. There's no shame in having to go back to the beginning either, Caleb. Some days it will be like it just happened."

"I have those days. Sometimes I have nightmares about that night. I dream that I was the one who drank too much, I was the one under that blue tarp. It's like I'm looking in from the outside and I can see my dad be notified about my death. I'm screaming to him it's not me, that I wasn't the one there, but then they pull back the tarp and it is. I wake up in a cold sweat, wondering what the hell happened."

A thought occurs to me, and I ask it slowly.

"Do you and the girl you were with, do you still talk?"

He rubs against the stubble on his jaw again. "Nah, we haven't spoken since the funeral. More her than me." His smile tilts. "Which sucks, because I really liked her, she's a nice girl."

"Maybe one day in the future, you and her can work it out?"

"Doubtful." He scrunches up his nose. "How do you look at Ace and not relive everything that went on here?"

I've wondered that myself more often than I care to admit. It was something that I always thought would rear its ugly head once we started moving forward, but it never has. I've never confused my feelings about Anthony with what happened here that day.

I shrug. "He saved me, and maybe that's part of it. But he and I were talking before then."

"Even though you were married?" He interrupts, a sly smile on his face.

"Yeah." I duck my head, not sure if I can take the intensity of his gaze. "I'm not exactly proud of that, but you have to understand the situation I was in."

He holds up his hands. "I'm not judging."

But many have. I see the looks, hear the whispers, and in the darkest of hours, I'm my own worst critic. I wasn't raised to cheat on my husband, I wasn't raised to give up on a marriage, but there comes a point where you can no longer take being abused. You want someone to touch you softly, you want someone to speak to you nicely, and you desperately want someone to love you. You realize you're worthy, and once you've hit that point, there's no going back.

"Fuck 'em." Caleb grins. "Whatever they think they know, they don't. Fuck 'em."

I wish it was that easy for me, but if this kid can have that attitude? Why can't I?

I'M tired when I get home from my shift today, but I force myself to check the mail, instead of walking straight into my bedroom and collapsing. I'm still trying to recover from the lake and all the fun we had. Shuffling through the mail that still comes for the people who used to live here and bills, a certified letter almost doesn't catch my attention.

Looking at the return address, my hands shake. It's from my attorney. Did the judge approve the divorce without Brent signing the papers? So much of this has been done without my input that I feel very disconnected. All I know is I feel like I've been waiting for this decision for most of my life. Using my fingernail, I tear through the top and drag the papers from where they're enclosed.

My eyes scan the document, waiting to see the words that will free me. My heart feels as if it's about to jump out of my chest as I skim through the paperwork that reads "Petition for Dissolution of Marriage".

I flip the page, ready to come out of my skin, when my gaze jumps to the bottom and I see the sentence I feel as if I've been waiting my whole life for. *Dissolution of marriage is granted.* I look to make sure the judge has signed it, and then I give a little shout of excitement. This wasn't what I expected today, but I'll take it any day of the week.

Running up the stairs of the front porch, I all but beat down Anthony's door, waiting for him to open it. When he does, I launch myself at him, taking his lips with mine, surprising the hell out of both of us. He catches me in his arms, and I give myself over to this kiss.

It's a melding of bodies, a melting of souls, and a promise of the future to come. I pour every bit of desire I've had not only for him, but for the life I felt everyone else always got to live into this kiss. His fingers dig into my hair, before he pulls back.

"What was that for?" he whispers, licking his lips, voice husky, eyes cloudy with what I've learned is passion.

"I'm free," I whisper back, and in that moment the tears come, rolling down my cheeks. "I'm free," I repeat, letting the tears fall. In my hands I hold the papers, and as he lets me, I pass them over to him.

"Is this what I think it is?" The excitement is apparent, hope is a living thing between us. This has been the one thing holding us back.

Nodding, I reach out to grab his forearms, as he reads them. "It's over, it's completely over."

"You know what this means right?" He reaches out, cupping my cheek in his hand.

"What?" I whisper, not quite believing what's happening. If I'm in a dream, I pray that no one wakes me up.

"I can do this anytime I want."

He leans in and takes the kiss I'm sure he's wanted since the first day he saw me. He pours as much emotion in this one as I poured into mine. Faintly, as if in the distance, I hear the door close, then I feel my body pressed against it. Easily, I take his weight and revel in it, loving the feel of it, wanting to have the experience of our naked skin against each other. I'm already imagining it – the slide of his sweaty skin against mine, the way his chin will feel against me. How my nails will rake down his back, what my fingers will feel like when I wrap them around his length. All things that have driven me crazy since I moved in here. Seconds or hours could have passed when he pulls away.

"While I would love to continue this, Vi, I have to be on shift in the next thirty minutes," he groans as he leans his forehead against the door.

"I'm sorry, I didn't plan this well." I giggle burying my face in his neck.

"Sometimes those are the best moments, don't you think?" He pushes the strands of hair that have fallen from my ponytail back, as he lifts my head off his shoulder. "I'll take any surprise you want to give me any day, Vi, and this is one of the best I've ever been given. If I knew someone could or would take my shift, I'd call them right now."

"I know." I turn my cheek into his palm. "But I couldn't help coming to tell you. I'll be here waiting for you when you get home."

"Those are the best words I've ever heard. Will you be here on my side of the duplex or yours?"

My heart pounds and my pulse speeds. This is a huge step for us, a big deal in the grand scheme of things. I've never allowed myself to come into his space with these intentions, not yet. I'm not sure if it's because I didn't trust men, or I didn't trust myself around him. But today, I know many things have changed. With the papers we hold, my entire life has changed. In some ways, it's finally beginning. The answer to this question means everything.

"I'll be right here when you get home, meaning I'll be on your side. I'll be sitting in your couch or lying in your bed." I wipe at the tears still silently streaming down my cheeks. "As long as that's okay with you."

Bringing me in for another kiss, he drops one on my lips, before he uses his thumbs to remove some of the moisture under my eyes. "Believe me when I say, nothing on this earth has ever sounded better to my ears."

I giggle, and it's the most carefree noise I've ever made. I feel as if I've lost the weight that's been bearing down on my shoulders, as if I'm the carefree adult I never got to be. This won't last forever, real life will make itself known, but I'm going to enjoy this for as long as I can.

"I've gotta get dressed and get going. The quicker I get going, the quicker I can get back. And knowing you're going to be here is going to make this the longest shift of my life," he groans as he throws his head back in frustration.

Pulling him in for a peck, I twine my arms around his neck. "Please be safe, Anthony. You got a woman here who desperately wants to live her life with you, and can't wait to get started."

He gives me the most magnificent smile. "I can't wait either. We're gonna take life by the balls and make it our bitch."

Those words are the best I've heard, and I'm vibrating with excitement to get started on our lives together. It looks like I'll have to wait at least nine hours though, and in those hours, I'll allow myself to mourn the life I had and plan for the life I'm anticipating. One thing is for sure. Anthony will make sure it's damn exciting.

PART 3

REALIZING LOVE

CHAPTER TWENTY-ONE

ACE

THIS SHIFT IS TAKING LONGER than I ever imagined it could, especially after the news that Violet shared with me. I'm riding with Tank, and thank God he's driving, because I can't seem to stop texting the woman I can still taste on my lips and tongue.

My imagination is wondering how far we would have taken it, had we not stopped. I'm definitely down for figuring it out.

A: Want to have dinner when I get done? Maybe go dancing? Like an honest-to-God date? Not this thing where we stay locked up in either of our homes. You dress nice, I dress nice, and we let other people see us together? Would you be up for that?

I know I'm up for that, I've wanted to show her off for a while, show other people who's stolen my heart, and how happy she makes me. I want to wear the smile on my face that so many of my friends wear on theirs. If anyone had asked me, I would have told them I was happy with the way things were, that it didn't matter I'm single. Fact is, it does matter. I've been waiting for over a year to have this woman as mine, and I can't believe the time is finally coming.

V: I would love to! Text me as you're heading home, and I'll be sure and be ready when you are.

A: I'll have to take a shower, but it shouldn't take long.

V: I'll wait as long as you need me to.

It strikes me as funny, the words she just gave to me. I've given them to her a few times. They feel just as good coming back to me, as they did leaving my lips.

A: See you in a few hours.

"Why are you sitting over there grinning like a fool? If I wasn't mistaken I'd think you had some type of woman in your life. You and Violet finally figure out that you're hot for each other?" Tank asks as we maneuver through the streets of Laurel Springs. We're working a mid-shift and these tend to be quieter than most.

I haven't told anyone what's happening with Violet, but I find myself wanting to talk with someone. I'm not like Renegade and Tank or even Mason and Holden, with a best friend on the team. With the four of them being completely up each other's asses most days, that leaves me as the odd man out. Typically I'm fine with it, because that means I can confide in any of them, at any given time without worrying I've hurt someone's feelings.

"Violet's divorce got finalized today." Saying the words brings a finality I haven't experienced yet. Knowing that this woman can now be all mine? It's something I always wished for, but never hoped would happen. I'm not into being disappointed.

Tank looks over, a huge smile on his face. "Does this mean you two are an item?"

"It means we're free to stop hiding like we're doing something wrong. I've never once been ashamed of the way we've acted with one another, but I know that it's bothered her," I admit to my friend. "She never felt right about it and wanted to keep it platonic until this went through."

He gives me a look, like he can't believe what I've told him. "So the two of you haven't ever done the deed? Seriously? Not even when we were down in Gulf Shores?"

I shake my head. "Most we've ever done is kiss and some heavy making out, and that's just been recent. You have to understand how she was those first few months, Trev. Nobody saw her like I did, and there was no way I could put my feelings onto her, until she was ready. It would have set her back years, I'm sure of it. Plus she'd just come from a hell of a relationship, I didn't want to pile on bullshit."

Neither one of us like reliving those months when she'd been scared of her own shadow, afraid of what would happen if she were left alone at night. Before I'd been able to get her the duplex next to mine, I'd parked my work car or personal vehicle in front of her shitty trailer to make sure she could sleep. I still remember the first night, she reluctantly gave me a hug. It felt like I'd won the lottery and killed a dragon all at the same time.

"That bad?" He stops at a four-way and turns his signal on to indicate we're going left.

"Worse than that." I shudder as I remember picking her up from the hospital. "I don't wish what happened to her on my worst enemy, and I have some motherfuckers in my life that did me wrong."

"How long was she in the hospital for? At the point all of that was happening, we were still trying to figure out what to do with Jefferson, and I'm ashamed to say I didn't pay much attention to what happened to her. We all knew you were taking care of her, and none of us wanted to step on your toes."

"A couple of days."

Those days bleed together in a fade of memories I haven't thought about since I brought her home. She'd insisted on going back to the home she'd shared with her husband and had been stubborn as hell. Never asked for help, even when she needed it. But with me she didn't have to ask for it, I knew and offered, expecting zero in return.

"You've been very patient with her," he comments.

"Not at all. She's the woman I see myself with. The one who can make me settle down and not have to do crazy shit anymore. So whether we've done the deed or not, really isn't that big of a deal. It'll happen when it's supposed to."

Tank gives me a smirk, looking sheepish. "Didn't mean to offend you."

"Didn't offend me, but I feel like everyone expects us to be so much further than we are. Both of us felt weird being anything other than friends while she was still married. We're going out on our first date tonight."

"You do you, man. We're all rooting for you."

"Which means you've all been talking about us like a couple of high school kids."

He doesn't deny it at all.

We tuck in behind a car, going about our routine. Sitting up a little straighter when we see them glance at us through their rearview. Something about the way they give us a look makes me take notice.

"Hey, the rest of us are completely settled, except for Mason. Now that's there's no drama in our lives, we have to gossip about you."

"And you're nosey as fuck," I supply as I snort. They'd gossip no matter if they were settled or not. He's just using it as an excuse.

"Well that too," he concedes.

And that's when the car in front of us takes off at a high rate of speed.

I'M CALLING in our position on the radio as Tank concentrates on navigating through the bottoms. After I call for backup, I hold on tightly, letting my body ease into the curves.

"You okay?" Trevor almost lost his life in a crash on this very stretch of road. If I could, I would reach over and take the wheel from him. I'm sure this is bringing back memories he'd rather forget. Hell, it's bringing back shit I'd rather forget.

"I'm good." His knuckles are white as he grips the steering wheel. I wonder if he really is, but his jaw is held strong, his mouth in a firm line. "This is about my job, not about what happened with me before." I'm unsure if he's telling me or trying to make himself believe the words.

The other responding unit is coming from the opposite direction. It makes me feel better when I hear the sirens and see the lights. I see Havoc attempting to box them in through a particularly sharp turn. The car in front of us has to slow down, and as they do, he pulls in front of them, blocking the way. We get behind them, not allowing them to move.

"Turn the car off!" I yell as I get out of my side of the cruiser. Leaving my door open to use for cover, I wait, just like everyone else does.

I listen as the engine of the car shuts off and watch as the driver puts their hands outside the window. "Drop the keys on the ground," I instruct, voice firm, hands strong as I watch him follow my instructions.

Havoc takes over and starts giving them motions to get out of the car. Once they're out and we have them cuffed, we get IDs and sit them against the door. My gaze hones in on the driver of the car. A quick flash goes back to where I've seen him before. I could have sworn he learned his lesson the first time.

"I know that kid," I tell Havoc as we meet in the middle. "He was the one Caleb was with the other night. The driver."

"Well then he shouldn't be driving again, because his license should be suspended."

When the license does come back as suspended, Havoc gets irritated.

"Damnit, go ahead and search the car, there's a reason he was running."

"Do I have consent?" I ask both the driver and the passenger. When the driver does nothing more than nod, I have to wonder what's caused the change in him.

Before I get started, I give them the respect of asking what's in it. "Is there anything you want to tell me about before I search it?" I ask as I put gloves on, to protect me in case I don't want to touch something. Luckily I've never been poked by a dirty needle, and I don't feel like having it happen today.

The kid sitting next to him is shaking, sweating profusely, and not meeting my eyes. The driver is stone cold. There's something in this car, and there's been an emotional change in the driver. He'd been amenable when I pulled him over before. Today he doesn't even glance at any of us. His dad had been apologetic when he came to get him, saying it was the first time he'd ever been in trouble. When I pulled him over the other day, he'd been almost polite, and quick to offer information. Today he's not. He's offering nothing and looking pretty fucking guilty.

Neither one of them have offered me any information, so I search thoroughly, expecting to find any number of things stashed in the vehicle. But when I find nothing in the front seat or back seat, I wonder if maybe I was quick to judge. Wouldn't be the first time, and definitely won't be the last.

However, as I open the trunk, I have a tingling at the back of my neck. I'm going to find something in this car. The question is what, and how is it going to affect the kids sitting here. "What am I going to find back here?" I ask one more time, giving them an option for an out. Neither one of them give me an answer, so I open the trunk, and whistle loudly when I get a good look at what they were transporting.

It's a trunk full of moonshine. Couple this with the rumors about what's going inside the school? I call Havoc over, wishing I didn't have to. I wish the person wasn't preying on the innocent, I wish there were some way we could stop this for good, and I hope like hell these kids are smart enough to realize how dangerous this is. All we need is another kid to die, and it'll tear a hole in this community as big as it's ever seen.

CHAPTER TWENTY-TWO

VIOLET

I FEEL like I've gone through every piece of clothing I own, but nothing feels good. Frustrated, I reach over to my phone and quickly FaceTime Leighton. If anyone can help me, it's going to be her.

"What's going on?" her smiling face asks as the connection is made.

"I have nothing to wear for a date with Anthony," I complain, as I show her the mess behind me. "I've tried on every piece of clothing I own and nothing looks or feels right." I plop down on the bed with a sigh. "Take pity on me and help me out."

"You're going out with him!" she screams.

"Yes," I laugh.

"Tonight?" She questions, more excited about this than I am, I think.

"Yes tonight." I roll my eyes. "Focus, Leigh."

"Right," She shakes her head. "Okay, you have plenty to wear, Vi. You have dresses, jeans, everything. Where are you two going?" I can see her situate herself on the couch, her stomach more visible as she enters her sixth month. My eyes watch with a soft smile as she caresses the bump in the tight shirt she wears.

"Out to eat and maybe dancing is where he said we were going."

Leighton's eyes light up, and I can almost feel her excitement through the video screen. "Then oh my God, Vi, wear a dress. Can you just imagine it? He pulls you close on the dance floor, pushes his hands up your thighs and grabs a handful of flesh? Sexiest thing ever."

Leighton and her dirty mind are starting to affect me. I'm completely and vividly imagining just what she's described. "You don't think that's too presumptuous?"

"You shared a bed with him at Whitney and Ryan's wedding. I mean either you want to be close to him, or you don't. And I kinda think you want to be close to him."

God, if she only knew. If she only knew how far we've come and how close we've gotten.

"I do have that black dress. Do you think that's too dressy?" I think back to the dress in the back of my closet, it could work.

"Oh hell no, it's sexy. Pair it with some fuck-me heels or some boots and you've got it. Curl your hair the way you do, or fishtail braid it, and he won't be able to keep his hands off you. Do that dramatic makeup look you're so good at."

I can't believe I'm talking to her about this and planning what I'm going to wear on a date with Anthony. For so long it's never seemed like it would be an option. My reality was darker, depressing, and didn't include this amazing guy in it.

Crazy how things change.

"Okay, I need to be shaving my legs then."

She winks at me through the screen, holding her lip between her teeth. "Shave it all girlfriend. Never know what you might be showing him tonight."

"You're a really bad influence. Talk to you later."

As I disconnect the call, she's giggling, and I'm shaking my head.

Sometimes I sit back and wonder why I was led to Laurel Springs, why I chose to stay here after the situation with Brent, even though it might have been easier for me to go somewhere else.

Every time, I come back to this being the place I'm meant to be. No other place I've ever lived has felt like home, and just maybe I'm finally ready to lay down some roots. The thought doesn't scare me as much as it once did, and that in itself is a powerful feeling. Glancing up at the clock, I realize I don't have much time before Anthony gets here. Letting out a little squeal, I run to the bathroom to shave my legs and hurry through my routine of getting ready. No way I want to be late.

MY HAIR IS STILL DAMP when I glance back at the clock again. I don't have time to dry and curl my hair like I'd wanted to. Curls would allow him to move his fingers freely – if we got around to it – but they don't look like they're gonna happen for me tonight.

Instead, I think back to my conversation with Leighton and remember what she said about a fishtail braid. Because I wear it on a regular basis, it doesn't take me long to do it. The look, however, gives the impression that it took hours to create. I have layers, and not all of them will go in neatly. A few well-placed bobby pins and I'm good to go.

Grabbing hold of my makeup bag, I go to work on my face. Typically Anthony see's the bare-bones version of my look. Tonight I want to be the girl he would take home from the bar if he saw me there. I do my eyeshadow with a much heavier hand than I normally do.

Just as I'm swiping on the last coat of the first metallic lip stain I've ever used in my life, there's a knock at the door. Inhaling deeply, I slowly let the breath out, not recognizing the person I see in the mirror. Having finally gotten around to getting all the new makeup products I wanted to try, my look is darker, more mature, and...alluring, if I had to give a description. I'm still messing with the braids, but this one is much more intricate, and I'm quite proud of myself for mastering it. Twirling in the mirror, the skirt flairs, showing off my thighs. Maybe Leighton was right.

"Coming." I slip into low-heeled ankle boots, ones that I'd bought on a whim a couple of months ago, but never wore. They're rose gold glitter and the flashiest things I've owned. I love them. One of the first things I bought when I realized my money was my money and no one could tell me how to spend it.

Checking the peephole, I make sure it's Anthony, and when I see his chiseled jawline, I realize tonight is a game changer. But this is a curveball in my life I'm willing to accept, swing at, and hopefully hit over the fence.

Ace

It's taking her a while to come to the door, and for a split second I wonder if she's changed her mind. Are we moving too fast? Have I pressured her into something she didn't really feel ready to do? I'm five seconds from reaching into the dark jeans I'm wearing and pulling out my cell phone to give her a call and tell her this is a bad idea, when her door opens. And my jaw hits the damn ground like a cartoon character from when I was a kid.

"Do I look okay?" she questions, looking shy. God, I hate that she even questions what she looks like. The woman standing in front of me is a wet dream and is so different from the woman I first met.

Somehow, I find my voice. "You're fucking gorgeous."

The black dress she's wearing skims her thighs, showing off surprisingly long legs for someone on the short side, encased in the sexiest pair of shoes I've seen her wear. Her eyes are dark and sultry. The lines around her lips are perfect in a way that's teasing me to smear the color. I hope whatever she's wearing on them is long-lasting. I definitely want that option later on tonight.

Her cheeks pinken, and I love the fact I was able to bring color to them. I'd like to bring color to many other parts of her body if she'd allow me to. We've been figuratively dancing around one another for a long time.

"Thank you." She smiles, her brown eyes moving up and down my body. "You're pretty hot yourself."

Those four little words please me in a way no others have. Hearing her admission does crazy things for my self-esteem. "These are for you," I remember the flowers I'm holding in my hands. They'd almost caused me to be late, but there's one thing I learned when I was first dating, and that's to make a good impression, even if you were friends to begin with.

"They're beautiful, you didn't have to." She steps aside, walking back into her portion of the duplex.

My feet follow of their own free will, watching as she walks in those shoes with a heel. Her ass sways as she balances and then takes another step. If Violet ever truly worked on strutting her stuff, she'd be a force to be reckoned with. And I'd be a fucking goner.

"Ready?" she asks after putting them in the water. "I've not been out on a date in a really long time. I'm kind of excited. I told myself not to get too excited, because I didn't want to be overbearing, but I can't help myself."

The smile she gives me is wide, full of promise, and unabashedly happy. I can't help but lean in and capture her lips with mine. She curls her hand around my wrist, where I hold her neck, but we keep it chaste. I want to coax her lips apart, push my tongue into her mouth, and get drunk on her taste. But I also want to take her out on the town and show her off too. Pulling back is one of the hardest things I've ever made myself do. Her lips chase me, but I stop her by pressing my thumb into her cheek with a little bit of force.

"We can do that later, right now, let's hit the town and show you off." And show her off is what I want to do. I'm not immune to the whispers and stares if someone sees us out together. While many people are happy for her, and for me, this is still the small-town south. There are upstanding members of our community who would rather see her stay with a man that abused her, than divorce and be happy. There are other women who would turn their back on her, tell her she deserved everything she got, and that in the eyes of the Lord she's still married to Brent. I'm here to give those people a great big *fuck you* when they see us out together.

Her eyes are clouded with what I hope is passion, but then a smile spreads across her face.

"Show me off?" Violet shakes her head. "Nah, we're gonna show you off. I don't remember when was the last time someone saw you around here in something other than faded jeans, a t-shirt, or your uniform. Remember, not many people came to the wedding. I'm excited to be on your arm tonight."

I wish I could tell her how lucky I am to have her. In fact, I would tell her, but I don't think she's ready to hear it. Instead, I give her a grin and offer her my arm. "Feeling's mutual."

We quickly lock up her side of the duplex and when we make our way to the truck, I open the door for her and lift her up. Deciding to throw caution to the wind, and see how far she'll let me go, I step up on the running board, spread her legs, and sneak my fingers beneath whatever pair of underwear she has on to give her a bit of a thrill. These are the types of liberties I've wanted to take with her, and I want Violet to be completely okay with them. Her eyes dilate, her legs spread a little further, and judging by the moan that resonates deep in her throat, she's totally down for this.

Later, I tell my libido. And as I step down, close the door, and make my way around to the driver's side, I hope like hell I can make it through this night.

No one has ever affected me the way she is right now, and if given the chance, she's the last one who will. Standing outside the driver's door, I take a deep breath, before I open it, and climb in.

"You good?" I ask as I buckle up and turn the truck on, putting it in gear.

"I'm great," she answers, reaching over to grab my hand.

And with her hand tucked in mine, we take off on this new adventure. I know where the end will be, have known since she moved in. The journey getting there? Worth all the time we've waited.

CHAPTER TWENTY-THREE

ACE

"I'M GETTING DIZZY." Violet giggles as I spin her around the dance floor.

This particular giggle is something I haven't heard from her before, not this carefree noise that bubbles up from her throat and explodes into a sound that puts goosebumps on my forearms. She's breathing heavily as I pull her into my arms, every part of our bodies touching. I'm breathing hard too, and as we share a breath, I push her away and then bring her back in. Sliding my hand down her back to cup her ass.

The song ends, and we break apart to clap. The house band that's playing announces they're going to slow it down a little bit. It's welcome, I'm getting tired. I haven't had a workout like this in a long time.

"You need to sit or are you good?" I put my mouth to her ear so she can hear me over the background racket.

She shakes her head, smile never leaving her face. "I'm good."

A slower tune starts playing from the band on the stage, and she easily slips into my arms. The sounds of everyone around us seems to quieten down as well as we sway to the beat. When I speak again, it's in a normal voice, and she's actually able to understand.

"You having a good time?"

"Best time ever." She slips her arms tighter around my neck. The laughing shine is gone from her eyes, and now she looks more serious, more passionate than I've seen her look. The beat the band is playing is a sexy rhythm, and as she starts circling her hips to it, I grit my teeth.

All night I've wanted to have my hands on her, and now that it's happening I'm not sure what to do. Violet's more receptive to my touch than she's ever been, and I insinuate my leg in between her thighs as we're making our way along the dance floor. As we approach a spot that's heavily shadowed, she releases one of her arms from around my neck, dragging her hand down my chest, and abdomen, hooking her hand along my waist. Subtly I can feel her starting to grind against my thigh.

"Ace," she whispers as I move us farther into the shadows, away from any prying eyes that may be watching. "Tell me to stop playing with fire."

I'm the wrong person to tell her to stop. There's a devil on my left that influences the next words out of my mouth. "Do whatever makes you feel good, baby."

"I can't here," she whispers back, running her hands up my chest.

My eyebrows are in my hairline as I look down at her. Am I mistaking what she's trying to tell me? I have to be completely sure, I don't want to make an assumption and have it set both of us back. "Where do you wanna go?

"Take me to your side?" she questions, a tilt to her head.

"C'mon." I grab her hand. "Let's get out of here."

Violet

The scenery as we drive back to the duplex we share passes by without me seeing much of it. I'm not questioning my decision. I knew tonight when I put this dress on, shaved my legs, and slipped into these heels where I wanted it to go. But I haven't slept with anyone else – ever – other than Brent. Not saying that's how this night will end up, but I've never done any of the other stuff either, and Anthony is the only other man I've ever kissed. I'm going into uncharted territory here, and I would be lying if I pretended I'm not nervous.

Anthony must have caught onto my nervousness, because he reaches over, grabbing my hand, bringing it up to his lips. He drops a kiss on our fingers. "Hey you know we don't have to do anything, right? Just because we're going back to my side doesn't mean I expect anything from you."

I slowly let out a breath, I'm expecting something from myself. "I know, and I wish I was one of those women who never second-guesses themselves, never lets the doubts in, and completely believes in every decision they make. But I'm not, and while I'm not second-guessing it, I'm kind of questioning it," I admit.

"Then let's talk it through."

My face burns as I open my mouth and try to put into words about what I'm feeling. Turning so I can see his profile in the dim glow of the dashboard, I close my eyes as I speak. "What if I'm not what you want? I've only ever been with one guy. What if I'm a disappointment to you? I don't think I can take it, Anthony. You're one person I don't want to exclude from my life. If I can't see you every day it's going to kill a little piece of my soul."

He glances over at me, his brow crinkled in a frown. "Woman, have you not felt the heat between us when we kiss? Have you not felt the reaction of my body when you're close to me? Because I sure as fuck have noticed how our breath speeds up, how your nipples harden behind those thin bras you wear, the way your gaze focuses on my lips." He reaches over, running his thumb over my bottom lip. "Like it's doing right now."

I let my tongue catch the pad of his thumb. "Mmm." He shifts in his seat. "There's no way we aren't going to be fire when we finally get together. I'm not saying that has to be tonight, but if you want some good old fashion necking and dry humping, I'm your guy too. Basically whatever you need, I'll give to you."

Mind blown. How has no one scooped this guy up? How has no one realized the type of person who hides behind the jokes and the ultimate dare-devil personality. He so badly wants to be a part of something, and all he's asking is to be a part of a unit called us. How can I ever deny him that?

AS WE ENTER Anthony's side of the duplex, my heart is pounding. I've obviously been here before, but in a much different set of circumstances than tonight. The sound of his keys hitting the catch-all next to the door is loud in the space. We both take our shoes off and set them by the door, then we stand awkwardly next to one another.

"This is your show, baby. You set the pace."

Anxiety bubbles up in my stomach as the reality of the situation hits me full force. I've taken my heels off and now I don't come up much higher than his chest. Now having been given the option, I'm not sure what I want to do with it. Lifting my eyes up to his, I inhale deeply. His normally clear eyes are darker with passion and desire. Tentatively I reach my hands out to smooth across his abdomen. The tension between us is thick, the air heavy with the weight of arousal that's been flowing between us for so long. Lifting up on my tiptoes, I lean in, pressing our lips together. Pushing my body against his, hoping to fit myself against all the nooks and crannies that are his.

It's a slow press, as we tilt into one another. Almost in a lazy haze, I pry his lips apart, before sneaking my tongue against his. Large male hands come up to the back of my neck, resting against the skin, not pushing or encouraging, just letting me know they're there. Nipping slightly at his lower lip, I love the sound he makes deep in his throat before he deepens the kiss. It's a growl, a moan, a sound of desperate hunger. It's everything I've wanted and more.

Now he's pushing against my lips, taking my mouth with his, giving me everything I want. Everything I crave. Clenching my fingers in his shirt, I pull at the fabric, lifting it above the waistband of his jeans. I push it up until I can't go any further. Separating our lips, he lets go of me, reaches behind him, and pulls it over his head. It's a total alpha male move, one I've seen in movies a hundred times. It gets me even hotter than it normally does. This is Anthony, and he's mine to do with whatever I please.

My gaze roams his body, taking in the ridges of his abs, and the smoothness of his chest. His jeans ride low on his hips, the "V" visible to my hungry eyes.

"You're killin' me, Vi." His voice is guttural, full of gravel and need. I love everything about it.

"I'm not sure what to do with you," I admit, my heart pounding.

He turns the tables on me. "I know exactly what to do with you, sweetness."

My breath hitches, voice husky as I speak. "Do it, please, just do it."

Leaning down, he grabs me around the thighs. His strong fingers dent my skin as he hitches me up to his waist, spreading me so that my bare skin is against his. Those full lips of his take control of mine as he carries me over to the couch, laying me down as he covers my body with his.

Pulling away for a second, I hear the question. "Is this okay?" Before he smears his mouth down my neck, nipping and sucking at the skin where it connects to my shoulder. We've been here before, but I appreciate the way he makes sure I'm good with whatever's happening. Brent never cared.

Get him out of your head, Violet. Anthony is nothing like Brent. They aren't even in the same area code.

"Perfect." I sigh, widening my thighs so he can rest more fully against my aching core.

"I'm not going to fuck you right now." He hooks his fingers in the neckline of my dress, pulling to expose the lace of my bra. "But I'm going to make you feel damn good."

While I'm disappointed he's not going to fuck me, I can live with it. "It's probably for the best." I sigh out a breath as he attaches his lips to my neck.

Pulling back, he nods. "Yeah, if I go in now, I'm not lasting three strokes. No kidding about it. You've got me right where you want me I'm sure, but I'd much prefer to give you a good time. I want to do all the things I've been wanting to do to you. Will you let me do that?"

One of his hands pushes up my thigh and rests against the matching lace of my panties. His other is still working to expose my bra.

"Yes," I agree, thrusting my chest into the palm of his hand. "Yes to all the things you want to do to me."

"All the things?" He lifts his head, eyebrow raised, sexy smirk on his face.

"All the things. Every single thing."

And that's when I hang on for dear life.

CHAPTER TWENTY-FOUR
ACE

Ace

VIOLET and I have been doing this delicate dance for a while. Since the first moment we met, for sure, but as we've gotten closer, it's been harder for me to ignore the way she makes me feel. The way I want to make her feel. Tonight, I don't have to and the fact is, I don't want to.

"Come with me." I grab her hand, leading her down the hallway to my bedroom. I'm sick of being on couches with her, cramped and pressed for time. Tonight we're taking this to my king-size bed. I want to lay her out, have room to work, and be able to show her what I can do.

Pushing her back against the mattress, I trail my hands up under her skirt, feeling for the barrier that's been holding her back from me all night. Once I find the lace of her panties, I tug them down her thighs, tossing them behind me.

"Ace," she moans when I come up on my knees, shoving her thighs apart. For a moment, I stare at her, wondering how I got to be so lucky, how this woman chose me out of anyone else she could have chosen. When she uses the name that my friends call me, it does things to me. The way her husky voice says it like a prayer.

Using my hands, I spread her thighs, hooking her legs over my shoulders and dive in, taking her pleasure with me. Using my thumbs, I make room for my tongue, licking at her clit, moving faster when she pushes against my face.

"Don't stop." She grabs hold of my hair, pulling me deeper into her body. "Please don't stop."

Like I would stop? Her taste is an aphrodisiac for me. Opening my mouth wide against her pussy, I give it my all. Using my index and middle fingers, I pump into her warmth, not letting up as she squirms beneath me. With one hand I hold her down, keep her steady so that I can get her off, so I can make her feel good.

"I'm there," she pants. "Oh my God, I'm there!" I feel her come against the flat of my tongue. Her thighs tighten against my face, and I keep up as she moves against me. As she all at once presses closer and tries to pull away.

I'm hard as fuck underneath the pants I wear. When I glance up at her from where I'm still laying between her thighs, our eyes meet, and the arousal I see in her depths is enough to make my cock jerk in response.

"I want you." She grabs me up by my shirt, pulling me on top of her. "You made me feel good, now let me return the favor."

I don't know what she means, but as she lifts the dress off her body, and pulls the cups of her lace bra down, I realize I can totally get with whatever the fuck this is going to entail.

"Take off your pants, Anthony. Everything down below the waist." With fucking pleasure.

I take off my shirt too, just in case. And then I wait. Wait for her to make a move, wait for her to continue this game. It's hard, but I be what I've been since the moment we've met. Patient.

When she presses me back against the headboard and then drops to her elbows in front of me, I don't think a lot of it, until she closes her mouth around my length. "Holy fuck." I lean my head against the wood, closing my eyes against the visual.

I don't expect the deep swallow, the swirl of her tongue, or her grabbing my balls. All of that is a surprise, but what's even more surprising is when she gets me nice and wet and then uses her hand to jack me. Getting back on her knees, she gets closer, and when she leans over, I nearly lose my fucking mind because I know what she's going to do.

Good little Violet, cups her tits and encloses them around my cock.

Mind and load completely blown in one fell swoop. As I pant and think of the easiest way to clean up this mess, I realize that I don't even care. All I care about is the woman who just rocked my world.

With someone else I might be embarrassed, I might be trying to make an excuse for her to get out here. Not with Violet. I want to know everything about her, I want to talk quietly for hours, and more than anything I want her to know how much she means to me.

"WHY DON'T YOU HAVE TATTOOS?" Her voice is quiet in the darkness of the room.

I grin, but I know she can't see it. Instead, I continue trailing my finger along the upper portion of her naked arm, causing her to snuggle in closer to me. My heart pounds against my chest wall as I feel the breath flutter against my skin. I hoped for this, but never dreamed it would come true. No matter how much I look like I believe in myself – most times I really don't.

"I'm scared of needles."

Her laugh gusts against my skin, causing shivers to ripple the flesh. "You laugh, but I'm serious."

"You've got to be kidding me. Every other guy in the MTF is basically covered in tattoos."

I roll my eyes. "I wouldn't call it covered in tattoos, but they have plenty for all of us."

"You're really scared of needles?" She sounds as if she doesn't believe me.

"Ask Menace, he had to hold my hand when the department got our flu shots." I shudder just thinking about it. "I've never been a huge fan of them."

"But you like to jump out of planes and stuff." She props her head up on her hand, gazing down at me. She's in a small sliver of light shining through the curtains.

"I get my thrills many other ways than having a tattoo done."

With the added light, I lift my arm, allowing my finger to trace the pattern the curtain makes on her skin. The way she's shifted, the blanket has exposed a small portion of her chest, allowing me to follow the sliver of light with the tips of my fingers. I hold her gaze as I open my palm to cup her breast in the darkness, flattening my hand against it as I rub back and forth, worrying the nub. The way her bottom lip pulls between her teeth is the sexiest thing I've discovered about her yet. She tilts her head back on her shoulders, thrusting her chest into my touch.

It was this way earlier when Violet finally surrendered to the electricity that's been building between us for months. When she gave herself over to it, she gave herself over to me. I toy with her, feeling my own body respond to her, but ignoring the need because I want her to feel all of the things she's never felt before.

"Feel good?" My voice is deep with arousal, I want her to hear it, want her to know what she does to me.

With other women I've been selfish, with her I want to be selfless. I want to show her the good things in life, prove to her that not everyone is a bastard. I want for this woman to experience nothing but pleasure. And more than anything, I want to be the man to bring her to the brink of a pleasure so great it almost hurts.

"Mmm hmmm," she moans when I situate myself against the head board, and reach down to grab her around the thighs. Once I've got a good grip, I spread them, bringing her to straddle my lap.

"Anthony." My name is a moan from her lips.

"Shhh, just let me play. *Now*, baby, *now* I'm going to fuck you. Are you protected?" I ask in a voice I don't even recognize as my own. "Do you trust me?"

She nods, gasping out on a breathless moan. "Yes, and yes."

With other women I'm not like this, I don't like to direct what their reactions are going to be. Typically I'm more worried about getting off, but with her, I want her pleasure first, last, and always.

Violet

My nipples go incredibly hard when I hear the ragged tone of his voice as he tells me he's going to fuck me. Every time Anthony has touched me, my body has responded in a way it never has before.

"I'm ready." I grasp his shoulders with my hands.

His hand curves around the globes of my ass, cupping it with his palm, as he scoots me up onto my knees. I look down to where he grips the base of his cock, and guides my body over his, and then down onto the length. Throwing my head back, I gasp loudly, because it just feels that damn good. Once I'm seated, his other hand grips the other ass cheek, and he pulls me forward, pushes me back, pulls me forward and pushes me back, setting the pace he wants me to use to ride him.

"Anthony," I whisper his name on a breath that gusts out between my open lips. "You feel." I inhale deeply, whining as he thrusts and withdraws, using my body to set the pace. "Amazing."

"So do you, Vi, so do you." He moves his hand to the front, pushing his palm down my stomach, using his thumb to rub at my clit. I'd thought I was done earlier, but now it throbs as he tilts his hips into mine, those abs of his rippling as he thrusts up into me.

Letting go of his shoulders, I lean back, putting my hands on his thighs, giving him free reign of my body below the waist. My eyes roll back and my head tilts as he strums my clit. My body moves of its own accord, going after the pleasure it wants, knowing that this is the man who can give it to me. Noises come from deep within my throat, noises I've never heard before, I didn't even know I could make them, as he plays my body.

"C'mon Vi," he growls as he lifts those thighs, letting me rest in the cradle of his knees. "Let go for me, come all over my cock, let me be the man to bring you this pleasure."

And with those final words, I do, he is. In the midst of it all I know he comes too, and I can't help but feel proud of myself. Trying to control my breathing, I fall down on his chest, purring contently when he wraps his arms around me and holds me tight.

Neither one of us says a word to the other as we both drift off, and I know without a doubt there's not a safer place for me than in his arms.

CHAPTER TWENTY-FIVE

VIOLET

FOOTBALL FRIDAY NIGHT.

The phrase is foreign to me. No matter where I've lived, I've never been a participant. Even last year. After everything that happened with Brent, I couldn't bring myself to come out and support Caleb, but with this being his senior year, I feel as if I kind of owe it to him.

Sitting next to Anthony on the bleachers, I have my shaker and we're ready to go. "How do I know when something good happens?" I ask as he looks at me like he doesn't want anyone to know we're even here together.

"The crowd will let you know, the team will let you know, hell I'll let you know. Do you know *anything* about football?"

"Other than the fact that Whitney loves it?" I shake my head. "No."

"Jesus Christ," he mumbles as he takes a drink of his Coke. "I brought you to a high school football game where these boys could end up state champs, and you have no idea what that even means."

"That they're good?" I giggle, laughing at how annoyed he is.

"Caleb will be playing for the University of Alabama, Vi. That's better than good."

I gaze out onto the field, trying to figure out what's going on. It's a little chilly tonight, which I use as an excuse to snuggle up next to Anthony. "Tell me, what's happening now."

He sighs good-naturedly, but slings his arm around my neck. "It's the opening kick-off. You see this line?" He points to a group of young men on the field. "They'll kick the ball, and one of those" – he points to the opposite end – "will return it."

"Who are we rooting for?"

Anthony points to the team set up to receive the kick-off. "Caleb's number fifty-four. It's Renegade's old number which burns Menace's ass up." He laughs as he drops a kiss on my cheek.

"Well Ryan was a great player, so he should be thankful." I hear Whitney's voice as she comes to sit next to us, holding Stella in her arms.

"Renegade working the game?" Anthony asks as he helps her get situated with the toddler.

"Yeah, but Trevor wanted to come to see Caleb, so we tagged along. Blaze is working the EMS truck tonight. It's a family affair." She screams as does the rest of the section we're sitting in. Her eyes having never left the field after she sat down.

"What happened?" I completely missed it, and I'm unsure as to why everyone's yelling and patting each other on the back like they had something to do with the play on the field.

"Caleb returned the kick-off for a touchdown. He's no match for these little boys, they may as well go home," Whitney yells through palms cupped over her mouth.

As I glance around, I think I may have just stepped into the Twilight zone.

"YOU OKAY?" Anthony asks at what I've learned is half-time.

"I'm good, just feeling a little out of my element."

"You're doing a great job." He tightens his arm around me. "Besides that whole rooting for the other team thing."

I defend myself. "I apologized, and Ernie promised not to dock my pay after I apologized. I got the colors mixed up."

He laughs, curling a lock of my hair around his finger. "You'll get it."

Beside me, Whitney stands, Stella in her arms. "We're going to the ladies' room, if you want to come with us."

"Sounds good."

"Maybe she can give you some tips on the game," Anthony throws out.

"Honey." Her voice is shot at this point. "There ain't enough tips in the world to help her, but if you stick around, we'll get ya fixed up. I'll have you in Tuscaloosa with me in no time. We gotta go see Caleb next year anyway. Do you realize how excited I am to know somebody on the team?"

I'm almost scared for Caleb, but I don't say anything. All I do is nod. "I'd appreciate anything you can do to help me."

As we descend the bleachers and make our way down to the bathrooms, Southern Belle Whitney is back.

"I wish we could go inside and not use these out here. They always stink to high Heaven."

Looking around, I notice Karina. "Karina!" I wave her over.

"Hey, it's good to see you." She gives me a smile. "Surprised to see you at the game though."

"No one is more surprised than I am, trust me. Is there any way we can go inside to use the bathroom?" I point to Whitney and Stella. "It might be difficult out here with her daughter."

"Oh yeah." Karina takes off for the school. "No problem. The alarm isn't on while the game goes on, but they do keep a close watch on the hallways and stuff. The back bathroom is always open, because it's handicap accessible."

"Thanks for the tip." Whitney puts Stella down on the ground. "Those stalls outside are so small, and while she's mobile, I can't always keep her in there with me. Last time, I ended up chasing her with my pants around my ankles. Thank God, the only person who came in there was my brother's girlfriend." She shudders. "Talk about embarrassing."

I laugh, glancing at my friend. "I can't even imagine you being that undignified."

"Oh yeah, when you have a baby and your hoo ha is laid out for everyone to see, you kinda just let some things go." She opens the door and we file in after her and Stella.

"She's really cute," Karina comments as she looks at Stella. "How old is she?"

"She'll be two in December. She's my little miracle." Whitney gazes down at the face that looks so much like Ryan it's scary. "We thought we might try for another, but I'm too old and too damn tired." She laughs.

"Now you can count on Holden and Leighton for your baby fix."

"Oh yeah." She nods. "And someday my brother will make it official with Blaze, then I can be the best aunt ever."

As she takes her stall, the words she's spoken roll through my mind. What would it be like to have roots like that? As a warmness penetrates my chest, I realize I'm looking forward to finding out.

Ace

"My wife around here?"

I glance up from my phone, seeing Renegade standing over me. He's wearing our typical uniform when we're out in public. Bullet proof vest, shirt, and tactical pants, with military boots. "She and Stella went to the bathroom with Violet. Have a seat and take a load off for a minute."

"Don't mind if I do." He sits down with a sigh, running his hands over his thighs.

"How's it going?"

"It's been a shitty night, let me just tell you that. Havoc was here with me for a while, but he had to go. I'm ready to get this night over with and go to bed."

Renegade isn't one to complain, not typically, so I know something has happened. "Care to fill me in?"

"Two things. We found some kids with moonshine before the kick-off, and they relayed the same story you got when you questioned the driver of that car. Whoever is dealing, is doing it within the school, and almost with the protection of the school, which is fucked up on all accounts."

I sigh, he's right. The question is, how do we figure out who our main source is. "And what is the second thing?"

"You remember finding that shallow grave out in the woods at the barn party last year? You know it got sent off for testing, to see if we could make an identification?"

My memory is a little fuzzy, but it's coming back, and I have a horrible feeling of dread. "Yeah, I remember."

"ID came back as Leighton's mom. Havoc left to go tell her." His voice is pitched low so no one else can hear the conversation we're having.

"Fuck," I breathe. We'd all been worried about that. Havoc had all but bet his career on it being Leighton's mom, but none of us wanted it to be true.

"He's requested a couple of days. Leighton didn't take it well, and with the baby due in about ten weeks, he was worried."

"No doubt, I would be too. I wish there was something we could do for them."

Renegade pulls his phone out of his pants pocket. "I already got a text about making them a casserole or some shit. You know how us Southern folk are. Somebody dies, you eat. Somebody is born, you eat. Check your phone; you're part of the group text."

Just as he says it, I feel the vibration. "I'll make sure we take something over."

"Keep it quiet for now, they don't want word to get out, in case it wasn't Jefferson."

We wrap the conversation up as the girls come back from the bathroom.

"Daddy!" Stella reaches for her dad as the girls make their way to their seats.

He grabs hold of his daughter and gives his wife a kiss on the cheek. "I can't stay, but I wanted to come and say hi to my girls."

Violet has a seat next to me, resting her head on my shoulder. "What would it be to have a life like that?" she questions as she watches them.

"If you wanna find out, I'd be game for it."

Her eyes are wide with surprise as she turns to face me.

"What?" I shrug. "You think I've been hanging around you for over a year because I feel sorry for you? Violet, I got it bad for you, you have to know that."

She reaches over, hooking her hand in my elbow, pulling me close. "I got it bad for you too."

Turning to face her on the bleachers, I hook my free arm around neck, pulling her in for a kiss.

"Kiss!"

Breaking apart, we laugh as we look down and see Stella clapping for us. As we separate, I reach down to grab her, sitting her on my lap as Whitney and Renegade continue talking for a few more minutes. Sitting with these friends, this woman at my side, in my town, watching our friend play football? I realize it's everything I've ever wanted in my life and I'm extremely grateful I didn't let that ring on Violet's finger dissuade me from going after exactly what I wanted.

CHAPTER TWENTY-SIX

VIOLET

"I FEEL like I'm going to explode," Leighton complains a week later as we clean up from a crazy breakfast rush at The Café.

"You're pregnant and due in a few weeks. You're supposed to feel that way," I remind her as I pull out a chair for her. "Have a seat, prop those feet up, and let me do the work."

"Funny, sometimes Holden says the same thing, only not about cleaning up." She has this naughty look on her face that is one hundred percent my friend.

I've been worried about her since they positively identified her mother's body. Especially with the holidays fast approaching, I'm wondering how she's going to handle it. Hopefully with a baby to care for, she won't dwell on it too much. I've watched her since she was given the information, and except for the first few days after it happened, she seems to be doing well. Leighton's a fighter, and I expected nothing less from her.

"Have you thought of a name yet?" I ask as I go around, wiping off the tables.

"You just want me to tell you if it's a boy or a girl," she accuses, a smile in her voice. "I'm not doing that until he or she is born."

They're refusing to let people in on the gender, and it's driving us all crazy. The nursery is in yellow and gray, so it could be either a boy or a girl. I've been trying to get it out of her for weeks now, but she's not slipping up and saying anything she shouldn't.

"Tell me about you and Ace," she requests, taking a drink of the water sitting in front of her. "You two still heating up the sheets?"

"Yeah." I grin back at her. "More than we probably should be."

"There can *never* be too much heating of the sheets, Violet. Mark my words."

Maybe she's on to something, but I'll never admit it. Just as I'm about to say something to her, Whitney comes in with her mom, both their faces white. "What's wrong?"

"There's been a wreck at the bottoms, and we don't know who's involved, but they say a cop was there."

I wasn't here when Trevor wrecked, but I've heard about it numerous times and just the things I've heard make my heart stop.

"We're just gonna wait here until we hear from people. Is that okay, Ernie?" Whitney asks as she and her mom take a seat at the same table Leighton sits at.

"Yeah, let me get you all some tea." He hustles out from behind the back and quickly motions for me to sit down.

Once the tea is delivered, we all glance at each other, and we do the only thing we can do. Wait.

Hours go by before we hear that the people who were in the wreck were elderly out-of-towners and some high school kids. The out-of-towners aren't doing well, and all I want to do is get home so I can see Anthony, so I can make sure he's okay.

A car pulls up, carrying Ryan. "Hey ladies." He comes through the threshold, picking Whitney up as she flings herself at him. "I came to make sure you two got home okay. Havoc and Ace were the officers in the car that responded." He points at me and Leighton. "They're fine, just dealing with some pretty serious issues at the crash site. Neither one is hurt though, I promise you that."

It helps me to breathe easier, knowing that Anthony isn't hurt and knowing that Holden is with him. "You can take her home, but I'm good. Holden drove her to work this morning." I point at Leighton. "I can make it on my own."

He looks like he wants to argue, but thinks better of it before herding the girls up and taking them home. As I watch them drive away, I know that I want to rush back to the duplex to be there for Anthony. I have no idea what he's faced tonight, but I definitely want to be the person who helps him make it better.

"Be careful, Violet," Ernie yells as I leave. I give him a wave, before I'm on the door.

FOUR HOURS LATER, I am sitting on the front porch, nursing a beer, and a plate of cookies when Ace comes home. I've texted with him a few times, but he seems off, as if he's more affected than he cares to let on. I won't let it bother me, won't let him shut me out the way I know he probably wants to.

When his squad car pulls in the driveway and he gets out, I don't run to him. I don't make a big fuss, or a scene. I let him come to me. Getting out of his car, I ache to put my arms around him. His shoulders are down-trodden and his demeanor is that of someone who's seen the worst in humanity today. The way he was a quiet strength when I needed it in the beginning, I'm that for him right now. As he gets out of the car, he gazes over the top of it, seeming to try and collect himself.

When he finally speaks, it's not at all what I expect to hear.

"Shit's not fair."

"What happened, Anthony?" I ask as I hold my hand out to him, letting him take mine as we enter my side of the duplex.

Grabbing the beer and cookies, I bring them in with us, before shutting the door. Walking over to the breakfast bar, I set them down and then look at him expectantly, waiting for him to let it all out.

Ace

"I act like shit doesn't bother me." I turn around so I don't have to face her, don't have to see those amazing eyes of hers look at me with sympathy in them. "But it does. It bothers the fuck out of me. Especially when people do stupid shit like this."

"What do you mean?" she asks, walking to me, reaching over to hold my hand.

There's dried blood on my uniform pants, and irrationally I don't want her to touch it. Flinching away from her touch, I put my fingers through my hair. It's longer than even I like it, but right now I use it as a distraction. "They aren't sure if the older couple will make it. Those kids that hit them? They were drunk. We found bottles of moonshine in the truck."

"But I thought..." She shakes her head, letting the words trail off.

"That we got rid of the threat when we arrested Jefferson?" I get up from where I'm sitting, wanting to rip my skin from my bones. This feeling is horrible, takes me back to the helplessness I felt when my unit came under fire, and I had to watch as my best friend died in my arms. "You'd think so right? But nah, sweetness, bad never stays gone forever. There's always another villain ready to step in."

The way the silence stretches between us kills me. I've never not been able to talk to Violet, but the way this feels is fucking foul. We're not connecting, and that's something we've never had a problem with. "What are you thinking?" The words are ripped out of my throat.

Lifting my hand up, I almost cup her cheek in my palm, but then I see a dark slash of oil or maybe dirt on my forearm. Hell, based on where they wrecked, it could be cow shit – I'm not sure. I drop my hand, feeling too dirty to touch her, too wrecked emotionally to be this bare in front of her.

"I'm thinking you're misinterpreting this look in my eyes." Her voice is strong, yet soft. "If anyone knows there's always a villain ready to take over, it's me. And if anyone knows what it's like to hurt, it's me. Don't hide how you're feeling, Anthony."

Nobody, except the shrink I got sent to after I started to venture into civilian life, has ever asked me how I'm feeling. "You sure you wanna make that statement, sweetheart? What I do for a living isn't all about directing traffic, community outreach, and helping damsels in distress change their flat tires. Sometimes what I do is the real fuckin' deal."

Violet looks like I slapped her, she literally and physically takes a step back from me. "I think I know better than most your job is the real fuckin' deal. Did you forget you came to my rescue while I was being beaten? While I was bleeding all over the floor of The Café and being flung around like I had no bones in my body? That you arrested my husband? You see the worst in humanity, nobody knows that better than I do."

"Ex-goddamn-husband," I growl because I can't stand to hear that he once had a claim on her.

"Does the title matter?"

"Yes." My voice is deadly calm. "He'll never have a claim on you again."

She straightens, showing that backbone I love. Standing tall and proud, she faces me, raising her chin. "And neither will you if you don't learn how to let me in. That's a hard limit for me, Anthony. We're in this together or we're just friends. Trust me and let me help you, the way you've helped me. Simple as that."

"Not so simple at all." I duck my head, feeling the weight of the world on my shoulders. "There are days I see the absolute worst humanity has to offer. I've done shit I can't ever talk about. Shit I would never want to admit to another human being. How do I deserve your help?"

"How about you let me decide what you deserve from me? What's got you so spooked?"

I don't want to tell her. Make myself that vulnerable? I swore to myself I'd never do it again, but she's right. I can't be strong all the time and expect her to lay it all out for me. If I want her trust, then I have to trust her with all the parts of me. Including the parts that I've never shared with anyone. The ugly, the sad, and the ones I'm not so proud of.

For the first time since I came home, I think maybe I do want to open myself up. And maybe this is the woman I want to open myself up to.

CHAPTER TWENTY-SEVEN

ACE

I GRAB hold of her shoulders, pushing her back into the hallway, leading to her bedroom. There's one thing I need right now, and that's to know she's mine. I need to bury all these feelings in her and let them come out as something better, something not tainted by the ugliness I see every night.

"What do you need from me?" she asks as we enter the bedroom, and I'm reaching down to undo the belt at my waist.

"You," I groan when her fingers push mine away. "I need to know this ugliness I see and experience is for something good. I need to know this won't beat or break me."

"It won't, because I won't let it." Violet drops to her knees before me, shoving my pants and underwear down around my ankles. Before I know what's happening, her warm heat has circled my dick, taking it down her throat.

I had been hard before, but now I'm granite as she slides her tongue up and down my length. There's no finesse tonight, nothing that remotely reminds me of the loving and caring guy I've been with her. She grabs hold of my ass cheeks holding me tightly as she works my length.

"Goddamn." I fist my fingers in her hair, holding onto her tight. Looking down at her, she looks up and our eyes meet. In that moment, I know I can't do this. While it feels good in the moment, I'll never take my anger out on her this way. Pushing her away from me, I lift her to her feet, cupping her jaw with my hand. "While I appreciate what you were doing, Vi, I can't ever use you like that."

"I want you to," she pants, putting her arms around my waist. "I want to be that for you."

"You are," I whisper, leaning in to kiss her, coaxing her mouth open with my tongue. I taste myself on her tongue, and the feeling is heady, makes me want to roar with approval that this woman is mine. "You are everything to me."

I don't know how we get our clothes off, but we do, and as she falls down onto the bed, I follow her, lying over top of her, covering her with my body. Using my hands, I push her wrists up over her head, pressing her down.

"Take what you need, Ace," she encourages me. "I saw the way you looked when you came home. You don't need pretty tonight."

She's right, I don't, but I'll never take anger out on her either.

"You don't have to hold back for me all the time, maybe I want you unrestrained and passionate." She hooks her feet behind my ass, pulling me to her. "Maybe sometimes I just want you to shove it in, give me a little bit of pain, and go to town."

Fuck, her words are making my cock harden further, making the tip leak, and sending all kinds of images to my brain. "Is that what you want?" I put my knees on the bed, prop myself up with my forearms. With my knees I spread her thighs wide.

"Yes!" she shoves her head against the comforter. "Let go, you don't always have to be so in control. Sometimes out of control is so much fun."

With those words, I plant myself home, grunting as I do. She responds to my grunt with a moan and groan of her own. Her nails are gripping at my fingers as she holds on. "Like this?"

"Yes, just like that. I love the way you thrust into me," she whispers at my ear. "Love the way your thighs make room in between mine, love the way you don't pull all the way out before you shove back in. Your chest rubbing against mine is hot, the way your hot breath pants onto my face. You unrestrained is the best."

With those words laying between us, I do as she asks. I bend my head down and fuck her in earnest. I don't withdraw every time, I leave the tip in before I press back into her body. She clenches tightly on me, thrusting against me. I can feel my body tightening, can feel myself about to let go, but I don't allow myself to.

Instead I put my thumb up to her mouth, let her suck it in, shiver when her tongue circles it like she did the head of my dick, and then I pull back so that I can watch myself slide in and out of her. Using my thumb, I worry it against her clit as I continue the slide into the heaven that is her body.

"Faster." She pumps against me, her hands moving up her chest to cup her tits and tweak her nipples.

"God, you look so sexy when you do that. Don't ever hold back what you need." I give her the words she gave to me.

"Don't stop." Her voice is high-pitched, her stomach muscles are clenched, and she's straining to get there. I know, because I am too.

We're pushing against each other, making lewd noises in the room, the bed is shaking along with my legs, but I won't stop until we both get there. And as I feel her tighten against me, and the hot heat jets out of my dick, I say the words that have been on the tip of my tongue for months now.

"I love you, Violet, love you so much. Please don't leave me."

I collapse, holding her tightly in my arms, emotion clogging my throat.

"Hey," she whispers as we pant against one another. "I love you too. I've loved you a long time Anthony 'Ace' Bailey."

And in that moment, all is right in my world.

THE NEXT DAY, I'm in a great mood, regardless of what I had to deal with the night before. Most everyone has commented on it, and even though it's raining, it's almost as if the sun is shining down everywhere I walk.

"God, you're annoying today," Havoc groans as we are packing up and heading back from what turned out to be a false alarm.

We'd gotten a tip from someone inside the high school telling us where a still was, and the same bottles of moonshine we'd found in the school were. What we ended up finding was nothing. So we'd suited up and gone out into the muddy woods for nothing.

"I'm not annoying, you've got a stick up your ass," I fire back at him.

The more pregnant Leighton's become, the more he's starting to get on everyone's nerves.

"Shut the fuck up before I take you and your smug attitude down," Havoc volleys back at me.

"Oh really? I'll take you down before you take me down."

He hands his gun over to Renegade. "Is that right?" he asks, taking his gloves off.

"That's right." I hand my gun over to Menace and take my gloves off too.

"Then you better prove it, smartass."

I groan as he hits first, knocking me down into the mud. But as we roll around, landing punches and generally having a great time, I thank God that I have a boss and men like this to look up to in my life.

CHAPTER TWENTY-EIGHT
VIOLET

"THIS WEATHER BLOWS." Leighton grimaces as we watch the rain come down in sheets outside The Café. It's made for a boring shift for both of us. "Since there's been no one in here, all I've done is eat." She puts another fry in her mouth, liberally dipped in ketchup. I'm not sure I've ever seen someone eat as much ketchup as she has since she found out she's pregnant.

I laugh, leaning my head against her shoulder. "You're doing great things, like growing a human. You're gonna be hungry. Plus, you're gonna have this baby very soon. You've already dropped."

"But if I gain a hundred pounds, Holden's not going to want me anymore." She pushes the fries away, but grabs another anyway.

"You're crazy, Leigh. I wish you could see what you look like right now. Like really see it." I turn to face her, ready to lay down some truth for her. Since she had to get a pair of maternity jeans, she's almost been having an identity crisis.

"Like a whale?"

"Absolutely gorgeous." I put my hand on her bump. "You glow, Leigh, I mean from the inside out, and when Holden walks in this place? The two of you could burn it down with the way he looks at you. There isn't anything for you to worry about when it comes to your husband."

She rolls her eyes and blows out a watery breath. "Nothing fits right anymore, my boobs are in the way, my belly is in the way, and I would kill for a little sunlight up in this place."

I laugh because I've thought the same thing about the sunlight. We've had more than enough rain to last us for a month. "Just a couple more months,

Leigh, and then you'll be able to hold that little boy who's probably going to be the spitting image of his dad." I take a guess at the gender, because they haven't told us, they haven't told anyone.

Her gaze lights up. "Can you imagine? Another Holden? Or maybe it'll be another me?"

Out of nowhere a pain hits me in the gut, because I imagine holding the spitting image of Anthony. Never in my life have I aspired to be a mom, I've never had the burning desire to have a child, but in this moment, I know if I ever did, it would be with him. Hoping I cover up my momentary bout of emotion, I shake my head. "I can't even begin to imagine."

She opens her mouth to speak, but the bell over the door rings, and we both whip our heads around. Sometimes when I'm not prepared to see him, Anthony completely takes my breath away. Take today for example.

The crew walking through the door are too good-looking to all be friends. When they run in a pack, I think panties drop everywhere. Holden, Anthony, and Mason walk through the place like they pay the rent.

"Afternoon, ladies." Mason grabs a menu and slides next to us at the counter.

I nod over to him, but my attention is firmly on Anthony as he walks over to me. I've turned in my seat so that I'm watching him as he approaches. For the longest time, I never truly understood what women meant by drooling. Today, it's like I've been given a crash course.

It's obvious he's been out in the rain. The dark hat he wears over his hair is turned backwards, exposing damp ends that drip onto his collar. I'm not sure what they were doing today, maybe something with the MTF? He's wearing a bulletproof vest that reads MTF across the chest, and the white shirt underneath is molded to what I can see of his biceps. My perusal doesn't stop when I get to the cargo pants that the moisture has caused to stick to him like a second skin. Dirt streaks his face and one of his forearms. He looks like a little kid who had fun in the mud. The look does things for me, but I will never tell him that.

"What happened to you?"

"My boss told me I couldn't take him down." He shrugs, glancing over with a smirk on his face to Holden.

Leighton has already made her way over to her husband, standing in between his spread thighs as he wraps his arms around her waist, pulling her close. I watch as he kisses her on the neck and she folds herself into his body. Those intimate gestures are my favorite things about being involved with a man like this.

"And did you?"

"We'll call it a tie." Holden rotates his shoulder, as he leans his forehead against Leighton's chest.

"Don't you dare make it so that he can't hold this baby," Leighton scolds him, throwing a glare in Anthony's direction.

"He started it," Anthony argues, pulling me into his arms. He's careful to keep the muddiness of his uniform off me, but even just feeling the heat coming from his body is worth it.

"And you finished it," Mason offers a smirk over his back at the two of us. It's like he's trying to hold in his chuckle, but fails in a big way as the laugh rips its way past his throat.

It's good to hear him laugh after the hell he's been through with Caleb. The four of us share a look, and we all join in, laughing with him. It's the first hint that maybe father and son are making it through the dark period they've been having. Caleb's smiles are easier, and now hearing Mason laugh, it's a healing balm for all of us.

"Can we get some food around here?" Holden grumbles.

I take pity on him, after reaching up to give Anthony a kiss on the cheek. "Burgers and fries all around?"

"And a milkshake," Holden adds. "Chocolate with a cherry."

"Eating your feelings?" Anthony continues picking at him.

"Did extra cardio last night, and again this morning." He winks at Leighton, a self-indulgent smile on his face. "I can afford to bulk on some calories. Don't be a hater, Ace."

He and I share a look. One that could do a little heating up of our own, if given the chance. "Trust me when I say I'm not hating any of what I'm getting, boss man."

Menace chuckles where he's sitting, looking slightly uncomfortable. "There's so much testosterone in this place, Jesus."

"Mostly from you, considering you haven't been laid in, like, thirteen years. Been a long build up, huh?" Holden delivers the low blow while Anthony laughs on.

"Y'all are so mean to each other." I hear Ernie ring the bell and go to grab their food.

"If we weren't mean to each other, we'd probably legit kill one another, which is why these two are dirty and hurting right now." Menace points to his co-workers. "Me on the other hand, I'm smart and know when to stay out of shit."

Delivering the food, I squeal when a corded forearm snakes around my waist, planting my ass on his lap. "Sit with me." Anthony's voice is deep, dark, and full of an erotic promise in my ear. He's taken off his vest, which held most of the dirt. Sitting with him won't hurt anything.

"For a minute." I relax back against him, glad that we aren't hiding ourselves anymore. I'm not exactly sure when it happened. A gradual progression maybe, where we decided we didn't want to be known how we started out. Gone are the married woman and the man who didn't care. Now we're just two people who genuinely care for and respect one another. It's taken us a long time to get to this point, but there's no one I'd rather have taken the journey with than him.

He lifts a french fry up to my mouth, letting me take a bite before he puts the rest of it in his mouth. Never did I believe we'd be like this. But I'd be lying if I said I didn't love it. To have a man who cares about me the way he does, I never dreamed I'd find it, but look at where I am now.

"What are your plans for Halloween?" Holden asks.

"We're dressing up and handing out candy since Anthony doesn't have to work." We'd gone over the things we could do, but neither one of us had wanted to be out on the roads with all the crazy people. In the end, that seemed like a tradition we could keep up for years to come.

Leighton claps her hands. "Like in matching costumes? A couple's costume? Because that would be awesome. If you are, I'll definitely come by and see you. Holden's gotta work."

"Come hand out candy with us," I encourage her. "We're gonna be Captain America and Wonder Woman! I'm really excited. It'll be so much fun."

"Oh great!" Leighton rolls her eyes, sighing. "Y'all will be superheroes, and I'll be a huge-ass gumball machine."

"Is that what you're gonna be? Those are so cute, especially with this belly you have."

She groans.

"I meant that as a compliment," I defend my choice of words.

"I know you did, I'm just so uncomfortable right now." She grabs hold of her back and attempts to stretch it. "I can't sleep, I can't stand, and I can't sit. I'm at the stage where absolutely nothing makes me happy."

"Not too much longer." Holden rubs her stomach while he places a kiss on her neck.

"He's right," I add. "Soon you'll be holding this *child*," I emphasize the word because neither one of them have told the secret yet. "So come have fun with us for one night."

"Oh alright." She sighs. "Why not?"

"I'll drop you off before I go on shift," Holden offers, seeming to be happy that she's going to have somewhere to go while he's working.

"And I'll take you home when we're done," I offer. "That way you don't have to be out by yourself, and you can still have a good time with us."

"Okay," she concedes, looking kind of excited. "Okay. If I show up tomorrow night dressed as a damn gumball machine, you better be dressed up."

I hold my hands up in surrender. "I promise." I laugh. "We'll have a good time."

Leighton doesn't look convinced, but I give her a huge smile and pray to the gods above that I'm right.

CHAPTER TWENTY-NINE

ACE

HALLOWEEN

"Come on, we gotta hurry up and get these done before they start showing up."

Violet and I are racing against the clock. Trick-or-treating starts at four p.m. and it's three-thirty. We're both changed, and Leighton's already here, helping us fill up the treat bags we'll be handing out. We'd starting filling them up when Violet got off work, but we'd gotten distracted when we got dressed in our costumes. If I'd known she was going to look as good as Wonder Woman herself, I would have had her try it on for me before today.

"You're a damn slave driver," Leighton grumbles as she situates herself on the couch. "If I knew you were going to be this bad, I would have said leave my ass at home."

Violet snickers, handing her friend a piece of chocolate. "Heie, eat this and you'll feel better."

Leighton does as told, and then grimaces, putting a hand to her back. "I've felt like shit all day. I didn't want to come, no offense to you all, but I'm just so uncomfortable. Holden didn't want me at the house by myself though, and we got into an argument about it. It's just not been a good day."

"Only a few more weeks," my girlfriend says as she leans over and rubs the felt balls on her friend's belly, "then you'll be able to at least sleep comfortably, just not much."

"So true." She sighs as she gets up and all but waddles to the kitchen.

I close the last of the bags and then put them in the container we have for easy access. "C'mon ladies, can Captain America get a selfie with Wonder Woman and the gum ball machine?"

"Ugh, you're too cheerful," Leighton gripes, grinning when I give her a look.

"I love Halloween, okay?"

"I love seeing my feet when I look down, but we can't all have what we want. Can we?" she retorts.

She turns to walk out of the living room, while I pull Violet to my side. "She's grouchy."

"She's carrying around thirty-five pounds on her frame that wasn't there nine months ago, of course she's grouchy." She puts her arms around my waist. "And I'm sorry if she hurt your feelings, but I'll take a selfie with you."

Leaning her cheek up to mine, I can see Violet smiling widely. God, I love this woman, and have I mentioned how hot she looks in this costume? With my hand that's not holding the phone, I reach up, using my index finger to grab her chin, and turn her into a kiss. As we deepen the connection, I capture a picture. One second in the lifetime that will be ours. Letting her go with one more tiny peck, I smirk at her. Violet wipes the lipstick off my mouth, a smirk of her own spreads across her face.

"You're the sexiest super hero I've ever seen." My ego takes a nice stroking when she says those words. I work out, so it's nice when she notices.

"Ain't nobody got anything on that ass." I smack it with the palm of my hand as she walks by.

Back when we first started with each other, I never thought she'd be this comfortable with me. Never thought I would be this comfortable with her. For everything we've gone through together, I realize we went through it to end up here. As the holidays approach, I know I'll be more thankful than I've ever been to have this woman by my side.

"Let's go give out some treat bags." She grabs my hand, dragging me onto our shared porch.

Kids are already arriving, and I can't help but be pleased when I see Violet sit down next to Leighton on the steps, oohing and aahing over all the cute costumes the kids are wearing. Maybe one day we'll have a kid of our own, and we'll be able to enjoy this rite of passage with them.

The thought doesn't scare me like it would have years ago. In fact, it's more exciting now than anything. Life is changing, and it's changing in a big way.

Violet

"I haven't seen this many cute kids, ever." I grin at the parents bringing them up as Leighton and I talk back and forth to one another.

"Just wait until the MTF kids get this age." Her eyes are sparkling with excitement. "We'll have Stella and ours, and probably by then you and Anthony will have one, Blaze and Tank will hopefully have one, and who knows with Mason."

"Wait a second." I laugh. "What makes you think that's going to happen with me and Anthony?" I glance over my shoulder, checking to see if he can hear this conversation going down. I don't want him to think I'm making plans or assumptions about him without his knowledge. While I would be interested in being married again if the circumstances were right, I don't want to set myself up for failure.

"Stop lying to yourself." Leighton grabs hold of her back, rubbing the middle deeply. "The two of you heat up any room you're in, and the way you look at each other? It's special, Vi, don't discount it. You're allowed to have the kind of romance people write about. You are." She puts her arm around me. "Just because your first attempt sucked ass, doesn't mean your whole life will be measured by your past. I'm the perfect example of that."

I think for a moment about what she's telling me. Leighton knows better than most anyone how past indiscretions (that aren't even yours) can ruin a life. If she's telling me to live for the moment, then who am I to tell her no?

We hand out another batch of bags, and she goes to stand up.

"My back is killing me, I've got to move." She grimaces as she tries to lift her weight up. "Even if it's just for a minute, I need to stand."

Offering her my arm, she stands, screams, and then falls back down beside me. In a flash, Anthony is over to us.

"Are you okay?" we ask at the same time. The fear is mirrored in both our voices.

Wide, scared eyes gaze back up at us, before they lower down to her lap. There I see a darkening of the leggings she wears.

"Leighton, did your water just break?" I gasp, my heart pounding.

"I think-I think so." She grips my hand in hers. "It's too early. He's not due for another two weeks," she cries.

It's a he – I'd been right. How does that not surprise me with her and Holden? Two weeks isn't a big deal, but I have a feeling she doesn't want to hear that from me right now. "Let's get you to the hospital and get Holden there to help you. You good to walk?" I stand up, holding onto her hand.

My eyes meet Anthony's. He's already on the phone, presumably with Holden. He's nodding, handing me his keys because his truck has more space than my compact car. As he ends his phone call, he grabs hold of Leighton, carrying her to the back cab of his truck.

"Holden's on his way, I'm gonna lock up here, and then I'll come join you two. Everything's going to be fine." He gets her situated, kisses me on the forehead, and off we go.

"I'm scared, Vi," Leighton says from the back seat. "I never had a mom, what if I'm a shitty one?"

"You take care of everybody in your life, Leigh. You're going to be fantastic. Now just lay back, relax, and get as much rest as you can. The next eighteen years of your life are going to be a whirlwind. Especially if your son is anything like your husband."

She groans. "I can't believe I caved."

"I think all will be forgiven as soon as you hold him in your arms."

"I hope Holden makes it," she worries. "What if he was on a stop, what if he gets into an accident trying to get to the hospital? This has been my fear since I found out I was pregnant. That he'd be on shift when I went into labor, and it'd put him in danger getting to me."

"Trust me." I reach back with my hand, grasping hold of hers. "He's going to get to you anyway he can."

We're quiet as we continue the journey to the hospital and as I pull up, I see Holden already waiting at the Emergency Room entrance.

"He's here, Leigh, you don't gotta worry."

Before I even have the truck stopped, he's opened the door and has his wife in his arms.

"Baby, are you okay?" The fear in his voice is palpable, and I feel as if I'm intruding on a private moment, but there's nowhere for me to go.

"Scared, but so glad you're here."

"I'm scared too, but I wouldn't miss this for the world and there's no one else I want to go through this with, other than you."

With a thank you to me, he picks her up, places her in a wheelchair, and they wheel her through the doors. I have to park the truck what feels like five miles from the entrance, because I can't park Anthony's truck that well. When I see my car pull up with Captain America driving it, I laugh harder than I probably should. He looks so uncomfortable.

"Did you by any chance grab us a change of clothes?" I giggle.

He looks down at himself and then at me. "Fuck no," he groans and laughs. "Well here's one for the record books. Welcome to the world baby Thompson." He entwines our fingers, and we proudly walk into the hospital as superheroes.

Seven hours later, as the MTF has gathered at the hospital and is crowded in the room with the new family, I know that all *is* forgiven. And I also know that I've never seen a boy as handsome as Ransom Thompson – named for Leighton's mom's maiden name. He's undoubtedly going to live up to that name, and I love knowing I'm going to be around to watch him grow up.

If anything, this has solidified my spot in Laurel Springs more than anything else ever could have.

CHAPTER THIRTY

VIOLET

Thanksgiving

MOST OF MY adult life I've been nervous. Nervous about what I would do to piss Brent off. Nervous about starting a brand-new job, nervous that someone would see right through the lies I wove around myself and my situation. What I've never been nervous about before is meeting parents. Back when I met Brent's, I was so numb to everything going on around me, I don't even remember it. Then after we high-tailed it out of town, we never went back.

Today, though, is a very important day; I'm meeting Anthony's family. The entire MTF crew has opened up their base of operations for everyone's family to share in the holiday together. Spearheaded by Blaze and Whitney, it's the first get together of its kind, but I can tell that most everyone is very excited about the families getting together. Anthony had to go help set up, so I'm grabbing the sweets I baked and the turkey we deep-fried last night that's now been sliced, for anyone who would prefer to have a cold sandwich.

A text message comes through, right as I'm about to head out.

A: Don't even be thinking about skipping this. I know you're nervous, but I'm telling you, my family will love you. It's just my parents.

V: Easy for you to say! I'm nervous, but I'll handle it well. I promise.

A: I have no doubt. Let me know when you get here, so I can help you.

V: I will. Love you!

A: Love you, Vi, you have no idea how much.

It's sentiments like those that prove to me what he and I have is the real thing. It's also the type of words that can sometimes put fear in my heart. Brent used love as a kind of bargaining chip. Like if you do this, I'll love you more, or if you loved me, you would do what I ask of you. I'm working hard on knowing there's a difference between this love and that love. It's hard, but I'm doing it.

DRIVING up to the headquarters makes my heart pound. I wasn't aware there were this many people in the MTF member's families. It looks like the high school football game parking lot. Caleb is literally out front directing traffic. When he sees me, he motions me into a more private part of the lot. Next to Anthony's truck is an empty space, which he motions for me to park in. When I turn the car off, I look up, seeing a sign that says "Ace's Woman" – which not only makes me laugh, but warms my heart. As I look down the row of cars, I see all of us have our own parking spots. These guys are nothing if not romantic.

Just as I'm about to let him know I'm here, Anthony's arms wrap around me from behind. "Hey." He drops a kiss on my exposed neck, tightening his arms around my waist. "I saw you pull in."

"Hey yourself." I turn in those arms, wrapping mine around his neck. "Are there as many people in there as I think there is?"

"It's not that bad." He chuckles as he leans in for a kiss. For a minute I let myself melt into his embrace, give myself over to the attraction and feelings we evoke in one another. "I see you didn't take my advice and wear a dress." He grabs my car keys and goes to unlock the trunk, where the food is.

My face heats thinking about the words he spoke to me while we were getting ready. "You said you'd have your hand up my skirt and your fingers in my panties. Jesus, I can't be having that meeting your parents for the first time, are you crazy?"

"About you? Yeah, but I guess I understand where you're coming from." He hefts one of the heavily-laden plates before whistling toward Caleb. "Come grab this other one."

"What am I supposed to carry?" I feel weird not doing any of the work, considering I serve people almost every day.

"Yourself, inside that door with your head held high."

I have to fight back tears. Anthony will never know what those words mean to me, and he'll never know how lucky I am. But I vow right now to make sure he knows how much I love him every day. Offering me his elbow, we walk into the building.

Ace

Inside, it's barely controlled chaos, which is to be expected when all of us, and our families get together. Not to mention, I kind of like it. This is where I'm at my best. Glancing around the room as I move to take the food over to one of the long tables we've set up, I realize how thankful I am for this day and this life. A few years ago I wasn't even home for Thanksgiving; today I'm celebrating with everyone who means everything to me. In one corner, I see Havoc with his wife and son. It looks like he's just finished feeding Ransom, because he's now burping him as Leighton looks on.

Tank is running around, chasing Stella and causing her to giggle and hide behind Menace's legs. The smile on Menace's face is enough to make Scrooge smile back. Then there's Whitney and Renegade, sitting at their table sharing some wine, watching their daughter have a great time. It's the stuff you see in Hallmark movies, but it's happening, right here in Laurel Springs, Alabama.

"I can't believe all the people here." Violet puts her arm around my waist, leaning against my chest.

And here we are, cozied up to one another without a care in the world.

"Anthony, is this your friend?" I hear the voice of my mom coming up behind us.

"It is. Mom, this is my girlfriend, Violet. Violet, this is my mom, Ellen. My dad was here, but he had to run and get some ice, because the ice machine can't keep up. You can meet him later."

My mom is the type of person who has never met a stranger, and she quickly pulls Violet into an all-encompassing hug. "I've heard so much about you. It's such a pleasure to meet the young woman who's putting a smile on Anthony's face."

"It's a pleasure to meet the woman who raised him to be such a good man."

I pinch Violet's side to let her know she did good, and my mom will eat this shit up like peanut butter on a spoon. The noise in the room is deafening as everyone is greeting everyone else, until we hear a very loud whistle.

All attention turns to Havoc, who now stands in the middle of the room. "Sorry, but I needed to get everyone's attention. I wanted to thank you all for coming out to this get together instead of hosting a bunch of separate ones. I know over the last couple of years, my team and I have thought of each other as family. We've seen a lot together, done a lot together, and lived through things other people can't fathom. For better or worse, they are my brothers. When we came up with the idea to bring all of you into this for the holiday, we wanted our two families to meet. Thank you all for agreeing to be here, we hope you enjoy the food, and the company. Hopefully this will be a tradition for years to come."

There's a very loud round of applause as everyone starts getting in line for food. "C'mon y'all, let's eat."

"DID YOU MAKE THIS TURKEY?" Mom asks as we sit at one of the long tables.

"The one for sandwiches? Yeah, I deep-friend it yesterday, carved it up, and we refrigerated it overnight. I was hoping there would be some left, but with this crew, I'm not sure that's possible."

"If you only knew how much you all eat, you should see Ernie's order every week," Violet jokes at my side.

"That's where I know you." My Mom snaps her fingers. "You waitress at The Café. I play Bridge in there once a month with my book club."

"Yes, I remember you." Violet is genuinely happy as the two realize they're more acquainted than they thought.

"I hope you don't mind me saying so. What happened to you was a shame, and I'm thankful you're with Anthony now. He may be a lot of things that aren't great, but he is a great man."

"Spoken like a mother who loves her son."

"No." I put my arm around Violet's chair. "Spoken like a mother who had to deal with a juvenile delinquent and still manages to love him after all these years."

"You're my favorite." Mom winks.

"Shit." I laugh. "I'm her favorite until I piss her off, and then my sister becomes her favorite," I say loudly to Violet.

"One of the perks of having two children. When you two get to that point, remember that two is better than one." She winks.

I share a look with the woman sitting next to me. All this togetherness, all this family, and all this love is almost too much to take sometimes. Especially for a man who lived so much of his life on the front line, but when I see her grin so hard her lips almost disappear I know I'm where I want to be, where I need to be, and where I'm supposed to.

In years past I couldn't say that, but now? It's one hundred percent the truth.

CHAPTER THIRTY-ONE

ACE

"DID YOU HAVE A GOOD TIME TODAY?" We're lying in bed, on my side of the duplex, snuggling together after working off some of the calories we consumed in the huge meal we ate.

"A great time, which surprised me, because I was so nervous about meeting your parents."

A grin spreads itself across my face and a happy warmth takes up residence in the middle of my chest at the pleased tone of her voice. "You and Mom got along like gangbusters as soon as the awkwardness wore off."

"The awkwardness didn't last as long as I thought it would." She stretches beside me, hooking her leg around my waist. Lifting it up with my hand so that it rests comfortably, I relax against the comfortableness of the bed.

She yawns as I push my hand through her hair, cuddling her up next to me. "When I first saw you, I imagined this," I whisper.

"What did you think when you first saw me?" she asks as I feel the smile against my shoulder.

"I'm starving." I rub my hand across my stomach as Havoc and I get out of the squad car and enter The Café. It's been a long day on shift and I ran late this morning, so I wasn't able to eat breakfast like I normally do.

"Same, but I'm excited to see my wife too."

I shake my head, a rueful look on my face. "Whipped dude, totally fucking whipped."

"You will be one day," he promises as we cross the street, coming to a stop in front of the glass doors of The Café. "You won't be expecting it, and it'll hit you like a right hook across the face."

"Yeah, okay."

We enter The Café and have a seat at one of the booths. Havoc goes to flirt with his wife, and that's when I see her. A woman I've never noticed before. She's about the same height as Leighton, but she's got hips for days. Her long, dark hair, is pinned severely behind her neck, giving her the look of someone much older than what she probably is. I'm checking her out as she brings food out to the table beside us. Her arms show strength as she lifts the heavy plates, setting them down on the table. And when she speaks, I feel goosebumps appear on my arms.

"Is there anything else I can get y'all?"

The voice is Southern, but not from around here, but it's the tone that gets me. It's a husky, just-had-sex sound that I want to hear every day of my life. When she gets done with them and comes back to our table? I face her, and I know immediately that I'm gone. This is the woman I've been waiting to meet for my whole life. My eyes rake her face, and I take in signs of unhappiness, stress, and fatigue. When they flit down to the ring on her finger, my good mood sinks, but as she uses that hand to push her hair back, I glimpse fingerprint bruises on her bicep under where her uniform comes to a stop. This woman is unhappy, and I make a vow to myself at some point I'll make her happy again. I'll show her what a good man is like, and I'll put a smile on that face. If it's the last thing I do. In this small exchange, she has my heart, and I know I'll never get it back. Because I don't want it back – I want her to have it all.

"You knew all that from like a three-minute glimpse of me?" She sounds like she doesn't believe me.

"Hand to God, Vi. I knew the minute I saw you. It just took me a long time to convince you, and that's okay because I'm patient. I would have waited another year for you."

"What did I do to deserve you?" She caresses my stomach.

"You dealt with a lot of shit you never should have, and I'm your prize for it." I turn us over so that I'm stretched over top of her.

"You're my prize? I think I won first place." She pushes her fingers up my skin, tightening them in my hair and yanking my face to hers for a kiss.

"Claim it baby, please."

And with a smile on her face, she does.

Violet

"Thank you all for being a great class for this semester, I'm pleased to say that you all passed," Karina tells the group of us who have gathered in the classroom that's become such a huge part of my life.

Here I got a piece of my life back, a part of me that Brent had tried to crush. I persevered, and continued with an education he tried to take away from me.

Thanks to this classroom and the things I learned here, I began the path to reclaiming myself and finding out exactly who Violet Miller truly is.

"I hope you all have continued success in whatever it is you choose to pursue, and I'll be seeing you all around." Karina gives us a wave. "That's all I have for the final class. Congratulations everyone."

The group of us begin to pack up and exit the room. As I make my way up there, Karina stops me. "Violet, can I talk to you for a minute?"

"Sure, what's wrong?"

"Nothing." She waits for the last person to leave. "I just wanted to say thanks for suggesting I try that dating app. I've been on a few dates. Nothing to write home about, but I'm hopeful."

"See, I told you there was life after getting your heart broken!"

"So what are you planning on doing?"

I think about what she's asking me. "I have one more class to take to finish this Associates. I'm gonna finish it and then apply at the county attorney's office. I saw where they were advertising for paralegals. Leighton won't be working at Ernie's forever I'm sure, and I really only enjoy working there because of her. It's time for me to make some changes and grow up. I have you to thank for a lot of that."

"Nonsense." She shoves my last paper in my hands. "You deserved this A, just like you deserve everything you're getting in life right now. I'll see you around at The Café, for as long as you're there, huh?"

"Yes, and here, give me your number. I'd love to keep getting tea with you."

As I leave this classroom that's meant so much to me, I'm leaving with a huge smile on my face, and a huge weight lifted off my shoulders. I'll be fine, I'll have friends, and I'll learn who I truly am. All with the help of the amazing group of people I've met in Laurel Springs.

CHAPTER THIRTY-TWO
ACE

CHRISTMAS

"Is it okay that we decided to wait to exchange gifts until we got back here?" Violet asks as she enters my side of the duplex. "It seemed so private, and I wasn't sure I wanted to do that in front of your parents."

"No, I'm okay with that." I pat the couch beside me, beckoning her to come sit beside me.

"You know this couch has held a pretty special place in my life since we made out on it that one time." She cuts her eyes over at me, desire and passion in them.

"Oh really?" I chuckle, slipping my arm against the back of the couch, pulling her closer to me.

"Yeah, that night was one of the first nights I felt like I could be myself with you, and you got me so hot." She closes her eyes.

"You got me hot too, but let's not talk about that right now. We're supposed to be exchanging gifts."

"Okay." She sighs. "You wanna go first?"

"How about we go together?"

"I'm good with that."

She hands me what looks like a gift certificate of some type, and I hand her my small box that I wrapped by myself. It's apparent that I wrapped it because it looks like Stella helped me. We both eye one another. Then we dig into the gifts.

I open the envelope and see two gift certificates for skydiving, and she jingles the keys I gave her at me, her eyebrow raised.

"I'll explain first, then you explain." I duck my head. Back when I'd thought of giving her this, it'd seemed like a great idea, but now that she doesn't understand what they are, I'm kind of second-guessing my idea. "They're keys to this place. I want you to move in with me when you feel like it's a good time. I want to move our relationship to the next level, and I want you to trust me enough to give me that part of you."

Tears slip from her eyes, and I'm confused. I didn't think this was one of those gifts that would make her cry. "Bad idea?"

"No," she sniffles. "Perfect. The reason I gave you two gift certificates? You know I'm scared of heights. Remember Gulf Shores when I wouldn't go parasailing with all of you? I know you love things that push the envelope, that give you a thrill and that's been me, but this is symbolic. With you by my side, I'm not scared of anything. I feel like I could do *anything* as long as you're right there next to me, Ace," she uses my call-sign. "And I'd be proud to live with you, to share your life, and to go skydiving with you. If you're with me, there's nothing I won't face."

This beautiful, perfect, amazing woman – she's come so far. In the blink of an eye, I'm across the couch, cupping her jaw with my hands, devouring her lips with mine. "You're the most amazing, fearless, badass woman I've ever met in my life and I can't wait to experience this adventure with you."

The smile she gives me transforms her face. "I can't either. There will be times when I test your patience, because that's who I am, but please don't ever give up on me."

"Never," I vow. "I'm never giving up on you. I know what it's like to have you. Somebody will have to rip what we have from my cold, dead hands. I mean that with every fiber of my being."

Together, in the colored lights of the Christmas tree we put up together, we snuggle on the couch. Both of us letting tears fall, making whispered promises to each other, and it's the best Christmas I've ever had. No one could have given me a better gift than what I got.

Her.

Violet

A Few Days Later

"This shit is legit." Caleb looks at me wide-eyed. "That table over there just gave me a twenty-five dollar tip. On a thirteen dollar bill."

"Are you kidding me?" I turn my head to stare at the table of older women. They give me five, if that.

"I could get used to being a waiter." He gives me a grin as he adjusts his apron. "I could take the whole place for you if you needed me to."

"Settle down, you stick to your own section and stay out of mine. You're about to get on my bad side." I give him a scowl. "And newsflash, those ladies only gave you that tip because they want you for your body."

"He's seventeen," I throw over at them as I deliver food to the table where Leighton, Holden, Ransom, Anthony and his parents are sitting at.

"Can you believe this?" I cross my arms over my chest, Leighton and I sharing a look. "He's raking in the dough."

Holden, takes a bite with one hand while he feeds Ransom with the other. "Hey, when ya got it, ya got it. Don't be a hater."

Leighton and I both give him a glare. "They gave him twenty-five dollars."

"What? The penny pinchers gave him actual paper money?"

"Yes." I take Anthony's coffee cup and give him a refresh, setting it down a little too hard. "It's ridiculous."

"What's ridiculous" – Anthony clears his throat – "is you two getting salty over a seventeen-year-old kid making more money than you do. From what I've heard through the grapevine, the girl he's talking to over there, he's taking out on a date next week."

Leighton and I whip our heads around. "Oh she's cute," we both say at the same time.

"Well if he's trying to take her out, I'll cut him some slack, but it's still not fair." I lean in, taking a bite of the bacon that Anthony is putting up to my mouth. "I gotta go, but I'll be back to check on y'all in a few minutes."

"Violet," Ellen's voice is quiet with the loud group she's sitting with. "Are we still on for the craft show later on today?"

"Yes," I answer, a smile on my face. "I get off here in about an hour, I'm gonna head home, take a shower, and then meet you out there. It starts at two, right?"

"Right. I'm excited to spend some time with you."

"I'm excited to spend time with you too." And I realize how true that statement is.

"Is it the one at the high school?" Leighton asks as she takes a bite of a biscuit.

"Yup," I answer, filling her coffee cup up to the brim.

"Could I tag along with y'all? I really need to get out of the house. I went last year, and I loved a lot of the stuff I saw. From what I remember, they have really cute baby stuff too."

Poor Leighton, she's not used to being cooped up in the house.

"I have no problem with it." I laugh. "Can Holden handle Ransom on his own?"

"Considering she handles him on her own while he's at work, I'd say he owes her an hour or two," Ellen mumbles as she takes a sip of her tea.

Leighton and I giggle as we both look at Anthony's mom. "Okay, now I see where you get your smart mouth from." I reach over the table, high-fiving his mom.

"Alright I really gotta go, but I'll see you out there. Leigh, want me to pick you up?"

"If you don't mind."

"We'll meet you there, Ellen."

And as I lean in, giving Anthony a chaste kiss, I love the way his arm comes around my waist. I love the way he silently lays claim on me there in front of everyone.

"Love you," he whispers.

"Love you too."

Making my way back over behind the counter, I top off the coffee of all the men sitting there, before I start filling out my tickets. Caleb comes over, asking me if he's doing his tickets right. I take a look at them, nodding in affirmative.

"Good job, bud. So are you really taking that girl out next week?"

Caleb's face turns bright red under the stubble on his cheek and chin. "Trying to. I fucked up before, Vi, messing with those girls who wanted one thing and that was it. She's a good girl, and she's heard about my reputation. It's up in the air."

"You'll be fine, Caleb, and she'll realize what a great person you are. We all make mistakes, but we can always come back from those mistakes."

His eyes roam my face as he leans against the counter. "You think so?"

"I know so. How else do you think I survived a shitty marriage and met the man I love now? Mistakes teach us what the good things are in life. They're necessary but they aren't forever."

"Here's hoping." He tosses a dishrag in my direction and I watch as he walks over to the girl.

She smiles up at him, turning her body toward his. He's respectful, doesn't crowd her, and helps her put her jacket on. I watch as he follows her out, and then gaze around at the inside of The Café, completely content with my life. It's abuzz with life, laughter, family and friendship.

I realize that's what this place has come to be for me. The epicenter of the life I have now, not the afternoon my husband came through the door and beat me. He may have smothered me, but he didn't put out my fire.

And maybe that's the best lesson I've learned this year.

That fire burns bright, and I have no doubt that Anthony Bailey and the town of Laurel Springs will continue to stoke it.

That's what happens when you find your person and you find your home. When you find both in one spot? That makes you an incredibly lucky person.

And no matter how unlucky I've been in the past, right now, I'm the luckiest person I know.

EPILOGUE

Violet

NEW YEAR'S **Eve**

"Abs of steel, did you eat the cookies?" I glare at him from the kitchen of my side of the duplex.

Next month we'll be packing it up so I can move into his side, but right now, I'm thinking about banishing him.

"Those weren't for me?" He gives me an innocent look.

"Not the *whole* container, what am I supposed to take to Holden and Leighton's?"

"There's a package of Oreo's up in the cabinet. I mean nobody's gonna give two shit's, Vi. They were amazing, by the way."

Unbelievable. "Okay, but when we get there empty handed you can tell everyone you ate all of them."

He struts over, opening his arms up to me, crushing me to him for a hug. "I'll tell them it was all me, nothing to do with you. I'll brag about how good they were, and then laugh inside because they won't be able to eat them."

"You're awful." I laugh, slapping him on that fuckin' ridged stomach of his. Which I still can't figure out how he maintains.

"Only awful for you." He dips his head, kissing my neck for longer than necessary. He licks a path to this one point I've found to be erogenous and then he nips slightly.

"Mmmm," I respond in kind. "We can't stay here can we?"

"Nope, we gotta go to the bonfire," he moans right along with me. "After the bonfire though, we can do whatever you want."

"Then that's definitely what I'm looking forward to."

"Who knows." He shrugs as we put on jackets and grab a blanket, since it's a cold night. "Maybe we'll have a little celebrating to do."

I'm confused, but Anthony is secretive like that sometimes. "Whatever you say."

But as he helps me into his truck, my mind is racing, wondering what the hell he's thinking.

LAUGHS AND DRINKS are flowing in turn, except for the ones who've been tapped to be designated drivers, as the group of us crowd around the bonfire at Holden and Leighton's. She wears Ransom on her chest, keeping him away from the smoke as much as she can, but we can all tell by the way he kicks his feet and makes noise, he loves being around the group.

"What are we doing?" Trevor asks as he sits in the circle, Blaze in his lap. He takes a drink of his beer. "Someone said something while we were eating about saying what we were thankful for this year and what we want for next year."

"I'm down for that." Anthony has a seat and pulls me into his lap as well. God, I love when he does that. I get to be surrounded by two-hundred pounds of man who smells like the outdoors and a musk that's all his. "You start Havoc, since it's your house."

We all turn to the leader of the team. "This has been the best year of my life, I'd be lying if I said it wasn't. I'm thankful for every bit of it. What I want for next year? To figure out where that moonshine is coming from within the school. That's the number one thing we get to work on, on Monday morning."

Leighton gazes up lovingly at her husband. "I'm thankful for the man sitting next to me, the baby strapped to my chest, the friends who surround us with nothing but peace and love. What I'm looking forward to is being this one's Mom and finishing my degree. I don't want to leave Ernie's because I love it, but it's time."

I feel a stutter in my heart as she says those words. She'll leave, and hopefully I will too, but there's a fear I'll stay, because there won't be anything better for me out there.

"I hope Dad uses the dating app and profile I put on his phone." Caleb chuckles as he looks over at his dad. "This summer I'll be leaving, I have to start football practice and I don't want him to be alone. It's time he had some love in his life that didn't come from his right hand."

"Oh my God." I snort as I look at Mason's face. Those two have a relationship I've never seen a parent and child have.

"Good talk, son." He takes a drink of the sweet tea he has in a tumbler. "I'll have you know, I've been getting messages for over a week. I've been looking at them, but I can't make any promises. I'm just glad you came back to me, and when you leave, I'll deal with it. I'm more excited about where life is taking you, and how proud I am of you."

They embrace, and I feel tears stinging my eyes. This whole group loves each other so much.

"I think I speak for both of us" – Renegade puts his arm around his wife – "in saying that we're hoping to get a little more sleep in the next year. No more getting up through the night, no more teething, potty training is almost done. We're looking to thoroughly enjoy the next year."

Whitney nods. "And of course, my wish is for Alabama to win the championship; we were fuckin' robbed this year."

Laughter sprouts up again because everyone knows how much Whitney loves her college football.

Trevor has a sweet smile on his face as he gazes at Blaze. He pushes her red hair back from her shoulder, resting his head on it. "I can't believe we've kept this a secret from all of you, but we're gonna roll into the New Year with a huge change."

All of us are looking around at one another, wondering what he's talking about. They flash their left hands to us, and in that moment, we all see the wedding bands on them.

"You got married?" I jump up to get a better look.

"Yeah." Blaze grins, "A few days ago. We just got a wild hair and decided to go for it."

I hug her as the rest of the group shouts congratulations and gives out hugs. "Y'all are crazy." I shake my head laughing.

When I turn to walk back to Anthony, I stop, because he's on one knee in front of me, holding out a ring box. "Am I crazy too?"

Ace

My heart is pounding within my chest, the muscle beating against the bone, as I try to remember the speech I've prepared.

"I had a million things I wanted to say to you." I lick my lips, adjusting my body from where I'm kneeling on the ground. "But right now, I'm damned if I can remember any of them. All I know is that I love coming home to you, waking up to you, watching you make your dreams come true. Hell, Violet, I love you – everything about you. I want to spend the rest of my life loving you. I want you to know what a real marriage is, what a real man can make you feel like. Do me the honor of letting me share my life with you. Marry me?"

She drops to her knees in front of me, tears streaming down her face, and she whispers the most perfect word I've ever heard.

"Yes."

And in that moment, she makes me the happiest man in the world.

Purchase Menace!

MENACE - BOOK V

SUMMARY

The sexy, single dad of the MTF finally gets his turn...

Mason "Menace" Harrison

"Single and ready to mingle."

Those are the words above every picture of almost every female that strikes my interest on this dating app my son talked me into getting. After being a single dad for seventeen years, I'm ready to spread my wings, just not with most of the co-eds who keep hitting on me and calling me daddy.

Now that Caleb's in his senior year of high school, I feel like I can let go of the iron-clad control I've had on myself without his mom in our lives. I've enjoyed raising him, love the relationship we have, and while he went off the rails for a bit last year, we're now closer than we've ever been. He's got a full ride to the University of Alabama, and I've settled into my spot with the Moonshine Task Force.

But my son isn't a substitute for a woman in my bed, he isn't someone I can share my dreams with, and he's not the person I want to grow old with by my side. I'm not sure who that is yet, but the smokin' hot lady going by the name BeachBum83 is definitely holding every single bit of my interest.

Karina Holland

"Looking for a good time, maybe more..."

Those were the lamest words I ever typed in my life, but it was the best I had for the dating app my friend Violet talked me into joining. I didn't have any high hopes for myself. As a high school teacher, I'm sick of pervy dads hitting on me when they come in to discuss their child's lack of motivation to understand business courses and apply themselves.

Until the day Mason Harrison walks into my classroom. I had no idea Caleb's dad was the man I met off that dating app who showed me how flexible I really am in the back of his Jeep. Within minutes of him speaking to my class, he proved the sparks weren't one-time only when we christened my desk.

Mason and Caleb? They touch a part of my heart that no one's ever touched before, and when a threat shows up, I prove just how tough I really am.

PROLOGUE

MENACE

JANUARY

"Jesus, please tell me that's not what you're wearing tonight."

At the sound of my eighteen-year-old's too deep voice, I turn around. Like I find myself doing more often than not now, I stop a second and take in the moment. In a few months, he won't be here to make fun of what I'm wearing.

God, when did Caleb get to be a man standing in front of me? Older than I was when he came into the world screaming and shaking. I can still remember when they placed him in my arms and told me I was responsible for his entire life. He was so small, and I remember looking up at the nurse, asking if it was okay to hold him. Like I needed permission or something. I've taken the responsibility of raising him seriously – because I wanted to – but also because there was no one else to do it. He and I, we've come a very long way together.

"What's wrong with it?" I press my hands against my chest, smoothing the shirt down.

He rolls his eyes, a grin tilting up the side of his mouth. With that move, it's like looking in a mirror and seeing myself. "Everything, Dad, everything."

"Then why don't you help me? I haven't been out on a date in more years than I care to count." At least on one where I asked the woman out and I wasn't set up by someone with good intentions. This date? It's all mine. "You went out on one last night. Work your magic."

Looking back, I realize this is probably the moment, where I completely lost control of the situation.

I'M NOT A NERVOUS GUY. Not usually. Being a member of the Moonshine Task Force requires I keep my cool, but tonight, as I stand in front of a restaurant in Birmingham, my hands shake, my palms sweat. Rubbing the heels of my hands on the jeans Caleb made me change into, I cross my booted ankles. The shoes he also recommended, because I *looked too much like a dad* in my own choices. I have to admit what he put me in shows the muscles off I work hard on, but at the same time I kinda feel like a douche. I've never been a flashy kind of guy with anything. Gripping my phone, I nervously look at it, searching for a text message that she may be running late, or even one that she may be calling this off.

However, when I hear the unmistakable click of high heels against the pavement, I glance up, and thank the heavens above Caleb shamed me into changing. Pushing off the wall, I slowly make my way toward the woman coming in my direction.

Karina – who I'm meeting tonight thanks to the dating profile Caleb set me up with – had been cute in her profile picture. Her other pictures had been playful, one or two of them sexy, but goddamn my jaw is about to hit the ground. Flesh and bone is so much more beautiful than photography in this instance. The woman walking toward me, with a sway to her hips in skin-tight jeans is sex on a stick. I'm the type of man who isn't into super feminine women. I'm not into dresses and florals, I'm into jeans, shirts, leather, and everything this woman is wearing turns me on.

For the first time in years, I allow my eyes to seriously feast on a woman, on the picture she makes in front of me as she eats up the distance between us. Starting at the top of her head, I approve of the just-been-fucked tousled curls. The lights from the parking lot give her an ethereal glow in the January early-evening darkness. She's one of those unicorns whose hair doesn't look truly blonde or naturally brown. Moving down, her face doesn't look painted on, and I give a silent prayer of thanks for that. The white shirt she wears underneath a black leather vest is tight enough for me to make out her curves underneath. Phone numbers and first names are all we've exchanged besides the pictures on the website, and I'm dying to hear her voice.

"Karina?" I approach her, my hand out.

She stops in front of me, extending her own hand out, a confident smile on her face. I love women who have confidence, yet still allow themselves to be vulnerable. Her poised demeanor is already winning her bonus points with me. "Mason?"

Her voice is raspy; sounding like we just had a round of break-the-bed sex, her accent not southern, more northern, but it suits her. She sounds almost like I imagined she would. Our hands clasp together and goddamn fireworks go off in the distance. Hand to God, I feel more chemistry when the palms of our hands touch than I have in the last three women I've been set up with. A few of those I'd taken out on more than one date, one I'd even slept with, but this woman; she excites me. Truthfully more than with any woman in my history.

"Glad you could make it." I release her hand, before tucking mine in the front pockets of my jeans to keep them from reaching out to touch her. She probably wouldn't enjoy being fondled within two minutes of us meeting one another.

"I've never met someone in person from the app." She pushes a curl that's sticking to her lip gloss back as we stand in the cool night air, staring at each other. The way she's slowly looking me up and down before her eyes settle on mine sends a thrill through my body.

"Me neither," I admit. "But I figure somebody's gotta pop my cherry. Might as well be a gorgeous woman like you."

Her eyes flutter up and down my body again, reminding me of the way mine had taken in hers. "Can't say that I'm disappointed either. Had I known they made single dads like you, I might have given it a shot before now."

Pleasure radiates in my stomach; I'll never admit it to anyone else, but I've disappointed so many in my life that her words make me feel like I've finally done something right.

"Shall we?"

Putting on my best manners, I open the door for her, slightly pressing my palm to her lower back as we walk through the entrance. As we're seated, I can't help but hope this night isn't the biggest waste of time ever.

"THEY'RE ABOUT TO CLOSE." I motion at the now empty dining room, watching as some of the waiters are already starting to vacuum their areas, wipe down tables, and stack chairs.

"I guess we should go." Karina uncrosses her legs and stands up from the table. We'd paid an hour before, but we'd been having such a good time talking about our favorite TV shows and music, neither one of us wanted to go. It was nice, not having the heavy first date stuff with her tonight. This was fun, the best first date I've ever had, and something I didn't realize I needed.

"Yeah, I guess we should." I stand along with her, digging my wallet out of my back pocket before throwing down a generous tip. We'd kept this table for the whole night, and not once had the waitress acted like we were an annoyance. "Let me walk you to your car."

The fact she's parked under a security light scores her points with me. We've never talked about professions, though, so I don't want to get into safety precautions. All she needs to hear is some jaded cop telling her about the do's and don'ts of safety at night. Nothing sexier, I'm sure.

"Mason." She stops me with a tug on my hand. "I don't know about you, but I don't want this night to end.

Dragging her into my arms, I circle an arm around her waist. "Take a ride with me?" I motion to my Jeep, hoping like hell she'll say yes but knowing that it's probably a bad idea. Fuck it; I've made worse decisions before.

The nod is almost imperceptible, but it's there. Holding hands, we go back across the lot to where my Jeep sits, also under a light. It's a beacon on this night, and something tells me my life is never going to be the same again.

Karina

My heart pounds as he pulls me across the parking lot to where the manliest Jeep I've ever seen sits. It's a four door with streaks of mud along the quarter panels; a large tire rests on the back door. There are bits of chrome, and it appears the colors are black and a dark cherry. All the way around, sexy.

"You like to get dirty, huh?" I didn't mean the phrase the way it came out, but now that it's there, I don't take it back either. I motion to the mud caked on strips of paint, tilting my head toward the tires that are covered in clay.

His dark eyes meet mine, and a smile slowly spreads across his stubble-covered face. I get the feeling he didn't shave for our date, and I'm one hundred percent okay with that. "I do." His voice is deep as he walks me around to the passenger side, opening the door for me. "But the dirt you're talking about is thanks to my son and some friends of his."

How cute is that? He took his son out mudding. It was probably that little guy's dream come true. Before I go any further, I want to make sure there's not some woman hiding in the background with a *Fatal Attraction* plot for her baby daddy. "Are you close with his mom? I know from your profile you aren't married or divorced."

A pained look crosses his face. "She's not in the picture, hasn't seen him since he was a baby. I'm a single dad in the truest sense of the word."

He helps me up into the Jeep, then I turn in my seat. "Well, I for one, am glad you could get away tonight." It's got to be hard for him to find a sitter – or a sitter who doesn't hit on him, because my God, this man is hot.

"Me too." He leans in so far that our bodies are touching. Finally completely touching. It's been over a year since a man has touched me. After I was humiliated before my wedding, I swore off men until I joined the dating app. But there's something about *this man*, about the way he touches me, about the way he looks at me, the giddiness I've had in my stomach since I first saw him waiting for me tonight. I'm craving that physical connection, and before I know it, I've bridged the gap between us and fused our lips together.

There's a surprised *mmm* from him deep in his throat. It's a growl, husky with the depth of its sexiness. It spreads goosebumps all over my body, and I know then, as I feel his big hands wrap around my hips, that I'm a goner.

ONE DAY IN THE FUTURE, someone will ask me how I ended up in the backseat of a Jeep, in a restaurant parking lot in Birmingham, Alabama with the hottest first date I've ever had. When they ask me that question, I'll be honest: I have absolutely no idea how it happened. One minute, we were necking, him standing outside the vehicle, propped up against my body, my legs spread to allow him room. The next, our fingers were fighting for the rights to undress as much and as fast as the space we occupied would allow in the backseat.

"I don't normally do this," I pant as his rough palm travels up my stomach, until it encounters the lace of my bra.

Removing his lips from my neck nibbling slightly with his teeth, he whispers in my ear. "Can I?"

It takes me much longer than I care to admit, to figure out he's asking for permission to move the lace down. What a fucking gentleman. "Oh, please." I tilt my head back giving him complete control over where he wants to put those lips of his. Exposing my neck, and any other part he wishes to gorge on.

"God I wish I was shorter," he moans as he moves one of his forearms under my thigh, lifting it to give him more room to work.

"No, fuck no, don't be shorter. Don't be smaller, don't be anything..." Oh Jesus, he's grinding into me now. I breathe out a short pant, grasp his shoulders with my nails, and wish we had a bed to do this in. "Don't be anything other than what you are." I wrap that leg around his waist, digging my heel into his ass, needing the friction of our bodies rubbing together.

He abandons my neck, moving down to where my hard nipple is pressing against the fabric of my shirt. I want to lift it, expose my entire body to his eyes, look down and see his lips wrapped around my flesh. But he stops my hands as I go to lift my shirt.

"Don't wanna get arrested for indecent exposure," he growls as he takes the turgid tip through the material, swirling his tongue around it.

The move is one of the most erotic ever done to me. I can feel the motion, but not the wetness of his saliva for a few moments as it soaks through the cotton. "Oh yes!" I grasp his hair in my fingers, thrusting up into his mouth, shivering when I feel the scrape of his teeth.

There's flurry of activity where in the space of a few minutes, one of my shoes is kicked off, one pant leg, one side of my panties is pushed down to allow me a little room to move, and his jeans are pushed down below his hips. When I feel the velvet hardness of his cock against my thigh, I reach down, circling my fingers around the girth. He's hot and hard, the skin stretched tightly along the crest of his head. Both of us moan loudly. Blindly, he's reaching into his back pocket. Hearing the unmistakable crinkle of a condom wrapper, I use my palm to jack the length.

"Don't go too fast." His voice is guttural, like he's swallowed gravel or smoked a pack of cigarettes.

"No such thing as too fast." I open my eyes, watching him, watching me as I continue pumping his erection.

"Yeah there is, sweetness. It'll be when I spill all over that smooth thigh of yours, because this is the hottest thing I've seen in a really long time."

I wonder how long it's been for him. Does he go straight home after work, and be a good dad to his son? Does he make do with showers and porn? I want him to make do with me.

My eyes widen as he licks the palm of his hand and slaps it against my pussy. My body jumps, vibrates, as I feel the shock all the way through my system and into my core. "I'm sufficiently wet," I assure him, needing him to hurry this up, needing him to get rid of the ache.

"So you are." He takes his index and middle fingers, pushing them in, stretching me. I pull them into my channel, no problem, all I want is more. More of anything and everything he wants to give me.

When I feel a trail of precum on my thigh, I lift my eyes to his. "Unless you want to lose it before you get it in me, now might be the perfect time."

His brown eyes flair with desire as he levers himself off of me, his forearm flexes as he pushes the condom down on his hard length. When he thrusts home, a cry erupts from the back of my throat. It's been so long since I felt the push of a man inside me, so long since I felt desirable, and an even longer time since I wasn't going through the motions.

As we push and pull against each other, as my nails dig into his forearms, as his sweat drips off his face onto me, I'm aware that what we're sharing isn't something people share every day. There's something hanging in the air, something I'm not ready to put a label to, but it's not just a one-night stand. I know in the end, that's what will scare me.

"Karina, you grip me so good." He digs his fingers into the globes of my ass, pulling me tighter against him, adding a grind when he pushes all the way in. He rubs against my clit, and my eyes roll back in my head as I let myself experience this. I don't question it, don't let my mind take me away from it. I feel it.

"Fuck me, Mason, just fuck me."

And as I give myself over to him, I let it wash over me. I let the orgasm take me like the tide at the beach. It comes crashing in, before it leaves a peaceful wreck in its wake.

It's a beautiful mess as we come and he groans into my neck, I wonder how I'm going to let my walls down, how I'm going to recover from opening myself up so wide to this man.

This man, who I just met, who has just given me the most body-depleting orgasm of my life. This man who obviously has a small child, and a life I know nothing about. My feverish skin feels clammy as I realize the repercussions of what we've done.

Quickly, I make my excuses, sliding from the back of the Jeep, clothes barely fastened, looking every bit like I just got fucked. He hurries to catch up with me, stuffing himself back into his pants and getting buttoned right as we reach my car.

I don't even remember what I say to him, but what doesn't leave me is the sad look on his face in the rearview mirror as I drive away. I'm sad too, but I'm totally not ready for the force of nature that is Mason – whatever his last name is – because we never shared that.

One thing, however, is for sure. I won't be forgetting Mason ever, or this night for at least a few weeks. The tingle in my thighs, the bruises on my neck, and the soreness in my core will be reminders of the onetime Karina Holland fucked some guy off a dating app in a parking lot.

A grin plays at my lips. Best mistake of my life.

CHAPTER ONE

KARINA

"I LOVE YOUR MAKEUP TODAY, Ms. H!" Jess, one of the senior cheerleaders compliments me as she runs into class, right before the bell rings, indicating hallways are supposed to be clear.

Little does this girl know my makeup looks different because I'm trying to hide the damage Mason did to my neck on Friday night. Three days later, and nothing is fading. If anything, I had to mix different colors of concealer as it's gotten darker. But that's not something you can talk about in a high school classroom. Instead, I grin. "Thank you, Jess! I'm always looking to try new stuff, you know? Trying to keep up with you gorgeous ladies."

"Whatever, you don't even need it."

I wish I had the blind confidence of this girl. Granted, I have it now, but it took me a long while to get it after my engagement fell apart, but I've never had as much as she does. "How's everybody doing today?" I lean against my desk. One more class to go after this one, and then we're out of here. These kids, though, they're sometimes the hardest ones to control.

"It's Monday, and I've got a case of them." One of the football players in the front row sighs heavily, putting his chin on his hand. "Worked all weekend, and now here I am."

Sometimes I feel bad for these kids, and then I remember we're raising our future leaders, they're learning values, and this is an economics class. It's good for him to talk about work.

"I get you, I worked all through college. And having said that, you've brought up a good point, Johnathan." I turn around to the whiteboard in the room, and show them what I've been working on. "Because I worked through college and was able to pay for some of my classes, as well as room and board, this total–," I point to a number figure I'd circled during the first class of the day, "–is what I paid back for my college education."

If there's one thing I believe in, it's transparency. These kids have got to know where their money is going. "That was the principal, add on interest, and this one is the total I paid." I point to another figure. "However, if I hadn't paid down almost fifteen hundred dollars a semester–," I point to another one, "–this is how much I would have paid. Do you get what I'm saying?"

The numbers are vastly different, and this group of kids ready to take on the world is understanding these principles; I can see it clicking in their faces.

"You sayin' I need to forget college and go on down to the gulf to work on an oil rig?" a guy in the back blurts out.

The group laughs, and I can't help but chuckle too. He does have a point; education this day and age is expensive, and everyone has to weigh the benefits. "I'm saying this is a choice that shouldn't be taken lightly. You need to be fully informed before you make that decision, and that's what I'm here to help you do."

As I'm about to continue through the lesson plan I have for today, an announcement comes over the intercom. "Faculty and students, be advised we are to execute lockdown and shelter-in-place protocol. This is a precaution; there is no threat to your person. Execute lockdown procedures immediately."

My heart is in my throat as I hear the voice of our school secretary over the intercom. As I've been trained to do, I go to my classroom door, lock it, and close the blinds covering the pane of glass that allows us to see who's coming in when it's closed. I'm in an interior room, so there are no windows for me to close, meaning there's no way of knowing what in the world is going on. Feigning a positivity I don't feel, I speak loudly so that I can be heard over the muttering of the kids.

"As she said, there is no threat, but obviously we won't be getting much done today. Why don't you all talk amongst yourselves and I'll get some work done."

Faster than I should, I move to my laptop on my desk. Under the guise of doing lesson plans, I check my school email account.

Teachers and Staff,

During a routine check of the grounds, one of our security guards located what he believes to be three large boxes containing moonshine in one of the supply closets. Laurel Springs MTF and local law enforcement has been called in to investigate. Due to the heartbreaking situation that happened last year, we'd like to keep this as quiet as we can. Please do not allow students to speculate.

You'll hear officers and possible K-9s running up and down the hallways as they also execute a locker search.

We hope to be able to release you soon, where we will expedite getting everyone home.

Principal Taggert

The death of a senior had happened during my first year in Laurel Springs, and it had torn this small community apart. Now that I'm more ingrained into this community and entering my second year, tears spring to my eyes as I think about any of these kids hurt because of a stupid decision made to drink a bad batch of moonshine. I feel anger at whoever is bringing this into our school, who's selling it cheap enough that these kids don't want to go down to the local liquor store and beg someone to buy them beer. But most of all, I fear for them, because I'm scared to death they're going to lose someone else, and there's nothing we can do about it.

Menace

I hate this. Hate being at this school, searching for moonshine while my son is locked in one of the classrooms. I loathe that we haven't been able to find the person responsible, and failure is weighing on me. We've been working our asses off following leads, but there just aren't many, and what we have isn't solid. It makes me feel like not only a failure as a parent, but also as an officer of the law, especially as a member of the specialized Moonshine Task Force.

Havoc, the commander of the task force, pulls me aside. "You go with the K-9 Officer as he searches lockers. Since your son is a student here, and you already have a relationship with educators, and the principal, I feel like they would respect and listen to you more than me. Especially if y'all find something in a locker, and the student needs to be confronted.

Everything he says is understandable, but every part of my body is wanting to go to the classroom Caleb is in, and make sure he's okay. But this is part of my job, part of what I signed on for, and how I make my living. Until we get the scene cleared and make sure it's safe for everyone, there will be no checking on my son. "Got it, we'll be in touch."

The K-9 Officer out of the next county over and I make our way down the hallways. I can never remember his name; all I can recall is the dog's name Jinx. Typically the officer answers to it, too.

"Your son goes here, doesn't he?" he asks as we wait for an indication of a hit from the dog.

"Yeah, I bet he's freaking the fuck out in whatever classroom he's in, he knows exactly what this shit means."

"Do you want to go reassure him it's okay? We can do that corridor next," he offers.

"No, I'm actually not sure what room he's in, and if he's scared, the rest of them have to be too. As soon was get the sweep done, I'll track him down and make sure he's good."

Thirty minutes later, ten bottles of moonshine, three baggies of weed, and a bag of what looks like meth rocks have been confiscated to go along with the initial finding. And now, the dog is pawing and scratching at a classroom door, begging to get in.

"Jinx, halt!" The dog goes down on his belly. He's wearing a muzzle, so there's no way he can accidentally bite someone, but he wants in the door bad. He's whining, which I've never heard him do in the many times we've worked with this department.

"That's an occupied classroom," I whisper to him. "What the fuck is in there?"

"No idea, but Jinx wants it bad. Get Havoc and see what he wants us to do. I'd say let's take the kids out, but what if it's something one of them carried through the door and it left a trace?"

Within minutes, Havoc is standing with us in front of the door. The principal is there too as we all discuss on what the proper protocol should be.

"Goddamn it." Havoc runs a palm over his buzz cut. "None of this shit is easy. We're damned if we do, damned if we don't. But if Jinx is picking up something in there, we've got to investigate it, Taggert."

"I do agree with you." The principal nods. "However, I ask that you allow me to be present if you do have to take a student."

"We can do that. Can you instruct them to open the door?"

My nerves are on edge as I barely listen to what's going on before the door opens and we're permitted inside the classroom. Out of the corner of my eye, I see Caleb. More than anything, I want to stop what I'm doing, go over and tell him it's okay, but I can't. I have a job to do, and a lot of people counting on us to do the job well. As Jinx moves up and down between the students, he gets nothing. However, this is a science room and there are a ton of cabinets. When he hits on one, Taggert asks the teacher, a Mr. Cartwright, to unlock it and let us look inside.

When he does, Jinx goes insane and I wonder what in the fuck could be in a science teacher's cabinet. For more than five minutes, they pull out bottle after bottle, but nothing illegal is found.

"Probably just the mixture of smells," Havoc apologizes to Mr. Cartwright and Principal Taggert. As I watch the teacher, I'm not so sure, but that's just a sense I'm getting. Since there's no proof to the contrary, we leave the room, but not before I wave at Caleb and give him a reassuring nod.

Now it's time to take care of what we *did* find. I have a feeling cleaning up this particular scene and dealing with parents is going to make for a very long afternoon.

CHAPTER TWO

KARINA

M: **The weekend was busy, and yesterday was a crap day at work, but I wanted to let you know I had a great night with you! Maybe we can do it again! Ya know, get each other's last names this time?**

Glancing down at the phone in my hand, I read the text message again, calling myself a fool millions of times over. This marked the fourth day since I had my date with Mason, and the second day he'd texted me. It would also mark the second day I'd ignore him.

Tilting my head back, I inspect my neck in the bathroom mirror. I won't have to be caking on the concealer and foundation for much longer. The love bites are finally starting to fade, but I still have bruises on my thighs and in between them I can still feel a twinge when I move a certain way. Mason definitely left an impression on me unlike anyone else has before. A part of me already wants to see him again, to make sure I never have to know what life is like without these love bites, without this soreness again. But that's only one part. The other part? Not so sure. Totally unsure if I want to open myself up to potential heartbreak again. Do I want to put myself out there, and trust someone, only to have that trust be thrown back in my face? Confidence? I got it. Trust? Not there yet.

Picking my toothbrush up from the bathroom sink, I go through the motions of my morning routine. Like every other day, I brush my teeth while I'm waiting for my moisturizer to dry, and just like every day since I had the Jeep escapade, my thoughts drift back to Mason. There's something about him, about the way he'd plunged into me, the way he hadn't treated me like I was going to break. He'd manhandled me, dented my flesh, thrusted like he couldn't get deep enough. God, I'd loved it all. While my body is begging to meet Mason for another hot night in the back of his Jeep, there's something holding me back.

"Just call it like it is, Karina. You're scared," I taunt my reflection in the mirror. I try not to see how bright my eyes are, how alive I look. I haven't looked this way in a long time, and the brightness has been shining since my date. I've seen a spark inside me that I haven't had in years – maybe ever – in my adult life.

The passion I felt with Mason, I've never felt before. Not with the man I was supposed to have married, not with my high school boyfriend, not with anyone. And that's what scares me. Shouldn't I have felt the searing desire for the man I was going to marry? It's got me questioning everything I thought I knew about my wants and desires. It's also got me very confused, which is why I completely ignore the next two messages he sends me. When all I really want to do is answer them and plan out our next date.

"QUIET DOWN EVERYBODY!"

I raise my voice attempting to shush the twenty teenagers I teach in the last class of the day. There are times when I want my English class back, the original class I taught when I came here and the class I still teach at night on occasion, but typically I love that I've been able to mix things up. This last class of the day, let's just say if they were my first, I'd probably have given up on teaching. On a good day they're hard to control; today, they're trying my patience. They've been this way since we came back from our Christmas break. This group of seniors is ready for the year to be over. If they continue on the way they have been, I'll be glad to see the ass-end of this school year too.

"Okay, next week we'll have a few of your family members coming in to talk about their jobs and realistic expectations regarding real-life wages and education. What I want from you all tomorrow is a two-page paper on what your dream occupation would be, comparing it to what Laurel Springs has to offer. If you were to be able to get your dream job, what would you need to do to achieve it? How would you make it happen? If you don't make it happen, where do you think you'll end up?"

There's groans throughout the room and a few giggles. Sitting on my desk, I look out amongst these kids, who are so close to adults, and try to remember back to how I felt at this time in my life. My dream hadn't been to be a teacher. I'd wanted to be an artist. As a teenager, I'd dabbled in drawing, pottery, painting, and anything else I could get my hands on. Some days I wish I had made the decision to keep going, but at the end of the day, I do love these kids.

"I need that tomorrow," I remind them as the bell rings, signaling the end of my day. Already I know which ones will turn it in, and which ones won't.

"Caleb," I call out to one of my students as they file out. "Your dad is still good with coming to talk to us?"

All I know is his dad is a member of the Moonshine Task Force here in the county, and given that the kids have had issues with drinking, I think it would be good for him to talk to all of us.

"Yeah." He nods, waving to a girl who tells him bye, giving her a smile. This kid is going to have so many women at college. "This will be his mid-shift, but he'll be here for the second half. They've got it cleared."

"I'll thank him when he's here, but please tell him as well. It could be a bit of a hostile environment, considering what he represents."

We both know I'm talking about the moonshine being shared in the school. The teachers have been warned, but the perpetrator still hasn't been caught.

"Ms. Holland, my dad's a strong dude; he knows what he's in for."

I give Caleb a smile. "You know your dad better than anybody, so I'll have to trust you on this."

He pulls his bag over his shoulder. "I gotta get to conditioning. I'll see you tomorrow."

Giving him my own wave, I watch him leave; excited for the opportunity I'm going to be able to give my students.

Menace

"What does it mean when a woman you had a good time with and thought for sure you'd see again, completely stops returning your texts and doesn't answer your phone calls?" I ask my son as we sit down to dinner together.

He chuckles, taking a drink of his water. "You mean she ghosted you, Dad? One date and she ghosted you?"

"What the hell does *ghosted* mean?"

Sometimes when he talks, I feel ninety years old.

"When someone totally disappears from your life, without a trace."

Exactly what hot-as-hell-Karina did to me? "Yeah, that's it, then. She even took her profile down on the site."

"Damn, Dad. Are you that bad of a date?"

Truthfully, I hadn't thought I was. But maybe I've been out of the game longer than I thought. "I didn't think so." I load my fork up with the steamed broccoli I made.

"Go for it again, I can tell you had a good time. You were smiling for a couple of days after. You seemed not so serious for a while. It looked good on you."

"I smile." I'm offended that my son acts like I don't.

He chews thoughtfully on the chicken he grilled for us, while I'd made the sides. "You do smile, but you smile like I did a few months ago. It's for appearances purpose; it doesn't meet your eyes. Face it, Dad, you're sick of living your life alone. It's not a bad thing but be honest with yourself. For those few days after your date, your smile reached your eyes and you didn't look like you had the weight of the world on your shoulders."

Caleb and I, we've come a long way in the past few months since he was pulled over with his friends for having moonshine and drugs in a car, and since he was caught drunk in public. We've gotten closer, we call each other on our shit, and there aren't secrets between us anymore. Except for our love lives, he knows all about safe sex, and as long as he's practicing it, I'm good. I have zero desire to know who or what my son is screwing, and I'm sure he feels the same way about me.

"Then that's something I'll work on. I'm not gonna lie and say there aren't days and nights when I'm not lonely. When you were younger, it was easier for me to stay busy, and even during the last few years. I've worked a lot of overtime to be able to provide you with options for college, unlike what I had. Only to find out, you didn't even need it." I give him a grin. He's been accepted to the University of Alabama on a full-ride football scholarship, and I've never been prouder of him. All the time I'd worked, all the money I'd saved, it's still worth it, because it'll give him a jumpstart on life I never had. But I'm quickly beginning to realize I've got to make myself happy too. He's not going to be here, and if my life is wrapped up in him? Then there's no life for me to live.

"Now's *your* time, Dad." He nods toward me. "You do you, I don't need you around all the time like I used to. As long as we get to eat dinner together a few times a week and get to spend a couple of days a month together, I'm good. If I have to share you with a woman, I will. You're gonna be lonely when I leave for Tuscaloosa in the summer."

My chest physically hurts at those words. "Don't remind me. I don't know what I'm going to do without you here."

"Now's the time to find out, don't waste it. I'm sure you'll find something or someone to occupy your time with." He flashes me a smartass grin.

"I'm sure I will too."

Truth was though; I really wanted to spend my time with Karina. If only I could get her to return my attempts to get in touch with her.

GROCERY SHOPPING IS my least favorite responsibility of being an adult. Always has been, always will be. I can do laundry, vacuum, dust furniture, passably cook – you name it, I do it all. The one thing I typically fail at?

Grocery shopping. I never go until we have absolutely nothing in our fridge. My list is literally a mile long on my phone, and I'm already over it.

"Hey Mason." I hear a female voice, as I round the corner into the produce section.

"Hey." I wave slightly at the woman speaking to me. I've seen her around town before, have spoken with her a few times, but I can never remember her name. And right now she's standing in front of the asparagus I need to go with one of the meals I have planned for the week. That's right, I'm a meal planner. If I wasn't, nothing would ever get cooked or we'd just have cereal every night. "Mind if I get in there." I point behind her. "I'm kinda in a hurry; it's been a long day."

She looks me up and down, taking in the uniform I'm wearing. I've gotten enough looks like this to know she appreciates the way I fill it out. She's probably thinking of an officer fantasy in her head, and I'm the star of the show. Today I don't have patience for it. All I want to do is get home, make dinner, and chill. The one woman I want the attention of still isn't paying any to me.

"I'm sure you did. Must be hard to go home and take care of your son at the end of the day by yourself."

It takes everything I have not to roll my eyes. "These days not so much, considering he's an adult. Turned eighteen at the beginning of the month. He doesn't need me all the time anymore." I make a lunge at a wrapped bunch of asparagus.

She grabs hold of it, yanking it to pull me closer to her. "Then maybe you need someone to take care of you? There's gotta be needs you have that aren't being fulfilled."

Her voice has dropped to levels that just aren't appropriate for the grocery store, and they aren't appropriate for me – ever. This isn't the woman I want, she's not the one who's been keeping me up at night with a hard-on. She's not the one I've been fantasizing about as I take care of business in the shower. Out of the corner of my eye I see hair and a body I would know anywhere. She's leaving the grocery store, and all I want to do is run after her, ask her exactly why she's been avoiding me.

Ignoring the woman still speaking to me, I move my cart toward the checkout lines, but we have people, carts, and checkout lanes in between us. I can't leave the food I've picked up; we need it at the house. With one last ditch effort, I yell her name.

"Karina!"

She glances back, her eyes widen in recognition, and just like that she's swallowed up in the afternoon rush of grocery shoppers. "Damnit." I beat my hand against the handle of the cart.

Something I do know for sure now, that I didn't know with certainty before: She lives here. No one else would be going to this hole-in-the-wall one stop shop if they didn't. Now I just have to figure out what it'll take for her to speak to me again – and maybe give me another shot.

One thing about me is that I don't give up easily. I felt something with this woman, something I've never felt before, not even with Caleb's mom, and I'll be damned if I just let it walk away without trying to explore it.

One way or another, hopefully I'll get an answer.

CHAPTER THREE

KARINA

MY HEART POUNDS as I throw my grocery bags into my trunk and then hop into my car speeding away from the grocery store. I'm not sure why it unnerves me so much that Mason was there, not sure why seeing him caused such a reaction within me, I'm seriously not sure of anything right now. All I know is the way he made me feel in those few hours I'll never forget. I want it again, but I'm not sure if I'm brave enough to invite this man back into my life. He could break me in ways my ex-fiancé never did.

Nothing I got at the grocery is in danger of spoiling, and right now I'm not looking to go home to an empty house. With my free hand, I pick my cell phone up from my cup holder and use the voice to text option to text one of the only friends I have here, Violet. Even being here for almost two years, it's been hard to make acquaintances. Most people don't come to Laurel Springs; most are born here and move away or are born here and stay here. It's not necessarily the destination of many graduates, but I've found a home here. One I enjoy, even if it's lonely sometimes.

K: Care to get a coffee? I really need someone to talk to.

V: Sure! Anthony's working tonight, and I just left The Café, it was totally dead tonight. If you don't care that I'm dressed like a waitress, I'll be there.

K: Meet you there in about five minutes.

I'm taking my coffee to an empty table in the back when Violet walks in, wearing her uniform and a warm jacket. Her hair is in one of the fancy braids she likes to wear, and I'm struck by how happy she looks. There's a glow to her face, a spring to her step, and an easy smile as she places her order. A year ago, she hadn't been happy, she hadn't worn her hair in a braid, and we hadn't even been friends. I was blessed to meet her at a time when we both needed one.

She waves at me and I wave back as I take off my coat, hanging it on the back of my chair. Having a seat in front of the window, I cross my legs and watch as families go about their nightly routines. Since I've been in Laurel Springs, it's been unusual for me to see people actually wearing jackets, but today they're dressed in hoodies, beanies, and gloves. A cold front moved in this afternoon, and if I didn't know better, I'd think I was back in Pennsylvania.

"How's it going?" Violet asks as she has a seat across from me, getting situated much the same way I did.

"Not too bad," I lie, wondering if it sounds forced to her like it sounds forced to me.

Violet tilts her head, pursing her lips, choosing to call me on my bullshit "You say that enough times and I might believe it. You're talking to *me*, Karina. What's happening?"

Taking a drink from my cup, I sigh. It's tortured, frustrated, and full of every emotion I've been feeling for the past year. "I went out on that date with the guy from the app."

"It went bad?"

I'd kept her out of the loop when I'd gotten back, because I'd been conflicted about my feelings, and a bit surprised that he and I had gone that far in the backseat of his vehicle. It's totally out of character for me, and I hadn't exactly wanted to hear her vocalize the things I already knew I was feeling. Why I worried, I'm not sure now, because if anyone *wouldn't* look upon me with judgement, it would be Violet. After all, she was married when she met her now fiancé.

"No." I shake my head, recalling just how much fun I had with Mason. Before the physical aspect had started, we'd laughed, told jokes, and generally had a great meal together. "It went amazing. We had dinner in Birmingham, shut the damn place down, and when it was over..." I trail off, not sure how much I want to share.

"What happened?" Violet presses me to continue. By looking at her, I know she can tell I'm holding something back.

"Me and this guy." I play with the lid on my coffee. My eyes not meeting hers, not because I'm ashamed, but I don't want her to know how much it affected me. "We had the most passionate encounter I've ever had. Like I didn't know I was capable of that kind of heat with someone. He made my body shake, made me forget who I was, where I was, and made me picture a future that wasn't alone."

"Sounds like he is an amazing guy. Why aren't you happy about it?"

"The things he made me feel." I shake my head, trying to articulate my fears. "They scare me. I mean I was engaged to another man, was ready to spend the rest of my life with him. My ex-fiancé, Braxton, never inspired the types of feelings this guy did. That's what scares me. If I were to give him the option, he'd have power over me. And I gave Braxton power, enough power to bring me to my knees and make me move thousands of miles to get away from the memories."

Violet is quiet for a few moments, fiddling with her container of coffee. She sighs, pulling her long-sleeve shirt over her fingers, and then bringing her arm up to push her hair behind her ear. "Take it from someone who knows, Rina. Sometimes giving another person that type of power is good. Sometimes it's the best present you can give yourself. Why not give it a shot and see what happens between the two of you?"

"He's a single dad." I use the excuse I've been running through my head for the past few days. I play with the bracelet on my wrist, smiling wistfully as I think about the things Mason told me about his day-to-day life. "The mother isn't in the picture, but I'm not sure he wants to bring another woman into his kid's life."

"Single dad's need love too," she giggles, winking at me. "Probably need more love than the average man, if he's been alone a long time. Get what I'm saying?"

He'd needed a lot of love. That I could categorically say for sure. "I don't know." I shrug, at a loss for words. "I just don't know. I saw him at the grocery tonight, and I ran from him."

"You ran?" Violet laughs. "I've never known you to run from anything, in the short amount of time we've known one another."

"I know this is totally not the person I am."

"He must have had a really nice dick," Violet mumbles, her cheeks turning a rosy red color.

I spurt my coffee out, before trying to wipe down the table. "Damn girl, Anthony has loosened that mouth of yours; I can't believe you just said that."

"Am I wrong?" She raises an eyebrow to me, daring me to tell her she is.

No she's not, and that's the bitch of the situation. She's totally right, and I want to know everything about the man I've had a taste of. The thing is, I just have to reach out, grab hold, and not let go. The question is – am I brave enough?

I'd like to think so, but sometimes the bravest can be the weakest. Given that fact, I have a lot to prove to myself.

Menace

Irritated with what went down at the grocery store, I'm angrily throwing my bags onto the counter, trying to slow my accelerated heartrate. For so long I lived like a damn monk, and the first time I try to get back out into the dating world, it backfires on me. Maybe I'm not cut out for this, maybe I'm just meant to be alone and have a booty call here and there.

But that's not true. I know it's not true.

If there's something I know about myself, it's that I truly want to share my life with a partner. I'd give up anything in the world for my son, but I'm tired. Tired of being alone, tired of not having anyone to discuss problems with, tired of not having someone to share my day with, and really fucking tired of my bed being empty.

Working on putting the groceries away, I think back to the day Caleb was born. Me and Maggie, his mom, were so young, we didn't know what to do. Hell, our parents weren't even there because they didn't agree with us keeping him. Throughout the entire seven months I was aware of the pregnancy, abortion and adoption were words thrown around every day from one of their mouths. I'd fought tooth and nail to get her to keep Caleb, and neither of my parents had been supportive. Eventually my mom came around, but my dad and I still have a strained relationship. I don't see that ever changing, which is why my relationship with my own son means so much to me.

When they put his little body into my shaking hands, he looked up at me, eyes wide, nose scrunched and I lost my heart to him in that moment. I knew without a doubt, at sixteen-years-old I would do whatever it took to make this boy of mine a success. It's been a hard eighteen years. We've faced struggles that neither of us were prepared for, crazy days of happiness, and lows that took us to the depths of anything we'd ever gone through. We've persevered, though, and I've done it all without Maggie's help. Together we've been a unit that no one could break, and in the summer that's exactly what's going to happen. He's going to leave and start a whole new life without me. Which means it's time for me to figure out what I'm going to do with mine for the next thirty years.

"What did that box of cereal do to you?"

Surprised, I turn around, seeing Caleb come through the garage door of our house. "I thought you were working tonight."

"Super slow." He leans into the fridge and grabs out one of the already-made salads I bought at the store. "Like literally in the two hours I was there, I waited a total of two tables. We called Ernie and he told us to go ahead and close for the night. Too cold." He shrugs off his hoodie, before opening a bottle of salad dressing, pouring some on, and then closes the lid on the salad. I watch as he shakes it around, something he's done since he started eating them, a smile ghosting across my face, before he sets it down, pops the container, and starts to chow down. Probably what I'm going to miss the most are the little quirks that are his, the ones that are familiar. Like the way he leaves his shoes at the front door, just slightly in the way so I trip over them at least twice a day. The way he will use the last of the shampoo and not tell me, but let me find out by grabbing the bottle and it being empty.

Empty-nest syndrome will hit me like a ton of bricks. That's one thing I can say for certain. I already know it, can already feel it.

"Hungry? I haven't eaten yet, I could cook."

He picks up the cell phone, flipping it over to check the time. "Nah, fix whatever you want. This'll be good for me. I don't need to eat again until tomorrow morning; this'll be my last meal. I didn't train today."

If there's one thing this kid is serious about, it's his training, and I thought he went right after school. "Did they cancel it?"

Caleb keeps his gaze on the food in front of him as he shakes his head. "Nah, I took Jess home, she didn't have a ride and missed the bus."

Two major things have happened to my son since Christmas. I bought him a truck, it isn't much but it gets him from point a to point b without me having worry about how he's getting there, and Jess. Jess kinda took me by surprise, but she's a senior heading to Ole Miss on a cheerleading scholarship the same time he leaves. The way his cheeks tinge pink, I wonder if taking her home is all he did.

"Took her home, huh? Shoulda left you at least an hour to get some training in." I mentally calculate the time in my head.

I can't help giving him shit. Hell, if he followed in my footsteps, I'd already be a grandfather. Every day I thank God he has more sense than I ever did.

"We just hung out." He shrugs, working really hard to swallow the bite of food he's taken.

Giving him a look, I can't help the grin that tugs on my lips. "Yeah, I'm sure you *just hung out*. You're so full of shit."

He sighs, refusing to meet my eyes. "Dad, she's hot and she likes me. It's nothing serious, we're both leaving in a few months."

"Just be smart about it." I open the fridge and grab out the other salad, doing the same thing Caleb did to get mine ready to eat.

"No kids until I got a ring on this finger." He holds up his ring finger, wagging it at me.

"Definitely, kiddo, make sure the girl makes an honest man out of you first."

Together we look at each other, smiles playing on both of our faces as we start laughing loudly. Damn, I'm gonna miss these moments when he moves away.

CHAPTER FOUR

KARINA

ONE MORE CLASS TO GO. That's what I keep telling myself as this day drags on, longer and longer. I've been hit on by two men and one woman already, thanks to the parents coming in to tell us about their jobs. It's all for the good of the kids. My mantra since this day started. They need the real-world experience that I hadn't had. I want this for them, so I'll make the best of whatever else we have coming our way today.

I just made an escape to the restroom, to wash my hands after one overzealous father shook it so hard, he left his sweat on me. Not one of the finer moments of my life. That's for damn sure. Typically, I'm speaking to students as I walk through the halls, but today, I just want to get this over with, go home, and indulge in an entire bottle of wine.

"Hey, Ms. Holland, my dad's here, is it okay if I go get him?" Caleb asks as I pass him in the hallway heading for our room.

Checking my watch, I see the bell is about to ring, but give him the permission he's seeking. "Sure, just make it quick. We're anxious to see what he's got for us."

Caleb gives me a salute and heads toward the office. I steel my reserves and head for my classroom. One more class to go.

I FEEL it the second he steps over the threshold. The hair on the back of my neck stands and I feel goosebumps along my forearms. The awareness in my body, the spark that ignited between us is still there. Even after me trying to ignore it since we found it. Chances are I'll always feel this spark, I will forever know when he's entered a room I'm in. I sit up straight from the slouch I had been in, as every part of my femininity stands at attention.

"Ms. Holland, this is my dad." Caleb brings him over to my desk, and I know before I look up who this is. I just know. And then our eyes meet, and I'm taken back to that night. His dark eyes clash with mine, and it's like he's stripped me naked in front of my classroom.

"Mason." He sticks out his hand for me to shake it, which is the very last thing I want to do. I want him to devour me, show me everything he showed me in the backseat of his Jeep. Screw this class I'm supposed to pay attention to. All I want to do is pay attention to the two of us.

I clear my throat, because I'm finding it a little hard to concentrate. "Karina," I answer back as I finally do shake the hand outstretched to me.

For longer than I care to admit, we stare at one another. "Class, please welcome Caleb's dad and listen as he speaks about what he does all day."

I watch as Mason waves to the class and every girl in the room eyes him like a piece of meat. Never mind that he's too old for every single one of them. A part of me wants to tell them to back off, I've had this man, and he's way too much for any of them.

"Hi, I'm Officer Mason Harrison with the Laurel Springs Police Department, and I'm also known as Menace with the Moonshine Task Force."

Fuck me, this guy is a cop. No wonder his body is to die for and he made me open up so easily on our date. I wish I could tell you that I paid attention to everything he said in the next forty-five minutes, but the truth is I don't. I just listen to his voice, watch his amazing ass, and try to figure out how to tell him I want to see him again. Every excuse I've given myself is now out the window. Now that I've had a chance to see him, touch him, and look into those amazing eyes of his again. I'm done running, done hiding. I want it all.

When the bell rings, I don't even bother to dismiss the class, all I want for them to do is get out so I can be alone with him. Part of me is excited, and part of me is scared when that exact scenario presents itself to us.

Menace

The bell rings, and with it being the last class of the day, they file out quickly. Caleb doesn't speak to me, but he gives me a wave. These days I know where he's going. Straight to The Café, and then he'll hit the gym by himself. Conditioning will be important for him when he gets to Tuscaloosa, even if it is mid-January right now. There's a slim possibility he'll give Jess a ride home, but I try not to think about that. The aftermath of them filing out leaves me alone with Karina Holland, star of every dream I've had since the date we went out on.

The door shuts and the two of us lock eyes. The tension and chemistry is enough to explode the entire school, much less this room. From where I stand, I can see her pulse throbbing at her neck. Her tongue swipes against her upper lip in a full lick before pulling the bottom one between her teeth. Her eyes break from mine, traveling down my chest, stopping at my hand, zeroing in on my fingers.

Oh Karina, I know exactly what you're remembering, and with the electricity literally popping between us, I know how you feel.

A smile spreads across my face, as I hold up one of the fingers she's staring at so hard. Many of the guys say I have no swagger, cause I'm older than they are, because I've been out of the game longer than they have, but they have another thing coming. I've got a lot of alphaness that's built up over my years of being alone, I'm *nothing* if not a hardass. Strutting over to the classroom door, I shut it, flipping the lock and closing the blinds.

"What are you doing, Mason?" The question is breathless. With anticipation? Maybe. Or remembrance of how we heated up the backseat of my Jeep. It doesn't matter to me, all that matters is I get a chance to make her miss me. To show her again what the two of us shared.

Not uttering a word, I advance on her. When I get to within arm's reach, I stop. Lifting an eyebrow, the permission I ask her for is silent. She's given plenty of time to walk away, but she doesn't. That's when I invite myself to get all up in her business.

Pushing her against the desk, I shove my thigh between hers, propping her up against the edge, barely taking her feet off the floor. Leaning in, I plant my hands on the wood, surrounding her with my body. My lips next to her ear, in this position; I tilt my neck and speak softly.

"Is there a reason you didn't return my calls, Karina? Why you didn't answer my texts? Why you all but ran from me in the goddamn grocery store two days ago?"

Her breath is hot against my neck. I can feel it coming in short pants against my skin. Can almost feel her arousal through the way her mouth opens, then closes, opens again as she gusts a breath against my flesh.

"I...I...I don't know," she stutters.

Taking my left hand off the desk, I pull back slightly so I can see her face. With my middle and index finger extended and the rest tucked into my palm, I run them against her lips, barely pressing on the moist flesh. Without much prompting she sucks, taking them up to the first knuckle. When I attempt to extricate them, she sucks harder.

"You like to try my patience." My voice is deep as I take my other hand off the desk, reaching up to her jaw. Softly I exert pressure, getting her to lessen the force enough so I can withdraw.

"Mmmm," she moans at the loss, chasing me as I pull away.

"Now tell me *why* you didn't return my attempts to get in touch with you."

She closes her eyes, leaning her head back on her shoulders. Taking the two fingers she slickened for me, I sneak my hand up the skirt she's wearing, bypass her lace panties, and thrust them into the heat I remember. She sighs heavily, bringing her head back up straight, before leaning it on my shoulder.

"Why?" I question again, going after her pleasure, knowing I don't have much time. Wanting her to feel everything we did that night.

"This scared me." She grips my ass in her hands, pulling my body close as she thrusts against my invasion.

"Me?" I take hold of the opening she left at her neck, pushing my lips against the tendons, working the skin with my lips.

"The way you–," she shoves against my fingers, chasing them when I withdraw again, breathing hard, twisting her hips, "–the way you, make me–" she opens her mouth, whining when I press in, then withdraw, anchoring her body with the weight of mine, not letting up with my teeth and tongue. "The way you make me feel," she finally rushes out in a tumble of words and breath, jumbled up as she thrusts hard against my fingers.

Lifting my mouth up from her neck, I grasp her earlobe between my teeth, nipping as I add my thumb to the mix down below. She's shoving against my fingers, trying to get purchase on her heels, but I'm still holding her just out of reach. "How do I make you feel?" I let my free hand drift up from her neck, grasping her hair tightly in my fist, positioning her how I want her.

"Out. Of. Control." She squirms against my ministrations. "Hot. Sexy. Horny," she finishes, kicking the heels off, planting her ass completely on the desk, and wrapping her legs around my waist as tightly as our position allows.

"Lose control for me then, Wild Girl, show me." I open my mouth against her neck, sucking harshly, as I feel her tighten around my fingers.

"Mason." She grabs hold of my shirt. "Don't stop, please don't stop."

The cramp in my forearm tells me I should, but I don't listen. I started this and now I'll finish it.

"Yes!" She pitches herself against my body, and I feel her let go against me.

This woman will never be able to fake an orgasm. Never. When she comes, her whole body is into it, and it leaves me with a big smile on my face. She's panting as I withdraw my fingers from her pussy and then attempt to straighten her out.

She reaches down to the erection tenting my tactical pants. Grabbing both her hands in one of mine, I stop her from making contact.

"While I'd love for you to reciprocate, Rina, I gotta get back to work."

Her dark eyes are bright with desire as she gives me a steamy smile. "You sure?"

I give her a wink before shoving the fingers I had inside her into my own mouth, making a presentation of licking them clean. My voice is raw when I answer. "Not what I wanna do, but I'll go back with your scent in my nose and your taste on my tongue. Maybe I'll see you tonight? Ya know, if you answer my call or text?"

She's still sitting on the desk when I get to the door, unlock it, and adjust my pants before I exit. I can see her reflection in the glass.

"Mason?"

"Yeah?" I turn around.

"Text me again. This time I'll answer."

Nodding, I smirk as I leave. Damn right she will.

CHAPTER FIVE

KARINA

I'M on my second glass of wine tonight, and my mind is still completely blown that Mason is Caleb Harrison's dad. I'm also still trying to recover from the way I orgasmed in my classroom. This man makes me do things I could lose my job over, but that fear pales in comparison to the way he makes me feel. Dear God, my face gets red as I think about it, body heats up as I relive it. I'm five minutes into the best daydream I've ever had when my phone rings. Glancing at the caller ID, I see that it's my mom.

"Hey Mom," I answer, sitting up straight and setting my wine over to the side. I'm doing my best to appear like I'm not half-way tipsy, but I'm not sure how well it's working.

"Hey," she answers, and I can hear the smile in her voice. "How's it going down south? We miss you."

I know she does. Every time she calls me, she doesn't necessarily lay on a guilt trip, but she lets me know how much they miss me at home. I haven't yet told her Philly doesn't feel like home anymore or that I'm happier in Laurel Springs than I ever was there. "It's going good. My students are getting restless, they're itching to graduate." I try to keep the topics we discuss safe. No way I can tell her what happened in my classroom today.

"Ready to get away from home, huh?"

Her words are met with my sigh. "Mom, I'm happy here. I know I'm far away, and I know that worries you, but I'm making friends and a new life here. I love it, even if it's not where you think I should be."

The disapproval is coming through the phone line, feeling like a boulder between us because of her judgement. "I just don't want you to forget you have a family here."

I'm glad she can't see my eye roll. "I'm not going to forget it, just please respect the fact that I have a new life here. I'm happy in Alabama."

The strained silence on the line is one of the reasons I left in the first place, but I can't tell her that. Just as I'm about to make my excuses and get off the phone call, she talks.

"Karina, there's something I need to tell you. I don't even know if you care anymore, but I feel like you need to know."

"Just spit it out, whatever it is, I'll deal with it."

She struggles, I can tell because it takes her longer than normal to lay whatever boom this is down on me. "Braxton and Sofie are getting married."

Those names are my ex-fiancé and my ex-best friend. I knew it had to do with them by the way she was beating around the bush. "Good for them." I let out a breath I hadn't been aware I was holding.

"This has to hurt, Karina." She keeps talking, but I stop listening.

In actuality, the pain I'd always assumed would be there when I found out this news isn't there. If they found love and they were able to keep it going, good on them. Not everyone can find someone to make them happy, and not everyone can make a commitment. I just hope Braxton doesn't do to her what he did to me. Either way, that's none of my business now.

"Are you okay, Karina?"

"I'm great, I'm happy for them. Mom, I've moved on."

"Have you met someone?"

Right now I'm not sure what Mason and I are, so I don't really want to talk about it with her. "It's very new, Mom. If it gets serious, I'll introduce you."

"I just want you to be happy."

"Mom, I am happy." And I realize I am. Back when I'd first moved here, I wasn't. The way I'd run had been a form of self-preservation, but now I'm in a place I love, teaching kids I love, and nothing else could be better.

"Love you, Mom. Talk to you again soon."

And as I get off the phone, I get a text from the man who's occupied my thoughts all afternoon.

Menace

Since I left the high school, I've been an uncomfortable and moody bastard. A part of my conscience berates itself for pulling that shit with Karina in her classroom, the other half of me congratulates myself for taking what we both wanted. It's been a long time since I did it, almost thought I'd forgotten how to assert myself, but I'm glad to know that part of me is very alive and well. My dick is still hard, but I know I'll have a semi until I'm deep inside her again. After making two rounds of the route I've been assigned and an hour before I go off-shift, I park on the side of the road, setting up my radar gun. With any luck, I won't have anyone speeding and it'll allow me to take care of some business.

For the first ten minutes, I catch up on paperwork, and then I can't wait anymore. I pick up my cell phone and send Karina a message.

M: Imagine my surprise when I walked into my son's classroom and saw you today.

The surprise had been immediate. Never had I imagined this hot-as-hell woman to be a teacher. We never had a teacher that looked like her when I was in school, that's for damn sure.

K: Surprise was mutual, big guy. When you talked about having a son, I imagined some cute little kid about six-years-old. Never in a million years did I think you were Caleb Harrison's dad. How old are you? Did you lie on the app?

I chuckle at her question. It's one that's routinely asked when I explain I'm his dad and he's my son. Sometimes it irritates me, because I've answered it so often, but I find I like sharing pieces of myself with her.

M: No, I'm 34...almost 35. Caleb was a very early in life surprise.

K: I can't wait to hear the story. Caleb's a special kid, he's been awesome to have in my class.

While I feel a twinge of pride, I know sometimes Caleb's a smartass and he's probably tried her patience a time or two.

M: No need to blow smoke, Teach. I know my son. He can be an ass, and he can have the smartest mouth on him, but he's intelligent when he puts his mind to it.

K: You know him well...

M: It's just been us for a long time we have to know each other well. When can I see you again?

The question is impulsive, but I know if I don't make an effort with this woman, she'll slip between my fingers. After waiting as long as I have to get back in the game, I don't want to let her go. Not after the time we had, not after she's monopolized my thoughts, and definitely not after I've found her again.

K: Tomorrow is Friday, are you free tomorrow night? Or do you work? I'm assuming you work some crazy shifts.

M: Sometimes, but I work a day shift tomorrow. I'm free for the night. Caleb's got a date and won't be home until late.

K: Where you taking me, big guy?

That's a good question, there aren't a lot of good places in Laurel Springs, but we can't drive to Birmingham every time we want to go out on a date.

M: Wherever you want to go, as long as it's in town. I have to work early on Saturday.

K: Is the Mexican place good? I've never eaten there. Only The Café and the fast food places, or I cook at home.

M: Yeah, it's one of the better ones I've been to, and I've lived all around the country.

K: Okay, I'll see you there tomorrow. Will you pick me up and take me home so I can have a margarita or two?

Immediately a smile spreads across my face. I've never had a woman ask that question before, and I kind of like it. She's cute and sexy at the same time. Hopefully she wants to get a little tipsy so we can take advantage of our situation.

M: It'll be my pleasure. Pick you up at six?

K: Sounds perfect! See you then, Mason.

As I put my phone back in the cup holder, I do it with the huge smile still on my face.

"DAD, why didn't you tell me you went out on a date with Ms. Holland?"

Caleb is waiting for me when I get off-shift, sitting in the living room, watching TV in the early-evening light. I don't know how he knows, but he's always been good at guessing things.

"I didn't realize she was Ms. Holland," I honestly tell him. "We didn't exchange last names, didn't tell each other what we did for a living. She knew I had a son, but she didn't know your name and didn't know how old you were."

"The chemistry was so hot between you two that most of the people in the classroom picked up on it. I think I know why you were smiling so much after your date with her. There's a lesson here." My son folds his arms over his chest. "Was this really the smartest thing you could have done? I mean she could have hurt you, abducted you, and left you on the side of the road."

He's giving me back everything I've told him about going with people he doesn't know. "It was careless of me, and irresponsible. I know, I know." But the truth is, I'd been so excited to go out with a woman who didn't know my life as a single dad, that I'd pushed all that away.

"I hope you've learned from your mistake. I won't say I'm angry about it, but I am disappointed in you." He uses the same voice I use with him when he's done something to disappoint me, and when I see the grin threatening across his face, I throw my jacket at him.

"You little shithead." I don't even know what to say to him.

"For real though, Dad, can I be real with you for a second? Dude's want to get with Ms. Holland. Like the new science teacher, he's been trying to hit it for at least the last few months. Coach has asked her out twice, and she's said no both times. But you, something about you got her to go out with you."

"Well I don't know what it was, I was myself when we emailed and texted."

"Don't let this go to your head, but you're kind of a cool guy when you aren't trying so hard."

"Gee thanks, Caleb."

"It's what I'm here for." He turns to look at me. "And real talk, Ms. Holland had some gnarly looking hickeys on her neck after the date the two of you went on. She tried to hide it, but you could tell. All of us were trying to figure out who hit that, because Ms. Holland is hot as hell. She doesn't know it, which makes her even hotter."

Now I've heard enough. "Look, if I'm going to date her, and I really would like to, I can't have you checking her out if I bring her around here."

"Dad." He rolls his eyes. "I check out lots of women, I'm a teenage guy. But I would never disrespect you, and if she's someone you want to spend time with, I want you to do it. You've lived your life for me, for a lot of years. I want you to live it for yourself now, make yourself happy."

"You know what? I'm going to. Wherever this goes with her, even if it doesn't end up lasting, I'm going to experience it."

Mind made up, I realize I'm ready for it. Completely ready to try my hand at an adult relationship, and no matter how it ends up, I'll be thankful for the experience. Because Karina Holland has fuckin' turned my life upside down, sideways, and destroyed my careful existence.

CHAPTER SIX
KARINA

"SHIT!" I hiss between clenched teeth as I put my finger a little too close to my curling wand, slightly burning the tip as I artfully arrange the last strand of hair I've curled around my face. Totally what I get for not using the glove provided, but I have more control with bare hands; and honestly, I like to live dangerously sometimes.

Giving myself a once-over, I admit, I'm pretty hot. Hopefully hot enough that Mason will want to do a little fooling around before he drops me off back home. I'm black on black and dark tonight. Black booties encase my feet, up to black ripped jeans, and a band t-shirt that's a little looser than I like it to be. Reaching behind me, I put a knot in the extra material, and when I do, it exposes a small swath of skin between the band of my jeans and the top of the cotton. Closing my eyes, I imagine Mason running those rough hands of his over the smooth skin. Insanity that I've been with this man once, been on one date with him, and he can have me this excited to see him.

The alarm on my phone goes off, telling me I have five minutes before he's supposed to arrive. Giving myself another glance, I take a little bit of concealer and dab at the edges of my eyes where I got the shadow a bit too dark. My look for tonight *is* dark with a plum matte lip color and plum shadow, but I'm not striving for the beaten look. Just the mysterious, sexy chick look. Grabbing my leather jacket, I put it over my shoulders, make sure I have my purse, and then take a deep breath. We've been out once, this is no different.

Except it is.

Before our date in Birmingham, I didn't know how he tasted, didn't know how the weight of his body felt on top of me, didn't realize how soft and hard lips could be at the same time. Didn't realize how a man could turn me inside out with a touch. That night in Birmingham opened my eyes to everything I've been missing, and I never want to miss it again. As I'm going through and shutting off lights, I hear someone pull into my driveway and see the shadows cast by a vehicle idling, before I hear footsteps on my front porch. Bonus points for him; he didn't honk and expect me to come meet him. The knock is strong and secure, resonating loudly through my living room. Definitely the knock of a cop. I laugh at the reference in my head.

Opening the door, I purse my lips at the man in front of me. Damn, I don't think I've ever been with a guy as hot as Mason Harrison.

"You look..." he trails off as his eyes rake over my body.

On impulse I do a little turn for him. Maybe wanting to show off what I have, maybe wanting him to see what's totally his if he wants to take it.

"There are no words," he finishes. "At least not in my vocabulary."

"You're not so bad yourself."

My eyes rake over him, the same way he did to me. Jeans that aren't too tight, but aren't too loose fit over long legs. A black t-shirt shows off his trim waist, a black and gray flannel sits over it, opened with the sleeves rolled up exposing strong forearms with a tattoo I didn't notice before. Just like everything else about him, it's hot.

"Nice." I run my hand over the ink. "Wouldn't have taken you for a guy with a tattoo. We didn't even get that shirt off of you last time, so I have no idea what's underneath."

His eyes flare dark with the passion I glimpsed during our night together and during our time in my classroom. It can quickly become an obsession of mine, seeing that look in his eyes. The blatant want on his face. To have it all directed at me? It's the stuff dreams are made of.

"I'd like to give you that opportunity as soon as possible." His voice is dark as he steps back, allowing me to turn and shut my door.

"We'll see." I flash him a grin and a look over my shoulder as I check the lock.

His brown eyes are on my porch lights. "What's wrong with that one?" he points to the one that's been out since I moved into the place.

"Don't know, I can't reach it. I keep telling the landlord, but he has yet to fix it for me." I shrug. "I'm pretty sure the bulb's just blown. I'm too short to reach it though, and I'm afraid I'll kill myself if I try to get a ladder. I hope this one doesn't go too."

"I'll take care of it for you in the next few days." He nods toward it. "It's not a good idea for a woman living by herself to have lights out like that. It goes against everything I've learned as a law enforcement officer."

Putting my hands on his chest, I lean up, giving him a chaste kiss. "I'm from Philly." My voice is soft. "I know how to take care of myself."

"I've been to war, and there are things that still give me pause. Safety of someone I'm interested in is one of those things. Just let me do it for you." He lets his hand slide along my back to cup the curve of my ass.

There's something arousing about a man who wants to take care of you, because he likes doing it, and truth be told I'll gladly let him. "If you insist."

"I do." He drops a kiss on my lips and then taps my ass before turning me to his Jeep. "Let's go, I'm starving."

Walking together, he escorts me to the passenger side of the Jeep, opening the door, and easily helps me into the seat. When he shuts the door, I breathe a calming sigh. There is something inherently sexy about this man, something that tells me I'm way in over my head if he ever decides to completely turn on the charm for me.

The drive to El Chico isn't long, but we keep up a steady stream of conversation as we go.

"How do you like being a member of the Moonshine Task Force? I didn't know you were a member. I know Leigh and Violet, but it never came up."

"Really?" He comes to a stop at the end of my street and motions for the person who stopped even with us to go. I try not to be mesmerized by the way his forearm flexes as he grips the steering wheel.

"Yeah, I tutored Leigh in a class she was having trouble with, and I teach night classes two nights a week. That's how I met Violet," I explain as we drive cautiously within the speed limit toward the restaurant. "Had I known they know you, I would have told them your name. Then I wouldn't have made an idiot of myself thinking you had a young child."

He chuckles. "I'm not real close with Ace, but if I had to say I have a best friend, it's Havoc."

"Leigh's husband, right?" I don't know their call signs off the top of my head.

"Right, they just had a baby, so I haven't seen him outside of work in a few weeks. It's actually why I decided to try the dating app."

Now we're getting somewhere. "This I'd love to hear. Why a man like you didn't have a line of women at your door."

Mason is quiet for a moment, and I think maybe I've overstepped when he shrugs and scratches the stubbly beard on his jaw. "I tried dating a few times when Caleb was younger, after I got back from my tour and honorably discharged. I really tried." He leans forward, checking both ways before he turns the truck to the right, taking us into the downtown area of Laurel Springs. "But so many women wanted to be Caleb's mom, they wanted to tell him what to do and pretend like they'd be around forever. After what happened with his mom, I couldn't just keep inviting women into his life. Half of them never lasted after a handful of dates, if they even made it that far, and it just felt unfair."

"Unfair to be living your life?"

"No, unfair to bring these women into Caleb's life when I knew it wouldn't last. Eventually, I gave up trying to date and settled for a few women who knew the score."

"Booty calls?" I supply, not sure I want to know the answer. I don't want to be categorized that way.

"We fulfilled needs that each other had." He's careful with his words. "Sometimes you just need a warm body beside you at night. Somedays you need someone to work off frustration with, and sometimes you just need that sexual release. If I hadn't had these things in my life, I would have gone crazy, because of all the stress I was under." He's talking, and I don't want to stop him. Even though this is our second official date, somehow I feel as if we've known each other our whole lives.

"Is that what I am?" I question quietly. "Someone who should know the score?"

Mason reaches over, entwining our fingers together, holding our palms in his lap as he continues to drive the streets of downtown. "No, you're different. You're the one I'm going to allow myself to truly be with. All those other women? They had no room in their lives for Caleb, because they didn't know him, they didn't want to get to know him. Even though he's an adult now, he needs a feminine presence in his life, and the two of you know one another. For the first time in years I feel like I can try to be a normal guy, take a girl out for a date, have her spend the night, and not worry about her hating me when I explain why we can't be together. Now, I can try to have a relationship." He pulls up to a stop at El Chico. "That is, if you want to try and have one with me."

I've listened to everything he's said, and I've let it all sink in. If I decide to be with Mason, Caleb comes with him.

"You're a package deal?" In my line of work, I see a lot of parents who don't love their children or their role as a parent half as much as Mason seems to. If he isn't the man I think he is, then I don't want to put myself in a relationship with him. Mason, though, I'm learning never disappoints.

"I am." He grips the steering wheel. "There's no one in this world I'm prouder of than my son, and there's no one who means more to me than him. If you're going to take me on, he comes with me, no matter where he is in life. He's leaving in the summer, so I plan on spending time with him, and if you come into our lives, you'll need to spend time with him, too. It's just how it's going to have to be."

It's a lot to digest, but I know the way I feel in the depths of my stomach, I know this flutter isn't something that comes along every day, and I also know how much I already care for Caleb. He's one of my favorite students, and I've enjoyed watching him mature during the school year. Getting out of the Jeep, I walk around, opening Mason's door and stepping on the running board. The shock is written plain as day across his face, when I lean in. "I'm in, fully and completely, with you. It might be stupid, considering we just met. It might be the biggest mistake of my life, it might blow up in our faces, but Mason, I want the experience."

Reaching up under my hair, he cups my neck, pulling me to kiss his lips. "I want the experience too, more than I've ever wanted it before."

CHAPTER SEVEN
MENACE

WALKING behind Karina has quickly become my favorite pastime. The way her jeans hug her ass should be fucking illegal in all fifty states and the District of Columbia.

"Two," I tell the hostess as we enter, holding up two fingers.

Fuck my life; I try to play it cool. The hostess is someone who's wanted me to take her out on a date for a while, and every time she drops the hint, I play it off. Needless to say, tonight when I walk in with my arm around Karina, I'm given the look of death.

"Hey Mason, didn't think you were really into dating." She gives me the evil eye.

"No, never said that," I correct her assumption, hating that I'm about to be a bit of a dick, but I don't want this woman to ruin what will be a great time between me and Karina. "I was just never into dating you."

Karina coughs, and I suspect it's hiding a laugh. Another glare is shot our way as we're taken to a booth in the back. Our menus are slapped on the table, before she turns, flinging her hair at us.

"Sorry about that." My face is red, hot with embarrassment, and I wonder how in the hell I forgot she worked here.

"It's okay, you've obviously been a hot cop and smoking single dad for a while, and I'm sure there are more women out there who wanted more time than you were willing to give."

She has a seat in the booth and I squeeze in next to her. I'm a same-side sitter with the person who has my attention, so I hope she's okay with me being handsy when the feeling strikes.

"You, I'm willing to give all my time to." I use my hand to push some of her curls over her shoulder. A smirk spreads across her face, and she scoots a little closer. "Some of these women, though, the minute I hit town, they were lined up." I run a hand through my hair as our waiter comes over.

He's a friend of Caleb's and I'm glad to see a friendly face.

"Mr. Harrison, Ms. Holland, how's it going?" He puts some chips in front of us and the cheese sauce I like.

"Good, Brad, how's it going with you?"

"School, training, work, repeat. Probably the same thing going on with Caleb."

Casually, I situate myself back against the booth, spreading my legs to give me room to kick them out before I curl my hand around Karina's neck. "Pretty much, at least I know you'll be in Tuscaloosa with him in the summer.'"

Brad nods before he takes our drink orders and disappears.

Karina leans into me. "Tell me why it's so embarrassing for a student to see me on a date."

"You have Brad in class?"

She nods, snickering. "At some point I have all the seniors in my class."

Brad delivers a pitcher of margaritas to her with a flourish and a Sprite for me. "Here ya go, Ms. Holland. Y'all ready to order?"

She opts for a taco salad while I get nachos that are bigger than my head. When he leaves, I watch her cautiously sip it.

"Careful, from what I've heard, those are strong," I warn her; secretly hoping it loosens her up. Not that she needs it, but I can tell she's a little nervous because a student has seen her.

"Trust me, I can hold my liquor."

Looking down at her, I can't help the grin that spreads across my face. She's cute as hell in her indignation. "Whatever you say."

"What's your call sign?" She asks out of nowhere. "I know you told the class, but I can't remember. I was too busy looking at your ass in your pants."

"Menace."

"Ooh big, bad, dangerous. It makes you sound like you can fuck shit up."

I laugh loudly as I reach forward, grabbing a chip and dipping it in the cheese sauce. "I *am* bad and dangerous, I *do* fuck shit up. You're right on all accounts."

"Modest, too." Her tone is sarcastic and playful as she takes another drink.

Chewing around the bite I've taken, I nod. "I mean I've been modest the last fourteen years, why shouldn't I give you all the impressive parts of me?"

She cuts her eyes my way. "Pretty sure I got to feel the most impressive part of you."

Coughing loudly as the chip goes down the wrong way, I struggle to get under control before turning in the seat and facing her. "Not what I expected to come out of your mouth."

"There's a lot about me you don't know, Menace, just like there's a lot about you I don't know. We're gonna have a good time getting there with each other."

"That we will." I lean forward, grabbing another chip and dipping it in the cheese dip. This time though, I hold it up to her lips and wait for her to take a bite. When she does, she makes a huge production of circling her tongue around my finger. I try but fail to hold back the groan that rips its way past my throat. "How are we going to do that? Get to know each other better?"

She situates herself in the seat, leaning a little closer to me. My eyes immediately go to the dark color of her lipstick or whatever it is. I can't wait to smear my lips across hers, see if I can disturb the harsh outline. "I don't know about you, but when I want to know something, I ask."

Immediately my mind goes to the questions she could ask. I'm not used to sharing my life, and if I'm honest, I haven't wanted to share my life with anyone before. This is a first for me, but it feels like a new beginning at the same time. This is the kind of relationship I should have had in my early twenties, but never got the chance to.

"Like twenty questions?" I don't know if we know each other that well yet.

She shrugs her shoulder, one of her curls brushing against my arm. I'm hyperaware of everything about her. "Or something like that. If it's a question we don't want to answer, we're allowed to pass. How's that sound?"

"Why the fuck not. You go first?" I give her the option. If I was taught anything, it's that ladies come first.

She twirls her straw in her glass, and I can feel her leg kicking beneath the table. Risking a glance, I see that she's crossed her legs, and there's something arousing about the way she's crossed them toward me. "How long have you lived here, and why Laurel Springs?"

Taking a drink and another chip, I start into the story about why we came here. Truth be told I haven't thought about it in a long time, so it's kind of odd to talk about it with another person. "I was working in a small sheriff's office in Texas, but I really wanted to put the training I got in the military to use. This place was small as hell; they didn't even have a damn SWAT team. There's places for law enforcement to apply for jobs, just like I'm sure there are for teachers. I applied everywhere I could. Laurel Springs was the first one to offer what I wanted, so Caleb and I packed up and moved here. We've been here for a number of years now, and I can honestly say I see myself retiring from here, unless something huge changes. I love the area, love the job, and love the people." I twist part of her hair around my index finger, pulling slightly. "What about you?"

She takes a healthy drink of her margarita before pouring another round. She blows out a breath in between her perfectly matte lips and puts her arms on the table before she lifts her head to look at me. "It's like some horrible country song." She snorts. "My fiancé and my best friend were fucking each other behind my back. I found out days before the wedding. Actually caught them doing it in the house I paid for. When I caught them, something inside me snapped. I kicked him out, kicked her out, cut off all my hair, and pawned my engagement ring. Within the week, I'd put the house on the market and had a job here. My family told me I was crazy to pick up everything and move south like I did, but honestly, I couldn't stand being around my ex-fiancé and ex-best friend anymore. When I saw either one of them, I got sick to my stomach. Couldn't stand to be in that house and was ready for a change. My family still asks me every time I talk to them when I'm coming home, but after almost two years, Laurel Springs feels more like home than Philly ever did."

She's quiet for a few minutes before she glances over, smiling at me. Her eyes are glassy and I think maybe she doesn't hold her liquor as well as she thinks. Karina Holland drunk and naked in the back of my Jeep would be fun, in my bed would be even more fun, but I don't want to press my luck and make any kind of plans before I know how the night is going to go.

"I'm glad you grew your hair back."

"So am I," she whispers. "I like when you grab hold of it."

This woman and this mouth of hers.

"Time for my question. Exactly how old are you, Karina Holland?"

She picks up her glass, puckering her mouth around her straw as she looks up at me from beneath hooded eyes. The motion is complete sex kitten, and I wonder if this woman knows how fucking hot she is.

"Don't you know it's rude to ask a woman her age."

I pull her closer with the arm around her neck. "Not when I've fucked her and plan on fucking her again. As an officer of the law, it's probably a smart thing for me to know."

"When you put it that way..." she trails off, putting her hand on my thigh below the table. Her nails dig slightly into the denim covering them, and in that moment I want to forget the dinner and the date. There's one thing we do well, and I'm ready to do it again with her as soon as possible. "I'm twenty-seven."

"Does it bother you that my son is nine years younger than you?" That had been a problem with one of the few women I had considered exploring things further with in the past. She couldn't get over the fact that Caleb was so close to her age, and like I'd told Karina before, we're a package deal. I can't be with someone who can't love Caleb at least a fraction of the way I do. If anyone deserves it, it's him.

"Does it bother you?" She turns it around on me. "Because it doesn't bother me. What would bother me is if you didn't pay attention to him, if you weren't a good dad, and if you raised him to be a brat. He's a good kid Mason, even though he had his issues. You should be proud of what you've done with him.

There are kids in his class with a ton of money and two parents that are holy terrors."

The praise warms me like nothing else has. "Thank you." I lower my head, kissing her on the cheek. "It means a lot that you say that."

"I say what I mean, Mason. You're raised a good son, and you should be proud."

When our food comes, I'm thankful for the reprieve in our conversation because the words she spoke hit a spot in me I wasn't sure any woman could ever touch. After Maggie, I'd held it closed, hidden it away. Luckily for me, this woman found it, and I don't think I'm ever going to ask her to give it back.

CHAPTER EIGHT
KARINA

WATCHING Mason drive has jumped to the top of my *favorite things in the world* list. There's something about watching his big hands rest on the steering wheel, his long fingers wrap around the cylindrical shape, and the way his forearms flex as he easily maneuvers through the streets of Laurel Springs.

"You okay?" His shit-eating grin is proof he knows exactly what I was looking at.

At dinner, I had a few margaritas, and I might possibly be replaying every second of what happened in the backseat of this Jeep the last time we were together. Crossing my legs to ease the ache between them, I let my gaze meet his. "Fine." The word is breathless and husky, even to my own ears. I sound like I should be on the other end of one of those sex-operator phone lines.

"You sure? A little tipsy?"

Maybe I am, slightly. He hadn't been lying when he told me those drinks were potent. "Mmmm." I make a non-committal sound in the back of my throat.

When he turns into my driveway, I want to extend the night, just like I did last time. My tongue is stuck to the roof of my mouth as I watch him get out and walk around to my side of the vehicle. The pair of worn jeans are delectable, loose enough to give him room to move, but tight enough so that I can see what he's packing underneath. The t-shirt he's pulled over his body tonight is just enough for me to see the smooth stomach lying just beneath. His hair? Tousled, but not as messed up as it would be if he'd give me half the chance to run my fingers through it. As he approaches and opens the passenger side door for me, I've gotten myself so worked up I can't stop the words that fly out of my mouth.

"The tattoo on your forearm has been turning me on all night."

There's a sharp intake of breath when he hears what I've said. His arms go up, gripping the doorframe, and those forearms of his flex in the muted light of the night. Here there's light given off by stars and the moon, and that glow makes him look like a dream come true. Given a moment, I quickly unbuckle my seatbelt. Faster than I've ever moved, I turn, open my thighs so he can stand in between them, and attack the man in front of me.

Sliding my hands along his waist, I push my fingers up under the t-shirt, welcoming the feel of his hot skin against the coolness of the night. Leaning up, I capture him in a kiss. Soft at first, we nip at each other's lips, before I hook my legs around him, pulling him into me. My hands travel up his back, still under his shirt, before I slide my nails down the smooth skin.

The kiss deepens, his tongue tangles with mine as we strain against each other. I'm feeling lightheaded as I realize I can't breathe, because he's literally kissed the breath from my body. Ripping my lips from his, I drag a breath into my lungs before I hone in on the pulse at the side of his neck, going to work on that stretch of skin. The deep moan in return causes a reaction I feel from the hard nipples thrusting against my bra to the pulsing I feel between my legs.

"Rina, fuck, we can't do this out here, and I have to be at work early," he pants as he tilts his head back, giving me more room to work.

"Rina?" I whisper, a question as to what the nickname means to him. It feels as if we're turning a corner.

"Yeah, my Rina. Is that okay?"

He's asking me if it's okay to give me a hot as fuck nickname while he's literally blowing my mind? "Perfection, big guy. Absolute perfection."

Opening my eyes, I pull away from him, taking in the picture he makes. His arms are up, gripping the doorframe of the Jeep where I sit, his forearms are straining, almost as if he's afraid to touch me. Beneath the t-shirt, I see his own nipples hard, begging for my touch. His stomach tenses and relaxes, tenses and relaxes as he tries to control the intake of air. Further down, I see his erection straining against the denim. Without thinking, I pull my hands from around his waist, fumbling them down to grasp his hard length.

"Fuckin' shit, Rina." He pulls out of my embrace.

As his heat leaves me, I take a look around. We're in the driveway of my home. I'm a teacher; he's a respected cop in our town. He's right. We need to rein this in and do it fast.

I take a cleansing inhale. "I'm sorry."

"No, don't be sorry." He cups my jaw with both hands, pushing his fingers up under my hair, forcing my gaze to meet his. "Don't ever be sorry for going after what you want. This–," he looks around, "–just isn't the right time or place."

"You're right." I lick my lips, tasting the flavor of his kisses on them.

"Goddamn, don't do that." His voice is tortured, tone guttural.

A feminine giggle escapes my throat. "I'm sorry."

He crowds against me, pushing his hardness against me. "You're not even a little bit." His grin is as boyish as the one I see Caleb sometimes give.

"You're right, not even a little bit."

Ducking his head, he gives me a chaste kiss. This time, he doesn't let it get out of hand, and neither do I. When he pulls away, he whispers an invitation. "Caleb and I are going to the fishing and hunting show in Birmingham on Sunday. Wanna come with us?"

My heart almost trips in my chest. He's inviting me to do something with his son and him. A smile spreads across my face. "I'd love to."

"Good." He noses my neck one more time. "When we come pick you up, we'll fix that porch light that's out. See you on Sunday?"

"Sunday." I nod as I hop out of the Jeep.

Ever the gentleman, Mason walks me to the door, making sure I'm safe before he turns, going back to his Jeep, and takes off for home. As I watch his taillights in the darkness of the night, I can't help but put my fingers up to my lips, feeling where his were such a short time ago. Tonight, I might go to bed frustrated, but I'll go to bed with a huge smile on my face.

Menace

"Made you coffee," Caleb mumbles as I stumble into the kitchen the next morning, rubbing the sleep out of my eyes.

"Thanks." I shuffle over to the coffee pot, thankful he had the forethought to go ahead and get me a cup out. "Shit this is gonna be a long day." I yawn loudly.

"Shouldn't have gone out on a work night." The sing-song voice of my teenager is enough to piss me off this morning. Honestly, he's not wrong. "Did you have a good time with Ms. Holland last night?"

Immediately I'm taken back to us making out in her driveway, where I almost forgot about us being in public and broke a couple laws myself. Never in my life have I been one of those men who thought about saying fuck it to being in public. I've always been the type of guy who kept most of my affection behind closed doors. The only person who I've even been comfortable hugging in public is my son, but Karina, she's challenging everything I thought I knew about myself. Even this early in the relationship. I would have given a lot just to pull her out of my Jeep, lie down on the ground, and let her ride me to the best orgasm of our lives. But that wasn't the way it had worked out, and I'll never be the type of person to put her in a potentially embarrassing or damaging situation.

"It was good." I swallow down a drink of the blessedly hot coffee.

Caleb squints at me as he takes a drink of his own. "Dude, it was so much better than good, I can tell by looking at you."

"I'm your dad, not your dude." I attempt to put some authority in my voice.

"Fair enough." He purses his lips. "But I'm also an adult, so don't pretend like I'm a little kid."

He's got me there; I've always treated him like an equal. Now that I have a woman I'm interested in, I shouldn't just turn it off and pretend as if he doesn't understand. "Karina..." I let my voice trail off, because I'm not sure how to describe her, not sure I want to let my son in on the thoughts and feelings I have for her "She makes me feel like I haven't felt before."

"You're hot for her," he supplies, a smile teasing his lips.

Fuck it. "I'm insanely hot for her." I groan as I run my hand along my neck, my voice gruffer than it should be while talking to my son, but our situation is what it is.

"Is that a bad thing?"

I think about it for a second, trying to allow myself to come to grips with what I've revealed to him. "It's not, but given the jobs we have, neither one of us need to do anything that could hurt our standing in the community."

"And you almost did that last night?"

Jesus why is he so smart? "I have no comment."

He laughs, a full-out, belly rolling laugh. "I'm glad, Dad. I'm glad she does that to you."

"Why?" I rub my eyes again, trying to figure out if I'm in some sort of alternate universe.

His cheeks pink as he has a seat at the breakfast bar. "As I've gotten older..." he trails off, face red. "I wondered how in the fuck you lived like a monk for so long. Especially this past year."

I think I get the gist of what he's telling me. My face is just as red, but I answer him honestly, because we've always been honest. "I'm not a teenager with teenage hormones rolling through my body, Caleb. Sometimes, it's lonely. Other times, like when I have a lot on my mind, I don't think about it."

"But you do think about Ms. Holland?"

We're quiet for a few minutes, until I sigh heavily. "Yeah, I do think about Ms. Holland."

And with that admission, I realize quickly I'm in a place I've never been before.

"Relax, Dad, you've waited for this your whole life."

I laugh, finding it amusing that my teenage son is the one talking me down, but truth be told he's probably smarter than most men my age. Walking over to him, I reach down, ruffling his hair. At least I'm still taller than he is. "Caleb, get to work."

He grins as he sets his coffee down on the counter.

"Dad, text her and tell her you like her."

I shake my head as he runs out the door to his truck. Little do I tell him I think Karina and I have moved past the I like you stage. What I'd rather tell her is that I don't want to go to bed at night lonely anymore. But it's too early for those words, and I have no desire to scare her away.

Instead, I grab my phone, text her a good morning, and then go about my routine. As I'm getting into my Jeep to make the drive to work, I get an answering text.

K: I barely slept at all last night, and when I did, I dreamed about all the things you could have been doing to me. Dream Mason is one of the hottest guys around.

Starting the Jeep, I take a minute to text her back.

M: Yeah? Real-life Mason has some tricks up his sleeve he hasn't showed you yet. Maybe we can make that happen sometime this week.

K: I'm going to be spending all day tomorrow with you. We will NEED to find some time to make it happen this week. Text me your schedule, and I'll let you know what mine is.

M: Will do when I get to work. I want this to work, Rina. More than I've wanted anything else in a really long time.

K: Same here, big guy.

And with a smile on my face, I head off to start my day. Having someone to share this stuff with? Doesn't suck at all.

CHAPTER NINE

MENACE

"WHAT'S that thing on the side of your neck?" Renegade asks as I duck into the squad car he and I are riding in today.

"What?" I pull the sun visor down and push back the plastic piece to look in the mirror. Son of a bitch, I got a hickey last night when Karina attacked my neck. "Must have cut myself shaving," I lie, knowing damn good and well I have a beard right now.

"Riiiigghhhtttt." He starts the car. As we pull out of the parking lot, I can feel his eyes on me.

"What, kid?"

"Don't give me that *kid* bullshit." He laughs as we drive up Main Street. "I have a wife, I have plenty of sex, and I know exactly what a hickey looks like. I've just never seen you with one before, so it's kind of weirding me out."

"Weirding you out?"

Renegade sighs. "I've always kind of seen you as a dad, but I also always thought of you as way older than the rest of us. Even though you and Whitney are close to the same age. I don't know, you've just been the one who had his shit together, and to see you with a hickey on your neck reminds me you're a guy ready to live his own life."

"That describes me pretty well. Seriously though, man, did you just call your wife old?" I watch the road as we slowly creep up Main Street until we get to the turn off for the state highway.

He gives me a scared glare when I mention what he's said about Whitney.

"You mention those words to her, I will cut you."

I laugh, because it's fun to get under his skin.

"Who is she?" Renegade immediately cuts to the heart of the matter and effectively changes the subject. "Anyone I know?"

I'm not sure if I want to invite this scrutiny into my life yet. If I tell Renegade, he'll tell Tank, who'll talk to Ace and Havoc about it, which means I'll be at the center of the gossip in this group. It's a place I've never been before. But at the same time I kinda wanna tell someone, kind of want to talk about the changes happening in my life. "I'm not sure if you know her or not. Karina Holland, the teacher."

"Believe it or not, I've met her before. It was quick and I didn't get a chance to talk to her very long, but from what I did see, she's cute."

"She's more than cute," I argue. "She's got these expressive as hell green eyes, her body is banging, and she laughs with this throaty laugh that sends goosebumps up and down my arms."

"Dude, you've got it bad. How did you meet her?"

He's right, I do have it bad, and I don't even know how it happened. Maybe it's just this time in my life is right. Maybe I'm ready to invite someone in to share my days and nights, and everything in between. Whatever the reason, she's turned my world upside-fuckin'-down.

"That dating app Caleb created me a profile for. She was one of the only ones who didn't ask me about being her daddy."

He chokes on his own spit. "Did a lot of women ask you?"

"You seriously have no idea, like none. I didn't know it was such a thing with this generation of woman. I'm already someone's dad; I don't want to treat the woman I'm with like that."

"I don't know how I would react if some woman came up to me and called me Daddy," Renegade snort-laughs as he says it. "See I can't even get it out without cracking up."

"Dating now is a totally different world from when I was a teenager or even a twenty-something," I concede. "But I was attracted to Karina's picture from the beginning. There was something about the way she smiled and the way the smile reached her eyes. We didn't have a whole lot of conversations back and forth – honestly, I think she liked the way I look. But within a week, we were making plans to meet one another for dinner in Birmingham."

"Oohhh, took her to the city, huh?"

"Where else was I gonna take her?" I give him a glare. "At the time I didn't know she lived right here in town, I thought she lived in the surrounding area. Anyway, we went to dinner, and we ended up having sex in the backseat of my Jeep. She ignored my attempts to get in touch with her after that for a week or so, and then I had to go talk to Caleb's class."

"No fucking way." Renegade snorts. "She was the teacher?"

"She was," I confirm. "Given the second chance, I wasn't going to let her get away. We came to an understanding, and we've seen each other once since then. Last night. And I invited her to come with me and Caleb to the hunting and fishing show tomorrow."

"Does Caleb know?"

"Yeah, and that's presented its own set of difficulties. She's his teacher, he kind of thinks she's hot, and while I don't think Caleb would ever do anything to make her uncomfortable, it might take us all a while to know how to interact with one another."

"That makes sense. I remember when Whitney and I first got together. It was easy for us, when it was just us. When you added the prying eyes of everyone else into the mix, that's when it became difficult to know what to do and how to react. The first time we had dinner with her family as a couple, we told them all she was pregnant. Talk about just throwing it out there." He shifts in his seat. "Tank decked me, and I worried that I'd fucked up our friendship, but everything worked out."

"I think that's kind of where I am," I admit. "There's so much that can go wrong. Like what if we don't make it? What if I fall hardcore for her, and it ends up being something she doesn't necessarily want? What if her and Caleb don't get along outside of her classroom? What if she gets in trouble for dating a student's parent?"

"What if it all works out and at this time next year you're still with her and happier than you've ever been? It can't be all gloom and doom my man."

I hear what he's saying, but so many things in my life have fucked up, I'm just not sure I can count on it.

My cell phone buzzes in the cup holder next to where I sit. Picking it up, a smile immediately spreads across my face.

K: So, I have one of those questions.

Fuck, my heart pounds just from seeing her name on my phone. When did I become this guy?

M: Which is?

K: What's your favorite type of music? Tickets for Shinedown go on sale next week, for their concert in January of next year. I know it's presumptuous, but if you like them and I like them? Maybe we can make plans. I'm being optimistic in our future here.

She sends me a picture of herself holding up a sign that says *go out on a date with me*? I can't help the laugh, even though it causes Renegade to glance over, a knowing look on his face.

M: I'm a rock fan, and I love them. Count me in! I say yes to your date.

The answer I get from her is a .gif with *YAASSSS* going across the bottom. The stupid smile on my face feels good, and it feels even better to know she's the one to put it there.

THINGS HAVE BEEN RELATIVELY quiet today as we've made our rounds through downtown and along the outlying areas of the county. We're an hour from going off-shift when a call comes through dispatch.

"We've got a report of what appears to the caller to be teenage kids drinking at Laurel Springs Park," our weekend dispatcher relates the information to use clearly. "She states they're loud, crude, and obnoxious. Two teenage boys making vulgar gestures and being all around inappropriate at a family park. She says they're drinking something out of bottles, but she doesn't know what it is."

"10-4," I answer back. "Show Renegade and I as responding, we're about five minutes out."

The lights on our cruiser pop on, as does the siren. When Renegade presses the accelerator, I hold on to the 'oh shit' handles as the engine responds. Being able to drive fast, be a little reckless, and the adrenaline spike I get as I'm about to answer a call – this right here is probably my favorite thing about being a cop, besides helping people. When I was in the Army, I lived off the dangerous aspect of some of the missions I took. My skill set was very specific, and nine things out of ten I did, I'll never be able to talk about to another human being. But it gave me purpose, it gave me something to do other than sit at home and wonder how I was going to feed my kid. No, that came later. After the Army, when I had to jump back into civilian life. Things weren't so easy then.

In a matter of what feels like seconds, we're pulling into the park, and immediately we see the teenagers the caller spoke about. Maddox Stanford and Billy Langston have played football with Caleb since he joined the team. They've been over to my house more times than I can count. I've sat in the stands with their dads, watching them play. Truth be told, I can barely believe what I'm seeing in front of me right now. Two kids who are in the prime of their lives are looking like two homeless bums on a park bench, drunk, in the middle of a Saturday.

"Maddox, Billy." I nod at the two of them as we approach. I have my thumbs hooked in my duty belt, giving them the appearance that I'm at ease. Really, I'm anything but. This scares me. I have a few more months to get Caleb out of here and keep him clean. With influences like this, it's going to be harder than I thought.

"Mr. Harrison." Maddox sits up straighter, trying to appear sober, but then a grin starts spreading across his face and the laughter of someone who's inebriated cuts through. "Or should I call you *Officer Harrison*?" He laughs, hitting Billy in the stomach.

They both laugh obnoxiously, and I do my best to remember I'm dealing with boys who aren't mature yet. "You should put the bottle down and stand up."

They do, both seeming to be somewhat reprimanded for the moment. I pull out my cuffs and secure Maddox's hands behind his back. "You're being detained, not arrested. I'm cuffing you for my and your safety."

Renegade does the same to Billy, and we start taking a look at what they brought to the park with them.

"Where'd you get this?" Renegade holds up a container of what we all know is moonshine.

"School," Billy answers, his face somber. "Are you going to call my parents?"

"You're drunk in public. That's the least of what's going to happen to you," I tell him as I start reading them both their rights.

As I sit them down, I realize one thing is growing more and more urgent. We need to get into that school and figure out who in the hell is making it so easy for these kids to come into contact with something that can kill them if they aren't careful.

CHAPTER TEN

KARINA

"THANKS FOR COMING WITH ME." Violet grins over at me as we sit in the only nail salon that Laurel Springs has to offer. "Whitney gave me this gift certificate for my birthday, and I haven't had time to come and use it yet."

"No problem." I watch as the nail technician cuts back my nails and starts painting the shellac I prefer on them. "I haven't had a manicure in a long time."

Vi looks at me, an inquisitive look on her face.

"What?"

"What's going on with that single dad? Did you get things straightened out? Decide to see him again?"

"Yeah, actually I'm seeing him tomorrow. I'm heading to the fishing and hunting show in Birmingham with him and his son tomorrow." I play it coy, while still giving her some of the details.

"Oh my God, Mason is taking Caleb, and they asked Anthony to go, but he's working, and I've never seen him so bummed. They have new boats there," she frowns. "But at least Caleb and Mason get to spend some time together."

"I know Caleb and Mason are going." I try to hint to her, about who the single dad was.

"That's right, Caleb's in your class." She shakes her head, as if to get her thoughts straight in her head.

"He is, but that's not how I know they're spending the day in Birmingham together tomorrow."

I dropped the bomb, now I'm waiting on her to respond to it.

"You're spending your day with Mason tomorrow?" Her eyes are wide as she looks over at me and she puts two and two together.

"Mason and Caleb, if you want to get technical." I decide to go for broke. "He invited me to the show with them in Birmingham."

"What? Wait a second." Her eyes are shining. "Is Mason the single dad? Like as in the Mason that works with my fiancé, Mason? Mason is the single dad and Caleb is my Caleb??"

A giggle bursts from my throat. "Yes!"

She shrieks as we get looks coming at us from all directions in the salon. "Shhhhh," I giggle, face flaming as she opens her mouth on a silent scream.

"I thought you said he had a little kid!"

"I *thought* it was a little kid, but I never asked either. Imagine my surprise when he walked into my classroom, ready to talk to the kids about jobs. Caleb was so happy to introduce us. Little did he know, we already knew each other *very well*."

She snorts as I'm sure she plays out the scene in her head. "Only you, K."

"I know," I reply, shaking my head. This stuff always happens to me, but I've never been so happy to have it happen before.

"So tell me all about it!"

"It's really new, Vi, I don't know if I want to jinx it. I'm enjoying hanging out with him, and I'm looking forward to getting to know Caleb better."

Her eyes are intense as she stares at me. "Why do I get the feeling you're already like knee deep into this, and you're just trying to manage your expectations?"

How the hell does this woman hit this shit on the head like this? "I got my heart broken once, I don't want it to happen again," I argue.

"I'm just gonna say this. Since I've started dating Anthony, I've gotten to know them all better. The one thing I *can* tell you about Mason is that he loves his son, he loves the guys he works with, and he doesn't give his heart half-way. He's not going to break yours, K. I can almost promise you that."

"There's just so many things he's seen and done, that I've never had to deal with." I pull my bottom lip between my teeth. "He was a dad as a teenager, he's sending his own teenager off to college this summer, he's had to deal with so many situations I've never even thought of," I trail off. "What if he gets bored with me, what if in the grand scheme of things I'm too immature for him, just because I don't have the same life experiences."

"That's bullshit and you know it." She uses her foot to jostle my chair slightly. "Stop looking for things that aren't there. How do you feel about him?"

The question is one nobody's ever asked, because I've not told anyone else we're dating. How do I feel about Mason Harrison? "He makes me laugh, he makes me hot, and throughout the day, I think about him. Probably way more than I should. I find myself texting him little snippets of conversations that I find funny. If I see a meme on Facebook and it reminds me of him, I'll screenshot it and text it to him. I've never done that with another guy." I realize as I'm talking, the words are the truth.

"What else, Karina? What else has he opened up inside of you that you never thought about."

"He cares so much about Caleb." I keep talking. "So many of our conversations when we're texting are about him. It's obvious Mason is so proud of his son."

"We all are," she interjects. "He's come a long way from being the annoying little shit he was a few months ago. He's grown up a lot in that time. I was afraid at one point of what would happen to him. Would we find him wrapped around a telephone pole? Would we find him dead at a barn party? Would he finally piss Mason off enough to where he'd actually do something detrimental to his son's future? Luckily Caleb pulled it together."

"I'm still waiting for Mason to tell me what happened between them, like what prompted the change, and how all of that came about. I'm sure I can ask other people in Laurel Springs, but I want that to come from his mouth."

As we put our fingers under the dryer, Violet glances at me again. "What else has been going on with the two of you?"

I can tell by the smile on her face, she knows we did the deed even though I never technically admitted to it when we met for coffee. Truth be told, I need a girlfriend sometimes. I need someone I can gossip with, talk about womanly things with. "We did the deed in the backseat of his Jeep. Hands down the best sex of my life," I giggle as I make the admission.

"There is something about Mason," Violet lets slip as she crosses her legs. "It's that daddy look he has."

"He told me that's why he asked me out." I laugh so hard I snort. "Because I didn't ask him to be my daddy on the dating app. So many women asked him to punish them. Oh my God, he showed me the messages." I laugh.

"I'm just saying, any man who has the look of concentration he does, can totally spank me anytime." She gives me a sly grin.

"Maybe that's something you can talk to Anthony about."

"Maybe so," she snickers.

When we leave the nail salon, I have a smile on my face and a spring in my step that wasn't there before. When I came to Laurel Springs, it was to get away from a past I didn't want to face. It was to escape the literally most embarrassing moments of my life. Now, I can't imagine living my life anywhere else. In the short time I've been here, this place has become ingrained in my body, a piece of me, and as I walk into one of the boutiques on the main square, I realize there's no other place I'd rather be.

My phone buzzes in the back pocket of my jeans, and when I see Mason's smiling face, I automatically unlock it, reading the text message like a junkie needing a hit.

M: Important question here. Coke or Pepsi?

A grin plays against my lips, as I quickly text out an answer.

K: Pepsi, is there any other brand?

M: Nooooo!!! You were the perfect woman, but our regional differences strike. There's no other brand than Coke.

K: Screw you, buddy, I'm still perfect. Truth be told, give me a Dr. Pepper any day.

I grin as I fire off the text.

M: Nice, a rebel. That's fuckin' hot.

K: That's me, big guy. A rebel, totally hot for you.

Glancing around to make sure no one's watching, I lift my phone up, and take a selfie with puckered lips.

M: Back at ya, babe.

He sends me an answering text with him and Holden giving me a thumbs up, big smiles on their faces. When I make it to my car, I have the biggest smile on my face, and the warmest spot in my heart. Laurel Springs is the best place to be.

Menace

"You're sure you're okay with Karina coming with us tomorrow?" I ask one more time as Caleb and I sit in front of the TV that night, watching a TV show we both like on Netflix.

"Yes, Dad, I'm fine with it. How many times do I have to tell you?"

I can tell he's getting irritated, but I've never pushed a woman on him before, and this is making me slightly nervous. He's never really seen me around a woman before, either. I kept all of my booty calls (as few of them as there were) far away from him, and the two women I'd seen in the past, we'd done minimal things together as a family. Something tells me, I won't be able to keep my hands off of Rina, and I don't want to embarrass him, me, or her.

I watch as he lifts his cell phone up, frowning as he starts furiously texting the other person on the other end of the phone. "Just checking." I watch as he continues to punch with unnecessary force. "Is something wrong?"

He continues texting, and then throws his phone on the table in front of him. "Jess is at a party with a friend. You know that's not my scene, especially not anymore. I didn't want her to go, but it's her friend's birthday. Now she's telling me she's not feeling comfortable there."

"Why not?" I'm immediately on alert. "What do you not want to tell me?"

"They've got moonshine," he whispers as he looks up at me. "I don't want you to go in there guns blazing, arresting everyone in the place. I don't need that on my conscience." He runs a hand over his stubbled face. "But I don't want her to stay there either. She wants to leave."

It takes everything I have to trust my son, to utter these words I hope like hell I don't end up regretting. "Then go get her."

"What? Dad are you sure? Her mom isn't home, and she doesn't want to stay by herself, that's one of the reasons she went out with them tonight. I don't want to take her home alone to an empty house. It sucks," he mumbles.

There's a pain in my chest at that mumble. I've left him alone more times than I care to count. I've had to let him take care of himself for a lot of years, not just because it was hard to find childcare, but also because the job I've been able to do as an officer offered us a lot more than a factory job would have. It killed me in certain circumstances to leave him by himself and for me to go do what I had to do, but it's the way the world has worked for us.

"Go get her and bring her back here. She can go with us tomorrow too, if you want."

He stares at me like I've grown an alien head, or like I spoke to him in a different language.

"What?"

"Who are you and what have you done with my dad?"

I don't miss the fact he's already getting up and walking toward his room. When he comes back he's wearing a pair of jeans, a hoodie, and he's going to the door to grab his shoes.

"I haven't done anything with your dad, I'm trying to make the best decision I can with the circumstances that have been laid out for us. If going to get her and bringing her back here is what needs to be done, then do it. I'm trusting you though, Caleb. Don't you have sex with that girl in this house." He gives me a shit-eating grin as I point to him. "I'm serious."

"Not even a little fuckin' around?" His smile is huge as he continues to needle at me.

"I swear to God, Caleb. I'll make you sleep on the couch, and I'll sleep on the floor in your bedroom while she sleeps in the bed. I'm not playing with you."

"Yes, sir." He stands up after putting on his shoes and grabs his truck keys. "I'll be back as soon as I can."

"Be careful, and if you need help, don't hesitate to call me. I know there are things you like to take care of on your own, since you're an adult and all, but you're my son. I'll severely injure anyone who touches you."

His look is serious as he walks across the living room, leaning down to give me a hug. "I know you will, that's why you're a great dad. Love you."

"Love you, too."

I watch his taillights in the drive until I can't see them anymore, before I pull out my cell phone and text Karina.

M: I think we're gonna have someone join us for the outing to Birmingham tomorrow.

It doesn't take her long to respond, which makes me smile. Maybe she was sitting by her phone, waiting to hear from me.

K: Oh really? Boy or girl?

M: Girl. Caleb's been seeing this cheerleader named Jess. She's at some party that he didn't want to go to, and I guess it's gotten out of hand for her. She's coming back here to spend the night.

K: You're letting two teenagers spend the night together in your house? I know Jess, she's cute.

M: I trust him.

It's hard for me to explain to someone who hasn't lived the life I have, why I trust him and why I give him so much freedom. Getting up as I wait for her to text me back, I switch out laundry, before going to clean up the kitchen.

M: The reason I snuck around as a kid was because no one trusted me. Had I been able to see his mom, we probably wouldn't have been sneaking around having sex in the fifteen minutes between the time we got home from school and the time her parents got home from work.

K: Fifteen minutes, big guy? Good thing your stamina has improved since then.

I love her sense of humor, love that she can take something so serious and lighten the mood. I wipe my hands on a towel before texting her back, and then going back to finish loading the dishwasher.

M: We can put my stamina to the test anytime you'd like to.

K: Hmmmmm. There's an offer I'll never be able to refuse. Next week we'll have to see what we can do.

M: We really need to talk about schedules, Rina. I hate not knowing when we'll actually get to see each other.

K: I agree. Maybe we can do that tomorrow?

I hear Caleb's truck coming up the drive and quickly end the conversation.

M: We will. Caleb's home, so I'll see you tomorrow.

K: Can't wait, big guy. Be nice to them!

I can't make any promises so I say nothing instead. As the two of them make their way from his truck to the front door, I can hear Caleb giving her a lecture.

"Jess, I told you this was a bad idea. Babe, you know I didn't want you to go without me, but you also know I can't be around that anymore."

"Caleb, please don't be mad at me. I asked you, but you didn't want to go. That was your decision, and I stood by you with it. I thought you were being paranoid, but now..." She has tears in her voice. "I get it. Thank you for not making me go home to an empty house."

When I can hear them kissing, I plop my ass down on the couch to give them some privacy. Three minutes later they come through the door. Introductions are made, and Jess thanks me for letting her stay. As they make their way back to Caleb's bedroom, I yell out.

"Remember what I said Caleb. I may be old, but my back can still take it."

He chuckles. "Got it, Dad. Good night."

And with trust in my child, I go to bed, sleeping so deep I don't wake up until the next morning, excited to spend a day with all the people I care about.

CHAPTER ELEVEN

KARINA

K: **How'd you sleep last night with two teenagers under your roof?**

I can't help but give Mason a hard time. Caleb's a good kid, I know that from having him in my class, but he's also a teenage boy, almost a man, with teenage hormones.

M: Slept like a baby, Rina. Told you I trust Caleb. Now had it been me and you'd been here? No doubt about it, there's no way I would have kept my hands off you last night.

I'm trying to think of what my reply will be when another message comes through; a picture of Mason's head against what I assume is his pillow. His eyes are heavy with sleep, his smile lazy, and his stubble is grown in more, adding to the beard on his face. Looking farther down, I can see his chest on full display. Immediately I wonder what he sleeps in.

K: You look cozy and fine as hell. What do you sleep in, Mase?

M: Last night? I slept in these.

The next thing I know, I get a picture angled a little further down, showing a flat stomach with light hair, leading to the waistband of what appear to be boxers. I'd have to be blind not to notice the bulge just below his waist. It makes me wonder what it would be like to wake up next to him, put my leg around his waist, feel his hardness, and bury my head in his neck, while we lay together. The outside world could wait while the two of us woke up and whispered quietly. I never even thought about these things with Braxton, my ex-fiancé. Can't even remember the last time I'd wanted to lounge around with him. Maybe the writing had been on the wall for us way before I found out he was sleeping with my best friend. The sound of another text coming through brings me out of my thoughts.

M: Usually I sleep in something a little different but with Jess here I didn't feel comfortable.

Dear Lord. This man...I have a feeling I know what he's suggesting.

K: Are you saying you usually sleep naked?

M: Wouldn't you like to know?

I love the way he teases me, the easy way in which we talk with one another.

K: Maybe one day I'll find out for sure. ::wink::

M: Fuck, I hope so! Hopefully sooner than we think. Let me get up and see if the kids are moving. Either way, we'll be there to get you in about an hour. That good for you, Rina?

K: Can't wait, big guy. See ya then.

With a squeal, I hop out of bed and run around trying to figure out just what the fuck I'm gonna wear.

Menace

I throw my phone down beside me on the bed, scrubbing my hands over my face and eyes. For all my talking to Caleb about not having teenage hormones, my dick sure is sporting morning wood. Karina gets me hard, no matter what she's doing. Just thinking about her is enough. I wonder if this is what people meant when they said there were honeymoon stages of relationships? With Caleb's mom, it really was the fact that I was a teenager, an errant wind could have gotten me hard. Now that I'm older, I honestly can't remember a woman I've had a reaction to like this.

Quickly, I take a shower, before getting dressed and cautiously walking into the kitchen. Last thing I want to do is interrupt a moment or some shit.

"Morning, Dad," Caleb talks around a mouthful of oatmeal. "Coffee's made, and your fave cup is over there." He gives me a huge, over-exaggerated smile.

I stare at him for a moment, but let it go as I get my coffee. "Morning to you two."

"Thanks for letting me stay here last night, Mr. Harrison. My mom texted me and told me that you'd sent her a message. I really appreciate it. Thanks for not letting her know where I really was."

Because of the job I have, I'd struggled with the decision as to what to tell Jess' mom, but in the end, I didn't want to worry another parent when things ended up being fine. After the way Caleb shared his disappointment, I have a feeling she won't be doing it again. Turning around, I stir the coffee I have with my sugar.

"It's no problem, I'm just glad you're okay, and please call me Mason, anything else makes me feel old as hell."

"You are old as hell," Caleb interjects.

"My mom is forty-five," Jess argues, as she takes a bite of her own oatmeal. "You're lucky to have a dad young enough to do cool stuff with." She puts her hand on Caleb's forearm.

The way they look at each other, I wonder if they did keep it PG last night, but as I told Rina, I trust my son. He's an adult, and accusing him of something he may or may not have done won't get me anywhere. I want us to enjoy the time we have left together. "Yeah Caleb, you're lucky to have a young dad who's awesome."

He coughs around the spoonful of oatmeal he's just put in his mouth. "I'm lucky to have you, but thirty-four seems so old."

It had seemed old to me too when I was his age, but now I'm coming to the realization that a new stage of my life is about to begin. At Christmas I'd been dreading Caleb going off to school, I'd been worried about how lonely I would be. Now? Now I'm kind of looking forward to seeing what happens, how I handle it, how Karina and I spend our time together. Instead of dreading summer, I'm looking at it with a realization that it might not be as bad as I had assumed.

"And eighteen seems so young," I throw back at him. "I've been old a long time; I had to grow up fast because of you." I tip my coffee cup at Caleb. "But I wouldn't change it, bud. Not at all."

"Yeah." He nods, finishing his bowl of oatmeal. "I'm not sure what I'd do if my dad was forty-five. Pretty sure your mom doesn't let you talk to her the way he lets me talk to him."

Jess laughs, looking between the two of us. "Not at all, but your relationship is different, and that's okay."

Finishing up my coffee, I put the cup in the sink, clapping my hands. "You two ready? Rina will be waiting on us."

"Dad's dating Ms. Holland." Caleb stands up, stretching as Jess looks over at me, eyes wide.

"She's the prettiest teacher we have, and you're way hotter than Mr. Cartwright." She clamps her hand over her mouth after the words escape.

"Who's Mr. Cartwright?" I ask, feeling jealousy like I haven't felt possibly ever.

"Science teacher who's asked her out a few times." Jess keeps talking, even though I have a feeling she doesn't mean to. "Honestly, he's a bit creepy, a lot of us girls think so. I'm glad Ms. Holland didn't go out with him. I'm sure the two of you have a lot more in common. His room is the one that the dog went into when we had the lockdown at school."

Immediately I've got my cop hat on. "Why does he make you feel creepy?"

Her eyes meet Caleb's and it looks like she doesn't want to speak, but he stares at her in the same way I do.

"Just the way he looks at us." She pushes her oatmeal away. "When we have practice, he's usually still at school, which is odd. By the time we leave, most teachers are gone. But he's hanging out by the locker rooms. He tells us it's because he wants to make sure we get out okay, since it's dark when we leave. I don't buy it."

"Why do you not buy it?" Caleb asks before I can question what she's said to me.

She shifts in her seat, almost as if she doesn't want to answer. Eventually she begins talking. "None of us ever stay alone in the locker room, because he's come in more than once to 'see if anyone's left'. I mean, not even Coach Williams comes in to check on us. She gives us our privacy and it used to be when the last person left, we'd text her and let her know, then lock up behind us. Now, since he's come in a few times, we don't ever stay by ourselves."

"Did he come in on you?" I ask her, already knowing I'm going to be talking to the principal about this as soon as I can.

"I was one of the ones who was changing when he came in." She looks down at her hands. "Thank God my back was to the door, otherwise, he would have seen more than most."

"Did he even fuckin' knock?" Caleb asks, grabbing hold of her hand.

"No." She shakes her head. "He said he assumed we were done because we weren't practicing anymore. Some of us take showers before we leave though. Regardless of what most everyone thinks, cheerleading is a sport, and depending on what we do, we sweat big time. If I have somewhere to be, I don't want to go stinking."

"Any of you report this?"

She shakes her head again, biting her bottom lip. "No, we were afraid no one would believe us. There aren't cameras in that part of the school, and we knew it would be our word against his. All of us who were there are seniors, and none of us want to get into that shit with a few months left in school. I have a scholarship and I don't want anyone to mess with it. I'm gonna get out of Laurel Springs and not come back."

And it's in that moment, I realize why she and Caleb won't last. If there's anything I know about my son, it's that he loves Laurel Springs. It's the home he always wanted, the place to put down roots he always craved. I have zero doubt that after he graduates, he'll come back here and live out the rest of his life. And when I look at him, I see he knows that too, but it doesn't stop him from giving everything he has to this girl. He leans over, kissing her on the cheek.

"One thing I can promise you is that my dad will take care of it."

"I will." I give her my promise. "There's no reason he should be scaring you ladies."

Not to mention it's not sat well with me that the dog picked up a scent in his classroom and nothing was ever found. I've now made it my mission to find out everything I can about Mr. Cartwright. If he has done something to hurt these kids, I'll make sure he's punished to the full extent of the law.

CHAPTER TWELVE

MENACE

AS WE'VE DRIVEN across town to Rina's house, I've been lost in thought, not paying attention to what's going on in the backseat of the Jeep. Feeling a little weird and guilty that my son and his girlfriend are sitting where Rina and I had sex, but there's nothing I can do about it now. I'm anxious to see her as evidenced by the way my fingers tap along to the radio on the steering wheel. Will this feeling of being excited to see her go away? God I hope not.

We pull up to Karina's house, and I can't get over how hard my heart is tripping at the thought of being around her. "You two sit tight, I'll be right back."

Slipping out of the driver's seat, I go up the porch steps two at a time, because I'm so excited to see her. Before I can knock on the door, she's opening it.

"Hey." My voice is breathless because I'm so excited to see her.

She smiles up at me, leaning in to give me a kiss.

So badly I want to reach in, wrap my arms around her waist, and give in to the overwhelming need I have to crush her to me. Instead I keep those feelings locked down and let her pull away.

"Hey, yourself." She steps back and I get a good look at her shirt.

I wish I was Felicia, she's always going somewhere.

The laugh that busts out of my gut causes her to giggle along with me. "You like it? I love shirts that have sayings on them. I even have one that says *Adios Pantalones*, but I didn't think that was appropriate for today." She turns on the porch light that works, placing a purse over her shoulder, and grabs her jacket.

"Oh yeah, that reminds me, leave the door open and I'll fix the lightbulb for you. Can you go to the Jeep and ask Caleb for the bag I packed?"

"No problem, big guy. Gotta say, you changing my porch light? Hot."

"That other dude you were with must not have done anything exciting."

She tilts her head to the side. "The thing with him was, he was a caller. He'd call someone to fix what was wrong. He wasn't a fixer, didn't like to get his hands dirty."

"Luckily for you, I like to get my hands dirty." I give her a wink, along with a smirk. I've missed seeing her, even though it's only been a few days. I've missed seeing the way her cheeks heat when I make a comment like this. The way her eyes light up and shine at me. Does something to my stomach that's never happened before.

"That is pretty lucky for me." She turns around, heading toward the Jeep.

When I look up again, Caleb is walking to me with the bag I requested. "Do we need to shut off the breaker?" he asks, digging through it to get the lightbulb.

"No, just do me a favor and turn off the switch from the inside." Rina's made her way back to where we are, and Jess is standing next to the Jeep, phone at her ear.

"Her mom called, she's probably telling her about the boring night she had at your house." She gives me a grin.

"Hey, I'm not boring," Caleb protests as he comes back to where we stand. "It's off, Dad."

"Not you." She throws a glance in my direction. "Your dad."

I don't miss the way her eyes travel my body as I extend to my full height, reaching up to unscrew the lightbulb. Feeling a breeze at my midsection, I can tell my t-shirt has risen over the waistband of my jeans. I shake the lightbulb, hearing the jingle of the piece that proves it's blown. Switching it with what Caleb holds in his hands, this time I watch Karina's face as I reach up to finishing replacing what we've taken out. Her eyes travel down my body and zero in on the spot that exposes itself again. I wonder briefly if she's looking at the skin or my package – either way I like it. When I finish, I tell Caleb to go turn the light back on, and then cut my gaze to her.

"You enjoy the show?"

She licks her lips, before flipping her hair over her shoulder. "Always do, big guy. Let's get this show on the road."

"Wait, I don't even get a thanks?"

"You will." She turns back around, walking over to me. Her eyes drop, as does the tone of her voice. "You'll get the best thanks ever later."

"Looking forward to it. Also looking forward to proving to you I'm not boring." I give her ass a smack as I help her into the passenger side of my Jeep.

Truth be told, I don't think I've ever looked more forward to anything else in my life.

"DOES it surprise you they didn't really wanna hang out with us?"

Karina pulls my arm closer to her, entwining our fingers together as we walk through the crowd that's gathered for the show. It's usually a huge one, and given the amount of people in the convention center, this year is no exception.

"Not at all," I answer loud enough for her to hear me. "Whenever Caleb has a friend with him, it's a toss-up though. Sometimes they hang out with me, other times they don't. Since I have someone to spend my time with today, I'm not surprised."

"Does it make you sad?"

"That he doesn't wanna hang out with me?" I shake my head. "Nah, we spend a lot of time together at home. I'm cool with it. Right now I want to spend the day with you." I tap her nose with my finger.

The look of adoration she gives me is everything I've ever wanted from the woman in my life. "You know I'd never get between you and him, I know he leaves soon."

"He does," I acknowledge. "But by the same token, I got a life to live, Rina, and I'm ready live it."

"I want to be the person you live it with." She turns, putting her arms around my waist.

"Same here." I lean down, brushing my lips against hers.

Karina

Never in my life have I been to a hunting and fishing show, never actually thought I would ever be at one. When I moved to Alabama it hadn't been high on my bucket list, but I'm quickly learning I want to do anything and everything I can with the man standing next to me. He's eyeing a tent set up with one of the displays.

"You like camping?"

I look behind me to make sure he's actually speaking to me. "Big guy, I'm from Philly, do I look like I'm made to camp?"

A gorgeous smile spreads across his face, reaching his eyes as he chuckles slightly. "You look like you're made for me, but not necessarily camping."

"Maybe I'd do it with you, once or twice, probably in the back yard of my or your house, but I wouldn't put much stock in me enjoying it." I bend down to glance inside the tent. It looks spacious, more spacious than I had given it credit for, but I'm still not feeling it. Where is my Netflix? Where do I plug in my hair dryer? These are all important questions I have.

"Not for you?" He rests his hand casually on my ass as I straighten up.

"I don't think so."

Putting his arm around my neck, he pulls me close as we navigate through the crazy crowd. "You don't have to camp," he assures me as he twists a piece of my hair with his finger.

Our eyes meet when I glance over. "I'd try it with you. I'd try most anything once with you."

"Anything, huh?" The wink he gives me is full of promise. The promise that we'll finally talk about our schedules and figure out a time when we can get together. "How about you share one of those bar-b-que platters with me?" He points over to a food vendor set up in the food court area.

Surprised at what he was really hinting at, I nod. "Sure, like I said, anything with you, big guy."

As he steers me through the people, his mouth tucks in close to my ear. "I'll hold you to that promise in a more carnal way later. No need for you to worry about that, Rina."

The tone and the promise send shivers down my body. I've never had a reaction like this to any other man I've ever dated. This man can own me, it wouldn't take much. Fuck, I'm basically already eating out of his hand. "I'm not worried." My answer is flippant with just a little bit of sass.

"You should be." He winks.

That wink? Travels all the way through my body. We've arrived at a commissary area, where they're selling more than bar-b-que. Looks like they have pizza, hot dogs, and hamburgers to go along with it.

"Want to split a pizza instead?" he asks as we walk toward the counter.

"Yes." I try to play it cool, but my stomach is growling, just thinking about it. "Walking all over this place has totally burned off the protein bar I had to start the day."

"You eat protein bars?"

"Sometimes." I shrug. "Depends on what I have going on in the morning. Typically I'm an oatmeal and banana girl, but when I don't have time, a protein bar will do in a pinch."

"Jesus, a woman after my own heart. I love oatmeal with bananas."

I turn around in his arms to face him. Hooking my fingers in his belt loops, I give him a smile. "Maybe one day we can have breakfast together."

He tucks me into his body. "I'm definitely putting that on the calendar."

As the two of us step forward and order a pepperoni pizza with a side salad and waters, I watch as the woman taking our food order looks Mason up and down. Tucking my hand in his back pocket, I give her my own look, letting her know this one's taken.

"Your number is one-thirty-four, and we'll call it when your order is ready," the girl tells him.

She reaches out, handing him a paper with the number on it. I grab it before her fingers can touch his. "We'll be up to get it." I turn us around and head toward an empty seat.

Mason laughs as he pulls out my chair for me. "Didn't know how jealous you are." He sits across from me.

"I found the awesomeness that is you first." I give him a grin. "You're mine, big guy."

"You'll find no arguments from me."

Pulling my phone out of my pocket, I glance over at him. "So about those schedules?"

By the time we get up, we have a date lined up for Wednesday night, and there's nothing else I'm looking forward to more.

CHAPTER THIRTEEN

KARINA

SINCE SUNDAY, I've been anxiously awaiting Wednesday. The week so far has been the slowest week of my life, but as the bell rings, I'm not hanging around; making sure no one needs me. No, I'm packing up my stuff and getting the fuck out of dodge.

Caleb gives me a little grin and wink as he leaves. I do have the decency to be a little embarrassed, but at the same time, I'm beyond ready to see Mason. As I shut down my computer and lock my classroom, I'm pulling my phone out of my purse and pausing to shoot off a quick message to him.

K: Leaving school right now. You're off shift in an hour, right?

M: Yeah, so expect to be at the house in about two hours. I want to take a shower. Caleb's working tonight, so we should have plenty of time to ourselves.

Given the way the two of us seem to behave with one another, I'm not sure if any amount of time will ever truly be enough.

K: See you there, big guy!

As I round the corner, heading toward the teacher's lot, I crash into someone. "Oh my God, I'm so sorry! I wasn't watching where I was going, shouldn't text and walk." I glance up, seeing Mr. Cartwright standing in front of me, he reaches out to steady me, and I pull away quickly.

"It's okay, do you need me to make sure you get to your car alright?"

Mr. Cartwright has given me the creeps since the first time we met. He put his hand on my shoulder and it was like someone had walked on my grave. Literally made my skin crawl. He's asked me out numerous times, and I've always turned him down. It's not that he's not cute. He is in a Spencer Reid, *Criminal Minds*, sort of way. But in all honesty, unless you're Mason Harrison, I'm in no way, shape, or form interested.

"No, I got it, just a little preoccupied tonight. Thanks for the offer." I do my best to be polite.

I wave; gazing back down at my phone, acting like what's on it is the most important thing in the world. As I leave the hallway and go out the doors, I look back. Mr. Cartwright is staring at me. This time, I turn around, not looking back, and head straight for my car. Once I get there, I lock the door, without a backward glance, and head for home.

ALMOST TWO HOURS LATER. Showered, changed, and freshly shaved, I'm heading toward Mason's home. He gave me the address and when I plugged it into my GPS, I realized we don't live far from one another at all. His house is in a little bit of an older section of town, but if given the choice, I would have bought a house there when I moved, just because of the gorgeous Craftsman style architecture. Within ten minutes I'm pulling up to the type of house I would have loved to buy, but instead, I got stuck renting the newer one I have.

Mason's Jeep sits in the driveway of a well-maintained and blue-gray house with white shutters. The landscaping is immaculate. The excited thumping of my heart is loud in my ears as I make my way up the front steps onto the porch. Before I can even knock, he's opened the door and pulled me through the entry way.

"I heard you pull up," he explains, as he tosses my purse onto a catch-all next to the door and takes off my jacket, hanging it on a coat rack in the hallway. He motions for me to kick off my shoes, which I do, and then I give myself a moment to take it all in.

For that moment, I get to look around the living room. It's dark, manly, and well-kept. Nothing like what I imagined with a teenager and a bachelor living here.

"I'll give you the tour next time, or a little later," he promises as he directs me down a hallway, pushing me through the threshold of a door into another room.

Immediately I know this is Mason's bedroom. The scent is unmistakable.

"Have you thought about this as much as I have?" I tilt my head to the side, asking him the question I've been dying to ask all day.

"Probably more," he admits as he pulls me into him. Grabbing hold of my hand, he brings it down to the tent in the athletic shorts he's wearing. "All day long, Rina. All fucking day long."

I know what he means. I've been horny all day long too, just thinking of the way he played my body last time. Thinking of how I felt the effects of him for days afterwards. Just knowing we can get naked this time? It's increasing my arousal tenfold.

Before I even ask him how we're going to play this, he reaches down, lifting my shirt off my head and over my body. I wore my favorite bra for this, and I can tell he appreciates it. It's a see-through mesh material with little flowers on it. The way he angles his hand to run his thumb over my nipples causes me to throw my head back and just feel. His big fingers are at my belly, unbuttoning my jeans, and when he pushes them down my thighs, I know we're getting completely serious.

"You're so damn beautiful." His voice is an octave lower, and when I tilt my head back up, his eyes are on my tits, right before he leans forward and takes one of my hard nipples in his mouth.

Gripping his hair, I hold him close with one hand, while I struggle to push down those shorts with the other. He helps as he breaks the suction on my flesh before pulling his shirt over his head. "God, Mase." I let my eyes travel over his body. "I don't think I've ever been with anyone as hot as you."

Encircling his arms around my waist, he picks me up, tossing me on his bed. "I know I've never been with anyone as hot as you."

And as he looks at me through those hooded eyes, I know I'm a goner.

"Spread those legs for me, baby. Let me see."

I know what he wants to see. How wet I am, how very much I want his cock deep inside me. I'm coy as I do it, inching my hand down my stomach to the lace band of the panties I wear. When my finger toys with the edge, his eyes zero in, and then his fingers are fighting with mine.

In seconds, I'm not sure where those panties are, and he's pressing between my legs with his body, his lips coming down on top of mine. When they meet, I moan deep in my throat as his chest rakes against my nipples, and his cock taunts my clit.

"Please, Mason," I beg, and when he grabs hold of my wrists, holding them over my head in one of his hands, my body rejoices.

Menace

"You don't have to beg, Rina. Just tell me what you want." My voice is deeper than normal. If I didn't know myself, I'd assume I'm a pack a day smoker who's been doing it for years.

Her legs catch the backs of my thighs. "You, inside me."

I wanna be there too, but I had hoped we'd be able to slow it down this time. Really explore each other's bodies. But maybe that's not in the cards right now. With my free hand, I reach up, pushing her bra up over her tits. As I do so, she lifts for me.

"Take it off."

Letting go of her wrists, I take note that she keeps them up where I had them, never makes a move to bring them down. When I get the bra off, I clamp my hands back around those wrists and bring my mouth down to those nipples begging for my touch. When I lightly use my teeth, her fingers grasp mine, her nails biting into my knuckles.

"Mason, oh God." She pushes against me, bucks against my hips with hers, cries out as I soothe the nip with my tongue. "I can't wait." Her head thrashes, the ends of her hair hitting our outstretched arms.

Using my free hand, I grab her ass, bringing our bodies into direct contact. Both of us moan loudly as her heat cups mine. "Gotta get a condom." I tap her hip, motioning for her to release me.

Getting up, I grab the condom off my nightstand, rip it open with my teeth, and look at the pretty picture she makes for me against my comforter. "Anyone ever tell you how sexy you look, Karina Holland?"

Her cheeks flush, and she bashfully shakes her head. I wonder why they haven't. She's sex on a stick as she watches me, her hand flitting down to her core. "You wanna touch yourself while I get ready?" She doesn't answer, just extends a finger and thrums her clit.

In response, I give my cock a few jerks, not missing the way her pulse beats at her neck, the way she tilts her head back to get a little of a better view, the way her mouth opens with no sound as I bring my palm over the head, and then cover it with the rubber. Using both hands, I grab her thighs and pull her to me, plunging into her wetness.

"Fuck, Mason," she groans, hooking a leg around me, digging her heel into my ass.

"Yes, fuck Mason," I agree. My tongue goes to work on her neck, kissing down her chest, grabbing hold of those sensitive nipples she has. Her fingers tangle in my hair, yanking on it, the way she loves to do as she arches into me.

She's moaning, but I can tell she's holding back. That's the one thing I don't want her to do. Not while I'm here with my abs flexed, thighs burning as I thrust in and out of her with every part of my body on high alert. "Give it to me, Karina, let me know how I make you feel."

I can see her glance at clock and I know what she's thinking. Caleb's probably home by now, but right now there are no fucks given in my mind. Using the flat of my hand, I pull us over onto our sides and deliver a smack to her ass cheek. "Don't hold back from me," I growl. "If he hears, he hears, I've lived like a monk for too long; I won't let you censor yourself. Give me what I do to you."

Our eyes meet, and I see the arousal that's flared. "You like that?"

She nods. "Mmm hmm." Her nails rake down my chest, tweaking my nipples as we strain against each other.

Pulling her leg over mine, I get deeper. She moans, groaning loudly.

"Oh my God," she moans, tilting her head back, her hands moving down to my waist to hold on as I fuck her hard.

Those hands move to my abdomen, and even that turns me on as I feel my cock elongate and harden further. Slapping her flesh again, she brings her head forward, resting it on my shoulder, her teeth biting deeply into my skin.

"That's it, I like that." She's humping against me allowing me to feel the wetness seeping from her body as she rotates her hips, and I plunge into her.

"You like that?" My voice is getting louder too; I'm being carried away by the way this woman makes me feel. "I fucking love the way you grip me." I navigate to where one hand is on her ass, lightly tapping it, before smacking it harder every few taps, and my other hand is in her hair, pulling and yanking to expose her throat to me.

"Mason." She reaches down from my abdomen, to hold the base of my cock. "I'm gonna come, I'm gonna come." She thrusts against me, jacking the part she can reach.

I'm at work on her neck; our bodies are sliding against one another. The heat in the room between us is almost unbearable as I maneuver her head the way I want it so I can get at the most sensitive part, where shoulder and neck meet. We're leaning on each other, and as I feel her begin to tighten around me, she screams. I moan, groaning so deep in my throat it hurts, as I pump into her, rolling her over onto her back. I can't stop my hips, can't stop from coming as I fill the condom full, as I suck open-mouthed on her neck, and all but devour her body with mine.

As I come down, my heart pounding, my hips still partially thrusting into her, and my lips lightly kissing her skin, I feel a peace I've never felt before. She's breathing heavily too, but I whisper my thoughts. "Can you stay tonight?"

Her gaze is surprised as our eyes meet. "I didn't pack a bag, big guy. Didn't know you might want that with me."

Entwining our fingers together, I capture her lips with mine. "Rina, I want it all with you, never fucking forget that."

CHAPTER FOURTEEN

KARINA

FEBRUARY

I'm watching the kids that just filed into my classroom. On Friday afternoons, typically *everyone* is hyped up, not paying attention and ready to go. This afternoon, I notice one person in particular, is pretty far off that game.

Caleb has a seat at the desk he normally occupies and puts his head down, burrowing deeply into the hoodie he wears, pulling it up over his head. I try to catch his eye, but he keeps his head down, eyes closed.

"How's it going today?" I ask the class as a whole.

"Long day, Ms. H," one of the guys sighs as he shakes his head. "Really long day. I can't speak for the rest of the class, but I had a freakin' pop quiz in Calculus that I'm ninety-nine percent sure I bombed. Happy Friday to me."

Reaching into my desk, I grab a chocolate bar. "Here ya go, Maddox. Bury your sorrows in chocolate, works for me."

He gives me a smile before he rips it open and eats half of it in one bite. "Anybody having a *good* day?" I prompt them.

There's a lot of frowning faces and dejected body language. "Nothing good? Y'all are downright depressing." I speak to them in their language.

"Welcome to our world," one of the girls sighs the same way Maddox did as she curls her hair around her finger. "But I could get happier if you have another chocolate bar."

I give her smile, grabbing another one out as I hand it to her. "I don't have enough chocolate to give to you all, so how about this? I'll take pity on you, and let you have a study hall today. Do whatever you need to do to make your weekend easier, and we'll start fresh on Monday. How's that sound?"

There's an audible and physical relief in the room. I watch as almost everyone grabs stuff out of their bags and starts working. Everyone except Caleb. As they all work, I notice that he drifts off to sleep. When the bell rings, he doesn't move. Getting up, I walk over to his desk, and lightly shake his shoulder. "Caleb, the bell rang, are you okay?"

He lifts glassy eyes up to me and for the first time I notice his cheeks are red. "I feel awful." He shivers, pulling the hoodie further around his body. "I called my dad." He puts his hands in his pockets. "But he's on shift and he's trying to find someone to take over for him. He asked me if I could drive myself to the Urgent Clinic, but my head hurts too bad and I'm a little dizzy. I'm scared to drive myself, even if he does meet me there."

There are few times when Caleb looks like a kid to me, and right now he looks like a very sick kid. Immediately the answer is in my mind, and I don't even think twice about it. "C'mon Caleb." I grab his arm, helping him get up from the desk.

He's struggling, trying to walk straight as we approach my desk. I lean him against it, as I grab my purse and jacket. "I'll call Mason on the way; I'm not going to let you suffer like this."

I don't expect him to say anything, and he doesn't as we slowly make our way out of the school. I've got my phone out, calling Mason as we walk.

"Rina, now's not a great time," he answers on the third ring.

"I know." With one hand I open the passenger side door, slipping Caleb inside. Shutting the door, I grab hold of the cell phone. "Caleb is really sick."

"Rina, I know, I'm trying to get someone to come cover my shift, but the weather is shit, and Caleb is technically an adult – or so I've been told five times already."

The worry and irritation in his voice is palpable. He was right about both of the things he said. The weather is shit; I would have to agree as I stand in the rain, shivering because of the cooler February temperatures. I also concede that Caleb is technically an adult, but it doesn't mean he doesn't need help right now. In this moment, I want to kick some ass of those who are making this difficult on Mason. "I know all of this." I keep my tone even, light, the way I soothe a student who's gotten a bad grade and is in the middle of an epic freak out because they're totally sure they won't be accepted to the college of their dreams. "Which is why I'm taking him to the Urgent Clinic. Finish your shift big guy; I got Caleb taken care of."

"Karina." The word is rough, like he can't believe what I'm telling him. Raw in the way it feels after something really salty is eaten. "You don't have to do this." His voice is quiet this time.

"I want to." I pull my jacket tighter around my body. "From just feeling his forehead, I can tell his temp is high, and sometimes you just need someone to take care of you. We'll be at the house when you get off shift."

He's quiet for longer than I like. "Mason?"

"Thank you isn't enough."

Even though he can't see it, I grin. "Thank you is plenty. I'll let you know what the doctor says."

"Please keep me informed."

We end the call as I get into the driver's seat. "You good, Caleb?"

He's leaned back in the seat with his arms wrapped around his chest shivering. "So cold."

Reaching over, I turn on the seat warmers and then crank the heat up. A part of me wants to leave him alone, let him rest until we get to the clinic, the other part of me is worried about how high his fever is, since we didn't take it with a thermometer. "When did you start feeling bad?"

Audibly he swallows, and I wonder if his throat hurts. "I didn't feel good this morning, but when the weather changes like this, I always feel like shit. Typically I get those pressure headaches, but around lunch I felt like a Mac Truck had hit me. That's when I texted Dad." He rolls his head on the headrest. "My body hurts so bad, and I wanted to leave, but I was scared to drive myself. Turns out three of the other MTF guys are sick, and Havoc is covering the shortage, so he was asking other officers to come in, but no one was responding."

"Caleb, I'm so sorry you had to sit through half a day feeling like that." I reach over, grabbing onto his clammy hand. Even the skin there is hot to the touch.

"S'ok." He pries his eyes open. "Kinda used to it. The only time I ever had someone to take care of me besides Dad was when my grandmother lived with us while Dad was deployed."

My heart breaks, literally breaks as I hear him tell the story of the two of them against all the odds. How many times has Mason needed help and had no one to turn to? How often has Caleb been sick and needed to feel the soft touch of a mother but had no one? Fighting back tears, I pull into the patient drop off for the clinic and then rush to park before hurrying inside. When I get there, Caleb is number three in line.

"My back is killing me," he moans as we move up.

Pushing my hand up under his jacket, I do my best to massage the tight muscles at his back and up around his shoulders. "It's where you've been shivering."

"So fuckin' sore." He coughs into the crook of his elbow.

When it's our turn, we move forward. Caleb, obviously a pro at this, tells them his name, tells him that his insurance hasn't changed, and his symptoms. They hand him a mask to wear, as well as one for me. Then the registration clerk asks a question, and I know the answer will completely change my relationship not only with Caleb, but with Mason as well.

"You've got a fifty-dollar co-pay, Caleb. You want us to bill it to your dad? And we need consent to treat too."

"I'm eighteen," he answers, fumbling in his wallet. "I can take care of this on my own."

Gently pushing him aside, I grab the pen from the clerk, sign my name, and dig through my purse before sliding my debit card toward her. "I'm responsible for him, and I'll pay the co-pay."

Later on when we're in the waiting room, Caleb turns to me. "Why did you do that?"

"Do what?" I glance up from where I'm texting Mason. There's still one person in front of Caleb and me, probably by the time Mason gets off shit, we'll be done.

"Sign as responsible for me and pay that money? Ms. Holland, it's too much." He stretches his legs out in front of him.

This right here, this is a loaded conversation we're about to have, and while I wouldn't choose to have it in the waiting area of a doctor's office, it needs to be said. "I think under the circumstances, you can probably call me Karina, or a nickname if you want. Your dad calls me Rina." I put my phone away. "Look, you aren't a child, so I'm not going to sugar coat this for you. There's something about Mason that's attracted me since the first time I saw him. He's considerate, a good dad to you, and a stand-up guy. I enjoy spending time with him." I push my hair back behind the mask they've had me wear. "And I enjoy spending time with you too. I know you aren't a little kid who needs someone to take care of him, but every once in a while, like when you're sick, everyone wants a little compassion. There was no way I was going to let you wait hours for Mason, not when I know it was killing him, and I could help the two of you out. That's just not who I am."

Caleb looks at me, his gaze so very much like his dad's. I almost feel as if I'm looking at younger version of Mason. "We've never had anyone in our lives like you, Karina."

"Good." I laugh. "Because I've never had anyone like the two of you in mine."

Folding his arms back over his chest, he levels me with his stare. "Don't hurt my dad, please don't hurt my dad. If there's anyone in this world who deserves love, it's him."

"That's a little further than we've gone." I squirm in my seat. My feelings for Mason are strong, which is why a little over a month after our first date I'm taking his son to the doctor, but love? I swore I'd never take that lightly again.

"I know my dad, and I know what kind of a woman you are. You two can fuck around with each other all you want, but feelings are involved. I'd have to be blind and deaf not to see or hear it." He flashes me a tired grin.

Hearing it. Good God. That night when Mason told me he didn't care who heard what he was doing to me. Caleb had heard it. Shit. I don't know what to say, I'm stunned, and then I'm saved as they call his name to be taken back. "Want me to go with you?"

"Yeah." He reaches down, grabbing my hand. "I've never been to a doctor by myself before, and honestly, it's a little scary."

The flashes of vulnerability are what endear this kid to me, and I question what in the hell kind of woman could abandon him. Quickly I follow him, wait as they take his weight, blood pressure, and temperature. "One hundred and two point nine," the nurse says as she looks at me. "Good thing you brought him in, he sounds a little dehydrated. Heart rate is a slightly elevated."

For the length of the visit, I'm a quiet reassurance to him, putting my hand on his back when they make him take a flu test, and grimacing when the test comes back positive.

"Good thing it's a Friday, right?" He tilts his head to me.

I agree with him. "Really good thing, sounds like you need to rest."

My phone buzzes in my hand, and I glance down to see who it is. "One second please, it's his dad."

M: Any update?

K: In with the doctor right now, I'll text you once we get home and he gets situated.

"And lots of fluids." The attending doctor hands me a prescription after I finish my text with Mason. "If his fever doesn't break in forty-eight hours, or gets higher, we need to see him back here. I can't stress enough the amount of fluids he needs, and here's an excuse for school. Don't send him back until Wednesday – this particular strain is not a laughing matter. Watch yourself and anyone else in the home. First sign of symptoms, call in here, and we'll get some of the Tamiflu called in for you too. Any questions?"

"Nope." I shake my head as I help Caleb back into his jacket and watch the doctor wash his hands. I do the same before we leave and head to the grocery store where the pharmacy is located to pick up his prescription.

"Do you have Gatorade at your house?" I ask him as we walk back to see if they have his medication ready yet.

"No." He shakes his head.

"Okay, you wait here, and I'll go grab some things you can eat and drink. If they call your name, tell them I'll be right back."

He nods, but has a seat with his head in his hands. I know the poor kid has to feel horrible. It's a work out as I practically run up and down the aisles getting Gatorade, orange juice, water, some jello, applesauce, the stuff to make grilled cheese, and some chicken noodle soup. When I glance at my phone, I see that I've done it all in fifteen minutes, and miracle of all miracles there's no one in the checkout line. Pushing my cart of bags back to the pharmacy location, they're just now calling Caleb's name. "Watch this stuff for me."

"Shit, Karina, did you buy the whole damn store?" His eyes are wide as he looks at the four, maybe five bags, in the cart.

"You're sick, you need things, and if you think this is me buying the whole store, you ain't seen nothing yet, kid."

I turn back to the pharmacy counter as they call his name again. When they ask me for sixty bucks for the medication, I get a stark dose of reality. This is what Mason's had to deal with his whole life. A simple visit to the doctor for a kid can sometimes cost over a hundred bucks when you factor in time off, food, medicine, doctor visit. I never want these two to have to go through something like this on their own again.

"Come on." I grab the cart, motioning to him. "Let's get you home."

"YOU'LL FEEL BETTER if you take a shower." I'm putting away the groceries I got while Caleb slowly takes his jacket off. "It'll make your muscles relax, and maybe it'll help break your fever."

"You're probably right." He looks like he's about to drop.

"You want some food? You should probably try to eat and drink something."

For a split second, he looks like I imagine he did as a little kid. "I wouldn't say no to one of those grilled cheeses you were talking about with some Gatorade."

"Then that's exactly what you'll have."

Watching his back as he leaves the kitchen, I pick up my phone, shooting off a quick text to Mason.

K: He tested positive for the flu. We got his prescription, doctor was very adamant that he push the fluids, so I got him some stuff to drink and some classic comfort food. We're home now, he's showering, I'm making him a grilled cheese, and I'm going to raid your dresser for something comfy to wear. Any objections?

I realize I'm not only being presumptuous, but I'm stepping on all kinds of boundaries with the message I just sent to Mason. I wonder how he'll respond to it.

M: Thank you so much for taking care of him. Thank you for taking that stress off me and being my partner when I really need one. Babe, get whatever you need. I'll be home in about an hour. Wait for me?

You can't knock the smile off my face with a two by four. Him requesting I stay, telling me it's okay to raid his clothes? We just moved into boyfriend and girlfriend territory, and I'm as giddy as I was when I was a teenager about it.

K: Me and your couch have a date with a blanket and a nap after Caleb lies down. Taking care of a teenager is tough work, but I think I handled it well.

M: You did, and we're grateful to you for it. When I get in, I'll lie down with you.

K: Seriously my favorite part of the day, and I can't wait.

No matter how stressful these last few hours may have been, I'm completely and totally looking forward to the rest of the night.

CHAPTER FIFTEEN
MENACE

WHEN I PULL into my driveway, the pit of my stomach warms, and my heart beats a little faster. Having another car parked next to where mine normally is, having someone inside, waiting on me? I never imagined there would be a time in my life that I could count on any of it. No one is more surprised than me, that I can now.

The house is quiet when I enter through the side door, but when I listen closely, I can hear the TV playing softly in the living room. It's seven at night when I check the clock, but obviously these two had a rough day. Taking off all my gear and slipping out of my boots, I make my way into the living room, and what greets me puts the biggest smile on my face.

Karina lies on the couch, wrapped up in a blanket, wearing one of my shirts, sleeping so soundly she hasn't noticed me come in. As quiet as I can, I walk over to where she lays, gently putting my hand on her shoulder.

"Rina, wake up, I'm home," I whisper.

She stirs slightly and then sits up when she realizes it's me. "Hey." Her voice is thick with sleep as she tries to acclimate to her surroundings. "I didn't mean to sleep that long."

"It's okay." I slide into the spot vacated by her, pulling her down across my lap. "You've had a rough day."

"So have you." She reaches up, pushing her fingers through my hair. The move is soothing rather than sexual. Grabbing her hand when she pulls it away, I bring her fingers to my mouth, kissing the tips.

"It's been a hell of a day." I sigh, kicking out my feet in front of me. "How's

Caleb? I don't want to wake him up, but I'll go check on him here in a few minutes."

"What time is it?" she asks, looking around for a clock. "It's probably almost time to take his temperature again."

"Little after seven. Give me a rundown of what the doctor said before we go check on him. Do you know how hard it was for me to leave his care to someone else?" I push her bangs back off her forehead, enjoying the rhythmic way I'm stroking her skin.

"Do you know how hard it was for your son to let me help him?" She laughs. "He kept apologizing. Saying he was costing me too much money and that he was an adult and he should be able to take care of all this by himself."

"He gets that from me." My tone is rueful. "I'm constantly telling him that it's time he take responsibility for his actions. But I never meant it was time for him to pay his medical bills on a busboy and waiter's tips. How much do I owe you, by the way? Between the medicine, doctor's visit, and food, I know this wasn't cheap."

She sits up, gazing at me long enough to make it uncomfortable. "Mason," she sighs, running her palm along the beard on my cheek. "You've done a lot on your own for so long. I can't believe what you've done on your own. It was mindboggling to me, and like I knew that you were strong, knew that you took your responsibilities seriously, but for as young as you were... Holy shit, I'm just..." she lets the words trail off in the silence of the room.

"Not gonna lie." I tilt my head into her palm. "When I was eighteen- nineteen, it was scary as hell. At least when I was a minor, Caleb got state health insurance, so I never had to worry about any of that stuff. Until I turned eighteen, and his mom left. Then it was up to me, that's why I joined the Army. You know how scary it was filling out the paperwork for a life insurance policy, knowing it was there in case something happened to me, but also trying to figure out who would take care of my child at the same time?"

"I can't even imagine." She puts her head on my shoulder. "I'm still stuck on a mother leaving a two-year-old child."

The chuckle I let escape is harsh. "I used to hate Maggie so much, especially on nights like this when Caleb was sick and I had to leave work, or had to find someone to help me take care of him. Or those school events where the 'Room Mom' is supposed to make sure there's cupcakes for all the kids. So many times I was embarrassed, not only because I sucked at that shit, but I was so young. I felt like I embarrassed him too, ya know? I wasn't perfect, and my cupcakes looked awful." I laugh again. "But the one thing I fuckin' hated her for more than anything, were the two years of deployments I had. One when he was five, and another when he was seven. He didn't know me when I came home. Back then there really wasn't internet, or things like that. I mean there were, but it's not the type of infrastructure there is today. He didn't even really know what I looked like. I remember breaking off from my line of guys and running up to him. I was so excited to see him. He'd just turned six, and he didn't even recognize me. Cried when I picked him up, because I'd had to grow a full beard over there. They put me in with the locals. Hardest damn time of my life." I clear my throat. "There are a lot of things I've forgiven that bitch for, but that? That's never gonna be one of them."

She's quiet as I stroke the back of her neck, the motion calming me as I think back to those hard first years of Caleb's life. We survived, because we had no other choice, but it wasn't thanks to anybody other than ourselves, a few friends, and a handful of family members.

"Is that why you left the Army?" she asks softly.

"The second deployment literally made me sick to my stomach. He started acting out, my mom couldn't handle him, he was in trouble at school, and no one knew what to do with him. By some miracle I was sent home a few weeks early and no one knew it. I watched him for two days, just sat back and watched, before I even told him I was home. He was a kid who was hurting, and I couldn't hurt him anymore. It would have been real easy for me to be career military, probably would have benefited us in ways I don't even know now, but it wasn't what was best for him. And since she didn't care, I had to." My mouth twists at the distaste of what I just said. "No, that's the wrong phrase. I didn't do it because I had to; I did it because I wanted to. But she also left me no option, ya know?"

"Do you know what ever happened to her?"

"Huh." I run my hand through my hair. "I've seen her twice since she left us. Both times she's wanted to come back, to see Caleb, just to make sure he's okay. I've never let her do it, and she never pushed me on it when he was a kid. Always figured if it meant that much to her, she'd take me to court, assert her rights, and if she was serious about it, that's what she would have done. But she never did. I get the feeling every time she showed up, it was because she had nowhere else to go and she thought I was hard up for her."

She turns in my arms, circling her arms around my neck. "Were you? Hard up for her? I mean-," she shrugs, "-the two of you had a child together, there must be some feelings there."

"There were, like eighteen years ago." I chuckle. "There's way too much water under that bridge. No lying to you though, the first time she showed back up, we fucked. But it felt awful. I told myself I'd never do it again, and I haven't. At this point it's been about seven years since I've seen her."

"One day she'll wake up and regret everything she's done, all the time she's lost and the relationship she doesn't have." Rina leans in, giving me a soft kiss on the lips.

Putting my arms around her waist, I pull her closer. "When she does, we aren't going to be here and there will be zero place for her in our lives."

"I shouldn't be happy about that." She gives me a smile. "But I am. I'm coming to think of the two of you as mine."

Those words echo my sentiment toward how I think of us too. She's got Caleb and me hook, line, and sinker.

"We're completely and totally yours, babe."

"Good, I don't want it to be any other way. How about we go check on Caleb and I can make you some dinner. I think I blew Caleb's mind with the mother of all grilled cheeses." She winks.

"You made him a grilled cheese?" God I love grilled cheese, but I always burn them. They're basically the bane of my existence.

"Sure did. You want one?"

"Two." I lean down, kissing her. "Definitely two. Be right back."

Making my way down the hallway to Caleb's room, I let myself believe this could be my future. This could be our future, if we just open ourselves up to it. There's been a lot of loneliness in our lives, with just the two of us, but if there's anyone we can welcome into our family, it's definitely Rina. Opening Caleb's door, I tiptoe in, and have a seat on the bed.

In sleep, he still reminds me of a little kid, only with some scruff on his face. When his features are relaxed, he's so innocent looking I almost forget about some of the shit he's done. Reaching over, I grab the thermometer, and then slightly shake him awake.

"Caleb, it's time to check that temp."

"Dad?" His eyes are glassy, and I have a feeling the temp is still gonna be there. He's shivering and burrowing deeper into his covers.

"Yeah, it's me. Just got home from work."

"Is Kari still here?"

"Kari?" My eyebrows pull together in confusion.

"Yeah, Ms. Holland said I had to figure out something to call her besides Ms. Holland when we aren't at school, and Rina's already taken." He gives me a pointed stare. "So I came up with Kari." He shrugs.

"Yeah." I shake my head, amazed he can even be thinking of this when he's so sick. "She's here. If I have anything to say about it, she'll stay tonight."

He closes his mouth around the tip of the thermometer I hold out while we wait for it to register. When it does, I whistle. Still almost a hundred and two.

"She was a lifesaver today, Dad. I don't know if she told you everything she did, but if it wasn't for her, I don't know what would have happened. She just took it upon herself to do the shit she thought was right."

"That's kinda her."

His voice is quieter when he speaks this time. "It was pretty cool, having someone besides you worry about me. Not like you don't worry and I don't appreciate it." He pulls the covers tighter. "I do, but her worry was different. She got me popsicles and made me food. It was a softer kind of worry."

"It was a mother's kind of worry," I supply for him, knowing he won't say the words aloud.

"There's not often I feel loss, like I missed out on something because she wasn't around." He swallows audibly. "But today, as she hung out with me and did everything I needed her to do, I felt that loss. Not that you don't do those things for me, but there was just something about having her do it."

"No, I get it. She's special, Caleb. I hope to have her around for a while."

He coughs harshly into his hand. "Would you marry her, Dad? If given the option?"

The question catches me off guard. I've never thought about marrying anyone other than his mom, right after we found out she was pregnant. Thank God that never worked out. I decide to answer honestly because I've always been that way with him. "Rina makes me do a lot of things I swore I would never do. I can't say either way, but I can say it doesn't scare me. Less than two months ago that wasn't even on my radar, but I can tell you without a doubt, I don't want her to leave."

"I don't either, Dad."

I lean down, kissing him on the forehead. "Then we'll do our best to make her stick around. Deal?"

He bumps my fist. "Deal."

"Now get some sleep, let the medicine work. If you need anything, we'll be in the living room. Don't hesitate to call either one of our phones if you can't get out of bed."

"Got it." He rolls over, hugging the pillow to his chest.

When I leave the room, I leave with a smile on my face.

CHAPTER SIXTEEN
MENACE

HAVOC YAWNS LOUDLY from where he sits beside me in the driver's seat. "Tired?" I rub my own eyes, having had a few late nights myself the past week.

"Exhausted man, I don't know how you did this as a teenager, going to school." He takes a drink of his coffee.

Even though it's almost four in the afternoon, he's still drinking java.

"Didn't have a choice." I shrug, nothing about what I did back then was special. No matter how many times people tell me it was amazing, I've never felt that way.

"No." He shakes his head, a firm tone to his voice. "You say that shit all the time. That you didn't have a choice. You had a choice, as evidenced by Caleb's mom. When are you going to stop acting like you've been a martyr and just admit you're a good man?"

Sighing, I push my head back against the leather seat. "I hate acting like what I did was some sort of sacrifice."

"It was a sacrifice. Fuck, you've been responsible since you were sixteen years old."

"Because I made a dumbass decision," I argue. "Did I really know what it meant to have sex with no condom? Yes. Did I really realize what the consequences to my actions were? No. Thank God for my mom, because without her I'd be a totally different person and Caleb wouldn't be who he is today. She saved me, but *my* dad? He never came around." I clear my throat because this is hard to talk about. Hard to admit that I disappointed a man I looked up to so highly. "He could never get over the fact I fucked up so bad."

"You never talk about him." Havoc seems to realize this for the first time.

"He doesn't deserve to be talked about. He and my mom are divorced, and they divorced because of the situation with Caleb. He never could seem to quite get over the fact I fucked up."

"Wait, so let me get this straight. Not only does Caleb not have a mom, but he doesn't have a grandfather, either?"

"Nope." I take a drink of the bottle of water sitting next to me. "And to be honest, I'm okay with that. From the time my dad found out about Caleb, he was a mean bastard. Kept telling me I'd completely ruined my life. I'd end up married, depressed, and alone, begging my wife for sex or even for a little bit of affection. Now, as an adult, I can see that's probably what happened to him. He and Mom were married eight months before I was born, so I guess the apple doesn't fall far from the tree." I run my fingers through my hair.

"I think you broke the cycle with Caleb." Havoc's voice is dead serious. "He's made it this far – he's got the scholarship, a good head on his shoulders. It's because you're a good man who understands what his son needs. It's what makes you a good cop, too. You listen, assess situations, and react accordingly. There's never been a moment where I wonder where your head is, even when all that shit was going down with him a few months ago. You're a good dad, Mason, but you're a great man. The people in your life who've left you are the ones missing out, not the other way around. Those of us that have you here in our circle are lucky as hell."

It means a lot to hear him say that, almost to the point that I become emotional. I've lived a lot of my life wondering when the other shoe will drop, when the next thing happens that makes me adjust my timeline. In all honesty, I've been doing that with Rina, too.

"You think Karina's lucky?" I throw the sentence out there, not sure why. Maybe today I need some confirmation on what I'm doing right in my life. It's not like Havoc and I need our egos stroked, but once in a while it's nice to know we're on the right track.

"Hell yeah. I can't speak for how you treat her as the man in her life, but I've seen the two of you together a few times now. The way she smiles at you? You've got that on lock down, whether you know it or not, whether you really wanted it or not."

"I wanted it, I want it," I interrupt him. "But like I said, it's hard to take shit at face value. I hear stuff. There's other teachers at school who want her, she's younger than I am. Caleb comes with me, and what woman her age wants a stepchild a few years younger than she is? I'm loaded with a shit ton of baggage."

"We all are, Mason. Don't act like you're special."

The chuckle that works its way past my throat is one I've needed to feel for a while. "Got it, I'm not a special snowflake."

"We all got shit in our pasts, some worse than others, but fuck, dude. She's into you. She loves your son, and I don't think anyone can miss she loves you too. I know it's hard for you to let things happen, I know it goes against every fiber of your being, but let this play out. Caleb leaves at the end of the school year. Then it's just the two of you. It's going to be important for you to have someone to share those lonely moments with, don't blow it yet."

"I'd rather not blow it period."

"Then don't." Havoc grins over at me. "Just don't. Tell her how you feel about her and move forward."

"Because that worked so well with you?" I quirk my eyebrow at my friend.

"Leigh knows I love her," he argues.

"She didn't, not at first."

"Exactly, I had to tell her, I had to show my feelings and let her know what was going on. Women aren't mind readers, just like we aren't. You've gotta let her in, Mason."

"It's hard," I admit. "So hard to let anyone in. Even when I think I'm ready, and I tell myself I am, it's hard. She's coming over to the house now, she's staying some nights. I just don't know if I can let her realize how important she is to me."

"You let me be your friend."

He's right, and he makes a good point. I let the MTF guys and their women into my life, and it has been amazing not only for me, but for Caleb too. I can only imagine what will happen if I let Rina in all the way. Something tells me it'll be one of the best decisions I've ever made, if I can just move past the fear.

Karina

"No, Caleb." I laugh as he demolishes a potato with the knife he's holding. "You have to cut it in quarters or strips, otherwise it won't get done."

"I don't know if I'm completely cut out for this cooking thing," he sighs. "I don't know how Dad does it."

He does it because he has to, and he does it because from what I can tell, he really only knows like five recipes well. "Mason's a jack of all trades."

Caleb makes a noise of affirmation in his throat. "Can I ask you a question, Kari?"

His voice is so serious, I'm not positive I want to know what the question is. "Are you gonna move in here when I'm gone?"

The knife I'm holding takes a sharp detour to the left. "I don't know, Caleb, your dad and I haven't really talked about it."

"I mean, you stay here at least part of the week now. You have since I got sick."

He's right. Since the middle of February I've spent more time here than I have at my own house. The feeling has been mutual; anytime I'm invited over I pack a bag and typically don't go home. With Mason not working a set shift, sometimes it's the only way we can see one another throughout the week. "It's something Mason and I will have to discuss, I just don't know how to answer your question, Caleb."

"I'm just sayin'." He shrugs. "I'd be okay if you did. Hell, I'd be okay if you did tomorrow."

"Thanks, Caleb. You'll never know how much your approval means to me. But we'll see what happens."

"I've gotta go switch out the laundry, it's my week." He runs his hands under the faucet, cleaning off the residue from the food. "Be right back."

I watch him as he leaves, before turning my attention back to the meal I'm cooking. I don't hear Mason until he speaks.

"He's right you know, you could move in here tomorrow, and I think we'd all be okay with it."

My hand stops chopping the vegetables, but I don't turn around, letting what he's said to me sink in. "Are you sure?"

"It's funny." He walks over to one of the stools at the breakfast bar and has a seat. "I was just talking to Havoc today about what you mean to me. And I was explaining to him about I'm not sure how to put into words what those feelings are because you know we haven't been together that long, but I know I feel strongly for you. It's not easy for me to let people in, and it's even harder for me to verbalize those feelings. Please understand what it means, me asking you to live here with me, with us."

Not able to stay away from him any longer, I eat up the distance between us with sure-footed steps. When I reach him, I circle my arms around his neck. "I know exactly what you mean, big guy, and I feel the same way. I'd like to live here with the two of you." I can't believe I'm taking this step. "I don't sleep as well without you anymore."

He leans forward, resting his forehead on mine, eyes closed. "I don't sleep so good without you anymore either."

"It'll be a few weeks before I can get moved in here. You understand, right? I gotta pack up all my shit."

"I'll help you," he vows. "I don't want us to be apart any longer than we need to be."

"Then I'll gladly accept your invitation. We'll get to work on it tomorrow. After we sleep good, and have a meal that's not grilled chicken."

He laughs as I mention what he and Caleb eat more of than should be legal.

"What is it you've got going over there? It smells amazing."

"Pot roast. I just put the veggies in, and I'm making cornbread. Should be done in about an hour."

His stomach growls. "Gonna have to do extra miles tomorrow, but fuck it."

"Yeah," Caleb mimics as he comes into the kitchen with us. "When a woman cooks you a meal that smells this good? Fuck it all."

I giggle, looking between the two of them. One thing I do know for sure? My life is going to be much fuller than it's been in years, and I have these two men in front of me to thank for it.

Never before have I been so glad I picked Laurel Springs as my destination on that fateful day when I decided to leave Philly.

CHAPTER SEVENTEEN
MENACE

TWO WEEKS **Later**

"You've got me so fuckin' hard," I moan as I run my hand up her thigh, spreading her legs around my waist. "All day long I've done nothing but think of you, and how you feel wrapped around me. Thank fuck we got you moved in today."

"What did it?" She giggles in a throaty voice. "The text last night telling you I was horny, but wouldn't take care of it until I see you, or the picture this morning?"

Karina, this sexy, almost nymph that I never imagined would show up and disrupt my existence is hell on my composure. When she asks questions like this, I feel compelled to tell the truth. "Both, I'm so fucking excited we got you moved in today. I don't have to deal with that shit anymore." My voice is deep as I situate her how I like her on my lap, leaning with my back against the headboard, taking some of the pressure off my core. "No woman I've ever been with is honest with her sexuality like you are. It's the biggest damn turn on."

She tilts her head, letting her hair fall to the side, exposing her neck to me. Taking the invitation, I dive in, suctioning my lips to her flesh, sucking ferociously, marking her for anyone she'll allow to see it. "I've never been this honest with anyone else before," she gasps, threading her fingers through my hair. "There's something about you, you bring out the sex kitten in me."

"You bring out the beast in me," I whisper as I smear my lips up her throat to her ear, twirling my tongue around the earring she wears, before using my teeth to tug on it. "Feel this." I bring her palm down to my erection. "Do you feel how hard I am? Feel that damp spot on my boxers?"

"Mmm hmm." She grinds her body against me, raking her nipples along my chest, letting the hair abrade what has to be impossibly sensitive flesh, given the tautness of the skin, the peak of the nubs. "I do," she breathes, as I dig my fingers into her thighs, seating her on top of me.

This is a new kind of hell. All I want is to bury myself as goddamn deep as I can go, but she needs to hear, needs to know what she does to me. Pulling my head back from her body, I tilt her chin with my index finger, forcing her unfocused eyes to meet mine. "Know what that's from?"

Her head shakes. "Mmm mmm."

"You baby, you." I push my free hand along her thigh, up her stomach, under her breast, and cup her tit as I talk to her, letting her nipple stab my palm. "That text last night got me so goddamn hard I couldn't even take the feel of the covers against my flesh. For over an hour I laid here, wondering if I should get dressed, go over there, and take care of what you need me to take care of for you. Finally, I drifted off, promising myself I'd seek you out today." I twist my hand, bringing my thumb and forefinger out to tweak the hard nub.

Karina shivers, shaking when I continue to manipulate it, continue to tell her about the hell I've been in all day.

"Woke up humping my mattress. Haven't done that since I was a teenager, Rina. Couldn't stop thinking about you all day." I'm grinding into her core now. "Almost came twice just from my pants rubbing against my hard-on. That's how fucking sensitive you got me. When I couldn't take it anymore, I'd give myself a rub with my palm, edge it out, and go until I almost couldn't take it anymore." I tilt her chin, forcing her to meet my eyes square. "Do you know what that feels like, baby?"

"Yeah," she whines, grinding right along with me. "Yeah big guy, I do, because that was me today. My fingers though-," she shakes her head, frustration in her eyes, "-aren't the same as your cock, and I couldn't get off."

I close my eyes, tilt my head back, and imagine for just a second, my Karina. Legs spread, hand between them, trying to give herself the satisfaction I give her. "You frustrated, sweetheart?"

"So frustrated." She pulls that full bottom lip between her teeth.

"Now you know why I've been a bastard today, why my boxers have a wet spot, and why I'm about to fuck you so hard." I reach down, pushing my boxers down my hips as she comes up on her knees.

"Yes, Mason, yes, I want that so much." She runs her hands up my chest, tweaking my nipples the same way I tweaked hers.

Nipple play has never been a thing for me – ever. But when she pulls on them, I feel more precum seep from my tip. Reaching over to the bedside table, I grab a condom, rip it open, and roll it onto my length. "Not gonna be sweet, Rina."

"Not what I need, Mason." She meets my gaze with hers. "Give me what you've got."

Sitting up, I situate us so that she's bent over the edge of the bed, feet on the floor, and head down, ass up. Using my index and middle finger, I test her to make sure she's ready. Feeling the wetness of her body, my knees give away slightly as I moan. "So damn ready for me."

Glancing down, I see everything I've ever wanted. Karina with her arms stretched out above her head, gripping the sheets with fingers curled into fists, waiting for the cock she so desperately wants. Taking a second, I run my hand over her firm ass cheeks, up her smooth back, under the fall of dark hair, and wrap some of it around my fist, tilting it up for me. With my other hand, I grasp her hips, pulling her back as I thrust my cock into her.

We both groan, loudly in the otherwise silence of the room. Caleb's out; we don't have to worry about being quiet, and it's the last thing I'm planning on being. Together, we get a rhythm going, one I know I won't be able to keep for long, but given the way she's slamming back to meet me, I don't think she'll be able to either. We've got each other so worked up in our heads, that this is just the culmination of our bodies finding release.

"You fuck me so good, Mason." She turns her head to look at me over her shoulder. Her eyes are hooded, mouth hanging open, body taut as I give her everything I've felt in the last twenty-four hours.

Her pussy grips me like a glove, sucking in as I pull out. Rocking on my feet, I keep the rhythm, thrusting harder as she meets me by scooting farther back into the cradle of my body.

"Shit," I hiss out between gritted teeth, loosening my hold on her hair, and instead using both hands to pull her back into me.

"Don't stop, Mason, please don't stop." She grips the sheets harder, stretches her body out farther.

That doesn't work for me; it doesn't let me thrust as hard as I need to. Grasping her around the thighs, I slam our bodies into one another, using the force to make her come up slightly on her knees. With one hand I reach around, grabbing a palm full of her tit. With the other, I close it around her neck, tilting her just the way I like, burying my face in the spot where neck and shoulder meet.

She whines as I tease her nipple, turning and twisting it in between my fingers, using everything I've learned about her to take her pleasure to the next level. Reaching behind her, she makes a grab for anything that can help her regain purchase. When her hands land on my thighs, she squeezes roughly, digging her nails into flesh. The bite of pain feels incredible as I continue to thrust, withdraw, thrust, and withdraw. My cock has been hard for far too long to keep this going, and I know without a doubt I'll blow soon.

Using my teeth, I worry the flesh on her shoulder, nipping with the pressure I know she likes, before I let my other hand work its way down her body. The tip of my finger finds her clit. It's seeking, looking for something to give it the ultimate pleasure, and when I drag my finger across it, Karina screams.

"Oh my God! Mason, I don't know if I can take it."

She's surrounded by me. By my body, my scent – everything. From being surrounded by her, I know it's a crazy feeling, and it's easy to let passion take over. "You can take it all," I promise her as I slide deeper into her body, her pussy loosening up as I work her clit with the pad of my finger. "You can take everything I'm going to give you."

"Mmmmmmm," she hums as she grips my thighs harder, digging her nails even deeper into the skin. "I can't," she pants, trying to catch her breath. "I don't..." she stops talking, removes her hands from me, and uses them on herself.

It's almost as if she can't stop touching herself, I feel her hand colliding with mine at her breast. Our fingers tangle as we both go for her nipple, her other hand stops overtop of mine at her pussy. Together we work on getting her off. I fuck her without limits, without care – all I want is for both of us to get off. I want to feel myself shoot inside this goddamn rubber, and I want to hear her scream so loud the neighbors know we just had sex.

"I can't," she's still saying.

"Can't what, Rina?" I breathe into her ear, as I don't stop my assault.

Fuck I couldn't stop it if I wanted to. Right now my cock is curved and ready for one thing, and that's fucking the woman who's had me crazy since the moment I met her.

"Can't believe how you're making me feel." She leans her head back against my shoulder, finally going limp, letting me have complete control over her body.

"I'm about to make you feel a whole lot better."

Whereas before she had been bracing against her knees, she just can't seem to take the force with which I'm going at her anymore. I literally pick her up in my arms as I thrust this time, pushing her across the bed as I do it. Her arms are reaching out in front of her, trying to find a way to get me to stop moving her, but I can't stop, I'm too close.

As she goes over the other side of the bed, she screams, reaching down to brace her arms on the floor.

"Oh fuck," she groans. "In this position-," she takes huge gulpfuls of air, "I'm rubbing against the bed. Jesus Christ."

And as she pushes back against me, I feel myself break as she breaks. I swear to God I come so much there's not enough room in the condom. "Fuck me, oh fuck." I withdraw quickly, strip the condom off, and finish coming against the sheets.

Glancing down, my dick is still hard, engorged, and looking like it's ready for action. A split-second decision is made by me as I see that Karina is still on her knees, arms still bracing her, pussy in the air.

I wrap my fingers around my cock, jacking it ferociously as I take two fingers and plunge into her tightness.

"Mason!" The scream is as loud as I've wanted to hear from her since we started. Her legs are shaking; I feel a gush of wetness against my palm as she literally collapses. And only then do I let myself completely go, only then do I let myself shoot against the blankets again and feel completely and utterly drained. Chest heaving, body a mess, my soul is healed, and I have one person to thank for that.

The woman who gave me a piece of myself back.

CHAPTER EIGHTEEN

KARINA

MARCH

"Do you have everything we're taking?" I ask Caleb and Mason as we grab bags we're taking to a Moonshine Task Force lunch.

I've never been to one of these before, but Violet told me a little of what would be going on. All the families are invited, and everybody gets to hang out with each other, without having to worry about working. Apparently, they try to have them once or twice a year, and it started after Trevor got hurt. Last night I was up late making potato salad and two different cakes. No matter if I'm tired this morning or not, it made me feel like a member of the team. I never had that sense of community with Braxton, or even with my own family, but here, I'm comfortable enough to pitch in and help whenever it's needed.

"Yeah." Mason holds up the bag he's carrying, nodding to Caleb who has the two cakes in his hands.

"Okay, let me grab the paper plates, and then we can be on our way."

"I thought Violet was bringing the plates," Mason yells over his shoulder as we all walk out to his Jeep.

"Oh she's been in a clusterfuck," Caleb answers before I can. "The duplex she and Ace live in had a massive flood night before last. She's been trying to rescue clothes and feeding the crew that came to dry them out."

Violet had called me and let me know what was going on, and I'd immediately offered to help. "What he said, so I offered to bring them so she didn't have to worry about it."

"Shit, that sucks. Ace and I don't typically work together, but it must not have made it through the grapevine yet."

Caleb stows everything in the back. "No, it happened super late. Leigh and I had to do some serious maneuvering to cover the Saturday morning crowd today. But as far as I know, everything's getting dried out, it's just been stressful. I think Ace may have lost some of his military stuff, and she lost some of her books. It's all material things, but those things meant a lot to them. Hopefully the company the insurance has called in can save some of it."

"Same." I nod. "The least I could do was bring the paper plates."

"Well I guess I can offer some muscle, if they need help moving stuff," Mason says as we get into the vehicle. "Somebody remind me to offer if they don't mention it at the lunch."

"Seeing you move my furniture was one of the highlights of my life, big guy. I am so totally there for you helping others."

He glances over at me, giving me a smile before he drops a kiss to my cheek. "Whatever makes you happy, babe."

And with an answering smile on my face, we pull out of the driveway, and ride as a family to the MTF gathering.

I GLANCE over to where Leighton holds Ransom in her arms, trying to shush the crying baby. He's howled since they got here, and given the way her back is tight with tension; her nerves can't take much more. My eyes find Holden, who's standing with Mason, sipping on a beer.

"You think he's going to go help her?" Violet asks as we watch the scene that's unfolding.

"I hope so, he's the father, but they both look completely exhausted."

"It can't be easy," Violet sighs. "With all the guys on rotation being sick lately, I know he's been pulling some doubles, which has left her at home alone with the baby."

Leighton comes back in, and even from where I stand, I can see the tears in her eyes, frustration written plainly across her face. It looks like she doesn't want to interrupt Holden, but Ransom takes care of that as he lets out a wail loud enough to bring the roof down. Interestingly enough, as Violet and I creep over to where they stand, I watch Mason set his bottle down and hold his hands out.

"Mind if I give it a try? Caleb had horrible colic. For a good three months none of us slept, until we learned a trick."

She all but tosses the baby into Mason's arms. "If you can make him stop screaming, I might kiss you."

Holden makes a noise in his throat at what she says while Mason laughs.

"When Caleb had it, everyone gave us all this information, like put the window up, humidifier, everything, but nothing helped. We drove him around and that kind of helped, but we were young and neither one of us had money to drive around for hours at a time until our son would fall asleep. This could totally be why Caleb cradles a football today." He gives them a grin as he turns Ransom around, draping him over his muscular forearm, belly and face down, resting in Mason's huge palm. With his other hand, he softly rubs Ransom's back. "When it was the worst, I'd have to rock Caleb too, but the pressure on the stomach seems to take care of whatever it is that makes them hurt so bad."

Within minutes, what had been wailing cries have subsided to sniffles, and it looks like he could go to sleep in Mason's arms.

"How hot is that?" Violet whispers to me as we watch the scene playing out in front of us.

There's absolutely no way for me to tell her how hot it is for me to watch my boyfriend hold a baby. He's self-assured, looks like he knows exactly what he's doing, and it's hot as hell. Back when he'd been a new parent with Caleb, I'm sure he hadn't been sure of anything, but right now he's showing what experience looks like, and it's sexy.

"So hot, he's getting laid tonight," I joke, as she laughs, spitting out part of the drink she's just taken.

"You two go get something to eat, enjoy your dinner. Ransom and I will be fine over here," Mason's telling them.

"Are you sure?" Leighton asks, probably scared to leave her son.

"It's been a really long time since I held one this small, but I got this." He gives her a wink.

"C'mon babe, let's enjoy a meal." Havoc turns her over to where the food has been set up.

As they excuse themselves, I excuse myself from Violet, walking toward where the two of them sit.

"Hey." I give him a smile as I have a seat next to him.

"Hey," he answers, his voice softer than normal.

"I had no idea you were the baby whisperer," I tease as I reach over, pushing a small tuft of hair out of Ransom's face.

He sighs in his sleep, pursing his lips, and in the blink of an eye I can see a child that looks like both Mason and I. Can see him holding the child like he's holding Ransom, and a longing with which I've never felt hits me hard.

Mason shrugs. "Even though I was young, I was good with him. Typically, it would be me up with him at night."

"Why does that not surprise me?" I try to keep my tone light, in case Caleb is anywhere around. I never want him to think I've said something about his mom, even if they don't have any kind of relationship.

"I always wanted more."

He blows my mind as he drops that bomb. "You did?"

"Yeah." He looks down at Ransom, a longing in his eyes I've never seen before. The side of his mouth tilts up, disrupting the smoothness of his face. "But I never found anyone I could see myself having one with, and now I feel like I'm too old. I mean, I've raised Caleb. Do I really want to start completely over?"

My stomach does a drop I'm not prepared for when I hear those words.

"But then I think, this time I could do all the things I wanted to do. I wouldn't be away for two years, I wouldn't be struggling to put a roof over his head the first few years of his life, and I wouldn't be growing up at the same time as him." Mason bites his lip. "I don't know, maybe I lost my chance."

"Do you think you did?" I ask quietly.

His dark eyes lift up to mine. "Do you want the truth?"

The air between us is heavy with something I can't name. It feels as if everything we've built, everything we've gone through with one another balances on this exchange. "I always want the truth; we haven't come this far by lying to each other. Even that first night."

"If I had the right woman with me, I wouldn't hesitate to do it again."

The words flow out before I can think to stop them, before I can force myself to stop them. "A woman like me?"

He reaches up, cupping my jaw in his hand, shoving his fingers behind my ear and up into my hair. "Yeah." He leans in, kissing me softly. "A woman like you. You're the only other person I've ever thought about having a kid with. There's something about you, Rina."

I close my eyes, leaning my forehead against his. "I never knew it was something I wanted until I saw you with Ransom, but fuck if my ovaries aren't aching right now," I giggle.

"That hot, huh?"

Pulling back, I give him a smile. "If you could see what I'm seeing, you'd get it, Mason."

"I'll remember this for later," he threatens. "When I'm on your nerves and I don't want you to put your cold feet on my legs, I'll remind you of how hot I am right now."

"Whatever works for you, big guy."

We're quiet for a few minutes, until he blows my mind again. "I'm serious, you know. I want more out of life than what I've been getting. The way I'm looking at it, that means a future with you, Rina. So if you aren't down for that, we should probably stop while we're ahead."

"I'm totally down for it. Maybe not kids this weekend, but I'm on the same wavelength as you."

He grins, one of those smiles that splits his face, showing off the experience there. Some would call them crow's feet and the laugh lines, but I love them. As much as I'm coming to love this man sitting beside me.

"So we'll hold kids off for a few weeks. No impregnating this weekend."

Truth be told, it sounds fun. Not having to worry about protection with him, being able to be as spontaneous as we want to be. Dear God, don't let me mess this up. If I'm not careful, I'll be completely and hopelessly in love with this man, and there won't be any going back from it.

CHAPTER NINETEEN

KARINA

APRIL

Today has been the longest day of the semester, I'm totally sure of that, and it's probably because Spring Break is right around the corner. It's sorely needed all the way around. From me to the kids, to the other teachers – I think we're all burnt out. One more week and I get to spend all Mason's free time with him. To say I'm giddy is an understatement. Lately things have kept us apart, and I need all the time with him I can get.

One more week – that's the mantra I keep repeating. I know it's bad. I love my job, really I do, but every once in a while the stress gets to me.

As I exit the school and head toward the teacher's lot, I notice someone lying against the concrete sign in the quad that sits in front of the school. From where I am, I can only see shoes, but immediately I'm on edge.

Hurrying along, pulling the strap of my purse up around my shoulder as I get to a position I can see. It's one of Caleb's teammates, Maddox, better known as Dox. He's one of the bigger guys who plays on the defensive line. Gazing down at him, I see he's completely out of it. His head tilts to the side, mouth open, and it almost looks like he's sleeping.

Leaning down, I shake his shoulder. "Dox?"

He makes a noise, letting me know that he's at least alive.

"Maddox!" I shake his shoulder harder, and for the first time notice a smell coming off of him that I shouldn't be noticing at school. Reaching down, I put my fingers to the pulse point on his neck. It's faint but there. Taking my phone out, I quickly dial 911.

"Yes, this is Karina Holland. I'm a teacher at Laurel Springs High School, and I've got a student passed out in front. He smells heavily of moonshine, and I can barely get him to come around."

The woman on the other end of the line talks like she believes everything is going to be okay, and I want to feel that in my bones, but right now I don't. All I can think about is keeping the students from seeing this. After what happened at the barn party and how it affected the school, the last thing I want to do is bring back bad memories or to have blood on my hands. I know I'm speaking, can feel my lips moving, can hear a hushed voice in the background that I know is mine, but I have zero idea of what I'm saying. My hands shake as I continue to make inconsequential noises. In the distance I can hear the wail of an ambulance.

We hang up as the paramedics hop down from the back of the ambulance, stretcher between them. One of them I recognize as Blaze. "What happened?" she questions as I go over what little bit I know. If someone asked me to tell them what exactly I said to her, I don't think I'd be able to repeat it.

"Is he going to be okay?" I finally find my voice; finally ask the real question of the day.

"His pulse is weak." She looks up to me, and I notice the fear in her eyes. "Did he have anything on him, anything nearby that we can attribute this to?"

I shake my head, my hair blowing against my lips in the breeze. "Absolutely nothing. I was walking to my car when I saw his feet, and I thought it was odd to see feet there. Like they were. Honestly I was thinking about Spring Break." My voice cracks. What if he doesn't get to enjoy the Spring Break of his senior year? What if he's ruined that for himself?

As fast as I can, I move back, allowing them room to work. An IV is put in his arm as a Laurel Springs police car comes to a screeching halt behind the ambulance. Mason gets out, all business. I've never seen him in uniform like this before, never seen him take command of a scene or investigation. He's quiet, authoritative, and assured as he starts asking questions and setting up a perimeter. Watching him make his way to me, my hands get sweaty, and I have to remind myself that this is the man I sleep with every night, except for when he works late shifts.

"You okay?" he asks quietly as he steps up to me, directing me out of the line of what's happening with Dox. He moves me over to the double doors that lead into the school.

"I thought he was dead." My voice is flat, tears in my eyes. "He looked dead."

"They don't think he got a bad batch of moonshine." He gives me a little piece of the information he's discovered. "They think he's drank too much. They'll flush him out and pump his stomach full of charcoal."

"How would he be doing it here at school?" My voice is a hushed whisper.

"He's a football player. Is he dragging around a gallon container of water with him to stay hydrated?" Mason asks.

This semester I don't have Maddox in class, but I put myself back to last semester when I had him, and I distinctly remember a large Yeti he carried, always drinking from it to keep from having muscle cramps because of dehydration. "He always had a silver Yeti he carried everywhere."

"Wonder where it is now." Mason jogs back over to where Maddox laid before they got him on the stretcher.

I watch, not allowing myself to breathe a sigh of relief until they have him in the back of the ambulance and they're on their way to the hospital. Only then do I let my eyes travel to where Mason is bent over, rifling through a book bag. "This it?" he holds up a silver Yeti, just like the one I remember Maddox drinking out of.

"That's it." I nod the affirmation.

He opens it, sniffing, before holding it back from his nose. "Good God, I can't stand the smell of that stuff, I will never get the fascination with it."

Truth be told, I don't either, but it's cheap and these kids like to have what they think is a good time. "I guess I'll go inside and make sure his parents are called."

"You seen anyone acting suspicious around here lately, Rina?" he asks as he crowds up into my space. "Anyone give you a weird feeling, make you uncomfortable? This shit is coming from inside this school, and we've got to figure out who and where before another kid dies."

The thought of something happening to any of the kids I think of as mine is enough to threaten tears falling. Immediately I tell him the one person who's always made me uncomfortable, in one way or another, since I came here. "Mr. Cartwright, the science teacher. We started around the same time together, and anytime I'm with him, I feel gross." I shiver. "There's no explanation for it, other than the fact he's asked me out a number of times and I've always said no. Sometimes he's more aggressive than others, but once in a while, he crosses a line."

"How does he cross a line?" Mason's voice is tight, his glare is intense.

"I just don't like the way he casually touches people around him. He did it to me a few times when he first moved here, and I just didn't like it," I'm at a loss to explain the way this man makes me feel. There are certain people who give off a vibe. Mr. Cartwright is one of them.

"Know where I might find him?"

"He tutors after school. Do you want me to take you to his classroom?"

He's got that *fuck shit up* look on his face, and I almost feel bad for Mr. Cartwright, but I also love when my man looks so fierce. "Lead the way baby, I have a few things I wanna talk to this guy about."

Menace

When she mentions the same teacher that Jess had mentioned to me, and the same person I had a talk to the principal about, I want to rage. There's no way in hell this guy should be allowed to do the things I think he's doing. Since that first day when the dog hit on his classroom, I've had a bad feeling; have wondered if this man is hiding something.

"Here's his room." Karina walks us in. "Mr. Cartwright?"

The son of a bitch pops up from behind the counter where the K-9 had indicated.

"I'm Officer Harrison," I walk over, introducing myself. "There's been an incident out on the front quad and I'd like to ask you a few questions."

When the guy gets a good look at me, I can tell he hates my guts. Call it intuition or whatever you want to, but immediately I can tell he doesn't like me. Maybe it's because he wanted Karina, maybe it's because he wanted to be a cop at one point in his life and couldn't swing it. Either way, he's not impressed.

"I don't know what I can do to help you. You're Caleb's dad, right?"

"That's right." And in my head I add *don't even think that you're going to be fucking up his scholarship, asshole.* "Have you noticed anything going on around here, anything out of the ordinary?"

"Can't say as I have." He shakes his head. "Kids are ready for Spring Break just like us. Right, Karina?"

She called him Mr. Cartwright, and now he's using her first name. This shit doesn't sit well with me at all. "You sure?" I bring his attention back to me. "Are you still waiting for the cheerleaders after they get done with practice?"

His eyes widen and I think I've shocked him. He opens his mouth, closes it, and then adjusts the sport coat he's wearing. "They aren't practicing right now, Officer Harrison, I have no idea what you're speaking of."

Now I'm getting a creepy feeling from him, an intuition that's never steered me wrong before. Walking over to where he is, I hook my thumbs in my utility belt, looking down at him. "You know exactly what I'm talking about, so don't play dumb with me. I can't prove anything, and I can't put my finger on it, Cartwright, but I think you know more about all of this than you're letting on. There's a reason that dog hit on your room, and there's a reason you were in the girls locker room. I don't have the answers yet, but I will, and when I do? You're gonna go down for this."

"You have a very active imagination Officer, but I can assure you, I'm innocent of what you're accusing me of."

"I'm not accusing, only stating facts as I see them. I'll be watching, Mr. Cartwright."

"Do whatever you feel like you need to." He gives me a smile that raises the hairs on my neck.

I've been doing this long enough now that I trust my gut, and my gut is telling me to watch this guy.

"Will do, sir." I hold my hand out for Karina. "C'mon, let's go to the hospital and make sure Maddox is okay."

As the two of us walk out of the classroom, I pull my cell from my pocket. "I'm calling Caleb; make sure he doesn't hear about this through the grapevine. That's the last thing he needs." I tap my fingers on my gun belt as I wait for him to answer. When he does, I lean against a locker. "Hey, I got some news, don't freak out on me..."

CHAPTER TWENTY
MENACE

"I SWEAR TO GOD, Mason, if you spray me with that water hose, it's on." Karina gives me a menacing (no pun intended) look. It's almost enough to make me want to spray her, just to see what she may do. Sometimes she's all talk, other times she's a force to be reckoned with.

A smile plays on the corners of my lips, as I hold my finger off the trigger of the hose we're using to wash her car. My tone, and look, is innocent. "Would I spray you on purpose?"

Her head tilts to the side, looking like she's trying to tell if I'm a calculating bastard today or not. "Given that it's the bowels of hell hot out here, I should be begging you to spray me, but I don't feel like having a wet t-shirt contest." She gestures down to the white tank top she's wearing.

Truth be told, I'm not into letting my neighbors see what's mine either. Never been the kind of guy who likes others to see what I have. Needless to say, I've never had and never wanted a threesome, which has, believe or not, been a make it or break it situation in some of the relationships I've been in. "Since I'm not into sharing, I'll keep my water over here to myself."

She gives me a look like she doesn't believe me, but it's the truth. I'm not into sharing, and even if I was, she's the one woman I would never want to.

"I heard from Maddox's mom earlier today," she mentions as she comes over to start washing the hood.

I watch as she bends over, using the rag to clean off dirt particles. So far it's been a dry spring, and if we don't get some rain soon, we'll be in a drought situation. Which means there may not be many more days like this with her.

Washing our cars in the sunlight, her wearing a bikini top under her shirt. These are the days I'm coming to live for.

"Oh really?" I haven't heard much about what happened to him since they put him in the back of the ambulance. Sometimes it's not easy to find out info either, given HIPAA laws and the amount of cases the Laurel Springs Police Department works. "How's he doing?"

"Okay. Really embarrassed. She said he suffered withdrawals the next day and they're moving him to a rehabilitation center, so that he can safely recover."

"Damn." I turn off the spray, trying to figure in my head how long he'd been abusing the alcohol for it to get to a point where he'd be going through withdrawals. "Did anyone know he was that bad?"

"No." She shakes her head. "None of us at school even noticed he was drunk half the time. What does that say about us as educators?"

"You can't take that on yourself, Rina. I mean, imagine what his parents feel like." From personal experience I know they feel like shit, and I'd never wish that on another parent – ever.

Neither one of us have approached the subject of Caleb and what happened with him. I know she's wanted to ask, I could feel it each time she almost did, but this time, I know she's going to.

"How did you feel? When Caleb hit his rough spot?"

"Like a fucking failure." I can still hear the hurt and pain in my voice. "He took his friend's death hard, I knew that, but I didn't realize how hard until I got a phone call from Ace telling me the shape my son was in. Not only was I embarrassed, but I was hurt. He and I have always been so close, and never before had he been the type of kid to lie to me. I still wonder, was he trying to tell me he needed help and I ignored it, or did I not see it? That's a period in time I don't ever want to repeat."

"I imagine." She grabs the hose from me, spraying off the rest of the car, and then entwines our fingers together, pulling me to the front porch. There we have a seat in the swing, while I prepare to tell her about the scariest moments of my life.

"He and I'd had conversations. I'd told him if he needed to see a counselor we'd do it, I asked him how he was handling it. Every time we'd talk, I'd get the same answer from him, *I'm good*. It wasn't until Ace called me and told me what was going on that I realized how 'good' he was. Fuck, he could have lost his ride to Alabama, he could have lost everything." I think back to how close he had been, how close we had been to losing it all, including our relationship with each other.

"What changed?" Her voice is soft as she asks. Part of me wonders if she really wants to know, or if she feels like she just has to see this through now that she's started it.

I think back to that night, on the side of the road. "He cried." My voice is hoarse as I remember the way he'd fallen in on himself, the way he'd seemed to try and hold the pieces of his flesh together. "I hadn't seen him cry since those deployments, Rina. There on the side of the road, he broke the fuck down that night. He didn't stop crying, not when I got him home, not when I put him to bed. We lay there together for hours, while he cried. While he got it all out. Goddamn, I'd never see him that emotional about anything before, and to know he'd been going through it all on his own? It liked to have killed me."

"It's breaking my heart right now, thinking about him silently suffering." Her voice is soft as she lays her head on my shoulder.

I pull her close, needing to feel her next to me. "That night we called Blaze and I explained to her what had been going on. She set us up with a counselor he saw for about a month. I'm not saying he's perfect, I'm sure he'll slip up again someday, because that's the nature of issues like what he had, but right now he's good. It's not to say I'm not nervous about when he leaves, but I have to trust him. If I don't trust him, then what kind of a relationship do we have?"

"You're a really good dad, Mason."

"Thanks." I kiss her on the forehead, happy that she still thinks so, after I've just told her about my worst failure at that title. "Sometimes it's nice to hear someone say it."

"You can always count on me, big guy."

And the best thing about it? I definitely know I can. There's no question. She'll be one hundred percent honest with me, even when it may be easier to lie. That's something I know I'll never have to worry about with her.

Karina

"I feel like we're an old married couple." I stretch out on the couch, curled up in Mason's arms as we watch *Riverdale* on Netflix. This hadn't been a show I wanted to watch, but Mason liked it, and after the first episode I was hooked. If that doesn't scream married couple, I don't know what does.

"If this is what it's like to be an old married couple, then I'm totally on board with it." He wraps his arm around my waist, holding me to his chest as we face the TV.

"I always wondered what people meant when they said they enjoyed staying in with their significant other. In my former life, I thought that meant the relationship was dying." I play with the t-shirt covering his chest, running my hands down his tapered waist.

The sound of a chuckle reverberates in his chest. "I never even knew what to expect, so you're doing better than me. I do admit, I wondered what all my friends were talking about when they said they were staying in, and how they liked it more than going out." He runs his hand up my back, cupping my neck. "I totally get it now."

"At least you aren't bored of me after living with me for a few weeks."

That had been one of my greatest fears, that the reason we got along so well was because we didn't spend a lot of time together. I haven't gotten bored of him, and I pray he feels the same for me.

"How could I ever get bored of you?" He tickles my side, and I come up on my knees, looking him in the eyes as I try to get away from his questing fingers. "When you love someone, you don't get bored. You just find new and better ways to hang out together and keep it exciting."

Immediately the teasing stops, and I stare at him, trying to decide if he meant what he said. When I look into the dark depths of his gaze, all I see there is the love that he just spoke of. "Are you serious, Mase?"

"So fucking serious." He holds me by the neck, forcing me to meet him head-on. "I've never told anyone besides my parents and son I love them. This is about as serious as you can get."

"You never told Maggie?" I can't help but ask; partially not believing what he's confessing can be true. I mean they had a child together and lived through a lot of things before she left.

"Never told her." His voice is rough. "I didn't know what love was when I was with her. I was a young kid who only knew what it meant to get his rocks off. I'm glad I didn't though, because that means I can save the important words for you, babe. Do you know how hard it is for me to tell you? To let someone in after I've had to protect me and my son our whole lives."

Tears are silently making their way down my face. "Yeah, I know exactly how hard it is, Mason. Please don't ever change. I'm sorry as hell you were hurt by her, but I'm so glad I'm the one who knows what it's like to have your love. I'll never take it for granted."

"I know," he whispers, pushing his hands up the nape of my neck, holding me close.

In turn, I push his hair out of his face, run my finger down his nose, and drop a kiss on the tip. "I love you too, big guy."

"I know," he whispers again, leaning up to give me a chaste kiss. It's one of those rare ones that don't get out of hand between us. It's exactly what it should be, and nothing more.

And as I lie back down against his chest, I realize with a clarity I've never had that this is the absolute happiest I've ever been.

CHAPTER TWENTY-ONE
MENACE

MAY

Sitting under the heat of the late-May sun in my backyard, I watch the group of friends that have become family congregate. All of the MTF, and a whole slew of Caleb's friends have come to celebrate his graduation.

"The sides are all set out," Rina swoops in to sit next to me. She's wearing a pair of cut-off shorts and a shirt that reads *Property of the MTF*. I have to completely agree with the sentiment. "You and Holden just need to get the grills going."

I reach over, grabbing her up and sitting her on my lap. She puts her arms around my neck and leans in close. "You okay?"

"Hittin' me hard today," I admit as I look over, seeing Caleb sit with a few friends and Jess. "He's not going to be here much longer."

She kisses me on the cheek as she crosses her legs. It's the most comfortable thing in the world for me to put my hands on her thighs and hold her tightly to me. "He's going to be fine, Mason. You raised a good son, you have nothing to worry about. You're going to be fine, I'll be here to make sure of it."

"I know." I take a drink of my beer. "I know you're right, but damn this is almost suffocating in the way it feels."

"It's fear, Mase, just fear. You won't be there to hold his hand any longer, and it's a scary situation. I feel it whenever I send my seniors off into the world," I admit. "The end of every year is like a stab in my heart. I only have them for a few short months, but they wiggle their way in, and I care about them deeply. When it's time to let them go, it's hard, but I have to believe they have bigger things to accomplish. I have to believe I've prepared them for what this world has to offer and that they can make good decisions," she runs her hands along my arms, soothing me. "I know you've raised Caleb to be one of those kids. You don't have to worry, big guy."

"Just gonna be weird not having him around, ya know? He used to be scared of the dark," I tell her quietly. "Especially after I came back from being deployed. He used to get up in the middle of the night, sneak into my room, and I'd wake up the next morning with him curled against my chest, holding his pillow. He did that until he was ten." I look out over the backyard, not seeing much of what's going on, as I get stuck in my memories. "At the time, I was so glad he stopped doing it because it'd scare the shit out of me when I woke up and saw him there. Now, I wish he'd done it just a few days longer."

"I'm sure every parent feels that way, Mase."

Letting out a deep breath, I tap her hip. "Havoc and I need to start these grills if we're gonna have time to eat before it gets too late."

"It's okay to be emotional, big guy." She wraps herself around me, after we get up. "It's actually a turn on."

"Then you should be dripping, because I don't think I've ever been this emotional in my life."

She winks up at me, before I bend down to give her a chaste kiss. Turning from her, I whistle at Havoc who's holding Ransom in his arms. "Let's get these grills going."

I watch as he hands the baby over to Leigh, and we get to work.

Karina

"He's getting so big," I reach out, running my finger down Ransom's cheek. He's in a sling around Leigh's body as she helps me make drinks for the entire crew that has showed up for Caleb's party.

"Girl, I know. That's why I'm wearing him. Whoever thought up these sling things is a freakin' genius. It leaves my hands and arms free so I can get work done. He's so heavy now, that it's hard to do things with him while I'm holding him, so this thing has been a lifesaver."

"I'm gonna run in and get the cake, I'll be right back."

Mason and Holden are done with the meat, and people are starting to fill their plates up, but I want to get the cake out so we can have a proper celebration for Caleb. Grabbing it out of the fridge, I fight my way through the crowd and set it on its own table, putting *graduate* napkins and plates out.

Violet has made herself event photographer, making sure there are pictures of everyone and everything to commemorate this event. "Caleb, Mason!" She yells for the two of them. "Come over here before someone cuts into this cake. We need a family picture."

I arrange it so that the *Congratulations Caleb* can be seen, and then start to step away as the two men come to stand behind it. Mason grabs my wrist. “Rina, where you goin’?”

“To stand over there, so you can get a picture,” I explain, the duh left unsaid in my tone.

“She asked for a family picture.” Mason levels me with a stare.

“And for us to have one of those, you’ll need to be in it,” Caleb finishes for him. “So, come get here in the middle and smile big, Kari.”

Tears prick the back of my eyes, and I have to bite my lip to keep from making an idiot of myself in front of all these people. I close my eyes, step in between them, and do my best to smile as Violet takes a bunch of pictures of the three of us. When she’s done, she comes over, showing us the back of the camera.

“I’m pretty sure–,” Caleb reaches in, cutting a small piece of his cake off and taking a bite, “–that’s the coolest first family picture in the history of the world.”

Seeing the happiness in all our eyes, I can’t help but agree with him.

CHAPTER TWENTY-TWO
KARINA

BEGINNING **of June**

Months ago when I accepted a request for a message from Mason Harrison on the dating app I'd recently signed up for; I couldn't have imagined this was where I'd be. Standing in his driveway, fighting to hold back tears as Caleb, the child I never knew I wanted, prepares to leave for college. Beside me, Mason is tense as we try to avert our eyes from the heartbreaking scene going on in front of us. Caleb is leaving for the University of Alabama today, and Jess leaves for Ole Miss two days from now. I'm not sure what the future holds for the couple, but it'll be almost impossible with them both on scholarships, to be able to keep their relationship going.

They spent the whole night out with one another last night, only showing up here at six-thirty a.m., to fall asleep on the couch wrapped up in each other's arms. When I woke them up at eight, because Caleb has to be in Tuscaloosa at noon, the stark sadness on both of their faces almost killed me.

"I know how she feels." Mason's voice is hoarse. "I know he'll only be a couple hours away, but you know as well as I do what's going to happen. He'll get a life there, trips home will be scarce, and he's not gonna give a shit about his old man."

"Now you're being dramatic," I whisper back. "Caleb worships the ground you walk on."

"He did," Mason concedes. "But he's his own man now; he won't need me as much as you think."

"He'll need you more than *you* think." I put my arms around his waist and rest my head on his shoulder. "I know you're having a hard time coming to grips with this, even though you've had months to prepare, but remember, you have me."

Menace

Months to prepare. If Rina only knew. I had eighteen years to prepare for the boy turned man in front of me to leave, but faced with it in this moment; I realize it wasn't long enough. I hold onto her, my anchor in this storm of emotions rioting through my body.

I'd asked him numerous times if he wanted me to go with him to Tuscaloosa, and he'd declined the offer. Saying all he was doing was reporting for summer workouts, he'd be staying in student housing, and there was no reason for me to drag ass there until he was in his dorm when the school year started. I'd fought against it every time, but eventually I had understood; he wanted to do this on his own, wanted to depend on himself, prove to himself he could get around in a place he'd only been a few times. Prove to me he could take care of himself. My fingers grip Karina tighter as Jess steps away from his embrace, gives us a wave, and runs to her car. Given the redness of her cheeks, it's going to be a few hours before she's finally calmed down.

"I'll call her later and make sure she's okay," Rina is telling Caleb as he walks toward us.

"Thanks Kari, you'll never know how much I appreciate it."

She breaks from me, throwing herself into Caleb's arms, burrowing her head into his shoulder as the man I raised from an infant holds her tightly against him. There are slight tracks down his cheeks, and he holds her head in the palm of his hand as she presses herself to him. Since the day she took care of him when he was sick, they've had a special relationship, and it's easy to see how much this is killing them too. "Take care of my dad," I hear him whisper to her. "Make sure he's happy, don't give him enough time to be sad."

"Hey." I step up. "Don't you worry about me. I've got life here to live, you concentrate on keeping that scholarship and kicking ass on the field. Your room is always open, anytime you want to come here and use it."

He lets go of her, standing in front of me. The son who fit on my forearm now stands in front of me, the top of his head at my vision line. He almost caught up with me before he stopped growing, but he'll definitely be more muscular than me when all is said and done. Looking at him, it's like looking into a mirror, seeing myself at his age, but seeing his future much brighter and full of hope than mine had ever been. For years I'd worried that I'd made the wrong decision when he'd been born. Maybe I should have given him up for adoption, let someone with more money and time than I had raise him, but in the end, I realized nobody loved him as much as I did. No one could, and I'd been happy with my sacrifices, had gladly made them. The pride I feel staring at my son right now is beyond anything I can describe. He and I? We made it. We made it through high school without him replicating my path, and the future is so fucking bright, I have to squint. I truly don't think there's ever been a prouder father than I am right now.

The two of us stare at each other for what feels like forever, then I open my arms like I used to when he was a kid. His eyes take one look and he falls into me, wrapping himself around me like he did then. I can hear sniffles from my left, and I know that Rina is losing it as she watches the two of us embrace out here for God and everyone to see. I'm about to lose it too as he tightens his grip around my waist, resting his forehead on my shoulder.

"You're gonna be..." my voice cracks as I try to give him reassurance. "You're gonna be fine, Caleb. You're gonna do amazing there." I clear my throat, trying to push back the tears I feel threatening to spill. I've never held my emotions back from my son, he's the one person who's needed to see them, and I'm proud I've raised one who doesn't shy away from his feelings.

"What if I don't?" His voice is quiet and deep at my ear, full of self-doubt, and holds the tiniest hint of the little boy who asked where his mom was and why he didn't have cute cupcakes in the second grade when all his friends did.

I stiffen my lip and tell him now the same thing I told him then. "They ain't any better than you are, Caleb. Nobody works as hard as you do, and nobody knows what sacrifice is more than you. Work hard, be a good person, and remember your manners. That's all you concentrate on. You need me? I'm a phone call away. I can be there in a few hours. Do not," I grasp his hair in my hands as I say these words, emphasizing again. "Do. Not. Hesitate. To. Call. Me."

He swallows, I can feel the motion against my shoulder, can feel the wetness staining my t-shirt where his face is buried. "I won't." His voice is muffled.

"You get in trouble, you call me. You need money? You use that credit card in your wallet; I'll take care of it. You miss us? You come home. It's easy as that, Son. There's nothing there that you don't have here, a few hours away."

"I'm gonna make you proud, do the shit I shoulda done instead of embarrassing you last year."

I pull him away from me, wiping away the tears streaming down his face. We haven't been separated since my deployments, and given our history with those, I know why he's scared and I know why I'm taking this so hard. "You've never embarrassed me, never. If anything, I probably embarrassed you with those ugly-ass cupcakes I took to your classes when it was your birthday. God, they were so bad." I laugh through my tears.

"You still remember that?" He laughs too, using his arm to wipe his nose, scrubs his hands down his face. "They were really bad, Dad, but then I remember you weren't much older than me, and I can barely cook Ramen Noodles." He laughs. "The thing that's always mattered is you were there. Nobody else was, but you stayed. You didn't abandon me when it would've been easier. And you dealt with all those looks, every time we did something and no one believed you were my dad. When I had that appendicitis at ten and the doctor waved you off, saying you were being paranoid. When I got my heart broken for the first time and you told me it was okay to be upset. When you listened to an ungrateful little shit few months ago, who didn't know what the fuck was going on in his head. You didn't let me stray, you stuck by me. I love you, Dad."

For a few minutes, I stare at him. Remembering this moment in time before everything changes and give myself a pat on the back for getting him here. There was a village. From my mom, who helped us whenever she could, to coaches, to Violet and the guys from the MTF, and especially Karina.

"It's your time now, make me proud." I cup his neck, forcing him to stare at me. "Have fun, but not too much. Study hard, but not all the time, and enjoy yourself."

"You too, Dad." His eyes flit to Karina. "Let me know when the wedding is." He gives us a smartass grin.

"Get outta here." I hug him one more time, before he bends down, hugging Karina again.

"I'll text you when I get there, let you know what house I'm in and stuff," he promises as he walks to his truck, loaded down with all he'll need.

"Please do." Karina worries at my side; I can feel her wringing her hands as I sling my arm around her shoulder, letting her bury her face into me. Before she inhales deeply and then forces herself to watch him go.

As we stand and watch his truck drive away, neither one of us move. We stand there for probably fifteen minutes after we can no longer see it. "He's gone," she whispers.

"C'mon, let's go inside, figure out what we're going to do." I hitch my head toward the house.

"Ice cream," she mumbles. "I need to drown my sorrows in lots of ice cream."

"And beer," I add. "Beer, ice cream, and Netflix. Today we wallow. Tomorrow we go do something fun," I promise as I kiss her head.

"You know it's okay to wallow for a few days, right?" Her fingers fist in my shirt. "I can't even imagine how that felt for you."

I'm still trying to process it, but I know it'll be good for him, I know he's going where he needs to. Those thoughts though, they don't ease this ache in my chest.

"One day at a time, Rina. That's all I can promise."

She grabs my hand entwining our fingers.

"We'll do it together, big guy. Always together."

Always together. During the hard times, I'll hold onto the words, and the memory of the pride I felt when I watched my son take his first step into adulthood and independence.

CHAPTER TWENTY-THREE

MENACE

JUNE

Karina is meeting up with some of her fellow teachers today at the high school. She mentioned something about helping to purge and clean some of the older rooms. They've been doing it for a while, a couple of the times some of the guys from the police department have been asked to go out and help move stuff, but I've never been one of them.

She looks cute as she's ready for her day, with her hair pulled back in braids, a hat over her head, a pair of old shorts, and one of my old t-shirts. I reach up, tugging on one of the braids. "Have fun today."

She gives me a look, one that says *kiss my ass*, before she grabs me around the waist.

"I'll see you later." She kisses me, squeezing the flesh of my stomach, before we part ways for the day. "Tell Caleb I miss him. I hope you two have a great day together."

"Ouch woman, that fuckin' hurt." I rub my side where she'd grabbed my fat.

"That'll teach you to pull on my hair."

I give her a hot grin. "Sometimes you like it, babe. Don't even act like you don't."

A grin plays along the corner of her lips too, but she doesn't say much. "Have fun with Caleb," she ends up telling me, as she puts her hand on the doorknob.

Conceding I won this battle of smartass comments, I blow her a kiss. "Will do, don't work too hard."

"Oh, trust me." She gives me a wink. "I won't."

I give her a tap on the ass as she leaves. As I watch her back out of the driveway, I can't help the smile that spreads across my face. Today I'm taking my son with me to do something I never thought I would do, but I know I want him with me when it happens. Flipping my keyring in my hand, I grab my wallet and hit the road for Tuscaloosa. It's going to be a great day.

CALEB IS WAITING out in front of the student housing he's been assigned to as I pull up. It takes everything I have not to open the door and embarrass him in front of anyone who walks by. I've missed this guy, more than I can express. As he hops in, I can't wipe the smile off my face.

"So what are we doing today?" He hands me a cup of coffee, much like the days of us living together.

Quickly I take a drink. "Damn, Son, nobody makes me coffee like you do, I don't know what you do differently, but not even the cups Rina makes me are as good."

He gives me a wink. "It's my little secret."

A part of me wants to know what that secret is, another part likes that we share something like this together. Back to his original question, I drop what's kind of a bomb on him. "I want to pick out an engagement ring for Rina, and I want you to help me. That cool with you?"

His surprised gaze clashes with mine, a wide smile brightening his features. "Are you serious?"

"Living with her has made me realize how much I love having her around. I don't see that ever changing, and I want her to be a part of our lives forever. I want her to be our family. But I also want you to be okay with it. If you aren't, please tell me."

Waiting for what feels like forever, he rubs at the stubble on his chin. "Do you know how popular I'll be in the locker room when I tell people she's my stepmom?"

I can't help but laugh when, as usual, he breaks everything down to the clearest of detail. I don't know why I worry about what his reaction will be, because he always surprises me. Caleb takes things in stride more than most adults do, and it's one of the things I love most about him.

"Do you know how proud I'll be when I tell people she's my wife?"

"Dad, I'm happy for you. Please don't get married without me."

Pulling my Jeep into the traffic, heading toward the nearest mall, I give him a glance over my sunglasses. "Are you serious? I want this to happen soon, but there's no way in hell it's happening without you. You've been a part of every major change of my life. This is no different. Plus, what a douche move, to include you in picking out the ring and then not inviting you to the wedding? What kind of a dad do you take me for?"

"A fucking amazing one." He laughs as we pull into the end of the mall that has a fancy jewelry store.

"Let's go get this ring and grab some lunch, I'm hungry."

He rubs his stomach. "I could eat."

Which we both know is a lie. Caleb could always eat, even if he had just eaten a large pizza by himself. Hooking my arm around his neck, I pull his head down and run my knuckles over his hair as he laughs. These are the moments I've missed with him being gone, but as long as I can have days like this, I know without a doubt I'll be fine.

WE'VE BEEN in the jewelry store for over forty-five minutes, but nothing is jumping out at me. The sales girl has been nice, giving me my space, but it looks like she can't take my indecision anymore.

"What metal are you looking for? That would at least narrow down your options. You look so confused, sir." She gives me a look of sympathy.

I motion Caleb over. "What metal do you think Rina would like."

"What's her personality?" the sales girl asks.

"She's a bit of a smartass," Caleb is quick to answer. "Nice, smart, cares about the people she loves, but she's classic too. She's got a beauty that comes from the inside."

Caleb is half-way in love with Rina. I realize it right now, but I know it's a platonic kind of love. "What he said, and God, she's just gorgeous. Everything I've ever wanted in a woman."

"Do you have a picture?" she asks.

I dig my phone out of my pocket, showing her a picture we took last week.

"Oh my, she is beautiful. With her coloring, I think she'd look best in rose gold. Why don't you come over here and let me show you what we have? From there, you can make a decision."

When she opens the case for us and I'm confronted with these rings, a contentment settles in my stomach, a peace. These are it, any of them are, but now that I feel that peace, I know Caleb and I can pick out the most awesome ring ever.

Karina

"How did we get stuck doing this?" Trinity, the new librarian who'll start in August, sighs as we move our mops and buckets to the girl's locker room.

"It's basically community service for the school. I was indoctrinated when I started, so they asked me to ease you into it. Honestly it's not that bad, and I think it makes teachers more aware of what the janitors have to go through. At least I feel like I pay more attention and do my best to help out when I now know what it takes just to clean a portion of the school."

She holds the door open as I push the mop and bucket in. It's hot out here. There isn't an air conditioner, and I wonder how the girls survive this, but then again they're younger than I am too.

"How did you and your boyfriend meet?" she asks, as she dips her rag and gets to work wiping off the lockers.

"On a dating app." I can't help the smirk. "He had the sexiest picture as his profile. I always thought that he was catfishing me, but then I met him for dinner and saw he was just as hot in real life. We moved in together not long ago."

Trinity makes a noise in her throat. "That's romantic, I wish shit like that would happen for me. I've not been lucky in love, ever." She laughs.

"How old are you?"

"Just turned twenty-one. I graduated high school early."

"What are you? Like a prodigy?" I gaze back at her, going to one of the seldom used supply closets out here to wipe down the walls and make sure there's no leaks from the roof.

"You could say that." She shrugs. "I'm smarter than average, but I was home-schooled so this will honestly be my first foray into high school life."

My eyes are wide as I look at her. "Oh honey, this is definitely going to surprise the hell outta you."

"I'm ready for a change." She pushes her hair out of her face. "Really ready for a change."

"You've come to the right place."

Taking my rag, I start washing the wall, but as I keep going, I hear water dripping from somewhere. "There's a leak in here, wonder if it's in the roof." I grab my phone, turning the flashlight on, trying to look and see if the tiles are discolored.

Trinity comes over, listening with me. "It's definitely going behind the wall, but I don't see any discoloration."

"Me neither." I take a look at it again, trying to figure out where the sound is coming from.

"Karina, it's not going all the way down the wall," she gasps, pointing at the wall.

"What?"

Then I see what she's telling me, the water is running down only so far, until it's making it's escape behind a crack, which makes no sense because I don't actually see where the wall separates.

"I'll hold the light, you see if you can get your fingers in there," I tell her as we crowd around, me holding the light over her head, her crouching and trying to peel the wood back with her fingers. Just as I think we're about to give up, the wood gives way. "What's in there?" I ask as she lifts a full piece of it away from the whole wall. Her head is a good portion in, as she glances down.

"Karina, we got a problem. It looks like a whole shit-ton of bottled up moonshine."

Immediately I realize what this means for the school. The fears that Mason had are founded – someone has been deliberately hurting the kids for the school year, and judging by the amount in there, they plan on continuing to do it. Putting my phone up to my ear, I dial 911. Other people besides us need to see this.

Even if the whole situation is doing nothing but making me sick to my stomach.

CHAPTER TWENTY-FOUR
MENACE

KARINA'S HEAD on my chest with her arms wrapped around my waist is my favorite place to be. Here, I don't worry about what Caleb's doing. If he's eating, if he's sleeping, are his coaches and teammates giving him a hard time, is he screwing around with girls he shouldn't be? I don't worry about what's going on in this town with the moonshine business. My brain isn't traveling fifty thousand miles an hour trying to unravel the mystery of how the moonshine is in the school. For the brief moments she's in my arms and I'm in hers, my brain is quiet, my thoughts are peaceful. The only thing I think about is how good it feels to have a partner. How warm and loved I feel with her beside me. It's an emotion I'd never known until I'd met her.

"You're quiet," she comments as she runs her foot up my leg.

"Just thinking." I roll over so that we're now facing each other, holding her in my arms.

"What are you thinking?" She smiles, running her finger along my jawline. Those green eyes of her are inquisitive and as bright as they always are. If there's one thing this woman has more than any other person I've ever met, it's a love of life.

My thoughts are more than likely not what she's assuming. In fact, I'm surprising myself with the direction my thoughts have taken. First and foremost, I'm wondering what it would be like to wake up with her next to me every morning. I'm trying to figure out why I've wasted so much of my life living one way, when I've always wanted to be the settled guy. I've always wanted to give Caleb the family he never had, always dreamed of having a partner. In the midst of this thing Karina and I have started, I've come to know what that actually means. How good it feels to have a partner, and I don't want to give it up. I've not planned any of this, but I feel such an urge, I blurt out the words that are on an infinite repeating scroll in my mind.

Voice hoarse, hands shaking, stomach in knots, I ask the question that's been rolling through my mind. "Marry me, Rina. Make me the happiest man in the world, and marry me."

Her surprise is written across her face, evident in the way her eyes widen, and the shock. "Mason, we haven't been together that long." She shakes her head. For the first time I see fear from her.

"I'm not like that other guy." I cup her face the palms of my hands, holding her steady, forcing her to look at me. "I'm not your ex-fiancé. I know what I would lose if I lost you, and I'm not planning on doing it." I tilt my head back in frustration for a second. "I'm just a guy, totally in love with a woman, who's waited more years than most to start that part of his life. I've never felt like this for anyone else, know deep down that I'll never feel like this for anyone ever again. Why wait, Rina? Why wait when I know I'm never going to love anyone else as much as I love you. My job is dangerous, and tomorrow is not promised." My voice is hoarse as I give her some reality. Every day when I leave the house, there's a possibility I won't come home. It's always mattered, because of Caleb, but now it's more acute. This woman has my heart; I don't want to leave her alone, should it come to that. More than anything I'm desperately wanting to spend whatever time I have left on this earth with her, making memories that last a lifetime, telling our grandkids about how we met, and how the attraction was so fucking instantaneous that I knew in the moment she would be mine forever.

"I just love you, and I just want to make memories with you, Rina. Fuck that other guy; he didn't know what he had. He let go of you so we could find each other. Don't you believe that?"

Our eyes meet, I can see the fear in the depths of those green orbs, but I can also see her wanting to say yes. There's a yearning I've never seen before.

"Let me give you everything I have. My love, my heart, my last name. It's all yours. All you have to do is say yes. Even if you don't say yes-," I lean my forehead into hers, "-I'll get it. It's only been a few months, but this feeling isn't going anywhere. You can guarantee that above everything else. This catch in my chest when I see you, the pounding of my heart, the smile that instantly spreads across my face? It's going to be there every fucking time I see you, no matter if we're together for a few months or a few dozen years."

"Yes." I faintly hear a whisper, feel wetness when I reach up with my thumbs. "Yes, I'll marry you."

"You will?" My stomach that's been doing somersaults since I asked is now gurgling with joy. My heart which has been nervously pumping is now happily pounding with excitement.

She chokes out a laugh. "If you didn't think I'd say yes, why did you ask?"

"I hoped you would." I let go of her and reach over to the bedside table, opening the drawer and grabbing out the ring Caleb helped me pick out when we were together over the weekend. "This is for you."

"You have a ring!!??" she squeals, sitting up, forgetting about being naked under the sheet.

"You think I'd ask without one? Caleb helped me pick it out. When he and I met for the afternoon, this is what we did."

"Then I know it's perfect." Her voice shakes as I open the box and show her the oval diamond set in rose gold. It's classic and timeless, everything she is wrapped up in a small trinket of my affection. The way she gasps when it comes into her view lets me know we've done a good job.

Sliding off the bed, in all my naked glory, I get down on one knee, holding out my hand for hers. "Karina Holland, will you share my life with me? Be my wife and come on this journey with me."

"Yes," she answers again, letting me slide the ring on her finger before she vaults off the bed, throwing her arms around my neck, kissing me, wrapping herself around me. "Yes, yes, yes!" She pulls back, and it's there in those eyes, where there had been fear minutes ago, I see the promise of my future.

"I'll make you happy, Rina, I swear."

"You already do, big guy." She plays with my hair, running the strands through her fingers. The goofy smile on her face, I know is mirrored in mine, and I'm not sure those will ever go away. "Nobody's ever made me happier, and I can't wait to do life with you."

Life with her? Going to be the best ever.

Karina

HAPPINESS WAS ALWAYS something that seemed to elude me. Something that seemed like everyone else had. I'd thought I was happy in Philly, until I came to Laurel Springs and realized what happiness really was. Now that I'm with Mason, I know I was content, but I wasn't happy. Every morning I wake up ready to face the day, ready to spend it with him, and to see what kind of trouble we can get into. Since the school year ended, there hasn't been much on the moonshine front, so it's allowed Mason to keep a regular schedule. It also affirms his thought that someone inside the school is the supplier. As I lie in bed this morning, all those thoughts are running through my head, but the one thing that outweighs all of it, is the new engagement ring sitting on my finger.

Lifting Mason's arm from around my waist, I carefully crawl out from under the blanket. Once I get to the kitchen, I do everything I can to contain a squeal, the squeal I'd wanted to give into last night when he'd proposed. When

I know I can't, I quickly make my way out to the back deck, run through the freshly cut yard and do a little dance while squealing to my heart's content. As I walk back to the house, I realize something else. I'm dying to share this momentous occasion with someone who will understand.

Grabbing my cell phone, I take a picture of my finger and attach it to a group message with Violet and Leigh.

K: So this happened last night.

I don't expect them to answer quickly, considering it's early in the morning. Earlier than I realized when I see it's barely pushing seven. But I'm surprised as they respond.

V: OMG, Karina!!! Is that what I think it is?? Did you and Mason get engaged???

L: What the what??? It's gorgeous! Congrats girl!

K: We did! Thank you all so much, it was completely unexpected, but I don't think I've ever been so happy in my life.

L: Girl, Whitney will be all over this!

K: I'm gonna let her, I've already planned one wedding that didn't take place. I'm not looking to do it again.

V: So many congratulations!! We need to get together to scream about this – all of us!

As I agree that we need to meet up, we end our conversation, and I decide there's one more person that I want to inform. The next people should probably be my parents, but Caleb has been such a large part of our relationship, I want him to be one of the first to know.

K: Thank you so much for helping your dad pick this out! I can't wait to officially be a part of your family.

I fire off the text to Caleb, feeling a little weepy, wishing he were here for me to hug. Quickly he became a part of my life I didn't know I was missing and if it hadn't been for him, Mason and I wouldn't be together now.

C: You've been a part of our family since Dad took you out on a date. Don't think you haven't. I can't wait to freak people out by calling you Mom.

K: LMAO!!

C: I gotta go to an early morning workout, but I love you, Kari. Thanks for completing our family. I can't wait to be an older brother.

K: Have a good practice! Love you too, kiddo.

And with the biggest smile on my face, I go about my day.

CHAPTER TWENTY-FIVE

KARINA

JULY

There have been a lot of times in my life when I imagined my wedding day, especially when I was engaged before. That day was supposed to be the most magical day of my life. It had been planned for almost a year. The dress had cost more than I'd been able to afford, but it had been a gift from my parents, and the honeymoon was more than my yearly salary. That had been a gift from his parents. I still wonder to this day if they'd known what was going on. If that had been their way of trying to buy me off. I should have known something was up when they'd been all too eager to spend what could have been a down payment on a nice home to send us away.

All of that though, it pales in comparison to what this day means to me. Last week when Mason had asked me to marry him, I'd imagined a long engagement. I'd thought maybe we'd get married next summer before Caleb started workouts for next year, but the more I'd thought about it, the more I realized I didn't want to wait.

Which is why, at this moment, everyone we hold dear to us is standing in the backyard of Whitney and Ryan's home, waiting to watch me walk down a makeshift aisle in a gorgeous dress I found two days ago.

"You sure you're ready for this?" my dad asks as he holds out his arm for me to take. He and mom have met all the important people to us in a whirlwind. They came in on Thursday and now Saturday I'm getting married. Thank God for being a teacher and having summers free.

"I've never been more ready for anything in my life," I assure him.

As my dad and especially with my track record, I know he's just making sure I'm ready, but at the same time he's seen me with Mason. Anyone who's seen me with Mason knows how much I adore him, how much he means to me, and the love and passion we share for one another.

"I have to say-," he nods, "-I was worried when you called us and told us you were getting married. I worried you were rushing into something because of what happened last time, but the more I'm around the two of you, the more I'm convinced this is the real deal."

"It is. I love him; I'm in love with him. I love Caleb, and we share some of the same friends. There isn't a better man for me to marry. He treats me better than I deserve."

"There's no such thing."

My dad never sees my flaws, never sees how I jump first without thinking, never sees how I don't care about the ripples I cause if I believe in something, and he sure doesn't see how wrong it probably was for me to sleep with Mason on the first date. But I'm beginning to learn that was the best impulse decision I've ever made.

"We're ready when you are." Whitney brings in a bouquet as she crouches to fix my train.

"Thank you again for getting this together on such short notice." I've thanked her profusely numerous times, and at some point, I have a feeling she's going to tell me to shut up.

"Are you kidding? This is what I live for. If I can't put a wedding together in a few days, I don't need to be a wedding planner. Sometimes it's fun for me to challenge my contacts and my skills. While it's a little stressful, romantic situations like this are my best to do. It makes my heart pitter-patter that the two of you can't wait to be married. That you don't want to have a long engagement because you just want to be married now. When Mason told me that, I knew I would do everything in my power to make it happen for the two of you."

"Still I appreciate it."

"The thanks I get is when I see the groom's face at the end of the aisle." She smiles. "It's my favorite part of weddings."

When I watch those videos on YouTube, they're my favorite part too, and I can't wait to see what Mason's reaction is to me.

"Alright, lady." She pulls my veil over my face. "Let's get you married."

With a gentle hand, my dad pulls me to the edge of the aisle that's been set up for the night in their yard. A plain white runner leads to where the ceremony will take place. Glancing down at my shoes, I take a moment to gather my breath. I inhale, exhale, and vow to myself I will never forget what this feels like.

Then I lift my head, look down the aisle, and stare directly into the eyes of the man I've come to love more than life itself, and as his gaze meets mine, the tears are almost instantaneous. I know without a doubt, this is the best decision I have ever made.

"Let's go, Dad, I have a groom you need to give me to."

I can feel him look over at me, but my eyes never leave Mason's, not once as we make our way down the aisle.

Menace

My Rina is the most beautiful bride I've ever seen. Not that I've seen a lot, but all of them pale in comparison to how she looks coming down the aisle toward me on her father's arm. I'd had to fight back tears when I'd first seen her, gripping my hands in front of me tightly, hanging on to whatever I could in order not to let the emotions spill out from me in front of the fifty guests we invited to the wedding.

"Dad, she looks amazing," Caleb whispers to me from where he stands as my best man.

"She's gorgeous," I answer back to him, my eyes never leaving her. So breathtaking I almost can't get air into my lungs.

Like a lot of things that have happened since she came into my life, I pinch myself, not sure I deserve it. Not at all sure I deserve the look of adoration she's giving me as she floats down the aisle toward where Caleb and I stand.

When her dad gives her hand over to me, I can't help but talk to her before we turn to face the preacher. "You look amazing."

"Not so bad yourself, big guy." She smirks, looking me up and down in the tux I wear.

Given the way she's eating me up with her eyes, maybe I'll need to dress like this more often during the marriage.

The ceremony is a blur. I know we exchange rings and repeat vows, but I can't tear my eyes away from her. Can't help but glance down at the neckline of the dress she wears, showing the upper swell of her breasts, can't wait to take it off her and see what kind of lingerie she's got covering herself underneath. There's a primal part of me that can't wait to claim my wife.

"Do you Karina, take this man to be your lawfully wedded husband?"

Those words bring me back to the present, they remind me that we have an audience, and me standing in front of a group of people with a hard-on is probably not the best thing for me to do right now.

"Do you, Mason, take this woman to be your lawfully wedded wife?"

"I do," I answer, the same way she had.

I let my eyes eat her up; don't hold back the desire I'm feeling from her, let her see all of it exposed. She's licking her lips, knowing what that does to me. And when we're pronounced husband and wife and I'm fucking finally told I can kiss her, I crush her body to mine. The kiss is borderline inappropriate, but

I've spent a lot of years of my life waiting for something like this to happen. If anyone deserves to do something inappropriate, it's me.

She takes the hand I hold out for her, and together we walk down the aisle as Caleb and Violet follow behind us. We try to get a moment alone, but immediately we're waylaid by different family members and then photographers want pictures.

It's an hour later, when we're finally getting into a limo taking us to the restaurant where we're having a reception.

"Finally got you alone." I pull her into my arms, planning on disrupting the careful up-do her hair is in, planning on smearing the lipstick she wears. Karina is never this put-together and it kind of unnerves me to see her this way.

"I never thought it would happen." She willingly comes to me, straddling my lap as she situates herself. "God, you look good." She runs her hands up my white tuxedo shirt.

"Me?" I move the skirt of her dress away, unzip my pants, and press up into her. "Do you feel what I've been dealing with since I saw you walk down the aisle? You know how hard it was to keep this shit contained for pictures? You think I want someone to ask us in twenty years why grandpa has a tent in the front of his tuxedo pants in the wedding pictures?"

"Yeah, well." She reaches up, pulling down the front of her dress, easing up on her knees so that her nipples are at mouth level. "Thank God for padded bras because these would have given me away quicker than your hard cock would have."

I see what she's talking about when I glance at the skin she's just exposed. Her nipples are hard, pulled taut and tight against the flesh, pointing out at attention, seeming to beg for it.

"And this," she adds as she sneaks a hand under her skirt, when she pulls it back out, I can see the moisture glistening on her two fingers. Feeling depraved and wanting to make a memory neither one of us will ever forget, I grab hold of her wrist and move her hand to where her nipple is still peaked.

"Touch it, Rina, rub your juices all over it," my quiet voice is a command. One I don't think she can refuse, even if she wanted to.

My girl, she pays attention, doing just as I asked her to. "Good girl," I growl before putting my hands on her back, pulling her forward to where that nipple smeared with her juices meets my tongue and mouth. With the flat of my tongue I lick everything off, rolling the flesh around before I nip, slightly using my teeth to scrape against the heat there.

"Fuck, Mason," she breathes. "We don't have much time, but I don't want to go to the reception. I want to go home, I want to get naked for you, and I want you to see what I wore for you underneath here."

Shhiiitttt. "I want that too, but we have a lot of people who came here to celebrate with us, and I'd feel bad if we didn't at least stick around to do cake and champagne." The guys had reworked schedules to be there, and even though I knew they would get it, it felt wrong to bypass all the hard work others had done to get the reception ready for us.

"Cake and champagne." Her breath is unsteady. "We can last through cake and champagne." The car comes to a stop. "Then you'll take me home and fuck me?"

"Like you even have to ask. You're my wife now; I'll do whatever it is you want me to." I tilt my head, kissing her neck as I help her pull her dress back up over her tits.

"I want you to take me home and fuck me." Her tone is soft, seductive. "I want to spend the night in your arms with your cock inside me. I want romantic and passionate, then I want hard and rough. I want us to finish as the sun comes up, and I want you to ruin me for any other man ever again."

"Thought I'd already done that baby, but challenge fucking accepted. Let's go get this over with, and I'll show you exactly the man you married, baby."

"Can't wait, big guy, fucking can't wait." She grabs my thumb between her teeth, sucking it like she does my cock, and I almost say screw it.

But the door to the limo opens, and I realize it's show time. This right here will be the most challenging performance of my life. Pretending like I want to be anywhere else other than between my wife's legs.

CHAPTER TWENTY-SIX

MENACE

AUGUST

Today very well could have been the longest day of my life. I've done nothing but write traffic tickets, try and track back the evidence that was found at the school during June, and run into fucking roadblock after roadblock in all of the above things. The only thing I'm legitimately looking forward to is going home and having a nice quiet night with my wife. Glancing at the silicone wedding ring I wear while I'm on shift, I imagine her waiting for me. She's been at home, waiting for me every night since we got married. I don't know what I'm going to do when she has to go back to work, besides miss the fuck out of her.

As I pull into our driveway, I feel the stresses of the day seep from my body. Something about parking next to her car and knowing she's there to greet me has done wonders for my stress level. Still doesn't mean I'm not tired as hell at the end of the day.

Getting out of my Jeep, I grab the mail, and shuffle through it as I stomp through the side door. "Rina, I'm home."

She comes out of the bedroom, wearing a small tank top and even smaller pair of shorts. I give thanks to the gods that it was hot as balls today. "Nice cheeks." I take a handful of her ass when she turns from me to go to the fridge. She playfully smacks my hand away as I make for another grab, before she gets just out of reach.

Looking at me over her shoulder, she gives me a wink. "You might think I'm hot, big guy, but you have no idea how delectable you look when you come off shift."

"Oh really?"

She winks as she grabs a bottle of water, taking a long drink. Splashes of the liquid she consumed are sticking to her lips, but she uses her tongue to wipe away the moisture and I have an instant hard-on. The way she runs her tongue along her bottom lip is the way she runs her tongue up my cock. "Really."

I have a seat at the kitchen table, extremely interested in this conversation. "What else do you find sexy about me?"

Ready to play my game, she walks over to where I am, raking her eyes over my body, and then kicks her hip out to the side. Her nipples are standing at attention and I know she's interested in getting naked with me. I know I have her, as I keep my feet out, feigning indifference.

"Do you know what I find sexy about you?" she asks, straddling my lap, throwing her legs over the chair I'm sitting in, before circling her arms around my neck.

In this position we're eye-level and I can't help the grin that plays at the corners of my mouth. "What's that?" I slip my hands down her back, settling them on the natural curve of her waist.

"So many things." She rolls her eyes playfully, sucking her bottom lip in between her teeth. That motion is giving me ideas too. "But there are a few that stand out. You might even think they're weird."

"Trust me." I lower my voice, let her hear the arousal. Push up against her, let her feel my hard length. "There are things I find sexy about you, that most people would commit me for. Borders on fetishes," my confession is whispered as I lean in, nipping lightly at her neck. "Do tell." I tap her hip, looking forward to hearing her sing my praises. It hasn't happened often enough in my personal life.

"The scruff on your chin." She puts her finger up to my chin, running the pad across the scruff she's speaking about. As she gets closer to my mouth, I make a motion, grab her finger with my lips and suck it deeply, running my tongue along the tip. She shivers and her eyes lower, get hooded as she goes on. "The way it teases my skin as you kiss my neck."

I let her finger go with an audible pop in the quiet room. "Mmm, tell me more." I run my hands along her thighs, denting the flesh with my fingers, knowing she likes things a little rougher when she's in a mood like this.

She leans in closer, grasping my hair in between her fingers. "The way you taste."

It makes my flesh pulse, makes it hot to the touch as I think of her tasting me. Lifting my hand up to her face, I caress her jawline before running my thumb over her lips. There's a wicked desire in her eyes, as they flicker down to my thumb, before she sucks it into her mouth, circling her tongue around the tip, much like she would other parts of my body.

"Son of a bitch," I moan, using my free hand to slip down and palm her ass, pressing her as close as we can get with these clothes separating us.

The fingers in my hair tug fiercely, tilting my head back on my shoulders, exposing my neck, and that's when Karina blows my mind. She's sucking, nipping, biting, licking, and grinding all at the same time. All I can do is push my hands up the back of her tank top, claw at her skin, growl as she makes contact with the erection in my tactical pants. Even between the clothes, I can feel her heat. She doesn't let up, as she moves from one side to the other, grabbing hold of my earlobe with her teeth, before she slips her hand between us, palming the flesh that's throbbing for her. I'm doing my best to keep from losing every ounce of self-respect I have, when she somehow manages to get her feet on the floor and stand over me. Because of my height, she's not much taller, but it puts those awesome tits of hers at eye-level. And that's when I decide turnabout is totally fair play.

Reaching forward, I slip one of those hard nipples into my mouth, nipping and sucking the same way she did my neck. Going to town on them through the cotton of her tank top. Immediately I realize she's not wearing a bra underneath, feeling the tightening of the flesh is enough to have pre-cum moistening the fabric of my boxers. My cock is punching at the zipper holding it back, hoping to get lose. What I wouldn't give to just reach down and pull it out, give it some relief.

"Mason, I want you," she moans, throwing her head back, thrusting those fingers of hers through my hair and holding me close to her.

With superhuman strength, I push her away, turn her around so that she's facing away from me, and slide those short shorts off her body, taking a scrap of lace with it. Before she can ask me what I'm doing, I've unzipped my pants, pushed them and my boxers down, so that the only thing I can get out is the only thing that matters. My rock-hard length. Pulling her hips back to me, I watch as those legs of hers straddle me, and then come down hard on my cock.

Her sexy back, that tapers down into two dimples over her ass, is a feast for me to look at. Her ass bounces as she uses those thighs of hers to push up and down on my dick. "Mason," she breathes loudly as I move my hands around to cup her tits up under the shirt, using my fingers to worry the evidence of her desire.

"Yeah, baby?" I pinch harder, causing her to lean slightly forward.

"You didn't get a condom."

I thought sinking into her had felt better than normal, but I don't freeze, I keep going. Using one hand to strum her clit, the other to twist the flesh begging for it at her chest. "I didn't," I confirm, knowing damn good and well she's not on birth control.

Her answer to my confirmation is to breathe deeper, ride me faster. "Is this what you want?" She puts one hand over mine at her clit, uses the other to help her ride me as she braces against the table.

What I want right now is to feel her pussy clamping my bare flesh, but I understand if kids aren't a priority for her. "I can pull out if you want me too, it's not that big of a deal," I assure her as I continue to work her flesh, loving the feel of her gripping me.

She's quiet for a few moments as we work against each other, as she swivels her hips and makes my cock hit places it's never hit before. "I don't want you to pull out," she whispers, gazing over her shoulder at me.

Our gazes lock and I stop what I'm doing. "You don't?"

"I don't. I mean-," she snickers, "-what are the chances of it happening the first time? Besides we're married, I want to feel what it's like for you to lose control inside me."

And that's all it takes, her giving me the option of doing exactly what I want to do. I go after her hard, bracing my booted feet on the floor as I pound into her, grabbing her hair up in one hand, pulling it back the way she likes. I don't stop working her clit furiously and she doesn't stop riding me, never slows down, never gives an inch.

When I feel her tighten against me, when I hear her scream of pleasure, I let go, moaning, groaning, grunting as I pull her back to my front, rest my forehead on her sweaty back, and ride out the conclusion of the best sex we've ever had.

"Fuck," I almost whimper as she gets off me, leaving my cock standing in the breeze.

"Feeling's mutual, big guy, wanna take a shower?"

As I look up at her body, naked on the lower half, nipples still hard on the upper half, hair a mess, I grin at her, knowing I made her look like a beautiful mess. Looking down at my lap, I see stains on my pants, my release running down my cock. For some reason I want to remember this moment, etch it into the database of memories I don't ever want to forget. When I do that, I reach out for her hand.

"Yeah, let's go get cleaned up."

She steps into my arms, kissing my throat. "I love you, Mase."

I grip her ass tight in my hand, giving it a squeeze as I kiss her forehead. "Love you more, Rina."

She smirks. "Nope, I love you *mas*!"

These little games are what I was missing in my life, and I thank God every day that I get to experience them with her.

CHAPTER TWENTY-SEVEN

KARINA

September

"I'm so tired." I yawn loudly as I lay on the couch, my feet in Mason's lap. We're watching something on TV, trying to avoid doing yard-work in the early September heat. "I feel like I'm coming down with something." I close my eyes, snuggling into the cushions.

"You were tired a lot this week," he comments as he grabs the cover off the back and covers me up with it. "Was it hectic at school?"

"Not particularly, which is why I think I'm coming down with something. My stomach wasn't happy with me this morning." I mention the other symptom I had. "Maybe if I just take a nap, I'll feel better." I turn into the couch, hugging one of the pillows.

The next thing I know, Mason's shaking my shoulder. "Rina, you've been asleep for two hours, time to get up."

I fight against the lethargy holding me down. Working against the exhaustion to prop myself up. "Two hours?"

"Yeah." He runs a hand down my face. It's my favorite hand. His left hand that holds the ring I put there a month and a half ago. The coolness feels good to the warmth of my skin. "Babe, are you okay?" His eyes are worried, a frown mars his gorgeous face as he stares hard at me. "I know we haven't been together years and years, but in the months I've known you, I haven't ever seen you be this tired or this rundown."

"I know." I push my hair back from my forehead, stomach growling. "I'm starving now, and I feel like I have a bit more energy."

"I made you a grilled cheese!" His voice is proud now that he's finally mastered it. "Even though I fuckin' learned *after* my kid is grown and out of the house." He has a seat next to me, as I pull my legs up to my chest.

"Just like I did for Caleb when he was sick?" I smile thinking of my stepson. "Have you talked to him lately?"

Mason takes a bite of one of the two sandwiches on the plate in front of him. "He called earlier while you were asleep. Said to tell you hi and he loves you, he'll text later."

Taking another bite of the food, I breathe through my nose as the food threatens to come back up. Throwing it down, I concentrate on trying to keep the food inside my body. When I know it won't work, I throw back the blanket I'm covered with and head for the trash can in the kitchen, right as I lose it all. Mason is behind me, holding my hair, trying to keep it from getting dirty, rubbing my back as I heave deeply. As I'm done, he directs me over to the sink where with shaking hands, I clean up and then turn to face Mason.

He looks lickable, leaning against the opposite cabinet, staring at me with those dark eyes of his. His arms are crossed over his chest, the ink on his forearm standing out to me as I make a feast of his body. When I get to his face, his mouth is set in a firm line.

"What?" I tilt my head to the side.

Pushing off the counter, he stands in front of me, grasping my chin with his thumb and index finger, making our gazes meet. "Rina." He stops speaking, using his other hand, he pushes it down my body, stopping on my stomach. "Have you even thought?" He lets the question hang there in the air.

"Before school started." I swallow hard, remembering that afternoon where we'd joked about getting pregnant. The one last hoorah of debauchery before we both had responsibilities and early wake up times. "Do you think? Mason, it couldn't have happened the first time we tried, right?"

"All it takes is once," he whispers as he crowds into my space. "You weren't on birth control before."

He's right, I wasn't, but I always assumed getting pregnant would be this long, drawn-out process, with plans, and charts, and temperature taking. But maybe when you're the happiest you've ever been, throwing caution to the wind and letting love encompass every part of your soul, you're given a miracle. "You really think so?"

"Only one way to find out, babe."

NOT EVEN IN my wild youth have I ever suspected I was pregnant. Me and my ex-fiancé never had a scare. I've always been more cautious than the next person, just because that's my personality. Mason is the first person I've ever been unprotected with. It strikes me as funny when I think of what that really means. I don't hide anything from him, he gets it all unfiltered and unprotected. The sex, the love, the heart, the mouth, and he accepts all of it. It's just the way he is.

And right this moment, I never imagined we'd be where we are. At a drugstore the next town over, picking up a pregnancy test. We'd decided to go this far out of our way because we didn't want to run into anyone we know and get a rumor started. But I can't help the way my hand shakes as we walk through the store.

"It's over there," I whisper as I point to the aisle with *Family Planning* hanging over it.

When we turn the corner, we're faced with more options than I ever thought possible.

"Jesus Christ." Mason glances at me. "Which one do we get?"

"You've done this before," I remind him as I start to feel queasy again.

"Oh, not this part," he's quick to correct me.

"How *did* you find out about Caleb?" I'm honestly curious, and this is something we haven't talked about before.

"This one of those questions, Rina?" He references back to our twenty-question type game we played when we first got together.

Do I really need to know how this happened to him before? Do I want to subject myself to what he went through with another woman? Before the answer would have been no, a very quick and adamant no. But today, starting what will hopefully be a new version of our family, I want to know.

"Yeah, I'd like to know."

He blows out a deep breath, running his free hand through his hair. "Her mom actually told me. I guess she had morning sickness and eventually they got it out of her. At ten in the morning, someone was beating on my bedroom door, screaming at me that I was a no-good piece of shit."

My heart breaks for him. To be as young as he was, and to be thrust into a situation such as that, with no planning and no warning – it was probably the scariest moment of his life.

"When I finally woke up, I was a heavy sleeper back then, and came out, her mom, my mom, and Maggie were standing there all facing me like I should have known what they were talking about."

"Where was your dad?" I ask quickly, the first thought that popped into my head.

"At the time he was at work, and then he wanted nothing to do with me because I'd ruined my life." He puts his hands in his pockets. "We talk every once in a while now, but I've made peace with it. He left me, not the other way around. Anyway, her mom pushes her toward me, tells me she's pregnant, and I'm responsible for the both of them now."

"What did you do?"

"I was panicked and shocked. I did probably what any kid my age would have done. I asked her if it was mine."

"Oh shit, Mason." I rub my face as those words come out of his mouth. "You didn't?"

"I did, and she slapped me, her mom slapped me, and my mom cried in the corner. It was all a hot mess. Eventually everyone calmed down, and the whole story came out. So to answer your question, I wasn't there for this part. I wasn't even there for the sonograms," he admits. "There's a lot of things I wanna do differently this go round, and the first one is to take care of you. So let's get a test and see what's happening."

My heart pounds as I grip his hand in mine, looking out over the tests that will potentially change our lives. Without even thinking, I grab one, not sure which one it is and not even caring.

"If I'm pregnant, it doesn't matter how much it costs or what brand it is, it'll still give me the answer I need." We make our way to the checkout; I reach in to a cooler, grabbing the biggest bottle of water I can find. "Gonna have to pee on it, right?"

Mason smiles, pulling me close as we stand in line. "You okay?" he asks softly, his breath pushing up tufts of my hair.

"Nervous, but good. If it happens, it happens. If this isn't it, we'll try again. It's still something you want, right?"

"I want it all with you, Rina, never ever think that I don't."

When it's our turn, I feel good as we put our purchase on the counter, pay for it, and quickly leave. As soon as we're in the Jeep, I'm cracking open the bottle of water and drinking it down. Determined not to have to wait much longer to find out what in the world is actually going on.

Menace

There have been times in my life when I've not been sure how to feel, how to react. This isn't one of them. Sitting on the bed and tapping my foot is all I can do though while I wait for Karina to come out of the bathroom. It'd be weird if I was in there while she peed on the stick. We aren't that type of couple yet. I'm not sure if we ever will be, if I'm honest. As she comes out, I stand. "How long do we have to wait?"

She's holding the test in her hands. "It says to wait three minutes, but unless this second line goes away in that time, we're pregnant."

Her eyes meet mine, and I rush across the room to pick her up in my arms. "Rina, you sure?"

Tears are quietly streaming down her face as she nods. "Look." She holds the test up for me to look. Sure enough there are two lines. Two lines means pregnant.

Even though I've been here before, I feel like my heart is going to beat out of my chest. It's different this time. Instead of feeling fear, all I feel is excitement.

"Should we tell Caleb?" she asks, wiping the tears from under her eyes.

"God I love you." I kiss her deeply, savoring the moment I have with her. The fact that in the middle of finding out she's pregnant for the first time, she thinks about Caleb. "Yes, but let's emphasize he should keep it quiet until we're ready to announce it to people."

"I love you, too." She smiles so brilliantly at me, and I lose my heart to her again. If anyone ever asked me, I literally wouldn't be able to list all the ways she's changed my life since she walked into it, heels clicking, hips swaying. "Should I text him or FaceTime? He might be in class, or he might be doing something important," she worries. His schedule changes up depending on what day and what he has going on.

"He'll love whatever you do," I try to reassure her.

Setting her down on the ground, I watch as she grabs her phone and takes a quick picture of the test as it sits on the bathroom counter. Coming over to her, I slide in behind, wrapping my arms around her waist, kissing her neck as she texts Caleb.

K: The reason I was asleep when you called.

She attaches a picture of the pregnancy test to the message. "How long do you think it'll be until he checks it?" she asks as she leans back into me.

"If it were me, a couple hours, maybe a full day. Since it's you, and you rank higher on his priority list than dear old dad does, he'll see it within the hour, or even minutes." My voice is dry as I make fun of how quickly he answers her, and how slowly he answers me.

When the phone rings, I give her a pointed look. "Told ya."

"You're on speaker." She sets the phone down as we listen to his voice on the other end.

"Are you two fucking kidding me? Seriously? I'm going to be an older brother?"

"Better late than never, right?" I joke with him, remembering how he used to ask for a sibling when he was younger.

"I'll be the best big brother on the planet, and whatever this is, brother or sister, couldn't ask for a better mom and dad."

Karina and I look at each other, her emotions plain as day in her eyes. Caleb's words have touched her, they've touched me too. Sometimes I'm not sure what I've done to deserve him. "Thanks, Son, we'll let you go, we're sure you're busy."

"Never too busy for news like this. I'm assuming I need to keep this quiet?"

"Please, until we have all the info and were sure things are fine."

I squeeze Karina in my arms as she buries her head in my shoulder.

"Will do, I gotta go to class, but please let me know what's going on. Just because I'm here doesn't mean I can't be home soon if I need to be."

We all hang up with plans to get together for the weekend, and as I'm left with Karina, we smile at one another. "I don't know about you, but I could use a nap. This has been an exciting day."

Wrapping her arms around me I hear her muffled voice. "Mason Harrison, you are speaking my language."

Standing up, I wrap her legs around my waist and walk us over to the bed. Wordlessly, we strip, and after I pull the sheets back, we fall in between them together. When we lie down, I curl around her, her back against my chest, and my hand on her stomach. In my arms lies everything I live for. The only thing missing is the other piece of my heart in Tuscaloosa, but I'm realizing more and more every day, it's time to let him go, let him live is own life.

As I drift off to sleep, I do so with one of the biggest smiles I've ever had spread across my face.

CHAPTER TWENTY-EIGHT
KARINA

OCTOBER

I'm beyond intimidated as I walk with my hand tucked into Mason's along the family section of the football stadium. This week we'd gotten the call that Caleb would be playing in the Auburn game and everyone who could in the MTF is with us. That includes Whitney, Ryan, and Stella. Part of my intimidation is watching this game with Whitney.

"Remember last time we were here?" She smiles over at Ryan as he carries Stella, wearing a cheerleading uniform. She's got stickers on her cheeks and carries a pom pom in her hand.

"I do." he gives her a look that says they only see each other.

"Yeah we have a lot in common with that." She hits elbows with me.

"We do?"

I know zero about football, and I have a feeling I'm way out of my element with the rest of them, including Stella. Pretty sure Stella knows more than I do, but I also know I wouldn't miss Caleb's debut for the world.

"Yeah." She gives me a grin. "I was pregnant last time I was here, too. Like close to popping, but it's always been my dream to go to a home game. Ryan made it happen for me, and it was one of the most special times in our life. Seriously, thanks for inviting us today."

Mason and I still haven't told everyone; we were waiting for November, and I've been careful not to let slip, so I'm speechless as to how she knows. Unless Mason's let it slip, and if he has, I might kill him, because keeping this secret is slowly killing me.

"You're glowing," she answers for me before I can ask the question. "And your boobs are huge. Same symptoms I had, and I kinda have a sixth sense about pregnant women now. I knew Leigh was before she told everybody too."

"We're gonna tell everybody in a few weeks. I have cute announcements picked out," I explain, wanting her to know that I'm not trying to keep it a secret forever. I'm not ashamed we're having a baby; I just want to make sure everything's good before I tell the world. "I just wanted to make sure everything was okay before we started telling."

"No, I get it." Whitney reaches over, taking Stella out of Ryan's arms as he and Mason go grab us some drinks and food. "I was scared to death to tell anyone I was pregnant. I worried constantly that something would happen and then I'd have to tell all those people I'd no longer be having a baby. Of course, I was older than you and I'd had problems conceiving before." She pushes Stella's bangs out of her face, using a wipe to clean up her mouth. "I love this one, and I'd like to have one more, but I just don't think it's in the cards for us. We've tried off and on since we had her, but still no positive pregnancy test." Her voice sounds wistful. "How many times did it take you and Mason?"

"Just once." I let a smirk play across my face. "Surprised us both, to be honest. I thought I was coming down with the flu or something."

"Same here." Whitney gives me a one-armed hug. "Ryan and I weren't even trying; I didn't think I could actually get pregnant. My ex-husband and I tried for years, but nothing happened. Luckily for us, Ryan had great little swimmers."

I snort as she talks about Ryan and his swimmers.

"Now I just think God is trying to tell us this one's gonna be a handful and we don't need another one." She bounces Stella in her arms.

Looking at the two of them, I hope I can have a relationship like they have with the child I'm having. Reaching down, I put my hand over my stomach as I watch Stella grab for the pearl earring in her ear, rubbing the stud. At the same time, Whitney reaches up and rubs her fingers along the pearl necklace she always wears. They are two peas in a pod, and it's easy to see how much they love each other. And when the boys return, the way Stella reaches for her daddy has my heart bursting. I can't wait to see our child reach for Mason like that.

"Let's go, ladies." Mason holds on to some of Ryan's food as he scoops Stella up in his arms, carrying her up the bleachers to where our seats are.

Whitney barely holds in the squeal as she sees how good they are. "I can't believe you all brought me to this, like I don't think you realize just how much I love you all."

"It was either you or Violet, and when we asked Violet, because of her relationship with Caleb, she threw the tickets at me and told me to ask you. Apparently you embarrassed her last time she watched a game with you?"

"Not my fault she didn't know which team to cheer for," Whitney defends herself.

"Will you protect me if I do the wrong thing?" I whisper over to Mason.

"With my life, babe." He puts his arm around me, kissing the side of my head as we anxiously await the kickoff.

Whitney gives me a high-five when they make a first down and I cheer loudly.

"I'm getting the hang of this!" I yell at Whitney, tweaking Stella's nose as they go back to the line of scrimmage.

"We're gonna score this time, I can feel it," Whitney screams loudly. "C'mon, boys! Show them who you are!"

Honestly, she scares me, but she's not judging me the way she judged Violet at the high school game, so I'll take it.

This time, the quarterback tosses the ball toward Caleb, jumping up his hands connect and he cradles it protectively, breaking a tackle. There's nothing but empty field in front of him.

"Run the ball, Cale!" Stella screams from where she's being held in Whitney's arms. Mom and daughter are screaming loudly.

The cheers and screams of the crowd are deafening as he runs faster than I imagine any other person can run. My heart is pounding as I watch him run to the end zone. Our group is literally losing their minds as they put the six points up on the scoreboard.

Beside me, I look at Mason, who's not losing his mind; he's just staring at his son with a proud smile on his face. Down on the field, the team is celebrating, smacking each other around and giving out high fives. Caleb takes off his helmet, holds the football in his hand and points to us. When I look out again he taps his chest twice, eyes connecting with ours. Given my hormones I sob like a baby while Mason holds me close.

Menace

It's completely different waiting after a college football game than it is a high school one. I don't know all the guys on this team, I haven't had the personal relationship with their parents, and not everyone knows me as "Caleb's dad". But that doesn't mean I'm not as excited to see him tonight as I was after those football games. In fact, tonight, I'm probably more excited than I've ever been.

"Caleb!" Whitney yells, and I realize he's walking toward us.

In the course of the months away from us, he's grown up more than I thought possible. He's muscular, filled out in a way he wasn't at home, he stands taller, and the scruff a little darker and fuller on his face.

"Hey, y'all." He makes a beeline for Stella who runs toward him.

"Cale, Cale!" she screams, so happy to see the friend who isn't around as much as he used to be.

He spends a few minutes with her, and then hugs Whitney and shakes Renegade's hand, thanking them for making the trip.

"I don't know if you know this about me or not," Whitney begins. "But this totally wasn't a problem for me to do," she deadpans. "In fact, if you have more tickets I could have, I'd take them off your hands in a jiffy."

"I'll keep that in mind, Whit."

"Just sayin' if you need me to do your laundry or something for them. I'd be happy to."

"Oohhh." Renegade throws his arm around her neck, pulling her back to his front. "Trust me; you do *not* want to be doing a teenage guy's laundry."

Caleb laughs and turns to us. "Thanks for coming, you two."

Karina encircles him in her arms, holding him tightly. "I'm super emotional right now, and you're just gonna have to deal with it." She wipes the tears from her eyes. "It's not something I can help, but I am so damn proud of you."

They speak quietly to each other for a moment, and then my son stands before me. There's a look on his face I've never seen before. "You did so good out there." I hold open my arms and let him step into them. Hugging him tightly, I say up a little prayer that he continues to be the man he is right now. That he continues to do the things I wasn't able to do and make the things he wants to happen, happen for himself.

"I brought something for you." He reaches into his bag, pulling out a football. "It's the one I made the touchdown with. I asked them to hold it so I could give it to you. If it weren't for you loving me enough to stick around, I wouldn't be here. I'll never know all the sacrifices you made, and I'll never understand what you went through in order to be the amazing dad you've been to me my whole life, but know I love you for every single one of them." He shrugs, putting the football in my hand. "I just thought it was important that you know that."

"You amaze me, Caleb, every single day, and if anyone's lucky, it's me." Those are the only words I can push past my tight throat.

His mom will never know what she missed when it comes to this kid. I used to feel sorry for him, because he missed out, or so I thought. No, now I'm sorry for her, because she'll never know what it's like to have this sort of relationship with him. There is nothing I would ever exchange for the bond we have, and I hope like hell I have it with this new child I'm having. I hug him tightly, before I push him away to arm's length. "You hungry? I know you probably don't wanna hang out with us old folks, but we'd love to hang out with you."

He winks at Stella. "I could eat, and it would be my pleasure to hang out with my family."

CHAPTER TWENTY-NINE
KARINA

November

School is routinely kicking my ass. Even though I've just passed my three-month mark in the pregnancy, I'm not feeling much better than when I started, and I'm still getting sick on a regular basis. It doesn't matter, though, the show must go on and I don't want to take time that I don't need yet. Because the due date is around the first week of May, I'll more than likely be taking maternity leave at Spring Break, so I don't want mess with any of the plans I already have.

It's taking me longer to finish grading papers and make lesson plans. Pregnancy brain is really a thing, and I'm suffering from it, all the time. I'm finding more often than not, it's easier for me to get things done at school, so I'm staying a little later than normal every night. The librarian keeps the library open since she does work too, and I've been finding going in there with her helps keep me on task. Grabbing my laptop and my water bottle, I close up my room and head to the front of the school.

"Hey Karina," she greets me as I come through the double doors.

Trinity has been a godsend for me, keeping me on track and allowing me to hang out with her as I've been fighting the effects of this pregnancy. This is her first year, but I've found her to be a breath of fresh air.

"How's it going, girlie?" I put my stuff down on one of the tables, spreading out everything I need to look at.

"Busy freaking day, and I've got a lot of stuff to shelve and catalogue. I don't want you to think I'm ignoring you, but I gotta do it back here." She scrunches up her nose as she points to the back room.

"You're good; I'll be okay out here by myself. I just have to get my brain wrapped around the fact I actually have to get this shit done." I motion to the stuff I have spread out.

"I know exactly what you mean. I should be about thirty minutes."

"Take your time, and when you're ready to lock up, let me know."

Just as I'm about to get down to business, I get a text from my husband.

M: Hey, I'm headed to the school. Where are you?

Immediately I smile, happy that I'll get to see my husband before we get home.

K: Are you coming to see me? I'm in the library getting some work done with Trinity.

M: Our proof came through on Cartwright, Rina. We have a warrant. Be safe. I love you.

K: Love you, too. I'll stay where I am.

M: Be sure that you do. As soon as I can, I'll get you.

The proof came through. I wonder what proof it is, but I also know that's probably something he can't tell me. I knew when I found the moonshine in the girl's locker room during our summer cleaning that Mr. Cartwright was responsible for it. All I had to do was wait until the MTF could prove it. God, I wish Mason were here right now.

Getting up from the table I'm at, I walk over to the window, gazing out over the teacher's parking lot. Mr. Cartwright's car is still there. I've often wondered how he could afford a Cadillac SUV, when the rest of the lot is littered with Toyotas and Kias, or cars that are at least ten years old. I noticed it, but I never questioned it. I wonder how much money he's made off these children; I also wonder how he sleeps at night knowing some of these kids have developed a habit so bad they've had to go to rehab. In the end, that's not for me to judge. He'll get his day in court, and he'll have to face his maker when he's ready. Still doesn't mean I'm not disappointed.

Moving my hand down my body, I cradle my stomach where the child Mason and I made out of love lies. I'm nervous as I wait for him to arrive. Only when he gets here will I feel safe. Until that moment, I'm worried, worried about what might happen, and how Mr. Cartwright will react once he knows he's been backed into a corner that he possibly won't make it out of.

Someone enters the library, and I'm hoping like hell it's my husband, but when I turn, I see Mr. Cartwright staring at me.

"It was you," he accuses, looking crazier than any person I've ever seen in my life. No actually, crazy isn't the way to describe how he looks. It's more desperation, and even I know desperate people do stupid things. "You're the one who found the moonshine in the girls' locker room; you're the one who found the moonshine in the false bottom of the cabinet in my classroom."

"No." I shake my head. "I didn't know anything about the false bottom on your cabinet." There's no place for me to go as he advances on me. I'm already against a wall, having gone here to look out the window. He stands between me and the door that would allow me to escape. "I did find the moonshine in the girls' locker room. It amazes me that you would let people think you were a creep, instead of just admitting that's where you hid most of your stash."

The smile he throws at me isn't pleasant, and my stomach turns at the look on his face. "It was easy to get it there, no cameras in the room or outside. When I'd run low in my classroom, I'd just go out there with my bag, put some in, and transport it. For the longest time no one asked any questions. Not until you and your husband started sniffing around."

I'm mentally trying to figure out what I can do to get out of this situation, and unfortunately, I'm fully aware there isn't much. "If you hurt me, he will kill you."

My heart pounds as I see him withdraw a gun from his waistband. "If he tries to hurt me, I'll kill you and that baby you're so proud of. You're my ticket out of here, Karina. Smile nicely for the cameras."

I make a run for it, but he grabs me around the neck, hooking me with his arm, pointing the gun too close to my head for comfort. Fear like I've never known envelopes me, and for the first time I'm scared for my life. I'm scared that I won't get to see my husband at the end of the day, that I'll never see Caleb play another football game, and I won't meet this child inside of me that is so loved. I throw up a prayer that it all works out, but there's a dread closing my throat and I lose something I've always had. Hope.

"Walk slowly," he instructs as we hear the sirens of police. "And if you do as I say, you might make it out of here today, but I wouldn't count on it."

Menace

"You can't be here," Havoc tells me as we set up a perimeter around the school.

"The fuck I can't, my wife is in there," I argue with him as he grabs me by the shoulders, pulling me away from the scene. Havoc looks at me, something in his eyes I don't normally see – a fear, a sadness. "Tell me, whatever it is, tell me," I beg, I know it's bad if he's hesitating. There's one thing Havoc Thompson does extremely well, and that's take control of a scene, run it like a well-oiled machine, and do so without personal feelings getting caught up in the mix. To see him this torn? It's killing me.

"A 911 call just came in. Trinity, the librarian, was in the back cataloguing. The indication bell that someone has entered the library came on. She knew Karina was out there, but she was afraid it was a student staying after school and Karina wouldn't be able to help them. It wasn't a student. It's Isaac Cartwright and he's holding a gun on Karina."

My world fucking crashes to my feet. Legitimately, I fall to the ground on my ass, my back against one of the cruisers. My life, as I know it, is ending at this moment. My throat is working double-time, swallowing back the bile as it threatens to come spewing out. I lean my head back, panting out deep breathes.

Havoc squats down to my level, putting his hand on my shoulder. "I'm not going to pretend like I know how you feel, because I don't. I'd be losing my goddamn mind if that was Leigh in there, but I'm going to tell you like I would tell anyone else. Let us do our job. If not, I'll have to remove you."

My eyes meet his. "Fuckin' try it, Holden."

"No, you try me, Mason. Let us get her out of there. Let us do what we're trained to do."

I know he's being honest with me, know he's speaking the truth, but none of this shit is easy. I want to be barging in there, guns blazing, beating the shit out of this motherfucker for even putting her in this situation. A shadow crosses my path, standing over me. I glance up when they don't move, and my eyes meet Ace's.

This is the first time I've ever seen Ace in sniper mode. I know he was one in the military, but I've never seen him ready to do battle. He's wearing his MTF uniform, but he carries a specialized rifle in his hands and a hat turned backwards – I know it's to keep his hair out of his face as he concentrates.

"I give you my word I'll make sure she goes home with you after this," he vows, his tone tight and deadly. "She's gonna be fine, I'll make sure of it."

I'm feeling like a bastard, not wanting them to know how this is affecting me. "Make sure that you do."

He nods and I think he knows I can't say anything else. If I give in to the fear, I'll be done for. They'll have to carry me out of here on a stretcher and take me to the mental health ward. I will break down, and I worry that there's no coming back. In my pocket, my phone vibrates.

Pulling it out, I read the text, forcing the palm of my hand into my eye, to rub the sting of tears away. It's a text from Caleb with an article attached to it, about the police presence at Laurel Springs High School.

C: Is Kari okay?

I hate myself for lying to him, but I know he can't do anything where he is except worry.

M: She's fine, I'll let you know when we're done here.

C: K, I was worried! I'm headed to class. Love you!

M: Pay attention and do great things. Love you, too!

Those tears finally break through, sliding down my cheeks as I drop my phone to the pavement and send up every version of a prayer I know. As I watch my teammates make shit happen, I sit next to the squad car, refusing to leave until I have my wife in my arms.

CHAPTER THIRTY
KARINA

"YOU DON'T HAVE to do this," I plead with him, trying to think of ways to get him to leave me alone and walk out on his own. I'm sure there are countless possibilities, but right now I'm coming up with nothing. The only thing I'm worried about is making sure my baby is okay. The baby we just announced that I'm having to our friends and family.

"No, I do." His hand shakes as he holds the gun on me. "You don't understand, I've been planning this for a long time."

"What?" I'm confused as I hear him speak.

His brows furrow as he looks at me, and it's almost as if I can see him arguing with himself, trying to decide if he wants to tell me the truth. A part of me doesn't want to know, because then it gives me hope. Hope that I'll make it out of here alive, and that he doesn't plan to kill me. If he's going to tell me everything, it would make sense he'd want to get rid of any evidence, but if he's not going to harm me, then why would he tell me anything? My stomach drops as he starts to talk.

"Five years ago, there was an article ran about the moonshine trade here in Alabama. I was living in Washington State at the time, trying to make ends meet, barely doing it, and eating whatever was on sale at the grocery store that week. For three years I figured out how to make my own moonshine. I worked hard, learned how to make the best, and right when I was ready to make my move, things started happening here in Laurel Springs. Remember? We got here about the same time, Karina."

I do remember. That's roughly about the time Leighton's dad was arrested and that whole operation went under. For a while moonshine had come in from a neighboring county and then it'd started in the school.

"I was sick of living paycheck-to-paycheck. These stupid backwoods kids didn't even realize what hit them when I started putting moonshine in the lockers, with instructions on how to get more. This little operation has funded my life, and I have enough now to go live on some beach in the tropics where there is zero extradition. You and your husband? You won't stop me."

"They were coming for you, I taunt him. They found proof and they were coming for you, that's why they're here now."

He pulls the ends of my hair with his fingers. "I know, they executed a search warrant on a storage unit I was using to store a bunch of my equipment. I thought I was being smart by registering it under a dummy corporation, but that came back to bite me in the ass. So now you, my dear, are going to get me out of this predicament I find myself in."

Every part of my body fights against what he wants me to do, but I also know that the MTF won't let him take me. If I can just make it outside, to where we have a chance, I know things will be okay. I make that promise to myself and work hard to convince my vaulting stomach that it's the truth.

"Look alive, Karina, it's time to put on a show."

And as we walk out into the waning sunlight, I close my eyes, praying to God that I get to walk away from this with every part of my body still attached.

Menace

"He's bringing her out!" I hear the chatter and immediately I'm on alert.

I jump up from where I've been sitting next to the cruiser and train my eyes on the motherfucker who's threatening the most precious thing in my life besides my son and the child she's carrying. I make sure he sees me, cross my arms over my chest and mean mug like I've never mean mugged before. Fuck, I want to vault myself over this damn car and take him out with my bare hands.

"Cartwright." Havoc's voice is clear and concise, in control of his emotions. "Let her go and we'll talk this out."

God I wish I was in control as much as he is, wish I could calm the pounding of my heart and convince myself that this is some sort of dream-like state I'm in. That I'm going to wake up and this hasn't happened at all, that I'm lying in bed with my wife, her stomach tucked protectively under my hand.

"No deal, she's my ticket out of here. I want a car, and I want a plane ticket."

"Just one?" Havoc questions.

The bastard runs a hand along her jaw, and that's when I let myself look at her. Her eyes are closed against the police presence in front of her; she's got her hands on her stomach. She looks almost serene as her right hand twists her wedding band around on her finger. She's not looking at any of this, and I thank the heavens for it. She doesn't have to see how many local and state police have converged to help; she won't have to see the bullet whiz by her face as Ace takes this fucker out.

I know she's not serene, though; I know she's got to be going crazy inside, the same way I'm going crazy. If they would just give me five minutes alone with this guy, he would never think about hurting another person for as long as he lives. If he makes it through this ordeal. Hell, if I make it through this ordeal. My chest is killing me, and I'm not sure if it's because I'm nervous or if it's because I'm having a possible fucking heart attack.

"I'm not that calculated," Cartwright answers. "Better make it two, and does a fetus need a ticket?"

Anger causes me to advance, but Renegade and Tank hold me back. I strain against their arms, pull at the hands physically keeping in my spot. Never did I think when we told people about the baby that it would be used against us. Fuck him for doing this to us, for being such a goddamn asshole. Right now I want to knock every single one of his teeth out of his mouth. I want to stomp a hole in his head and make him drink soup for the rest of his natural life.

"Trust me when I say I know exactly what you want to do right now, but you can't," Tank whispers in my ear. "Let Ace do what he does best. We're gonna take care of her, brother, just let us."

Knowing he's telling the truth and actually letting it happen are two different things. I drown out whatever Havoc is telling him as I focus on Karina. Different parts of our life together so far run through my mind like a highlight reel.

The first time I saw her walking up to me on our first date. The way she looked as she came against me the first time. Watching her sleep on the couch after she took care of Caleb. The way she took care of me when Caleb left. Her walking down the aisle toward me at our wedding. The surprise in her face when we found out we were expecting, and just this morning, the kiss she gave me as she left for work.

It wrenches my heart, and just when I'm not sure I can take much more, I hear a shot from above us. I know immediately it's coming from a building across the street. It's the shot Ace is taking to either wound this man significantly or it will end his life. Without a doubt it will pass mere millimeters from my wife's flesh, but I trust Ace with everything, and as Cartwright's shoulder kicks back, I watch him fall to the ground.

Karina with her eyes still closed, starts to go with him, but I run, dig my feet into the ground, and make it before she falls. I catch her just like I promised myself I always would. I pull her away from the danger and hold her tightly in my arms.

"Open those eyes for me, let me know you're okay, Rina." My voice is shot, my nerves are shot, and the only thing I can do is run my hands over her body, feel for anything that's hurt or broken. If there's one thing on her that's not like it was when she went to school this morning, I'll murder him. No jury in the world would make me do jail time, and even if they did, for her, I'd be happy to do it.

She opens her eyes, trying to get her bearings. Those green orbs connect with mine, and then I see the fear. It eats at me, makes me feel so foul that she had to endure this because of my job. Never again will she be put in any danger, I vow it myself right then and there. "Is it over?"

"Completely and totally over." I crush her to me as we're approached by Blaze, and Violet breaks the perimeter around the area, running to us.

"Oh my God, I thought you were dead. I trust Ace with everything, but I thought...oh my God." Violet crouches in front of us as Blaze immediately starts taking her vitals. Violet holds her hand, as it appears she wants to assure herself Karina really is alright. I know the feeling.

"I thought I was too," she admits as tears come and she begins to shake. Her teeth are chattering, and I wrap her tighter in my arms, hoping to transfer the body heat.

"She's in shock," Blaze speaks calmly and quietly. "Things are gonna be fine, let's just take you in and get you checked out."

She grabs my hand, her fingers entwining in mine. Her voice as she lets the words slip out are damn near my undoing. "Don't leave me, please don't leave me."

"Not a chance, babe, never a chance." It's a vow I'll spend the rest of my life making come true. This woman will never be in this kind of danger again if I can help it.

Holding her in my arms, I carry her out to the ambulance, climb inside and refuse to let go until we get to the hospital. After a scare like that, I'm sure no one would blame me.

As we drive off for the hospital I get a message from Caleb.

C: Really fuckin' pissed you lied to me but kind of okay with it, too. Had I known what was going on I would have been a wreck. I love you both, please call me tomorrow after you've both processed this and let me know you're okay.

M: Will do, love you too. We're headed to the hospital. And trust me, nobody was gonna hurt her on my watch.

And they never will again.

CHAPTER THIRTY-ONE

KARINA

"CAN you cut this off of me?" I ask Mason after he's laid me down in our bed.

His eyes flash to the hospital bracelet I'm wearing, and I can tell it annoys him as much as it annoys me. I don't like the reminder of what went down earlier today and honestly could do without anything ever reminding me again. After the hospital had pronounced me and the baby, which after some testing they told me they think is a girl, were okay, Mason had brought us home.

"I'm so sorry this happened to you," he whispers as he cuts it off, rubbing at the irritation the plastic edges had left on my skin.

"Look at me." I give him my most stern teacher's voice. "This wasn't your fault. He was an unhinged psychopath who thought he'd get away with potentially killing kids. This isn't you, Mason. This is him."

"You could have died," he argues.

Grabbing his chin with my fingers, I force him to meet my eyes. "You could have too. What if he'd turned the gun on y'all? What if he'd decided to go down in a blaze of glory? Suicide by cop and he'd gotten one of you?"

"We wear vests," he argues again.

Rolling my eyes, I sigh. I'm refusing to let him take the blame for this. None of this has been because of who he is, it's been the work of someone who wasn't balanced. I will make him see this if it's the last thing I do.

"You don't wear vests on your legs, which have a pretty crucial artery running through it. Not to mention your damn head. You're not going to win in this case, big guy, so you might as well just give it to me. What happened today was unfortunate, but it could have happened to anyone. I'm glad and lucky that we're all okay, he's going to go away for a long time, and now hopefully you'll have some sort of reprieve before moonshine shows up again."

He realizes he can't argue with me on these points, I can tell by the way his eyes soften. "I don't want to get your blood pressure up by arguing, so I won't." He tucks a piece of my hair behind my ear.

Wrapping my arms around his waist, I make a proposition in his ear. "I don't know about you, but after he touched me, I feel dirty. I need a shower, and I need you to get my blood pressure up in a totally different way."

He answers me in the most delicious way. A deep moan in my ear, followed by the best words ever. "Let me take care of you, Rina."

"YOU RELAXED?" he asks after the shower, as I'm lying on my side in the bed. He's behind me, big hands all over my body, and as he gently pushes into me, I moan.

"As relaxed as I'm ever gonna be." I grasp the comforter in my fingers, holding on tightly as he pushes and pulls out of me.

Unlike our normal crazy and chaotic couplings, this one is slow. He takes his time, showing me with our bodies how much he loves me, how scared he'd been for me. His hands move up and down my flesh, almost in a reverent way. This time there's no gasping, and even no talking between us. All I need him to do is let me know I'm alive. All I need is to feel his love and know I'll never have to live without it.

"Love you so fuckin' much," he whispers in my ear as his finger sinks down to where we're joined.

"Love you too," I whisper back just as softly as we work toward our goal. His other hands glides over my stomach, where our child is safely held.

"Nothing means more to me than this." His voice is so low I almost can't hear him, but I know he's worshiping me. Worshipping us. "Don't know what I would do if I didn't have you with me."

"Don't think about that, never think about it." I push against him, clawing at the covers as we push toward the end together.

"Lost years off my life." He buries his face in my neck. "When I saw him walk you out, for a brief minute I thought maybe you wouldn't go home with me today."

"No way was I going to let him take me out." The promise is in my voice.

We strain against each other, both fighting for the orgasm that will prove that we're still here. That Isaac Cartwright didn't break us. I move one of my hands down, to where it rests over his. Together we hold my stomach as he pushes against my back. There's something about him wrapping me up in his warmth, his feet braced under mine, his arm up over my head. I'm completely surrounded by my man. My man. The one who makes my heart pump, the one who makes me want him more than I've ever wanted anything, and the one who showed me what true love is.

"I'm gonna come, Mason." I bring my hand up to cup my breast, he lays his hand over top of mine, directing me on how to hard to squeeze, and as I feel the end start to break through, he moves that same hand down to where our bodies are joined.

As he spills inside of me, we both groan as my orgasm hits hard. Together our bodies jump, and we do it in a choreographed dance. As his chest heaves against my back, I think about how different this day could have been and pray for many more years with this man. A lifetime will never be enough, but less than one? That would have been criminal.

And in this moment, I know, Mason Harrison? He's my life. The one I've been searching for and the reason I was hurt, but not heartbroken. Had I not been hurt, I wouldn't have moved here, and I never would have found the love of my life.

Breathless, I mouth a *thank you* and close my eyes, resting in the shelter that is his arms. The place that has now become my home.

CHAPTER THIRTY-TWO
KARINA

APRIL

"Are you ready?" I ask my two guys as they both shuffle into the kitchen, both wearing suits. "Damn, don't y'all look good?"

"I need help with this tie, Dad." Caleb holds his tie up in his hands.

Mason motions for him to bring it over. "Who does this for you when you're at school? You wear a suit to the game."

"My roommate, Slater," he answers. "He's there on a baseball scholarship. We're keeping each other out of trouble."

"Well, at least someone's there to keep you under control." I run my hand over my stomach, grimacing. Baby girl is dropping and my hips feel it like no other.

"You okay?" Mason asks as he eyes me.

"I'm fine," I assure him. "High heels may not have been the best idea, but I want to look like my old self today. Especially on Easter." I curl my lip up. "But I may have to change into flats."

Mason finishes up Caleb's tie. "Someone told me that you might have to, and they also gave me a heads up on a pair of shoes you wanted." He winks at me as he walks back to our bedroom.

"What did he do?" I look at Caleb for answers.

"Don't look at me, I have zero idea on this one, Kari."

Having a seat at the kitchen table, I feel anything but pretty as my belly presses against the black fabric of my dress. For Easter, I wanted to dress in something Spring-ish, but maternity fashion leaves a lot to be desired, and I didn't want to spend a fortune on a dress I'd only wear once. Even though I feel kind of cute in this little black dress, those high heels were my splash of color, and now I'll just look frumpy, even if my hair is curled and my makeup is on point. Mason comes out of the bedroom, holding a wrapped box.

"What's this?" I roll it around in my hands as I look up at him.

"Your Easter gift, Mama. I think you'll like it."

Ripping into the wrapping paper, I try to feel excitement as I open the box, but truthfully, I'm just tired. I know this day is an important one in the South, and I'm glad I have my family with me, but I'm bummed. I can't lie, I'm totally bummed. Inside the box is a label I'm familiar with, and I sit up a little straighter, a smile plays at the corners of my mouth. "You didn't!"

"You can thank Leigh for this." He kneels down in front of me. "She said that toward the end of her pregnancy, she just wanted a little color and sparkle in her life. Then she sent me a link to these."

My fingers fumble as I push the tissue paper back and then I squeal as I see the pink sparkles of the shoes in front of me. "I can't believe you went on the Kate Spade website and ordered these." I lean forward with difficulty and kiss him soundly on the mouth.

"Anything that will put that smile on your face, baby. Hand them over, and I'll tie them for you."

Be still my heart. This man is more than I ever could have asked for. "This is a great splash of color and makes me feel as if I'm not so frumpy."

"You're anything but frumpy, Rina. I've never seen a woman look more beautiful than you." He reaches up, running a hand over my belly. "You're sexy, hot, everything I've ever wanted in a woman, and if it takes a pair of crazy looking shoes to bring a smile to your face right now, then that's what it takes. Stand up and see how they feel."

He helps me, by holding out his hands for me, and as I let my weight shift onto my feet, I groan. "They feel so much better than those heels. I love these." I look down, barely able to see them, but the sunlight coming through the kitchen window catches the material and sparkles show on both Caleb and Mason. "You don't know how happy this makes me."

"Anything to make you happy, Rina, anything."

"Not to be outdone." Caleb hands me a box.

"What did *you* do?"

"Well I can tell you it's not ninety-dollar shoes because I'm a broke college student, but I did pick this up the other day." His tone is dry as he looks at Mason.

"Neither one of you had to do anything," I protest.

"Rina." Mason laughs. "You made us Easter baskets. I'm thirty-six years old and he's nineteen. I mean, you obviously love the holiday."

"I love any holiday." My tone is smart as I pucker my lips at him. "You know this about me already."

Opening the box, I squeal as I see the pink shirt Caleb's purchased for me. It says *Hatching in May* with an Easter egg on it. "This is the cutest thing ever, thank you so much." I pull him into my arms.

"Okay." I wipe my eyes, emotional as hell about everything. "Let's go to church and then meet the rest of the MTF for Easter dinner. We gotta get this show on the road if we're gonna make it."

As a family we walk to the Jeep, and Mason easily helps me inside. As I buckle in and watch Mason walk around the front, I glance back, seeing Caleb take his seat.

The moment is perfect, as we drive to the church. My husband, my son, and my soon-to-be-born daughter are all together as a family. When I moved to Laurel Springs, I never dreamed this could happen, but as we travel across town, I think, like I do a lot these days, just how lucky I am.

EPILOGUE

MENACE

MAY

There have been four days that have been the most important in my life. When Caleb was born, I joined the Moonshine Task Force, married Karina, and now this moment. When our daughter entered the world.

"Caleb should be here in the next fifteen minutes." I read the text I just got from him so Karina knows what's going on. "There was a wreck on I-65 and he got stuck in the traffic coming home. I told him we won't let anyone else meet her until he does."

Karina looks up at me, smiling. "Sounds good, I want him to be the first."

This woman, looking at me the way she is, has blown my mind today. After waking up at three a.m. with her water breaking, she went through seven hours of active labor, refusing to call anyone until it was time to start pushing. She didn't want anyone to have to wait around on her. By the time I called Caleb, I knew he wouldn't be here in time, but I figured that saved us all from some major embarrassment. I'm a hundred percent positive he didn't want to be in the same room as the person he sees as his mom with her legs spread for everyone to see what was going on between them. I had wanted to be able to concentrate on her, make sure things were fine, and there were no complications before we'd let Caleb know. Hell, more than anything, I wanted to make sure it wasn't a false alarm. We'd had one of those last week, and he'd sleepily made the drive at two in the morning, only to end up sleeping in his bedroom at our house.

"You look beautiful," I whisper as I lean into her, kissing her on the lips.

"I'm sure I look like a hot mess, Mason, but I love you for acting like I don't."

In between us, my daughter makes a noise, bringing my attention to her. Fuck, I'd thought Caleb was small when he was born. His little sister was smaller, by a full pound, but Jesus she has a set of lungs on her. One day she'll either be a cheerleader or a singer, with the way she can scream.

"She looks so much like you," Rina comments as she runs her fingers along the smooth face, scrunched up at the moment.

"Hopefully she'll grow out of that," I joke as I reach down, running my own finger along her skin. "Honestly, she looks like Caleb, I'll have to get some of his baby pictures out and let you see. They're definitely related."

"He'll fall in love with her," she predicts, holding our daughter close, rubbing her nose along the blanket she's swaddled in. "I know he will. He's going to be the most amazing big brother the world has ever seen. Nobody will be able to touch her."

"That's the way it should be, and if he can't take care of it, I will." I feel myself getting irritated; just thinking someone could hurt this little girl of mine.

"Calm down, big guy. She's a whopping hour old. I think you can hold off on having to harm someone as they come to the front door for a date. You have a few years before that happens."

I grab her hand, bringing it to my lips for a kiss, a show of appreciation for all she's given me. When I moved to Laurel Springs, never in a million years did I imagine this would be my life. Fuck, when we met in January of last year I'd never imagined this could be how I'm living. I'd assumed I would be eating microwave meals and trying to figure out how to fill my free time with Caleb gone. Instead, I'm doing things I wasn't able to do the first time around, I'm experiencing all new life situations, and I'm living the way I want to.

"I'm almost scared to hold her," I admit. "She's smaller than Ransom, too."

"Yeah, but I'm sure she'll want her daddy to hold her as soon as possible."

Daddy. A word I thought I'd never hear again. One I assumed I was done with. Fact is I'm not done, and I can't wait to experience what this round will be like with a girl. Quickly I take my shirt off so she and I can do skin-to-skin, just like she and Karina had done. Grabbing her up from Karina's arms, I hold her close, knowing she can feel my heartbeat coming through the distance between us.

Immediately, the smell takes me back to the first time I held Caleb. I remember how unsure I was, how scared I was. I realize I'm not scared this time, that I'm completely prepared for what's coming my way. This child I'll enjoy, this child will have those fucking cute cupcakes when it's her birthday because she has a mother who loves her. One who loves me, and one who stuck around, who will stick around, even when times get tough. "I love you." I lean down, kissing her small nose.

There's a knock at the door, and when Caleb enters, he's carrying flowers and a pink teddy bear. "I bought this for her as soon as you found out it was a girl," he explains as he approaches the bed, setting the flowers on the bedside table for Karina. "For you, Kari. You look amazing for just giving birth." He leans in, hugging her, but his eyes never stray from his sister's face.

"You wanna hold her?" I ask him, motioning to the rocking chair in the corner.

"She's so little." His voice is as awestruck as mine had felt the first moment I saw her.

"You'll be fine," I reassure him.

He makes his way over to the rocking chair, having a seat, and I carefully place my daughter in his arms. In that moment Caleb does fall in love with his baby sister. It's written plainly across his face. The look of complete and total devotion fills a spot in my heart I didn't even know was empty.

From her spot on the bed, I see Karina take a picture of the moment in front of her. Our eyes meet, and as two parents I don't think we can be more pleased with what's transpiring in front of us. Caleb is counting her toes, making sure they're all there.

"Ten fingers, ten toes, gorgeous eyes, and hair like Kari's. I think you're just about perfect, Kelsea." He grins to her and as he tucks the blanket a little tighter around her, I watch her reach up and grab his finger. He doesn't stop speaking. "I'll protect you with everything I have. I've waited a long time to have a sibling, and I'll make sure you never have to worry about anything. You'll never worry if you have a friend, because I'll only be a phone call away. You'll never worry if you need a confidant because I'll never judge. And by God, you will have the most amazing cupcakes for your birthday, I will personally see to it."

The group of us laugh, knowing what those words mean to him. He looks up at us smiling, and I take a seat on the bed next to Karina.

"You good?" she asks as she leans in to my side. I wrap my arm around her waist, pulling her to me. My heart is so full as I look at the picture in front of me. I know eventually her parents will show up, my mom will make an appearance, and I'll make an effort with my dad by sending him a picture. None of that matters more than the other three people in the room with me. Regardless of anything that's happened. My wife, my son, my daughter – they are my family. They are my legacy, and no one will ever be able to take that away from me. Secure in that knowledge, I'm happy as I look out over my family

As the door to the room opens and the guys from the MTF pour in, their own kids with them, I kiss her, giving her a smile. "No babe, I'm great."

And as everyone starts cooing over Kelsea, welcoming Caleb back, and congratulating us on a job well done, I know without a doubt it will never get much better than this."

The teenage fuckup, the single dad, and the loner of the crew – none of those labels apply any more.

The one that does?

Mason Harrison: happy man.

Purchase Cruise at the vendor of your choice below!
Amazon
Amazon AU
Amazon CA
Amazon UK
Apple
B&N
Google Play
Kobo

CRUISE - BOOK VI

SUMMARY

The kid is now a man, and he's got something to prove.....

Caleb "Cruise" Harrison

"A dad is a son's first hero..."

All my life I've looked up to my dad, there's nothing I ever wanted to do more than be a member of the Moonshine Task Force right next to him. I said no to playing football professionally to stay in Laurel Springs and fulfill my dream.

I'm biding my time, paying my dues, and learning from the elder MTF members. To most of them I'm the kid they watched grow up, and while they're proud of me, they don't take me seriously.

Life is status quo until the morning all hell breaks loose in our small town threatening everyone I know and love – including the one woman I can't get out of my head.

Ruby Carson

"My favorite place? In his arms..."

Caleb saved me from the worst date of my life, swooping in like the fixer he is. Smiling his panty-melting grin, he grabbed my hand and extricated me from the longest ninety minutes known in the history of the world. After saving me, he took me on the best date I've ever had. We've been inseparable since that crazy night.

It hasn't been picture-perfect. His job is dangerous; it worries me, even when he tells me not to. One gorgeous summer day, it all comes crashing down on us.

The man who has my heart is in the middle of a FUBAR situation that has no good ending. My hope is when the smoke clears Caleb will be walking toward me, arms outstretched, with that grin on his face, before he envelopes my body into the hug only he can give.

That's what would happen in a perfect world – but I've never known a perfect world – not even with Caleb...

PROLOGUE
CRUISE

"DISPATCH, be advised I'm stuck on the railroad tracks." I bang my head against the steering wheel as I hear the snickering answering my admission.

I can literally hear every single one of the MTF members laughing – my damn dad being the loudest. His loud chuckle could be heard in a group of hyenas.

Dispatch manages to hold it together, as she speaks to me. "Do you need a wrecker..." She trails off, and then I hear it. "Newbie?"

Pushing my fingers through my hair, I lean against the hand holding the radio. I groan before I press the button. "Yes, I'd rather not get my squad car crushed by a train."

"Help is headed your way," she answers, and again I can hear the laughter in her voice.

It's not long that I have to wait until another squad car pulls up. It parks a safe distance away, and as the two get out, I let out a short breath. "Fuck my life."

Not one to back down from anything, not anymore, I get out, facing the proverbial firing squad.

"Caleb." Havoc runs his hand over his chin. "What the fuck did you do?" He laughs as he observes the way my car sits across the tracks, the tires in such a way I can't get out.

"Don't even ask." I put my hands on my hips as I shake my head. "Renegade got the guy, and that's all that matters."

I shoot my dad a look. "You wanna say something?"

He saunters over to me, clapping his hand against my shoulder, squeezing tightly. "Welcome to the team, Rookie."

The twitching of his mouth at the corners causes me to lose control, and I let go with a loud laugh, not able to catch my breath as I bend at the waist. When I finally get it under control, I give them a smirk. "Fifth day on the job, and I'm already a fucking legend."

CHAPTER ONE
CRUISE

FIVE YEARS **Later**

September

It's a rainy night in Laurel Springs as I pull my Rubicon into one of the only empty spots in front of The Café. For just a moment, I turn off the ignition and sit, still amazed at how many people can fit inside. My rookie year on the MTF, Ernie passed away and Leighton had used her business smarts and degree, purchasing the place that meant so much to all of us. Ernie had no family, and her stepping in to keep an important part of the community alive had brought us all closer together.

We'd had an old-fashioned type of barn raising. People from two counties over in each direction came to help us remodel and expand The Café. It's now doubled in size, with updated everything, and I knew from talking to Havoc that Leighton was doing very well for herself. So well, in fact, she'd brought Brooks into the business two years ago, and they have become a formidable team. Once their family name was known for moonshine. Now? The Strathers are known throughout the six-county area for having the best food, desserts, and the most hospitality anyone could ask for. The establishment is alcohol free and caters to anyone who wants to have fun without being impaired.

Truth be told, it's where I eat most of my meals these days.

Today has been a long fucking day, and there's not going to be any break in this weather for at least the next two. Reaching over, I grab my hoodie, shrugging it over my head, making sure I'm covered before I duck out of the safety of the vehicle and make a run for it. My combat boots beat against the stone of the sidewalk, splashing water against the back of my legs, but at least they're covered by my tactical pants. As I get to the door, I hold it open for an elderly couple making their way as quickly up the sidewalk as they can.

"Thank you." The woman gives me a wide smile, while the man pats me on the side.

"No problem, I hope y'all have a good night." I let the door shut behind me and shake the droplets off my hoodie as I look around for my food partner tonight.

Morgan Santana is my food partner almost every night, if I'm honest. He joined the EMT squad right around the time I joined the MTF, we're the same age, and we share a lot of the same interests. I'd never had a best friend besides my dad before I met him, but I can honestly say Morgan is the closest friend I've ever had. I'd been close with my college roommate, Slater, but our friendship revolved around homesickness and college sports. Morgan and I talk about everything.

"Over here." He waves through the crowd. Looks as if he's secured us a booth away from a lot of the families and amongst older couples and younger ones on date nights. Fuck my life; it gets old being a single guy all the time.

"Thanks for putting us over here in loved-up central," I say as I take a look around, sliding into the booth across from him.

"Cut me a break, Harrison, it was the only seat that didn't have babies around it." He glances over the top of his menu.

"I don't know why you're even looking." I toss my menu aside. "It's fried chicken night, and that's what both of us always get."

"Maybe I'm watching my weight." He pats his stomach, which is probably tighter than mine.

"Yeah," I chuckle. "Okay, sounds about right."

"Hey, guys." Leighton smiles as she strolls up to our table. "What's going on tonight?"

I put my arm out, pulling her to my side. "Oh, you know, arresting bad guys, writing tickets, fucking shit up. Normal stuff."

"Maybe for him." Morgan throws me a glare. "I got puked on today, by a baby. That was so not normal stuff for me." Which explains why he didn't want to sit next to any tonight.

"Ewwww." She curls her lip up in disgust. "I don't miss those days. Thank God Ransom and Cutter are out of that stage," she mentions her and Havoc's two boys.

"Where are they at?" I look around the building for them. Typically, when she works nights, they're with her.

"Ransom had football practice earlier today, so Holden took them out for pizza. Y'all ready to order?"

Their son is huge. He'll be playing college ball before we all know it. "I'd much rather have the fried chicken and mashed potatoes with gravy," I tell her as she writes down my order.

"Brown gravy?"

"Hell yes, and some water too, please."

Nodding she turns to Morgan. "What do you want tonight?"

"Give me a vegetable plate with grilled chicken and a water. Some of us are watching what we eat."

I shake my head as he tries to guilt me. "I weigh ten pounds more than I did when I played college football, and five of those pounds are probably muscle. You're not getting me to admit I shouldn't be eating this. Do you know how many years of my life I spent making sure I was within my macros? I try not to worry about it so much now."

"Gotcha." She leans in and says in a lowered voice, "Can you all watch the table beside you? The guy is giving me some creeptastic vibes and the girl is eating that appetizer like she hasn't eaten in the last six years."

Leighton turns away and immediately my attention goes to the couple at the table beside us. I can't see the woman's face, but one of my strengths is reading body language. Hers says she's highly tense, uncomfortable, and possibly scared, given the way her foot taps against the floor. Her back is ramrod straight, one hand is gripping the table, and there's an iciness in the way she's holding herself.

Quietly I watch as she all but shovels a potato skin in her mouth, then grabs for the last one on the plate. Any person with eyes can see either she's starving or trying to get this night over with. Given the vibes this guy is throwing off, I'm assuming it's the latter.

"Well, at least I know you like to swallow." He gives her a lecherous smile, licking his lips.

The move is creepy enough that it even makes my skin crawl. I shift around so I can see her profile; she looks young and way too innocent to be messing with this guy.

"Not typically." Her dry answer makes me grin.

"I woulda found out in a few hours anyway." He gives her a wink.

"Don't flatter yourself. I hadn't even planned on inviting you in, and given the way you've acted so far during this date, I'm not inclined to do so."

I love the way she's affected an ice princess tone. Very quickly, she's setting boundaries, and my cop senses totally approve of what's going on.

"Sweetheart." He tilts his head toward her, the grin now gone from her face. "You forget I picked you up? I know where you live. I can get in anytime I want."

The fork she'd been using to cut her potato skin falls to the plate with a loud bang, and that's when I get pissed enough to get up. "Be back." I tap the table at Morgan.

There's four chairs at the table they're occupying. I grab one, turn it around and straddle it.

"Hey fuck face, who do you think you are?" the guy asks, irritation in his voice.

Reaching into the hoodie, I pull the badge on a chain around my neck off and slam it down on the Formica. "Hey fuck face, I'm the police, and I think I just heard you threaten this young lady. Who do you think *you* are is the appropriate question here."

Ruby

"Hey fuck face, I'm the police and I think I just heard you threaten this young lady. Who the fuck do you think you are is the appropriate question here."

I hear the scrape of the chair as the man who just spoke the words yanks it out from under the table and has a seat. Thank God he's showed up; the last line of conversation scared me more than I'd even like to admit to myself.

As my eyes take in the badge that's been slammed on the surface of the table, I want to kiss this man who's interrupted the date from hell. However, I can't seem to make my eyes move from the badge, I'm somewhat shaking as I hear what's being said between the two of them.

"I didn't mean anything by it." My date is stumbling over his words, fidgeting, sweat sprinkling his forehead. Besides being a cop, this officer is an intimidating figure all his own.

"No, I'm pretty sure you told her if she didn't perform oral sex on you, you were going to break into her house and get it. I could charge you with a pretty good amount of shit right now. Give me your ID."

The smooth voice, laced with power and authority, washes over me. This man, this officer, doesn't have as strong an accent as most people around here, and I wonder if he's born and bred.

My date fumbles with his wallet, finally producing an ID, handing it over with shaking hands. Finally, I allow myself to look up at the man who's saved me from who knows what. He's gorgeous. His features are strong, a close-cropped beard covers his face, and soulful brown eyes glance my way as he looks between the two of us. Pushing the sleeves of the hoodie he wears up, I see ink on his forearm, but the way he's moving it, doesn't allow me to get a good look. So badly, I want to reach over, still the movement, and feast on whatever it is he cared enough about to permanently mark himself.

"Seth Donovan," he rolls the name of my date around on his tongue, almost as if he's trying it on for size. "Is this address correct?" He pulls his cell phone from his pocket, tapping in a few numbers.

"Ye....ye.....yes," he finally answers, nodding excessively.

My knight in shining armor is talking to someone on the other end of the line, and I realize he's running Seth's name. For what, I'm not sure, but I've seen enough cop reality shows that I'm figuring it's for warrants.

"Is that right?" Those brown eyes land on the other man at the table, and the full lips, spread in a tight line. "Send a uniform, I'm off-duty. We're at The Café."

He disconnects the call, sets the phone down, stands up, and motions for Seth to do the same. "You my friend, have a warrant. Stand up, a uniform is on the way to get you."

"You're full of shit!"

My savior leans in close, whispering, but it's loud enough for me to hear it. "This is a family establishment, and you'll respect the people who work hard. Unlike you, who seems to like breaking and entering and stealing things that aren't yours. Put your hands behind your back or I'll do it for you."

This officer has at least twenty-five pounds of pure muscle on Seth, and for about thirty seconds, it looks like this disaster is going to get even worse. I get the feeling in the pit of my stomach that Seth will run, and he'll make a spectacle of himself when he does. Instead, he puts his hands behind his back, his head hanging low.

It's all a blur as he's read his rights, cuffed, and hauled out front. I'm fully aware of everyone's eyes on me, which is embarrassing, but I also worry about my job. I'll have to do damage control on Monday. Right now though, I just want to get out of here, which is going to prove difficult because Seth was my ride. Not long after they've walked outside, I see the flash of blue lights through the plate glass window. And a few minutes later, the man who did his civic duty is strutting back over to my table.

Oh this officer, whoever he is, doesn't walk like mere mortals, no. He struts. Every eye in the room is glued to him, and I'm impressed with the easy way he handles the attention. The soft roll of his hips. It's obvious that the women in the room wonder what it's like to be me, the men in the room wonder what it's like to be him. He stops in front of me, and I get a look at how tall he is, how powerful the body under his clothes must be. He sits back down in the chair he vacated.

"You alright, ma'am?"

There's a boyish quality to the way he's asked the question, along with the easy smile that's spread across his face. It sends butterflies from the pit of my stomach up my throat. I have to focus on my words as I say them. "I am. Thank you so much for coming to my rescue. My name is Ruby."

"No problem. Where the hell did you find that piece of work?"

"A friend from work." I think back to the librarian, Trinity, telling me what a nice guy she thought Seth was. I guess the two of us have totally different definitions of nice guys.

He runs a hand through thick, dark hair, and gives me a grin. "Not much of a friend, huh?" Tapping his knuckles on the table, he motions over to the booth he left, to the man sitting there by himself, watching this all play out. "My friend and I were getting some dinner, and since you're kind of stuck here, would it be okay if we ate with you? I'll take you home when we're done."

I want to say yes, but after what's just happened to me, I'm hesitant. Right then, Leighton, comes over, carrying three plates. "Trust me, honey. He's a good one, I've known Caleb since he was a teenager. He'll get ya home safe, or I can call Holden and have him take you. But Caleb works with Holden as part of the Moonshine Task Force; you're in good hands."

The Moonshine Task Force. I've heard of them, one of the fellow teachers I work with has a husband who's a member. I know they're trustworthy, and for the first time this night, I relax.

CHAPTER TWO
RUBY

"THIS IS ME." I point to the duplex I'm renting while trying to figure out how to live on a first-year teacher's salary. It's not as easy as I assumed it would be back when I was still in the dorms taking classes.

He chuckles as he pulls his Jeep into the gravel lot. This Jeep is the manliest thing I've seen. Completely blacked out with all the bells and whistles anyone could ask for. The glow of the dashboard is blue, and the contrast between the light, his coloring, and those soulful brown eyes of his is almost my undoing as we sit here in the dark, alone.

"Why the laugh? I know it's not much." I'm slightly offended by the way he's reacting to where I live. And really disappointed.

"I'm not laughing at you, Ruby." He grips the steering wheel with those long fingers of his, causing his forearms to flex tight. "It's just that back in the day, a couple of my co-workers lived in this duplex before they fell in love and got married."

"They allow women on the Moonshine Task Force?" I've never heard of it before, but it doesn't mean that it isn't true.

"No." He laughs again. "When I was a teenager I worked at The Café, and there was a waitress who worked there too. She had a bad experience with her husband, and Ace, now my co-worker with the MTF helped her out of it. They ended up living here next to each other, and when her divorce was final, they admitted their feelings for one another and got married."

The sigh that comes from deep within me is light. I'm a helpless romantic, and while that's sometimes played against me, I do love when two people come together in the face of adversity. "That's a sweet story."

"They're a sweet couple." He runs a hand over his chin. "Do you want me to come in and make sure everything's okay? Given the way Seth threatened you tonight, I asked the arresting officer to fill out a temporary protection order, especially since he's wanted for breaking and entering. He won't be getting out of jail tonight, and I have no idea what's going to happen when he goes before the judge. If you give me your phone number, I can text you and let you know. Chances are he'll be given bail, but if he can't make the amount, he'll be sitting in lockup until he's arraigned. I don't think you have anything to worry about." He shrugs. "But I'm also not God, so if you feel that something's off, please give us a call."

"Or I can text you?" I raise an eyebrow because I don't really want this whole town to know my embarrassment at being caught in this situation.

"Absolutely."

Within a few minutes, we have each other's numbers and he's walking me to my front door. "Thank you again." I turn, looking up at him. He's taller, so much taller than me that he dwarfs my body. If he wanted to surround me, it wouldn't be that hard, and I'd probably let him. I'm a sucker for a man who can take control of a situation and not back down. That's the epitome of what Caleb has done for me tonight.

"Just doin' my job." He puts his hands in his hoodie, rocking back and forth on his heels.

I don't know why, but those words hurt slightly. A part of me hoped he'd come to my rescue because he'd actually wanted to, not because he felt like he had to. The last thing I want to be is someone's job.

"I'm sorry to have ruined your night," I try to keep the emotion out of my voice. This has been the weirdest few hours of my life and telling myself the reaction I'm having is emotional isn't helping the lump I feel in my throat.

"You didn't." He pulls one of those hands out of his hoodie, bracing it against the door. "It was my pleasure to rescue you, Ruby. I'm glad you're okay, I'm beyond glad that asshole didn't hurt you, and what I'd really like to see again is that smile on your face you gave me a few times tonight."

My heart pounds in my chest, my throat dry as I try to swallow, and my stomach has those butterflies again. The smile he's asking about spreads across my face without me even thinking about it. "I'm lucky you rescued me; today could have ended pretty shitty for me," I admit, pulling my gaze away from his intense brown stare.

"It could have." His voice is sober. "But it didn't. I know this is crazy, but I had a good time with you tonight, even if it did start off kind of weird. Could I see you again? Maybe show you what a real man does to woo a woman?"

That heart of mine speeds up to double-time. My palms get slightly sweaty and I'm embarrassed to say my knees knock just a little. "I'd like that," I manage not to sound like an idiot.

"I work nights all weekend." His tone is apologetic. "But I'm available for breakfast in about ten hours, if that's not too soon." The look on his face is so hopeful that I can't help but be impressed.

A laugh bubbles up from my stomach, and I throw my head back with the force of it. "Breakfast it is."

"I know a place, over in Calvert City," he mentions a town about an hour away. "They have one of the best breakfasts around, and there's a nice little section of downtown we can explore, before I have to come back and take a nap before work. Is that okay?"

"Sounds great." I nod, thinking that I'll like the chance to spend some time with him. Even though maybe I should be apprehensive after what happened to me tonight, I inherently trust the man standing in front of me. Something tells me to trust my gut with this one, and my gut is giving me nothing but signals to go along with whatever this man is asking of me.

"I'll pick you up around eight? We should get there in enough time that we get breakfast but most of the rush is gone."

"I'll see you then." I lean in, kissing him on the cheek, before turning around, unlocking my door, and walking inside.

"Be sure and lock it, Ruby. Be safe."

"You too, Officer." I give him a little wave before doing exactly what he asked me to do.

Cruise

Jogging back to my Jeep, I get in and execute a three-point turn to get out of the drive, before I allow the smile to spread all the way across my face. I do a little dance in my seat and gleefully beat a hand against the steering wheel.

There are lots of things that have happened in my life that I can't explain. Why my mom left me at such a young age, why I was blessed to get another one in the form of Kari, why my little sister is nine and I'm twenty-eight, how my dad and I have such a great relationship even though we're only sixteen years apart in age. I've had tough times, and I've had great times, but there's always been parts I've never been able to explain. Much like what just happened.

From the moment I sat down at the table in The Café, I felt something drawing me to Ruby. I wanted to protect her, to make sure she got home safe, to be sure this dumbass she'd been set up with didn't try something he shouldn't have. The feeling increased as she had dinner with me and Morgan. We laughed, we joked, a meal that should have lasted an hour extended to almost two, and I could tell that none of us wanted to leave when we got our checks. There's been few times in my life when I had such a great meal with someone of the opposite sex who wasn't obviously trying to get into my pants. The invitation to breakfast tomorrow was spur of the moment, but now that I've extended it, I can't get it off my mind.

Turning the radio up, I sing along to the country song, tinged with a little bit of rock. If anyone had to ask me to describe myself, that's probably the best way. I love the simple things in life, they're my favorite. I don't like to make anything complicated, but at the same time I like to ride the edge – more sexual than anything – but I have a past, and sometimes I just gotta let it out.

The song is interrupted as a call comes through my Bluetooth. Mason Harrison. Probably checking up on his son. I allow the call through. "Hey, Dad!"

"You arrested someone at The Café tonight?" He goes right into the reason he called without even offering pleasantries.

I roll my eyes. Should have known he'd hear about it first thing in this small town. "No, I didn't arrest them, but Renegade did. I was sitting there having dinner with Morgan when I heard the guy she was on a date with threaten her. It was a fuckin' shitty move and I couldn't sit there and listen to it. She was obviously uncomfortable."

"He threatened her?"

I relate back the story, and my dad whistles through his teeth. "What a douche."

"Yeah, so when I called in his name, he had warrants for breaking and entering. I actually just took her home because she was stranded."

I leave out the detail that I'm seeing her tomorrow. Since Jess, who I dated during my senior year in high school, I don't introduce women to my parents unless I know they're going to stick around. In ten years, they've met one other woman, and that had been a huge mistake. I'd let her meet my family, and when we agreed to go our separate ways, it was sad for everyone involved. Unfortunately, she and I just weren't meant to be. There were no hard feelings, still isn't, it just wasn't right for either of us.

"Yeah, so that's my night in a nutshell. How's the fam?" I turn his attention away from me, onto the women in our lives.

"Good, Rina is already in bed and so is Kels, but I was still up because I worked a little over and wanted to check in with you after I heard what happened. I'm hitting the hay here soon." He yawns loudly in my ear. "You know you don't have to eat with Morgan all the time, you can come have dinner here."

"I have dinner there plenty," I argue. "At least three times a week."

"I'm just saying, it doesn't matter how many times a week you're here. We love to see you whenever that is."

"I know, and Morgan knows he's invited too, but sometimes we just want to be dudes."

"I get it," Dad laughs. "Your mom wanted me to tell you, in case you didn't know."

The transition from calling my stepmother Karina to Mom had happened slowly. It wasn't something that one day I woke up and just blurted out. It was a decision I made and then had to put into execution. But as Kelsea had gotten older, I was afraid she'd ask questions – why did she call her Mom and I called her Kari? The reality of the situation would be way too much for a little kid to comprehend, much less handle, and I'd made the decision on my own to take it out of the equation.

Never having called anyone Mom before, I had to try to the word out on my tongue. I had to practice saying it, really let the motion of moving my lips to form the word become second nature. I'd called her Mom in my head for months before I'd actually tried the word out in person. The day I had, she'd stopped what she was doing, turned to me, and cried like the emotional woman she is. She'd hugged me, clung to me, and thanked me for letting her be a part of my life. It's tough to admit, but even I cried that day, and a huge burden had been lifted off my shoulders. Karina Harrison is my mom, no matter if she gave birth to me or not. She's always loved me more than the actual woman who gave birth to me did.

"Tell her I'm fine." I pull into the apartment complex I'm living at for the moment and park my Jeep in my designated space. "I'm home, so I'm gonna go. I have to work night shift tomorrow," I groan.

"Good luck getting your sleep in."

The one good thing about having a parent with the same job as you? They get your sleep habits. "Will do, Dad. Love you."

"Love you too. Be safe, kiddo."

CHAPTER THREE

RUBY

LISTENING to the rain beat against the roof has always been one of my favorite pastimes. And now that I live on my own, not at my parents' house and not at a dorm full of loud roommates, I can be lazy and listen to it whenever I want to.

On mornings like this, I think. And since I'm thinking, I'm rehashing everything that happened last night in my mind. To me, life has never been lived in hours. It's been lived in moments, goals, achievements, and special occasions. Hours though, hours mean a lot too. Take roughly ten hours ago.

If Caleb hadn't been there to save me last night, who knows where I'd be at this hour. I could be lying in this bed hurting, contemplating an entirely different trip today. It might be one to the ER, instead of a few counties over. It could be spent making police reports, rather than trying to decide what I want to wear. Last night I was taught a valuable lesson. I'll never take hours for granted again.

Throwing my covers off, I shiver at the chill in the room. This fall has been colder than most, and if I remember correctly, it's not supposed to get above fifty today. Perfect book weather, if you were to ask me. Getting up and doing my daily business is exciting because I know I'm going to get to spend at least part of my day with Caleb. As I'm brushing my teeth, I hear my phone go off on my night stand.

When I'm done, I rush over, wondering which of my friends is texting me on a Saturday morning. When I see that it's Caleb's number, I get both excited and worried. What if he's canceling on me?

***C:** Just wanted to make sure we're still on for today and give you an update.*

They denied bail because Seth had warrants in three other counties. He's actually going to be extradited. You dodged a bullet, Ruby.

I feel how lucky I am, know how fortunate I was that people were watching out for me last night, and grateful to live in the small town I do.

R: *Thanks for letting me know. Kinda makes me feel better, knowing he's not around anymore. And of course we're still on!*

C: *Understandable. I'll be by to pick you up in about thirty minutes. I just have to drop my little sister off at a friend's house. She's having a sleepover tonight.*

Caleb has a little sister? Immediately I'm wondering how much younger she is than him, and I decide since he appears at least a few years older than me, she's probably a teenager.

Thirty minutes doesn't give me much time, but I spring into action, doing the best I can with what I have. Putting on a little bit of makeup, I run my fingers through my naturally curly hair. Because it's raining, it goes every which way, and I know the only way I'm going to be able to tame it is by putting it in a braid. Which makes me look all of ten years old.

It can't be helped; I think I'll always look young for my age. Even now, having my own classroom, people assume I'm a student and not a teacher. Swiping a little mascara on my lashes, I put my pearl studs in my ears, and opt for a deep plum lip stain. At least maybe he'll be drawn to my lips for most of the day. With my golden blonde hair, it makes a striking contrast. Besides full lips and big eyes, about the only thing I have to work is my ample chest, which nobody will be able to see underneath my rain coat today, but that's okay. I'll tuck it away for a surprise, in case we go out on another date. Glancing out the window as I go for my rain boots, I see him.

The Rubicon, which I'd found so sexy the night before, pulls up into my drive. He doesn't turn it off, but he bails out, running to my front porch. And the brief glimpse I get of him is enough to send my pulse racing. Caleb wears a very worn pair of jeans, a t-shirt with a flannel unbuttoned over it, rolled up those forearms of his, with a hat pulled low over his eyes.

The knock that announces he's here is enough to set me on edge.

Calming myself, I open the door, as I'm slipping my rain jacket on. "Hey," I greet him, not able to wipe the smile off my face at seeing him again. It's crazy, we met last night, but I've never had a connection with someone the way I have a connection with him.

"Hey." He grins back. "Sorry about the weather. I ordered sunshine with a high of seventy. Instead I got this." He shrugs. "We can make the best of it, right?"

"How dare mother nature not listen to you?" I grab my cross-body bag, slinging it over my chest.

"That's what I'm saying." He plays along, his voice playful. "I mean doesn't she know I'm trying to impress you?"

He takes my elbow as we descend the porch, then he walks me over to the passenger side of the Jeep where he helps me in, before he jogs around the front. The inside is nice and warm, a familiar rock song plays on the radio, and the gentle thump of the windshield wipers cocoon me in a feeling of rightness like I've never had before.

"You don't have to try, Caleb, you're already impressing me pretty hard-core." I buckle up as he checks his blind spot and then begins backing out. "The guy last night honked the horn. He didn't even come to my door."

"Fuck that," he says the words like they taste bad. "My dad would have my ass if I didn't go get a woman at her door. He's chivalrous like that. Any kid who ever wants to date my sister will have to go through both of us," he preaches as he turns toward Calvert City.

"She's lucky to have a brother like you." I think of my own brother.

Cruise

"Nah, I'm lucky to have a little sister like her. I waited a long time for one," I admit as I turn onto the county highway that will take us to Calvert City.

I'm usually not a talker. Typically I have to get to know someone before I start belting out my life story, but there's something about this girl. Since I saw her sitting there last night, so stoic, so unsure of the situation she was in, I've wanted to talk to her. I've wanted to tell her everything will be okay and explain to her that even though things might seem a little scary now, they won't always.

"You ever been out here?" I change the subject from my family. For people who don't know where I come from, it's a little difficult to explain.

"I'm assuming we're going to The Hen Lays The Egg?" She mentions the name of the most popular breakfast joint in these parts.

"Is there any other place to go?" I question.

"The Café." She giggles as she slides her gaze over at me.

"Oh, you got jokes? I see how it is." I adjust my seat to make it a little more comfortable with my long legs and then sit back to enjoy the ride. "I go there all the time."

"I do too, I can't believe I've never seen you there before." She looks like she might be trying to place me. "But I do feel like maybe I have seen you before last night."

As a cop, especially as a member of the MTF, I'm recognized a lot. We're required to be at many functions, some of them are attended by the whole town, some by a certain population. Either way, we're seen a lot. "Probably in one of my official capacities."

"I don't think so." She shakes her head, her lips pursed, eyebrows together. "I've been trying to put my finger on it since I saw you last night. You're a member of the Moonshine Task Force, right?"

"Yup." No one will ever know how proud I am to carry on the tradition my dad started. When I'd been offered a contract in the draft to play pro ball, he'd argued with me for days about what I was giving up. The truth is, I've never wanted to do anything other than follow in his footsteps. The things I've aspired to do are to make a difference in my community, get alcohol off the streets, and not to let kids be in the same position I was in as a teenager. All of those things mean something to me. They mean something ball never did. Football gave me opportunities, but it wasn't my one true love.

"My co-worker has a husband who's on the Moonshine Task Force. You'd probably know him."

"Considering there's six of us? I'm almost positive I do." I chuckle as I think about who she could possibly know. We never discussed her job last night.

"Karina Harrison is a teacher at the same school as me."

I laugh as I look across the console into the passenger's seat. "No shit, huh?" I can't stop the laugh. Reaching into the cup holder, I grab my phone and show her my lock screen.

"She's your sister-in-law? That's awesome, she's such a nice lady. She's helped me so much in figuring out what I need to do."

I've never known anyone who truly knew Kari, so this should be interesting when I drop this bomb on her. "No, she's not my sister-in-law. She's married to my dad, but I call her Mom."

Ruby's mouth slams shut. She looks at me, looks at the road, looks at me again, opens her mouth, and then closes it. Her eyebrows come together in confusion, she opens her mouth, shuts it, then reaches into the cup holder, grabs the phone and looks at the lock screen again. "No way." She shakes her head. Looks at it again, and then shakes it again. "No way."

"It's true." I make a cross motion over my chest.

"There's no way that's your dad." She glances at the picture again. "Brother maybe, but not dad."

"I swear to God," I say with a laugh. She's cute in her confusion. "You wanna see my birth certificate? He's my dad."

"Did he have you at like fourteen?"

"Sixteen," I correct her. "Dad had me at sixteen and raised me by himself after my biological mom left. Kari and Dad got married almost eleven years ago. She got pregnant with my sister within a month of them getting married, while I was in my freshman year of college."

"Shut the front door. Are you shitting me?"

"I'm totally not, you can ask Kari next time you see her at work. In fact, it's probably where you've seen me. Sometimes I pick Kelsea up and take her to the school so Mom doesn't have to make more than one trip," I explain as I pass a slower moving car once we come to a passing spot in the road.

"You call her Mom?"

"I call her Kari sometimes, but mostly Mom. I used to not, but then Kelsea got old enough to where I was afraid she'd question it. And to be honest with you, Kari did more for me than my real mom ever did. If there was a woman who earned the title, it's her."

"I can see that." She glances out the window, gazing at the scenery as it passes by. "She does have a way about her. She makes everyone want to be her friend, everyone tells her their secrets, and if you ever need a shoulder to cry on or someone to tell you all the good things about yourself, she's the person to go to."

"Yes, exactly. Her and my dad, they have the type of marriage I want one day."

"I've seen them together." Her smile is huge, almost as if she's relieving a memory. "He came to work not long ago to bring her a coffee after school had let out. We were doing parent/teacher conferences and it was a really long night. He brought me one too, because I work in the same module as her. When he walked into the room, she lit up. I've never seen a couple so freaking happy to see one another before."

"That's them." I shake my head. "Kind of so sweet it's sickening. Back when I was in college, it used to embarrass me, but as I've gotten older, I realize how lucky they are to have it. My dad didn't have anything for a lot of years, and he hit the lottery with her. Hell, I did too."

"She told me once, when she was talking about her family, that she not only fell in love with her husband, but with her husband's son too. I thought she was talking about some little kid." She giggles.

"Nope, totally me." If I could strut, I would. I like when she says good things about me, and it makes it even better that it hopefully impressed Ruby. Kari and I, we have a special relationship. "I had the flu and she took care of me. From that point on, I never had to wonder if anyone besides my dad cared about me."

"That's a sweet story, Caleb. You're blessed to be able to call her Mom."

As we enter Calvert City proper, I reflect on her words. I know she's right. But I'm also blessed that this woman was somehow dropped into my life. Call it a sixth sense, maybe obsession, or a premonition. Call it anything you want, but I know this day is going to be the start of something good, and if I can stay the course, maybe I will have a relationship like my parents. Maybe I won't be the one member of the MTF who seems to be cursed when it comes to the women in his life.

"Looks like we'll have to park along the side streets and walk down. That okay with you?" The rain hasn't let up, and I worry for a second that she's a girlie girl who can't stand for her hair to get wet, who's worried about her makeup running, and her clothes getting damp.

"Nope, I figured we might, that's why I dressed the way I did. You don't have to worry about me, Caleb. I'm not gonna melt because I got a little wet."

Immediately those words go to a place they probably shouldn't, but I'm a guy and it's been awhile since I got laid. I tell my dick that she didn't mean it the way it sounded, but as she turns to get out of the Jeep and her ass is framed by a tight pair of jeans, I take a minute to thank my own lucky stars that this woman came with me today. After her scare last night, she could have told me to fuck off, but she didn't, and if I'm smart, I'll keep my body under control and my thoughts in safe places.

As I get out, I adjust my package, and pray nobody can tell just how much I want this woman.

CHAPTER FOUR

CRUISE

"DO YOU LIKE TEACHING?"

We've gotten our drinks, ordered our food, and now we're just waiting for everything to be delivered. I'm going to use my time wisely and ask her about anything that comes to mind. Anything that will let me learn more about this woman who's intrigued me.

"I love it," she answers, happiness shining from her eyes. "It's hard being a high school teacher at my age though," she sighs. "At twenty-four, I'm not much older than they are, and I look younger than I am."

"You do," I agree. "But there's something about those blue eyes of yours that kind of drag me in. With a look, they tell anyone that you're old enough to know what you like."

I've caught her looking at me like that a few times. Like she wants to know all my secrets and what I look like without a shirt on. Can't say I don't want to know all of that about her too.

"You think so? This is my first year, but last year when I was a student teacher, it was a struggle to ask them to call me Ms. Carson, and that was my thing not theirs, but it's not gotten any easier yet."

"You get hit on?" I throw that in there. If she were my teacher, I'd totally hit on her.

She averts her eyes. "Yes, typically by guys who are young enough to send me to jail, which was why I was out on that date last night."

"Whoever your friend was that set you up should have known better." I take a drink of my coffee that's been brought to the table. "You should tell her she needs better friends."

"I'll definitely be speaking to Trinity on Monday morning." She takes an answering drink from her glass. "It's just so hard to date." She shrugs, sighing with what sounds like frustration. "I grew up in Laurel Springs, actually saw you play in a few football games, but I didn't recognize you at The Café. Even though I grew up here though, I didn't have a high school boyfriend, and college was fun, but I didn't find anyone there to spend the rest of my life with, ya know? My friends are in two groups. Single and ready to party it up or married and having their first kid. I'm single, but I want to be committed," she explains. "Probably just scared you off with that admission," she laughs nervously.

"No." I shake my head. Little does she know I've wanted this a long time, and I've been looking too. "You didn't scare me off. Kinda said some of the things I've been thinking about myself lately. I didn't grow up in Laurel Springs, but when we moved here, it was home. At my age, everybody is basically a bachelor for life, or they're on child number two. I didn't want to follow in my dad's footsteps – having me so young. So I think I've kinda stunted my own relationship growth, if that makes sense."

"It does." She nods vigorously. "When you have a goal you're concentrating on, you don't want anything to get in the way. Then when you reach that goal, you realize everyone passed you by."

"You get it."

"I do." She smiles over her cup at me. "Thank you for saving me last night."

I smile back at her. "Thank you for needing saving."

Ruby

I lean back in the seat I've occupied for the last hour, managing to stuff one last bite of apple streusel in my mouth, before I moan and push the plate away from me.

"Where the hell do you put it all?" I ask Caleb as he reaches over and grabs what was left on my plate, demolishing it in one bite.

"I work out," he defends himself. "Less than I should, but I run at least five miles every other day."

"So you're a distance runner?" I take a drink of my iced coffee. "Lots of stamina."

"I got all the stamina you need." He licks the fork he'd used to cut the sweet pastry, before he laughs at himself. I eye his tongue, hoping he doesn't notice, thinking about what it would feel like against my skin. "That was a really bad joke."

"Effective though." I give him a wink. "Do you just run or do you lift weights too?"

"I'm not a huge fan of lifting, like I used to be. Back when I was in college and in high school that was my thing. Bulk up, and cut, bulk up and cut. These days," – he pats his stomach – "I prefer to be lean. It's easier on my body, healthier for my mind. I indulge when I want, within reason, and if it gets out of control, I rein it back in."

"Spoken like a man who's never had a weight problem."

There's a sharp edge to my voice, and I wonder if he picked up on it. It's not his fault I'd been overweight my freshman year of high school and had worked hard to lose a total of thirty pounds. Joining the cheerleading squad had helped, but it'd not really changed the way people looked at me. It's not his fault I'd been passed over by every guy in high school I'd liked, and then still passed over once I lost the weight. It'd taken me a long time to come to terms with the fact that I had to have confidence in myself before anyone else would see it.

"Never have, and I don't believe for a second you have either," he admits. "To me, you're perfect. But if you listen to my buddy, Morgan, talk about me. He'll tell you I need to lose at least ten pounds."

"From where I'm looking, you look mighty fine." I give him a once over, and then let my eyes travel back up and down again, blushing when he notices me.

"Thanks for your vote of confidence." He pats his stomach again. "I will say this. We gotta get up and move, otherwise I'm gonna fall asleep before I even get home."

"You might have to roll me out of here," I groan as I lift myself up out of the chair and start putting my jacket on again, digging in my purse for some cash. When I hand him part of what the bill should be, he looks down at the money, almost like he's scared it's going to bite him.

"You remember that thing about my dad kicking my ass cause he's chivalrous? This is another one of those things. We eat, I pay."

Not used to this, I still want to do my part. "Then I pay the tip." I throw down part of my cash. "No arguing."

He holds his hands up. "Mom taught me never to argue with a lady. If you want to leave the tip, you go on and leave the tip."

We slowly walk toward the entrance of the restaurant, dodging people as we do. Even though it's after breakfast rush on a Saturday, there are still people milling about and there's a wait for a table. When we finally get past all the people, I turn to him. "It's still raining, but I'm up for a little window shopping if you are."

"Whatever you wanna do, I'm good with." He zips up his jacket and puts his hat back on. "As long as I get back home in time to take a nap, I don't care what we do. I just want to spend some more time with you."

The heat I feel on my cheeks says a blush is working its way up my neck, but surprisingly I'm okay with it. Caleb Harrison can embarrass me any day. "You ready?" he asks, reaching out for my hand.

"Sure am," I clasp our fingers together as we take off into the soggy mid-morning weather.

"Ya know I like rain like this. A soft drizzle, coating the streets, washing everything new again." He holds onto me tighter as I step down from the curb and we cross the street.

Downtown Calvert City looks like it could have been plucked from any postcard in the nineteen fifties. Mom and Pop shops have their doors open, even though the weather is wet and cool. Many of them have cider available or hot cocoa as we browse through their wares.

"I like this too," I admit, entwining my fingers in his. "A nice, steady, drizzle, it's my favorite. I have a tin roof on my duplex and I was listening to it come down this morning before you came to get me. It's the most relaxing sound." I turn him toward a small store I've been to a few times. "Over here, they have the best shampoo for curly hair. She handmakes it and it's got essential oils in it that curly hair needs. If I hadn't run out, my hair wouldn't look so insane today." I touch my braid with my free hand.

"Not insane, kinda cute." He tugs on the end of the braid. "I like this look on you."

When he smiles, the hint of a dimple shows on his left cheek, and I can't help but smile back. "Whatever you say," I laugh.

When we walk inside, he separates, looking at some of the stuff this shop has for men. He picks up some moisturizing oil I bought my dad not long ago. "I got that for my dad to use instead of aftershave." I glance at the bottle to make sure it's the right one. "Yeah, this one, and he loves it. Says it doesn't dry his face out, and it smells like the beach." I pick up another one. "I liked this one too; it smells a little spicier, sexier than the one I gave my dad."

I reach over, grab the bottle and lift it up to Caleb's nose. The hint of teakwood is enough to make me inhale deeply as I bring it under mine next.

It's one of my favorite scents, and I'd love to smell it on him.

"You like the way this smells, huh?"

"Yeah." I nod, blushing again. "Huge turn-on." I smack my hand over my mouth as I realize what I've just said. It's a little too early in whatever this is to be talking about turn-off's and turn-on's, but there's something about this guy and his deep brown eyes that makes me just want to keep talking.

A slow grin spreads across his face. "Is that right?"

"Ruby, I got your shampoo and conditioner." The cashier and part-owner of the store yells from across the room.

Saved by the bell, I turn around, thankfully hiding myself from his direct gaze to go and purchase what I need. When I feel him stand behind me, I turn around and get the bottle of oil. "Add this to it too." Deciding to go for broke, I am as direct as I can. "I'm the one who wants to smell it on your neck, I might as well be the one to pay for it."

His eyes darken when I lick my suddenly dry lips and I wonder just what the hell I'm doing. This direct person isn't me. Typically I play coy, make a guy chase me, and in the end, I push them away because they come on too strong and suffocate me. But this guy? Maybe I want to chase him a little bit, maybe I'm feeling like it could be mutual, and when he catches me, I want him to take me. I want him to show me what I've been missing with these college guys, because there is no doubt in my mind, as I watch his big hand grab his bag, he's a man.

We walk back out into the weather, this time quieter with one another, but there's a tension that wasn't there before. It's not unwelcome. It's a string of sexual awareness we didn't have when we'd walked in. I can't even bring myself to regret I created the tension there, because I've never gone after what I want before. This will be the first time and hopefully it won't be a bust.

"You wanna head back?" I tilt my head toward his Jeep.

He pulls his phone out of his pocket and glances at the time. "We should, even though I'm having a really good time with you. I do need to get that nap in. If not, I won't be worth shit tonight."

The whole way back to my apartment, I grapple with what I want to ask. I want to see him again, but I've never been the type of woman to be forward. To ask the guy out on the date, more for fear that I'll get shot down, but I'm worried I'll let this moment pass me by.

Caleb takes the decision out of my hands, when he pulls up to my duplex and cuts the ignition. "I'd like to see you again, the next couple of days might be a little crazy for me after the weather we've had, so can we plan something for Friday night? Would that be okay with you?"

Inside my heart is pounding, I want to jump up and down and give the finger to the part of my personality that always expects the worst. But I don't, I keep it together. "Sounds good, what do you want to do?"

"We can check out the new bar, if that's okay?"

Recently a brewery opened up a few streets over from The Café, boasting its own bar. I've wanted to check it out, but I never wanted to go by myself. "Text me the time, when you get your schedule?"

We're staring at one another, so badly I want to lean over the seat and kiss him. Press my lips to his and know exactly what it feels like.

"What the hell," he mumbles as he takes the decision out of my hands once again, grasping my neck in his palm and pulling me close. His lips are soft as they coax mine open. His tongue tastes like the syrup he had on his pancakes and there's a hint of the coffee he drank. I moan softly in the back of my throat, wishing the console didn't separate us. When he pulls away, we're both breathing slightly faster than we were before.

"I gotta go." His voice is husky.

Mine is partially breathless. "That nap, huh?"

"Yeah." He sounds as if he regrets his job at this moment. "I'll text you though?"

"I'd like that a lot."

"Let me walk you." He makes to get out, but I stop him.

"Nah, I like to run." I give him a grin.

Getting out of the Jeep, I run to the front porch, dodging puddles as I go. He waits until I open the door and wave at him. As I make it safely inside, I can't help but feel like today was a life changer.

CHAPTER FIVE

RUBY

SUNDAY MORNING SERVICE is a tradition in my family, has been since I was a little kid. I'm not particularly religious, but even if you aren't, you're still expected to make an appearance.

"I promise, Mom, I'm fine!" I assure my mom for probably the nineteenth time since I showed up this morning. "The cop who helped me was nice, and there's nothing to worry about. He took me home, took care of everything, and made sure I didn't have to be scared. You don't have to worry."

"I'm just not used to you living on your own," she worries, pushing my hair back, out of my face. "It's an adjustment period for us, I'm not trying to crowd you, but please remember, you're still our little girl."

I want to tell her I've been on my own a while. When I was in college no one was there to make sure I came home at a decent hour, to make sure I went to class, or that I ate at a certain time. Funny how that worked out. I even had to make sure I did my own laundry. There was no one there to do that either. Moving back here has partially suffocated me, because now I have a whole family who's worried about me constantly. I know I should appreciate it, but at the same time, it's starting to get annoying.

"You were introduced to him from someone you work with?" my dad asks as he comes to stand next to us, resting his hands in his slacks pockets. "You didn't meet him off of one of those dating sites, did you, Ruby? That's so dangerous. I hope you have a better head on your shoulders than that."

Jesus Christ. All I want to do is get out of here, and away from the inquisition. If they think all of these things about me, how do they think I managed to make it through college? It's almost as if they still see me as a teenager.

"I promise I met him through a co-worker. I don't even have a profile on those sites, Dad, and believe it or not, I managed to take care of myself for almost five years and get a degree. I'm good!" I try to hold the irritation out of my voice, but I don't quite manage it.

My mom looks like she wants to say more, but wisely keeps it to herself. "I know we're a little overbearing, but you're our only daughter."

I've heard this my entire life. My older brother, Lance, could legit go impregnate the entire town and they would throw a celebration party, but me? I should have sensibilities. It makes me wonder what they would say if they knew I've thought about Caleb since he left, wondered what would have happened if I'd been bold enough to invite him in yesterday.

"You coming over to the house for lunch?" Dad asks as he and Mom start walking to their car.

"Not today, I have a lot of papers to grade, laundry to do and all that adult stuff."

I want to roll my eyes, but I keep from it. One day. One day they'll see me as the capable person I am. Education isn't the easiest program to go through, and I did it, graduating with honors. But nobody ever said anything about that, nope. Seems like they never will either.

As I wave goodbye to them, I get in my car, taking my hair down from where it's pinned up. Driving through town, I stop at one of the three fast food places we have, and as I pull out, I see a Laurel Springs cop car blowing past, lights blazing. I wonder if that's Caleb, or his dad. According to the text he sent this morning, he's working a double today, and as I see the car navigate traffic, see people not get out of the way when they should, my heart is in my throat. I've never had anyone I care about have a job where they could get hurt. This is going to take some getting used to.

SUNDAY NIGHT GRADING papers has never been my idea of a fun time, so when my cell buzzes, I hope it's Caleb. I know that he's what they call on-shift, and because of the crazy amounts of rain we've had, they're dealing with flooding. I don't think I ever realized the hours other professions put in. He had to do a double today after working the late shift on Saturday. No wonder he naps when he can. I'd be a walking zombie if someone had me mixing up my days and nights like that. What I don't expect to see is Karina sending me a message.

K: *I heard through the grapevine you had a problem with the date that Trinity set you up on. My son was there to save the day?*

R: *Yeah, it was a hot mess in front of everyone at The Café. I'll explain to Principal Taggert tomorrow morning, just in case. It was really embarrassing,* *but your son did save me. You should have heard how that conversation went he told me you're his mom.*

K: *Ha! I bet there was a lot of explaining going on. I'm glad he was there though, I just wanted to check on you. See you tomorrow!*

As I say my goodbyes to Karina, I throw my phone on my coffee table. I haven't seen Caleb since we parted ways yesterday. I'm not even sure how late he's working today.

What I am sure of is that I want to see him again. Tucking my lip between my teeth and going to sit on my couch, I send a text with my heart in my throat.

R: *How was your day?*

My hands shake as I wait for him to answer, and I wonder if this is the newness of our relationship, or if this is *the guy* I'll have this with for the rest of my life. I don't have the experience to know which is which, but what I do know is I like it. I like the fluttery feeling in my stomach, and I like the fact that he's the one to give it to me.

Cruise

I'm cold, wet, fucking hungry, and really done with this goddamn day when I get the text from Ruby asking how my day is going. For a few brief minutes I don't answer it. I contemplate lying to her, telling her it's been a good one, and then forgetting she even made the attempt to text. Then I look at my team, realize that every single one of them has had a shitty day too, and they have women at home they care about. They lay those problems down at the feet of the women they share their lives with. They don't sugar coat shit, they're partners in the ways that matter, and I know that if I want this to go anywhere with Ruby, we've got to be partners.

C: *Really fuckin' shitty. I can't talk about it right now, and I might not be able to text the rest of the night, but I want to see you. Soon.*

"Where the fuck did this shit wash up from?" Havoc stands to his full height from his crouched position. He's got his hands on his hips, looking down at a crate full of moonshine.

Over the past few years, we've almost eradicated the illegal sale and distribution of the shit that kills people. We've made huge strides and we've worked diligently with the state and county to get this shit off the street. This? This is a kick in the gut.

We responded to a call that said water had run over Pond Creek Road, and when we got here, that wasn't a lie. What we didn't expect to find were about five cases of moonshine floating for anyone to take. "You think it was hidden somewhere?" I crouch down to get a better look at it.

The bottles look old, reminiscent of the night when a friend of mine died after drinking a bad batch. To this day I can't look at glass bottles like this and not relive portions of that night. Most everything we see these days is in some fancy bottle, not many people embrace the old ways anymore. Just looking at it makes me shiver, gets me emotional, and makes me wonder what he'd be doing now. Would he be working with us? Would he have a family? That's the shit that sometimes keeps me up at night.

"It's got mud caked on it." Dad comes over to us. "But if it was in that creek bed, I mean it could have happened during the flood." He runs a hand through his hair. "What makes you think it's old?" He looks at Havoc, questioning the same thing I am.

"Don't know." He shakes his head. "A hunch maybe? This isn't the product we've seen around here the past few years."

"If you wanna get technical, we ain't seen this product since Jefferson went to jail. We can send it off for testing, see where it came from," Dad throws the suggestion out there. "For the most part we've eradicated production like this. If it comes into this town, it comes from out of state. We all know that."

"Jefferson's in jail," I protest. "He's still got a few more years left on his sentence, and Brooks is straight and narrow now. I mean he's not gonna fuck up what he's got with Trinity." Everyone who's seen them together and knows how happy they are knows he's not going to mess it up. He's worked hard to have a stable life; I don't see him doing anything to ever fuck it up again.

Havoc gazes out over the raging creek that's rushed it's banks and now sits over the road. "Doesn't mean he hasn't taught someone else on the inside and then instructed them on what to do once they got out. I don't know, I don't like the feel of this. Maybe he had all that stashed, and somebody was waiting for it to be found."

"I think you're paranoid." Dad claps him on the shoulder, leveling with his friend. "I think you're looking for something that isn't there. I mean we can investigate it, don't get me wrong, but don't let it consume your life. Things are going well for you and Leigh right now."

"That's why I'm worried about it. I don't want anything to mess up what we've got." He runs a hand over his mouth, almost like he can't believe he let the words come out. He and Leighton have been through hell and back with her family, and I completely understand why he's worried, but I'm with Dad; I don't think it's a source for concern at this point.

"Don't let shit like this in your head and it won't."

I'm watching the two of them, constantly amazed at how their friendship works. Forever impressed with the way they speak to one another and how they take each other's feelings into account, even when they don't agree with one another. That's the way mine and Morgan's friendship works, only we don't have a job together. Sometimes I'm thankful for that, because we do get a little shitty with one another now and again.

"So what do you want us to do with it?" I turn to Havoc for instruction. Ace and I found it when we responded, so it's up to us to take care of it.

"Take it to evidence, send off some to the state lab, and see what they come back with. Once the water recedes, we'll come out here and see if there are any clues or anything left. Right now you've worked nineteen hours straight, kid. Go home and get some sleep."

He's right, and I'm dead on my feet, but as I walk to my squad car, I realize I don't want to go home to my empty apartment. I want to go to Ruby's, have someone to talk to about this day. I wonder what she'd say if I laid my worries and my tiredness down at her feet. Would she make me dinner and put me to bed? Would she lay with me until I fall sleep? After long shifts like this, I sometimes have a really hard time turning my brain off. As evidenced by how it's running a mile a minute right now.

I wonder what the answers are to all these questions. Would she be the person who holds me when I can't sleep through the night? I want the answer, want it badly.

But tonight the answer won't come. School is in session tomorrow, and all I need to do is crash.

CHAPTER SIX

RUBY

"I'M SO SORRY!"

As soon as I walk into the library on Monday morning after going to see Principal Taggert, the apology is already coming from Trinity's mouth.

"I had no idea Seth was like that. We've known each other a while, he was my next door neighbor." She runs to me, enveloping me in a hug. "Brooks always says I'm too trusting, but I just never imagined he would be like that. And to think I could have gotten you hurt. I'm really, really sorry, Ruby."

"It's okay," I assure her. "All's well that ends well. I ended up having a great time anyway."

"It's all over town, that you left with Caleb."

My cheeks heat, I can feel it flush up my neck. There's no telling what people in this town are saying. "I did leave with him, he was kind of my knight in shining armor. If it hadn't been for him and his friend, things would have probably turned out a lot differently."

"Thank God he was there." She squeezes my hand. "Again, I'm so sorry. I never meant for it to happen, and I promise I'll never set you up on a date again."

I'm almost relieved, not to mention, I have a good feeling about Caleb. "Maybe I won't need you to set me up anymore." I shrug. Glancing up at the clock, I realize the bell will ring in a few minutes. "Gotta go. We'll talk later."

Hurrying along the same hallways I walked as a student, I wave and call out random hello's to the students I now teach. Turning down my side of the building, I run right into Karina.

"I was coming to find you." She steadies me as I hold my coffee in front of me, praying that it won't slosh.

When it doesn't, I breathe a sigh of relief. "I made it." I give her a smile.

"Honestly, I wanted to check on you. I know you told me you were okay and Caleb told me you were okay when I asked, but what happened to you had to be scary."

Karina is the mother hen to everyone in our module, but she's never overbearing about it. "It was." I'm never going to lie to her. She's been my mentor since I was a student here. "But Caleb saved me. Like I told you in the text, had he not listened to what was going on, it would have been a whole other story. I probably would have made the news, and not in a good way." A shiver runs through my body as I think about it.

"Have you talked to Principal Taggert yet?"

I take a drink of my coffee before answering. "I stopped by on my way in and explained what happened. He said as long as I wasn't arrested, we're all good."

A smirk tilts Karina's mouth as she leans in, her eyes twinkling. "Trust me, honey. You can get arrested in your bedroom anytime, and it's fun as hell."

It's hard for me to swallow the coffee, but I do. For a full minute I struggle with what to say to her. "I don't even know how to respond to that considering all Caleb and I have done is kiss, but I'll keep it in mind."

She winks. "He didn't even tell me you kissed."

When the bell rings I quickly make my escape.

Cruise

"Think you can spot me?" I ask Morgan as the two of us workout in the gym at our apartment complex. I don't lift heavy anymore, but I do like to have a little bulk in case I have to throw some weight around with someone I'm trying to arrest.

"Yeah." He comes over to where I'm waiting on the bench and helps me lift the bar before I start, counting my reps. "So what happened with you and the girl from The Café?" he asks as we get started.

"I took her out the next day," I admit, a smile on my face as I think about our breakfast. "For breakfast, since I had to work the night shift."

"Wow dude, really? You ever had a date that fast?" Morgan asks as he holds his hands close to the bar, there to catch it in case I lose my grip.

"No, but there was something about her. How unsure she looked when I sat down at that table, how cute she looked in her porch light. I don't know, I thought she was hot, and I hadn't had a date in a while, so I thought I'd take it." I try to play it off. Truth of the matter was, she kept me going when all I'd wanted to do was go to sleep during my long-ass shift.

"Look at you, sounding like your pops." Morgan switches places with me, adding weight to his bar, before he starts his reps.

"My pops is a happy man," I remind him, thinking of how just about every day he's got a smile on his face.

"He is, and a damn lucky one," Morgan grunts as he pushes the bar up. "I don't know how you lucked out with a stepmom who looks like yours, Harrison, but fuck."

I roll my eyes, used to this. "She was my teacher before; I already had respect for her. Plus I mean, ewwww. This isn't porno, it's real life, man."

He chuckles as he sits up, panting. "I don't know about you, but I gotta get going. I'm working the night shift tonight."

"I'm in serious overtime because of the weather the last few days. They switched my shift with someone else tonight. I think I'm gonna go have dinner at my parents, if they're having something good," I tell Morgan as I watch him packing up his bag.

"Tell your mom I said hey." He says the "hey" in a really deep voice, coupling it with a wink.

"Dude, come on. My dad would kick your ass, let's not even joke around. You *know* he would kick your ass from here to next week."

Morgan laughs as he puts his hoodie on, shouldering his duffel and grabbing his bottle of water. We leave the fitness center and then walk up the stairs. Being next door neighbors also helps keep our friendship grounded, and it's nice to have someone who understands your job. "Your pops would throw down, and probably almost kill me."

Of that I have no doubt. "See you around." I give him a wave as we go to our separate spaces.

I'm about to climb into the shower when my phone rings, and because of who's calling, I answer it.

"Hey Caleb, it's your mom."

I roll my eyes. "Yeah, your picture shows up when you call, along with your name in my phone."

She laughs, because she knows it annoys me when she starts a conversation like that. "I made pot roast and corn bread," she says it in a sing-song voice. That had been one of the first meals Kari made us when she started staying with Dad, and to this day it's one of my favorites.

"You did, huh?"

"I did." I can hear her smile through the phone. "I thought you might like to join us tonight."

"I could eat." I rub my stomach that's already clenching at the thought of the meal I love so much.

"You're so full of shit." I hear my Dad's voice in the background. "Just get over here, we'll eat in an hour."

"Gotta take a shower, I just worked out with Morgan, but I'll be there very soon," I promise into the phone, reaching out to test the water. "In fact, my water's hot, I'll see you in a few."

"Great! Can't wait to see you and hear all about what's going on with Ruby!"

She hangs up before I can say anything, and I realize with great clarity that she played me like a drum. I soothe myself with the knowledge that while I'm facing the great inquisition, at least I'll be eating one of my favorite meals, and sometimes, that's the price you have to pay to get something you really want.

"WHO'S RUBY?" Kelsea asks as soon as I enter the house through the side door. She runs, jumps up, and locks her arms around my neck.

"Who've you been talkin' to Cupcake?" I tug on her braid as I sit her down. Damn I hope she has a growth spurt soon. She's way too short, and I don't want other kids picking on her.

"Nobody." She walks over to the breakfast bar, hitches herself up in the chair, and starts working on what appears to be homework. "I just heard Mom talking to someone else."

"Kels, you're not supposed to listen to my private conversations." Kari comes into the kitchen, wearing a MTF shirt and a pair of sweatpants. "That's why they're private."

"But you said it loud enough for me to hear it." She gives a look, as if that should solve everything.

"She's got a point." Dad says as he comes in the same side door that I just came through.

"Stop ganging up on me, or no one's getting dinner."

Wisely, we all shut up. Dad comes through, clapping his hand on my shoulder, giving Kelsea a kiss on the forehead, and then walking up to Mom. She puts her hands on her hips. "You think you deserve food after you sided against me?"

"You're not gonna tell me no, Rina, and I think we both know that. Doesn't matter what it is, you never tell me no." He cups the side of her neck and leans in for a kiss.

The two of them, at one time, embarrassed me with their displays of how they feel for one another. Growing up without a mother figure in my life, I hadn't known how to react to the public displays of affection they enjoyed with one another. Now though, as a grown man, I know I want a life like this, a wife who will let me cop a feel when she bends over to get something out of the fridge, one who won't stop me when I come up behind her while she's at the sink and press my body into hers. I want all of it, and I send up a little prayer, thanking God for letting Kari come into our lives, because without her I wouldn't be the man I am today.

"C'mon, Kels, if they're going to suck face and be all lovey dovey, we can do your homework in the living room."

She grabs her stuff quickly and hops down, following me as we get her stuff spread out on the coffee table. "What are we working on tonight?" I ask as we get comfortable.

"Just some history, I have to answer these three questions, and I'm almost done." She points to the questions. "I just have one more sentence to write, then I expect you to tell me who Ruby is." She grins.

I groan as I think about how I'm being annoyed by every single member of my family right now. "I guess I could talk to you about it."

She pulls her bottom lip between her teeth, hurriedly writing the last sentence, throws her pen down, and then looks at me, excitement in her eyes. "Now, who's Ruby?"

I chuckle, shaking my head. "Cupcake, she and I have only been out on one date." I try to manage her expectations. The only other woman I've introduced her to didn't work out so well.

"But you like her right?"

"How do you know that?

"Because you get a smile on your face when you talk about her."

I try to think back. What are my facial expressions when I talk about Ruby? Do I really smile when I talk about her? "You think?"

"I saw it when Mom was asking you about her. Tell me about her." Kels turns around on her knees, looking at me. "Is she pretty?"

"She's super pretty, she's got blue eyes and blonde hair. She's short, but she fits right here." I put my hand at my collarbone, and that's when I realize it. I'm smiling as I talk about her.

"I'm smiling, aren't I?" I shake my head at Kels.

She giggles. "You are."

And that's when I realize that after one date, one moment in a lifetime of moments with this woman, I'm completely and totally fucked. It's finally happened to me. I've met the person who brings a smile to my face, and while on one hand, I'm scared to death – I'm also so fucking ready.

Hitching my head back against the couch cushions, I say a little "bring it on" to the big man upstairs.

CHAPTER SEVEN
RUBY

I'VE NEVER BEEN SO excited for a Friday night in my life. This week has passed slowly, with numerous text messages between Caleb and me. Even if we can't see each other much, at least we have this as a means to get to know each other. We haven't been able to get together, and maybe that's why I'm so excited. He's busy, I'm busy, and we don't have just a ton of free time to devote to one another.

It's a commitment; I know I'm serious when I make one, and he seems to be serious too. This must be the difference in dealing with a man, rather than a boy who's unsure of what he wants.

So far, I have to admit I'm liking it. Grabbing my phone, I scroll back through our messages, grinning as I see some of them, thinking back to our conversations.

C: *What's your favorite TV show?*

R: *Whatever I can watch on Netflix and don't have to wait for. I like shows that are already over.*

C: *Into that instant gratification, huh?*

I grin as I think about what he's saying. To most people I'm not the least bit naughty. No one's ever seen me as a bad girl, but Caleb didn't know me in high school, he didn't know the girl who didn't believe in herself. With him I can be anything I want to be, and that is a heady feeling.

R: *Guilty as charged. I'm not a patient person at all.*

C: *I'll file that away for a later date. I'd love to try your patience out.*

Is he flirting with me? Not many people have flirted with me, and I haven't returned the favor, which is why I can't spot it out in the wild.

C: *Delaying gratification can make the ending that much sweeter, hotter, and offer so much more satisfaction.*

He's definitely flirting with me, and I squirm in my seat.

R: *Maybe with you, I'll give it a shot.*

C: *It would be my pleasure, Ruby. To try your patience out, see how you handle it.*

My face is burning with the heat of what he's suggesting.

R: *I'd like that.*

C: *I'll definitely keep that in mind. But right now I gotta go Ruby, I got a call.*

R: *Be careful!*

As soon as I send the text, I say a little prayer that he's safe tonight.

I grin as I look at one of our other text conversations. In college, I never did the whole text conversation thing with any of the guys I dated. I saw them often enough between the dorms, what parties I went to, and study groups. But Caleb? He's a man with an important job, one he's got to work more than most people, and he's dedicated. His time isn't exactly his own. So when he's able to give me a little bit of it, I take all I can get.

R: *Please tell me why I'm such a dork.*

C: *I don't know you super well yet, but I can categorically say someone who looks like you isn't a dork, sweetheart.*

Little does he know, but he will totally learn. It's weird, the feeling that we've known each other for years, and I'm perfectly okay sharing things with him.

R: *So today in front of my class, I was using the projector to demonstrate something I was doing, and I was typing. I was supposed to type dart, and I typed fart.*

I give him a moment to let that sink in. Let him see how sometimes I stick my foot in my mouth, even when I don't mean to. How I even do it in a classroom full of kids.

R: *You don't realize how immature your class is until they crack up at the word fart.*

C: *If you only knew how immature I am, because I'm cracking the fuck up.*

A giggle escapes from my throat as I remember the entire situation. It had been hard for me to keep it together, but I'd managed to until I turned my back.

R: *Confession: I laughed too!*

C: *Perfect answer, gorgeous. Perfect answer.*

I'm dying, waiting for him to get here to pick me up. As we've talked this week, and I've gotten to know him better, I like him even more than I did when he saved me. When I hear his Jeep pull up outside, I grab my bag, fluff my hair, and do a quick breath check. The knock literally makes my heart beat triple time. I've never had a reaction to a man like this before, but honestly, the few relationships I've been in haven't been with a man. Not a real one like Caleb Harrison.

I force myself to slow down and walk to the door, not run. When I open it, I feel that same spark I felt the other night at The Café. He's wearing a pair of black jeans, with a pair of black Timberlands, the laces lazily done up on his feet, a wallet chain hangs out of his back pocket, and a white thermal long-sleeve shirt covers his torso. Hand to God, this guy could be a cover model if he wanted to be. His dark hair is mussed, face covered with a day's growth of beard, those brown eyes of his dark and roaming my body just like I'm roaming his, and those pink lips? Kissable and full. Finally I speak. "Hey."

His lips hitch in a grin. "Hey yourself." His arm curls around my waist before he dips down, stealing a kiss. The feel of his lips against mine is something I've craved since I last saw him. He's warm, comforting, and everything I remember him being. Inhaling deeply I smell the oil I got him. It gives me a little thrill that he's decided to use it.

The kiss isn't long, or even very involved, but it's enough to interest me, and want to try it again. "How was work?" I know he worked an early shift today. I'm new at this, I'm not sure if he wants to talk about what happened, or not, but I figure he'll let me know if the subject is off limits.

"Blissfully slow." He escorts me out of the door and down toward his Jeep.

"Good, then hopefully you won't be too tired to hang out with me tonight." I bite my lip as he helps me in.

"I don't work until tomorrow night, so you've got me a while if you want me." His smile he gives me is pure bad boy, like he knows how hot he is, and makes no excuses about it.

I do want him, and I feel like there's always this undercurrent of need between us. Even though this is only the third time we've been together, only the second date we've been on. "Sounds good to me." I decide maybe that's a better way of putting it, rather than the creepy way.

He shuts the door, and as he walks around the front end of the vehicle, I admire the way he walks, his swagger, and the way his hair lays to the side probably from where he's run his fingers through it. When he climbs in behind the wheel, I almost hold my breath, hoping I enjoy watching him drive as much as I did last time.

Cruise

Goddamn she's hot, with that curly blond hair, clear blue eyes, and ruby red lips. Ruby. Just like her. The sweater she wears shows off her curves, but not too much. It hugs everything in a way that makes me want to see more, but doesn't show everything she's got. If I'm honest, though, it's the jeans she wears that are driving me insane. There's a rip in the thigh. It's giving me a glimpse of smooth skin, and fuck if I don't want to see that skin with nothing hiding it.

Getting onto the main road, I keep with the flow of traffic, but I can't wait any longer. Her skin is calling me. I reach over, hooking my finger in the spot where the rip is. "I like this." My voice is gruffer than I mean for it to be.

She grabs at my fingers, holding them tightly in hers. Looking down I see her nails are painted either a dark gray or black. I like that, too. "My jeans?"

"No." I shake my head. "The skin it shows. It's a fucking cock tease, but I like to be teased. Now all I'm gonna be able to think about all night is what you look like with nothing covering that smooth skin."

She's quiet and I wonder for a minute if I've come on too strong. I've been accused of that before, but I'm an intense guy and I'm honest to a fault.

"Hopefully we can work that out for you soon." She lifts her eyes up to mine. Blue meets brown, and I see something flare in hers. Her tongue sneaks out to lick her lips. "I'd like to know what it feels like to have your hands touching my bare skin."

Her cheeks turn bright red, and as we come to a stop at a light, I reach over, dragging my finger down her cheek. It's hot to the touch. "What's wrong, Ruby? Embarrassed to admit that to me?"

"A little." She ducks her head, breaking our gaze.

"Don't ever worry about being embarrassed with me, Ruby Red," I say the words, and I know this woman is always going to be my Red. She'll be my passion, the desire to be around her, the color of her lips.

"Ruby Red?" She grins over at me.

"That okay with you?"

My dad's always called Mom *Rina*, and I've wanted a woman who deserved a nickname since she came into our lives. I learned the specialness of it from their relationship, and I've wanted that for so long. The nickname for her rolls off my tongue, and I know it's perfect. Waiting for her to answer is like waiting for paint to dry.

"I love it." Her smile is white behind those red lips, and in this moment, everything is right.

"WHY DO THEY CALL YOU CRUISE?" She grins at me, over the mouth of her beer bottle. We've had a good time people watching, eaten some bar food, and now we're discussing our lives.

"How do you know my call sign?"

She shrugs, an impish look on her face. "Maybe, just maybe, I asked Karina."

I run a hand through hair that's a little shaggy. I'm at least three months behind on a haircut. Something my dad likes to bitch at me for every time he sees me. It's a thing we have. "When I played football at the University of Alabama, I was a running back. At one point, when I ran, I kicked it into a gear that everybody called cruise control. Once I was there, nobody could stop me." I shrug. "The nickname stuck, even if I haven't played ball in six years."

"You didn't go pro? Everyone in this town knows how good you were." She questions, her eyes bright from the liquor she's consumed.

Swallowing my drink, I shake my head. I've been asked this before, but never by someone like her. "Nah, I was actually drafted, but I turned the contract down. It wasn't something I ever wanted to do. I got the degree for my dad, but I never wanted to do anything other than be a cop. I was a good football player, but I think I can be a great cop. It's taken me longer than it would take others, because I entered after I'd already been on the force for a year. Everyone else had been in the military before they got on the force, so they automatically went onto the Moonshine Task Force. It's understandable, ya know? I don't have that military experience and I had to do some specialized tests to show I can handle myself, but I think in the last five years, I've more than proven I can."

"Hmmm." She slides closer to me, putting her hand on my thigh, caressing it slowly. I take notice, and love that she seems to like to touch me. "Football player, cop, and now a member of a highly specialized task force? You must have speed, and an extremely motivated personality to go with the stamina we've already determined you have."

Flashing her the smile that's gotten me into a ton of panties, I play the bashful guy, ducking my head. Straight up though, this girl does make me blush. "Little bit."

"Maybe one day I'll find out all about it. After all, you've been my knight in shining armor since you rescued me at the restaurant."

"Kinda my duty, ma'am." I give her my full southern drawl. "Ya know, protect and serve."

She leans in, whispering close to my ear. "How about you protect and I'll serve?"

CHAPTER EIGHT

RUBY

HE HASN'T GONE HOME, and I haven't wanted him to. We've been sitting on my back porch, watching the sun come up, talking about everything and nothing at all. Truth be told, I keep trying to come up with questions to keep him here. I don't want this night to end, don't want to let him go.

"You want kids?" I ask him, pulling a blanket around my shoulders that I went to get an hour and a half ago once it got too cold. My legs are in his lap and he's still playing with the rip in my thigh. He hasn't stopped doing it since we sat down, and I'd be lying if I said I wasn't feeling it in every part of my body. Each time he makes a trip forward and back, my nipples peak and my core throbs.

"At least two, probably three or four, if I'm given a chance. I want a family, something I didn't have until I was eighteen, when Karina came into our lives." His voice is deep with what sounds like the need to sleep. We've talked for hours, and even I have to lick my dry lips.

"I'm there for the two. I have a brother who's two years older than me," I reveal. "Our relationship isn't like you and your sister's, though. We're tough on each other, and he's a fuck up. I find myself cleaning up his messes, and my parents constantly make excuses for him. It drives me up the damn wall, but he's my older brother and I like to give him chances."

"Men mature slower than women." He plays with the skin of my thigh again, causing my breath to catch and my thighs to press together.

I laugh loudly because that's what my mom has told me almost every time I've complained about them coddling Preston. "Trust me, I know all about that. I hear it every time I complain about him."

Caleb chuckles deep in his throat. "Look at that sunrise." He extends his finger toward the sun coming up. I follow his finger, as it traces the horizon.

We sit there for a few more minutes, both yawning as we put our heads together. At this point I've been up for twenty-four hours and I'm pretty sure he has been too.

"I need to get out of here–" his words are broken up by a stretch, dislodging my head and legs from his grasp-"if I'm going to make it home before I fall asleep."

There's an idea floating around in my head, and I'm wondering if I want to ask it. Rejection is a thing, and I'm scared of it, but we're running out of time because I'm tired, and I know he is too. I don't want him to get hurt on his way home, so I go ahead and decide that it's time to grow a pair. We turn quiet, each lost in our own thoughts. With a deep breath, I work up the courage to throw it out there.

"You can stay here with me, if you want to. We can sleep, and then when you're rested enough, you can go home," I invite him, almost cringing at the way I sound. Not confident at all.

His eyes are wide, like it's the last thing he expected me to ask, and the silence stretches for too long. It embarrasses me and all my insecurities seep into my thoughts. If he'd really wanted to stay, he would have jumped on the chance. And now I feel stupid.

"Forget it." I reach down, grabbing a bottle of water one of us has gone in and gotten during our long night of conversation. I'm getting it so that I have a reason to get up and leave. So he can leave me without having to save face and make a quick exit. "Bad idea."

"No." He reaches out, stopping me. "Great idea. I haven't slept with a woman in a long time. I'd be honored to break that drought with you."

Little does he know, the pleasure is all mine.

Cruise

"If at any time you don't feel comfortable, just tell me." I follow Ruby into the back of the duplex, and immediately I feel as if I've been placed in a time warp. Earlier when I came in, I didn't pay much attention, but now I do, remembering us all moving Violet in when she'd been able to leave her husband. "Not much has changed since Violet lived here."

"Is it weird she lived here and now you're here with me?" She takes off her shoes, motioning for me to do the same and stick them next to the doorway.

"No, I wasn't here very often. I helped her a few times, move in, move across to Ace's side, and then when they bought a house all of us moved them out. It's been years since I've been in here, but I remember how proud she was of it."

She turns toward me, holding her hand out for my jacket. "That's kinda how I feel." She shrugs. "I went from my parents' house to the dorms, and now I'm here. I'm lucky though, so many of my classmates weren't able to find jobs, and they've had to move back home. Even if Laurel Springs doesn't pay a lot, I didn't have to move back home. I'll always be thankful that it worked out this way."

"Oh my God, isn't that the truth? I live in an apartment across town, it's a really small two-bedroom, but I would rather live there than live with my parents again," I commiserate with her. "I sleep naked now, and there's no way I could do that under my parents' roof."

She laughs loudly, putting her hands over her face, as she runs her eyes up and down my body. "You sleep naked?"

"Well, once we get to know each other well enough, you'll find out for sure." I give her a wink. I'd like both of us to sleep naked right now, wrapped up in one another. After talking to her about anything and everything, I feel closer to her than I have anyone else I've been with in a long time. It's just I don't know how she'd handle the request. Soon though, we'll know each other that well. Until then, I tell my wayward dick to calm down.

"I don't know what I'm going to do with you." She walks farther into the living room, and I follow her like a puppy.

"Just let me stick around. I'm gonna end up being one of those things you can't live without," I say, making her a promise.

"You think so?" Ruby asks, stepping close to me this time, hooking her arms around my waist.

"Count on it." I loop my arms around her waist, holding her close.

"SURE YOU DON'T WANT to take your jeans off?" she asks as we get situated in her bed. She's changed into a pair of the shortest damn shorts I've seen, and a shirt that slips off her shoulder. When she moves a certain way, it shows the lace of a black bra underneath. I run my hand down my stomach, barely able to stop myself from reaching down and adjusting my package.

"I think they should stay on, I don't want to pressure you into moving too fast, because of how I react to you." I let my eyes do the talking as she flits around the room, closing the curtains.

"I kinda like how you react to me."

When she gets done, she comes back over to where I'm lying and slides in next to me. "You set your alarm, right?"

"Yep." I pick up my phone and make sure one more time I set it correctly. "We can sleep almost eight hours, then I have to get out of here and go change for work."

Slowly, she scoots over to where her head lays on my chest. Circling my arm around her neck, I hold her close.

"You're the first guy I've ever had in this bed," she whispers softly a few minutes after we cuddle up with one another.

"What about in this apartment?" My voice is deeper than it should be, the answer she's about to give me means more than it should.

I've always been the guy who's taken my responsibilities seriously, and I've been accused of having a hero complex more than once. But the night when I saw her scared to death, it did something to me. The first glance I had at her, I saw a future. One I've never let myself think about, one I wasn't really sure was ever for me. Everyone always told me when I met my match I'd know it, and damn if I don't know it right now.

"No men besides family have ever been in the living room, much less the bedroom." She scoots in closer to me. Maybe she's like me, feeling more comfortable because of the darkness of the room, the quietness encompassing us.

"That makes me happy." I run my finger up and down her arm.

"You should go to sleep," she says quietly before tucking her face into my neck, hooking her leg over my abdomen.

Chancing her pulling away, I put my hand on her thigh, squeezing, where it lays against a cock that's starting to pay attention to what's happening between us. "I should," I agree with her. My eyes are heavy, words a little slurred, because I'm starting to drift off. I have presence of mind to lightly push my fingers through her hair, and level her gaze to mine. "But what I really want to do–" I stop, letting her pull away if she wants. When she doesn't I go forward with what I've been wanting to say all day. "–is kiss you. Is that okay with you?"

Her smile is lazy, and she doesn't open her eyes, but she tilts her mouth to mine, letting me take control. Control is something I like, it's something I crave, and her giving it to me so easily? Maybe Ruby's made for me in more ways than one. Leaning slightly into her, I brush my lips against hers, slightly pressing for entry. When she allows it, I take. My tongue dances with hers as I slightly tighten my grasp in her hair. Slowly she melts into me, hugging me tighter with her hip across my waist. My hand there tightens on her thigh, and it takes everything I have not to pull her across me, sit her up, strip her of her shirt and bra, and end up with her tits in my mouth. She strains against me, digging her fingers into my skin, moaning softly in the back of her throat. When I pull away, she chases me, but I hold her back.

"As much as I would love to explore this mouth, and making out with you, I seriously gotta get some sleep."

My voice is wrecked, deep and regretful.

"I know."

"If I didn't have to work tonight..." I release her hair from my grip and let my hand fall to the front of her shirt. Through the material, I cup her breast, running my thumb over a nipple that's peaked against my touch. "I would explore all the ways we could both make each other feel good, but I do have to be decently rested to work a shift."

She moans, easing back from me, grabbing my thumb. "Then don't tease me, Caleb. Get some sleep so I don't have to worry about you so much."

"You gonna worry about me?" The thought spreads a warmth across my chest and into the pit of my stomach.

"Yeah, hot stuff," she sighs as she situates herself against me again. "I'm gonna worry a lot about you."

"I didn't see you coming," I whisper in the stillness.

"Didn't see you coming either."

And as I listen to the sound of her even breathing, I drift off into the best nap I've ever had before a shift.

CHAPTER NINE
CRUISE

I'M DREAMING, wrapped in the fogginess of whatever my subconscious wants me to know. My mouth is slanted, claiming the mouth of another, my fingers are thrust into hair I know, blonde and a mass of curls, as I tilt her face to the side so I can get in deeper.

"Caleb," she moans, and as I feel her hands at my biceps, I know this isn't a dream.

"Ruby," I hiss as I feel her legs part, allowing me to slide in between them.

Sometime in the afternoon we've spent sleeping, we've rolled toward one another and started kissing. The kissing must have been going on for a while, because my cock is hard, pressing against the zipper of my jeans, and as I pry my eyes open I see love bites on her chest and neck. The belt at my waist is undone, and the button on my jeans has been popped. I'm thick against my boxers, searching for her core.

"Don't stop," she whispers as I lever myself away from her body. With the admission, she's bold, reaching back for me. "I've wanted this all night while we talked. I initiated while you were asleep," she admits as she wraps her legs around me.

She may have initiated, but I'm sure as fuck gonna finish it. I don't have as much control as I like to have as I reach in between us and work on pushing both sets of clothing we're wearing down. I may have teased her earlier, but now she's teasing the fuck out of me. Somehow I strip us both of the barriers between us and manage to reach into my jeans to grab the condom I keep there for those "just in case" times.

"Take off your shirt." My voice is strangled as I push the latex down over my length. When she's left in just her bra, I realize I want that gone, too. "Bra too, let me see you Ruby."

Her gaze is on my thick hardness as she takes the bra off, licking her lips as she sees me give myself a few strokes. "God, I can't wait." Her eyes are hooded.

"I can't either." I push up on my knees, allowing her to fall back against the pillows. "How long has it been for you?" I ask her before I position myself at her entrance, my fingers in front of my cock.

"Few months." She bites her lip as I slowly work a finger inside her. She accepts it, moaning as I push all the way in. "Keep going," she begs.

With two fingers, and then three fingers down, I know she's ready. And I definitely know I'm ready. Removing my hand, I slowly press into her, and we both moan, straining against each other. "Feels so good, so tight around me," I pant against her neck.

Her nails score up and down my back as she pulls me closer to her, and as she opens wider, I know I'm completely lost to this woman.

Ruby

There's a part of me that really should be ashamed. I knew he was asleep, knew I was playing with fire when I started kissing his neck and rubbing against his stomach. I've never been the type of person to literally take what I want, but I want Caleb, and I know he wants me too. So when he responded, I gave myself a small pat on the back.

Now though? I know I'm in over my head. No one else has ever played my body the way this man is. Ever made me feel like I could break apart with just a few thrusts, and here I am, opening wider, giving him more access to my body.

"Don't stop," I beg him. Most of the guys I've been with always stop before it feels really good. But with Caleb, it's been feeling magnificent for a while. "Please don't stop."

"I'm not going to, Red, not until you come all over me," he whispers darkly in my ear.

Reaching up, he grasps my hand and pulls it down in between us where we're connected. "Make yourself feel good, Ruby, show me what you like."

Getting over the embarrassment I would normally feel when asked to do things like this, because I want it so fucking much, I reach down and work my clit as he presses into and then pulls out of my body.

"Yeah, loosen up for me, let yourself go there," he encourages me.

When I lift my eyes up to his, I see him looking down to where I'm working myself. He's propped up on his arms, watching everything that's going on between us, his eyes glued to where we're connected. The flush of his face says he likes what he sees.

"You like it?" I ask, surprised at the question coming from in between my lips.

"Fucking turns me on, can't you tell?" His length grows, presses deeper into me.

I wonder what would happen if I took my other free hand and cupped my breast with it. With that idea in my head, I do exactly what I'm thinking, but before I do, I reach forward to his mouth, holding a finger up to his lips. He obliges sucking it deep, twirling his tongue around it, before letting me go. Knowing I have his attention, I make a production out of bringing that finger to my nipple, flicking it, circling around it, and moaning deeply as I arch my back. The show I'm putting on for him is turning me on too as I see his eyes darken, as I feel his pace quicken.

I realize that we're both in the driver's seat for each other. Hooking my legs tighter around his waist, I bounce against him, thrust up, closing my eyes and throw my head back. I'm feeling him touch, rub, and slide along every part of my body, letting him and my fingers play me like an orchestra.

"Ruby, you're so fucking hot." His hand goes to my other breast, palming it as he buries himself deeply inside of me.

No one has ever called me hot before, and hearing it come off his lips is enough to turn me on even more. "You're hot too," I whisper. "Everything about you."

When the pace quickens again, his angle changes, hitting a spot inside my body that no one else has ever managed to reach. "Oh fuck, Caleb, right there!"

With a few more thrusts, I feel his body stiffen, and as he pulses into the condom, I'm right there with him. We're both moaning, groaning, scratching, and completely decimated by what we've experienced as we lay beside each other, trying to slow our breathing.

Eventually there's a sound that breaks into my conscious. "Caleb, is that your alarm?"

"Oh fuck." He scrambles, trying to find where the noise is coming from.

The sheets and covers, along with our clothes are everywhere, and eventually we find his phone under his jeans, which are under the bed. The alarm has been going off for over an hour, and he's officially late. There's two missed calls, and he's trying like hell to get rid of the condom and put his pants on.

"I hate to run, Ruby, I really do, but fuck I'm late."

I laugh as I watch him try to put his clothes back on and kiss me at the same time. "I wish I had the whole afternoon here with you." He cups my face.

"I understand. You've gotta go. I'll see you soon?"

He nods, before his face gets serious and he stops rushing. He palms my neck and forces my eyes to meet his. "I don't take what we did here lightly, and just because I have to rush off doesn't mean shit in the grand scheme of things. Thank you for giving me a piece of you."

I lean in kissing him on those lips of his. "Thanks for giving me a piece of you too."

He blushes, the first time I've ever seen him do that, before he goes back to putting his clothes on and then rushes off to work. When the door closes, I lean back against my bed and smile the biggest smile ever. I'm a supremely happy woman.

CHAPTER TEN

RUBY

TODAY HAS BEEN one of the longest days ever. It feels like every teenager I've spoken to has been a smartass to me, and I'm beyond ready to go home. Unfortunately, I have to submit my grades for the quarter, and it has to be done before I leave.

My kids are doing well, and that makes me smile. History has always been one of my loves, and to know my kids are doing well with it, makes me incredibly happy. Maybe I'm doing something right. On days when I totally question it, I can look at these grades and know I've helped them accomplish this success.

As a first-year teacher, this is everything I can hope for. Maybe I'm not changing lives, but more than anything, they're listening to me. It's enough to bring a smile to my face. Glancing at the clock on my computer, I give myself a goal of getting these all entered within the next hour. If I do, then I still have time to take a spin class at the gym. Putting in my earbuds, I crank the music on my phone and get to work.

I'm into it, moving my head to beat as Justin Timberlake talks about summer love (hey, I like the oldies), when I feel lips on the side of my neck, the scrape of stubble against my smooth skin. I jump, but don't scream as I smell the beard oil I gave Caleb. His arm snakes around my neck, my eyes fluttering down to check for the ink on his arm to confirm it's him. Closing my eyes, I lean my head back against him, exposing my neck to his lips. Reaching up, I take out my earbuds.

"Hey." My voice is hoarse, as I feel his tongue play against the pulse beating just beneath.

His moan is a deep sound in my ear that causes goose bumps to pop out on my arms, all the way down my body. I feel it in every part he's touched of me. My nipples harden against the cups of my bra, my core hums with the knowledge of how only he can possess me. I've only had him once, but I want him again, again, and again.

"Hey yourself."

God that deep growl of his is enough to make any mere mortal fall to his feet and offer to worship the ground he walks on. When he loosens his hold on me, I physically feel the loss, but turn in my chair, to look up at him as he extends to his full height. Sitting here, I'm eye level with his flat stomach, just below is his belt buckle and I can see he's just as affected by me as I am by him. My lips are dry, and my tongue sneaks out to moisten the bottom one. He groans, reaching forward with his hand to curve it around my jaw, his thumb swipes against the wet flesh. "So, is this how it's going to be?" Caleb asks, that voice of his is deep, hoarse, dark.

"What do you mean?" I'm genuinely confused, fighting to make sense of what he's asked. Pushing back the brain fog only this man can give me, I glance up, my eyes meeting his.

He leans down so that we're even with one another. Immediately my gaze goes to the pink fullness of his lips. I'm hit with a memory of them being wrapped around my nipple as he thrust into my body. As his eyes flash, it's like he knows what I'm thinking.

"I mean–" He tilts my chin forward "–now that we've had a piece of each other, is this how it's going to be all the time? Sparks flying, heart pounding, goose bump-inducing awareness between the two of us? It'll calm down, right? Because if I get hard every time I see you, this is gonna be a problem."

"I don't know," I admit as I shake my head in his grip. "I've never experienced it before, you're the first, hot stuff." I give him a grin.

The side of his mouth tilts in a smirk, before a brilliant smile spreads across his face. "Yeah?"

"Yeah."

He nods. "I like that shit."

A giggle rips from deep in my throat. "I like that shit, too."

He laughs along with me, before he straightens up and we physically take a step apart from one another.

"What are you doing here?" It's not very often I see him at school.

"Picked up Kels after her play practice at the elementary school and brought her over for Mom. Dad's working, and Mom said something about having to get quarter grades in. I'm assuming that's why you're here."

He drags an empty chair over and has a seat. "It's been a long day," he sighs. "It's nice to sit down, I've been on my feet forever."

"It has been a long day," I agree with him, and suddenly I'm happy that I have the option of basically sitting down whenever I want.

"What's your plans?" He leans forward, putting his hand on my thigh.

I love that he always seems to have to touch me, to want to be connected whenever we're together. "I have about ten more minutes to go here, and then I was going to hit up a spin class, but it looks like I'm not going to make it." I frown as I check the clock. Caleb interrupting has put me behind, but I can't be sorry to see him today.

"Well that's easy, come work out with me and Morgan," he says as if it's no big deal.

"Have you lost your damn mind?" My voice is as high-pitched as I've ever heard it. "Why would I want to go embarrass myself like that?"

He tilts his head to the side, before he huffs out a breath. "Yeah, you do spin class, we don't. To do spin, you have to be in decent shape. Trust me, you'll do fine with us, and you'll get to spend time with me," he says with a cocky grin.

"Okay," I agree. "Don't make me regret this, but give me a few minutes and then we can go."

Cruise

"It's not much," I warn Ruby as we stand at the front door of my apartment. "But I don't really need much, since I'm not here half the time."

"It's fine," she laughs. "What you have can't be much different than what I have."

What she says is true, but for some reason, I'm a little embarrassed to show her where I live. Opening the door, I enter and hold it open for her. I left a light on before I went to work, in case I had to stay late. I hate coming in to a dark house.

"It's very you." Her eyes are taking in the sparse furnishings. "There's not a lot of clutter, very no-nonsense," she teases me.

"You're so funny. I'll have you know I spend most of my time in the bedroom."

"Oh, I bet you do." She winks.

"Look at you, getting that personality." I crowd her into the door I just closed. I allow myself a moment to capture her lips, to let my tongue tangle with hers, to feel the grip of her nails in my shoulders as she hangs on. When I pull back, we both seemed dazed, and that's honestly the way I like it.

"We should probably change and get that work out in." She licks her lips, and I imagine she's tasting me.

"Yeah, c'mon. Maybe we should change separately."

"Sounds like a good idea."

"You take Kelsea's room. It's hers when she's here."

Showing her to Kelsea's room, I leave, to give her privacy before I go to my room. When I shut the door, I take a deep breath, leaning my head against it. No woman has ever affected me the way she does, and it's throwing me off. Groaning, I let my forehead hit the door, before I go grab some clothes, and hope to God I'm not tortured for the next hour.

"I THOUGHT you said you weren't in good shape," I huff as I run on the treadmill next to Ruby's.

She's keeping pace with me, possibly going a little faster. Morgan has abandoned us to work on his abs; he's not much of a runner.

"I didn't think I was." She gives me a look.

"You just don't give yourself enough credit. Obviously you're in good shape." I let my eyes linger on her ass in the pair of leggings she wears. I'm not a huge fan of workout clothes as regular clothes on women, but if she wore those all the time, I wouldn't complain. When we finally break the five-mile mark, I slow the pace down, holding my sides as we cool our bodies and stealing glances at her as she does the same.

"So what else do you normally do?" she asks as she holds her arms above her head, stretching them behind her back.

"Today is pull-up day. You can hang out with us for a few more minutes and then we can go grab some dinner, or you can head back to my apartment and get changed. Your call."

Her eyes show interest. "I think I'd like to watch you do some pull-ups."

I'd be lying if I didn't admit the fact she wants to watch this is a turn-on for me. I like that she likes my body; I enjoy hers, I want her to enjoy mine. I try to keep my head in the game as I walk over to where Morgan is, and he helps me strap the weight around my waist. He and I have been working out together a long time, we move like a well-oiled machine. I jump up, grabbing the bar and start counting my reps, feeling the burn in my arms and abs.

"Is that as hard as it looks?" Ruby questions from where she sits in front of me. "I mean the way all your muscles are rippling, the way your veins are showing. It looks like you're working pretty damn hard."

"It's not easy," I huff out. "But this is the best way for me to stay lean and take down those guys who like to run away."

"Plus he likes showing off for you," Morgan inserts his voice in the conversation.

"He's not wrong, but he should totally shut the fuck up," I groan as I finish up my reps.

The three of us are taking a rest, drinking water, and trying to let our bodies recover slightly when Morgan looks over at the two of us. "So dinner, or did you two have something planned?"

"When he says dinner, he means The Café," I clue her in on what we do most nights. "You want to come with us?"

"Sure, I was going to eat a frozen organic pizza, but I'll take The Café any day."

When the two of us get back into my apartment, I grip her hand in mine. "Thanks for coming with us. It's weird to say, but neither Morgan nor I have had a woman in our lives for a while and it's been the two of us as best friends for the last six years."

"Since you joined the MTF?"

"No, I had to do a year on the police force before I could move to the MTF. I don't have military training like everyone else, so there were special qualifications I had to fulfill to be a part of it. Not that it really matters, I would have done whatever, but..." I shrug. "Morgan and I have always had each other's backs when no one else was around, ya know?"

"I get it. He's important to you." She wraps her arms around my neck, leaning in for a peck on the lips.

"You're important to me too." I hug her around the waist.

"We can co-exist, I promise."

And right then it hits me how lucky I am to have her in my life. Someone who gets it. Some women would be pissed, but not Ruby, and I'm beyond thankful she chose me.

CHAPTER ELEVEN

CRUISE

OCTOBER

"You sure you're okay spending the evening with my family?" I ask Ruby as she climbs into my Jeep and gets situated. "I know this is kind of moving a little quickly for us, but Halloween is a family affair in my house."

"No, I'm excited!" She reaches back to put her bag down in the back seat. "Plus I'm super excited to see that you're wearing your old football uniform. And I'm excited to wear my old cheerleading one for you."

Truth be told, I'm kind of excited to wear it for her. I can only imagine what life would have been like when we were in high school if she had been my girlfriend. Maybe we would have fucked under the bleachers, maybe I would have had the guts to actually go all the way with someone in my house. I like to think I wouldn't have paid attention to the rules my dad laid down, and I would've done whatever it took to be with her. "So is that what you're really wearing tonight?" I question as I turn from her duplex toward my parents' house.

"Isn't that obvious?"

"With you, not a damn thing is obvious." I give her a grin.

"I'm really gonna be the head cheerleader to your captain of the football team. When you told me, I dug out my old cheerleading uniform, and I'll be damned if it actually fit."

Immediately I'm hard thinking of the role-playing that could go in this scenario. Maybe tonight I *will* get a chance to fuck her under the bleachers. Not able to help it, I put my hand on her thigh. "Oh really? Where'd you come up with that idea?"

"Like I said, as soon as you told me you were pulling out your old football jersey and stuff, it was the only thing I could think of." She puts her hand on top of mine. "I went back and forth on whether I should be a cheerleader or not, because let's face it, I don't really have the body I used to have for it, but I think I found one of my old uniforms that was flattering."

"Get the fuck outta here with you saying you don't have the body for it. Your body is fucking bangin', Ruby. Don't let anyone tell you different. You're perfect for me, I don't want you to change a damn thing." I pull her hand in between my legs, letting her feel my length. "I'm already hard thinking about you wearing it, and I haven't even seen you in it yet."

I wonder if anyone's ever told her that before, because she doesn't quite meet my eyes. I know she had issues with how she looked before, but I want her to know without a doubt she turns me on.

"I can't wait to see you in it tonight." I lean over, giving her a kiss as we stop at a red light. "Actually, I can't wait to get you out of it, and get in you tonight." I move my nose along her jawline, nipping at her skin.

"Anyone ever tell you you're a bad boy with a one-track mind?"

"Only for you, Red, only for you." I pull her hand up to my lips and drop a kiss on the back.

"I kinda like how you do it only for me."

He pulls his sunglasses down so I can see those brown eyes of his. "I kinda like it how you lose all your inhibitions with me, and even when you try to keep it from happening, it happens. You trust me with your pleasure, and there's nothing I value more."

I AM IN HELL.

That's the first thought that comes to my mind as Ruby walks out of what once was my room. The skirt is shorter than I imagined it would be, and the top hugs her body like a motherfucking glove.

Kelsea grabbed her hand and begged her to help with her outfit as soon as she saw Ruby's. They've been in Kelsea's room for the last thirty minutes, and all I can think about is how she looked in that costume. It's giving me thoughts I shouldn't have around my little sister, much less my mother.

"You sure you're okay to take her while I sit here and hand out candy?" Kari snaps me out of my thoughts as she empties bags of chocolate into bowls. Snagging a Snickers to give me something to do, I pop it into my mouth, chewing as I talk around it. I'm chomping harder than I should, just to take my mind off those smooth legs. "Yeah, we don't mind. Honestly this is probably the last year for Kels anyway."

"Bubba, I'm ready." She comes running out of her room dressed as a University of Alabama cheerleader. Ruby following behind her.

"Hang on," she cautions. "Let me put your sticker on your face."

The sticker is my old number, and I can't help but grin when I see Ruby's got one on her face too. I watch as Ruby quickly puts it on, before she hands Kels her pom poms.

"You two lovely ladies ready?" I ask as I take a good look at them.

"We are when you are, hot stuff." Ruby leans in, giving me a chaste kiss.

It's the first time we've kissed in front of my family, and Kari gives me a knowing smile when she and I pull away from one another. "Okay Mom, we're leaving. We'll be back in a bit."

"Have fun, y'all. Mason should be home by the time you get home, so we'll grill some burgers and hot dogs, if that's okay?"

My stomach growls as I think about eating. It's been a super busy day and I barely got lunch. "Okay with you?" I look back at Ruby.

"You're drivin', I'm ridin'." She winks.

Immediately I have a vision of her riding my dick in my head. It's the fucking skirt, everything about the skirt and seeing so much leg exposed is driving me nuts. Hopefully I'll be able to get through this night without embarrassing myself.

"Grab your bucket Kels and let's get out of here."

She does as she's told and the three of us walk out of the house, down the porch steps, and to my Jeep.

"Are we going downtown?" Kels asks as she straps herself into the back.

All the businesses downtown set up a row of sorts that any kid can use as a one-stop shop to completely fill their buckets up. Because it's so crowded, many parents still choose the old way of trick-or-treating, which is why Mom is at home with a bucket and bags of candy, but this, this is more my speed. "Yup, I'm gonna do my best to park as close as we can, and then we'll hoof it over. I heard Leigh say she's giving out goodie bags. Not gonna lie, I'm down for that too, so we're definitely hitting up The Café."

Kelsea giggles. "I can't wait until I look like the type of cheerleader Ruby does," she mentions out of the blue. "Right now my chest doesn't fill out this top," she pouts, her voice letting us both know how upset she is.

"What the fuck, Kels? You're ten. Your chest isn't supposed to fill out the top." I glance at her in the rearview mirror, my heart racing like I've run five miles. These type of words shouldn't be coming from my little sister. I don't want her to grow up on me, because then I'll have to fight the boys off.

"Don't worry, Kelsea." Ruby turns around to face her. "My chest didn't fill out this top until my freshman year of college."

"How old were you?" she asks, awe in her voice.

"Almost eighteen, so you've got a way to go, chick. You're perfect just the way you are, Kels. Don't compare yourself to others. There's a quote that says comparison is the thief of joy. If you spend your whole life wondering why you don't look like someone else, you're going to miss out on a lot of good times. Trust me, I did."

It looks like Kelsea is taking her words to heart, and I'm so happy Ruby is here with me to help me through this process. I wouldn't have known what to say if it had just been the two of us, and right now I'm thanking my lucky stars she's with us. Reaching over, I grip her hand in mine.

"Thank you," I whisper.

She grins over at me. "Believe it or not, I've been through this more than once in my life, and I'd hate to see her almost kill herself trying to be perfect the way I did."

Ruby

I've never met Mason officially and to say I'm nervous is an understatement. A part of me had hoped to change before I got to meet him; I'm still in this damn cheerleading uniform, and it makes me self-conscious as hell. Although this is only the first time I've hung out with Kelsea, I have a feeling she's easier to win over than her dad.

"Why are you so quiet over there?" Caleb asks as we drive slowly through the remaining kids trick or treating.

"I'm nervous about meeting your dad." I've met more people than I care to remember since the school year has started, but somehow, not Mason. We've seen each other in passing, but never had an introduction. I'm more nervous than I thought I would be, and I'm having a hard time explaining why.

"Oh babe," he laughs as he reaches over and grabs my hand, bringing it up to his lips. "Don't be nervous to meet my dad. He's like the quintessential dad. You'll be fine. There's nothing super special about Mason Harrison, other than the fact he's a regular guy who loves his family."

"So not true. He's your dad, Caleb, and that right there makes him super special."

Our eyes meet, and I can tell what I've said touches him, the way his eyes dilate, the way he can't force words out of his mouth.

"Ohhhh she's good," we hear from the backseat.

I laugh as I turn around and look at Kelsea. "It's true though. I like your brother and I want all of you to like me too." I've never thought about it so much, but these people mean a lot to Caleb, I want them to know they mean as much to me. It's obvious he's a family man and he likes to spend a lot of time with them. It makes sense that I want to make a good impression too.

"I like you," she assures me. "He's only ever introduced me to one other girl. Cassie was nice," she mentions what I'm assuming is the name of the ex-girlfriend. "But she couldn't handle the stress of being with a cop. It made her too nervous."

I didn't exactly expect those words to come out of her mouth, but she's surprising the hell out of me. Obviously her brother has taught her well, and not to hold her tongue.

"What the fuck, Kels?" He sounds as if he can't believe what his sister has said.

"It's true! Ruby though, she can handle it, I can already tell."

My grin almost breaks my face. This kid is one of the best kids I've ever met in my life.

"What do you know about any of that? You were five," Caleb meets her eyes in the rearview mirror.

"Doesn't mean people don't say things around me, and I'm not stupid," she reminds him.

From the mouths of babes. They recognize so many things that none of us give them credit for.

"Well I'll promise you something here and now." I turn around so that I can look at Kelsea. "If you're ever worried I can't handle your brother's lifestyle, call me on it. Because I want to be what he needs, and I'd really like to hang around and be your friend."

She holds out her small hand and we shake on it.

CHAPTER TWELVE
RUBY

WE PULL into Karina and Mason's home, and immediately I see a Jeep that reminds me of Caleb's. Glancing over at him, I give him a grin. "Exactly how much are you and your dad alike?"

"So much!" Kelsea says as she jumps out of the backseat. "Sometimes I think Bubba and Dad share a brain."

"She's not wrong." He hitches his chin toward the house. "C'mon."

I'm slow getting out of the passenger's side, and I'm not sure why. I've seen Mason around school before, and I know we've said "Hi" a few times, but I'm nervous. After Caleb and I spent the night talking, I know how much his dad means to him. I know the relationship they've had with one another and just how much he seeks approval from Mason. It makes me want that approval too, and also gives me a fear that I won't live up to what Mason sees as the woman for his son.

Caleb comes around to meet me, taking my hand in his. He turns me so that we're facing one another. His free hand comes up under my chin, tucking a finger there, tilting me up to meet his gaze. "It's gonna be fine, babe. Trust me."

I take a deep breath wondering just how fine it'll be. We follow Kelsea in through the side door, and she yells for her dad as soon as she sees him.

"Daddy! You're here."

He turns from where he'd been talking to Karina, and once his eyes land on Kelsea, he scoops her up in his arms, holding her tightly. I don't know this man, but the way he closes his eyes and hangs on to her, it worries me slightly. He's still wearing his uniform, and it's obvious he just got off-shift.

Karina locks eyes with me, and I can see she's been crying. Discreetly she wipes her fingers under her eyes, and as Mason sits Kelsea back on the ground, she pushes Kelsea's hair back. "Why don't you go get changed and we'll cook some dinner. Then you can show us all the candy you got."

"Dad?" Caleb asks, standing behind me, sticking his arm around my neck and pulling my back to his front.

I can tell by the energy in the room that something has happened, I'm just not sure what it is. I'm nervous as I wait for either one of them to speak, and when they finally do, I'm not prepared for what I hear.

"Be thankful you didn't have your radio on you tonight. A teenager got hit over on Calhoun by a drunk driver. He Was life-flighted to Birmingham. The scene was a fucking mess. In all the years I've done this, I've never seen so much damn blood, never heard someone scream so loud."

"You responded?" Caleb moves from behind me, walking up to his dad.

Seeing the two of them there, facing one another, I'm struck with how much alike they look. Mason's only a few inches taller than his son, but Caleb's more muscular, wider, and just seems to take up a little more room than his dad.

"Yeah." He holds a hand behind his neck, his voice hoarse as he answers. "I was first on scene. It wasn't anything I'd wish on my worst enemy."

"Shit." He leans in, wrapping his arms around his dad, comforting him because they both know what this feels like.

"It was Tanner." Karina pushes between her lips, her throat sounding like it won't let the words come out.

"No..." I feel tears come to my eyes. Tanner Sumner is loved by everyone in our school. He's the heart of Laurel Springs High, a sixteen-year-old with special needs, he's doted on and everyone has taken him under their wing. He helps the football team, the cheerleaders, he runs the concession stand – where no one gets annoyed with him when it takes him a few seconds longer to count change; he's everything good about everyone. The tears are slipping down my face. "Is he gonna make it?"

Mason clears his throat, as he looks at me for the first time. "They aren't sure. Blaze was on scene, and I know she'd do whatever it takes to stabilize him until they could get him to the heli-pad. The asshole had Moonshine in his trunk, was drinking it in a water bottle." He puts his palms to his eyes and rubs hard.

All of us adults are trying to get our emotions under control when we hear Kelsea running back through the hallway. It's obvious by the way she's quiet and unsure of whether to approach her dad that she knows something has happened.

"I'm gonna go take a shower, Kels, and I'll fire up the grill when I'm done," he tells her as he quickly walks back to what I assume is their bedroom.

Karina glances at the two of us, her eyes pleading. Caleb looks as wrecked as the rest of us, and he seems to be having trouble figuring out what needs to be done. Glancing around, I notice Kelsea's bare nails, and on impulse I reach into my purse. I have an assortment of nail polish in there, it's what I do when I'm bored, but I have a favorite. Rose gold glitter – I always feel like a million bucks when I'm wearing it. "How about we go outside, wait for your dad, and I paint your nails? This color would look so great on you." I shake it up and hand it to her.

"Mom?" she glances at Karina, who has such relief in her eyes.

"That would be so much fun! You go out there with Ruby, and I'm gonna go check on your dad."

Caleb snaps out of it when she mentions Mason. "I'll go ahead and get the stuff ready to grill, Mom. Tell him to take his time."

She comes over, kissing him on the cheek, before she all but runs to the bedroom. Karina's a strong woman, and I can't even begin to imagine how many times she's had to comfort her husband after he's come home from a rough shift. It makes me wonder if I have what it takes. Immediately, I know I do. I'll never give up on what Caleb and I could build together.

"Is he okay?" Kelsea asks, glancing at the two of us, shuffling on her feet, putting her hands in her pockets.

"He had a rough day, Kels. You know sometimes, we just do." Caleb squats in front of her, pulling her into his arms. "But he'll be fine because he's got us, and he'll definitely want to see how awesome your nails look when Ruby gets done with them."

She pulls back from him, and then motions for me to follow her out onto the back porch. As I'm about to leave the kitchen I hear Caleb's voice.

"Ruby?"

"Yeah?" I glance back at him, waiting to hear what he wants to say.

"Thanks, you don't know how much you taking her mind off of how he acted when he came home helps. She gets really upset when she can't figure out what's going on with him."

He's right, I'm new to this. I don't know what it's like to deal with the hard, emotional stuff that comes with being someone who dates a cop, but I do know the toll has to be enormous. If I can't handle this, how can I handle things that may or may not happen to Caleb? That's the thought that runs through my head; this was a test and I've passed. I don't know how I'll handle it when it's him, but I hope I do as well as I have today.

"No need to thank me, hot stuff. When you're ready, we'll be out here waiting on you."

"NOW?" Kelsea asks as she looks at me.

"Few more minutes." I giggle when she squirms in her seat. "Beauty takes time, girlfriend, but if you like this and it's okay with your mom and dad, I'll take you to get your nails done sometime. They have little dryers that fix you up in no time at all."

"We'll have to ask." She nods to me, her tone very serious. "I'm not sure I can handle this every freakin' time."

"Be right back." I get up and go to where Caleb is manning the grill for his dad. "You okay?" I ask as I stand beside him, running my hand up and down his back.

He wraps his arm around my shoulders, pulling me in close. "Should probably be asking if you're okay, I didn't know Tanner."

"Yeah, we'll definitely have to do some counseling at school. He's a big part of Laurel Springs High. Right now, though, I'm more worried about you and your dad. While you don't know him, I don't know what it's like to see someone who's been hit by a car, so I think in the grand scheme of things, we're even. Plus it can't be easy to see your dad affected by things."

"It never is." He flips the burgers, sighing heavily. "He's always been such a strong person, and it never occurs to me that this shit bothers him, until I see it bother him. None of what we do is easy, but that is the hardest. Especially when moonshine's involved. We take that personally, and it just hurts me to see him hurt. He's always been this larger-than-life guy who never lets anything get to him, it just hurts," he explains.

"I can see that." I curl into his chest, wrapping my arms around his waist. I lay my head on his chest, listening to the strong beat of his heart. "I can handle this," I assure him, at the same time assuring myself. None of what's happened here tonight has scared me away from being with him.

"I know you can, you did amazing today."

I preen under the praise he's given me. To know he understands that I'm willing to do whatever it takes to prove to him I'm serious about our relationship means everything to me.

He drops a kiss to my forehead as his parents come out the back door. Karina sends Kelsea inside to wash up, and Mason walks toward the two of us.

"Sorry you walked into a shit storm." His lips tilt to the side, and the move is so much like Caleb's, I feel like I'm seeing my boyfriend in sixteen years."

"It's okay." I return his grin. "Life isn't always rainbows and unicorns."

"No, it's not. I'm Mason." He holds out his hand.

I untangle myself from Caleb, holding my hand out too. "Ruby, nice to meet you."

We talk for a few minutes about how we've seen each other around school, and then Mason smacks his son in the stomach. "Move over and let your old man work."

Caleb hands him the spatula. "I'll have you know I had this shit locked down. Don't need you coming out here and telling me what to do."

They share a grin, and I know this is their way of making sure the other is okay. It's endearing and totally makes me want to melt that Caleb can be this way with the man he looks up to so much.

"Ruby, can you help me bring the sides out?" Karina yells from the door as Kelsea comes back out, her hair out of her face and it looks like her hands washed.

As we assemble the meal and I have a seat next to Caleb, I look around thinking I definitely could belong here if given the chance.

CHAPTER THIRTEEN
CRUISE

"YOU SEEM TENSE," Ruby comments as we pull out of my parent's driveway.

She's right, I am. There are some days I hate what I do because of the emotional toll it takes on me and the men on my team. Then there are days I love what I do because of all the shit we take off the streets. We make life safer for the citizens of the town we live in. No day is perfect, but this one was super shitty for my dad. I hate that he had to see what he had to see, and now he's gotta live with it. He'll need to process it and figure out how to not take it with him the next time he goes out on the streets.

"Just the stress of the job sometimes. Even though it didn't happen to me, I know what my dad's going through, and I worry about him." I shrug as I drive us along the deserted streets of Laurel Springs.

At this hour everyone's closed up shop, the candy's all gone, and what's left are the reminders of a Halloween that's over. There are jack-o-lanterns sitting on steps, candy wrappers here and there on the ground, and a couple of teenage stragglers walking the streets.

"How do you deal with the stress when it's you?" she asks softly as she reaches over, running her nails along my neck.

Do I want to be completely honest with her? Do I want to tell her exactly how I deal with it? There's a part of me that realizes this is more than she bargained for. But if I want this woman to know me, the real me, I have to be honest, don't I? If not, we'll never make it, and I desperately want to make it.

I stop at a red light, grip the steering wheel, and decide to fucking go for it.

My voice is soft, rough, wrecked when I answer her. "Sex, but not just any sex. I like it a little rough and a little adventurous."

Her blue eyes widen, her mouth is slightly open, those teeth of hers taking her lip between them. "How have all your other girlfriends dealt with it?" she asks softly.

"They haven't." I shrug. "I've never told anyone else. Like I told you, I haven't really had a girlfriend for a long time. You're the first one I've trusted enough to tell."

Her eyes lift up to the light, still glowing red. She leans forward, turning her body to me. "Thank you for trusting me, Caleb."

"You trusted me from the first moment we met," I remind her.

"Which is why I want to be everything you need."

She takes my hand in hers, pulling it between her skirt-covered legs. "Is this adventurous enough for you?" she asks as her fingers move her panties aside and place mine against her bare skin.

I lick my lips as I feel her arousal. Behind us a car horn honks, but I don't remove my fingers as the costumes we're wearing gives me an idea. "Ruby Red, we're gonna see exactly how adventurous you can be."

"HERE?" Her voice is almost a shriek as I pull around the back of the high school.

"I use the football field sometimes to work out on; I run the edges, trust me no one *ever* comes back here." I remove my hand from between her legs. "C'mon, you don't even know what I want."

She moans as I put the Jeep in park and get out, coming around to her side. Reaching into the back, I grab a blanket I keep behind the passenger's seat for emergencies.

"Where are we going?" She unbuckles, turns, and spreads her legs to let me in between them.

I allow myself to capture her lips, before I put the blanket over my shoulder and grasp her around the thighs. "You'll see, head cheerleader."

A blush works its way up her neck. As I carry us under the bleachers. "Caleb." She wraps her arms around my neck, burying her face there.

When I get us deep enough under the bleachers so that we can't be seen, but we can see, I tell her to put the blanket down behind her, on a small concrete seat.

"Back when I was in high school, I'd come out here and smoke," I admit to her, as I set her down.

"You smoked? God, you're just every girl's dream guy. Dark, brooding, smoker – the ultimate bad boy." She runs her hand down my chest, until she encounters my belt buckle.

"You're about to see how bad I can be." I close my eyes, enjoying the feel of her fingers on my body. My cock punches against my zipper. Opening my eyes, I look down at her. "You okay with this? I don't want to do anything you aren't okay with."

I'm unbuckling my belt as I gaze down at her, waiting for her to tell me yes or no.

"I'm okay. I told you, I want to be whatever you need me to be," she answers as she spreads her thighs wide. "I want whatever it is you want to give me."

It's all I need to hear as I push my pants down far enough to extract my cock. She breathes deeply as she sees how hard I am, licks her lips when she notices the drop on the tip. "This won't be pretty, Red," I warn her as I take myself in hand, stroking up and down. "Not everything in the world is pretty."

Understanding sparks in her eyes. She gets this is how I get rid of those desperate feelings. I fuck them out, let them go as I cum, and bury myself in something that's good and decent. "I don't want pretty," she whispers.

Her blue eyes are now closed as she leans her head back, and I watch as she moves her hand down her body, pulling aside those panties for me. Her skirt is hitched to her waist, and underneath the tight top she wears, I can see her nipples peaked. This is turning her on as much as it's turning me on. Maybe she has to fuck a little of the bad in the world out too.

My hands are shaking, and I'm fumbling with the condom I've taken out of my back pocket. Shaking because I can't wait to get inside her, fumbling because I'm about to lose my cool. I move the hand that's holding her panties to the side to her core, extend her finger and encourage her to play with her clit. "Make sure you're ready, baby."

There's a noise in the back of her throat, and I'm surprised as fuck when she goes for it. She's not shy in the least, maybe it's because of where we are, what this situation is, and what we're doing, or maybe it's because she wants me as much as I want her. Pushing the condom down my length is literally almost enough to undo me, but I grit my teeth and move on. Holding the base, I push my legs apart to put me level with her, and then press my cock inside her.

We both moan loudly as I press home. "Shhhhh."

"You moaned too," she points out as she grabs hold of my biceps when I start to pound.

"I know, I know." I lean my head against her shoulder, letting her take my weight since she's sitting down. "But we have to try and be–" I grunt when she widens her legs. "*Fuck me.*" My eyes roll back in my head slightly. "Quiet."

She buries her face in my shoulder, just like I've done to her. Both of us moaning, grunting, groaning, fucking like something you see on Tumblr. My hands grip her hips, my fingers tilt her ass as I use her and she uses me. It's the most primitive fuck I've ever had. Her breath is hot against the shirt I wear, and I know mine's hot against her skin.

"Caleb." She runs her hands up and down my arms. "Feels so good, I didn't know this would feel so good," she breathes out.

I can't speak in full sentences, not with the way her pussy is gripping my dick, but I do my best. "Forbidden. Could get caught. No finesse. Just fucking. Sometimes it's better."

"Yes." she tilts her head back, exposing her neck, and I go to town. Nipping and biting, flicking my tongue against the wild pulse there. Open-mouthed, I suck at the flesh, knowing I'll mark her. Knowing that tomorrow when she wakes up, she'll bear proof this night happened.

"Ahhh," she groans out. I hit a particularly sensitive spot.

Taking one of my hands off her body, I move it to her mouth, gently covering it, so that it muffles the noise of what we're doing. Not that it helps a whole lot, the sound of my balls slapping against her is loud in the still of the night, but if I absolutely have to, I can slow down. She can't seem to stop voicing her approval of what I'm doing to her, and truth be told, I don't want her to.

"I'm gonna come," I whisper in her ear, pushing my thumb against her clit as I work the both of us. In that instant, I can feel her tighten against me, can feel her let go, and it makes me want to beat my chest and scream to the world I did this to her.

But instead, I thrust. Once, twice, and on the third withdrawal, I come. Hard. Fast. More. With a ragged grunt, I feel the release everywhere. My stomach muscles and ass jerk as I empty into the condom. We both look down, watching me fill it as I can't seem to stop myself. My nipples are tight and I have to throw my head back as I continue to thrust into the air, my cock searching out her warmth again as my fingers grip her thighs tight. My mouth is open, heaving in deep pulls of air, trying to come down from whatever this orgasm is. My body is trembling, my skin is sensitive, and my dick is still fucking hard when my gaze falls on Ruby.

Her makeup is smeared, those panties are now ripped, and her hair is a mess. She's trembling too. I step closer, because I don't want to leave her so exposed, using my body to block hers, in case anyone were to happen upon us.

What I don't expect, is for her to reach around me, stick her hand in my jeans pocket and pull out another condom. I watch in a blur as she takes the first one off, using those wrecked panties to clean me up, and then puts another one on.

"I need you again, Caleb. Having you that wild one time wasn't enough.

It'll never be enough." She scoots closer to the edge, angles my cock down, and pulls me into her using her hands.

Fuck me, this woman. She's everything, literally everything.

And minutes later, when we both come again, I know without a doubt, I'm never letting her go.

CHAPTER FOURTEEN
RUBY

November

When I wake up the next morning, I feel like I'm a different person. Not only am I a different person, but I'm closer to Caleb than I've ever been to anyone else. Rolling over, I grab my cell phone, seeing I have a text from him. For a moment, I inhale the scent of the pillow he slept on, loving that now my bed smells like him.

Glancing up at the clock, I see it's past ten; he's already been at work for a few hours.

C: *Morning, Red. You okay? You looked peaceful, and I didn't want to wake you up before I left.*

R: *I'm good! I promise I would let you know if you hurt me. You so could have woken me up, it would have been fine.*

The way he commanded my body last night did frighten me, but not in the way he thinks. I've never had someone make me so aware of how another person can pleasure you so much.

C: *Did you like it?*

I contemplate lying to him. I really do. Not because I'm embarrassed at what we did, but I'm a little self-conscious at how I reacted to him. One thing I'm learning though, is I have a need to be honest.

R: *I did, but only with you. I don't think I would have trusted anyone else as much as I trusted you last night.*

C: *That's good, and I'm glad I didn't scare you off.*

R: *No! Not at all, I wouldn't mind doing it again.*

C: *All good to hear, Red. I gotta go, I'll talk to you later.*

Sighing, I fall back against my bed and let the smile spread across my face. I'm lazy as I contemplate getting up and moving. My plan before what happened last night was to do some shopping today, but I'm having a hard time motivating myself. When my phone beeps beside me again, I make a grab for it, hoping it's Caleb. Instead, I see Karina.

K: *Hey! Mason's working today, so Kelsea and I are doing some shopping. I was wondering if you want to go with us? We're going to Birmingham.*

Karina and I have been friendly since I started student-teaching. I was lucky enough to do my rotation at Laurel Springs and then slipped into a full-time job there, so the two of us have known each other for almost two years. We, however, haven't been what I would call the type of friends who get together outside of work. We're acquaintances who help each other out when we need it. I know she's making an effort to get to know me outside of work because of Caleb, and I find I want to get to know her as well. Which is why I text back an *I'd love to* when before I may have made an excuse and not moved from my bed.

K: *Great! We'll pick you up in about an hour if that's okay with you?*

R: *I'll be ready! I've been told it's the old duplex where Ace and Violet lived, if that means anything to you.*

K: *Perfect! I know exactly where that is.*

And with that motivation, I hop out of bed, and get ready to go about my day.

"THANKS FOR COMING WITH US," Karina says as she backs out of the driveway of my duplex. "When I mentioned we were going, Kels threw out the idea to invite you and I got excited about it too. Typically it's just the two of us, and she falls asleep on the way home." She shoots a glare through the rearview to her daughter.

"It's just because you make me shop 'til I drop."

"Pretty sure it's the other way around, kiddo."

In the back seat, I watch as Kelsea puts on a pair of ear buds and starts watching her iPad.

"Another reason I needed another adult to come," Karina laughs. "I get bored on the drive with no one to talk to. She'll be engrossed in that thing until we get to the mall."

"No problem." I situate myself in my seat, and put the drink I brought with me into the cupholder. "I tend to go by myself, so it'll be fun to go with someone else."

"By yourself?" I can tell she wants to ask why.

"Most of the friends I had in high school have either taken longer to finish college than I did, or they've moved on from Laurel Springs, and me being the youngest teacher doesn't help. There aren't a lot of women around my age, if you think about it."

I can see her doing the math in her head, going over who's around my age. "You're right, I never thought of that. Well, never fear, we're here now. We're actually meeting a couple of the MTF wives in Birmingham. I hope that doesn't scare you off."

Scares the fuck out of me. "No, I'm good," I answer, reaching over to take a drink from my to-go cup. At least she didn't tell me before I agreed to come, then I may have backed out.

"How did last night go, after what happened with Mason? Sometimes that kind of stuff affects Caleb too, I'm glad he had you to help him."

I can literally feel the warmth in my neck, working up to my face. "He was upset, but he's okay now, we worked it out."

She gives me a knowing glance. "Yeah, I can tell you did. You missed a little spot on your neck where you tried to cover up that beard rash."

My hand immediately flies to where Caleb had been biting and nuzzling my skin. Immediately I want the attention off me, so I turn to her.

"How did you and Mason meet?" It's something I've wondered since I found out who she was married to. I want to know how she came to be Caleb's mom.

"Smooth," she giggles.

Her gaze shifts back to where Kelsea is still watching her iPad. Karina says her name once, and when she doesn't even flinch, she starts talking. "We met off a dating app. We talked for maybe two weeks before we met in person, at a restaurant in Birmingham, actually." She gets a nostalgic smile on her face.

"What happened then?"

She turns to face me, whispering. "We had an amazing date, then we fucked in the parking lot in the back seat of his Jeep, and I ran because I was scared of how he made me feel."

"Holy shit, Karina!"

"Yeah." She grins. "He's still got that Jeep. It's not the one he drives now, but he refuses to trade it in. Every once in a while, he and I take it out for a spin." She winks.

"How did you get to know Caleb?" I intentionally put a curve in the conversation, just because I'm not sure how much I want to hear about her and Mason's sex life.

"That's a funny story, I thought Caleb was a little kid. Mase had mentioned being a single dad, and I just assumed it was to a little kid. Caleb was my student, and when I had a career day, in walked Mase wearing his uniform."

"Oh hell." I can just imagine, because I know what Caleb looks like in his.

"Yeah." She nods, obviously remembering the situation well. "He confronted me about running and told me I wouldn't be running any longer. Then when I realized Caleb was basically an adult, Mason and I had some serious conversations about what he was doing as a teenager."

I laugh loudly at that. "Obviously not what I was doing," I mumble.

"Me neither, not at least until I was eighteen." She checks her blind spot as we merge into the lane that will take us to Birmingham. "But I mean, come on, you see what my husband looks like. You see what Caleb looks like. Even as a teenager, Caleb had girls who wanted to be with him."

"I bet he did." Now this I'm curious about.

"I don't know what his college life was like," Karina continues speaking. "Because he never really talked to me much about the girls he was dating or screwing around with while he was there. But he did have a high school girlfriend. That ended when she went to Ole Miss and he went to Alabama. She didn't love Laurel Springs though and said she'd never live there. I always knew he'd be back to Laurel Springs."

"Yeah, we had a conversation not long ago about how he was drafted, but all he ever wanted to do was follow in his dad's footsteps."

She sighs. "He's always had a huge case of hero worship for his dad. Mason doesn't understand it. Like any parent, he wants better for his son than what he was able to give him. I don't know the full story, but they had some really lean years when Caleb was little, Mason was away serving, and things just went to shit. But I'd say Caleb is a very well-adjusted grown up today."

Unless you count the fact he likes rough sex to take the edge off. But that's our secret to keep, and I'll guard it with my life.

"He is, he's a good man," I agree with her. "Mason did a great job with him."

"I can't wait for you to hang out with him more. Last night was awful and he wasn't himself. Usually those three have me in stitches, and the way Caleb talks to his dad? They're best friends, and you can tell. Back when I first started dating Mason, I was kind of amazed at the conversations the two of them had together. Eventually I realized it was because they'd actually grown up with one another, and while Mase did lay down the law when he needed to, more than anything they were friends. It's how I try to raise Kels, but it's harder because of the age difference and she's a girl."

"Girls are so different than boys."

"Oh my God, I know. There are things that are completely different for her and Caleb. Even though Caleb was older, there are still some parallels for the two of them, and the way she handles it is like night and day. He's really good with her, though."

"I noticed that last night. There's nothing hotter than a guy who's good with his little sister and even has a bedroom for her at his apartment."

She flashes me a grin. "If he gets wind you said that he'll totally use it to his advantage."

"Trust me when I say, he doesn't have to do much."

She giggles as we take the exit to the mall and begin the search for parking.

Cruise

I'm sitting in the MTF headquarters doing some paperwork I'm behind on when my phone vibrates next to where it's sitting on the desk. When I see a picture of Kelsea, Ruby, and Karina, I can't help but smile.

R: *Wish me luck! I'm going shopping with them and with the MTF wife crew.*

C: *You're gonna need it! Stay strong, don't let them pull you into discussing shit you don't wanna discuss. Those ladies and even the kids are sneaky. Before you know it, you've agreed to host a sleepover at your apartment for Stella and Kels, along with feeding them, and letting them watch scary movies they have zero business watching.*

R: *You're a good brother.*

C: *I'm a sucker....don't make my mistakes, Red. Learn to say no!*

R: *LOL!*

I glance up, when the main door opens and in walk my dad and Renegade.

"What's up?" I yell at them from where I'm seated.

We've been so busy, I'm behind by at least a few weeks, so much that I'm not out patrolling today. After last night though, I can't say that I'm completely sad to not be on the streets.

"We got back the sample from the creek bed," Renegade says as the two of them have a seat in front of my desk.

"Oh yeah, and what was it?"

"Really old 'shine," Dad supplies the answer. "Like probably from back when Jefferson was hiding it. There are some markers in it that can date it, and it's not new product. Which is a relief."

We've basically eradicated most of the big operations that have come and gone since Jefferson and the Strathers were making big money selling their supply. A few suppliers have come and gone, but for the most part, we dismantle any of the operations before they can get too big. It's why they keep us together, and it's why we all still have jobs. Nine times out of ten anyone we catch with moonshine now is from out of state, moving it in, or they're working on their own. It doesn't mean we don't still have some sometimes, and it doesn't mean that it still isn't dangerous. People can still die, and dealers can still kill. We're proud of what we're doing here.

"Anyway, we don't want to interrupt you, just wanted to come by and let you know." Renegade gets up from where he's had a seat. "I'm gonna hit the head and then we can be back out." He lifts a chin to my dad.

I wait until he's gone before I turn my gaze onto the man who's raised me my entire life. "You good after last night?"

His answer is slow, and I can tell he thinks about it for a few minutes. "I'm good. I'm glad you and Ruby were there last night, it helped with Kelsea. Really sorry I didn't get more of a chance to talk to her."

"Nah, it's okay, she gets it."

"She's pretty," he needles at me. "I've see her around school before."

"Dad..."

"What? I'm just saying."

"It's new," I warn him. "It's new and I don't know where it's going."

"Yeah well, at one point Rina and I were new too, and you see how that ended up."

Before I can say anything else, Renegade comes out, and the two of them head out. Leaving me alone with thoughts of a blonde haired, blue-eyed vixen that, after last night, has me all tied in knots.

CHAPTER FIFTEEN

RUBY

"GET IT!"

I'm not sure who's talking to me. I'm surrounded by a group of women, all telling me I need to get this dress I just impulsively grabbed and tried on.

"Whitney, don't pressure her if she doesn't want to," the red-head who we met at the mall, I think they called her Blaze, tells her friend.

"No, someone needs to pressure her, because if Caleb saw her in that? Oh my God, he'd be all over her. It'd be great for Valentine's Day. I mean he could take the skirt off and still keep the top on. Ya know, some men like that!"

"Hello! I'm his mother!"

There's too much noise around me, but I do like the way this dress I picked up looks. It's on clearance for much less than its original price tag, and the deep pink color shows off the little bit of a tan I keep year-round. What's throwing me is the fact that it's a two-piece and where they meet in the middle, you can see a good portion of my stomach.

As I listen to everyone voice their opinions behind me, I quickly take a picture and send it to Caleb, wanting his opinion to what he thinks I should do.

R: *Toss or buy? What do you think? As you can see by the peanut gallery's faces behind me, there's a heated debate going on.*

I hope he's not busy, and it doesn't take him too long to get back to me. I'm pretty sure Whitney will throw down in a minute, just to prove a point. She's very, very loud in her belief I should buy this dress.

C: *Fuck, Ruby! Get it! I love everything about it. Especially the little strip of skin you see between the two pieces. Please, get it.*

R: *Will do! Thank you, hot stuff.*

C: *Wear it for me? Soon.*

I would probably wear it for him tonight, but I do like Whitney's idea of wearing it on Valentine's Day. So instead of just telling him that, I decide to play a little coy.

R: *Ehhh, we'll see. Thanks for telling me to get it!*

"Alright." I turn around, facing what has almost become a firing squad. "I'm getting it. You can all stop pleading your cases."

A cheer goes up, and people in the store look at us. I'm not used to being the center of attention, but I've had a good time with these ladies today.

"I love it," Kelsea tells me as I come out of the dressing room, after putting my own clothes back on.

"Thanks, Kels! I love it too."

As we're standing in line to pay for it, she puts her head on my thigh and wraps her arms around my waist. It's a show of trust I'm not exactly prepared for, but as my eyes meet the group of women who are waiting for me to check out, I can almost hear them welcoming me to the group.

"LET ME ASK HER," Karina is saying into her cell phone as we're walking out of the mall. She got a phone call from Mason, and she's been talking to him the last few minutes.

"Mase wants to know if you want to have dinner with us. He and Caleb are prepared to make some spaghetti, if you do. Caleb's over at the house with him. After last night, I think we'd all like a little bit of a do-over."

"I'd love to," I answer immediately. One, because that means I get to see Caleb. Two, because I really would like to get to know Mason. He's a huge part of Caleb's life, and I'd never dream of holding what happened last night against him, but I'd like to see him on a normal day.

"We'll be there in the next hour or two, depending on traffic. I'll let you know when we get closer." She finishes up the phone call, and we all head out to the parking lot to make the trek home.

Cruise

C: *Thanks for agreeing to dinner tonight. I can't wait to see you.*

Does that make me whipped? I saw her last night, but now I'm dying to see her again. More than anything, I want to see her relaxed and in the home I shared with my dad for so long. It's important to me that they like each other. More important than I ever thought it would be.

R: *I'm excited to hang out with you all again tonight. Plus, I'm really excited to see you, and see what you can cook.*

C: *Hey, Dad and I are capable of cooking a few meals. We may not be gourmet chefs, but we're passable.*

R: *That remains to be seen, hot stuff.*

She sends a little winky emoticon, and again she's surprised me. There are certain things she does, almost two months into this relationship, that surprise me.

"Rina just texted that they should be here in about thirty minutes." Dad comes into the kitchen, fresh from the shower. I took one before I came over, and it's obvious he wants to get dinner started.

"What do you want me to do?" I go over to the sink and wash my hands.

"Start the salad and garlic bread while I get the other stuff going?"

"Can do."

For a few minutes the two of us work in silence, both concentrating on the tasks at hand, until Dad breaks the silence. "So you like this girl?"

Like is too weak of a word, but I don't think I've fully admitted it to myself yet. I've never been much a liar to my dad, and I don't want to start now. "You remember you telling me you were insanely hot for Mom? Well that's how I am with her."

"I remember those days." Dad gives me a grin. "Happy you're having them."

"Kinda never thought it would happen," I confide in him. "Just wasn't sure."

"Caleb, it hadn't happened because you weren't ready for it. Cassie," he mentions the last relationship I had, "would have probably given you whatever you wanted, but you weren't ready for it."

"I don't think she could have handled it," I admit. "Like what happened to you last night, she would have crumbled. There would have been no helping Kelsea get over it, none of that. But Ruby, she's got what it takes, she gets every part of me."

"Every part?" Dad asks, the eyes so much like mine looking at me.

After last night, I can definitely say an affirmative. "Yeah, every part. I'm a lucky man to have found her."

"Hold on tight to her, woman like her don't come along every day."

"I know. I got it, and I don't plan on letting her go."

"WHAT ARE YOU DOIN' here?" Kelsea asks as she walks in through the garage, looking at me with a smile on her face.

"We're makin' dinner. What are you doing here?"

"I live here...duh!"

"Well I lived here before you," I argue with her. "Sometimes I like to come back and have dinner, ya know?"

"Just didn't expect to see you tonight."

I crouch down to her. "Just couldn't wait to see you again." I grip her nose between my pointer finger and middle finger, pulling on it.

"Stop!" She giggles as she runs down the hallway with her bags in her hand.

When I stand up, I'm face-to-face with Ruby. "Hey." I reach out, pulling her into my arms, hugging her around the neck.

Her hey is muffled by the cotton of my t-shirt. When I release her, she sniffs. "Something smells really good in here."

Kari laughs from where she's standing next to Dad. "That's because Mase can cook like five things well, and one of them is spaghetti. He's passed that on to Caleb, and I daresay, it's some of the best spaghetti you'll ever eat."

"C'mon, Rina, give credit where credit is due. We even make our own sauce from scratch," He slings an arm around her neck, pulling her close, almost the same way I did to Ruby. The similarities are sometimes fucking scary.

She rolls her eyes. "You make it using a can of tomato paste."

"We mix multiple ingredients together to make a sauce that's not readily available in a jar. Hence, we make our sauce from scratch. I challenge you to tell me that's not the definition, Mrs. Harrison."

I glance over at Ruby who's grinning at the two of them.

Dad makes a production of looking at his watch. "Still waiting, babe."

"Oh shut the fuck up, Mason, and just get the stuff on the table."

He chuckles as she turns her back to him and smacks her on the ass.

"Ouch!" She turns giving him a glare.

He tilts his head to the side. "Don't even, Rina."

I put my mouth next to Ruby's ear. "Welcome to a *real* dinner at my house."

"I think I'm gonna like it here."

LATER ON, Kelsea's gone to bed, while the four of us adults sit on the back porch, each enjoying a beer. It's cold, but a few years ago, they put in a fire pit, so it's warm enough.

"Do we have to tell Ruby about all the stupid shit I've done?" I groan as we sit snuggled together in one of the chairs. She's on my lap, curled into my chest, and I'm burying my face in her hair.

"You've done plenty," Dad busts my balls as he takes a drink of his beer.

"Getting my squad car stuck on the railroad tracks was probably the most embarrassing," I admit.

Dad laughs loudly. "They had to call the train company, because one was headed that way. It stopped a good twenty feet from Caleb's car. I mean we all stood there watching. Me, him, and Havoc. We were screaming and waving our arms, hoping like hell this guy wouldn't hit this car and it would blow up. When he put the brakes on, the train smoked. We thought we were all fucked."

"And they never let me live it down."

"Oh hell no." Dad shakes his head. "You will never, ever live that down, just like Havoc will never live down when Dale asked to speak to a supervisor, knowing damn good and well Havoc is the supervisor."

"I bet you get some really belligerent people," I make an observation.

"We do," we both say.

"There was a guy not long ago, who was threatening to kill Renegade's whole family."

"Oh my God," Mom inhales deeply. "Why?"

"Because–" Dad's gaze settles on the two women with us "–Renegade told him to drop his weapon. It turned out the weapon was a small flashlight, that in the dark, looked like a gun. The guy didn't take too kindly to being arrested for resisting and started spewing a shit ton of threats. Said he'd kill all our entire families and he'd do it with a smile on his face, anyone we cared about would be dead."

"What did they do with him?" Ruby asks softly.

"He's in the psych ward of the prison right now. Luckily the judge agreed with the doctor who gave the evaluation. That's not always the case." My voice is somber as I again remind her of what she's signed up for. "None of what we do is easy."

"It's just like being a teacher, hot stuff. It's not glamorous and you don't make a lot of money doing it, but without any of us, the future of this nation wouldn't have a future."

I tighten my grip around her, because she does get it. Out of anyone, she gets it, and it's nice to know the person I want to share my time with, doesn't begrudge the civic duty I owe to this community.

I just have to prove that when the time comes, I can love them both equally.

CHAPTER SIXTEEN
RUBY

LATE NOVEMBER

"I'm warning you, my house isn't like yours." I fidget with my fingers as I hold my hands in my lap.

Caleb's driving us to my parents' house for Thanksgiving dinner. Because of my extended family, we're actually having it on the Saturday after Thanksgiving. Which is good, since he wasn't scheduled to work today.

"I know, in the years I've been hanging out with friends and stuff, I've come to realize my family situation is way different than most. I'll be able to handle it, Red, it's okay."

My parents are so much less laid back than Mason and Karina, they take things way too seriously when it comes to me, and let Lance run around like he has no responsibilities, or any kind of care in the world. It isn't fair, but it's what I live with. "I just hope you won't want to say fuck it with me after this."

He reaches over, grabbing my hand. "I'll always want to fuck you, Red; you're hot as hell."

My face flames. I'm still not used to the way he talks, even a few months into this relationship. I think Caleb will always heat me up, and even I know that's something most people never get. "Ditto." I grip his fingers in mine now.

I direct him down a tree-lined road on the opposite side of town from where his parents' house is. My parent's own a farm, and even though there isn't much money in it anymore, they still work the land like it's the best gift they've ever been given. As the white house I grew up in comes into view, I try to look at it from Caleb's eyes. It's old, been in my family for generations, and while there have been a few upgrades, most of what's there has been there since the early 1900s. It used to embarrass me, but I learned it's a part of our heritage.

"Wow," he breathes deeply as he gets a good look at the wrap around porch.

"It's mostly the original design." I give him a brief history. "Of course they've had to replace the wood over the years, but mostly, this is the house my great-great-grandfather built for his family."

"Do you know what I would give to have that kind of history for my family?" he whispers.

And in this moment, I realize that maybe the two of us are fulfilling roles in our lives that both of us needed filled. He makes me not take myself so seriously, makes me push at the boundaries both myself and my parents have set for me my whole life, and I give him the history, the sense of belonging he's always needed.

"I never thought about how truly important that is, but you can bet I am now. C'mon, Caleb." I hitch my head toward the front door as we park. "Be your normal charming self and my mom will love you. Don't worry about my dad and brother; once they find out you played for Alabama, you're golden."

"HE'S REALLY CUTE," Mom whispers to me as we finish up the last of the side dishes.

Caleb had offered to help, but the men in the family had commandeered him and not let go.

"He is." I look back at the living room, hearing his deep voice explain why the team on the television had run a play opposite of what the consensus had been they would run.

"He seems to be a good man too, good manners, I like the way he held the door open for you when you came in the house. Seems like he's very polite."

I fight the snicker that wants to come out. He's polite all right, until we get naked and then Caleb can be downright demanding, but I'd be lying if I said I didn't need that in my life.

"He's everything and more, Mom. I'm lucky he was there that night, at The Café."

"Yes you are," she agrees as she wipes her hands on her apron. "Maybe we should invite him to Sunday service. You think he'd come?"

I think he would probably do anything I asked him to do. "I can, if you want me to. It's not a promise he'll be there, but I'll put the invitation out, because I know that's important to you. He's busy and it would depend on his schedule."

She smiles at me and calls the men to the table, while we set the dishes out. As I'm lifting the big platter of turkey, Caleb swoops in, grabbing it from my hands. "I got it, Red. Where does it go?"

I literally fucking swoon at how hot he is when he's being a gentleman to impress my family. "Over there." I point to a bare spot on the table. "Thank you."

"Any time." He gives me a wink over his shoulder.

As we have a seat and my dad prays over the meal, I'm starting to relax.

"What's it like being a cop here?" my brother asks, being as polite as I've ever seen him be. "There was a time when I thought about trying out at the academy, but I'm needed to work around here."

I know he doesn't mean it as a slight to me, but I feel it as Lance reminds us all he's expected to work the land. He hadn't really been given an option, as the male child, and maybe that's why he is how he is. He wasn't really given a choice. I had no idea that had ever been something he wanted to do. While I've been judgmental of him, maybe I should listen instead when he speaks.

"We aren't a big town, so we don't have a lot of the problems other cities do. That's not to say there aren't situations that are dangerous. We have our fair share of domestics, drugs, and just people who are mean, but I'd never want to do this anywhere else. My home is here, my heart is here."

"Was the academy hard?" my mom asks, as she fills his plate with stuffing.

"Not any harder than playing football was." He shrugs. "I kind of had a physical advantage because I was already used to most of the fitness stuff. My dad taught me to shoot when I was young, so I had that advantage too. I had a hard time with the ten-codes and statutes. Other cadets gave me a hard time because of who my dad is and thought that I'd be treated differently. I wasn't; I had to pass all my classes and do everything else that the rest of them did. But, in the end I figured it out and graduated. It was one of the proudest moments I've ever had."

"Watching Ruby graduate from college was one of our proudest moments." Dad looks over at me. "As a family, it was one of our proudest days ever. Even though it wasn't that long ago, it'll be one of our better memories."

"Really?" I ask, genuinely surprised.

"Yeah." He smiles. "It wasn't easy to get you there. Just like most everything else, there were sacrifices that had to be made, but we knew we wanted to do it for you. It was a decision we made as a family. Me, your mom, your brother. We wanted you to have your dream."

I'm speechless as I think about what that probably meant for Lance. Now, I understand why they give him such leeway, why they let him do the things he wants to do. He sacrificed so much for me, and I never gave him credit for it.

"I'll make you proud," I promise them all.

Lance gives me a grin from across the table. "You already do."

As we all get back to our food, I realize that without Caleb being here, without him starting this conversation, we never would have had it. It's just one other way he's brought new perspective to my life, and I grow more thankful for it every single day.

Cruise

"Thanks for inviting me," I tell Ruby's parents as she and I prepare to leave. "And thanks for having your dinner on another day, to help accommodate. Unfortunately in my line of work, sometimes I'm not available on holidays."

"You're talking to a family of farmer's son, I think we get it." Phillip puts my mind at ease.

One of the things I had been most worried about when it came to meeting her family was them thinking I couldn't give her everything. My job has been a deterrent for most of my adult life, but I'm willing to admit the deterrent has been because of me. Because of what I've wanted, not because of what they've wanted. Now I'm ready to give in and experience it all.

Ruby stands next to me as her mom reaches in and gives me a hug. "Hopefully we'll see you at church?"

I've never gone to church in my life, not regularly, but I'll do whatever's expected of me to get in the good graces of this family. Just so they know I'm serious about their daughter.

"As soon as I can make it," I promise as Ruby and I head out the door, down the porch steps and to the Jeep.

Once we get in and shut the door, we both breathe a sigh of relief.

She leans over, kissing me fully on the mouth. "We made it!"

We sure did.

CHAPTER SEVENTEEN

CRUISE

MID-DECEMBER

"Sorry I couldn't come and pick you up," I apologize as Ruby meets me outside the only Baptist Church in town.

I had been cutting it close, working overnight. As it is, I've made it with ten minutes to spare, after going home, taking a shower, and changing into a pair of khakis and a button-down. My hair is still wet, and I didn't have time to shave, but they'll have to take me how I am.

"It's okay, I had Mom and Dad pick me up so I could ride back with you." She smiles up at me, leaning in for a kiss. She's wearing a modest dress with a cardigan over it, her hair half up in braid across the crown of her head, her curls a little unruly, just the way I like it. I like this buttoned up version of her; it makes me want to mess her up.

It's been a few days since I've seen her, and if I let myself, I'd take what she's offering right now way too far for the church parking lot.

"You look tired." She runs the palm of her hand against the stubble on my face, her eyes concerned.

"Been up for about fifteen hours, will probably pull a full twenty-four by the time we hit the parade," I admit. "But I've got a couple of cans of Red Bull in the Jeep, and since school's out for the break, I'm hoping I can convince you to take a nap with me when we get done."

"In your bed?" she asks. "It smells like you."

God, this woman. "If that's what you want." I rub my thumb against her pink lips, before leaning down to take another kiss from her.

"It's definitely what I want." She tilts her head toward the two doors that are starting to close. "We better get inside before the service starts."

Her hand in mine, she leads me up the steps and through the doors, directly to the pew her family sits in. We exchange quiet greetings, before having a seat. I get comfortable, putting my arm around her shoulders, pulling her hand with my free one onto my thigh. She crosses her legs toward me and leans in, as we both look ahead and pay attention to whatever's being preached today.

I've done my best to keep my attention focused on the pulpit at the front of the church, but I'm having a hard time not wanting to close my eyes for just a few minutes.

"He's almost done," Ruby assures from beside me.

"Now we have an update on Tanner, a young teenager that was hit at Halloween. We've been praying for him, and I heard from his mama the other day he'll be heading home at the end of next week. We'd like to get together, provide them with meals for the their first couple of weeks back, along with some gift cards to help with day-to-day purchases. I'll post something about it in the church's Facebook group tonight," he finishes off.

"Oh thank God," Ruby whispers. "I was worried about him, and we hadn't had an update in a while."

Leaning in, I kiss her on the forehead. Knowing that she's relieved, makes me relieved too.

"ARE you all coming to the parade?" I ask her mom and dad as we stand outside the church, waiting for Ruby to change into something warmer. It's colder today than it has been in the past few weeks, and it rained last night, leaving a chill to the air. I've changed into some jeans, a long-sleeve shirt, grabbing an old hunting jacket and put a beanie on my head.

"Nah, too cold for us." Susan smiles as she takes Phillip's hand in hers. "But hopefully we'll get to see you again soon, young man?"

"I hope so too," I tell her as she leans in to give me a kiss on the cheek. Phillip gives my hand a shake, and they are off.

Going over to my Jeep, I lean against the passenger side door, waiting for Ruby to come down the steps. When she does, I can't help but smile at the picture she makes. She's wearing those jeans I like, with the rip in the thigh, and a North Face jacket, along with a beanie on her head too.

"I love those jeans." I pull her into my arms, looping them around her waist. My hands itch to reach down, and palm her ass cheeks, pull her so close to me that there's no space between us. My mind warns me that this isn't the place for that.

"Just like I love this chain you wear." She reaches down, grabbing the wallet chain I have.

"Yeah? You never told me that."

She shrugs. "Always kinda been my little secret. Here's the thing though, for most everyone else you're this officer of the law, you uphold all the rights, punish all the wrongs. All of that inherently makes you this really good guy, but for me? You're a bad boy, you make me do all the things I always told myself I would never have the courage to do. You make me drop all my inhibitions and encourage me to trust you. So the tattoo on your arm" – she runs her fingers along where she knows the ink is – "and this chain you wear" – she tugs on it, and for some reason that tug goes to my groin too – "they're some of my favorite parts of you. I consider them mine." She leans up on her tiptoes, circling her other arm around my neck, pulling me down.

Before our lips meet, I let her know the truth. "They're completely and totally yours. No one else gets this side of me."

"Good." I can feel the smile against my lips. "No one else gets this side of me either."

There, in the parking lot of the church, I take the kiss I've wanted all morning. Tongue, nipping, even a little teeth involved, and for the life of me, I can't help but think since God knows what's in our hearts, he's probably, definitely okay with this little public display of affection.

"YOU WANT A HOT CHOCOLATE?" I ask as we exit the Jeep and start walking to what will be the main thoroughfare of the parade. I've got my Red Bull in one hand, her hand in my other.

"Oh yes, that would be awesome." She snuggles next to my body, allowing me to block the wind that's coming between the buildings.

When we round the corner, there's a line, but Leighton is working the hot chocolate booth. She sees my head over the sea of people and gives me a smile. "Officer Harrison, how many you want?"

I hold up one finger, and she sends Ransom over with one for me. "Mom says it's on the house."

"Tell her I said thank you." I hand it over to Ruby.

"Come watch me play and we'll call it even?"

The kid drives a hard bargain. There's still a few games left in the football season, and I can't tell him no. "Have your mom or dad text me your schedule, and I'll be sure and make it to one."

Ransom gives a smile and a thumbs up.

"You're such a good guy, Caleb. You do your best to make time for everybody."

"They make time for me." I shrug. "So many times in my childhood nobody had the time to give to me, they didn't care whether I had it or not. I do my best to let people know they matter. Even if it's just showing up to some football game."

She leans up, kissing me on the cheek. "Whether you want to admit it or not, you're special. I'm so happy to be here with you today."

And those words? They make me happier than anything else has made me in a long time. "C'mon, let's go find Mom and Kels."

After a text conversation and a little walk around where we are, we eventually find them.

"Bubba!" Kels greets me, running up to us and throwing her arms around the both of us. You would think she hasn't seen us in months.

I give her a hug and then go over to where Mom sits in one of her camping chairs. "How's it going?"

"Cold, why is it so cold?"

I laugh. "You're from Philly, you should be used to this."

"Nope, in the years I've been here, I've lost what I used to be able to tolerate. Now the temp gets below forty and it's freezing."

"Where's Dad?"

"He's at the roadblock, keeping traffic from coming down here. I'm surprised you made it, didn't you work last night?"

"I went to church with Ruby and her parents." I hold up the Red Bull. "And I brought reinforcements."

Her gaze cuts to me, surprise across her face and in her voice. "You? Went to church?"

Somehow, I feel like I'm never going to hear the end of this. "I did. Can we drop it?"

"She's more special than you want anyone to know, isn't she? Damn, Caleb. You went to church. You know what that means, don't you?"

That I'm completely and totally serious about her. Everyone saw us there today, together. It was the equivalent of giving her my letterman's jacket in high school.

"Yeah, I know, and I'm good with it."

Her mouth is hanging open as she reaches in and grabs my hand. "I'm happy for you. I'm so happy that you've finally decided to let someone else in. I know with the fear your mom put in you about people leaving."

"You're my mom," I remind her. "And you gave me zero fear."

She knows by the way I've spoken that I don't want to talk about the woman who gave birth to me any longer.

"Then I'll just say I'm happy for you, and we'll leave it at that?"

"That I'll gladly take."

The crowd shifts as the parade is about to start. Kelsea sits in her chair next to Mom's and I have a seat on the curb, motioning for Ruby to come sit in my lap. She does so without hesitation, sitting sideways so that my arms go around her thighs. As we watch the parade, I play with that patch of bare skin, grinning when she giggles, burying her head in my neck.

"That tickles." She kisses me softly on my Adam's apple.

"Where?" I whisper.

We're around hundreds of people, but it feels like we're totally and completely alone.

"Everywhere," she answers, those blue eyes of hers shining bright.

With her newfound boldness, I know I won't lose the smile I have for the rest of the day.

"WHY DON'T you let me drive?" Ruby questions as we make our way back to my Jeep. I've already been through the two Red Bulls and I'm dead on my feet.

"You sure you can handle this big boy?"

"I can handle you, can't I?"

Catching her around the waist, I pull her to me. "This mouth you've got." I cup her jaw. "What am I going to do with it?"

"Kiss it, own it."

Looking around, I see we don't have an audience. My lips to her ear, I whisper. "Fuck it? Cause I think you'd kinda like that too."

"You'll never know until you try, hot stuff."

With those words, she takes off at a run for my Jeep, sliding into the driver's side.

"Be careful with him." I hand her the keys.

"I'll be as careful with him as I am with you," she promises as I let my seat lay back.

Before we're even out of the parking lot, I'm asleep. Content in the knowledge I trust this woman with everything.

CHAPTER EIGHTEEN
CRUISE

NEW YEAR'S **Eve**

"She needs to be in bed by eight," Karina tells me as Ruby and I wait for her and Dad to leave for their date.

I shoot Ruby a look, before I put my hand over Karina's mouth. "Mom, I've watched my sister before, in fact, I watch her probably more often than most brothers do. I think I got this."

"I know." She wraps her finger around her curl, before her eyes cut to Dad's. "It's just... I feel bad asking you to watch her on New Year's, especially when you have Ruby," she admits, looking apologetically at the both of us.

"I think we'll be fine." I roll my eyes. "You and Dad go out, have a blast, rent a room if you want. We got this."

"Listen to your son." Dad puts his arm around Mom, pulling her toward the door. "He's got this."

"I know he does," she worries again, biting on her nail. "I'm just really sorry you're spending your first New Year's together, watching your little sister."

"Karina," Ruby laughs. "It's fine, I promise. We're gonna have a good time here. You two go out and have fun, like he said, we got this."

"Okay, okay, I'll stop apologizing. If you need anything we have our phones on."

"Rina." Dad's voice is soft, but commanding. "If you don't stop, we're gonna miss our reservation. Trust me when I say, we'll make it up to them. Let's go, babe."

"Okay, I got it!" She grabs her phone and purse. "You two have fun."

Dad looks at me, a twinkle in his eye. "You remember what I told you the last time you stayed here with a girl? Same rules apply."

"Fuck that," I laugh, giving him the finger. "I'm watching your offspring so you can go have a good time, you can forget it."

He laughs loudly as he looks at me. "Just keep it quiet." He winks.

"Whatever, Dad. Get outta here."

They finally leave, and I lean my back against the door. "I never thought they would leave. Cupcake, where are you?" I yell for my sister.

"Did they finally go, Bub?" she asks as she comes in the kitchen. "I never thought they would leave. What are we doing tonight? Is Ruby staying with us?"

"She is." I reach down, picking her up in my arms. At ten, she's still small for her age, and I'll hate the day that I can't hold her like the little girl she is. "What do you want to do tonight?"

"Since Ruby's here, do you think we can paint my nails?" She glances down at Ruby's, which are a bright pink, glittering in the light.

"You're in luck, I brought my nail stuff, because we had such a good time talking about it last time." Ruby lifts up the bag she brought with her.

"While you ladies are doing your nails, I'll order us a pizza and find something to watch on TV. Sound good?"

"Yeah." Kelsea grins, and by her look, I know she's excited to spend time with us.

I watch as Kelsea and Ruby go into the living room and start setting their stuff up on the coffee table. "Is pepperoni okay with you two?"

"Sounds good to me." Ruby gives me a thumbs up.

"Cupcake, you want the apple streusel dessert?" Kelsea is a sucker for all things sweet. She's a lot like me.

"You know me, you know I do," she answers as I log into my account on my phone. Within minutes, I've ordered pizza, cheese bread, and a dessert for us.

I think twice about it, but I still go ahead and make Ruby and I drinks. We're not planning on going anywhere for at least a few hours, so I feel like it's okay for us to have some Jack and Cokes. Walking back into the living room, I watch as Ruby and my sister play on Kelsea's phone.

"Stick your tongue out" Ruby grins as they take a picture. "I love these filters, I keep trying to get your brother to try them with me, but he won't." She shoots me a look.

"Forgive me if I don't want to look like a dog or a panda bear. I'm good the way I am."

"You sure are." She shoots me a wink.

Turning the TV on, I queue up *Pitch Perfect*, because I know it's a favorite in this household. Basically I check my man card at the door, when it comes to Kelsea. Ruby and my sister sit down on the floor with their nail stuff spread out across the coffee table, I lay on the couch, so that I'm close to them. As I situate myself, I put my arm around Ruby's neck, laying on my stomach so I can touch her as she helps Kelsea do her nails. I've never been the type of guy who's had to be touchy-feely with a woman, but Ruby's changed all of that for me.

"I *love* this movie," Kelsea looks back at me, giving me a grin.

"I know you do, Cupcake, it's why I picked it."

Situating myself on the couch, I sigh, but it's a content sigh. Never in my adult life have I felt so settled, felt like I was where I should be. That's what Ruby gives me; she gives me a peace I've never had. There's always been this anxiety bubbling under the surface. It's been there since I was a kid, constantly at the back of my mind, always making me wonder when things are going to go bad. Finally, I'm not waiting for the other shoe to drop, I'm comfortable in living my life and being happy in it. Curling my hand against her neck, I lean in, kissing her softly.

"What's that for?" She turns slightly so I can see her face.

"Just for being you, Red. Just for being you."

When the doorbell rings, I gladly go get the pizza for these ladies in my life, and I love that I'll get to spend my New Year's Eve with them.

"DOES THIS TAKE YOU BACK?" Ruby asks as we lay on the couch wrapped up in each other. My hands are on her ass, and she's turned into my body, touching each part of me she can. Kelsea went to bed, and it was like game on with my lady.

"Not really," I admit. "There's only one other girl I've ever had in this house. She and I didn't curl up on the couch. We spent the night in my room." I drop a kiss on her forehead.

"Ohh really?" She lifts herself up on her elbow. "This I gotta hear." My girl is inquisitive about almost everything, has been since we spent the night after Halloween together.

"Long story short, she was at a party and things got a little too serious for her. She called me and asked me to come and get her. Her parents weren't home and she didn't want to go home to an empty house. Dad offered to let her come here, but he warned me that we better not sleep together, or fuck around." I chuckle, remembering him warning me. "But we slept in my room with the door shut that night."

"And what did you do with her?" She puts her hand under her hair, looking down at me, her blue eyes shining bright. Seeming to dare me to tell her the entire truth. I have nothing to hide, so I have no problem with telling her all about my night of rebellion.

I think back to that night, remembering Jess with fondness, a smile on my face. She and I saw each other once or twice when we were in college and Alabama played Ole Miss, but we never managed to recapture what we had those few months in high school. "We fucked around," I admit. "She gave me the best blowjob I'd had up to that point in my life, and I had to keep quiet for fear my dad would hear. It was kinda hot."

The memory of us messing around while trying to keep quiet is fresh in my mind. As a teenager that had been the hottest thing I'd ever done, as an adult, it cracks me up that I'd had the guts to do it, knowing my dad would have beat my ass.

"Such a bad boy." Ruby grins before she leans down, placing an open mouth kiss on my neck. Her tongue and lips are a huge turn on as she nips, nibbles, and soothes.

"Maybe I was." I thread my fingers through her hair, holding her tightly to my flesh as she begins nibbling.

Pulling back, she licks her lips. "The question is, are you still?"

"Now? Now I'm adult who takes my pleasure seriously."

"Hmmmm, funny enough, I take my pleasure seriously too." She kisses me again, running her hand down my chest and stomach, stopping when she encounters the buckle of my belt. "And maybe I feel like this Jess girl, laid down a challenge for all the girls to come after her."

Immediately, I stiffen, grabbing her around the neck, tilting her chin up to meet mine. "I can promise you, I'm not the type of man to compare, but at the same time I can tell you no one has ever made me feel the way you do. You get me off harder than I've ever gotten off, and I wake up every morning wanting to bury myself so deeply inside you we don't know where each other begins and ends. Whatever happened in my past, there is legitimately no comparison to what I have with you."

It's important she know what she means to me. That when I fall, I don't fall easily, but at the same time I fall hard and completely.

Ruby

This man constantly turns me on and makes me want to explore the edges I have within myself. I want to be the first, the last, and the only thing he thinks of. So I feel slightly that there is a challenge that's been thrown down when he tells me what happened in this house with his high school girlfriend. That's on me, not on him, but I still want to blow his mind. It's a point of personal pride.

"Trust me, Caleb, whatever I do, is something I want to do. To prove to myself I can, and to prove to myself that there aren't any boundaries between us."

He inhales deeply, the inhale sharp and encompassing his whole body.

"You don't have to prove anything to me, baby, but if you want to prove something to yourself, far be it from me to stop you."

I fumble with the buckle of his belt, but I eventually get it unhooked, and his jeans unbuttoned and unzipped. A sly smile on my face, I lean in, claiming his lips for my own, before I pull away and work my way down his body. When I realize how tall he is will encumber what I have planned, I get up off the couch and kneel in front of it. He gets the idea, sitting up so that his legs are spread with me in the middle.

"Remember you don't have to do this." He cups my neck in his hand as he situates himself, pulling his jeans and boxers down.

His cock stands erect before me, hard and tall. Licking my lips, I lean forward, grasping the base and closing my lips around the head, testing the resistance against my tongue.

"Son of a bitch, Red," he groans out as his head falls against the back of the couch and he spreads his legs farther, putting his feet flat on the floor. "Baby." He tangles his fingers through my hair, as I come up and then go back down.

Using my tongue, I lick down and then up, circling the head, before I pull my mouth off and use my hand to jack the length while I glance up at him. Our eyes meet, and my body heats up as I see what I've done to him. "Feel good?"

"Fucking amazing." His eyes are already hooded, chest already heaving, and I can tell how excited he is. It's obvious he's a fan of head, and I can't believe he's never told me.

Taking him down my throat, he moans loudly, pushing his hips up at the same time.

"Shhhh," I giggle. "Don't wake up Kelsea."

"If you knew how warm, wet, and absolutely amazing your mouth felt around my dick, you'd know it's almost impossible to keep the sounds to myself. God you get it so wet." His head lolls against the couch as he digs his fingers in my hair.

Lifting my eyes up to his, I pull his cock out of my mouth, my hand around the base. If there's one thing I've learned, he likes to be in control. "Show me, Caleb. Show me what you want."

His eyes darken and those fingers in my hair grip harder as he pushes me down on his length. The excitement of proving to him what I can do helps me take him deep. Saliva helps to lubricate his way as he pushes his hips up and my head down.

"Yeah, Ruby, just like that." He pushes my hair back from my face, moving his hand down to my jaw, tilting me the way he wants me to go.

Turning my head to the side, I make a huge production of taking him, as my eyes flutter up to his. I feel like a fucking porn star as I put on a show for him.

"Oh God, yeah, look at me as you take my cock down your throat. Get it wet, Red," he encourages as our pace picks up. My jaw hurts because he's so large, so thick in my mouth.

Pulling him loose, I pant heavily. "You're so thick, my jaw." I point, my chest heaving, my heart pounding.

He chuckles as he grips the end of his cock, lazily stroking it as he glances down at me. "I never wanna hurt you," he assures.

And I never wanna leave him wanting. Reaching to the hem of my shirt, I grasp it, pulling it over my head, before I pull the cups of my bra down.

"Oh fuck, Red, seriously?"

Leaning with my hand against the back of the couch, I dangle my nipples in front him. He grabs one in his mouth, twirling his tongue around the peak. Taking my knees again, I lean over his cock, grasping the sides of my tits.

"Oh fucking shit," he moans deep in his throat as I enclose his hard length in between my flesh and start to move up and down around his cock.

Another thing I've learned about Caleb is he's very visual and he's a very dirty boy. He likes sex, he doesn't mind getting messy, and he loves telling me what to do. "Like this?" I gaze up at him, taking in the passion on his face, the sweat dripping off, and the way he's pulled his bottom lip in between his teeth.

"Fuck yeah, Red, don't stop." He's given up the façade of trying to hold his shit together as his hands come down over where mine are, pressing my tits around his cock. The way he's pressing up into them, he's got no rhythm, no finesse. It's as if he's lost all semblance of the guy who normally fucks me until I can't see straight. I've finally done it, finally made him lose his control.

"Give it to me, Caleb," I hiss out in between my teeth, rubbing my tits up and down his length, enjoying the slippery feel of him there.

His head punches back against the couch as he runs a hand up his t-shirt covered chest. He's grabbing his nipple in between his fingers, tugging roughly on it. I wish I could reach up and take it into my mouth, the way he takes mine. Right now I wish I could swirl my tongue around the hard nub, bite his flesh the way he bites mine. Doubling up my efforts, I go after his orgasm hard, stopping once to push his length back into my mouth, to replace the moisture lost by him jacking it between my tits.

"You want it?" His neck is strained, his words breathless as he pushes up in between the tight space.

"Yes!" And I realize I don't know what he's asking, but I want whatever he's willing to give me. His pleasure is my pleasure.

Caleb pulls back, taking himself in his free hand, jacking up and down furiously. "Push those tits together, Ruby," he hisses between clenched teeth.

Immediately I know what he wants, and I want it too. To feel his pleasure across my skin? It's what I've been aiming for since we started this rendezvous with one another. "You want it?" he asks me again, his eyes open wide as he looks down at me.

"Yeah." I give him a grin as my eyes drift down to where he's holding himself, his big hand running up and down his length. It always amazes me when I watch him jack off, he's much rougher on his flesh than I dare be. Probably because he knows what he can handle. Offering my flesh up to him, I lean in close as his hand goes up and down in a blur. "C'mon, Cruise," I use his callsign. The only time I use it is when we're getting intimate like this, and as such it affects him like no other. His hand goes faster, his hips push harder. The veins in his neck are standing out, and his whole body is tightening as he works for relief.

"Ahhh yeah." The words come out in a rush as I feel the heat of his release on my skin. His lip is clenched between his teeth, and I'm panting as he paints my tits with the evidence of his pleasure.

CHAPTER NINETEEN
CRUISE

I'M WRECKED as I lay panting, my head resting against the back of the couch, trying to figure out exactly where I am. If I've ever come that fucking hard, it's been a long time. When I hear a giggle, I pry my eyes open, seeing Ruby still kneeling in front of me. Her breasts are wet with me, and I wish we were alone, back in my apartment or her duplex. I would think nothing of jerking my shirt off and pressing our skin together. We aren't alone though, and we're lucky Kels hasn't woken up yet. I struggle out of my shirt, using it to clean her off, since we don't have anything around to do so. As good as I can, I stuff myself back into my jeans, before zipping, buttoning won't be happening for a while. I sigh, running my hands through my hair.

"You okay?" she asks, raking her nails along my stomach muscles. They contract roughly against her touch and my body instinctively wants to seek more from her.

Leaning down, I capture the edge of her jaw with my fingers, holding her still for me. "Fucking perfect."

"Did you come harder?" she asks, those blue eyes dark in the flicker of the TV playing behind us. "Ya know, than you did with her?"

I see this is a point of pride for her, and instead of getting annoyed she brought up Jess again, I drag my hand down her neck, over the swell of her breast and press her nipple in between the pads of my fingers. "I always come harder for you than I ever have anyone else. That's what happens when you care about the person who's blowing your mind, or your dick." I give her a grin. "There's no comparison, please don't think there is. You get me more than any other woman ever has, and because of that, you get a part of me that no other woman ever has. Fuck, you're so special to me..." I trail off as I capture her lips with mine.

She moans deep in her throat as I coax her tongue out to tangle with mine. When I pull away, her lips chase mine, and I can feel her warm breath on my skin. "C'mon, let's take this someplace a little more private?"

She nods, grabbing my hand when I stand up, reaching for her. Together, we make a path through the house, turning off lights, checking on locks, and then quietly we look in on Kels. When I see she's slept through our living room blow job, I close the door and drag Ruby to my teenage bedroom. When we get inside, I flip the lock, and push her up against the door, shoving my thigh in between her legs.

"You're in luck, Red, there's a small bathroom attached to this bedroom. The shower is tiny, but it'll work for what we need to do. Which is clean you off." I run my finger along the swell of her tits, feeling a bit of the stickiness of me left behind. She moans, closing her eyes and licking her lips as I let my palm caress the weight. Not able to stop myself, I give into the urge to lean forward and take one of those nipples into my mouth. My tongue circles the hard nub and I suck hard, hollowing out my cheeks as she grabs my hair and holds me tightly to her.

The cry she gives when I nip slightly is guttural and that's when I make a decision. My hands on her ass, I pick her up, carrying us to the bathroom, not removing my mouth from her flesh until I have to sit her down.

She's breathing heavily as she watches me turn the water on, and then a slight film of steam fills the room.

Without words, we disrobe and step into the shower. Once we're there, it's comical how small it is. We manage to get shampoo and body wash on us, but it's a tight fit. I have to hold my arms up and she has to stand in the shadow of my body, almost putting her arms around my waist. I love being this close to her, love sharing this moment, and I know it's one I'll never forget.

"How did you even jack-off in here?" she asks as she grins up at me.

My face scrunches together in a laugh. "That's a seriously personal question."

"I got seriously up close and personal with you a few minutes ago, so I think you can answer it." We switch places as she gets under the flow of water and quickly washes off.

"I didn't." I wink. "That's what laying in my bed was for. Then I'd come take a shower. You have to make do with what you've got."

"Oh is that how it is?" she laughs as she tilts her head back to get the shampoo out of her locks.

When she does, she offers her tits up to me, and I'm an enterprising man. I take what's offered. Swirling my tongue around the tip, I reach down to her ass, grab her up, putting her legs around my waist. As I reach to turn the shower off, she squeals when I turn with her in my arms, taking us to my bed. "That's exactly how it is." I toss her on the mattress I spent most of my teenage years on, and then look my fill. Her legs are slightly parted as she looks up at me, her elbows holding her weight. "And just so we're clear, Ruby Red." I get down on my knees, ignoring the hardwood under my wet skin, spreading those thighs to make room for my shoulders. "I'm about to get seriously up close and personal with you."

For a few moments, I stare at the feast before me. Letting my gaze travel from the top of her head to where I'm situated between her thighs. Her blue eyes meet my brown ones, her eyebrow raised. "Do you need a roadmap?"

My grin tilts into a smirk. I love the sassiness of her, the way she tells me what she wants in her own way. "Nope, just takin' my time."

Her legs widen farther, a smirk covers her face. "Then maybe I can entice you." Her hand scoots down her body, her pink nail extending, almost touching her clit before I reach up, grabbing it in my grasp.

"Oh no, babe, this is all mine." I run the flat of my hand along her pussy, covering it completely, before running my index finger along the little piece of skin that's begging for my touch.

"Then take it." She thrusts toward my mouth. "Please, take it."

At that loss of control, I angle my head to the side, use my free hand to expose her clit, and dive in for a taste of what I know will become an obsession. "Caleb," she whispers as she reaches down and threads her fingers through my hair, holding my mouth as close to her as it can be. I give her what she wants, circling her nub with my tongue and then suctioning hard and deep.

Pulling back with a loud pop, I let go of the fingers I'd captured, placing them on her breast. "Make yourself feel good." I bring my other hand back down to where my mouth is. Extending two fingers and pulling the rest back into my palm, I test the tightness of her channel, moaning deep in my throat when I feel how fucking wet she is. Blowing me turned her on, and mother fuck if that doesn't turn *me* on. Even though I just came not long ago, I can feel my dick hardening again, the head bumping the edge of the bed. It feels good, so I keep thrusting as I continue to work her.

Using the tip of my tongue, I circle her nub, flicking the flesh as I push my fingers in and out of her body. Her moans are loud in the room, and I worry that Kelsea is going to hear, but I also can't stop the way I feel, the way she's feeling. When I push even deeper, she lets out a guttural cry, forcing me to remove my mouth. "Red? Kels, remember?"

"Fuck Caleb, you do that so good." She extends her leg and hooks me around the neck, bringing me back down to her. When I give her a pointed stare, she grabs a pillow, shoving it over her face. There's a chuckle in my throat, but when I get back to the business at hand, I find I have to tell myself to stop moaning.

She's so sweet, everything I've ever wanted in a woman, and her taste was made for me. Her pussy too, almost completely bare, just a little patch of hair at the top, neatly trimmed. Makes me glad I take my time to do my own trimming. With everything I have, ignoring the pain in my knees, the cramp in my forearm, I go after her, because I can feel her tightening, can feel her getting close. I want to give her what she gave to me. And that's when I hear her, even through the pillow. I can't wipe the smile from my face, even when I wipe my mouth. She puts the pillow to the side, chest heaving, stomach going concave as she looks down at me, running her hands up and down her body.

"Where did you learn that little tongue and then suction, and then thrust gimmick? Because, oh my God!" She's gripping her skin, almost like she has to touch herself, and it's hot as fuck.

"I've got a few tricks you haven't seen yet," I assure her, as I walk over to where I left my jeans, going into the back pocket and fumbling with my wallet. This is one of those times where I wish we'd had the birth control discussion, where I wish I could sink into her bare, and not worry about any consequences. Feel myself shoot inside her body, feel her take every bit of myself I have to give her. It's something we'll need to discuss in the future, but right now, the cock against my stomach is demanding fucking relief.

"God, Caleb Harrison." She looks over at me, eyes hooded, lips pink, face flushed with the orgasm I just gave her. I'm going to give her more, and she's going to look like my very own porn star before I'm done. "If I knew your middle name, I'd call you by that too." She shakes her head. "You're amazing at what you do."

"It's Matthew. My middle name is Matthew."

The smile she gives me is dazzling. "Mine is Josephine."

I stop what I'm doing and give her a smile back. "That's you, an old soul."

The tender moment is completely unexpected, but it's everything I've come to understand makes up Ruby.

I snag the condom I'm looking for and suit up as I walk back over to where she lays, spread out for me like an all you can eat buffet. Pushing her thighs apart, I dive into the space that's been left for me, curling my arms around her head, putting my palms flat and pushing up. She accepts me easily, a small grunt leaving her throat as she adjusts to my size.

"Okay?" I strangle out, feeling her squeeze against my fullness. It's almost enough to set me off, but I hold back, clenching my ass, trying to focus on anything other than the way she feels.

"Yeah." She nods, lifting her head off the bed, pressing our lips together.

Pushing deeper, I pull back, and bury my head in her neck. "Hang on, Red, I can't wait any longer."

And as we both groan into each other's skin, I realize with everything I have, I don't want to let this woman go.

CHAPTER TWENTY

RUBY

FEBRUARY

I'm nervous as I smooth the dress down my torso, examining the way it shows the bare patch of skin at my stomach. Caleb is supposed to be here to pick me up in an hour. Excitement bubbles up in my throat as I think about how he's going to play my body after our dinner reservation. I bought special lingerie for tonight, and I can't wait to show it to him.

I'm finishing up my hair when my phone rings. Seeing his smiling face, my stomach immediately sinks. Foreboding hits me hard, and I know he's about to cancel.

"Hey," I answer, trying to sound much more positive than I feel.

"Red." The regret is deep in his voice, like he wants to tell me anything other than what he's about to.

"You have to cancel don't you?"

He sighs heavily. "I do. There's been a bad wreck on sixty-five, and they've called everybody in. There's some fatalities, Ruby. Dad and I are both responding."

Carefully I control my emotions, because I don't want him to know I'm upset. There's nothing he can do about this, and honestly, it's the reality of our relationship. If I let this get to me, I'll never be able to handle anything, and there's no point in us even being with one another anymore. "It's okay," I soothe him. "We can plan for something else; it's not a huge deal."

"It *is* a huge deal," he argues. "And I feel like shit that I'm doing this to you."

"I know what getting involved with you entails, and there are sacrifices that sometimes have to be made. It'll be okay."

He's quiet for longer than I like before he speaks again. "I bet you look gorgeous. Can you at least send me a picture?"

He's killing me. "I'll do it as soon as we hang up. I'm not mad, or disappointed. This is life, babe."

"Okay." He sounds resigned.

"Just let me know when you're safe, and done. Maybe we can hang out later."

"I'll keep you informed," he promises, and I can hear people in the background telling him they're leaving.

"Go, Caleb. I'll see you soon."

"Bye, Red. I'm sorry," he apologizes again.

"No need, be safe."

"Always," and then he's gone.

When I make sure the phone's been hung up, I let out a little cry, because I am disappointed and upset. Not at him, but at the situation. Then I feel awful, people have died, and I'm feeling sorry for myself for not going out on a date. "Suck it up, Ruby."

My phone vibrates with a text. After the news I just got, I wonder if I want to see whose messaging me now. When I look over, I see Karina's name.

K: *Wanna come hang out with me and Kels? We lost our V-Day date too.*

R: *Be right there!*

And in this moment, I'm so thankful to be a part of this family.

Cruise

The scene we've encountered is awful. A couple obviously on their way to a date for the night. She's wearing a dress, he's dressed up in a suit, and as we search the scene, trying to find ID so that we can notify next of kin, we find an engagement ring in his pocket.

This is the shit I hate. People who get stopped in the tracks of their lives. I'm sure they started this night, especially the guy, thinking that it would be the best night of his life. It's a reminder of how quickly life can turn in the complete opposite direction of what you assume it will.

"Caleb, I need you to go over there and start directing traffic around some of that debris." Dad throws me a vest and points to where there's a bottle neck.

I put the yellow vest on and move quickly to get to work.

"LOOKS like Ruby is at the house." Dad comes over as we're finishing clearing up the scene.

"Is she?"

"Yeah, Rina invited her over. The three of them decided to spend V-Day together, since we ended up having to work."

At least she didn't have to sit at home by herself, and I'm thankful she had my family to be with. "Good, then I'll head to the house with you. I'll follow behind."

I'm beyond tired and beyond ready to see my family as we pull up into the driveway of the only house I've ever been able to call a home. Dad gets out of his Jeep slowly, just like I do. He puts his arm around my neck, pulling me into his side.

"You don't gotta turn it off just because you've had a rough night and you have a woman in there waiting for you. It's okay to feel whatever it is you feel. You start lying to yourself and her, then you're fucked. Whatever we walk in to, is what we walk in to. She may be upset, she may be angry, but then again she may be okay. This sets the tone for the rest of what you two have, but don't let it ruin anything. Got it?"

I nod, thankful for the advice he's given me. "Love you, Dad."

He gives me a grin. "Love you too. You're a good man, Caleb. The two of you will figure this relationship shit out."

We enter the kitchen through the side door where the three women in our lives look to be having the best time ever. Kari and Ruby are drinking margaritas, and Kelsea's got what looks like a slushy in her glass.

"You're home!" Kelsea yells as she hops down from her chair at the bar, running to me and Dad. We both hug her before we each go to the respective woman in our life.

As I greet Ruby, my gaze lands on some flowers and cupcakes on the bar. "Good job, Dad. Those flowers and cupcakes look amazing."

"I will take credit all day for the flowers." He wraps his arms around mom's neck from behind. "But the cupcakes, I didn't do."

"Ruby did them," Kelsea lets us know as she bites into one. "And they are totally amazeballs. Chocolate covered strawberry."

I let go of Ruby, moving in to inspect the cupcakes sitting on the counter. They look like they were bought at a bakery. The chocolate frosting layered on, with little pearls on top, sitting in Valentine's day cupcake sleeves. "You did these?"

"Yeah." She looks at me like I'm crazy. "We never bought desserts at my house, you've met my parents. I can bake, if I do say so myself."

My eyes flutter to Mom and Dad, both standing there, looking at me with looks on their faces. Dad gives me a grin before he speaks. "No ugly-ass cupcakes for birthday parties, am I right?"

The pounding of my heart inside my chest seizes, as I wrap my arms tightly around this woman who's changed so many things in my life.

"What in the world are you two talking about?" she laughs as I bury my face in her hair.

"Just a little inside joke," Dad saves me from having to put voice to my feelings.

Kissing her on the temple, I pull myself together. "Let's give one a try."

Reaching forward, I devour the sweet treat, moaning as the flavors hit my tongue. My eyes almost roll into the back of my head, it tastes so good. "That's it. Cupcakes every night, forever."

"Not happening," she laughs, smacking the stomach I'm so proud of. "You'd have to be way more dedicated to working out than you are right now."

She's not wrong, and I concede defeat easily.

WE'VE DECIDED to spend the night here because I'm tired and she's a little tipsy. I hand her a shirt to wear, watching as she takes off her jeans and gets comfortable.

"Oh, I almost forgot." She reaches into her purse, pulling out a card. "Happy Valentine's Day." She pushes back her hair nervously. "I've never had a Valentine, so I wasn't sure what to get you."

Going over to my bag, I pull out a card for her too. "My big present was the dinner we had to cancel, so I'm sorry you're getting just the card now." And I feel like complete shit over it, but as Dad said earlier, there's nothing that can be done.

"Just promise me we'll go back sometime?"

"That I can promise." I lean in, kissing her softly.

I slip between the covers and pull her into my side, curling my arm around her shoulders, holding her close. Her fingers play with my bare skin, trailing her nails back and forth. "Can I ask a question?"

"Anything." I kiss her forehead, grasping her fingers in mine, just wanting to feel close to this absolutely amazing person who's come into my life.

"What was the deal with the cupcakes?"

My throat works hard as it swallows roughly, but I know I have to be honest with her. Even if I don't tell her the whole story, I have to give her what this means to me. "You know some of the situation with my birth mom. One thing that always bothered me, that seriously sucked was Dad couldn't make cupcakes for the class on my birthday. I mean he did," I amend my statement, "but they sucked. They were so shitty," I laugh. "Somehow over time, that became something that stuck out to me. You were a very lucky person if you had someone to make you cupcakes that didn't suck."

She pushes herself up on her elbow. "Caleb, if you want me to, I'll make you cupcakes every day."

I laugh loudly. "How about on my birthday and maybe on a few holidays? It's really not that big of a deal."

"It is a big deal." She sees right through me trying to joke this out. "And what's a big deal to you, is a big deal to me. You'll have those cupcakes whenever you want them."

She comes off her elbow, pressing herself to me, holding me tightly around the waist. And for the first time, in a very long time, I feel like I can breathe. I inhale deeply, the scent of her shampoo, and drift off into one of the best sleeps I've had in years.

CHAPTER TWENTY-ONE

CRUISE

MARCH

It's been a somewhat quiet night on shift, and I have less than an hour to go. I'm really looking forward to going home and crashing, this is my third twelve-hour night his week.

"We have a report of shots fired from a silver colored Impala, in the vicinity of Callahan and Miller."

The info from dispatch makes my ears perk up, I'm two streets over from Callahan. "Dispatch, do we have plates?"

"The only thing anyone got was a possible W as in water, and a H as in Harry."

Up ahead of me, a silver Impala turns into my line of vision. I accelerate, until I can see their license plate. There in the glow cast by my headlights is a W and an H. "Dispatch, can you run this plate? I believe I have the vehicle in sight."

Giving them the plate number, I know this is the shooter in question. I can feel it in the way my body tenses, the way my hands grip the wheel, the acceleration of my heartbeat. It's an intuition everyone told me I would get once I'd been on the force long enough – and they were right.

"They're driving on suspension, Caleb."

"10-4, I'm initiating the stop." I flip on my lights and hope they pull over. When they take off like a bat out of hell, I groan.

The police package in the Camaro I drive responds as I punch the gas. "They took off, traveling north," I calmly relay to the hub of the station, hoping other officers can respond.

"I'm coming south." I hear my dad's voice respond. Typically we aren't on shift together, but his is starting right as mine is ending.

We take a left, and I keep the information coming. My heart is pounding, but my voice is calm. It was probably the hardest thing for me to learn, to not let what other people are doing affect me. I have to keep a level head about me, have to be the voice of reason, even when speeds are topping ninety miles an hour. This time we take a right, and I have to slow down to keep from hitting the car in front of me.

"He's gonna lose it," I warn everyone listening.

And as he pushes the limits of the car he's driving, making a sharp left, he loses control and rolls over. "Roll over," I quickly shout into my radio.

Hopping out of my car, blue lights and sirens blaring, I see that the driver has gotten out and is turning to run. I lunge forward, pushing us both against a chain-link fence.

"Don't resist me," I groan as he does just that, stiffening his arm so I can't get it behind his back. He flings my hand off and sprints to the left, but I manage to tackle him and we hit the asphalt hard.

"I can't go back," he's screaming. "I can't go back, just let go."

"Stop resisting!"

I've got him down on the ground, but he's strong, trying to flip me over, and I can't get his arms behind his back. We're still for a moment, each of us trying to get the upper hand on the other. I use my feet to brace against the asphalt, put the legs that managed to almost let me be a pro football player as leverage.

Risking it for a moment, I manage to key my radio. "I need assistance, I can't get him cuffed."

It's the longest seconds of my life as I hear other officers calling out where they are, and I almost cry with joy when I hear the stomping of boots in my direction. "I'm here, I'm here!" It's my dad, and I've never been more thankful in my life.

He and Tank were riding together, both take over as I roll off the guy, completely wasted of strength, and trying to regain my surroundings. Adrenaline is flowing through my body, and I'm shaking with the exertion it took to hold him still. As Tank and my dad get him cuffed, other officers arrive.

"You okay?" Dad asks me quietly as he bends down so that we're eye-level. He reaches out his hand, helping me up.

"Yeah," I pant. "He was strong, I just couldn't get him cuffed."

He pulls me into a hug while Tank waits his turn. "Lost fuckin' years off my life when you said you couldn't get him cuffed and we didn't hear anything else on the radio. Thought he'd hurt you."

"I'm a big guy, but he was strong." I lean over, pressing my hands against my knees.

"Not wanting to go back to jail makes you do things. You're bleeding, and your pants are torn. You sure you're okay?"

"I think so."

"Let Blaze check you out." Tank grabs me in for a hug around the neck. "Fuck that was scary, man."

"Yeah, try being there," I laugh, because now that's all I can do.

"C'mon over here, let me check you out, stud muffin," Blaze yells from her ambulance.

I'm not even sure when they got here, but as I have a seat, I'm feeling very lucky that I wasn't hurt. This could have gone a very different way.

Ruby

"Are you okay?" I ask Caleb, as he walks through my front door.

We were supposed to meet after work, and while I was at the grocery store, I ran into Morgan who asked me how Caleb was doing. It was a shock to find out what had happened, and I've been losing my mind ever since.

"I'm fine," he answers, enveloping me into his arms. "I've never had a scare like that before though. I couldn't get him cuffed, and I was scared I wasn't going to get him cuffed."

"When Morgan told me what happened, I was worried he was going to tell me you'd been injured."

I'm shaking as I hold him in my arms, running my hands all along his body, making sure he's okay.

"It's just part of the job, Ruby. There are days like this when things happen, and then there are days when nothing happens. I'm glad to get to come home to you, though. It made filling out all the reports and waiting to get checked out worth it."

"What do you need from me?" I ask, my eyes searching his, looking to see if he needs me to be what I was after the hard night his dad had.

"I need you," he answers, his voice hoarse. "I need you to be exactly who you are, and us to be exactly who we are."

He's got the stench of sweat on him, probably from the adrenaline that pumped through his body and the exertion of trying to save his own life. "C'mon." I grab his hand, leading him to my bathroom.

I sit him down on the toilet, as I start to fill my bathtub up. He's despondent as he gazes off to the side, not focusing on much of anything. I can understand he's got a lot going on in his head, and I want to help him work through all of it. But I know him, he's not ready to talk about any of it. What he's ready to do is not have to think.

Once the tub is full, I go to work on taking his shoes off, then his pants, and finally his vest and shirt. When he's naked in front of me, he seems to come back to the present. "Sorry, I'm a little out of it."

I kiss the space over his heart. Before I move to the road rash spots on his arms and knees. I'm so thankful he wasn't hurt worse. The reality of the situation is scary, but I also realize how lucky we are. "You're fine, let me help you."

When we're both naked and I've put him the bathtub, I kneel next to it, taking the time to wash him off. I massage the tight muscles and do my best to ignore the one between his thighs that's now resting on his flat stomach. Every once in a while, I watch as he reaches down and gives himself a few strokes, but I want him relaxed before I do anything. Finally, his head leans back against the tub, and his eyes close.

His hand is still on his cock, jerking slowly, to a rhythm only he hears in his head. It's hot, watching him do this, knowing that he's doing it for me. Knowing that he's completely lost all inhibitions around me. Quickly I jump into the tub, hoping to not disturb him. I know I've accomplished that when I learn forward, take his length down my throat, and he levers up out of the water.

"Son of a bitch, Ruby, I wasn't expecting that."

It doesn't take him long to get with the program though. His thick fingers dig into my hair, pushing me up and lifting me down. "Stop, stop," he pants, pulling me up by the thighs to straddle him.

"We've never..." he swallows roughly. "We've never had the conversation, but I would really like to go bareback in you tonight. Can I do that? Are you protected?"

God, just the words he uses is enough to turn me on.

"Yeah, I am. I'd love to do that with you."

There's no hesitation, in one push he's inside my body, mouth at my breast, and the world as I know it has completely turned on its axis. Because unprotected sex with Caleb? Feeling him with absolutely nothing between us? Better than I ever imagined it could be.

CHAPTER TWENTY-TWO

RUBY

MAY

"Okay ladies and gents, you have five minutes before the bell rings, and that's all I have for the class. Talk amongst yourselves, but please keep it down," I tell the juniors that make up my history class.

History isn't my first love. If given the choice, I would have taught English, but I can do both and there was a need for a History teacher, so here I am. Using my five minutes wisely, I go ahead and start in on next week's lesson plans, because I plan to spend as much of this weekend as I can with Caleb. A smile toys against my lips as I think about the guy who has so unexpectedly come into my life. We've been going strong for months now, definitely longer than any other relationship I've ever had. With other guys, I didn't stay at their places, they didn't stay at mine. I know part of that is growing up, not being in the dorms anymore, and not having to worry about roommates, but I feel adult in this with him. Like he and I could make a go of this, if we continue to travel down the path we are. I've never felt that with another man.

The bell rings and my class dismisses. As is my custom, I watch them as they leave, and then stand out in the hall until most of the crowd disperses. I broke up a fight once, and since then I've continued to do this. It's important that none of the students get hurt on my watch. I take it very seriously.

"Ruby!" I hear a loud voice coming down the hallway, and it's a voice I'd know anywhere, one that's started to make me smile.

"Hey Kels." I wave as I see her and Caleb coming down the hallway.

Lord I love to watch Caleb approach, it's nice to watch him leave too, but watching him approach legitimately makes my heart beat faster. The asshole, he knows it too, I can see his smirk from where I stand.

He's working today, wearing his MTF uniform of tactical pants and a t-shirt with a bullet-proof vest reading MTF on the chest in bright yellow letters. His badge hangs around his neck, and goddamn if he isn't sex on a stick. I watch as he slows his walk down, the loose-legged gait becoming lazy as he eats up the distance between us. Kelsea beats him to me, and I reach down to give her a hug.

"See ya, Ruby, I gotta go find Mom."

"See ya." But my eyes aren't on her, they're on her older brother.

He hasn't shaved today, and it makes his brown eyes pop against his tan face. When he's finally within a few inches of me, he reaches out with his left hand, the exposed ink on his arm catching in my peripheral, and cups my jaw, before shoving his fingers into my hair, tilting my head to the side and claiming my lips with his. The kiss, compared to many of the others we share isn't even steamy, but this is Caleb. Everything he does is a turn on. When he breaks away, his voice is deep, rough. "Missed you today."

Not able to take it, I step forward, wrapping my arms around his waist. "Missed you too," I answer, before leaning in for another kiss.

When we break apart again, he pulls his bottom lip in between his teeth after he licks the fullness. "Sucked not waking up next to you this morning. We're gonna have to do something about that, Ruby Red."

"At some point we will," I agree, because I hate waking up alone too.

"Soon?" he moves his hand forward, using his thumb to wipe at my bottom lip.

"Soon, hot stuff, really soon."

He sighs. "I'm gonna go say hi to my mom, wanna come with me?"

"Yeah, just let me lock up my classroom."

He's a gentleman, standing in the door until I've done everything I need to do and then shutting off the light and closing the door for me. I fumble with the key because he's standing so close. There's something about his presence that rattles me, but in a good way. As we walk down the hallway, he puts his arm around my neck, pulling me close.

For a moment, I flash back in time, wondering what it would be like to walk these halls with him when I was in high school, if I had been just a little older. He and I would have at least been in this school at the same time. Chances are he wouldn't have even noticed me, but I can still imagine what it would have been like walking these halls with him.

"Did you walk down this hall with your high school girlfriend?" I tease him.

He throws back his head, groaning. "Yeah, we walked down this hall, but I wasn't nearly as excited to see her as I am to see you."

I'll take what he's giving me, even if sometimes I don't fully believe it. Unfortunately I'm a cynic, but it's gotten me this far in life, so I'll take what I can get.

Cruise

"I've never told a woman about my past, never managed to get close enough one to trust her enough with the information. Opening up about how I grew up isn't easy, at all." I hold her close, kissing her forehead to give me comfort as I consider opening up and baring myself to Ruby. I'm not even sure why I'm doing it tonight, but the things we've been through recently have made me want to share every part of my life with her. Knowing she doesn't judge me and she doesn't blame me are huge parts of why I trust her.

"You and your dad seem like you had a decent life before Karina came along." She leans up, kissing me on the neck.

I'm torn between her believing these things about me and being completely honest about the path I took to adulthood. "My parents had me at sixteen and my mom left before my second birthday. I've only ever seen her once, and never officially met her." I lay my dirty secret down at her feet, wondering if this will change her perception of me.

She pushes herself up on her elbow, her blue eyes moving up and down my body. I wish I knew her thoughts, could see inside her mind and see if it surprises her. "She left?"

"Yeah." I reach over, running my fingers through her hair. "She left. Which is why Dad and I are so close now. It was just us for a long time, except when I was little and he was deployed."

"Who took care of you then?" she questions softly, running her fingers along my bare skin.

"My grandmother. We don't have a relationship now because of some things that went down between my dad and his dad, but at least I had someone to take care of me when he was gone."

"Did you like staying with her?"

I swallow roughly, tightening my arms around her. "No, I hated it. The only thing I wanted back then was my dad. I didn't understand why he was gone, what he was doing, and why I had to share him with the world. I remember him and other people trying to explain it to me, but I could never get it to compute in my head. I always thought he was *my* dad, and there was absolutely no reason I should have to share him. I felt the sacrifice early, and I reacted badly to it. The second time he was deployed, I was a complete shit. I acted out, got into fights, and was literally a holy terror. After that, Dad didn't take another deployment and got out."

"From there, where did you go?"

It's hard to explain this vagabond life to someone who's only known me as a person who's had a stable existence, but I want her to know me. The real me. "We lived in a few different towns in Texas before we ended up settling in Laurel Springs. It wasn't until we came here that I realized what a home was and felt like I belonged."

"I'm glad you did." She finally relaxes, putting her head on my shoulder. "If you hadn't, I never would have met you. I'm a firm believer, given the way I grew up, that everything happens for a reason. Your mom leaving directly brought you and your dad here. To the Moonshine Task Force. To Laurel Springs, and in the end, to me. I can't hate her for that, Caleb. I just can't. I can tell you she missed out on knowing an amazing man, but I can't hate a life that directly affected bringing you into mine."

Wrapping my arms around her, I realize how blessed I truly am.

CHAPTER TWENTY-THREE

CRUISE

JUNE

"**W**ow!" Her gaze falters on me as she hops into the Jeep and gets a good look at the shirt I'm wearing. "That shirt is bright."

"Yeah, I know." I look down at the hot pink shirt covering my body. "The Hurricanes got to pick out their colors, and they decided on hot pink and black. I'm very well aware that I look like a goddamn highlighter. The perks of coaching *and* having to attend softball games."

She laughs, covering her mouth with her hand. "Mason wears it too?"

"What can I say? Kels makes us do shit we never thought we'd do. Like wear hot pink and spend our weekends during the summer and fall with ten-year-old girls. But I'd rather them be with us than some tyrannical coach who doesn't give two shits. I did that enough in football. These girls are learning valuable lessons. Even if I do catch a few of their moms checking out my ass."

Her blonde hair whips around. "I'm sorry? What? They're checking out your ass?"

"Well I mean, it's a nice ass." I give her a wink. "But just in case, I got you a little something to wear today." We come to a stop at a red light, and I reach into the backseat of the Jeep, holding another hot pink shirt.

She opens it up, smiling big as she sees that it has the team name on it, and then turns it around where it sports Kelsea's number and it says *Coach's Girl* on it. "Great, so now people will think I'm with your dad."

"We're both coaches," I correct her.

"Aren't you assistant?" She giggles, busting my balls.

"Fuck that, I'm out there on the field, in the hot sun every day. Besides,

Mom has one that says *Coach's Wife*; he wouldn't have a wife and a girlfriend. Everyone knows that. Mom would cut his dick off. Everybody will know you're mine. Especially when we walk in together and you give all those women the evil eye for staring at my ass."

She reaches down, managing to grab a little bit of skin to pinch. "Damn right, Harrison. That ass is mine, and they may as well just get used to it."

Damn, I love this woman. Love the way she makes me feel, the way she's fully integrated into my family, and the fact she's not ashamed to be with me. If I'm honest that's something that's hindered me for a lot of years. Because my mom left, I always got the feeling people were ashamed to be seen with me. That they didn't love me as much as I loved them. Ruby is showing me that I'm capable of being loved. I'm capable of accepting love, and maybe just maybe, I can take it at face value and not question it. After all, I was able to get it with Karina, I give it to Kels, and my dad with no question. To a point I give it to Ruby too, but opening myself up is hard. I'm learning though, with this woman, and it's worth it.

Ruby

"I see you graduated to the official shirt," Karina greets me as I make my up in the stands to sit next to her.

"I did." I take a drink of my water bottle and pull my sunglasses down further on my face. "When he gave it to me, I had to give him shit and tell him that people will think Mason has both a wife and a girlfriend."

Karina laughs, throwing her head back. "Oh my God, I told him that too. I told him he should have put assistant on there."

"He got made fun of by both of us." I smile softly as I gaze out onto the field.

"It's cool, he's used to being made fun of." She smirks. "That's basically our relationship."

"At least he's a good sport."

"Caleb's always been a good sport about everything. When I tell him and other people that Kelsea's lucky she got the brother she did, I'm not kidding at all."

The two of us people watch as other parents, friends and family members arrive for the game that's about to start. I want to talk to Karina about Caleb, but I'm not sure how to approach the subject.

"So I went by Caleb's the other day, but I saw your car parked beside his Jeep and was scared I'd interrupt something if I went in." She gives me a grin.

I try to think back to what day she's talking about, wondering if she would have really interrupted anything. Chances are, with us, she would have, but I don't want to tell her that.

"It was Saturday, and I knew he had to work that night. It was late enough in the afternoon that he was probably taking a nap."

Immediately my face burns, because I do remember that day. He'd tied me up and shown me what nipple clamps can do, something I'd never experienced before, and probably never will with anyone but him. Instead of taking the nap he'd wanted, he'd ended up being fifteen minutes late to work.

"Feel good, Ruby?" he whispers into my ear as he circles my nipple with his finger. The clamps have been on long enough that I can't feel anything anymore, but I'm straining against the Velcro he's wrapped around my wrists. If I can just get my finger underneath, I can get loose and take the clamp off, feel the explosion of pleasure that borders on pain he's told me I'll feel when he does.

"Yes, God yes, please," I fight against the restraints again. "I want this."

"You sure?" His brown eyes are almost black, his cheeks red underneath the stubble. He's as excited as I am. I nod, wrapping my legs around his waist.

When he fingers the metal release on the clamp, and then presses it, I about come up off the bed. The rush of feeling is overwhelming and I'm not sure I can deal with it, until he clasps his mouth over the tight bud, soothing it with his tongue. His other hand goes down to my pussy, where I'm as wet as I've ever been. And when he bites roughly on the sensitized skin, I come, in a shivering quivering mess against him. It takes me by surprise, and I scream loudly.

"Yes," he encourages me. "Let the whole fuckin' complex know."

And when he takes off the other clamp, I'm pretty damn sure I do just that.

"You would have interrupted something," I whisper under my breath.

"Things are going good with the two of you? He doesn't really talk much to me about it, which makes sense. I'm the mother figure in his life, but I'd like to know he's happy."

"I'm happy, and I hope he is. I haven't ever been with someone like him before. He's something else." I shake my head.

"He's a lot like his dad. I'd never met anyone like him before either, and he blew my carefully laid plans and world totally up.

"That's Caleb if I ever had to describe him. He's definitely blowing up my plans and rocking my world."

"Girl, I know all about the world rocking when it comes to a Harrison boy."

And that's when Caleb and the girls take the field. He's coaching the third base line which is where we're sitting, and as he bends over, hands on his knees, I get the best look at his ass. Today is definitely a damn good day.

CHAPTER TWENTY-FOUR

CRUISE

FOURTH OF JULY

"Do you need my help?" I ask Tank as I sit around a patio table at his parent's house. The entire MTF and their families have descended upon their pool, and have taken over their bar-b-cue. Somehow all of us got the afternoon and night off. Many of us worked the early morning and previous overnight hours, so there's some tired faces but we're all extremely happy to be spending this holiday together.

"Nah, I got it." He closes the lid to the grill and heads back into the kitchen.

I'm glancing around, half paying attention, with my arm around Ruby, when a conversation starts that gets my interest. Renegade and Whitney are talking about a teenage boy Renegade found stealing at a local department store.

"I don't doubt that," Ruby is saying at my side, in response to whatever is being discussed. My girl is fired up about whatever this is, because she's leaned forward in her seat, away from my arm around her shoulder. The tank top she wears pulls at the back, and shows the skin between the edge of it, and the beginning of her bikini bottoms. I rub the exposed flesh, trying to calm her down. "I taught Nickolas." She sits her glass down on the table. "He was in my class and I tried to get his piece of shit parents in there, I reported them to Principal Taggart and made a CPS complaint."

"I'm sorry." I lean forward with her. "I totally missed what happened, can somebody fill me in real quick. Why's Red so pissed?"

Renegade takes a drink of his beer. "It's that kid I picked up the other night.

The one who was stealing? He was stealing food, socks, and underwear, man. It wasn't like he picked up a video game system. When I got there–" Renegade takes a moment to shake his head "–he reminded me of me, at his age. I asked him, ya know, why are you taking this stuff?"

Ruby interrupts him. "He's takin' it because school is out, he has no food to eat, and I can guarantee you the kid hasn't had new clothes since my freshman year of college. He's Caleb's size." She hooks her thumb at me. "Remember when I asked you if you had anything you weren't gonna keep? The stuff you gave to me, I gave to him."

My heart breaks for this kid as I listen to everyone talk about him. "Did you charge him?"

"Nah, I talked to the owner, told him what the kid told me, and paid for what he'd stolen."

"You paid for it?" That's big. It happens every once in a while with us, but we really have to believe the situation.

"Yeah, and I took him home, where I witnessed some not so great things happening."

Whitney picks up the story as she grabs hold of her husband's hand. "We've spoken with some people we know, and we've contacted a lawyer. He's going to be emergency placed in our home as a foster child next week. That's how bad it was."

"No shit?" I'm amazed that this has gone so fast, but it couldn't have happened to anyone better than these two.

"Yeah." Renegade smiles at his wife, as he runs his hand along her arm, and then they clasp them together. "We wanted more kids and it never happened for whatever reason. Maybe this was it. When I presented what I had to the supervisor over at CPS, she made things happen. Nickolas was taken out of their care yesterday. He'll get looked at today, have all the paperwork filled out tomorrow, and we'll take custody of him after the hearing on Monday."

"I wish we could have just taken him today. So he could have met all of you and everything." Whitney worries her bottom lip between her teeth.

"I know, Princess, but we gotta do stuff by the book."

Beside me, Ruby speaks again. "If he needs some help to get to where he should be for the upcoming school year, my summer class is almost over. I'll do anything I can to help him. I'm positive he wasn't getting the help he needed at home."

"Thank you, I'll text you and set something up." Whitney grins over at my girlfriend.

Having her willingly put herself in our group is one of the best feelings I've ever felt. As we all go back to talking to one another, I lean in. "You wanna go get in the pool?"

"Sure!"

We get up and go over to the lounge chairs, me taking off my shirt, kicking off my flip flops. I watch as she puts her hair in a ponytail and kicks off her own flip flops, but never moves to take the tank top off. "You gonna get in with that."

She nods. "I've never been fully comfortable with my stomach."

That pisses me off. Walking over to her, I tilt her chin up to look at me. "If you're uncomfortable, then you're uncomfortable, but know I think you're fucking gorgeous, perfect, and everything I've ever wanted."

"Thank you." She leans her forehead against my chin. "I'll think about it."

"You do that."

A few hours later, when I come out of the house from using the bathroom, I see my brave girl has finally taken that tank top off, and damned if she doesn't look amazing playing volleyball with all the other ladies.

Ruby

"Sometimes, I sit back, look at you, and wonder how in the hell I got so lucky." I lean my head against Caleb's shoulder, wrapping myself around his body. His big hand rubs against my back, and I can't help but feel the goose bumps appear.

We're sitting in the bed of Ryan's truck, waiting on the Fourth of July fireworks to start. He laughs deep in his throat as he takes a drink from his beer bottle. "You wonder that? Babe, that's my life. Like why in the hell did you decide to even go out with me after what happened to you that night. I'm a lucky motherfucker."

"I think we're both pretty lucky." I reach over, taking a drink from his bottle of beer. It tastes better when it's his; I can't explain it, but there's a taste that's just Caleb's.

His eyes follow the motion of my throat, and I can tell by the way his eyes dilate, he approves of me sharing it with him. Wrapping his arm around my neck, he pulls me into him. "That's sexy as fuck," he whispers in my ear.

"What is?" I'm not sure what he's talking about.

"Sharing my beer with me, not being afraid to do what feels good. I've never been with a woman like you before." He pulls me closer into his body.

Glancing around at the group with us, I notice no one's really paying any attention. He picks me up, sitting me cross-ways over his lap. I circle my arms around his neck, leaning in to take his lips with mine. It's a hot night, but I don't mind being close to him, don't mind being in his lap sitting so close. "You think I'm sexy?" I question, when he tugs on the end of my hair.

"Always, you're always sexy. Doesn't matter what you're doing, you just being you is the sexiest thing I've ever seen."

My cheeks heat at the mention of him thinking I'm sexy. This relationship that the two of us have, is so different than anything else I've ever experienced.

"Bubba." I hear Kelsea's small voice beside us and pull back, respecting the fact she wants her brother's attention.

"Yeah, Cupcake?"

"Will you go ride the Ferris Wheel with me?"

"You want Red to go with us?" He gives me a wink.

I pinch him on the side. "You know I hate heights."

"I'll be there with you and..." he trails off. "Cupcake's going, so I mean you'd be hanging out with a ten-year-old."

"Oh, so that's how it's going to be?" I give him a saucy smile. "You're trying to shame me into riding the Ferris wheel with your little sister by acting like she's braver than me."

"Actions speak way louder than words, Red."

"Alright then." I stand up, holding my hand out for Caleb. "Let's get this show on the road."

"C'mon, Kelsea." He jumps down from the tailgate of the truck, holding his hands up to help me down too.

It's the annual Fourth of July celebration for Laurel Springs, and while I have no intentions of riding the Ferris Wheel, I'm really happy to be here with Caleb and Kelsea. He holds my hand as we walk through the crowd of people.

"I can't believe we walked these same paths, did all this same shit, but a few years apart, and we never knew each other." He lets go of my hand and pulls me by the neck into his side.

"You were older, and away at college," I remind him. "What would you be interested in a high school kid like me for?"

"Young Caleb was fuckin' dumb Caleb," he growls as he nips at my ear.

"And I wouldn't have had the confidence back then to let you make a play for me. I would have just faded into the background," I try to explain to him. "Even though I was a cheerleader, I totally hid in the back row."

"You're my cheerleader, babe. You would have been front and center, right here for me." His eyes heat as he looks at me.

Where we are on the main thoroughfare isn't far from the football field, and I can tell by the heated look we exchange, we're both thinking of Halloween. But tonight we have someone else with us.

"Can we get some cotton candy?" Kelsea asks as we see a line waiting to get the sugary treat.

"Yes!" I let go of Caleb and run up to walk next to her. "We can get all the cotton candy there is."

As we walk away, I turn around, throwing a smirk and a wink back at Caleb.

Cruise

I love the way she's taken to my sister and my sister has taken to her. They're two peas in a pod, and I've always known if I wanted to keep someone in my life, Kelsea would have to love them. Right now, I'm pretty sure she loves Ruby more than she loves me. After all, what do I know about nail polish, braids, and clothes? It makes me think things though, as I watch the two of them walking ahead of me.

They look almost related, because Kelsea has a major case of hero worship right now. She wants to do everything Ruby does, and that includes wearing whatever clothes she can find that match any of my girlfriend's. They're both wearing cut-off shorts and tank tops. The thing it makes me think about? What if in ten years that's Ruby with our kid?

Never, in the almost twenty-nine years I've been on this planet, have I thought long-term about anything other than the Moonshine Task Force. Never have I thought past what I wanted to do once I made it. After I said goodbye to a pro football career, all my time and energy was spent making my dad proud. Making him see I understood the sacrifice he made for me, for us as family.

Now? I'm thinking about my future, what I want out of life. And I'm more sure than I've ever been that it's a curvaceous blonde spitfire, small enough for me to rest my chin on her head, bold enough to make me hard with just a look. She's sweetness mixed with sassy, and her blue eyes can see right through my soul. And she's completely perfect for me. She fits me, she fits my family, and without me even realizing it, she's become one of the most important people in my life.

"Hey ladies," I yell as they've gotten ahead of me, standing in line for what looks like the largest cotton candy I've ever seen. "Wait for me!"

"Hurry up then, slow poke," Ruby yells back as she and Kelsea giggle, sharing what appears to be a private joke between the two of them.

When I get there, they're next in line. I pay for what they order, and then wait with them while it's being made. I watch in awe as the person makes cotton candy fucking art. He gives a small heart to Kelsea, which makes her immediately fall in love, and then I watch as the fucker makes a flower for Ruby, handing it to her with a flourish.

"For the beautiful lady."

She smiles at him, gratefully accepting it, before she takes a bite. I scowl at him over her head, mouth a *WTF dude*, and turn them toward the rides.

"How did that guy know my favorite flowers are pansies?" she wonders as she continues picking at the different colors, before putting them in her mouth.

I watch as she licks her lips to rid them of the sugar, and then I wonder, why the fuck didn't *I* know pansies were her favorite flower? Why the fuck haven't I gotten her flowers before, and why am I so jealous of some guy who works at a carnival?

God, love is a crazy fuckin' thing.

"C'mon let's go to the Ferris Wheel." Kels directs us through the crowd, to where we stand in line.

"Are you really going to go?" I ask Ruby, knowing from a few conversations we've had, she truly hates heights.

"No." She grins as she shakes her head. "The two of you have totally got this taken care of. There's no way." She puts her arms around my waist. "Even with you, I'd probably pee my pants and get so scared I wouldn't be able to physically get off the ride."

I can't imagine this woman that's come to mean so much to me would ever be that scared of something, but we all have our quirks. "I'd keep you safe," I remind her.

"You're not God, Caleb, and there's no safety net under this thing. Sorry, but you're not getting me up there. I'll gladly watch the two of you with my feet safely on the ground down here."

She's still eating her cotton candy, and it's turned her lips a different color. Unable to help myself, I lean forward, licking the sweetness off of them. Glancing around, I see that Kelsea is talking to one of her friends from school. "I wonder what that would taste like around your other lips." My voice is pitched low, and I can tell the moment she understands what I'm saying. Her gaze becomes heated and she stops with a piece of the candy half-way to her mouth.

"Caleb Matthew." Her voice is scandalized. "I can't believe you just said that to me."

"Believe it." I lean in, getting a taste of the sweetness myself. The line is moving and it's our turn. "And you best believe I'm picking up another bag before we leave. Tonight, Ruby Red? We're gonna have some fun."

TWO ORGASMS and a bag of cotton candy later, we're both laying in her bed, trying to get our breath back.

"You're gonna kill me one day," she accuses as she rolls over to rest her head on my shoulder.

"Nope." I hold my hand to my chest. "Pretty sure my heart is going to beat out of my chest. That, was one of the best ideas I've ever had."

She makes a noise in her throat. "True, but it's sticky."

I snort, tilting my head down so that I can see her. "Newsflash babe, most everything that's fun without clothes on is sticky. If that's your only complaint, I'm not accepting it."

"Then don't." She shrugs. "Just come join me in the shower."

She gets up, slipping out from under the covers. My gaze is immediately drawn to her naked ass and the two dimples above it. When she turns around, looking at me over her shoulder, I'm a goner. I'm out of bed so quickly I almost trip over the covers, and all I know is one thing: I'm gonna clean her up, just so I can dirty her up again. It's become one of my favorite things about being in a relationship.

CHAPTER TWENTY-FIVE

RUBY

IT'S A HOT SUMMER DAY, as I walk onto the practice field. Since school let out in early June, I've been catching up on sleep, taking a summer class, and spending as much time with the man in my life as I can. Neither Mason nor Caleb are here today. Both are on duty, so another parent has offered to help the girls practice. Karina is sick with a summer cold and me? I'm here, not sure what the hell I've gotten myself into. Kelsea and I are spending the afternoon together, beginning with me picking her up. So we'll see how this goes.

"Ruby!" I hear as I shield my eyes and look out along the field. Kelsea is running toward me, her backpack bouncing as she runs.

"Hey Kels," I greet her, a real smile on my face. She and I haven't had a ton of time with one another, but as Caleb and I have gotten closer, the same has been true for the two of us. "You ready?" I wave to today's coach as she walks beside me.

"I am, it's hot out here." She pushes her hair back from her forehead.

Taking a good look at her, I see her face is beet red, and she's sweated a good deal. "You wanna go take a shower before we go do our thing?"

She looks up at me, nodding. "I feel so gross."

"No problem, your brother's apartment is closer than mine. Is it okay if we go there?"

"How are we going to get in if he's not there?" she questions as we get to my car.

"I have a key," I say the words off-handedly, as we get to my car. He gave me one not long ago, and it had been a turning point in our relationship. Whatever this is between us, is serious.

"He gave you a key?" Her eyes are wide. "Ruby, does that mean you're gonna get married?"

I'm taken aback by her question, but I can understand how she probably came to that conclusion. A kid doesn't understand the way things like this work. "I don't know Kels, maybe one day, but definitely not tomorrow."

"I wouldn't mind it," she announces. "I've always wanted a sister and I'd love it if you were mine."

I'm overcome with more emotion than I want to admit. This little girl with a heart so much like her brother's, has totally worked her way into mine.

"I've always wanted a sister too, Kels, and if I had to choose, you would be it."

She seems happy with the answer as she sings along to the radio. Meanwhile I'm trying to hold my shit together, pleased beyond all belief that she sees me as worthy of Caleb. A part of me always wonders if I will be, because he's had such a hard life, I want to make sure I'm the one he wants to come home to at the end of the day. The one he always wants to confide in, and I want him to know he's the most important person in my life, because I want to be one of the most important in his.

This is definitely a good start.

"ALRIGHT CHICK, when you get done with your shower, we'll head out for some lunch and then we can go get our nails done if you want?" I offer. Getting my nails done is something I truly enjoy, and given the amount of times Kels asks me about it, I'm pretty sure she likes it too.

"Just gonna go grab my clothes." She runs into the room that Caleb calls hers when she spends the night.

Sitting down on the couch, I pull up a girlie show on Netflix I've been watching the last few weeks, before texting Caleb.

R: *Kels and I are using your apartment so she can take a shower before we go get our nails done. She was really hot when I went to pick her up.*

I expect for it to take a little time for him to text me back, but to my surprise it doesn't. Must be a slow day for him.

C: *Do whatever you need to, baby. That's why I gave you a key.*

Most days I can't get over the way he talks to me, and today is no exception to that. I haven't seen him in two days and I miss him. Our schedules have been off a little from one another.

C: *Maybe you can come back when you get done? Not seeing you for two days is not working for me.*

R: *Funny, hot stuff, it's not working for me either. I miss you.*

Texting isn't the same as hearing his deep voice, not the same as feeling his fingers against my skin, feeling the warmth of his body pressed to mine.

C: *I miss your face too, Red. Send me a pic?*

The smile that's spread across my face can't be denied. The fluttery feeling in my stomach can't be denied either. I've waited my whole life for a man to make me feel this way, and I'm so happy the man to do it is Caleb Harrison. Holding my phone up, I give him my best smile, along with a wink into the camera. Hitting a few buttons, I send it, and wait for him to get back with me. A few minutes later, I get a response from him. A picture of his smiling face.

I allow a smile back at him, wanting to pinch myself to make sure I'm not dreaming. His brown eyes, the color of bourbon, sparkle as he grins. There's a small dimple in his left cheek, and he's got a five-o'clock shadow coloring his deeply tanned skinned, even though it's only early afternoon. His lips are full, like he's been licking them most of the day, and I can't wait until I put a kiss on them. If anyone had told me when I went into The Café that day, that I'd end up with Caleb, I would have told them they were crazy. Yet, here I am, having the time of my life.

"Ruby, can you braid my hair?" Kelsea asks as she comes into the living room, carrying a brush and a hair tie.

"Sure, let me finish this, and then we'll get it done."

R: *Kelsea is done. I'll see you tonight?*

We hadn't been planning on seeing one another, but now that I know we're both thinking the same thing, I can't help but want to see him.

C: *Be at my apartment when I get off, babe. I go off-shift at 6:30*

Looking at the clock, I know Kelsea and I will have plenty of time to get our stuff done together.

"Alright, come over here, and we'll get you fixed up."

Kelsea sits in front of me, crossing her legs. "Can you do a braid in the front?"

"So you don't want all your hair braided? Just some of it?" I verify as I brush her hair.

"I want it the way you had your hair the other day."

I wish I had my curling wand with me, because then I could curl the rest that's not going in the braid, and she could look like me. "We'll get it right." I motion for her to turn around and get to work. Because I do my hair like this all the time, I'm done in a few minutes. "There ya go!"

We grab our stuff and leave Caleb's apartment, setting out for our adventure.

"The Café good for lunch?" I question as we head toward downtown.

"It's where we always go." She nods. "I love their chocolate milkshakes."

"I think after the afternoon you had at practice, you probably deserve a milkshake."

"Caleb always lets me get them too," she admits, a smile on her face. "Mom and Dad don't like for me to have so much sugar, but it's my favorite."

"That's because Caleb and I are the cool couple." I think of Karina and Mason.

Something tells me they aren't as serious as they like to make people think they are. They probably have a damn good time when it's just them, but they try to set a good example for Kelsea.

"You are, you two let me do everything my parents won't let me do."

That's the fun part of not being the parent, but I don't tell her that. Parking at The Café, I turn the car off. "Let's go eat!"

"YOU HOME?" I announce myself as I enter Caleb's apartment. I saw his Jeep outside, but that doesn't mean he's not with Morgan working out. Since our texts earlier, I've wanted nothing more than to see him.

"Yeah." He comes out of his bedroom, towel around his waist, water making rivers along the ripples in his skin. "Just got here."

"I can see that." I lick my lips as I make a feast out of his body.

"You see something you like, Red?" His grin is mischievous. He knows I like his body, knows I love to explore it, and knows exactly what it can do to me.

"Sometimes I just can't believe you're all mine," I inhale deeply as I say the words.

"Believe it, babe, you got me."

For some reason those words affect me in a way that I have to cross the room, fold him into my arms, and hold him close to me. Every day he goes out into the field to protect the people of this town, I worry about him, know that no matter what he's doing, he's living his dream, but when I get to see him at the end of a shift? It's the best feeling, because I know he's okay. I know he's made it, and we're going to have more seconds, minutes, hours, and days together.

"Hey, what's wrong?" He tilts my face up to his, those brown eyes searching mine.

"Nothing." I shake my head, voice thick. "Just really happy to see you today."

The smile he gives me is my favorite kind. It's huge, shows a small dimple in his cheek and works it's way up to his eyes. "I'm happy to see you too. Favorite part of any day I have, Red. You've gotta know that. You've made my life better."

Resting my head against his chest, I close my eyes and breathe in the after shave he still uses. Somehow those words seem like an omen, but I'm not sure if it's good or bad. All I know is I want tonight and every other night with him, and I'll make sure he always knows it.

CHAPTER TWENTY-SIX

CRUISE

I LOVE the smile on Kelsea's face, love even more that I'm the one who put it there. "You excited Kels?" I grin into the rearview as we make the drive to Birmingham.

"So excited, like I knew you knew him." She bounces in her seat. "But I didn't really *know*!"

Him references my college roommate Slater Harlow, known by everyone who watches professional baseball as *Savage*. He's a formidable force on the baseball diamond, having the best season of his career. We're not as close as we once were, because life took us two totally different directions, but we still hang out every once in a while. Typically I like to keep the fact I know him from just about everyone, because I know he values his privacy. Now though? Kels is old enough to go to a major league game, and I'm doing my best to impress Ruby.

"I've known him a long time." I think back to our college days, how both of us had been so damn homesick. Him more than me, since I could at least head home on the weekend. Slater was from Georgia, his parents not well-off at all, and he'd never been able to afford a quick trip home. Hell, he barely went home in the summer, instead choosing to stay on-campus and work odd jobs to make money for the next semester. It was no surprise to me that our senior year he'd opted himself for the draft and gone pro. Within two years, he was the starting right-fielder for the Birmingham Bandits, racking up hits, RBIs, and a ton of fans. Now, it's my pleasure to see my good friend do as well as he is.

"He was your roommate?" Ruby asks as she reaches over and grabs my hand.

I love when she grabs my hand on any drive we make together. Being connected to her makes me calmer than I've ever been. Something about the connection quiets my brain and eases any anxiety I feel. "Yup, up until our senior year, then he opted to join the draft and I got a single room. Which worked out perfect for all that booty I got being a football player." I grin over at Ruby who shakes her head, now used to the way I talk.

"You're so bad, and you're so lucky I'm not jealous anymore over what you did before you met me."

"What does booty mean?" Kelsea asks from the backseat.

"Yeah, babe." Ruby gives me a smart-ass grin. "Why don't you tell her what booty means?"

Fuck my life. "It means spending time with someone you really like." I glance over at Ruby, sticking my tongue out at her for putting me in this position. "Like I spend time with Ruby."

"You mean like Mom and Dad spend time together?"

"Kind of, but whatever you do, don't say anything to them about getting booty. This will be one of our sibling secrets." I reach back, my pinky finger extended to her. "Got it?"

"Got it." She grabs hold of my pinky in hers and we swear on it.

For the rest of the drive, I keep my damn mouth shut about college.

AS WE APPROACH THE STADIUM, I follow the signs that go with the parking pass I was given from Slater. I can feel the excitement in the Jeep as we are told to break apart from the pack and follow a much smaller line of cars to a private parking area.

"Are we in the family parking?" Ruby asks, glancing around at the cars surrounding us. They're definitely nicer than my Rubicon, but I refuse to feel like I don't belong.

"I think so." I put it in park, grab my hat and sunglasses, before I hop out. "C'mon, ladies, let's get this show on the road."

Opening the back, I help Kelsea down, and then go around to Ruby's side, doing the same with her.

"Look at you being such a gentleman," Ruby teases, reaching in and grabbing her bag. She's a teacher, for sure. My mom carries the same bag everywhere. I call it a GO bag, because no matter what you might need, it's probably inside that bag. You need a band-aid? They got it. A bottle of water? No problem. A poncho? Definitely in there. A sewing kit? No big deal, it's fucking secured to the side with a magnet. Teachers are better than any Boy Scout I've ever met. When the world ends, I don't need a prepper, give me a damn teacher, any day of the week. Securing it crossbody, she pushes her hair back behind her ears. "We're ready."

"What do you mean, look at me being a gentleman? I'm always polite. You know this." I put my hand out for Kelsea to hold it as we cross the parking lot. I don't want to lose her here, so she's gonna have to be embarrassed by holding her big brother's hand. "C'mon, Cupcake, you got your stuff?"

She holds up the shirt she wants signed and the pink sharpie she wants it signed in. "Got it!"

"Let's go." I hitch my chin to the gate.

Ruby

My heart is so full as I watch the two of them cross the parking lot, Kelsea's hand in his. They're speaking to one another, Caleb leaning down so he can hear her. Quickly, I take my phone out and capture a picture of the two of them, sending it over to Karina, since she's not here to witness this.

As they get to the gate, Kelsea turns around. "C'mon, Ruby!"

I jog to catch up with them. It's a blur as Caleb leads us through some corridors, flashing a badge here and there. Eventually we come to a hallway and standing there is the guy I recognize as *Savage* Harlow. He's almost dressed for the game, wearing a pair of baseball pants, cleats, and a shirt with the arms cut out. It's probably too hot for him to wear the full uniform right now. Kelsea stops in her tracks, letting go of Caleb's hand, turning back to me.

"Kels." He reaches back for her, but she comes to me, hiding behind my leg. I've never seen her do this before, but I recognize it. This is something I did when I was a small child and I was shy to meet someone who meant a lot to me.

"She's a little shy." I run my hand over her hair. "I think she'll be good in a few minutes."

The way she clings to me, makes my heart flutter, my stomach clinch. If Caleb and I ever have a child, is this what it's going to be like? I can see it in the future, but I know I don't want to get ahead of myself.

"It's good to see you, man." Caleb walks up to Slater, giving his hand a shake and pulling him in for a hug.

"You too." Slater slaps him on the shoulder. He glances over at us. "Is that Kelsea? I haven't seen her since she was a baby."

"You knew me as a baby?" That makes her move from behind my leg and causes her to speak up.

"Yeah." He squats down so that he's at eye-level with her. "Last time I saw you, you were about two years old. We used to hang out with you all the time. Your mom and dad would bring you when they came to visit your brother."

She looks up at me. "I think I'm okay, I've known him a long time." She holds out her shirt and her sharpie. "Can you sign this for me?"

Caleb and I share a laugh and a grin over her head. All the shyness that was there before is gone now. She's asking him questions and asked to be taken out onto the field. "Yeah." Slater stands. "We can go toss a ball real quick, if that's okay with your brother."

"Sounds good to me," he answers when everyone looks at him.

As we walk to the field, Slater turns around. "I don't know your name yet and I'm sorry to have been rude, I'm Slater."

"This is my girlfriend, Ruby," Caleb introduces us, putting an arm around my shoulder.

"He's gonna marry her." Kelsey giggles before she runs off.

"Is that right?" Slater gives Caleb a look, before he turns around and runs off after her.

"I know she's kidding and pushing what she wants, off onto you," I tell him, letting him know that as much as my heart wants it to happen, I'm putting no pressure on him.

"Slater will take her mind off of it, he doesn't like to talk about relationships," he tells me as we walk to the field. "He and his high school girlfriend couldn't make the long-distance thing work. As far as I know, he's never gotten over it and given having a relationship another shot."

I watch Slater as he throws a ball back and forth between him and Kelsea. Her smile is huge, as is his when they laugh at something one of them say.

"Hopefully one day he'll find what we have." I hook my arms around his waist, holding him tightly.

"That's my hope too." He leans down, kissing me on the forehead.

"ONE MORE OUT!" I look over at Kelsea, who's literally vibrating in the seat between me and Caleb. "Can you believe it? They're going to win your first ever Major League Baseball game. How exciting is this?"

She jumps up and down as the final out is made and fireworks erupt over the stadium. We'd had great seats, given to us by Slater, behind the Bandit's dugout. As we're gathering our stuff to leave, I hear someone yell *Harrison*.

We all turn around and see Slater standing there. He motions for Kelsea to come down, holding out a ball to her. I'm not sure what he says, but it gets him a huge smile, and when she comes back holding the ball, I'm beyond thankful to have experienced this day with the two of them.

"Y'all ready?" he asks after waving to his friend. "It'll be at least a few hours before we get home, and the longer we put it off, the worse it will be."

"Let's go." I grab some of the stuff we bought and we slowly make our way up the stands as the massive group of people begin filing out.

It's been a great day, I realize as we hit the interstate, heading north. The

Bandits won by two runs, we got to spend time together, and I got to experience my first baseball game. As I lean back with a huge smile on my face, I don't know that this is the last day everything will be normal for us, and reality is about to make itself known in a big way.

CHAPTER TWENTY-SEVEN
CRUISE

THE JULY SUN is beating down on the pavement as I make my drive around the streets that make up Laurel Springs. It's been a boring day, for the most part, but I'm not stupid enough to think it'll last. Lately it's been slow and I've been feeling a lot like the other shoe might drop. This nagging feeling hasn't let go for the last week, but I know eventually either that shoe will drop or I'll get over it.

Rain came through over an hour ago, but it did nothing to cool the day down. It's now a sauna outside. In certain parts there's actually steam coming up off the road. Behind the sun that's moved in, you can see more clouds behind. A dark hazy threat looming in the background, more storms are moving in. The stillness of the day threatens to break wide open when they do.

Because of the heat that's been baking the ground and asphalt for days, most people are inside this afternoon, enjoying the air conditioning and not wanting to have heatstroke. Probably one of the reasons the radio has been quiet for the most part. As I make a turn onto the state highway, I hear dispatch come over the radio.

"Calvert County is requesting assistance. They initiated a traffic stop on a blue Tahoe. When they opened the back, it was full of moonshine. Be advised the suspect shot the officer who pulled him over, and they are traveling at a high rate of speed toward Laurel County. He should be entering in the next few minutes. The officer was pronounced dead on scene. Proceed with extreme caution."

My ears perk up, because I'm the one who's going to cut him off. I'm right where Laurel and Calvert counties intersect. Immediately I feel my adrenaline start to kick in. I grip the steering wheel so hard my knuckles are white. Controlling my breathing is easy, it's something I've conditioned myself to do, but the pounding in my heart? It's a rhythm that doesn't slow as I hit the button and speak to dispatch on the other end of the line.

"Dispatch, I'm where the suspect will enter. Should I deploy spike strips?"

"Negative." I hear Havoc's voice come over the radio. "He's moving too fast for you to get them out. With the road conditions it's risky and he might hit you. He'll be to you in the next two minutes. Take over the pursuit from Calvert County. Make sure that dashboard cam is on and activate that body cam, Cruise. I'll be there as soon as I can."

Doing as my boss has instructed me, I make sure everything is on and recording. My adrenaline pumps harder and I realize I had just been thinking about how boring this day was. Seems like business is about to pick up. I shoot up a little prayer that we all make it out of this as I get ready to take over.

I can hear the sirens before I can see them, but the Tahoe is a blur of blue as it passes in front of me. Like I was instructed to do, I pick up the pursuit. The Calvert County Deputies respectfully stop, and the police package is going through the gears as we pick up speed. Road conditions are hazardous, but I'm used to driving in them; I've been trained on how to handle any situation that presents itself to me. I have no doubt I can handle this one. "Heading east, toward the downtown district," I give the other guys my position, knowing that on this day everyone is spread out around the county. However, they'll all be making their way toward me, now that they know the chase has entered Laurel County.

"Caleb," dispatch comes across. "Be careful, they're trying to get to you. Havoc is closest, but according to GPS he's still ten minutes away."

I know this means I have to take care of whatever happens myself. This is what I've been training for since I started. I don't need anyone to help take up the slack. If I can't handle this, then this shouldn't be my job.

Calmly I relay the directions in which we're moving toward downtown, and I realize soon he's going to be in front of The Café, and there's construction going on down there. He'll be pinned in, but he won't realize it until he's right up on it. I start motioning with my arm, but he doesn't notice, and as we round the corner, there's a sickening thud as he hits the concrete barrier, the front-end of the SUV taking the brunt of the impact. Because of the slick roads, he slid right into it. There's smoke billowing from under the hood, the front crunched in a way that I wonder if the driver's legs are broken. I can see the airbag has been deployed from where I am, but I can also see movement, and I don't want him to get the drop on me. Taking cover behind my own driver's door, I steel my nerves and put some authority in my voice.

"GET out of the car with your hands up!"

The driver's side door is open, and all I want is for them to put their hands up and get out of the car. Or at least hold off until my backup can get here. I don't have time to assess injuries, because I'm hesitant to move forward without the safety of the door protecting me.

"Driver!" I yell again. "Get out of the vehicle and put your hands up!"

There's authority in my voice. I'm doing what I'm trained to do. In my peripheral vision I can see that everyone in The Café is crowded around the plate glass window, looking out at what's going on. For a split second, I let my attention move to the window. There, I see my mom and Kelsea standing there, both with shock written across their faces, fear in their eyes. Desperately I want them to move back, I want Leigh to grab them and take them away from whatever this potential danger might be. This man supposedly has a gun and they're standing like open targets at a shootout. When I get out of this, me and Dad are going to have a discussion with both of them.

"Fuck you!" I hear from the smoking vehicle. The voice is as strong as mine, so I have to assume the driver isn't hurt. He's here to put up a fight, and I have to take whatever fight that may be seriously.

"Driver!" I try again. This time adding, "Come out with your hands up, facing away from me."

It's a split second. Literally five seconds out of an entire lifetime that happens in front of me. He comes from behind the driver's side door, holding his gun pointed on me. It's like a movie flashes through my brain. Meeting Kari for the first time, graduating, winning my first football game at Alabama, meeting Kelsea, watching her take her first steps, say Caleb for the first time, and then my dad. I remember all the things my dad has done for me. In my mind I hear him say I love you, and finally it's Ruby. The way she smiled up at me last night as I sheathed myself inside her. The way her head tilted back as she gave herself over to the feelings we invoke in each other. I never told her I love her, and right now, I might never get the chance to. I have to push all those things out of my head and concentrate on what's happening in front of me right now. Taking control of the situation is of the utmost importance, and I can't have all of the noise. Locking all of it away, I put some bass in my voice this time.

"Put it down," I command.

He doesn't though, he holds what looks to be a glock up, takes aim, and I know the second he decides to fire. It's like I can see across the hood of my vehicle into his eyes. I see there's no other way this can go. He's not going down without a fight, and there's a choice I have to make. It's either him or me. If I want to go home to my family tonight, I have to decide if I'm willing to take this shot. All those people in The Café are in danger, they're counting on me to protect them. The enormity of the situation sends rivulets of sweat down the back of my bullet proof vest. There's not time to second guess my decision because it's then that I hear the crack of the gun firing explode against the stillness of the day.

When he fires, I shift my weight, take aim, and fire too. His shot hits me in the vest, and I'm propelled a few feet backward as I take the impact of the handgun he was in possession of. My shot hits him in the chest, and as he falls, I think it's fatal. I struggle to my feet as I get up, walking over to where he is, my gun still drawn, pain radiating from where I've been hit. I hear the murmurs of patrons, I'm assuming that have come out from the businesses on Main Street. When I get to him, I can see he's not breathing, but I reach down and check his pulse anyway. As I suspected, my shot was fatal. Kicking the gun out of his reach, I finally key the mic.

"Dispatch, be advised, shots fired," I'm panting into the radio.

"Caleb!" I hear Havoc's voice on the radio. "Are you okay?"

I'm trying to get my breath to answer him, unhooking the vest from around my ribs, inhaling a deep gasp of air. I sink to the asphalt, letting the concrete barrier hold me up, as I try to get my surroundings, try to breathe without it shooting pain through my ribs and as I tilt my head back to the sky, thunder cracks loudly and rain falls in sheets, covering everything.

"Caleb?" This time it's Renegade's voice.

I can't make myself get up, can't make myself move from where I am. Shock is a crazy thing, and I'm so damn tired. It's the adrenaline high coming down, my body trying to absorb the crazy amounts that were flowing through me as the situation unfolded.

"I'm okay, he got me in the vest, but I need an investigator on scene. Suspect is deceased."

I'm in shock as I say the words, not fully able to believe this has just happened. I'm not stupid. I know the risk I take every day, the potential for something like this to happen every time I go on shift. I just honestly didn't think today would be the day. Which I guess no one ever thinks it'll be the day, but I can't help but think about how I was bemoaning the fact it'd been a slow day.

It's a blur as people start pouring out of The Café and backup finally arrives. My gun is taken away from me, and as per protocol, I'm placed on administrative leave immediately. Morgan is there though, checking me over, making sure the vest did its job. And it's in that moment, I hear a small voice screaming my name.

Kelsea is running from The Café toward me at full speed, Karina is on her heels, and both are crying as they hit me hard, each taking me in their arms.

I allow myself to bury my head in my mom's neck, allow my baby sister to hold me around the legs, and as they pull me back behind the side wall of The Café, away from prying eyes I let it go. I cry, I cry like I haven't cried since I was pulled over by Ace and I had to face my dad with all the shit I'd done as a teenager. Huge sobs wrack my body and out of nowhere, I feel strong arms wrap around us, and I know Dad is there. He's holding us all as I cry like a baby in my mom's arms.

"I'm sorry," I choke out. "So damn sorry."

His voice is near my ear, and I hear every word he says. "Don't you be sorry, Caleb. You saved a lot of people today, including your mom and sister. Never apologize for doing your job."

But I know me, and I know it's going to take me a while to be okay with this. And I know something else too – I'm fucked up, and I have no idea how to process any of this.

Ruby

"What happened today?" My voice is shrill to my own ears, but I've heard rumors all day. I hadn't been anywhere near The Café when the incident happened with Caleb, so I've had to hear it second hand each time. Right now, all I want is to be with the man I love and make sure he's okay. I tried to be polite and knock on his door, but when he wouldn't answer, I used the key he gave me and let myself in. What I'd found scared me.

Caleb sitting on the couch, nursing a beer, still wearing his clothes from this afternoon, some of them still partially wet.

"He pointed a gun at me," he says the words blankly, without emotion, and that's what's bothering me more than anything. The lack of emotion. I'm pretty sure he's still in shock, but I don't know how to help him, not sure how I can make this better for him. Part of me wants to call Morgan, the other part of me is scared to leave Caleb alone long enough for me to do that.

"He was going to kill me." He swallows hard. "All I could think about was you and my family. What would happen with you all if I wasn't here anymore. Would you find someone to take my place? Would Kelsea remember me in ten years? How would Dad take it? I mean so much shit went through my head. It was like a highlight reel of my life, like someone was playing it at my funeral. Every bit of it was so surreal, Ruby Red. Every bit of it. It was like an out of body experience that I couldn't get away from. A dream I couldn't wake up from."

"What can I do to help you, Caleb?" I grab his cheeks, forcing him to face me. "What do you need from me?"

"I'm so fucked up right now." He gets up from the couch, quickly going to the kitchen and grabbing another beer. "I don't know what I need. All I know is I fucking killed a man, Ruby. I killed a man. You want me touching you? Do you want to go to bed with a man who ended another life? Can you honestly say you can live with me knowing I did that? Because I'm not sure I can live with myself right now."

"You killed a criminal who had warrants out of five counties and an attempted murder charge, along with the fact he killed another deputy today. You saved what could have been a mass killing situation, you're a hero, Caleb."

"A hero?" I see tears pool in his eyes. "I don't feel like a damn hero right now."

"You're in shock, you have to give yourself time to work through this, to recover. You've got to give yourself a break. No one says you have to digest this whole situation tonight, right now."

He takes another drink of his beer, and I'm at a loss on how to help him. I'm not sure what I can do to break through the bullshit he seems to be stuck on. He's looking at this the wrong way.

"How's that going to help his family recover?" His voice is hoarse as he asks me this question. I can tell it bothers him, and to be honest it bothers me too, but I can't let him stay locked in his head like this. It isn't healthy.

"How do we even know he had a family?" I point out. Not much has been released about the man Caleb took down today.

"Well then that just makes it all better, doesn't it?" He gives me a look that so smartass I'd like to smack him across the face. This isn't the man I know, the man I've fallen in love with. I've never told him, but I do love him. Love everything about him.

"You don't have to be so mean, Caleb."

The look on his face isn't one I've ever seen before, and suddenly I'm scared. More scared and worried than I had been this afternoon. I wonder what it's going to take to make him believe he's not a monster. Am I strong enough to pull him out of this? Will my love be enough to make him see? Right now I'm doubting it, but I can't let him know that. I can't let him know that I'm scared. Right now I have to be the strong one for him, because he's always been the strong one for me.

"Sweetheart, this is the real Caleb, he's just been on his best behavior so he can fuck the shit out of you. Surprise and sorry about your luck."

And that's when I know that not only is my heart broken, but his is too, and I have zero idea how to fix it or make it right. I refuse to believe this is him, and tonight, I also refuse to let him wallow in his pity alone. He wants to drink himself silly? Then I'll drink right along with him. Kicking my shoes off, I stalk over to the fridge and grab my own beer.

"You're not doing this alone, Caleb."

"You're cute if you think you're gonna stop me."

"Try me, because maybe I've been on my best behavior too. You push me, and I'll push back. You might not like it, but you're not going to be alone tonight."

"Fuck it." He takes a drink from his bottle. "Do whatever you think you have to, but this changes nothing."

"That's where you're wrong. This afternoon, it changed everything."

"Good that you found out now, Ruby."

It doesn't escape me that he doesn't call me Ruby Red, but that's okay. I'll get my name back, just like I'll get him back. With patience and love.

CHAPTER TWENTY-EIGHT

RUBY

I'M SITTING in my car watching Morgan and Caleb eat through The Café window. This is what I've been reduced to. It's been a week since the shooting, and so far, Caleb's refused to see me. I went to see him the other night, and it was a bad scene.

"What are you doing here?" Caleb opens his door, arms crossed over his chest. "I figured me not answering any of your calls let you know I'm not up to talking to anyone right now. Including you."

Not gonna lie, this hurts. Seeing him like this hurts, hearing him talk to me the way he is hurts. But I won't give up on him. I promised Kelsea months ago that I would be here if he needed me, that I could handle whatever was thrown at me.

"You need me," I talk against the tightness in my throat.

"I need to be left the fuck alone. You. Mom. Dad. You all need to leave me the fuck alone."

"We won't," I shake my head standing my ground. "We won't leave you alone to deal with this by yourself."

"Fine, then if you won't leave, I will."

I watch helplessly as he puts his shoes on, grabs his wallet, and storms out. Once I'm there by myself, I clean up, making myself busy until I realize he's not coming back. Finally I take myself to his bed, tuck his pillow under my chin, and cry it all out.

When I wake up alone the next morning, I know he hasn't been back, and I know he won't until I'm gone. It's sobering, and it's not the best feeling in the world. But he won't push me away that easily.

That fear of rejection is still here, but I've finally decided that I don't care. He's sent every one of my calls to voicemail. Any text I've sent has gone unanswered, and I'm beyond frustrated.

I can't understand why he's pushing me away, when even sitting here like I am, staring at him from a distance, I can see he needs me. He and Morgan drove separately; I see both their vehicles. I plan on confronting him when he leaves – I'm beyond sick of being ignored.

Some may say I'm crazy, and maybe that's a fact, but I know this man. I know him better than I know myself, and he needs me, I need him, and I've got to get him to see reason. Before we have nothing else to fight for.

Morgan gets up, throwing some money on the counter, before he walks out to his vehicle and leaves. He's in his EMT uniform, so he must either be reporting for duty, or he's got to be somewhere. Caleb is slower, and I can't help but think maybe that's a little help from the big guy upstairs, maybe he's helping me get this man I care for so much alone.

As I see Caleb start to come outside, I get out of my car and go over to his driver's side door, waiting patiently until he can see me.

"Red?"

The nickname slips from his lips, I can tell because it looks like he wants to put it back where it came from. But I don't let him. "Yeah, it's me. Ya know, the person who's been by your side for the past few months. Ruby Red?"

A wall is erected between the two of us. He switches off his emotions, holding himself rigid as he looks at me. "We have nothing to talk about."

"We have *everything* to talk about, starting with why you won't see me, why you won't talk to me, and what the fuck's going on inside your head right now."

"Nothing you want to get involved in."

"How do you know, Caleb? You won't tell me, you won't talk to me. I have literally zero idea what's going on there, and it's all because you've decided I can't handle it."

"You can't," he yells. "Because I can't."

"Don't decide what I can and can't do. I don't appreciate it."

He fumes, I can tell by the way his face is red, the way his hands clench into fists at his sides. "I can't live with myself, Ruby, how can I expect you to live with me?"

"What you need to do is realize this is when you need me, not when you need to push me away. Please Caleb," I beg. I break down and beg, something I promised myself I wouldn't do. "I don't want to see you hurt like this, please just let me be there for you."

"So people can talk about you behind your back? I know people are talking. Mom and Kelsea are upset about it. I don't want you to be upset about it too. What if we had kids, Ruby? How would they handle it?" His voice is hoarse. "How would they be able to separate their dad from the man I was?"

"Easy! The same way you do. What the fuck is going on here?"

"I don't know." He puts his hands up to his forehead. "All I know is I can't stand for you to look at me with that fucking pity in your eyes. It reminds me too much of how people looked at me when they realized I didn't have a mom. I don't want to be that poor, pitiful guy, twice in my life."

"You aren't, you idiot, and if you'd get your head out of your ass, you would see that."

I'm losing the battle, I can tell. He's retreating and there's nothing I can do to bring him back. The Caleb I know isn't there right now; he's somewhere untouchable, and all I can hope for is that we can bring him back.

"I'll wait for you," I tell him. "Wait until you can figure out what's going on in your head, wait until you see it's all clear."

"Don't." He holds up his hand, like he wants to run his thumb along my lip, the way he always used to. "Don't wait for me."

"Why can't you touch me?" The tears pool and fall. I miss it, miss his touch, the easy way he had to be touching me all the time. I crave it, want it badly, can't understand why he's punishing both of us.

"Because I can't touch you with this blood on my hands. Red, you're everything good and pure. I'll fuck you up too."

"You're not fucked up," I argue. "You're in shock over what you did, and you're trying to process it. Stop pushing me away and let me help you."

I reach out to grab his arm and he pulls it away, pushing me when I get too close. "Don't push me away."

"Don't make me hurt you." His voice is deep, dark, and full of something I've never heard before.

"You're already hurting me." I pull my arms around my waist. "I gave it all to you, Caleb, everything. The good, the bad, and the ugly. And you only want to give me the good, how is that fair?"

"Life isn't fair, Ruby, and it's better you learn that now, rather than five years from now when we're married and you hate me enough to divorce me."

"Where is this shit even coming from in your head?"

"I've seen it."

"And you've also seen your parents have a great relationship. Don't lump me in with people who can't handle it. Do you not remember who I was the first night I met your dad? The person I was the night you almost didn't get that guy cuffed." I wipe the tears out of my eyes, wipe them off my face. "I understand that you're drifting right now. You don't have a job you can go to, you're worried people are going to label you something you aren't. I get that, but don't you give up on me."

"How can I not give up on you, when I've already given up on myself."

That's when he gets in his Jeep, leaving me there crying. Letting me watch the taillights in the darkness of the night as he drives out of my life. As I look at the people watching me, I feel like a freakshow. Like everyone knows something I don't.

He'll come back, he has to, because what we have is too good to throw away. He'll see he's a hero, he'll believe it, and then he'll realize just how much he needs me.

That's what I keep telling myself as I walk to my car, compose myself, and drive away.

Cruise

It's hard to explain to everyone who keeps asking what exactly is going on in my head. There are so many thoughts and emotions I have swimming through the noise. It reminds me how I felt when my friend died in high school, and I'm trying desperately not to let myself turn down that destructive path again. I'm feeling guilt for taking another man's life. Pride for making sure my community is safe. Denial in what I did could have been prevented, and partially dirty at the blood on my hands.

I don't want to corrupt Ruby or anyone else with what I've done, but it's hard to live with. Knowing I ended another man's life is inherently shocking, and while I wait for the internal review, I'm increasingly worried they're going to say I had another option.

That's what's driving me right now. The fear that I did have another option.

The fear that I made the wrong decision.

The fear that I'm one of those cops who didn't think about the consequences before he committed an action that can't be reversed.

Until I know where I stand on what I've done, I can't come to Ruby clean, I can't be at peace with my decision, and I sure as fuck can't be expected to go on with my day-to-day like nothing happened.

Because it did. A man is dead. I shot him.

And I still have no idea whether it was justifiable or not.

My career and life lay in the balance of what the internal investigators find. They hold my entire life in their hands, and I'm nervous as fuck that they won't see it the way I did.

If they don't, my life and career as I know it is over, and I definitely won't be the man that Ruby thought I was. That's possibly the hardest part I'll ever have to come to terms with. So right now, it's easier to think I'm a fucker, rather than letting her know I care way more than I should.

CHAPTER TWENTY-NINE

CRUISE

"HOW'D YOU GET IN HERE?"

My dad is waiting on me, probably ready to rip me a new one, just like Ruby did. I'm so not in the mood for it tonight.

"You don't need to know how I got in here." He gets up from where he's sitting on my couch. "Instead, what we need to do is talk about how we're going to get you to where you need to be."

"What the fuck is that supposed to mean? This is me."

"This isn't you, we both know that. I didn't raise you to be a fuck face. You haven't been answering my calls, your mom's, Kelsea's, or come to find out Ruby's, so let's talk about this Caleb. What the fuck is going on?"

"Nothing." I grind my teeth together, not wanting to do this with him.

"We've done this once before son, and we won't do it again. Do you remember when your friend died? Remember when you pushed everyone away? How'd that work out for you?"

"How does having a murderer for a son work out for you?" I fire back at him. "Because I'm on administrative leave for committing murder."

"No." He shakes his head. "You aren't. You're on administrative leave for using deadly force related to your job. They are two different things, Caleb. Two very different things."

"They don't feel like different things," I argue as the door opens behind me.

I turn around, seeing Morgan standing there. His inked arms folded over his chest. His eyes meet my dad's. "Figured you might need some help and wanted to offer it in case you did."

"So what? You two gonna gang up on me, confront me like Ruby just did?

Let me cut you to the bone with the venom I'm gonna spew? We all know I'm a fucker when backed into a corner. I strike first, ask questions later. You wanna confront me? You better be ready to take it."

Dad comes to stand in front of me. "You've been like this since you were a kid. Always trying to strike first, always trying to deliver that blow before it's dealt to you, but I swear to you, that's not what's happening here. Let me explain."

"There's nothing to explain," I yell. "I shot a man and it's fucked me up."

"It's not the first thing that's ever fucked you up, Caleb," Dad starts. "You wanna go back to the beginning? Lay this shit down at my feet. Blame me. I'm the one who started it. I've told you before I shoulda given you away and not kept you for my own selfish reasons. I kept you, even when I deployed to a war I wasn't sure I was going to come back from. I wasn't a perfect parent, I put you through shit you're probably still trying to deal with today. You wanna *start* at the beginning? Blame me. Let's get this all out. If you ain't gonna listen to me, then fuckin' cut me down, and when you're done, I'll tell you what you need to know. I've been here, I've done this. Maybe not as a member of the MTF, but I've killed to live. When you're faced with the decision, you make it. I'm a big man." He sits down on my couch and spreads his arms wide. "I can take it. Whatever you want to dish out. I can take."

He points at his chest. "Give it to me, don't give it the women you love."

"I never told her I love her." My throat gets tight. "That was the one thing that kept rolling through my head when that guy pointed that gun at me," I admit. "I never told her I love her."

"And if you keep pushing her away–" Morgan's voice is gentle at my back "–you're never going to be able to. Now I know what your dad's gonna tell you. Shut the fuck up and listen. Then you'll get a chance to make this shit right with Ruby, and this fucker won't win. Just give him a chance."

I look between the two of them.

"If you still feel the need to let loose when I'm done, I'm here," Dad says, his words strained. "I'm always here. Just give me five minutes."

"Okay," I agree. "What is it you need to tell me?"

"The deputies in Calvert County are familiar with him, they've dealt with him on numerous occasions. He's been threatening suicide by cop for the last two months, but they've been able to deescalate the situation every time it's arisen. We didn't have that background info, man. None of us knew it, and all you knew was a man was pointing a gun at you. You did what you're trained to do, you did what any of us would have done. If it hadn't happened when it did, it would have happened later. He would have kept putting himself into situations that escalated to where no one had a choice. He left Calvert County knowing what he was doing."

The admission hits me straight in the chest. It does make it easier, but it doesn't fully erase all of my guilt. "At least I know I was never going to have a choice, but it still doesn't change the fact I killed a man."

"No, you weren't, and it doesn't," Dad agrees. "He was going to force someone to do it, and you were that person. If you hadn't of, who knows what he would have done to force someone. There were all those innocent people at The Café, including your mother and sister. Would you have been happier if he pulled his gun on one of them? Or God forgive, shot one of them?"

I swallow roughly, not wanting to comprehend what he's asking me. "No, God no. I couldn't live with myself if I didn't protect them."

"Regardless of if you want to hear it or not, you saved lives. You saved a lot of lives, and you'll get medal for it."

"I don't feel like I deserve a medal."

"You will." Morgan claps his hand on my back. "When the shock wears off and it can all sink in, you'll realize that what you did was heroic. You'll realize that not many people would have acted as quickly as you did, and in acting that quickly you were a hero. No one blames you man, we just want to see you get better. We want to see you with Ruby, and happy."

Ruby. Her name affects me unlike anything else ever has. "She hates me."

"She doesn't hate you," Dad and Morgan say at the same time.

"She's a good woman," Dad keeps on. "She'll forgive you, but that doesn't mean you won't have to work for it."

I'll have to get her trust back, because right now I've walked all over it without even thinking about how this affected her.

"For God's sakes," Morgan chuckles. "Tell her you love her. All of us have known how you feel about her for at least the past five months, let her in on the secret."

I tilt my head back, my emotions getting the better of me.

"Before I leave..." Dad reaches beside him on the couch. "Here's your gun and badge back. You've been cleared. Havoc said to give you a few more days off work, but if you want it, your spot is still available. Look–" he puts his hands on my face, forcing me to meet his eyes. "I know this shit's hard. It's never easy, but it's important. The work we do is important, and you'll never know how proud I am that you chose to follow in my footsteps, but if it's not for you Caleb, there's no shame in getting out. I'm not gonna love you any less. You're my first-born, my only son. Having you turned me into the person I am today, and you're always gonna be my best friend, no matter what you do."

Now I'm really trying to keep the emotions from getting to me. "I just want to make you proud, and I felt like what I did wasn't honorable. Maybe I could have done something else, ended it peacefully."

"You. Could. Not. Have. You did everything right, son."

I sniffle slightly because this has been weighing so heavily on my heart.

"Then I'll call Havoc and let him know I'll be back the first of next week. There's some things I have to do. Like get Ruby back."

"Hey," I yell at Dad as he turns to leave. He stops, cocking his head to the side. "Thank you."

"No problem. I love you, son."

"Love you too." I'm finding those words mean so much more now than they ever did.

"You got this?" Morgan asks as we watch Dad leave. "You know what you're gonna do and shit?"

"Yeah, thanks for being here, I..." my voice trails as I try to think of some way to repay him for what he's helped give me.

"Don't even say it, man." We clasp hands, hugging each other. "If anyone gets it, it's me. Now go get your girl back."

As they leave my apartment, I breathe for the first time since this whole situation went down. Damn it feels good to inhale and exhale without the weight of the world on your chest.

I'VE LET myself have a little breakdown, allowed myself to purge all the emotions that have been so close to the surface since the day of the shooting, and I've come to a few realizations. I need Ruby to live my life, more than I ever imagined. She kind of makes my world go round.

And if there's one thing I have to do, it's show her how much she means to me. The first order of business to accomplish that is to go get something that means a lot to both of us and show up on her doorstep. There's nothing more romantic than that. Right?

When I get there and she lets me in without a word, just steps aside and lets me enter, I know I have one chance and I better not fucking blow this. If I do, I'll always wonder what would have happened if I wasn't such a dumbass.

CHAPTER THIRTY
RUBY

I'M LYING on my couch, re-watching some TV show I've seen a million times, trying to figure out how to get through to Caleb when the doorbell rings. At first I ignore it, not wanting to disturb my brooding, but then I hear his voice.

"Red?" It's unsure and soft as he knocks on the door this time. "I know I don't deserve for you to let me in, but I'm asking you to. Please?"

For a moment I think about ignoring him, I think about letting him sit out there and sweat. Give him the same type of reaction he's given me, but I realize quickly one of us has to be the bigger person. That person is me, because I know he's hurting and I know he's dealt with the situation he's been thrust into the best way he knows how.

Opening the door, I stand there with my arms crossed. Until I see what he's carrying in his hands.

The ugliest looking cupcakes I've ever seen in my life.

"I finally realized why he made them, even though they looked like shit," he gives me a slight smile. "It's the thought that counts, and the selflessness that he knew I'd hate them because of what they looked like. He did it because he loved me, and he wanted to try and make me happy."

Tears are already pouring from my eyes, as I step back and let Caleb in.

A little while later, we've moved to the bedroom. We're laying with my head on his chest, and while it feels good to be wrapped up in his arms, I'm feeling anger. He did fuck up, it did hurt, and I'm not over it yet. We lay with one another, comforting each other against whatever it is that's bothering us. It's a familiar place to be, but now it's been slightly tainted by the way he's acted.

"I know I've broken your trust, Ruby, because I didn't let you be there for me, but I want to prove to you I'm worthy of it now."

I hear what Caleb is saying, and while I'm willing to give him a free pass on what happened after the shooting, it doesn't mean that I'm not still upset with him. It hurts, to know that he didn't trust me, and yeah in a way, my trust is broken now too. "Caleb..." I let the word fall off because I don't know how to explain, don't know what I can say to change it.

"No, I get it. I hurt you when I didn't need to. Instead of coming to you for help, I pushed you away, and then I gave you mixed signals. I fucked up, I fucked up in a big way."

The frustration and anger seeps over. I fold my arms across my chest, fix him with a stare, and let him have it. "I told you I'd be here for you. I'm glad you're here now and I want to help you. What I don't want is for you to just think that when things get hard, you can be a fuck face, say you're sorry, make me cupcakes, and all will be forgiven. That's not how this is going to work, babe. I need to know if I put my trust in you again, I won't regret it."

I've said my peace, and he nods, accepting it.

"C'mere." He motions for me to lay on him. "Let me prove you can trust me."

"How?" I'm suspicious as I look down at him, wondering if he's playing some sort of game. I'm not sure my heart can take it if he is. These last few days have been difficult, at best.

"Give me your hands." He holds his to me, palms up.

For a split second I think about it, but then I place mine in his.

"Brace against me," he instructs.

And that's when I feel him lift me up, propping me with his hands and feet in the air. "Caleb you know I'm scared of heights." The fear is making my heart pound, even though I'm literally inches away from him.

"I know, Ruby Red, but trust me to make sure you don't fall. Let go and have fun, enjoy the feeling in your stomach and the excitement in your throat."

"More like I'm about to puke on you," I ground out between clenched teeth. I'm scared, shaking, not trusting him to take care of me, not trusting him not to let me fall.

"Relax," he instructs, his dark eyes boring into mine. "Relax and trust me, Red. Please, just trust me."

There's hysterical fear in my body right now, most of it is unfounded. Even if he does drop me, I'm only going to fall off the bed, but the fear is real. It's there. It's a war within myself as I try to determine if I'm going to forgive him. If I'm going to trust him. If anyone had asked me before the incident, I would have said with zero hesitation that Caleb was mine, I was his, and we were going to be together. I thought he believed in me, believed in us, but he threw all of that into my face, and didn't give a shit.

Another part of me argues that he'd been through a traumatic experience, and none of us ever know how we're going to react when that happens. Maybe he was doing the best he could with what he had, emotionally, and maybe what I'm here to do is be the person who supports him no matter what. Who stands behind him and is strong when he doesn't believe he can be. Who picks him up when he falls down or forgets what he has. Looking inside myself, I wonder if holding the grudge is worth missing out on everything we've shared together. I've given many things to this man that I've never given anyone else, and I'm not about to throw it all away, because times got a little rough.

Decision made, I close my eyes, relax, and trust him. I feel like I'm flying as he props me up on him, holding me with his palms against mine. "I trust you," I whisper.

He holds me aloft for a few seconds, then rolls me over in his arms. "Thank you." He holds me tight, wrapping his arms around me, burying his face in my hair. "I'm so fuckin' sorry, Ruby. So sorry that I couldn't get out of my own head." His voice is hoarse as he finally...fucking finally spills his guts.

"I felt like shit, ya know? Like there was some way I could have prevented what happened, if I would have done something differently." His voice is deep as he talks. "It was my first kill." There's tears in his eyes. "All the other guys on the team, they have that military experience, but all I did was ROTC in college. I didn't go to war, I didn't know what it was like to end a human life. It's a lot to take in, Red, a lot to forgive yourself for. I couldn't look at myself in the mirror. How could I think you or Kels, or Mom and Dad could look at me?"

"Who got to you?" I ask softly, holding him against me, running my hands up and down his back.

"Morgan. He said some things that make a lot of sense. Dad too. They found out that the guy had threatened suicide by cop before. There was no way he was being taken without a fight. I literally had no choice."

I breathe deeply, so happy that he's forgiven himself. Elated that he's overcome this speed bump that's been hindering us for the past few weeks. At the same time, it scares me even more. There will be a next time, there always is. Will he push me away? Will he let me help? "Promise me," I whisper digging my nails into his shirt, holding him tightly against my body.

"What? What promise do you need?"

"I need you to promise that next time you won't shut me out. Next time you show me, next time you let me see the ugly, the vulnerable. And there will be a next time, Caleb, in your line of work, we both know that. You can show me the anger too, but not to push me away, to let it out. I can take whatever you have to throw at me. I'm not letting you go, and I don't run away that easily."

His brown eyes cloud, when he puts a hand to my face, cupping my cheek. I turn into the caress, kissing his palm. "I forgot that some people do stick around when things get tough."

"Most people do, and you can count on me to always be one. Love doesn't mean you're around when everything's perfect. Love means you see the ugly, you comfort the hurt, and you fix the broken. Love isn't always easy and it's not always beautiful, but that's what makes it worth it."

"I don't deserve you, Red. As much as you lost your trust in me, I flat out didn't trust you."

I fight back the tears that are threatening to fall. "I forgive you, and that's all that matters."

He moves his hands around to the nape of my neck, pushing our foreheads together. "The whole time, the only thing running through my head was *I never told Ruby I love her*, even after eight months together, I never told you. I wanna tell you now, I don't want you to ever doubt it."

My face is breaking apart in one of the biggest smiles I've ever had. "I love you, Ruby Red, you're my everything."

"You're my everything too, don't ever forget that."

And as we lie there with one another, I let all the tears fall, let all the hurt go, and look forward to what the future holds for us.

CHAPTER THIRTY-ONE

RUBY

September

Back when I bought this dress so many months ago, I had assumed I would wear it for Valentine's Day, but because of Caleb's schedule we were never able to make a special date work. He never did take me to that dinner, but we've had so many other special moments that I truly can't complain. Tonight, however, I'm thrilled to be wearing this dress to watch him get an award for bravery.

"You look absolutely gorgeous." He comes up behind me in the mirror as I'm applying a layer of lipstick.

"You don't look so bad yourself." I turn around in his arms, helping to straighten his dress uniform.

I don't think Caleb has ever looked as hot as he does right now. There's something about him being so buttoned-up that I'm loving. "It's cutting off my circulation." He pulls at the fabric around his neck.

"You're fine." I slap his hands away. "Are you nervous?"

"Not really," he says with a shake of his head. "Nerves was playing for the college football championship. This is more anxious than anything. What if someone thinks I don't deserve this award?"

"Then they'll have to deal with me." She gives me a grin. "Nobody's gonna talk shit about the man I love."

"Don't I know it? I think you've become my most vocal supporter, even more vocal than Mom and Kels."

The blush covers her cheeks and neck. It's the one I love. The one that says she's embarrassed, but not really. "I'm sorry."

"Don't be." I lean in, kissing her. "I appreciate you looking out for me. I love that you will do whatever it takes to defend me. You're one of a kind, Ruby Red."

Her eyes glaze over and immediately a frown comes to my face. "What's wrong?"

"There was a time last month when I wasn't sure if you'd ever call me Ruby Red again, hell I wasn't sure if you'd actually even see me again."

"I was stupid," I assure her. "There was so much shit rolling around in my head, that I couldn't figure out what was real and what was noise. It took talking to family, friends, and the work appointed therapist, but I'm good now. I'm over whatever it was holding me back. You're never going to get rid of me."

"Good." She grins. "There's no way I'd ever want to."

"Now, we've gotta get this show on the road, if we're going to make it in time."

Ruby

Proud doesn't even begin to describe how I'm feeling as I watch Caleb accept his award from Holden. There's not a dry eye at our table between me, my mom, Karina, and Kelsea. I guess they were smart to sit most of the women together.

I watch as he's interviewed by the local news station, and then the newspaper before he comes back over to join us. "You did so good up there," I whisper, leaning in to kiss his neck. "I love you."

"Love you too, Red."

I'm still not used to him saying the words to me, but every time he says them they seem more real. As a few more officers line up to receive their awards, Caleb puts his arm around my shoulders and leans back, enjoying the rest of the ceremony.

"We're hosting a little get together," Holden says as the group stands together after the ceremony is complete. "If anyone wants to come hang out with us."

Caleb and I look at one another, I don't know what his plans are, but judging by the look in his eyes, he doesn't want to hang out with his friends from work.

"Nah, we got plans," he answers. "Thanks, though."

Cruise

"Where are we going?" Ruby asks as she sits in the passenger seat of my Jeep.

"You'll see," I deflect the question, hoping that she won't notice where we're headed. Which direction I went in, when I got on the interstate and just how long we've been driving and talking.

Luckily for me, she doesn't, until we pull up to the gate. "Caleb, isn't this where they practice?"

"Yeah," I answer as we look at Alabama's summer practice field. I still have some connections from when I played here, and for some just the mention of my name can get me exactly what I want. "It's where I practiced too."

"What are we doing here?" She gets out when I come around to her side of the Jeep, opening her door.

"Little fantasy I've always had." I shrug. "And you in that dress tonight, is giving me so many ideas."

"Fantasy?"

"Yeah." I let a smile play at the corners of my lips. "There was this thing all the seniors did, but I never got to do, because I didn't have a girlfriend at the time, or really any girl I trusted to bring out here."

"What kind of thing?" She raises an eyebrow in my direction.

I hold her had as we walk toward the locker rooms, using a key that was given to me to enter. Above the lockers, there are names, along with seats to sit on. I glance around, memories coming back to me as I think about the four years I spent here. The good times, the tough times, the times I wanted to give up. It hits me square in the chest that those four years aren't any different than these last five on the MTF. Life will always be trying to knock you down in some way or another, it's up to you if you want to keep standing tall or not.

When my gaze lands on what was my locker, I tilt my head toward it. "Every senior player brought their girlfriend out here to christen their locker for luck, before the season started."

She giggles as she looks at me like I've lost my mind. "Are you serious?"

"Dead."

"But this isn't your locker anymore."

"Nope, looks like we'll be giving Walker, whoever that is, a free round of good luck for his season."

She bites that full bottom lip. "Why is this such a thing for you?"

I pull her into me. "I think I've proven to you just how much I like sex that's risky, and back then, this was as risky as it got. Had I known you back then? We would have been here the first day of spring practice."

It looks like she's thinking about it, wondering if I'm telling her the truth or not. "Trust me, we would have done it more than once."

"More than once?"

"Oh yeah." I run my hand along the slice of skin that's visible at her mid-section. "Any chance we would have gotten. I would have shown you the stamina a running back has."

"Well then, when you throw down a challenge like that?" She takes her top off, throwing it in my direction. "How can I say no?"

I watch as she steps out of her skirt before I grab her around the waist, pulling her up against me, carrying her over, before I tilt her chin to look at me. "Easy, Ruby Red. You can never say no to me, just like I can't say no to you."

When I dip my head, running my tongue along the flesh that's exposed over the top of her bra, all I hear is her whispered, "Yes."

"See? Never say no..."

CHAPTER THIRTY-TWO

RUBY

"WHERE ARE YOU TAKING ME?" I watch as Caleb drives through the streets of downtown. This fall night is cool as rain falls from the sky. It's not sheets like the day he shot the armed man, but a steady drumming against the roof of the Jeep.

"You'll see." His deep voice has a secretive lilt to it, one that I've come to know well in the year we've been together. He's not great at keeping secrets, but when he does, they're the best kind.

As he turns in front of The Café, I grin. No matter what's happened inside the building or in front of it, this is still one of our favorite places to go, to be. On any given night, we can walk inside and find any number of friends or family inside. It's darkish in there tonight, but I figure maybe the electricity is flickering because of the rain storm we're in. Earlier in the day, the school had lost power.

He snags a parking spot near the door. "Don't touch the door, I'll come around for you. I don't want you get wet."

Since the first night I met him, he's been a gentleman. I mean, don't get me wrong, he can be pretty demanding too, but no one has ever taken care of me like Caleb does. He comes around to my side of the Jeep, holding his jacket over our heads as we make a dash for the front door.

As we enter, I realize there's something off about what we've walked in to. Typically The Café is almost so loud you have to speak with some bass to be heard, and the tables are usually jam-packed. Taking a look around tonight, I notice the only people here are our friends and family. People who have come to mean a lot to us in the year we've been together. People we've made memories with.

My parents and brother, Caleb's parents, and Kelsea sit in one booth. Behind them Morgan, Brooks, and Trinity look at us, small smiles on their faces. In all the other booths I see members of the Moonshine Task Force and their families, as well as a few of the teachers I'm friends with and roommates from college. I have no idea how they all came to be here tonight, or why they even are, but I do have an idea that Caleb is probably behind it.

"What's going on?" I whisper to Caleb as everyone watches us walk to the middle of the room. We're the center of attention, and it makes me a little self-conscious, but I also want to know what's going on.

"Nothing." He shakes his head, as he leads me to the table.

It's almost like everyone is holding their breath as they watch us, and it makes me nervous. But I trust Caleb, with everything I have. We've been through a lot together. There's no one I trust more than him, and no one I want to do life with more than him.

"You remember this table?" he asks quietly when we get to the middle of the room. It's the one I sat at while I listened to that awful date of mine make disparaging remarks about me.

Glancing around, I'm hit with a flashback of the first night we met. Giving him a huge smile, I nod. "I do."

Cruise

"Morgan and I were sitting right there–" he points to where his parents and mine sit. "–when Leigh came over to us and told us the couple sitting right here–" he touches the Formica top with his finger "–weren't having a good night. That the girl seemed scared out of her mind, and the guy was creeping even Leigh out. I kinda thought maybe Leigh was overreacting, because that's kind of what she does, but then I listened."

"Hey!" Leigh yells. Whatever else she says is muffled as Holden pulls her to him, covering her mouth up with the palm of his hand. I laugh, thankful as hell I did listen.

"I remember." She puts her arms around my waist, tilting her head as she looks up at me. "He really was creepy," she says loud enough for everyone to hear. "I was eating our appetizer like I hadn't eaten it weeks, just trying to choke it down to get out of the situation. At one point, he looked at me, and told me at least I could swallow."

She makes a face, looking around at all the people who have gathered. There's a sound in the room as everyone gets offended for her, at least the people old enough to realize what he'd meant.

"Then the jerk made a comment about knowing where she lived because he'd picked her up, and how he was going to invite himself in." I pick up the story. "At that point, I knew I had to step in."

She giggles. "I remember him pulling up a chair, and when I glanced over I was in shock. I'd never seen a guy as gorgeous as you, hot stuff."

"That's right, eat your heart out." I give a wink as I look around. Moving my hands up from her waist, I cup her jawline. "But I'd honestly never seen anyone as beautiful as you. And it pissed me off that this guy was scaring you and didn't realize what he had sitting there right in front of him. I knew pretty quickly that I wanted you in my life."

"You did?" she asks softly, almost as if she doesn't believe I knew almost immediately, and I can tell why she wonders. It took me forever to tell her my feelings. But that was more me than it ever was her.

"I did." I lean down kissing her lightly on the lips. "Then the months of amazingness came, and I wondered what I'd done to deserve it, waited for the bad thing – whatever it was going to be – to happen. Because, babe, with me, there's always something right around the corner."

I hear sniffles in the room, can see tears in Ruby's eyes, and I know she's thinking back to the summer. How I pushed her away, how I was a fucking asshole, just trying to cope with the bullshit that was handed to me. "But you didn't leave me, Ruby Red. You kept fighting for me, for us. It wasn't long after that, I knew you were the one."

"It took that long?" She pinches my arm as everyone laughs through their tears.

"I knew it before then, but it took me longer to admit it. Sometimes, I'm slow. You know this."

She leans in, kissing my jawline. "Doesn't matter, Caleb, I love you just the way you are."

My heart pounds in my chest so loudly I'm surprised she and everyone around, doesn't hear it. "You do love me. Anyone who didn't, wouldn't have been able to put up with me for those weeks while I did everything I could to push you away." I swallow roughly. "They wouldn't have stayed, they wouldn't have listened to the shit I spewed and still kept coming back for more."

"Caleb..."

"No." I put my finger up to her lips. "Let me finish. You're the strongest woman I know besides my mom, it takes a strong woman to love me. For all my goodness, I have a lot of faults. For all my strengths, baby, I have a ton of weaknesses. But with you beside me, they don't cripple me. Not like they used to. I've learned that instead of pushing you away, I need to lean on you. That when I'm not strong, you are. When I'm faced with a mountain of self-doubt, you're right there beside me when we scale it, go over it, and conquer that bitch."

She laughs, as does everyone else. It makes me feel like I'm doing a good job, and I'm not fucking this completely up.

"You love me, you love my sister, and that means more to me than anything in this world. I waited a long time for her, as you've come to know." I grin. "But I've waited even longer for you, Ruby Red. I didn't know it, didn't realize it, but everyday we're together I'm reminded of what my life could be like without you. I smile so much now, I laugh, I get this fluttery feeling in my stomach and chest when I see you."

"I get it too," she whispers, standing up on tiptoe to kiss the dimple in my cheek. "Every time I see that strut you have, the swagger, the attitude. Every damn time."

"You're beautiful, and you're too good for me, but I don't want to ever let you go, don't think I ever can let you go." I lean my forehead into hers, closing my eyes as I breathe deeply.

It takes a lot of courage to bare yourself in front of your friends and family, in front of the woman you want to spend the rest of your life with. But I'll do it anytime I need to for the woman whose forehead touches mine. Taking a big inhale, I remove my forehead from hers, reach into my pocket for the ring, and take a knee in front of her.

The whole place loses it, as does she. There's already tears streaming down her face, and fuck it, I'm feeling choked up too. This is the culmination of a lifetime of not feeling like I'm good enough, and I'm about to ask this woman if I truly am good enough for her. There's a chance she could say no. I don't think she will, but there's always a fucking chance. I push that thought out of my head and forge on with what I want, more than anything.

"Ruby Red, will you do me the absolute privilege of letting me take care of you the rest of your life? You can take care of me too." I bite my lip, trying to hold back the emotion. It's threatening though, threatening to break free and show everyone just how much this woman means to me. "We can do this thing you've taught me – ya know? Take care of each other. We can wake up together every day, go to sleep together most nights – when Havoc doesn't have me working night shift."

The guys laugh, and so does she.

"But more than anything, I'll have a partner. We can eat junk food, watch stupid TV, walk in the rain, and do everything either of us have ever wanted to. Bonus is we don't have to do it alone."

She leans down, caressing my face. "You're never gonna be alone again, hot stuff."

"Do life with me? Be my best friend? Be the amazing mom to my kids I know you'll be? Marry me?"

"Yes!" she screams loudly as she launches herself at me, knocking me to my back on the floor.

I close my arms around her, holding her tightly to me, whispering so many words, I don't even know what they are. She's straddling my waist, kissing my neck, mouth, every piece of skin she can get to. I'm kissing her too, giving her everything she's giving me. Eventually as everyone surrounds us, they pick us up, and I put the ring on her finger.

Eventually I feel someone tugging at my waist. I look down and see Kels. "Yeah?"

She reaches up, hugging me tight. I pick her up, so that I can hear her above all the noise. Ruby comes to us. With a huge smile on Kels face, she says what I'm sure she's wanted to say a long time. "Told you both you were gonna get married, and now she really is going to be my sister!"

A while later, Dad pulls me aside. "How does it feel?"

I look up at him, because he's still a little taller than me. "Just like you said it would. It feels good to be wanted."

"You'll never know what it's like to be alone again." He hugs me tightly.

And I realize he's right. What my mom did to me, didn't define me. It never has, and with Ruby Red by my side, I'm never going to feel like the kid who wasn't good enough again.

As I walk over to her, scooping her up in my arms, twirling her around, Leigh brings out the food she's prepared. I realize this is the beginning of my journey. It's not the end, not the middle.

This is where Caleb Harrison beats the odds and becomes the man he's always been meant to be.

EPILOGUE

CRUISE

FIVE YEARS **Later**

"Molly's asleep." I press my wife up against the door to our bedroom, spreading open-mouth kisses along her neck as we grind against one another. Pulling back, I push my hands up her tank top, palming her breasts, moaning as I feel her nipples peak against her bra. "I paid Kelsea her stupid-ass babysitting fee, she's gone. We're alone." I can hear the annoyance in my voice. It's been an on-going argument between the two of us, how I'd watched her for free as a kid, and now she charges us.

We've been out with friends and family, had a DD, and both of us have had a little too much to drink. Her with the margaritas she likes to indulge in with the ladies, and me with the whiskey Morgan and I were shooting straight with my dad.

"God, I want you." She rakes her nails across my neck, down my back, and fists my shirt in her hands.

I want her too. Molly is three now, born within the first two years of us getting married, and we've finally got this parenting thing down. But for the last few years, we've been winging it, quickies while she's napping, weekend fuck fests when we can both get the time off and grandparents are willing to take her, but all of it is planned. There's really no spontaneity anymore, except tonight. This right here, is the most spontaneous we've been since we brought Molly home from the hospital. It's not planned, set aside time to be with one another. It's this crazy passionate moment where she's been teasing my cock all night, and as soon as the bedroom door had shut, I couldn't wait to get my mouth and hands on her, cock inside her.

"Fuck, I want you too," I moan as I finish pushing the tank top up and over her head. My hands are clumsy as I pull down the lace cups of her bra, those tight nipples calling to me, making my mouth water as I lean my head down and take first one, then the other deep, twirling my tongue around them. When I lean back to admire my handiwork, I see the evidence of the moisture of my mouth there, bringing my thumbs up to worry the nubs into even harder points.

"Damn it, I ache for you." She's pushing her core hard against my cock.

I haven't been this drunk in a long time, and all I know is I want to fuck. It's the only thing I want to do when I get this far gone. "I ache for you too." I hold her against the door with one hand, while with the other I tear at my belt, push my boxers down, and free my engorged dick. "Shit, that feels better." I lick the palm of my hand, bringing it in between her thighs, where the only thing covering her is a short skirt, and some skimpy as fuck lace panties. My girl knew what she wanted tonight when she got dressed.

"Really, Red? Lace bra and panties? Were you horny? Did you want to tempt me? Is that why you couldn't keep your hands off me under the table tonight?"

Her head falls back against the door, a loud bang, that I pray to God doesn't wake up our daughter. "Yeah." She thrusts against my fingers. "I need you, hot stuff, need you so bad."

When I push inside her, throwing my head back, because every time with her is always like the first time, she gasps loudly.

"Babe, do you have a condom?"

What the fuck? "No, we're married. What the hell Ruby?"

"I'm late in getting my birth control renewed. You know, with us having two more-than-full-time-jobs, a child, life. I don't have an appointment until the end of next month."

But that doesn't stop her from grinding on my length. "You keep doing that, and there's no chance in hell I'll be able to pull out," I groan loudly, wrapping my forearms around her thighs, as I walk us over to the bed, throwing her down as I climb on top of her, and really give my hips room to work.

"Feels so good." She claws at my shirt, fisting it as she pulls it off my body, running her hands along my chest, tweaking my nipples how I like it.

"Fuck, Red." I'm trying to keep it together here, but she's not making things easy. She's thrusting against me, and I'm pushing into her, the bed is hitting against the wall, and neither one of us are caring about the noise we're making. That's when I feel it, the tingle in my lower back. Separating from a kiss that's out of control, I pant. "Gotta stop, babe, we need to stop. I'm gonna come." I try to prevent my dick from pushing inside her, try to pull away. I give it a valiant effort, but at the last second, she thrusts up. "Gotta come." And right as I feel my cock pulse, she encloses me with her wet heat. "Fuck," I groan out for more reasons than one, as she trembles around my body, holding me tightly.

Long minutes later, we're still lying connected, each panting as we try to get our breath back. "I tried," I breathe into her neck. "I love you, so I tried."

"I know." Her breath tickles the skin of my ear as she giggles in that way tipsy people do. "I don't think the timing was right anyway. I've only been without birth control for a week or so, it's probably still in my system. We're good, hot stuff. Either way, I love you for trying."

Ruby: A Few Weeks Later

"Before I give you the prescription. is there any chance you could be pregnant?" My OB/GYN asks as I sit in her office, having already done all the other examinations I need to get my birth control refilled.

"No," I answer, but then that super-hot night where Caleb and I didn't use anything comes to the forefront of my mind. "Wait, yes. There was one time, a week after my birth control ran out, but I figured it'd still be in my system, and it was only once," I shrug. "Although I haven't had a period since then, and I have been feeling a little off the past few days, I just figured it was stress."

"Once is all it takes," she laughs. "Let me go ahead and take some blood. We'll run the test, call, and let you know."

Sitting in the chair, waiting to have my blood drawn, is the most nerve-wracking experience ever. Molly had been planned; we'd gone into it with the decision we wanted a baby, had bought a house in preparation of her coming, not too far from either one of our parents' and had done it by the book. This is giving me anxiety. This, if it turns out to be positive, has not been planned. As I get up from the chair, I'm a little dizzy, causing me to sit back down for a minute while they wrap my arm with gauze. "I haven't eaten today," I explain when they look at me funny.

When I leave, I head straight for The Café, where Caleb and I are meeting for a rare lunch date. As I walk in and look around for my husband, I'm struck with how hot he looks sitting in the booth, Molly on his lap, him holding his phone, so they can watch something. He's got his chin resting on her head, and they're engrossed in whatever it is. Fuck he's hot when he's being such a good dad. As I get closer, his head lifts, and the smile that spreads across his face makes my heart pound faster. Getting up out of the booth, he carefully sets Molly down, before meeting me and wrapping his arms around me.

"Hey, Red, what's with the arm?" I kiss him softly before we snuggle into the booth together, sitting next to one another. "By the way, I already ordered for you."

That's the good thing about having a husband that knows you so well. He knows what you like, when you're freaking out, and when something is going on. The waitress comes, dropping off a water for me with lemon. I offer her a smile, before I turn to my husband.

"They had to do blood work."

Immediately, those brown eyes of his are worried. "Something wrong?"

Looking around, to make sure none of our families are here, I lean in. "I had to take a pregnancy test. Ya know, because of that night?"

"Shit, it was once, I mean that doesn't happen, right?"

"Karina said it happened for her and your dad." I push my hand through my hair. "It wouldn't be an awful thing, I've been thinking about it." I hook my arm into his elbow. "Granted it wasn't planned like Molly, but if it happens, it happens."

EIGHT MONTHS later as I'm holding my son, Levi, in my arms waiting for my in-laws and Molly to come meet him, I glance up at my husband and smile.

"Are you happy, Red?" He leans down, pushing the blanket back from Levi's face.

"Very! Tired, but happy."

When the door opens and they walk in, Molly slowly makes her way over, before I reach out with my hand, smiling at her. She smiles back at me, the same smile her dad has. "Come meet your little brother," I encourage her, glancing at her "Big Sister" shirt.

Caleb stands next to his dad, the two of them patting each other on the back. Mason folds his arms over his chest. "What did y'all end up naming him?"

"Levi Mason Harrison," he says the words like they're no big deal, but when we get to his middle name, Mason and Karina gasp, and I can feel the emotion in the room.

My husband looks at his dad. "A strong name for my son that matches the strongest man I know."

As I watch them embrace and hand Levi over to Kelsea, I reach down to my phone and take a picture.

Two men, thrown away by one woman, who overcame every obstacle to be the amazing people they are today. If that's not a testament to love, I don't know what is.

In this moment, Caleb and Mason Harrison, they set the bar for this baby held in his aunt's arms, and they show Kelsea who real men are. And the one on the left who wears the ring I put on his finger? He shows me loyalty, compassion, and the love of a great man every day.

If anyone asked me to describe him?

Caleb Harrison. Good man, wonderful father, and the greatest love of my life.

The End
Click here for a bonus Cruise scene!

Continue on with the next generation of the MTF!
Book #1 of the Laurel Springs Emergency Response Team is Ransom!

www.ingramcontent.com/pod-product-compliance
Lightning Source LLC
Chambersburg PA
CBHW020326030826
48979CB00020B/184

* 9 7 9 8 9 8 5 8 6 4 9 0 8 *